The Works of William Makepeace Thackeray

General Editor: Peter L. Shillingsburg

———◇———

THE NEWCOMES

The Works of William Makepeace Thackeray
General Editor: Peter L. Shillingsburg
Editorial Board
  Edgar F. Harden
  John Sutherland

The History of Henry Esmond
  edited by Edgar F. Harden
Vanity Fair: A Novel without a Hero
  edited by Peter L. Shillingsburg
The History of Pendennis
  edited by Peter L. Shillingsburg
*Flore et Zypher, The Yellowplush Papers,
  Major Gahagan*
  edited by Peter L. Shillingsburg
The Newcomes
  edited by Peter L. Shillingsburg

WILLIAM MAKEPEACE THACKERAY

———◇———

THE NEWCOMES

MEMOIRS OF A MOST RESPECTABLE FAMILY

———◇———

edited by

PETER L. SHILLINGSBURG

with a historical essay by

R. D. McMASTER

ANN ARBOR

THE UNIVERSITY OF MICHIGAN PRESS

1996

Support for research and production costs was provided by the
National Endowment for the Humanities, Division of Research
Grants.

∞ Printed on acid-free paper

1999   1998   1997   1996   4   3   2   1

A CIP catalog record for this book is available from the British Library.

Library of Congress Cataloging-in-Publication Data

Thackeray, William Makepeace, 1811–1863.
    The Newcomes : memoirs of a most respectable family /
William Makepeace Thackeray ; edited by Peter L. Shillingsburg
; with a historical essay by R.D. McMaster.
        p.   cm.   — (The Works of W.M. Thackeray ; 5)
    ISBN 0-472-10675-9 (hardcover : alk. paper)
    1. Family—England—Fiction. I. Shillingsburg, Peter L. II.
McMaster, Rowland. III. Title. IV. Series: Thackeray, William
Makepeace, 1811–1863. Works. 1989 ; 5.
PR5614.A1   1996
823'.8—dc20   96-4229
                                                              CIP

CONTENTS

Note on the Text and Textual Apparatus

Previous collections of Thackeray's Works (over a dozen since the first collection published by Smith, Elder, and Co. in London in 1868–69) and the continuing appearance of single volumes of his works attest to Thackeray's stature as a major Victorian novelist. But the textual corruptions of these editions and the general lack of knowledge about Thackeray's methods of composition and revision have increased the distance between readers and Thackeray's texts.

The purpose of this new edition is, first, to present the text as much as possible as Thackeray produced it and, second, to show the composition and revision of the work. This edition results from a comparative study of all extant documents from the now fragmented manuscript to the last edition touched by the author. The reading text here presented is based on the manuscript where it is extant and on the first edition where there is no manuscript. Verbal changes introduced in the first edition have been adopted for the present text unless they appear to be inadvertent or the result of faulty revision. Number 6 (chapters 17–20) forms an exception to this general rule; number 6 is based on the manuscript and does not introduce the changes from the first edition because in the editor's opinion they were made by someone other than the author, as is explained in the Textual Commentary.

The readings reported in the footnotes and in the record of emendations represent texts *as silently emended,* as described in the Textual Introduction under "Silent Emendations," where there is also a full discussion of this policy. Thus, the record in these two areas is not a strictly accurate report of the very routine accidentals of the document. The purpose of the reports given in these two areas is to enable a cleaner representation of substantive and semi-substantive readings: those that affect the meaning of the text. A full report of all silent emendations is made in the electronic files available with the book from the publisher.

The reports of manuscript alterations, at the back of the book, do not incorporate any silent emendations.

Emendations are listed in the Textual Apparatus. Notes on the Text explain some emendations and some decisions not to emend. Evidence bearing on other forms of the text is described in the Textual Introduction and detailed in the Record of Text Variants in such a way that, in so far as evidence has survived, the text as Thackeray intended it at any point in its history can be educed for study and comparison.

The Newcomes was published serially and then in two volumes. This edition indicates the division into monthly installments and maintains the two-volume division. Consequently pagination and chapter numbering begin anew in the second volume.

Acknowledgments

For permission to use manuscripts, drawings, proofs, and rare books in their collections, I am grateful to the Charterhouse School; the British Library; the Henry W. and Albert A. Berg Collection and the Manuscripts Division of the New York Public Library, Astor, Lennox, and Tilden Foundations; the Harry Ransom Humanities Center, University of Texas; the Houghton Library, Harvard University; the Henry E. Huntington Library, San Marino, California; and the Robert H. Taylor Collection, Princeton. For permission to quote from unpublished material I am indebted to Mrs. Belinda Norman-Butler.

This volume would have been incomparably more difficult to produce were it not for the pioneering scholarship of Gordon N. Ray, Edgar F. Harden, and John Sutherland. I am particularly grateful for the support and collaboration offered by R. D. McMaster.

For encouragement and advice, I am grateful to Paul Eggert, Edgar F. Harden, Elizabeth James, John Sutherland, and James L. W. West. For clerical and research assistance I am grateful to Laurie Buchholz, Mike Denton, Genevieve Fager West, Jennifer Hughes, Andy Lowry, Mike Molloy, and Ann Taylor.

For financial assistance, I am grateful to the Mississippi State University Office of Research and to the National Endowment for the Humanities, Division of Research Grants.

List of Symbols

Ms = manuscript

Ms1 = draft manuscript of penultimate page of the novel

Ms2 = revised manuscript of same page

E1 = first edition, printed from standing type

P1 = first edition, printed from plates

HM = *Harper's Magazine*

NY = Harper's New York edition (1849–50)

R = revised London edition (1856)

~~word~~ = marks material deleted

« » = encloses manuscript material deleted within a deletion

↑ ↓ = encloses manuscript material inserted

↑↑ ↓↓ = encloses manuscript material added within an insertion

+ += encloses material not actually deleted but replaced by revision

++ ++= encloses material cancelled by mistake

[ ] = encloses information supplied by the editor

[text over text] = indicates a correction made by writing the new letter or word in the same space as the old. This differs in appearance from a deletion and insertion; it is like a strikeover.

[illeg] = illegible letter or word

-/ = end-of-line hyphen

J. J. in Dreamland

THE NEWCOMES

MEMOIRS OF A MOST Respectable FAMILY

Vol. I.

EDITED by

A. PENDENNIS ESQre

ILLUSTRATED by RICHARD DOYLE.

LONDON

BRADBURY & EVANS WHITEFRIARS

CONTENTS.

———◇———

CONTENTS

LIST OF PLATES.

———◇———

THE NEWCOMES.

Chapter I.

THE OVERTURE—AFTER WHICH THE CURTAIN RISES UPON A DRINKING CHORUS.

CROW, who had flown away with a cheese from a dairy window, sate perched on a tree looking down at a great big frog in a pool underneath him. The frog's hideous large eyes were goggling out of his head in a manner which appeared quite ridiculous to the old black-a-moor, who watched the splay-footed slimy wretch with that peculiar grim humour belonging to crows. Not far from the frog a fat ox was[1] browsing; whilst a few lambs frisked about the meadow, or nibbled the grass and buttercups there.

Who should come in to the farther end of the field but a wolf? He was so cunningly dressed up in sheep's clothing, that the very lambs did not know master wolf; nay, one of them, whose dam the wolf had just eaten, after which he had thrown her skin over his shoulders, ran up innocently towards the devouring monster, mistaking him for her mamma.

"He he!" says a fox sneaking round the hedge-paling, over which the tree grew, whereupon the crow was perched looking down on the frog who was staring with his goggle eyes fit to burst with envy, and croaking abuse[2] at the ox. "How absurd those lambs are! Yonder silly little knock-kneed baah-ling does not know the old wolf dressed in the sheep's fleece. He is the same old rogue who gobbled up little Red Riding Hood's grandmother for lunch, and swallowed little Red Riding Hood for supper. *Tirez la bobinette et la chévillette cherra.* He he!"

---

[1] a fat ox was *E1*] was a fat ox *HM*
[2] abuse *E1*] above *HM*

An owl that was hidden in the hollow of the tree, woke up. "O ho, master fox," says she, "I cannot see you, but I smell you! If some folks like lambs, other folks like geese," says the owl.

"And your ladyship is fond of mice," says the fox.

"The Chinese eat them," says the owl, "and I have read that they are very fond of dogs," continued the old lady.

"I wish they would exterminate every cur of them off the face of the earth," said the fox.

"And I have also read in works of travel, that the French eat frogs," continued the owl. "Aha, my friend Crapaud! are you there? That was a very pretty concert we sang together last night!"

"If the French devour my brethren; the English eat beef," croaked out the frog,—"great, big, brutal, bellowing oxen."

"Ho, whoo!" says the owl, "I have heard that the English are toad-eaters too!"

"But who ever heard of them eating an owl or a fox, Madam?" says Reynard, "or their sitting down and taking a crow to pick," adds the polite rogue with a bow to the old crow who was perched above them with the cheese in his mouth. "We are privileged animals, all of us; at least we never furnish dishes for the odious orgies of man."

"I am the bird of wisdom," says the owl; "I was the companion of Pallas Minerva: I am frequently represented in the Egyptian monuments."

"I have seen you over the British barn-doors," said the fox, with a grin. "You have a deal of scholarship, Mrs. Owl. I know a thing or two myself; but am, I confess it, no scholar—a mere man of the world—a fellow that lives by his wits—a mere country gentleman."

"You sneer at scholarship," continues the owl, with a sneer on her venerable face. "I read a good deal of a night."

"When I am engaged deciphering the cocks and hens at roost," says the fox.

"It's a pity for all that you can't read; that board nailed over my head would give you some information."

"What does it say?" says the fox.

"I can't spell in the daylight," answered the owl; and giving a yawn, went back to sleep till evening in the hollow of her tree.

"A fig for her hieroglyphics!" said the fox, looking up at the crow in the tree. "What airs our slow neighbour gives herself! She pretends to all the wisdom; whereas, your reverences, the crows, are endowed with gifts far superior to those benighted old big-wigs of owls, who blink in the darkness, and call their hooting singing. How noble it is to hear a chorus of crows! There are twenty-four brethren of the Order of St. Corvinus, who have builded themselves a convent near a wood which I frequent; what a droning and a chanting they keep up! I protest their reverences' singing is nothing to yours! You sing so deliciously in parts, do for the love of harmony favour me with a solo!"

While this conversation was going on, the ox was chumping the grass; the frog was eyeing him in such a rage at his superior proportions, that he would have spurted venom at him if he could, and that he would have burst, only that is impossible, from sheer envy; the little lambkin was lying unsuspiciously at the side of the wolf in fleecy hosiery, who did not as yet molest her, being replenished with the mutton her[3] mamma. But now the wolf's eyes began to glare, and his sharp white teeth to show, and he rose up with a growl, and began to think he should like lamb for supper.

"What large eyes you have got!" bleated out the lamb, with rather a timid look.

"The better to see you with, my dear."

"What large teeth you have got!"

"The better to ——"

At this moment such a terrific yell filled the field, that all its inhabitants started with terror. It was from a donkey, who had somehow got a lion's skin, and now[4] came in at the hedge, pursued by some men and boys with sticks and guns.

When the wolf in sheep's clothing heard the bellow of the ass in the lion's skin, fancying that the monarch of the forest was near, he ran away as fast as his disguise would let him. When the ox heard the noise he dashed round the meadow-ditch, and with one trample of his hoof squashed the frog who had been abusing him. When the crow saw the people with guns coming, he instantly dropped the cheese out of his mouth, and took to wing. When the fox saw the cheese drop, he immediately made a jump at it (for he knew the donkey's voice, and that his asinine bray was not a bit like his royal master's roar), and making for the cheese, fell into a steel-trap, which snapped off his tail; without which he was obliged to go into the world, pretending, forsooth, that it was the fashion not to wear tails any more; and that the fox-party were better without 'em.

Meanwhile, a boy with a stick came up, and belaboured master donkey, until he roared louder than ever. The wolf, with the sheep's clothing drag-gling about his legs, could not run fast, and was detected and shot by one of the men. The blind old owl, whirring out of the hollow tree, quite amazed at the disturbance, flounced into the face of a ploughboy, who knocked her down with a pitchfork. The butcher came and quietly led off the ox and the lamb; and the farmer, finding the fox's brush in the trap, hung it up over his mantel-piece, and always bragged that he had been in at his death.

"What a farrago of old fables is this! What a dressing up in old clothes!" says the critic. (I think I see such a one—a Solomon that sits in judgment over us authors and chops up our children.) "As sure as I am just and wise, modest, learned, and religious, so surely I have read something very like this stuff and nonsense about jackasses and foxes before. That wolf in sheep's clothing?—do I not know him? That fox discoursing with the crow?—have I not previously heard of him? Yes, in Lafontaine's fables: let us get the Dictionary and the Fable and the Biographie Universelle, article Lafontaine, and confound the impostor."

"Then in what a contemptuous way," may Solomon go on to remark, "does this author speak of human nature! There is scarce one of these characters he represents but is a villain. The fox is a flatterer; the frog is an emblem of impotence and envy; the wolf in sheep's clothing, a blood-thirsty

[3] mutton her *E1*] mutton of her *HM*
[4] now *E1*] [absent] *HM*

hypocrite, wearing the garb of innocence; the ass in the lion's skin, a quack trying to terrify, by assuming the appearance of a forest monarch (does the writer, writhing under merited castigation, mean to sneer at critics in this character? We laugh at the impertinent comparison); the ox, a stupid common-place—the only innocent being in the writer's (stolen) apologue is a fool,—the idiotic lamb, who does not know his own mother!" And then the critic, if in a virtuous mood, may indulge in some fine writing regarding the holy beauteousness of maternal affection.

Why not? If authors sneer, it is the critic's business to sneer at them for sneering. He must pretend to be their superior, or who would care about his opinion? And his livelihood is to find fault. Besides he is right sometimes; and the stories he reads, and the characters drawn in them, are old sure enough. What stories are new? All types of all characters march through all fables: tremblers and boasters; victims and bullies; dupes and knaves; long-eared Neddies, giving themselves leonine airs; Tartuffes wearing virtuous clothing; lovers and their trials, their blindness, their folly and constancy. With the very first page of the human story do not love and lies too begin? So the tales were told ages before Æsop: and asses under lions' manes roared in Hebrew; and sly foxes flattered in Etruscan; and wolves in sheep's clothing gnashed their teeth in Sanscrit, no doubt. The sun shines to-day as he did when he first began shining; and the birds in the tree overhead, while I am writing, sing very much the same note they have sung ever since there were finches. Nay, since last he besought good-natured friends to listen once a month to his talking, a friend of the writer[5] has seen the New World, and found the (featherless) birds there exceedingly like their brethren of Europe. There may be nothing new under and including the sun; but it looks fresh every morning, and we rise with it to toil, hope, scheme, laugh, struggle, love, suffer, until the night comes and quiet. And then will wake Morrow and the eyes that look on it; and so *da capo*.

This, then, is to be a story, may it please you, in which jackdaws will wear peacocks' feathers, and awaken the just ridicule of the peacocks; in which, while every justice is done to the peacocks themselves, the splendour of their plumage, the gorgeousness of their dazzling necks, and the magnificence of their tails, exception will yet be taken to the absurdity of their ricketty strut, and the foolish discord of their pert squeaking; in which lions in love will have their claws pared by sly virgins; in which rogues will sometimes triumph, and honest folks, let us hope, come by their own; in which there will be black crape and white favours; in which there will be tears under orange-flower wreaths and jokes in mourning-coaches; in which there will be dinners of herbs with contentment and without, and banquets of stalled oxen where there is care and hatred—ay, and kindness and friendship too, along with the feast. It does not follow that all men are honest because they are poor; and I have known some who were friendly and generous, although they had plenty of money. There are some great landlords who do not grind down their tenants; there are actually bishops who are not hypocrites; there are liberal men even among the Whigs, and

[5] a friend of the writer *E1*] the writer *HM*

the Radicals themselves are not all Aristocrats at heart. But who ever heard of giving the Moral before the Fable? Children are only led to accept the one after their delectation over the other: let us take care lest our readers skip both; and so let us bring them on quickly—our wolves and lambs, our foxes and lions, our roaring donkies, our billing ringdoves, our motherly partlets, and crowing chanticleers.

There was once a time when the sun used to shine brighter than it appears to do in this latter half of the nineteenth century; when the zest of life was certainly keener; when tavern wines seemed to be delicious, and tavern dinners the perfection of cookery; when the perusal of novels was productive of immense delight, and the monthly advent of magazine-day was hailed as an exciting holiday; when to know Thompson, who had written a magazine-article, was an honour and a privilege; and to see Brown, the author of the last romance in the flesh, and actually walking in the Park with his umbrella and Mrs. Brown, was an event remarkable, and to the end of life to be perfectly well remembered; when the women of this world were a thousand times more beautiful than those of the present time; and the houris of the theatres especially so ravishing and angelic, that to see them was to set the heart in motion, and to see them again was to struggle for half an hour previously at the door of the pit; when tailors called at a man's lodgings to dazzle him with cards of fancy-waistcoats; when it seemed necessary to purchase a grand silver dressing-case, so as to be ready for the beard which was not yet born (as yearling brides provide lace caps, and work rich clothes, for the expected darling); when to ride in the Park on a ten-shilling hack seemed to be the height of fashionable enjoyment, and to splash your college tutor as you were driving down Regent Street in a hired cab the triumph[6] of satire; when the acme of pleasure seemed to be to meet Jones of Trinity at the Bedford, and to make an arrangement with him, and with King of Corpus (who was staying at the Colonnade), and Martin of Trinity Hall (who was with his family in Bloomsbury Square) to dine at the Piazza, go to the play and see Braham in "Fra Diavolo," and end the frolic evening by partaking of supper and a song at the Cave of Harmony.—It was in the days of my own youth then that I met one or two of the characters who are to figure in this history, and whom I must ask leave to accompany for a short while, and until, familiarised with the public, they can make their own way. As I recal them the roses bloom again, and the nightingales sing by the calm Bendemeer.

Going to the play then, and to the pit, as was the fashion in those honest[7] days, with some young fellows of my own age, having listened delighted to the most cheerful and brilliant of operas, and laughed enthusiastically at the farce, we became naturally hungry at twelve o'clock at night, and a desire for welsh-rabbits and good old glee-singing led us to the Cave of Harmony, then kept by the celebrated Hoskins, among whose friends we were proud to count.

We enjoyed such[8] intimacy with Mr. Hoskins that he never failed to greet

---

[6] triumph *E1*] delight and triumph *HM*
[7] honest *E1*] merry *P1 R*
[8] such *E1*] that *HM*

us with a kind nod; and John the waiter made room for us near the President of the convivial meeting. We knew the three admirable glee-singers, and many a time they partook of brandy-and-water at our expense. One of us gave his call dinner at Hoskins's, and a merry time we had of it. Where are you, O Hoskins, bird of the night? Do you warble your songs by Acheron, or troll your chorusses by the banks of black Avernus?

The goes of stout, the Chough and Crow, the welsh-rabbit, the Red-Cross Knight, the hot brandy-and-water (the brown the strong!) the Bloom is on the Rye (the bloom isn't on the Rye any more!) the song and the cup in a word passed round merrily, and I daresay the songs and bumpers were encored. It happened that there was a very small attendance at the Cave that night, and we were all more sociable and friendly because the company was select. The songs were chiefly of the sentimental class; such ditties were much in vogue at the time of which I speak.

There came into the Cave a gentleman with a lean brown face and long black mustachios, dressed in very loose clothes, and evidently a stranger to the place. At least he had not visited it for a long time. He was pointing out changes to a lad who was in his company; and calling for sherry-and-water, he listened to the music, and twirled his mustachios with great enthusiasm.

At the very first glimpse of me the boy jumped up from the table, bounded across the room, ran to me with his hands out, and blushing, said, "Don't you know me?"

It was little Newcome, my school-fellow, whom I had not seen for six years, grown a fine tall young stripling now, with the same bright blue eyes which I remembered when he was quite a little boy.

"What the deuce brings you here?" said I.

He laughed and looked roguish. "My father—that's my father—would come. He's just come back from India. He says all the wits used to come here,—Mr. Sheridan, Captain Morris, Colonel Hanger, Professor Porson. I told him your name, and that you used to be very kind to me when I first went to Smithfield. I've left now; I'm to have a private tutor. I say, I've got such a jolly poney! It's better fun than old Smiffle."

Here the whiskered gentleman, Newcome's father, pointing to a waiter to follow him with his glass of sherry-and-water, strode across the room twirling his mustachios, and came up to the table where we sate, making a salutation with his hat in a very stately and polite manner, so that Hoskins himself was, as it were, obliged to bow; the glee-singers murmured among themselves (their eyes rolling over their glasses towards one another as they sucked brandy-and-water), and that mischievous little wag, little Nadab the Improvisatore (who had just come in), began to mimick him, feeling his imaginary whiskers, after the manner of the stranger, and flapping about his pocket-handkerchief in the most ludicrous manner. Hoskins checked this ribaldry by sternly looking towards Nadab, and at the same time called upon the gents to give their orders, the waiter being in the room, and Mr. Bellew about to sing a song.

Newcome's father came up and held out his hand to me. I daresay I blushed, for I had been comparing him to the admirable Harley in the Critic, and had christened him Don Ferolo Whiskerandos.

He spoke in a voice exceedingly soft and pleasant, and with a cordiality so simple and sincere, that my laughter shrank away ashamed; and gave place to a feeling much more respectful and friendly. In youth, you see, one is touched by kindness. A man of the world may, of course, be grateful or not as he chooses.

"I have heard of your kindness, Sir," says he, "to my boy. And whoever is kind to him is kind to me. Will you allow me to sit down by you? and may I beg you to try my cheroots?" We were friends in a minute—young Newcome snuggling by my side, his father opposite, to whom, after a minute or two of conversation, I presented my three college friends.

"You have come here, gentlemen, to see the wits," says the Colonel. "Are there any celebrated persons in the room? I have been five-and-thirty years from home, and want to see all that is to be seen."

King of Corpus (who was an incorrigible wag) was on the point of pulling some dreadful long bow, and pointing out a half-dozen of people in the room, as R. and H. and L.,[9] &c., the most celebrated wits of that day: but I cut King's shins under the table, and got the fellow to hold his tongue.

"*Maxima debetur pueris,*" says Jones, (a fellow of very kind feeling, who has gone into the Church since,) and writing on his card to Hoskins hinted to him that a boy was in the room, and a gentleman, who was quite a green-horn: hence that the songs had better be carefully selected.

And so they were, A lady's school might have come in, and but for the smell of the cigars and brandy-and-water have taken no harm by what happened. Why should it not always be so? If there are any Caves of Harmony now, I warrant Messieurs the landlords, their interests would be better consulted by keeping their singers within bounds. The very greatest scamps like pretty songs, and are melted by them: so are honest people. It was worth a guinea to see the simple Colonel, and his delight at the music. He forgot all about the distinguished wits whom he had expected to see in his ravishment over the glees.

"I say, Clive: this is delightful. This is better than your aunt's concert with all the Squallinis, hey? I shall come here often. Landlord; may I venture to ask those gentlemen if they will take any refreshment? What are their names? (to one of his neighbours) I was scarcely allowed to hear any singing before I went out; except an oratorio, where I fell asleep: but this, by George, is as[1] fine as Incledon!" He became quite excited over his sherry-and-water—("I'm sorry to see you, gentlemen, drinking brandy-pawnee," says he. "It plays the deuce with our young men in India.") He joined in all the chorusses with an exceedingly sweet voice. He laughed at the Derby Ram so that it did you good to hear him: and when Hoskins sang (as he did admirably) the Old English Gentleman, and described, in measured cadence, the death of that venerable aristocrat, tears trickled down the honest[2] warrior's cheek, while he held out his hand to Hoskins and said, "Thank you, Sir, for that song; it is an honour to human nature." On which Hoskins began to cry too.

And now young Nadab having been cautioned, commenced one of those surprising feats of improvisation with which he used to charm audiences.

[9] R. and H. and L. *E1*] Rogers and Hook and Luttrel, *R*
[1] this, by George, is as *E1*] this must be quite as *HM*
[2] honest *E1*] [omitted] *P1*

He took us all off, and had rhymes pat about all the principal persons in the room; King's pins (which he wore very splendid), Martin's red waistcoat, &c. The Colonel was charmed with each feat, and joined delighted with the chorus—Ritolderolritolderol ritolderolderay, (*bis*).[3] And when coming to the Colonel himself, he burst out—

> "A military gent I see—and while his face I scan,
> I think you'll all agree with me—He came from Hindostan.
> And by his side sits laughing free—A youth with curly head,
> I think you'll all agree with me—that he was best in bed. Ritolderol," &c.

The Colonel laughed immensely at this sally, and clapped his son, young Clive, on the shoulder, "Hear what he says of you, Sir? Clive, best be off to bed, my boy—ho, ho! No, no. We know a trick worth two of that. 'We won't go home till morning, till daylight does appear.' Why should we? Why shouldn't my boy have innocent pleasure? I was allowed none when I was a young chap, and the severity was nearly the ruin of me. I must go and speak with that young man—the most astonishing thing I ever heard in my life. What's his name? Mr. Nadab? Mr. Nadab; Sir, you have delighted me. May I make so free as to ask you to come and dine with me to-morrow at six. Colonel Newcome, if you please, Nerot's Hotel, Clifford Street. I am always proud to make the acquaintance of men of genius, and you are one, or my name is not Newcome!"

"Sir, you do me Hhonour," says Mr. Nadab, pulling up his shirt-collars, "and perhaps the day will come when the world will do me justice,—may I put down your hhonoured name for my book of poems?"

"Of course, my dear Sir," says the enthusiastic Colonel, "I'll send them all over India. Put me down for six copies, and do me the favour to bring them to-morrow when you come to dinner."

And now Mr. Hoskins asking if any gentleman would volunteer a song, what was our amazement when the simple Colonel offered to sing himself, at which the room applauded vociferously; whilst methought poor Clive Newcome hung down his head, and blushed as red as a peony. I felt for the young lad, and thought what my own sensations would have been, if, in that place, my own uncle, Major Pendennis, had suddenly proposed to exert his lyrical powers.

The Colonel selected the ditty of "Wapping Old Stairs" (a ballad so sweet and touching that surely any English poet might be proud to be the father of it), and he sang this quaint and charming old song in an exceedingly pleasant voice, with flourishes and roulades in the old Incledon manner, which has pretty nearly passed away. The singer gave his heart and soul to the simple ballad, and delivered Molly's gentle appeal so pathetically that even the professional gentlemen hummed and buzzed a sincere applause; and some wags who were inclined to jeer at the beginning of the performance, clinked their glasses and rapped their sticks with quite a respectful enthusiasm. When the song was over, Clive held up his head too; after the shock of the first verse, looked round with surprise and pleasure in his eyes; and we, I need not say, backed our friend, delighted to see him come

---

[3] (*bis*). *E1*] ritolderolritolderol ritolderolderay. *HM*

out of his queer scrape so triumphantly. The Colonel bowed and smiled with very pleasant good nature at our plaudits. It was like Dr. Primrose preaching his sermon in the prison. There was something touching in the naïveté and kindness of the placid and simple gentleman.

Great Hoskins, placed on high, amidst the tuneful choir, was pleased to signify his approbation, and gave his guest's health in his usual dignified manner. "I am much obliged to you, Sir," says Mr. Hoskins; "the room ought to be much obliged to you: I drink your ealth and song, Sir;" and he bowed to the Colonel politely over his glass of brandy-and-water, of which he absorbed a little in his customer's honour. "I have not heard that song," he was kind enough to say, "better performed since Mr. Incledon sung it. He was a great singer, Sir, and I may say, in the words of our immortal Shakspere, that, take him for all in all, we shall not look upon his like again."

The Colonel blushed in his turn, and turning round to his boy with an arch smile, said, "I learnt it from Incledon. I used to slip out from Grey Friars to hear him, Heaven bless me, forty[4] years ago; and I used to be flogged afterwards, and served me right too. Lord! Lord! how the time passes!" He drank off his sherry-and-water, and fell back in his chair; we could see he was thinking about his youth—the golden time—the happy, the bright, the unforgotten. I was myself nearly two-and-twenty years of age at that period, and felt as old as, ay,[5] older than the Colonel.

Whilst he was singing his ballad, there had walked, or rather reeled, into the room, a gentleman in a military frock coat and duck trowsers of dubious hue, with whose name and person some of my readers are perhaps already acquainted. In fact it was my friend Captain Costigan, in his usual condition at this hour of the night.

Holding on by various tables, the Captain had sidled up without accident to himself or any of the jugs and glasses round about him, to the table where we sat, and had taken his place near the writer, his old acquaintance. He warbled the refrain of the Colonel's song, not inharmoniously; and saluted its[6] pathetic conclusion with a subdued hiccup, and a plentiful effusion of tears. "Bedad it is a beautiful song," says he, "and many a time I heard poor Harry Incledon sing it."

"He's a great character," whispered that unlucky King of Corpus to his neighbour the Colonel; "was a Captain in the army. We call him the General. Captain Costigan, will you take something to drink?"

"Bedad I will," says the Captain, "and I'll sing ye a song tu."

And having procured a glass of whiskey-and-water from the passing waiter, the poor old man, settling his face into a horrid[7] grin, and leering, as he was wont, when he gave what he called one of his prime songs, began his music.

The unlucky wretch, who scarcely knew what he was doing or saying, selected one of the most outrageous performances of his *répertoire,* fired off a tipsey howl by way of overture, and away he went. At the end of the

---

[4] forty *E1*] thirty *HM*
[5] as old as, ay,] as old, as ay, *E1*] as old, ay, *HM*
[6] its *E1*] his *R*
[7] a horrid *E1*] that horrid *HM*

second verse the Colonel started up, clapping on his hat, seizing his stick, and looking as ferocious as though he had been going to do battle with a Pindaree, "Silence!" he roared out.

"Hear, hear!" cried certain wags at a farther table. "Go on, Costigan!" said others.

"Go on!" cries the Colonel, in his high voice, trembling with anger. "Does any gentleman say 'Go on?' Does any man who has a wife and sisters, or children at home, say 'Go on' to such disgusting ribaldry as this? Do you dare, Sir, to call yourself a gentleman, and to say that you hold the king's commission, and to sit down amongst Christians and men of honour, and defile the ears of young boys with this wicked balderdash?"

"Why do you bring young boys here, old boy?" cries a voice of the malcontents.

"Why? Because I thought I was coming to a society of gentlemen," cried out the indignant Colonel. "Because I never could have believed that Englishmen could meet together and allow a man, and an old man, so to disgrace himself. For shame, you old wretch! Go home to your bed, you hoary old sinner! And for my part, I'm not sorry that my son should see, for once in his life, to what shame and degradation and dishonour, drunkenness and whiskey may bring a man. Never mind the change, Sir!—Curse the change!" says the Colonel, facing the amazed waiter. "Keep it till you see me in this place again; which will be never[8]—by George, never!" And shouldering his stick, and scowling round at the company of scared bacchanalians, the indignant gentleman stalked away, his boy after him.

Clive seemed rather shame-faced; but I fear the rest of the company looked still more foolish.

"*Aussi que diable venait-il faire dans cette galère?*" says King of Corpus to Jones of Trinity; and Jones gave a shrug of his shoulders, which were smarting, perhaps; for that uplifted cane of the Colonel's had somehow fallen on the back of every man in the room.

---

[8] be never *E1*] never be *HM*

THE EFFECT OF THE GENERAL'S SONG

Chapter II.

COLONEL NEWCOME'S WILD OATS.

S the young gentleman who has just[1] gone to bed is to be[2] the hero of the following pages, we had best[3] begin our account of him with his family history, which luckily is not very long.

When pig-tails still grew on the backs of the British gentry, and their wives wore cushions on their heads, over which they tied their own hair, and disguised it with powder and pomatum: when ministers went in their stars and orders to the House of Commons, and the orators of the Opposition attacked nightly the noble lord in the blue ribbon: when Mr. Washington was heading the American rebels with a courage, it must be confessed, worthy of a better cause: there came up to London out of a Northern county, Mr. Thomas Newcome, afterwards Thomas Newcome, Esq., and sheriff of London, afterwards Mr. Alderman Newcome, the founder of the family whose name has given the title to this history. It was but in the reign of George III. that Mr. Newcome first made his appearance in Cheapside; having made his entry into London on a waggon, which landed him and some bales of cloth, all his fortune, in Bishopsgate Street: though if it could be proved that the Normans wore pig-tails under William the Conqueror, and Mr. Washington fought against the English under King Richard in Palestine, I am sure some of the present Newcomes would pay the Heralds' Office handsomely, living, as they do, amongst the noblest of the land, and giving entertainments to none but the very highest nobility and élite of the fashionable and diplomatic world, as you may read any day in the newspapers. For though these Newcomes have got a pedigree from the College, which is printed in Budge's "Landed Aristocracy of Great Britain," and which proves that the Newcome of Cromwell's army, the Newcome who was among the last six who were hanged by Queen Mary for protestantism, were ancestors of this house; of which a member distinguished himself at Bosworth Field; and the founder slain by King Harold's side at Hastings had been surgeon-barber to King Edward the Confessor; yet, between ourselves, I think that

[1] who has just *E1*] just *HM*
[2] is to be *E1*] at such an untimely hour is *HM*
[3] we had best *E1*] let us *HM*

Sir Brian Newcome, of Newcome, does[4] not believe a word of the story, any more than the rest of the world does, although a number of his children bear names out of the Saxon Calendar.

Was Thomas Newcome a foundling—a workhouse child out of that village, which has now become a great manufacturing town, and which bears his name? Such[5] was the report set about at the last election, when Sir Brian, in the Conservative interest, contested the borough; and Mr. Yapp, the out-and-out Liberal candidate, had a picture of the old workhouse placarded over the town as the birth-place of the Newcomes; with placards ironically exciting freemen to vote for Newcome and *union*—Newcome and the *parish* interests, &c. Who cares for these local scandals? It matters very little to those who have the good fortune to be invited to Lady Ann Newcome's parties whether her beautiful daughters can trace their pedigrees no higher than to the alderman their grandfather; or whether, through the mythic[6] ancestral barber-surgeon, they hang on to the chin of Edward Confessor and King.

Thomas Newcome, who had been a weaver in his native village, brought the very best character for honesty, thrift, and ingenuity with him to London, where he was taken into the house of Hobson Brothers, cloth-factors; afterwards Hobson and Newcome. This fact may suffice to indicate Thomas Newcome's story. Like Whittington and many other London apprentices, he began poor and ended by marrying his master's daughter, and becoming sheriff and alderman of the City of London.

But it was only *en secondes noces* that he espoused the wealthy, and religious, and eminent (such was the word applied to certain professing Christians in those days) Sophia Alethea Hobson—a woman who, considerably older than Mr. Newcome, had the advantage of surviving him many years. Her mansion at Clapham was long the resort of the most favoured amongst the religious world. The most eloquent expounders, the most gifted missionaries, the most interesting converts from foreign islands, were to be found at her sumptuous table, spread with the produce of her magnificent gardens. Heaven indeed blessed those gardens with plenty, as many reverend gentlemen remarked; there were no finer grapes, peaches, or pine-apples, in all England. Mr. Whitfield himself christened her; and it was said generally in the City, and by her friends, that Miss Hobson's two christian names, Sophia and Alethea, were two Greek words, which, being interpreted, meant wisdom and truth. She, her villa and gardens, are now no more; but Sophia Terrace, Upper and Lower Alethea Road, and Hobson's Buildings, Square, &c., show, every quarter-day, that the ground sacred to her (and freehold) still bears plenteous fruit for the descendants of this eminent woman.

We are, however, advancing matters. When Thomas Newcome had been some time in London, he quitted the house of Hobson, finding an opening, though in a much smaller way, for himself. And no sooner did his business prosper, than he went down into the north, like a man, to a pretty girl whom he had left there, and whom he had promised to marry.

[4] does *E1*] could *P1 R*
[5] Such *E1*] That *HM*
[6] mythic *E1*] mystic *HM*

What seemed an imprudent match (for his wife had nothing but a pale face, that had grown older and paler with long waiting), turned out a very lucky one for Newcome. The whole country side was pleased to think of the prosperous London tradesman returning to keep his promise to the penniless girl whom he had loved in the days of his own poverty; the great country clothiers, who knew his prudence and honesty, gave him much of their business when he went back to London. Susan Newcome would have lived to be a rich woman had not fate ended her career, within a year after her marriage, when she died giving birth to a son.

Newcome had a nurse for the child, and a cottage at Clapham, hard by Mr. Hobson's house, where he had often walked in the garden of a Sunday, and been invited to sit down to take a glass of wine. Since he had left their service, the house had added a banking business, which was greatly helped by the Quakers and their religious connection, and Newcome keeping his account there, and gradually increasing his business, was held in very good esteem by his former employers, and invited sometimes to tea at the Hermitage; for which entertainments he did not in truth much care at first, being a City man, a good deal tired with his business during the day, and apt to go to sleep over the sermons, expoundings, and hymns, with which the gifted preachers, missionaries, &c., who were always at the Hermitage, used to wind up the evening before supper. Nor was he a supping man (in which case he would have found the parties pleasanter, for in Egypt itself there were not more savoury fleshpots than at Clapham); he was very moderate in his meals, of a bilious temperament, and, besides, obliged to be in town early in the morning, always setting off to walk an hour before the first coach.

But when his poor Susan died, Miss Hobson, by her father's demise, having now become a partner in the house, as well as heiress to the pious and childless Zachariah Hobson, her uncle; Mr. Newcome, with his little boy in his hand, met Miss Hobson as she was coming out of meeting one Sunday; and the child looked so pretty (Mr. N. was a very personable, fresh-coloured man, himself; he wore powder to the end, and top-boots and brass buttons, in his later days, after he had been sheriff—indeed, one of the finest specimens of the old London merchant), Miss Hobson, I say, invited him and little Tommy into the grounds of the Hermitage; did not quarrel with the innocent child for frisking about in the hay on the lawn, which lay basking in the Sabbath sunshine, and at the end of the visit gave him a large piece of pound-cake, a quantity of the finest hot-house grapes, and a tract in one syllable. Tommy was ill the next day; but on the next Sunday his father was at meeting.

He became very soon after this an awakened man; and the tittling and tattling, and the sneering and gossiping, all over Clapham, and the talk on 'Change, and the pokes in the waistcoat administered by the wags to Newcome, "Newcome, give you joy, my boy;" "Newcome, new partner in Hobson's;" "Newcome, just take in this paper to Hobson's, they'll do it, I warrant;" &c., &c.; and the groans of the Rev. Gideon Bawls, of the Rev. Athanasius O'Grady, that eminent convert from Popery, who, quarreling with each other, yea, striving one against another, had yet two sentiments in common, their love for Miss Hobson, their dread, their hatred of the worldly Newcome; all these squabbles and jokes, and pribbles and prabbles, look you, may be omitted. As gallantly as he had married[7] a woman without a penny, as gallantly as he had conquered his poverty and achieved his own independence, so bravely he went in and won the great City prize with a fortune of a quarter of a million. And every one of his old friends, and every honest-hearted fellow who likes to see shrewdness, and honesty, and courage, succeed, was glad of his good fortune, and said, "Newcome, my boy (or "Newcome, my buck," if they were old City cronies, and very familiar), I give you joy."

Of course Mr. Newcome might have gone into parliament: of course before the close of his life he might have been made a Baronet: but he eschewed honours senatorial or blood red hands. "It wouldn't do," with his good sense he said; "the Quaker connexion wouldn't like it." His wife never cared about being called Lady Newcome. To manage the great house of Hobson Brothers and Newcome; to attend to the interests of the enslaved negro; to awaken the benighted Hottentot to a sense of the truth; to convert Jews, Turks, Infidels, and Papists; to arouse the indifferent and often blasphemous mariner; to guide the washerwoman in the right way; to head all the public charities of her sect, and do a thousand of secret[8] kindnesses that none knew of; to answer myriads of letters, pension endless ministers, and supply their teeming wives with continuous baby-linen; to hear preachers daily bawling for hours, and listen untired on her knees after a long day's labour, while florid rhapsodists belaboured cushions above her with wearisome benedictions; all these things had this woman to do, and for near fourscore years she fought her fight womanfully: imperious but deserving to rule, hard but doing her duty, severe but charitable, and untiring in generosity as in labour: unforgiving in one instance—in that of her husband's eldest son, Thomas Newcome; the little boy who had played on the hay, and whom at first she had loved very sternly and fondly.

Mr. Thomas Newcome, the father of his wife's twin boys, the junior partner of the house of Hobson Brothers, & Co., lived several years after winning the great prize about which all his friends so congratulated him. But he was after all only the junior partner of the house. His wife was manager in Threadneedle Street and at home—when the clerical gentlemen prayed they importuned Heaven for that sainted woman a long time before they thought of asking any favour for her husband. The gardeners touched their hats, the clerks at the bank brought him the books, but they took their orders from her, not from him. I think he grew weary of the prayer-meetings, he yawned over the sufferings of the negroes, and wished the converted Jews at Jericho. About the time the French Emperor was meeting with his Russian reverses Mr. Newcome died: his mausoleum is in Clapham Church Yard, near the modest grave where his first wife reposes.

When his father married, Mr. Thomas Newcome, jun., and Sarah his nurse were transported from the cottage where they had lived in great comfort to the palace hard by, surrounded by lawns and gardens, pineries, graperies, aviaries, luxuries of all kinds. This paradise, five miles from the standard at Cornhill, was separated from the outer world by a thick hedge of tall trees, and an ivy-covered porter's-gate, through which they

---

[7] had married *E1*] had gone and married *HM*
[8] of secret *E1*] secret *R*

A SERIOUS PARADISE

who travelled to London on the top of the Clapham coach could only get a glimpse of the bliss within. It was a serious paradise. As you entered at the gate, gravity fell on you; and decorum wrapped you in a garment of starch. The butcher-boy who galloped his horse and cart madly about the adjoining lanes and common, whistled wild melodies (caught up in abominable play-house galleries), and joked with a hundred cook-maids, on passing that lodge fell into an undertaker's pace, and delivered his joints and sweet-breads silently at the servant's[9] entrance. The rooks in the elms cawed sermons at morning and evening; the peacocks walked demurely on the terraces; the guinea-fowls looked more quaker-like than those savoury-birds usually do. The lodge-keeper was serious, and a clerk at a neighbour-ing chapel. The pastors who entered at that gate, and greeted his comely wife and children, fed the little lambkins with tracts.[1] The head-gardener was a Scotch Calvinist, after the strictest order, only occupying himself with the melons and pines provisionally, and until the end of the world, which event he could prove by infallible calculations, was to come off in two or three years at farthest. Wherefore he asked should the butler brew strong ale to be drunken three years hence; or the housekeeper (a follower of Joanna Southcote), make provisions of fine linen and lay up stores of jams? On a Sunday (which good old Saxon word was scarcely known at the Her-mitage), the household marched away in separate couples or groups to at least half-a-dozen of religious edifices, each to sit under his or her favourite minister, the only man who went to Church being Thomas Newcome, ac-companied by Tommy his little son, and Sarah his nurse, who was I believe also his aunt, or at least his mother's first cousin. Tommy was taught hymns very soon after he could speak, appropriate to his tender age, pointing out to him the inevitable fate of wicked children, and giving him the earliest possible warning and description of the punishment of little sinners. He re-peated these poems to his step-mother after dinner, before a great, shining mahogany table, covered with grapes, pine-apples, plum-cake, port-wine, and Madeira, and surrounded by stout men in black, with baggy white

neckcloths, who took the little man between their knees, and questioned him as to his right understanding of the place whither naughty boys were bound. They patted his head with their fat hands if he said well, or rebuked him if he was bold as he often was.

Nurse Sarah or Aunt Sarah would have died had she remained many years in that stifling garden of Eden. She could not bear to part from the child whom her mistress and kinswoman had confided to her (the women had worked in the same room at Newcome's, and loved each other always, when Susan became a merchant's lady and Sarah her servant). She was nobody in the pompous new household but Master Tommy's nurse. The honest soul never mentioned her relationship to the boy's mother, nor indeed did Mr. Newcome acquaint his new family with that circumstance. The housekeeper called her an Erastian: Mrs. Newcome's own serious maid informed against her for telling Tommy stories of Lancashire witches and believing in the same. The black footman (Madam's maid and the butler were of course privately united) persecuted her with his addresses, and was even encouraged by his mistress, who thought of sending him as a missionary to the Niger. No little love, and fidelity, and constancy did honest Sarah show and use during the years she passed at the Hermitage, and until Tommy went to school. Her master, with many private prayers and entreaties, in which he passionately recalled his former wife's memory and affection, implored his friend to stay with him, and Tommy's fondness for her and artless caresses, and the scrapes he got into, and the howls he uttered over the hymns and catechisms which he was bidden to learn (by Rev. T. Clack, of Highbury College, his daily tutor, who was commissioned to spare not the rod neither to spoil the child), all these causes induced Sarah to remain with her young master until such time as he was sent to school.

Meanwhile an event of prodigious importance, a wonderment, a blessing and a delight, had happened at the Hermitage. About two years after Mrs. Newcome's marriage, the lady being then forty-three years of age, no less than two little cherubs appeared in the Clapham Paradise—the twins, Hobson Newcome and Brian Newcome, called after their uncle and late grandfather, whose name and rank they were destined to perpetuate. And now there was no reason why young Newcome should not go[2] to school. Old Mr. Hobson and his brother had been educated at that school of Grey Friars, of which mention has been made in former works: and to Grey Friars Thomas Newcome was accordingly sent, exchanging—O ye Gods! with what delight—the splendour of Clapham for the rough, plentiful fare of the place, blacking his master's shoes with perfect readiness, till he rose in the school, and the time came when he should have a fag of his own: tibbing out and receiving the penalty therefor: bartering a black eye, per bearer, against a bloody nose drawn at sight, with a schoolfellow, and shaking hands the next day; playing at cricket, hockey, prisoners' base, and football, according to the season, and gorging himself and friends with tarts when he had money (and of this he had plenty) to spend. I have seen

[2] reason why young Newcome should not go *E1*] objection why young Newcome should go *HM*

his name carved upon the Gown Boys' arch: but he was at school long before my time; his son showed me the name when we were boys together, in some year when George the Fourth was king.

The pleasures of this school-life were such to Tommy Newcome, that he did not care to go home for a holiday: and indeed, by insubordination and boisterousness; by playing tricks and breaking windows; by marauding upon the gardener's peaches and the housekeeper's jam; by upsetting his two little brothers in a go-cart (of which wanton and careless injury the present[3] Baronet's nose bears marks to this very[4] day);—by going to sleep during the sermons, and treating reverend gentlemen with levity, he drew down on himself the merited wrath of his stepmother; and many punishments in this present life, besides those of a future and much more durable kind, which the good lady did not fail to point out that he must undoubtedly inherit. His father, at Mrs. Newcome's instigation, certainly whipped Tommy for upsetting his little brothers in the go-cart; but upon being pressed to repeat the whipping for some other peccadillo performed soon after, Mr. Newcome refused at once, using a wicked, worldly expression, which well might shock any serious lady; saying, in fact, that he would be deed[5] if he beat the boy any more, and that he got flogging enough at school, in which opinion Master Tommy fully coincided.

The undaunted woman, his step-mother, was not to be made to forego her plans for the boy's reform by any such vulgar ribaldries; and Mr. Newcome being absent in the City on his business, and Tommy refractory as usual, she summoned the serious butler and the black footman (for the lashings of whose brethren she felt an unaffected pity) to operate together in the chastisement of this young criminal. But he dashed so furiously against the butler's shins as to draw blood from his comely limbs, and to

3 present *E1*] [omitted] *P1 R*
4 this very *E1*] his dying *P1 R*
5 deed *E1*] damned *HM*

cause that serious and overfed menial to limp and suffer for many days after; and seizing the decanter, he swore he would demolish blackey's ugly face with it; nay, he threatened to discharge it at Mrs. Newcome's own head before he would submit to the coercion which she desired her agents to administer.

High words took place between Mr. and Mrs. Newcome that night on the gentleman's return home from the City, and on his learning the events of the morning. It is to be feared he made use of further oaths, which hasty ejaculations need not be set down in this place; at any rate he behaved with spirit and manliness as master of the house, vowed that if any servant laid a hand on the child, he would thrash him first and then discharge him; and I daresay expressed himself with bitterness and regret, that he had married a wife who would not be obedient to her husband; and had entered a house of which he was not suffered to be the master. Friends were called in— the interference, the supplications, of the Clapham Clergy, some of whom dined constantly at the Hermitage, prevailed to allay this domestic quarrel, and no doubt the good sense of Mrs. Newcome, who though imperious, was yet not unkind; and, who excellent as she was, yet could be brought to own that she was sometimes in fault, induced her to make at least a temporary submission to the man whom she had placed at the head of her house, and whom it must be confessed she had vowed to love and honour. When Tommy fell ill of the scarlet fever, which afflicting event occurred presently after the above dispute, his own nurse, Sarah, could not have been more tender, watchful and affectionate, than his stepmother showed herself to be. She nursed him through his illness: allowed his food and medicine to be administered by no other hand; sat up with the boy through a night of his fever, and uttered not one single reproach to her husband (who watched with her) when the twins took the disease (from which we need not say they happily recovered), and though young Tommy, in his temporary delirium, mistaking her for nurse Sarah, addressed her as his dear Fat Sally—whereas[6] no whipping-post to which she ever would have tied him could have been leaner than Mrs. Newcome—and under this feverish delusion actually abused her to her face; calling her an old cat, an old Methodist, and jumping up in his little bed forgetful of his previous fancy, vowing that he would put on his clothes and run away to Sally. Sally was at her northern home by this time, with a liberal pension which Mr. Newcome gave her, and which his son and his son's son after him, through all their difficulties and distresses, always found means to pay.

What the boy threatened in his delirium he had thought of no doubt more than once in his solitary and unhappy holidays. A year after he actually ran away, not from school, but from home; and appeared one morning gaunt and hungry at Sarah's cottage two hundred miles away from Clapham, who housed the poor prodigal, and killed her calf for him— washed him, with many tears and kisses, and put him to bed and to sleep; from which slumber he was aroused by the appearance of his father, whose sure instinct, backed by Mrs. Newcome's own quick intelligence, had made

[6] whereas *E1*] though *HM*

him at once aware whither the young runaway had fled. The poor father came horsewhip in hand—he knew of no other law or means to maintain his authority—many and many a time had his own father, the old weaver, whose memory he loved and honoured, strapped and beaten him—seeing this instrument in the parent's hand, as Mr. Newcome thrust out the weeping trembling Sarah and closed the door upon her, Tommy, scared out of a sweet sleep and a delightful dream of cricket, knew his fate; and getting up out of bed received his punishment without a word. Very likely the father suffered more than the child, for when the punishment was over, the little man, yet trembling and quivering with the pain, held out his little bleeding hand and said, "I can—I can take it from you, Sir;" saying which his face flushed, and his eyes filled, for the first time—whereupon the father burst into a passion of tears, and embraced the boy and kissed him, besought and prayed him to be rebellious no more—flung the whip away from him and swore, come what would, he would never strike him again. The quarrel was the means of a great and happy reconciliation. The three dined together in Sarah's cottage. Perhaps the father would have liked to walk that evening in the lanes and fields where he had wandered as a young fellow: where he had first courted and first kissed the young girl he loved—poor child—who had waited for him so faithfully and fondly, who had passed so many a day of patient want and meek expectance to be repaid by such a scant holiday and brief fruition.

Mrs. Newcome never made the slightest allusion to Tom's absence after his return, but was quite gentle and affectionate with him, and that night read the parable of the Prodigal in a very low and quiet voice.

This however was only a temporary truce. War very soon broke out again between the impetuous lad and his rigid domineering mother-in-law. It was not that he was very bad, or she perhaps more stern than other ladies, but the two could not agree. The boy sulked and was miserable at home. He fell to drinking with the grooms in the stables. I think he went to Epsom races, and was discovered after that act of rebellion. Driving from a most interesting breakfast at Roehampton (where a delightful Hebrew convert had spoken, oh! so graciously!) Mrs. Newcome—in her state carriage, with her bay horses—met Tom, her son-in-law, in a tax-cart, excited by drink, and accompanied by all sorts of friends, male and female. John the black man was bidden to descend from the carriage and bring him to Mrs. Newcome. He came; his voice was thick with drink. He laughed wildly: he described a fight at which he had been present: it was not possible that such a castaway as this should continue in a house where her two little cherubs were growing up in innocence and grace.

The boy had a great fancy for India; and Orme's History, containing the exploits of Clive and Lawrence, was his favourite book of all in his father's library. Being offered a writership, he scouted the idea of a civil appointment, and would be contented with nothing but a uniform. A cavalry cadetship was procured for Thomas Newcome; and the young man's future career being thus determined, and his step-mother's unwilling consent procured, Mr. Newcome thought fit to send his son to a tutor for military instruction, and removed him from the London school, where in truth he had made but very little progress in the humaner letters. The lad was placed with a professor who prepared young men for the army, and received rather a better professional education than fell to the lot of most young soldiers of his day. He cultivated the mathematics and fortification with more assiduity than he had ever bestowed on Greek and Latin, and especially made such a progress in the French tongue as was very uncommon among the British youth his contemporaries.

In the study of this agreeable language, over which young Newcome spent a great deal of his time, he unluckily had some instructors who were destined to bring the poor lad into yet farther trouble at home. His tutor, an easy gentleman, lived at Blackheath, and, not far from thence, on the road to Woolwich, dwelt the little Chevalier de Blois, at whose house the young man much preferred to take his French lessons rather than to receive them under his tutor's own roof.

For the fact was that the little Chevalier de Blois had two pretty young daughters, with whom he had fled from his country along with thousands of French gentlemen at the period of revolution and emigration. He was a cadet of a very ancient family, and his brother, the Marquis de Blois, was a fugitive like himself, but with the army of the princes on the Rhine, or with his exiled sovereign at Mittau. The chevalier had seen the wars of the great Frederic: what man could be found better to teach young Newcome the French language, and the art military? It was surprising with what assiduity he pursued his studies. Mademoiselle Léonore, the chevalier's daughter, would carry on her little industry very undisturbedly in the same parlour with her father and his pupil. She painted card-racks; laboured at embroidery; was ready to employ her quick little brain or fingers in any way by which she could find means to add a few shillings to the scanty store on which this exiled family supported themselves in their day of misfortune. I suppose the chevalier was not in the least unquiet about her, because she was promised in marriage to the Comte de Florac, also of the emigration—a distinguished officer like the chevalier,—than whom he was a year older, and, at the time of which we speak, engaged in London in giving private lessons on the fiddle. Sometimes on a Sunday he would walk to Blackheath with that instrument in his hand, and pay his court to his young fiancée, and talk over happier days with his old companion in arms. Tom Newcome took no French lessons on a Sunday. He passed that day at Clapham generally, where, strange to say, he never said a word about Mademoiselle de Blois.

What happens when two young folks of eighteen, handsome and ardent, generous and impetuous, alone in the world, or without strong affections to bind them elsewhere,—what happens when they meet daily over French dictionaries, embroidery frames, or indeed upon any business whatever? No doubt Mademoiselle Léonore was a young lady perfectly *bien élevée*, and ready as every well elevated young Frenchwoman should be, to accept a husband of her parents' choosing; but while the elderly M. de Florac was fiddling in London, there was that handsome young Tom Newcome ever present at Blackheath. To make a long matter short, Tom declared his passion, and was for marrying Léonore off-hand, if she would but come with him to the little Catholic chapel at Woolwich. Why should they not go out to India together and be happy ever after?

The innocent little amour may have been several months in transaction, and was discovered by Mrs. Newcome, whose keen spectacles nothing could escape. It chanced that she drove to Blackheath to Tom's tutor's. Tom was absent taking his French and drawing lessons of M. de Blois. Thither Tom's step-mother followed him, and found the young man sure enough with his instructor over his books and plans of fortification. Mademoiselle and her card-screens were in the room, but behind those screens she could not hide her blushes and confusion from Mrs. Newcome's sharp glances. In one moment the banker's wife saw the whole affair;—the whole mystery which had been passing for months under poor M. de Blois' nose, without his having the least notion of the truth.

Mrs. Newcome said she wanted her son to return home with her upon private affairs; and before they had reached the Hermitage a fine battle had ensued between them. His mother had charged him with being a wretch and a monster, and he had replied fiercely, denying the accusation with scorn, and announcing his wish instantly to marry the most virtuous, the most beautiful of her sex. To marry a papist! This was all that was wanted to make poor Tom's cup of bitterness run over. Mr. Newcome was called in, and the two elders passed a great part of the night in an assault upon the lad. He was grown too tall for the cane; but Mrs. Newcome thonged him with the lash of her indignation for many an hour that evening.

He was forbidden to enter M. de Blois' house, a prohibition at which the spirited young fellow snapped his fingers, and laughed in scorn. Nothing he swore but death should part him from the young lady. On the next day his father came to him alone and plied him with entreaties, but he was as obdurate as before. He would have her; nothing should prevent[7] him. He cocked his hat and walked out of the lodge gate, as his father, quite beaten by the young man's obstinacy, with haggard face and tearful eyes, went his own way into town. He was not very angry himself: in the course of their talk overnight the boy had spoken bravely and honestly, and Newcome could remember how in his own early life, he too[8] had courted and loved a young lass. It was Mrs. Newcome the father was afraid of. Who shall depict her wrath at the idea that a child of her house was about to marry a popish girl?

So young Newcome went his way to Blackheath, bent upon falling straightway down upon his knees before Léonore, and having the chevalier's blessing. That old fiddler in London scarcely seemed to him to be an obstacle: it seemed monstrous that a young creature should be given away to a man older than her own father. He did not know the law of honour, as it obtained amongst French gentlemen of those days, or how religiously their daughters were bound by it.

But Mrs. Newcome had been beforehand with him, and had visited the Chevalier de Blois almost at cock-crow. She charged him insolently with

7 should prevent *E1*] could part her from *HM*
8 too *E1*] [absent] *HM*

being privy to the attachment between the young people; pursued him with vulgar rebukes about beggary, popery, and French adventurers. Her husband had to make a very contrite apology afterwards for the language which his wife had thought fit to employ. *"You* forbid me," said the Chevalier, "you forbid Mademoiselle de Blois to marry your son, Mr. Thomas! No, Madam, she comes of a race which is not accustomed to ally itself with persons of your class; and is promised to a gentleman whose ancestors were dukes and peers when Mr. Newcome's were blacking shoes!" Instead of finding his pretty blushing girl on arriving at Woolwich, poor Tom only found his French master, livid with rage and quivering under his *ailes de pigeon.* We pass over the scenes that followed; the young man's passionate entreaties, and fury and despair. In his own defence, and to prove his honour to the world, M. de Blois determined that his daughter should instantly marry the Count. The poor girl yielded without a word, as became her; and, it was with this marriage effected almost before his eyes, and frantic with wrath and despair, that young Newcome embarked for India, and quitted the parents whom he was never more to see.

Tom's name was no more mentioned at Clapham. His letters to his father were written to the City; very pleasant they were, and comforting to the father's heart. He sent Tom liberal private remittances to India, until the boy wrote to say that he wanted no more. Mr. Newcome would have liked to leave Tom all his private fortune, for the twins were only too well cared for; but he dared not on account of his terror of Sophia Alethea, his wife; and he died, and poor Tom was only secretly forgiven.

Chapter III.

COLONEL NEWCOME'S LETTER-BOX.

I.

ITH the most heartfelt joy, my dear Major, I take[1] up my pen to announce to you the happy arrival of the Ram Chunder, and the *dearest and handsomest* little boy who, I am sure, ever came from India. Little Clive is in *perfect health.* He speaks English *wonderfully* well. He cried when he parted from Mr. Sneid, the supercargo, who most kindly brought him from Southampton in a postchaise, but these tears in childhood are *of very brief duration!* The voyage, Mr. Sneid states, was most favourable, occupying only four months and eleven days. How different from that more lengthened and dangerous passage of eight months, and almost perpetual seasickness, in which my poor dear sister Emma went to Bengal, to become the wife of the best of husbands and the mother of the dearest of little boys, and to enjoy these inestimable blessings for so brief an interval! She has quitted this wicked and wretched world for one where all is peace. The misery and ill-treatment which she endured from Captain Casey,[2] her first odious husband, were, I am sure, amply repaid, my dear Colonel, by your subsequent affection. If the most sumptuous dresses which London, even Paris, could supply, jewellery the most costly, and elegant lace, and *everything lovely and fashionable* could content a woman, these, I am sure, during the last four years of her life, the poor girl had. Of what avail are they when this scene of vanity is closed?

"Mr. Sneid announces that the passage was most favourable. They stayed a week at the Cape, and three days at St. Helena, where they visited Bonaparte's tomb, (another instance of the vanity of all things!) and their voyage was enlivened off Ascension by the taking of some delicious turtle!

[1] WITH the most heartfelt joy, my dear Major, I take *E1*] "MY DEAR MAJOR—I most joyfully take *HM*
[2] Casey *E1*] Closky *HM*

"You may be sure that *the most liberal* sum which you have placed to my credit with the Messrs. Hobson & Co., shall be faithfully expended on my dear little charge. Mrs. Newcome can scarcely be called his grandmamma, I suppose; and I daresay her methodistical ladyship will not care to see the daughters and grandson of a clergyman of the Church of England! My brother Charles took leave to wait upon her when he presented your last *most generous* bill at the bank. She received him *most rudely*, and said a fool and his money are soon parted; and when Charles said, 'Madam, I am the brother of the late Mrs. Major[3] Newcome.' 'Sir,' says she, 'I judge nobody; but from all accounts, you are the brother of a very vain, idle, thoughtless, extravagant woman; and Thomas Newcome was as foolish about his wife as about his money.' Of course, unless Mrs. N. writes to invite dear Clive, I shall not think of sending him to Clapham.

"It is such hot weather that I cannot wear the *beautiful shawl* you have sent me, and shall keep it *in lavender* till next winter! My brother, who thanks you for your continuous bounty, will write next month, and report progress as to his dear pupil. Clive will add a postscript of his own, and I am, my dear Major,[4] with a thousand thanks for your kindness to me,

"Your grateful and affectionate,
"MARTHA HONEYMAN."

In a round hand and on lines ruled with pencil:—

"Dearest Papa i am very well i hope you are Very Well. Mr. Sneed brought me in a postchaise i like Mr. Sneed very much. i like Aunt Martha i like Hannah. There are no ships here i am your affectionate son Clive Newcome."

II.

"RUE ST. DOMINIQUE ST. GERMAIN, PARIS, *Nov.* 15, 1820.

"LONG separated from the country which was the home of my youth, I carried from her tender recollections, and bear her always a lively gratitude. The Heaven has placed me in a position very different from that in which I knew you. I have been the mother of many children. My husband has recovered a portion of the property which the Revolution tore from us; and France, in returning to its legitimate sovereign, received once more the nobility which accompanied his august house into exile. We, however, preceded his Majesty, more happy than many of our companions. Believing farther resistance to be useless; dazzled, perhaps, by the brilliancy of that genius which restored order, submitted Europe, and governed France; M. de Florac, in the first days, was reconciled to the Conqueror of Marengo and Austerlitz, and held a position in his Imperial Court. This submission, at first attributed to infidelity, has subsequently been pardoned to my husband. His sufferings during the Hundred Days made to pardon his adhesion to him who was Emperor. My husband is now an old man.

---

[3] Major *E1*] Colonel *HM*
[4] Major *E1*] Colonel *HM*

He was of the disastrous campaign of Moscow, as one of the chamberlains of Napoleon. Withdrawn from the world he gives his time to his feeble health—to his family—to Heaven.

"I have not forgotten a time before those days, when, according to promises given by my father, I became the wife of M. de Florac. Sometimes I have heard of your career. One of my parents, M. de F., who took service in the English India, has entertained me of you; he informed me how yet a young man you won laurels at Argom and Bhartpour; how you escaped to death at Laswari. I have followed them, Sir, on the map. I have taken part in your victories[5] and your glory. Ah! I am not so cold, but my heart has trembled for your dangers;—not so aged, but I remember the young man who learned from the pupil of Frederic the first rudiments of war. Your great heart, your love of truth, your courage were your own. None had to teach you those qualities, of which a good God had endowed you. My good father is dead since many years. He, too, was permitted to see France before to die.

"I have read in the English journals not only that you are married, but that you have a son. Permit me to send to your wife, to your child, these accompanying tokens of an old friendship. I have seen that Mistress Newcome was widow, and am not sorry of it. My friend, I hope there was not that difference of age between your wife and you that I have known in other unions. I pray the good God to bless yours. I hold you always in my memory. As I write the past comes back to me. I see a noble young man, who has a soft voice, and brown eyes. I see the Thames, and the smiling plains of Blackheath. I listen and pray at my chamber-door as my father talks to you in our little cabinet of studies. I look from my window, and see you depart.

"My sons are men: one follows the profession of arms, one has embraced the ecclesiastical state; my daughter is herself a mother. I remember this was your birthday; I have made myself a little fête in celebrating it, after how many years of absence, of silence!

"COMTESSE DE FLORAC.
"(*Née L. de Blois*)."

III.

"MY DEAR THOMAS,—Mr. Sneid, supercargo of the 'Ramchunder,' East Indiaman, handed over to us yesterday your letter, and, to-day, I have purchased three thousand three hundred and twenty-three pounds 6 and 8d. three per cent. Consols, in our joint names (H. and B. Newcome), held for your little boy. Mr. S. gives a very favourable account of the little man, and left him in perfect health two days since, at the house of his aunt, Miss Honeyman. We have placed £200 to that lady's credit, at your desire.

"Lady Ann is charmed with the present which she received yesterday, and says the white shawl is a great deal too handsome. My mother is also greatly pleased with hers, and has forwarded, by the coach to Brighton, to-

---

5 victories *E1*] victory *HM*

day, a packet of books, tracts, &c., suited for his tender age, for your little boy. She heard of you lately from the Rev. T. Sweatenham, on his return from India. He spoke of your kindness, and of the hospitable manner in which you had received him at your house, and alluded to you in a very handsome way in the course of the thanksgiving that evening. I daresay my mother will ask your little boy to the Hermitage; and when we have a house of our own, I am sure Ann and I will be very happy to see him. Yours affectionately,

"B. NEWCOME.

"MAJOR NEWCOME."

IV.

"MY DEAR COLONEL,—Did I not know the generosity of your heart, and the bountiful means which Heaven has put at your disposal in order to gratify that noble disposition; were I not certain that the small sum I required will permanently place me beyond the reach of the difficulties of life, and will infallibly be repaid before six months are over, believe me I never would have ventured upon that bold step which our friendship (carried on epistolarily as it has been), our relationship, and your admirable disposition, have induced me to venture to take.

"That elegant and commodious chapel, known as Lady Whittlesea's, Denmark Street, May Fair, being for sale, I have determined on venturing my all in its acquisition, and in laying, as I hope, the foundation of a competence for myself and excellent sister. What is a lodging-house at Brighton but an uncertain maintenance? The mariner on the sea before those cliffs is no more sure of wind and wave, or of fish to his laborious net, than the Brighton houseowner (bred in affluence, she may have been, and used to unremitting plenty) to the support of the casual travellers who visit the city. On one day they come in shoals, it is true, but where are they on the next? For many months my poor sister's first floor was a desert, until occupied by your noble little boy, my nephew and pupil. Clive is everything that a father's, an uncle's (who loves him as a father), a pastor's, a teacher's, affections could desire. He is not one of those premature geniuses whose much vaunted infantine talents disappear along with adolescence; he is not, I frankly own, more advanced in his classical and mathematical studies than some children even younger than himself, but he has acquired the rudiments of health; he has laid in a store of honesty and good-humour, which are not less likely to advance him in life than mere science and language, than the *as in præsenti,* or the *pons asinorum.*

"But I forget, in thinking of my dear little friend and pupil, that the subject of this letter—namely, the acquisition of the proprietary chapel[6] to which I have alluded, and the hopes, nay, certainty of a fortune, if aught below is certain, which that acquisition holds out. What is a curacy, but a synonym for starvation? If we accuse the Eremites of old of wasting their lives in unprofitable wildernesses, what shall we say to many a hermit of protestant, and so-called civilised times, who hides his head in a solitude

6 chapel *E1*] church *HM*

in Yorkshire, and buries[7] his probably fine talents in a Lincolnshire fen? Have I genius? Am I blessed with gifts of eloquence to thrill and soothe, to arouse the sluggish, to terrify the sinful, to cheer and convince the timid, to lead the blind groping in darkness, and to trample the audacious sceptic in the dust? My own conscience, besides a hundred testimonials from places of popular, most popular worship, from revered prelates, from distinguished clergy, tell me I have these gifts. A voice within me cries 'Go forth, Charles Honeyman, fight the good fight; wipe the tears of the repentant sinner; sing of hope to the agonised criminal; whisper courage, brother, courage, at the ghastly death-bed, and strike down the infidel with the lance of evidence and the shield of reason!' In a pecuniary point of view I am confident, nay, the calculations may be established as irresistibly as an algebraic equation, that I can realise, as incumbent of Lady Whittlesea's chapel, the sum of *not less* than one thousand pounds per annum. Such a sum, with economy (and without it what sum were sufficient?) will enable me to provide amply for my wants, to discharge my obligations to you, to my sister, and some other creditors, very, very unlike you, and to place Miss Honeyman in a home more worthy of her than that which she now occupies, only to vacate it at the beck of every passing stranger!

"My sister does not disapprove of my plan, into which enter some modifications which I have not, as yet, submitted to her, being anxious at first that they should be sanctioned by you. From the income of the Whittlesea chapel I propose to allow Miss Honeyman the sum of two hundred pounds per annum, *paid quarterly*. This, with her private property, which she has kept more thriftily than her unfortunate and confiding brother guarded his (for whenever I had a guinea a tale of distress would melt it into half a sovereign), will enable Miss Honeyman to live in a way becoming my father's daughter.

"Comforted with this provision as my sister will be, I would suggest that our dearest young Clive should be transferred from her petticoat government, and given up to the care of his affectionate uncle and tutor. His present allowance will most liberally suffice for his expenses, board, lodging, and education while under my roof, and I shall be able to exert a paternal, a pastoral influence over his studies, his conduct, and his *highest welfare*, which I cannot so conveniently exercise at Brighton, where I am but Miss Honeyman's stipendiary, and where I often have to submit in cases where I know, for dearest Clive's own welfare, it is I, and not my sister, should be paramount.

"I have given then to a friend, the Rev. Marcus Flather, a draft for two hundred and fifty pounds sterling, drawn upon you at your agent's in Calcutta, which sum will go in liquidation of dear Clive's first year's board with me, or, upon my word of honour as a gentleman and clergyman, shall be paid back at three months after sight, if you will draw upon me. As I never, no, were it my last penny in the world,—would dishonour your draft,—I implore you, my dear Colonel, not to refuse mine. My credit in

---

[7] and buries *E1*] who buries *HM*

this city where credit is *everything,* and the awful future so little thought of, my engagements to Mr. Flather, my own prospects in life, and the

comfort of my dear sister's declining years, all—all depend upon this bold, this *eventful* measure.   My ruin or my earthly happiness lies entirely in your hands.   Can I doubt which way your kind heart will lead you, and that you will come to the aid of your affectionate brother-in-law,

"CHARLES HONEYMAN.

"Our little Clive has been to London on a visit to his uncle's and to the Hermitage, Clapham, to pay his duty to his step-grandmother, the wealthy Mrs. Newcome. I pass over words disparaging of myself which the child in his artless prattle subsequently narrated. She was very gracious to *him,* and presented him with a five pound note, a copy of Kirk White's Poems, and a work called Little Henry and his Bearer, relating to India, and the excellent Catechism of our Church. Clive is full of humour, and I enclose you a rude scrap representing the bishopess of Clapham, as she is called,—the other figure is a rude though entertaining sketch of some other droll personage.

"LIEUTENANT-COLONEL NEWCOME, &c."

V.

"MY DEAR COLONEL,—The Rev. Marcus Flather has just written me a letter at which I am greatly shocked and perplexed, informing me that my brother Charles has given him a draft upon you for two hundred and fifty pounds, when goodness knows it is not you but we who are many, many hundred pounds debtors to you. Charles has explained that he drew the bill at your desire, that you wrote to say you would be glad to serve him in any way, and that the money is wanted to make his fortune. Yet I don't know, poor Charles is always going to make his fortune and has never done it. That school which he bought, and for which you and me between us paid the purchase-money, turned out no good, and the only pupils left at the end of the first half-year were two woolly-headed poor little mulattos, whose father was in gaol at St. Kitt's, and whom I kept actually in my own second floor back-room whilst the lawyers were settling things, and Charles was away in France, and until my dearest little Clive came to live with me.

"Then as he was too small for a great school, I thought Clive could not do better than stay with his old aunt and have his uncle Charles for a tutor, who is one of the finest scholars in the world. I wish you could hear him in the pulpit. His delivery is grander and more impressive than any divine now in England. His sermons you have subscribed for, and likewise his book of elegant poems, which are pronounced to be *very fine.*

"When he returned from Calais, and those horrid lawers had left off worritting him, I thought as his frame was much shattered and he was too weak to take a curacy, that he could not do better than become Clive's tutor, and agreed to pay him out of your handsome donation of 250*l.* for Clive, a sum of one hundred pounds per year, so that when the board of the two and Clive's clothing are taken into consideration, I think you will see that no great profit is left to Miss Martha Honeyman.

"Charles talks to me of his new church in London, and of making me some grand allowance. The poor boy is very affectionate, and always building castles in the air, and of having Clive to live with him in London, *now this musn't be and I won't hear of it.* Charles is too kind to be a schoolmaster, and Master Clive laughs at him. It was only the other day, after his return from his grandmamma's, regarding which I wrote you, per Burrampooter, the 23rd ult., that I found a picture of Mrs. Newcome and Charles too, and of both their spectacles, quite like. I put it away, but some rogue, I suppose, has stolen it. He has done me and Hannah too. Mr. Speck, the artist, laughed and took it home, and says he is a wonder at drawing.

"Instead then of allowing Clive to go with Charles to London next month where my brother is bent on going, I shall send Clivey to Dr. Timpany's school, Marine-parade, of which I hear the best account, but I hope you will think of soon sending him to a great school. My father always said it was the best place for boys, and I have a brother to whom my poor mother spared the rod, and who, I fear, has turned out but a spoilt child.

"I am, dear Colonel, your most faithful servant,

"MARTHA HONEYMAN.

"LIEUTENANT-COLONEL NEWCOME, C.B."

VI.

"MY DEAR BROTHER,—I hasten to inform you of a calamity which, though it might be looked for in the course of nature, has occasioned deep grief not only in our family but in this city. This morning, at half-past four o'clock, our beloved and respected mother, Sophia Alethea Newcome expired, at the advanced age of eighty-three years. On the night of Tuesday-Wednesday, the 12-13th, having been engaged reading and writing in her library until a late hour, and having dismissed the servants, who she never would allow to sit up for her, as well as my brother and his wife, who always are in the habit of retiring early, Mrs. Newcome extinguished the lamps, took a bed-chamber candle to return to her room, and must have fallen on the landing, where she was discovered by the maids, sitting with her head reclining against the balustrades, and endeavouring to staunch a wound in her forehead, which was bleeding profusely, having struck in a fall against the stone step of the stair.

"When Mrs. Newcome was found she was speechless, but still sensible, and medical aid being sent for, she was carried to bed. Mr. Newcome and Lady Ann both hurried to her apartment, and she knew them, and took the hands of each, but paralysis had probably ensued in consequence of the shock of the fall; nor was her voice ever heard, except in inarticulate moanings, since the hour on the previous evening, when she gave them her blessing, and bade them good night. Thus perished this good and excellent woman, the truest Christian, the most charitable friend to the poor and needful, the head of this great house of business, the best and most affectionate of mothers.

"The contents of her will have long been known to us, and that document was dated one month after our lamented father's death. Mr. Thomas Newcome's property being divided equally amongst his three sons, the property of his second wife naturally devolves upon her own issue, my brother Brian and myself. There are very heavy legacies to servants and to charitable and religious institutions, of which, in life, she was the munificent patroness; and I regret, my dear brother, that no memorial to you should have been left by my mother, because she often spoke of you latterly in terms of affection, and on the very day on which she died, commenced a letter to your little boy, which was left unfinished on the library-table. My brother said that on that same day, at breakfast, she pointed to a volume of Orme's Hindostan, the book, she said, which set poor dear Tom wild to go to India. I know you will be pleased to hear of these proofs of returning good-will and affection in one who often spoke latterly of her early regard for you. I have no more time, under the weight of business which this present affliction entails, than to say that I am yours, dear brother, very sincerely,

"H. NEWCOME.

"LIEUTENANT-COLONEL NEWCOME, &c."

Chapter IV.

IN WHICH THE AUTHOR AND THE HERO RESUME THEIR ACQUAINTANCE.

F WE are to narrate the youthful history not only of the hero of this tale, but of the hero's father, we shall never have done with nursery biography. A gentleman's grandmother may delight in fond recapitulation of her darling's boyish frolics and early genius; but shall we weary our kind readers by this infantile prattle, and set down the revered British public for an old woman? Only to two or three persons in all the world are the reminiscences of a man's early youth interesting—to the parent who nursed him, to the fond wife or child mayhap afterwards who loves him,—to himself always and supremely whatever may be his actual prosperity or ill fortune, his present age, illness, difficulties, renown, or disappointments, the dawn of his life still shines brightly for him; the early griefs and delights and attachments remain with him ever faithful and dear. I shall ask leave to say, regarding the juvenile biography of Mr. Clive Newcome, of whose history I am the Chronicler, only so much as is sufficient to account for some peculiarities of his character, and for his subsequent career in the world.

Although we were schoolfellows, my acquaintance with young Newcome at the seat of learning where we first met was very brief and casual. He had the advantage of being six years the junior of his present biographer, and such a difference of age between lads at a public school puts intimacy out of the question—a junior ensign being no more familiar with the commander-in-chief at the Horse-Guards; or a barrister on his first circuit with my Lord Chief Justice on the bench, than the newly-breeched infant in the Petties with a senior boy in a tailed coat. As we[1] "knew each other at home," as our school phrase was, and our families being somewhat acquainted,[2] Newcome's maternal uncle, the Rev. Charles Honeyman (the highly-gifted preacher, and incumbent of Lady Whittlesea's chapel, Denmark Street, May Fair), when he brought the child after the Christmas vacation of 182—

[1] As we *E1*] We *R*
[2] being somewhat acquainted, *E1*] were somewhat acquainted: *R*

to the Grey Friars' school, recommended him in a neat complimentary speech to my superintendence and protection. My uncle, Major Pendennis, had for a while a seat in the chapel of this sweet and popular preacher, and professed, as a great number of persons of fashion did, a great admiration for him—an admiration which I shared in my early youth, but which has been modified by maturer judgment.

Mr. Honeyman told me, with an air of deep respect, that his young nephew's father, Colonel Thomas Newcome, C.B., was a most gallant and distinguished officer in the Bengal establishment of the Honourable East India Company; and that his uncles, the Colonel's half-brothers, were the eminent bankers, heads of the firm of Hobson Brothers & Newcome, Hobson Newcome, Esquire, Brianstone Square, and Marble Head, Sussex, and Sir Brian Newcome, of Newcome, and Park Lane, "whom to name," says Mr. Honeyman, with the fluent eloquence with which he decorated the commonest circumstances of life, "is to designate two of the merchant princes of the wealthiest city the world has ever known; and one, if not two, of the leaders of that aristocracy which rallies round the throne of the most

elegant and refined of European sovereigns." I promised Mr. Honeyman to do what I could for the boy; and he proceeded to take leave of his little nephew in my presence in terms equally eloquent, pulling out a long and very slender green purse from which he extracted the sum of two and sixpence, which he presented to the child, who received the money with rather a queer twinkle in his blue eyes.

After that day's school, I met my little protégé in the neighbourhood of the pastry-cook's, regaling himself with raspberry tarts. "You must not spend all that money, Sir, which your uncle gave you," said I (having perhaps even at that early age a slightly satirical turn), "in tarts and gingerbeer."

The urchin rubbed the raspberry jam off his mouth, and said, "It don't matter, Sir, for I've got lots more."

"How much?" says the Grand Inquisitor: for the formula of interrogation used to be, when a new boy came to the school, "What's your name? Who's your father? and how much money have you got?"

The little fellow pulled such a handful of sovereigns out of his pocket as might have made the tallest scholar feel a pang of envy. "Uncle Hobson," says he, "gave me two; Aunt Hobson gave me one—no, Aunt Hobson gave me thirty shillings; Uncle Newcome gave me three pound; and Aunt Ann gave me one pound five; and Aunt Honeyman sent me ten shillings in a letter. And Ethel wanted to give me a pound, only I wouldn't have it, you know; because Ethel's younger than me, and I have plenty."

"And who is Ethel?" asks the senior boy, smiling at the artless youth's confessions.

"Ethel is my cousin," replies little Newcome; "Aunt Ann's daughter. There's Ethel and Alice, and Aunt Ann wanted the baby to be called Boadicea, only Uncle wouldn't; and there's Barnes and Egbert and little Alfred; only he don't count, he's quite a baby you know. Egbert and me was at school at Timpany's; he's going to Eton next half. He's older than me, but I can lick him."

"And how old is Egbert?" asks the smiling senior.

"Egbert's ten, and I'm nine, and Ethel's seven," replies the little chubby-faced hero, digging his hands deep into his trowser's pockets, and jingling all the sovereigns there. I advised him to let me be his banker; and, keeping one out of his many gold pieces, he handed over the others, on which he drew with great liberality till his whole stock was expended. The school-hours of the upper and under boys were different at that time; the little

fellows coming out of their hall half an hour before the Fifth and Sixth Forms; and many a time I used to find my little blue jacket in waiting, with his honest square face, and white hair, and bright blue eyes, and I knew that he was come to draw on his bank. Ere long one of the pretty blue eyes was shut up, and a fine black one substituted in its place. He had been engaged, it appeared, in a pugilistic encounter with a giant of his own Form, whom he had worsted in the combat. "Didn't I pitch into him, that's all?" says he in the elation of victory; and when I asked whence the quarrel arose, he stoutly informed me that "Wolf Minor, his opponent, had been bullying a little boy, and that he (the gigantic Newcome) wouldn't stand it."

So, being called away from the school, I said farewell and God bless you to the brave little man, who remained awhile at the Grey Friars, where his career and troubles had only just begun. Nor did we meet again until I was myself a young man occupying chambers in the Temple, where our rencontre took place in the manner already described.

Poor Costigan's outrageous behaviour had caused my meeting with my schoolfellow of early days to terminate so abruptly and unpleasantly, that I scarce expected to see Clive again, or at any rate to renew my acquaintance with the indignant East Indian warrior who had quitted our company in such a huff. Breakfast however was scarcely over in my chambers the next morning, when there came a knock at the outer door, and my clerk introduced, "Colonel Newcome and Mr. Newcome."

Perhaps the (joint) occupant of the chambers in Lamb Court, Temple, felt a little pang of shame at hearing the name of the visitors; for, if the truth must be told, I was engaged pretty much as I had been occupied on the night previous, and was smoking a cigar over the *Times* newspaper. How many young men in the temple smoke a cigar after breakfast as they read the *Times*? My friend and companion of those days, and all days, Mr. George Warrington, was employed with his short pipe, and was not in the least disconcerted at the appearance of the visitors, as he would not have been had the Archbishop of Canterbury stepped in.

Little Clive looked curiously about our queer premises, while the Colonel shook me cordially by the hand. No traces of yesterday's wrath were visible on his face, but a friendly smile lighted his honest[3] bronzed countenance, as he too looked round the old room with its dingy curtains and prints and book-cases, its litter of proof-sheets, blotted manuscripts, and books for review, empty sodawater bottles, cigar boxes, and what not.

"I went off in a flame of fire last night," says the Colonel, "and being cooled this morning, thought it but my duty to call on Mr. Pendennis and apologise for my abrupt behaviour. The conduct of that tipsy old Captain.—What is his name?—was so abominable, that I could not bear that Clive should be any longer in the same room with him, and I went off without saying a word of thanks or good night to my son's old friend. I owe you a shake of the hand for last night, Mr. Pendennis." And, so saying, he was kind enough to give me his hand a second time.

"And this is the abode of the Muses, is it, Sir?" our guest went on. "I know your writings very well. Clive here used to send me the *Pall Mall Gazette* every month."

"We took it at Smiffle, regular," says Clive. "Always patronise Grey Friars men." "Smiffle," it must be explained, is a fond abbreviation for Smithfield, near to which great mart of mutton and oxen, our school is situated, and old Cistercians, often playfully designate their place of education by the name of the neighbouring market.

"Clive sent me the *Gazette* every month; and I read your romance of Walter Lorraine in my boat as I was coming down the river to Calcutta."

"Have Pen's immortal productions made their appearance on board Bengalee Budgerows; and are their leaves floating on the yellow banks of Jumna?" asks Warrington, that sceptic, who respects no work of modern genius.

"I gave your book to Mrs. Timmins, at Calcutta," says the Colonel, simply. "I daresay you have heard of *her*. She is one of the most dashing women

[3] honest *E1*] [omitted] *R*

in all India. She was delighted with your work; and I can tell you it is not with every man's writing that Mrs. Timmins is pleased," he added, with a knowing air.

"It's capital!" broke in Clive. "I say, that part you know where Walter runs away with Neæra, and the General can't pursue them, though he has got the postchaise at the door, because Tim O'Toole has hidden his wooden-leg! By Jove, it's capital!—All the funny part.—I don't like the sentimental stuff, and suicide and that: and as for poetry, I hate poetry."

"Pen's is not first chop," says Warrington. "I am obliged to take the young man down from time to time, Colonel Newcome. Otherwise he would grow so conceited there would be no bearing him."

"I say?" says Clive.

"What were you about to remark?" asks Mr. Warrington, with an air of great interest.

"I say, Pendennis," continued the artless youth, "I thought you were a great swell. When we used to read about the grand parties in the *Pall Mall Gazette,* the fellows used to say you were at every one of them, and you see, I thought you must have chambers in the Albany and lots of horses to ride, and a valet and a groom, and a cab at the very least."

"Sir," says the Colonel, "I hope it is not your practice to measure and estimate gentlemen by such paltry standards as those. A man of letters follows the noblest calling which any man can pursue. I would rather be the author of a work of genius, than be Governor-General of India. I admire genius. I salute it wherever I meet it. I like my own profession better than any in the world, but then it is because I am suited to it. I couldn't write four lines in verse, no, not to save me from being shot. A man cannot have all the advantages of life. Who would not be poor if he could be sure of possessing genius, and winning fame and immortality, Sir? Think of Dr. Johnson, what a genius he had, and where did he live? In apartments that I daresay were no better than these, which I am sure, gentlemen, are most cheerful and pleasant," says the Colonel, thinking he had offended us. "One of the great pleasures and delights which I had proposed to myself on coming home was to be allowed to have the honour of meeting with men of learning and genius, with wits, poets, and historians, if I may be so fortunate; and of benefitting by their conversation. I left England too young to have that privilege. In my father's house money was thought of I fear rather than intellect: neither he nor I had the opportunities which I wish you to have; and I am surprised you should think of reflecting upon Mr. Pendennis's poverty, or of feeling any sentiment but respect and admiration when you enter the apartments of the poet and the literary man. I have never been in the rooms of a literary man before," the Colonel said, turning away from his son to us, "excuse me, is that—that paper really a proof-sheet?" We handed over to him that curiosity, smiling at the enthusiasm of the honest gentleman who could admire what to us was as unpalatable as a tart to a pastrycook.

Being with men of letters he thought proper to make his conversation entirely literary, and in the course of my subsequent more intimate acquaintance with him, though I knew he had distinguished himself in twenty actions, he never could be brought to talk of his military feats or experience, but passed them by, as if they were subjects utterly unworthy of notice.

I found he believed Dr. Johnson to be the greatest of men: the doctor's words were constantly in his mouth; and he never travelled without Boswell's Life. Besides these, he read Cæsar and Tacitus "with translations, Sir, with translations—I'm thankful that I kept *some* of my Latin from Grey Friars"—and he quoted sentences from the Latin Grammar, apropos of a hundred events of common life, and with perfect simplicity and satisfaction to himself. Besides the above-named books the "Spectator," "Don Quixote," and "Sir Charles Grandison," formed a part of his travelling library. "I read these, Sir," he used to say, "because I like to be in the company of gentlemen; and Sir Roger de Coverley, and Sir Charles Grandison, and Don Quixote are the finest gentlemen in the world." And when we asked him his opinion of Fielding,—

"'Tom Jones,' Sir; 'Joseph Andrews!' Sir," he cried, twirling his mustachios. "I read them when I was a boy, when I kept other bad company, and did other low and disgraceful things, of which I'm ashamed now. Sir, in my father's library I happened to fall in with those books; and I read them in secret, just as I used to go in private and drink beer, and fight cocks, and smoke pipes with Jack and Tom, the grooms in the stables. Mrs. Newcome found me, I recollect, with one of those books; and thinking it might be by Mrs. Hannah More, or some of that sort, for it was a grave-looking volume: and though I wouldn't lie about that or anything else—never did, Sir; never, before Heaven, have I told more than three lies in my life—I kept my own council;—I say, she took it herself to read one evening; and read on gravely—for she had no more idea of a joke than I have of Hebrew—until she came to the part about Lady B— and Joseph Andrews; and then she shut the book, Sir; and you should have seen the look she gave me! I own I burst out a laughing, for I was a wild young

rebel, Sir. But she was in the right, Sir, and I was in the wrong. A book, Sir, that tells the story of a parcel of servants, of a pack of footmen and ladies' maids fuddling in ale-houses! Do you suppose I want to know what my kitmutgars and cousomahs are doing? I am as little proud as any man in the world: but there must be distinction, Sir; and as it is my lot and Clive's lot to be a gentleman, I won't sit in the kitchen and boose in the servants' hall. As for that Tom Jones—that fellow that sells himself, Sir— by Heavens, my blood boils when I think of him! I wouldn't sit down in the same room with such a fellow, Sir. If he came in at that door, I would say, 'How dare you, you hireling ruffian, to sully with your presence an apartment where my young friend and I are conversing together? where two gentlemen, I say, are taking their wine after dinner? How dare you, you degraded villain!' I don't mean you, Sir. I—I—I beg your pardon."

The Colonel was striding about the room in his white[4] garments, puffing his cigar fiercely anon, and then waving his yellow bandanna; and it was by the arrival of Larkins, my clerk, that his apostrophe to Tom Jones was interrupted; he, Larkins, taking care not to show his amazement, having been schooled not to show or feel surprise at anything he might see or hear in our chambers.

"What is it, Larkins?" said I. Larkins' other master had taken his leave some time before, having business which called him away, and leaving me with the honest Colonel, quite happy with his talk and cigar.

"It's Bretts' man," says Larkins.

I confounded Bretts' man and told the boy to bid him call again. Young Larkins came grinning back in a moment, and said,—

"Please, Sir, he says, his orders is not to go away without the money."

"Confound him, again," I cried. "Tell him I have no money in the house. He must come to-morrow."

As I spoke, Clive was looking in wonder, and the Colonel's countenance assumed an appearance of the most dolorous sympathy. Nevertheless, as with a great effort, he fell to talking about Tom Jones again, and continued:

"No, Sir, I have no words to express my indignation against such a fellow as Tom Jones. But I forgot that I need not speak. The great and good Dr. Johnson has settled that question. You remember what he said to Mr. Boswell about Fielding?"

"And yet Gibbon praises him, colonel," said the Colonel's interlocutor, "and that is no small praise. He says that Mr. Fielding was of the family that drew its origin from the Counts of Hapsburg; but ——"

"Gibbon! Gibbon was an infidel; and I would not give the end of this cigar for such a man's opinion. If Mr. Fielding was a gentleman by birth, he ought to have known better; and so much the worse for him that he did not. But what am I talking of, wasting your valuable time? No more smoke, thank you. I must away into the City, but would not pass the Temple without calling on you, and thanking my boy's old protector. You will have the kindness to come and dine with us—to-morrow, the next day, your own day? Your friend is going out of town? I hope, on his return, to have the pleasure of making his farther acquaintance. Come, Clive."

Clive, who had been deep in a volume of Hogarth's engravings during the above discussion, or rather, oration of his father's, started up and took leave, beseeching me, at the same time, to come soon and see his poney; and so, with renewed greetings, we parted.

[4] white *E1*] loose *R*

I was scarcely returned to my newspaper again, when the knocker of our door was again agitated, and the Colonel ran back, looking very much agitated and confused.

"I beg pardon," says he; "I think I left my—my—" Larkins had quitted the room by this time, and then he began more unreservedly. "My dear young friend," says he, "a thousand pardons for what I am going to say, but as Clive's friend, I know I may take that liberty. I have left the boy in the court. I know the fate of men of letters and genius: when we were here just now, there came a single knock—a demand—that, that you did not seem to be momentarily able to meet. Now do, do pardon the liberty, and let me be your banker. You said you were engaged in a new work: it will be a masterpiece, I am sure, if it's like the last. Put me down for twenty copies, and allow me to settle with you in advance. I may be off, you know. I'm a bird of passage—a restless old soldier."

"My dear Colonel," said I, quite touched and pleased by this extreme kindness, "my dun was but the washerwoman's boy, and Mrs. Brett is in my debt, if I am not mistaken. Besides, I already have a banker in your family."

"In my family, my dear Sir?"

"Messrs. Newcome, in Threadneedle Street, are good enough to keep my money for me when I have any, and I am happy to say they have some of mine in hand now. I am almost sorry that I am not in want in order that I might have the pleasure of receiving a kindness from you." And we shook hands for the fourth time that morning, and the kind gentleman left me to rejoin his son.

Chapter V.

CLIVE'S UNCLES.

THE dinner so hospitably offered by the Colonel was gladly accepted, and followed by many more entertainments at the cost of that good-natured friend. He and an Indian chum of his lived at this time at Nerot's Hotel, in Clifford Street, where Mr. Clive, too, found the good cheer a great deal more to his taste than the homely, though plentiful, fare at Grey Friars, at which of course, when boys, we all turned up our noses, though many a poor fellow, in the struggles of after-life, has looked back with regret very likely to that well-spread youthful table. Thus my intimacy with the father and the son grew to be considerable, and a great deal more to my liking than my relations with Clive's City uncles which have been mentioned in the last chapter, and which were, in truth, exceedingly distant and awful.

If all the private accounts, kept by those worthy bankers, were like mine, where would have been Newcome Hall and Park Lane, Marble Head and Brianstone Square? I used, by strong efforts of self-denial, to maintain a balance of two or three guineas untouched at the bank, so that my account might still remain open; and fancied the clerks and cashiers grinned when I went to draw for money. Rather than face that awful counter, I would send Larkins, the clerk, or Mrs. Flanagan, the laundress. As for entering the private parlour at the back, wherein behind the glazed partition I could see the bald heads of Newcome Brothers engaged with other capitalists or peering over the newspaper, I would as soon have thought of walking into the Doctor's own library at Grey Friars, or of volunteering to take an arm-chair in a dentist's studio, and have a tooth out, as of entering into that awful precinct. My good uncle, on the other hand, the late Major Pendennis, who kept naturally but a very small account with Hobsons', would walk into the parlour and salute the two magnates who governed there with the ease and gravity of a Rothschild. "My good fellow," the kind old gentleman would say to his nephew and pupil: "*Il faut se faire valoir.* I tell you, Sir, your bankers like to keep *every* gentleman's account. And it's a mistake to suppose they are only civil to their great moneyed clients. Look at me. I go in to them, and talk to them whenever I am in the City. I hear the news of 'Change, and carry it to our end of the town. It looks well, Sir, to be well with your banker; and at *our* end of London, perhaps, I can do a good turn for the Newcomes."

It is certain that in his own kingdom of May Fair and St. James's my revered[1] uncle was at least the banker's equal. On my coming to London, he was kind enough to procure me invitations to some of Lady Ann Newcome's evening parties in Park Lane, as likewise to Mrs. Newcome's entertainments in Brianstone Square; though, I confess, of these latter, after a while, I was a lax and negligent attendant. "Between ourselves, my good fellow," the shrewd old Mentor of those days would say, "Mrs. Newcome's parties are not altogether select; nor is she a lady of the very highest breeding; but it gives a man a good air to be seen at his banker's house. I recommend you to go for a few minutes whenever you are asked." And go I accordingly did sometimes, though I always fancied, rightly or wrongly, from Mrs. Newcome's manner to me, that she knew I had but thirty shillings left at the bank. Once and again, in two or three years, Mr. Hobson Newcome would meet me, and ask me to fill a vacant place that day or the next evening at his table; which invitation I might accept or otherwise. But one does not eat a man's salt, as it were, at these dinners. There is nothing sacred in this kind of London hospitality. Your white waistcoat fills a gap in a man's table, and retires filled for its service of the evening. "Gad," the dear old Major used to say, "if we were not to talk freely of those we dine with, how mum London would be! Some of the pleasantest[2] evenings I have ever spent have been when we have sate after a great dinner, *en petit comité*, and abused the people who are gone. You have your turn, *mon cher;* but why not? Do you suppose I fancy my friends haven't found out *my* little faults and peculiarities? And as I can't help it, I let myself be executed and offer up my oddities *de bonne grace. Entre nous,* Brother Hobson Newcome is a good fellow, but a vulgar fellow; and his wife—his wife exactly *suits* him."

Once a year Lady Ann Newcome (about whom my Mentor was much more circumspect; for I somehow used to remark that as the rank of persons grew higher, Major Pendennis spoke of them with more caution and respect)—once or twice in a year Lady Ann Newcome opened her saloons for a concert and a ball, at both of which the whole street was crowded with carriages, and all the great world, and some of the small, were present. Mrs. Newcome had her ball too, and her concert of English music in opposition to the Italian singers of her sister-in-law. The music of her country, Mrs. N. said was good enough for *her.*

The truth must be told, that there was no love lost between the two ladies. Brianstone Square could not forget the superiority of Park Lane's rank; and the catalogue of grandees at dear Ann's parties filled dear Maria's heart with envy. There are people upon whom rank and worldly goods make such an impression, that they naturally fall down on their knees and worship the owners; there are others to whom the sight of Prosperity is offensive, and who never see Dives' chariot but to growl and hoot at it. Mrs. Newcome, as far as my humble experience would lead me to suppose, is not only envious, but proud of her envy. She mistakes it for honesty and public spirit. *She* will not bow down to kiss the hand of a haughty aristocracy. She is a merchant's wife and an attorney's daughter. There is no pride about her. Her brother-in-law, poor dear Brian—considering everybody

---

[1] revered *E1*] reverend *R*
[2] pleasantest *HM*] pleasant *E1*

knows everything in London, was there ever such a delusion as his?—was welcome, after banking-hours, to forsake his own[3] friends for his wife's fine relations, and to dangle after lords and ladies in May Fair. She had no such absurd vanity; not she. She imparted these opinions pretty liberally to all her acquaintances in almost all her conversations. It was clear that the two ladies were best apart. There are some folks who will see insolence in persons of rank, as there are others who will insist that all clergymen are hypocrites, all reformers villains, all placemen plunderers, and so forth; and Mrs. Newcome never, I am sure, imagined that she had a prejudice, or that she was other than an honest, independent, high-spirited woman. Both of the ladies had command over their husbands, who were of soft natures easily led by woman, as, in truth, are all the males of this family. Accordingly, when Sir Brian Newcome voted for the Tory candidate in the City, Mr. Hobson Newcome plumped for the Reformer. While Brian, in the House of Commons, sat among the mild Conservatives, Hobson unmasked traitors and thundered at aristocratic corruption, so as to make the Marylebone Vestry thrill with enthusiasm. When Lady Ann, her husband, and her flock of children fasted in Lent, and declared for the High Church doctrines, Mrs. Hobson had paroxysms of alarm regarding the progress of

<hr />

[3] own *E1*] old *R*

Popery, and shuddered out of the chapel where she had a pew, because the clergyman there, for a very brief season, appeared to preach in a surplice.

Poor bewildered Honeyman! it was a sad day for you, when you appeared in your neat pulpit with your fragrant pocket-handkerchief (and your sermon likewise all millefleurs), in a trim, prim freshly mangled surplice, which you thought became you! How did you look aghast, and pass your jewelled hand through your curls, as you saw Mrs. Newcome, who had been as good as five-and-twenty pounds a-year to you, look up from her pew, seize hold of Mr. Newcome, fling open the pew-door, drive out with her parasol, her little flock of children, bewildered but not ill-pleased to get away from the sermon, and summon John from the back seats to bring away the bag of prayer-books! Many a good dinner did Charles Honeyman lose by assuming that unlucky ephod. Why did the high-priest of his diocese order him to put it on? It was delightful to view him afterwards, and the airs of martyrdom which he assumed. Had they been going to tear him to pieces with wild beasts next day, he could scarcely have looked more meek, or resigned himself more pathetically to the persecutors. But I am advancing matters. At this early time of which I write, a period not twenty years since, surplices were not even thought of in conjunction with sermons: clerical gentlemen have appeared in them, and under the heavy hand of persecution have sunk down in their pulpits again, as Jack pops back into his box. Charles Honeyman's elegant discourses were at this time preached in a rich silk Master of Arts gown, presented to him, along with a teapot full of sovereigns, by his affectionate congregation at Leatherhead.

But that I may not be accused of prejudice in describing Mrs. Newcome and her family, and lest the reader should suppose that some slight offered to the writer by this wealthy and virtuous banker's lady was the secret reason for this unfavourable sketch of her character, let me be allowed to report, as accurately as I can remember them, the words of a kinsman of her own, — Giles, Esquire, whom I had the honour of meeting at her table, and who, as we walked away from Brianstone Square, was kind enough to discourse very freely about the relatives whom he had just left.

"That was a good dinner, Sir," said Mr. Giles, puffing the[4] cigar which I offered to him, and disposed to be very social and communicative— "Hobson Newcome's table is about as good a one as any I ever put my legs under. You didn't have twice of turtle, Sir, I remarked that—I always do, at that house especially, for I know where Newcome gets it. We belong to the same livery in the City, Hobson and I, the Oystermongers' Company, Sir, and we like our turtle good, I can tell you—good and a great deal of it you say,—Hay, hay, not so bad.

"I suppose you're a young barrister, sucking lawyer, or that sort of thing. Because you was put at the end of the table and nobody took notice of you. That's my place too, I'm a relative: and Newcome asks me if he has got a place to spare. He met me in the City to-day, and says, 'Tom,' says he, 'there's some dinner in the square at half-past seven; I wish you would go and fetch Louisa, whom we haven't seen this ever so long.' Louisa is my wife, Sir—Maria's sister—Newcome married that gal from my house. 'No, no, Hobson,' says I, 'Louisa's [5] engaged nursing number eight'—that's our number, Sir—the truth is between you and me, Sir, my missis won't come any more at no price. She can't stand it; Mrs. Newcome's dam patronising airs is enough to choke off any body. 'Well, Hobson, my boy,' says I, 'a good dinner's a good dinner: and I'll come though Louisa won't, that is, can't.'"

While Mr. Giles, who was considerably enlivened by claret, was discoursing thus candidly, his companion was thinking how he, Mr. Arthur Pendennis, had been met that very afternoon on the steps of the Megatherium Club by Mr. Newcome, and had accepted that dinner, which Mrs. Giles, with more spirit, had declined. Giles continued talking—"I'm an old stager, I am. I don't mind the rows between the women. I believe Mrs. Newcome and Lady Newcome's just as bad too; I know Maria is always driving at her one way or the other, and calling her proud and aristocratic, and that; and yet my wife says Maria, who pretends to be such a radical, never asks us to meet the Baronet and his lady. 'And why should she, Loo, my dear?' says I. 'I don't want to meet Lady Newcome, nor Lord Kew, nor any of 'em.' Lord Kew, ain't it an odd name? Tearing young swell, that Lord Kew: tremendous wild fellow.

"I was a clerk in that house, Sir, as a young man; I was there in the old woman's time, and Mr. Newcome's—the father of these young men—as good a man as ever stood on 'Change." And then Mr. Giles, warming with his subject, enters at large into the history of the house. "You see, Sir," says he, "the banking-house of Hobson Brothers, or Newcome Brothers, as the partners of the firm really are, is not one of the leading banking firms of the City of London, but a most respectable house of many years' standing, and doing a most respectable business, especially in the Dissenting connection." After the business came into the hands of the Newcome Brothers, Hobson Newcome, Esq., and Sir Brian Newcome, Bart., M.P., Mr. Giles shows how a considerable West-end connection was likewise established, chiefly through the aristocratic friends and connections of the above-named Bart.

But the best man of business, according to Mr. Giles, whom the firm of Hobson Brothers ever knew, better than her father and uncle, better than her husband Sir T. Newcome, better than her sons and successors above-mentioned, was the famous Sophia Alethea Hobson, afterwards Newcome—of whom might be said what Frederick the Great said of his sister, that she was *sexu fœmina, vir ingenio*—in sex a woman, and in mind a man. Nor was she, my informant told me, without even manly personal characteristics; she had a very deep and gruff voice, and in her old age a beard which many a young man might envy; and as she came in to the bank out of her carriage from Clapham, in her dark green pelisse with fur trimmings, in her gray beaver hat, beaver gloves, and great gold spectacles, not a clerk in that house did not tremble before her, and it was said she only wanted a pipe in her mouth, considerably to resemble the late Field Marshal Prince Blucher.

Her funeral was one of the most imposing sights ever witnessed in Clapham. There was such a crowd you might have thought it was a Derby-day. The carriages of some of the greatest City firms, and the wealthiest

[5] 'No, no, Hobson,' says I, 'Louisa's *HM*] 'No, no,' says I, 'Hobson; Louisa's *E1*

Dissenting houses; several coaches full of ministers of all denominations, including the Established Church; the carriage of the Right Honourable the Earl of Kew, and that of his daughter, Lady Ann Newcome, attended that revered lady's remains to their final resting-place. No less than nine sermons were preached at various places of public worship regarding her end. She fell up-stairs at a very advanced age, going from the library to the bed-room, after all the household was gone to rest, and was found by the maids in the morning, inarticulate, but still alive, her head being cut frightfully with the bed-room candle[6] with which she was retiring to her apartment. "And," said Mr. Giles with great energy, "besides the empty carriages at that funeral, and the parson in black, and the mutes and feathers and that, there were hundreds and hundreds of people who wore no black, and who weren't present; and who wept for their benefactress, I can tell you. She had her faults, and many of 'em; but the amount of that woman's charities are unheard of, Sir—unheard of—and they are put to the credit side of her account up yonder.

"The old lady had a will of her own," my companion continued. "She would try and know about everybody's business out of business hours: got to know from the young clerks what chapels they went to, and from the clergyman whether they attended regular; kept her sons, years after they were grown men, as if they were boys at school,—and what was the consequence? They had a quarrel with Sir Thomas Newcome's own son, a harum-scarum lad, who ran away, and then was sent to India! and between ourselves, both Mr. Hobson and Mr. Brian,[7] the present Baronet, though at home they were as mum as Quakers at a meeting, used to go out on the sly, Sir, and be off to the play, Sir, and sowed their wild oats like any other young men, Sir, like any other young men. Law bless me, once, as I was going away from the Haymarket, if I didn't see Mr. Hobson coming out

of the Opera, in tights and an Opera-hat, Sir, like 'Froggy would a wooing

6 candle *E1*] candlestick *HM*
7 both Mr. Hobson and Mr. Brian,] Mr. Hobson and Mr. Brian both, *E1*

go,' of a Saturday night, too, when his ma thought him safe in bed in the
City! I warrant he hadn't *his Opera-hat* on when he went to chapel with her
ladyship the next morning—that very morning, as sure as my name's John
Giles.

"When the old lady was gone, Mr. Hobson had no need of any more
humbugging, but took his pleasure freely. Fighting, tandems, four-in-
hand, anything. He and his brother—his elder brother by a quarter of
an hour—were always very good friends; but after Mr. Brian married, and
there was only court cards at his table, Mr. Hobson couldn't stand it. They
weren't of his suit, he said; and for some time he said he wasn't a marrying
man—quite the contrary; but we all come to our fate, you know, and his
time came as mine did. You know we married sisters? It was thought a
fine match for Polly Smith, when she married the great Mr. Newcome; but
I doubt whether my old woman at home hasn't had the best of it, after all;
and if ever you come Bernard Street way on a Sunday, about six o'clock,
and would like a slice of beef and a glass of port, I hope you'll come and
see."

Do not let us be too angry with Colonel Newcome's two most respectable
brothers, if for some years they neglected their Indian relative, or held
him in slight esteem. Their mother never pardoned him, or at least by
any actual words admitted his restoration to favour. For many years, as
far as they knew, poor Tom was an unrepentant prodigal, wallowing in
bad company, and cut off from all respectable sympathy. Their father had
never had the courage to acquaint them with his more true, and kind, and
charitable version of Tom's story. So he passed at home for no better than
a black sheep; his marriage with a penniless young lady did not tend to
raise him in the esteem of his relatives at Clapham; it was not until he was
a widower, until he had been mentioned several times in the *Gazette* for
distinguished military service, until they began to speak very well of him
in Leadenhall Street, where the representatives of Hobson Brothers were
of course East India proprietors, and until he remitted considerable sums
of money to England that the bankers his brethren began to be reconciled
to him.

I say, do not let us be hard upon them. No people are so ready to give
a man a bad name as his own kinsfolk; and having made him that present,
they are ever most unwilling to take it back again. If they give him nothing
else in the days of his difficulty, he may be sure of their pity, and that he
is held up as an example to his young cousins to avoid. If he loses his
money they call him poor fellow, and point morals out of him. If he falls
among thieves, the respectable Pharisees of his race turn their heads aside
and leave him penniless and bleeding. They clap him on the back kindly
enough when he returns, after shipwreck, with money in his pocket. How
naturally Joseph's brothers made salaams to him, and admired him, and
did him honour, when they found the poor outcast a prime minister, and
worth ever so much money! Surely human nature is not much altered
since the days of those primeval Jews. We would not thrust brother Joseph
down a well and sell him bodily, but—but if he has scrambled out of a well of
his own digging, and got out of his early bondage into renown and credit,
at least we applaud him and respect him, and are proud of Joseph as a
member of the family.

Little Clive was the innocent and lucky object upon whom the increasing affection of the Newcomes for their Indian brother was exhibited. When he was first brought home a sickly child, consigned to his maternal aunt, the kind old maiden lady at Brighton, Hobson Brothers scarce took any notice of the little man, but left him to the entire superintendence of his own family. Then there came a large remittance from his father, and the child was asked by Uncle Newcome at Christmas. Then his father's name was mentioned in general orders, and Uncle Hobson asked little Clive at midsummer. Then Lord H., a late governor-general, coming home, and meeting the brothers at a grand dinner at the Albion, given by the Court of Directors to his late Excellency, spoke to the bankers about that most distinguished officer their relative; and Mrs. Hobson drove over to see his aunt, where the boy was; gave him a sovereign out of her purse, and advised strongly that he should be sent to Timpany's along with her own boy. Then Clive went from one uncle's house to another; and was liked at both; and much preferred poneys to ride, going out after rabbits with the keeper, money in his pocket (charged to the debit of Lieut.-Col. T. Newcome), and clothes from the London tailor, to the homely quarters and conversation of poor kind old Aunt Honeyman at Brighton. Clive's uncles were not unkind, they liked each other; their wives who hated each other united in liking Clive when they knew him and petting the wayward handsome boy; they were only pursuing the way of the world, which huzzays all[8] prosperity, and turns away from misfortune as from some contagious disease. Indeed, how can we see a man's brilliant qualities if he is what we call in the shade?

The gentlemen, Clive's uncles, who had their affairs to mind during the day, society and the family to occupy them of evenings and holidays, treated their young kinsman, the Indian Colonel's son, as other wealthy British uncles treat other young kinsmen. They received him in his vacations kindly enough. They tipped him when he went to school; when he had the hooping cough, a confidential young clerk went round by way of Grey Friars Square to ask after him: the sea being recommended to him

[8] all *E1*] at *R*

Mrs. Newcome gave him change of air in Sussex, and transferred him to his maternal aunt at Brighton. Then it was *bonjour.* As the lodge gates closed upon him, Mrs. Newcome's heart shut up too and confined itself within the firs, laurels, and palings which bound the home precincts. Had not she her own children and affairs? her brood of fowls, her Sunday school, her melon-beds, her rose-garden, her quarrel with the parson, &c. to attend to? Mr. Newcome, arriving on a Saturday night, hears he is gone; says "Oh!" and begins to ask about the new gravel-walk along the cliff, and whether it is completed, and if the China pig fattens kindly upon the new feed.

Clive, in the avuncular gig, is driven over the downs to Brighton to his maternal aunt there; and there he is a king. He has the best bed-room, Uncle Honeyman turning out for him; sweetbreads for dinner—no end of jam for breakfast; excuses from church on the plea of delicate health; his aunt's maid to see him to bed—his aunt to come smiling in when he rings his bell of a morning. He is made much of, and coaxed, and dandled and fondled, as if he were a young duke. So he is to Miss Honeyman. He is the son of Colonel Newcome, C.B., who sends her shawls, ivory chessmen, scented sandal-wood work-boxes and kincob scarfs; who, as she tells Hannah the maid, has fifty servants in India; at which Hannah constantly exclaims, "Lor, mum, what can he do with 'em, mum?" who, when in consequence of her misfortunes, she resolved on taking a house at Brighton, and letting part of the same furnished, sent her an order for a hundred pounds towards the expenses thereof; who gave Mr. Honeyman, her brother, a much larger sum of money at the period of his calamity. Is it gratitude for past favours? is it desire for more? is it vanity of relationship? is it love for the dead sister—or tender regard for her offspring which makes Mrs. Martha Honeyman so fond of her nephew? I never could count how many causes went to produce any given effect or action in a person's life, and have been for my own part many a time quite misled in my own case, fancying some grand, some magnanimous, some virtuous reason, for an act of which I was proud, when, lo, some pert little satirical monitor springs up inwardly, upsetting the fond humbug which I was cherishing—the peacock's tail wherein my absurd vanity had clad itself— and says, "Away with this boasting! *I* am the cause of your virtue, my lad. You are pleased that yesterday at dinner you refrained from the dry champagne; my name is Worldly Prudence, not Self-denial, and *I* caused you to refrain. You are pleased, because you gave a guinea to Diddler; I am Laziness, not Generosity, which inspired you. You hug yourself because you resisted other temptation? Coward! it was because you dared not run the risk of the wrong! Out with your peacock's plumage! walk off in the feathers which Nature gave you, and thank Heaven they are not altogether black." In a word Aunt Honeyman was a kind soul, and such was the splendour of Clive's father, of his gifts, his generosity, his military services, and companionship of the battles[9] that the lad did really appear a young duke to her. And Mrs. Newcome was not unkind: and if Clive had been really a young duke, I am sure he would have had the best bed-room at Marble Head, and not one of the far-off little rooms in the boys' wing; I am sure

[9] battles *E1*] Bath *R*

he would have had jellies and Charlottes Russes, instead of mere broth, chicken and batter pudding as fell to his lot; and when he was gone (in the carriage, mind you, not in the gig driven by a groom), I am sure Mrs. Newcome would have written a letter that night to Her Grace the Duchess Dowager, his mamma, full of praise of the dear child, his graciousness, his beauty, and his wit, and declaring that she must love him henceforth and for ever after as *a son of her own*. You toss down the page with scorn, and say, "It is not true. Human nature is not so bad as this cynic would have it to be. *You* would make no difference between the rich and the poor." Be it so. *You* would not. But own that your next door neighbour would. Nor is this, dear Madam, addressed to you; no, no, we are not so rude as to talk about you to your face; but, if we may not speak of the lady who has just left the room, what is to become of conversation and society?

We forbear to describe the meeting between the Colonel and his son— the pretty boy from whom he had parted more than seven years before with such pangs of heart; and of whom he had thought ever since with such a constant longing affection. Half an hour after the father left the boy, and in his grief and loneliness was rowing back to shore, Clive was at play with a dozen of other children on the sunny deck of the ship. When two bells rang for their dinner, they were all hurrying to the cuddy-table, and busy over their meal. What a sad repast their parents had that day! How their hearts followed the careless young ones home across the great ocean! Mothers' prayers go with them. Strong men, alone on their knees, with streaming eyes and broken accents, implore Heaven for those little ones, who were prattling at their sides but a few hours since. Long after they are gone, careless and happy, recollections of the sweet past rise up and smite those who remain: the flowers they had planted in their little gardens, the toys they played with, the little vacant cribs they slept in as fathers' eyes looked blessings down on them. Most of us who have passed a couple of score of years in the world, have had such sights as these to move us. And those who have, will think none the worse of my worthy Colonel for his tender and faithful heart.

With that fidelity which was an instinct of his nature, this brave man thought ever of his absent child and longed after him. He never forsook the native servants and nurses who had had charge of the child but endowed them with money sufficient (and indeed little was wanted by people of that frugal race) to make all their future lives comfortable. No friends went to Europe, nor ship[1] departed, but Newcome sent presents and remembrances to the boy, and costly tokens of his love and thanks to all who were kind to his son. What a strange pathos seems to me to accompany all our Indian story! Besides that official history which fills Gazettes, and embroiders banners with names of victory; which gives moralists and enemies cause to cry out at English rapine; and enables patriots to boast of invincible British Valour—besides the splendour and conquest, the wealth and glory, the crowned ambition, the conquered danger, the vast prize, and the blood freely shed in winning it—Should not one remember the tears too? Besides the lives of myriads of British men, conquering on a

---

[1] nor ship *E1*] nor ships *R*] a ship *Ms*

hundred fields,[2] from Plassy to Meanee, and bathing them[3] *cruore nostro*: think of the women and the tribute which they perforce must pay to those victorious achievements.[4] Scarce a soldier goes to yonder shores but leaves a home and grief in it behind him. The lords of the subject province find wives there: but their children cannot live on the soil. The parents bring their children to the shore, and part from them: the family must be broken up—keep the flowers of your home beyond a certain time and the sickening buds[5] wither and die. In America it is from the breast of a poor slave that a child is taken: in India it is from the wife and from under the palace of a splendid prōconsul.

The experience of this grief made Newcome's naturally kind heart only the more tender, and hence he had a weakness for children which made him the laughing-stock of old maids, old bachelors, and sensible persons; but the darling of all nurseries to whose little inhabitants he was uniformly kind; were they the Collectors' progeny in their palanquins or the Serjeants' children tumbling about the cantonment, or the dusky little heathens in the huts of his servants round his gate.

It is known that there is no part of the world where ladies are more fascinating than in British India. Perhaps the warmth of the sun kindles flames in the hearts of both sexes, which would probably beat quite coolly in their native air; else why should Miss Brown be engaged ten days after her landing at Calcutta? or why should Miss Smith have half a dozen proposals before she has been a week at the Station? And it is not only bachelors on whom the young ladies confer their affections; they will take widowers without any difficulty: and a man so generally liked as Major Newcome, with such a good character, with a private fortune of his own, so chivalrous, generous, good-looking, eligible in a word—you may be sure would have found a wife easily enough, had he any mind for replacing the late Mrs. Casey.

The Colonel, as has been stated, had an Indian chum or companion, with whom he shared his lodgings; and from many jocular remarks of this latter gentleman (who loved good jokes and uttered not a few) I could gather that the honest widower Colonel Newcome had been often tempted to alter his condition, and that the Indian ladies had tried numberless attacks upon his bereaved heart, and devised endless schemes of carrying it by assault, treason, or other mode of capture. Mrs. Casey (his defunct wife) had overcome it by sheer pity and helplessness. He had found her so friendless, that he took her in to the vacant place, and installed her there as he would have received a traveller into his bungalow. He divided his meal with her, and made her welcome to his best. "I believe Tom Newcome married her," sly Mr. Binnie used to say, "in order that he might have permission to pay her milliner's bills;" and in this way he was amply gratified until the day of her death. A feeble miniature of the lady, with yellow ringlets and a guitar, hung over the mantelpiece of the Colonel's bed-chamber, where I have often seen that work of art; and subsequently,

---

[2] conquering on a hundred fields, *E1*] conquering *MS*
[3] to Meanee, and bathing them *E1*] to those of Meanee and bathing a hundred fields *MS*
[4] to ...achievements. *E1*] for ...armies. *MS*
[5] sickening buds *E1*] poor wan flowers *MS*

when he and Mr. Binnie took a house, there was hung up in the spare bed-
room a companion portrait to the miniature—that of the Colonel's predecessor, Jack Casey, who in life used to fling plates at his Emma's head,
and who perished from a fatal attachment to the bottle. I am inclined to
think that Colonel Newcome was not much cast down by the loss of his
wife, and that they lived but indifferently together. Clive used to say in his
artless way that his father scarcely ever mentioned his mother's name; and
no doubt the union was not happy, although Newcome continued piously
to acknowledge it, long after death had brought it to a termination, by
constant benefactions and remembrances to the departed lady's kindred.

Those widows or virgins who endeavoured to fill Emma's place found
the door of Newcome's heart fast and barred, and assailed it in vain. Miss
Billing sat down before it with her piano, and, as the Colonel was a practitioner on the flute, hoped to make all life one harmonious duet with him;
but she played her most brilliant sonatas and variations in vain; and, as
everybody knows, subsequently carried her grand piano to Lieutenant and
Adjutant Hodgkin's house, whose name she now bears. The lovely widow
Wilkins, with two darling little children, stopped at Newcome's hospitable
house, on her way to Calcutta; and it was thought she might never leave
it: but her kind host, as was his wont, crammed her children with presents
and good things, consoled and entertained the fair widow, and one morning, after she had remained three months at the station, the Colonel's
palanquins and bearers made their appearance, and Elvira Wilkins went
away weeping as a widow should. Why did she abuse Newcome ever after
at Calcutta, Bath, Cheltenham, and wherever she went, calling him selfish, pompous, Quixotic, and a Bahawder? I could mention half-a-dozen
other names of ladies of most respectable families connected with Leadenhall Street, who, according to Colonel Newcome's chum—that wicked
Mr. Binnie—had all conspired more or less to give Clive Newcome a step-
mother.

But he had had an unlucky experience in his own case; and thought
within himself, "No, I won't give Clive a stepmother. As Heaven has taken
his own mother from him; why, I must try to be father and mother too
to the lad." He kept the child as long as ever the climate would allow of
his remaining, and then sent him home. Then his aim was to save money
for the youngster. He was of a nature so uncontrollably generous, that to
be sure he spent five rupees where another would save them, and make a
fine show besides; but it is not a man's gifts or hospitalities that generally
injure his fortune. It is on themselves that prodigals spend most. And as
Newcome had no personal extravagances, and the smallest selfish wants;
could live almost as frugally as a Hindoo; kept his horses not to race but to
ride; wore his old clothes and uniforms until they were the laughter of his
regiment; did not care for show, and had no longer an extravagant wife;
he managed to lay by considerably out of his liberal allowances, and to find
himself and Clive growing richer every year.

"When Clive has had five or six years at school"—that was his scheme—
"he will be a fine scholar, and have at least as much classical learning as a
gentleman in the world need possess. Then I will go to England, and we
will pass three or four years together, in which he will learn to be intimate
with me, and, I hope, to like me. I shall be his pupil for Latin and Greek,

A Letter from Clive

and try and make up for lost time. I know there is nothing like a knowledge of the classics to give a man good breeding—'*Ingenuas didicisse fideliter
artes emollunt mores, nec sinuisse feros.*' I shall be able to help him with my
knowledge of the world, and to keep him out of the way of sharpers and
a pack of rogues who commonly infest young men. I will make myself his
companion, and pretend to no superiority; for, indeed, isn't he my superior? Of course he is, with his advantages. *He* hasn't been an idle young
scamp as I was. And we will travel together, first through England, Scotland, and Ireland, for every man should know his own country, and then
we will make the grand tour. Then, by the time he is eighteen, he will be
able to choose his profession. He can go into the army, and emulate the
glorious man after whom I named him; or if he prefers the church, or the
law, they are open to him; and when he goes to the university, by which
time I shall be in all probability a major-general, I can come back to India
for a few years, and return by the time he has a wife and a home for his
old father; or if I die, I shall have done the best for him, and my boy will
be left with the best education, a tolerable small fortune, and the blessing
of his old father."

Such were the plans of our kind schemer. How fondly he dwelt on them,
how affectionately he wrote of them to his boy! How he read books of
travels and looked over the maps of Europe! and said "Rome, Sir, glorious
Rome; it won't be very long, major, before my boy and I see the Colosseum,
and kiss the Pope's toe. We shall go up the Rhine to Switzerland, and over
the Simplon, the work of the great Napoleon. By Jove, Sir, think of the
Turks before Vienna, and Sobieski clearing eighty thousand of 'em off the
face of the earth! How my boy will rejoice in the picture-galleries there, and
in Prince Eugene's prints! You know, I suppose, that Prince Eugene, one
of the greatest generals in the world, was also one of the greatest lovers of
the fine arts. '*Ingenuas didicisse,*' hey, Doctor? you know the rest,—'*emollunt
mores nec.*'"

"'*Emollunt mores!*' Colonel," says Doctor McTaggart, who perhaps was
too canny to correct the commanding officer's Latin. "Don't ye noo that
Prence Eugene was about as savage a Turrk as iver was? Have ye niver rad
the mimores of the Prants de Leen?"

"Well, he was a great cavalry officer," answers the Colonel, "and he left a
great collection of prints—*that* you know. How Clive will delight in them!
The boy's talent for drawing is wonderful, Sir, wonderful. He sent me
a picture of our old school—the very actual thing, Sir; the cloisters, the
school, the head gown-boy going in with the rods, and the doctor himself.
It would make you die of laughing!"

He regaled the ladies of the regiment with Clive's letters, and those of
Miss Honeyman, which contained an account of the boy. He even bored
some of his bearers[6] with this prattle; and sporting young men would give
or take odds that the Colonel would mention Clive's name, once before
five minutes, three times in ten minutes, twenty-five times in the course
of dinner and so on. But they who laughed at the Colonel laughed very
kindly; and everybody who knew him, loved him; everybody that is, who
loved modesty, and generosity, and honour.

---

[6] bearers *E1*] hearers *HM*

At last the happy time came for which the kind father had been longing more passionately than any prisoner for liberty, or school-boy for holiday. Colonel Newcome has taken leave of his regiment, leaving Major Tomkinson, nothing loth, in command. He has travelled to Calcutta; and the Commander-in-Chief, in general orders, has announced that in giving to Lieutenant-Colonel Thomas Newcome, C.B., of the Bengal Cavalry, leave[7] for the first time, after no less than thirty-four years' absence from home, "he (Sir George Husler) cannot refrain from expressing his sense of the great and meritorious services of this most distinguished officer, who has left his regiment in a state of the highest discipline and efficiency." And now the ship has sailed, the voyage is over, and once more, after so many long years, the honest soldier's foot is on his native shore.

[7] Cavalry, leave *E1*] Cavalry, *HM*

Chapter VI.

NEWCOME BROTHERS.

BESIDES his own boy, whom he worshipped, this kind Colonel had a score, at least, of adopted children, to whom he chose to stand in the light of a father. He was for ever whirling away in post-chaises to this school and that, to see Jack Brown's boys, of the Cavalry; or Mrs. Smith's girls, of the Civil Service; or poor Tom Hicks's orphan, who had nobody to look after him now that the cholera had carried off Tom, and his wife, too. On board the ship in which he returned from Calcutta were a dozen of little children, of both sexes, some of whom he actually escorted to their friends before he visited his own; and though his heart was longing for his boy at Grey Friars. The children at the schools seen, and largely rewarded out of his bounty (his loose white trousers had great pockets, always heavy with gold and silver, which he jingled when he was not pulling his mustachios— to see the way in which he tipped children made one almost long to be a boy again): and when he had visited Miss Pinkerton's establishment, or Doctor Ramshorn's adjoining academy at Chiswick, and seen little Tom Davis or little Fanny Holmes, the honest fellow would come home and write off straightway a long letter to Tom's or Fanny's parents, far away in the Indian country; whose hearts he made happy by his accounts of their children, as he had delighted the children themselves by his affection and bounty. All the apple and orange-women (especially such as had babies as well as lollypops at their stalls), all the street-sweepers on the road be- tween Nerot's and the Oriental, knew him, and were his pensioners. His brothers in Threadneedle Street cast up their eyes at the cheques which he drew.

One of the little people of whom the kind Newcome had taken charge, luckily dwelt near Portsmouth; and when the faithful Colonel consigned Miss Fipps to her grandmother, Mrs. Admiral Fipps, at Southampton, Miss Fipps clung to her guardian, and with tears and howls was torn away from him. Not until her maiden aunts had consoled her with strawberries, which she never before had tasted, was the little Indian comforted for the de- parture of her dear Colonel. Master Cox, Tom Cox's boy, of the Native Infantry, had to be carried asleep from the George to the mail that night. Master Cox woke up at the dawn wondering, as the coach passed through the pleasant green roads of Bromley. The good gentleman consigned the little chap to his uncle, Dr. Cox, Bloomsbury Square, before he went to his own quarters, and then on the errand on which his fond heart was bent.

He had written to his brothers from Portsmouth, announcing his arrival, and three words to Clive, conveying the same intelligence. The letter was served to the boy along with one bowl of tea and one buttered roll, of eighty such which were distributed to fourscore other boys, boarders of the same house with our young friend. How the lad's face must have flushed, and his eyes brightened, when he read the news! When the master of the house, the Rev. Mr. Popkinson, came into the long-room, with a good-natured face, and said, "Newcome, you're wanted," he knows who is come. He does not heed that notorious bruiser, old Hodge, who roars out, "Confound you, Newcome; I'll give it you for upsetting your tea over my new trousers." He runs to the room where the stranger is waiting for him. We will shut the door, if you please, upon that scene.

If Clive had not been as fine and handsome a young lad as any in that school or country, no doubt his fond father would have been just as well pleased, and endowed him with a hundred fanciful graces; but, in truth, in looks and manners he was everything which his parent could desire; and I hope the artist who illustrates this work will take care to do justice to his portrait. Mr. Clive himself, let that painter be assured, will not be too well pleased if his countenance and figure do not receive proper attention. He is not yet endowed with those splendid mustachios and whiskers which he has himself subsequently depicted, but he is the picture of health, strength, activity, and good-humour. He has a good forehead, shaded with a quantity of waving light hair; a complexion which ladies might envy; a mouth which seems accustomed to laughing; and a pair of blue eyes, that sparkle with intelligence and frank kindness. No wonder the pleased father cannot refrain from looking at him. He is, in a word, just such a youth as has a right to be the hero of a novel.

The bell rings for second school, and Mr. Popkinson, arrayed in cap and gown, comes in to shake Colonel Newcome by the hand, and to say he supposes it's to be a holiday for Newcome that day. He does not say a word about Clive's scrape of the day before, and that awful row in the bedrooms, where the lad and three others were discovered making a supper off a pork pie and two bottles of prime old port from the Red Cow public-house in Grey Friars Lane. When the bell has done ringing, and all these busy little bees have swarmed into their hive, there is a solitude in the place. The Colonel and his son walked the playground together, that gravelly flat, as destitute of herbage as the Arabian desert, but, nevertheless, in the language of the place called the green. They walk the green, and they pace the cloisters, and Clive shows his father his own name of Thomas Newcome carved upon one of the arches forty years ago. As they talk, the boy gives sidelong glances at his new friend, and wonders at the Colonel's loose trousers, long mustachios, and yellow face. He looks very odd, Clive thinks, very odd and very kind, and he looks like a gentleman, every inch of him:—not like Martin's father, who came to see his son lately in highlows, and a shocking bad hat, and actually flung coppers amongst the boys for a scramble. He bursts out a laughing at the exquisitely ludicrous idea of a gentleman of his fashion scrambling for coppers.

And now, enjoining the boy to be ready against his return (and you may be sure Mr. Clive was on the look-out long before his sire appeared), the Colonel whirled away in his cab to the City to shake hands with his brothers, whom he had not seen since they were demure little men in blue jackets, under charge of a serious tutor.

He rushed through the clerks and the banking-house, he broke into the parlour where the lords of the establishment were seated. He astonished those trim quiet gentlemen by the warmth of his greeting, by the vigour of his hand-shake, and the loud high tones of his voice, which penetrated the glass walls of the parlour, and might actually be heard by the busy clerks in the hall without. He knew Brian from Hobson at once—that unlucky little accident in the go-cart having left its mark for ever on the nose of Sir Brian Newcome, the elder of the twins. Sir Brian had a bald head and light hair, a short whisker cut to his cheek, a buff waistcoat, very neat boots and hands. He looked like the Portrait of a Gentleman at the Exhibition, as the worthy is represented: dignified in attitude, bland, smiling, and statesmanlike, sitting at a table unsealing letters, with a despatch-box and a silver inkstand before him, a column and a scarlet curtain behind, and a park in the distance, with a great thunder-storm lowering[1] in the sky. Such a portrait, in fact, hangs over the great side-board at Newcome to this day; and above the three great silver waiters, which the gratitude of as many Companies has presented to their respected director and chairman.

In face, Hobson Newcome, Esq., was like his elder brother, but was more portly in person. He allowed his red whiskers to grow wherever nature had planted them, on his cheeks and under his chin. He wore thick shoes with nails in them, or natty round-toed boots, with tight trousers and a single strap. He affected the country-gentleman in his appearance. His hat had a broad brim, and the ample pockets of his cut-away coat were never destitute of agricultural produce, samples of beans or corn, which he used to bite and chew even on 'Change, or a whip-lash, or balls for horses: in fine, he was a good old country-gentleman. If it was fine in Threadneedle Street, he would say it was good weather for the hay; if it rained, the country wanted rain; if it was frosty, "No hunting, to-day, Tomkins, my boy," and so forth. As he rode from Brianstone Square to the City you would take him—and he was pleased to be so taken—for a jolly country squire. He was a better man of business than his more solemn and stately brother, at whom he laughed in his jocular way; and he said rightly, that a gentleman must get up very early in the morning who wanted to take *him* in.

The Colonel breaks into the sanctum of these worthy gentlemen; and each receives him in a manner consonant with his peculiar nature. Sir Brian regretted that Lady Ann was away from London, being at Brighton with the children, who were all ill of the measles. Hobson said, "Maria can't treat you to such good company as my lady could give you, but when will you take a day and come and dine with us? Let's see, to-day's Wednesday; to-morrow we've a party. No, we're engaged." He meant that his table was full, and that he did not care to crowd it; but there was no use in imparting this circumstance to the Colonel. "Friday, we dine at Judge Budge's—queer name, Judge Budge, ain't it? Saturday, I'm going down to Marble Head, to look after the hay. Come on Monday, Tom, and I'll introduce you to the misses and the young uns."

[1] lowering *E1*] louring *R*

"I will bring Clive," says Colonel Newcome, rather disturbed at this reception. "After his illness my sister-in-law was very kind to him."

"No, hang it, don't bring boys; there's no good in boys; they stop the talk down-stairs, and the ladies don't want 'em in the drawing-room. Send him to dine with the children on Sunday, if you like, and come along down with me to Marble Head, and I'll show you such a crop of hay as will make your eyes open. Are you fond of farming?"

"I have not seen my boy for years," says the Colonel; "I had rather pass Saturday and Sunday with him, if you please, and some day we will go to Marble Head together."

"Well, an offer's an offer. I don't know any pleasanter thing than getting out of this confounded City and smelling the hedges, and looking at the crops coming up, and passing the Sunday in quiet." And his own tastes being thus agricultural, the honest[2] gentleman thought that everybody else must delight in the same recreation.

"In the winter, I hope we shall see you at Newcome," says the elder brother, blandly smiling. "I can't give you any tiger-shooting, but I'll promise you that you shall find plenty of pheasants in our jungle," and he laughed very gently at this mild sally.

The Colonel gave him a queer look. "I shall be at Newcome before the winter. I shall be there, please God, before many days are over."

"Indeed!" says the Baronet, with an air of great surprise. "You are going down to look at the cradle of our race. I believe the Newcomes were there before the Conqueror. It was but a village in our grandfather's time, and it is an immense flourishing town now, for which I hope to get—I expect to get—a charter."

"Do you?" says the Colonel. "I am going down there to see a relation."

"A relation! What relatives have we there?" cries the Baronet. "My children, with the exception of Barnes. Barnes, this is your uncle, Colonel Thomas Newcome. I have great pleasure, Brother, in introducing you to my eldest son."

A fair-haired young gentleman, languid and pale, and arrayed in the very height of fashion, made his appearance at this juncture in the parlour, and returned Colonel Newcome's greeting with a smiling acknowledgment of his own. "Very happy to see you, I'm sure," said the young man. "You find London very much changed since you were here. Very good time to come—the very full of the season."

Poor Thomas Newcome was quite abashed by this strange reception. Here was a man, hungry for affection, and one relation asked him to dinner next Monday, and another invited him to shoot pheasants at Christmas. Here was a beardless young sprig, who patronised him, and vouchsafed to ask him whether he found London was changed.

"I don't know whether it's changed," says the Colonel, biting his nails; "I know it's not what I expected to find it."

"To-day, it's really as hot as I should think it must be in India," says young Mr. Barnes Newcome.

"Hot!" says the Colonel, with a grin. "It seems to me you are all cool enough here."

[2] honest *E1*] worthy *R*

"Just what Sir Thomas de Boots said, Sir," says Barnes, turning round to his father. "Don't you remember when he came home from Bombay? I recollect his saying, at Lady Featherstone's, one dooced hot night, as it seemed to us; I recklect his saying that he felt quite cold. Did you know him in India, Colonel Newcome? He's liked at the Horse Guards, but he's hated in his regiment."

Colonel Newcome here growled a wish regarding the ultimate fate of Sir Thomas de Boots, which we trust may never be realised by that distinguished cavalry officer.

"My brother says he's going to Newcome, Barnes, next week," said the Baronet, wishing to make the conversation more interesting to the newly-arrived Colonel. "He was saying so just when you came in, and I was asking him what took him there?"

"Did you ever hear of Sarah Mason?" says the Colonel.

"Really, I never did," the Baronet answered.

"Sarah Mason? No, upon my word, I don't think I ever did," said the young man.

"Well, that's a pity too," the Colonel said with a sneer. "Mrs. Mason is a relation of your's—at least by marriage. She is my aunt or cousin—I used to call her Aunt, and she and my father and mother all worked in the same mill at Newcome together."

"I remember—God bless my soul—I remember now!" cries the Baronet. "We pay her forty pound a year on your account—don't you know, Brother? Look to Colonel Newcome's account—I recollect the name quite well. But I thought she had been your nurse, and—and an old servant of my father's."

"So she was my nurse, and an old servant of my father's," answered the Colonel. "But she was my mother's cousin too: and very lucky was my mother to have such a servant, or to have a servant at all. There is not in the whole world a more faithful creature or a better woman."

Mr. Hobson rather enjoyed his brother's perplexity, and to see, when the Baronet rode the high horse, how he came down sometimes. "I am sure it does you very great credit," gasped the courtly head of the firm, "to remember a—a humble friend and connexion of our father's so well."

"I think, Brother, you might have recollected her too," the Colonel growled out. His face was blushing: he was quite angry and hurt at what seemed to him Sir Brian's hardness of heart.

"Pardon me if I don't see the necessity," said Sir Brian. "*I* have no relationship with Mrs. Mason, and do not remember ever having seen her. Can I do anything for you, Brother? Can I be useful to you in any way? Pray command me and Barnes here, who after City hours will be delighted if he can be serviceable to you—*I* am nailed to this counter all the morning, and to the House of Commons all night;—I will be with you in one moment, Mr. Quilter. Good bye, my dear Colonel. How well India has agreed with you! how young you look! the hot winds are nothing to what we endure in Parliament. Hobson," in a low voice, "you saw about that hm, that power of attorney—and hm and hm will call here at 12 about that hm. I am sorry I must say good bye—it seems so hard after not meeting for so many years."

"Very," says the Colonel.

"Mind and send for me whenever you want me, now."

"O of course," said the elder brother, and thought when will that ever be!

"Lady Ann will be too delighted at hearing of your arrival. Give my love to Clive—a remarkable[3] fine boy, Clive—good morning;" and the Baronet was gone, and his bald head might presently be seen alongside of Mr. Quilter's confidential grey poll, both of their faces turned into an immense ledger.

Mr. Hobson accompanied the Colonel to the door, and shook him cordially by the hand as he got into his cab. The man asked whither he should drive? and poor Newcome hardly knew where he was or whither he should go. "Drive! a—oh—ah—damme, drive me anywhere away from this place!" was all he could say; and very likely the cabman thought he was a disappointed debtor who had asked in vain to renew a bill. In fact, Thomas Newcome had overdrawn his little account. There was no such balance of affection in that bank of his brothers, as the simple creature had expected to find there.

When he was gone, Sir Brian went back to his parlour, where sate young Barnes perusing the paper. "My revered uncle seems to have brought back a quantity of cayenne pepper from India, Sir," he said to his father.

"He seems a very kind-hearted simple man," the Baronet said: "eccentric, but he has been more than thirty years away from home. Of course you will call upon him to-morrow morning. Do everything you can to make him comfortable. Whom would he like to meet at dinner? I will ask some of the Directors.[4] Ask him, Barnes, for next Wednesday or Saturday—no; Saturday I dine with the Speaker. But see that every attention is paid him."

"Does he intend to have our relation up to town, Sir? I should like to meet Mrs. Mason of all things. A venerable washerwoman I dare say, or perhaps keeps a public-house," simpered out young Barnes.

"Silence, Barnes; you jest at everything, you young men do—you do. Colonel Newcome's affection for his old nurse does him the greatest honour," said the Baronet, who really meant what he said.

"And I hope my mother will have her to stay a good deal at Newcome. I'm sure she must have been a washerwoman, and mangled my uncle in early life. His costume struck me with respectful astonishment. He disdains the use of straps to his trowsers, and is seemingly unacquainted with gloves. If he had died in India, would my late aunt have had to perish on a funeral pile?" Here Mr. Quilter, entering with a heap of bills, put an end to these sarcastic remarks, and young Newcome, applying himself to his business (of which he was a perfect master), forgot about his uncle till after City hours, when he entertained some young gentlemen of Bays's Club with an account of his newly arrived relative.

Towards the City whither he wended his way, whatever had been the ball or the dissipation of the night before, young Barnes Newcome might be seen walking every morning, resolutely and swiftly with his neat umbrella. As he passed Charing Cross on his way westwards, his little boots trailed slowly over the pavement, his head hung languid, (bending lower still, and

[3] remarkable *E1*] remarkably *HM*
[4] Directors. *HM*] Direction. *E1*

smiling with faded sweetness as he doffed his hat and saluted a passing carriage), his umbrella trailed after him. Not a dandy on all the Pall Mall pavement seemed to have less to do than he.

Heavyside, a large young officer of the household troops—old Sir Thomas de Boots—and Horace Fogey, whom every one knows—are in the window of Bays's, yawning as widely as that window itself. Horses under the charge of men in red jackets are pacing up and down St. James's Street. Cabmen on the stand are regaling with beer. Gentlemen with grooms behind them pass towards the park. Great dowager barouches roll along emblazoned with coronets, and driven by coachmen in silvery wigs. Wistful provincials gaze in at the clubs. Foreigners chatter and show their teeth, and look at the ladies in the carriages, and smoke and spit refreshingly round about. Policeman X slouches along the pavement. It is 5 o'clock, the noon in Pall Mall.

"Here's little Newcome coming," says Mr. Horace Fogey. "He and the muffin-man generally make their appearance in public together."

"Dashed little prig," says Sir Thomas de Boots, "why the dash did they ever let him in here? If I hadn't been in India, by dash—he should have been black-balled twenty times over, by dash." Only Sir Thomas used words far more terrific than dash, for this distinguished cavalry officer swore very freely.

"He amuses me; he's such a mischievous little devil," says good-natured Charley Heavyside.

"It takes very little to amuse you," remarks Fogey.

"*You* don't, Fogey," answers Charley. "I know every one of your demd old stories, that are as old as my grandmother. How-dy-do, Barney. (Enter Barnes Newcome.) How are the Three per Cents. you little beggar? I wish you'd do me a bit of stiff: and just tell your father if I may overdraw my account, I'll vote with him—hanged if I don't."

Barnes orders absinthe-and-water, and drinks: Heavyside resuming his elegant raillery. "I say, Barney, your name's Barney, and you're a banker. You must be a little Jew, hey? Vell, how mosh vill you to my little pill for?"

"Do hee-haw in the House of Commons, Heavyside," says the young man with a languid air. "That's your place: you're returned for it. (Captain the Honourable Charles Heavyside is a member of the legislature, and eminent in the House for asinine imitations which delight his own, and confuse the other party.) Don't bray here. I hate the shop out of shop hours."

"Dash the little puppy," growls Sir de Boots, swelling in his waistband.

"What do they say about the Russians in the City?" says Horace Fogey, who has been in the diplomatic service. "Has the fleet left Cronstadt, or has it not?"

"How should I know?" asks Barney. "Ain't it all in the evening paper?"

"That is very uncomfortable news from India, General," resumes Fogey —"there's Lady Doddington's carriage, how well she looks—that movement of Runjeet-Singh[5] on Peshawur: that fleet on the Irrawaddy. It looks doocid queer, let me tell you, and Penguin is not the man to be Governor-General of India in a time of difficulty."

---

[5] Runjeet-Singh *E1*] Runjet-Singh *R*

"And Hustler's not the man to be Commander-in-Chief: dashder old fool never lived: a dashed old psalm-singing, blundering old woman," says Sir Thomas, who wanted the command himself.

"*You* ain't in the psalm-singing line, Sir Thomas?" says Mr. Barnes, "quite the contrary." In fact Sir de Boots in his youth used to sing with the Duke of York, and even against Captain Costigan, but was beaten by that superior Bacchanalian artist.

Sir Thomas looks as if to ask what the dash is that to you? but wanting still to go to India again, and knowing how strong the Newcomes are in Leadenhall Street, he thinks it necessary to be civil to the young cub, and swallows his wrath once more into his waistband.

"I've got an uncle come home from India—upon my word I have," says Barnes Newcome. "That is why I am so exhausted. I am going to buy him a pair of gloves, number fourteen—and I want a tailor for him—not a young man's tailor. Fogey's tailor rather. I'd take my father's; but he has all his things made in the country—all—in the borough, you know—he's a public man."

"Is Colonel Newcome, of the Bengal Cavalry, your uncle?" asks Sir Thomas de Boots.

"Yes; will you come and meet him at dinner next Wednesday week, Sir Thomas? and Fogey, you come; you know you like a good dinner. You don't know anything against my uncle, do you, Sir Thomas? Have I any Brahminical cousins? Need we be ashamed of him?"

"I tell you what, young man, if you were more like him it wouldn't hurt you. He's an odd man; they call him Don Quixote in India; I suppose you've[6] read *Don Quixote*."

"Never heard of it, upon my word; and why do you wish I should be more like him? I don't wish to be like him at all, thank you."

"Why, because he is one of the bravest officers that ever lived," roared out the old soldier. "Because he's one of the kindest fellows; because he gives himself no dashed airs, although he has reason to be proud if he chose. That's why, Mr. Newcome."

"A topper for you, Barney, my boy," remarks Charles Heavyside, as the indignant general walks away gobbling and red. Barney calmly drinks the remains of his absinthe.

"I don't know what that old muff means," he says innocently, when he has finished his bitter draught. "He's always flying out at me, the old turkey-cock. He quarrels with my play at whist, the old idiot, and can no more play than an old baby. He pretends to teach me billiards, and I'll give him fifteen in twenty and beat his old head off. Why do they let such fellows into clubs? Let's have a game at piquet till dinner, Heavyside? Hallo! That's my uncle, that tall man with the mustachios and the short trowsers walking with that boy of his. I dare say they are going to dine in Covent Garden, and going to the play. How-dy-do, Nunky"—and so the worthy pair went up to the card-room, where they sate at piquet until the hour of sunset and dinner arrived.

---

[6] you've *E1*] you have *R*

Mr. Barnes Newcome at his Club

Chapter VII.

IN WHICH MR. CLIVE'S SCHOOL-DAYS ARE OVER.

UR good Colonel had luckily to look forward to a more pleasant meeting with his son, than that unfortunate interview with his other near relatives.

He dismissed his cab at Ludgate Hill, and walked thence by the dismal precincts of Newgate, and across the muddy pavement of Smithfield, on his way back to the old school where his son was, a way which he had trodden many a time in his own early days. There was Cistercian Street, and the Red Cow of his youth: there was the quaint old Greyfriars Square, with its blackened trees and garden, surrounded by ancient houses of the build of the last century, now slumbering like pensioners in the sunshine.

Under the great archway of the hospital he could look at the old gothic building; and a black-gowned pensioner or two crawling over the quiet square, or passing from one dark arch to another. The boarding-houses of the school were situated in the square, hard by the more ancient buildings of the hospital. A great noise of shouting, crying, clapping forms and cupboards, treble voices, bass voices, poured out of the schoolboys' windows: their life, bustle, and gaiety, contrasted strangely with the quiet of those old men, creeping along in their black gowns under the ancient arches yonder, whose struggle of life was over, whose hope and noise and bustle had sunk into that grey calm. There was Thomas Newcome arrived at the middle of life, standing between the shouting boys and the tottering seniors, and in a situation to moralise upon both, had not his son Clive, who has espied him from within Mr. Hopkinson's, or let us say at once Hopkey's house, come jumping down the steps to greet his sire. Clive was dressed in his very best; not one of those four hundred young gentlemen had a better figure, a better tailor, or a neater boot. School-fellows, grinning through the bars, envied him as he walked away: senior boys made remarks on Colonel Newcome's loose clothes and long mustachios, his brown hands and unbrushed hat. The Colonel was smoking a cheroot as he walked; and the gigantic Smith, the cock of the school, who happened to be looking majestically out of window, was pleased to say that he thought Newcome's governor was a fine manly-looking fellow.

"Tell me about your uncles, Clive," said the Colonel, as they walked on arm in arm.

"What about them, Sir?" asks the boy. "I don't think I know much."

"You have been to stay with them. You wrote about them. Were they kind to you?"

"O, yes, I suppose they are very kind. They always tipped me: only you know when I go there I scarcely ever see them. Mr. Newcome asks me the oftenest—two or three times a quarter when he's in town, and gives me a sovereign regular."

"Well, he must see you to give you the sovereign," says Clive's father, laughing.

The boy blushed rather.

"Yes. When it's time to go back to Smithfield on a Sunday night, I go into the dining-room to shake hands, and he gives it me; but he don't speak to me much, you know, and I don't care about going to Brianstone Square, except for the tip, of course that's important, because I am made to dine with the children, and they are quite little ones; and a great cross French governess, who is always crying and shrieking after them, and finding fault with them. My uncle generally has his dinner-parties on Saturday, or goes out; and Aunt gives me ten shillings and sends me to the play; that's better fun than a dinner party." Here the lad blushed again. "I used," says[1] he, "when I was younger, to stand on the stairs and prig things out of the dishes when they came out from dinner, but I'm past that now. Maria (that's my cousin) used to take the sweet things and give 'em to the governess. Fancy! she used to put lumps of sugar into her pocket and eat them in the school-room! Uncle Hobson don't live in such good society as Uncle Newcome. You see, Aunt Hobson, she's very kind you know, and all that, but I don't think she's what you call *comme il faut.*"

"Why, how are you to judge?" asks the father, amused at the lad's candid prattle, "and where does the difference lie?"

"I can't tell you what it is, or how it is," the boy answered, "only one can't help seeing the difference. It isn't rank and that; only somehow there are some men gentlemen and some not, and some women ladies and some not. There's Jones now, the fifth form master, every man sees *he's* a gentleman, though he wears ever so old clothes; and there's Mr. Brown, who oils his hair, and wears rings, and white chokers—my eyes! such white chokers! and yet we call him the handsome snob! And so about Aunt Maria, she's very handsome and she's very finely dressed, only somehow she's not—she's not the ticket you see."

"O, she's not the ticket," says the Colonel, much amused.

"Well, what I mean is—but never mind," says the boy, "I can't tell you what I mean. I don't like to make fun of her you know, for after all, she is very kind to me; but Aunt Ann is different, and it seems as if what she says is more natural; and though she has funny ways of her own too, yet somehow she looks grander,"—and here the lad laughed again. "And do you know, I

---

[1] says *E1*] said *HM*

often think that as good a lady as Aunt Ann herself, is old Aunt Honeyman at Brighton—that is, in all essentials, you know. For she is not proud, and she is not vain, and she never says an unkind word behind anybody's back, and she does a deal of kindness to the poor without appearing to crow over them you know; and she[2] is not a bit ashamed of letting lodgings, or being poor herself, as sometimes I think some of our family—"

"I thought we were going to speak no ill of them," says the Colonel, smiling.

"Well, it only slipped out unawares," says Clive, laughing; "but at Newcome when they go on about the Newcomes, and that great ass, Barnes Newcome, gives himself his airs, it makes me die of laughing. That time I went down to Newcome, I went to see old Aunt Sarah, and she told me everything, and showed me the room where my grandfather—you know; and do you know I was a little hurt at first, for I thought we were swells till then. And when I came back to school, where perhaps I had been giving myself airs, and bragging about Newcome, why you know I thought it was right to tell the fellows."

"That's a man," said the Colonel, with delight; though had he said 'that's a boy,' he had spoken more correctly. Indeed, how many men do we know in the world without caring to know who their fathers were? and how many more who wisely do not care to tell us? "That's a man," cries the Colonel, "never be ashamed of your father, Clive."

"Ashamed of *my* father!" says Clive, looking up to him, and walking on as proud as a peacock. "I say," the lad resumed, after a pause—

"Say what you say," said the father.

"Is that all true what's in the peerage—in the baronetage, about Uncle Newcome and Newcome; about the Newcome who was burned at Smithfield; about the one that was at the battle of Bosworth; and the old old Newcome who was bar—that is, who was surgeon to Edward the Confessor, and was killed at Hastings? I am afraid it isn't; and yet I should like it to be true."

"I think every man would like to come of an ancient and honourable race," said the Colonel, in his honest way. "As you like your father to be an honourable man, why not your grandfather, and his ancestors before him? But if we can't inherit a good name; at least we can do our best to leave one, my boy; and that is an ambition which, please God, you and I will both hold by."

With this simple talk the old and young gentlemen beguiled their way, until they came into the Western quarter of the town, where the junior member of the firm of Newcome Brothers had his house—a handsome and roomy mansion in Brianstone Square. Colonel Newcome was bent on paying a visit to his sister-in-law, and as he knocked at the door, where the pair were kept waiting some[3] little time, he could remark through the opened windows of the dining-room, that a great table was laid and every preparation made for a feast.

[2] For she is not proud, and she is not vain, and she never says an unkind word behind anybody's back, and she does a deal of kindness to the poor without appearing to crow over them you know; and she *E1*] And she *R*
[3] some *E1*] for some *HM*

"My brother said he was engaged to dinner to-day," said the Colonel. "Does Mrs. Newcome give parties when he is away?"

"She invites all the company," answered Clive. "My uncle never asks anyone without Aunt's leave."

The Colonel's countenance fell. He has a great dinner, and does not ask his own brother! Newcome thought. Why, if he had come to me in India with all his family, he might have staid for a year, and I should have been offended if he had gone elsewhere.

A hot menial, in a red waistcoat, came and opened the door; and without waiting for preparatory queries, said, "Not at home."

"It's my father, John," said Clive; "my aunt will see Colonel Newcome."

"Missis not at home," said the man. "Missis is gone in carriage—Not at this door!—Take them things down the area steps, young man!" bawls out the domestic. This latter speech was addressed to a pastry-cook's boy, with a large sugar temple and many conical papers containing delicacies for dessert. "Mind the hice is here in time; or there'll be a blow up with your governor,"—and John struggled back closing the door on the astonished Colonel.

"Upon my life, they actually shut the door in our faces," said the poor gentleman.

"The man is very busy, Sir. There's a great dinner. I'm sure my aunt would not refuse you," Clive interposed; "She is very kind. I suppose it's different here to what it is in India. There are the children in the square,— those are the girls in blue,—that's the French governess, the one with the mustachios and the yellow parasol. How d'ye do, Mary? How d'ye do, Fanny? This is my father,—this is your uncle."

"Mesdemoiselles! Je vous défends de parler à qui que ce soit hors du Squar!" screams out the lady of the mustachios; and she strode forward to call back her young charges.

The Colonel addressed her in very good French. "I hope you will permit me to make acquaintance with my nieces," he said, "and with their instructress, of whom my son has given me such a favourable account."

"Hem!" said Mademoiselle Lebrun, remembering the last fight she and Clive had had together, and a portrait of herself (with enormous whiskers) which the young scapegrace had drawn. "Monsieur is very good. But one cannot too early inculcate *retenue* and decorum to young ladies in a country where demoiselles seem for ever to forget that they are young ladies of condition. I am forced to keep the eyes of lynx upon these young persons, otherwise Heaven knows what would come to them. Only yesterday, my back is turned for a moment, I cast my eyes on a book, having but little time for literature, Monsieur—for literature, which I adore—when a cry makes itself to hear. I turn myself, and what do I see? Mesdemoiselles, your nieces, playing at criquette, with the Messieurs Smees—sons of Doctor Smees—young galopins, Monsieur!" All this was shrieked with immense volubility and many actions of the hand and parasol across the square-railings to the amused Colonel, at whom the little girls peered through the bars.

"Well, my dears, I should like to have a game at cricket with you, too," says the kind gentleman, reaching them each a brown hand.

"You, Monsieur, c'est différent—a man of your age! Salute Monsieur your uncle, Mesdemoiselles. You conceive, Monsieur, that I also must be cautious when I speak to a man so distinguished in a public squar." And she cast down her great eyes and hid those radiant orbs from the Colonel.

Meanwhile, Colonel Newcome, indifferent to the direction which Miss Lebrun's eyes took, whether towards his hat or his boots, was surveying his little nieces with that kind expression which his face always wore when it was turned towards children. "Have you heard of your uncle in India?" he asked them.

"No," says Maria.

"Yes," says Fanny. "You know Mademoiselle said (Mademoiselle at this moment was twittering her fingers, and, as it were, kissing them in the direction of a grand barouche that was advancing along the square)—you know Mademoiselle said that if we were *méchantes* we should be sent to our uncle in India. I think I should like to go with you."

"O you silly child!" cries Maria.

"Yes I should, if Clive went too," says little Fanny.

"Behold Madam, who arrives from her promenade!" Miss Lebrun exclaimed; and, turning round, Colonel Newcome had the satisfaction of beholding, for the first time, his sister-in-law.

A stout lady, with fair hair and a fine bonnet and pelisse (who knows what were the fine bonnets and pelisses of the year 183—?), was reclining in the barouche, the scarlet-plush integuments of her domestics blazing before and behind her. A pretty little foot was on the cushion opposite to her; feathers waved in her bonnet; a book was in her lap; an oval portrait of a gentleman reposed on her voluminous bosom. She wore another picture of two darling heads, with pink cheeks and golden hair, on one of her wrists, with many more chains, bracelets, bangles, and knicknacks. A pair of dirty gloves marred the splendour of this appearance; a heap of books from the library strewed the back seat of the carriage, and showed that her habits were literary. Springing down from his station behind his mistress, the youth clad in the nether garments of red sammit discharged thunderclaps on the door of Mrs. Newcome's house, announcing to the whole square that his mistress had returned to her abode. Since the fort saluted the governor-general at ——, Colonel Newcome had never heard such a cannonading.[4]

Clive, with a queer twinkle of his eyes, ran towards his aunt. She bent over the carriage languidly towards him. She liked him. "What, you, Clive!" she said. "How come you away from school of a Thursday, Sir?"

"It is a holiday," says he. "My father is come; and he is come to see you."

She bowed her head with an expression of affable surprise and majestic satisfaction. "Indeed, Clive!" she was good enough to exclaim, and with an air which seemed to say, "Let him come up and be presented to me." The honest gentleman stepped forward and took off his hat and bowed, and stood bare-headed. She surveyed him blandly; and with infinite grace put forward one of the pudgy little hands in one of the dirty gloves. Can you fancy a twopenny-halfpenny baroness of King Francis's time patronis-

---

[4] Since the fort ... cannonading. *E1*] [omitted] *R*

ing Bayard? Can you imagine Queen Guinever's lady's maid's lady's maid being affable to Sir Lancelot? I protest there is nothing like the virtue of English women.

"You have only arrived to-day; and you came to see me? That was very kind. N'est ce pas que c'étoit bong de Mouseer le Collonel, Mademoiselle? Madamaselle Lebrun le Collonel Newcome, mong frère." (In a whisper, "My children's governess and my friend, a most superior woman.") "Was it not kind of Colonel Newcome to come to see me? Have you had a pleasant voyage? Did you come by St. Helena? O, how I envy you[5] seeing the tomb of that great man! Nous parlong de Napolleong, Mademoiselle, dong voter père a été le Général favvory."

"O Dieu! que n'ai-je pu le voir," interjaculates Mademoiselle. "Lui dont parle l'univers, dont mon père m'a si souvent parlé?" but this remark passes quite unnoticed by Mademoiselle's friend, who continues—

"Clive, donnez-moi voter bras. These are two of my girls. My boys are at school. I shall be so glad to introduce them to their uncle. *This* naughty boy might never have seen you, but that we took him home to Marble Head, after the scarlet fever, and made him well, didn't we, Clive? And we are all very fond of him; and you must not be jealous of his love for his aunt. We feel that we quite know you through him, and we know that you know us; and we hope you will *like* us. Do you think your papa will like us, Clive? Or perhaps you will like Lady Ann best. Yes; you have been to her first, of course? Not been? Oh! because she is not in town." Leaning fondly on the arm of Clive, Mademoiselle standing grouped with the children hard by, while John, with his hat off, stood at the opened door, Mrs. Newcome slowly uttered the above remarkable remarks to the Colonel, on the threshold of her house, which she never asked him to pass.

"If you will come in to us at about ten this evening," she then said, "you will find some men, not undistinguished, who honour me of an evening. Perhaps they will be interesting to you, Colonel Newcome, as you are newly arrived in Europe. Not men of worldly rank, necessarily, although some of them are amongst the noblest of Europe. But *my* maxim is, that genius is an illustration, and merit is better than any pedigree. You have heard of Professor Bodgers? Count Poski? Doctor Mac Guffog, who is called in his native country the Ezekiel of Clackmannan? Mr. Shaloo, the great Irish patriot? our papers have told you of *him*. These and some more have been good enough to promise me a visit to-night. A stranger coming to London could scarcely have a better opportunity of seeing some of our great illustrations of science and literature. And you will meet our own family—not Sir Brian's, who—who have other society and amusements— but mine. I hope Mr. Newcome and myself will never forget *them*. We have a few friends at dinner, and now I must go in and consult with Mrs. Hubbard, my housekeeper. Good bye, for the present. Mind, not later than ten, as Mr. Newcome must be up betimes in the morning, and *our* parties break up early. When Clive is a little older, I dare say we shall see him, too. *Good* bye!" And again the Colonel was favoured with a shake of the glove, and the lady and her suite sailed up the stair, and passed in at the door.

[5] you *E1*] your *HM*

She had not the faintest idea but that the hospitality which she was offering to her kinsman was of the most cordial and pleasant kind. She fancied everything she did was perfectly right and graceful. She invited her husband's clerks to come through the rain at ten o'clock from Kentish Town; she asked artists to bring their sketch-books from Kensington, or luckless pianists to trudge with their music from Brompton. She rewarded them with a smile and a cup of tea, and thought they were made happy by her condescension. If, after two or three of these delightful evenings, they ceased to attend her receptions, she shook her little flaxen head, and sadly intimated that Mr. A. was getting into bad courses, or feared that Mr. B. found merely *intellectual* parties too quiet for him. Else, what young man in his senses could refuse such entertainment and instruction?

Chapter VIII.

O push on in the crowd, every male or female struggler must use his shoulders. If a better place than yours presents itself just beyond your neighbour, elbow him and take it. Look how a steadily-purposed man or woman at court, at a ball, or exhibition, wherever there is a competition and a squeeze, gets the best place; the nearest the sovereign, if bent on kissing the royal hand; the closest to the grand stand, if minded to go to Ascot; the best view and hearing of the Rev. Mr. Thumpington, when all the town is rushing to hear that exciting divine; the largest quantity of ice, champagne, and seltzer, cold pâté, or other his or her favourite flesh-pot, if gluttonously minded, at a supper whence hundreds of people come empty away. A woman of the world will marry her daughter and have done with her; get her carriage and be at home and asleep in bed; whilst a timid mamma has still her girl in the nursery, or is beseeching the servants in the cloak-room to look for her shawls, with which some one else has whisked away an hour ago. What a man has to do in society is to assert himself. Is there a good place at table? Take it. At the Treasury or the Home Office? Ask for it. Do you want to go to a party to which you are not invited? Ask to be asked. Ask A., ask B., ask Mrs. C., ask everybody you know: you will be thought a bore; but you will have your way. What matters if you are considered obtrusive, provided that you obtrude? By pushing steadily, nine hundred and ninety-nine people in a thousand will yield to you. Only command persons, and you may be pretty sure that a good number will obey. How well your shilling[1] will have been laid out, O gentle reader, who purchase this; and, taking the maxim to heart, follow it through life! You may be sure of success. If your neighbour's foot obstructs you, stamp on it; and do you suppose he won't take it away?

The proofs of the correctness of the above remarks I show in various members of the Newcome family. Here was a vulgar little woman, not

[1] shilling *E1*] money *R*

clever nor pretty, especially; meeting Mr. Newcome casually, she ordered him to marry her, and he obeyed; as he obeyed her in everything else which she chose to order through life. Meeting Colonel Newcome on the steps of her house, she orders him to come to her evening party; and though he has not been to an evening party for five-and-thirty years—though he has not been to bed the night before—though he has no mufti-coat except one sent him out by Messrs. Stultz to India in the year 1821, he never once thinks of disobeying Mrs. Newcome's order, but is actually at her door at five minutes past ten, having arrayed himself, to the wonderment of Clive, and left the boy to talk with his friend and fellow passenger, Mr. Binnie, who has just arrived from Portsmouth, who has dined with him, and who, by previous arrangement, has taken up his quarters at the same hotel.

This Stultz coat, a blue swallow-tail, with yellow buttons, now wearing a tinge of their native copper, a very high velvet collar, on a level with the tips of the Captain's ears, with a high waist, indicated by two lapelles, and a pair of buttons high up in the wearer's back, a white waistcoat and scarlet under-waistcoat, and a pair of the never-failing duck trousers, complete Thomas Newcome's costume, along with the white hat in which we have seen him in the morning, and which was one of two dozen purchased by him some years since at public outcry, Burrumtollah. We have called him Captain purposely, while speaking of his coat, for he held that rank when the garment came out to him; and having been in the habit of considering it a splendid coat for twelve years past, he has not the least idea of changing his opinion.

Doctor Mac Guffog, Professor Bodgers, Count Poski, and all the lions present at Mrs. Newcome's *réunion* that evening, were completely eclipsed by Colonel Newcome. The worthy soul, who cared not the least about adorning himself, had a handsome diamond brooch of the year 1801, given him by poor Jack Cutler, who was knocked over by his side at Argaum, and wore this ornament in his desk for a thousand days and nights at a time; in his shirt-frill, on such parade-evenings, as he considered Mrs. Newcome's to be. The splendour of this jewel, and of his flashing buttons, caused all eyes to turn to him. There were many pairs of mustachios present; those of Professor Schnurr, a very corpulent martyr, just escaped from Spandau, and of Maximilien Tranchard, French exile and apostle of liberty, were the only whiskers in the room capable of vying in interest with Colonel Newcome's. Polish chieftains were at this time so common in London, that nobody (except one noble member for Marylebone, and, once a year, the Lord Mayor) took any interest in them. The general opinion was, that the stranger was the Wallachian Boyar, whose arrival at Mivart's, the *Morning Post* had just announced. Mrs. Miles, whose delicious every other Wednesdays in Montague Square, are supposed by some to be rival entertainments to Mrs. Newcome's alternate Thursdays in Brianstone Square, pinched her daughter Mira, engaged in a polyglot conversation with Herr Schnurr, Signor Carabossi, the guitarist, and Monsieur Pivier, the celebrated French chess-player, to point out the Boyar. Mira Miles wished she knew a little Moldavian, not so much that she might speak it, but that she might be heard to speak it. Mrs. Miles, who had not had the educational advantages of her daughter, simpered up with "Madame Newcome pas ici—votre excellence nouvellement arrivé—avez vous fait ung bong voyage? Je reçois chez moi Mercredi prochaing; lonnure de vous voir—Madamasel Miles ma fille;" and Mira, now reinforcing her mamma, poured in a glib little oration in French, somewhat to the astonishment of the Colonel, who began to think however, that perhaps French was the language of the polite world, into which he was now making his very first *entrée*.

Mrs. Newcome had left her place at the door of her drawing-room, to walk through her rooms with Rummun Lall, the celebrated Indian merchant, otherwise His Excellency Rummun Lall, otherwise His Highness Rummun Lall, the chief proprietor of the diamond mines in Golconda, with a claim of three millions and a half upon the East India Company; who smoked his hookah after dinner when the ladies were gone, and in whose honour (for his servants always brought a couple or more of hookahs with them) many English gentlemen made themselves sick, while trying to emulate the same practice. Mr. Newcome had been obliged to go to bed himself in consequence of the uncontrollable nausea produced by the chillum; and Doctor Mac Guffog, in hopes of converting his Highness, had puffed his till he was as black in the face as the interesting Indian—and now, having hung on his arm—always in the dirty gloves, flirting a fan whilst his Excellency consumed betel out of a silver box; and having promenaded him and his turban, and his shawls, and his kincab pelisse, and his lacquered moustache, and keen brown face, and opal eyeballs through her rooms, the hostess came back to her station at the drawing-room door.

As soon as his Excellency saw the Colonel, whom he perfectly well knew, his Highness's princely air was exchanged for one of the deepest humility. He bowed his head and put his two hands before his eyes, and came creeping towards him submissively, to the wonderment of Mrs. Miles; who was yet more astonished when the Moldavian magnate exclaimed in perfectly good English, "What Rummun, you here?"

The Rummun, still bending and holding his hands before him, uttered a number of rapid sentences in the Hindustani language, which Colonel Newcome received twirling his mustachios with much hauteur. He turned on his heel rather abruptly and began to speak to Mrs. Newcome, who smiled and thanked him for coming—on his first night after his return.

The Colonel said, "to whose house should he first come but to his brother's?" How Mrs. Newcome wished she could have had room for him at dinner! And there was room after all, for Mr. Shaloony was detained at the House. The most interesting conversation. The Indian Prince was so intelligent!

"The Indian what?" asks Colonel Newcome. The heathen gentleman had gone off, and was seated by one of the handsomest young women in the room, whose fair face was turned towards him, whose blond ringlets touched his shoulder, and who was listening to him as eagerly as Desdemona listened to Othello.

"His Highness"

The Colonel's rage was excited as he saw the Indian's behaviour. He curled his mustachios up to his eyes in his wrath. "You don't mean that that man calls himself a Prince? That a fellow who wouldn't sit down in an officer's presence is . . ."

"How do you do, Mr. Honeyman?—Eh, bong soir, Monsieur—You are very late, Mr. Pressly. What, Barnes! is it possible that you do me the honour to come all the way from May Fair to Marylebone. I thought you young men of fashion never crossed Oxford Street. Colonel Newcome, this is your nephew."

"How do you do, Sir," says Barnes, surveying the Colonel's costume with inward wonder, but without the least outward manifestation of surprise. "I suppose you dined here to meet the black Prince. I came to ask him and my uncle to meet you at dinner on Wednesday. Where's my uncle, Ma'am?"

"Your uncle is gone to bed ill. He smoked one of those hookahs which the Prince brings, and it has made him very unwell indeed, Barnes. How is Lady Ann? Is Lord Kew in London? Is your sister better for Brighton air? I see your cousin is appointed Secretary of Legation. Have you good accounts of your aunt Lady Fanny?"

"Lady Fanny is as well as can be expected, and the baby is going on perfectly well, thank you," Barnes said drily; and his aunt, obstinately gracious with him, turned away to some other new comer.

"It's interesting, isn't it, Sir," says Barnes, turning to the Colonel, "to see such union in families? Whenever I come here, my aunt trots out all my relations; and I send a man round in the mornin to ask how they all are. So Uncle Hobson is gone to bed sick with a hookah. I know there was a deuce of a row made when I smoked at Marble Head. You are promised to us for Wednesday, please. Is there anybody you would like to meet? Not our friend the Rummun. How the girls crowd round him! By Gad, a fellow who's rich in London may have the pick of any gal—not here—not in this sort of thing; I mean in society, you know," says Barnes confidentially. "I've seen the old dowagers crowdin round that fellow, and the girls snugglin up to his India-rubber face. He's known to have two wives already in India; but, by Gad, for a settlement, I believe some of 'em here would marry—I mean of the girls in society."

"But isn't this society?" asked the Colonel.

"Oh, of course. It's very good society and that sort of thing—but it's not, you know—you understand. I give you my honour there are not three people in the room one meets anywhere, except the Rummun. What is he at home, Sir? I know he ain't a Prince, you know, any more than I am."

"I believe he is a rich man now," said the Colonel. "He began from very low beginnings, and odd stories are told about the origin of his fortune."

"That may be," says the young man; "of course, as business men, that's not our affair. But has he got the fortune? He keeps a large account with us; and, I think, wants to have larger dealings with us still. As one of the family we may ask you to stand by us, and tell us anything you know. My father has asked him down to Newcome, and we've taken him up; wisely or not I can't say. I think otherwise; but I'm quite young in the house, and of course the elders have the chief superintendence." The young man of business had dropped his drawl or his languor, and was speaking quite unaffectedly, good-naturedly, and selfishly. Had you talked to him for a week, you could not have made him understand the scorn and loathing with which the Colonel regarded him. Here was a young fellow as keen as the oldest curmudgeon; a lad with scarce a beard to his chin that would pursue his bond as rigidly as Shylock. "If he is like this at twenty, what will he be at fifty?" groaned the Colonel. "I'd rather Clive were dead than have him such a heartless worldling as this." And yet the young man was not ungenerous, not untruth-telling, not unserviceable. He thought his life was good enough. It was as[2] good as that of other folks he lived with. You don't suppose he had any misgivings, provided he was in the City early enough in the morning; or slept badly, unless he indulged too freely over night; or twinges of conscience that his life was misspent? He thought his life a most lucky and reputable one. He had a share in a good business, and felt that he could increase it. Some day he would marry a good match, with a good fortune; meanwhile he could take his pleasure decorously, and sow his wild oats as some of the young Londoners sow them, not broadcast after the fashion of careless scatter-brained youth, but trimly and neatly, in quiet places, where the crop can come up unobserved, and be taken in without bustle or scandal. Barnes Newcome never missed going to church, or dressing for dinner. He never kept a tradesman waiting for his money. He never drank too much, except when other fellows did, and in good

---

[2] young man was not ungenerous, not untruth-telling, not unserviceable. He thought his life was good enough. It was as *E1*] young man's life was as *R*

company. He never[3] was late for business, or huddled over his toilet, however brief had been his sleep, or severe his headache. In a word, he was as scrupulously whited as any sepulchre in the whole bills of mortality.

Whilst young Barnes and his uncle were thus holding parley, a slim gentleman of bland aspect, with a roomy forehead, or what his female admirers called "a noble brow," and a neat white neckcloth tied with clerical skill, was surveying Colonel Newcome through his shining spectacles, and waiting for an opportunity to address him. The Colonel remarked the eagerness with which the gentleman in black regarded him, and asked Mr. Barnes who was the padre? Mr. Barnes turned his eyeglass towards the spectacles, and said "he didn't know any more than the dead; he didn't know two people in the room." The spectacles nevertheless made the eyeglass a bow, of which the latter took no sort of cognisance. The spectacles advanced; Mr. Newcome fell back with a peevish exclamation of "Confound the fellow, what is he coming to speak to *me* for?" He did not choose to be addressed by all sorts of persons in all houses.

But he of the spectacles, with an expression of delight in his pale blue eyes, and smiles dimpling his countenance, pressed onwards with outstretched hands, and it was towards the Colonel he turned these smiles and friendly salutations. "Did I hear aright, Sir, from Mrs. Miles," he said, "and have I the honour of speaking to Colonel Newcome?"

"The same, Sir," says the Colonel; at which the other, tearing off a glove of lavender-coloured kid, uttered the words "Charles Honeyman," and seized the hand of his brother-in-law. "My poor sister's husband," he continued; "my own benefactor; Clive's father. How strange are these meetings in the mighty world! How I rejoice to see you, and know you!"

"You are Charles, are you?" cries the other. "I am very glad, indeed, to shake you by the hand, Honeyman. Clive and I should have beat up your quarters to-day, but we were busy until dinner-time. You put me in mind of poor Emma, Charles," he added, sadly. Emma had not been a good wife to him; a flighty silly little woman, who had caused him when alive many a night of pain and day of anxiety.

"Poor, poor Emma!" exclaimed the ecclesiastic, casting his eyes towards the chandelier, and passing a white cambric pocket-handkerchief gracefully before them. No man in London understood the ring business or the pocket-handkerchief business better, or smothered his emotion more beautifully. "In the gayest moments, in the giddiest throng of fashion, the thoughts of the past will rise; the departed will be among us still. But this is not the strain wherewith to greet the friend newly arrived on our shores. How it rejoices me to behold you in old England! How you must have joyed to see Clive!"

"D—— the humbug," muttered Barnes, who knew him perfectly well. "The fellow is always in the pulpit."

The incumbent of Lady Whittlesea's chapel smiled and bowed to him. "You do not recognise me, Sir; I have had the honour of seeing you in your public capacity in the City, when I have called at the bank, the bearer of my brother-in-law's generous——"

---

[3] He never drank too much, except when other fellows did, and in good company. He never *E1*] He seldom drank too much, and never *R*

"Never mind that, Honeyman!" cried the Colonel.

"But I *do* mind, my dear Colonel," answers Mr. Honeyman. "I should be a very bad man, and a very ungrateful brother if I *ever* forgot your kindness."

"For God's sake leave my kindness alone."

"He'll never leave it alone as long as he can use it," muttered Mr. Barnes in his teeth, and turning to his uncle. "May I take you home, Sir? my cab is at the door; and I shall be glad to drive you." But the Colonel said he must talk to his brother-in-law for a while, and, Mr. Barnes bowing very respectfully to him, slipped under a dowager's arm in the doorway, and retreated silently down-stairs.

Newcome was now thrown entirely upon the clergyman, and the latter described the personages present to the stranger who was curious to know how the party was composed. Mrs. Newcome herself would have been pleased had she heard Honeyman's discourse regarding her guests and herself. Charles Honeyman so spoke of most persons that you might fancy they were listening over his shoulder. Such an assemblage of learning, genius, and virtue, might well delight and astonish a stranger. "That lady in the red turban, with the handsome daughters, is Lady Budge, wife of the eminent judge of that name—everybody was astonished that he was not made Chief Justice, and elevated to the Peerage—the only objection (as I have heard confidentially) was on the part of a late sovereign, who said he never could consent to have a peer of the name of Budge. Her ladyship was of humble, I have heard even menial station originally, but becomes her present rank, dispenses the most elegant hospitality at her mansion in Connaught Terrace, and is a pattern as a wife and a mother. The young man talking to her daughter is a young barrister, already becoming celebrated as a contributor to some of our principal reviews."

"Who is that cavalry officer in a white waistcoat talking to the Jew with the beard?" asks the Colonel.

"He—he! That cavalry officer is another literary man of celebrity, and by profession an attorney. But he has quitted the law for the Muses, and it would appear that the Nine are never wooed except by gentlemen with mustachios."

"Never wrote a verse in my life," says[4] the Colonel laughing, and stroking his own.

"For I remark so many literary gentlemen with that decoration. The Jew with the beard, as you call him, is Herr von Lungen, the eminent hautboy-player. The three next gentlemen are Mr. Smee, of the Royal Academy (who is shaved as you perceive), and Mr. Moyes, and Mr. Cropper, who are both very hairy about the chin. At the piano, singing, accompanied by Mademoiselle Lebrun, is Signor Mezzocaldo, the great barytone from Rome. Professor Quartz and Baron Hammerstein, celebrated geologists from Germany, are talking with their illustrious *confrère*, Sir Robert Craxton, in the door. Do you see yonder that stout gentleman with snuff on his shirt? the eloquent Dr. Mac Guffog, of Edinburgh, talking to Dr. Ettore, who lately escaped from the Inquisition at Rome in the disguise of a

---

[4] says *E1*] said *HM*

washerwoman, after undergoing the question several times, the rack and the thumbscrew. They say that he was to have been burned in the Grand Square the next morning; but between ourselves, my dear Colonel, I mistrust these stories of converts and martyrs. Did you ever see a more jolly-looking man than Professor Schnurr, who was locked up in Spielberg, and got out up a chimney, and through a window. Had he waited a few months there are very few windows he could have passed through. That splendid man in the red fez is Kurbash Pasha—another renegade I deeply lament to say—a hairdresser from Marseilles, by name Monsieur Ferchaud, who passed into Egypt, and laid aside the *tongs* for the turban. He is talking with Mr. Palmer, one of our most delightful young poets, and with Desmond O'Tara, son of the late revered bishop of Ballinafad, who has lately quitted ours for the errors of the Church of Rome. Let me whisper to you that your kinswoman is rather a searcher after what we call here *notabilities*. I heard talk of one I knew in better days—of one who was the comrade of my youth, and the delight of Oxford—poor Pidge of Brasenose, who got the Newdegate in my third year, and who, under his present name of Father Bartolo, was to have been here in his capuchin dress with a beard and bare feet; but I presume he could not get permission from his Superior. That is Mr. Huff, the political economist, talking with Mr. Macduff, the member for Glenlivat. That is the Coroner for Middlesex conversing with the great surgeon Sir Cutler Sharp, and that pretty little laughing girl talking with them is no other than the celebrated Miss Pinnifer, whose novel of Ralph the Resurrectionist created such a sensation after it was abused in the Trimestrial Review. It was a little bold certainly—I just looked at it at my club—after hours devoted to parish duty a clergyman is sometimes allowed, you know, *desipere in loco*—there are descriptions in it certainly startling—ideas about marriage not exactly orthodox—but the poor child wrote the book actually in the nursery, and all England was ringing with it before Dr. Pinnifer, her father, knew who was the author. That is the Doctor asleep in the corner by Miss Rudge, the American authoress, who I daresay is explaining to him the difference between the two Governments. My dear Mrs. Newcome, I am giving my brother-in-law a little sketch of some of the celebrities who are crowding your salon to-night. What a delightful evening you have given us!"

"I try to do my best, Colonel Newcome," said the lady of the house. "I hope many a night we may see you here; and, as I said this morning, Clive, when he is of an age to appreciate this kind of entertainment. Fashion I do not worship. You may meet that amongst other branches of our family; but genius and talent I do reverence. And if I can be the means—the *humble* means—to bring men of genius together—mind to associate with mind—men of all nations to mingle in *friendly unison*—I shall not have lived *altogether* in vain. They call us women of the world *frivolous*, Colonel Newcome. So some may be; I do not say there are not in our own family persons who worship mere worldly rank, and think but of fashion and gaiety; but such, I trust, will never be the objects in life of me and *my* children. We are but merchants; we seek to be *no more*. If I can look around me and see as I do" (she waves her fan round, and points to the illustrations scintillating round the room), "and see as I do now—a Poski, whose name is

ever connected with Polish history—an Ettore, who has exchanged a ton-
sure and a rack for our own free country—a Hammerstein, and a Quartz, a
Miss Rudge, our Transatlantic sister (who I trust will not mention *this* modest salon in her forthcoming work on Europe), and Miss Pinnifer, whose
genius I acknowledge, though I deplore her opinions; if I can gather together travellers, poets, and painters, princes and distinguished soldiers
from the East, and clergymen, remarkable for their eloquence, *my* humble
aim is attained, and Maria Newcome is not altogether useless in her generation. Will you take a little refreshment? Allow *your sister* to go down
to the dining-room supported by your *gallant* arm." She looked round to
the admiring congregation, whereof Honeyman, as it were, acted as clerk,
and flirting her fan, and flinging up her little head, Consummate Virtue
walked down on the arm of the Colonel.

The refreshment was rather meagre. The foreign artists generally
dashed down-stairs, and absorbed all the ices, creams, &c. To those coming late there were chicken bones, table-cloths puddled with melted ice,
glasses hazy with sherry, and broken bits of bread. The Colonel said he
never supped; and he and Honeyman walked away together, the former
to bed, the latter, I am sorry to say, to his club; for he was a dainty feeder,
and loved lobster, and talk late at night, and a comfortable little glass of
something wherewith to conclude the day.

He agreed to come to breakfast with the Colonel, who named eight or
nine for the meal. Nine Mr. Honeyman agreed to with a sigh. The incumbent of Lady Whittlesea's chapel seldom rose before eleven. For to tell
the truth, no French Abbé of Louis XV. was more lazy and luxurious, and
effeminate, than our polite bachelor preacher.

One of Colonel Newcome's fellow-passengers from India was Mr. James
Binnie of the civil service, a jolly young bachelor of two or three and forty,
who, having spent half of his past life in Bengal, was bent upon enjoying the remainder in Britain or in Europe, if a residence at home should
prove agreeable to him. The nabob of books and tradition is a personage
no longer to be found among us. He is neither as wealthy nor as wicked
as the jaundiced monster of romances and comedies, who purchases the
estates of broken down English gentlemen, with rupees tortured out of
bleeding rajahs, who smokes a hookah in public, and in private carries
about a guilty conscience, diamonds of untold value, and a diseased liver;
who has a vulgar wife, with a retinue of black servants whom she maltreats,
and a gentle son and daughter with good impulses and an imperfect education, desirous to amend their own and their parents' lives, and thoroughly
ashamed of the follies of the old people. If you go to the house of an Indian
gentleman now, he does not say, "Bring more curricles," like the famous
Nabob of Stanstead Park. He goes to Leadenhall Street in an omnibus,
and walks back from the City for exercise. I have known some who have
had maid-servants to wait on them at dinner. I have met scores who look
as florid and rosy as any British squire who has never left his paternal beef
and acres. They do not wear nankeen jackets in summer. Their livers are
not out of order any more; and as for hookahs, I dare swear there are not

two now kept alight[5] within the bills of mortality; and that retired Indians would as soon think of smoking them, as their wives would of burning themselves on their husbands' bodies at the cemetery, Kensal Green, near to the Tyburnian quarter of the city which the Indian world at present inhabits. It used to be Baker Street and Harley Street; it used to be Portland Place, and in more early days Bedford Square, where the Indian magnates flourished; districts which have fallen from their pristine state of splendour now, even as Agra, and Benares, and Lucknow, and Tippoo Sultan's city are fallen.

After two-and-twenty years' absence from London, Mr. Binnie returned to it on the top of the Gosport coach with a hat-box and a little portmanteau, a pink fresh-shaven face, a perfect appetite, a suit of clothes like everybody else's, and not the shadow of a black servant. He called a cab at the White Horse Cellar, and drove to Nerot's Hotel, Clifford Street; and he gave the cabman eightpence, making the fellow, who grumbled, understand that Clifford Street was not two hundred yards from Bond Street, and that he was paid at the rate of five shillings and fourpence per mile—calculating the mile at only sixteen hundred yards. He asked the waiter at what time Colonel Newcome had ordered dinner, and finding there was an hour on his hands before the meal, walked out to examine the neighbourhood for a lodging where he could live more quietly than in a hotel. He called it a hotal. Mr. Binnie was a North Briton, his father having been a Writer to the Signet, in Edinburgh, who had procured his son a writership in return for electioneering services done to an East Indian Director. Binnie had his retiring-pension, and, besides, had saved half his allowances ever since he had been in India. He was a man of great reading, no small ability, considerable accomplishment, excellent good sense and good humour. The ostentatious said he was a screw; but he gave away more money than far more extravagant people: he was a disciple of David Hume (whom he admired more than any other mortal), and the serious denounced him as a man of dangerous principles, though there were among the serious men much more dangerous than James Binnie.

On returning to his hotel, Colonel Newcome found this worthy gentleman installed in his room in the best arm-chair sleeping cosily; the evening paper laid decently over his plump waistcoat, and his little legs placed on an opposite chair. Mr. Binnie woke up briskly when the Colonel entered. "It is you, you gad-about, is it?" cried the civilian. "How has the beau monde of London treated the Indian Adonis? Have you made a sensation, Newcome? Gad, Tom, I remember you a buck of bucks when that coat first came out to Calcutta—just a Barrackpore Brummel—in Lord Minto's reign was it, or when Lord Hastings was Satrap over us?"

"A man must have one good coat," says the Colonel; "I don't profess to be a dandy; but get a coat from a good tailor, and then have done with it." He still thought his garment was as handsome as need be.

"Done with it—ye're never done with it!" cries the civilian.

"An old coat is an old friend, old Binnie. I don't want to be rid of one or the other. How long did you and my boy sit up together—isn't he a

5 alight *E 1*] alive *HM*

fine lad, Binnie? I expect you are going to put him down for something handsome in your will."

"See what it is to have a real friend now, Colonel! I sate up for ye, or let us say more correctly, I waited for you—because I knew you would want to talk about that scapegrace of yours. And if I had gone to bed, I should have had you walking up to No. 26, and waking me out of my first rosy slumber. Well, now confess; avoid not. Haven't ye fallen in love with some young beauty on the very first night of your arrival in your sister's salong, and selected a mother-in-law for young[6] Scapegrace?"

"Isn't he a fine fellow, James?" says the Colonel, lighting a cheroot as he sits on the table. Was it joy, or the bed-room candle with which he lighted his cigar, which illuminated his honest features so, and made them so to shine?

"I have been occupied, Sir, in taking the lad's moral measurement: and have[7] pumped him as successfully as ever I cross-examined a rogue in my court. I place his qualities thus.—Love of approbation sixteen. Benevolence fourteen. Combativeness fourteen. Adhesiveness two. Amativeness is not yet of course fully developed, but I expect will be prodeegiously strong. The imaginative and reflective organs are very large—those of calculation weak. He may make a poet or a painter, or you may make a sojor of him, though worse men than him's good enough for that—but a bad merchant, a lazy lawyer, and a miserable mathematician. He has wit and conscientiousness, so ye[8] mustn't think of making a clergyman of him."

"Binnie!" says the Colonel, gravely, "you are always sneering at the cloth."

"When I think that but for my appointment to India, I should have been a luminary of the faith and a pillar of the church! grappling with the ghostly enemy in the pulpit, and giving out the psawm. Eh, Sir, what a loss Scottish Divinity has had in James Binnie!" cries the little civilian with his most comical face. "But that is not the question. My opinion, Colonel, is, that young scapegrace will give you a deal of trouble; or would, only you are so absurdly proud of him that you think everything he does is perfaction. He'll spend your money for you: he'll do as little work as need be. He'll get into scrapes with the sax. He's almost as simple as his father, and that is to say that any rogue will cheat him: and he seems to me to have got your obstinate habit of telling the truth, Colonel, which may prevent his getting on in the world, but on the other hand will keep him from going very wrong. So that though there is every fear for him, there's some hope and some consolation."

"What do you think of his Latin and Greek?" asks the Colonel. Before going out to his party, Newcome had laid a deep scheme with Binnie, and it had been agreed that the latter should examine the young fellow in his humanities.

"Wall," cries the Scot, "I find that the lad knows as much about Greek and Latin as I knew myself when I was eighteen years of age."

---

[6] young E1] your R
[7] and have E1] and I have R
[8] ye E1] you R

"My dear Binnie, is it possible? You, the best scholar in all India!"

"And which amounted to exactly nothing. He has acquired in five years, and by the admirable seestem purshood at your public schools, just about as much knowledge of the ancient languages, as he could get by three months' application at home. Mind ye, I don't say he would apply; it is most probable he would do no such thing. But at the cost of—how much? two hundred pounds annually—for five years—he has acquired about five and twenty guineas worth of classical leeterature—enough I daresay to enable him to quote Horace respectably through life, and what more do ye[9] want from a young man of his expectations? I think I should send him into the army, that's the best place for him—there's the least to do, and the handsomest clothes to wear. *Acce segnum!*" says the little wag, daintily taking up the tail of his friend's coat.

"There's never any knowing whether you are in jest or in earnest, Binnie," the puzzled Colonel said.

"How should you know, when I don't know myself?" answered the Scotchman.[1] "In earnest now, Tom Newcome, I think your boy is as fine a lad as I ever set eyes on. He seems to have intelligence and good temper. He carries his letter of recommendation in his countenance: and with the honesty—and the rupees, mind ye—which he inherits from his father, the deuce is in it if he can't make his way. What time's the breakfast? Eh, but it was a comfort this morning not to hear the holy-stoning on the deck. We ought to go into lodgings, and not fling our money out of the window of this hotel. We must make the young chap take us about and show us the town in the morning, Tom. I had but three days of it five-and-twenty years ago, and I propose to reshoome my observations to-morrow after breakfast. We'll just go on deck and see how's her head before we turn in, eh Colonel?" and with this the jolly gentleman nodded over his candle to his friend, and trotted off to bed.

The Colonel and his friend were light sleepers and early risers, like most men that come from the country where they had both been so long sojourning, and were awake and dressed long before the London waiters had thought of quitting their beds. The housemaid was the only being stirring in the morning when little Mr. Binnie blundered over her pail as she was washing the deck. Early as he was, his fellow-traveller had preceded him. Binnie found the Colonel in his sitting-room arrayed in what are called in Scotland his stocking-feet, already puffing the cigar, which in truth was seldom out of his mouth at any hour of the day.

He had a couple of bed-rooms adjacent to this sitting-room, and when Binnie, as brisk and rosy about the gills as Chanticleer, broke out in a morning salutation, "Hush," says the Colonel, putting a long finger up to his mouth, and advancing towards him as noiselessly as a ghost.

"What's in the wind now?" asks the little Scot; "and what for have ye not got your shoes on?"

"Clive's asleep," says the Colonel, with a countenance full of extreme anxiety.

---

[9] ye *E1*] you *R*
[1] "There's never any knowing ... Scotchman. *E1*] [omitted] *R*

"The darling boy slumbers, does he?" said the wag; "mayn't I just step in and look at his beautiful countenance whilst he's asleep, Colonel?"

"You may if you take off those confounded creaking shoes," the other answered, quite gravely; and Binnie turned away to hide his jolly round face, which was screwed up with laughter.

"Have ye been breathing a prayer over your rosy infant's slumbers, Tom," asks Mr. Binnie.

"And if I have, James Binnie," the Colonel said, gravely, and his sallow face blushing somewhat, "if I have I hope I've done no harm. The last time I saw him asleep was nine years ago, a sickly little pale-faced boy in his little cot, and now, Sir, that I see him again, strong and handsome, and all that a fond father can wish to see a boy, I should be an ungrateful villain, James, if I didn't—if I didn't do what you said just now, and thank God Almighty for restoring him to me."

Binnie did not laugh any more. "By George, Tom Newcome," said he, "you're just one of the saints of the earth. If all men were like you there'd be an end of both our trades; there would be no fighting and no soldiering, no rogues, and no magistrates to catch them." The Colonel wondered at his friend's enthusiasm, who was not used to be complimentary; indeed what so usual with him as that simple act of gratitude and devotion about which his comrade spoke to him? To ask a blessing for his boy was as natural to him as to wake with the sunrise, or to go to rest when the day was over. His first and his last thought was always the child.

The two gentlemen were home in time enough to find Clive dressed, and his uncle arrived for breakfast. The Colonel said a grace over that meal: the life was begun which he had[2] longed and prayed for, and the son smiling before his eyes who had been in his thoughts for so many fond years.

---

[2] had *E1*] [omitted] *R*

Chapter IX.

N Steyne Gardens, Brighton, the lodging-houses are among the most frequented in that city of lodging-houses. These mansions have bow-windows in front, bulging out with gentle prominences, and ornamented with neat verandahs, from which you can behold the tide of human kind as it flows up and down the Steyne, and that blue ocean over which Brittannia is said to rule, stretching brightly away eastward and westward. The chain-pier, as everybody knows, runs intrepidly into the sea, which sometimes, in fine weather, bathes its feet with laughing wavelets, and anon, on stormy days, dashes over its sides with roaring foam. Here, for the sum of two-pence, you can go out to sea and pace this vast deck without need of a steward with a basin. You can watch the sun setting in splendour over Worthing, or illuminating with its rising glories the ups and downs of Rottingdean. You see the citizen with his family inveigled into the shallops of the mercenary native mariner, and fancy that the motion cannot be pleasant; and how the hirer of the boat, *otium et oppidi laudat*[1] *rura sui*, haply sighs for ease, and prefers Richmond or Hampstead. You behold a hundred bathing-machines put to sea; and your naughty fancy depicts the beauties splashing under their white awnings. Along the rippled sands (stay, are they rippled sands or shingly beach?) the prawn-boy seeks the delicious material of your breakfast. Breakfast—meal in London almost unknown, greedily devoured in Brighton! In yon vessels now nearing the shore the sleepless mariner has ventured forth to seize the delicate whiting, the greedy and foolish mackarel, and the homely sole. Hark to the twanging horn! it is the early coach going out to London. Your eye follows it, and rests on the pinnacles built by the beloved GEORGE. See the worn-out London roué pacing the pier, inhaling the sea air, and casting furtive glances under the bonnets of the pretty girls who trot here before lessons! Mark the bilious lawyer, escaped for a day from Pump Court, and

---

[1] *laudat E1] laudans R*

sniffing the fresh breezes before he goes back to breakfast and a bag full of briefs at the Albion! See that pretty string of prattling school girls, from the chubby-cheeked, flaxen-headed, little maiden just toddling by the side of the second teacher, to the arch damsel of fifteen, giggling and conscious of her beauty, whom Miss Griffin, the stern head-governess, awfully reproves! See Tomkins with a telescope and marine-jacket; young Nathan and young Abrams, already bedizened in jewellery, and rivalling the sun in oriental splendour—yonder poor invalid crawling along in her chair—yonder jolly fat lady examining the Brighton pebbles (I actually once saw a lady buy one), and her children wondering at the sticking-plaister portraits with gold hair, and gold stocks, and prodigious high-heeled boots, miracles of art, and cheap at seven-and-sixpence! It is the fashion to run down George IV., but what myriads of Londoners ought to thank him for inventing Brighton! One of the best of physicians our city has ever known, is kind, cheerful, merry Doctor Brighton. Hail thou purveyor of shrimps and honest prescriber of South Down mutton! There is no mutton so good as Brighton mutton; no flys so pleasant as Brighton flys; nor any cliff so pleasant to ride on; no shops so beautiful to look at as the Brighton gimcrack shops, and the fruit shops, and the market. I fancy myself in Mrs. Honeyman's lodgings in Steyne Gardens, and in enjoyment of all these things.

If the gracious reader has had losses in life, losses not so bad as to cause absolute want, or inflict upon him or her the bodily injury of starvation, let him confess that the evils of this poverty are by no means so great as his timorous fancy depicted. Say your money has been invested in West Diddlesex bonds, or other luckless speculations—the news of the smash comes; you pay your outlying bills with the balance at the banker's; you assemble your family and make them a fine speech; the wife of your bosom goes round and embraces the sons and daughters seriatim; nestling in your own waistcoat finally, in possession of which, she says (with tender tears and fond quotations from Holy Writ, God bless her!), and of the darlings round about, lies all *her* worldly treasure: the weeping servants are dismissed, their wages paid in full, and with a present of prayer and hymn books from their mistress; your elegant house in Harley Street is to let, and you subside into lodgings in Pentonville, or Kensington, or Brompton. How unlike the mansion where you paid taxes and distributed elegant hospitality for so many years!

You subside into lodgings, I say, and you find yourself very tolerably comfortable. I am not sure that in her heart your wife is not happier than in what she calls her happy days. She will be somebody hereafter: she was nobody in Harley Street: that is, everybody else in her visiting book, take the names all round, was as good as she. They had the very same entrées, plated ware, men to wait, &c., at all the houses where you visited in the street. Your candlesticks might be handsomer (and indeed they had a very[2] fine effect upon the dinner-table), but then Mr. Jones's silver (or electroplated) dishes were much finer. You had more carriages at your door on the evening of your delightful soirées than Mrs. Brown (there is no phrase more elegant, and to my taste, than that in which people are described as

[2] very *E1*] [omitted] *R*

Londin super Mare

"seeing a great deal of carriage company"); but yet Mrs. Brown, from the circumstance of her being a baronet's niece, took precedence of your dear wife at most tables. Hence the latter charming woman's scorn at the British baronetcy, and her many jokes at the order. In a word, and in the height of your social prosperity, there was always a lurking dissatisfaction, and a something bitter, in the midst of the fountain of delights at which you were permitted to drink.

There is no good (unless your taste is that way) in living in a society where you are merely the equal of everybody else. Many people give themselves extreme pains to frequent company where all around them are their superiors, and where, do what you will, you must be subject to continual mortification—(as, for instance, when Marchioness X. forgets you, and you can't help thinking that she cuts you on purpose; when Duchess Z. passes by in her diamonds, &c.). The true pleasure of life is to live with your inferiors. Be the cock of your village; the queen of your coterie; and, besides very great persons, the people whom Fate has specially endowed with this kindly consolation, are those who have seen what are called better days— those who have had losses. I am like Cæsar, and of a noble mind: if I cannot be first in Piccadilly, let me try Hatton Garden, and see whether I cannot lead the *ton* there. If I cannot take the lead at White's or the Traveller's, let me be president of the Jolly Sandboys at the Bag of Nails, and blackball everybody who does not pay me honour. If my darling Bessy cannot go out of a drawing-room until a baronet's niece (ha! ha! a baronet's niece, forsooth!) has walked before her, let us frequent company where we shall be the first; and how *can* we be the first unless we select our inferiors for our associates? This kind of pleasure is to be had by almost everybody, and at scarce any cost. With a shilling's worth of tea and muffins you can get as much adulation and respect as many people cannot purchase with a thousand pounds' worth of plate and profusion, hired footmen, turning their houses topsy-turvy, and suppers from Gunter's. Adulation!—why, the people who come to you give as good parties as you do. Respect!—the very menials, who wait behind your supper-table, waited at a duke's yesterday, and actually patronise you! O you silly spendthrift! you can buy flattery for twopence, and you spend ever so much money in entertaining your equals and betters, and nobody admires you!

Now Aunt Honeyman was a woman of a thousand virtues; cheerful, frugal, honest, laborious, charitable, good-humoured, truth-telling, devoted to her[3] family, capable of any sacrifice for those she loved; and when she came to have losses of money, Fortune straightway compensated her by many kindnesses which no income can supply. The good old lady admired the word gentlewoman of all others in the English vocabulary, and made all around her feel that such was her rank. Her mother's father was a naval captain; her father had taken pupils, got a living, sent his son to college, dined with the squire, published his volume of sermons, was liked in his parish, where Miss Honeyman kept house for him, was respected for his kindness and famous for his port-wine; and so died, leaving about two hundred pounds a year to his two children, nothing to Clive Newcome's mother, who had displeased him by her first marriage (an elope-

---

[3] her *E1*] the *HM*

ment with Ensign Casey), and subsequent light courses. Charles Honeyman spent his money elegantly in wine parties at Oxford, and afterwards in foreign travel;—spent his money, and as much of Miss Honeyman's as that worthy soul would give him. She was a woman of spirit and resolution. She brought her furniture to Brighton (believing that the whole place still fondly remembered her grandfather, Captain Nokes, who had resided there, and his gallantry in Lord Rodney's action with the Count de Grasse), took a house and let the upper floors to lodgers.

The little brisk old lady brought a maid-servant out of the country with her, who was daughter to her father's clerk, and had learned her letters and worked her first sampler under Miss Honeyman's own eye, whom she adored all through her life. No Indian begum rolling in wealth, no countess mistress of castles and town-houses, ever had such a faithful toady as Hannah Hicks was to her mistress. Under Hannah was a young lady from the workhouse, who called Hannah, "Mrs. Hicks, mum," and who bowed in awe as much[4] before that domestic as Hannah did before Miss Honeyman. At five o'clock in summer, at seven in winter (for Mrs. Honeyman, a good economist, was chary of candlelight), Hannah woke up little Sally, and these three women rose. I leave you to imagine what a row there was in the establishment if Sally appeared with flowers under her bonnet, gave signs of levity or insubordination, prolonged her absence when sent forth for the beer, or was discovered in flirtation with the baker's boy or the grocer's young man. Sally was frequently renewed. Miss Honeyman called all her young persons Sally; and a great number of Sallies were consumed in her house. The qualities of the Sally for the time being formed a constant and delightful subject of conversation between Hannah and her mistress. The few friends who visited Miss Honeyman in her back-parlour, had *their* Sallies, in discussing whose peculiarities of disposition these good ladies passed the hours agreeably over their tea.

Many persons who let lodgings in Brighton have been servants themselves—are retired housekeepers, tradesfolk, and the like. With these surrounding individuals Hannah treated on a footing of equality, bringing to her mistress accounts of their various goings on; "how No. 6 was let; how No. 9 had not paid his rent again; how the first-floor at 27 had game almost every day, and made-dishes from Mutton's; how the family who had taken Mrs. Bugsby's had left as usual after the very first night, the poor little infant blistered all over with bites on its little dear[5] face; how the Miss Learys was going on shameful with the two young men, actially in their setting-room, mum, where one of them offered Miss Laura Leary a cigar; how Mrs. Cribb *still* went cuttin' pounds and pounds of meat off the lodgers' jints, emptying their tea-caddies, actially reading their letters. Sally had been told so by Polly, the Cribbs' maid, who was kep, how that poor child was kep, hearing language perfectly hawful!" These tales and anecdotes, not altogether redounding to their neighbours' credit, Hannah copiously collected and brought to her mistress's tea-table, or served at her frugal little supper when Miss Honeyman, the labours of the day over, partook of that cheerful meal. I need not say that such horrors as occurred at Mrs.

---

[4] in awe as much *E1*] as much in awe *R*
[5] little dear *E1*] dear little *R*

Bugsby's never befel in Mrs. Honeyman's establishment. Every room was fiercely swept and sprinkled, and watched by cunning eyes which nothing could escape; curtains were taken down, mattresses explored, every bone in bed dislocated and washed as soon as a lodger took his departure. And as for cribbing meat or sugar, Sally might occasionally abstract a lump or two, or pop a veal-cutlet into her mouth while bringing the dishes downstairs:—Sallies would—giddy creatures bred in workhouses—but Hannah might be entrusted with untold gold and uncorked brandy, and Miss Honeyman would as soon think of cutting a slice off Hannah's nose and devouring it, as of poaching on her lodgers' mutton. The best mutton-broth, the best veal-cutlets, the best necks of mutton and French beans, the best fried fish and plumpest partridges, in all Brighton, were to be had at Miss Honeyman's—and for her favourites the best Indian currie and rice, coming from a distinguished relative, at present an officer in Bengal. But very few were admitted to this mark of Miss Honeyman's confidence. If a family did not go to church they were not in favour: if they went to a dissenting meeting she had no opinion of them at all. Once there came to her house a quiet Staffordshire family who ate no meat on Fridays, and whom Miss Honeyman pitied as belonging to the Romish superstition: but when they were visited by two corpulent gentlemen in black, one of whom wore a purple under waistcoat, before[6] whom the Staffordshire lady absolutely sank down on her knees as he went into the drawing-room; Mrs. Honeyman sternly gave warning to these idolaters. She would have no Jesuits in *her* premises. She showed Hannah the picture in Howell's Medulla of the martyrs burning at Smithfield: who said, "Lord bless you, mum," and hoped it was a long time ago. She called on the curate: and many and many a time, for years after, pointed out to her friends, and sometimes to her lodgers, the spot on the carpet where the poor benighted creature had knelt down. So she went on respected by all her friends, by all her tradesmen, by herself not a little, talking of her previous "misfortunes" with amusing equanimity; as if her father's parsonage house had been a palace of splendour, and the one horse chaise (with the lamps for evenings) from which she had descended, a noble equipage. "But I know it is for the best, Clive," she would say to her nephew in describing those grandeurs, "and, thank Heaven, can be resigned in that station in life to which it has pleased God to call me."

The good lady was called the Duchess by her fellow tradesfolk in the square in which she lived. (I don't know what would have come to her had she been told she was a tradeswoman!) Her butchers, bakers, and market-people, paid her as much respect as though she had been a grandee's housekeeper out of Kemp Town. Knowing her station, she yet was kind to those inferior beings. She held affable conversations with them, she patronised Mr. Rogers, who was said to be worth a hundred thousand—two hundred thousand pound, (or lbs. was it?) and who said, "Law bless the old Duchess, she do make as much of a pound of veal-cutlet as some would of a score of bullocks, but you see she's a lady born and a lady bred: she'd die before she'd owe a farden, and she's seen better days, you know." She went to see the grocer's wife on an interesting occasion, and won the heart of the family by tasting their caudle. Her fishmonger (it was fine to hear

6 before *E1*] and before *R*

her talk of "my fishmonger") would sell her a whiting as respectfully as if she had called for a dozen turbots and lobsters. It was believed by those good folks that her father had been a Bishop at the very least: and the better days which she had known were supposed to signify some almost unearthly prosperity. "I have always found, Hannah," the simple soul would say, "that people know their place, or can be very very[7] easily made to find it if they lose it; and if a gentlewoman does not forget herself, her inferiors will not forget that she is a gentlewoman." "No indeed, mum, and I'm sure they would do no such thing, mum," says Hannah, who carries away the teapot for her own breakfast, (to be transmitted to Sally for her subsequent refection) whilst her mistress washes her cup and saucer, as her mother had washed her own China many scores of years[8] ago.

If some of the surrounding lodging-house keepers, as I have no doubt they did, disliked the little Duchess for the airs which she gave herself, as they averred; they must have envied her too her superior prosperity, for there was scarcely ever a card in her window, whilst those ensigns in her neighbours' houses would remain exposed to the flies and the weather, and disregarded by passers by for months together. She had many regular customers, or what should be rather called constant friends. Deaf old Mr. Cricklade came every winter for fourteen years, and stopped until the hunting was over; an invaluable man, giving little trouble, passing all day on horseback, and all night over his rubber at the club. The Misses Barkham, Barkhambury, Tunbridge Wells, whose father had been at college with Mr. Honeyman, came regularly in June for sea air, letting Barkhambury for the summer season. Then, for many years, she had her nephew as we have seen; and kind recommendations from the clergymen of Brighton, and a constant friend in the celebrated Dr. Goodenough of London, who[9] had been her father's private pupil, and of his college afterwards,[1] who sent his patients from time to time down to her, and his fellow physician, Dr. H——, who on his part would never take any fee from Miss Honeyman, except a packet of India currie-powder, a ham cured as she only knew how to cure them, and once a year, or so, a dish of her tea.

"Was there ever such luck as that confounded old Duchess's," says Mr. Gawler, coal-merchant and lodging-house keeper, next door but two, whose apartments were more odious in some respects than Mrs. Bugsby's own. "Was there ever such devil's[2] own luck, Mrs. G.? It's only a fortnight ago as I read in the *Sussex Advertiser* the death of Miss Barkham, of Barkhambury, Tunbridge Wells, and thinks I there's a spoke in *your* wheel, you stuck-up little old Duchess, with your cussed airs and impudence. And she ain't put her card up three days; and look yere, yere's two carriages, two maids, three children, one of them wrapped up in a Hinjar shawl— man hout a livery,—looks like a foring cove I think—lady in satin pelisse, and of course they go to the Duchess, be hanged to her. Of course it's our luck, nothing ever was like our luck. I'm blowed if I don't put a pistol to my

[7] very very *E1*] very *R*
[8] many scores of years *E1*] many score years *HM*
[9] London, who *E1*] London (who *R*
[1] afterwards, *E1*] afterwards), *R*
[2] devil's *E1*] a devil's *HM*

'ead, and end it, Mrs. G. There they go in—three, four, six, seven on 'em, and the man. That's the precious child's physic I suppose he's a carryin' in the basket. Just look at the luggage. I say! There's a bloody hand on the first carriage. It's a baronet, is it? I 'ope your ladyship's very well; and I 'ope Sir John will soon be down yere to join his family." Mr. Gawler makes sarcastic bows over the card in his bow-window whilst making this speech. The little Gawlers rush on to the drawing-room verandah themselves to examine the new arrivals.

"This is Mrs. Honeyman's?" asks the gentleman designated by Mr. Gawler as "the foring cove," and hands in a card on which the words "Mrs. Honeyman, 110, Steyne Gardens. J. Goodenough," are written in that celebrated physician's handwriting. "We want five bet-rooms, six bets, two or three sitting-rooms. Have you got dese?"

"Will you speak to my mistress?" says Hannah. And if it is a fact that Miss Honeyman *does* happen to be in the front parlour looking at the carriages, what harm is there in the circumstance, pray? Is not Gawler looking, and the people next door? Are not half a dozen little boys already gathered in the street (as if they started up out of the trap-doors for the coals), and the nursery maids in the stunted little garden, are not they looking through the bars of the square? "Please to speak to mistress," says Hannah, opening the parlour-door, and with a curtsey, "a gentleman about the apartments, mum."

"Five bet-rooms," says the man, entering. "Six bets, two or dree sitting-rooms? We gome from Dr. Goodenough."

"Are the apartments for you, Sir?" says the little Duchess, looking up at the large gentleman.

"For my Lady," answers the man.

"Had you not better take off your hat?" asks the Duchess, pointing out of one of her little mittens to 'the foring cove's' beaver, which he has neglected to remove.

The man grins, and takes off the hat. "I beck your bardon, Ma'am," says he. "Have you fife bet-rooms?" &c. The Doctor has cured the German of an illness, as well as his employers, and especially recommended Miss Honeyman to Mr. Kuhn.

"I have such a number[3] of apartments. My servant will show them to you." And she walks back with great state to her chair by the window, and resumes her station and work there.

Mr. Kuhn reports to his mistress, who descends to inspect the apartments, accompanied through them by Hannah. The rooms are pronounced to be exceedingly neat and pleasant, and exactly what are wanted for the family. The baggage is forthwith ordered to be brought from the carriages. The little invalid wrapped in his shawl is brought up-stairs by the affectionate Mr. Kuhn, who carries him as gently as if he had been bred all his life to nurse babies. The smiling Sally (the Sally for the time being happens to be a very[4] fresh pink-cheeked pretty little Sally) emerges from the kitchen and introduces the young ladies, the governess, the maids, to their apartments. The eldest, a slim black-haired young lass of thirteen,

---

[3] such a number *E1*] that number *R*
[4] very *E1*] [absent] *HM*

frisks about the rooms, looks at all the pictures, runs in and out of the verandah, tries the piano, and bursts out laughing at its wheezy jingle (it had been poor Emma's piano, bought for her on her seventeenth birthday, three weeks before she ran away with the ensign; her music is still in the stand by it: the Rev. Charles Honeyman has warbled sacred melodies over it, and Miss Honeyman considers it a delightful instrument), kisses her languid little brother laid on the sofa, and performs a hundred gay and agile motions suited to her age.

"O what a piano! Why it is[5] as cracked as Miss Quigley's voice!"

"My dear!" says Mamma. The little languid boy bursts out into a jolly laugh.

"What funny pictures, Mamma! Action with Count de Grasse; the Death of General Wolfe; a portrait of an officer, an old officer in blue, like Grandpapa; Brazen Nose[6] College, Oxford: what a funny name."

At the idea of Brazen Nose[7] College, another laugh comes from the invalid. "I suppose they've all got *brass noses* there," he says; and explodes at this joke. The poor little laugh ends in a cough, and Mamma's travelling basket, which contains everything, produces a bottle of syrup, labelled "Master A. Newcome. A tea-spoonful to be taken when the cough is troublesome."

"O the delightful sea! the blue, the fresh, the ever free," sings the young lady, with a shake. (I suppose the maritime song from which she quoted was just written at this time.) "How much better this is than going home and seeing those horrid factories and chimnies! I love Doctor Goodenough for sending us here. What a sweet house it is! Everybody is happy in it, even Miss Quigley is happy, Mamma. What nice rooms! What pretty chintz. What a—O what a—comfortable sofa!" and she falls down on the sofa, which, truth to say, was the Rev. Charles Honeyman's luxurious sofa from Oxford, presented to him by young Cibber Wright[8] of Christchurch, when that gentleman-commoner was eliminated from the University.

"The person of the house," Mamma says, "hardly comes up to Dr. Goodenough's description of her. He says he remembers her a pretty little woman when her father was his private tutor."

"She has grown very much since," says the girl. And an explosion takes place from the sofa, where the little man is always ready to laugh at any joke, or anything like a joke, uttered by himself or by any of his family or friends. As for Doctor Goodenough, he says laughing has saved that boy's life.

"She looks quite like a maid," continues the lady. "She has hard hands, and she called me mum always. I was quite disappointed in her." And she subsides into a novel, with many of which kind of works, and with other volumes, and with work-boxes, and with wonderful inkstands, portfolios, portable days of the month, scent-bottles, scissor-cases, gilt miniature easels displaying portraits, and countless gim-cracks of travel, the rapid Kuhn has covered the tables in the twinkling of an eye.

[5] it is *E1*] is it *HM*
[6] Brazen Nose *E1*] Brazenose *R*
[7] Brazen Nose *E1*] Brazenose *R*
[8] Cibber Wright *E1*] Downy *R*

The person supposed to be the landlady enters the room at this juncture, and the lady rises to receive her. The little wag on the sofa puts his arm round his sister's neck, and whispers, "I say, Eth, isn't she a pretty girl? I shall write to Doctor Goodenough and tell him how much she's *grown.*" Convulsions follow this sally to the surprise of Hannah, who says, "Pooty little dear!—what time will he have his dinner, mum?"

"Thank you, Mrs. Honeyman, at two o'clock," says the lady with a bow of her head. "There is a clergyman of your name in London; is he a relation?" The lady in her turn is astonished, for the tall person breaks out into a grin, and says, "Law, mum, you're speakin' of Master Charles. He's in London."

"Indeed!—of Master Charles?"

"And you take me for missis, mum. I beg your pardon, mum," cries Hannah. The invalid hits his sister in the side with a weak little fist. If laughter can cure, *Salva est res.* Doctor Goodenough's patient is safe. "Master Charles is missis's brother, mum. I've got no brother, mum—never had no brother. Only one son, who's in the Police, mum, thank you. And law bless me, I was going to forget! If you please, mum, missis says, if you are quite rested, she will pay her duty to you, mum."

"O indeed," says the lady, rather stiffly; and taking this for an acceptance of her mistress's visit, Hannah retires.

"This Miss Honeyman seems to be a great personage," says the lady. "If people let lodgings, why do they give themselves such airs?"

"We never saw Monsieur de Boigne at Boulogne, Mamma," interposes the girl.

"Monsieur de Boigne, my dear Ethel! Monsieur de Boigne is very well. But—" here the door opens, and in a large cap bristling with ribbons, with her best chesnut front, and her best black silk gown, on which her gold watch shines very splendidly, little Miss Honeyman makes her appearance, and a dignified curtsey to her lodger.

That lady vouchsafes a very slight inclination of the head indeed, which she repeats when Miss Honeyman says, "I am glad to hear your ladyship is pleased with the apartments."

"Yes, they will do very well, thank you," answers the latter person, gravely.

"And they have such a beautiful view of the sea!" cries Ethel.

"As if all the houses hadn't a view of the sea, Ethel! The price has been arranged, I think? My servants will require a comfortable room to dine in—by themselves, Ma'am, if you please. My governess and the younger children will dine together. My daughter dines with me—and my little boy's dinner will be ready at two o'clock precisely, if you please. It is now near one."

"Am I to understand?" interposed Miss Honeyman.

"O! I have no doubt we shall understand each other, Ma'am," cried Lady Ann Newcome, (whose noble presence the acute reader has no doubt ere this divined and saluted). "Doctor Goodenough has given me a most satisfactory account of you—more satisfactory perhaps than—than you are aware of." Perhaps Lady Ann's sentence was not going to end in a very satisfactory way for Mrs. Honeyman; but, awed by a peculiar look of resolution in the little lady, her lodger of an hour paused in whatever offensive remark she might have been about to make. "It is as well that I at last have the pleasure of seeing you, that I may state what I want, and that we may, as you say, understand each other. Breakfast and tea, if you please, will be served in the same manner as dinner. And you will have the kindness to order fresh milk every morning for my little boy—ass's milk—Doctor Goodenough has ordered ass's milk. Anything further I want I will communicate through the person who spoke to you—Kuhn, Mr. Kuhn, and that will do."

A heavy shower of rain was descending at this moment, and little Mrs. Honeyman looking at her lodger, who had sate down and taken up her book, said, "Have your ladyship's servants unpacked your trunks?"

"What on earth, Madam, have you—has that to do with the question?"

"They will be put to the trouble of packing again, I fear. I cannot provide—three times five are fifteen—fifteen separate meals for seven persons—besides those of my own family. If your servants cannot eat with mine, or in my kitchen, they and their mistress must go elsewhere. And the sooner the better, Madam, the sooner the better!" says Mrs. Honeyman, trembling with indignation, and sitting down in a chair spreading her silks.

"Do you know who I am?" asks Lady Ann, rising.

"Perfectly well, Madam," says the other. "And had I known, you should never have come into my house, that's more."

"Madam!" cries the lady, on which the poor little invalid, scared and nervous, and hungry for his dinner, began to cry from his sofa.

"It will be a pity that the dear little boy should be disturbed. Dear little child, I have often heard of him, and of you, Miss," says the little householder rising. "I will get you some dinner, my dear, for Clive's sake. And meanwhile your ladyship will have the kindness to seek for some other apartments—for not a bit shall my fire cook for any one else of your company." And with this the indignant little landlady sailed out of the room.

"Gracious goodness! Who *is* the woman?" cries Lady Ann. "I never was so insulted in my life."

"O Mamma, it was you begun!" says downright Ethel. "That is—Hush, Alfred, dear.—Hush, my darling!"

"O it was Mamma began! I'm so hungry! I'm so hungry!" howled the little man on the sofa—or off it rather—for he was now down on the ground, kicking away the shawls which enveloped him.

"What is it, my boy? What is it, my blessed darling? You *shall* have your dinner! Give her all, Ethel. There are the keys of my desk—there's my watch—there are my rings. Let her take my all. The monster! the child must live! It can't go away in such a storm as this. Give me a cloak, a parasol, anything—I'll go forth and get a lodging. I'll beg my bread from house to house—if this fiend refuses me. Eat the biscuits, dear! A little of the syrup, Alfred darling; it's very nice, love! and come to your old mother—your poor old mother."

Alfred roared out "No—it's not n—ice: it's n—a—a—asty! I won't have syrup. I *will* have dinner." The mother, whose embraces the child repelled with infantine kicks, plunged madly at the bells, rang them all four vehemently, and ran down-stairs towards the parlour, whence Miss Honeyman was issuing.

The good lady had not at first known the names of her lodgers, but had taken them in willingly enough on Dr. Goodenough's recommendation. And it was not until one of the nurses entrusted with the care of Master Alfred's dinner informed Miss Honeyman of the name of her guest, that she knew she was entertaining Lady Ann Newcome: and that the pretty girl was the fair Miss Ethel; the little sick boy, the little Alfred of whom his cousin spoke, and of whom Clive had made a hundred little drawings in his rude way, as he drew everybody. Then bidding Sally run off to St. James's Street for a chicken—she saw it put on the spit, and prepared a bread sauce, and composed a batter-pudding as she only knew how to make batter-puddings. Then she went to array herself in her best clothes, as we have seen—as we have heard rather (Goodness forbid that we should *see* Miss Honeyman arraying herself, or penetrate that chaste mystery, her toilette!): then she came to wait upon Lady Ann, not a little flurried as to the result of that queer interview; then she whisked out of the drawing-room as before has been shown; and, finding the chicken roasted to a turn, the napkin and tray ready spread by Hannah the neat-handed, she was bearing them up to the little patient when the frantic parent met her on the stair.

"Is it—is it for my child?" cried Lady Ann, reeling against the bannister.

"Yes, it's for the child," says Mrs. Honeyman, tossing up her head. "But nobody else has anything in the house."

"God bless you—God bless you! A mother's bl—l—essings go with you," gurgled the lady, who was not, it must be confessed, a woman of strong moral character.

It was good to see the little man eating the fowl. Ethel, who had never cut anything in her young existence, except her fingers now and then with her brother's and her governess's pen-knives, bethought her of asking Miss Honeyman to carve the chicken. Lady Ann, with clasped hands and streaming eyes, sate looking on at the ravishing scene.

"Why did you not let us know you were Clive's aunt?" Ethel asked, putting out her hand. The old lady took hers very kindly, and said, "Because you didn't give me time. And do you love Clive, my dear?"

The reconciliation between Miss Honeyman and her lodger was perfect. Lady Ann wrote a quire of note-paper off to Sir Brian for that day's post— only she was too late, as she always was. Mr. Kuhn perfectly delighted Miss Honeyman that evening by his droll sayings, jokes, and pronunciation, and by his praises of Master Glife, as he called him. He lived out of the house, did everything for everybody, was never out of the way when wanted, and never in the way when not wanted. Ere long Mrs. Honeyman got out a bottle of the famous Madeira which her Colonel sent her, and treated him to a glass in her own room. Kuhn smacked his lips and held out the glass again. The honest rogue[9] knew good wine.

---

[9] honest rogue *E1*] rogue *R*

Chapter X.

ETHEL AND HER RELATIONS.

OR four-and-twenty successive hours Lady Ann Newcome was perfectly in raptures with her new lodgings and every person and thing[1] which they contained. The drawing-rooms were fitted with the greatest taste: the dinner was exquisite. Were there ever such delicious veal cutlets, such verdant French beans? "Why do we have those odious French cooks, my dear, with their shocking principles —the principles of all Frenchmen are shocking— and the dreadful bills they bring us in; and their consequential airs and graces? I am determined to part with Brignol. I have written to your father this evening to give Brignol warning. When did he ever give us veal cutlets? What can be nicer?"

"Indeed they were very good," says[2] Miss Ethel who had mutton five times a week at one o'clock. "I am so glad you like the house and Clive's— and Mrs. Honeyman."

"Like her! the dear little old woman! I feel as if she had been my friend all my life! I feel quite drawn towards her. What a wonderful coincidence that Dr. Goodenough should direct us to this very house! I have written to your father about it. And to think that I should have written to Clive at this very house, and quite forgotten Mrs. Honeyman's name—and

[1] person and thing *E1*] thing and person *Ms*
[2] says *Ms*] said *E1*

ETHEL

such an odd name too. I forget everything, everything. You know I forgot your Aunt Louisa's husband's name: and when I was Godmother to her baby, and the clergyman said, "What is this[3] infant's name?" I said, "Really I forget." And so I did. He was a London clergyman but I forget at what church. Suppose it should be this very Mr. Honeyman! It may have been you know: and then the coincidence would be still more droll. That tall old nice-looking respectable person with a mark on her nose, the housekeeper—what is her name?—seems a most invaluable person. I think I shall ask her to come to us. I am sure she would save me I don't know how much money every week, and I am certain Mrs. Trotter is making a fortune by us. I shall write to your Papa and ask him permission to ask this person." Ethel's mother was constantly falling in love with her new acquaintances: her man-servants and her maid-servants, her horses and ponies, and the visitor within her gates. She would ask strangers to Newcome, hug and embrace them on Sunday, not speak to them on Monday, and on Tuesday behave so rudely to them that they were gone before Wednesday. Her daughter had had so many governesses, all darlings during the first week and monsters afterwards: that the poor child possessed none of the accomplishments of her age. She could not play on the piano: she could not speak French well: she could not tell you when gunpowder was invented: she had not the faintest idea of the date of the Norman conquest, or whether the earth went round the sun or *vice versâ*. She did not know the number of counties in England, Scotland and Wales let alone Ireland: she did not know the difference between latitude and longitude. She had had so many governesses: their accounts differed: poor Ethel was bewildered by a multiplicity of teachers and thought herself a monster of ignorance. They gave her a book at a Sunday school and little girls of eight years old answered questions of which she knew nothing. The place swam before her. She could not see the sun shining on their fair flaxen heads and pretty faces; the rosy little children holding up their eager hands, and crying the answer to this question and that, seemed mocking her. She seemed to read in the book, "O Ethel, you Dunce Dunce Dunce." She went home silent in the carriage and burst into bitter tears on her bed. Naturally a haughty girl of the highest spirit, resolute and imperious, this little visit to the parish school taught Ethel lessons[4] more valuable than ever so much arithmetic and geography.[5] Clive has told me a story of her in her youth, which perhaps may apply to some others of the youthful female aristocracy. She used to walk, with other select young ladies and gentlemen, their nurses and governesses, in a certain reserved plot of ground railed off from Hyde Park; whereof some of the lucky dwellers in the neighbourhood of Apsley House have a key. In this garden at the age of nine or thereabout she had contracted an intimate friendship with the Lord Hercules O'Ryan—as every one of my gentle readers knows, one of the sons of the Marquess of Ballyshannon. The Lord Hercules was a year younger than Miss Ethel Newcome, which may account for the passion which grew

---

[3] this *Ms*] the *E1*
[4] lessons *E1*] much that was *Ms*
[5] [The remainder of this and the next paragraph are omitted from *R*.]

up between these young persons: it being a provision in nature that a boy always falls in love with a girl older than himself, or rather perhaps that a girl bestows her affections on a little boy, who submits to receive them.

One day Sir Brian Newcome announced his intention to go to Newcome that very morning, taking his family and, of course, Ethel with him. She was inconsolable. "What will Lord Hercules do when he finds I am gone?" she asked of her nurse. The nurse endeavouring to soothe her, said, "Perhaps his lordship would know nothing about the circumstance." "He will," said Miss Ethel—*"he'll read it in the newspaper."* My Lord Hercules, it is to be hoped, strangled this infant passion in the cradle; having long since married Isabella, only daughter of —— Grains, Esq., of Drayton Windsor, a partner in the great brewery of Foker and Co.[6]

When Ethel was thirteen years old she had grown to be such a tall girl that she overtopped her companions by a head or more and morally perhaps also felt herself too tall for their society. "Fancy myself," she thought, "dressing a doll like Lily Putland; or wearing a pinafore like Lucy Tucker!" She did not care for their sports. She could not walk with them: it seemed as if every one stared; nor dance with them at the Academy, nor attend the Cours de Littérature Universelle et de Science Compréhensive of the professor then the mode—the smallest girls took her up in the class. She was bewildered by the multitude of things they bade her learn. At the youthful little assemblies of her sex; when, under the guide of their respected governesses, the girls came to tea at six o'clock, dancing, charades and so forth, Ethel herded not with the children of her own age, nor yet with the teachers who sit apart at these assemblies imparting to each other their little wrongs, but Ethel romped with the little children, the rosy little trots

6 Clive has told me a story ... Foker and Co. *E1*] [omitted] *R*

and took them on her knees and told them a thousand stories. By these she was adored; and loved like a mother almost, for as such the hearty kindly girl showed herself to them; but at home she was alone *farouche* and intractable, and did battle with the governesses and overcame them one after another. I break the promise of a former page, and am obliged to describe the youthful days of more than one person who is to take a share in this story. Not always doth the writer know whither the Divine Muse leadeth him. But of this be sure: she is as inexorable as Truth. We must tell our tale as she imparts it to us: and go on or turn aside at her bidding.

Here she ordains that we should speak of other members of this family whose history we chronicle and it behoves us to say a word regarding the Earl of Kew, the head of the noble house into which Sir Brian Newcome had married.

When we read in the fairy stories that the King and Queen who lived once upon a time, build a castle of steel, defended by moats and sentinels innumerable in which they place their darling only child, the Prince or Princess whose birth has blest them after so many years of marriage and whose christening feast has been interrupted by the cantankerous humour of that notorious old fairy who always persists in coming although she has not received any invitation to the baptismal ceremony——when Prince Prettyman is locked up in the steel tower provided only with the most wholesome food, the most edifying educational works and the most venerable old tutor to instruct and to bore him, we know as a matter of course that the steel bolts and brazen bars will one day be of no avail.—The old tutor will go off in a doze, and the moats and drawbridges will either be passed by his Royal Highness's implacable enemies; or crossed by the young scapegrace himself who is determined to outwit his guardians, and see the wicked world. The old King and Queen always come in and find the chambers empty; the saucy heir-apparent flown; the porters and sentinels drunk; the ancient tutor asleep. They tear their venerable wigs in anguish, they kick the major-domo down-stairs, they turn the duenna out of doors, the toothless old dragon—There is no resisting fate—The Princess *will* step out of window by the rope ladder: the Prince *will* be off to pursue his pleasures and sow his wild oats at the appointed season. How many of our English Princes have been coddled at home by their fond papas and mammas, walled up in inaccessible castles with a tutor and a library, guarded by cordons of sentinels, sermoners, old aunts, old women from the world without;—and have nevertheless escaped from all these guardians and astonished the world by their extravagance and their frolics! What a wild rogue was that Prince Harry, son of the austere sovereign who robbed Richard the Second of his crown—the youth who took purses on Gadshill; frequented Eastcheap taverns with Colonel Falstaff and worse company; and boxed Chief Justice Gascoigne's ears! What must have been the venerable Queen Charlotte's state of mind, when she heard of the courses of *her* beautiful young prince—of his punting at gambling-tables, of his dealings with horse jockeys, of his awful doings with Perdita? Besides instances taken from our Royal Family, could we not draw examples from our respected nobility? There was that young Lord Warwick, Mr. Addison's step-son. We know that his mother was severe, and his step-father a most eloquent moralist, yet the young gentleman's career was shocking, positively shocking. He boxed the watch, he fuddled himself at taverns, he was no better than a Mohock. The chronicles of that day contain accounts of many a mad prank which he played, as we have legends of a still earlier date of the lawless freaks of the wild Prince and Poyns. Our people has never looked very unkindly on these frolics. A young nobleman full of life and spirits, generous of his money, jovial in his humour, ready with his sword, frank, handsome, prodigal, courageous, always finds favour. Young Scapegrace rides a steeple-chase or beats a bargeman and the crowd applauds him, sages and seniors shake their heads, and look at him not unkindly, even stern old female moralists are disarmed at the sight of youth and gallantry and beauty. I know very well that Charles Surface is a sad dog and Tom Jones no better than he should be, but in spite of such critics as Dr. Johnson and Colonel Newcome, most of us have a sneaking regard for honest Tom, and hope Sophia will be happy and Tom will end well at last.

Five-and-twenty years ago the young Earl of Kew came upon the town which speedily rang with the feats of his lordship. He began life time enough to enjoy certain pleasures from which our young aristocracy of the present day seem, alas! to be cut off, so much more peaceable and polished do we grow; so much does the spirit of the age appear to equalise all ranks; so strongly has the good sense of society, to which in the end gentlemen of the very[7] highest fashion must bow, put its veto upon practices and amusements with which our fathers were familiar. At that time the Sunday newspapers contained many and many exciting reports of boxing matches. Bruising was considered a fine manly old English custom. Boys at public schools fondly perused histories of the noble science, from the redoubtable days of Broughton and Slack to the heroic times of Dutch Sam and the Game Chicken. Young gentlemen went eagerly to Moulsey to see the Slasher punch the Pet's head or the Negro beat the Jew's nose to[8] a jelly. The island rang as yet with the tooting horns and rattling teams of mail coaches; a gay sight was the road in Merry England in those days before steam-engines arose and flung its hostelry and chivalry over. To travel in coaches, to drive coaches, to know coachmen and guards, to be familiar with inns along the road, to laugh with the jolly hostess in the bar, to chuck the pretty chamber-maid under the chin, were the delight of men who were young not very long ago. Who ever thought of writing to the *Times* then? "Biffin," I warrant, did not grudge his money and "A Thirsty Soul" paid cheerfully for his drink.[9] The road was an institution, the ring was an institution. Men rallied round them; and, not without a kind conservatism, expatiated upon the benefits with which they endowed the country, and the evils which would occur when they should be no more:—decay of English spirit—decay of manly pluck, ruin of the breed of horses and so forth and so forth. To give and take a black eye was not unusual nor derogatory in a gentleman; to drive a stage coach the enjoyment, the emulation of

---

7 very *E1*] [absent] *HM*
8 to *E1*] into *HM*
9 Who ever thought ... for his drink. *E1*] [omitted] *R*

generous youth. Is there any young fellow of the present time who aspires to take the place of a stoker? You see occasionally in Hyde Park one dismal old drag with a lonely driver. Where are you, charioteers.[1] Where are you, O rattling Quicksilver, O swift Defiance? You are passed[2] by racers stronger and swifter than you—Your lamps are out. And the music of your horns has died away—

Just at the ending of that old time, Lord Kew's life began. That kindly middle-aged gentleman whom his county knows—that good landlord and friend of all his tenantry round about; that builder of churches and indefatigable visitor of schools; that writer of letters to the Farmers of Kewshire so full of sense and benevolence, who wins prizes at agricultural shows and even lectures at county town institutes in his modest pleasant[3] way, was the wild young Lord Kew of a quarter of a century back, who kept race horses; patronised boxers; fought a duel; thrashed a Life Guardsman; gambled furiously at Crockford's and did who knows what besides?

His mother, a devout lady, nursed her son and his property carefully during the young gentleman's minority: keeping him and his younger brother away from all mischief, under the eyes of the most careful pastors and masters. She learnt Latin with the boys, she taught them to play on the piano. She enraged old Lady Kew, the children's grandmother, who prophesied that her daughter-in-law would make milksops of her sons, to whom the old lady was never reconciled until after mylord's entry at Christchurch where he began to distinguish himself very soon after his first term. He drove tandems, kept hunters, gave dinners, scandalised the Dean, screwed up the tutor's door, and agonised his mother at home by his lawless proceedings. He quitted the University after a very brief sojourn at[4] that seat of learning. It may be the Oxford authorities requested his lordship to retire; let byegones be byegones. His youthful son, the present Lord Walham, is now at Christchurch reading with the greatest assiduity. Let us not be too particular in narrating his father's unedifying frolics of a quarter of a century ago.

Old Lady Kew, who in conjunction with Mrs. Newcome had made the marriage between Mr. Brian Newcome and her daughter, always despised her son-in-law and, being a frank open person uttering her mind always, took little pains to conceal her opinion regarding him or any other individual. "Sir Brian Newcome," she would say, "is one of the most stupid and respectable of men. Ann is clever but has not a grain of common sense. They make a very well-assorted couple. Her flightiness would have driven any man crazy who had an opinion of his own. She would have ruined any poor man of her own rank. As it is I have given her a husband exactly suited for her. He pays the bills, does not see how absurd she is, keeps order in the establishment and checks her follies. She wanted to marry her cousin, Tom Poyntz, when they were both very young and proposed to die of a broken heart when I arranged her match with Mr. Newcome. A

---

[1] Charioteers. *Ms*] charioteers? *E1*
[2] passed *E1*] past *Ms*
[3] pleasant *E1*] kindly *Ms*
[4] at *E1*] it *Ms*

broken fiddlestick! She would have ruined Tom Poyntz in a year and has no more idea of the cost of a leg of mutton than I have of Algebra."

The Countess of Kew loved Brighton; and preferred living there even at the season when Londoners find such especial charms in their own city. "London after Easter," the old lady said, "was intolerable. Pleasure becomes a business then so oppressive, that all good company is destroyed by it. Half the men are sick with the feasts which they eat day after day. The women are thinking of the half-dozen parties they have to go to in the course of the night. The young girls are thinking of their partners and their toilettes. Intimacy becomes impossible, and quiet enjoyment of life. On the other hand, the crowd of *bourgeois* has not invaded Brighton. The drive is not blocked up by flies full of stock-brokers' wives and children; and you can take the air in your chair upon the Chain-pier without being stifled by the cigars of the odious shop-boys from London." So Lady Kew's name was usually amongst the earliest which the Brighton newspapers recorded amongst the arrivals.

Her only unmarried daughter, Lady Julia, lived with her ladyship. Poor Lady Julia had suffered early from a spine-disease, which had kept her for many years to her couch. Being always at home, and under her mother's eyes—she was the old lady's victim—her pincushion, into which Lady Kew plunged a hundred little points of sarcasm daily. As children are sometimes brought before magistrates: and their poor little backs and shoulders laid bare, covered with bruises and lashes which brutal parents have inflicted— so I daresay, if there had been any tribunal or judge, before whom this poor patient lady's heart could have been exposed, it would have been found scarred all over with numberless ancient wounds, and bleeding from yesterday's castigation. Old Lady Kew's tongue was a dreadful thong which made numbers of people wince. She was not altogether cruel; but she knew the dexterity with which she wielded her lash, and liked to exercise it. Poor Lady Julia was always at hand, when her mother was minded to try her powers.

Lady Kew had just made herself comfortable at Brighton: when her little grandson's illness brought Lady Ann Newcome and her family down to the sea. Lady Kew was almost scared back to London again, or blown over the water to Dieppe. She had never had the measles. "Why did not Ann carry the child to some other place? Julia, you will on no account go and see that little pestiferous swarm of Newcomes—unless you want to send me out of the world, which I daresay you do—for I am a dreadful plague to you, I know, and my death would be a release to you."

"You see Doctor H. who visits the child every day," cries poor Pincushion. "You are not afraid when he comes."

"Doctor H.? Doctor H. comes to cure me—or to tell me the news—or to flatter me, or to feel my pulse, and to pretend to prescribe, or to take his guinea; of course Dr. H. must go to see all sorts of people in all sorts of diseases. You would not have me be such a brute as to order him not to attend my own grandson.[5] I forbid you to go to Ann's house. You will send one of the men every day to inquire. Let the groom go—Yes, Charles—

[5] grandson. *Ms*] grandson? *E1*

He will not go into the house. He will ring the bell and wait outside. He had better ring the bell at the area—I suppose there is an area—and speak to the servants through the bars: and bring us word how Alfred is." Poor Pincushion felt fresh compunctions. She had met the children, and kissed the baby, and held kind Ethel's hand in her's that day as she was out in her chair. There was no use, however, to make this confession—Is she the only good woman or man of whom domestic tyranny has made a hypocrite?

Charles, the groom, brings back perfectly favourable reports of Master Alfred's health that day: which Doctor H. in the course of his visit confirms. The child is getting well rapidly: eating like a little ogre. His cousin Lord Kew has been to see him. He is the kindest of men, Lord Kew: he brought the little man Tom and Jerry with the pictures. The boy is delighted with the pictures.

"Why has not Kew come to see me? When did he come? Write him a note and send for him instantly, Julia. Did you know he was here?"

Julia says that she had but that moment read in the Brighton paper, the arrival of the Earl of Kew and the Honourable J. Belsize at the Albion.

"I am sure they are here for some mischief," cries the old lady, delighted. "Whenever George and John[6] Belsize are together I know there is some wickedness planning. What do you know, Doctor? I see by your face you know something. Do tell it me that I may write it to his odious psalm-singing mother."

Doctor H.'s face does indeed wear a knowing look. He simpers and says, "I did see Lord Kew driving this morning, first with the Honourable Mr. Belsize, and afterwards—" Here he glances towards Lady Julia, as if to say, "Before an unmarried lady I do not like to tell your ladyship with whom I saw Lord Kew driving, after he had left the Honourable Mr. Belsize who went to play a match with Captain Huxtable at tennis."

"Are you afraid to speak before Julia?" cries the elder lady. "Why, bless my soul, she is forty years old; and has heard everything that can be heard. Tell[7] me about Kew this instant, Doctor H."

The Doctor blandly acknowledges that Lord Kew had been driving Madame Pozzoprofondo, the famous contralto of the Italian Opera, in his phaeton for two hours in the face of all Brighton.

"Yes, Doctor—" interposes Lady Julia blushing, "but Signor Pozzopro-fondo was in the carriage too—a—a-sitting behind with the groom. He was indeed, Mamma."

"Julia, *vous n'êtes qu'une ganache*,"[8] says Lady Kew shrugging her shoulders, and looking at her daughter from under her bushy black eyebrows. Her ladyship, a sister of the late lamented Marquis of Steyne, possessed no small share of the wit and intelligence, and a considerable resemblance to the features of that distinguished nobleman.

Lady Kew bids her daughter take a pen and write. *"Monsieur le mauvais sujet.* Gentlemen who wish to take the sea air in private or to avoid their

---

[6] John *E1*] Charles *R*

[7] heard everything that can be heard. Tell *E1*] heard a thousand times worse things than you are going to tell her. He He! That she has: and I have told them too:" cries Lady Kew rapping her knuckles on the table. "Tell *Ms*

[8] *ganache E1*] *bête R*

relations had best go to other places than Brighton, where their names are printed in the newspapers. If you are[9] not drowned in a pozzo—"

"Mamma," interposes the secretary—

"—in a pozzoprofondo—you will please come to dine with two old women at half past seven. You may bring Mr. Belsize and must tell us a hundred stories.   "Your etcetera,   L. Kew."

Julia wrote all the letter as her mother dictated it, save only one sentence, and the note was sealed and dispatched to my Lord Kew, who came to dinner with Jack Belsize. Jack Belsize liked to dine with Lady Kew. He said she was an old dear and the wickedest old woman in all England: and he liked to dine with Lady Julia, who was a poor suffering dear, and the best woman in all England. Jack Belsize liked every one and every one liked him.

Two evenings afterwards the young men repeated their visit to Lady Kew—and this time Lord Kew was loud in praises of his cousins of the house of Newcome.

"Not of the eldest cub, Barnes? Surely,[1] my dear," cries Lady Kew.

"No, confound him, not Barnes."

"No, d—— it, not Barnes. I beg your pardon, Lady Julia," broke in Jack Belsize. "I can get on with most men: but that little Barney is too odious a little snob."

"A little what? Mr. Belsize."

"A little snob, Ma'am—I have no other word: though he is your grandson. I never heard him say a good word of any mortal soul or do a kind action."

"Thank you, Mr. Belsize," says the lady.

"But the others are capital. There is that little chap who has just had the measles. He's a dear little brick. And as for Miss Ethel."

"Ethel is a trump, Ma'am," says Lord Kew slapping his hand on his knee.

"Alfred is a brick and Ethel is a trump I think you say," remarks Lady Kew nodding approval, "and Barnes is a snob—This is very satisfactory to know."

"We met the children out to-day," cries the enthusiastic Kew, "as I was driving Jack in the drag. And I got out and talked to 'em."

"Governess an uncommonly nice woman—oldish but—I beg your pardon, Lady Julia," cries the inopportune Jack Belsize—"I'm always putting my foot in it."

"Putting your foot into what? Go on, Kew."

"Well, we met the whole posse of children; and the little fellow wanted a drive and I said I would drive him and Ethel too if she would come. Upon my word she is as pretty a girl as you can see on a summer's day—and the governess said 'No,' of course—Governesses always do—But I said I was her uncle; and Jack paid her such a fine compliment that the young woman was mollified and the children took their seats beside me, and Jack went behind—"

"Where Monsieur Pozzoprofondo sits, *bon.*"

---

[9] are *E1*] do *Ms*
[1] eldest cub, Barnes? surely *Ms*] eldest, Barnes, surely, *E1*

"We drove on to the Downs and we were nearly coming to grief. My horses are young: and when they get on the grass they are as if they were mad. It was very wrong, I know it was."

"D——d rash," interposes Jack. "He had nearly broken all our necks."

"And my brother Frank would have been Lord Kew," continued the young Earl with a quiet smile. "What an escape for him! The horses ran away—ever so far—and I thought the carriage must upset. The poor little boy who has lost his pluck in the fever began to cry; but that young girl though she was as white as a sheet, never gave up for a moment, and sate in her place like a man. We met nothing, luckily: and I pulled the horses in after a mile or two—and I drove 'em into Brighton as quiet as if I had been driving a hearse. And that little trump of an Ethel, what do you think she said? She said, 'I was not frightened, but you must not tell Mamma.' My aunt, it appears, was in a dreadful commotion—I ought to have thought of that."

"Lady Ann is a ridiculous old dear—I beg your pardon, Lady Kew," here breaks in Jack the Apologizer—

"There is a brother of Sir Brian Newcome's staying with them," Lord Kew proceeds, "an East India Colonel, a very fine-looking old boy—"

"Smokes awfully, row about it in the hotel—Go on, Kew, beg your . . ."

"This gentleman was on the look out for us, it appears, for when we came in sight he dispatched a boy who was with him, running like a lamplighter back to my aunt to say all was well. And he took little Alfred out of the carriage, and then helped out Ethel and said, 'My dear, you are too pretty to scold; but you have given us all a *belle peur*.' And then he made me and Jack a low bow and stalked into the lodgings."

"I think you do deserve to be whipped, both of you," cries Lady Kew.

"We went up and made our peace with my aunt—and were presented in form to the Colonel, and his youthful cub."

"As fine a fellow as ever I saw: and as fine a boy as ever I saw," cries Jack Belsize. "The[2] young chap is a great hand at drawing—upon my life the best drawings I ever saw. And he was making a picture for little what-dyoucallem. And Miss Newcome was looking over them. And Lady Ann pointed out the group to me, and said how pretty it was. She is uncommonly sentimental you know, Lady Ann."

"My daughter Ann is the greatest fool in the three kingdoms," cried Lady Kew, looking fiercely over her spectacles. And Julia was instructed to write that night to her sister; and desire that Ethel should be sent to see her grandmother:—Ethel, who rebelled against her grandmother, and always fought on her Aunt Julia's side, when the weaker was oppressed by the older and stronger lady.

2 "The *E1*] "Lady Ann pointed it out to us. The *Ms*

Chapter XI.

AINT PETER of Alcantara, as I have read in a life of St. Theresa, informed that devout lady that he had passed forty years of his life sleeping only an hour and a half each day; his cell was but four feet and a half long so that he never lay down: his pillow was a wooden log in the stone wall: he ate but once in three days; he was for three years in a convent of his order without knowing any one of his brethren except by the sound of their voices, for he never during this period took his eyes off the ground: he always walked barefoot: and this blessed old man was[1] but skin and bone when he died. The eating only once in three days, so he told his sister Saint, was by no means impossible if you began the regimen in your youth. To conquer sleep was the hardest of all austerities which he practised:—I fancy the pious individual so employed: day after day, night after night, on his knees or standing up in devout meditations in the cupboard, his dwelling place, bareheaded and barefooted, walking over rocks, briars, mud, sharp stones (picking out the very worst places, let us trust, with his downcast eyes) under the bitter snow or the drifting rain or the scorching sunshine—I fancy Saint Peter of Alcantara and contrast him with such a personage as the Incumbent of Lady Whittlesea's chapel, May Fair—

His hermitage is situated in Walpole[2] Street let us say, on the second floor of a quiet mansion, let out to hermits by a nobleman's butler, whose wife takes care of the lodgings. His cells consist of a refectory, a dormitory, and an adjacent oratory where he keeps his shower-bath and boots—the pretty boots trimly stretched on boot-trees and blacked to a nicety (not varnished) by the boy who waits on him. The bare-footed business may suit superstitious ages and gentlemen of Alcantara, but does not become

---

[1] barefoot: and this blessed old man was *Ms*] barefoot, and was *E1*

[2] Walpole *E1*] Queen *Ms* [*Ms* continues to use Queen until 117.41, after which Walpole appears in the *Ms*]

May Fair and the Nineteenth Century. If Saint Pedro walked the earth now with his eyes to the ground, he would know fashionable divines by the way in which they were shod. Charles Honeyman's is a sweet foot—I have no doubt as delicate and plump and cosy[3] as the white hand with its two rings, which he passes in impassioned moments through his slender flaxen hair.

A sweet odour pervades his sleeping apartment—not that peculiar and delicious fragrance with which the Saints of the Roman Church are said to gratify the neighbourhood where they repose—but oils, redolent of the richest perfumes of Macassar, essences (from Truefitt's or Delcroix's) into which a thousand flowers have expressed their sweetest breath: await his meek head on rising; and infuse the pocket-handkerchief with which he dries and draws so many tears. For he cries a good deal in his sermons, to which the ladies about him contribute showers of sympathy.

By his bedside are slippers lined with blue silk and worked of an ecclesiastical pattern, by some of the faithful who sit at his feet. They come to him in anonymous parcels: they come to him in silver paper: boys in buttons (pages who minister to female grace!) leave them at the door for the Revd. C. Honeyman, and skip[4] away without a word. Purses are sent to him—pen-wipers—a portfolio with the Honeyman arms (azure on a bend or, three bees sable between three beehives of the second)—yea,[5] braces have been known to reach him by the post (in his days of popularity) and flowers, and grapes, and jelly when he was ill, and throat-comforters—and lozenges for his dear bronchitis. In one of his drawers is the rich silk cassock presented to him by his congregation at Leatherhead (when the young curate quitted that parish for London duty) and on his breakfast-table the silver tea-pot once filled with sovereigns and presented by the same devotees. The devoteapot[6] he has, but the sovereigns, where are they?

What a different life this is from our honest friend of Alcantara who eats once in three days! At one time if Honeyman could have drunk tea three times in an evening, he might have had it. The glass on his chimney-piece is crowded with invitations, not merely cards of ceremony, of which there are plenty; but dear little confidential notes from sweet friends of his congregation. "O dear Mr. Honeyman!" writes Blanche, "what a sermon that was! I cannot go to bed to-night without thanking you for it!" "Do, *do* dear Mr. Honeyman," writes Beatrice "lend me that delightful sermon. And can you come and drink tea with me and Selina and my aunt? Papa and Mamma dine out, but you *know*, I am always your faithful Chesterfield Street." And so on. He has all the domestic accomplishments; he plays on the violoncello: he sings a delicious second, not only in sacred but in secular music. He has a thousand anecdotes, laughable riddles, droll stories (of the utmost correctness, you understand) with which he entertains females of all ages; suiting his conversation to stately matrons, deaf old dowagers (who can hear his clear voice better than the loudest roar of their stupid

---

[3] cosy *Ms*] rosy *E1*
[4] skip *Ms*] slip *E1*
[5] arms (azure ... the second)—yea, *Ms*] arms—yea, *E1*
[6] devoteapot *Ms E1 R*] tea-pot *HM NY*

sons-in-law), mature spinsters, young beauties dancing through the season, even rosy little slips out of the nursery who cluster round his beloved feet. Societies fight for him to preach their charity sermons. You read in the papers—"The Wapping Hospital for Wooden-legged Seamen. On Sunday the 23rd, Sermons will be preached in behalf of this charity by the Lord BISHOP OF TOBAGO in the morning, in the afternoon by the REVD. C. HONEYMAN, A.M., Incumbent of &c., CGF. Clergyman's Grandmothers' Fund. Sermons in aid of this Admirable Institution will be preached on Sunday, 4th May, by the Very Revd. The Dean of Pimlico, and the Revd. C. Honeyman, A.M." When the Dean of Pimlico has his illness, many people think Honeyman will have the Deanery; that he ought to have it, a hundred female voices vow and declare: though it is said that a right reverend head at headquarters shakes dubiously when his name is mentioned for preferment: his fame is spread wide and not only women but men come to hear him. Members of Parliament, even Cabinet Ministers, sit under him: Lord Dozeley of course is seen in a front pew: where was a public meeting without Lord Dozeley? The men come away from his sermons and say, "It's very pleasant, but I don't know what the deuce makes all you women crowd so to hear the man." "O Charles! if you would but go oftener!" sighs Lady Anna Maria. "Can't you speak to the Home Secretary.[7] Can't you do something for him?" "We can ask him to dinner next Wednesday if you like," says Charles. "They say he's a pleasant fellow out of the wood. Besides there is no use in doing anything for him," Charles goes on. "He can't make less than a thousand a year out of his chapel: and that is better than any thing any one can give him.—A thousand a year—besides the rent of the wine-vaults below the chapel."

"Don't Charles!" says his wife with a solemn look. "Don't ridicule things in that way."

"Confound it, there *are* wine-vaults under the chapel!" answers downright Charles. "I saw the name Sherrick & Co. offices and a green door and a brass plate. It's better to sit over vaults with wine in them than coffins. I wonder if it's the Sherrick with whom Kew and Jack Belsize had that ugly row?"

"What ugly row—don't say ugly row—It is not a nice word to hear the children use—Go on, my darlings. What was the dispute of Lord Kew and Mr. Belsize and this Mr. Sherrick?"

"It was all about pictures and about horses and about money and about one other subject which enters into every row that I ever heard of."

"And what is that, dear?" asks the innocent lady hanging on her husband's arm and quite pleased to have led him to church and brought him thence. "And what is it that enters into every row, as you call it, Charles?"

"*A woman*, my love," answers the gentleman, behind whom we have been in imagination walking out from Charles Honeyman's church on a Sunday in June: as the whole pavement blooms with artificial flowers and fresh bonnets; as there is a buzz and cackle all around regarding the sermon; as carriages drive off; as lady-dowagers[8] walk home; as prayer books and footmen's sticks gleam in the sun; as little boys with baked mutton and potatoes

---

[7] Secretary. *Ms*] Secretary? *E1*
[8] lady-dowagers *E1*] ladies *Ms*

pass from the courts; as children issue from the public-houses with pots of beer; as the Reverend Charles Honeyman who has been drawing tears in the sermon, and has seen, not without complacent throbs, a Secretary of State in the pew beneath him; divests himself of his rich silk cassock in the vestry, before he walks away to his neighbouring hermitage—where have we placed it?—in Walpole Street. I wish St. Pedro of Alcantara could have some of that shoulder of mutton with the baked potatoes, and a drink of that frothing beer. See, yonder trots little Lord Dozeley who has been asleep for an hour with his head against the wood like St. Pedro of Alcantara.

An East Indian gentleman and his son wait until the whole chapel is clear, and survey Lady Whittlesea's monument at their leisure, and other hideous slabs erected in memory of defunct frequenters of the chapel. Whose was that face which Colonel Newcome thought he recognised—that of a stout man who came down from the organ gallery? Could it be Broff the bass singer who delivered the Red-Cross Knight with such applause at the Cave of Melody, and who has been singing in this place?—There are some chapels in London, where, the function over, one almost expects to see the sextons put brown-hollands over the pews and galleries as they do at the Theatre Royal, Covent Garden.[9]

The writer of these veracious pages was once walking through a splendid English palace, standing amidst parks and gardens than which none more magnificent have been seen[1] since the days of Aladdin, in company with a melancholy friend who viewed all things darkly through his gloomy eyes. The housekeeper, pattering on before us from chamber to chamber, was expatiating upon the magnificence of this picture; the beauty of that statue; the marvellous richness of these hangings and carpets: the admirable likeness of the late Marquis by Sir Thomas; of his father the fifth Earl by Sir Joshua and so on; when, in the very richest room of the whole castle, Hicks, such was my melancholy companion's name, stopped the Cicerone in her prattle, saying in a hollow voice, "And now, Madam, will you show us the closet *where the Skeleton* is?" The scared functionary paused in the midst of her harangue: that article was not inserted in the catalogue which she daily utters to visitors for their half-crown. Hicks's question brought a darkness down upon the hall where we were standing. We did not see the room: and yet I have no doubt there is such an one; and ever after when I have thought of the splendid castle towering in the midst of shady trees, under which the dappled deer are browsing—of the terraces gleaming with statues and bright with a hundred thousand flowers, of the bridges and shining fountains and rivers wherein the castle windows reflect their festive gleams when the halls are filled with happy feasters and over the darkling woods comes the sound of music—always, I say, when I think of Castle Bluebeard:—it is to think of that dark little closet which I know is there, and which the lordly owner opens shuddering—after midnight—when he is sleepless and *must* go unlock it, when the palace is hushed, when beauties are sleeping around him unconscious, and revellers are at rest. O Mrs. Housekeeper: all the other keys hast thou: but that key thou hast not!

[9] Theatre Royal, Covent Garden *E1*] Royal Covent Garden Theatre. *Ms*
[1] seen *E1*] [omitted] *R*

Have we not all such closets, my jolly friend, as well as the noble Marquess of Carabas? At night, when all the house is asleep but you, don't you get up and peep into yours? When you in your turn are slumbering: up gets Mrs. Brown from your side, steals down-stairs like Amina to her ghoul, clicks open the secret door, and looks into *her* dark depository. Did she tell you of that little affair with Smith long before she knew you?—Psha! who knows any one save himself alone? Who, in showing his house to the closest and dearest, doesn't keep back the key of a closet or two? I think of a lovely reader laying down the page and looking over at her unconscious husband, asleep perhaps after dinner. Yes, Madam, a closet he hath: and you who pry into everything shall never have the key of it: I think of some honest Othello pausing over this very sentence in a railroad carriage, and stealthily gazing at Desdemona opposite to him, innocently administering sandwiches to their little boy.—I am trying to turn off the sentence with a joke you see—I feel it is growing too dreadful, too serious.

And to what, pray, do these serious, these disagreeable, these almost personal observations tend?—to this simply that Charles Honeyman the beloved and popular preacher, the elegant divine to whom Miss Blanche writes sonnets and whom Miss Beatrice[2] invites to tea: who comes with smiles on his lip, gentle sympathy in his tones, innocent gaiety in his accent; who melts, rouses, terrifies in the pulpit; who charms over the tea urn and the bland bread and butter—Charles Honeyman has one or two skeleton closets in his lodgings, Walpole Street, May Fair, and many a wakeful night whilst Mrs. Ridley his landlady and her tired husband the nobleman's major-domo, whilst the lodger on the first floor, whilst the cook and housemaid and weary little bootboy are at rest (mind you, they have all got *their* closets which they open with their skeleton-keys): he wakes up, and looks at the ghastly occupant of that receptacle. One of the Reverend Charles Honeyman's grisly[3] night-haunters is—but stop, let us give a little account of the lodgings and of some of the people frequenting the same.

First floor Mr. Bagshot. Member for a Norfolk borough. Stout jolly gentleman: dines at the Carlton Club: greatly addicted to Greenwich and Richmond in the season: bets in a moderate way: does not go into Society except now and again to the chiefs of his party when they give great entertainments: and once or twice to the houses of great County Dons who dwell near him in the country. Is not of very good family: was in fact an Apothecary: married a woman with money much older than himself who does not like London and stops at home at Hummingham not much to the displeasure of Bagshot: gives every now and then nice little quiet dinners, which Mrs. Ridley cooks admirably, to exceedingly stupid jolly old Parliamentary fogies; who absorb with much silence and cheerfulness a vast quantity of wine. They have just begun to drink '24 claret now: that of '15 being scarce and almost drunk up. Writes daily and hears every morning from Mrs. Bagshot: does not read her letters always, does not rise till long past eleven o'clock of a Sunday and has *John Bull* and *Bell's Life* in bed: frequents the Blue Posts sometimes: rides a stout cob out of his country,[4]

---

[2] Beatrice *E1*] Emily *Ms HM*
[3] grisly *Ms*] grizzly *E1*
[4] country *Ms*] county *E1*

and pays like the Bank of England.

The house is a Norfolk house. Mrs. Ridley was housekeeper to the great Squire Bayham, who had the estate before the Conqueror, and who came to such a dreadful crash in the year 1825, the year of the panic. Bayham still belongs to the family, but in what a state, as those can say who recollect it in its palmy days! Fifteen hundred acres of the best land in England were sold off, all the timber cut down as level as a billiard board—Mr. Bayham now lives up in one corner of the house, which used to be filled with the finest company in Europe—Law bless you! the Bayhams have seen almost all the nobility of England come in and go out: and was[5] gentlefolks, when many a fine lord's father of the present day was sweeping a counting-house.

The house will hold genteelly no more than these two inmates, but in the season it manages to accommodate Miss Cann, who too was from Bayham's, having been a governess there to the young lady who is dead, and who now makes such a livelihood as she can best raise, by going out as a daily teacher.[6] Miss Cann dines with Mrs. Ridley in the adjoining little back parlour. Ridley but seldom can be spared to partake of the family dinner, his duties in the house and about the person of my Lord Todmorden keeping him constantly near that[7] nobleman. How little Miss Cann can go on and keep alive on the crumb she eats for breakfast,[8] and the scrap she picks at dinner, du astonish Mrs. Ridler that it du! She declares that the two canary birds encaged in her window (whence is a cheerful prospect of the back of Lady Whittlesea's chapel) eat more than Miss Cann. The two birds set up a tremendous singing and chorussing when Miss Cann, spying the occasion of the first-floor lodger's absence, begins practising her music-pieces—such trills, roulades, and flourishes go on from the birds and Miss Cann[9]—it is a wonder how any fingers can move over the jingling ivory so quickly as Miss Cann's. Excellent a woman as she is, admirably virtuous, frugal, brisk, honest and cheerful, *I* would not like to live in lodgings where there was a lady so addicted to playing variations—No more does Honeyman. On a Saturday, when he is composing his valuable sermons (the rogue, you may be sure, leaves his work to the last day, and there are, I am given to understand, among the clergy many better men than Honeyman, who are as dilatory as he), he begs, he entreats with tears in his eyes that Miss Cann's music may cease. I would back little Cann to write a sermon against him, for all his reputation as a popular preacher.

Old and weazened as that piano is, feeble and cracked her[1] voice, it is wonderful what a pleasant concert she can give in that parlour of a Saturday evening: to Mrs. Ridley who generally dozes a good deal, and to a lad who listens with all his soul, with tears sometimes in his great eyes, with crowding fancies filling his brain and throbbing at his heart as the Artist plies her humble instrument. She plays old music of Handel or[2] Haydn,

5 was *Ms*] were *E1*
6 teacher. *E1*] governess. *Ms*
7 near that *E1*] near the person of that *Ms*
8 breakfast, *E1*] her breakfast, *R*
9 Miss Cann *Ms*] the lodger *E1*
1 her *E1*] as is her *R*
2 or *Ms*] and *E1*

and the little chamber anon swells into a cathedral; and he who listens beholds altars lighted, priests ministering, fair children swinging censers, great oriel windows gleaming in sunset, and seen through arched columns, and avenues of twilight marble. The young fellow who hears her has been often and often to the opera and the theatres. As she plays *Don Juan,* Zerlina comes tripping over the meadows and Masetto after her, with a crowd of peasants and maidens; and they sing the sweetest of all music, and the heart beats with happiness and kindness and pleasure: Piano Pianissimo! the city is hushed. The towers of the great cathedral rise in the distance, its spires lighted by the broad moon. The statues in the moonlit place cast long shadows athwart the pavement: but the fountain in the midst is dressed out like Cinderella for the night, and sings and wears a crest of diamonds. That great sombre street all in shade, can it be the famous Toledo? or is it the Corso? Or is it the great street in Madrid, the one which leads to the Escurial where the Rubens and Velasquez are? It is Fancy Street: Poetry Street. Imagination Street—the street where lovely ladies look from balconies, where cavaliers strike mandolins and draw swords and engage, where long processions pass and venerable hermits with long beards bless the kneeling people: where the rude soldiery swaggering through the place with flags and halberts, and fife and dance, seize the slim waists of the daughters of the people, and bid the pifferari play to their dancing—Blow, bagpipes, a storm of harmony! become, trumpets, trombones, ophycleides, fiddles and bassoons! Fire, guns! Sound, tocsins, shout, people: louder, shriller and sweeter than all, sing, thou ravishing heroine! and see on his cream coloured charger Massaniello prances in and Fra Diavolo leaps down the balcony, carabine in hand and Sir Huon of Bordeaux sails up to the quay with the Sultan's daughter of Babylon. All these delights and sights and joys and glories, these thrills of sympathy, movements of unknown longing, and visions of beauty, a young sickly lad of eighteen enjoys in a little dark room where there is a bed disguised in the shape of a wardrobe, and a little old woman is playing under a gas-lamp on the jingling keys of an old piano.

    For a long time Mr. Samuel Ridley, Butler and Confidential Valet to the Right Honourable John James Baron Todmorden, was in a state of the greatest despair and gloom about his only son, the little John James, a sickly and almost deformed child of whom there was "no making nothink," as Mr. Ridley said. His figure precluded him from following his father's profession and waiting upon the British nobility; who naturally require large and handsome men to skip up behind their rolling carriages, and hand their plates at dinner. When John James was six years old, his father remarked with tears in his eyes, he wasn't higher than a plate-basket. The boys jeered at him in the streets—some wapped him spite[3] of his diminutive size. At school he made but little progress. He was always sickly and dirty and timid and crying: whimpering in the kitchen away from his mother who, though she loved him, took Mr. Ridley's view of his character and thought him little better than an idiot until such time as little Miss Cann took him in hand, when at length there was some hope of him.

---

[3] spite *Ms E1*] in spite *HM*

"Half-witted, you great stupid big man!" says Miss Cann, who had a fine spirit of her own. "That boy half-witted! He has got more wit in his little finger than you have in all your great person! You are a very good man, Ridley, very good-natured I'm sure and bear with the teazing of a waspish old woman; but you are not the wisest of mankind. Tut Tut, don't tell *me!* You know you spell out the words when you read the newspaper still, and what would your bills look like, if I did not write them in my nice little hand? I tell you that boy is a genius. I tell you that one day the world will hear of him. His heart is made of pure gold. You think that all the wit belongs to the big people. Look at me, you great tall man! Am I not a hundred times cleverer than you are? Yes, and John James is worth a thousand such insignificant little chits as I am: and he is as tall as me too, Sir. Do you hear that? One day I am determined he shall dine at Lord Todmorden's table, and he shall get the prize at the Royal Academy and be famous, Sir, famous!"

"Well, Miss C., I wish he may get it; that's all I say," answers Mr. Ridley. "The pore feller[4] does no harm, that I agnowledge:[5] but *I* never see the good he was up to yet. I wish he'd begin in it; I wish he would now": and the honest gentleman relapsed[6] into the study of his paper.

All those beautiful sounds and thoughts which Miss Cann conveys to him out of her charmed piano, the young artist straightway translates into forms: and knights in armour with plume and shield and battle axe, and splendid young noblemen with flowing ringlets and bounteous plumes of feathers and rapiers and russet boots—and fierce bandittoes with crimson tights, doublets profusely illustrated with large brass buttons, and the dumpy basket-hilted claymores known to be the favourite weapon with which these whiskered ruffians do battle—wasp-waisted peasant girls and young countesses with O such large eyes and cherry lips!—all these splendid forms of war and beauty crowd to the young draughtsman's pencil, and cover letter-backs, copy-books, without end. If his hand strikes off some face peculiarly lovely and to his taste—some fair vision that has shone on his imagination; some houri of a dancer, some bright young lady of fashion in an opera-box whom he has seen, or fancied he has seen (for the youth is short-sighted though he hardly as yet knows his misfortune)—if he has made some effort extraordinarily successful, our young Pygmalion hides away the masterpiece, and he paints the beauty with all his skill—the lips a bright carmine; the eyes a deep deep cobalt, the cheeks a dazzling vermillion, the ringlets of a golden hue, and he worships this sweet creature of his in secret, fancies a history for her—a castle to storm, a tyrant Usurper who keeps her imprisoned, and a Prince in black ringlets and a spangled cloak who scales the tower, who slays the tyrant and then kneels gracefully at the Princess's feet and says, "Lady wilt thou be mine?"

There is a kind lady in the neighbourhood, who takes in dressmaking for the neighbouring maid-servants and has a small establishment of lollipops, theatrical characters and ginger-beer for the boys in Little Craggs's Buildings, hard by the Running Footman public-house, where Father and other

4 pore feller *Ms*] poor fellow *E1*
5 agnowledge: *Ms*] acknowledge; *E1*
6 relapsed *Ms*] relapses *E1*

gentlemen's gentlemen have their club;—this good soul also sells Sunday
newspapers to the footmen of the neighbouring gentry, and besides has
a stock of novels for the ladies of the upper servants' table. Next to Miss
Cann, Miss Flinders is John James's greatest friend and benefactor. She has
remarked him when he was quite a little man, and used to bring his father's
beer of a Sunday. Out of her novels he has taught himself to read, dull
boy at the day-school though he was, and always the last in his class there.
Hours, happy hours, has he spent cowering behind her counter; or hug-
ging her books under his pinafore when he had leave to carry them home.
The whole library has passed through his hands, his long lean tremulous
hands, and under his eager eyes. He has made illustrations to every one
of those books, and been frightened at his own pictures of Manfroni or the
One-handed Monk, Abellino the Terrific, Bravo of Venice, and Rinaldo Rinaldini, Captain of Robbers. How he has blistered *Thaddeus of Warsaw* with
his tears; and drawn him in his Polish cap and tights and Hessians! William
Wallace, the Hero of Scotland, how nobly he has depicted him! with what
whiskers and bushy ostrich plumes!—in a tight-kilt and with what magnificent calves to his legs, laying about him with his battle-axe and bestriding
the bodies of King Edward's prostrate cavaliers! At this time Mr. Honeyman comes to lodge in Walpole Street and brings a set of Scott's novels, for
which he subscribed when at Oxford: and young John James who at first
waits upon him and does little odd jobs for the reverend gentleman, lights
upon the volumes and reads them with such a delight and passion of pleasure as all the delights of future days will scarce equal. A fool, is he? an idle
feller out of whom no good will ever come—as his father says. There was a
time, when, in despair of any better chance for him, his parents thought of
apprenticing him to a tailor; and John James was waked up from a dream
of Rebecca and informed of the cruelty meditated against him.—I forbear
to describe the tears and terror and frantic desperation in which the poor
boy was plunged. Little Miss Cann rescued him from that awful board, and
Honeyman likewise interceded for him, and Mr. Bagshot promised that as
soon as his party came in, he would ask the Minister for a tide-waitership
for him:—for every body liked the solemn, soft-hearted, willing little lad,
and no one knew him less than his pompous and stupid and respectable
father.

Miss Cann painted flowers and card-screens elegantly and "finished"
pencil-drawings most elaborately for her pupils. She could copy prints so
that at a little distance you would scarcely know that the copy in stumped
chalk was not a bad mezzotinto engraving. She even had a little old paint-
box and showed you one or two ivory miniatures out of the drawer. She
gave John James what little knowledge of drawing she had, and handed
him over her invaluable recipes for mixing water-colours—"for trees in
foregrounds, burnt sienna and indigo"—"for very dark foliage, ivory black
and gambouge"—"for flesh-colour," &c. &c. John James went through her
poor little course, but not so brilliantly as she expected. She was forced to
own that several of her pupils' "pieces" were executed much more dexterously than Johnny Ridley's. Honeyman looked at the boy's drawings from
time to time and said, "Hm ha—very clever—a great deal of fancy, really."
But Honeyman knew no more of the subject than a deaf and dumb man

knows of music. He could talk the art-cant very glibly, and had a set of Morghens and Madonnas as became a clergyman and a man of taste: but he saw not with eyes such as those wherewith Heaven had endowed the humble little butler's boy, to whom splendours of Nature were revealed to vulgar sight invisible, and beauties manifest in forms, colour, shadows of common objects, when most of the world saw only what was dull and gross and familiar. One reads in the magic story-books of a charm or a flower which the wizard gives, and which enables the bearer to see the fairies. O enchanting boon of Nature which reveals to the possessor the hidden spirits of Beauty round about him! spirits which the strongest and most gifted masters[7] compel into painting or song. To others, it is granted but to have fleeting glimpses of that fair art-world; and tempted by ambition or barred by faint-heartedness or driven by necessity, to turn away thence to the vulgar life-track, and the light of common day.

The reader who has passed through Walpole Street scores of times knows the discomfortable architecture of all save the great houses built in Queen Anne's and George 1st., his time:[8] and while some of the neighbouring streets, to wit, Great Craggs Street, Bolingbroke Street and others, contain mansions fairly coped with stone, with little obelisks before the doors, and great extinguishers wherein the torches of the nobility's running footmen were put out a hundred and thirty or forty years ago:—houses which still remain abodes of the quality, and where you shall see a hundred carriages gather of a public night;—Walpole Street has quite faded away into lodgings, private hotels, doctors' houses and the like: nor is No. 23 (Ridley's) by any means the best house in the street. The parlour furnished and tenanted by Miss Cann as has been described:—the first floor—Bagshot Esquire, M.P. The second floor, Honeyman. What remains but the garrets and the ample staircase and the kitchens, and the family being all put to bed, how can you imagine there is room for any more inhabitants?

And yet there is one lodger more, and one who like almost all the other personages mentioned up to the present time (and some of whom you have no idea yet) will play a definite part in the ensuing history. At night when Honeyman comes in he finds on the hall table three wax bed-room candles—his own, Bagshot's and another. As for Miss Cann, she is locked into the parlour and in bed long ago, her stout little walking shoes being on the mat at the door. At 12 o'clock at noon, sometimes at 1, nay at 2 and 3—long after Bagshot is gone to his committees, and little Cann to her pupils—a voice issues from the very topmost floor, from a room where there is no bell; a voice of thunder calling out "Slavey! Julia! Julia, my love! Mrs. Ridley!" And this summons not being obeyed, it will not unfrequently happen that a pair of trowsers inclosing a pair of boots with iron heels, and known by the name of the celebrated Prussian General who came up to help the other christener of boots at Waterloo, will be flung down from the topmost story even to the marble floor of the resounding hall. There[9]

7 masters *E1*] master *Ms*
8 George 1st., his time: *Ms*] George the First's time; *E1*
9 There *Ms*] Then *E1*

the boy Thomas, otherwise called Slavey, may say, "There he goes agin": or Mrs. Ridley's own back parlour bell rings vehemently, and Julia the cook will exclaim, "Lor, it's Mr. Frederick."

If the breeches and boots are not understood, the owner himself appears in great wrath dancing on the upper story, dancing down to the lower floor; and loosely enveloped in a ragged and flowing robe de chambre.[1] In this costume and condition he will dance into Honeyman's apartment where that meek divine may be sitting with a headache or over a novel or a newspaper, dance up to the fire flapping his robe tails, poke it and warm himself there, dance up to the cupboard where his reverence keeps his sherry and help himself to a glass.

"*Salve! Spes fidei, lumen ecclesiæ,*" he will say; "here's towards you, my buck. I knows the tap. Sherrick's Marsala bottled three months after date at two hundred and forty-six shillings the dozen."

"Indeed. Indeed it's not," (and now we are coming to an idea of the skeleton in poor Honeyman's closet—not that this huge handsome jolly Fred Bayham[2] is the skeleton—far from it—Mr. Frederick weighs fourteen stone). "Indeed. Indeed it isn't, Fred, I'm sure," sighs the other. "You exaggerate, indeed you do. The wine is not dear, not by any means so expensive as you say."

"How much a glass, think you?" says Fred, filling another bumper. "A half-crown, think ye? a half-crown, Honeyman? By cock and pye, it is not worth a bender." He says this in the manner of the most celebrated trage-dian of the day. He can imitate any actor tragic or comic; any known parlia-mentary orator or clergyman: any saw, cock, cloop of a cork wrenched from a bottle and guggling of wine into the decanter afterwards, bee buzzing, lit-tle boy up a chimney, &c.; he imitates people being ill[3] on board a steam-packet so well that he makes you die of laughing: his uncle the Bishop could not resist this comic exhibition and gave Fred a cheque for a comfort-able sum of money; and Fred, getting cash for the cheque at The Cave of Harmony, imitated his uncle the Bishop and his Chaplain, winding up with his lordship and Chaplain being unwell at sea—the Chaplain and Bishop quite natural and distinct.

"How much does a glass of this sack cost thee, Charley," resumes Fred after this parenthesis. "You say it is not dear? Charles Honeyman, you had ever[4] from your youth up a villainous habit. And I perfectly well remem-ber, Sir, that in boyhood's breezy hour when I was the delight of his school you[5] used to tell lies to your venerable father. You did, Charles. Excuse the frankness of an early friend, it's my belief you'd rather lie than not. Hm—" he looks at the cards in the chimney-glass; invitations to dinner, proffers of muffins. "Do lend me your sermon—O you old imposter! you hoary old Ananias!—I say Charley, why haven't you picked out some nice girl for

---

[1] floor; and loosely enveloped in a ragged and flowing robe de chambre. *E1*] floor, and with the exception of a flowing robe de chambre and a slight interior garment in the *simple appareil* of an Ancient Briton. *Ms*
[2] Fred Bayham *E1*] Ancient Briton *Ms*
[3] ill *E1*] sick *Ms*
[4] ever *Ms*] even *E1*
[5] Sir, that in . . . school you *Ms*] Sir, in . . . school, that you *E1*

yours truly? one with lands and beeves, with rents and consols, mark you? I have no money 'tis true, but then I don't owe as much as you. I am a handsomer man than you are, look at this chest (he slaps it), these limbs, they are manly, Sir, manly—"

"For Heaven's sake, Bayham," cries Mr. Honeyman, white with terror— "If any body were to come . . ."

"What did I say anon, Sir? that I was manly, ay, manly—let any ruffian save a bailiff come and meet the doughty arm of Frederick Bayham."

"O Lord Lord, here's somebody coming into the room!" cries Charles sinking back on the sofa as the door opens.

"Ha, dost thou come with murderous intent?" and now he advances in an approved offensive attitude, and then, "Caitiff,[6] come on, come on!"— and he walks off with a tragic laugh, crying, "Ha ha ha, 'tis but the slavey!"

The slavey has Mr. Frederick's hot water, and a bottle of soda water on the same tray. He has been instructed to bring soda whenever he hears the word Slavey pronounced from above—The bottle explodes and Frederick drinks, and hisses after his drink as though he had been all hot within.

"What's o'clock now, Slavey—half-past three?[7] Let me see, I breakfasted exactly ten hours ago, in the rosy morning off a modest cup of coffee in Covent Garden Market. Coffee a penny, bread a simple halfpenny. What has Mrs. Ridley for dinner? Please, Sir, Roast Pork?[8] Get me some. Bring it into my room, unless, Honeyman, you insist upon my having it here, kind fellow!"

At this[9] moment a smart knock comes to the door and Fred says, "Well, Charles, it may be a friend or a lady come to confess and I'm off. Knew you'd be sorry I was going. Tom, bring up my things, brush 'em gently, you scoundrel, and don't take the nap off; bring up the roast pork and plenty of apple sauce, tell Mrs. Ridley with my love; and one of Mr. Honeyman's shirts and one of his razors. Adieu, Charles! Amend! Remember me!" And he vanishes into the upper chambers.

[6] attitude, and then, "Caitiff, *Ms*] attitude. "Caitiff, *E1*
[7] three? *E1*] one *Ms*; cf. 119.17
[8] Please, . . . Pork? *Ms*] ¶"Please, . . . Pork."¶*E1*
[9] this *Ms*] the *E1*

Chapter XII.

OHN JAMES had opened the door hastening to welcome a friend and patron the sight of whom always gladdened the youth's eyes;—no other than Clive Newcome: in young Ridley's opinion, the most splendid fortunate beautiful high-born and gifted youth this Island contained. What generous boy in his time has not worshipped somebody? Before the female enslaver makes her appearance, every lad has a friend of friends, a crony of cronies, to whom he writes immense letters in vacation, whom he cherishes in his heart of hearts; whose sister he proposes to marry in after life; whose purse he shares; for whom he will take a thrashing if need be: who is his hero. Clive was John James's youthful Divinity: when he wanted to draw Thaddeus of Warsaw, a Prince, Ivanhoe, or someone splendid and egregious, it was Clive he took for a model. His heart leapt when he saw the young fellow. He would walk cheerfully to Grey Friars with a letter or message for Clive: on the chance of seeing him, and getting a kind word from him, or a shake of the hand. An ex-butler of Lord Todmorden was a pensioner in the Grey Friars Hospital, (it has been said that at that ancient Establishment is a College for old men as well as for boys,) and this old man would come sometimes to his successor's Sunday dinner, and grumble from the hour of that meal until nine o'clock when he was forced to depart so as to be within Grey Friars' gates before ten—grumble about his dinner, grumble about his beer, grumble about the number of chapels he had to attend, about the gown he wore, about the Master's treatment of him, about the want of plums in the pudding, as old men and schoolboys grumble. It was wonderful what a liking John James took to this odious, querulous, graceless, stupid and snuffy old man, and how he would find pretexts for visiting him at his lodging in the Old Hospital. He actually took that journey that he might have a chance of seeing Clive. He sent Clive notes and packets of drawings, thanked him for books lent—asked advice about future reading—anything so that he might have a sight of his pride, his patron, his paragon.

[1] *Ms* lacks title

I am afraid Clive Newcome employed him to smuggle rum-shrub and cigars into the premises—giving him appointments in the school precincts where young Clive would come and stealthily receive the forbidden goods. The poor lad was known by the boys and called Newcome's Punch. He was all but hunchbacked; long and lean in the arm; sallow, with a great forehead and waving black hair and large melancholy eyes.

"What, is it you, J.J.?" cries Clive gaily when his humble friend appears at the door. "Father, this is my friend Ridley. This is the fellow what *can* draw."

"I know who[1] I will back against any young man of his size at *that*," says the Colonel looking at Clive fondly. He considered there was not such a genius in the world; and had already thought of having some of Clive's drawings published by McLean of the Haymarket.

"This is my father just come from India—and Mr. Pendennis, an old Grey Friars' man. Is my uncle at home?" Both these gentlemen bestow rather patronising nods of the head on the lad introduced to them as J.J. His exterior is but mean-looking. Colonel Newcome, one of the humblest-minded men alive, has yet his old-fashioned military notions; and speaks to a butler's son as to a private soldier, kindly but not familiarly.

"Mr. Honeyman is at home, gentlemen," the young lad says humbly. "Shall I show you up to his room?" And we walk up the stairs after our guide. We find Mr. Honeyman deep in study on his sofa, with "Pearson on the Creed" before him. The novel has been whipped under the pillow. Clive found it there some short time afterwards during his uncle's temporary absence in his dressing-room. He has agreed to suspend his theological studies, and go out with his brother-in-law to dine.

As Clive and his friend were at Honeyman's door and just as we were entering to see the divine seated in state before his folio—Clive whispers, "J.J., come along, old fellow, and show us some drawings. What are you doing?"

"I was doing some Arabian Nights," says J.J., "up in my room: and hearing a knock which I thought was yours, I came down."

"Shew us the pictures. Let's go up into your room," cries Clive.

"What, *will* you?" says the other. "It is but a very small place."

"Never mind. Come along," says Clive: and the two lads disappear together, leaving the three grown gentlemen to discourse together, or rather two of us to listen to Honeyman who expatiates upon the beauty of the weather, the difficulties of the clerical calling, the honour Colonel Newcome does him by a visit, &c.—with his usual eloquence.

After a while Clive comes down without J.J. from the upper regions. He is greatly excited. "O, Sir," he says to his father, "you talk about my drawings—You should see J.J.'s! By Jove, that fellow is a genius. They are beautiful, Sir. You seem actually to read the Arabian Nights, you know—only in pictures—There is Scheherazade telling the stories, and—what do you call her?—Dinarsade and the Sultan sitting in bed and listening. Such a grim old cove! You see he has cut off ever so many of his wives' heads. I can't think where that chap gets his ideas from. I can beat him in drawing

[1] who *E1*] whom *R*

horses, I know, and dogs: but I can only draw what I see. Somehow he seems to see things we don't, don't you know? O, Father, I'm determined I'd rather be a painter than anything." And he falls to drawing horses and dogs at his uncle's table, round which the elders are seated.[2]

"I've settled it up-stairs with J.J.," says Clive, working away with his pen. "We shall take a studio together; perhaps we will go abroad together. Won't that be fun, father?"

"My dear Clive," remarks Mr. Honeyman, with bland dignity, "there are degrees in society which we must respect. You surely cannot think of being a professional artist. Such a profession is very well for your young protégé; but for you—"

"What for me?" cries Clive. "We are no such great folks that I know of; and if we were, I say a painter is as good as a lawyer, or a doctor, or even a soldier. In Dr. Johnson's Life, which my father is always reading—I like to read about Sir Joshua Reynolds best: I think he is the best gentleman of all in the book. My! wouldn't I like to paint a picture like Lord Heathfield in the National Gallery! *Wouldn't* I just? I think I would sooner have done that, than have fought at Gibraltar. And those Three Graces—oh, aren't they graceful! And that Cardinal Beaufort at Dulwich!—it frightens me so, I daren't look at it. Wasn't Reynolds a clipper, that's all! and wasn't Rubens a brick? He was an ambassador and Knight of the Bath; so was Vandyck. And Titian, and Raphael, and Velasquez?—I'll just trouble you to show me better gentlemen than them, Uncle Charles."

"Far be it from me to say that the pictorial calling is not honourable," says Uncle Charles; "but as the world goes there are other professions in greater repute; and I should have thought Colonel Newcome's son—"

"He shall follow his own bent," said the Colonel; "as long as his calling is honest it becomes a gentleman; and if he were to take a fancy to play on the fiddle—actually on the fiddle—I shouldn't object."

"Such a rum chap there was up-stairs!" Clive resumes, looking up from his scribbling. "He was walking up and down on the landing in a dressing-gown with scarcely any other clothes on—holding a plate in one hand, and a pork chop he was munching with the other—Like this—(and Clive draws a figure). What do you think, Sir? He was in the Cave of Harmony, he says, that night you flared up about Captain Costigan. He knew me at once: and he says, 'Sir, your father acted like a gentleman, a Christian and a man of honour. *Maxima debetur pueris reverentia.* Give him my compliments— I don't know his highly respectable name.' His highly respectable name," says Clive cracking with laughter. "Those were his very words. 'And inform him that I am an orphan myself—in needy circumstances'—he said he was in needy circumstances—'and I heartily wish he'd adopt me.'"

The lad puffed out his face, made his voice as loud and as deep as he could; and from his imitation and the picture he had drawn, I knew at once that Fred Bayham was the man he mimicked.

"And does the Red Rover live here," cried Mr. Pendennis, "and have we earthed him at last?"

---

[2] table, round which the elders are seated. *E1*] table while the elders continue their conversation. *Ms.* The next five paragraphs, not in the *Ms*, were added to *E1* at proof stage.

"He sometimes comes here," Mr. Honeyman said with a careless manner. "My landlord and landlady were butler and housekeeper to his father, Bayham of Bayham, one of the oldest families in Europe. And Mr. Frederick Bayham, the exceedingly eccentric person of whom you speak, was a private pupil of my own dear father in our happy days at Saint Bonhambury."[3]

He had scarcely spoken when a knock was heard at the door: and before the occupant of the lodgings could say "Come in," Mr. Frederick Bayham made his appearance; arrayed in that peculiar costume which he affected. In those days we wore very tall stocks, only a very few poetic and eccentric persons venturing on the Byron collar: but Fred Bayham confined his neck by a simple ribbon, which allowed his great red whiskers to curl freely round his capacious jowl. He wore a black frock and a large broad-brimmed hat, and looked somewhat like a Dissenting preacher—At other periods you would see him in a green coat and a blue neckcloth, as if the turf or the driving of coaches was his occupation.

"I have heard from the young man of the house who you were, Colonel Newcome," he said, with the greatest gravity, "and happened to be present, Sir, the other night: for I was aweary, having been toiling all the day in

[3] Saint Bonhambury." *Ms*] Borehambury." *E1*; cf. 244.

literary labour and needed some refreshment—I happened to be present, Sir, at a scene which did you the greatest honour, and of which I spoke, not knowing you, with something like levity to your son. He is an *ingenui vultus puer ingenuique pudoris*—Pendennis how are you?—And I thought, Sir, I would come down and tender an apology if I had said any words that might savour of offence to a gentleman who was in the right, as I told the room when you quitted it—as Mr. Pendennis, I am sure, will remember."

Mr. Pendennis looked surprise and perhaps negation.

"You forget, Pendennis? Those who quit that room, Sir, often forget on the morrow what occurred during the revelry of the night. You did right in refusing to return to that scene. We public men are obliged often to seek our refreshment at hours when luckier individuals are lapt in slumber."

"And what may be your occupation, Mr. Bayham?" asks the Colonel rather gloomily: for he had an idea that Bayham was adopting a strain of *persiflage* which the Indian gentleman by no means relished. Never saying aught but a kind word to any one, he was on fire at the notion that any should take a liberty with him.

"A barrister, Sir, but without business—a literary man who can but seldom find an opportunity to sell the works of his brain—a gentleman, Sir, who has met with neglect, perhaps merited, perhaps undeserved, from his family. I get my bread as best I may. On that evening I had been lecturing on the genius of some of our comic writers at the Parthenopæon, Hackney. My audience was scanty—perhaps equal to my deserts. I came home on foot to an egg and a glass of beer after midnight—and witnessed the scene which did you so much honour. What is this? I fancy a ludicrous picture of myself—" He had taken up the sketch which Clive had been drawing. "I like fun even at my own expense, and can afford to laugh at a joke which is meant in good humour."

This speech quite reconciled the honest Colonel. "I am sure the author of that, Mr. Bayham, meant you nor any man any harm.[4] Why! the rascal, Sir, has drawn me, his own father; and I have sent the drawing to Major Hobbs who is in command of my regiment. Chinnery himself, Sir, couldn't hit off a likeness better: he has drawn me on horseback and he has drawn me on foot and he has drawn my friend Mr. Binnie who lives with me. We have scores of his drawings at my lodgings and if you will favour us by dining with us to-day, and these gentlemen, you shall see that you are not the only person caricatured by Clive here."

"I just took some little dinner up-stairs, Sir. I am a moderate man and can live if need be like a Spartan: but to join such good company I will gladly use the knife and fork again. You will excuse the traveller's dress? I keep a room here which I use only occasionally and am at present lodging—in the country."

When Honeyman was ready, the Colonel who had the greatest respect for the Church, would not hear of going out of the room before the Clergyman: and took his arm to walk. Bayham then fell to Mr. Pendennis's lot, and they went together. Through Hill Street and Berkeley Square their course was straight enough: but at Hay Hill, Mr. Bayham made an abrupt

[4] meant you nor any man any harm. *Ms*] means you or any any no harm. *E1*

tack larboard, engaging in a labyrinth of stables and walking a long way round from Clifford Street whither we were bound. He hinted at a cab, but Pendennis refused to ride, being in truth anxious to see which way his eccentric companion would steer. "There are reasons," growled Bayham, "which need not be explained to one of your experience why Bond Street must be avoided by some men peculiarly situated. The smell of Truefitt's pomatums makes me ill. Tell me, Pendennis, is this Indian warrior a Rajah of large wealth? Could he, do you think, recommend me to a situation in the East India Company? I would gladly take any honest post in which fidelity might be useful: genius might be appreciated, and courage rewarded. Here we are. The hotel seems comfortable. I never was in it before."

When we entered the Colonel's sitting-room at Nerot's, we found the waiter engaged in extending the tables. "We are a larger party than I expected," our host said. "I met my brother Brian on horseback leaving cards at that great house in —— Street."

"The Russian Embassy," says Mr. Honeyman, who knew the town quite well.

"And he said he was disengaged, and would dine with us," continues the Colonel.

"Am I to understand, Colonel Newcome," says Mr. Frederick Bayham, "that you are related to the eminent banker, Sir Brian Newcome, who gives such uncommonly swell parties in Park Lane?"

"What is a swell party?" asks the Colonel laughing. "I dined with my brother last Wednesday: and it was a very grand dinner certainly. The Governor-General himself could not give a more splendid entertainment. But, do you know, I scarcely had enough to eat? I don't eat side dishes; and as for the roast beef of old England, why, the meat was put on the table, and whisked away like Sancho's inauguration feast at Barataria. We did not dine till nine o'clock. I like a few glasses of claret and a cosy talk after dinner; but—well, well—" (no doubt the worthy gentleman was accusing himself of telling tales out of school and had come to a timely repentance). "*Our* dinner, I hope, will be different. Jack Binnie will take care of that. That fellow is full of anecdote and fun. You will meet one or two more of our service: Sir Thomas de Boots who is not a bad chap over a glass of wine; Mr. Pendennis's chum, Mr. Warrington, and my nephew, Barnes Newcome—a dry fellow at first but I daresay he has good about him when you know him:—almost every man has," said the good-natured philosopher. "Clive, you rogue, mind and be moderate with the Champagne, Sir!"

"Champagne's for women," says Clive. "I stick to claret."

"I say, Pendennis," here Bayham remarked, "it is my deliberate opinion that F.B. has got into a good thing."

Mr. Pendennis, seeing there was a great party, was for going home to his chambers to dress. "Hm!" says Mr. Bayham. "Don't see the necessity. What right-minded man looks at the exterior of his neighbour? He looks *here*, Sir, and examines *there*," and Bayham tapped his forehead which was expansive, and then his heart, which he considered to be in the right place.

"What is this I hear about dressing?" asks our host. "Dine in your frock, my good friend, and welcome: if your dress-coat is in the country."

"It is at present at an uncle's," Mr. Bayham said with great gravity, "and I take your hospitality as you offer it, Colonel Newcome—cordially and frankly."

Honest Mr. Binnie made his appearance a short time before the appointed hour for receiving the guests, arrayed in a tight little pair of trowsers and white silk-stockings and pumps, his bald head shining like a billiard-ball, his jolly gills rosy with good humour. He was bent on pleasure. "Hey, lads," says he, "but we'll make a night of it. We haven't had a night since the farewell dinner off Plymouth."

"And a jolly night it was, James!" ejaculates the Colonel.

"Egad, what a song that Tom Norris sings."

"And your Jock o'Hazeldean is as good as a play, Jack."

"And I think you beat iny one I iver hard in Tom Bowling yourself, Tom!" cries the Colonel's delighted chum. Mr. Pendennis opened the eyes of astonishment at the idea of the possibility of renewing these festivities but he kept the lips of prudence closed.[5]

And now the carriages began to drive up, and the guests of Colonel Newcome to arrive.

[5] The next paragraph and the chapter break were added at proof stage for *E1*. The first paragraph of the next chapter was also heavily revised for *E1* in proof. The *Ms* continues without a paragraph or chapter break: closed. ¶One by one the guests now began to arrive: There was the first mate and the medical officer of the ship in which the two gentlemen had come to England— The mate was a healthy-looking mariner with a broad brown face and red whiskers and a great pair of hands covered with freckles, who looked sadly uncomfortable in his shore-going clothes. The mate was a Scotchman: the Doctor was a Scotchman: of the gentlemen from the Oriental Club, three were Scotchmen. These were, of course, Mr. Binnie's guests: the South-Britons were invited by his chum the Colonel.

Chapter XIII.

HE earliest comers were the first mate and the medical officer of the ship in which the two gentlemen had come to England. The mate was a Scotchman: the Doctor was a Scotchman: of the gentlemen from the Oriental Club, three were Scotchmen.[1]

The Southrons, with one exception, were the last to arrive: and for a while we stood looking out of the windows awaiting their coming. The first mate pulled out a pen-knife and arranged his nails. The Doctor and Mr. Binnie talked of the progress of medicine. Binnie had walked the hospitals of Edinburgh before getting his civil appointment to India.[2] The three gentlemen from Hanover Square and the Colonel had plenty to say about Tom Smith of the Cavalry, and Harry Hall of the Engineers, how Topham was going to marry poor little Bob Wallis's widow: how many lakhs Barker had brought home and the like. The tall grey-headed Englishman, who had been in the East too, in the king's service—joined for a while in this conversation, but presently left it, and came and talked with Clive.[3] "I knew your father in India," said the gentleman to the lad, "there is not a more gallant or respected officer in that service. I have a boy too: a step-son who has just gone into the army. He is older than you: he was born at the end of the Waterloo year, and so was a great friend of his and mine, who was at your school, Sir Rawdon Crawley."

"He was in Gown Boys, I know," says the boy: "succeeded his uncle, Pitt, fourth Baronet. I don't know how his mother—her who wrote the Hymns, you know, and goes to Mr. Honeyman's chapel—comes to be Rebecca, Lady Crawley. His father, Colonel Rawdon Crawley, died at Coventry Island in

[1] End of revision reported at end of previous chapter.
[2] India *E1*] India; where he had doctored himself very freely. *Ms*
[3] Clive.] Clive; *E1*] Clive about his school and his doings. *Ms*

August 182—,[4] and his uncle, Sir Pitt, not till September here. I remember we used to talk about it at Grey Friars when I was quite a little chap: and there were bets whether Crawley, I mean the young one, was a Baronet or not."

"Whin I sailed to Rigy, Cornel"—the first mate was speaking, nor can any spelling nor combination of letters of which I am master reproduce this gentleman's accent when he was talking his best. "I racklackt they used always to sairve us a drem before denner. And as your frinds are kipping the denner and as I've no watch to-night, I'll just do as we used to do at Rigy. James, my fine fellow, jist look alive and breng me a small glass of brendy will ye? Did ye iver try a brandy-cock-tail, Cornel? When I sailed on the New York line we used jest to make bits before denner: and—thank ye, James"; and he tossed off a glass of brandy.[5]

Here a waiter announces in a loud voice, "Sir Thomas de Boots," and the General enters scowling round the room according to his fashion, very red in the face, very tight in the girth, splendidly attired with a choking white neckcloth, a voluminous waistcoat and his orders on.

"Stars and Garters by Jingo!" cries Mr. Frederick Bayham, "I say, Pendennis, have you any idea, is the Duke coming? I wouldn't have come in these Bluchers if I had known it. Confound it, no—Hoby himself, my own bootmaker, wouldn't have allowed poor F.B. to appear in Bluchers if he had known that I was going to meet the Duke. My[6] linen's all right, any how," and F.B. breathed a thankful prayer for that. Indeed who but the

---

[4] 182—, *E1*] 18—, *Ms*

[5] *Ms* contains an additional paragraph at this point, deleted from *E1*: "I wish I was implicated in that transaction," whispers Mr. Bayham, who had been keeping as close to Mr. Pendennis as a sheriff's officer to a debtor. "I think yonder weather-beaten mariner shows proof of his good sense. I say—tst! you! hi!—is his name James? another little glass of"

[6] Duke. My *E1*] Duke—" and poor FB here looked down disconsolately at his lower extremities which were clothed in kerseymere shining with old age, and in boots whereof the extremities curled upwards like those of the Turks. "My *Ms*

test

very curious could tell that not F.B.'s, but C.H.'s, Charles Honeyman's, was the mark upon that decorous linen?

Colonel Newcome introduced[7] Sir Thomas to every one in the room, as he had introduced us all to each other previously—and as Sir Thomas looked at one after another, his face was kind enough to assume an expression which seemed to ask, "And who the Devil are *you*, Sir?" as clearly as though the General himself had given utterance to the words. With the gentleman in the window talking to Clive he seemed to have some acquaintance and said not unkindly, "How d'you do, Dobbin."

The carriage of Sir Brian Newcome now drove up, from which the Baronet descended in state, leaning upon the arm of the Apollo in plush and powder, who closed the shutters of the great coach, and mounted by the side of the coachman, laced and periwigged. The Bench of Bishops has given up its wigs—cannot the box, too, be made to resign that insane decoration? Is it necessary for our comfort that the men who do our work in stable or household should be dressed like Merry Andrews? Enter Sir Brian Newcome smiling blandly. He greets his brother affectionately, Sir Thomas gaily; he nods and smiles to Clive and graciously permits Mr. Pendennis to take hold of two fingers of his extended right hand. That gentleman is charmed, of course, with the condescension. What man could be otherwise than happy to be allowed a momentary embrace of two such precious fingers? When a gentleman so favours me, I always ask mentally why he has taken the trouble at all; and regret that I have not had the presence of mind to poke one finger against his two. If I were worth ten thousand a year, I cannot help inwardly reflecting, and kept a large account in Threadneedle Street, I cannot help thinking he would have favoured me with the whole palm.[8]

The arrival of these two grandees has somehow cast a solemnity over the company—The weather is talked about: brilliant in itself it does not occasion very brilliant remarks among Colonel Newcome's guests. Sir Brian really thinks it must be as hot as it is in India—Sir Thomas de Boots, swelling in his white waistcoat in the armholes of which his thumbs are engaged, smiles scornfully, and wishes Sir Brian had ever felt a good sweltering day in the hot winds in India—Sir Brian withdraws the untenable proposition that London is as hot as Calcutta. Mr. Binnie looks at his watch: and at the Colonel. "We have only your nephew Tom to wait for," he says, "I think we may make so bold as to order the dinner," a proposal heartily seconded by Mr. Frederick Bayham.

The dinner appears steaming, borne by steaming waiters. The grandees take their places one on each side of the Colonel. He begs Mr. Honeyman to say grace, and stands reverentially during that brief ceremony, while De Boots looks queerly at him from over his napkin. All the young men take their places at the farther end of the table round about Mr. Binnie: and at the end of the second course Mr. Barnes Newcome makes his appearance.

Mr. Barnes does not show the slightest degree of disturbance although he disturbs all the company. Soup and fish are brought for him, and meat which he leisurely eats, while twelve other gentlemen are kept waiting. We mark Mr. Binnie's twinkling eyes as they watch the young man. "Eh," he seems to say, "but that's just about as free and easy a young chap as ever I set eyes on." And so Mr. Barnes *was* a cool young chap. That dish is so good he must really have some more. He discusses the second supply leisurely and turning round simpering to his neighbour says, "I really hope I'm not keeping every body waiting."

"Hm," grunts the neighbour, Mr. Bayham. "It doesn't much matter, for we had all pretty well done dinner." Barnes takes a note of Mr. Bayham's dress—his long frock-coat, the ribbon round his neck; and surveys him with an admirable impudence. Who are these people, thinks he, my uncle has got together. He bows graciously to the honest[9] Colonel who asks him to take wine. He is so insufferably affable, that every man near him would like to give him a beating.

All the time of the dinner the host was challenging every body to drink wine in his honest old-fashioned way, and Mr. Binnie seconding the chief entertainer. Such was the way in England and Scotland when they were young men. And when Binnie, asking Sir Brian, receives for reply from the Baronet, "Thank you, no, my dear Sir. I have exceeded already, positively exceeded"; the poor discomfited gentleman hardly knows whither to apply but luckily Tom Norris the first mate comes to his rescue and cries out, "Mr. Binnie, *I*'ve not had enough, and I'll drink a glass of any thing ye like with ye." The fact is, that Mr. Norris *has* had enough. He has drunk bumpers to the health of every member of the company: his glass has been filled scores of times by watchful waiters. So has Mr. Bayham absorbed great quantities of drink: but without any visible effect on that veteran toper. So has young Clive taken more than is good for him. His cheeks are flushed and burning, he is chattering and laughing loudly at his end of the table—Mr. Warrington eyes the lad with some curiosity; and then regards Mr. Barnes with a look of scorn, which does not scorch that affable young person.

I am obliged to confess that the mate of the Indiaman at an early period of the dessert and when nobody had asked him for any such public expression of his opinions, insisted on rising and proposing the health of Colonel Newcome whose virtues he lauded outrageously and whom he pronounced to be one of the best of mortal men. Sir Brian looked very much alarmed at the commencement of this speech, which the mate delivered with immense shrieks and gesticulation; but the Baronet recovered during the course of the rambling oration, and at its conclusion gracefully tapped the table with one of those patronising fingers; and lifting up a glass containing at least a thimble-full of claret, said, "My dear brother, I drink your health with all my heart, I'm su-ah." The youthful Barnes had uttered many "hear hears" during the discourse with an irony which, with every fresh glass of wine he drank, he cared less to conceal. And though Barnes had come late he had drunk largely, making up for lost time.

[9] honest *E1*] [omitted] *R*

Those ironical cheers, and all his cousin's behaviour during dinner had struck young Clive who was growing very angry. He growled out remarks uncomplimentary to Barnes. His eyes as he looked towards his kinsman flashed out[1] challenges, of which we who were watching him could see the warlike purport. Warrington looked at Bayham and Pendennis[2] with glances of apprehension. We saw that danger was brooding unless the one young man could be restrained from his impertinence and the other from his wine.

Colonel Newcome said a very few words in reply to his honest friend the chief mate: and there the matter might have ended: but I am sorry to say Mr. Binnie now thought it necessary to rise and deliver himself of some remarks regarding the king's service coupled with the name of Major General Sir Thomas de Boots, K.C.B. &c.—the receipt of which that gallant officer was obliged to acknowledge in a confusion amounting almost to apoplexy. The glasses went whack whack upon the hospitable board; the evening set in for public speaking. Encouraged by his last effort, Mr. Binnie now proposed Sir Brian Newcome's health; and that Baronet rose and uttered an exceedingly lengthy speech delivered with his wine glass on his bosom.

Then that sad rogue Bayham must get up, and call earnestly and respectfully for silence and the chairman's hearty sympathy for the few observations which he had to propose. Our armies had been drunk with proper enthusiasm—such men as he beheld around him deserved the applause of all honest hearts, and merited the cheers with which their names had been received. (Hear Hear! from Barnes Newcome sarcastically. Hear Hear HEAR! fiercely from Clive.) "But whilst we applaud our army, should we forget a profession still more exalted?—yes still more exalted, I say in the face of the gallant General opposite—and that profession, I need not say, is the Church. (Applause.) Gentlemen, we have among us one who, while partaking largely of the dainties on this festive board, drinking freely of the sparkling wine-cup which our gallant friend's[3] hospitality administers to us—sanctifies by his presence the feast of which he partakes, inaugurates with appropriate benedictions, and graces it, I may say, both before and after meat. Gentlemen, Charles Honeyman was the friend of my childhood, his father the instructor of my early days. If Frederick Bayham's latter life has been chequered by misfortune, it may be that I have forgotten the precepts which the venerable parent of Charles Honeyman poured into an inattentive ear. He too as a child, was not exempt from faults; as a young man, I am told, not quite free from youthful indiscretions: but in this present Anno Domini we hail Charles Honeyman as a precept and an example, as a *decus fidei* and a *lumen ecclesiæ* (as I told him in the confidence of the private circle this morning, and ere I ever thought to publish my opinion in this distinguished company). Colonel Newcome and Mr. Binnie! I drink to the health of the Reverend Charles Honeyman, A.M. May we listen to many more of his sermons, as well as to that

[1] out *E1*] [omitted] *R*
[2] at Bayham and Pendennis *E1*] at Pendennis *Ms*
[3] friend's *R*] [absent] *E1*

admirable discourse with which I am sure he is about to electrify us now.
May we profit by his eloquence! And cherish in our memories the truths
which come mended from his tongue!" He ceased; poor Honeyman had
to rise on his legs, and gasp out a few incoherent remarks in reply. Without a book before him, the incumbent of Lady Whittlesea's chapel was no
prophet, and the truth is he made poor work of his oration.

At the end of it, he, Sir Brian, Colonel Dobbin and one of the Indian
gentlemen quitted the room in spite of the loud outcries of our generous
hosts[4] who insisted that the party should not break up. "Close up, gentlemen," called out honest Newcome, "we are not going to part just yet.
Let me fill your glass, General. You used to have no objection to a glass
of wine," and he poured out a bumper for his friend which the old Campaigner sucked in with fitting gusto. "Who will give us a song? Binnie,
give us the Laird of Cockpen. It's capital, my dear General—Capital," the
Colonel whispered to his neighbour.

Mr. Binnie struck up the Laird of Cockpen, without, I am bound to say,
the least[5] reluctance. He bobbed to one man, and he winked to another,
and he tossed his glass, and gave all the points of his song in a manner
which did credit to his simplicity and his humour. You haughty Southern-
ers little know how a jolly Scotch gentleman can *desipere in loco* and how he
chirrups over his honest cups. I do not say whether it was with the song
or with Mr. Binnie that we were most amused. It was a good commonty as
Christopher Sly says; nor were we sorry[6] when it was done.

Him the first mate succeeded: after which came a song from the redoubted F. Bayham; which he sang with a bass voice which Lablache might
envy—and of which the chorus was frantically sung by the whole company.
The cry was then for the Colonel; on which Barnes Newcome who had been
drinking much, started up with something like an oath, crying, "O—I can't
stand this."

"Then leave it, confound you!" said young Clive, with fury in his face.
"If our company is not good for you why do you come into it?"

"Whas that?" asks Barnes who was evidently affected by wine. Bayham
roared, "Silence," and Barnes Newcome looking round with a tipsy toss of
the head, finally sate down.

The Colonel sang as we have said with a very high voice, using freely
the falsetto after the manner of the tenor-singers of his day. He chose one
of his maritime songs, and got through the first verse very well, Barnes
wagging his head at the chorus with a "bravo" so offensive that Fred Bayham his neighbour gripped the young man's arm and told him to hold his
confounded tongue.

The Colonel began his second verse: and here, as will often happen to
amateur singers, his falsetto broke down. He was not in the least annoyed,
for I saw him smile very good-naturedly; and he was going to try the verse
again, when that unlucky Barnes first gave a sort of crowing imitation of

[4] hosts *Ms*] host *E1*
[5] Cockpen, without, I am bound to say, the least *E1*] Cockpen I am bound to say without
the least *Ms*
[6] sorry *E1*] very sorry *Ms*

the song and then burst into a yell of laughter. Clive dashed a glass of wine in his face at the next minute, glass and all; and no one who had watched the young man's behaviour was sorry for the insult.

I never saw a kind face express more terror than Colonel Newcome's. He started back as if he had himself received the blow from his son. "Gracious God!" he cried out. "My boy insult a gentleman at my table!"

"I'd like to do it again," says Clive whose whole body was trembling with anger.

"Are you drunk, Sir?" shouted his father.

"The boy served the young fellow right, Sir" growled Fred Bayham in his deepest voice. "Come along, young man. Stand up straight and keep a civil tongue in your head next time, mind you, when you dine with gentlemen. It's easy to see," says Fred, looking round with a knowing air, "that this young man hasn't got the usages of society—he's not been accustomed to it"; and he led the dandy out.

Others had meanwhile explained the state of the case to the Colonel; including Sir Thomas de Boots who was highly energetic and delighted with Clive's spirit and some were for having the song to continue; but the Colonel puffing his cigar said, "No. My pipe is out. I will never sing again." So this history will record no more of Thomas Newcome's musical performances.

Chapter XIV.

PARK LANE.

LIVE woke up the next morning to be aware of a racking headache, and by the dim light of his throbbing eyes to behold his father with solemn face at his bed-foot,—a reproving conscience to greet his waking.

"You drank too much wine last night, and disgraced yourself, Sir," the old soldier said. "You must get up and eat humble pie this morning, my boy."

"Humble what, Father?" asked the lad hardly aware of his words or the scene before him. "O, I've got such a headache!"

"Serve you right, Sir. Many a young fellow has had to go on parade in the morning with a headache earned overnight. Drink this water—now jump up—Now, dash the water well over your head— There you come! Make[1] your toilette quickly and let us be off, and find Cousin Barnes before he has left home."

Clive obeyed the paternal orders; dressed himself quickly, and descending, found his father smoking his morning cigar, in the apartment where they had dined the night before and where the tables still were covered with the relics of yesterday's feast—the emptied bottles, the blank lamps, the scattered ashes and fruits, the wretched heel-taps that have been lying exposed all night to the air—who does not know the aspect of an expired feast?[2]

"The field of action strewed with the dead, my boy," says Clive's father. "See, here's the glass on the floor yet and a great stain of claret on the carpet."

"O Father!" says Clive hanging his head down, "I know I shouldn't have done it. But Barnes Newcome would provoke the patience of Job, and I couldn't bear to have my father insulted."

"I am big enough to fight my own battles, my boy," the Colonel said good-naturedly putting his hand on the lad's damp head. "How your head

[1] Make *E1*] Wide awake, and feeling your coppers hot, eh Sir? Have a cold-bath, make *Ms*

[2] feast? *E1*] feast—the appearance of a theatre when the play is over and the daylight comes streaming in over the vacant benches? *Ms*

throbs! If Barnes laughed at my singing, depend upon it, Sir, there was something ridiculous in it, and he laughed because he could not help it. If he behaved ill:—we should not: and to a man who is eating our salt too, and is of our blood."

"He is ashamed of our blood, Father," cries Clive still indignant.

"We ought to be ashamed of doing wrong. We must go and ask his pardon. Once when I was a young man in India," the father continued very gravely, "some hot words passed at mess—not such an insult as that of last night—I don't think I could have quite borne that—and people found fault with me for forgiving the youngster who had uttered the offensive expressions over his wine. Some of my acquaintance sneered at my courage, and that is a hard imputation for a young fellow of spirit to bear. But providentially, you see, it was war-time, and very soon after, I had the good luck to show that I was not a *poule mouillée* as the French call it, and the man who insulted me and whom I forgave became my fastest friend—and died by my side—it was poor Jack Cutler—at Argaum. We must go and ask Barnes Newcome's pardon, Sir; and—forgive other people's trespasses, my boy, if we hope forgiveness of our own." His voice sank down as he spoke, and he bowed his honest[3] head reverently—I have heard his son tell the simple story years afterwards with tears in his eyes.

Piccadilly was hardly yet awake the next morning, and the sparkling dews and the poor homeless vagabonds still had possession of the grass of Hyde Park, as the pair walked up to Sir Brian Newcome's house, where the shutters were just opening to let in the day. The housemaid, who was scrubbing the steps of the house, and washing its trim feet in a manner which became such a polite mansion's morning toilet, knew Master Clive and smiled at him from under her blowsy curl-papers, admitting the two gentlemen into Sir Brian's dining-room, where they proposed to wait until Mr. Barnes should appear. There they sate for an hour looking at Lawrence's picture of Lady Ann, leaning over a harp, attired in white muslin; at Harlowe's portrait of Mrs. Newcome, with her two sons, simpering at her knees, painted at a time when the Newcome brothers were not the bald-headed, red-whiskered British merchants with whom the reader has made acquaintance, but chubby children with hair flowing down their backs, and quaint little swallow-tailed jackets and nankeen trowsers. A splendid portrait of the late Earl of Kew in his peer's robes hangs opposite his daughter and her harp. We are writing of George the Fourth's reign; I daresay there hung in the room a fine framed print of that great sovereign. The chandelier is in a canvas bag; the vast side-board, whereon are erected open frames for the support of Sir Brian Newcome's grand silver trays, which on dinner-days gleam on that festive board, now groans under the weight of Sir Brian's blue-books. An immense receptacle for wine, shaped like a Roman sarcophagus, lurks under the side-board. Two people sitting at that large dining-table must talk very loud so as to make themselves heard across those great slabs of mahogany covered with damask. The butler and servants who attend at the table, take a long time walking round it. I picture to myself two persons of ordinary size sitting in that great room at

---

[3] honest *E1*] [omitted] *R*

that great table, far apart in neat evening costume sipping a little sherry, silent, genteel, and glum, and think, the great and wealthy are not always to be envied and that there may be more comfort and happiness in a snug parlor, where you are served by a brisk little maid than in a great dark, dreary dining-hall, where a funereal major-domo and a couple of stealthy footmen minister to you your mutton-chop. They come and lay the cloth presently, wide as the main sheet of some tall ammiral. A pile of news-papers and letters for the master of the house, the *Newcome Sentinel,* old county paper, moderate conservative, in which our worthy townsman and member is praised, his benefactions recorded and his speeches given at full length: the *Newcome Independent,* in which our precious member is weekly described as a ninny and informed almost every Thursday morning that he is a bloated aristocrat, as he munches his dry toast.——Heaps of letters, county papers, *Times* and *Morning Herald* for Sir Brian Newcome; little heaps of letters, (dinner and soirée cards most of these) and *Morning Post* for Mr. Barnes. Punctually as eight o'clock strikes, that young gentleman comes to breakfast; his father will lie yet for another hour; the Baronet's prodigious labours in the House of Commons keeping him frequently out of bed till sunrise.

As his cousin entered the room, Clive turned very red, and perhaps a faint blush might appear on Barnes's pallid countenance. He came in, a handkerchief in one hand, a pamphlet in the other, and both hands being thus engaged, he could offer neither to his kinsmen.—"You are come to breakfast? I hope," he said, calling it "bweakfast,"[4] and pronouncing the words with a most languid drawl—"or perhaps you want to see my father; he is never out of his room till half-past nine. Harper, did Sir Brian come in last night before or after me?"—Harper, the butler, thinks Sir Brian came in after Mr. Barnes.

When that functionary had quitted the room, Barnes turned round to his uncle in a candid smiling way and said:—"The fact is, Sir, I don't know when I came home myself very distinctly, and can't of course tell about my father. Generally you know, there are two candles left in the hall, you know; and if there are two, you know, I know of course that my father is still at the House. But last night after that capital song you sang, hang me if I know what happened to me. I beg your pardon, Sir, I'm shocked at having been so overtaken. Such a confounded thing doesn't happen to me once in ten years. I do trust I didn't do any thing rude to any body, for I thought some of your friends the pleasantest fellows I ever met in my life; and as for the claret, 'gad, as if I hadn't had enough after dinner, I brought a quantity of it away with me on my shirt-front and waistcoat!"

"I beg your pardon, Barnes," Clive said blushing deeply, "and I'm very sorry indeed for what passed. I threw it."

The Colonel, who had been listening with a queer expression of wonder and doubt on his face, here interrupted Mr. Barnes, "It was Clive that— that spilled the wine over you last night," Thomas Newcome said; "the young rascal had drunk a great deal too much wine and had neither the use of his head nor his hands, and this morning I have given him a lecture,

[4] bweakfast *Ms R*] weakfast *E1*

and he has come to ask your pardon for his clumsiness: and if you have forgotten your share in the night's transaction, I hope you have forgotten his: and will accept his hand and his apology."

"Apology! There's no apology," cries Barnes holding out a couple of fingers of his hand but looking towards the Colonel. "I don't know what happened any more than the dead. Did we have a row? were there any glasses broken? the best way in such cases is to sweep 'em up. We can't mend them."[5]

The Colonel said gravely—"that he was thankful to find that the disturbance of the night before had no worse result."[6] He pulled the tail of Clive's coat when that unlucky young blunderer was about to trouble his cousin with indiscreet questions or explanations and checked his talk. "The other night you saw an old man in drink, my boy;" he said, "and to what shame and degradation the old wretch had brought himself. Wine has given you a warning too, which I hope you will remember all your life; no one has ever seen me the worse for drink these forty years, and I hope both you young gentlemen will take counsel by an old soldier, who fully preaches what he practises, and beseeches you to beware of the bottle."

After quitting their kinsman, the kind Colonel farther improved the occasion with his son; and told him out of his own experience many stories of quarrels and duels and wine: how the wine had occasioned the brawl,[7] and the foolish speech over night the bloody meeting at morning: how he had known widows and orphans made by hot words uttered in idle orgies: how the truest honour was the manly confession of wrong; and the best courage the courage to avoid temptation. The humble-minded speaker whose advice contained the best of all wisdom, that which comes from a gentle and reverent spirit and a pure and generous heart, never for once thought of the effect which he might be producing but uttered his simple say according to the truth within him. Indeed he spoke out his mind pretty resolutely on all subjects which moved or interested him; and Clive his son, and his honest chum Mr. Binnie who had a great deal more reading and much keener intelligence than the Colonel, were amused often at his naïve opinions[8] about men or books or morals. Mr. Clive had a very fine natural sense of humour which played perpetually round his father's simple philosophy, with kind and smiling comments.[9] Between this pair of friends

---

[5] them." *E1*] them,"—and here Barnes could not help giving a little look at his cousin, which caused the latter young gentleman to feel sure that Barnes was perfectly aware of the previous night's transaction, in spite of all his assertions to the contrary. *Ms*

[6] result." *E1*] result;" and as Barnes did not seem in the least inclined to press for any precise account of the transactions of the previous night, the prudent negociator of peace did not choose to bring them forward. *Ms*

[7] brawl, *Ms*] brawls *E1*

[8] opinions *Ms*] opinion *E1*

[9] comments. *E1*] comments. Lad as he was he had a shrewdness and experience which the elder's fifty years had never attained. Clive with his young eyes looked more clearly at men and the world than his father who had seen it so long and so little: and the boy very soon began to keep his own opinion and to question the experience of which his artless sire never doubted the value. In truth Thomas Newcome was but a child in the understanding of the world although he fancied himself becomingly versed in that science; imagining that a man of necessity acquired experience by age and took steps in knowledge, as he did in military rank, by seniority. You who have children round

the superiority of wit lay, almost from the very first, on the younger man's side; but on the other hand Clive felt a tender admiration for his father's goodness, a loving delight in contemplating his elder's character, which he has never lost and which in the trials of their future life inexpressibly cheered and consoled both of them. *Beati illi!* O man of the world, whose wearied eyes may glance over this page, may those who come after you so regard you! O generous boy who read in it, may you have such a friend to trust and cherish in youth, and in future days fondly and proudly to remember!

Some four or five weeks after the quasi reconciliation between Clive and his kinsman, the chief[1] part of Sir Brian Newcome's family were assembled at the breakfast-table together, where the meal was taken in common and at the early hour of eight (unless the senator was kept too late in the House of Commons overnight): and Lady Ann and her nursery were now returned to London again, little Alfred being perfectly set up by a month of Brighton air. It was a Thursday morning, on which day of the week, it has been said, the *Newcome Independent* and the *Newcome Sentinel* both made their appearance upon the Baronet's table.[2] The household from above and from below, the maids and footmen from the basement, the nurses, children and governess from the attics, all poured into the room at the sound of a certain bell.[3]

I do not sneer at the purpose for which, at that chiming eight o'clock bell, the household is called together. The urns are hissing; the plate is shining; the father of the house standing up reads from a gilt book for three or four minutes in a measured cadence: the members of the family are around the table in an attitude of decent reverence: the younger children whisper responses at their mother's knees: the governess worships a little apart: the maids and the large footmen are in a cluster before their chairs, the upper servants performing their devotion on the other side of the side-board: the nurse whisks about the unconscious last-born and tosses it up and down during the ceremony. I do not sneer at that:—at the act at which all these people are assembled:—it is at the rest of the day

---

your firesides would you rather have them humble and silent and obedient, or frank and trustful? *Ms*

[1] kinsman, the chief *E1*] on the morning when the young heir of Newcome and Park Lane had professed such repentance for his excesses in wine, the chief *Ms*

[2] table. *E1*] table: When the family were in London the breakfast-room naturally presented a much more cheerful appearance than it wore when we were first introduced to it. Sir Brian discharged the domestic duties with stately regularity. A public man was separated from his family so much and by such constant interruptions! He is bound to be an example to those around him. Sir Brian had a weak but fine voice, he thought, and an impressive manner of elocution. *Ms*

[3] *Ms* contains an additional paragraph, omitted from *E1*: ¶The Newcome house in London was always up many hours before its fashionable neighbours whose masters had no banks in the city which they were obliged to attend. In March Lady Ann would rise every morning by candle light so as to be at breakfast at eight o'clock. Her daughter was not out yet; and her ladyship could get away from her balls and parties before midnight. But when Ethel should come out, though they might have to go to four balls of a night and might not get to bed till four o'clock, Lady Ann vowed and declared she would do the same thing, she *would* be present at her husband's breakfast—she would have the family assembled at the commencement of the day.

I marvel,—at the rest of the day and what it brings. At the very instant when the voice has ceased speaking and the gilded book is shut, the world begins again, and for the next twenty-three hours and fifty-seven minutes all that household is given up to it. The servile squad rises up and marches away to its basement, whence, should it happen to be a gala day, those tall gentlemen at present attired in Oxford mixture will issue forth with flour plastered on their heads, yellow coats, pink breeches, sky-blue waistcoats, silver lace, buckles in their shoes, black silk bags on their backs and I don't know what insane emblems of servility and absurd bedizenments of folly. Their very manner of speaking to what we call their masters and mistresses will be a like monstrous masquerade. You know no more of that race which inhabits the basement floor, than of the men and brethren of Timbuctoo to whom some among us send missionaries. If you met some of your servants in the streets (I respectfully suppose for a moment that the reader is a person of high fashion and a great establishment), you would not know their faces. You might sleep under the same roof for half a century and know nothing about them. If they were ill you would not visit them, though you would send them an apothecary and of course order that they lacked for nothing. You are not unkind. You are not worse than your neighbours. Nay, perhaps if you did go into the kitchen or to take tea[4] in the servants' hall, you would do little good and only bore the folks assembled there. But so it is. With those fellow Christians who have just been[5] saying Amen to your prayers, you have scarcely the community of charity. They come you don't know whence: they think and talk you don't know what; they die and you don't care, or *vice versâ*. They answer the bell for prayers as they answer the bell for coals, for exactly three minutes in the day you all kneel together on one carpet and, the desires and petitions of the servants—and masters—over, the rite called family worship is ended.

Exeunt servants, save those two who warm the newspapers, administer the muffins and serve out the tea. Sir Brian reads his letters and chumps his dry toast. Ethel whispers to her mother, she thinks Eliza is looking very ill. Lady Ann asks which is Eliza? is it the woman that was ill before they left town? If she is ill Mrs. Trotter[6] had better send her away. Mrs. Trotter[7] is only a great deal too good-natured—she is always keeping people who are ill. Then her ladyship begins to read the *Morning Post* and glances over the names of the persons who were present at Baroness Bosco's ball and Mrs. Toddle Tompkyns's *soirée dansante* in Belgrave Square.

"Every body was there," says Barnes looking over from his paper. "But who is Mrs. Toddle Tompkyns?" asks Mamma. "Who ever heard of a Mrs. Toddle Tompkyns? What do people mean by going to such a person?"

"Lady Popinjoy[8] asked the people," Barnes says gravely. "The thing was really doosed well done. The woman looked frightened: but she's pretty and I am told the daughter will have a great pot[9] of money."

[4] take tea *Ms*] take the tea *E1*
[5] just been *Ms E1*] been just *R*
[6] Trotter *E1*] Hicks *Ms*
[7] Trotter *E1*] Hicks *Ms*
[8] Popinjoy *Ms E1*] Popinjay *R*
[9] pot *Ms*] lot *E1*

An astounding Piece of Intelligence

"Is she pretty and did you dance with her?" asks Ethel.

"Me dance!" says Mr. Barnes. We are speaking of a time before Casinos were, and when the British youth were by no means so active in dancing practice as at this[1] present period. Barnes resumed the reading of his county paper, but presently laid it down with an execration so brisk and loud that his mother gave a little outcry and even his father looked up from his letters to ask the meaning of an oath so unexpected and ungenteel.

"My uncle the Colonel of sepoys and his amiable son have been paying a visit to Newcome—that's the news which I have the pleasure to announce to you," says Mr. Barnes.

"You are always sneering about our uncle," breaks in Ethel with impetuous voice, "and saying unkind things about Clive. Our uncle is a dear good kind man and I love him. He came to Brighton to see us and went out every day for hours and hours with Alfred. And Clive too drew pictures for him. And he is good and kind and generous and honest as his father. And Barnes is always speaking ill of him behind his back."

"And his aunt lets very nice lodgings and is altogether a most desirable acquaintance," says Mr. Barnes. "What a shame it is that we have not cultivated that branch of the family."

"My dear fellow," cries Sir Brian. "I have no doubt Miss Honeywood[2] is a most respectable person. Nothing is so ungenerous as to rebuke a gentleman or a lady on account of their poverty, and I coincide with Ethel in thinking that you speak of your uncle and his son in terms which to say the least are disrespectful."

"Miss Honeyman is a dear little old woman," breaks in Ethel. "Was not she kind to Alfred, Mamma, and did not she make him nice jelly. And a Doctor of Divinity,—you know Clive's grandfather was a Doctor of Divinity, Mamma, there's a picture of him in a wig—is just as good as a banker, you know he is."

"Did you bring some of Miss Honeyman's lodging-house cards with you, Ethel?" says her brother, "and had we not better hang up one or two in Lombard Street:—hers, and our other relation's, Mrs. Mason?"

"My darling love, who is Mrs. Mason?" asks Lady Ann.

"Another member of the family, Ma'am. She was cousin——"

"She was no such thing, Sir," roars Sir Brian.

"She was relative and housemaid of my grandfather during his first marriage. She acted I believe as dry nurse to the distinguished Colonel of sepoys, my uncle. She has retired into private life in her native town of Newcome, and occupies her latter days by the management of a mangle. The Colonel and young Pothouse have gone down to spend a few days with their elderly relative. It's all here in the paper, by Jove." Mr. Barnes clenched his fist and stamped upon the newspaper with much energy.

"And so they should go down and see her; and so the Colonel should love his nurse, and not forget his relations if they are old and poor," cries Ethel with a flush on her face and tears starting into her eyes.

"Hear what the Newcome papers say about it," shrieks out Mr. Barnes—his voice quivering, his little eyes flashing out scorn. "It's in both the pa-

[1] this *Ms E1*] the *R*
[2] Honeywood *Ms*] Honeyman *E1*

pers. I daresay it will be in the *Times* to-morrow. By —— it's delightful. Our paper only mentions the gratifying circumstance; here is the paragraph. 'Lieutenant Colonel Newcome, C.B., a distinguished Indian officer and elder[3] brother of our respected townsman and representative Sir Brian Newcome, Bart., has been staying for the last week at the King's Arms in our city. He has been visited by the principal inhabitants and leading gentlemen of Newcome and has come among us as we understand in order to pass a few days with an elderly relative who has been living for many years past in great retirement in this place.'"

"Well I see no great harm in that paragraph," says Sir Brian. "I wish my brother had gone to the Roebuck and not to the King's Arms as the Roebuck is our house, but he could not be expected to know much about the Newcome Inns as he is a *new comer himself*.[4] And I think it was very right of the people to call on him."

"Now hear what the *Independent* says, and see if you like that, Sir," cries Barnes grinning fiercely and he began to read as follows:

"'Mr. Independent. I was born and bred a Screwcomite and am naturally proud of *Everybody* and *Everything* which bears the revered name of Screwcome. I am a Briton and a man though I have not the honour of a vote for my native borough: if I had you may be sure I would give it to our *admired* and *talented* representative Don Pomposo Lickspittle Grindpauper Poor-house Agincourt Screwcome: whose ancestors fought with Julius Caesar against William the Conqueror, and whose father certainly wielded *a cloth yard shaft* in London not fifty years ago.

"'Don Pomposo, as you know, seldom favours the town of Screwcome with a visit. Our gentry are not of *ancient birth* enough to be welcome to a Lady Screwcome. Our manufactories make their money by Trade, O fie! how can it be supposed that such *vulgarians* should be received among the *aristocratic society* of Screwcome House! Two balls in the season, and ten dozen of Gooseberry are enough for *them*.'"

"It's that scoundrel, Parrot," burst out Sir Brian, "because I wouldn't have any more wine of him—No, it's Vidler the apothecary. By Heaven, Lady Ann, I told you it would be so. Why didn't you ask the Miss Vidlers to your ball?"

"They were on the list," cries Lady Ann—"three of them. I did every thing I could. I consulted Mr. Vidler for poor Alfred and he actually stopped and saw the dear child take the physic—Why were they not asked to the ball?" cries her ladyship bewildered. "I declare to gracious goodness I don't know."

"Barnes scratched their names," cries Ethel, "out of the list, Mamma. You know you did, Barnes. You said you had gallipots enough."

"I don't think it is like Vidler's writing," said Mr. Barnes perhaps willing to turn the conversation. "I think it must be that villain Duff the baker who made the song about us at the last election. But hear the rest of the paragraph," and he continued to read.

"'The Screwcomites are at this moment favoured with a visit from a gentleman of the Screwcome family who having passed all his life *abroad*

---

3 elder *R*] younger *Ms E1*
4 *new comer himself.*] *new comer* himself *E1*] *Newcomer himself Ms*

is somewhat different from his relatives whom we all so *love and honour!* This distinguished gentleman, this gallant soldier, has come among us, not merely to see our manufactures—in which Screwcome can vie with any city in the North—but an old servant and relation of his family whom he is not above recognising; who nursed him in his early days; who has been living in her native place for many years, supported by the generous bounty of Colonel N——. The gallant officer accompanied by his son, a fine youth, has taken repeated drives round our beautiful environs in one of friend Taplow's (of the King's Arms) open drags, and accompanied by Mrs. M——, now an aged lady, who speaks with tears in her eyes of the goodness and gratitude of her gallant soldier!

"'One day last week they drove to Screwcome House. Will it be believed that though the house is only four miles distant from our city—though Don Pomposo's family have inhabited it these twelve years for four or five months every year—Mrs. M—— saw her cousin's house for the first time; and has[5] never set her eyes upon those grandees, except in public places, since the day when they *honoured* the County, by purchasing the estate which they own!

"'I have, as I repeat, no vote for the borough: but if I had, O wouldn't I show my respectful gratitude at the next election, and plump for Pomposo! I shall keep my eye upon him and am, Mr. Independent,

"'Your constant reader
"'PEEPING TOM.'"[6]

"The spirit of radicalism abroad in this country," said Sir Brian Newcome, crushing his egg-shell desperately, "is dreadful, really dreadful. We are on the edge of a positive volcano." Down went the egg-spoon into its crater. "The worst sentiments are everywhere publicly advocated; the licentiousness of the press has reached a pinnacle which menaces us with ruin; there is no law which these shameless newspapers respect; no rank which is safe from their attacks; no ancient landmark which the lava flood of democracy does not threaten to overwhelm and destroy."

"When I was at Spielburg," Barnes Newcome remarked kindly, "I saw three long-bearded, putty-faced blaguards pacin[7] up and down a little court-yard, and Count Keppenheimer[8] told me they were three damned editors of Milanese newspapers, who had had seven years of imprisonment already; and last year when Keppenheimer came to shoot at Newcome, I showed him that old thief, old Batters, the proprietor of the *Independent,* and Potts, his infernal ally, driving in a dog-cart; and I said to him, Keppenheimer, I wish we had a place where we could lock up some of our infernal radicals of the press, or that you could take off those two villains to Spielburg; and as we were passin, that infernal Potts burst out laughin in my face, and cut one of my pointers over the head with his whip. We must do something with that *Independent,* Sir."

---

[5] and has *Ms*] has *E1*

[6] The remainder of this chapter was added at proof stage. *Ms* continues without a break with the next chapter.

[7] blaguards pacin *E1*] blackguards pacing *R*

[8] Keppenheimer *E1*] Kettenheimer *R* [Also twice more in this paragraph.]

"We must," says the father, solemnly, "we must put it down, Barnes, we must put it down."

"I think," says Barnes, "we had best give the railway advertisements to Batters."

"But that makes the man of the *Sentinel* so angry," says the elder persecutor of the press.

"Then let us give Tom Potts some shootin at any rate; the ruffian is always poachin about our covers as it is. Speers should be written to, Sir, to keep a look out upon Batters and that villain his accomplice, and to be civil to them, and that sort of thing; and, damn it, to be down upon them whenever he sees the opportunity."

During the above conspiracy for bribing or crushing the independence of a great organ of British opinion, Miss Ethel Newcome held her tongue; but when her papa closed the conversation, by announcing solemnly that he would communicate with Speers, Ethel turning to her mother said, "Mamma, is it true that Grandpapa has a relation living at Newcome who is old and poor?"

"My darling child, how on earth should I know?" says Lady Ann. "I dare say Mr. Newcome had plenty of poor relations."

"I am sure some on your side, Ann, have been good enough to visit me at the bank," says Sir Brian, who thought his wife's ejaculation was a reflection upon his family, whereas it was the statement of a simple fact in Natural History. "This person was no relation of my father's at all. She was remotely connected with his first wife, I believe. She acted as servant to him, and has been most handsomely pensioned by the Colonel."

"Who went to her, like a kind, dear, good, brave uncle as he is," cried Ethel; "the very day I go to Newcome I'll go to see her." She caught a look of negation in her father's eye, "I will go—that is if Papa will give me leave," says Miss Ethel.

"By Gad, Sir," says Barnes, "I think it is the very best thing she could do; and the best way of doing it, Ethel can go with one of the boys and take Mrs. Whatdoyoucallem a gown, or a tract, or that sort of thing, and stop that infernal *Independent*'s mouth."

"If we had gone sooner," said Miss Ethel, simply, "there would not have been all this abuse of us in the paper." To which statement her worldly father and brother perforce agreeing, we may congratulate good old Mrs. Mason upon the new and polite acquaintances she is about to make.

Chapter XV.

THE OLD LADIES.

HE above letter and conversation will show what our active Colonel's movements and history had been since the last chapter in which they were recorded. He and Clive took the Liverpool Mail[1] and travelled from Liverpool to Newcome with a post-chaise and a pair of horses, which landed them at the King's Arms. The Colonel delighted in post-chaising—the rapid transit through the country amused him and cheered his spirits. Besides, had he not Dr. Johnson's word for it, that a swift journey in a post-chaise was one of the greatest enjoyments in life and a sojourn in a comfortable inn one of its chief pleasures? In travelling he was as happy and noisy as a boy. He talked to the waiters and made friends with the landlord, got all the information which he could gather, regarding the towns into which he came, and drove about from one sight or curiosity to another with indefatigable good humour and interest. It was good for Clive to see men and cities, to visit mills, manufactories, country seats, cathedrals. He asked a hundred questions— regarding all things round about him, and anyone caring to know who Thomas Newcome was and what his rank and business, found no difficulty in having his questions answered by the simple and kindly traveller.

Mine host of the King's Arms, Mr. Taplow aforesaid, knew in five minutes who his guest was and the errand on which he came. Was not Colonel Newcome's name painted on all his trunks and boxes? Was not his servant ready to answer all questions regarding the Colonel and his son? Newcome pretty generally introduced Clive to my landlord, when the latter brought his guest his bottle of wine. With old-fashioned cordiality the

---

[1] recorded. He and Clive took the Liverpool Mail *E1*] recorded. ¶The active gentleman as before has been stated was constantly on the whirl to visit one friend or the other and his boy's guardian and the kind and aged woman who had been the mother of his own earliest days were among the first persons in this country whom he hastened to embrace. He and Clive took the Liverpool Mail whence Newcome is distant not many miles *Ms*

Colonel would bid the landlord drink a glass of his own liquor and seldom failed to say to him "This is my son, Sir. We are travelling together to see the country. Every English gentleman should see his own country first before he goes abroad as we intend to do afterwards,—to make the Grand Tour. And I will thank you to tell me what there is remarkable in your town and what we ought to see. Antiquities, manufactories and seats in the neighbourhood. We wish to see everything, Sir. Everything." Elaborate diaries of these home tours are still extant in Clive's boyish manuscript and the Colonel's dashing handwriting. Quaint records of places visited and alarming accounts of inn bills paid.

So Mr. Taplow knew in five minutes that his guest was a brother of Sir Brian, their member; and saw the note dispatched by an hostler to "Mrs.[2] Sarah Mason, Jubilee Row," announcing that the Colonel had arrived and would be with her after his dinner. Mr. Taplow did not think fit to tell his guest that the house Sir Brian used—the Blue House—was the Roebuck, not the King's Arms. Might not the gentlemen be of different politics? Mr. Taplow's wine knew none.

Some of the jolliest fellows in all Newcome use the Boscawen Room at the King's Arms as their club and pass numberless merry evenings and crack countless jokes there.

Duff the baker, Old Mr. Vidler when he can get away from his medical labours (and his hand shakes, it must be owned, very much now and his nose is very red), Parrot the auctioneer and that amusing dog Tom Potts the talented reporter of the *Independent* were pretty constant attendants at the King's Arms and Colonel Newcome's dinner was not over before some of these gentlemen knew what dishes he had had, how he had called for a bottle of sherry and a bottle of claret like a gentleman; how he had paid the post-boys and travelled with a servant like a top-sawyer; and[3] that he was come to shake hands with an old nurse and relative of his family. Every one of those jolly Britons thought well of the Colonel for his affectionateness and liberality and contrasted it with the behaviour of the Tory Baronet— their representative.

His arrival made a sensation in the place. The Blue Club at the Roebuck discussed it as well as the uncompromising Liberals at the King's Arms. Mr. Speers,[4] Sir Brian's agent, did not know how to act, and advised[5] Sir Brian by the next night's mail. The Reverend Dr. Bulders, the Rector, left his card.[6]

Meanwhile it was not gain or business but only love and gratitude which brought Thomas Newcome to his father's native town. Their dinner over, away went the Colonel and Clive guided by the hostler their previous messenger to the humble little tenement which Thomas Newcome's earliest

[2] to "Mrs. *E1*] Mrs. *Ms*
[3] and *Ms R*] [omitted] *E1*
[4] King's Arms. Mr. Speers, *E1*] King's Arms. Scared by the intelligence and perhaps not liking to meet the Buffs in their stronghold at the Arms, Mr. Speers, *Ms*
[5] act, and advised *E1*] act, waited for the return of Mr. Hookham his partner who was gone to Manchester on business, and advised *Ms*
[6] card. *E1*] card. It will be time to speak more fully regarding Newcome and its inhabitants when we come to have farther business in that place. *Ms*

friend inhabited. The good old woman put her spectacles into her Bible and flung herself into her boy's arms, her boy who was more than fifty years old. She embraced Clive still more eagerly and frequently than she kissed his father. She did not know her Colonel with them whiskers. Clive was the very picture of the dear boy as he had left her almost two score years ago. And as fondly as she hung on the boy, her memory had ever clung round that early time when they were together. The good soul told endless tales of her darling's childhood, his frolics and beauty. To-day was uncertain to her, but the past was still bright and clear. As they sat prattling together over the bright tea-table attended by the trim little maid whose service[7] the Colonel's bounty secured for his old nurse, the kind old creature insisted on having Clive by her side. Again and again she would think that he[8] was actually her own boy, forgetting in that sweet and pious hallucination that the bronzed face and thinned hair and melancholy eyes of the veteran before her were those of her nursling of old days. So for near half the space of man's allotted life he had been absent from her, and day and night wherever he was, in sickness or wealth,[9] in sorrow or danger, her innocent love and prayers had attended the absent darling. Not in vain[1] does he live whose course is so befriended. Let us be thankful for our race, as we think of the love that blesses some of us. Surely it has something of Heaven in it and angels celestial may rejoice in it and admire it.[2]

Having nothing whatever to do, our Colonel's movements are of course exceedingly rapid, and he has the very shortest time to spend in any single place. He can spare but that evening,[3] Saturday, and the next day, Sunday, when he will faithfully accompany his dear old nurse to church. And what a festival is that day for her, when she has her Colonel and that beautiful brilliant boy of his by her side, and Mr. Hicks, the curate, looking at him, and the venerable Dr. Bulders himself eyeing him from the pulpit, and all the neighbours fluttering and whispering to be sure, who can be that fine military gentleman, and that splendid young man sitting by old Mrs. Mason, and leading her so affectionately out of church? That Saturday and Sunday the Colonel will pass with good old Mason, but on Monday he must be off; on Tuesday he must be in London, he has important business in London,—in fact, Tom Hamilton, of his regiment, comes up for election at the Oriental on that day, and on such an occasion could Thomas Newcome be absent? He drives away from the King's Arms through a row of smirking chambermaids, smiling waiters, and thankful ostlers, accompanied to the post-chaise, of which the obsequious Taplow shuts the door, and the Boscawen Room pronounces him that night to be a trump; and the whole of the busy town, ere the next day is over, has heard of his coming and departure, praised his kindliness and generosity, and no doubt

---

[7] service *Ms*] services *E1*
[8] think that he *Ms*] think he *E1*
[9] wealth, *Ms*] health *E1*
[1] vain *Ms*] vain, not in vain, *E1*
[2] The next two paragraphs, "Having nothing . . . in the last chapter." were added at proof stage.
[3] He can spare but that evening, *R*] That evening, *E1*

contrasted it with the different behaviour of the Baronet, his brother, who has gone for some time by the ignominious sobriquet of Screwcome, in the neighbourhood of his ancestral hall.

Dear old nurse Mason will have a score of visits to make and to receive, at all of which you may be sure that triumphal[1] advent of the Colonel's will be discussed and admired. Mrs. Mason will show her beautiful new India shawl, and her splendid Bible with the large print, and the affectionate inscription, from Thomas Newcome to his dearest old friend; her little maid will exhibit her new gown; the curate will see the Bible, and Mrs. Bulders will admire the shawl; and the old friends and humble companions of the good old lady, as they take their Sunday walks by the pompous lodge-gates of Newcome Park, which stand with the Baronet's new-fangled arms over them, gilded, and filagreed, and barred, will tell their stories too about the kind Colonel and his hard brother. When did Sir Brian ever visit a poor old woman's cottage, or his bailiff exempt from the rent? What good action, except a few thin blankets and beggarly coal and soup-tickets, did Newcome Park ever do for the poor? And as for the Colonel's wealth, lord bless you, he's been in India these five and-thirty years; the Baronet's money is a drop in the sea to his. The Colonel is the kindest, the best, the richest of men. These facts and opinions, doubtless, inspired the eloquent pen of "Peeping Tom," when he indited the sarcastic epistle to the *Newcome Independent,* which we perused over Sir Brian Newcome's shoulder in the last chapter.

And you may be sure Thomas Newcome had not been many weeks in England before good little Miss Honeyman at Brighton was favoured with a visit from her dear Colonel. The envious Gawler scowling out of his bow-window where the flyblown card still proclaimed that his lodgings were un-occupied, had the mortification to behold a yellow post-chaise drive up to Miss Honeyman's door and having discharged two gentlemen from within, trot away with servant and baggage to some house of entertainment other than Gawler's. Whilst this wretch was cursing his own ill fate and exe-crating yet more deeply Miss Honeyman's better fortune, the worthy little lady was treating her Colonel to a sisterly embrace and a solemn reception. Hannah, the faithful housekeeper, was presented and had a shake of the hand. The Colonel knew all about Hannah: ere he had been in England a week, a basket containing pots of jam of her confection and a tongue of Hannah's curing had arrived for the Colonel. That very night when his servant had lodged Colonel Newcome's effects at the neighbouring hôtel, Hannah was in possession of one of the Colonel's shirts, she and her mis-tress having previously conspired to make a dozen of those garments for the family benefactor.

All the presents which Newcome had ever transmitted to his sister-in-law from India had been taken out of the cotton and lavender in which the faithful creature kept them. It was a fine hot day in June but I promise you Miss Honeyman wore her blazing scarlet Cachemire shawl; her great brooch representing the Taj of Agra was in her collar and her bracelet (she used to say, "I am given to understand they are called Bangles, my dear,

[1] triumphal *E1*] triumphant *HM*

by the natives,") decorated the sleeves round her lean old hands which trembled with pleasure as they received the kind grasp of the Colonel of Colonels. How busy those hands had been that morning! What custards they had whipped, what a triumph of pie-crusts they had achieved! Before Colonel Newcome had been ten minutes in the house, the celebrated veal-cutlets made their appearance. Was not the whole house adorned in expectation of his coming? Had not Mr. Kuhn, the affable foreign gentleman of the first floor lodgers, prepared a French dish? Was not Betty on the look out and instructed to put the cutlets on the fire at the very moment when the Colonel's carriage drove up to her mistress's door? The good woman's eyes twinkled, the kind old hand and voice shook as, holding up a bright glass of Madeira, Miss Honeyman drank the Colonel's health. "I promise you, my dear Colonel," says she nodding her head adorned with a bristling superstructure of lace and ribbands, "I promise you that I can drink your health in good *wine*!" The wine was of his own sending; and so were the China fire-screens, and the sandalwood workbox, and the ivory card-case, and those magnificent pink and white chessmen, carved like little sepoys and mandarins with the castles on elephants' backs, George the Third and his Queen in pink ivory, against the Emperor of China and lady in white—the delight of Clive's childhood, the chief ornament of the old spinster's sitting-room.[2]

Miss Honeyman's little feast was pronounced to be the perfection of cookery. And when the meal was over came a noise of little feet at the parlour door which being opened there appeared, first, a tall nurse with a dancing baby, second and third, two little girls with little frocks, little trowsers, long ringlets, blue eyes and blue ribbons to match, fourth, Master Alfred now quite recovered from his illness and holding by the hand, fifth, Miss Ethel Newcome blushing like a rose.

Hannah, grinning, acted as mistress of the ceremonies calling out the names of Miss Newcomes, Master Newcomes "to see the Colonel if you please, Ma'am," bobbing a curtsey and giving a knowing nod to Master Clive as she smoothed her new silk apron. Hannah too was in new attire all crisp and rustling in the Colonel's honour. Miss Ethel did not cease blushing as she advanced towards her uncle. And the honest campaigner started up, blushing too. Mr. Clive rose also as little Alfred of whom he was a great friend ran towards him—Clive rose, laughed, nodded at Ethel and eat gingerbread nuts all at the same time. As for Colonel Thomas Newcome and his niece, they fell in love with each other instantaneously like Prince Camaralzaman and the Princess of China.

I have turned away one artist: the poor creature was utterly incompetent to depict the sublime, graceful and pathetic personages and events with which this history will most assuredly abound, and I doubt whether even the designer engaged in his place can make such a portrait of Miss Ethel Newcome as shall satisfy her friends and her own sense of justice.

[2] sitting-room. *E1*] sitting room. Here was another aging woman, a grateful recipient of Thomas Newcome's gentle charity. May those of us whom fortune has endowed liberally be able to count such a client or two, and to think now and again of a stricken wayfarer helped and soothed in his misfortune, or a widow's cruise replenished. *Ms*

That blush which we have indicated, he cannot render. How are you to copy it with a steel point and a ball of printers' ink?[3] That kindness which lights up the Colonel's eyes; gives an expression to the very wrinkles round about them; shines as a halo round his face—what artist can paint it? The painters of old when they pourtrayed sainted personages were fain to have recourse to compasses and gold-leaf[4]—as if celestial splendours could be represented by Dutch metal! As[5] our artist cannot come up to this task, the reader[6] will be pleased to let his fancy paint for itself the look of courtesy for a woman, admiration for a young beauty, protection for an innocent child, all of which are expressed upon the Colonel's kind face, as his eyes are set upon Ethel Newcome.

"Mamma has sent us to bid you welcome to England, Uncle," says Miss Ethel advancing, and never thinking for a moment of laying aside that fine blush which she brought into the room, and which is *her* pretty symbol of youth and modesty and beauty.

He took a little slim white hand and laid it down on his brown palm, where it looked all the whiter: he cleared the grizzled mustachio from his mouth and stooping down he kissed the little white hand with a great

deal of grace and dignity.[7] There was no point of resemblance, and yet

---

[3] I have turned away ... printers' ink? *Ms E1*] [omitted] *R*

[4] gold-leaf *E1*] gold-leafs *Ms*

[5] metal! As *E1*] metal. Does not one see sometimes in the faces of the good and charitable; the just and pure those expressions bright sweet and beatific, those Insignia of Love? it makes a mean home bright and pleasant: it changes a dish of herbs to a feast—it causes a plain face to look beautiful—as *Ms*

[6] The painters of old when they pourtrayed sainted personages were fain to have recourse to compasses and gold-leaf—as if celestial splendours could be represented by Dutch metal! As our artist cannot come up to this task, the reader *E1*] The reader *R*

[7] The rest of this paragraph, the sketch, the next four paragraphs, and the fifth paragraph through "beside him during his visit." were added in proof stage.

a something in the girl's look, voice, and movements, which caused his heart to thrill, and an image out of the past to rise up and salute him. The eyes which had brightened his youth (and which he saw in his dreams and thoughts for faithful years afterwards, as though they looked at him out of Heaven), seemed to shine upon him after five-and-thirty years. He remembered such a fair bending neck and clustering hair, such a light foot and airy figure, such a slim hand lying in his own—and now parted from it with a gap of ten thousand long days between. It is an old saying, that we forget nothing; as people in fever begin suddenly to talk the language of their infancy: we are stricken by memory sometimes, and old affections rush back on us as vivid as in the time when they were our daily talk, when their presence gladdened our eyes, when their accents thrilled in our ears, when with passionate tears and grief we flung ourselves upon their hopeless corpses. Parting is death, at least as far as life is concerned. A passion comes to an end; it is carried off in a coffin, or, weeping in a post-chaise, it drops out of life one way or other, and the earth-clods close over it, and we see it no more. But it has been part of our souls, and it is eternal. Does a mother not love her dead infant? a man his lost mistress? with the fond wife nestling at his side,—yes, with twenty children smiling round her knee. No doubt, as the old soldier held the girl's hand in his, the little talisman led him back to Hades, and he saw Leonora. . . .

"How do you do, Uncle," say girls No. 2 and 3, in a pretty little infantile[8] chorus. He drops the talisman, he is back in common life again—the dancing baby in the arms of the bobbing nurse babbles a welcome. Alfred looks up for awhile at his uncle in the white trowsers, and then instantly proposes that Clive should make him some drawings; and is on his knees at the next moment. He is always climbing on somebody or something, or winding over chairs, curling through bannisters, standing on somebody's head, or his own head,—as his convalescence advances, his breakages are fearful. Miss Honeyman and Hannah will talk about his dilapidations for years after the little chap has left them. When he is a jolly young officer in the Guards, and comes to see them at Brighton, they will show him the blue dragon Chayny jar on which he *would* sit, and which he cried so fearfully upon breaking.

When this little party has gone out smiling to take its walk on the seashore, the Colonel sits down and resumes the interrupted dessert. Miss Honeyman talks of the children and their mother, and the merits of Mr. Kuhn, and the beauty of Miss Ethel, glancing significantly towards Clive, who has had enough of gingerbread-nuts and dessert and wine, and whose youthful nose is by this time at the window. What kind-hearted woman, young or old, does not love match-making?

The Colonel, without lifting his eyes from the table, says "she reminds him of—of somebody he knew once."

"Indeed!" cries Miss Honeyman, and thinks Emma must have altered very much after going to India, for she had fair hair, and white eyelashes, and not a pretty foot certainly—but, my dear good lady, the Colonel is not thinking of the late Mrs. Casey.

---

[8] infantile *E1*] infantine *R*

He has taken a fitting quantity of the Madeira, the artless greeting of the people here, young and old, has warmed his heart, and he goes up-stairs to pay a visit to his sister-in-law, to whom he makes his most courteous bow as becomes a lady of her rank. Ethel takes her place quite naturally beside him during his visit. Where did he learn those fine manners, which all of us who knew him admired in him?—He had a natural simplicity; an habitual practice of kind and generous thoughts; a pure mind and therefore above hypocrisy and affectation—perhaps those French people with whom he had been intimate in early life had imparted to him some of the traditional graces of their *vieille cour*—certainly his half-brothers had inherited none such. "What is this that Barnes has written about his uncle, that the Colonel is ridiculous," Lady Ann said to her daughter that night. "Your uncle is adorable. I have never seen a more perfect grand seigneur. He puts me in mind of my grandfather, though Grandpapa's grand manner was more artificial, and his voice spoiled by snuff. See the Colonel. He smokes round the garden, but with what perfect grace! This is the man Uncle Hobson and your poor dear Papa have represented to us as a species of bear! Mr. Newcome, who has himself the *ton* of a waiter! The Colonel is perfect. What can Barnes mean by ridiculing him? I wish Barnes had such a distinguished air: but he is like his poor dear Papa. *Que voulez vous*, my love? The Newcomes are honourable: the Newcomes are wealthy: but distinguished; no. I never deluded myself with that notion when I married your poor dear Papa. At once I pronounce Colonel Newcome a person to be in every way distinguished by us—On our return to London I shall present him to all our family: poor good man! let him see that his family have some presentable relations besides those whom he will meet at Mrs. Newcome's in Brianstone Square. You must go to Brianstone Square immediately we return to London—You must ask your cousins and their governess, and we'll give them a little party. Mrs. Newcome is insupportable, but we must never forsake our relatives, Ethel. When you come out you will have to dine there and to[9] go to her ball. Every young lady in your position in the world has sacrifices to make: and duties to her family to perform. Look at me. Why did I marry your poor dear Papa? from duty. Has your Aunt Fanny who ran away with Captain Canonbury been happy? They have eleven children and are starving at Boulogne. Think of three of Fanny's boys in yellow stockings at the Bluecoat School! Your Papa got them appointed. I am sure my Papa would have gone mad if he had seen that day! She came with one of the poor wretches to Park Lane: but I could not see them. My feelings would not allow me. When my maid, I had a French maid then—Louise you remember? her conduct was *abominable*: so was Préville's—when she came and said that my lady Fanny was below with a young gentleman *qui portait des bas jaunes*—I could not see the child. I begged her to come up to me in[1] my room: and, absolutely that I might not offend her, I went to bed. That wretch Louise met her at Boulogne and told her afterwards—Good night, we must not stand chattering here any more. Heaven bless you, my darling! Those are

9 to *Ms E1*] [omitted] *R*
1 up to me in *Ms*] up in *E1*

the Colonel's windows! Look, he is smoking on his balcony—that must be Clive's room. Clive is a good kind boy. It was very kind of him to draw so many pictures for Alfred. Put the drawings away, Ethel. Mr. Smee saw some in Park Lane and said they showed remarkable genius. What a genius your Aunt Emily had for drawing! but it was flowers! I had no genius in particular, so Mamma used to say—and Doctor Belper said, 'My dear Lady Walham' (it was before my grandpapa's death), 'has Miss Ann a genius for sewing buttons and making puddens?'—puddens he pronounced it—Good night my own love. Blessings, blessings on my Ethel!"

The Colonel from his balcony saw the slim figure of the retreating girl, and looked fondly after her: and as the smoke of his cigar floated in the air, he formed a fine castle in it, whereof Clive was lord, and that pretty Ethel, lady. What a frank generous bright young creature is yonder! thought he. How cheery and gay she is! how good to Miss Honeyman to whom she behaved with just the respect that was the old lady's due—how affectionate

with her brothers and sisters—What a sweet voice she has! What a pretty little white hand it is! When she gave it me—it looked like a little white bird lying in mine—I must wear gloves, by Jove I must, and my[2] coat *is*

[2] must, and my *E1*] must and perhaps my *Ms*

old-fashioned as Binnie says! What a fine[3] match might be made between that child and Clive! She reminds me of a pair of eyes I haven't seen these forty years. I would like to have Clive married to her: to see him out of the scrapes and dangers that young fellows encounter, and safe with such a sweet girl as that. If God had so willed it: I might have been happy myself and could have made a woman happy. But the Fates were against me. I should like to see Clive happy: and then say *Nunc Dimittis*. "I shan't want anything more to-night, Kean, and you can go to bed."

"Thank you Colonel," says Kean who enters having prepared his master's bed-chamber—and is retiring when the Colonel calls after him.

"I say, Kean, is that blue coat of mine very old?"

"Uncommon white about the seams, Colonel," says the man.

"Is it older than other people's coats?"—Kean is obliged gravely to confess that the Colonel's coat is very queer.

"Get me another coat then. See that I don't do anything or wear anything unusual. I have been so long out of Europe, that I don't know the customs here and am not above learning." Kean retires vowing that his Master is a old trump; which opinion he had already expressed to Mr. Kuhn, Lady Hann's man, over a long potation which those two gentlemen had taken together. And, as all of us, in one way or another, are subject to this domestic criticism, from which not the most exalted can escape, I say, lucky is the man whose servants speak well of him.

[3] fine *E1*] nice *Ms*

AN EVENING AT ASTLEY'S

Chapter XVI.

IN WHICH MR. SHERRICK LETS HIS HOUSE IN FITZROY SQUARE.

IN spite of the sneers of the *Newcome Independent,* and the Colonel's unlucky visit to his nurse's native place, he still remained in high favour in Park Lane; where the worthy gentleman paid almost daily visits, and was received with welcome and almost affection, at least by the ladies and the children of the house. Who[1] was it that took the children to Astley's but Uncle Newcome? I saw him there in the midst of a cluster of these little people, all children together. He laughed delighted at Mr. Merryman's jokes in the ring. He beheld the Battle of Waterloo with breathless interest and was amazed—amazed, by Jove, Sir—at the prodigious likeness of the principal actor to the Emperor Napoleon, whose tomb he had visited on his return from India, as it pleased him to tell his little audience who sat clustering round him: the little girls, Sir Brian's daughters, holding each by a finger of his honest[2] hands, young masters Alfred and Edward clapping and hurrahing by his side, while Mr. Clive and Miss Ethel sat in the back of the box enjoying the scene but with that decorum which belonged to their superior age and gravity. As for Clive, he was in these matters much older than the grizzled old warrior his father. It did one good to hear the Colonel's honest laughs at clowns' jokes, and to see[3] the tenderness and simplicity with which he watched over this happy brood of young ones. How lavishly did he supply them with sweetmeats between the acts! There he sat in the midst of them and ate an orange himself with perfect satisfaction. I wonder what sum of money Mr. Barnes Newcome would have taken to sit for five hours with his young brothers and sisters in a public box at the theatre and eat an orange in the face of the audience?[4] When little Alfred went to Harrow, you may be sure Colonel Newcome and Clive galloped

---

[1] house. Who *E1*] house; whose good will he secured by those means of corruption to which the kind soul usually resorted when dealing with children;—purchasing their little votes by all sorts of bribery and treating; and securing their suffrages by every kind of toy, picture book, sweetmeat and diversion. Who *Ms*

[2] honest *Ms E1*] [omitted] *R*

[3] see *E1*] watch *Ms*

[4] audience? *E1*] audience? The great family Coach was in waiting with the flaming lamps, the magnificent horses and the huge footman in powder to convey this happy party back to Park Lane. Even Miss Quigley the governess forgot her wrongs for that night and owned to Lady Jones's governess next door that Colonel Newcome's behaviour to her was that of a perfect gentleman. As for Ethel we have stated that she and her uncle fell in love at first sight. She showed her regard for him by a thousand pretty kindnesses, looks and gestures. She used to blush when he came; her honest eyes lighting up with love and welcome when she beheld him, or when she thought of him. If she had had a friend,

over to see the little man and tipped him royally. What money is better bestowed than that of a schoolboy's tip? How the kindness is recalled[5] by the recipient in after days! It blesses him that gives and him that takes. Remember how happy such benefactions made you in your own early time and go off on the very first free[6] day and tip your nephew at school!

The Colonel's organ of benevolence was so large, that he would have liked to administer bounties to the young folks his nephews and nieces in Brianstone Square as well as to their cousins in Park Lane; but Mrs. Newcome was a great deal too virtuous to admit of such spoiling of children. She took the poor gentleman to task for an attempt upon her boys when those lads came home for their holidays and caused them ruefully to give back the shining gold sovereign with which their uncle had thought to give them a treat.[7] "I do not quarrel with *other* families," says she, "I do not *allude* to other families," meaning of course that she did not allude to Park Lane.[8] "There *may* be children who are allowed to receive money from their fathers' grown-up friends. There *may* be children who hold out their hands for presents, and thus become mercenary in early life. I make no reflections with regard to *other* households. *I* only look and think and pray for the welfare of my *own* beloved ones. They want for nothing. Heaven has bounteously furnished us with every comfort, with every elegance, with every luxury—Why need we be bounden to others, who have been ourselves so amply provided? I should consider it ingratitude, Colonel Newcome, want of proper spirit to allow *my* boys to accept money. Mind, I make *no allusions*. When they go to school, they receive a sovereign a-piece from their father and a shilling a week which is *ample* pocket-money. When they are at home, I desire that they may have rational amusements: I send them to the Polytechnic with Professor Hickson who kindly explains to them some of the marvels of science and the wonders of machinery. I send them to the picture galleries and the British Museum. I go with them myself to the delightful lectures at the Institution in Albemarle Street. I do not desire that they should attend theatrical exhibitions. I do not quarrel with those who go to plays: far from it!—Who am I that I should venture to judge the conduct of others? When you wrote from India expressing a wish that your boy should be made acquainted with the works of Shakespeare, I gave up my own opinion at once—Should *I* interpose between a

a dear dear darling friend as most young ladies of that age have I have no doubt, she would have covered quires of letter paper in discribing him, But that blessing had been denied to Miss Ethel as yet. She loved Mamma of course and Papa of course too, but until Uncle Newcome came it seemed as if nobody had been found to love her. She actually undertook ornamental feminine works in order to make him presents. She endowed him with mysterious book markers, cords for his watch, antimacassars and such like useful articles. She learned to net from the housekeeper, in order to make Uncle Newcome a purse, an immense purse with the most refulgent lapels and the grandest gold rings. *Ms*
5 tip? How the kindness is recalled *E1*] tip? What a deal of happiness can you confer, worthy Sir who have the coin to spare with that little piece of gold! How it is recalled *Ms*
6 free *Ms*] fine *E1*
7 treat. *E1*] treat. She made both uncle and nephews fine speeches upon the occasion, warning the discomfited elder of the great evil resulting from the practise of giving money to children; of the sinfulness of bribing their little affections; creating avaricious desires in their young minds, and so forth. *Ms*
8 Lane. *E1*] Lane, the goings on in which house formed the constant subject of her most virtuous animadversion. *Ms*

child and his father? I encouraged the boy to go to the play and sent him to the pit with one of our footmen."

"And you tipped him very handsomely, my dear Maria, too," said the good-natured Colonel breaking in upon her sermon, but Virtue was not to be put off in that way.

"And why, Colonel Newcome," Virtue exclaimed laying a pudgy little hand on its heart, "why did I treat Clive so? Because I stood towards him *in loco parentis,* because he was as a child to me and I to him as a mother. I indulged him more than my own. I loved him with a true maternal tenderness—*Then* he was happy to come to our house: *then* perhaps Park Lane was not so often open to him as Brianstone Square: but I make *no allusions. Then* he did not go six times to another house for once that he came to mine. He was a simple confiding generous boy. He was not dazzled by worldly rank or titles of splendour. He could not find *these* in Brianstone Square. A merchant's wife, a country lawyer's daughter. I could not be expected to have my humble board surrounded by titled aristocracy. I would not if I could. I love my own family too well—I am too honest, too simple, let me own it at once, Colonel Newcome, too *proud*! And now, now his father has come to England and I have resigned him, and he meets with no titled aristocrats at my house and he does not come here any more." Tears welled[9] out of her little eyes as she spoke and she covered her round face with her pocket-handkerchief.[1]

Had Colonel Newcome read the paper that morning he might have seen amongst what are called the fashionable announcements the cause perhaps why his sister-in-law had exhibited so much anger and virtue. The *Morning Post* stated that yesterday Sir Brian and Lady Newcome entertained at dinner His Excellency the Persian Ambassador and Bucksheesh Bey; the Right Honourable Cannon Rowe, President of the Board of Control, and Lady Louisa Rowe; the Earl of H—, the Countess of Kew, the Earl of Kew, Sir Curry Baughton, Major General and Mrs. Hooker, Colonel Newcome and Mr. Horace Fogey. Afterwards her ladyship had an assembly which

---

[9] welled *Ms*] rolled *E1*

[1] pocket-handkerchief. ¶Had *E1*] pocket handkerchief. ¶The little woman had no idea as usual but that she was perfectly virtuous and influenced by the noblest motives. No reasoning could have convinced her that she was jealous, or vulgar, or wrong. She never was wrong in her own mind; she was all humility, honesty, simplicity; and imbued with the most virtuous sentiments, and uttering them in fine language for the benefit of others. Considering that she never meddled with other people's affairs, it was wonderful how well she knew them; and, though she went so seldom to Park Lane, how intimate she was with all the transactions which occurred in that unlucky house. The Colonel went thither oftener than he came to her—of course—poor dear Colonel! She was afraid, afraid that he had the weakness of almost all Englishmen—a love for titles and persons of rank. The Colonel took the Park Lane children to the play;—Of course, when people have that unfortunate weakness for rank the commonest artifice which they employ is to ingratiate themselves with the children of great families. Did he ever ask to take *her* children out, poor dear darlings. Her father was but a country lawyer &c. &c. Meanwhile the object of all this sarcasm and scorn and suspicion and anger, was simply the kindest soul alive, and went to see one kinswoman often because her home was pleasant; and visited the other seldom, because she patronised him and bored him. Very likely the worthy man had not made the confession to himself, but the result was so. In the one house he was welcome and at home, in the other he was received with ceremony and a sermon: and he could not but perceive that while Mrs. Hobson was always never alluding to Park Lane, Park Lane left Mrs. Hobson, and her doings and her friends and her parties, alone. ¶Had *Ms*

was attended by &c. &c.

This catalogue of illustrious names had been read by Mrs. Newcome to her spouse at breakfast with such comments as she was in the habit of making. "The President of the Board of Control, the Chairman of the Court of Directors, an Ex-Governor General of India and a whole regiment of Kews! By Jove, Maria, the Colonel is in good company," cries Mr. Newcome with a laugh. "That's the sort of dinner you should have given him. Some people to talk about India. When he dined with us he was put between old Lady Wormly and Professor Roots. I don't wonder at his going to sleep after dinner. I was off myself once or twice during that confounded long argument between Professor Roots and Dr. Windus. That Windus is the deuce to talk."

"Dr. Windus is a man of science and his name is of European celebrity!" says Maria solemnly. "Any intellectual person would prefer such company to the titled nobodies into whose family your brother has married."

"There you go, Polly: you are always having a shy at Lady Ann and her relations," says Mr. Newcome good-naturedly.

"A shy. How can you use such vulgar words, Mr. Newcome—What have I to do with Sir Brian's titled relations? *I* do not value nobility. I prefer people of science—people of intellect—to all the rank in the world."

"So you do," says Hobson her spouse. "You have your party—Lady Ann has her party—You take your line—Lady Ann takes her line—You are a superior woman, my dear Polly, every one knows that. I'm a plain country farmer, I am. As long as you are happy, I am happy too. The people you get to dine here may talk Greek or Algebra for what I care. By Jove, my dear, I think you can hold your own with the best of them."

"I have endeavoured by assiduity to make up for time lost, and an early imperfect education," says Mrs. Newcome. "You married a poor country lawyer's daughter. You did not seek a partner in the Peerage, Mr. Newcome."

"No. No. Not such a confounded flat as that," cries Mr. Newcome surveying his plump partner behind her silver teapot, with eyes of admiration.

"I had an imperfect education, but I knew its blessings and have, I trust, endeavoured to cultivate the humble talents which Heaven has given me, Mr. Newcome."

"Humble by Jove!" exclaims the husband. "No gammon of that sort, Polly. You know well enough that you are a superior woman—I ain't a superior man. I know that. One is enough in a family.[2] I leave the reading to you, my dear. Here comes my horses. I say, I wish you'd call on Lady Ann to-day. Do go and see her, now. That's a good girl. I know she is flighty and that; and Brian's back is up a little. But he ain't a bad fellow and I wish I could see you and his wife better friends."

On his way to the City Mr. Newcome rode to look at the new house, No. 120, Fitzroy Square,[3] which his brother the Colonel had taken in conjunction with that Indian friend of his, Mr. Binnie. Shrewd old cock, Mr. Binnie. Has brought home a good bit of money from India. Is looking out

---

[2] family. *E1*] family. But I am a good man of business. I know a good horse, and I think I ain't a bad farmer. *Ms*
[3] house, No. 120, Fitzroy Square, *E1*] house, *Ms*

for safe investments. Has been introduced to Newcome Brothers.[4] Mr. Newcome thinks very well of the Colonel's friend.[5]

The house is vast but, it must be owned, melancholy. Not long since, it was a ladies' school in an unprosperous condition. The scar left by Madame Latour's brass plate may still be seen on the tall black door, cheerfully ornamented in the style of the end of the last century with a funereal urn in the centre of the entry and garlands and the skulls of rams at each corner.[6] Madame Latour who at one time actually kept a large yellow coach and drove her parlour young ladies in the Regents Park was an exile from her native country (Islington was her birthplace and Grigson her paternal name) and an outlaw at the suit of Samuel Sherrick: that Mr. Sherrick whose wine vaults undermine Lady Whittlesea's chapel where the eloquent Honeyman preaches.

The House is Mr. Sherrick's house, to whom our two Indian gentlemen were introduced by the Colonel's brother-in-law, Mr. Honeyman. Some say his name is Shadrach and pretend to have known him as an orange boy, afterwards as a chorus singer in the theatres, afterwards as secretary to a great tragedian. I know nothing of these stories. He[7] may or he may not be a partner of Mr. Campion,[8] of Shepherd's Inn. He has a handsome Villa, Abbey Road, St. John's Wood, entertains good company rather loud, of the sporting sort, rides and drives very showy horses. Has boxes at the Opera whenever he likes and free access behind the scenes. Is handsome dark bright-eyed with a quantity of jewellery and a tuft to his chin. Sings sweetly sentimental songs after dinner. Who cares a fig what was the religion of Mr. Sherrick's ancestry, or what the occupation of his youth. Mr. Honeyman a most respectable man surely introduced Sherrick to the Colonel and Binnie.

Mr. Sherrick[9] stocked their cellar with some of the wine over which Hon-

[4] Newcome Brothers. *E1*] Hobson brothers. *Ms*

[5] friend. *E1*] friend.¶He rides to the door of that handsome stone fronted, roomy, gloomy mansion No. 120. Fitzroy Square which Mr. Binnie and the Colonel had just engaged together. The house is so spacious that there is ample room for the three establishments which are about to occupy it. There is a large backparlour for Mr. Binnie's library which he has been gathering with great care for twenty years past and which now consists of several thousand serviceable volumes. This room is considered to be his own and whenever he may have a fancy to retire to it, his castle which no man may enter. The books which cover the wall presently make it the most comfortable room in the mansion. *Ms*

[6] corner. *E1*] corner. Faint traces of the ladies' school still linger about the mansion. In the dingy upper chambers are marks against the walls of many beds. The scholars ceased to come; the parlour boarders did not pay. The teachers could not get their salaries, *Ms*

[7] stories. He *E1*] stories—I do not know in the least who Mr. Sherrick's father was. He *Ms*

[8] *Ms* left a blank for this name.

[9] Binnie. ¶Mr. Sherrick *E1*] Binnie whom he treated to a little entertainment at his lodgings. Mr. Sherrick asked these gentlemen to dinner at St. John's Wood where they met Lord Bareacres, General O'Locmy of the Portuguese service, Philip Barnes, Lord Kew's brother—all gentlemen of rank and station and Mr. Boss the celebrated Bass singer. T. R. D. L. and T. R. C. G. and Galpin the delightful tenor. They had a very pleasant evening. A great deal of after dinner music, though the Colonel steadfastly refused to sing. Clive was not of this dinner. He and his friend Digby finding better amusement at the play. ¶Well. The result of this new acquaintance was that Mr. Sherrick having a large and commodious house, No. 120, Fitzroy Square, to let on very reasonable terms, Colonel Newcome and Mr. Binnie agreed to take it between them, and Mr. Sherrick *Ms*

eyman preached such lovely sermons. It was not dear, it was not bad when you dealt with Mr. Sherrick for wine alone. Going into his market with ready money in your hand, as our simple friends did, you were pretty fairly treated by Mr. Sherrick.

The house being taken, we may be certain there was fine amusement for Clive, Mr. Binnie and the Colonel, in frequenting the sales, in the inspection of upholsterers' shops, and the purchase of furniture for the new mansion.[1] It was like nobody else's house. There were three masters with four or five servants over them. Kean for the Colonel and his son, a smart boy with boots for Mr. Binnie, Mrs. Kean to cook and keep house with a couple of maids under her. The Colonel himself was great at making hash mutton, hot pot, curry and pillau. What cosy pipes did we not smoke in the dining-room, in the drawing-room or where we would. What pleasant evenings did we not have with Mr. Binnie's books and Schiedam. Then there were the solemn state dinners at most of which the writer of this biography had a corner.[2]

Clive had a tutor, Grindley of Corpus, whom we recommended to him and with whom the young gentleman did not fatigue his brains very much but his great *forte* decidedly lay in drawing. He sketched the horses, he sketched the dogs, all the servants from the blear-eyed boot-boy to the rosy-cheeked lass, Mrs. Kean's niece, whom that virtuous housekeeper was always calling to come down-stairs. He drew his father in all postures— asleep, on foot, on horseback—and jolly little Mr. Binnie with his plump legs on a chair or jumping briskly on the back of the cob which he rode. He should have drawn the pictures for this book but that he no longer condescends to make sketches. Young Ridley was his daily friend now and Clive, his classics and mathematics over in the morning and the ride with Father over, this pair[3] of young men would constantly attend Gandish's Drawing Academy where, to be sure, Ridley passed many hours at work on his art before his young friend and patron could be spared from his books to his pencil.

"O," says Clive if you talk to him now about those early days, "it was a jolly time." I do not believe there was any young fellow in London so happy and there hangs up in his painting-room now a head painted at one sitting of a man rather bald with hair touched with grey, with a large moustache and a sweet mouth half smiling beneath it and melancholy eyes, and Clive shows that portrait of their grandfather to his children and tells them that the whole world never saw a nobler gentleman.

---

[1] A portion of manuscript (*Ms* pp. 54.9-56.26) originally meant to continue at this point in installment number 5 (*E1*, p. 160.15) was cut when the installment overflowed its allotted 32 printed pages. When copy for installment 6 ran short, the passage was inserted (text corresponding to pages 172.1–173.18, below: had received a coat ... so comfortless so pleasant.). The transfer and the revisions it entailed were undertaken, apparently, by Percival Leigh in Thackeray's absence on the Continent.

[2] corner. *E1*] corner; for those who read this simple story may understand how my acquaintance with Colonel Newcome speedily ripened into a friendship and in what a sincere regard I held him. *Ms*

[3] and Clive, his classics and mathematics over in the morning and the ride with Father over, this pair] and Grindley, his classics and mathematics over in the morning and the ride with father over, this pair *Ms E1*] and Grindley, his classics and mathematics over in the morning, this pair *P1*] after Grindley's classics and mathematics in the morning, this pair *R*

Chapter XVII.

A SCHOOL OF ART.[1]

RITISH art either finds her[2] peculiar nourishment in melancholy, and loves to fix her[3] abode in desert-places, or it may be her purse is but[4] slenderly furnished, and she is forced to put up with accommodations rejected by more prosperous callings. Some of the most dismal quarters of the town are colonised by her disciples and professors. In walking through streets which may have been gay and polite in days[5] when ladies' chairmen jostled each other on the pavement, and link-boys with their torches lighted the beaux over the mud; who has not marked[6] the artist's invasion of those regions once devoted to fashion and gaiety? Centre windows of drawing-room floors[7] are enlarged so as to reach up into bed-rooms—bed-rooms where Lady Betty has had her hair powdered, and where the painter's north-light now takes possession of the place which her toilet-table occupied a hundred years ago. There are degrees in decadence: after the Fashion chooses another quarter[8] and retreats from Soho and[9] Bloomsbury, let us say, to

1 Title not in *Ms*
2 her *E1*] its *Ms*
3 her *E1*] its *Ms*
4 is but *E1*] is *Ms*
5 polite in days *Ms*] polite *E1*
6 marked *Ms*] remarked *E1*
7 drawing-room floors *Ms*] drawing rooms *E1*
8 chooses another quarter *Ms*] chooses to emigrate, *E1*
9 and *Ms*] or *E1*

Cavendish Square, physicians come and occupy the vacant houses; which still have a respectable look, the windows being cleaned and the knockers and plates kept bright, and the doctor's carriage almost[1] as fine as the countess's which has wheeled away elsewhere:—the physician rolls away presently after her ladyship.[2] A boarding-house succeeds[3] the physician,[4] and then Dick Tinto comes with his dingy brass plate, and breaks in his north window; and sets up his sitter's throne. I love his honest moustache and jaunty velvet-jacket; his queer figure; his queer vanities; his kind heart. Why should he not suffer his ruddy ringlets to fall over his falling collar?[5] Why should he not wear a hat like Guy Fawkes and a beard like the Saracen Snow Hill?[6] Why should he deny himself velvet?[7] It is only a sort[8] of fustian which costs[9] eighteen pence a yard. He cannot help himself:[1] and breaks out into costume naturally[2] as a bird sings or a bulb produces[3] a tulip. And as Dick under yonder terrific appearance of bristling beard, waving cloak,[4] and shadowy sombrero is a good kindly simple creature got up at a very cheap rate: so his life is consistent with his dress: he clothes his honest ideas in whiskers penny-velvet and Guy Fawkes hats,[5] he gives his genius a darkling swagger and a romantic envelope; which, being removed, you find not a bravo but a kind chirping Soul, not a moody poet avoiding mankind for the nobler[6] company of his own great thoughts, but a jolly little chap who has an aptitude for painting brocade gowns and bits[7] of armour (with figures inside them): or trees and cattle, or gondolas and buildings or what not;—an instinct for the picturesque which exhibits itself in his works and outwardly on his person—beyond this, a gentle creature loving his friends, his cups, feasts, children,[8] merry-makings and all good things. The kindest folks alive I have found among those scowling whiskeradoes. They open oysters with their yataghans, toast muffins on their rapiers; and fill their Venice glasses with half-and-half: If they have money in their lean purses, be sure they have a friend to share it: What innocent gaiety! What genuine human kindness,[9] what jovial suppers on thread-bare cloths and wonder-

---

[1]carriage almost *Ms*] carriage rolling round the square, almost *E1*
[2]wheeled away ... her ladyship. *Ms*] whisked away her ladyship to other regions. *E1*
[3]succeeds *Ms*] mayhap succeeds *E1*
[4]physician, *Ms*] physician, who has followed after his sick folks into the new country: *E1*
[5]falling collar? *Ms*] shirt-collar? *E1*
[6]Why should he not wear ... Snow Hill? *Ms*] [omitted] *E1*
[7]velvet? *Ms*] his velvet? *E1*
[8]only a sort *Ms*] but a kind *E1*
[9]costs *Ms*] costs him *E1*
[1]cannot help himself *Ms*] is naturally what he is, *E1*
[2]naturally *Ms*] as spontaneously *E1*
[3]produces *Ms*] bears *E1*
[4]bristling beard, waving cloak, *Ms*] waving cloak, bristling beard, *E1*
[5]he clothes ... Guy Fawkes hats, *Ms*] [omitted] *E1*
[6]nobler *Ms*] better *E1*
[7]and bits *Ms*] a bit *E1*] or bits *R*
[8]children, *Ms*] [omitted] *E1*
[9]What genuine human kindness, *Ms*] [omitted] *E1*

ful songs after! What pathos, merriment, humour does not a man enjoy, who frequents their company!—Mr. Clive Newcome, who has long
since shaved his beard, who has become a family man, and has seen the
world in a thousand different phases, avers that his life as an art student
at home and abroad was the pleasantest part of his whole existence. It
may not be more amusing in the telling, than the chronicle of a feast,
or the accurate report of two lovers' conversation: but the biographer
having brought his hero to this period of his life, is bound to describe it
before he passes[1] to other occurrences which are to be narrated in their
turn.

We may be sure the boy had many conversations with his affectionate guardian as to the profession which he should follow. As regarded
mathematical and classical learning the elder Newcome was forced to
admit that out of every hundred boys there were fifty as clever as his
own, and at least fifty more industrious: the army in time of peace
Colonel Newcome thought a bad trade for a young fellow so fond of ease
and pleasure as his son was:[2] his delight in the pencil was manifest to
all eyes: were[3] not all[4] his school-books full of caricatures of the masters: whilst his tutor Grindley was lecturing him did he not draw Grindley instinctively and[5] under his very nose? A painter Clive was determined to be and nothing else:—The father acquiesced in the lad's decision;[6] and Clive being then about[7] sixteen years of age, began to study
the rudiments of the[8] art *en règle*, under the eminent Mr. Gandish of
Soho.

It was that well-known portrait-painter, Alfred[9] Smee, Esq., R.A., who
recommended Gandish's to Colonel Newcome one day when the two gentlemen met at Lady Ann's table.[1] Mr. Smee happened to examine some of
Clive's drawings which the young fellow had executed for his little cousins;
he[2] found no better amusement than making[3] pictures for them and would
cheerfully pass evening after evening in that diversion. He had made a
thousand sketches of Ethel before a year was over: a year every day of
which seemed to increase the attractions of the fair young creature, develop
her nymph-like form and give her figure fresh graces. Also of course Clive[4]
drew Alfred and the nursery;[5] Aunt Ann and the Blenheim spaniels, Mr.

---

[1] describe it before he passes *Ms*] relate it, before passing *E1*
[2] son was: *Ms*] son: *E1*
[3] all eyes: were *Ms*] all. Were *E1*
[4] all *Ms*] [omitted] *E1*
[5] and *Ms*] [omitted] *E1*
[6] The father ... decision; *Ms*] [omitted] *E1*
[7] about *Ms*] some *E1*
[8] rudiments of the *Ms*] [omitted] *E1*
[9] Alfred *E1*] Frederick *Ms*] Andrew *R*
[1] at Lady Ann's table] at Lady Anne's table *Ms*] at dinner at Lady Anne Newcome's table.
E1
[2] his little cousins; he *Ms*] his cousins. Clive *E1*
[3] than making *Ms*] than in making *E1*
[4] Clive *Ms R*] [omitted] *E1*
[5] nursery; *Ms*] nursery in general, *E1*

Kuhn with[6] his earrings, the majestic John bringing in the coalscuttle; the melancholy Miss Quigley;[7] and all persons or objects in that establishment with which he was familiar. "What a genius the lad has!" the complimentary Mr. Smee averred, "What a force and individuality there is in all his drawings! Look at these[8] horses, capital, by Jove, capital! and Alfred on his poney and Miss Ethel in her Spanish hat with her hair flowing in the wind! I must take this sketch, I positively must now—and show it to Landseer." And the courtly artist daintily enveloped the drawing in a sheet of paper and put it away in his hat and vowed subsequently that the great painter had been delighted with the young man's performance. Smee was not only charmed with Clive's skill as an artist but thought his head would be an admirable one to paint. Such a rich complexion! such fine tones[9] in his hair! such eyes! to see real blue eyes was so rare now-a-days!—And the Colonel too!—if the Colonel would but give him a few sittings—the French grey[1] uniform of the Bengal Cavalry—the silver lace—the little bit of red ribbon just to warm up the picture—it was seldom, Mr. Smee declared, that an artist could get such an opportunity for colour. With our hideous vermilion uniforms there was no chance of doing anything. Rubens himself could scarcely manage scarlet. Look at the horseman in Cuyp's famous picture at the Louvre! The red was a positive blot upon the whole picture. There was nothing like French grey and silver. All which did not prevent Mr. Smee from painting Sir Brian in a flaring deputy-lieutenant's uniform and entreating all military men whom he met to sit to him in scarlet. Clive Newcome, Mr. Smee[2] succeeded in painting, of course for mere friendship's sake and because he liked the subject, though he could not refuse the cheque which Colonel Newcome sent him for the frame and the picture. But[3] no cajoleries could induce the old campaigner to sit to any artist save one. He said he should be ashamed to pay fifty guineas for the likeness of his homely face. He jocularly proposed to James Binnie to have his head put upon[4] the canvas, and Mr. Smee enthusiastically caught at the idea: but honest James winked his droll eyes saying his was a beauty that did not want any paint, and when Mr. Smee took his leave after dinner in Fitzroy Square where this conversation was held, James Binnie hinted that the Academician was no better than an old humbug, in which surmise he was probably not altogether incorrect. Certain young men who frequented the kind Colonel's house were also somewhat of this opinion; and made endless jokes at the portrait painter's expense. He[5] plastered his sitters with adulation, as methodically as he covered his canvas. He waylaid gentlemen at dinner; he inveigled unsuspecting folks into his studio, and had their heads off their shoulders before they were aware. One

---

6 Mr. Kuhn with *Ms*] and Mr. Kuhn and *E1*] Mr. Kuhn and *R*
7 the melancholy Miss Quigley; *Ms*] [omitted] *E1*
8 these *Ms*] his *E1*
9 tones *Ms*] turns *E1*
1 French grey *Ms*] gray *E1*
2 Mr. Smee *Ms*] the Academician *E1*
3 the picture. But *Ms*] picture; but *E1*
4 upon *Ms*] on *E1*
5 the portrait painter's expence. He *Ms*] the painter's expense. Smee *E1*

day on our way from the Temple through Howland Street to the Colonel's house, we beheld Major-General Sir Thomas de Boots in full fig[6] rushing from Smee's door to his brougham. The coachman was absent refreshing

himself at a neighbouring tap. The little street-boys cheered and hurrayed Sir Thomas, as he sat arrayed in gold and scarlet[7] in his chariot. He blushed purple when he beheld us: no artist would have dared to imitate those violet[8] tones: he was one of the numberless[9] victims of Mr. Smee.

One day then, day to be noted with a white stone, Colonel Newcome and his son, with[1] Mr. Smee, R.A., walked from their[2] house to Gandish's which was not far removed thence: and young Clive who was a perfect mimic, described to his friends, and illustrated as his wont was[3] by diagrams, the interview which he had with that Professor. "By Jove, you must see Gandish, Pen," says[4] Clive, "Gandish is worth the whole world. Come and be an art student—you'll find such jolly fellows there—Gandish calls it Hart-student, and says, 'Hars est celare Hartem,' by Jove he does. He gave us[5] a little Latin as he brought out a cake and a bottle of wine, you know.

[6] fig *Ms*] uniform *E1*
[7] as he sat arrayed in gold and scarlet *Ms*] as, arrayed in gold and scarlet, he sate *E1* [Compositor misread the caret for the insertion.]
[8] violet *Ms*] purple *E1*
[9] numberless *Ms*] numerous *E1*
[1] and his son with *Ms*] with his son and *E1*
[2] their *Ms*] the Colonel's *E1*
[3] as his wont was *Ms*] as was his wont, *E1*
[4] Pen,' says *Ms*] Pa!" cries *E1*] Pen!" cries *R*
[5] gave us *Ms*] treated us to *E1*

"The Governor was splendid, Sir. He wore gloves, you know he only puts 'em[6] on on Parade days; and turned out[7] spick and span. He ought to be a general officer—he looks like a Field Marshal, don't he? You should have seen him bowing to Mrs.[8] Gandish and the Miss Gandishes dressed all in their best, round the tray with the cake![9] He takes his glass of wine and he[1] sweeps them all round with a bow. 'I hope, young ladies,' says he, 'you don't often go into[2] the students' room—I am afraid the young gentlemen would leave off looking at the statues, if *you* came in.' And so they would: for you never saw such Guys, but the dear old boy fancies every woman is a beauty.

"'Mr. Smee, you are looking at my pictur[3] of Boadishia?' says Gandish (wouldn't he have caught it for his quantities at Grey Friars, that's all?)—

"'Yes—ah—yes,' says Smee,[4] putting his hand over his eyes and standing before it—looking steady, you know, as if he was going to see whereabouts he should hit[5] Boadishia.

"'It was painted when you were a young man—four year before you were an Associate, Smee. It ad[6] some success in its time and there's good

6 'em *Ms*] them *E1*
7 out *Ms*] out for the occasion *E1*
8 Mrs. *E1*] the ~~three~~ Mrs. *Ms*
9 tray with the cake! *Ms*] cake-tray! *E1*
1 he *Ms*] [omitted] *E1*
2 into *Ms*] to *E1*
3 pictur *Ms*] picture *E1*
4 Smee, *Ms*] Mr. Smee, *E1*
5 hit *Ms*] *hit E1*
6 It ad *Ms*] Had *E1*

pints about that picture—But[7] I never could git a[8] price for it: and here it hangs in my own room—Igh Art won't do in this country, Colonel, it's a melancholy fact.'

" 'High Art—I should think it *is* high Art,' whispers old Smee, 'fourteen feet high at least'—and then out loud he says, 'It[9] has very fine points in it indeed,[1] Gandish, as you say—Foreshortening of that arm, capital—capital—That[2] red drapery carried off into the right of the picture, very skilfully managed.'

" 'It's not like portrait painting, Smee—High Art,' says Gandish. 'The models of the hancient Britons in that pictur alone cost me thirty pound, when I was a struggling man; and had just married my Bessy[3] here. You reckonise Boadishia, Colonel: with the Roman 'elmet, cuirass and javeling of the period—all studied from the hantique, Sir—the glorious hantique.'

" 'All but Boadicea,' says Father, 'who[4] remains always young.' And he began to speak the lines out of Cowper, he did, waving his stick like an old trump, and famous verses[5] they are," cries the lad.

" 'When the British warrior queen,
Bleeding from the Roman rods—'

"Jolly verses! Haven't I translated them into Alcaics?" says Clive, with a merry laugh, and resumes his history.[6]

" 'O I must have those verses in my album!' cries one of the young ladies—but Gandish, you see, was not thinking[7] about any works but his own: and goes on. 'Study of my eldest daughter, exhibited 1816.'

" 'No Pa—not '16,' cries Miss Gandish. 'She don't look like a chicken, I can tell you.'

" 'Admired. I[8] can show you what the papers said of it at the time. *Morning Chronicle* and *Examiner* spoke most ighly of it. My son as an infant, Ercules Stranglin the Serpent, over the piano. Fust conception of my pictur of *Non Hangli sed Hangeli.*'[9]

" 'For which I can guess who were the angels that sate,' says Father—upon my word that old Governor. He goes[1] a little too strong! But Mr.

[7] picture—But *Ms*] pictur,' Gandish goes on. 'But *E1*
[8] git a *Ms*] get my *E1*
[9] 'It *Ms*] 'The picture *E1*
[1] indeed *Ms*] [omitted] *E1*
[2] capital—capital—That *Ms*] capital! That *E1*
[3] Bessy *Ms*] Betsey *E1*
[4] 'who *Ms*] 'She *E1*
[5] verses *Ms*] [omitted] *E1*
[6] " 'When the British warrior queen, / Bleeding from the Roman rods—' ¶"Jolly verses! Haven't I translated them into Alcaics?" says Clive, with a merry laugh, and resumes his history. *E1*] When the [blank] ~~Roman~~ ↑British↓ Queen. [blank] / Trochaic Tetrameter—*I* remember," and he broke into a merry laugh. *Ms*
[7] ladies—but Gandish you see was thinking *Ms*] ladies. 'Did you compose them, Colonel Newcome?' But Gandish, you see, was not thinking *E1*
[8] " 'Admired. I *Ms*] " 'Admired,' Gandish goes on, never heeding her,—'I *E1*
[9] pictur of *Non Hangli sed Hangeli.*' *Ms*] picture of Non Hangli said Hangeli.' *E1*
[1] goes *Ms*] is *E1*

Gandish listened no more to him than to Mr. Smee; and went on,[2] 'Myself at thirty-three years of age—I[3] could have been a portrait painter, Mr. Smee.'

" 'Indeed it was lucky for us[4] you devoted yourself to high art, Gandish,' says Mr. Smee;[5] and sips the wine and puts it down again making a face;—it wasn't[6] first-rate tipple you see.

" 'Two girls,' continues that indomitable Mr. Gandish. 'Highdea[7] for Babes in the Wood—View of Pæstum taken on the spot by myself when travelling with the late lamented Hearl of Kew—Beauty, Valour, Commerce and Liberty condoling with Britannia on the Fall of Nelson[8]— allegorical piece, drawn at a very early age, after Trafalgar—Mr. Fuseli saw that piece[9] when I was a student of the Academy, and said to me, Mr. Gandish, study[1] the antique. There's nothing like it—Those were his[2] very words. If you do me the favour to walk into the Hatrium you'll remark my great pictur[3] also from English Istory—an English Historical[4] painter, Sir, should be employed chiefly in English History. That's what *I* would have done. Why ain't there temples for us, where the people might read their History[5] at a glance and without knowing how to read? Why is my Alfred 'anging up in this 'all? because there is no patronage for a man who devotes himself to Igh Art. You know the anecdote, Colonel? King Alfred flying from the Danes took refuge in a neaterd's 'ut. The shepherd's[6] wife told him to bake a cake and the Fugitive Sovering[7] set down to his ignoble task, and forgitting it in the cares of State let the cake burn, on which the woman struck him—The moment chosen[8] is when she is lifting her 'and to deliver the blow—The King receives it with majesty mingled with meekness—In the background the door is hopening,[9] letting in the king's officers to say[1] the Danes are defeated. The daylight breaks in at the aperture, signifying the dawning of 'Ope. That story, Sir, which I found in my researches in Istory has since become so popular, Sir, that hundreds of artists have painted it, hundreds! I who discovered the leg-

---

[2] on *Ms*] on, buttering himself all over, as I have read the Hottentots do. *E1*
[3] age—I *Ms*] age!' says he, pointing to a portrait of a gentleman in leather breeches and mahogany boots; 'I *É1*
[4] us *Ms*] some of us *E1*
[5] says Mr. Smee; *Ms*] Mr. Smee says, *E1*
[6] wasn't *Ms*] was not *E1*
[7] Highdea *Ms*] Hidea *E1*
[8] Fall of Nelson *Ms*] death of Admiral Viscount Nelson *E1*
[9] piece *Ms*] piece, sir, *E1*
[1] me Mr. Gandish, study *Ms*] me, Young man, stick to *E1*
[2] his *Ms R*] 'is *E1*
[3] pictur *Ms*] pictures *E1*
[4] Historical *Ms*] historical *E1*] istorical *R*
[5] History *Ms*] history *E1*] istory *R*
[6] shepherd's *Ms*] rustic's *E1*
[7] Sovering *Ms*] sovering *E1*] sovereign *R*
[8] chosen *Ms*] chose *E1*
[9] is hopening *Ms*] of the 'ut is open, *E1*
[1] king's officers to say *Ms*] royal officers to announce *E1*

end, have my pictur—here—now, Colonel, let me[2] lead you through the Statue Gallery—Apollo, you see—the Venus Hanadyomene, the glorious Venus of the Louvre, the[3] Laocoon—my friend Gibson's Nimth, you see, is the only Figure I admit amongst the Antiques—now up this stair to the students' room, where I trust my young friend Mr. Newcome will labour assidiously. *Ars longa est,* Mr. Newcome, *Vita—*'

"I[4] trembled," Clive said, "lest my father should introduce a certain favourite quotation beginning *'Ingenuas didicisso'*—but he refrained and we went into the room, where a score of students were assembled, who all looked away from their drawing-boards at the New Comer.[5]

" 'Here will be your place, Mr. Newcome, and[6] here that of your young friend—what did you say was his name?' I told him Ridley—for my dear old Governor has promised to pay for J.J. too, you know. 'Mr. Chivers is the senior pupil and custos of the room in the habsence of myself or my son.[7] Mr. Chivers, Mr. Newcome—gentlemen, Mr. Newcome, a new pupil. My son, Charles Gandish—Colonel Newcome. Assiduity, gentlemen. Assiduity, gentlemen.[8] *Ars longa, Vita brevis et linea recta brevissima est*—This way, Colonel, down these steps across the court yard to my own studio, where I beg to ave your opinion of a little work on which I am at present occupied. There,[9] gentlemen!' and pulling aside a curtain Gandish says, 'There! ...' "   •

"And what was the work, Clive?" we ask[1] after we have done laughing at his imitation.

"Hand round the hat, J.J.!" cries Clive. "Now, ladies and gentlemen, pay your money!—Now walk in, for the performance is 'just a-going to begin!' " Nor would the rogue ever tell us what Gandish's curtained masterpiece[2] was.

Not a successful painter, Mr. Gandish was an excellent master; and regarding all artists save one perhaps, a good critic. Clive and his friend J.J. came soon after, and commenced their studies together.[3] The one took his humble seat at the drawing-board, a poor mean-looking lad with worn out[4] clothes, downcast features, a[5] figure almost deformed; the other adorned by good health, good looks, and the best of tailors; ushered into the studio with his father and Mr. Smee as his aides-de-camp on his entry; and previously announced there with all the eloquence of honest Gandish. "I bet he's

---

[2] here—now, Colonel, let me *Ms*] here!' ¶" 'Now, Colonel,' says the showman, 'let me—let me *E1*

[3] Louvre, the *Ms*] Louvre, which I saw in 1814, Colonel, in its glory—the *E1*

[4] *Vita—*' ¶"I *E1*] *Vita;* I *Ms*

[5] drawing [end of page] at the New Comer. *Ms*] drawing-boards as we entered. *E1*

[6] Newcome, and *Ms*] Newcome,' says the Professor, 'and *E1*

[7] habsence of myself or my Son. *Ms*] absence of my son. *E1*

[8] Assiduity gentlemen. Assiduity gentlemen. *Ms*] Assiduity, gentlemen, assiduity. *E1*

[9] Studio, where ... occupied. There *Ms*] studio. There, *E1*

[1] the work, Clive?" we ask*Ms*] the masterpiece behind it? we ask of Clive *E1*

[2] masterpiece *Ms*] picture *E1*

[3] together *Ms*] under him. *E1*

[4] out *Ms*] [omitted] *E1*

[5] a *Ms*] and a *E1*

'ad cake and wine," says one youthful student, of an epicurean and satirical turn. "I bet he might have it every day if he liked." In fact Gandish was

always handing him sweetmeats of compliments and cordials of approbation. He had coat sleeves with silk linings—he had studs in his shirt. How different was the texture and colour of that garment, to the sleeves Bob Grimes displayed when he took his coat off to put on his working-jacket! Horses used actually[6] to come for him to Gandish's door which was situated in a certain lofty street in Soho. The Miss G.'s would smile at him from the parlour window as he mounted and rode splendidly away:[7] and those opposition beauties, the Miss Levisons, daughters of the professor of dancing over the way, seldom failed to greet the young gentleman with an admiring ogle from their great black eyes. Master Clive was pronounced an "out-and-outer," a "swell and no mistake" and complimented with scarce one dissentient voice by the simple academy assembled[8] at Gandish's. Besides he drew very well: there could be no doubt about that. In revenge for a caricature which that[9] huge red-haired Scotch student, Sandy[1] M'Collop,

[6] deformed; the other adorned ... Horses used actually *E1*] deformed. He was the butt of the young students round about him. His face and person were caricatured by those jovial young satirists, a score of times, before he had been a week in the school: whereas Clive arrived splendid in fine raiment with his father and Mr. Smee as aides de camp on the first day; Mr. Gandish showing them over his establishment and having previously informed Mrs. Gandish and the Miss Gandishes and all the Gentlemen of the academy of the wealth and fashion of his pupil. Horses actually used *Ms*

[7] away: *Ms*] off, *E1*

[8] assembled *Ms*] [omitted] *E1*

[9] In revenge for a caricature which that *Ms*] Caricatures of the students of course were passing constantly among them, and in revenge for one which a *E1*

[1] Sandy *Ms*] Mr. Sandy *E1*

GANDISH'S

had made, of John James, Clive perpetrated a picture of Sandy which set the pupils'[2] room in a roar; and when the Caledonian giant uttered satirical remarks against the assembled company averring that they were a parcel of sneaks, a set of leck-spettles,[3] and using other[4] epithets still more vulgar, Clive pulled[5] off his coat[6] in an instant, invited Mr. M'Collop into the back yard, instructed him in a science which Clive[7] himself had acquired at Grey Friars, and administered to him two black eyes[8] which prevented the young artist from seeing the head of the Laocoon which he was copying, for some days after.[9] The Scotchman's superior weight and age might have given the combat a different conclusion, had it endured long after Clive's brilliant opening attack with his right and left. But Professor Gandish came out of his painting-room at the sound of battle, and could hardly[1] credit his own eyes when he beheld[2] those of Mr. M'Collop. The young Scotchman was a generous enemy: to do him justice,[3] he bore Clive no rancour. They became friends then: and afterwards at Rome whither they subsequently went to pursue their studies. The fame of Mr. M'Collop as an artist has long since been established. His pictures of Lord Lovat in Prison and Hogarth Painting Him, of the Blowing up of the Kirk of Field (painted for M'Collop of M'Collop), of the Torture of the Covenanters, the Murder of the Regent, the Murder of Rizzio and other historical pieces all of course from Scotch history, have established his reputation in South as well as in North Britain. No one would suppose from the gloomy character of his works that Sandy M'Collop is one of the most jovial souls alive. Within six months after their little difference Clive and he were the greatest friends[4] and it was by the former's suggestion that Mr. James Binnie gave Sandy his first commission for which he[5] selected the cheerful subject of the young Duke of Rothsay starving in prison.

During this period Mr. Clive assumed the *toga virilis* and beheld with inexpressible satisfaction the first growth of those mustachios which have since given him such a martial[6] appearance. Being at Gandish's and so near the dancing academy, what must he do but take lessons in the Terpsichorean art too, making himself as popular with the dancing folks as with

---

[2] pupils' *Ms*] whole *E1*
[3] leck spettles *Ms*] lick-spittles *E1*
[4] other *Ms*] [omitted] *E1*
[5] pulled *Ms*] slipped *E1*
[6] coat *Ms*] fine silk-sleeved coat *E1*
[7] Clive *Ms*] the lad *E1*
[8] to him two black eyes *Ms*] two black eyes to Sandy *E1*
[9] from seeing the head ... copying, for some days after. *Ms*] from seeing for some days after the head ... copying. *E1*
[1] hardly *Ms*] scarcely *E1*
[2] beheld *Ms*] saw *E1*
[3] of Mr. Mc.Collop. ... justice, *Ms*] of poor Mr. M'Collop so darkened. To do the Scotchman justice, *E1*
[4] friends *Ms*] of friends *E1*
[5] commission for which he *Ms*] commission, who *E1*
[6] martial *Ms*] marked *E1*

the drawing folks and the jolly young king[7] of his company every where. He gave entertainments to his fellow-students in the Upper Chambers in Fitzroy Square which were devoted to his use, inviting his father and Mr. Binnie to these[8] parties now and then. And songs were sung, and pipes were smoked, and many a pleasant supper eaten: There was no stint, but no excess. No young man was ever seen to quit those apartments "the worse" as it is called "for drink"—for[9] the Colonel made that one of the conditions of his son's hospitality, that nothing like intoxication should ensue from it. The good gentleman did not frequent the parties of the juniors: he saw that his presence rather silenced the young men; and left them to themselves confiding in Clive's parole, and went away to play his honest rubber[1] at the Club; and many a time heard[2] the young fellows' departing steps[3] tramping by his bed-chamber door, as he lay within[4] happy to think that his[5] son was happy.

[7] young King *Ms*] king *E1*
[8] these *Ms*] those *E1*
[9] called 'for drink'—for *Ms*] called, for liquor. Fred Bayham's uncle the bishop, could not be more decorous than F.B. as he left the Colonel's house, for *E1*
[1] honest rubber *Ms*] honest rubber of whist *E1*] rubber of whist *R*
[2] heard *Ms*] he heard *E1*
[3] fellows' departing steps *Ms*] fellow's steps *E1*
[4] within *Ms*] wakeful within, *E1*
[5] think that his *Ms*] think his *E1*

Chapter XVIII.

LIVE used to give us[1] droll accounts of the young disciples at Gandish's; who were of various ages and conditions, and in whose company the young fellow took his place with that good-temper and gaiety which have seldom deserted him in life and have put him at ease wherever his fate has led him. He is in truth as much at home in a fine drawing-room as in a public-house parlour; and can talk as pleasantly to the polite mistress of the mansion, as to the jolly landlady dispensing her drinks from her bar. Not one of the Gandishites but was after a while well-inclined to the young fellow; from Mr. Chivers the senior pupil, down to the little imp Harry Hooker who knew as much mischief at twelve years old, and could draw as cleverly as many a student of five-and-twenty; and Bob Trotter the diminutive fag of the studio who ran on all the young men's errands, and fetched them in apples, oranges and walnuts. Clive opened his eyes with wonder when he first beheld these simple feasts, and the pleasure with which some of the young men partook of them. They were addicted to polonies: they did not disguise their love for Banbury cakes: they made bets in ginger-beer and gave and took the odds in that frothing liquor. There was a young Hebrew amongst the pupils, upon whom his brother students used playfully to press ham-sandwiches, pork sausages and the like. This young man (who has risen to great wealth subsequently, and was bankrupt only three months since) actually brought[2] cocoa-nuts, and sold them at a profit amongst the lads. His pockets were never without pencil-cases, French chalk, garnet-brooches for which he was willing to bargain. He behaved very rudely to Gandish, who seemed to be afraid before him. It was whispered that the Professor was not altogether easy in his circumstances, and that the elder Moss had some mysterious hold over him.

---

[1] give us *Ms*] give *E1*
[2] brought *Ms*] bought *E1*

Honeyman and Bayham who once came to see Clive at the studio, seemed each disturbed at beholding young Moss (seated there making a copy of the Marsyas). "Pa knows both those gents," he informed Clive afterwards with a wicked twinkle of his Oriental eyes. "Step in, Mr. Newcome, any day you are passing down Wardour Street; and see if you want[3] any thing in our way." (He pronounced the words in his own way, saying "Step id Bister Doocob, ady day idto Vorder Street," &c.) This young gentleman could get tickets for almost all the theatres, which he gave or sold; and gave splendid accounts at Gandish's of the brilliant masquerades. Clive was greatly diverted at beholding Mr. Moss at one of these entertainments, dressed in a scarlet coat and top-boots, and calling out, "Yoicks! Hark forward" fitfully to another Orientalist his younger brother, attired like a midshipman. Once Clive bought a half-dozen of theatre tickets from Mr. Moss, which he distributed to the young fellows of the studio—but when this nice young man tried farther to tempt him on the next day, "Mr. Moss," Clive said[4] with much dignity, "I am very much obliged to you for your offer, but when I go to the play, I prefer paying at the door."[5]

The Senior Student,[6] Mr. Chivers, used to sit in one corner of the room occupied over a lithographic stone. He was an uncouth and peevish young man; for ever finding fault with the younger pupils, whose butt he was. Next in rank and age was M'Collop, before named: and these two were at first more than usually harsh and captious with Clive, whose prosperity offended them; and whose dandyfied manners, free and easy ways, and evident influence over the junior[7] scholars, gave umbrage to these laborious[8] elderly apprentices. Clive at first returned Mr. Chivers war for war, controlment for controlment: but when the lad found that[9] Chivers was the son of a helpless widow; that he maintained her by his lithographic vignettes for the music-sellers, and by the scanty remuneration of some lessons which he gave at a school at Highgate:—when Clive saw or fancied he saw, the lonely senior eyeing with hungry glances[1] the luncheons of bread and cheese and sweetstuff[2] which the young lads of the studio enjoyed, I promise you Mr. Clive's wrath against Chivers was speedily turned into kindness and compassion,[3] and he sought, and no doubt found, means of feeding Chivers without offending his testy independence.

Nigh to Gandish's was and perhaps is another establishment for teaching the arts of design—Barker's; which had the additional dignity of a Life and Costume Academy;[4] frequented by a class of students usually[5] more

[3] want *Ms*] don't want *E1*
[4] said *Ms*] said to him *E1*
[5] door. *Ms*] doors. *E1*
[6] The Senior Student *Ms*] [omitted] *E1*
[7] Junior *Ms*] younger *E1*
[8] laborious *Ms*] [omitted] *E1*
[9] the lad found that *Ms*] he found *E1*
[1] glances *Ms*] eyes *E1*
[2] bread and cheese and sweet stuff *Ms*] cheese and bread and sweetstuff, *E1*
[3] kindness and compassion, *Ms*] compassion and kindness, *E1*
[4] Life and Costume Academy; *Ms*] life academy and costume; *E1*] life and costume academy; *R*
[5] usually *Ms*] [omitted] *E1*

advanced than the Gandishites.[6] Between these and the Barkerites there was constant[7] rivalry and emulation in and out of doors. Gandish sent more pupils to the Royal Academy: Gandish had brought up three medallists; and the last R.A. student sent to Rome was a Gandishite. Barker on the contrary scorned and loathed Trafalgar Square; and laughed at its Art, and pretensions.[8] Barker exhibited in Pall Mall and Suffolk Street. He laughed at old Gandish and his pictures, made minced-meat[9] of his *Angli and Angeli,* and tore King Alfred and his muffin[1] to pieces. The young men of the respective schools used to meet at Lundy's coffee house and billiard-room, and smoke there and do battle. Before Clive and his friend J.J. came to Gandish's, the Barkerites were having the best of that constant match which the two academies were playing. Fred Bayham who knew every coffee-house in town; and whose initials were scored on a thousand tavern-doors; was for a while a pretty[2] constant visitor at Lundy's—played pool with the young men, did[3] not disdain to dip his beard into their porter-pots when invited to partake of their drink, treated them handsomely when he was in cash himself; and was an honorary member of Barker's Academy. Nay when the Guardsman was not forthcoming, who was standing for one of Barker's heroic pictures; Bayham bared his immense arms, and brawny shoulders; and stood as Prince Edward with Philippa sucking the poisoned wound. He would take his friends up to the picture at[4] the Exhibition, and proudly point to it. "Look at that biceps, Sir, and now look at this—That's Barker's masterpiece, Sir, and that's the muscle of F.B., Sir." In no company was F.B. greater than in the society of the artists; in whose smoky haunts and airy parlours he might often be found. It was from F.B. that Clive heard of Mr. Chivers's struggles and honest industry—A great deal of shrewd advice could F.B. give on occasion: and many a kind action and gentle office of charity was the[5] jolly outlaw known to do and cause to be done. His advice to Clive was most edifying at this time of our young gentleman's life, and he owns that he was kept from much mischief by this queer counsellor.

A few months after Clive and J.J. had entered at Gandish's, that academy began to hold its own against its rival. That[6] silent young disciple was pronounced to be a genius. His copies were beautiful in delicacy and finish. His designs were exquisite for grace and richness of fancy. Mr. Gandish took to himself all[7] the credit for J.J.'s genius: Clive ever and fondly acknowledged the benefit he got from his friend's skill and[8] taste and bright

[6] the Gandishites. *Ms*] those of Gandish's. *E1*

[7] constant *Ms*] a constant *E1*

[8] Art, and pretensions. *Ms*] art. *E1*

[9] minced-meat *Ms*] mince-meat *E1*

[1] muffin *Ms*] muffins *E1*

[2] pretty *Ms*] [omitted] *E1*

[3] did *Ms*] and did *E1*

[4] at *Ms*] in *E1*

[5] the *Ms*] this *E1*

[6] That *Ms*] The *E1*

[7] all *Ms*] [omitted] *E1*

[8] skill and *Ms*] [omitted] *E1*

enthusiasm and sure skill. As for Clive, if he was successful in the academy he was doubly victorious out of it. His person was handsome his courage high, his gaiety and frankness delightful and winning. His money was plenty, and he spent it like a young king. He could speedily beat all the club at Lundy's at billiards: and give points to the redoubted F.B. himself. He sang a famous song at their jolly supper-parties: and J.J. had no greater delight than to listen to his fresh voice: and watch the young conqueror at the billiard-table where the balls seemed to obey him.

Clive was not the most docile of Mr. Gandish's young[9] pupils. If he had not come to the studio on horseback, several of the young students averred, Gandish would not always have been praising him and quoting him as that professor certainly did. It must be confessed that the young ladies read the history of Clive's uncle in the Book of Baronets and that Gandish Junior, possibly[1] with an eye to business, made a design of a picture in which, according to that veracious volume, one of the Newcomes was represented as going cheerfully to the stake at Smithfield, surrounded by some very ill-favoured Dominicans whose arguments did not appear to make the least impression upon the martyr of the Newcome family. Sandy M'Collop devised a counter picture wherein the barber surgeon of King Edward the Confessor was drawn operating upon the beard of that Monarch—to which piece of satire, Clive gallantly replied by a design representing Sawney Bean M'Collop, Chief of the clan of that name, descending from his mountains into Edinburgh and his astonishment at beholding a pair of breeches for the first time. These playful jokes passed constantly amongst the young men of Gandish's studio. There was no one there who was not caricatured in one way or other.[2] He whose eyes looked not very straight was depicted with a most awful squint. The youth whom nature had endowed with somewhat lengthy nose was drawn by the caricaturists with a prodigious proboscis; little Bobby Moss the young Hebrew artist from Wardour Street was delineated with three hats and an old clothes bag, nor were poor J.J.'s round shoulders spared until Clive indignantly remonstrated at the hideous hunchback pictures which the lads[3] made of his friend and vowed that[4] it was a shame to make jokes at such a deformity.

Our friend, if the truth must be told regarding him, though one of the most frank generous and kind-hearted persons, is of a nature somewhat haughty and imperious, and very likely the course of life which he now led and the society which he was compelled to keep served to increase some original defects in his character and to fortify a certain disposition to think well of himself with which his enemies not unjustly reproach him. He has been known very pathetically to lament that he was withdrawn from school too early, where a couple of years' further course of thrashings from his tyrant, Old Hodge, he avers, would have done him good. He laments that he was not sent to college, where if a young man receives no other discipline, at least he acquires that of meeting with his equals in society, and

[9] young *Ms*] [omitted] *E1*
[1] Junior possibly *Ms*] junr., probably *E1*
[2] other. *Ms*] another. *E1*
[3] lads *Ms*] boys *E1*
[4] that *Ms*] [omitted] *E1*

of assuredly finding his betters. Whereas[5] in poor Mr. Gandish's Studio of Art, our young gentleman scarcely found a comrade that was not in one way or other his flatterer, his inferior, his honest or dishonest admirer. The influence of his family's rank and wealth acted more or less on all those simple folks. He had two or three humble friends who[6] would run on his errands, and vied with each other in winning the young nabob's favour. His very goodness of heart rendered him a more easy prey to their flattery, and his kind and jovial disposition led him into company from which he had been much better away. I am afraid that artful young Moss, whose parents dealt in pictures, furniture, jimcracks and jewellery, victimised Clive sadly with rings, chains, shirt-studs, flaming shirt-pins,[7] and such vanities: which the poor young rogue locked up in his desk generally, only venturing to wear them when he was out of his father's sight and[8] of Mr. Binnie's whose shrewd eyes watched him very keenly.

Mr. Clive used to leave home every day shortly after noon when he was supposed to betake himself to Gandish's studio: but was the young gentleman always at the drawing-board copying from the antique when his father thought he was so severely[9] engaged? I fear his place was sometimes vacant. His friend J.J. worked every day and all day; many a time the steady little student remarked his patron's absence and no doubt gently remonstrated with him; but when Clive did come to his work he executed it with remarkable skill and rapidity; and Ridley was too fond of him to say a word at home regarding the shortcomings of the youthful scapegrace. Candid readers may sometimes have heard their friend Tom's[1] mother lament that her darling was working too hard at College: or Harry's sisters express their anxiety lest his too rigorous attendance in Chambers (after which he will persist in sitting up all night reading those dreary law books which cost such an immense sum of money) should undermine dear Henry's health: and to such acute persons a word is sufficient to indicate young Mr. Clive Newcome's proceedings. Meanwhile his father, who knew no more of the world than Harry's simple sisters or Tom's[2] fond mother, never doubted but[3] that all Clive's doings were right, and that his boy was the best of boys.

"If that young man goes on as charmingly as he has begun," Clive's cousin Barnes Newcome said of his kinsman, "he will be a paragon. I saw him last night at Vauxhall in company with young Moss, whose father does bills, and keeps the bric-a-brac shop in Wardour Street; two or three other gentlemen, probably young old-clothes-men, who had concluded for the day the labours of the bag, joined Mr. Newcome and his friend, and they partook of rack-punch in an arbour. He is a delightful youth, Cousin Clive, and I feel sure is[4] about to be an honour to our family."

[5] betters. Whereas *Ms*] betters: whereas *E1*
[6] folks. He ... who *Ms*] folks, who *E1*
[7] rings, chains, shirt-studs, flaming shirt-pins,] rings chains shirtstuds flaming shirt pins *Ms*] rings and chains, shirt-studs and flaming shirt-pins, *E1*
[8] and *Ms*] or *E1*
[9] thought he was so severely *Ms*] supposed him to be so devotedly *E1*
[1] Tom's *Ms*] Jones's *E1*
[2] Tom's *Ms*] Jones's *E1*
[3] but *Ms*] [omitted] *E1*
[4] sure is *Ms*] sure he is *E1*

Chapter XIX.

THE COLONEL AT HOME.[1]

UR good Colonel's house had[2] received a coat of paint, which like Madame Latour's rouge in her latter days only served to make her careworn face look more ghastly. The kitchens were gloomy. The stables were gloomy. Great black passages, cracked conservatory, dilapidated bathroom with melancholy waters mourning[3] and fizzing from the cistern, the great large blank stone staircase were all so many melancholy features in the general countenance of the house, but the Colonel thought it perfectly cheerful and pleasant and set about furnishing it[4] in his rough and ready way. One day a[5] cartload of chairs, the next a waggon full of fenders, fire irons and glass and crockery—a quantity of supplies, in a word, he poured into the place. There was a yellow curtain[6] in the back drawing-room and green curtains in the front. The carpet was an immense bargain bought dirt cheap, Sir, at a sale in Euston Square. He was against the purchase of a carpet for the stairs. What was the good of it? What did men want with stair-carpets? His own apartment contained a wonderful assortment of lumber: shelves which he nailed himself, old Indian garments, camphor trunks. What did he want with gewgaws. Anything was good enough for an old soldier. But the spare bed-room was endowed with all sorts of splendour—a bed as big as a general's tent, a cheval glass—whereas the Colonel shaved in a little cracked mirror which cost him no more than King Stephen's breeches—and a handsome new carpet, while the boards of the Colonel's bed-chamber were as bare—as bare as old Miss Scragg's

[1] The first paragraph and the first two sentences of the second paragraph of this chapter were originally intended for the last page of chapter 16 (page 154, above), but were moved to this point when installment No. 5 overflowed and No. 6 ran short of copy.
[2] Our good Colonel's house had *E1*] It had *Ms*
[3] mourning *Ms*] moaning *E1*
[4] and set about furnishing it *Ms*] and furnished it *E1*
[5] day a *Ms E1*] day came a *R*
[6] was a yellow curtain *Ms*] were a yellow curtain *E1*] were yellow curtains *R NY*

shoulders which would be so much more comfortable were they covered up. Mr. Binnie's bed-chamber was neat snug and appropriate. And Clive had a study and bed-room at the top of the house which he was allowed to furnish entirely according to his own taste. How he and Ridley revelled in Wardour Street. What delightful coloured prints of hunting, racing and beautiful ladies did they not purchase, mount with their own hands, cut out for screens, frame and glaze and hang up on the walls. When the rooms were ready they gave a party inviting the Colonel and Mr. Binnie by note of hand, two gentlemen from Lamb Court, Temple, Mr. Honeyman and Fred Bayham. We must have Fred Bayham. Fred Bayham frankly asked, "Is Mr. Sherrick with whom you have become rather intimate lately—and mind you I say nothing but I recommend strangers in London to be cautious about their friends—is Mr. Sherrick coming to you, young 'un, because if he is F.B. must respectfully decline."

Mr. Sherrick was not invited and accordingly F.B. came. But Sherrick was invited on other days and a very queer society did our honest Colonel gather together in that queer house, so dreary, so dingy, so comfortless, so pleasant.[7] He, who[8] was one of the most hospitable men alive, loved to have his friends constantly[9] around him; and it must be confessed that the evening-parties now occasionally given in Fitzroy Square were composed[1] of the oddest assemblage of people—the correct East India gentlemen from Hanover Square: the artists, Clive's friends, gentlemen of all ages with all sorts of beards, in every variety of costume; now and again a stray schoolfellow from Grey Friars who stared, as well he might, at the company in which he found himself—Sometimes a few ladies were brought to these entertainments. The immense politeness of the good host compensated some of them, for the strangeness of the[2] company. They had never seen such odd-looking hairy men as those young artists nor such wonderful women as Colonel Newcome assembled together. He was good to all old maids, and poor widows. Retired Captains with large families of daughters found in him their best friend. He sent carriages to fetch them and bring them back from the suburbs where they dwelt. Gandish, Mrs. Gandish and the four Miss Gandishes in scarlet robes were constant attendants of[3] the Colonel's soirées. "I delight, Sir, in the hospitality[4] of my distinguished military friend," Mr. Gandish would say: "the Harmy has always been my passion. I served in the Soho Volunteers three years myself—till the conclusion of the war, Sir, till the conclusion of the war."

It was a great sight to see Mr. Frederick Bayham engaged in the waltz or the quadrille with some of the elderly houris at the Colonel's parties. F.B., like a good-natured F.B. as he was, always chose the plainest women for[5] partners and entertained them with profound compliments and sump-

---

[7] Here ends the passage originally intended for Chapter 16.
[8] He, who *E1*] Our good Colonel who *Ms*
[9] constantly *Ms*] [omitted] *E1*
[1] composed *Ms*] [omitted] *E1*
[2] the *Ms*] his *E1*
[3] of *Ms*] at *E1*
[4] hospitality *Ms*] 'ospitality *E1*
[5] for *Ms*] as *E1*

tuous conversation. The Colonel likewise danced quadrilles with the utmost gravity. Waltzing had been invented long since his time: but he had[6] practised quadrilles when they first came in about 1817 in Calcutta. To see him leading up a little old maid, and bowing to her when the dance was ended, and performing Cavalier seul with stately simplicity— was a sight indeed to remember. If Clive Newcome had not such a fine sense of humour: he would have blushed for his father's simplicity—As it was, the elder's guileless goodness and childish[7] trustfulness endeared him immensely to his son. "Look at the old boy, Pendennis," he would say. "Look at him leading up that old Miss Tidswell to the piano. Doesn't he do it like an old duke? I lay a guinea[8] she thinks she is going to be my mother-in-law—all the women are in love with him, young and old. 'Should he upbraid'—There she goes—'I'll own that he[9] prevail, And sing as sweetly as a nigh-tin-gale!' O you old warbler! Look at Father's old head[1] bobbing up and down! Wouldn't he do for Sir Roger de Coverley? How do you do, Uncle Charles—I say, M'Collop, how goes[2] on the Duke of Whatdyecallem starving in the Castle—Gandish says it's very good." The lad retires to a group of artists. Mr. Honeyman comes up, with a

6 had *Ms*] [omitted] *E1*
7 childish *Ms*] childlike *E1*
8 guinea *Ms*] wager *E1*
9 he *Ms*] he'll *E1*
1 head *Ms R*] heart *E1* [compositor's error]
2 goes *Ms*] gets *E1*

faint smile playing on his features like moonlight on the façade of Lady Whittlesea's chapel.

"These parties are the most singular I have ever seen," Honeyman whispers.[3] "In entering one of these assemblies one is struck by[4] the immensity of London; and by[5] the sense of one's own insignificance—without, I trust, departing from my clerical character, nay from my very avocation as Incumbent of a London chapel—I have seen a good deal of the world—And here is an assemblage, no doubt of most respectable persons on scarce one of whom I ever set eyes till this evening. Where does my good brother find such characters. Who can be that extraordinary man with the collars of his shirt turned down who is just now going to sing?"[6]

"That," says Mr. Honeyman's interlocutor, "that[7] is the celebrated though neglected artist, Professor Gandish, whom nothing but jealousy has kept out of the Royal Academy. Surely you have heard of the Great Gandish."

"Indeed I am ashamed to confess my ignorance—But a clergyman busy with his duties, knows little, too little perhaps,[8] of the Fine Arts."

"Gandish, Sir, is one of the greatest geniuses on whom an[9] ungrateful country ever trampled. He exhibited his first celebrated picture of Alfred in the Neatherd's Hut (he says he is the first who ever touched that subject) in 180–: but Lord Nelson's death and victory of Trafalgar occupied the public attention at that time, and Gandish's work went unnoticed. In the year 1816 he painted his great work of Boadicea. You see her before you, that lady in yellow with a light front and a turban. Boadicea became Mrs. Gandish in that year. So late as '27 he brought before the world his '*Non Angli sed Angeli*'—two of the angels are yonder in sea green dresses, the Misses Gandish—the youth in the[1] Berlin gloves was the little male Angel[2] of that piece."

"How come you to know all this, you strange man?" asks[3] Mr. Honeyman.

"Simply because Gandish has told me twenty times. He tells the story to everybody every time he sees them. He told it to-day at dinner. Boadicea and the Angeli[4] came afterwards."

"Satire! Satire! Mr. Pendennis!" says the divine holding up a reproving finger of lavender kid. "Beware of a wicked wit!—But when a man has that tendency—I know how difficult it is to restrain! My dear Colonel, good evening! You have a great reception to-night—That gentleman's bass voice is very fine. Mr. Pendennis and I were admiring it anon.[5] The Wolf

---

3 Honeyman whispers. *Ms*] whispers Honeyman. *E1*
4 by *Ms*] with *E1*
5 by *Ms*] with *E1*
6 Who can be ... sing? *Ms*] [omitted] *E1*
7 that *Ms*] [omitted] *E1*
8 too little perhaps, *Ms*] perhaps too little *E1*
9 an *Ms*] our *E1*
1 the *Ms*] [omitted] *E1*
2 Angel *Ms*] angelus *E1*
3 asks *Ms*] says *E1*
4 Angeli *Ms*] angels *E1*
5 it anon— *Ms*] it. *E1*

is a song admirably adapted to show its capabilities."

Mr. Gandish's autobiography had occupied the whole time after the retirement of the ladies from Colonel Newcome's dinner-table. Mr. Hobson
Newcome had been asleep during the performance, Sir Curry Baughton
and one or two of the Colonel's professional and military guests silent and
puzzled, honest Mr. Binnie with his shrewd good-humoured face sipping
his claret as usual and delivering a sly joke now and again to the gentlemen
at his end of the table. Mrs. Newcome had sat by him in sulky dignity. Was
it that Lady Baughton's diamonds offended her?—her ladyship and her
daughter being attired in great splendour for a court ball which they were
to attend that evening. Was she hurt because *she* was not invited to that
Royal Entertainment while others were asked.[6] As these festivities take[7]
place at an early hour the ladies bidden were obliged to quit the Colonel's
house before his[8] evening party commenced, from which Lady Ann declared she was quite vexed to be obliged to run away.

Lady Ann Newcome had been as gracious on this occasion as her sister-
in-law[9] had been out of humour. Everything pleased her in the house.
She had no idea that there were such fine houses in that quarter of the
town. She thought the dinner so very nice. That Mr. Binnie such a
good-humoured looking gentleman. That stout gentleman with his collars
turned down like Lord Byron, so exceedingly clever and full of information. A celebrated artist, was he? (Courtly Mr. Smee had his own opinion
upon that point but did not utter it.) All those artists are so eccentric and
amusing and clever! Before dinner she insisted upon seeing Clive's den
with its pictures and casts and pipes. "You horrid young wicked creature,
have you began[1] to smoke already?" she asked as she admired[2] his room.
She admired everything; nothing could exceed her satisfaction.

The sisters-in-law kissed on meeting with that cordiality so delightful
to witness in sisters who dwell together in unity. It was, "My dear Maria,
what an age since I have seen you!" "My dear Ann, our occupations are
so engrossing, our circles are so different!" in a languid response from the
other. "Sir Brian is not coming, I suppose? Now Colonel!" She turns in a
frisky manner towards him and taps her fan. "Did I not tell you Sir Brian
would not come?"

"He is kept at the House of Commons, my dear. Those dreadful committees you know.[3] He was quite vexed at not being able to come."

"I know, I know, dear Ann. There are always excuses to gentlemen in
Parliament. I have received many such. Mr. Shaloo and Mr. McSheny,[4]
the leaders of our party often and often disappoint me. I *knew* Brian would
not come. *My* husband came from[5] Marble Head on purpose this morning.

---

6 Entertainment while others were asked. *Ms*] Entertainment? *E1*
7 take *Ms*] were to take *E1*
8 his *Ms*] the *E1*
9 sister-in-law *E1*] sester *Ms*
1 began *Ms*] begun *E1*
2 asked . . . admired *Ms*] asks . . . admires *E1*
3 committees you know. *Ms*] committees. *E1*
4 Shaloo and Mr. McSheny, *E1*] Shaloo Mr. McSheng, *Ms*
5 from *Ms*] down from *E1*

Nothing would have induced *us* to give up our brother's party."

"I believe you. I did come from[6] Marble Head this morning, and I was four hours in the hayfield before I came away, and in the city till five and I've been to look at a horse afterwards at Tattersall's, and I'm as hungry as a hunter and as tired as a hodman," says Mr. Newcome with his hands in his pockets. "How do you do, Mr. Pendennis. Maria, you remember Mr. Pendennis, don't you?"

"Perfectly," replies the languid Maria. Mr.[7] Gandish, Colonel Topham, Major M'Cracken are announced, and then in diamonds, feathers and splendour, Lady Baughton and Miss Baughton who are going to the Queen's Ball and Sir Curry Baughton not quite in his deputy-lieutenant's uniform as yet, looking very shy in a pair of blue trowsers with a glistering[8] stripe of silver down the seams. Clive looks with wonder and delight at these ravishing ladies rustling in fresh brocades, with feathers, diamonds and every magnificence. Aunt Ann has not her court-dress on as yet, and Aunt Maria blushes as she beholds the new comers, having thought fit to attire herself in a high dress with a Quaker-like simplicity and a pair of gloves more than ordinarily dingy. The pretty little foot she has, it is true, and sticks it out from habit; but what is Mrs. Newcome's foot compared with that sweet little chaussure which the lovely[9] Miss Baughton exhibits and withdraws; the sheeny,[1] white satin slipper, the dazzling[2] pink stocking which ever and anon peeps from the rustling folds of her robe and timidly retires into its covert? That foot, light as it is, crushes Mrs. Newcome. No wonder she winces and is angry. There are some mischievous persons who rather like to witness that discomfiture. All Mr. Smee's flatteries that day failed to soothe her. She was in the state in which his canvases sometimes are when he cannot paint on them.[3]

What happened to her alone in the drawing-room when the ladies invited to the dinner had departed and those convoked to the soirée began to arrive,—what happened to her or to them I do not like to think. The Gandishes arrived first, Boadicea and the Angels; we judged so from the fact that young Mr. Gandish came blushing into the dessert. Name after name was announced of persons of whom Mrs. Newcome knew nothing. The young and the old, the pretty and homely, they were all in their best dresses and no doubt stared at Mrs. Newcome so obstinately plain in her attire. When we came up-stairs from dinner we found her seated entirely by herself tapping her fan at the fireplace; timid groups of persons were round about, waiting for the irruption of the gentlemen, until the pleasure should begin. Mr. Newcome who came up-stairs yawning was heard to say to his wife, "O dam—let's cut," and they went down-stairs and waited until their carriage arrived[4] when they quitted Fitzroy Square.

[6] from *Ms*] down from *E1*
[7] Mr. *Ms*] Mrs. *E1*
[8] glistering *Ms*] glittering *E1*
[9] the lovely *Ms*] [omitted] *E1*
[1] sheeny, *Ms*] shiny *E1*
[2] dazzling *Ms*] [omitted] *E1*
[3] She was in ... paint on them. *Ms E1*] [omitted] *R*
[4] arrived *Ms*] had arrived *E1*

Mr. Barnes Newcome presently arrived looking particularly smart and lively, with a large flower in his button-hole, and leaning on the arm of a friend. "How doyoudo, Pendennis," he says with a peculiarly dandyfied air. "Did you dine here? you look as if you had[5] dined here, (and Barnes certainly as if he had dined elsewhere). I was only asked to the cold soirée. Who[6] did you have for dinner? You had my mamma and the Baughtons, and my uncle and aunt, I know, for they are down below in the library waiting for the carriage. He is asleep and she is as sulky as a bear."

"Why did Mrs. Newcome say I should find nobody I knew up here?" asks Barnes's companion; "on the contrary there are lots of fellows I know. There's Fred Bayham dancing like a harlequin. There's old Gandish who used to be my drawing-master: and my Brighton friends, your uncle and cousin, Barnes. What relations are they to me? must be some relations— Fine fellow your cousin."

"Hm!"[7] growls Barnes, "very fine boy, not spoiled[8] at all, not fond of flattery, not surrounded by toadies, not fond of drink—delightful boy. See yonder! the young fellow is in conversation with his most intimate friend, a little crooked fellow, with long hair. Do you know who he is? He is the son of old Todmorden's butler: upon my life it's true."

"And suppose it is, what the deuce do I care?" cries Lord Kew. "A man must be somebody's son:[9] Who can be more respectable than a butler? When I am a middle-aged man, I humbly hope I shall look like a butler myself. Suppose you were to put ten of Gunter's men into the House of Lords, do you mean to say they[1] would not look as well as any average ten peers in the House? Look at Lord Westcot. He is exactly like a butler. That's why the country has such confidence in him. I never dine with him but I fancy he ought to be at the sideboard. Here comes that insufferable little old Smee. How do you do, Mr. Smee."

Mr. Smee smiles his sweetest smile—With his rings, diamond shirt studs and red velvet waistcoat, there are few more elaborate and killing[2] middle-aged bucks than Alfred[3] Smee. "How do you do, my dear lord," cries this[4] bland one. "Who would ever have thought of seeing your lordship here?"

"Why the deuce not? Mr. Smee?" asks Lord Kew abruptly. "Is it wrong to come here? I have been in the house only five minutes, and three people have said the same thing to me—Mrs. Newcome who is sitting downstairs in a rage waiting for her carriage, the condescending Barnes, and yourself—Why do *you* come here, Smee? How are you, Mr. Gandish— How do the fine arts go?"

"Your lordship's kindness in asking[5] will cheer them if any thing will,"

[5] had *Ms*] [omitted] *E1*
[6] Who *Ms E1*] Whom *R*
[7] Hm! *Ms R*] Him, *E1*
[8] spoiled *Ms*] spirited *E1*
[9] "A man ... son *Ms*] *misplaced after* butler? *E1*
[1] they *Ms*] that they *E1*
[2] and killing *Ms*] [omitted] *E1*
[3] Alfred *Ms E1*] Andrew *R* [See note at 157.25.]
[4] this *Ms*] the *E1*
[5] asking *Ms*] asking for them *E1*

says Mr. Gandish. "Your noble family has always patronised them. I am proud to be reckonised by your lordship in this house; where the distinguished father of one of my pupils entertains us this evening. A most promising young man, is young Mr. Clive—talents for a hamateur really most remarkable."

"Excellent upon my word, excellent," cries Mr. Smee. "I'm not an animal-painter myself and perhaps don't think much of that branch of the profession, but it seems to me the young fellow draws horses with the most wonderful spirit. I hope Lady Walham is very well and that she was satisfied with her son's portrait—Stockholm, I think, your brother is appointed to? I wish I might be allowed to paint the elder as well as the younger brother, my lord."

"I am an historical painter but whenever Lord Kew is painted I hope his lordship will think of the old servant of his lordship's family, Charles Gandish," cries the professor.

"I am like Susannah between the two Elders," says Lord Kew. "Let my innocence alone, Smee. Mr. Gandish, don't persecute my modesty with your addresses. I won't be painted. I am not a fit subject for a historical painter, Mr. Gandish."

"Halcibiades sate to Praxiteles and Pericles to Phidjas," remarks Gandish.

"The cases are not quite similar," says Lord Kew languidly. "You are no doubt fully equal to Praxiteles, Gandish;[6] but I don't see my resemblance to—to[7] the other party. I should not look well as a hero: and Smee could not paint me handsome enough."

"I would try, my dear lord," cries Mr. Smee.

"I know you would, my dear fellow," Lord Kew answered looking at the painter with a lazy scorn in his eyes. "Where is Colonel Newcome, Mr. Gandish?" Mr. Gandish replied that our gallant Ost[8] was dancing a quadrille in the next room; and the young gentleman walked on towards that apartment to pay his respects to the giver of the evening's entertainment.

Newcome's behaviour to the young peer was ceremonious but not in the least servile. He saluted the other's superior rank, not his person, as he turned the guard out for a general officer. He never could be brought to be otherwise than cold and grave in his behaviour to John James: nor was it without difficulty, when young Ridley and his son became pupils at Gandish's, he could be induced to invite the former to his parties. "An artist is any man's equal," he said. "I have no prejudices[9] of that sort, and think that Sir Joshua Reynolds and Doctor Johnson were fit company for any person of whatever rank. But a young man whose father may have to[1] wait behind me at dinner should not be brought into my company." Clive compromised[2] the dispute with a laugh. "First," says he, "I will wait till I am asked and then I promise I will not go to dine with Lord Todmorden."

[6] Praxiteles, Gandish; *Ms*] Praxiteles; *E1*
[7] to—to *Ms*] to *E1*
[8] Ost *Ms*] host *E1*
[9] prejudices *Ms*] prejudice *E1*
[1] have to *Ms*] have had to *E1*
[2] compromised *Ms*] compromises *E1*

Chapter XX.

CLIVE'S pleasures,[1] studies or occupations, such as they were, filled his day pretty completely, and caused the young gentleman's time to pass rapidly and pleasantly, his father, it must be owned, had no such resources, and the good Colonel's idleness hung rather[2] heavily upon him. He submitted very kindly to this infliction, however, as he would have done to any other for Clive's sake: and though he may have wished himself back with his regiment again, and engaged in the pursuits in which all[3] his life had been spent; he chose to consider these desires as very selfish and blameable on his part; and sacrificed them resolutely for his son's welfare. The young fellow, I daresay, gave his parent no more credit for this[4] long self-denial than many other children award to their's. We take such life-offerings as our due commonly. The old French satirist avers that in a love affair, there is usually one person who loves, and the other *qui se laisse aimer*: it is only in later days perhaps, when the treasures of love are spent, and the kind hand cold which ministered them, that we remember how tender it was; how soft to caress;[5] how eager to shield; how ready to support and caress. The ears may no longer hear, which would have received our words of thanks so delightedly. Let us hope those fruits of Love, though tardy, are yet not all too late; and though we bring our tribute of reverence and gratitude, it may be, but[6] to a gravestone; there is an acceptance even there, for the stricken heart's oblation of fond remorse, contrite memo-

---

[1]pleasures, *Ms*] amusements, *E1*
[2]rather *Ms*] [omitted] *E1*
[3]all *Ms*] [omitted] *E1*
[4]this *Ms*] his *E1*
[5]caress; *Ms*] soothe; *E1*
[6]be but *Ms*] be *E1*

ries and pious tears. I am thinking of the love of Clive Newcome's father for him; (and perhaps, young reader, of yours and mine[7])—how the old man lay awake, and devised kindnesses, and gave his all for the love of his son; and the young man took, and spent, and slept, and made merry. Did we not say at our tale's commencement that all stories were old? Careless prodigals and anxious elders have been from the beginning;—and so may love and repentance and forgiveness endure even till the end.

The stifling fogs, the slippery mud, the dun-dreary November mornings when the Regent's Park where the Colonel took his early walk was wrapped in yellow mist; must have been a melancholy exchange for the splendour of Eastern sunrise and the invigorating gallop at dawn, to which, for so many years of his life, Thomas Newcome had accustomed himself. His obstinate habit of early waking accompanied him to England, and occasioned the despair of his London domestics, who if Master wasn't so awful early would have found no fault with him, for a gentleman as gives less trouble to his servants; as scarcely ever rings the bell for hisself; as will brush his own clothes; as will even boil his own shaving water, in the little Hetna which he keep[8] up in his dressing-room; as pays so regular, and as[9] never looks twice at the accounts;—such a man deserved to be beloved[1] by his household; and I daresay comparisons were made between him and his son, who do ring the bells; and scold if his boots ain't nice; and horder about like a young lord. But Clive though imperious was very liberal and good-humoured; and not the worse liked or[2] served because he insisted upon exerting his youthful authority. As for friend Binnie, he had a hundred pursuits of his own which made his time pass very comfortably. He had all the lectures at the British Institution; he had the Geographical Society, the Asiatic Society, and the Political-Economy Club; and though he talked year after year of going to visit his relations in Scotland; the months and seasons passed away and his feet still beat the London pavement.

In spite of the cold reception which[3] his brothers gave him, duty was duty, and Colonel Newcome still proposed or hoped to be well with the female members of the Newcome family. And having, as we have said, plenty of time on his hands: and, living at no very great distance from either of his brothers' town-houses; when their wives were in London, the elder Newcome was for paying them pretty constant visits. But after the good gentleman had called twice or thrice in the forenoon[4] upon his sister-in-law in Brianstone Square; bringing, as was his wont, a present for this little niece, or a book for that: Mrs. Newcome with her usual virtue gave

---

[7] of yours and mine *Ms*] that of yours and mine for ourselves *E1*
[8] keep *Ms*] keeps *E1*
[9] as *Ms*] [omitted] *E1*
[1] beloved *Ms*] loved *E1*
[2] liked or *Ms*] [omitted] *E1*
[3] which *Ms*] [omitted] *E1*
[4] in the forenoon *Ms*] [omitted] *E1*

him to understand that the occupations[5] of an English matron, who besides her multifarious family duties, had her own intellectual culture to mind, would not allow her to pass her[6] mornings in idle gossip;[7] and of course took great credit to herself for having so rebuked him. "I am not above instruction at[8] *any* age," says she thanking Heaven (or complimenting it rather for having created a being so virtuous and humble-minded). "When Professor Schroff comes, I sit with my children and take lessons in German—and I say my verbs with Maria and Fanny[9] in the same class." Yes, with curtsies and fine speeches, she actually bowed her brother out of doors: and the honest gentleman as he meekly left her, thought with bewilderment[1] of the different hospitality to which he had been accustomed in the East; where no friend's house was ever closed to him; where no neighbour was so busy but he had time to make Thomas Newcome welcome.

When Hobson Newcome's boys came home for their holydays their kind uncle was for treating them to the sights of the town—but here again Virtue interfered[2] and laid its interdict upon pleasure. "I thank[3] you very much, my dear Colonel," says Virtue: "there never was surely such a kind affectionate unselfish creature as you are, and so dangerous[4] for children—but my boys and yours are brought up on a *very different* plan—Excuse me for saying that I do not think it is adviseable that they should even see too much of each other. Clive's company is not good for them."

"Great Heavens, Maria!" cries the Colonel starting up, "do you mean that my boy's society is not good enough for any boy alive."

Maria turned very red. She had said not more than she meant but more than she meant to say. "My dear Colonel! How hot we are! How angry you Indian gentlemen become with us poor women! Your boy is much older than mine. He lives with Artists—with all sorts of eccentric people. Our children are bred in quite a different fashion.[5] Hobson will succeed his father in the bank; and dear Samuel I trust will go into the Church—I told you before, the views I had regarding the darling[6] boys: but it was most kind of you to think of them—most kind and generous."[7]

"That nabob of ours' is a queer fish," Hobson Newcome remarked to

---

5 occupations *Ms*] occupation *E1*
6 her *Ms*] the *E1*
7 gossip; *Ms*] gossips: *E1*] gossip: *R*
8 at *Ms*] of *E1*
9 Fanny *Ms*] Tommy *E1*
1 gentleman … bewilderment *Ms*] gentleman meekly left her, though with bewilderment as he thought *E1*
2 again Virtue interfered *Ms*] virture again interposed *E1*
3 'I thank *Ms*] "Thank *E1*
4 dangerous *Ms*] indulgent *E1*
5 in quite a different fashion. *Ms*] on *quite a different plan. E1*
6 darling *Ms*] [omitted] *E1*
7 kind and generous.' *Ms*] generous and kind." *E1*

his nephew.[8] "He's[9] as proud as Lucifer, he's[1] always taking huff about something[2] or the other. He went off in a fury[3] the other day[4] because your aunt objected to his taking the boys to the play. She don't like their going to the play—your[5] aunt is a woman who is deuced[6] wide awake I can tell you."

"I always knew, Sir, my[7] aunt was perfectly aware of the time of[8] day," says Barnes.[9]

"And then the Colonel flies out about his boy, and said[1] that my wife insulted him—I used to like that boy. Before his father came he was a good lad enough—a jolly little[2] brave little fellow."

"I didn't know him[3] at that interesting period of his existence," remarks Barnes.

"But since he has taken this mad-freak[4] of turning painter," the uncle continues, "there's[5] no understanding the chap. Did you ever see such a set of fellows as the Colonel had got together at his party the other night? Dirty chaps in velvet coats and beards? They looked like a set of mountebanks. And this young Clive is going to turn painter—"

"Very nice[6] thing for the family, Sir.[7] I always said he was a darling boy," says[8] Barnes.

"Darling Jackass!" cries Mr. Hobson.[9] "Confound it, why doesn't my brother set him up in some respectable trade.[1] I ain't proud. *I* haven't[2] married an earl's daughter—no offence to you, Barnes—"

"I[3] can't help it, you know,[4] if my grandfather is a gentleman, Sir,"[5] says Barnes with a bow and a[6] fascinating smile.

[8] nephew. *Ms*] nephew Barnes. *E1*
[9] 'He's *Ms*] "He is *E1*
[1] he's *Ms*] he is *E1*
[2] something *Ms*] one thing *E1*
[3] fury *Ms*] fume *E1*
[4] day *Ms*] night *E1*
[5] play—your *Ms*] play. My mother didn't either. Your *E1*
[6] deuced *Ms*] uncommon *E1*
[7] my *Ms*] that my *E1*
[8] of *Ms R*] of the *E1*
[9] Barnes. *Ms*] Barnes with a bow. *E1*
[1] said *Ms*] says *E1*
[2] little *Ms*] [omitted] *E1*
[3] I didn't know him *Ms*] "I confess I did not know Mr. Clive *E1*
[4] mad-freak *Ms*] mad-cap freak *E1*
[5] 'there's *Ms*] "there is *E1*
[6] nice *Ms*] advantageous *E1*
[7] family, Sir. *Ms*] family. He'll do our pictures for nothing. *E1*
[8] says *Ms*] simpered *E1*
[9] cries Mr. Hobson.] ...Hodson. *Ms*] growled out the senior. *E1*
[1] trade. *Ms*] business? *E1*
[2] *I* haven't *Ms*] I have not *E1*
[3] I *Ms*] Not at all, Sir. I *E1*
[4] you know *Ms*] [omitted] *E1*
[5] Sir,' *Ms*] [omitted] *E1*
[6] bow and a *Ms*] [omitted] *E1*

The uncle laughs—"I mean, I don't care what a fellow is if he is a good fellow. But a painter! Hang it—a painter's no trade at all. I don't fancy seeing one of our family sticking up pictures for sale—I don't like it, Barnes."

"Here[7] comes his distinguished friend, Mr. Pendennis," whispers Barnes: and the uncle growling out, "Dam all literary fellows, and artists the whole lot of 'em," turns away: and little Tom Eaves who has overheard the conversation at the Club repeats it with embellishments to the present reporter.[8]

Very soon Mrs. Newcome announced that their Indian brother found the society of Brianstone Square little[9] to his taste as indeed how should he, being a man of a good harmless disposition certainly but of small intellectual culture? It could not be helped. She had done *her* utmost to make him welcome and grieved that their pursuits were not congenial.[1] She heard that he was much more intimate in Park Lane. Possibly the superior rank of Lady Ann's family might present charms to Colonel Newcome who fell asleep at her assembly.[2] His boy, she was afraid, was leading the most *irregular* life.[3] He was growing a pair of mustachios: and going about with all sorts of wild associates. She found no fault—who was she to find fault with *any one*?[4] But she had been compelled to hint that *her*[5] children must not be too intimate with him. And so between one brother who at least[6] meant no unkindness, and another who was all affection and good will, this undoubting woman created distrust, difference,[7] dislike which one day was possibly to[8] lead to open rupture. The wicked are wicked no doubt; and they go astray, and they fall, and they come by their deserts: but who can measure[9] the mischief which the very virtuous do?

To his[1] sister-in-law, Lady Ann, the Colonel's society was more welcome. The affectionate gentleman never tired of doing kindnesses to his brother's many children; and as Mr. Clive's pursuits now separated him a good deal from his father, the Colonel, not perhaps without a sigh that Fate should so separate[2] him from the society which he loved best in the world, consoled himself as best he might with his nephews and nieces, especially with

---

[7] Here *Ms*] "Hush! here *E1*

[8] fellows, and artists the whole lot of 'em ... present reporter. *Ms*] fellows—all artists—the whole lot of them!" turns away. Barnes waves three languid fingers of recognition towards Pendennis: and when the uncle and nephew have moved out of the club newspaper room, little Tom Eaves comes up and tells the present reporter every word of their conversation. *E1*

[9] little *Ms*] very little *E1*

[1] congenial. *Ms*] more congenial. *E1*

[2] assembly. *Ms*] assemblies. *E1*

[3] *irregular* life. *Ms*] *irregular life. E1*

[4] *any one*? *Ms*] any one? *E1*

[5] *her Ms*] her *E1*

[6] at least *Ms*] [omitted] *E1*

[7] distrust, difference, *Ms*] difference, distrust, *E1*

[8] which one day was possibly to *Ms*] which might one day possibly *E1*

[9] measure *Ms*] tell *E1*

[1] his *Ms*] her *E1*

[2] separate *Ms E1*] sever *R*

Ethel for whom his *belle passion,* conceived at first sight, never diminished. "If Uncle Newcome had a hundred children," Ethel said, who was rather jealous of disposition, "he would spoil them all." He found a fine occupation in breaking a pretty little horse for her; of which he made her a present—and there was no horse in the park that was handsomer,[3] and surely no girl who looked more beautiful, than Ethel[4] with her broad hat, and her[5] red ribbon, with her thick black locks waving round her bright face, galloping along the ride on Bhurtpore. Occasionally Clive was of[6] their riding parties; when the Colonel would fall back, and fondly survey the two[7] young people cantering side by side over the grass: but by a tacit convention it was arranged that the cousins should be but seldom together; the Colonel might be his niece's companion; and no one could receive him with a more joyous welcome; but when Mr. Clive made his appearance with his father at the Park Lane door, a certain *gêne* was visible in Miss Ethel: who would never mount except with Colonel Newcome's assistance: and who, especially after Mr. Clive's famous mustachios made their appearance, rallied him and remonstrated with him regarding those ornaments—and treated him with much distance and ceremony.[8] She asked him if he was going into the Army?—She could not understand how any but military men could wear mustachios; and then she looked fondly and archly at her uncle, and said she liked none that were not grey.

Clive set her down as a very haughty aristocratic spoiled[9] young creature. If he had been in love with her, no doubt he would have sacrificed even those beloved new-born whiskers for the charmer. Had he not already bought on credit the necessary implements in a fine dressing-case from young Moss? But he was not in love with her: otherwise he would have found a thousand opportunities of riding with her, walking with her, meeting her in spite of all prohibitions tacit or expressed, all governesses, guardians, mammas,[1] punctilios, and kind hints from friends. For a while Mr. Clive thought himself in love with his cousin; than whom no more beautiful young girl could be seen in any park, ball or drawing-room: and he drew a hundred pictures of her; and discoursed about her beauties to J.J. who fell in love with her on hearsay. But at this time Mademoiselle Saltarelli was dancing at Drury Lane Theatre, and it certainly may be said that Clive's first love was bestowed upon that beauty, whom he worshipped chastely from the pit-benches:[2] whose picture of course he drew in most of her favourite characters: and for whom his passion lasted until the end of the sea-

---

[3] handsomer, *Ms*] so handsome, *E1*
[4] Ethel *Ms*] Ethel Newcome *E1*
[5] hat, and her *Ms*] hat and *E1*
[6] of *Ms*] at *E1*
[7] two *Ms*] [omitted] *E1*
[8] ceremony. *Ms*] dignity. *E1*
[9] aristocratic spoiled *Ms*] spoiled, aristrocratic *E1*
[1] mammas, *Ms*] mamma's *E1*
[2] beauty, . . . pit-benches: *Ms*] beauty: *E1*

son: when her 'night' was announced, tickets to be had at the theatre or of Mademoiselle Saltarelli, Buckingham Street, Strand. Then it was that going[3] with a throbbing heart and a five pound note, to engage places for the Houri's benefit, Clive beheld Madame Rogomme, Mademoiselle Saltarelli's mother, who entertained him in the French language in a dark parlour smelling of onions. And oh! issuing from the adjoining dining-room (where was a dingy vision of a feast and pewterpots upon a darkling tablecloth)—could that lean, scraggy, old, beetle-browed, yellow face,[4] who cried "*Où es tu donc, Maman?*" with such a shrill nasal voice—could that elderly vixen, be the[5] blooming and divine Saltarelli? Clive drew her picture as she was; and a likeness of Madame Rogomme, her mamma. A Mosaic youth, profusely jewelled, and scented at once with tobacco and Eau de Cologne, occupied Clive's stall, on Mademoiselle Saltarelli's night. It was young Mr. Moss of Gandish's to whom Newcome ceded his place: and who laughed (as he did

at all[6] Clive's jokes,) when the latter told the story of his interview with the dancer. "Paid five pound to see that woman. I could have took you behind the scenes (or *beide* the *seeds*, Mr. Moss said) and showed her to you for dothig!" Did he take Clive behind the scenes?—Over this part of the young gentleman's life without implying the least harm to him, for have not others been behind the scenes, and can there be more[7] dreary objects than those whitened and raddled old women who shudder at the slips?—over this stage of Clive Newcome's life we may surely drop the curtain.

It is pleasanter to contemplate that[8] kind old face of Clive's father, that

3 going *Ms*] [omitted] *E1*
4 yellow face, *E1*] yellow-faced, *Ms*
5 the *Ms R*] that *E1*
6 he did at all *Ms*] he always did at *E1*
7 more *Ms*] any more *E1*
8 that *Ms E1*] the *R*

"Have you killed many Men with this Sword, Uncle?"

sweet young blushing lady by his side as the two ride homewards at sunset: the grooms behind in quiet conversation; talking about horses[9] as men never tire in[1] talking about horses. Ethel wants to know about battles: about lovers' lamps which she has read of in *Lallah Rookh*. "Have you ever seen them, Uncle, floating down the Ganges of a night?"—about Indian widows—"Did you actually see one burning, and hear her scream as you rode up?"—She wonders whether he will tell her anything about Clive's mother: how she must have loved Uncle Newcome! Ethel can't bear somehow to think that her name was Mrs. Casey—perhaps he was very fond of her; though he scarcely ever mentions her name. She was nothing like that good old funny Miss Honeyman at Brighton. Who could the person be, a lady whom[2] her uncle knew ever so long ago—a French lady, whom her uncle says Ethel often resembles? That is why he speaks French so well. He can recite pages[3] out of Racine—Perhaps it was the French lady who taught him. And he was not very happy at the Hermitage, (though Grandpapa was a very kind good man): and he upset Papa in a little carriage and got into disgrace and was wild,[4] and was sent to India? He could not have been very bad, Ethel thinks looking at him with her honest eyes. Last week he went to the Drawing-Room and Papa presented him. His uniform of grey and silver was quite old: but yet[5] he looked much grander than Sir Brian in his new deputy-lieutenant's dress. "Next year when I am presented you must come too, Sir," says Ethel. "I insist upon it that[6] you must come too."

"I will order a new uniform, Ethel," says her uncle.

The girl laughs. "When little Egbert took hold of your sword, Uncle, and asked[7] how many people you had killed with it—Do[8] you know I had the same question in my mind? And I thought when you went to the Drawing-Room, perhaps the King will knight him. But instead he knighted Mamma's apothecary, Sir Danby Jilks,—that horrid little man: and I won't have you knighted any more."

"I hope Egbert won't ask Sir Danby Jilks, how many people *he* has killed," says the Colonel laughing. But thinking this joke too severe upon Sir Danby and the profession he forthwith apologises by narrating many anecdotes he knows to the credit of surgeons—how when the fever broke out on board their[9] ship going to India: their surgeon devoted himself to the safety of the crew; and died himself leaving directions for the treatment of the patients when he was gone: what heroism the doctors showed during the cholera in India; and what courage he had seen some of them

---

9 conversation; talking about horses *Ms*] conversation about horses, *E1*
1 in *Ms*] of *E1*
2 be, a lady whom *Ms*] be?—a person that *E1*
3 pages] ~~whole~~ pages *Ms*] whole pages *E1*
4 and got into disgrace and was wild *Ms*] and was wild, and got into disgrace *E1*
5 old: but yet *Ms*] old, yet *E1*
6 it that *Ms*] it, *E1*
7 asked *Ms*] asked you *E1*
8 killed with it—Do *Ms*] killed, do *E1*
9 their *Ms*] the *E1*

exhibit in action, attending the wounded[1] under the hottest fire, and exposing themselves as readily as the bravest troops. Ethel declares that her
uncle always will talk about[2] other people's courage, and never say a word
about his own. "And the only reason," she says, "which made me like that
odious Sir Thomas de Boots; who laughs so, and looks so red, and pays
such horrid compliments to all ladies: was that he praised you, Uncle, at
Newcome last year, when Barnes—when he came to us at Christmas. Why
did you not come? Mamma and I went to see your old nurse; and we
found her such a nice old lady." So the pair talk kindly on, riding homewards through the pleasant summer twilight. Mamma had[3] gone out to
dinner; and there were cards for three parties afterwards. "O how I wish
it was next year!" says Miss Ethel.

Many a splendid assembly, and many a brilliant next year will the ardent
and hopeful young creature enjoy: but in the midst of her splendours
and triumphs, buzzing flatterers, conquered rivals, prostrate admirers; no
doubt she will think some times of that quiet season, before the world began
for her; and that dear old friend on whose arm she leaned while she was
yet a young girl.

The Colonel comes to Park Street early in the afternoon[4] when the mistress of the house, surrounded by her little ones, is administering dinner to
them. He behaves with splendid courtesy to Miss Quigley, the governess,
and makes a point of taking wine with her, and of making a most profound
bow during that ceremony. Miss Quigley cannot help thinking Colonel
Newcome's bow very fine. She has an idea that his late Majesty must have
bowed in that way: she flutteringly imparts this opinion to Lady Ann's
maid; who tells her mistress, who tells Miss Ethel, who watches the Colonel
the next time he takes wine with Miss Quigley: and then[5] they laugh, and
then Ethel tells him; so that the gentleman and the governess have to blush
ever after when they drink wine together. When she is walking with her
little charges in the Park, (or their[6] before-mentioned reserved[7] Paradise
nigh to Apsley House) faint signals of welcome appear in[8] her wan cheeks.
She knows the dear Colonel amongst a thousand horsemen. If Ethel makes
for her uncle purses, guard-chains, antimacassars and the like beautiful
and useful articles, I believe it is in reality Miss Quigley who does four-
fifths of the work,—as she sits alone in her[9] school-room—high high up
in that lone house, when the little ones are long since asleep, before her
dismal little tea-tray, with her poor little work-baskets,[1] and her little desk,
containing her mother's letters and her mementos of home.

[1] wounded *Ms*] wounded men *E1*
[2] about *Ms*] of *E1*
[3] had *E1*] has *Ms*
[4] afternoon *Ms*] forenoon, *E1*
[5] then *Ms*] [omitted] *E1*
[6] their *Ms*] in that *E1*
[7] reserved *Ms*] [omitted] *E1*
[8] in *Ms*] on *E1*
[9] her *Ms*] the *E1*
[1] with her poor little work-baskets, *Ms*] [omitted] *E1*

There are of course numberless fine parties in Park Lane, where the Colonel knows he would be very welcome. But to these[2] grand assemblies he does not care to come. "I like to go to the club best," he says to Lady Ann. "We talk there as you do here about persons; and about Jack marrying and Tom dying and so forth. But we have known Jack and Tom all our lives and so are interested in talking about them, just as you are in speaking of your own friends and habitual society. They are people whose names I have sometimes read in the newspaper, but whom I never thought of meeting until I came to your house. What has an old fellow like me to say to your young dandies, or old dowagers?"

"Mamma is very odd, and sometimes very captious, my dear Colonel," said Lady Ann with a blush—"She suffers so frightfully from tic, that we all are[3] bound to pardon her—"

"Poor dear old lady!" cries the Colonel. "It was not what she said to me, but what she said about Clive that hurt me. I am sure I should not have replied so hastily had I known she was in pain."[4]

Truth to tell, old Lady Kew had been particularly rude to Colonel New-come and Clive; Ethel's birthday befel in the spring, on which anniversary[5] she was accustomed[6] to have a juvenile assembly; chiefly of girls of her own age and condition, who came accompanied by a few governesses; and they played and sang their little duets and choruses[7] together; and enjoyed a gentle refection of sponge-cakes, jellies, tea and the like—The Colonel, who was invited to this little party, sent a fine present to his favourite Ethel; and Clive and his friend J.J. made a funny series of drawings representing the life of a young lady, as they imagined it—and drawing her progress, from her cradle upwards; now engaged with her doll, then with her dancing-master; now marching in her back-board, now crying over her German lessons; dressed[8] for her first ball finally, and bestowing her hand upon a dandy of preternatural hideousness,[9] who was kneeling at her feet as the happy man. This picture was the delight of the laughing happy girls—except perhaps the little cousins from Brianstone Square, who were invited to Ethel's party; but were so overpowered by the prodigious new dresses in which their mamma had attired them; that they could admire nothing but their rustling pink frocks, their enormous sashes, their lovely new silk stockings.

Lady Kew coming to London attended[1] the party: and presented her granddaughter with a sixpenny pincushion. The Colonel had sent Ethel a beautiful little gold watch and chain. Her aunt had complimented her with that refreshing work, *Alison's History of Europe*, richly bound—Lady Kew's

---

2 to these *Ms*] if there be *E1*
3 all are *Ms*] are all *E1*
4 This paragraph was omitted from *E1*.
5 anniversary *Ms*] occasion *E1*
6 accustomed *Ms*] wont *E1*
7 duets and choruses *Ms*] duetts and chorusses *E1*
8 dressed *Ms*] and dressed *E1*
9 hideousness, *Ms*] ugliness, *E1*
1 attended *Ms*] attended on *E1*

pincushion made rather a poor figure among the gifts; whence probably arose her ladyship's ill humour.

Ethel's grandmother became exceedingly testy, when, the Colonel arriving, Ethel ran up to him and thanked him for the beautiful watch in return for which she gave him a kiss: which I daresay amply repaid Colonel Newcome; and shortly after him, Mr. Clive arrived, looking uncommonly handsome, with that smart little beard and mustachio, with which nature had recently gifted him. As he entered, all the girls who had been admiring his pictures began to clap their hands. Mr. Clive Newcome blushed and looked none the worse for that indication of modesty.

Lady Kew had met Colonel Newcome a half-dozen times at her daughter's house: but on this occasion she had quite forgotten him, for when the Colonel made her a bow, her ladyship regarded him steadily, and beckoning her daughter to her, asked who the gentleman was who had[2] just kissed Ethel? Trembling as she always did before her mother, Lady Ann explained. Lady Kew said "O": and left Colonel Newcome blushing and rather *embarrassé de sa personne* before her.

With the clapping of hands which[3] greeted Clive's arrival, the Countess was by no means more good-humoured—Not aware of her wrath, the young fellow who had also previously been presented to her, came forward presently to make her his compliments. "Pray, who are you?" she said looking him[4] very calmly[5] in the face—He told her his name.

"Hm," said Lady Kew. "I have heard of you and I have heard very little good of you."

"Will your ladyship please to give me[6] your informant?" cried out Colonel Newcome.[7] Barnes Newcome who had condescended to attend his sister's little fête, and had been languidly watching the frolics of the young people, looked very much alarmed.

---

[2] had *Ms NY*] has *E1 R*
[3] which *Ms*] that *E1*
[4] him *Ms*] at him *E1*
[5] calmly *Ms*] earnestly *E1*
[6] me *E1*] my *Ms*
[7] *E1* inserts paragraph break here.

Chapter XXI.

IS SENTIMENTAL BUT SHORT.

ITHOUT wishing to disparage the youth of other nations, I think a well-bred English lad has this advantage over them, that his bearing is commonly more modest than theirs. He does not assume the tailcoat and the manners of manhood too early: he holds his tongue, and listens to his elders: his mind blushes as well as his cheeks: he does not know how to make bows and pay compliments like the young Frenchman: nor to contradict his seniors as I am informed American striplings do. Boys, who learn nothing else at our public schools, learn at least good manners, or what we consider to be such—and, with regard to the person at present under consideration, it is certain that all his acquaintances, excepting perhaps his dear cousin Barnes Newcome, agreed in considering him as a very frank, manly, modest, and agreeable young fellow. My friend Warrington found a grim pleasure in his company; and his bright face, droll humour, and kindly laughter, were always welcome in our chambers. Honest Fred Bayham was charmed to be in his society; and used pathetically to aver that he himself might have been such a youth, had he been blest with a kind father to watch, and good friends to guide, his early career. In fact, Fred was by far the most didactic of Clive's bachelor acquaintances, pursued the young man with endless advice and sermons, and held himself up as a warning to Clive, and a touching example of the evil consequences of early idleness and dissipation. Gentlemen of much higher rank in the world took a fancy to the lad. Captain Jack Belsize introduced him to his own mess, as also to the Guard dinner at St. James's; and my Lord Kew invited him to Kewbury, his lordship's house in Oxfordshire, where Clive enjoyed hunting, shooting, and plenty of good company. Mrs. Newcome groaned in spirit when she heard of these proceedings; and feared, feared very much that that unfortunate young man was going to ruin; and Barnes Newcome amiably disseminated reports amongst his family that the lad was plunged in all sorts of debaucheries: that he was tipsy every night: that he was engaged, in his sober moments, with dice, the turf, or worse amusements: and that his head was so turned by living with Kew and Belsize, that the little rascal's pride and arrogance were perfectly insufferable. Ethel would indignantly deny these charges; then perhaps credit a few of them; and she looked at Clive with melancholy eyes when he came to visit his aunt; and I hope prayed that Heaven might mend his wicked ways. The truth is, the young fellow enjoyed life, as one of his age and spirit might be expected to do; but he did very little harm, and meant less; and was quite unconscious of the reputation which his kind friends were making for him.

There had been a long-standing promise that Clive and his father were to go to Newcome at Christmas: and I daresay Ethel proposed to reform the young prodigal, if prodigal he was, for she busied herself delightedly in preparing the apartments which they were to inhabit during their stay—speculated upon it in a hundred pleasant ways, putting off her visit to this pleasant neighbour, or that pretty scene in the vicinage, until her uncle should come and they should be enabled to enjoy the excursion together. And before the arrival of her relatives, Ethel, with one of her young brothers, went to see Mrs. Mason; and introduced herself as Colonel Newcome's niece; and came back charmed with the old lady, and eager once more in defence of Clive (when that young gentleman's character happened to be called in question by her brother Barnes), for had she not seen the kindest letter, which Clive had written to old Mrs. Mason, and the beautiful drawing of his father on horseback and in regimentals, waving his sword in front of the gallant —th Bengal Cavalry, which the lad had sent down to the good old woman?—He could not be very bad, Ethel thought, who was so kind and thoughtful for the poor. His father's son could not be altogether a reprobate. When Mrs. Mason seeing how good and beautiful Ethel was, and thinking in her heart, nothing could be too good or beautiful for Clive, nodded her kind old head at Miss Ethel, and said she should like to find a husband for her—Miss Ethel blushed, and looked handsomer than ever; and at home, when she was describing the interview, never mentioned this part of her talk with Mrs. Mason.

But the *enfant terrible,* young Alfred, did: announcing to all the company at dessert, that Ethel was in love with Clive—that Clive was coming to marry her—that Mrs. Mason, the old woman at Newcome, had told him so.

"I daresay she has told the tale all over Newcome!" shrieked out Mr. Barnes. "I daresay it will be in the *Independent* next week. By Jove, it's a pretty connexion—and nice acquaintances this uncle of ours brings us!" A fine battle ensued upon the receipt and discussion of this intelligence: Barnes was more than usually bitter and sarcastic: Ethel haughtily recriminated, losing her temper, and then her firmness, until, fairly bursting into tears, she taxed Barnes with meanness and malignity in for ever uttering stories to his cousin's disadvantage; and pursuing with constant slander and cruelty one of the very best of men. She rose and left the table in great tribulation—she went to her room and wrote a letter to her uncle, blistered with tears, in which she besought him not to come to Newcome.—Perhaps she went and looked at the apartments which she had adorned and prepared for his reception. It was for him and for his company that she was eager. She had met no one so generous and gentle, so honest and unselfish, until she had seen him.

Lady Ann knew the ways of women very well; and when Ethel that night, still in great indignation and scorn against Barnes, announced that she had written a letter to her uncle, begging the Colonel not to come at Christmas, Ethel's mother soothed the wounded girl, and treated her with peculiar gentleness and affection; and she wisely gave Mr. Barnes to understand, that if he wished to bring about that very attachment, the idea of which made him so angry, he could use no better means than those which he chose to employ at present, of constantly abusing and insulting poor Clive, and awakening Ethel's sympathies by mere opposition. And Ethel's sad little letter was extracted from the post-bag: and her mother brought it to her, sealed, in her own room, where the young lady burned it: being easily brought by Lady Ann's quiet remonstrances to perceive that it was best no allusion should take place to the silly dispute which had occurred that evening; and that Clive and his father should come for the Christmas holidays, if they were so minded. But when they came, there was no Ethel at Newcome. She was gone on a visit to her sick aunt, Lady Julia. Colonel Newcome passed the holidays sadly without his young favourite, and Clive consoled himself by knocking down pheasants with Sir Brian's keepers: and increased his cousin's attachment for him by breaking the knees of Barnes's favourite mare out hunting. It was a dreary entertainment; father and son were glad enough to get away from it, and to return to their[1] own humbler quarters in London.

Thomas Newcome had now been for three years in the possession of that felicity which his soul longed after; and had any friend of his asked him if he was happy, he would have answered in the affirmative no doubt, and protested that he was in the enjoyment of everything a reasonable man could desire. And yet, in spite of his happiness, his honest face grew more melancholy: his loose clothes hung only the looser on his lean limbs: he ate his meals without appetite: his nights were restless: and he would sit for hours silent in the midst of his family, so that Mr. Binnie first began jocularly to surmise that Tom was crossed in love; then seriously to think that his health was suffering and that a doctor should be called to see him; and at last to agree that idleness was not good for the Colonel, and that he missed the military occupation to which he had been for so many years accustomed.

The Colonel insisted that he was perfectly happy and contented. What could he want more than he had—the society of his son, for the present; and a prospect of quiet for his declining days? Binnie vowed that his friend's days had no business to decline as yet; that a sober man of fifty ought to be at his best; and that Newcome had grown older in three years in Europe, than in a quarter of a century in the East—all which statements were true, though the Colonel persisted in denying them.

He was very restless. He was always finding business in distant quarters of England. He must go visit Tom Barker who was settled in Devonshire, or Harry Johnson who had retired and was living in Wales. He surprised

---

[1] their *E1*] his *R*

Mrs. Honeyman by the frequency of his visits to Brighton, and always came away much improved in health by the sea air, and by constant riding with the harriers there. He appeared at Bath and at Cheltenham, where, as we know, there are many old Indians. Mr. Binnie was not indisposed to accompany him on some of these jaunts—'provided,' the Civilian said, 'you don't take young Hopeful, who is much better without us; and let us two old fogies enjoy ourselves together.'

Clive was not sorry to be left alone. The father knew that only too well. The young man had occupations, ideas, associates, in whom the elder could take no interest. Sitting below in his blank, cheerless bed-room, Newcome could hear the lad and his friends talking, singing, and making merry, overhead. Something would be said in Clive's well-known tones, and a roar of laughter would proceed from the youthful company. They had all sorts of tricks, bye-words, waggeries, of which the father could not understand the jest nor the secret. He longed to share in it, but the party would be hushed if he went in to join it—and he would come away sad at heart, to think that his presence should be a signal for silence among them; and that his son could not be merry in his company.

We must not quarrel with Clive and Clive's friends, because they could not joke and be free in the presence of the worthy gentleman. If they hushed when he came in, Thomas Newcome's sad face would seem to look round—appealing to one after another of them, and asking, "why don't you go on laughing?" A company of old comrades shall be merry and laughing together, and the entrance of a single youngster will stop the conversation—and if men of middle age feel this restraint with our juniors, the young ones surely have a right to be silent before their elders. The boys are always mum under the eyes of the usher. There is scarce any parent, however friendly or tender with his children, but must feel sometimes that they have thoughts which are not his or hers; and wishes and secrets quite beyond the parental control: and, as people are vain, long after they are fathers, aye, or grandfathers, and not seldom fancy that mere personal desire of domination is overweening anxiety and love for their family; no doubt that common outcry against thankless children might often be shown to prove, not that the son is disobedient, but the father too exacting. When a mother (as fond mothers often will) vows that she knows every thought in her daughter's heart, I think she pretends to know a great deal too much;—nor can there be a wholesomer task for the elders, as our young subjects grow up, naturally demanding liberty and citizen's rights, than for us gracefully to abdicate our sovereign pretensions and claims of absolute control. There's many a family chief who governs wisely and gently, who is loth to give the power up when he should. Ah, be sure, it is not youth alone that has need to learn humility! By their very virtues, and the purity of their lives, many good parents create flatterers for themselves, and so live in the midst of a filial court of parasites—and seldom without a pang of unwillingness, and often not at all, will they consent to forego their autocracy, and exchange the tribute they have been wont to exact of love and obedience for the willing offering of love and freedom.

Our good Colonel was not of the tyrannous, but of the loving order of fathers: and having fixed his whole heart upon this darling youth, his son, was punished, as I suppose such worldly and selfish love ought to be punished (so Mr. Honeyman says, at least, in his pulpit), by a hundred little mortifications, disappointments, and secret wounds, which stung not the less severely, though never mentioned by their victim.

Sometimes he would have a company of such gentlemen as Messrs. Warrington, Honeyman, and Pendennis, when haply a literary conversation would ensue after dinner; and the merits of our present poets and writers would be discussed with the claret. Honeyman was well enough read in profane literature, especially of the lighter sort; and, I daresay, could have passed a satisfactory examination in Balzac, Dumas, and Paul de Kock himself, of all whose works our good host was entirely ignorant,—as indeed he was of graver books, and of earlier books, and of books in general—except those few which we have said formed his travelling library. He heard opinions that amazed and bewildered him. He heard that Byron was no great poet, though a very clever man. He heard that there had been a wicked persecution against Mr. Pope's memory and fame, and that it was time to reinstate him: that his favourite, Dr. Johnson, talked admirably, but did not write English: that young Keats was a genius to be estimated in future days with young Raphael: and that a young gentleman of Cambridge who had lately published two volumes of verses, might take rank with the greatest poets of all. Doctor Johnson not write English! Lord Byron not one of the greatest poets of the world! Sir Walter a poet of the second order! Mr. Pope attacked for inferiority and want of imagination; Mr. Keats and this young Mr. Tennyson of Cambridge, the chief of modern poetic literature! What were these new dicta, which Mr. Warrington delivered with a puff of tobacco-smoke: to which Mr. Honeyman blandly assented and Clive listened with pleasure? Such opinions were not of the Colonel's time. He tried in vain to construe Œnone; and to make sense of Lamia. Ulysses he could understand; but what were these prodigious laudations bestowed on it? And that reverence for Mr. Wordsworth, what did it mean? Had he not written Peter Bell, and been turned into deserved ridicule by all the reviews? Was that dreary Excursion to be compared to Goldsmith's Traveller, or Doctor Johnson's Imitation of the Tenth Satire of Juvenal? If the young men told the truth, where had been the truth in his own young days; and in what ignorance had our forefathers been brought up?—Mr. Addison was only an elegant essayist, and shallow trifler! All these opinions were openly uttered over the Colonel's claret: as he and Mr. Binnie sate wondering at the speakers, who were knocking the Gods of their youth about their ears. To Binnie the shock was not so great; the hard-headed Scotchman had read Hume in his college days, and sneered at some of the Gods even at that early time. But with Newcome the admiration for the literature of the last century was an article of belief: and the incredulity of the young men seemed rank blasphemy. "You will be sneering at Shakspeare next," he said: and was silenced, though not better pleased, when his youthful guests told him, that Doctor Goldsmith sneered at him too; that Dr. Johnson did not understand him, and that Congreve, in his own day and afterwards, was considered to be, in some points, Shakspeare's superior. "What do you think a man's criticism is worth, Sir," cries Mr. Warrington, "who says those lines of Mr. Congreve, about a church?—

> 'How reverend is the face of yon tall pile,
> Whose ancient pillars rear their marble heads,
> To bear aloft its vast and ponderous roof,
> By its own weight made stedfast and immovable;
> Looking tranquillity. It strikes an awe
> And terror on my aching sight'—et cætera—

what do you think of a critic who says those lines are finer than anything Shakspeare ever wrote?" A dim consciousness of danger for Clive, a terror that his son had got into the society of heretics and unbelievers, came over the Colonel—and then presently, as was the wont with his modest soul, a gentle sense of humility. He was in the wrong, perhaps, and these younger men were right. Who was he, to set up his judgment against men of letters, educated at College? It was better that Clive should follow them than him, who had had but a brief schooling, and that neglected, and who had not the original genius of his son's brilliant companions. We particularise these talks, and the little incidental mortifications which one of the best of men endured, not because the conversations are worth the remembering or recording, but because they presently very materially influenced his own and his son's future history.

In the midst of the artists and their talk the poor Colonel was equally in the dark. They assaulted this academician and that; laughed at Mr. Haydon, or sneered at Mr. Eastlake, or the contrary—deified Mr. Turner on one side of the table, and on the other scorned him as a madman—nor could Newcome comprehend a word of their jargon. Some sense there must be in their conversation: Clive joined eagerly in it and took one side or another. But what was all this rapture about a snuffy brown picture called Titian, this delight in three flabby nymphs by Rubens, and so forth? As for the vaunted Antique, and the Elgin marbles—it might be that that battered torso was a miracle, and that broken-nosed bust a perfect beauty. He tried and tried to see that they were. He went away privily and worked at the National Gallery with a catalogue: and passed hours in the Museum before the ancient statues desperately praying to comprehend them, and puzzled before them as he remembered he was puzzled before the Greek rudiments as a child when he cried over ὁ καὶ ἡ ἀληθης καὶ το ἀληθες. Whereas when Clive came to look at these same things his eyes would lighten up with pleasure, and his cheeks flush with enthusiasm. He seemed to drink in colour as he would a feast of wine. Before the statues he would wave his finger, following the line of grace, and burst into ejaculations of delight and admiration. "Why can't I love the things which he loves?" thought Newcome; "why am I blind to the beauties which he admires so much—and am I unable to comprehend what he evidently understands at his young age?"

So, as he thought what vain egotistical hopes he used to form about the boy when he was away in India—how in his plans for the happy future, Clive was to be always at his side; how they were to read, work, play, think, be merry together—a sickening and humiliating sense of the reality came over him: and he sadly contrasted it with the former fond anticipations.

A STUDENT OF THE OLD MASTERS

Together they were, yet he was alone still. His thoughts were not the boy's: and his affections rewarded but with a part of the young man's heart. Very likely other lovers have suffered equally. Many a man and woman has been incensed and worshipped, and has shown no more feeling than is to be expected from idols. There is yonder statue in St. Peter's, of which the toe is worn away with kisses, and which sits, and will sit eternally, prim and cold. As the young man grew, it seemed to the father, as if each day separated them more and more. He himself became more melancholy and silent. His friend the Civilian marked the ennui, and commented on it in his laughing way. Sometimes he announced to the club, that Tom Newcome was in love: then he thought it was not Tom's heart but his liver that was affected, and recommended blue-pill. O thou fond fool! who art thou, to know any man's heart save thine alone? Wherefore were wings made, and do feathers grow, but that birds should fly? The instinct that bids you love your nest, leads the young ones to seek a tree and a mate of their own. As if Thomas Newcome by poring over poems or pictures ever so much could read them with Clive's eyes!—as if by sitting mum over his wine, but watching till the lad came home with his latch-key (when the Colonel crept back to his own room in his stockings), by prodigal bounties, by stealthy affection, by any schemes or prayers, he could hope to remain first in his son's heart!

One day going into Clive's study, where the lad was so deeply engaged that he did not hear the father's steps advancing, Thomas Newcome found his son, pencil in hand, poring over a paper, which blushing he thrust hastily into his breast-pocket, as soon as he saw his visitor. The father was deeply smitten and mortified. "I—I am sorry you have any secrets from me, Clive," he gasped out at length.

The boy's face lighted up with humour. "Here it is, Father, if you would like to see:"—and he pulled out a paper which contained neither more nor less than a copy of very flowery verses, about a certain young lady, who had succeeded (after I know not how many predecessors), to the place of *prima-donna assoluta* in Clive's heart. And be pleased, Madam, not to be too eager with your censure—and fancy that Mr. Clive or his Chronicler would insinuate any thing wrong. I daresay you felt a flame or two before you were married yourself: and that the Captain or the Curate, and the interesting young foreigner with whom you danced, caused your heart to beat, before you bestowed that treasure on Mr. Candour. Clive was doing no more than your own son will do when he is eighteen or nineteen years old himself—if he is a lad of any spirit and a worthy son of so charming a lady as yourself.

Chapter XXII.

R. CLIVE, as we have said, had now begun to make acquaintances of his own; and the chimney-glass in his study was decorated with such a number of cards of invitation, as made his ex-fellow student of Gandish's, young Moss, when admitted into that sanctum, stare with respectful astonishment. "Lady Bary Rowe at obe," the young Hebrew read out; "Lady Baughton at obe, dadsig! By eyes! what a tip-top swell you're a gettid to be, Newcome! I guess this is a different sort of business to the hops at old Levison's, where you first learned the polka; and where we had to pay a shilling a glass for negus!"

"*We* had to pay! *You* never paid anything, Moss," cries Clive, laughing; and indeed the negus imbibed by Mr. Moss did not cost that prudent young fellow a penny.

"Well, well; I suppose at these swell parties you ave as buch champade as ever you like," continues Moss. "Lady Kicklebury at obe—small early party. Why I declare you know the whole peerage! I say, if any of these swells want a little tip-top lace, a real bargain, or diamonds, you know, you might put in a word for us, and do us a good turn."

"Give me some of your cards," says Clive; "I can distribute them about at the balls I go to. But you must treat my friends better than you serve me. Those cigars which you sent me were abominable, Moss; the groom in the stable won't smoke them."

"What a regular swell that Newcome has become!" says Mr. Moss to an old companion, another of Clive's fellow-students: "I saw him riding in the Park with the Earl of Kew, and Captain Belsize, and a whole lot of 'em—*I* know 'em all—and he'd hardly nod to me. I'll have a horse next Sunday, and *then* I'll see whether he'll cut me or not. Confound his airs! For all he's such a count, I know he's got an aunt who lets lodgings at Brighton, and an uncle who'll be preaching in the Bench if he don't keep a precious good look-out."

"Newcome is not a bit of a count," answers Moss's companion,

indignantly. "He don't care a straw whether a fellow's poor or rich; and he comes up to my room just as willingly as he would go to a duke's. He is always trying to do a friend a good turn. He draws the figure capitally: he *looks* proud, but he isn't, and is the best-natured fellow I ever saw."

"He ain't been in our place this eighteen months," says Mr. Moss: "I know that."

"Because when he came, you were always screwing him with some bargain or other," cried the intrepid Hicks, Mr. Moss's companion for the moment. "He said he couldn't afford to know you: you never let him out of your house without a pin, or a box of Eau de Cologne, or a bundle of cigars. And when you cut the arts for the shop, how were you and Newcome to go on together, I should like to know?"

"I know a relative of his who comes to our 'ouse every three months, to renew a little bill," says Mr. Moss, with a grin: "and I know this, if I go to the Earl of Kew in the Albany, or the Honourable Captain Belsize, Knightsbridge Barracks, *they* let me in soon enough. I'm told his father ain't got much money."

"How the deuce should I know? or what do I care?" cries the young artist, stamping the heel of his blucher on the pavement. "When I was sick in that confounded Clipstone Street, I know the Colonel came to see me, and Newcome too, day after day, and night after night. And when I was getting well, they sent me wine and jelly, and all sorts of jolly things. I should like to know how often *you* came to see me, Moss, and what you did for a fellow?"

"Well, I kep away, because I thought you wouldn't like to be reminded of that two pound three you owe me, Hicks: that's why I kep away," says Mr. Moss, who, I daresay, was good-natured too. And when young Moss appeared at the billiard-room that night, it was evident that Hicks had told the story; for the Wardour Street youth was saluted with a roar of queries, "How about that two pound three that Hicks owes you?"

The artless conversation of the two youths will enable us to understand how our hero's life was speeding. Connected in one way or another with persons in all ranks, it never entered his head to be ashamed of the profession which he had chosen. People in the great world did not in the least trouble themselves regarding him, or care to know whether Mr. Clive Newcome followed painting or any other pursuit: and though Clive saw many of his schoolfellows in the world, these entering into the army, others talking with delight of college, and its pleasures or studies; yet, having made up his mind that art was his calling, he refused to quit her for any other mistress, and plied his easel very stoutly. He passed through the course of study prescribed by Mr. Gandish, and drew every cast and statue in that gentleman's studio. Grindly, his tutor, getting a curacy,

Clive[1] did not replace him; but he took a course of modern languages, which he learned with considerable aptitude and rapidity. And now, being strong enough to paint without a master, it was found that there was no good light in the house in Fitzroy Square; and Mr. Clive must needs

[1] The illustration, which seems more appropriate at this point, appeared in next paragraph after "He spoke about".

have an atelier hard by, where he could pursue his own devices independently.

If his kind father felt any pang even at this temporary parting, he was greatly soothed and pleased by a little mark of attention on the young man's part, of which his present biographer happened to be a witness; for having walked over with Colonel Newcome to see the new studio, with its tall centre window, and its curtains, and carved wardrobes, china jars, pieces of armour, and other artistical properties, the lad, with a very sweet smile of kindness and affection lighting up his honest face, took one of two Bramah's house-keys with which he was provided, and gave it to his father: "That's *your* key, Sir," he said to the Colonel; "and you must be my first sitter, please, Father; for though I'm a historical painter, I shall condescend to do a few portraits, you know." The Colonel took his son's hand, and grasped it; as Clive fondly put the other hand on his father's shoulder. Then Colonel Newcome walked away into the next room for a minute or two, and came back wiping his moustache with his handkerchief, and still holding the key in the other hand. He spoke about some trivial subject when he returned; but his voice quite trembled; and I thought his face seemed to glow with love and pleasure. Clive has never painted anything better than that head, which he executed in a couple of sittings; and wisely left without subjecting it to the chances of farther labour.

It is certain the young man worked much better after he had been inducted into this apartment of his own. And the meals at home were gayer; and the rides with his father more frequent and agreeable. The Colonel used his key once or twice, and found Clive and his friend Ridley engaged in depicting a life-guardsman,—or a muscular negro,—or a Malay from a neighbouring crossing, who would appear as Othello, conversing with a Clipstone Street nymph, who was ready to represent Desdemona, Diana, Queen Ellinor (sucking poison from the arm of the Plantagenet of the Blues), or any other model of virgin or maiden excellence.

Of course our young man commenced as a historical painter, deeming that the highest branch of art; and declining (except for preparatory studies) to operate on any but the largest canvases. He painted a prodigious battle-piece of Assaye, with General Wellesley at the head of the 19th Dragoons charging the Mahratta Artillery, and sabring them at their guns. A piece of ordnance was dragged into the back-yard, and the Colonel's stud put into requisition to supply studies for this enormous picture. Fred Bayham (a stunning likeness) appeared as the principal figure in the foreground, terrifically wounded, but still of undaunted courage, slashing about amidst a group of writhing Malays, and bestriding the body of a dead cab-horse, which Clive painted, until the landlady and rest of the lodgers cried out, and for sanitary reasons the knackers removed the slaughtered charger. So large was this picture that it could only be got out of the great window by means of artifice and coaxing; and its transport caused a shout of triumph among the little boys in Charlotte Street. Will it be believed that the Royal Academicians rejected the Battle of Assaye? The master-piece was so big that Fitzroy Square could not hold it; and the

Colonel had thoughts of presenting it to the Oriental Club; but Clive (who had taken a trip to Paris with his father, as a *délassement* after the fatigues incident on his great work), when he saw it, after a month's interval, declared the thing was rubbish, and massacred Britons, Malays, Dragoons, Artillery and all.

"HOTEL DE LA TERRASSE, RUE DE RIVOLI.
"April 27—*May* 1, 183—

"MY DEAR PENDENNIS,—You said I might write you a line from Paris; and if you find in my correspondence any valuable hints for the *Pall-Mall Gazette* you are welcome to use them gratis. Now I am here, I wonder I have never been here before; and that I have seen the Dieppe packet a thousand times at Brighton pier without thinking of going on board her. We had a rough little passage to Boulogne. We went into action as we cleared Dover pier; when the *first gun* was fired, and a stout old lady was carried off by a steward to the cabin; half a dozen more dropped immediately, and the crew bustled about, bringing basins for the wounded. The Colonel smiled as he saw them fall. 'I'm an old sailor,' says he to a gentleman on board. 'As I was coming home, Sir, and we had plenty of rough weather on the voyage, I never thought of being unwell. My boy here, who made the voyage twelve years ago last May, may have lost his sea-legs; but for me, Sir ——' Here a great wave dashed over the three of us; and would you believe it? in five minutes after, the dear old Governor was as ill as all the rest of the passengers. When we arrived, we went through a line of ropes to the custom-house, with a crowd of snobs jeering at us on each side; and then were carried off by a bawling commissioner to an hotel, where the Colonel, who speaks French beautifully, you know, told the waiter to get us a *petit déjeuner soigné*; on which the fellow, grinning, said, 'a nice fried sole, Sir,—nice mutton chop, Sir,' in regular Temple-bar English; and brought us Harvey sauce with the chops, and the last *Bell's Life* to amuse us after our luncheon. I wondered if all the Frenchmen read *Bell's Life,* and if all the inns smell so of brandy-and-water.

"We walked out to see the town, which I daresay you know, and therefore shan't describe. We saw some good studies of fishwomen with bare legs; and remarked that the soldiers were very dumpy and small. We were glad when the time came to set off by the diligence; and having the *coupé* to ourselves, made a very comfortable journey to Paris. It was jolly to hear the postillions crying to their horses, and the bells of the team, and to feel ourselves really in France. We took in provender at Abbeville and Amiens, and were comfortably landed here after about six-and-twenty hours of coaching. Didn't I get up the next morning and have a good walk in the Tuileries? The chestnuts were out, and the statues all shining; and all the windows of the palace in a blaze. It looks big enough for the king of the giants to live in. How grand it is! I like the barbarous splendour of the architecture, and the ornaments profuse and enormous with which it is overladen. Think of Louis XVI. with a thousand gentlemen at his back, and a mob of yelling ruffians in front of him, giving up his crown without a fight for it; leaving his friends to be butchered, and himself sneaking into prison! No end of little children were skipping and playing in the sunshiny walks, with dresses as bright and cheeks as red as the flowers and roses in the parterres. I couldn't help thinking of Barbaroux and his bloody pikemen swarming in the gardens, and fancied the Swiss in the windows yonder; where they were to be slaughtered when the King had turned his back. What a great man that Carlyle is! I have read the battle in his 'History' so often, that I knew it before I had seen it. Our windows look out on the obelisk where the guillotine stood. The Colonel doesn't admire Carlyle. He says Mrs. Graham's 'Letters from Paris' are excellent, and we bought 'Scott's Visit to Paris,' and 'Paris Re-visited,' and read them in the diligence. They are famous good reading; but the Palais Royal is very much altered since Scott's time: no end of handsome shops; I went there directly,—the same night we arrived, when the Colonel went to bed. But there is none of the fun going on which Scott describes. The *laquais de place* says Charles X. put an end to it all.

"Next morning the governor had letters to deliver after breakfast; and left me at the Louvre door. I shall come and live here I think. I feel as if I never want to go away. I had not been ten minutes in the place before I fell in love with the most beautiful creature the world has ever seen. She was standing silent and majestic in the centre of one of the rooms of the statue gallery; and the very first glimpse of her struck one breathless with the sense of her beauty. I could not see the colour of her eyes and hair exactly, but the latter is light, and the eyes I should think are grey. Her complexion is of a beautiful warm marble tinge. She is not a clever woman, evidently; I do not think she laughs or talks much—she seems too lazy to do more than smile. She is only beautiful. This divine creature has lost her arms, which have been cut off at the shoulders,[2] but she looks none the less lovely for the accident. She may be some two-and-thirty years old; and she was born about two thousand years ago. Her name is the Venus of Milo. O, Victrix! O, lucky Paris! (I don't mean this present Lutetia, but Priam's son.) How could he give the apple to any else but this enslaver,— this joy of gods and men? at whose benign presence the flowers spring up, and the smiling ocean sparkles, and the soft skies beam with serene light! I wish we might sacrifice. I would bring a spotless kid, snowy-coated, and a pair of doves, and a jar of honey—yea, honey from Morel's in Piccadilly, thyme-flavoured, narbonian, and we would acknowledge the Sovereign Loveliness, and adjure the Divine Aphrodite. Did you ever see my pretty young cousin, Miss Newcome, Sir Brian's daughter? She has a great look of the huntress Diana. It is sometimes too proud and too cold for me. The blare of those horns is too shrill, and the rapid pursuit through bush and bramble too daring. O, thou generous Venus! O, thou beautiful bountiful calm! At thy soft feet let me kneel—on cushions of Tyrian purple. Don't show this to Warrington, please: I never thought when I began that Pegasus was going to run away with me.

"I wish I had read Greek a little more at school: it's too late at my age; I

---

[2] lost her arms, which have been cut off at the shoulders, *R*] lost an arm which has been cut off at the shoulder, *E1*

shall be nineteen soon, and have got my own business; but when we return
I think I shall try and read it with Cribs. What have I been doing, spending six months over a picture of Sepoys and Dragoons cutting each other's
throats? Art ought not to be a fever. It ought to be a calm; not a screaming
bull-fight or a battle of gladiators, but a temple for placid contemplation,
rapt[3] worship, stately rhythmic ceremony, and music solemn and tender.
I shall take down my Snyders' and Rubens' when I get home; and turn
quietist. To think I have spent weeks in depicting bony Life Guardsmen
delivering cut one, or Saint George, and painting black beggars off a crossing!

"What a grand thing it is to think of half a mile of pictures at the Louvre! Not but that there are a score under the old pepper-boxes in Trafalgar
Square as fine as the best here. I don't care for any Raphael here, as much
as our own St. Catharine. There is nothing more grand. Could the pyra-
mids of Egypt or the Colossus of Rhodes be greater than our Sebastian;
and for our Bacchus and Ariadne, you cannot beat the best you know. But
if we have fine jewels, here there are whole sets of them: there are kings
and all their splendid courts round about them. J.J. and I must come and
live here. O, such portraits of Titian! O such swells by Vandyke! I'm sure
he must have been as fine a gentleman as any he painted! It's a shame
they haven't got a Sir Joshua or two. At a feast of painters he has a right
to a place, and at the high table too. Do you remember Tom Rogers, of
Gandish's? He used to come to my rooms—my other rooms in the Square.
Tom is here with a fine carotty beard, and a velvet jacket, cut open at the
sleeves, to show that Tom has a shirt. I daresay it was clean last Sunday. He
has not learned French yet, but pretends to have forgotten English; and
promises to introduce me to a set of the French artists his *camarades*. There
seems to be a scarcity of soap among these young fellows; and I think I shall
cut off my mustachios; only Warrington will have nothing to laugh at when
I come home.

"The Colonel and I went to dine at the Café de Paris, and afterwards to
the opera. Ask for *huitres de Marenne* when you dine here. We dined with
a tremendous French swell, the Vicomte de Florac, *officier d'ordonnance* to
one of the princes, and son of some old friends of my father's. They are
of very high birth, but very poor. He will be a duke when his cousin, the
Duc d'Ivry, dies. His father is quite old. The vicomte was born in England. He pointed out to us no end of famous people at the opera—a few of
the Fauxbourg St. Germain, and ever so many of the present people:—M.
Thiers, and Count Molé, and Georges Sand, and Victor Hugo, and Jules
Janin—I forget half their names. And yesterday we went to see his mother,
Madame de Florac. I suppose she was an old flame of the Colonel's, for
their meeting was uncommonly ceremonious and tender. It was like an elderly Sir Charles Grandison saluting a middle-aged Miss Byron. And only
fancy! the Colonel has been here once before since his return to England!
It must have been last year, when he was away for ten days, whilst I was
painting that rubbishing picture of the Black Prince waiting on King John.

[3] rapt *R*] wrapt *E1*

Madame de F. is a very grand lady, and must have been a great beauty in her time. There are two pictures by Gerard in her salon—of her and M. de Florac. M. de Florac, old swell, powder, thick eyebrows, hooked nose; no end of stars, ribbons, and embroidery. Madame also in the dress of the Empire—pensive, beautiful, black velvet, and a look something like my cousin's. She wore a little old-fashioned brooch yesterday, and said, '*Voila, la reconnoissez-vous?* Last year when you were here, it was in the country;' and she smiled at him: and the dear old boy gave a sort of groan and dropped his head in his hand. I know what it is. I've gone through it myself. I kept for six months an absurd ribbon of that infernal little flirt Fanny Freeman. Don't you remember how angry I was when you abused her?

" 'Your father and I knew each other when we were children, my friend,' the Countess said to me (in the sweetest French accent). He was looking into the garden of the house where they live, in the Rue Saint Dominique. 'You must come and see me often, always. You remind me of him,' and, she added, with a very sweet kind smile, 'Do you like best to think that he was better-looking than you, or that you excel him?' I said I should like to be like him. But who is? There are cleverer fellows, I daresay; but where is there such a good one? I wonder whether he was very fond of Madame de Florac? The old Count doesn't show. He is quite old, and wears a pigtail. We saw it bobbing over his garden chair. He lets the upper part of his house; Major-General the Honourable Zeno F. Pokey, of Cincinnati, U.S., lives in it. We saw Mrs. Pokey's carriage in the court, and her footmen smoking cigars there; a tottering old man with feeble legs, as old as old Count de Florac, seemed to be the only domestic who waited on the family below.

"Madame de Florac and my father talked about my profession. The Countess said it was a *belle carrière.* The Colonel said it was better than the army. '*Ah oui, Monsieur,*' says she very sadly. And then he said, 'that presently I should very likely come to study at Paris, when he knew there would be a kind friend to watch over *son garçon.*'

" 'But you will be here to watch over him yourself, *mon ami?*' says the French lady.

"Father shook his head. 'I shall very probably have to go back to India,' he said. 'My furlough is expired. I am now taking my extra leave. If I can get my promotion, I need not return. Without that I cannot afford to live in Europe. But my absence in all probability will be but very short,' he said. 'And Clive is old enough now to go on without me.'

"Is this the reason why Father has been so gloomy for some months past? I thought it might have been some of my follies which made him uncomfortable; and you know I have been trying my best to amend—I have not half such a tailor's bill this year as last. I owe scarcely anything. I have paid off Moss every halfpenny for his confounded rings and gimcracks. I asked Father about this melancholy news as we walked away from Madame de Florac.

"He is not near so rich as we thought. Since he has been at home he says he has spent greatly more than his income, and is quite angry at his own extravagance. At first he thought he might have retired from the army altogether; but after three years at home, he finds he cannot live upon his income. When he gets his promotion as full Colonel, he will be entitled to a thousand a year; that, and what he has invested in India, and a little in this country, will be plenty for both of us. He never seems to think of my making money by my profession. Why, suppose I sell the Battle of Assaye for £500? that will be enough to carry me on ever so long, without dipping into the purse of the dear old father.

"The Viscount de Florac called to dine with us. The Colonel said he did not care about going out: and so the Viscount and I went together. *Trois Frères Provençaux*—he ordered the dinner and of course I paid. Then we went to a little theatre, and he took me behind the scenes—such a queer place! We went to the *loge* of Mademoiselle Finette, who acted the part of 'Le petit Tambour,' in which she sings a famous song with a drum. He asked her and several literary fellows to supper at the Café Anglais. And I came home ever so late, and lost twenty Napoleons at a game called Bouillotte. It was all the change out of a twenty pound note which dear old Binnie gave me before we set out with a quotation out of Horace you know, about *Neque tu choreas sperne puer.* Oh me! how guilty I felt as I walked home at ever so much o'clock to the Hôtel de la Terrasse, and sneaked into our apartment! But the Colonel was sound asleep. His dear old boots stood sentries at his bed-room door, and I slunk into mine as silently as I could.

"PS. Wednesday. There's just one scrap of paper left. I have got J.J.'s letter. He has been to the private view of the Academy (so that his own picture is in), and the 'Battle of Assaye' is refused. Smee told him it was too big. I daresay it's very bad. I'm glad I'm away, and the fellows are not condoling with me.

"Please go and see Mr. Binnie. He has come to grief. He rode the Colonel's horse; came down on the pavement and wrenched his leg, and I'm afraid the grey's. Please look at his legs; we can't understand John's report of them. He, I mean Mr. B., was going to Scotland to see his relations when the accident happened. You know he has always been going to Scotland to see his relations. He makes light of the business, and says the Colonel is not to think of coming to him: and *I* don't want to go back just yet, to see all the fellows from Gandish's, and the Life Academy, and have them grinning at my misfortune.

"The governor would send his regards I daresay, but he is out, and I am always yours affectionately,

"CLIVE NEWCOME.

"PS. He tipped me himself this morning; isn't he a kind dear old fellow?"

ARTHUR PENDENNIS, ESQ., TO CLIVE NEWCOME, ESQ.

"PALL MALL GAZETTE, JOURNAL OF POLITICS, LITERATURE, AND FASHION.
"225, CATHERINE STREET, STRAND.

"DEAR CLIVE,—I regret very much for Fred Bayham's sake (who has lately taken the responsible office of Fine Arts Critic for the P. G.) that your extensive picture of the 'Battle of Assaye' has not found a place in the Royal Academy Exhibition. F.B. is at least fifteen shillings out of pocket by its rejection, as he had prepared a flaming eulogium of your work, which of course is so much waste paper in consequence of this calamity. Never mind. Courage, my son. The Duke of Wellington you know was beat back at Seringapatam before he succeeded at Assaye. I hope you will fight other battles, and that fortune in future years will be more favourable to you. The town does not talk very much of your discomfiture. You see the parliamentary debates are very interesting just now, and somehow the 'Battle of Assaye' does not seem to excite the public mind.

"I have been to Fitzroy Square; both to the stables and the house. The Houyhnhm's legs are very well; the horse slipped on his side and not on his knees, and has received no sort of injury. Not so Mr. Binnie, his ancle is much wrenched and inflamed. He must keep his sofa for many days, perhaps weeks. But you know he is a very cheerful philosopher, and endures the evils of life with much equanimity. His sister has come to him. I don't know whether that may be considered as a consolation of his evil or an aggravation of it. You know he uses the sarcastic method in his talk, and it was difficult to understand from him whether he was pleased or bored by the embraces of his relative. She was an infant when he last beheld her, on his departure to India. She is now (to speak with respect) a very brisk, plump, pretty little widow; having, seemingly, recovered from her grief at the death of her husband, Captain Mackenzie, in the West Indies. Mr. Binnie was just on the point of visiting his relatives who reside at Musselburgh, near Edinburgh, when he met with the fatal accident which prevented his visit to his native shores. His account of his misfortune and his lonely condition was so pathetic that Mrs. Mackenzie and her daughter put themselves into the Edinburgh steamer, and rushed to console his sofa. They occupy your bed-room and sitting-room, which latter Mrs. Mackenzie says no longer smells of tobacco smoke, as it did when she took possession of your den. If you have left any papers about, any bills, any billets-doux, I make no doubt the ladies have read every single one of them, according to the amiable habits of their sex. The daughter is a bright little blue-eyed fair-haired lass, with a very sweet voice, in which she sings (unaided by instrumental music, and seated on a chair in the middle of the room) the artless ballads of her native country. I had the pleasure of hearing the 'Bonnets of Bonny Dundee,' and 'Jock of Hazeldean,' from her ruby lips two evenings since; not indeed for the first time in my life, but never from such a pretty little singer. Though both ladies speak our language with something of the tone usually employed by the inhabitants of the northern part of Britain, their accent is exceedingly pleasant, and indeed by no means so strong as Mr. Binnie's own; for Captain Mackenzie was an Englishman for whose sake his lady modified her native Musselburgh pronunciation. She tells many interesting anecdotes of him, of the West Indies, and of the distinguished regiment of Infantry to which the captain belonged. Miss Rosa is a great favourite with her uncle, and I have had the good fortune to make their stay in the metropolis more pleasant, by sending them orders, from the *Pall Mall Gazette,* for the theatres, panoramas, and the principal sights in town. For pictures they do not seem to care much; they thought the National Gallery a dreary exhibition, and in the Royal Academy could be got to admire nothing but the picture of M'Collop of M'Collop, by our friend of the like name, but they think Madame Tussaud's interesting exhibition of Waxwork the most delightful in London; and there I had the happiness of introducing them to our friend Mr. Frederick Bayham; who, subsequently, on coming to this office with his valuable contributions on the Fine Arts, made particular enquiries as to their pecuniary means, and expressed himself instantly ready to bestow his hand upon the mother or daughter, provided old Mr. Binnie would make a satisfactory settlement. I got the ladies a box at the opera, whither they were attended by Captain Goby of their regiment, god-father to Miss, and where I had the honour of paying them a visit. I saw your fair young cousin Miss Newcome in the lobby with her grandmamma Lady Kew. Mr. Bayham with great eloquence pointed out to the Scotch ladies the various distinguished characters in the house. The opera delighted them, but they were astounded at the ballet, from which mother and daughter retreated in the midst of a fire of pleasantries of Captain Goby. I can fancy that officer at mess, and how brilliant his anecdotes must be[4] when the company of ladies does not restrain his genial flow of humour.

"Here comes Mr. Baker with the proofs. In case you don't see the P. G. at Galignani's, I send you an extract from Bayham's article on the Royal Academy, where you will have the benefit of his opinion on the works of some of your friends:—

" '617. "Moses Bringing Home the Gross of Green Spectacles." Smith, R.A.—Perhaps poor Goldsmith's exquisite little work has never been so great a favourite as in the present age. We have here, in a work by one of our most eminent artists, an homage to the genius of him "who touched nothing which he did not adorn:" and the charming subject is handled in the most delicious manner by Mr. Smith. The chiaroscuro is admirable: the impasto is perfect. Perhaps a *very* captious critic might object to the foreshortening of Moses's left leg; but where there is so much to praise justly, the *Pall-Mall Gazette* does not care to condemn.

" '420. Our (and the public's) favourite, Brown, R.A., treats us to a subject from the best of all stories, the tale "which laughed Spain's chivalry away," the ever new Don Quixote. The incident which Brown has selected is the "Don's Attack on the Flock of Sheep;" the sheep are in his best manner, painted with all his well-known facility and *brio*. Mr. Brown's friendly rival, Hopkins, has selected Gil Blas for an illustration this year; and the "Robber's Cavern" is one of the most masterly of Hopkins's productions.

" 'Great Rooms. 33. "Portrait of Cardinal Cospetto." O'Gogstay, A.R.A.; and "Neighbourhood of Corpodibacco—Evening—a Contadina and a Trasteverino dancing at the door of a Locanda to the music of a Pifferaro."— Since his visit to Italy Mr. O'Gogstay seems to have given up the scenes of Irish humour with which he used to delight us; and the romance, the poetry, the religion of "Italia la bella" form the subjects of his pencil. The

[4] be *E1*] have been *R*

scene near Corpodibacco (we know the spot well, and have spent many a happy month in its romantic mountains) is most characteristic. Cardinal Cospetto, we must say, is a most truculent prelate, and not certainly an *ornament* to his church.

" '49, 210, 311. Smee, R.A.—Portraits which a Reynolds might be proud of; a Vandyke or Claude[5] might not disown. "Sir Brian Newcome, in the costume of a Deputy-Lieutenant," "Major-General Sir Thomas de Boots, K.C.B.," painted for the 50th Dragoons, are triumphs, indeed, of this noble painter. Why have we no picture of the sovereign and her august consort from Smee's brush? When Charles II. picked up Titian's mahl-stick, he observed to a courtier, "A king you can always have; a genius comes but rarely." While we have a Smee among us, and a monarch whom we admire,—may the one be employed to transmit to posterity the beloved features of the other! We know our lucubrations are read in *high places*, and respectfully insinuate *verbum sapienti*.

" '1906. "The M'Collop of M'Collop,"—A. M'Collop,—is a noble work of a young artist, who, in depicting the gallant chief of a hardy Scottish clan, has also represented a romantic Highland landscape, in the midst of which, "his foot upon his native heath," stands a man of splendid symmetrical figure and great facial advantages. We shall keep our eye on Mr. M'Collop.

" '1367. "Oberon and Titania." Ridley.—This sweet and fanciful little picture draws crowds round about it, and is one of the most charming and delightful works of the present exhibition. We echo the universal opinion in declaring that it shows not only the greatest promise, but the most delicate and beautiful performance. The Earl of Kew, we understand, bought the picture at the private view; and we congratulate the young painter heartily upon his successful *début*. He is, we understand, a pupil of Mr. Gandish. Where is that admirable painter? We miss his bold canvases and grand historic outline.'

"I shall alter a few inaccuracies in the composition of our friend F.B., who has, as he says, 'drawn it uncommonly mild in the above criticism.' In fact, two days since, he brought in an article of quite a different tendency, of which he retains only the two last paragraphs; but he has, with great magnanimity, recalled his previous observations; and, indeed, he knows as much about pictures as some critics I could name.

"Good bye, my dear Clive! I send my kindest regards to your father; and think you had best see as little as possible of your bouillotte-playing French friend and *his* friends. This advice I know you will follow, as young men always follow the advice of their seniors and well-wishers. I dine in Fitzroy Square to-day with the pretty widow and her daughter, and am, yours always, dear Clive, A. P. "

---

[5] Claude *E1*] a Claude *R*

Chapter XXIII.

HE most hospitable and polite of Colonels would not hear of Mrs. Mackenzie and her daughter quitting his house when he returned to it, after six weeks' pleasant sojourn in Paris; nor, indeed, did his fair guest show the least anxiety or intention to go away. Mrs. Mackenzie had a fine merry humour of her own. She was an old soldier's wife, she said, and knew when her quarters were good; and I suppose, since her honeymoon, when the captain took her to Harrogate and Cheltenham, stopping at the first hotels, and travelling in a chaise and pair the whole way, she had never been so well off as in that roomy mansion near Tottenham Court Road. Of her mother's house at Musselburgh she gave a ludicrous but dismal account. "Eh, James," she said, "I think if you had come to Mamma, as you threatened, you would not have staid very long. It's a wearisome place. Dr. M'Craw boards with her; and it's sermons and psalm-singing from morning till night. My little Josey takes kindly to the life there, and I left her behind, poor little darling! It was not fair to bring three of us to take possession of your house, dear James; but my poor little Rosey was just withering away there. It's good for the dear child to see the world a little, and a kind uncle, who is not afraid of us now he sees us, is he?" Kind Uncle James was not at all afraid of little Rosey; whose pretty face and modest manners, and sweet songs, and blue eyes, cheered and soothed the old bachelor. Nor was Rosey's mother less agreeable and pleasant. She had married the captain (it was a love-match, against the will of her parents, who had destined her to be the third wife of old Dr. M'Mull) when very young. Many sorrows she had had, including poverty, the captain's imprisonment for debt, and his demise;[1] but she was of a gay and lightsome spirit. She was but three-and-thirty years old, and looked five-and-twenty. She was active, brisk, jovial, and alert; and so

---

[1] demise; *E1*] decease; *R*

good-looking, that it was a wonder she had not taken a successor to Captain Mackenzie. James Binnie cautioned his friend the Colonel against the attractions of the buxom syren; and laughingly would ask Clive how he would like Mrs. Mackenzie for a mamaw?

Colonel Newcome felt himself very much at ease regarding his future prospects. He was very glad that his friend James was reconciled to his family, and hinted to Clive that the late Captain Mackenzie's extravagance had been the cause of the rupture between him and his brother-in-law, who had helped that prodigal captain repeatedly during his life; and in spite of family quarrels, had never ceased to act generously to his widowed sister and her family. "But I think, Mr. Clive," said he, "that as Miss Rosa is very pretty, and you have a spare room at your studio, you had best take up your quarters in Charlotte Street as long as the ladies are living with us." Clive was nothing loth to be independent; but he showed himself to be a very good home-loving youth. He walked home to breakfast every morning, dined often, and spent the evenings with the family. Indeed, the house was a great deal more cheerful for the presence of the two pleasant ladies. Nothing could be prettier than to see the two ladies tripping down-stairs together, Mamma's pretty arm round Rosey's pretty waist. Mamma's talk was perpetually of Rosey. That child was always gay, always good, always happy! That darling girl woke with a smile on her face, it was sweet to see her! Uncle James, in his dry way, said, he dared to say it *was* very pretty. "Go away, you droll, dear old kind Uncle James!" Rosey's mamma would cry out. "You old bachelors are wicked old things!" Uncle James used to kiss Rosey very kindly and pleasantly. She was as modest, as gentle, as eager to please Colonel Newcome as any little girl could be. It was pretty to see her tripping across the room with his coffee-cup; or peeling walnuts for him after dinner with her white plump little fingers.

Mrs. Irons, the housekeeper, naturally detested Mrs. Mackenzie, and was jealous of her: though the latter did everything to soothe and coax the governess of the two gentlemen's establishment. She praised her dinners, delighted in her puddings, must beg Mrs. Irons to allow her to see one of those delicious puddings made, and to write the receipt for her, that Mrs. Mackenzie might use it when she was away. It was Mrs. Irons' belief that Mrs. Mackenzie never intended to go away. She had no ideer of ladies, as were ladies, coming into her kitchen. The maids vowed that they heard Miss Rosa crying, and Mamma scolding in her bed-room, for all she was so soft-spoken. How was that jug broke, and that chair smashed in the bed-room, that day there was such a awful row up there?

Mrs. Mackenzie played admirably, in the old-fashioned way, dances, reels, and Scotch and Irish tunes, the former of which filled James Binnie's soul with delectation. The good mother naturally desired that her darling should have a few good lessons of the piano while she was in London. Rosey was eternally strumming upon an instrument which had been taken up-stairs for her special practice; and the Colonel, who was always seeking to do harmless jobs of kindness for his friends, bethought him of little Miss Cann, the governess at Ridley's, whom he recommended as an instructress. "Anybody whom *you* recommend I'm sure, dear Colonel, we shall like," said Mrs. Mackenzie, who looked as black as thunder, and had probably intended to have Monsieur Quatremains or Signor Twankeydillo; and the little governess came to her pupil. Mrs. Mackenzie treated her very gruffly and haughtily at first; but as soon as she heard Miss Cann play, the widow was pacified, nay charmed. Monsieur Quatremains charged a guinea for three quarters of an hour; while Miss Cann thankfully took five shillings for an hour and a half; and the difference of twenty lessons, for which dear Uncle James paid, went into Mrs. Mackenzie's pocket, and thence probably on to her pretty shoulders and head in the shape of a fine silk dress and a beautiful French bonnet, in which Captain Goby said, upon his life, she didn't look twenty.

The little governess trotting home after her lesson would often look in to Clive's studio in Charlotte Street, where her two boys, as she called Clive and J.J., were at work each at his easel. Clive used to laugh, and tell us who joked him about the widow and her daughter, what Miss Cann said about them. Mrs. Mack was not all honey it appeared. If Rosey played incorrectly, Mamma flew at her with prodigious vehemence of language; and sometimes with a slap on poor Rosey's back. She must make Rosey wear tight boots, and stamp on her little feet if they refused to enter into the slipper. I blush for the indiscretion of Miss Cann; but she actually told J.J., that Mamma insisted upon lacing her so tight, as nearly to choke the poor little lass. Rosey did not fight: Rosey always yielded; and the scolding over and the tears dried, would come simpering down-stairs with Mamma's arm round her waist, and her pretty artless happy smile for the gentlemen below. Besides the Scottish songs without music, she sang ballads at the piano very sweetly. Mamma used to cry at these ditties. "That child's voice brings tears into my eyes, Mr. Newcome," she would say. "She has never known a moment's sorrow yet! Heaven grant, Heaven grant, she may be happy! But what shall I be when I lose her?"

"Why, my dear, when ye lose Rosey, ye'll console yourself with Josey," says droll Mr. Binnie from the sofa, who perhaps saw the manœuvre of the widow.

The widow laughs heartily and really. She places a handkerchief over her mouth. She glances at her brother with a pair of eyes full of knowing mischief. "Ah, dear James," she says, "you don't know what it is to have a mother's feelings."

"I can partly understand them," says James. "Rosey, sing me that pretty little French song." Mrs. Mackenzie's attention to Clive was really quite affecting. If any of his friends came to the house, she took them aside and praised Clive to them. The Colonel she adored. She had never met with such a man or seen such a manner. The manners of the Bishop of Tobago were beautiful, and he certainly had one of the softest and finest hands in the world; but not finer than Colonel Newcome's. "Look at his foot!" (and she put out her own, which was uncommonly pretty and suddenly withdrew it, with an arch glance meant to represent a blush) "my shoe would fit it! When we were at Coventry Island, Sir Peregrine Blandy, who succeeded poor dear Sir Rawdon Crawley—I saw his dear boy was gazetted to a lieutenant-colonelcy in the Guards last week—Sir Peregrine, who was one of the Prince of Wales's most intimate friends, was always said to have the finest manner and presence of any man of his day; and very grand and noble he was, but I don't think he was equal to Colonel Newcome; I really don't think so. Do you think so, Mr. Honeyman? What a charming discourse that was last Sunday! I know there were *two* pair of eyes not dry in the church. I could not see the other people just for crying myself. O, but I wish we could have you at Musselburgh! I was bred a Presbyterian of course; but in much travelling through the world with my dear husband, I came to love his church. At home we sit under Dr. M'Craw, of course; but he is so awfully long! Four hours every Sunday at least, morning and afternoon! It nearly kills poor Rosey. Did you hear her voice at your church? The dear girl is delighted with the chants. Rosey, were you not delighted with the chants?"

If she is delighted with the chants, Honeyman is delighted with the chantress and her mamma. He dashes the fair hair from his brow: he sits down to the piano, and plays one or two of them, warbling a faint vocal accompaniment, and looking as if he would be lifted off the screw music-stool, and flutter up to the ceiling.

"O, it's just seraphic!" says the widow. "It's just the breath of incense, and the pealing of the organ at the Cathedral at Montreal. Rosey doesn't remember Montreal. She was a wee wee child. She was born on the voyage out, and christened at sea. *You* remember, Goby."

" 'Gad, I promised and vowed to teach her her catechism; but 'gad, I haven't," says Captain Goby. "We were between Montreal and Quebec for three years with the Hundredth, the Hundred and Twentieth Highlanders; and the Thirty-third Dragoon Guards a part of the time; Fipley commanded them, and a very jolly time we had. Much better than the West Indies, where a fellow's liver goes to the deuce with hot pickles and sangaree. Mackenzie was a dev'lish wild fellow," whispers Captain Goby to his neighbour (the present biographer indeed), "and Mrs. Mack was—was as pretty a little woman as ever you set eyes on." (Captain Goby winks, and looks peculiarly sly as he makes this statement.) "Our regiment wasn't on your side of India, Colonel."

And in the interchange of such delightful remarks, and with music and song the evening passes away. "Since the house had been adorned by the fair presence of Mrs. Mackenzie and her daughter," Honeyman said, always gallant in behaviour and flowery in expression, "it seemed as if spring had visited it. Its hospitality was invested with a new grace; its ever welcome little *réunions* were doubly charming. But why did these ladies come, if they were to go away again? How—how would Mr. Binnie console himself (not to mention others), if they left him in solitude?"

"We have no wish to leave my brother James in solitude," cries Mrs. Mackenzie, frankly laughing. "We like London a great deal better than Musselburgh."

"O, that we do!" ejaculates the blushing Rosey.

"And we will stay as long as ever my brother will keep us," continues the widow.

"Uncle James is so kind and dear," says Rosey. "I hope he won't send me and Mamma away."

"He were[2] a brute—a savage, if he did!" cries Binnie,[3] with glances of rapture towards the two pretty faces. Everybody liked them. Binnie received their caresses very good-humouredly. The Colonel liked every woman under the sun. Clive laughed and joked and waltzed alternately with Rosey and her mamma. The latter was the briskest partner of the two. The unsuspicious widow, poor dear innocent, would leave her girl at the painting-room, and go shopping herself; but little J.J. also worked there, being occupied with his second picture: and he was almost the only one of Clive's friends whom the widow did not like. She pronounced the quiet little painter a pert, little, obtrusive, under-bred creature.

In a word, Mrs. Mackenzie was, as the phrase is, 'setting her cap' so openly at Clive, that none of us could avoid seeing her play: and Clive laughed at her simple manœuvres as merrily as the rest. She was a merry little woman. We gave her and her pretty daughter a luncheon in Lamb Court, Temple; in Sibwright's chambers—luncheon from Dick's Coffee House—ices and dessert from Partington's in the Strand. Miss Rosey, Mr. Sibwright, our neighbour in Lamb Court, and the Reverend Charles Honeyman sang very delightfully after lunch; there was quite a crowd of porters, laundresses, and boys to listen in the Court; Mr. Paley was disgusted with the noise we made—in fact, the party was perfectly successful. We all liked the widow, and if she did set her pretty ribbons at Clive, why should not she? We all liked the pretty, fresh, modest Rosey. Why, even the grave old benchers in the Temple church, when the ladies visited it on Sunday, winked their reverend eyes with pleasure, as they looked at those two uncommonly smart, pretty, well-dressed, fashionable women. Ladies, go to the Temple church. You will see more young men, and receive more respectful attention there than in any place, except perhaps at Oxford or Cambridge. Go to the Temple church—not, of course, for the admiration which you will excite and which you cannot help; but because the sermon is excellent, the choral services beautifully performed, and the church so interesting as a monument of the thirteenth century, and as it contains the tombs of those dear Knights Templars!

Mrs. Mackenzie could be grave or gay, according to her company: nor could any woman be of more edifying behaviour when an occasional Scottish friend bringing a letter from darling Josey, or a recommendatory letter from Josey's grandmother, paid a visit in Fitzroy Square. Little Miss Cann used to laugh and wink knowingly, saying, "You will never get back your bed-room, Mr. Clive. You may be sure that Miss Josey will come in a few months; and perhaps old Mrs. Binnie, only no doubt she and her daughter do not agree. But the widow has taken possession of Uncle James; and

---

[2] were *E1*] was *R*
[3] Binnie, *E1*] Honeyman, *R*

she will carry off somebody else if I am not mistaken. Should you like a stepmother, Mr. Clive, or should you prefer a wife?"

Whether the fair lady tried her wiles upon Colonel Newcome the present writer has no certain means of ascertaining: but I think another image occupied his heart: and this Circe tempted him no more than a score of other enchantresses who had tried their spells upon him. If she tried she failed. She was a very shrewd woman, quite frank in her talk when such frankness suited her. She said to me, "Colonel Newcome has had some great passion, once upon a time, I am sure of that, and has no more heart to give away. The woman who had his must have been a very lucky woman: though I daresay she did not value what she had; or did not live to enjoy it—or—or something or other. You see tragedies in some people's faces. I recollect when we were in Coventry Island—there was a chaplain there— a very good man—a Mr. Bell, and married to a pretty little woman who died. The first day I saw him I said, 'I know that man has had a great grief in life. I am sure that he left his heart in England.' You gentlemen who write books, Mr. Pendennis, and stop at the third volume, know very well that the real story often begins afterwards. My third volume ended when I was sixteen, and was married to my poor husband. Do you think all our adventures ended then, and that we lived happy ever after? I live for my darling girls now. All I want is to see them comfortable in life. Nothing can be more generous than my dear brother James has been. I am only his half-sister, you know, and was an infant in arms when he went away. He had differences with Captain Mackenzie who was headstrong and imprudent, and I own my poor dear husband was in the wrong. James could not live with my poor mother. Neither could by possibility suit the other. I have often, I own, longed to come and keep house for him. His home, the society he sees, of men of talents like Mr. Warrington and—and I won't mention names, or pay compliments to a man who knows human nature so well as the author of 'Walter Lorraine': this house is pleasanter a thousand times than Musselburgh—pleasanter for me and my dearest Rosey, whose delicate nature shrunk and withered up in poor Mamma's society. She was never happy except in my room, the dear child! She's all gentleness and affection. She doesn't seem to show it; but she has the most wonderful appreciation of wit, of genius, and talent of all kinds. She always hides her feelings, except from her fond old mother. I went up into our room yesterday, and found her in tears. I can't bear to see her eyes red or to think of her suffering. I asked her what ailed her, and kissed her. She is a tender plant, Mr. Pendennis! Heaven knows with what care I have nurtured her! She looked up smiling on my shoulder. She looked so pretty! 'O, Mamma,' the darling child said, 'I couldn't help it. I have been crying over 'Walter Lorraine!'" (Enter Rosey.) "Rosey, darling! I have been telling Mr. Pendennis what a naughty, naughty child you were yesterday, and how you read a book which I told you you shouldn't read; for it is a very *wicked* book; and though it contains some sad sad truths, it is a great deal too misanthropic (is that the right word? I'm a poor soldier's wife, and no scholar, you know,) and a great deal too *bitter*; and though the reviews praise it, and the clever people—*we* are poor simple country people—*we* won't praise it. Sing, dearest, that little song" (profuse kisses to Rosey) "that pretty thing that Mr. Pendennis likes."

"I am sure that I will sing any thing that Mr. Pendennis likes," says Rosey, with her candid bright eyes—and she goes to the piano and warbles Batti, Batti, with her sweet fresh artless voice.

More caresses follow. Mamma is in a rapture. How pretty they look—the mother and daughter—two lilies twining together. The necessity of an entertainment at the Temple—lunch from Dick's (as before mentioned), dessert from Partington's, Sibwright's spoons, his boy to aid ours, nay, Sib himself, and his rooms, which are so much more elegant than ours, and where there is a piano and guitar: all these thoughts pass in rapid and brilliant combination in the pleasant[4] Mr. Pendennis's mind. How delighted the ladies are with the proposal! Mrs. Mackenzie claps her pretty hands, and kisses Rosey again. If osculation is a mark of love, surely Mrs. Mack is the best of mothers. I may say, without false modesty, that our little entertainment was most successful. The champagne was iced to a nicety. The ladies did not perceive that our laundress, Mrs. Flanagan, was intoxicated very early in the afternoon. Percy Sibwright sang admirably, and with the greatest spirit, ditties in many languages. I am sure Miss Rosey thought him (as indeed he is) one of the most fascinating young fellows about town. To her mother's excellent accompaniment Rosey sang her favourite songs (by the way her stock was very small—five, I think, was the number). Then the table was moved into a corner, where the quivering moulds of jelly seemed to keep time to the music; and whilst Percy played, two couple of waltzers actually whirled round the little room. No wonder that the court below was thronged with admirers, that Paley the reading man was in a rage, and Mrs. Flanagan in a state of excitement. Ah! pleasant days, happy old dingy chambers illuminated by youthful sunshine! merry songs and kind faces—it is pleasant to recall you. Some of those bright eyes shine no more: some of those smiling lips do not speak. Some are not less kind, but sadder than in those days: of which the memories revisit us for a moment, and sink back into the grey past. The dear old Colonel beat time with great delight to the songs; the widow lit his cigar with her own fair fingers. That was the only smoke permitted during the entertainment—George Warrington himself not being allowed to use his cutty-pipe—though the gay little widow said that she had been used to smoking in the West Indies, and I daresay spoke the truth. Our entertainment lasted actually until after dark: and a particularly neat cab being called from St. Clement's by Mr. Binnie's boy, you may be sure we all conducted the ladies to their vehicle: and many a fellow returning from his lonely club that evening into chambers must have envied us the pleasure of having received two such beauties.

The clerical bachelor was not to be outdone by the gentlemen of the bar; and the entertainment at the Temple was followed by one at Honeyman's lodgings, which, I must own, greatly exceeded ours in splendour, for Honeyman had his luncheon from Gunter's; and if he had been Miss Rosey's

---

4 pleasant *E1*] pleased *R*

mother, giving a breakfast to the dear girl on her marriage, the affair could not have been more elegant and handsome. We had but two bouquets at our entertainment; at Honeyman's there were four upon the breakfast-table, besides a great pine-apple, which must have cost the rogue three or four guineas, and which Percy Sibwright delicately cut up. Rosey thought the pine-apple delicious. "The dear thing does not remember the pine-apples in the West Indies!" cries Mrs. Mackenzie; and she gave us many exciting narratives of entertainments at which she had been present at various colonial governors' tables. After luncheon, our host hoped we should have a little music. Dancing, of course, could not be allowed. "That," said Honeyman, with his "soft-bleating sigh," "were scarcely clerical. You know, besides, you are in a *hermitage*; and (with a glance round the table) must put up with Cenobite's fare." The fare was, as I have said, excellent. The wine was bad, as George, and I, and Sib agreed; and in so far we flattered ourselves that *our* feast altogether excelled the parson's. The champagne especially was such stuff, that Warrington remarked on it to his neighbour, a dark gentleman, with a tuft to his chin, and splendid rings and chains.

The dark gentleman's wife and daughter were the other two ladies invited by our host. The elder was splendidly dressed. Poor Mrs. Mackenzie's simple gimcracks, though she displayed them to the most advantage, and could make an ormolu bracelet go as far as another woman's emerald clasps, were as nothing compared to the other lady's gorgeous jewellery. Her fingers glittered with rings innumerable. The head of her smelling-bottle was as big as her husband's gold snuff-box, and of the same splendid material. Our ladies, it must be confessed, came in a modest cab from Fitzroy Square; these arrived in a splendid little open carriage with white ponies, and harness all over brass, which the lady of the rings drove with a whip that was a parasol. Mrs. Mackenzie, standing at Honeyman's window, with her arm round Rosey's waist, viewed this arrival perhaps with envy. "My dear Mr. Honeyman, whose are those beautiful horses?" cries Rosey, with enthusiasm.

The divine says with a faint blush—"It is—ah—it is Mrs. Sherrick and Miss Sherrick, who have done me the favour to come to luncheon."

"Wine merchant. Oh!" thinks Mrs. Mackenzie, who has seen Sherrick's brass-plate on the cellar-door of Lady Whittlesea's chapel; and hence, perhaps, she was a trifle more magniloquent than usual, and entertained us with stories of colonial governors and their ladies, mentioning no persons, but those who "had handles to their names," as the phrase is.

Although Sherrick had actually supplied the champagne which Warrington abused to him in confidence, the wine-merchant was not wounded; on the contrary, he roared with laughter at the remark, and some of us smiled who understood the humour of the joke. As for George Warrington, he scarce knew more about the town than the ladies opposite to him; who, yet more innocent than George, thought the champagne very good. Mrs. Sherrick was silent during the meal, looking constantly up at her husband, as if alarmed and always in the habit of appealing to that gentleman, who gave her, as I thought, knowing glances and savage winks, which made me augur that he bullied her at home. Miss Sherrick was exceedingly handsome: she kept the fringed curtains of her eyes constantly down; but when she lifted them up towards Clive, who was very attentive to her (the rogue never sees a handsome woman, but to this day he continues the same practice)—when she looked up and smiled, she was indeed a beautiful young creature to behold,—with her pale forehead, her thick arched eyebrows, her rounded cheeks, and her full lips slightly shaded,—how shall I mention the word?—slightly pencilled, after the manner of the lips of the French governess, Mademoiselle Lenoir.

Percy Sibwright engaged Miss Mackenzie with his usual grace and affability. Mrs. Mackenzie did her very utmost to be gracious; but it was evident the party was not altogether to her liking. Poor Percy, about whose means and expectations she had in the most natural way in the world asked information from me, was not perhaps a very eligible admirer for darling Rosey. She knew not that Percy can no more help gallantry than the sun can help shining. As soon as Rosey had done eating up her pine-apple, artlessly confessing (to Percy Sibwright's inquiries) that she preferred it to the rasps and hinnyblobs in her grandmamma's garden, "Now, dearest Rosey," cries Mrs. Mack, "now, a little song. You promised Mr. Pendennis a little song." Honeyman whisks open the piano in a moment. The widow takes off her cleaned gloves (Mrs. Sherrick's were new, and of the best Paris make), and little Rosey sings, No. 1 followed by No. 2, with very great applause. Mother and daughter entwine as they quit the piano. "Brava! brava!" says Percy Sibwright. Does Mr. Clive Newcome say nothing? His back is turned to the piano, and he is looking with all his might into the eyes of Miss Sherrick.

Percy sings a Spanish seguidella, or a German lied, or a French romance, or a Neapolitan canzonet, which, I am bound to say, excites very little attention. Mrs. Ridley is sending in coffee at this juncture, of which Mrs. Sherrick partakes, with lots of sugar, as she has partaken of numberless things before. Chickens, plover's eggs, prawns, aspics, jellies, creams, grapes, and what-not. Mr. Honeyman advances, and with deep respect asks if Mrs. Sherrick and Miss Sherrick will not be persuaded to sing? She rises and bows, and again takes off the French gloves, and shows the large white hands glittering with rings, and, summoning Emily her daughter, they go to the piano.

"Can she sing?" whispers Mrs. Mackenzie, "can she sing after eating so much?" Can she sing, indeed! O, you poor ignorant Mrs. Mackenzie! Why, when you were in the West Indies, if you ever read the English newspapers, you must have read of the fame of Miss Folthorpe. Mrs. Sherrick is no other than the famous artist,[5] who, after three years of brilliant triumphs at the Scala, the Pergola, the San Carlo, the opera in England, forsook her profession, rejected a hundred suitors, and married Sherrick, who was Mr. Cox's lawyer, who failed, as every body knows, as manager of Drury Lane. Sherrick, like a man of spirit, would not allow his wife to sing in public after his marriage; but in private society, of course, she is welcome to perform: and now with her daughter, who possesses a noble contralto voice,

[5] artist, *E1*] artiste, *R*

MR. HONEYMAN AT HOME

she takes her place royally at the piano, and the two sing so magnificently that everybody in the room, with one single exception, is charmed and delighted; and that[6] little Miss Cann herself creeps up the stairs, and stands with Mrs. Ridley at the door to listen to the music.

Miss Sherrick looks doubly handsome as she sings. Clive Newcome is in a rapture; so is good-natured Miss Rosey, whose little heart beats with pleasure, and who says quite unaffectedly to Miss Sherrick, with delight and gratitude beaming from her blue eyes, "Why did you ask me to sing, when you sing so wonderfully, so beautifully yourself? Do not leave the piano, please, do sing again." And she puts out a kind little hand towards the superior artist,[7] and, blushing, leads her back to the instrument. "I'm sure me and Emily will sing for you as much as you like, dear," says Mrs. Sherrick, nodding to Rosey good-naturedly. Mrs. Mackenzie, who has been biting her lips and drumming the time on a side-table, forgets at last the pain of being vanquished in admiration of the conquerors. "It was cruel of you not to tell us, Mr. Honeyman," she says, "of the—of the treat you had in store for us. I had no idea we were going to meet professional people; Mrs. Sherrick's singing is indeed beautiful."

"If you come up to our place in the Regent's Park, Mr. Newcome," Mr. Sherrick says, "Mrs. S. and Emily will give you as many songs as you like. How do you like the house in Fitzroy Square. Anything wanting doing there? I'm a good landlord to a good tenant. Don't care what I spend on my houses. Lose by 'em sometimes. Name a day when you'll come to us; and I'll ask some good fellows to meet you. Your father and Mr. Binnie came once. That was when you were a young chap. They didn't have a bad evening, I believe. You just come and try us—I can give you as good a glass of wine as most, I think," and he smiles, perhaps thinking of the champagne which Mr. Warrington had slighted. "I've ad the close carriage for my wife this evening," he continues, looking out of window at a very handsome brougham which has just drawn up there. "That little pair of horses steps prettily together, don't they? Fond of horses? I know you are. See you in the park; and going by our house sometimes. The Colonel sits a horse uncommonly well: so do you, Mr. Newcome. I've often said, 'Why don't they get off their horses and say, Sherrick, we're come for a bit of lunch and a glass of sherry?' Name a day, Sir. Mr. P., will you be in it?"

Clive Newcome named a day, and told his father of the circumstance in the evening. The Colonel looked grave. "There was something which I did not quite like about Mr. Sherrick," said that acute observer of human nature. "It was easy to see that the man is not quite a gentleman. I don't care what a man's trade is, Clive. Indeed, who are we, to give ourselves airs upon that subject? But when I am gone, my boy, and there is nobody near you who knows the world as I do, you may fall into designing hands, and rogues may lead you into mischief: keep a sharp look out, Clive. Mr. Pendennis, here, knows that there are designing fellows abroad" (and the dear old gentleman gives a very knowing nod as he speaks). "When I am

---

[6] that *E1*] [omitted] *R*
[7] artist, *E1*] artiste, *R*

gone, keep the lad from harm's way, Pendennis. Meanwhile Mr. Sherrick has been a very good and obliging landlord; and a man who sells wine may certainly give a friend a bottle. I am glad you had a pleasant evening, boys. Ladies! I hope you have had a pleasant afternoon. Miss Rosey, you are come back to make tea for the old gentlemen? James begins to get about briskly now. He walked to Hanover Square, Mrs. Mackenzie, without hurting his ancle in the least."

"I am almost sorry that he is getting well," says Mrs. Mackenzie, sincerely. "He won't want us when he is quite cured."

"Indeed, my dear creature!" cries the Colonel, taking her pretty hand and kissing it. "He will want you, and he shall want you. James no more knows the world than Miss Rosey here; and if I had not been with him, would have been perfectly unable to take care of himself. When I am gone to India, somebody must stay with him; and—and my boy must have a home to go to," says the kind soldier, his voice dropping. "I had been in hopes that his own relatives would have received him more, but never mind about that," he cried more cheerfully. "Why, I may not be absent a year! perhaps need not go at all—I am second for promotion. A couple of our old generals may drop any day; and when I get my regiment I come back to stay, to live at home. Meantime, whilst I am gone, my dear lady, you will take care of James; and you will be kind to my boy."

"That I will!" said the widow radiant with pleasure, and she took one of Clive's hands and pressed it for an instant; and from Clive's father's kind face there beamed out that benediction, which always made his countenance appear to me among the most beautiful of human faces.

Chapter XXIV.

IN WHICH THE NEWCOME BROTHERS ONCE MORE MEET TOGETHER IN
UNITY.

HIS narrative, as the judicious reader no doubt is aware, is written maturely and at ease, long after the voyage is over, whereof it recounts the adventures and perils; the winds adverse and favourable; the storms, shoals, shipwrecks, islands, and so forth, which Clive Newcome met in his early journey in life. In such a history events follow each other without necessarily having a connection with one another. One ship crosses another ship, and after a visit from one captain to his comrade, they sail away each on his course. The Clive Newcome meets a vessel which makes signals that she is short of bread and water; and after supplying her, our captain leaves her to see her no more. One or two of the vessels with which we commenced the voyage together, part company in a gale, and founder miserably; others, after being wofully battered in the tempest, make port; or are cast upon surprising islands where all sorts of unlooked-for prosperity awaits the lucky crew. Also, no doubt, the writer of the book, into whose hands Clive Newcome's logs have been put, and who is charged with the duty of making two octavo volumes out of his friend's story; dresses up the narrative in his own way; utters his own remarks in place of Newcome's; makes fanciful descriptions of individuals and incidents with which he never could have been personally acquainted; and commits blunders, which the critics will discover. A great number of the descriptions in "Cook's Voyages," for instance, were notoriously invented by Dr. Hawkesworth, who "did" the book: so in the present volumes, where dialogues are written down, which the reporter could by no possibility have heard, and where mo-

tives are detected which the persons actuated by them certainly never confided to the writer, the public must once for all be warned that the author's individual fancy very likely supplies much of the narrative; and
that he forms it as best he may, out of stray papers, conversations reported to him, and his knowledge, right or wrong, of the characters of
the persons engaged. And, as is the case with the most orthodox histories, the writer's own guesses or conjectures are printed in exactly the
same type as the most ascertained patent facts. I fancy, for my part,
that the speeches attributed to Clive, the Colonel, and the rest, are as
authentic as the orations in Sallust or Livy, and only implore the truth-
loving public to believe that incidents here told, and which passed very
probably without witnesses, were either confided to me subsequently as
compiler of this biography, or are of such a nature that they must have
happened from what we know happened after. For example, when you
read such words as Q V E R O M A N V S on a battered Roman stone, your
profound antiquarian knowledge enables you to assert that S E N A T V S
P O P V L V S was also inscribed there at some time or other. You take
a mutilated statue of Mars, Bacchus, Apollo, or Virorum, and you pop
him on a wanting hand, an absent foot, or a nose, which time or bar-
barians have defaced. You tell your tales as you can, and state the facts
as you think they must have been. In this manner, Mr. James (historiographer to her Majesty),[1] Titus Livius, Professor Alison, Robinson Cru-
soe, and all historians proceeded. Blunders there must be in the best of
these narratives, and more asserted than they can possibly know or vouch
for.

To recur to our own affairs, and the subject at present in hand. I am
obliged here to supply from conjecture a few points of the history, which
I could not know from actual experience or hearsay. Clive, let us say is
Romanus, and we must add Senatus Populusque to his inscription. After Mrs. Mackenzie and her pretty daughter had been for a few months
in London, which they did not think of quitting, although Mr. Binnie's
wounded little leg was now as well and as brisk as ever it had been; a
redintegration of love began to take place between the Colonel and his
relatives in Park Lane. How should we know that there had ever been a
quarrel, or at any rate a coolness? Thomas Newcome was not a man to talk
at length of any such matter; though a word or two occasionally dropped
in conversation by the simple gentleman might lead persons who chose
to interest themselves about his family affairs to form their own opinions
concerning them. After that visit of the Colonel and his son to Newcome,
Ethel was constantly away with her grandmother. The Colonel went to
see his pretty little favourite at Brighton, and once, twice, thrice, Lady
Kew's door was denied to him. The knocker of that door could not be
more fierce than the old lady's countenance, when Newcome met her in
her chariot driving on the cliff. Once, forming the loveliest of a charming Amazonian squadron, led by Mr. Whiskin, the riding-master, when
the Colonel encountered his pretty Ethel, she greeted him affectionately

[1] James (historiographer to her Majesty) *E1*] James, *R*

it is true; there was still the sweet look of candour and love in her eyes; but when he rode up to her she looked so constrained, when he talked about Clive so reserved, when he left her, so sad, that he could not but feel

pain and commiseration. Back he went to London, having in a week only caught this single glance of his darling.

This event occurred while Clive was painting his picture of the Battle of Assaye, before mentioned, during the struggles incident on which composition he was not thinking much about Miss Ethel, or his papa, or any other subject but his great work. Whilst Assaye was still in progress Thomas Newcome must have had an explanation with his sister-in-law, Lady Ann, to whom he frankly owned the hopes which he had entertained for Clive, and who must as frankly have told the Colonel that Ethel's family had very different views for that young lady to those which the simple Colonel had formed. A generous early attachment, the Colonel thought, is the safeguard of a young man. To love a noble girl; to wait awhile and struggle, and haply do some little achievement in order to win her; the best task to which his boy could set himself. If two young people so loving each other were to marry on rather narrow means, what then? A happy home was better than the finest house in May Fair; a generous young fellow, such as, please God, his son was,—loyal, upright, and a gentleman, might pretend surely to his kinswoman's hand without derogation; and the affection he bore Ethel himself was so great, and the sweet regard with which she returned it, that the simple father thought his kindly project was favoured by Heaven, and prayed for its fulfilment, and pleased himself to think, when his campaigns were over, and his sword hung on the wall, what a beloved daughter he might have to soothe and cheer his old age. With such a wife for his son, and child for himself, he thought the happiness of his last years might repay him for friendless boyhood, lonely manhood, and cheerless exile; and he imparted his simple scheme to Ethel's mother, who no doubt was touched as he told his story; for she always professed regard and respect for him, and in the differences which afterwards occurred in the family, and the quarrels which divided the brothers, still remained faithful to the good Colonel.

But Barnes Newcome, Esquire, was the head of the house, and the governor of his father and all Sir Brian's affairs, and Barnes Newcome, Esquire, hated his cousin Clive, and spoke of him as a beggarly painter, an impudent snob, an infernal young puppy, and so forth; and Barnes with his usual freedom of language imparted his opinions to his Uncle Hobson at the bank, and Uncle Hobson carried them home to Mrs. Newcome in Brianstone Square; and Mrs. Newcome took an early opportunity of telling the Colonel her opinion on the subject, and of bewailing that love for aristocracy which she saw actuated some folks; and the Colonel was brought to see that Barnes was his boy's enemy, and words very likely passed between them, for Thomas Newcome took a new banker at this time, and, as Clive informed me, was in very great dudgeon, because Hobson Brothers wrote to him to say that he had overdrawn his account. "I am sure there is some screw loose," the sagacious youth remarked to me; "and the Colonel and the people in Park Lane are at variance, because he goes there very little now; and he promised to go to Court when Ethel was presented, and he didn't go."

Some months after the arrival of Mr. Binnie's niece and sister in Fitzroy Square, the fraternal quarrel between the Newcomes must have come to an end—for that time at least—and was followed by a rather ostentatious reconciliation. And pretty little Rosy Mackenzie was the innocent and unconscious cause of this amiable change in the minds of the three brethren, as I gathered from a little conversation with Mrs. Newcome, who did me the honour to invite me to her table. As she had not vouchsafed this hospitality to me for a couple of years previously, and perfectly stifled me with affability when we met,—as her invitation came quite at the end of the season, when almost everybody was out of town, and a dinner to a man is no compliment—I was at first for declining this invitation, and spoke of it with great scorn when Mr. Newcome orally delivered it to me at Bays's Club.

"What," said I, turning round to an old man of the world, who happened to be in the room at the time, "what do these people mean by asking a fellow to dinner in August, and taking me up after dropping me for two years?"

"My good fellow," says my friend—it was my kind old Uncle Major Pendennis indeed—"I have lived long enough about town never to ask myself questions of that sort. In the world people drop you and take you up every day. You know Lady Cheddar by sight? I have known her husband for forty years. I have stayed with them in the country for weeks at a time. She knows me as well as she knows King Charles at Charing Cross, and a doosid deal better, and yet for a whole season she will drop me—pass me by, as if there was no such person in the world. Well, Sir, what do I do? I never see her. I give you my word I am never conscious of her existence; and if I meet her at dinner, I'm no more aware of her than the fellows in the play are of Banquo. What's the end of it? She comes round—only last Toosday she came round—and said Lord Cheddar wanted me to go down to Wilt-shire. I asked after the family (you know Henry Churningham is engaged to Miss Rennet?—a doosid good match for the Cheddars). We shook hands and are as good friends as ever. I don't suppose she'll cry when I die, you know (said the worthy old gentleman with a grin). Nor shall I go into *very* deep mourning if anything happens to her. You were quite right to say to Newcome that you did not know whether you were free or not, and would look at your engagements when you got home, and give him an answer. A fellow of that rank *has* no right to give himself airs. But they will, Sir. Some of those bankers are as high and mighty as the oldest families. They marry noblemen's daughters, by Jove, and think nothing is too good for 'em. But I should go, if I were you, Arthur. I dined there a couple of months ago; and the bankeress said something about you: that you and her nephew were much together, that you were sad wild dogs, I think—something of that sort. ''Gad, Ma'am,' says I, 'boys will be boys.' 'And they grow to be men!' says she, nodding her head. Queer little woman, devilish pompous. Dinner confoundedly long, stoopid, scientific."

The old gentleman was on this day inclined to be talkative and confidential, and I set down some more remarks which he made concerning my friends. "Your Indian Colonel," says he, "seems a worthy man." The Major quite forgot having been in India himself, unless he was in company with some very great personage. "He don't seem to know much of the world, and we are not very intimate. Fitzroy Square is a dev'lish long way off for a fellow to go for a dinner, and, *entre nous*, the dinner is rather queer and the company still more so. It's right for you who are a literary man to see all sorts of people; but I'm different you know, so Newcome and I are not very thick together. They say he wanted to marry your friend to Lady Ann's daughter, an exceedingly fine girl; one of the prettiest girls come out this season. I hear the young men say so. And that shows how monstrous ignorant of the world Colonel Newcome is. His son could no more get that girl than he could marry one of the royal princesses. Mark my words, they intend Miss Newcome for Lord Kew. Those banker-fellows are wild after grand marriages. Kew will sow his wild oats, and they'll marry her to him; or if not to him to some man of high rank. His father Walham was a weak young man; but his grandmother, old Lady Kew, is a monstrous clever old woman, too severe with her children, one of whom ran away and married a poor devil without a shilling. Nothing could show a more deplorable ignorance of the world than poor Newcome supposing his son could make such a match as that with his cousin. Is it true that he is going to make his son an artist? I don't know what the dooce the world is coming to. An artist! By gad, in my time a fellow would as soon have thought of making his son a hair-dresser, or a pastry-cook, by gad." And the worthy Major gives his nephew two fingers, and trots off to the next club in St. James's Street, of which he is a member.

The virtuous hostess of Brianstone Square was quite civil and good-humoured when Mr. Pendennis appeared at her house; and my surprise was not inconsiderable when I found the whole party from Saint Pancras there assembled;—Mr. Binnie; the Colonel and his son; Mrs. Mackenzie, looking uncommonly handsome and perfectly well-dressed; and Miss

Rosey, in pink crape, with pearly shoulders and blushing cheeks, and beautiful fair ringlets—as fresh and comely a sight as it was possible to witness. Scarcely had we made our bows, and shaken our hands, and imparted our observations about the fineness of the weather, when behold! as we look from the drawing-room windows into the cheerful square of Brianstone, a great family coach arrives, driven by a family coachman in a family wig, and we recognise Lady Ann Newcome's carriage, and see her ladyship, her mother, her daughter, and her husband, Sir Brian, descend from the vehicle. "It is quite a family party," whispers the happy Mrs. Newcome to the happy writer conversing with her in the niche of the window. "Knowing your intimacy with our brother, Colonel Newcome, we thought it would please him to meet you here. Will you be so kind as to take Miss Newcome to dinner?"

Everybody was bent upon being happy and gracious. It was "My dear brother, how do you do?" from Sir Brian. "My dear Colonel, how glad we are to see you! how well you look!" from Lady Ann. Miss Newcome ran up to him with both hands out, and put her beautiful face so close to his that I thought, upon my conscience, she was going to kiss him. And Lady Kew, advancing in the frankest manner, with a smile, I must own, rather awful playing round her many wrinkles, round her ladyship's hooked-nose, and displaying her ladyship's teeth (a new and exceedingly handsome set), held out her hand to Colonel Newcome, and said briskly, "Colonel, it is an age since we met." She turns to Clive with equal graciousness and good humour, and says, "Mr. Clive, let me shake hands with you; I have heard all sorts of good of you, that you have been painting the most beautiful things, that you are going to be quite famous." Nothing can exceed the grace and kindness of Lady Ann Newcome towards Mrs. Mackenzie: the pretty widow blushes with pleasure at this greeting; and now Lady Ann must be introduced to Mrs. Mackenzie's charming daughter, and whispers in the delighted mother's ear, "She is lovely!" Rosey comes up looking rosy indeed, and executes a pretty curtsey with a great deal of blushing grace.

Ethel has been so happy to see her dear uncle, that as yet she has had no eyes for any one else, until Clive advancing, those bright eyes become brighter still with surprise and pleasure as she beholds him. For being absent with his family in Italy now, and not likely to see this biography for many many months, I may say that he is a much handsomer fellow than our designer has represented; and if that wayward artist should take this very scene for the purpose of illustration, he is requested to bear in mind that the hero of this story will wish to have justice done to his person.[2] There exists in Mr. Newcome's possession a charming little pencil drawing of Clive at this age, and which Colonel Newcome took with him when he went— whither he is about to go in a very few pages—and brought back with him to this country. A florid apparel becomes some men, as simple raiment suits others; and Clive in his youth was of the ornamental class of mankind—a customer to tailors, a wearer of handsome rings, shirt-studs, mustachios,

---

[2] For being absent with his family . . . done to his person. *E1*] And, as she looks, Miss Ethel sees a very handsome fellow. *R*

long hair, and the like; nor could he help, in his costume or his nature, being picturesque and generous and splendid. He was always greatly delighted with that Scotch man-at-arms in "Quentin Durward," who twists off an inch or two of his gold chain to treat a friend and pay for a bottle. He would give a comrade a ring or a fine-jewelled pin, if he had no money. Silver dressing-cases, and brocade morning-gowns were in him a sort of propriety at this season of his youth. It was a pleasure to persons of colder temperament to sun themselves in the warmth of his bright looks and generous humour. His laughter cheered one like wine. I do not know that he was very witty; but he was pleasant. He was prone to blush: the history of a generous trait moistened his eyes instantly. He was instinctively fond of children, and of the other sex from one year old to eighty. Coming from the Derby once—a merry party—and stopped on the road from Epsom in a lock of carriages, during which the people in the carriage a-head saluted us with many vituperative epithets, and seized the heads of our leaders,— Clive in a twinkling jumped off the box, and the next minute we saw him engaged with a half-dozen of the enemy: his hat gone, his fair hair flying off his face, his blue eyes flashing fire, his lips and nostrils quivering with wrath, his right and left hand hitting out, *que c'étoit un plaisir à voir.* His father sat back in the carriage, looking with delight and wonder—indeed it was a great sight. Policeman X separated the warriors. Clive ascended the box again with a dreadful wound in the coat, which was gashed from the waist to the shoulder. I hardly ever saw the elder Newcome in such a state of triumph. The post-boys quite stared at the gratuity he gave them, and wished they might drive his lordship to the Oaks.

All the time we have been making this sketch Ethel is standing, looking at Clive; and the blushing youth casts down his eyes before her's. Her face assumes a look of arch humour. She passes a slim hand over the prettiest lips, and a chin with the most lovely of dimples, thereby indicating her admiration of Mr. Clive's mustachios and imperial. They are of a warm yellowish chestnut colour, and have not yet known the razor. He wears a low cravat; a shirt front of the finest lawn, with ruby buttons. His hair of a lighter colour, waves almost to "his manly shoulders broad." "Upon my word, my dear Colonel," says Lady Kew, after looking at him, and nodding her head shrewdly, "I think we were right."

"No doubt right in everything your ladyship does, but in what particularly?" asks the Colonel.

"Right to keep him out of the way. Ethel has been disposed of these ten years. Did not Ann tell you? How foolish of her! But all mothers like to have young men dying for their daughters. Your son is really the handsomest boy in London. Who is that conceited-looking young man in the window? Mr. Pen—what? Has your son really been very wicked? I was told he was a sad scapegrace."

"I never knew him do, and I don't believe he ever thought anything that was untrue, or unkind, or ungenerous," says the Colonel. "If any one has belied my boy to you, and I think I know who his enemy has been—"

"The young lady is very pretty," remarks Lady Kew, stopping the Colonel's further outbreak. "How very young her mother looks! Ethel, my dear! Colonel Newcome must present us to Mrs. Mackenzie and Miss Mackenzie;" and Ethel, giving a nod to Clive, with whom she has talked for a minute or two, again puts her hand in her uncle's, and walks towards Mrs. Mackenzie and her daughter.

And now let the artist, if he has succeeded in drawing Clive to his liking, cut a fresh pencil, and give us a likeness of Ethel.[3] She is seventeen years old; rather taller than the majority of women; of a countenance somewhat grave and haughty, but on occasion brightening with humour or beaming with kindliness and affection. Too quick to detect affectation or insincerity in others, too impatient of dulness or pomposity, she is more sarcastic now than she became when after years of suffering had softened her nature. Truth looks out of her bright eyes, and rises up armed, and flashes scorn or denial perhaps too readily, when she encounters flattery, or meanness, or imposture. After her first appearance in the world, if the truth must be told, this young lady was popular neither with many men, nor with most women. The innocent dancing youth who pressed round her, attracted by her beauty, were rather afraid, after a while, of engaging her. This one felt dimly that she despised him; another, that his simpering common-places (delights of how many well-bred maidens!) only occasioned Miss Newcome's laughter. Young Lord Crœsus, whom all maidens and matrons were eager to secure, was astounded to find that he was utterly indifferent to her, and that she would refuse him twice or thrice in an evening, and dance as many times with poor Tom Spring, who was his father's ninth son, and only at home till he could get a ship and go to sea again. The young women were frightened at her sarcasm. She seemed to know what *fadaises* they whispered to their partners as they paused in the waltzes; and Fanny, who was luring Lord Crœsus towards her with her blue eyes, dropped them guiltily to the floor when Ethel's turned towards her; and Cecilia sang more out of time than usual; and Clara, who was holding Freddy, and Charley, and Tommy round her enchanted by her bright conversation and witty mischief, became dumb and disturbed when Ethel passed her with her cold face; and old Lady Hookham, who was playing off her little Minnie now at young Jack Gorget of the Guards, now at the eager and simple Bob Bateson, of the Coldstreams, would slink off when Ethel made her appearance on the ground; whose presence seemed to frighten away the fish and the angler. No wonder that the other Mayfair nymphs were afraid of this severe Diana, whose looks were so cold and whose arrows were so keen.

But those who had no cause to heed Diana's shot or coldness might admire her beauty; nor could the famous Parisian marble which Clive said she resembled, be more perfect in form than this young lady. Her hair and eyebrows were jet black (these latter may have been too thick according to some physiognomists, giving rather a stern expression to the eyes, and hence causing those guilty ones to tremble who came under her lash),

---

[3] And now let the artist, if he has succeeded in drawing Clive to his liking, cut a fresh pencil, and give us a likeness of Ethel. *E1*] We must say a word respecting the rise and progress of Miss Ethel. *R*

A FAMILY PARTY

but her complexion was as dazzlingly fair and her cheeks as red as Miss Rosey's own, who had a right to those beauties, being a blonde by nature. In Miss Ethel's black hair there was a slight natural ripple, as when a fresh breeze blows over the *melan hudor*—a ripple such as Roman ladies nineteen hundred years ago, and our own beauties a short time since, endeavoured to imitate by art, paper, and I believe crumpling irons. Her eyes were gray; her mouth rather large; her teeth as regular and bright as Lady Kew's own; her voice low and sweet; and her smile, when it lighted up her face and eyes, as beautiful as spring sunshine; also they could lighten and flash often, and sometimes, though rarely, rain. As for her figure— but as this tall slender form is concealed in a simple white muslin robe, (of the sort which I believe is called *demie-toilette,*) in which her fair arms are enveloped; and which is confined at her slim waist by an azure ribbon, and descends to her feet—let us make a respectful bow to that fair image of Youth, Health, and Modesty, and fancy it as pretty as we will. Miss Ethel made a very stately curtsey to Mrs. Mackenzie, surveying that widow calmly; so that the elder lady looked up and fluttered; but towards Rosey she held out her hand, and smiled with the utmost kindness, and the smile was returned by the other; and the blushes with which Miss Mackenzie was always ready at this time, became her very much. As for Mrs. Mackenzie— the very largest curve that shall not be a caricature, and actually disfigure the widow's countenance—a smile so wide and steady—so exceedingly ri- dent, indeed, as almost to be ridiculous, may be drawn upon her buxom face, if the artist chooses to attempt it as it appeared during the whole of this summer evening—before dinner came (when people ordinarily look very grave), when she was introduced to the company: when she was made known to our friends Julia and Maria, the darling child, lovely little dears! how like their papa and mamma! when Sir Brian Newcome gave her his arm down-stairs to the dining-room: when any body spoke to her: when John offered her meat, or the gentleman in the white waistcoat, wine: when she accepted or when she refused these refreshments; when Mr. Newcome told her a dreadfully stupid story: when the Colonel called cheerily from his end of the table, "My dear Mrs. Mackenzie, you don't take any wine to-day: may I not have the honour of drinking a glass of champagne with you?": when the new boy from the country upset some sauce upon her shoulder: when Mrs. Newcome made the signal for departure; and I have no doubt in the drawing-room, when the ladies retired thither. "Mrs. Mack is perfectly awful," Clive told me afterwards, "since that dinner in Brian- stone Square. Lady Kew and Lady Ann are never out of her mouth; she has had white muslin dresses made just like Ethel's for herself and her daughter. She has bought a peerage, and knows the pedigree of the whole Kew family. She won't go out in a cab now without the boy on the box; and in the plate for the cards which she has established in the drawing-room, you know, Lady Kew's pasteboard always *will* come up to the top, though I poke it down whenever I go into the room. As for poor Lady Trotter, the Governess of St. Kitt's, you know, and the Bishop of Tobago, they are quite bowled out: Mrs. Mack has not mentioned them for a week."

During the dinner it seemed to me that the lovely young lady by whom

I sate cast many glances towards Mrs. Mackenzie, which did not betoken particular pleasure. Miss Ethel asked me several questions regarding Clive, and also respecting Miss Mackenzie: perhaps her questions were rather downright and imperious, and she patronised me in a manner that would not have given all gentlemen pleasure. I was Clive's friend, his schoolfellow? had seen him a great deal? know him very well—very well, indeed? Was it true that he had been very thoughtless? very wild? Who told her so? That was not her question (with a blush). It was not true, and I ought to know? He was not spoiled? He was very good-natured, generous, told the truth? He loved his profession very much, and had great talent? Indeed she was very glad. Why do they sneer at his profession? It seemed to her quite as good as her father's and brother's. Were artists not very dissipated? Not more so, nor often so much as other young men. Was Mr. Binnie rich, and was he going to leave all his money to his niece? How long have you known them? Is Miss Mackenzie as good-natured as she looks? Not very clever, I suppose. Mrs. Mackenzie looks very—No thank you, no more. Grandmamma (she is very deaf, and cannot hear) scolded me for reading the book you wrote; and took the book away. I got it afterwards, and read it all. I don't think there was any harm in it. Why do you give such bad characters of women? Don't you know any good ones? Yes, two as good as any in the world. They are unselfish: they are pious; they are always doing good; they live in the country? Why don't you put them into a book? Why don't you put my uncle into a book? He is so good, that nobody could make him good enough. Before I came out, I heard a young lady (Lady Clavering's daughter Miss Amory), sing a song of yours. I have never spoken to an author before. I saw Mr. Lyon at Lady Popinjoy's, and heard him speak. He said it was very hot, and he looked so I am sure. Who is the greatest author now alive? You will tell me when you come up-stairs after dinner:—and the young lady sails away following the matrons, who rise and ascend to the drawing-room. Miss Newcome has been watching the behaviour of the author, by whom she sate; curious to know what such a person's habits are; whether he speaks and acts like other people; and in what respect authors are different from persons "in society."

When we had sufficiently enjoyed claret and politics below stairs, the gentlemen went to the drawing-room to partake of coffee and the ladies' delightful conversation. We had heard previously the tinkling of the piano above, and the well-known sound of a couple of Miss Rosey's five songs. The two young ladies were engaged over an album at a side table, when the males of the party arrived. The book contained a number of Clive's drawings made in the time of his very early youth for the amusement of his little cousins. Miss Ethel seemed to be very much pleased with these performances, which Miss Mackenzie likewise examined with great good nature and satisfaction. So she did the views of Rome, Naples, Marble Head, in the county of Sussex, &c., in the same collection: so she did the Berlin cockatoo and spaniel which Mrs. Newcome was working in idle moments: so she did the Books of Beauty, Flowers of Loveliness, and so forth. She thought the prints very sweet and pretty: she thought the poetry very pretty and sweet. Which did she like best, Mr. Niminy's "Lines to a bunch

of violets," or Miss Piminy's "Stanzas to a wreath of roses?" Miss Mackenzie was quite puzzled to say which of these masterpieces she preferred;
she found them alike so pretty. She appealed, as in most cases, to Mamma.
"How, my darling love, can I pretend to know?" Mamma says. "I have been
a soldier's wife, battling about the world. I have not had your advantages.
I had no drawing masters: nor music masters as you have. You, dearest
child, must instruct *me* in these things." This poses Rosey: who prefers to
have her opinions dealt out to her like her frocks, bonnets, handkerchiefs,
her shoes and gloves, and the order thereof; the lumps of sugar for her
tea, the proper quantity of raspberry jam for breakfast; who trusts for all
supplies corporeal and spiritual to her mother. For her own part, Rosey
is pleased with everything in nature. Does she love music? O, yes. Bellini
and Donizetti? O, yes. Dancing? They had no dancing at Grandmamma's,
but she adores dancing, and Mr. Clive dances very well, indeed. (A smile
from Miss Ethel at this admission). Does she like the country? O, she is so
happy in the country! London? London is delightful, and so is the sea-
side. She does not know really which she likes best, London or the country,
for Mamma is not near her to decide, being engaged listening to Sir Brian,
who is laying down the law to her, and smiling, smiling with all her might.
In fact, Mr. Newcome says to Mr. Pendennis in his droll, humorous way,
"That woman grins like a Cheshire cat." Who was the naturalist who first
discovered that peculiarity of the cats in Cheshire?

In regard to Miss Mackenzie's opinions, then, it is not easy to discover
that they are decided, or profound, or original; but it seems pretty clear
that she has a good temper, and a happy contented disposition. And the
smile which her pretty countenance wears shows off to great advantage
the two dimples on her pink cheeks. Her teeth are even and white, her
hair of a beautiful colour, and no snow can be whiter than her fair round
neck and polished shoulders. She talks very kindly and good-naturedly
with Julia and Maria (Mrs. Hobson's precious ones) until she is bewildered
by the statements which those young ladies make regarding astronomy,
botany, and chemistry, all of which they are studying. "My dears, I don't
know a single word about any of these abstruse subjects, I wish I did,"
she says. And Ethel Newcome laughs. She too is ignorant upon all these
subjects. "I am glad there is some one else," says Rosey, with naïveté, "who
is as ignorant as I am." And the younger children with a solemn air say
they will ask Mamma leave to teach her. So everybody, somehow, great
or small, seems to protect her; and the humble, simple, gentle little thing
wins a certain degree of good will from the world, which is touched by
her humility and her pretty sweet looks. The servants in Fitzroy Square
waited upon her much more kindly than upon her smiling bustling mother.
Uncle James is especially fond of his little Rosey. Her presence in his study
never discomposes him; whereas his sister fatigues him with the exceeding
activity of her gratitude, and her energy in pleasing. As I was going away,
I thought I heard Sir Brian Newcome say "It (but what 'it' was of course
I cannot conjecture) . . it will do very well. The mother seems a superior
woman."

Chapter XXV.

I HAD no more conversation with Miss Newcome that night, who had forgotten her curiosity about the habits of authors. When she had ended her talk with Miss Mackenzie, she devoted the rest of the evening to her uncle Colonel Newcome: and concluded by saying, "And now you will come and ride with me tomorrow, Uncle, won't you?" which the Colonel faithfully promised to do. And she shook hands with Clive very kindly: and with Rosey very frankly, but as I thought with rather a patronising air: and she made a very stately bow to Mrs. Mackenzie, and so departed with her father and mother. Lady Kew had gone away earlier. Mrs. Mackenzie informed us afterwards that the Countess had gone to sleep after her dinner. If it was at Mrs. Mack's story about the Governor's ball at Tobago, and the quarrel for precedence between the Lord Bishop's lady, Mrs. Rotchet, and the Chief Justice's wife, Lady Barwise, I should not be at all surprised.

A handsome fly carried off the ladies to Fitzroy Square, and the two worthy Indian gentlemen in their company; Clive and I walking with the usual Havannah to light us home. And Clive remarked that he supposed there had been some difference between his father and the bankers: for they had not met for ever so many months before, and the Colonel always had looked very gloomy when his brothers were mentioned. "And I can't help thinking," says the astute youth, "that they fancied I was in love with Ethel (I know the Colonel would have liked me to make up to her) and that may have occasioned the row. Now, I suppose, they think I am engaged to Rosey. What the deuce are they in such a hurry to marry me for?"

Clive's companion remarked, "that marriage was a laudable institution: and an honest attachment an excellent conservator of youthful morals." On which Clive replied, "Why don't you marry yourself?"

This it was justly suggested was no argument, but a merely personal allusion foreign to the question, which was, that marriage was laudable, &c.

Mr. Clive laughed. "Rosey is as good a little creature as can be," he said. "She is never out of temper, though I fancy Mrs. Mackenzie tries her. I don't think she is very wise: but she is uncommonly pretty, and her beauty grows on you. As for Ethel, anything so high and mighty I have never seen, since I saw the French giantess. Going to court: and about to parties every night where a parcel of young fools flatter her, has perfectly spoiled her. By Jove, how handsome she is! How she turns with her long neck, and looks at you from under those black eye-brows! If I painted her hair, I think I should paint it almost blue, and then glaze over with lake. It *is* blue. And how finely her head is joined on to her shoulders!"—And he waves in the air an imaginary line with his cigar. "She would do for Judith, wouldn't she? Or how grand she would look as Herodias's daughter sweeping down a stair—in a great dress of cloth of gold like Paul Veronese—holding a charger before her with white arms you know—with the muscles accented like that glorious Diana at Paris—a savage smile on her face and a ghastly solemn gory head on the dish—I see the picture, Sir, I see the picture!" and he fell to curling his mustachios—just like his brave old father.

I could not help laughing at the resemblance, and mentioning it to my friend. He broke, as was his wont, into a fond eulogium of his sire, wished he could be like him—worked himself up into another state of excitement, in which he averred, "that if his father wanted him to marry, he would marry that instant. And why not Rosey? She is a dear little thing. Or why not that splendid Miss Sherrick? What a head!—a regular Titian! I was looking at the difference of their colour at Uncle Honeyman's that day of the *déjeuner.* The shadows in Rosey's face, Sir, are all pearly tinted. You ought to paint her in milk, Sir!" cries the enthusiast. "Have you ever remarked the gray round her eyes, and the sort of purple bloom of her cheek? Rubens could have done the colour: but I don't somehow like to think of a young lady and that sensuous old Peter Paul in company. I look at her like a little wild flower in a field—like a little child at play, Sir. Pretty little tender nursling. If I see her passing in the street, I feel as if I would like some fellow to be rude to her, that I might have the pleasure of knocking him down. She is like a little song bird, Sir,—a tremulous, fluttering little linnet that you would take into your hand, *pavidam quærentem matrem,* and smooth its little plumes, and let it perch on your finger and sing. The Sherrick creates quite a different sentiment—the Sherrick is splendid, stately, sleepy, . . ."

"Stupid," hints Clive's companion.

"Stupid! Why not? Some women ought to be stupid. What you call dulness I call repose. Give me a calm woman, a slow woman,—a lazy, majestic woman. Show me a gracious virgin bearing a lily: not a leering giggler frisking a rattle. A lively woman would be the death of me. Look at Mrs. Mack, perpetually nodding, winking, grinning, throwing out signals which you are to be at the trouble to answer! I thought her delightful for three days, I declare I was in love with her—that is, as much as I can be after—but never mind that, I feel I shall never be really in love again. Why shouldn't the Sherrick be stupid, I say? About great beauty there should always reign a silence. As you look at the great stars, the great ocean, any great scene of nature: you hush, Sir. You laugh at a pantomime, but you are still in a temple. When I saw the great Venus of the Louvre, I thought wert thou alive, O goddess, thou should'st never open those lovely lips but to speak lowly, slowly: thou should'st never descend from that pedestal but to walk stately to some near couch, and assume another attitude of beautiful calm. To be beautiful is enough. If a woman can do that well: who shall demand more from her? You don't want a rose to sing. And I think wit is out of place where there's great beauty; as I wouldn't have a Queen to cut jokes on her throne. I say, Pendennis,"—here broke off the enthusiastic youth,— "have you got another cigar? Shall we go in to Finch's, and have a game at billiards? Just one—it's quite early yet. Or shall we go in to the Haunt? It's Wednesday night you know, when all the boys go." We tap at a door in an old, old street in Soho: an old maid with a kind, comical face opens the door, and nods friendly, and says, "How do, Sir, aint seen you this ever so long. How do, Mr. Noocom." "Who's here?" "Most everybody's here." We pass by a little snug bar, in which a trim elderly lady is seated by a great fire, on which boils an enormous kettle; while two gentlemen are attacking a cold saddle of mutton and West India pickles: hard by Mrs. Nokes, the landlady's elbow—with mutual bows—we recognise Hickson, the sculptor, and Morgan, intrepid Irish chieftain, chief of the reporters of the *Morning Press* newspaper. We pass through a passage into a back room, and are received with a roar of welcome from a crowd of men, almost invisible in the smoke.

"I am right glad to see thee, boy!" cries a cheery voice (that will never troll a chorus more). "We spake anon of thy misfortune, gentle youth! and that thy warriors of Assaye have charged the Academy in vain.—Mayhap thou frightenedst the courtly school with barbarous visages of grisly war. Pendennis, thou dost wear a thirsty look! Resplendent swell! untwine thy choker white, and I will either stand a glass of grog: or thou shalt pay the like for me, my lad, and tell us of the fashionable world." Thus spake the brave old Tom Sarjent,—also one of the Press, one of the old boys: a good old scholar with a good old library of books, who had taken his seat anytime these forty years by the chimney fire in this old Haunt: where painters, sculptors, men of letters, actors, used to congregate, passing pleasant hours in rough kindly communion, and many a day seeing the sunrise lighting the rosy street ere they parted, and Betsy put the useless lamp out, and closed the hospitable gates of the Haunt.

The time is not very long since: though to-day is so changed. As we think of it: the kind familiar faces rise up, and we hear the pleasant voices and singing. There are they met, the honest hearty companions. In the days when the Haunt *was* a haunt, stage coaches were not yet quite over. Casinos were not invented: clubs were rather rare luxuries: there were sanded floors, triangular sawdust-boxes, pipes, and tavern parlours. Young Smith and Brown, from the Temple, did not go from chambers to dine at the Polyanthus, or the Megatherium, off potage à la Bisque, turbot au gratin, cotelettes à la Whatdyoucallem, and a pint of St. Emilion: but ordered their beef-steak and pint of port from the "plump head-waiter at the Cock:" did not disdain the pit of the theatre; and for a supper a homely refection at the tavern. How delightful are the suppers in Charles Lamb to read of even now!—the cards—the punch—the candles to be snuffed—the social oysters—the modest cheer! Whoever snuffs a candle now? What man has a domestic supper whose dinner-hour is eight o'clock? Those little meetings, in the memory of many of us yet, are gone quite away into the past. Five and twenty years ago is a hundred years off—so much has our social life changed in those five lustres. James Boswell himself, were he to revisit London, would scarce venture to enter a tavern. He would find scarce a respectable companion to enter its doors with him.[1] It is an institution as extinct as a hackney-coach. Many a grown man who peruses this historic page, has never seen such a vehicle, and only heard of rum-punch as a drink which his ancestors used to tipple.

Cheery old Tom Sarjent is surrounded at the Haunt by a dozen of kind boon companions. They toil all day at their avocations of art, or letters, or law, and here meet for a harmless night's recreation and converse. They talk of literature, or politics, or pictures, or plays, socially banter one another over their cheap cups: sing brave old songs sometimes when they are especially jolly; kindly ballads in praise of love and wine; famous maritime ditties in honour of old England. I fancy I hear Jack Brent's noble voice rolling out the sad generous *refrain* of "The Deserter," "Then for that reason and for a season we will be merry before we go," or Michael Percy's clear tenor carolling the Irish chorus of "What's that to any one, whether or no," or Mark Wilder shouting his bottle song of "Garryowen na gloria." These songs were regarded with affection by the brave old frequenters of the Haunt. A gentleman's property in a song was considered sacred. It was respectfully asked for: it was heard with the more pleasure for being old. Honest Tom Sarjent! how the times have changed since we saw thee! I believe the present chief of the reporters of the —— newspaper (which responsible office Tom filled) goes to parliament in his brougham, and dines with the ministers of the crown.

Around Tom are seated grave Royal Academicians, rising gay Associates; writers of other Journals besides the *Pall Mall Gazette*; a barrister maybe, whose name will be famous some day: a hewer of marble perhaps; a surgeon whose patients have not come yet, and one or two men about town who like this queer assembly better than haunts much more splendid. Captain Shandon has been here and his jokes are preserved in the tradition of the place. Owlet, the philosopher, came once and tried, as his wont is, to lecture, but his metaphysics were beaten down by a storm of banter. Slatter, who gave himself such airs because he wrote in the —— *Review,* tried to air himself at the Haunt but was choked by the smoke, and silenced by the unanimous poohpooping of the assembly. Dick Walker, who rebelled secretly at Sarjent's authority, once thought to give himself consequence by bringing a young lord from the Blue Posts, but he was so unmercifully "chaffed" by Tom, that even the young lord laughed at him. His lordship has been heard to say he had been taken to a monsus queeah place, queeah

---

[1] He would find scarce a respectable companion to enter its doors with him. *E1*] [omitted] *R*

set of folks, in a tap somewhere, though he went away quite delighted with
Tom's affability, but he never came again. He could not find the place
probably. You might pass the Haunt in the daytime and not know it in the
least. "I believe," said Charley Ormond, (A. R. A. he was then) "I believe in
the day there's no such place at all: and when Betsy turns the gas off at the
door lamp as we go away the whole thing vanishes, the door, the house, the
bar, the Haunt, Betsy, the beer-boy, Mrs. Nokes and all." It has vanished:
it is to be found no more: neither by night nor by day—unless the ghosts
of good fellows still haunt it.

As the genial talk and glass go round, and after Clive and his friend have
modestly answered the various queries put to them by good old Tom Sarjent, the acknowledged Præses of the assembly and Sachem of this venerable wigwam; the door opens and another well known figure is recognised
with shouts as it emerges through the smoke. "Bayham all hail!" says Tom.
"Frederick I am right glad to see thee!"

Bayham says he is disturbed in spirit, and calls for a pint of beer to
console him.

"Hast thou flown far thou restless bird of night?" asks Father Tom, who
loves speaking in blank verses.

"I have come from Cursitor Street," says Bayham in a low groan. "I have
just been to see a poor devil in quod there. Is that you Pendennis? You
know the man—Charles Honeyman."

"What!" cries Clive starting up.

"O my prophetic soul, my uncle!" growls Bayham. "I did not see the
young one: but 'tis true."

The reader is aware that more than three[2] years have elapsed, of
which time the preceding pages contain the harmless chronicle; and while
Thomas Newcome's leave has been running out and Clive's mustachios
growing, the fate of other persons connected with our story has also had
its development, and their fortune has experienced its natural progress,
its increase or decay. Our tale, such as it has hitherto been arranged, has
passed in leisurely scenes wherein the present tense is perforce adopted;
the writer acting as chorus to the drama, and occasionally explaining by
hints or more open statements, what has occurred during the intervals of
the acts; and how it happens that the performers are in such or such a
posture. In the modern theatre, as the play-going critic knows, the ex-
planatory personage is usually of quite a third-rate order. He is the two
walking gentlemen friends of Sir Harry Courtly, who welcome the young
baronet to London, and discourse about the niggardliness of Harry's old
uncle, the Nabob; and the depth of Courtly's passion for Lady Annabel
the *première amoureuse.* He is the confidant in white linen to the heroine
in white satin. He is, "Tom, you rascal," the valet or tiger, more or less impudent and acute—that well-known menial in top-boots and a livery frock
with red cuffs and collar, whom Sir Harry always retains in his service, addresses with scurrilous familiarity and pays so irregularly: or he is Lucetta,
Lady Annabel's waiting maid, who carries the *billets-doux* and peeps into
them; knows all about the family affairs; pops the lover under the sofa;

---

[2] three *HM NY*] the three *E1 R*

and sings a comic song between the scenes. Our business now is to enter into Charles Honeyman's privacy, to peer into the secrets of that reverend gentleman, and to tell what has happened to him during the past months, in which he has made fitful though graceful appearances on our scene.[3]

While his nephew's whiskers have been budding, and his brother-in-law has been spending his money and leave, Mr. Honeyman's hopes have been withering, his sermons growing stale, his once blooming popularity drooping and running to seed. Many causes have contributed to bring him to his present melancholy strait. When you go to Lady Whittlesea's chapel now, it is by no means crowded. Gaps are in the pews: there is not the least difficulty in getting a snug place near the pulpit, whence the preacher can look over his pocket handkerchief and see Lord Dosely no more: his lordship has long gone to sleep elsewhere; and a host of the fashionable faithful have migrated too. The incumbent can no more cast his fine eyes upon the French bonnets of the female aristocracy and see some of the loveliest faces in Mayfair regarding his[4] with expressions of admiration. Actual dowdy tradesmen of the neighbourhood are seated with their families in the aisles: Ridley and his wife and son have one of the very best seats. To be sure Ridley looks like a nobleman with his large waistcoat, bald head, and gilt book: J.J. has a fine head, but Mrs. Ridley! cook and housekeeper is written on her round face. The music is by no means of its former good quality. That rebellious and ill-conditioned basso Bellew has seceded, and seduced the four best singing boys, who now perform glees at the Cave of Harmony. Honeyman has a right to speak of persecution and to compare himself to a hermit in so far that he preaches in a desert. Once, like another hermit, St. Hierome, he used to be visited by lions. None such come to him now. Such lions as frequent the clergy are gone off to lick the feet of other ecclesiastics. They are weary of poor Honeyman's old sermons.

Rivals have sprung up in the course of these three years—have sprung up round about Honeyman and carried his flock into their folds. We know how such simple animals will leap one after another and that it is the sheepish way. Perhaps a new pastor has come to the church of St. Jacob's hard by—bold, resolute, bright, clear, a scholar and no pedant: his manly voice is thrilling in their ears, he speaks of life and conduct, of practice as well as faith; and crowds of the most polite and most intelligent, and best informed, and best dressed, and most selfish people in the world come and hear him twice at least. There are so many well informed and well dressed &c. &c. people in the world that the succession of them keeps St. Jacob's full for a year or more. Then, it may be, a bawling quack, who has neither knowledge, nor scholarship, nor charity, but who frightens the public with denunciations and rouses them with the energy of his wrath, succeeds in bringing them together for a while till they tire of his din and curses. Meanwhile the good quiet old churches round about ring their accustomed bell: open their sabbath gates:[5] receive their tranquil congregations and sober priest, who has been busy all the week, at schools and sick beds with watchful teaching, gentle counsel and silent alms.

---

[3] scene. *E1*] stage. *R*
[4] his *E1*] him *R*
[5] gates: *E1*] gates; and *R*

Though we saw Honeyman but seldom, for his company was not altogether amusing, and his affectation when one became acquainted with it
very tiresome to witness, Fred Bayham, from his garret at Mrs. Ridley's,
kept constant watch over the curate, and told us of his proceedings from
time to time. When we heard the melancholy news first announced, of
course the intelligence damped the gaiety of Clive and his companion; and
F.B., who conducted all the affairs of life with great gravity, telling Tom Sarjent that he had news of importance for our private ear, Tom with still more
gravity than F.B.'s said, "Go my children, you had best discuss this topic in
a separate room apart from the din and fun of a convivial assembly;" and
ringing the bell he bade Betsy bring him another glass of rum and water,
and one for Mr. Desborough to be charged to him.

We adjourned to another parlour then, where gas was lighted up: and
F.B. over a pint of beer narrated poor Honeyman's mishap. "Saving your
presence, Clive," said Bayham, "and with every regard for the youthful
bloom of your young heart's affections, your uncle Charles Honeyman, Sir,
is a bad lot. I have known him these twenty years, when I was at his father's
as a private tutor. Old Miss Honeyman is one of those cards which we call
trumps—so was old Honeyman a trump; but Charles and his sister——"

I stamped on F.B.'s foot under the table. He seemed to have forgotten
that he was about to speak of Clive's mother.

"Hem! of your poor mother, I—hem—I may say *vidi tantum.* I scarcely
knew her. She married very young: as I was when she left Borhambury.
But Charles exhibited his character at a very early age—and it was not
a charming one—no, by no means a model of virtue. He always had a
genius for running into debt. He borrowed from every one of the pupils—
I don't know how he spent it except in hardbake and alycompaine—and
even from old Nosey's groom, pardon me, we used to call your grandfather
by that playful epithet (boys will be boys, you know), even from the doctor's
groom he took money, and I recollect thrashing Charles Honeyman for
that disgraceful action.

"At college, without any particular show, he was always in debt and difficulties. Take warning by him, dear youth! By him and by me, if you like.
See me—me, F. Bayham, descended from the ancient kings that long the
Tuscan sceptre swayed, dodge down a street to get out of sight of a boot
shop, and my colossal frame tremble if a chap puts his hand on my shoulder, as you did, Pendennis, the other day in the Strand, when I thought a
straw might have knocked me down! I have had my errors, Clive. I know
'em. I'll take another pint of beer, if you please. Betsy, has Mrs. Nokes
any cold meat in the bar? and an accustomed pickle? Ha! Give her my
compliments, and say F.B. is hungry. I resume my tale. Faults F.B. has,
and knows it. Humbug he may have been sometimes; but I'm not such a
complete humbug as Honeyman."

Clive did not know how to look at this character of his relative, but Clive's
companion burst into a fit of laughter, at which F.B. nodded gravely, and
resumed his narrative. "I don't know how much money he has had from
your governor, but this I can say, the half of it would make F.B. a happy
man. I don't know out of how much the reverend party has nobbled his
poor old sister at Brighton. He has mortgaged his chapel to Sherrick, I

suppose you know, who is master of it, and could turn him out any day. I don't think Sherrick is a bad fellow. I think he's a good fellow; I have known him do many a good turn to a chap in misfortune. He wants to get into society: what more natural? That was why you were asked to meet him the other day—and why he asked you to dinner. I hope you had a good one. I wish he'd ask me.

"Then Moss has got his[6] bills, and Moss's brother-in-law in Cursitor Street has taken possession of his revered person. He's very welcome. One Jew has the chapel, another Hebrew has the clergyman. It's singular, ain't it? Sherrick might turn Lady Whittlesea into a synagogue and have the Chief Rabbi into the pulpit, where my uncle the Bishop has given out the text.

"The shares of that concern ain't at a premium. I have had immense fun with Sherrick about it. I like the Hebrew, Sir. He maddens with rage when F.B. goes and asks him whether any more pews are let over-head. Honeyman begged and borrowed in order to buy out the last man. I remember when the speculation was famous, when all the boxes (I mean the pews) were taken for the season, and you couldn't get a place, come ever so early. Then Honeyman was spoilt, and gave his sermons over and over again. People got sick of seeing the old humbug cry, the old crocodile! Then we tried the musical dodge. F.B. came forward, Sir, there. That *was* a coup: I did it, Sir. Bellew wouldn't have sung for any man but me— and for two-and-twenty months I kept him as sober as Father Matthew. Then Honeyman didn't pay him: there was a row in the sacred building, and Bellew retired. Then Sherrick must meddle in it. And having heard a chap out Hampstead way who Sherrick thought would do, Honeyman was forced to engage him, regardless of expense. You recollect the fellow, Sir. The Reverend Simeon Rawkins, the lowest of the low church, Sir, a red-haired dumpy man, who gasped at his h's and spoke with a Lancashire twang—he'd no more do for Mayfair than Grimaldi for Macbeth. He and Honeyman used to fight like cat and dog in the vestry: and he drove away a third part of the congregation. He was an honest man and an able man too, though not a sound churchman (F.B. said this with a very edifying gravity): I told Sherrick this the very day I heard him. And if he had spoken to me on the subject I might have saved him a pretty penny— a precious deal more than the paltry sum which he and I had a quarrel about at that time—a matter of business, Sir—a pecuniary difference about a small three-months' thing which caused a temporary estrangement between us. As for Honeyman, he used to cry about it. Your uncle is great in the lachrymatory line, Clive Newcome. He used to go with tears in his eyes to Sherrick, and implore him not to have Rawkins, but he would. And I must say for poor Charles that the failure of Lady Whittlesea's has not been altogether Charles's fault; and that Sherrick has kicked down that property.

"Well then Sir, poor Charles thought to make it all right by marrying Mrs. Brumby;—and she was very fond of him and the thing was all but done, in spite of her sons who were in a rage as you may fancy. But Charley,

---

[6] his *E1*] Honeyman's *R*

Sir, has such a propensity for humbug that he will tell lies when there is no earthly good in lying. He represented his chapel at twelve hundred a year, his private means as so and so; and when he came to book up with Briggs, the lawyer, Mrs. Brumby's brother, it was found that he lied and prevaricated so that the widow in actual disgust would have nothing more to do with him. She was a good woman of business and managed the hat shop for nine years whilst poor Brumby was at Doctor Tokely's. A first-rate shop it was too. I introduced Charles to it. My uncle, the bishop, had his shovels there: and they used for a considerable period to cover *this* humble roof with tiles," said F.B., tapping his capacious forehead; "I am sure he might have had Brumby," he added in his melancholy tones, "but for those unlucky lies. She didn't want money. She had plenty. She longed to get into society and was bent on marrying a gentleman.

"But what I can't pardon in Honeyman is the way in which he has done poor old Ridley and his wife. I took him there you know, thinking they would send their bills in once a month: that he was doing a good business: in fact that I had put 'em into a good thing. And the fellow has told me a score of times, that he and the Ridleys were all right. But he has not only not paid his lodgings, but he has had money of them: he has given dinners: he has made Ridley pay for wine. He has kept paying lodgers out of the house and he tells me all this with a burst of tears, when he sent for me to Lazarus's to-night, and I went to him Sir because he was in distress—went into the lion's den, Sir!" says F.B., looking round nobly. "I don't know how much he owes them: because of course you know the sum he mentions aint the right one. He never *does* tell the truth—does Charles. But think of the pluck of those good Ridleys never saying a single word to F.B. about the debt! 'We are poor, but we have saved some money and can lie out of it. And we think Mr. Honeyman will pay us,' says Mrs. Ridley to me this very evening. And she thrilled my heart-strings, Sir; and I took her in my arms, and kissed the old woman," says Bayham, "and I rather astonished little Miss Cann and young J.J. who came in with a picture under his arm. But she said she had kissed Master Frederick long before J.J. was born—and so she had: that good and faithful servant—and my emotion in embracing her was manly, Sir, manly."

Here old Betsy came in to say that the supper was a waitin' for Mr. Bayham and it was a gettin' very late: and we left F.B. to his meal and bidding adieu to Mrs. Nokes, Clive and I went each to our habitation.

Chapter XXVI.

T an hour early the next morning I was not surprised to see Colonel Newcome at my chambers, to whom Clive had communicated Bayham's important news of the night before. The Colonel's object, as any one who knew him need scarcely be told, was to rescue his brother-in-law; and being ignorant of lawyers, sheriffs' officers, and their proceedings, he bethought him that he would apply to Lamb Court for information, and in so far showed some prudence, for at least I knew more of the world and its ways than my simple client, and was enabled to make better terms for the unfortunate prisoner, or rather for Colonel Newcome who was the real sufferer, than Honeyman's creditors might otherwise have been disposed to give.

I thought it would be more prudent that our good Samaritan should not see the victim of rogues whom he was about to succour; and left him to entertain himself with Mr. Warrington in Lamb Court, while I sped to the lock-up-house, where the May Fair pet was confined. A sickly smile played over his countenance as he beheld me when I was ushered to his private room. The reverend gentleman was not shaved; he had partaken of breakfast. I saw a glass which had once contained brandy on the dirty tray whereon his meal was placed: a greasy novel from a Chancery Lane library lay on the table: but he was at present occupied in writing one or more of those great long letters, those laborious, ornate, eloquent statements, those documents so profusely underlined, in which the *machinations of villains* are laid bare with italic fervour; the coldness, to use no *harsher* phrase, of friends on whom reliance *might have been placed*; the outrageous conduct of Solomons; the astonishing failure of Smith to pay a sum of money on which he had counted as *on the Bank of England*; finally, the *infallible certainty* of repaying (with what heartfelt thanks need not be said) the loan of so many pounds *next Saturday week at farthest*. All this, which some readers in the course of their experience have read no doubt in many handwritings, was duly set forth by poor Honeyman. There was a wafer in a wine-glass on the table, and the bearer no doubt below to carry the missive. They always send these letters by a messenger, who is introduced in the postscript; he is always sitting in the hall when you get the letter, and is "a young man waiting for an answer, please."

No one can suppose that Honeyman laid a complete statement of his affairs before the negociator, who was charged to look into them. No creditor does confess all his debts, but breaks them gradually to his man of business, factor or benefactor, leading him on from surprise to surprise; and when he is in possession of the tailor's little account, introducing him to the bootmaker. Honeyman's schedule I felt perfectly certain was not correct. The detainers against him were trifling. "Moss of Wardour Street, one hundred and twenty—I believe I have paid him thousands in this very transaction," ejaculates Honeyman. "A heartless West End tradesman hearing of my misfortune—these people are all linked together, my dear Pendennis, and rush like vultures upon their prey! Waddilove, the tailor, has another writ out for ninety-eight pounds—a man whom I have made by my recommendations! Tobbins, the bootmaker, his neighbour in Jermyn Street, forty-one pounds more, and that is all—I give you my word, all. In a few months, when my pew-rents will be coming in, I should have settled with those cormorants; otherwise, my total and irretrievable ruin, and the disgrace and humiliation of a prison attend me. I know it; I can bear it; I have been wretchedly weak, Pendennis: I can say *mea culpa, mea maxima culpa*, and I can—bear—my—penalty." In his finest moments he was never more pathetic. He turned his head away, and concealed it in a handkerchief not so white as those which veiled his emotions at Lady Whittlesea's.

How by degrees this slippery penitent was induced to make other confessions; how we got an idea of Mrs. Ridley's account from him, of his dealings with Mr. Sherrick, need not be mentioned here. The conclusion to which Colonel Newcome's ambassador came was, that to help such a man would be quite useless; and that the Fleet Prison would be a most wholesome retreat for this most reckless divine. Ere the day was out Messrs. Waddilove and Tobbins had conferred with their neighbour in St. James's, Mr. Brace; and there came a detainer from that haberdasher for gloves, cravats, and pocket-handkerchiefs, that might have done credit to the most dandified young Guardsman. Mr. Warrington was on Mr. Pendennis's side, and urged that the law should take its course. "Why help a man," said he, "who will not help himself? Let the law sponge out the fellow's debts; set him going again with twenty pounds when he quits the prison, and get him a chaplaincy in the Isle of Man."

I saw by the Colonel's grave kind face that these hard opinions did not suit him. At all events, Sir, promise us, we said, that you will pay nothing yourself—that *you* won't see Honeyman's creditors, and let people, who know the world better, deal with him. "Know the world, young man!" cries Newcome; "I should think if I don't know the world at my age, I never shall." And if he had lived to be as old as Jahaleel a boy could still have cheated him.[1]

"I do not scruple to tell you," he said, after a pause, during which a plenty of smoke was delivered from the council of three, "that I have— a fund—which I had set aside for mere purposes of pleasure, I give you my word, and a part of which I shall think it my duty to devote to poor Honeyman's distresses. The fund is not large. The money was intended in fact:—however, there it is. If Pendennis will go round to these tradesmen, and make some composition with them, as their prices have been no doubt enormously exaggerated, I see no harm. Besides the tradesfolk there is good Mrs. Ridley and Mr. Sherrick—we must see them; and, if we can, set this luckless Charles again on his legs. We have read of other prodigals who were kindly treated; and we may have debts of our own to forgive, boys."

Into Mr. Sherrick's account we had no need to enter. That gentleman had acted with perfect fairness by Honeyman. He laughingly said to us, "You don't imagine I would lend that chap a shilling without security? I will give him fifty or a hundred. Here's one of his notes, with what-do-

---

[1] The illustration belongs two paragraphs above, but would not fit on the previous page, either in this edition or in the first, where it follows the paragraph ending "Isle of Man."

you-call-'em's—that rum fellow Bayham's—name as drawer. A nice pair, aint they? Pooh! *I* shall never touch 'em. I lent some money on the shop overhead," says Sherrick, pointing to the ceiling (we were in his counting-house in the cellar of Lady Whittlesea's chapel), "because I thought it was a good speculation. And so it was at first. The people liked Honeyman. All the nobs came to hear him. Now the speculation aint so good. He's used up. A chap can't be expected to last for ever. When I first engaged Mademoiselle Bravura at my theatre, you couldn't get a place for three weeks together. The next year she didn't draw twenty pounds a week. So it was with Pottle, and the regular drama humbug. At first it was all very well. Good business, good houses, our immortal bard, and that sort of game. They engaged the tigers and the French riding people over the way; and there was Pottle bellowing away in my place to the orchestra and the orders. It's all a speculation. I've speculated in about pretty much everything that's going: in theatres, in joint-stock jobs, in building ground, in bills, in gas and insurance companies, and in this chapel. Poor old Honeyman! *I* won't hurt him. About that other chap I put in to do the first business—that red-haired chap, Rawkins—I think I was wrong. I think he injured the property. But I don't know everything, you know. I wasn't bred to know about parsons—quite the reverse. I thought, when I heard Rawkins at Hampstead, he was just the thing. I used to go about, Sir, just as I did to the provinces, when I had the theatre—Camberwell, Islington, Kennington, Clapton, all about, and hear the young chaps. Have a glass of sherry; and here's better luck to Honeyman. As for that Colonel, he's a trump, Sir! I never see such a man. I have to deal with such a precious lot of rogues: in the city and out of it, among the swells and all you know, that to see such a fellow refreshes me; and I'd do anything for him. You've made a good thing of that *Pall Mall Gazette*! I tried papers too; but mine didn't do. I don't know why. I tried a Tory one, moderate Liberal, and out-and-out uncompromising Radical. I say, what d'ye think of a religious paper, the *Catechism*, or some such name? Would Honeyman do as editor? I'm afraid it's all up with the poor cove at the chapel." And I parted with Mr. Sherrick, not a little edified by his talk, and greatly relieved as to Honeyman's fate. The tradesmen of Honeyman's body were appeased; and as for Mr. Moss, when he found that the curate had no effects, and must go before the Insolvent Court, unless Moss chose to take the composition, which we were empowered to offer him; he too was brought to hear reason, and parted with the stamped paper on which was poor Honeyman's signature. Our negotiation had like to have come to an end by Clive's untimely indignation, who offered at one stage of the proceedings to pitch young Moss out of window; but nothing came of this most ungentlebadlike beayviour on Noocob's part, further than remonstrance and delay in the proceedings; and Honeyman preached a lovely sermon at Lady Whittlesea's the very next Sunday. He had made himself much liked in the sponging-house, and Mr. Lazarus said, "If he hadn't a got out time enough, I'd a let him out for Sunday, and sent one of my men with him to show him the way ome, you know; for when a gentleman behaves as a gentleman to me, I behave as a gentleman to him."

Mrs. Ridley's account, and it was a long one, was paid without a single question, or the deduction of a farthing; but the Colonel rather sickened of Honeyman's expressions of rapturous gratitude, and received his professions of mingled contrition and delight very coolly. "My boy," says the father to Clive, "you see to what straits debt brings a man, to tamper with truth, to have to cheat the poor. Think of flying before a washerwoman, or humbling yourself to a tailor, or eating a poor man's children's bread!" Clive blushed, I thought, and looked rather confused.

"O, Father," says he, "I—I'm afraid I owe some money too—not much; but about forty pound, five-and-twenty for cigars, and fifteen I borrowed of Pendennis, and—and—I've been devilish annoyed about it all this time."

"You stupid boy," says the father, "I knew about the cigars bill, and paid it last week. Anything I have is yours you know. As long as there is a guinea, there is half for you. See that every shilling we owe is paid before—before a week is over. And go down and ask Binnie if I can see him in his study. I want to have some conversation with him." When Clive was gone away, he said to me in a very sweet voice, "In God's name, keep my boy out of debt when I am gone, Arthur. I shall return to India very soon."

"Very soon, Sir! You have another year's leave," said I.

"Yes, but no allowances you know; and this affair of Honeyman's has pretty nearly emptied the little purse I had set aside for European expenses. They have been very much heavier than I expected. As it is, I overdrew my account at my brother's, and have been obliged to draw money from my agents in Calcutta. A year sooner or later (unless two of our senior officers had died, when I should have got my promotion and full colonel's pay with it, and proposed to remain in this country)—a year sooner or later, what does it matter? Clive will go away and work at his art, and see the great schools of painting while I am absent. I thought at one time how pleasant it would be to accompany him. But *l'homme propose,* Pendennis. I fancy now a lad is not the better for being always tied to his parent's apron-string. You young fellows are too clever for me. I haven't learned your ideas or read your books. I feel myself very often an old damper in your company. I will go back, Sir, where I have some friends, and where I am somebody still. I know an honest face or two, white and brown, that will lighten up in the old regiment when they see Tom Newcome again. God bless you, Arthur. You young fellows in this country have such cold ways that we old ones hardly know how to like you at first. James Binnie and I, when we first came home, used to talk you over, and think you laughed at us. But you didn't, I know. God Almighty bless you, and send you a good wife, and make a good man of you. I have bought a watch, which I would like you to wear in remembrance of me and my boy, to whom you were so kind when you were boys together in the old Grey Friars." I took his hand, and uttered some incoherent words of affection and respect. Did not Thomas Newcome merit both from all who knew him?

His resolution being taken, our good Colonel began to make silent but effectual preparations for his coming departure. He was pleased during these last days of his stay to give me even more of his confidence than

I had previously enjoyed, and was kind enough to say that he regarded me almost as a son of his own, and hoped I would act as elder brother and guardian to Clive. Ah! who is to guard the guardian? The younger brother had many nobler qualities than belonged to the elder. The world had not hardened Clive, nor even succeeded in spoiling him. I perceive I am diverging from his history into that of another person, and will return to the subject proper of the book.

Colonel Newcome expressed himself as being particularly touched and pleased with his friend Binnie's conduct, now that the Colonel's departure was determined. "James is one of the most generous of men, Pendennis, and I am proud to be put under an obligation to him, and to tell it too. I hired this house, as you are aware, of our speculative friend Mr. Sherrick, and am answerable for the payment of the rent till the expiry of the lease. James has taken the matter off my hands entirely. The place is greatly too large for him, but he says that he likes it, and intends to stay, and that his sister and niece shall be his housekeepers. Clive (here, perhaps, the speaker's voice drops a little) Clive will be the son of the house still, honest James says, and God bless him. James is richer than I thought by near a lakh of rupees—and here is a hint for you, Master Arthur. Mr. Binnie has declared to me in confidence that if his niece, Miss Rosey, shall marry a person of whom he approves, he will leave her a considerable part of his fortune."

The Colonel's confidant here said that his own arrangements were made in another quarter, to which statement the Colonel replied knowingly, "I thought so. A little bird has whispered to me the name of a certain Miss A. I knew her grandfather, an accommodating old gentleman, and I borrowed some money from him when I was a subaltern at Calcutta. I tell you in strict confidence, my dear young friend, that I hope and trust a certain young gentleman of your acquaintance may be induced to think how good and pretty and sweet-tempered a girl Miss Mackenzie is, and that she may be brought to like him. If you young men would marry in good time good and virtuous women—as I am sure—ahem!—Miss Amory is—half the temptations of your youth would be avoided. You would neither be dissolute, as many of you seem to me, or cold and selfish, which are worse vices still. And my prayer is, that my Clive may cast anchor early out of the reach of temptation, and mate with some such kind girl as Binnie's niece. When I first came home I formed other plans for him which could not be brought to a successful issue; and knowing his ardent disposition, and having kept an eye on the young rogue's conduct, I tremble lest some mischance with a woman should befal him, and long to have him out of danger."

So the kind scheme of the two elders was, that their young ones should marry and be happy ever after, like the Prince and Princess of the Fairy-Tale: and dear Mrs. Mackenzie, (have I said that at the commencement of her visit to her brother she made almost open love to the Colonel?) dear Mrs. Mack was content to forego her own chances so that her darling Rosey might be happy. We used to laugh and say, that as soon as Clive's father was gone, Josey would be sent for to join Rosey. But little Josey being under her grandmother's sole influence took a most gratifying and serious turn; wrote letters, in which she questioned the morality of operas, Towers of London, and wax-works; and, before a year was out, married Elder Bogie, of Mr. M'Craw's church.

Presently was to be read in the *Morning Post* an advertisement of the sale of three horses (the description and pedigree following), "the property of an officer returning to India. Apply to the groom, at the stables, 150, Fitzroy Square."

The Court of Directors invited Lieutenant-Colonel Newcome to an entertainment given to Major-General Sir Ralph Spurrier, K.C.B., appointed Commander-in-Chief at Madras. Clive was asked to this dinner too, "and the governor's health was drunk, Sir," Clive said, "after dinner, and the dear old fellow made such a good speech, in returning thanks!"

He, Clive and I made a pilgrimage to Grey Friars, and had the Green to ourselves, it being the Bartlemytide vacation, and the boys all away. One of the good old Poor Brothers whom we both recollected accompanied us round the place; and we sate for a while in Captain Scarsdale's little room (he had been a peninsular officer, who had sold out, and was fain in his old age to retire into this calm retreat). And we talked, as old schoolmates and lovers talk, about subjects interesting to schoolmates and lovers only.

One by one the Colonel took leave of his friends, young and old; ran down to Newcome, and gave Mrs. Mason a parting benediction; slept a night at Tom Smith's, and passed a day with Jack Brown; went to all the boys' and girls' schools where his little protégés were, so as to be able to take the very last and most authentic account of the young folks to their parents in India; spent a week at Marble Head, and shot partridges there, but for which entertainment, Clive said, the place would have been intolerable; and thence proceeded to Brighton to pass a little time with good Miss Honeyman. As for Sir Brian's family, when parliament broke up of course they did not stay in town. Barnes, of course, had part of a moor in Scotland, whither his uncle and cousin did not follow him. The rest went abroad. Sir Brian wanted the waters of Aix-la-Chapelle; the brothers parted very good friends; Lady Ann, and all the young people, heartily wished him farewell. I believe Sir Brian even accompanied the Colonel down-stairs from the drawing-room, in Park Lane, and actually came out and saw his brother into his cab (just as he would accompany old Lady Bagges when she came to look at her account at the bank, from the parlour to her carriage). But as for Ethel *she* was not going to be put off with this sort of parting: and the next morning a cab dashed up to Fitzroy Square, and a veiled lady came out thence, and was closeted with Colonel Newcome for five minutes, and when he led her back to the carriage there were tears in his eyes.

Mrs. Mackenzie joked about the transaction (having watched it from the dining-room windows), and asked the Colonel who his sweetheart was? Newcome replied very sternly, that he hoped no one would ever speak lightly of that young lady, whom he loved as his own daughter; and I thought Rosey looked vexed at the praises thus bestowed. This was the day before we all went down to Brighton. Miss Honeyman's lodgings were taken for Mr. Binnie and his ladies. Clive and her dearest Colonel had apartments next door. Charles Honeyman came down and preached one of his very best sermons. Fred Bayham was there, and looked particularly grand and noble on the pier and the cliff. I am inclined to think he had had some explanation with Thomas Newcome, which had placed F.B. in a state of at least temporary prosperity. Whom did he not benefit whom he knew, and what eye that saw him did not bless him? F.B. was greatly affected at Charles's sermon, of which our party of course could see the allusions. Tears actually rolled down his brown cheeks; for Fred was a man very easily moved, and as it were a softened sinner. Little Rosey and her mother sobbed audibly, greatly to the surprise of stout old Miss Honeyman, who had no idea of such watery exhibitions, and to the discomfiture of poor Newcome, who was annoyed to have his praises even hinted in that sacred edifice. Good Mr. James Binnie came for once to church; and, however variously their feelings might be exhibited or repressed, I think there was not one of the little circle there assembled who did not bring to the place a humble prayer and a gentle heart. It was the last sabbath-bell our dear friend was to hear for many a day on his native shore. The great sea washed the beach as we came out, blue with the reflection of the skies, and its innumerable waves crested with sunshine. I see the good man and his boy yet clinging to him, as they pace together by the shore.

The Colonel was very much pleased by a visit from Mr. Ridley, and the communication which he made (My Lord Todmorden has a mansion and park in Sussex, whence Mr. Ridley came to pay his duty to Colonel Newcome). He said he "never could forget the kindness with which the Colonel have a treated him. His lordship have taken a young man, which Mr. Ridley had brought him up under his own eye, and can answer for him, Mr. R. says, with impunity; and which he is to be his lordship's own man for the future. And his lordship have appointed me his steward, and having, as he always hev been, been most liberal in point of sellary. And me and Mrs. Ridley was thinking, Sir, most respectfully, with regard to our son, Mr. John James Ridley—as good and honest a young man, which I am proud to say it, that if Mr. Clive goes abroad we should be most proud and happy if John James went with him. And the money which you have paid us so handsome, Colonel, he shall have it; which it was the excellent ideer of Miss Cann; and my lord have ordered a pictur of John James in the most libral manner, and have asked my son to dinner, Sir, at his lordship's own table, which I have faithfully served him five and thirty years." Ridley's voice fairly broke down at this part of his speech, which evidently was a studied composition, and he uttered no more of it, for the Colonel cordially shook him by the hand, and Clive jumped up clapping his, and saying that it was the greatest wish of his heart that J.J. and he should be companions in France and Italy. "But I did not like to ask my dear old father," he said, "who has had so many calls on his purse, and besides, I knew that J.J. was too independent to come as my follower."

The Colonel's berth has been duly secured ere now. This time he makes the overland journey; and his passage is to Alexandria, taken in one of the noble ships of the Peninsular and Oriental Company. His kit is as simple as a subaltern's; I believe, but for Clive's friendly compulsion, he would

"Farewell"

have carried back no other than the old uniform which has served him for so many years. Clive and his father travelled to Southampton together by themselves. F.B. and I took the Southampton coach: we had asked leave to see the last of him, and say a "God bless you" to our dear old friend. So the day came when the vessel was to sail. We saw his cabin, and witnessed all the bustle and stir on board the good ship on a day of departure. Our thoughts, however, were fixed but on one person—the case, no doubt, with hundreds more on such a day. There was many a group of friends closing wistfully together on the sunny deck, and saying the last words of blessing and farewell. The bustle of the ship passes dimly round about them; the hurrying noise of crew and officers running on their duty; the tramp and song of the men at the capstan bars; the bells ringing, as the hour for departure comes nearer and nearer, as mother and son, father and daughter, husband and wife, hold hands yet for a little while. We saw Clive and his father talking together by the wheel. Then they went below; and a passenger, her husband, asked me to give my arm to an almost fainting lady, and to lead her off the ship. Bayham followed us, carrying their two children in his arms, as the husband turned away, and walked aft. The last bell was ringing, and they were crying, "Now for the shore." The whole ship had begun to throb ere this, and its great wheels to beat the water, and the chimneys had flung out their black signals for sailing. We were as yet close on the dock, and we saw Clive coming up from below, looking very pale; the plank was drawn after him as he stepped on land.

Then, with three great cheers from the dock, and from the crew in the bows, and from the passengers on the quarter deck, the noble ship strikes the first stroke of her destined race, and swims away towards the ocean. "There he is, there he is," shouts Fred Bayham, waving his hat. "God bless him, God bless him!" I scarce perceived at the ship's side, beckoning an adieu, our dear old friend, when the lady, whose husband had bidden me to lead her away from the ship, fainted in my arms. Poor soul! Her, too, has fate stricken. Ah, pangs of hearts torn asunder, passionate regrets, cruel, cruel partings! Shall you not end one day, ere many years; when the tears shall be wiped from all eyes, and there shall be neither sorrow nor pain?

Chapter XXVII.

YOUTH AND SUNSHINE.

LTHOUGH Thomas Newcome was gone back to India in search of more money, finding that he could not live upon his income at home, he was nevertheless rather a wealthy man; and at the moment of his departure from Europe had two lakhs of rupees invested in various Indian securities. "A thousand a year," he thought, "more, added to the interest accruing from my two lakhs, will enable us to live very comfortably at home. I can give Clive ten thousand pounds when he marries, and five hundred a-year out of my allowances. If he gets a wife with some money, they may have every enjoyment of life; and as for his pictures he can paint just as few or as many of those as he pleases." Newcome did not seem seriously to believe that his son would live by painting pictures, but considered Clive as a young prince who chose to amuse himself with painting. The Muse of Painting is a lady whose social station is not altogether recognised with us as yet. The polite world permits a gentleman to amuse himself with her, but to take her for better or for worse! forsake all other chances and cleave unto her! to assume her name! Many a respectable person would be as much shocked at the notion, as if his son had married an opera dancer.

Newcome left a hundred a-year in England, of which the principal sum was to be transferred to his boy as soon as he came of age. He endowed Clive farther with a considerable annual sum, which his London bankers would pay: "And if these are not enough," says he kindly, "you must draw upon my agents, Messrs. Franks and Merryweather, at Calcutta, who will receive your signature just as if it was mine." Before going away, he introduced Clive to F. and M.'s corresponding London house, Jolly and Baines, Fog Court—leading out of Leadenhall—Mr. Jolly, a myth as regarded the firm, now married to Lady Julia Jolly—a park in Kent—evangelical interest—great at Exeter Hall meetings—knew Clive's grandmother—that is, Mrs. Newcome, a most admirable woman. Baines represents a house in the Regent's Park, with an emigrative tendency towards Belgravia— musical daughters—Herr Moscheles, Benedick, Ella, Osborne, constantly at dinner—sonatas in P flat (op. 936), composed and dedicated to Miss Euphemia Baines, by her most obliged, most obedient servant, Ferdinando Blitz. Baines hopes that his young friend will come constantly to York Terrace, where the girls will be most happy to see him; and mentions at home a singular whim of Colonel Newcome's, who can give his son twelve or fifteen hundred a-year, and makes an artist of him. Euphemia and Flora adore artists; they feel quite interested about this young man. "He was scribbling caricatures all the time I was talking with his father in my parlour," says Mr. Baines, and produces a sketch of an orange-woman near the Bank, who had struck Clive's eyes, and been transferred to the blotting-paper in Fog Court. "*He* needn't do anything," said good-natured Mr. Baines. "I guess all the pictures he'll paint won't sell for much."

"Is he fond of music, Papa?" asks Miss. "What a pity he had not come to our last evening; and now the season is over!"

"And Mr. Newcome is going out of town. He came to me to-day for circular notes—says he's going through Switzerland and into Italy—lives in Charlotte Street, Fitzroy Square. Queer place, ain't it? Put his name down in your book, and ask him to dinner next season."

Before Clive went away, he had an apparatus of easels, sketching-stools, umbrellas, and painting-boxes, the most elaborate and beautiful that Messrs. Soap and Isaac could supply. It made J.J.'s eyes glisten to see those lovely gimcracks of art; those smooth mill-boards, those slab-tinted sketching-blocks, and glistening rows of colour-tubes lying in their boxes, which seemed to cry, "Come, squeeze me." If painting-boxes made painters; if sketching-stools would but enable one to sketch, surely I would hasten this very instant to Messrs. Soap and Isaac! but, alas! these pretty toys no more make artists than cowls make monks.

As a proof that Clive did intend to practise his profession, and to live by it too, at this time he took four sporting sketches to a print-seller in the Haymarket, and disposed of them at the rate of seven shillings and sixpence per sketch. His exultation at receiving a sovereign and half a sovereign from Mr. Jones was boundless. "I can do half a dozen of these things easily in a morning," says he. "Two guineas a day is twelve guineas—say ten guineas a week, for I won't work on Sundays, and may take a holiday in the week besides. Ten guineas a week is five hundred a-year. That is pretty nearly as much money as I shall want, and I need not draw the dear old governor's allowance at all." He wrote an ardent letter, full of happiness and affection, to the kind father, which he shall find a month after he has arrived in India, and read to his friends in Calcutta and Barrackpore. Clive invited many of his artist friends to a grand feast in honour of the thirty shillings. The King's Arms, Kensington, was the hotel selected (tavern beloved of artists for many score years!). Gandish was there, and the Gandishites and some chosen spirits from the Life Academy, Clipstone Street, and J.J. was vice-president, with Fred Bayham by his side, to make the speeches and carve the mutton; and I promise you many a merry song was sung, and many a health drunk in flowing bumpers; and as jolly a party was assembled as any London contained that day. The *beau monde* had quitted it; the Park was empty as we crossed it; and the leaves of Kensington Gardens had begun to fall, dying after the fatigues of a London season. We sang all the way home through Knightsbridge and by the Park railings, and the Covent Garden carters halting at the Half-way House were astonished at our choruses. There is no half-way house now; no merry chorus at midnight.

Then Clive and J.J. took the steam-boat to Antwerp; and those who love pictures may imagine how the two young men rejoiced in one of the most picturesque cities of the world; where they went back straightway into the sixteenth century; where the inn at which they staid (delightful old Grand Laboureur, thine ancient walls are levelled! thy comfortable hospitalities exist no more!) seemed such a hostelry as that where Quentin Durward first saw his sweetheart; where knights of Velasquez or burgomasters of Rubens seemed to look from the windows of the tall-gabled houses and the quaint porches; where the Bourse still stood, the Bourse of three hundred years ago, and you had but to supply figures with beards and ruffs, and rapiers and trunk-hose, to make the picture complete; where to be awakened by the carillon of the bells was to waken to the most delightful sense of life and happiness; where nuns, actual nuns, walked the streets, and every figure in the Place de Meir, and every devotee at church kneeling and draped in black, or entering the confessional (actually the confessional!), was a delightful subject for the new sketch-book. Had Clive drawn as much everywhere as at Antwerp, Messrs. Soap and Isaac might have made a little income by supplying him with materials.

After Antwerp, Clive's correspondent gets a letter dated from the Hotel de Suède at Brussels, which contains an elaborate eulogy of the cookery and comfort of that hotel, where the wines, according to the writer's opinion, are unmatched almost in Europe. And this is followed by a description of Waterloo, and a sketch of Hougoumont, in which J.J. is represented running away in the character of a French grenadier, Clive pursuing him in the life-guard's habit, and mounted on a thundering charger.

Next follows a letter from Bonn. Verses about Drachenfels of a not very superior style of versification: account of Crichton, an old Grey Friars man, who has become a student at the university; of a commerz, a drunken bout; and a students' duel at Bonn. "And whom should I find here," says Mr. Clive, "but Aunt Ann, Ethel, Miss Quigley, and the little ones, the whole detachment under the command of Kuhn? Uncle Brian is staying at Aix. He is recovered from his attack. And, upon my conscience, I think my pretty cousin looks prettier every day.

"When they are not in London," Clive goes on to write, "or I sometimes think when Barnes or old Lady Kew are not looking over them, they are quite different. You know how cold they have latterly seemed to us, and how their conduct annoyed my dear old father. Nothing can be kinder than their behaviour since we have met. It was on the little hill at Godesberg, J.J. and I were mounting to the ruin, followed by the beggars who waylay

A Meeting in Rhineland

you, and have taken the place of the other robbers who used to live there, when there came a procession of donkeys down the steep, and I heard a little voice cry 'Hullo! it's Clive! hooray, Clive!' and an ass came pattering down the declivity, with a little pair of white trowsers at an immensely wide angle over the donkey's back, and behold there was little Alfred grinning with all his might.

"He turned his beast and was for galloping up the hill again, I suppose to inform his relations; but the donkey refused with many kicks, one of which sent Alfred plunging amongst the stones, and we were rubbing him down just as the rest of the party came upon us. Miss Quigley looked very grim on an old white poney; my aunt was on a black horse that might have turned grey, he is so old. Then come two donkeysful of children, with Kuhn as supercargo; then Ethel on donkey back, too, with a bunch of wild flowers in her hand, a great straw hat with a crimson ribbon, a white muslin jacket you know, bound at the waist with a ribbon of the first, and a dark skirt, with a shawl round her feet which Kuhn had arranged. As she stopped, the donkey fell to cropping greens in the hedge; the trees there chequered her white dress and face with shadow. Her eyes, hair, and forehead were in shadow too—but the light was all upon her right cheek: upon her shoulder down to her arm, which was of a warmer white, and on the bunch of flowers which she held, blue, yellow and red poppies, and so forth.

"J.J. says 'I think the birds began to sing louder when she came.' We have both agreed that she is the handsomest woman in England. It's not her form merely, which is certainly as yet too thin and a little angular—it is her colour. I do not care for woman or picture without colour. O ye carnations! O ye *lilia mista rosis!* O such black hair and solemn eyebrows! It seems to me the roses and carnations have bloomed again since we saw them last in London; when they were drooping from the exposure to night air, candle light, and heated ball-rooms.

"Here I was in the midst of a regiment of donkeys, bearing a crowd of relations; J.J. standing modestly in the back ground—beggars completing the group, and Kuhn ruling over them with voice and gesture, oaths and whip. Throw in the Rhine in the distance flashing by the Seven Mountains—but mind and make Ethel the principal figure: if you make her like—she certainly *will* be—and other lights will be only minor fires. You may paint her form, but you can't paint her colour; that is what beats us in nature. A line *must* come right; you can force that into its place, but you can't compel the circumambient air. There is no yellow I know of will make sunshine; and no blue that is a bit like sky. And so with pictures: I think you only get signs of colour, and formulas to stand for it. That brickdust which we agree to receive as representing a blush, look at it—can you say it is in the least like the blush which flickers and varies as it sweeps over the down of the cheek—as you see sunshine playing over a meadow? Look into it and see what a variety of delicate blooms there are! a multitude of flowerets twining into one tint! We may break our colour pots and strive after the line alone: that is palpable and we can grasp it—the other is impossible and beyond us." Which sentiment I here set down, not on account of its worth (and I think it is contradicted—as well as asserted—in more than one of the letters I subsequently had from Mr. Clive), but it may serve to show the ardent and impulsive disposition of this youth, by whom all beauties of art and nature, animate or inanimate, (the former especially,) were welcomed with a gusto and delight whereof colder temperaments are incapable. The view of a fine landscape, a fine picture, a handsome woman, would make this harmless young sensualist tipsy with pleasure. He seemed to derive an actual hilarity and intoxication as his eye drank in these sights; and, though it was his maxim that all dinners were good, and he could eat bread and cheese and drink small beer with perfect good humour, I believe that he found a certain pleasure in a bottle of claret, which most men's systems were incapable of feeling.

This spring-time of youth is the season of letter-writing. A lad in high health and spirits, the blood running briskly in his young veins, and the world, and life, and nature bright and welcome to him, looks out, perforce, for some companion to whom he may impart his sense of the pleasure which he enjoys, and which were not complete unless a friend were by to share it. I was the person most convenient for the young fellow's purpose; he was pleased to confer upon me the title of friend *en titre*, and confidant in particular; to endow the confidant in question with a number of virtues and excellences which existed very likely only in the lad's imagination; to lament that the confidant had no sister whom he, Clive, might marry out of hand; and to make me a thousand simple protests of affection and admiration, which are noted here as signs of the young man's character, by no means as proofs of the goodness of mine. The books given to the present biographer by "his affectionate friend, Clive Newcome," still bear on the title-pages the marks of that boyish hand and youthful fervour. He had a copy of "Walter Lorraine," bound and gilt with such splendour as made the author blush for his performance, which has since been seen at the book-stalls at a price suited to the very humblest purses. He fired up and fought a newspaper critic (whom Clive met at the Haunt one night) who had dared to write an article in which that work was slighted; and if, in the course of nature, his friendship has outlived that rapturous period; the kindness of the two old friends, I hope, is not the less because it is no longer romantic, and the days of white vellum and gilt edges have passed away. From the abundance of the letters which the affectionate young fellow now wrote, the ensuing portion of his youthful history is compiled. It may serve to recal passages of their early days to such of his seniors as occasionally turn over the leaves of a novel; and in the story of his faults, indiscretions, passions, and actions, young readers may be reminded of their own.

Now that the old Countess, and perhaps Barnes, were away, the barrier between Clive and this family seemed to be withdrawn. The young folks who loved him were free to see him as often as he would come. They were going to Baden: would he come too? Baden was on the road to Switzerland, he might journey to Strasbourg, Basle, and so on. Clive was glad enough to go with his cousins—and travel in the orbit of such a lovely girl as Ethel Newcome. J.J. performed the second part always when Clive was present: and so they all travelled to Coblentz, Mayence, and Frankfort together, making the journey which everybody knows, and sketching the mountains and castles we all of us have sketched. Ethel's beauty made all the passengers on all the steamers look round and admire. Clive was proud of being in the suite of such a lovely person. The family travelled with a pair of those carriages, which used to thunder along the continental roads a dozen years since, and from interior, box, and rumble discharge a dozen English people at hotel gates.

The journey is all sunshine and pleasure and novelty: the circular notes with which Mr. Baines of Fog Court has supplied Clive Newcome, Esquire, enabled that young gentleman to travel with great ease and comfort. He has not yet ventured upon engaging a valet de chambre, it being agreed between him and J.J. that two travelling artists have no right to such an aristocratic appendage, but he has bought a snug little britzska at Frankfort, (the youth has very polite tastes, is already a connoisseur in wine, and has no scruple in ordering the best at the hotels,) and the britzska travels in company with Lady Ann's caravan, either in its wake so as to be out of reach of the dust, or more frequently a-head of that enormous vehicle, and its tender, in which come the children and the governess of Lady Ann Newcome, guarded by a huge and melancholy London footman, who beholds Rhine and Neckar, valley and mountain, village and ruin, with a like dismal composure. Little Alfred and little Egbert are by no means sorry to escape from Miss Quigley and the tender, and ride for a stage or two in Clive's britzska. The little girls cry sometimes to be admitted to that privilege. I daresay Ethel would like very well to quit her place in the caravan, where she sits circumvented by Mamma's dogs, and books, bags, dressing boxes, and gimcrack cases, without which apparatus some English ladies of condition cannot travel; but Miss Ethel is grown up, she is out, and has been presented at Court, and is a person of too great dignity now to sit anywhere but in the place of state in the chariot corner. I like to think for my part of the gallant young fellow taking his pleasure and enjoying his holiday, and few sights are more pleasant than to watch a happy manly English youth, free-handed and generous-hearted, content and good-humour shining in his honest face, pleased and pleasing, eager, active, and thankful for services, and exercising bravely his noble youthful privilege to be happy and to enjoy. Sing, cheery spirit, whilst the spring lasts; bloom whilst the sun shines, kindly flowers of youth! You shall be none the worse to-morrow for having been happy to-day, if the day brings no action to shame it. As for J.J., he too had his share of enjoyment; the charming scenes around him did not escape his bright eye, he absorbed pleasure in his silent way, he was up with the sunrise always, and at work with his eyes and his heart if not with his hands. A beautiful object too is such a one to contemplate, a pure virgin soul, a creature gentle, pious, and full of love, endowed with sweet gifts, humble and timid, but for truth's and justice's sake inflexible, thankful to God and man, fond, patient, and faithful. Clive was still his hero as ever, his patron, his splendid young prince and chieftain. Who was so brave, who was so handsome, generous, witty as Clive? To hear Clive sing as the lad would whilst they were seated at their work, or driving along on this happy journey, through fair landscapes in the sunshine, gave J.J. the keenest pleasure: his wit was a little slow, but he would laugh with his eyes at Clive's sallies, or ponder over them and explode with laughter presently, giving a new source of amusement to these merry travellers, and little Alfred would laugh at J.J.'s laughing: and so, with a hundred harmless jokes to enliven, and the ever changing, ever charming smiles of nature to cheer and accompany it, the happy day's journey would come to an end.

So they travelled by the accustomed route to the prettiest town of all places where Pleasure has set up her tents; and where the gay, the melancholy, the idle or occupied, grave or naughty, come for amusement, or business, or relaxation; where London beauties, having danced and flirted all the season, may dance and flirt a little more; where well-dressed rogues from all quarters of the world assemble; where I have seen severe London lawyers, forgetting their wigs and the Temple, trying their luck against fortune and M. Bénazet; where wistful schemers conspire and prick cards down, and deeply meditate the infallible coup; and try it, and lose it, and borrow a hundred francs to go home; where even virtuous British ladies venture their little stakes, and draw up their winnings with trembling rakes, by the side of ladies who are not virtuous at all, no not even by name; where young prodigals break the bank sometimes, and carry plunder out of a place which Hercules himself could scarcely compel; where you meet wonderful countesses and princesses, whose husbands are almost always absent on their vast estates—in Italy, Spain, Piedmont—who knows where their lordship's possessions are?—while trains of suitors surround those wandering Penelopes their noble wives; Russian Boyars, Spanish Grandees of the Order of the Fleece, Counts of France, and Princes Polish and Italian innumerable, who perfume the gilded halls with their tobacco-smoke, and swear in all languages against the Black and the Red. The famous English monosyllable by which things, persons, luck, even eyes, are devoted to the infernal gods, we may be sure is not wanting in that Babel. Where does one not hear it? "D— the luck," says Lord Kew, as the croupier sweeps off his lordship's rouleaux. "D— the luck," says Brown, the bagman, who has been backing his lordship with five franc pieces. "Ah, body of Bacchus!" says Count Felice, whom we all remember a courier. *"Ah, sacré coup,"* cries M. le Vicomte de Florac, as his last louis parts company from him—each cursing in his native tongue. O sweet chorus!

That Lord Kew should be at Baden is no wonder. If you heard of him at the Finish, or at Buckingham Palace ball, or in a watch-house, or at the Third Cataract, or at a Newmarket meeting, you would not be surprised. He goes everywhere; does everything with all his might; knows everybody. Last week he won who knows how many thousand louis from the bank (it appears Brown has chosen one of the unlucky days to back his lordship). He will eat his supper as gaily after a great victory as after a signal defeat; and we know that to win with magnanimity requires much more constancy than to lose. His sleep will not be disturbed by one event or the other. He will play skittles all the morning with perfect contentment, romp with children in the forenoon (he is the friend of half the children in the place), or he will cheerfully leave the green-table and all the risk and excitement there, to take a hand at sixpenny whist with General Fogey, or to give the six Miss Fogeys a turn each in the ball-room. From H. R. H. the Prince Royal of ——, who is the greatest guest at Baden, down to Brown the bagman, who does not consider himself the smallest, Lord Kew is hail fellow with everybody, and has a kind word from and for all.

Chapter XXVIII.

I N the company assembled at Baden, Clive found one or two old acquaintances; among them his friend of Paris, M. de Florac, not in quite so brilliant a condition as when Newcome had last met him on the Boulevard. Florac owned that Fortune had been very unkind to him at Baden; and, indeed, she had not only emptied his purse, but his portmanteaus, jewel box, and linen closet—the contents of all of which had ranged themselves on the red and black against Monsieur Bénazet's crown pieces: whatever side they took was, however, the unlucky one. "This campaign has been my Moscow, *mon cher,*" Florac owned to Clive. "I am conquered by Bénazet; I have lost in almost every combat. I have lost my treasure, my baggage, my ammunition of war, everything but my honour, which, *au reste,* Mons. Bénazet will not accept as a stake: if he would, there are plenty here, believe me, who would set it on the Trente et Quarante. Sometimes I have had a mind to go home; my mother, who is an angel all forgiveness, would receive her prodigal, and kill the fatted veal for me. But what will you? He annoys me—the domestic veal. Besides, my brother the Abbé, though the best of Christians, is a Jew upon certain matters; a Bénazet who will not *troquer* absolution except against repentance; and I have not for a sou of repentance in my pocket! I have been sorry, yes—but it was because odd came up in place of even, or the reverse. The accursed *après* has chased me like a remorse, and when black has come up I have wished myself converted to red. Otherwise I have no repentance—I am *joueur*—nature has made me so, as she made my brother *dévot.* The Archbishop of Strasbourg is of our parents; I saw his grandeur when I went lately to Strasbourg, on my last pilgrimage to the Mont de Piété. I owned to him that I would pawn his cross and ring to go play: the good prelate laughed, and said his chaplain should keep an eye on them. Will you dine with me? The landlord of my hotel was the intendant of our cousin, the Duc d'Ivry, and will give me credit to the day of judgment. I do not abuse his noble confidence. My dear! there are covers of silver put upon my table every day with which I could retrieve my fortune, did I listen to the suggestions of Satanas; but I say to him, *Vade retro.* Come and dine with me—Duluc's kitchen is very good."

These easy confessions were uttered by a gentleman who was nearly forty years of age, and who had indeed played the part of a young man in Paris and the great European world so long, that he knew or chose to perform no other. He did not want for abilities; had the best temper in the world; was well bred and gentlemanlike always; and was gay even after Moscow. His courage was known, and his character for bravery and another kind of gallantry probably exaggerated by his bad reputation. Had his mother not been alive, perhaps he would have believed in the virtue of no woman. But this one he worshipped, and spoke with tenderness and enthusiasm of her constant love and patience and goodness. "See her miniature!" he said, "I never separate myself from it—O, never! It saved my life in an affair about—about a woman who was not worth the powder which poor Jules and I burned for her. His ball struck me here, upon the waistcoat, bruising my rib and sending me to my bed, which I never should have left alive but for this picture. O, she is an angel, my mother. I am sure that Heaven has nothing to deny that saint, and that her tears wash out my sins."

Clive smiled. "I think Madame de Florac must weep a good deal," he said.

"*Enormément*, my friend! My faith! I do not deny it! I give her cause, night and evening. I am possessed by demons! This little Affenthaler wine of this country has a little smack which is most agreeable. The passions tear me, my young friend! Play is fatal, but play is not so fatal as woman. Pass me the écrévisses, they are most succulent. Take warning by me, and avoid both. I saw you *rôder* round the green-tables, and marked your eyes as they glistened over the heaps of gold, and looked at some of our beauties of Baden. Beware of such syrens, young man! and take me for your Mentor; avoiding what I have done—that understands itself. You have not played as yet? Do not do so; above all avoid a martingale, if you do. Play ought not to be an affair of calculation, but of inspiration. I have calculated infallibly; and what has been the effect? Gousset empty, tiroirs empty, nécessaire parted for Strasbourg! Where is my fur pelisse, Frédéric?"

"*Parbleu vous le savez bien, Monsieur le Vicomte,*" says Frédéric, the domestic, who was waiting on Clive and his friend.

"A pelisse lined with true sable, and worth three thousand francs, that I won of a little Russian at billiards. That pelisse is at Strasbourg (where the infamous worms of the Mount of Piety are actually gnawing her). Two hundred francs and this *reconnaissance*, which Frédéric receive, are all that now represents the pelisse. How many chemises have I, Frédéric?"

"*Eh, parbleu, Monsieur le Vicomte sait bien que nous avons toujours vingt-quatre chemises,*" says Frédéric, grumbling.

Monsieur le Vicomte springs up shrieking from the dinner-table. "Twenty-four shirts," says he, "and I have been a week without a louis in my pocket! *Bélître! Nigaud!*" He flings open one drawer after another, but there are no signs of that superfluity of linen of which the domestic spoke, whose countenance now changes from a grim frown to a grim smile.

"Ah, my faithful Frédéric, I pardon thee! Mr. Newcome will understand my harmless *supercherie*. Frédéric was in my company of the Guard, and remains with me since. He is Caleb Balderstone and I am Ravenswood. Yes, I am Edgard. Let us have coffee and a cigar, Balderstoun."

"Plait-il Monsieur le Vicomte?" says the French Caleb.

"Thou comprehendest not English. Thou readest not Valtare Scott, thou!" cries the master. "I was recounting to Monsieur Newcome thy history and my misfortunes. Go seek coffee for us, *Nigaud.*" And as the two gentlemen partake of that exhilarating liquor, the elder confides gaily to his guest the reason why he prefers taking coffee at the Hotel to the coffee at the great Café of the Redoute, with a *duris urgéns in rébūs égestâss!* pronounced in the true French manner.

Clive was greatly amused by the gaiety of the Viscount after his misfortunes and his Moscow; and thought that one of Mr. Baines's circular notes might not be ill laid out in succouring this hero. It may have been to this end that Florac's confessions tended; though to do him justice the incorrigible young fellow would confide his adventures to any one who would listen; and the exact state of his wardrobe, and the story of his pawned pelisse, dressing-case, rings and watches, were known to all Baden.

"You tell me to marry and range myself," said Clive, (to whom the Viscount was expatiating upon the charms of the *superbe* young *Anglaise* with whom he had seen Clive walking on the promenade). "Why do you not marry and range yourself too?"

"Eh, my dear! I am married already. You do not know it? I am married since the Revolution of July. Yes. We were poor in those days, as poor we remain. My cousins the Duc d'Ivry's sons and his grandson were still alive. Seeing no other resource and pursued by the Arabs, I espoused the Vicomtesse de Florac. I gave her my name, you comprehend, in exchange for her own odious one. She was Miss Higg. Do you know the family Higg of Manchesterre in the comté of Lancastre? She was then a person of a ripe age. The Vicomtesse is now—ah! it is fifteen years since, and she dies not. Our union was not happy, my friend—Madame Paul de Florac is of the reformed religion—not of the Anglican church, you understand—but a dissident I know not of what sort. We inhabited the Hôtel de Florac for a while after our union, which was all of convenience, you understand. She filled her salon with ministers to make you die. She assaulted my poor father in his garden-chair, whence he could not escape her. She told my sainted mother that she was an idolatress—she who only idolatrises her children! She called us other poor catholics who follow the rites of our fathers, *des Romishes;* and Rome, Babylon; and the Holy Father—a scarlet—eh! a scarlet abomination. She outraged my mother, that angel; essayed to convert the antechamber and the office; put little books in the Abbé's bed-room. Eh, my friend! what a good king was Charles IX. and his mother what a wise sovereign! I lament that Madame de Florac should have escaped the St. Barthélemi, when no doubt she was spared on account of her tender age. We have been separated for many years; her income was greatly exaggerated. Beyond the payment of my debts I owe her nothing. I wish I could say as much of all the rest of the world. Shall we take a turn of promenade? *Mauvais sujet!* I see you are longing to be at the green-table."

Clive was not longing to be at the green-table: but his companion was never easy at it or away from it. Next to winning, losing M. de Florac said was the best sport—next to losing, looking on. So he and Clive went down to the Redoute where Lord Kew was playing with a crowd of awe-struck amateurs and breathless punters admiring his valour and fortune; and Clive saying that he knew nothing about the game took out five Napoleons from his purse, and besought Florac to invest them in the most profitable manner at roulette. The other made some faint attempts at a scruple: but the money was speedily laid on the table, where it increased and multiplied amazingly too; so that in a quarter of an hour Florac brought quite a handful of gold pieces to his principal. Then Clive, I daresay blushing as he made the proposal, offered half the handful of napoleons to M. de Florac to be repaid when he thought fit. And fortune must have been very favourable to the husband of Miss Higg that night: for in the course of an hour he insisted on paying back Clive's loan; and two days afterwards appeared with his shirt-studs (of course with his shirts also), released from captivity, his watch, rings, and chains, on the parade; and was observed to wear his celebrated fur pelisse as he drove back in a britzska from Strasbourg. "As for myself," wrote Clive, "I put back into my purse the five Napoleons with which I had begun; and laid down the whole mass of winnings on the table, where it was doubled and then quadrupled, and then swept up by the croupiers, greatly to my ease of mind. And then Lord Kew asked me to supper and we had a merry night."

This was Mr. Clive's first and last appearance as a gambler. J.J. looked very grave when he heard of these transactions. Clive's French friend did not please his English companion at all, nor the friends of Clive's French friend, the Russians, the Spaniards, the Italians, of sounding titles and glittering decorations, and the ladies who belonged to their society. He saw by chance Ethel escorted by her cousin Lord Kew passing through a crowd of this company one day. There was not one woman there who was not the heroine of some discreditable story. It was the Comtesse Calypso who had been jilted by the Duc Ulysse. It was the Marquise Ariane to whom the Prince Thésée had behaved so shamefully, and who had taken to Bacchus as a consolation. It was Madame Médée, who had absolutely killed her old father by her conduct regarding Jason: she had done everything for Jason: she had got him the *toison d'or* from the Queen Mother, and now had to meet him every day with his little blonde bride on his arm! J.J. compared Ethel, moving in the midst of these folks, to the Lady amidst the rout of Comus. There they were, the Fauns and Satyrs: there they were, the merry Pagans: drinking and dancing, dicing and sporting; laughing out jests that never should be spoken; whispering rendezvous to be written in midnight calendars; jeering at honest people who passed under their palace windows—jolly rebels and repealers of the law. Ah, if Mrs. Brown, whose children are gone to bed at the Hotel, knew but the history of that calm dignified-looking gentleman who sits under her, and over whose patient back she frantically advances and withdraws her two-franc piece, whilst his own columns of louis d'or are offering battle to fortune—how she would shrink away from the shoulder which she pushes! That man so calm and well-bred, with a string of orders on his breast, so well-dressed, with such white hands, has stabbed trusting hearts; severed family ties; written lying vows; signed false oaths; torn up pitilessly tender appeals for redress, and tossed away into the fire supplications blistered with tears; packed cards and cogged dice; or used pistol or sword as calmly and dexterously as he now ranges his battalions of gold pieces.

Ridley shrank away from such lawless people with the delicacy belonging to his timid and retiring nature, but it must be owned that Mr. Clive was by no means so squeamish. He did not know in the first place the mystery of their iniquities; and his sunny kindly spirit, undimmed by any of the cares which clouded it subsequently, was disposed to shine upon all people alike. The world was welcome to him: the day a pleasure: all nature a gay feast: scarce any dispositions discordant with his own (for pretension only made him laugh, and hypocrisy he will never be able to understand if he lives to be a hundred years old): the night brought him a long sleep, and the morning a glad waking. To those privileges of youth what enjoyments of age are comparable? what achievements of ambition? what rewards of money and fame? Clive's happy friendly nature shone out of his face; and almost all who beheld it felt kindly towards him. As those guileless virgins of romance and ballad, who walk smiling through dark forests charming off dragons and confronting lions; the young man as yet went through the world harmless; no giant waylaid him as yet; no robbing ogre fed on him: and (greatest danger of all for one of his ardent nature) no winning enchantress or artful syren coaxed him to her cave, or lured him into her waters—haunts into which we know so many young simpletons are drawn, where their silly bones are picked and their tender flesh devoured.

The time was short which Clive spent at Baden, for it has been said the winter was approaching, and the destination of our young artists was Rome; but he may have passed some score of days here, to which he and another person in that pretty watering place possibly looked back afterwards, as not the unhappiest periods of their lives. Among Colonel Newcome's papers to which the family biographer has had subsequent access, there are a couple of letters from Clive dated Baden at this time, and full of happiness, gaiety, and affection. Letter No. 1 says, "Ethel is the prettiest girl here. At the assemblies all the princes, counts, dukes, Parthians, Medes and Elamites, are dying to dance with her. She sends her dearest love to her uncle." By the side of the words "prettiest girl," was written in a frank female hand the monosyllable "*Stuff;*" and as a note to the expression "dearest love," with a star to mark the text and the note, are squeezed in the same feminine characters at the bottom of Clive's page, the words "*That I do. E. N.*"

In letter No. 2, the first two pages are closely written in Clive's handwriting, describing his pursuits and studies, and giving amusing details of the life at Baden, and the company whom he met there—narrating his *rencontre* with their Paris friend, M. de Florac, and the arrival of the Duchesse d'Ivry, Florac's cousin, whose titles the Vicomte will probably inherit. Not a word about Florac's gambling propensities are mentioned in the letter; but Clive honestly confesses that he has staked five napoleons, doubled them, quadrupled them, won ever so much, lost it all back again, and come away from the table with his original five pounds in his pocket—proposing never to play any more. "Ethel," he concludes, "is looking over my shoulder. She thinks me such a delightful creature that she is never easy without me. She bids me to say that I am the best of sons and cousins, and am, in a word, a darling du . . ." The rest of this important word is not given, but *goose* is added in the female hand. In the faded ink, on the yellow paper that may have crossed and recrossed oceans, that has lain locked in chests for years, and buried under piles of family archives, while your friends have been dying and your head has grown white—who has not disinterred mementoes like these—from which the past smiles at you so sadly, shimmering out of Hades an instant but to sink back again into the cold shades, perhaps with a faint, faint sound as of a remembered tone—a ghostly echo of a once familiar laughter? I was looking of late at a wall in the Naples' museum, whereon a boy of Herculaneum eighteen hundred years ago had scratched with a nail the figure of a soldier. I could fancy the child turning round and smiling on me after having done his etching. Which of us that is thirty years old has not had his Pompeii? Deep under ashes lies the Life of Youth,—the careless Sport, the Pleasure and Passion, the darling Joy. You open an old letter-box and look at your own childish scrawls, or your mother's letters to you when you were at school; and excavate your heart. O me for the day when the whole city shall be bare and the chambers unroofed—and every cranny visible to the Light above, from the Forum to the Lupanar!

Ethel takes up the pen. "My dear uncle," she says, "while Clive is sketching out of window, let me write you[1] a line or two on his paper, though *I know you like to hear no one speak* but him. I wish I could draw him for you as he stands yonder, looking the picture of good health, good spirits, and good-humour. Every body likes him. He is quite unaffected; always gay; always pleased. He draws more and more beautifully every day; and his affection for young Mr. Ridley, who is really a most excellent and astonishing young man, and actually a better artist than Clive himself, is most romantic, and does your son the greatest credit. You will order Clive not to sell his pictures, won't you? I know it is not wrong, but your son might look higher than to be an artist. It is a rise for Mr. Ridley, but a fall for him. An artist, an organist, a pianist, all these are very good people, but you know not *de notre monde*, and Clive ought to belong to it.

"We met him at Bonn on our way to a great family gathering here; where, I must tell you, we are assembled for what I call the Congress of Baden! The chief of the house of Kew is here, and what time he does not devote to skittles, to smoking cigars, to the *jeu* in the evenings, to Madame d'Ivry, to Madame de Cruchecassée, and the foreign people (of whom there are a host here of the worst kind, as usual), he graciously bestows on me. Lord and Lady Dorking are here, with their meek little daughter, Clara Pulleyn; and Barnes is coming. Uncle Hobson has returned to Lombard Street to relieve guard. I think you will hear before very long of Lady Clara Newcome. Grandmamma, who was to have presided at the Congress of Baden, and still you know reigns over the house of Kew, has been stopped at Kissingen with an attack of rheumatism; I pity poor Aunt Julia who can never leave her. Here are all our news. I declare I have filled the whole

[1] you *E1*] to you *R*

page; men write closer than we do. I wear the dear brooch you gave me, often and often; I think of you always, dear, kind uncle as your affectionate Ethel."

Besides roulette and trente et quarante, a number of amusing games are played at Baden, which are not performed, so to speak, *sur table*. These little diversions and *jeux de société* can go on anywhere; in an alley in the park; in a picnic to this old schloss, or that pretty hunting lodge; at a tea-table in a lodging house or hotel; in a ball at the Redoute; in the play-rooms, behind the backs of the gamblers whose eyes are only cast upon rakes and rouleaux, and red and black; or on the broad walk in front of the Conversation Rooms, where thousands of people are drinking and chattering, lounging and smoking, whilst the Austrian brass band, in the little music pavilion, plays the most delightful mazurkas and waltzes. Here the widow plays her black suit, and sets her bright eyes against the rich bachelor, elderly or young as may be. Here the artful practitioner, who has dealt in a thousand such games, engages the young simpleton with more money than wit; and knowing his weakness and her skill, we may safely take the odds, and back rouge et couleur to win. Here Mamma, not having money perhaps, but metal more attractive, stakes her virgin daughter against Count Fettacker's forests and meadows; or Lord Lackland plays his coronet, of which the jewels have long since been in pawn, against Miss Bags' three per cents. And so two or three funny little games were going on at Baden amongst our immediate acquaintance; besides that vulgar sport round the green-table, at which the mob, with whom we have little to do, was elbowing each other. A hint of these domestic prolusions has been given to the reader in the foregoing extract from Miss Ethel Newcome's letter: likewise some passions have been in play, of which a modest young English maiden could not be aware. Do not, however, let us be too prematurely proud of our virtue. That tariff of British virtue is wonderfully organised. Heaven help the society which made its laws! Gnats are shut out of its ports, or not admitted without scrutiny and repugnance, whilst herds of camels are let in. The law professes to exclude some goods, (or bads shall we call them?)—well, some articles of baggage, which are yet smuggled openly under the eyes of winking officers, and worn every day without shame. Shame! What is shame? Virtue is very often shameful according to the English social constitution, and shame honourable. Truth, if yours happens to differ from your neighbour's, provokes your friend's coldness, your mother's tears, the world's persecution. Love is not to be dealt in, save under restrictions which kill its sweet healthy free commerce. Sin in man is so light, that scarce the fine of a penny is imposed; while for woman it is so heavy, that no repentance can wash it out. Ah! yes; all stories are old. You proud matrons in your May Fair markets, have you never seen a virgin sold, or sold one? Have you never heard of a poor wayfarer fallen among robbers, and not a Pharisee to help him? of a poor woman fallen more sadly yet, abject in repentance and tears, and a crowd to stone her? I pace this broad Baden walk as the sunset is gilding the hills round about, as the orchestra blows its merry tunes, as the happy children laugh and sport in the alleys, as the lamps of the gambling palace are lighted up, as the throngs of pleasure-hunters stroll, and smoke, and flirt, and hum: and wonder sometimes, is it the sinners who are the most sinful? Is it poor Prodigal yonder amongst the bad company, calling black and red and tossing the champagne; or brother Straightlace that grudges his repentance? Is it downcast Hagar that slinks away with poor little Ishmael in her hand; or bitter old virtuous Sarah, who scowls at her from my demure Lord Abraham's arm?

One day of the previous May, when of course everybody went to visit the Water-colour Exhibitions, Ethel Newcome was taken to see the pictures by her grandmother, that rigorous old Lady Kew, who still proposed to reign over all her family. The girl had high spirit, and very likely hot words had passed between the elder and the younger lady; such as I am given to understand will be uttered in the most polite families. They came to a piece by Mr. Hunt, representing one of those figures which he knows how to paint with such consummate truth and pathos—a friendless young girl, cowering in a door-way, evidently without home or shelter. The exquisite fidelity of the details, and the plaintive beauty of the expression of the child, attracted old Lady Kew's admiration, who was an excellent judge of works of art; and she stood for some time looking at the drawing, with Ethel by her side. Nothing, in truth, could be more simple or pathetic; Ethel laughed, and her grandmother looking up from her stick on which she hobbled about, saw a very sarcastic expression in the girl's eyes.

"You have no taste for pictures, only for painters, I suppose," said Lady Kew.

"I was not looking at the picture," said Ethel, still with a smile, "but at the little green ticket in the corner."

"Sold," said Lady Kew. "Of course it is sold; all Mr. Hunt's pictures are sold. There is not one of them here on which you won't see the green ticket. He is a most admirable artist. I don't know whether his comedy or tragedy are the most excellent."

"I think, Grandmamma," Ethel said, "we young ladies in the world, when we are exhibiting, ought to have little green tickets pinned on our backs, with 'Sold' written on them; it would prevent trouble and any future haggling, you know. Then at the end of the season the owner would come to carry us home."

Grandmamma only said, "Ethel, you are a fool," and hobbled on to Mr. Cattermole's picture hard by. "What splendid colour; what a romantic gloom; what a flowing pencil and dexterous hand!" Lady Kew could delight in pictures, applaud good poetry, and squeeze out a tear over a good novel too. That afternoon, young Dawkins, the rising water-colour artist, who used to come daily to the gallery and stand delighted before his own piece, was aghast to perceive that there was no green ticket in the corner of his frame, and he pointed out the deficiency to the keeper of the pictures. His landscape, however, was sold and paid for, so no great mischief occurred. On that same evening, when the Newcome family assembled at dinner in Park Lane, Ethel appeared with a bright green ticket pinned in the front of her white muslin frock, and when asked what this queer fancy meant, she made Lady Kew a curtsey, looking her full in the face, and turning round to her father, said, "I am a *tableau-vivant*, Papa. I am number 46 in the Exhibition of the Gallery of Painters in Water-colours."

"My love, what do you mean?" says Mamma; and Lady Kew, jumping up on her crooked stick with immense agility, tore the card out of Ethel's bosom, and very likely would have boxed her ears, but that her parents were present and Lord Kew was announced.

Ethel talked about pictures the whole evening, and would talk of nothing else. Grandmamma went away furious. "She told Barnes, and when everybody was gone there was a pretty row in the building," said Madam Ethel, with an arch look, when she narrated the story. "Barnes was ready to kill me and eat me; but I never was afraid of Barnes." And the biographer gathers from this little anecdote narrated to him, never mind by whom, at a long subsequent period, that there had been great disputes in Sir Brian Newcome's establishment, fierce drawing-room battles, whereof certain pictures of a certain painter might have furnished the cause, and in which Miss Newcome had the whole of the family forces against her. That such battles take place in other domestic establishments, who shall say or shall not say? Who, when he goes out to dinner, and is received by a bland host with a gay shake of the hand, and a pretty hostess with a gracious smile of welcome, dares to think that Mr. Johnson up-stairs, half-an-hour before, was swearing out of his dressing-room at Mrs. Johnson, for having ordered a turbot instead of a salmon, or that Mrs. Johnson, now talking to Lady Jones so nicely about their mutual darling children, was crying her eyes out as her maid was fastening her gown, as the carriages were actually driving up? The servants know these things, but not we in the dining-room. Hark with what a respectful tone Johnson begs the clergyman present to say grace!

Whatever these family quarrels may have been, let bygones be bygones, and let us be perfectly sure, that to whatever purpose Miss Ethel Newcome, for good or for evil, might make her mind up, she had quite spirit enough to hold her own. She chose to be Countess of Kew because she chose to be Countess of Kew; had she set her heart on marrying Mr. Kuhn, she would have had her way, and made the family adopt it, and called him dear Fritz, as by his godfathers and godmothers, in his baptism, Mr. Kuhn was called. Clive was but a fancy, if he had even been so much as that, not a passion, and she fancied a pretty four-pronged coronet still more.

So that the diatribe wherein we lately indulged, about the selling of virgins, by no means applies to Lady Ann Newcome, who signed the address to Mrs. Stowe, the other day, along with thousands more virtuous British matrons; but should the reader haply say, "Is thy fable, O Poet, narrated concerning Tancred Pulleyn, Earl of Dorking, and Sigismunda, his wife," the reluctant moralist is obliged to own that the cap *does* fit those noble personages of whose lofty society you will however see but little.

For though I would like to go into an Indian Brahmin's house and see the punkahs and the purdahs and tattys, and the pretty brown maidens with great eyes, and great nose-rings, and painted foreheads, and slim waists cased in Cashmir shawls, Kincob scarfs, curly slippers, gilt trowsers, precious anklets and bangles; and have the mystery of Eastern existence revealed to me, (as who would not who has read the Arabian Nights in his youth?) yet I would not choose the moment when the Brahmin of the house was dead, his women howling, his priests doctoring his child of a widow, now frightening her with sermons, now drugging her with bang, so as to push her on his funeral pile at last, and into the arms of that carcase, stupefied, but obedient and decorous. And though I like to walk, even in fancy, in an earl's house, splendid, well ordered, where there are feasts and fine pictures and fair ladies and endless books and good company; yet there are times when the visit is not pleasant; and when the parents in that fine house are getting ready their daughter for sale, and frightening away her tears with threats, and stupefying her grief with narcotics, praying her and imploring her, and dramming her and coaxing her, and blessing her, and cursing her perhaps, till they have brought her into such a state as shall fit the poor young thing for that deadly couch upon which they are about to thrust her. When my lord and lady are so engaged I prefer not[2] to call at their mansion, number 1000 in Grosvenor Square, but to partake of a dinner of herbs rather than of that stalled ox which their cook is roasting whole. There are some people who are not so squeamish. The family comes of course; the most reverend the Lord Arch-Brahmin of Benares will attend the ceremony; there will be flowers and lights and white favours; and quite a string of carriages up to the pagoda; and such a breakfast afterwards; and music in the street and little parish boys hurrahing; and no end of speeches within and tears shed (no doubt), and his grace the Arch-Brahmin will make a highly appropriate speech, just with a faint scent of incense about it as such a speech ought to have, and the young person will slip away unperceived, and take off her veils, wreaths, orange flowers, bangles and finery, and will put on a plain dress more suited for the occasion, and the house-door will open—and there comes the SUTTEE in company of the body: yonder the pile is waiting on four wheels with four horses, the crowd hurrahs and the deed is done.

This ceremony amongst us is so stale and common that to be sure there is no need to describe its rites, and as women sell themselves for what you call an establishment every day to the applause of themselves, their parents, and the world, why on earth should a man ape at originality and pretend to pity them? Never mind about the lies at the altar, the blasphemy against the godlike name of love, the sordid surrender, the smiling dishonour. What the deuce does a *mariage de convenance* mean but all this, and are not such sober Hymeneal torches more satisfactory often than the most brilliant love matches that ever flamed and burnt out? Of course. Let us not weep when everybody else is laughing: let us pity the agonised duchess when her daughter, Lady Atalanta, runs away with the doctor—of course, that's respectable; let us pity Lady Iphigenia's father when that venerable chief is obliged to offer up his darling child; but it is over *her* part of the business that a decorous painter would throw the veil now. Her ladyship's sacrifice is performed, and the less said about it the better.

2 not *E1*] [omitted] *R*

Such was the case regarding an affair which appeared in due subsequence in the newspapers not long afterwards under the fascinating title of "Marriage in High Life," and which was in truth the occasion of the little family Congress of Baden which we are now chronicling. We all know, everybody at least who has the slightest acquaintance with the army list; that, at the commencement of their life, my Lord Kew, my Lord Viscount Rooster, the Earl of Dorking's eldest son, and the Honourable Charles Belsize, familiarly called Jack Belsize, were subaltern officers in one of his Majesty's regiments of cuirassier guards. They heard the chimes at midnight like other young men, they enjoyed their fun and frolics as gentlemen of spirit will do; sowing their wild oats plentifully, and scattering them with boyish profusion. Lord Kew's luck had blessed him with more sacks of oats than fell to the lot of his noble young companions. Lord Dorking's house is known to have been long impoverished; an excellent informant, Major Pendennis, has entertained me with many edifying accounts of the exploits of Lord Rooster's grandfather "with the wild Prince and Poyns," of his feats in the hunting field, over the bottle, over the dice-box. He played two nights and two days at a sitting with Charles Fox, when they both lost sums awful to reckon. He played often with Lord Steyne, and came away, as all men did, dreadful sufferers from those midnight encounters. His descendants incurred the penalties of the progenitor's imprudence, and Chanticlere, though one of the finest castles in England, is splendid but for a month in the year. The estate is mortgaged up to the very castle windows. "Dorking cannot cut a stick or kill a buck in his own park:" the good old Major used to tell with tragic accents: "he lives by his cabbages, grapes, and pine-apples, and the fees which people give for seeing the place and gardens, which are still the show of the county, and among the most splendid in the island. When Dorking is at Chanticlere, Ballard, who married his sister, lends him the plate and sends three men with it. Four cooks inside, and four maids and six footmen on the roof, with a butler driving, come down from London in a trap, and wait the month. And as the last carriage of the company drives away, the servants' coach is packed, and they all bowl back to town again. It's pitiable, Sir, pitiable."

In Lord Kew's youth, the names of himself and his two noble friends appeared on innumerable slips of stamped paper, conveying pecuniary assurances of a promissory nature; all of which promises, my Lord Kew singly and most honourably discharged. Neither of his two companions in arms had the means of meeting these engagements. Ballard, Rooster's uncle, was said to make his lordship some allowance. As for Jack Belsize; how he lived; how he laughed; how he dressed himself so well, and looked so fat and handsome; how he got a shilling to pay for a cab or a cigar; what ravens fed him; was a wonder to all. The young men claimed kinsmanship with one another, which those who are learned in the peerage may unravel.

When Lord Dorking's eldest daughter married the Honourable and Venerable Dennis Gallowglass, Archdeacon of Bullintubber, (and at present Viscount Gallowglass and Killbrogue, and Lord Bishop of Ballyshannon), great festivities took place at Chanticlere, whither the relatives of the high contracting parties were invited. Among them came poor Jack Belsize, and hence the tears which are dropping at Baden at this present period of our history. Clara Pulleyn was then a pretty little maiden of sixteen, and Jack a handsome guardsman of six- or seven-and-twenty. As she had been especially warned against Jack as a wicked young rogue, whose *anté-cédents* were wofully against him; as she was never allowed to sit near him at dinner, or to walk with him, or to play at billiards with him, or to waltz with him; as she was scolded if he spoke a word to her, or if he picked up her glove, or touched her hand in a round game, or caught him when they were playing at blindman's-buff; as they neither of them had a penny in the world, and were both very good-looking, of course Clara was always catching Jack at blindman's-buff; constantly lighting upon him in the shrubberies or corridors, &c., &c., &c. She fell in love (she was not the first) with Jack's broad chest and thin waist; she thought his whiskers, as indeed they were, the handsomest pair in all his majesty's Brigade of Cuirassiers.

We know not what tears were shed in the vast and silent halls of Chanticlere, when the company were gone, and the four cooks, and four maids, six footmen, and temporary butler had driven back in their private trap to the metropolis, which is not forty miles distant from that splendid castle. How can we tell? The guests departed, the lodge gates shut; all is mystery:—darkness with one pair of wax candles blinking dismally in a solitary chamber; all the rest dreary vistas of brown hollands, rolled Turkey carpets, gaunt ancestors on the walls, scowling out of the twilight blank. The imagination is at liberty to depict his lordship, with one candle, over his dreadful endless tapes and papers; her ladyship with the other, and an old, old novel, wherein, perhaps, Mrs. Radcliffe describes a castle as dreary as her own; and poor little Clara sighing and crying in the midst of these funereal splendours, as lonely and heart-sick as Oriana in her moated grange:—poor little Clara!

Lord Kew's drag took the young men to London; his lordship driving, and the servants sitting inside. Jack sat behind with the two grooms, and tooted on a cornet-à-piston in the most melancholy manner. He partook of no refreshment on the road. His silence at his clubs was remarked: smoking, billiards, military duties, and this and that, roused him a little, and presently Jack was alive again. But then came the season, Lady Clara Pulleyn's first season in London, and Jack was more alive than ever. There was no ball he did not go to; no opera (that is to say, no opera of *certain* operas) which he did not frequent. It was easy to see by his face, two minutes after entering a room, whether the person he sought was there or absent; not difficult for those who were in the secret, to watch in another pair of eyes the bright kindling signals which answered Jack's fiery glances. Ah! how beautiful he looked on his charger on the birthday, all in a blaze of scarlet, and bullion, and steel. O Jack! tear her out of yon carriage, from the side of yonder livid, feathered, painted, boney dowager! place her behind you on the black charger; cut down the policeman, and away with you! The carriage rolls in through St. James's Park; Jack sits alone with his sword dropped to the ground, or only *atra cura* on the crupper behind him; and Snip, the tailor, in the crowd thinks it is for fear of him Jack's head droops. Lady Clara Pulleyn is presented by her mother, the Countess of Dorking;

and Jack is arrested that night as he is going out of White's to meet her at the Opera.

Jack's little exploits are known in the Insolvent Court, where he made his appearances as Charles Belsize, commonly called the Honourable Charles Belsize, whose dealings were smartly chronicled by the indignant moralists of the press of those days. The "Scourge" flogged him heartily. The "Whip," (of which the accomplished editor was himself in Whitecross Street prison,) was especially virtuous regarding him; and the "Penny Voice of Freedom" gave him an awful dressing. I am not here to scourge sinners; I am true to my party; it is the other side this humble pen attacks; let us keep to the virtuous and respectable, for as for poor sinners they get the whipping-post every day. One person was faithful to poor Jack through all his blunders and follies and extravagance and misfortunes, and that was the pretty young girl of Chanticlere, round whose young affections his luxuriant whiskers had curled. And the world may cry out at Lord Kew for sending his brougham to the Queen's Bench prison, and giving a great feast at Grignon's to Jack on the day of his liberation, but I for one will not quarrel with his lordship. He and many other sinners had a jolly night. They said Kew made a fine speech, in hearing and acknowledging which Jack Belsize wept copiously. Barnes Newcome was in a rage at Jack's manumission, and sincerely hoped Mr. Commissioner would give him a couple of years longer; and cursed and swore with a great liberality on hearing of his liberty.

That this poor prodigal should marry Clara Pulleyn, and by way of a dowry lay his schedule at her feet, was out of the question. His noble father, Lord Highgate, was furious against him; his eldest brother would not see him; he had given up all hopes of winning his darling prize long ago, and one day there came to him a great packet bearing the seal of Chanticlere, containing a wretched little letter signed C. P. , and a dozen sheets of Jack's own clumsy writing delivered who knows how, in what crush rooms, quadrilles, bouquets, balls, and in which were scrawled Jack's love and passion and ardour. How many a time had he looked into the dictionary at White's, to see whether eternal was spelt with an e, and adore with one a or two! There they were, the incoherent utterances of his brave longing heart; and those two wretched, wretched lines signed C., begging that C.'s little letters might too be returned or destroyed. To do him justice he burnt them loyally every one along with his own waste paper. He kept not one single little token which she had given him, or let him take. The rose, the glove, the little handkerchief which she had dropped to him, how he cried over them! The ringlet of golden hair—he burnt them all, all in his own fire in the prison, save a little, little bit of the hair, which might be any one's, which was the colour of his sister's. Kew saw the deed done; perhaps he hurried away when Jack came to the very last part of the sacrifice, and flung the hair into the fire, where he would have liked to fling his heart and his life too.

So Clara was free, and the year when Jack came out of prison and went abroad, she passed the season in London dancing about night after night, and everybody said she was well out of that silly affair with Jack Belsize.

It was then that Barnes Newcome, Esq., a partner of the wealthy banking firm of Hobson Brothers and Newcomes, son and heir of Sir Brian Newcome, of Newcome, Bart., and M.P., descended in right line from Bryan de Newcomyn, slain at Hastings, and barber-surgeon to Edward the Confessor, &c., &c., cast the eyes of regard on the Lady Clara Pulleyn, who was a little pale and languid certainly, but had blue eyes, a delicate skin, and a pretty person, and knowing her previous history as well as you who have just perused it, deigned to entertain matrimonial intentions towards her ladyship.

Not one of the members of these most respectable families, excepting poor little Clara perhaps, poor little fish (as if she had any call but to do her duty, or[3] to ask *à quelle sauce elle serait mangée*), protested against this little affair of traffic; Lady Dorking had a brood of little chickens to succeed Clara. There was little Hennie, who was sixteen, and Biddy, who was fourteen, and Adelaide, and who knows how many more. How could she refuse a young man, not very agreeable it is true, nor particularly amiable, nor of good birth, at least on his father's side, but otherwise eligible, and heir to so many thousands a-year? The Newcomes, on their side, think it a desirable match. Barnes, it must be confessed, is growing rather selfish, and has some bachelor ways which a wife will reform. Lady Kew is strongly for the match. With her own family interest, Lord Steyne and Lord Kew, her nephews, and Barnes's own father-in-law, Lord Dorking, in the Peers; why shall not the Newcomes sit there too, and resume the old seat which all the world knows they had in the time of Richard III.? Barnes and his father had got up quite a belief about a Newcome killed at Bosworth, along with King Richard, and hated Henry VII. as an enemy of their noble race. So all the parties were pretty well agreed. Lady Ann wrote rather a pretty little poem about welcoming the white Fawn to the Newcome bowers, and "Clara" was made to rhyme with "fairer," and "timid does and antlered deer to dot the glades of Chanticlere," quite in a picturesque way. Lady Kew pronounced that the poem was very pretty indeed.

The year after Jack Belsize made his foreign tour he returned to London for the season. Lady Clara did not happen to be there; her health was a little delicate, and her kind parents took her abroad; so all things went on very smoothly and comfortably indeed.

Yes, but when things were so quiet and comfortable, when the ladies of the two families had met at the Congress of Baden, and liked each other so much, when Barnes and his papa the Baronet, recovered from his illness, were actually on their journey from Aix-la-Chapelle, and Lady Kew in motion from Kissingen to the Congress of Baden, why on earth should Jack Belsize, haggard, wild, having been winning great sums, it was said, at Hombourg—forsake his luck there, and run over frantically to Baden? He wore a great thick beard, a great slouched hat—he looked like nothing more or less than a painter or an Italian brigand. Unsuspecting Clive, remembering the jolly dinner which Jack had procured for him at the Guards' mess in St. James's, whither Jack himself came from the Horse

[3] or *E1*] and *R*

Guards—simple Clive, seeing Jack enter the town, hailed him cordially, and invited him to dinner, and Jack accepted, and Clive told him all the news he had of the place, how Kew was there, and Lady Ann Newcome, and Ethel; and Barnes was coming. "I am not very fond of him either," says Clive, smiling, when Belsize mentioned his name. So Barnes was coming to marry that pretty little Lady Clara Pulleyn. The knowing youth! I daresay he was rather pleased with his knowledge of the fashionable world, and the idea that Jack Belsize would think he, too, was somebody.

Jack drank an immense quantity of champagne, and the dinner over, as they could hear the band playing from Clive's open windows in the snug clean little Hotel de France, Jack proposed they should go on the promenade. M. de Florac was of the party; he had been exceedingly jocular when Lord Kew's name was mentioned, and said, *"Ce petit Kiou! M. le Duc d'Ivry, mon oncle, l'honore d'une amitié toute particulière."* These three gentlemen walked out; the promenade was crowded, the band was playing "Home, sweet Home," very sweetly, and the very first persons they met on the walk were the Lords of Kew and Dorking, on the arm of which latter venerable peer his daughter Lady Clara was hanging.

Jack Belsize, in a velvet coat, with a sombrero slouched over his face, with a beard reaching to his waist, was, no doubt, not recognised at first by the noble Lord of Dorking, for he was greeting the other two gentlemen with his usual politeness and affability; when, of a sudden, Lady Clara looking up, gave a little shriek and fell down lifeless on the gravel-walk. Then the old earl recognised Mr. Belsize, and Clive heard him say, "You villain, how dare you come here?"

Belsize had flung himself down to lift up Clara, calling her frantically by her name, when old Dorking sprang to seize him.

"Hands off, my lord," said the other, shaking the old man from his back. "Confound you, Jack, hold your tongue," roars out Kew. Clive runs for a chair, and a dozen were forthcoming. Florac skips back with a glass of water. Belsize runs towards the awakening girl: and the father, for an instant, losing all patience and self-command, trembling in every limb, lifts his stick, and says again, "Leave her, you ruffian." "Lady Clara has fainted again, Sir," says Captain Belsize. "I am staying at the Hotel de France. If you touch me, old man," (this in a very low voice), "by Heaven I shall kill you. I wish you good morning;" and taking a last long look at the lifeless girl, he lifts his hat and walks away. Lord Dorking mechanically takes his hat off, and stands stupidly gazing after him. He beckoned Clive to follow him, and a crowd of the frequenters of the place are by this time closed round the fainting young lady.

Here was a pretty incident in the Congress of Baden!

An Incident in the Life of Jack Belsize

Chapter XXIX.

THEL had all along known that her holiday was to be a short one, and that, her papa and Barnes arrived, there was to be no more laughing and fun and sketching and walking with Clive; so she took the sunshine while it lasted, determined to bear with a stout heart the bad weather.

Sir Brian Newcome and his eldest born arrived at Baden on the very night of Jack Belsize's performance upon the promenade; of course it was necessary to inform the young bridegroom of the facts. His acquaintances of the public, who by this time know his temper, and are acquainted with his language, can imagine the explosions of the one and the vehemence of the other; it was a perfect *feu d'artifice* of oaths which he sent up. Mr. Newcome only fired off these volleys of curses when he was in a passion, but then he was in a passion very frequently.

As for Lady Clara's little accident, he was disposed to treat that very lightly. "Poor dear Clara of course, of course," he said, "she's been accustomed to fainting fits; no wonder she was agitated on the sight of that villain, after his infernal treatment of her. If I had been there" (a volley of oaths comes here along the whole line) "I should have strangled the scoundrel; I should have murdered him."

"Mercy, Barnes," cries Lady Ann.

"It was a mercy Barnes was not there," says Ethel gravely; "a fight between him and Captain Belsize would have been awful indeed."

"I am afraid of no man, Ethel," says Barnes fiercely with another oath.

"Hit one of your own size, Barnes," says Miss Ethel, (who had a number of school-phrases from her little brothers, and used them on occasions skilfully). "Hit Captain Belsize, he has got no friends."

As Jack Belsize from his height and strength was fitted to be not only an officer but actually a private in his former gallant regiment, and brother Barnes was but a puny young gentleman, the idea of a personal conflict between them was rather ridiculous. Some notion of this sort may have passed through Sir Brian's mind, for the Baronet said with his usual solemnity, "It is the cause, Ethel, it is the cause, my dear, which gives strength; in such a cause as Barnes's, with a beautiful young creature to protect from a villain, any man would be strong, any man would be strong." "Since his last attack," Barnes used to say, "my poor old governor is exceedingly shaky, very groggy about the head;" which was the fact. Barnes was already master at Newcome and the bank, and awaiting with perfect composure the event which was to place the blood-red hand of the Newcome baronetcy on his own brougham.

Casting his eyes about the room, a heap of drawings, the work of a well-known hand which he hated, met his eye. There were a half-dozen sketches of Baden. Ethel on horseback again. The children and the dogs just in the old way. "D— him, is he here?" screams out Barnes. "Is that young pot-house villain here? and hasn't Kew knocked his head off? Clive Newcome is here, Sir," he cries out to his father. "The Colonel's son. I have no doubt they met by——"

"By what, Barnes?" says Ethel.

"Clive is here, is he?" says the Baronet; "making caricatures, hey? You did not mention him in your letters, Lady Ann."

Sir Brian was evidently very much touched by his last attack.

Ethel blushed; it was a curious fact, but there had been no mention of Clive in the ladies' letters to Sir Brian.

"My dear, we met him by the merest chance, at Bonn, travelling with a friend of his; and he speaks a little German, and was very useful to us, and took one of the boys in his britzska the whole way."

"Boys always crowd in a carriage," says Sir Brian. "Kick your shins; always in the way. I remember, when we used to come in the carriage from Clapham, when we were boys, I used to kick my brother Tom's shins. Poor Tom, he was a devilish wild fellow in those days. You don't recollect Tom, my Lady Ann?"

Farther anecdotes from Sir Brian are interrupted by Lord Kew's arrival. "How dydo, Kew," cries Barnes. "How's Clara?" and Lord Kew walking up with great respect to shake hands with Sir Brian, says, "I am glad to see you looking so well, Sir," and scarcely takes any notice of Barnes. That Mr. Barnes Newcome was an individual not universally beloved, is a point of history of which there can be no doubt.

"You have not told me how Clara is, my good fellow," continues Barnes. "I have heard all about her meeting with that villain, Jack Belsize."

"Don't call names, my good fellow," says Lord Kew. "It strikes me you don't know Belsize well enough to call him by nicknames or by other names. Lady Clara Pulleyn, I believe, is very unwell indeed."

"Confound the fellow! How dared he to come here?" cries Barnes, backing from this little rebuff.

"Dare is another ugly word. I would advise you not to use it to the fellow himself."

"What do you mean?" says Barnes, looking very serious in an instant.

"Easy, my good friend. Not so very loud. It appears, Ethel, that poor

Jack—*I* know him pretty well, you see, Barnes, and may call him by what names I like—had been dining to-day with cousin Clive; he and M. de Florac; and that they went with Jack to the promenade, not in the least aware of Mr. Jack Belsize's private affairs, or of the shindy that was going to happen."

"By Jove, he shall answer for it," cries out Barnes in a loud voice.

"I daresay he will, if you ask him," says the other drily; "but not before ladies. He'd be afraid of frightening them. Poor Jack was always as gentle as a lamb before women. I had some talk with the Frenchman just now," continued Lord Kew gaily, as if wishing to pass over this side of the subject. "'Mi Lord Kiou,' says he, 'we have made your friend Jac to hear reason. He is a little *fou*, your friend Jack. He drank champagne at dinner like an ogre. How is the *charmante* Miss Clara?' Florac, you see, calls her Miss Clara, Barnes; the world calls her Lady Clara. You call her Clara. You happy dog, you."

"I don't see why that infernal young cub of a Clive is always meddling in our affairs," cries out Barnes, whose rage was perpetually being whipped into new outcries. "Why has he been about this house? Why is he here?"

"It is very well for you that he was, Barnes," Lord Kew said. "The young fellow showed great temper and spirit. There has been a famous row, but don't be alarmed, it is all over. It is all over, everybody may go to bed and sleep comfortably. Barnes need not get up in the morning to punch Jack Belsize's head. I'm sorry for your disappointment, you Fenchurch Street fire-eater. Come away. It will be but proper, you know, for a bridegroom elect to go and ask news of *la charmante* Miss Clara."

"As we went out of the house," Lord Kew told Clive, "I said to Barnes, that every word I had uttered up-stairs with regard to the reconciliation was a lie. That Jack Belsize was determined to have his blood, and was walking under the lime-trees by which we had to pass with a thundering big stick. You should have seen the state the fellow was in, Sir. The sweet youth started back, and turned as yellow as a cream cheese. Then he made a pretext to go into his room, and said it was for his pocket handkerchief, but I know it was for a pistol; for he dropped his hand from my arm into his pocket, every time I said 'Here's Jack,' as we walked down the avenue to Lord Dorking's apartment."

A great deal of animated business had been transacted during the two hours subsequent to poor Lady Clara's mishap. Clive and Belsize had returned to the former's quarters, while gentle J.J. was utilising the last rays of the sun to tint a sketch which he had made during the morning. He fled to his own apartment on the arrival of the fierce-looking stranger, whose glaring eyes, pallid looks, shaggy beard, clutched hands and incessant gasps and mutterings as he strode up and down, might well scare a peaceable person. Very terrible must Jack have looked as he trampled those boards in the growing twilight, anon stopping to drink another tumbler of champagne, then groaning expressions of inarticulate wrath, and again sinking down on Clive's bed with a drooping head and breaking voice, crying, "Poor little thing, poor little devil."

"If the old man sends me a message, you will stand by me, won't you,

Newcome? He was a fierce old fellow in his time, and I have seen him shoot straight enough at Chanticlere. I suppose you know what the affair is about?"

"I never heard of it before, but I think I understand," says Clive, gravely.

"I can't ask Kew, he is one of the family; he is going to marry Miss Newcome. It is no use asking him."

All Clive's blood tingled at the idea that any man was going to marry Miss Newcome. He knew it before—a fortnight since, and it was nothing to him to hear it. He was glad that the growing darkness prevented his face from being seen. "I am of the family, too," said Clive, "and Barnes Newcome and I had the same grandfather."

"Oh, yes, old boy—old banker, the weaver, what was he? I forgot," says poor Jack, kicking on Clive's bed, "in that family the Newcomes don't count. I beg your pardon," groans poor Jack.

They lapse into silence, during which Jack's cigar glimmers from the twilight corner where Clive's bed is; whilst Clive wafts his fragrance out of the window where he sits, and whence he has a view of Lady Ann Newcome's windows to the right, over the bridge across the little rushing river, at the Hotel de Hollande hard by. The lights twinkle in the booths under the pretty lime avenues. The hum of distant voices is heard; the gambling palace is all in a blaze; it is an assembly night, and from the doors of the conversation-rooms, as they open and close, escape gusts of harmony. Behind on the little hill the darkling woods lie calm, the edges of the fir-trees cut sharp against the sky, which is clear with a crescent moon and the lambent lights of the starry hosts of heaven. Clive does not see pine-robed hills and shining stars, nor think of pleasure in its palace yonder, nor of pain writhing on his own bed within a few feet of him, where poor Belsize was groaning. His eyes are fixed upon a window whence comes the red light of a lamp, across which shadows float now and again. So every light in every booth yonder has a scheme of its own: every star above shines by itself; and each individual heart of ours goes on brightening with its own hopes, burning with its own desires, and quivering with its own pain.

The reverie is interrupted by the waiter, who announces M. le Vicomte de Florac, and a third cigar is added to the other two smoky lights. Belsize is glad to see Florac, whom he has known in a thousand haunts. He will do my business for me. He has been out half-a-dozen times, thinks Jack. It would relieve the poor fellow's boiling blood that some one would let a little out. He lays his affair before Florac, he expects a message from Lord Dorking.

"*Comment donc?*" cries Florac; "*il y avait donc quelque chose! Cette pauvre petite Miss! Vous voulez tuer le père, après avoir délaissé la fille? Cherchez d'autres témoins, Monsieur. Le Vicomte de Florac ne se fait pas complice de telles lâchetés.*"

"By Heaven," says Jack, sitting up on the bed, with his eyes glaring, "I have a great mind, Florac, to wring your infernal little neck, and to fling you out of the window. Is all the world going to turn against me? I am half mad as it is. If any man dares to think anything wrong regarding that little angel, or to fancy that she is not as pure, and as good, and as gentle, and as innocent, by Heaven, as any angel there,—if any man thinks I'd be the villain to hurt her, I should just like to see him," says Jack. "By the Lord, Sir, just bring him to me. Just tell the waiter to send him up-stairs. Hurt her! I hurt her! O! I'm a fool! a fool! a d——d fool! Who's that?"

"It's Kew," says a voice out of the darkness from behind cigar No. 4, and Clive now, having a party assembled, scrapes a match and lights his candles.

"I heard your last words, Jack," Lord Kew says bluntly, "and you never spoke more truth in your life. Why did you come here? What right had you to stab that poor little heart over again, and frighten Lady Clara with your confounded hairy face? You promised me you would never see her. You gave your word of honour you wouldn't, when I gave you the money to go abroad. Hang the money, I don't mind that; it was on your promise that you would prowl about her no more. The Dorkings left London before you came there; they gave you your innings. They have behaved kindly and fairly enough to that poor girl. How was she to marry such a bankrupt beggar as you are? What you have done is a shame, Charley Belsize. I tell you it is unmanly, and cowardly."

"Pst," says Florac, *"numero deux, voila le mot lâché."*

"Don't bite your thumb at me," Kew went on. "I know you could thrash me, if that's what you mean by shaking your fists; so could most men. I tell you again—you have done a bad deed; you have broken your word of honour, and you knocked down Clara Pulleyn to-day as cruelly as if you had done it with your hand."

With this rush upon him, and fiery assault of Kew, Belsize was quite bewildered. The huge man flung up his great arms, and let them drop at his side as a gladiator that surrenders, and asks for pity. He sank down once more on the iron bed.

"I don't know," says he, rolling and rolling round, in one of his great hands, one of the brass knobs of the bed by which he was seated, "I don't know, Frank," says he, "what the world is coming to, or me either; here is twice in one night I have been called a coward by you, and by that little what-d'-you-call'm. I beg your pardon, Florac. I don't know whether it is very brave in you to hit a chap when he is down: hit again, I have no friends. I have acted like a blackguard, I own that; I did break my promise; you had that safe enough, Frank, my boy; but I did not think it would hurt her to see me," says he, with a dreadful sob in his voice. "By — I would have given ten years of my life to look at her. I was going mad without her. I tried every place, every thing; went to Ems, to Wiesbaden, to Hombourg, and played like hell. It used to excite me once, and now I don't care for it. I won no end of money,—no end for a poor beggar like me, that is; but I couldn't keep away. I couldn't, and if she had been at the North Pole, by Heavens I would have followed her."

"And so just to look at her, just to give your confounded stupid eyes two minutes' pleasure, you must bring about all this pain, you great baby," cries Kew, who was very soft-hearted, and in truth quite torn himself by the sight of poor Jack's agony.

"Get me to see her for five minutes, Kew," cries the other, griping his comrade's hand in his; "but for five minutes."

"For shame," cries Lord Kew, shaking away his hand, "be a man Jack, and have no more of this puling. It's not a baby, that must have its toy, and cries because it can't get it. Spare the poor girl this pain, for her own sake, and balk yourself of the pleasure of bullying and making her unhappy."

Belsize started up with looks that were by no means pleasant. "There's enough of this chaff. I have been called names, and blackguarded quite sufficiently for one sitting. I shall act as I please. I choose to take my own way, and if any gentleman stops me he has full warning." And he fell to tugging his mustachios, which were of a dark tawny hue, and looked as warlike as he had ever done on any field-day.

"I take the warning!" said Lord Kew. "And if I know the way you are going, as I think I do, I will do my best to stop you, madman as you are! You can hardly propose to follow her to her own doorway and pose yourself before your mistress as the murderer of her father, like Rodrigue in the French play. If Rooster were here it would be his business to defend his sister; in his absence I will take the duty on myself, and I say to you, Charles Belsize, in the presence of these gentlemen, that any man who insults this young lady, who persecutes her with his presence, knowing it can but pain her, who persists in following her when he has given his word of honour to avoid her, that such a man is——"

"What, my Lord Kew?" cries Belsize, whose chest began to heave.

"You know what," answers the other. "You know what a man is who insults a poor woman, and breaks his word of honour. Consider the word said, and act upon it as you think fit."

"I owe you four thousand pounds, Kew," says Belsize, "and I have got four thousand on the bills, besides four hundred when I came out of that place."

"You insult me the more," cries Kew flashing out, by alluding to the money. "If you will leave this place to-morrow, well and good; if not, you will please to give me a meeting. Mr. Newcome, will you be so kind as to act as my friend? We are connexions you know, and this gentleman chooses to insult a lady who is about to become one of our family."

"*C'est bien, milord. Ma foi! c'est d'agir en vrai gentilhomme,*" says Florac delighted. "*Touchez-là, mon petit Kiou. Tu as du cœur.* Godam! you are a brave! A brave fellow!" and the Viscount reached out his hand cordially to Lord Kew.

His purpose was evidently pacific. From Kew he turned to the great guardsman, and taking him by the coat began to apostrophise him. "And you, *mon gros,*" says he, "is there no way of calming this hot blood without a *saignée?* Have you a penny to the world? Can you hope to carry off your Chimène, O Rodrigue, and live by robbing afterwards on the great way? Suppose you kill ze Fazér, you kill Kiou, you kill Roostere, your Chimène will have a pretty moon of honey."

"What the devil do you mean about your Chimène and your Rodrigue? What do[1] you mean, Viscount?" says Jack Belsize[2] once more, and he

---

[1] What do] Do *E1*
[2] Jack Belsize] Belsize, Jack Belsize *E1*

dashed his hand across his eyes. "Kew has riled me and he drove me half wild. I ain't much of a Frenchman, but I know enough of what you said, to say it's true, by Jove, and that Frank Kew's a trump. That's what you mean. Give us your hand, Frank. God bless you, old boy; don't be too hard upon me, you know I'm d——d miserable, that I am. Hullo. What's this?" Jack's pathetic speech was interrupted at this instant, for the Vicomte de Florac in his enthusiasm rushed into his arms, and jumped up towards his face and proceeded to kiss Jack. A roar of immense laughter, as he shook the little Viscount off, cleared the air and ended his[3] quarrel.

Everybody joined in this chorus, the Frenchman with the rest who said, "he loved to laugh *même* when he did not know why." And now came the moment of the evening, when Clive, according to Lord Kew's saying, behaved so well and prevented Barnes from incurring a great danger. In truth, what Mr. Clive did or said amounted exactly to nothing. What moments can we not all remember in our lives when it would have been so much wittier and wiser to say and do nothing?

Florac, a very sober drinker like most of his nation, was blessed with a very fine appetite, which, as he said, renewed itself thrice a day at least. He now proposed supper, and poor Jack was for supper too, and especially more drink, champagne and seltzer water; "bring champagne and seltzer water, there is nothing like it." Clive could not object to this entertainment, which was ordered forthwith, and the four young men sat down to share it.

Whilst Florac was partaking of his favourite écrevisses, giving not only his palate but his hands, his beard, his mustachios and cheeks a full enjoyment of the sauce which he found so delicious, he chose to revert now and again to the occurrences which had just past, and which had better perhaps have been forgotten, and gaily rallied Belsize upon his warlike humour. "If ze petit prétendu was here, what would you have done wiz him, Jac? You would croquer im, like zis écrevisse, hein? You would mache his bones, hein?"

Jack, who had forgotten to put the seltzer water into his champagne, writhed at the idea of having Barnes Newcome before him, and swore, could he but see Barnes, he would take the little villain's life.

And but for Clive, Jack might actually have beheld his enemy. Young Clive after the meal went to the window with his eternal cigar, and of course began to look at That Other window. Here, as he looked, a carriage had at the moment driven up. He saw two servants descend, then two gentlemen, and then he heard a well-known voice swearing at the couriers. To his credit be it said, he checked the exclamation which was on his lips, and when he came back to the table, did not announce to Kew or his right-hand neighbour Belsize, that his uncle and Barnes had arrived. Belsize, by this time, had had quite too much wine: when the Viscount went away, poor Jack's head was nodding; he had been awake all the night before; sleepless for how many nights previous. He scarce took any notice of the Frenchman's departure.

[3] his *E1*] this *R*

Lord Kew remained. He was for taking Jack to walk, and for reasoning with him farther, and for entering more at large than perhaps he chose to do before the two others upon this family dispute. Clive took a moment to whisper to Lord Kew, "My uncle and Barnes are arrived, don't let Belsize go out; for goodness' sake let us get him to bed."

And lest the poor fellow should take a fancy to visit his mistress by moonlight, when he was safe in his room, Lord Kew softly turned the key in Mr. Jack's door.

Chapter XXX.

A RETREAT.

A S Clive lay awake revolving the strange incidents of the day and speculating upon the tragedy in which he had been suddenly called to take a certain part, a sure presentiment told him that his own happy holiday was come to an end, and that the clouds and storm which he had always somehow foreboded were about to break and obscure this brief pleasant period of sunshine. He rose at a very early hour, flung his windows open, looked out no doubt towards those other windows in the neighbouring hotel where he may have fancied he saw a curtain stirring, drawn by a hand that every hour now he longed more to press. He turned back into his chamber with a sort of groan, and surveyed some of the relics of the last night's little feast which still remained on the table. There were the champagne flasks which poor Jack Belsize had emptied, the tall Seltzer-water bottle, from which the gases had issued and mingled with the hot air of the previous night's talk. Glasses with dregs of liquor, ashes of cigars, or their black stumps strewing the cloth. The dead men, the burst guns, of yesterday's battle. Early as it was, his neighbour J.J. had been up before him. Clive could hear him singing as was his wont when the pencil went well, and the colours arranged themselves to his satisfaction over his peaceful and happy work.

He pulled his own drawing-table to the window, set out his board and colour-box, filled a great glass from the Seltzer-water bottle, drank some of the vapid liquor, and[1] plunged his brushes in the rest with which he began to paint. The work all went wrong—There was no song for him over his labour; he dashed brush and board aside after a while, opened his drawers, pulled out his portmanteaus from under the bed and fell to packing mechanically. J.J. heard the noise from the next room and came in smiling with a great painting brush in his mouth.

"Have the bills in, J.J.," says Clive. "Leave your cards on your friends, old boy; say good bye to that pretty little strawberry girl whose picture you have been doing; polish it off to-day and dry the little thing's tears. I read PPC in the stars last night and my familiar spirit came to me in a vision and said, 'Clive, son of Thomas, put thy travelling boots on.'"

Lest any premature moralist should prepare to cry fie against the good pure-minded little J.J., I hereby state that his strawberry girl was a little village maiden of seven years old whose sweet little picture a bishop purchased at the next year's Exhibition.

"Are you going already?" cries J.J. removing the bit[2] out of his mouth. "I thought you had arranged parties for a week to come and that the princesses and the duchesses had positively forbidden the departure of your lordship."

"We have dallied at Capua long enough," says Clive, "and the legions have the route for Rome. So wills Hannibal the son of Hasdrubal."

"The son of Hasdrubal is quite right," his companion answered; "the sooner we march the better. I have always said it. I will get all the accounts in. Hannibal has been living like a voluptuous Carthaginian prince, one two three champagne bottles. There will be a deuce of a bill to pay."

"Ah! there will be a deuce of a bill to pay," says Clive with a groan whereof J.J. knew the portent; for the young men had the confidence of youth one in another. Clive was accustomed to pour out his full heart to any crony who was near him; and indeed had he spoken never a word, his growing attachment to his cousin was not hard to see. A hundred times and with the glowing language and feelings of youth, with the fire of his twenty years, with the ardour of a painter, he had spoken of her and described her. Her magnanimous simplicity, her courage and lofty scorn, her kindness towards her little family, her form, her glorious colour of rich carnation and dazzling white, her queenly grace when quiescent and in motion had constantly formed the subjects of this young gentleman's ardent eulogies. As he looked at a great picture or statue, at the Venus of Milo, calm and deep, unfathomably beautiful as the sea from which she sprung, as he looked at the rushing Aurora of the Rospigliosi or the Assumption of Titian, more bright and glorious than sunshine or that divine Madonna and divine Infant of Dresden whose sweet faces must have shone upon Raphael out of Heaven, his[3] heart sang hymns as it were, before these gracious altars; and somewhat as he worshipped these masterpieces of his art he admired the beauty of Ethel.[4]

[1] and *E1*] [not present] *Ms*
[2] bit *Ms E1*] brush *R*
[3] his *Ms E1*] Clive's *R*
[4] altars; and ... Ethel. *E1*] altars. *Ms*

J.J. felt these things exquisitely after his manner, and enjoyed honest Clive's mode of celebration and rapturous fioriture of song; but Ridley's natural note was much gentler, and he sang his hymns in plaintive minors. Ethel was all that was bright and beautiful, but,—but she was engaged to Lord Kew. The shrewd kind confidant used gently to hint the sad fact to the impetuous hero of this piece. The impetuous hero knew this quite well. As he was sitting over his painting-board, he would break forth frequently, after his manner, in which laughter and sentiment were mingled and roar out with all the force of his healthy young lungs—

"But her heart it is another's, she never—can—be——mine."

And then hero and confidant would laugh each at his drawing-table. Miss Ethel went between the two gentlemen by the name of Alice Grey.

Very likely Night, the Grey Mentor, had given Clive Newcome the benefit of his sad counsel: poor Belsize's agony, and the wretchedness of the young lady who shared in the desperate passion, may have set our young man a thinking: and Lord Kew's frankness and courage and honour whereof Clive had been a witness during the night, touched his heart with a generous admiration and manned him for a trial which he felt was indeed severe. He thought of the dear old father ploughing the seas on the[5] way to his duty and was determined by Heaven's help to do his own. Only[6] three weeks since, when strolling careless about Bonn he had lighted upon Ethel and the laughing group of little cousins, he was a boy as they were, thinking but of the enjoyment of the day and the sunshine, as[7] careless as those children. And now the thoughts and passions which had sprung up in a week or two had given him an experience such as years do not always furnish, and our friend was to show, not only that he could feel love in his heart, but that he could give proof of courage and self-denial and honour.

"Do you remember, J.J.," says he, as boots and breeches went plunging into the portmanteau and with immense energy he pummels down one upon the other, "do you remember (a dig into the snowy bosom of a dress cambric shirt) my dear old father's only campaign story of his running away (a frightful blow into the ribs of a waistcoat), running away at Asseer-Ghur?—"

"Asseer-What?" says J.J. wondering—

"The siege[8] of Asseer-Ghur," says Clive, "fought in the eventful year 1803; Lieutenant Newcome,[9] who has very neat legs, let me tell you, which also he has imparted to his descendants, had put on a new pair of leather breeches, for he likes to go handsomely dressed into action. His horse was shot; the enemy were upon him: and the governor had to choose between death and retreat. I have heard his brother officers say that my dear old father was the bravest man they ever knew,

---

[5] the *E1*] his *Ms*

[6] Only *E1*] But *Ms*

[7] as *E1*] was *Ms*

[8] siege *E1*] battle *Ms*

[9] in the eventful year 1803; Lieutenant Newcome *E1*] on the eventful day Lieutenant Thomas Newcome *Ms*

the coolest hand, Sir. What do you think it was Lieutenant Newcome's

duty to do under these circumstances? To remain alone as he was, his troop having turned about, and to be cut down by the Mahratta horsemen—To perish or to run, Sir?"

"I know which I should have done," says Ridley.

"Exactly. Lieutenant Newcome adopted that course. His bran new leather breeches were exceedingly tight, and greatly incommoded the rapidity of his retreating movement, but he ran away, Sir, and afterwards begot your obedient servant. That is the history of the battle of Asseer-Ghur."

"And now for the moral," says J.J. not a little amused.

"J.J., old boy, this is my battle of Asseer-Ghur. I am off. Dip into the money bag: pay the people: be generous, J.J., but not too prodigal. The chamber-maid is ugly, yet let her not want for a crown to console her at our departure. The waiters have been brisk and servile. Reward the slaves for their labours. Forget not the humble Boots, so shall he bless us when we depart. For Artists is[1] gentlemen though Ethel does not think so. De— No—God bless her, God bless her," groans out Clive cramming his two fists into his eyes. If Ridley admired him before, he thought none the worse of

[1] is *Ms*] are *E1*

him now. And if[2] any generous young fellow in life reads the Fable which may possibly concern him, let him take a senior's counsel and remember that there are perils in our battle, God help us, from[3] which the bravest had best run away.

Early as the morning yet was, Clive had a visitor and the door opened to let in Lord Kew's honest face. Ridley retreated before it into his own den, the appearance of earls scared the modest painter though he was proud and pleased that his Clive should have their company. Lord Kew indeed lived in more splendid apartments on the first floor of the hotel, Clive and his friend occupying a couple of spacious chambers on the second story. "You are an early bird," says Kew. "I got up myself in a panic before daylight almost. Jack was making a deuce of a row in his room and fit to blow the door out. I have been coaxing him for this hour; I wish we had thought of giving him a dose of laudanum last night, if it finished him poor old boy it would do him no harm." And then, laughing, he gave Clive an account of his interview with Barnes on the previous night. "You seem to be packing up to go, too," says Lord Kew with a momentary glance of humour darting from his keen eyes. "The weather is breaking up here and if you are going to cross the St. Gothard, as the Newcomes told me, the sooner the better. It's bitter cold over the mountains in October."

"Very cold," says Clive biting his nails.

"Post or Vett.?" asks my lord.

"I bought a carriage at Frankfort," says Clive in an offhand manner.

"Hulloh!" cries the other who was perfectly kind and entirely frank and pleasant and showed no difference in his conversation with men of any degree except perhaps that to his inferiors in station he was a little more polite than to his equals but who would as soon have thought of a young artist leaving Baden in a carriage of his own as of his riding away on a dragon.

"I only gave twenty pounds for the carriage, it's a little light thing, we are two, a couple of horses carry us and our traps, you know, and we can stop where we like. I don't depend upon my profession," Clive added with a blush, "I made three guineas once and that is the only money I ever gained in my life."

"Of course, my dear fellow, have not I been to your father's house? At that pretty ball, and seen no end of fine people there? We are young swells. I know that very well. We only paint for pleasure."

"We are artists, and we intend to paint for money, my lord," says Clive. "Will your lordship give me an order?"

"My lordship serves me right," the other said, "I think, Newcome, as you are going, I think you might do some folks here a good turn though the service is rather a disagreeable one. Jack Belsize is not fit to be left alone. I can't go away from here just now for reasons of state. Do be a good fellow and take him with you. Put the Alps between him and this confounded business, and if I can serve you in any way I shall be delighted

---

[2] And if *E1*] If *Ms*
[3] from *E1*] in *Ms*

if you will furnish me with the occasion. Jack does not know yet that our amiable Barnes is here. I know how fond you are of him. I have heard the story, glass of claret and all. We all love Barnes. How that poor Lady Clara can have accepted him the Lord knows. We are fearfully and wonderfully made, especially women."

"Good Heavens," Clive broke out, "can it be possible that a young creature can have been brought to like such a selfish insolent coxcomb as that, such a cocktail as Barnes Newcome? You know very well, Lord Kew, what his life is. There was a poor girl whom he brought out of a Newcome factory when he was a boy himself and might have had a heart one would have thought, whom he ill-treated, whom he deserted, and flung out of doors without a penny, upon some pretence of her infidelity towards him, who came and actually sat down on the steps of Park Lane with a child on each side of her, and not their cries and their hunger but the fear of his own shame and a dread of a police court forced him to give her a maintenance. I never see the fellow but I loathe him and long to kick him out of window and this man is to marry a noble young lady because forsooth he is a partner in a bank and heir to seven or eight thousand a year. O, it is a shame, it is a shame! It makes me sick when I think of the lot which the poor thing is to endure."

"It is not a nice story," said Lord Kew, rolling a cigarette. "Barnes is not a nice man. I give you that in. You have not heard it talked about in the family, have you?"

"Good Heavens! you don't suppose that I would speak to Ethel, to Miss Newcome, about such a foul subject as that?" cries Clive. "I never mentioned it to my own father. He would have turned Barnes out of his doors if he had known it."

"It was the talk about town, I know," Kew said dryly. "Every thing is told in those confounded clubs. I told you I give up Barnes. I like him no more than you do. He may have treated the woman ill, I suspect he has not an angelical temper: but in this matter he has not been so bad, so very bad as it would seem. The first step is wrong of course:—those factory towns, that sort of thing you know:—well well, the commencement of the business is a bad one. But he is not the only sinner in London. He declared on his honour to me when the matter was talked about and he was coming on for election at Bays's and was as nearly pilled as any man I ever knew in my life,—he declared on his word that he only parted from Mrs. DeLacy (Mrs. DeLacy the poor devil used to call herself) because he found that she had served him—as such women will serve men. He offered to send his children to school in Yorkshire:—rather a cheap school,—but she would not part with them. She made a scandal in order to get good terms and she succeeded. He was anxious to break the connexion: he owned it had hung like a millstone round his neck and caused him a great deal of remorse— annoyance you may call it. He was immensely cut up about it. I remember when that fellow was hanged for murdering a woman, Barnes said he did not wonder at his having done it. Young men make those connexions in their early lives and rue them all their days after. He was heartily sorry, that we may take for granted. He wished to lead a proper life. My grandmother managed this business with the Dorkings. Lady Kew still pulls stroke oar in our boat, you know, and the old woman will not give up her place. They know everything, the elders do. He is a clever fellow. He is witty in his way. When he likes he can make himself quite agreeable to some people. There has been no sort of force. You don't suppose young ladies are confined in dungeons and subject to tortures, do you? But there is a brood of Pulleyns at Chanticlere, and old Dorking has nothing to give them. His daughter accepted Barnes of her own free will: he knowing perfectly well of that previous affair with Jack. The poor devil bursts into the place yesterday and the girl drops down in a faint. She will see Belsize this very day if he likes. I took a note from Lady Dorking to him at five o'clock this morning. If he fancies that there is any constraint put upon Lady Clara's actions she will tell him with her own lips that she has acted of her own free will. She will marry the husband she has chosen and do her duty by him. You are quite a young un who boil and froth up with indignation at the idea that a girl hardly off with an old love should take on with a new—"

"I am not indignant with her," says Clive, "for breaking with Belsize but for marrying Barnes."

"You hate him: and—you know he is your enemy and indeed, young fellow, he does not compliment you in talking about you: A pretty young scapegrace he has made *you* out to be and very likely thinks you to be. It depends on the colours in which a fellow is painted. Our friends and our enemies draw us: and I often think both pictures are like," continued the easy world-philosopher. "You hate Barnes and cannot see any good in him. He sees none in you. There have been tremendous shindies in Park Lane *apropos* of your worship and of a subject which I don't care to mention," said Lord Kew with some dignity, "and what is the upshot of all this malevolence? I like you, I like your father, I think he is a noble old boy. There are those who represented him as a sordid schemer. Give Mr. Barnes the benefit of common charity at any rate; and let others like him, if you do not.

"And as for this romance of love," the young nobleman went on, kindling as he spoke and forgetting the slang and colloquialisms with which we garnish all our conversation—"This fine picture of Jenny and Jessamy falling in love at first sight, billing and cooing in an arbour and retiring to a cottage afterwards to go on cooing and billing—Pshaw! what folly is this! It is good for romances and for Misses to sigh about: but any man who walks through the world with his eyes open knows how senseless is all this rubbish. I do not[4] say that a young man and woman are not to meet and to fall in love that instant and to marry that day year and love each other till they are a hundred. That is the supreme lot: but that is the lot which the gods only grant to Baucis and Philemon and a very very few besides. As for the rest, they must compromise; make themselves as comfortable as they can, and take the good and the bad together. And as for Jenny and Jessamy; by Jove! look round among your friends: count up the love matches, and see what has been the end of most of them! Love in a cottage! Who is to pay the landlord for the cottage? Who is to pay for

---

[4] do not *Ms*] don't *E1*

Jenny's tea and cream and Jessamy's mutton chops? If he has cold mutton, he will quarrel with her: if there is nothing in the cupboard, a pretty meal they make! No, you cry out against people in our world making money marriages! Why, kings and queens marry on the same understanding. My butcher has saved a stocking full of money: and marries his daughter to a young salesman. Mr. and Mrs. Salesman prosper in life and get an alderman's daughter for their son. My attorney looks out amongst his clients for an eligible husband for Miss Deeds: sends his son to the bar, into Parliament, where he cuts a figure and becomes attorney-general, makes a fortune, has a house in Belgrave Square, and marries Miss Deeds of the second generation to a peer. Do not accuse us of being more sordid than our neighbours. We do but as the world does: and a girl in our society accepts the best party which offers itself, just as Miss Chummey when entreated by two young gentlemen of the order of costermongers inclines to the one who rides from market on a moke, rather than to the gentleman who sells his greens from a handbasket."

This tirade which his lordship delivered with considerable spirit was intended no doubt to carry a moral for Clive's private hearing. And which to do him justice the youth was not slow to comprehend. The point was, "Young man! if certain persons of rank chose to receive you very kindly who have but a comely face, good manners and three or four hundred pounds a-year: do not presume upon their good nature or indulge in certain ambitious hopes which your vanity may induce you to form. Sail down the stream with the brass nobs,[5] Master Earthenpot, but beware of coming too near! You are a nice young man, but there are some prizes which are too good for you and are meant for your betters and you might as well ask the prime minister for the next vacant garter as expect to wear on your breast such a star as Ethel Newcome."

Before Clive made his accustomed visit to his friends at the hotel opposite, the last great potentiary had arrived who was to take part in the Family Congress of Baden. In place of Ethel's flushing cheeks and bright eyes Clive found on entering Lady Ann Newcome's sitting-room, the parchment-covered features and the well-known hooked beak of the old Countess of Kew. To support the glances from beneath the bushy black eyebrows on each side of that promontory was no pleasant matter. The whole family cowered under Lady Kew's eyes and nose, and she ruled by force of them. It was only Ethel whom these awful features did not utterly subdue and dismay.

Besides Lady Kew, Clive had the pleasure of finding his lordship, her grandson, Lady Ann and children of various sizes, and Mr. Barnes. Not one of whom was the person whom Clive desired to behold.

The queer glance in Kew's eye directed towards Clive who was himself not by any means deficient in perception informed him that there had just been a conversation in which his own name had figured. Having been abusing Clive extravagantly as he did whenever he mentioned his cousin's name, Barnes must needs hang his head when the young fellow came in.

[5] nobs *Ms*] pots *E1*

His hand was yet on the chamber-door and Barnes was calling him miscreant and scoundrel within. So no wonder Barnes had a hangdog look. But as for Lady Kew that veteran diplomatist allowed no signs of discomfiture or any other emotion to display themselves on her ancient countenance. Her bushy eyebrows were groves of mystery, her unfathomable eyes were wells of gloom.

She gratified Clive by a momentary loan of two knuckly old fingers, which he was at liberty to hold or to drop. And then he went on to enjoy the felicity of shaking hands with Mr. Barnes, who, observing and enjoying his confusion over Lady Kew's reception, determined to try Clive in the same way and he gave Clive at the same time a supercilious "How de dah" which the other would have liked[6] to drive down his throat. A constant desire to throttle Mr. Barnes; to beat him on the nose; to send him flying out of window; was a sentiment with which this singular young man inspired many persons whom he accosted. A biographer ought to be impartial, yet I own, in a modified degree, to have partaken of this sentiment. He looked very much younger than his actual time of life and was not of a commanding stature: but patronised his equals, nay let us say his betters, so insufferably that a common wish for his suppression existed amongst many persons in society.

Clive told me of this little circumstance and I am sorry to say of his own subsequent ill behaviour. "We were standing apart from the ladies," so Clive narrated, "when Barnes and I had our little passage of arms.[7] He had tried the finger business upon me before, and[8] I had before told him either to shake hands or to leave it alone. You know the way in which the impudent little beggar stands astride and sticks his little feet out. I brought my heel well down on his confounded little varnished toe, and gave it a scrunch which made Mr. Barnes shriek out one of his loudest oaths."

" 'D— clumsy Be—,' "[9] screamed out Barnes.

Clive said in a low voice, "I thought you only swore at women, Barnes."

"It is you that say things before women, Clive," cries his cousin looking very furious.

Mr. Clive lost all patience. "In what company, Barnes, would you like me to say, that I think you are a snob? Will you have it on the Parade. Come out and I'll[1] speak to you."

"Barnes can't go out on the Parade," cries Lord Kew bursting out laughing, "there's another gentleman there wanting him." And two of the three young men enjoyed this joke exceedingly. I doubt whether Barnes Newcome Newcome, Esq., of Newcome, was one of the persons amused.

"What wickedness are you three boys laughing at?" cries Lady Ann perfectly innocent and good-natured: "no good I will be bound. Come here, Clive." Our[2] young friend, it must be premised, had no sooner received

6 would have liked *E1*] was obliged *Ms*
7 "We were standing . . . passage of arms. *E1*] [not present] *Ms*
8 before, and *E1*] before," Clive said, "and *Ms*
9 Be— *Ms*] —— *E1*
1 I'll *Ms*] I will *E1*
2 Our *E1*] For our *Ms*

the thrust of Lady Kew's two fingers on entering, than it had been intimated to him that his interview with that gracious lady was at an end. For she had instantly called her daughter to her with whom her ladyship fell a-whispering; and then it was that Clive retreated from Lady Kew's hand, to fall into Barnes's.

"Clive trod on Barnes's toe," cries out cheery Lord Kew "and has hurt Barnes's favourite corn so that he cannot go out, and is actually obliged to keep the room. That's what we were laughing at."

"Hm," growled Lady Kew. She knew to what her grandson alluded. Lord Kew had represented Jack Belsize and his thundering big stick in the most terrific colours to the family council. The joke was too good a one not to serve twice.

Lady Ann in her whispered conversation with the old Countess had possibly deprecated her mother's anger towards poor Clive, for when he came up to the two ladies the younger took his hand with great kindness and said, "My dear Clive, we are very sorry you are going. You were of the greatest use to us in the journey. I am sure you have been uncommonly good-natured and obliging and we shall all miss you very much." Her gentleness smote the generous young fellow, and an emotion of gratitude towards her for being so compassionate to him in his misery caused his cheeks to blush and his eyes perhaps to moisten. "Thank you, dear Aunt," says he. "You have been very good and kind to me. It is I that will[3] feel lonely—but—but it is quite time that I should go to my work."

"Quite time," said the severe possessor of the eagle beak. "Baden is a bad place for young men. They make acquaintances here of which very little good can come. They frequent the gambling-tables and live with the most disreputable French Viscounts. We have heard of your goings on, Sir. It is a great pity that Colonel Newcome did not take you with him to India."

"My dear Mamma," cries Lady Ann. "I am sure Clive has been a very good boy indeed." The old lady's morality put a stop to Clive's pathetic mood and he replied with a great deal of spirit, "Dear Lady Ann, you have been always very good, and kindness is nothing surprising from you; but Lady Kew's advice which I should not have ventured to ask is an unexpected favour. My father knows the extent of the gambling transactions to which your ladyship was pleased to allude: and introduced me to the gentleman whose acquaintance you don't seem to think eligible."

"My good young man, I think it is time you were off," Lady Kew said this time with great good-humour; she liked Clive's spirit and as long as he interfered with none of her plans was quite disposed to be friendly with him. "Go to Rome, go to Florence, go wherever you like and study very hard and make very good pictures and come back again and we shall all be very glad to see you. You have very great talents—these sketches are really capital."

"Is not he very clever, Mamma," said kind Lady Ann eagerly. Clive felt the pathetic mood coming on again and an immense desire to hug Lady

3 will *Ms*] shall *E1*

Ann in his arms and to kiss her. How grateful are we—how touched a frank and generous heart is for a kind word extended to us in our pain! The pressure of a tender hand nerves a man for an operation and cheers him for the dreadful interview with the surgeon.

That cool old Operator who had taken Mr. Clive's case in hand now produced her shining knife and executed the first cut with perfect neatness and precision. "We are come here as I suppose you know, Mr. Newcome, upon family matters, and I frankly tell you that I think for your own sake you would be much better away. I wrote my daughter a great scolding when I heard that you were in this place."

"But it was by the merest chance, Mamma, indeed it was," cries Lady Ann.

"Of course by the merest chance and by the merest chance I heard of it too. A little bird came and told me at Kissingen. You have no more sense, Ann, than a goose. I have told you so a hundred times. Lady Ann requested you to stay and I, my good young friend, request you to go away."

"I needed no request," said Clive. "My going, Lady Kew, is my own act. I was going without requiring any guide to show me to the door."

"No doubt you were, and my arrival, is the signal for Mr. Newcome's *bonjour.* I am Bogey and I frighten every body away. By the scene which you witnessed yesterday, my good young friend, and all that painful *esclandre* on the promenade, you must see how absurd and dangerous and wicked, yes wicked it is, for parents to allow intimacies to spring up between young people which can only lead to disgrace and unhappiness. Lady Dorking was another good-natured goose. I had not arrived yesterday ten minutes when my maid came running in to tell me of what had occurred on the promenade, and tired as I was I went that instant to Jane Dorking and passed the evening with her and that poor little creature to whom Captain Belsize behaved so cruelly. She does not care a fig for him—not one fig. Her childish inclination is passed away these two years, whilst Mr. Jack was performing his feats in prison: and if the wretch flatters himself that it was on his account she was agitated yesterday, he is perfectly mistaken and you may tell him Lady Kew said so. She is subject to fainting fits. Dr. Finck[4] has been attending her ever since she has been here. She fainted only last Tuesday at the sight of a rat walking about their lodgings (they have dreadful lodgings, the Dorkings) and no wonder she was frightened at the sight of that great coarse tipsy wretch! She is engaged, as you know, to your connexion, my grandson Barnes,—in all respects a most eligible union. The rank of life of the parties suits them to one another. She is a good young woman, and Barnes has experienced from persons of another sort such horrors that he will know the blessing of domestic virtue. It was high time he should.

"I say all this in perfect frankness to you.

"Go back again and play in the garden, little brats (this to the innocents who came frisking in from the lawn in front of the windows), You have

4 Finck *E1*] Strumpf *Ms*

been? And Barnes sent you in here? Go up to Miss Quigley. No stop. Go and tell Ethel to come down, bring her down with you. Do you understand?"

The unconscious infants toddle up-stairs to their sister; and Lady Kew blandly says, "Ethel's engagement to my grandson, Lord Kew, has long been settled in our family, though these things are best not talked about until they are quite determined, you know, my dear Mr. Newcome. When we saw you and your father in London we heard that you too,—that you too were engaged to a young lady in your own rank of life, a Miss—what was her name?—Miss MacPherson, Miss Mackenzie. Your aunt Mrs. Hobson Newcome, who I must say is a most blundering silly person, had set about this story. It appears there is no truth in it. Do not look surprised that I know about your affairs. I am an old witch and know numbers of things." And, indeed, how Lady Kew came to know this fact, whether her maid corresponded with Lady Ann's maid;—what her ladyship's means of information were, avowed or occult,—this biographer has never been able to ascertain. Very likely, Ethel, who in these last three weeks had been made aware of that interesting circumstance, had announced it to Lady Kew in the course of a cross-examination, and there may have been a battle between the granddaughter and the grandmother, of which the family chronicler of the Newcomes has had no precise knowledge. That there were many such I know—skirmishes, sieges and general engagements. When we hear the guns and see the wounded, we know there has been a fight. Who knows had there been a battle royal and was Miss Newcome having her wounds dressed up-stairs?

"You will like to say good bye to your cousin, I know," Lady Kew continued with imperturbable placidity. "Ethel, my dear, here is Mr. Clive Newcome who has come to bid us all good bye." The little girls came trotting down at this moment, each holding a skirt of their elder sister. She looked rather pale but her expression was haughty—almost fierce.

Clive rose up as she entered, from the sofa by the old Countess's side which place she had pointed him to take during the amputation. He rose up and put his hair back off his face and said very calmly, "Yes, I am come to say good bye. My holidays are over, and Ridley and I are off for Rome; good bye and God bless you, Ethel."

She gave him her hand and said, "Good bye, Clive," but her hand did not return his pressure, and dropped to her side, when he let it go.

Hearing the words good bye little Alice burst into a howl and little Maude who was an impetuous little thing stamped her little red shoes and said, "It sant be good bye. Tive sant go." Alice roaring, clung hold of Clive's trowsers. He took them up gaily, each on an arm as he had done a hundred times and tossed the children on to his shoulders where they used to like to pull his yellow mustachios. He kissed the little hands and faces, and a moment after was gone.

"*Qu'as tu,*" says M. de Florac meeting him going over the bridge to his own hôtel. "*Qu'as tu, mon petit Claive. Est-ce qu'on vient de t'arracher une dent?*"

"*C'est ça,*" says Clive and walked into the Hôtel de France. "Hulloh! J.J.! Ridley!" he sang out. "Order the trap out and let's be off." "I thought we

FAREWELL

"To Rome"

were not to march till to-morrow," says J.J. divining perhaps that some catastrophe had occurred. Indeed, Mr. Clive was going a day sooner than he had intended. He woke at Fribourg the next morning. It was the grand old cathedral he looked at, not Baden of the pine-clad hills, of the pretty walks and the lime-tree avenues. Not Baden, the prettiest booth of all Vanity Fair. The crowds and the music, the gambling-tables and the cadaverous croupiers and chinking gold were far out of sight and hearing. There was one window in the Hôtel de Hollande that he thought of, how a fair arm used to open it in the early morning, how the muslin curtain, in the morning air swayed to and fro. He would have given how much to see it once more. Walking about at Fribourg in the night away from his companions, he had thought of ordering horses, galloping back to Baden and once again under that window, calling Ethel, Ethel. But he came back to his Inn and the quiet J.J. and to poor Jack Belsize who had had his tooth taken out, too.

We had almost forgotten Jack who took a back seat in Clive's carriage as befits a secondary personage in this history. And Clive in truth had almost forgotten him too. But Jack having his own cares and business, and having rammed his own carpet-bag, brought it down without a word, and Clive found him environed in smoke when he came down to take his place in the little britzka. I wonder whether the window at the Hôtel de Hollande saw him go: there are some curtains behind which no historian however prying is allowed to peep.

"*Tiens, le petit part,*" says Florac of the cigar who was always sauntering. "Yes, we go," says Clive. "There is a fourth place, Viscount, will you come too."

"I would love it well," replies Florac, "but I am here in faction. My cousin and Seigneur M. le Duc d'Ivry is coming all the way from Bagnères de Bigorre. He says he counts on me:—*affaires d'état, mon cher, affaires d'état.*"

"How pleased the Duchess will be—Easy with that bag!" shouts Clive. "How pleased the Princess will be!" In truth he hardly knew what he was saying.

"*Vous croyez. Vous croyez,*" says M. de Florac. "As you have a fourth place I know who had best take it."

"And who is that?" asked the young traveller. Lord Kew and Barnes, Esq., of Newcome,[5] came out of the Hôtel de Hollande at this moment. Barnes slunk back, seeing Jack Belsize's hairy face. Kew ran over the bridge. Good bye Clive, Good bye Jack, Good bye Kew. It was a great handshaking, away goes the postillion blowing his horn, and young Hannibal has left Capua behind him.

---

5 Barnes Esq of Newcome *Ms*] Barnes, Esq., of Newcome, *E1*] Barnes Newcome, Esq., *R*] Barnes Newcome, Esq., of Newcome, *HM NY*

Chapter XXXI.

ONE of Clive Newcome's letters from Baden, the young man described to me with considerable humour and numerous illustrations as his wont was, a great lady to whom he was presented at that watering-place by his friend Lord Kew. Lord Kew had travelled in the East with Monsieur le Duc and Madame la Duchesse d'Ivry; the Prince being an old friend of his lordship's family. He is the Q of Madame d'Ivry's book of travels, "Footprints of the Gazelles; by a daughter of the Crusaders," in which she prays so fervently for Lord Kew's conversion. He is the Q who rescued the Princess from the Arabs, and performed many a feat which lives in her glowing pages. He persists in saying that he never rescued Madame la Princesse from any Arabs at all, except from one beggar who was bawling out for bucksheesh, and whom Kew drove away with a stick. They made pilgrimages to all the holy places: and a piteous sight it was, said Lord Kew, to see the old Prince in the Jerusalem processions at Easter pacing with bare feet and a candle. Here Lord Kew separated from the Prince's party. His name does not occur in the last part of the "Footprints"; which in truth are filled full of strange rhapsodies, adventures which nobody ever saw but the princess, and mystic disquisitions. She hesitates at nothing, like other poets of her nation: not profoundly learned, she invents where she has not acquired: mingles together religion and the opera: and performs Parisian pas-de-ballet before the gates of monasteries and the cells of anchorites. She describes, as if she had herself witnessed the catastrophe, the passage of the Red Sea: and, as if there were no doubt of the transaction, an unhappy love-affair between Pharaoh's eldest son and Moses's daughter. At Cairo *apropos* of Joseph's granaries, she enters into a furious tirade against Putiphar, whom she describes as old[1] sav-

[1] describes as old *Ms*] paints as an old *E1*

age suspicious and a tyrant. They generally have a copy of the "Foot-prints of the Gazelles" at the Circulating Library at Baden; as Madame d'Ivry constantly visits that watering-place. M. le Duc was not pleased with the book: which was published entirely without his concurrence; and which he described as one of the ten thousand follies of Madame la Duchesse.

This nobleman was five and forty years older than his Duchess. France is the country where that sweet Christian institution of *mariages de conve-nance* (which so many folks of the family about which this story treats are engaged in arranging) is most in vogue. There the newspapers daily an-nounce that M. de Foy[2] has a *bureau de confiance* where families may ar-range marriages for their sons and daughters in perfect comfort and se-curity. It is but a question of money on one side and the other. Made-moiselle has so many francs of *dot*: Monsieur has such and such *rentes* or lands in possession or reversion, an *étude d'avoué*, a shop with a cer-tain *clientèle* bringing him such and such an income which may be dou-bled by the judicious addition of so much capital,—and the pretty little matrimonial arrangement is concluded (the agent touching his percent-age) or broken off and nobody unhappy and the world none the wiser. The consequences of the system I do not pretend personally to know: but if the light literature of a country is a reflex of its manners, and French novels are a picture of French life, a pretty society must that be into the midst of which the London reader may walk in twelve hours from this time of perusal and from which only twenty miles of sea separate us.

When the old Duke d'Ivry of the ancient ancient nobility of France, an emigrant with Artois, a warrior with Condé, an exile during the reign of the Corsican usurper, a grand Prince, a great nobleman afterwards, though shorn of nineteen-twentieths of his wealth by the revolution—when the Duc d'Ivry lost his two sons, and his son's sons likewise died,—as if fate had determined to end the direct line of that noble house which had fur-nished queens to Europe and renowned chiefs to the Crusaders,—being of an intrepid spirit the Duke was ill-disposed to yield to his redoubtable enemy in spite of the cruel blows which the latter had inflicted upon him; and when he was more than sixty years of age, three months before the July Revolution broke out, a young lady of a sufficient nobility, a virgin of sixteen, was brought out of the convent of the Sacré Cœur at Paris and married with immense splendour and ceremony to this princely widower. The most august names signed the book of the civil marriage. Madame la Dauphine and Madame la Duchesse de Berri complimented the young bride with royal favours. Her portrait by Dubufe was in the Exhibition of the[3] next year, a charming young Duchess indeed with black eyes and black ringlets, pearls on her neck and diamonds in her hair, as beauti-ful as a princess of a fairy tale. M. d'Ivry whose early life may have been rather oragious was yet a gentleman perfectly well conserved. Resolute

---

[2] M. de Foy *E1*] M. Foy *Ms*
[3] of the *Ms*] [omitted] *E1*

against fate his enemy, (one would fancy fate was of an aristocratic turn, and took special[4] delight in combats with princely houses, the Atridæ, the Borbonidæ, the Ivrys—the[5] Browns and Jones's being of no account) the Duke seemed to be determined not only to secure a progeny, but to defy age. At sixty he was still young, or seemed to be so. His hair was as black as the Princess's own, his teeth as white: If you saw him on the Boulevard de Gand sunning among the youthful exquisites there, or riding au Bois with a grace worthy of old Franconi himself, you would take him for one of the young men, of whom indeed up to his marriage he retained a number of the graceful follies and amusements, although his manners had a dignity acquired in the old days of Versailles and the Trianon which the moderns cannot hope to imitate. He was assiduous behind the scenes of the opera as any journalist or any young dandy of twenty years. He "ranged himself," as the French phrase is, shortly before his marriage, just like any other young bachelor; took leave of Phryne and Aspasie in the coulisses, and proposed to devote himself henceforth to his charming young wife.

The *affreux catastrophe* of July arrived. The ancient Bourbons were once more on the road to exile, save one wily old remnant of the race, who rode grinning over the Barricades and distributing *poignées de main* to the stout fists that had pummelled his family out of France.[6] M. le Duc d'Ivry who lost his place at Court, his appointments which helped his income very much, and his peerage, would no more acknowledge the usurper of Neuilly than him of Elba. The ex-peer retired to his *terres*. He barricaded his house in Paris against all supporters of the citizen King, his nearest kinsman,[7] M. de Florac among the rest who for his part cheerfully took his oath of fidelity, and his seat in Louis Philippe's house of peers, having indeed been accustomed to swear to all dynasties for some years past.

In due time Madame la Duchesse d'Ivry gave birth to a child—a daughter, whom her noble father received with but small pleasure. What the Duke desired was an heir to his house[8]—a Prince de Montcontour, to fill the place of the sons and grandsons gone before him to join their ancestors in the tomb. No more children however blessed the old Duke's union. Madame d'Ivry went the round of all the watering places: pilgrimages were tried: vows and gifts to all saints supposed to be favourable to the d'Ivry family, or to families in general. But the saints turned a deaf ear: they were inexorable since the True Religion and the elder Bourbons were banished from France.

Living by themselves in their ancient castles, or their[9] dreary mansion of the Faubourg St. Germain, I suppose the Duke and Duchess grew tired of one another, as persons who enter into a *mariage de convenance*, sometimes, nay, as those who light a flaming lovematch and run away with one another

---

4 special *Ms*] especial *E1*
5 the Ivrys—the *E1*] the ~~Montaigns~~ ↑d'Ivrys↓ and so on,—the *Ms*
6 exile, save one wily . . . family out of France. *Ms E1*] exile. *R*
7 his nearest kinsman, *E1*] his cousin *Ms*
8 ~~name~~house *Ms*] name *E1*
9 their *E1*] the *Ms*

will be found to do. A lady of one-and-twenty and a gentleman of sixty-six alone in a great Castle which they cannot afford to fill with company,[1] have not unfrequently a third guest at their table who comes without a card, and whom they cannot shut out, though they keep their doors closed ever so. His name is Ennui, and many a long hour and weary weary night must such folks pass in the unbidden society of this Old Man of the Sea; this daily guest at the board; this watchful attendant at the fireside; this assiduous companion who *will* walk out with you, this sleepless restless bedfellow.

At first, M. d'Ivry, that well conserved nobleman who never would allow that he was not young exhibited no sign of doubt regarding his own youth except an extreme jealousy and avoidance of all other young fellows. Very likely Madame la Duchesse may have thought men in general dyed their hair, wore stays and had the rheumatism. Coming out of the Convent of the Sacré-Cœur, how was the innocent young lady to know better? You see in these *mariages de convenance,* though a coronet may be convenient to a beautiful young creature; and a beautiful young creature may be convenient to an old gentleman, there are articles which the marriage-monger cannot make to convene at all: tempers over which M. de Foy and his like have no control: and tastes which cannot be put into the marriage settlements. So this couple were unhappy and the Duke and Duchess quarreled with one another like the most vulgar pair who ever fought across a table.

In this unhappy state of home affairs, Madame took to literature, Monsieur to politics. She discovered that she was a great unappreciated soul: and when a woman finds that treasure in her bosom, of course she sets her own price on the article. Did you ever see the first poems of Madame la Duchesse d'Ivry, "Les cris de l'âme?" She used to read them to her very intimate friends, in white, with her hair a good deal down her back. They had some success. Dubufe having painted her as a Duchess: Scheffer depicted her as a Muse. That was in the third year of her marriage, when she rebelled against the Duke her husband, insisted on opening her saloons to Art and Literature; and, a fervent devotee still, proposed to unite Genius and Religion. Poets had interviews with her. Musicians came and twangled guitars to her. Her husband entering her room would fall over the sabre and spurs of Count Almaviva from the boulevard, or Don Basilio with his great sombrero and shoe-buckles. The old gentleman was breathless and bewildered in following her through all her vagaries. He was of old France, she of new. What did he know of the École Romantique, and these *jeunes gens* with their Marie Tudors and Tours de Nesle: and sanguineous histories of queens who sowed their lovers into sacks, Emperors who had interviews with robber captains in Charlemagne's tomb, Buridans and Hernanis and stuff? Monsieur le Vicomte de Chateaubriand was a man of genius as a writer, certainly immortal; and M. de Lamartine was a young man extremely *bien pensant,* but ma foi give him *Crébillon fils* or a bonne farce of M. Vadé to make laugh: for the great sentiments, for the beautiful style, give him M. de Lormian (although Bonapartist) or the Abbé de Lille—And for the new school. Bah!—these little Dumases and

---

[1] which they cannot . . . company, *Ms*] [omitted] *E1*

Hugos and Mussets, what is all that? "M. de Lormian shall be immortal, Monsieur," he would say, "when all these *fréluquets* are forgotten." After his marriage he frequented the coulisses of the Opera no more; but he was a pretty constant attendant at the Théâtre Français, where you might hear him snoring over the chefs-d'œuvre of French tragedy.

For some little time[2] after 1830, the Duchess was as great a Carlist as her husband could wish; and they conspired together very comfortably at first. Of an adventurous turn, eager for excitement of all kinds, nothing would have better pleased the Duchess than to follow MADAME in her adventurous courses in La Vendée, disguised as a boy above all. She was persuaded to stay at home, however, and aid the good cause at Paris: while Monsieur le Duc went off to Brittany to offer his old sword to the mother of his king. But MADAME was discovered up the chimney at Rennes, and all sorts of things were discovered afterwards—The world said that our silly little Duchess of Paris was partly the cause of the discovery. Spies were put upon her; and to some people she would tell anything. M. le Duc, on paying his annual visit to august exiles at Goritz, was very badly received; Madame la Dauphine gave him a sermon. He had an awful quarrel with Madame la Duchesse on returning to Paris. He provoked Monsieur le Comte Tiercelin—le beau Tiercelin—an officer of ordonnance of the Duke of Orleans into a duel, *apropos* of a cup of coffee in a salon: he actually wounded the beau Tiercelin—he sixty-five years of age! his nephew, M. de Florac, was loud in praise of his kinsman's bravery.

That pretty figure and complexion which still appear so captivating in M. Dubufe's portrait of Madame la Duchesse d'Ivry have long existed—it must be owned—only in paint. "*Je la préfère à l'huile,*" the Vicomte de Florac said of his cousin—"She should get her blushes from Monsieur Dubufe—those of her present furnishers are not near so natural." Sometimes the Duchess appeared with these postiches roses, sometimes of a mortal paleness. Sometimes she looked plump, on other occasions wofully thin. "When she goes into the world," said the same chronicler, "ma cousine surrounds herself with *jupons*—c'est pour défendre sa vertu: when she is in a devotional mood, she gives up rouge, roast-meat and crinoline, and *fait maigre absolument.*" To spite the Prince her husband, she took up with the Vicomte de Florac: and to please herself she cast him away. She took his brother, the Abbé de Florac, for a director and presently parted from him. "Mon frère, ce saint homme, ne parle jamais de Madame la Princesse—maintenant," said the Vicomte. "She must have confessed to him des choses affreuses—oh oui!—affreuses ma parole d'honneur!"

The Duke d'Ivry[3] being archiroyaliste, Madame la Duchesse[4] must make herself ultraphilippiste. "O oui! tout ce qu'il-y-a de plus Madame-Adélaïde au monde!" cried Florac. "She raffoles of M. le Régent: she used to keep a fast of the day of the supplice of Philippe Égalité, Saint and Martyr. I say used for to make to enrage her husband, and to recal the Abbé

---

2 For some little time *E1*] During the first years *Ms*
3 Duke d'Ivry *E1*] Prince de Montaign *Ms*
4 la Duchesse *E1*] de Montaign *Ms*

my brother, did she not advise herself to consult M. le Pasteur Grigou, and to attend the preach at his Temple? When this sheep had brought her shepherd back, she dismissed the Pasteur Grigou. Then she tired of M. l'Abbé again, and my brother is come out from her shaking his good head. Ah! She must have put things into it which astonished the good Abbé! You know he has since taken the Dominican robe? My word of honour! I believe it was terror of her that drove him into a convent. You shall see him at Rome, Clive. Give him news of his elder: and tell him this gross prodigal is repenting amongst the swine. My word of honour! I desire but the death of Madame la Vicomtesse de Florac, to marry and range myself!

"After being Royalist, Philippist, Catholic, Huguenot: Madame d'Ivry must take to Pantheism, to bearded philosophers who believe in nothing not even in clean linen, eclecticism, republicanism, what know I? All her changes have been chronicled by books of her composition. *Les Démons*, poem Catholic: Charles IX is the hero: and the Demons are shot for the most part at the Catastrophe of Saint-Bartholomew. My good mother, all good Catholic as she is, was startled by the boldness of this doctrine. Then there came *Une Dragonnade* par Mme. La Duchesse d'Ivry,[5] which is all on your side. That was of the time of the Pastor Grigou: that one. The last was *Les Dieux déchus*, poeme en 20 chants par Mme. la D—— d'I: Guard yourself well from this Muse!—If she takes a fancy to you, she will never leave you alone. If you see her often, she will fancy you are in love with her, and tell her husband. She always tells my uncle—afterwards—after she has quarreled with you and grown tired of you—Eh! being in London once, she had the idea to make herself a *Quakre*; wore the costume, consulted a minister of that culte, and quarreled with him as of rule. It appears the Quakers do not beat themselves, otherwise my poor uncle must have payed of his person.

"The turn of the philosophers then came—the chemists—the natural historians, what know I? She made a laboratory in her hotel and rehearsed poisons like Madame de Brinvilliers—she spent hours in the Jardin des Plantes. Since she has grown *affreusement maigre* and wears mounting robes, she has taken more than ever to the idea that she resembles Mary Queen of Scots. She wears a little frill and a little cap. Every man she loves, she says, has come to misfortune. She calls her lodgings Lochleven. Eh! I pity the landlord of Lochleven! She calls ce gros Blackball vous savez[6]—that pillar of Estaminets, that Prince of Mauvais-ton, her Bothwell: little Mijaud the poor little pianist, she named her Rizzio: young Lord Greenhorn who was here with his Governor, a Monsieur of Oxfort, she christened her Darnley, and the minister Anglican, her John Knox! The poor man was quite enchanted! Beware of this haggard Syren, my little Clive!—mistrust her dangerous song! Her cave is *jonché* with the bones of her victims. Be you not one!" Far from causing Clive to avoid Madame la Duchesse, these cautions very likely would have made him only the more eager to make her acquaintance,

---

5 Duchesse d'Ivry, *E1*] Princesse de Montaign, *Ms*
6 vous savez *Ms E1*] [omitted] *R*

but that a much nobler attraction drew him elsewhere. At first, being introduced to Madame d'Ivry's salon, he was pleased and flattered, and behaved himself there merrily and agreeably enough. He had not studied Horace Vernet for nothing: he drew a fine picture of Kew rescuing her from the Arabs with a plenty of sabres, pistols, burnouses and dromedaries. He made a pretty sketch of her little girl Antoinette; and a wonderful likeness of Miss O'Grady, the little girl's governess, the mother's dame de compagnie—Miss O'Grady with the richest Milesian brogue, who had been engaged to give Antoinette the pure English accent. But the French lady's great eyes and painted smiles would not bear comparison with Ethel's natural brightness and beauty. Clive, who had been appointed painter in ordinary to the Queen of Scots, neglected his business; and went over to the English faction: so did one or two more of the Princess's followers, leaving her Majesty by no means well pleased at their desertion.

There had been many quarrels between M. d'Ivry and his next of kin—Political differences, private differences—a long story. The Prince who had been wild himself could not pardon the Vicomte de Florac for being wild. Efforts at reconciliation had been made which ended unsuccessfully. The Vicomte de Florac had been allowed for a brief space to be intimate with the chief of his family and then had been dismissed for being too intimate. Right or wrong, the Prince was jealous of all young men who approached the Princess. "He is suspicious," Madame de Florac indignantly said, "because he remembers: and he thinks other men are like himself." The Vicomte discreetly said, "My cousin has paid me the compliment to be jealous of me," and acquiesced in his banishment with a shrug.

During the emigration the old Lord Kew had been very kind to the[7] exiles: M. d'Ivry amongst the number: and that nobleman was anxious to return to all Lord Kew's family when they came to France the hospitality which he had received himself in England. He still remembered or professed to remember Lady Kew's beauty. How many women are there, awful of aspect, at present, of whom the same pleasing legend is not narrated? It must be true, for do not they themselves confess it? I know of few things more remarkable or suggestive of philosophic contemplation than those physical changes. When[8] the old Prince and the old Countess met together and talked confidentially, their conversation bloomed into a jargon wonderful to hear. Old scandals woke up, old naughtinesses rose out of their graves, and danced and smirked and gibbered again like those wicked nuns whom Bertram and Robert le Diable evoke from their sepulchres whilst the bassoon performs a diabolical incantation. The Brighton Pavilion was tenanted: Ranelagh and the Pantheon swarmed with dancers and masks: Perdita was found again, and walked a minuet with the Prince of Wales: Mrs. Clarke and the Duke of York danced together—a pretty dance: the old Duke wore a *jabot* and *ailes-de-pigeon*, the old Countess a hoop and a cushion on her head. If haply the

7 the *Ms*] [omitted] *E1*
8 When *Ms NY*] ¶When *E1 R*

young folks came in, the elders modified their recollections, and Lady Kew brought honest old King George, and good old ugly Queen Charlotte to

the rescue. Her ladyship was sister of the Marquess of Steyne: and in some respects resembled that lamented nobleman. Their family had relations in France (Lady Kew had always a pied-à-terre at Paris, a bitter little scandal-shop where les *bien-pensants* assembled and retailed the most awful stories against the reigning dynasty). It was she who handed over le petit Kiou when quite a boy to Monsieur and Madame d'Ivry, to be *lancé* into Parisian society. He was treated as a son of the family by the Duke, one of whose many Christian names his lordship, Francis George Xavier, Earl of Kew and Viscount Walham, bears. If Lady Kew hated any one (and she could hate very considerably) she hated her daughter-in-law, Walham's widow, and the methodists who surrounded her. Kew remain among a pack of psalm-singing old women and parsons with his mother! Fi donc! Frank was Lady Kew's boy: she would form him: marry him: leave him her money if he married to her liking: and show him life. So she showed it to him.

Have you taken your children to the National Gallery in London, and shown them the Mariage à la Mode? Was the Artist exceeding the privilege of his calling in painting the Catastrophe in which those guilty people all suffer? If this fable were not true: if many and many of our young men of pleasure had not acted it, and rued the moral, I would tear the page. You know that in our nursery tales there is commonly a Good Fairy to counsel, and a bad one to mislead the young Duke. You perhaps feel that in your own life there is a Good Principle imploring you to come into its kind bosom, and a Bad Passion which tempts you into its arms. Be of easy minds, good-natured people! Let us disdain surprises and *coups-de-théâtre* for once; and tell those good souls who are interested about him, that there is a Good Spirit coming to the rescue of our young Lord Kew.

Surrounded by her Court and royal attendants, La Reine Marie used graciously to attend the play-table, where luck occasionally declared itself for and against her Majesty. Her appearance used to create not a little excitement in the Saloon of Roulette, the game which she patronised as being more "fertile of emotions" than the slower *trente et quarante*. She dreamed of numbers: had favourite incantations by which to conjure them: noted the figures made by peels of peaches and so forth, the numbers of houses, on hackney-coaches—was superstitious *comme toutes les âmes poétiques*. She commonly brought a beautiful agate bonbonnière full of gold pieces which she played. It was wonderful to see her grimaces: to watch her behaviour: her appeals to Heaven, her delight and despair. Madame la Baronne de la Cruchecassée played on one side of her: Madame la Comtesse de Schlangenbad on the other. When she had lost all her money her Majesty would condescend to borrow—not from these ladies—knowing the Royal peculiarity they never had any money; they always lost; they swiftly pocketed their winnings and never left a mass on the table, or quitted it as Courtiers will when they saw luck was going against their Sovereign. The officers of her household were Count Punter, a Hanoverian, the Cavaliere Spada, Captain Blackball of a mysterious English regiment which might be any one of the hundred and twenty in the army list: and other noblemen and gentlemen, Greeks, Russians and Spaniards. Mr. and Mrs. Jones (of England) who had made the Princess's acquaintance at Bagnères[9] (where her lord still remained in the gout) and perseveringly followed her all the way to Baden; were dazzled by the splendour of the company in which they found themselves. Miss Jones wrote such letters to her dearest friend Miss Thompson,[1] Cambridge Square, London, as caused that young person to crêver with envy. Bob Jones, who had grown a pair of mustachios since he left home, began to think slightingly of poor little Fanny Thompson,[2] now he had got into "the best continental society." Might not he[3] quarter a Countess's coat on his brougham along with the Jones' arms, or more slap-up still, have the two shields painted on the panels with the coronet over?[4] "Do you know the Princess calls herself the Queen of Scots and she calls me Julian Avenel!" says Jones delighted to Clive: who wrote me about the transmogrification of our schoolfellow, an attorney's son whom I recollected a snivelling little boy at Grey Friars. "I say Newcome! The Princess is going to establish an order," cried Bob in extacy. Every one of her aides-de-camp had a bunch of orders at his button: excepting, of course, poor Jones.

Like all persons who beheld her, when Miss Newcome and her party made their appearance at Baden, Monsieur de Florac was enraptured with her beauty. "I speak of it constantly before the Princess. I know it pleases her so," the Vicomte said. "You should have seen her looks when your friend M. Jone praised Mees Newcome! She ground her teeth with fury.

[9] Bagnères *E1*] Vichy *Ms*
[1] Thompson, *E1*] Smith, *Ms*
[2] Thompson, *E1*] Smith, *Ms*
[3] Might not he *E1*] Why he might *Ms*
[4] over? *E1*] over! *Ms*

Tiens, ce petit sournois de Kiou! He always spoke of her as a mere sac d'argent that he was about to marry—an ingot of the cité—une fille de Lord Maire. Have all English bankers such pearls of daughters? If the Vicomtesse de Florac had but quitted the earth, dont elle fait l'ornement—I would present myself to the charmante Mees and ride a steeple chase with Kiou!" That he should win it, the Viscount never doubted.

When Lady Ann Newcome first appeared in the ball-room at Baden, Madame la Duchesse d'Ivry begged the Earl of Kew (notre filleul she called him) to present her to his aunt, Miladi, and her charming daughter. "My filleul had not prepared me for so much grace," she said turning a look towards Lord Kew which caused his lordship some embarrassment. Her kindness and graciousness were extreme. Her caresses and compliments never ceased all the evening. She told the mother and the daughter too that she had never seen any one so lovely as Ethel. Whenever she saw Lady Ann's children in the walks she ran to them (so that Captain Blackball and Count Punter, A.D.C., were amazed at her tenderness). She étouffed them with kisses. What lilies and roses! What lovely little creatures! what companions for her own Antoinette. "This is your governess, Miss Quigli? Mademoiselle, you must let me present you to Miss O'Grédi your compatriot and I hope your children will be always together." The Irish Protestant governess scowled at the Irish Catholic—there was a Boyne Water between them.

Little Antoinette, a lonely little girl, was glad to find any companions. "Mamma kisses me on the promenade," she told them in her artless way. "She never kisses me at home." One day when Lord Kew with Florac and Clive were playing with the children, Antoinette said, "Pourquoi ne venez vous plus chez nous, M. de Kew? And why does Mamma say you are a lâche? She said so yesterday to ces Messieurs. And why does Mamma say thou art only a vaurien, mon cousin? Thou art always very good for me. I love thee better[5] than all those Messieurs. Ma tante Florac a été bonne pour moi à Paris aussi—Ah! qu'elle a été bonne!"

"C'est que les anges aiment bien les petits chérubins and my mother is an angel, seest thou," cries Florac kissing her.

"Thy mother is not dead," said little Antoinette, "then why dost thou cry, my cousin?" And the three spectators were touched by this little scene and speech.

Lady Ann Newcome received the caresses and compliments of Madame la Duchesse d'Ivry,[6] with marked coldness on the part of one commonly so very good-natured. Ethel's instinct told her that there was something wrong in this woman and she shrunk from her with haughty reserve. The girl's conduct was not likely to please the French lady, but she never relaxed in her smiles and her compliments, her caresses and her professions of admiration. She was present when Clara Pulleyn fell; and, prodigal of *câlineries* and consolation, and shawls and scent bottles to the unhappy young lady, she *would* accompany her home. She inquired perpetually af-

[5] better *E1*] much better *Ms*
[6] Duchesse d'Ivry,] Princess, de Montaign, *Ms*] Duchesse, *E1*

ter the health of *cette pauvre petite Miss Clara.* O how she railed against *ces Anglaises*, and their prudery! Can you fancy her and her circle, the tea-table set in the twilight that evening, the court assembled, Madame de la Cruchecassée and Madame de Schlangenbad and their whiskered humble servants, Baron Punter and Count Spada and Marquis Iago and Prince Iachimo and worthy Captain[7] Blackball? Can you fancy a moonlight con-clave, and ghouls feasting on the fresh corpse of a reputation? The jibes and sarcasms, the laughing and the gnashing of teeth? How they tear the dainty limbs and relish the tender morsels . . . "The air of this place is not good for you, believe me my little Kew, it is dangerous: Have pressing af-fairs in England, let your chateau burn down, or your intendant run away and pursue him. Partez, mon petit Kiou. Partez or evil will come of it." Such was the advice which a friend of Lord Kew gave the young nobleman.

---

[7] Captain *E1*] ~~Capt.~~ †Colonel† *Ms*

Chapter XXXII.

THEL had made various attempts to become intimate with her future sister-in-law; had walked and ridden and talked with Lady Clara before Barnes's arrival. She had come away not very much impressed with respect for Lady Clara's mental powers. Indeed we have said that Miss Ethel was rather more prone to attack women than to admire them and was a little hard upon the fashionable young persons of her acquaintance and sex. In after life, care and thought subdued her pride and she learned to look at society more good-naturedly, but at this time and for some years after she was impatient of common-place people and did not choose to conceal her scorn. Lady Clara was very much afraid of her. Those timid little thoughts which would come out and frisk and gambol with pretty graceful antics and advance confidingly at the sound of Jack Belsize's jolly voice, and nibble crumbs out of his hand, shrank away before Ethel, severe nymph with the bright eyes, and hid themselves under the thickets and in the shade. Who has not overheard a simple couple of girls, or of lovers possibly, pouring out their little hearts, laughing at their own little jokes, prattling and prattling away unceasingly until Mamma appears with her awful didactic countenance or the governess with her dry moralities and the colloquy straightway ceases, the laughter stops, the chirp of the harmless little birds is hushed. Lady Clara being of a timid nature stood in as much awe of Ethel as of her father and mother; whereas her next sister, a brisk young creature of seventeen who was of the order of romps or tomboys, was by no means afraid of Miss Newcome and indeed a much greater favourite with her than her placid elder sister.

Young ladies may have been crossed in love and have had their sufferings, their frantic moments of grief and tears, their wakeful nights and so forth, but it is only in very sentimental novels that people occupy themselves perpetually with that passion and I believe what are called broken hearts are very rare articles indeed. Tom is jilted, is for a while in a dreadful state, bores all his male acquaintance with his groans and his frenzy, rallies from the complaint, eats his dinner very kindly, takes an interest in the next turf event and is found at Newmarket as usual bawling out the odds which he will give or take. Miss has her paroxysm and recovery. Madame Crinoline's new importations from Paris interest the young creature. She deigns to consider whether pink or blue will become her most. She conspires with her maid to make the spring morning dresses answer for the autumn. She resumes her books, piano, and music (giving up certain songs perhaps that she used to sing). She waltzes with the Captain, gets a colour, waltzes longer better and ten times quicker than Lucy who is dancing with the Major, replies in an animated manner to the Captain's delightful remarks, takes a little supper and looks quite kindly at him before she pulls up the carriage windows.

Clive may not like his cousin Barnes Newcome and many other men share in that antipathy, but all ladies do not. It is a fact that Barnes when he likes can make himself a very pleasant fellow. He is dreadfully satirical, that is certain, but many persons are amused by those dreadful satirical young men, and to hear fun made of our neighbours, even of some of our friends, does not make us very angry. Barnes is one of the very best waltzers in all society, that is the truth; whereas it must be confessed Some One Else[1] was very heavy and slow, his great foot always crushing you, and he always begging your pardon. Barnes whirls a partner round a room ages after she is ready to faint. What wicked fun he makes of other people when he stops! he is not handsome but in his face there is something odd-looking and distinguished. It is certain he has beautiful small feet and hands.

He comes every day from the city, drops in in his quiet unobtrusive way and drinks tea at five o'clock; always brings a budget of the funniest stories with him, makes Mamma laugh, Clara laugh, Henrietta who is in the school-room still die of laughing. Papa has the highest opinion of Mr. Newcome as a man of business: if he had had such a friend in early life his affairs would not be where they now are, poor dear kind Papa! Do they want to go anywhere, is not Mr. Newcome always ready? Did he not procure that delightful room for them to witness the Lord Mayor's show; and make Clara die of laughing at those odd city people at the Mansion House ball? He is at every party; and never[2] tired though he gets up so early. He waltzes with nobody else, he is always there to put Lady Clara in the carriage. At the drawing-room he looked quite *handsome* in his uniform of the Newcome Hussars, bottle-green and silver lace: he speaks politics so *exceedingly* well with Papa and gentlemen after dinner. He is a sound conservative, full of practical good sense and information, with no dangerous newfangled ideas, such as young men have.

[1] Some One Else *E1*] some one else *Ms*
[2] and never *E1*] never *Ms*

When poor dear Sir Brian Newcome's health gives way quite Mr. Newcome will go into Parliament and then he will resume the old Barony which has been in abeyance in the family since the reign of Richard the Third. They had fallen quite quite low. Mr. Newcome's grandfather came to London with a satchel on his back, like Whittington. Isn't[3] it romantic?

This process has been going on for months.[4] It is not in one day that poor Lady Clara has been made to forget the past and to lay aside her mourning. Day after day, very likely, the undeniable faults and many peccadilloes of—of that other person, have been exposed to her. People around the young lady may desire to spare her feelings, but can have no interest in screening poor Jack from condign reprobation: a wild prodigal—a disgrace to his order—a son of old Highgate's leading such a life and making such a scandal! Lord Dorking believes Mr. Belsize to be an abandoned monster and fiend in human shape: gathers and relates all the stories that ever have been told to the young man's disadvantage and of these be sure there are enough, and speaks of him with transports of indignation. At the end of months of unwearied courtship Mr. Barnes Newcome is honestly accepted and Lady Clara is waiting for him at Baden not unhappy to receive him: when walking on the promenade with her father, the ghost of her dead love suddenly rises before her, and the young lady faints to the ground.

When Barnes Newcome thinks fit he can be perfectly placable in his demeanour and delicate in his conduct. What he said upon this painful subject was delivered with the greatest propriety. He did not for one moment consider that Lady Clara's agitation arose from any present feeling in Mr. Belsize's favour, but that she was naturally moved by the remembrance of the past and the sudden appearance which recalled it. "And but that a lady's name should never be made the subject of dispute between men," Newcome said to Lord Dorking with great dignity, "and that Captain Belsize has opportunely quitted the place, I should certainly have chastised him. He and another adventurer against whom I have had to warn my own family, have quitted Baden this afternoon. I am glad that both are gone, Captain Belsize especially; for my temper, my lord, is hot and I do not think I should have commanded it."

Lord Kew, when this elder lord informed him of this admirable speech of Barnes Newcome's, upon whose character, prudence and dignity the Earl of Dorking pronounced a fervent eulogium, shook his head gravely and said, "Yes, Barnes was a dead shot and a most determined fellow:" and did not burst out laughing until he and Lord Dorking had parted. Then to be sure he took his fill of laughter, he told the story to Ethel, he complimented Barnes on his heroic self denial, the joke of the thundering big stick was nothing to it. Barnes Newcome laughed too, he had

---

[3] Whittington. Isn't *E1*] Whittington; is not *Ms*
[4] months. *E1*] many months. *Ms*

plenty of humour, Barnes. "I think you might have wapped[5] Jack when he came out from his interview with the Dorkings," Kew said: "the poor devil was so bewildered and weak, that Alfred might have thrashed him. At other times you would find it more difficult, Barnes my man." Mr. B. Newcome resumed his dignity, said a joke was a joke and there was quite enough of this one, which assertion we may be sure he conscientiously made.

This[6] meeting and parting between the old lovers passed with a great deal of calm and propriety on both sides. Miss's parents of course were present when Jack, at their summons, waited upon them and their daughter and made his hangdog bow. My Lord Dorking said (Poor Jack in the anguish of his heart, had poured out the story to Clive Newcome afterwards), "Mr. Belsize, I have to apologise for words which I used in my heat yesterday and which I recall and regret as I am sure you do that there should have been any occasion for them."

Mr. Belsize looking at the carpet said he was very sorry.

Lady Dorking here remarked that as Captain Belsize was now at Baden, he might wish to hear from Lady Clara Pulleyn's own lips that the[7] engagement into which she had entered was formed by herself, certainly with the consent and advice of her family. "Is it not so, my dear?"

Lady Clara said "Yes Mamma," with a low curtsey.

"We have now to wish you good bye, Charles Belsize," said my lord with some feeling. "As your relative and your father's old friend I wish you well. I hope your future course in life may not be so unfortunate as the past year. I request that we may part friends. Good bye, Charles. Clara, shake hands with Captain Belsize. My Lady Dorking, you will please to give Charles your hand. You have known him since he was a child, and, and—we are sorry Jack to be obliged to part in this way." In this wise Mr. Jack Belsize's tooth was finally extracted and for the moment we wish him and his brother patient a good journey.

Little lynx-eyed Dr. Von Finck who attends most of the polite company at Baden drove ceaselessly about the place that day with the *real* version of the fainting-fit story, about which we may be sure the wicked and malicious and the uninitiated had a hundred absurd details. Lady Clara ever engaged to Captain Belsize—Fiddle-dee-dee! Every body knew the Captain's affairs and that he could no more think of marrying than flying. Lady Clara faint at seeing him! she fainted before he came up. She was always fainting and had done so thrice in the last week to his knowledge. Lord Dorking, had a nervous affection of his right arm and was always shaking his stick. He did not say Villain, he said William. Captain Belsize's name is William, It is not so in the peerage? Is he called Jack[8] in the peerage? Those peerages are always wrong. These candid explanations of course had their effect. Wicked tongues were of course

5 wapped *Ms*] whopped *E1*
6 This *Ms*] That *E1*
7 that the *E1*] the *Ms*
8 Jack *Ms E1*] Charles *R*

instantaneously silent. People were entirely satisfied: they always are. The next night being assembly night Lady Clara appeared at the Rooms and danced with Lord Kew and Mr. Barnes Newcome. All the society was as gracious and good-humoured as possible and there was no more question

of fainting than of burning down the Conversation house. But Madame de Cruchecassée and Madame de Schlangenbad and those horrid people whom the men speak to, but whom the women salute with silent curtseys, persisted in declaring that there was no prude like an English prude and to Dr. Finck's oaths, assertions, explanations only replied with a shrug of their bold shoulders, "Taisez-vous, Docteur, vous n'etes[9] qu'une vieille bête."

Lady Kew was at the rooms uncommonly gracious. Miss Ethel took a few turns of the waltz with Lord Kew but this nymph looked more *farouche* than upon ordinary days. Bob Jones who admired her hugely asked leave to waltz with her and entertained her with recollections of Clive Newcome at school. He remembered a fight in which Clive had been engaged and re-counted that action to Miss Newcome who seemed to be interested. He was pleased to deplore Clive's fancy for turning artist, and that[1] Miss Newcome recommended him to have his likeness taken. For she said his appearance was exceedingly picturesque. He was going on with farther prattle, but she suddenly cut Mr. Jones short making him a bow and going to sit down by Lady Kew. "And the next day, Sir," said Bob with whom the present writer had the happiness of dining at a mess dinner at the Upper Temple, "when

---

[9] n'etes *Ms*] n'ete *E1*
[1] that *Ms E1*] [omitted] *R*

I met her on the walk, Sir, she cut me as dead as a stone. The airs those swells give themselves is enough to make any man turn republican."

Miss Ethel indeed was haughty, very haughty and of a difficult temper. She spared none of her party except her kind mother, to whom Ethel always was kind and her father whom since his illnesses she tended with much benevolence and care. But she did battle with Lady Kew repeatedly, coming to her Aunt Julia's rescue, on whom the Countess[2] as usual exercised her powers of torturing. She made Barnes quail before her by[3] the shafts of contempt which she flashed at him and she did not spare Lord Kew whose good nature was no shield against her scorn. The old Queen Mother was fairly afraid of her. She even left off beating Lady Julia when Ethel came in, of course taking her revenge in the young girl's absence, but trying in her presence to soothe and please her. Against Lord Kew the young girl's anger was most unjust and the more cruel because the kindly young nobleman never spoke a hard word of any mortal soul, and carrying no arms should have been assaulted by none. But his very good nature seemed to make his young opponent only the more wrathful. She shot because his honest breast was bare. It bled at the wounds which she inflicted. Her relatives looked at her surprised[4] at her cruelty, and the young man himself was shocked in his dignity and best feelings by his cousin's wanton ill humour.

Lady Kew fancied she understood the cause of this peevishness and remonstated with Miss Ethel. "Shall we write a letter to Lucerne and order Dick Tinto back again?" said her ladyship. "Are you such a fool, Ethel, as to be hankering after that young scapegrace and his yellow beard? His drawings are very pretty. Why, I think he might earn a couple of hundred a year as a teacher and nothing would be easier than to break your engagement with Kew and whistle the drawing-master back again."

Ethel took up the whole heap of Clive's drawings, lighted a taper, carried the drawings to the fireplace and set them in a blaze. "A very pretty piece of work," says Lady Kew, "and which proves satisfactorily that you don't care for the young Clive at all. Have we arranged a correspondence? We are cousins you know; we may write pretty cousinly letters to one another." A month before the old lady would have attacked her with other arms than sarcasm, but she was scared now, and dared to use no coarser weapons. "O," cried Ethel in a transport, "what a life ours is, and how you buy and sell and haggle over your children. It is not Clive I care about poor boy. Our ways of life are separate. I cannot break from my own family and I know very well how you would receive him in it. Had he money it would be different. You would receive him and welcome him, and hold out your hands to him: but he is only a poor painter and we forsooth are bankers in the City and he comes among us on sufferance like those concert-singers whom Mamma treats with so much politeness and who go down and have supper by themselves. Why should they not be as good as we are?"

---

[2] the Countess *R*] her mother *Ms E1*
[3] her by *Ms E1*] [omitted] *R*
[4] looked at her surprised *Ms E1*] looked, surprised *R*

"M. de C——, my dear, is of a noble family," interposed Lady Kew; "when he has given up singing and made his fortune, no doubt he can go back into the world again."

"Made his fortune, yes," Ethel continued, "that is the cry. There never were, since the world began, people so unblushingly sordid! we own it and are proud of it. We barter rank against money and money against rank day after day. Why did you marry my father to my mother? was it for his wit? you know he might have been an angel and you would have scorned him. Your daughter was bought with Papa's money as surely as ever Newcome was. Will there be no day when this Mammon worship will cease among us?"

"Not in my time or yours, Ethel," the elder said not unkindly; perhaps she thought—of a day long ago before she was sold herself.

"We are sold," the young girl went on, "we are as much sold as Turkish women. The only difference being that our masters may have but one Circassian at a time. No, there is no freedom for us. I wear my green ticket and wait till my master comes. But every day as I think of our slavery, I revolt against it more. That poor wretch, that poor girl whom my brother is to marry, Why did she not revolt and fly? I would, if I loved a man sufficiently, loved him better than the world, than wealth, than rank, than fine houses and titles and I feel I love these best,—I would give up all to follow him. But what can I be with my name and my parents? I belong to the world like all the rest of my family. It is you who have bred us up: you who are answerable for us. Why are there no convents to which we can fly. You make a fine marriage for me. You provide me with a good husband, a kind soul, not very wise, but very kind; you make me what you call happy and I would rather be at the plough like the women here."

"No you wouldn't, Ethel," replies the grandmother drily. "These are the fine speeches of school girls. The showers of rain would spoil your complexion. You would be perfectly tired in an hour and come back to luncheon. You belong to your belongings, my dear, and are no better than the rest of the world:—very good looking as you know perfectly well, and not very good tempered: it is lucky that Kew is. Calm your temper, at least before marriage; such a prize does not fall to a pretty girl's lot every day. Why, you sent him away quite scared by your cruelty; and if he is not playing at roulette or at billiards, I daresay he is thinking what a little termagant you are and that he had best pause while it is yet time. Before I was married your poor grandfather never knew I had a temper. Of after-days I say nothing, but trials are good for all of us and he bore his like an angel."

Lady Kew too, on this occasion at least, was admirably good-humoured. She also when it was necessary could put a restraint on her temper and having this match very much at heart chose to coax and to soothe her granddaughter rather than to endeavour to scold and frighten her.

"Why do you desire this marriage so much, Grandmamma," the girl asked. "My cousin is not very much in love at least I should fancy not," she added blushing. "I am bound to own Lord Kew is not in the least eager and I think if you were to tell him to wait for five years he would be quite willing. Why should you be so very anxious?"

"Why, my dear? Because[5] I think young ladies who want to go and work in the fields should make hay while the sun shines, because I think it is high time that Kew should *ranger* himself, because I am sure he will make the best husband and Ethel the prettiest Countess in England." And the old lady seldom exhibiting any signs of affection looked at her granddaughter very fondly. From her Ethel looked up into the glass which very likely repeated on its shining face the truth her elder had just uttered. Shall we quarrel with the girl for that dazzling reflection: for owning that charming truth, and submitting to that conscious triumph? Give her her part of vanity, of youth, of desire to rule and be admired. Meanwhile Mr. Clive's drawings have been crackling in the fireplace at her feet and the last spark of that combustion is twinkling out unheeded.

[5] dear? Because *E1*] dear because *Ms*

Chapter XXXIII.

LADY KEW AT THE CONGRESS.

HEN Lady Kew heard that Madame d'Ivry was at Baden, and was informed at once of the French lady's graciousness to- wards the Newcome family, and of her fury against Lord Kew, the old Count- ess gave a loose to that energetic tem- per with which na- ture had gifted her; a temper which she tied up sometimes and kept from barking and biting; but which when unmuzzled was an ani- mal of whom all her ladyship's family had a just apprehension. Not one of them but in his or her time had been wounded, lacerated, tumbled over, otherwise frightened or injured by this unruly brute. The cowards brought it sops and patted it; the prudent gave it a clear berth, and walked round so as not to meet it; but woe be to those of the family who had to bring the meal, and prepare the litter, and (to speak respectfully) share the kennel with Lady Kew's "Black Dog!" Surely a fine furious temper, if accompa- nied with a certain magnanimity and bravery which often go together with it, is one of the most precious and fortunate gifts with which a gentleman or lady can be endowed. A person always ready to fight is certain of the greatest consideration amongst his or her family circle. The lazy grow tired of contending with him; the timid coax and flatter him; and as almost ev- ery one is timid or lazy, a bad-tempered man is sure to have his own way. It is he who commands, and all the others obey. If he is a gourmand, he has what he likes for dinner; and the tastes of all the rest are subservient to him. She (we playfully transfer the gender, as a bad temper is of both sexes) has the place which she likes best in the drawing-room; nor do her parents, nor her brothers and sisters, venture to take her favourite chair.

If she wants to go to a party, Mamma will dress herself in spite of her head-ache; and Papa, who hates those dreadful soirées, will go up-stairs after dinner and put on his poor old white neckcloth, though he has been toil-ing at chambers all day, and must be there early in the morning—he will go out with her, we say, and stay for the cotillon. If the family are taking their tour in the summer, it is she who ordains whither they shall go, and when they shall stop. If he comes home late, the dinner is kept for him, and not one dares to say a word though ever so hungry. If he is in a good humour, how every one frisks about and is happy! How the servants jump up at his bell and run to wait upon him! How they sit up patiently, and how eagerly they rush out to fetch cabs in the rain! Whereas for you and me, who have the tempers of angels, and never were known to be angry or to complain, nobody cares whether we are pleased or not. Our wives go to the milliners and send us the bill, and we pay it; our John finishes reading the newspaper before he answers our bell, and brings it to us; our sons loll in the arm-chair which we should like; fill the house with their young men, and smoke in the dining-room; our tailors fit us badly; our butchers give us the youngest mutton; our tradesmen dun us much more quickly than other people's, because they know we are good-natured; and our servants go out whenever they like, and openly have their friends to supper in the kitchen. When Lady Kew said *Sic volo, sic jubeo*, I promise you few persons of her ladyship's belongings stopped, before they did her biddings, to ask her reasons.

If, which very seldom happens, there are two such imperious and dom-ineering spirits in a family, unpleasantries of course will arise from their contentions; or, if out of doors, the family Bajazet meets with some other violent Turk, dreadful battles ensue, all the allies on either side are brought in, and the surrounding neighbours perforce engaged in the quarrel. This was unluckily the case in the present instance. Lady Kew, unaccustomed to have her will questioned at home, liked to impose it abroad. She judged the persons around her with great freedom of speech. Her opinions were quoted, as people's sayings will be; and if she made bitter speeches, depend on it they lost nothing in the carrying. She was furious against Madame la Duchesse d'Ivry, and exploded in various companies whenever that lady's name was mentioned. "Why was she not with her husband? Why was the poor old duke left to his gout, and this woman trailing through the country with her vagabond court of billiard-markers at her heels? She to call herself Mary Queen of Scots, forsooth!—well, she merited the title in some respects, though she had not murdered her husband as yet. Ah! I should like to be Queen Elizabeth if the Duchess is Queen of Scots!" said the old lady, shaking her old fist. And these sentiments being uttered in public, upon the Promenade, to mutual friends, of course the Duchess had the benefit of Lady Kew's remarks a few minutes after they were uttered; and her Grace, and the distinguished princes, counts, and noblemen in her court, designated as billiard-markers by the old Countess, returned the lat-ter's compliments with pretty speeches of their own. Scandals were dug up respecting her ladyship, so old that one would have thought them forgot-ten these forty years,—so old that they happened before most of the Newcomes now extant were born, and surely therefore out[1] of the province of this contemporary biography. Lady Kew was indignant with her daughter (there were some moments when *any* conduct of her friends did not meet her ladyship's approbation) even for the scant civility with which Lady Ann had received the Duchess's advances. "Leave a card upon her!—yes, send a card by one of your footmen; but go in to see her—because she was at the window and saw you drive up.—Are you mad, Ann? That was the very reason you should not have come out of your carriage. But you are so weak and good-natured, that if a highwayman stopped you, you would say, 'Thank you, Sir,' as you gave him your purse: yes, and if Mrs. Macheath called on you afterwards you would return the visit!"

Even had these speeches been made *about* the Duchess, and some of them not addressed to her, things might have gone on pretty well. If we quarrelled with all the people who abuse us behind our backs, and began to tear their eyes out as soon as we set ours on them, what a life it would be, and when should we have any quiet? Backbiting is all fair in society. Abuse me, and I will abuse you; but let us be friends when we meet. Have not we all entered a dozen rooms, and been sure, from the countenances of the amiable persons present, that they had been discussing our little peculiarities, perhaps as we were on the stairs? Was our visit, therefore, the less agreeable? Did we quarrel and say hard words to one another's faces? No—we wait until some of our dear friends take their leave, and then comes our turn. My back is at my neighbour's service; as soon as that is turned let him make what faces he thinks proper: but when we meet we grin and shake hands like well-bred folk, to whom clean linen is not more necessary than a clean sweet-looking countenance, and a nicely got-up smile, for company.

Here was Lady Kew's mistake. She wanted, for some reason, to drive Madame d'Ivry out of Baden; and thought there were no better means of effecting this object than by using the high hand, and practising those frowns upon the Duchess which had scared away so many other persons. But the Queen of Scots was resolute, too, and her band of courtiers fought stoutly round about her. Some of them could not pay their bills, and could not retreat: others had courage, and did not choose to fly. Instead of coaxing and soothing Madame d'Ivry, Madame de Kew thought by a brisk attack to rout and dislodge her. She began on almost the very first occasion when the ladies met. "I was so sorry to hear that Monsieur le Duc was ill at Bagnères, Madame la Duchesse," the old lady began on their very first meeting, after the usual salutations had taken place.

"Madame la Comtesse is very kind to interest herself in Monsieur d'Ivry's health. Monsieur le Duc at his age is not disposed to travel. You, dear Miladi, are more happy in being always able to retain the *gout des voyages!*"

"I come to my family! my dear Duchess."

"How charmed they must be to possess you! Miladi Ann, you must be inexpressibly consoled by the presence of a mother so tender! Permit me to

[1] out *E1*] are out *R*

present Madame la Comtesse de la Cruchecassée to Madame la Comtesse de Kew. Miladi is sister to that amiable Marquis of Steyne, whom you have known, Ambrosine! Madame la Baronne de Schlangenbad, Miladi Kew. Do you not see the resemblance to Milor? These ladies have enjoyed the hospitalities—the splendours of Gaunt House. They were of those famous routs of which the charming Mistress Crawly, *la sémillante Becki*, made part! How sad the Hôtel de Gaunt must be under the present circumstances! Have you heard, Miladi, of the charming Mistress Becki? Monsieur le Duc describes her as the most spirituelle Englishwoman he ever met." The Queen of Scots turns and whispers her lady of honour, and shrugs and taps her forehead. Lady Kew knows that Madame d'Ivry speaks of her nephew, the present Lord Steyne, who is not in his right mind. The Duchess looks round, and sees a friend in the distance whom she beckons. "Comtesse, you know already Monsieur the Captain Blackball? He makes the delight of our society!" A dreadful man with a large cigar, a florid waistcoat, and billiards written on his countenance, swaggers forward at the Duchess's summons. The Countess of Kew has not gained much by her attack. She has been presented to Cruchecassée and Schlangenbad. She sees herself on the eve of becoming the acquaintance of Captain Blackball.

"Permit me, Duchess, to choose my *English* friends at least for myself," says Lady Kew, drumming her foot.

"But, Madam, assuredly! You do not love this good Monsieur de Blackball? Eh! the English manners are droll, pardon me for saying so. It is wonderful how proud you are as a nation, and how ashamed you are of your compatriots!"

"There are some persons who are ashamed of nothing, Madame la Duchesse," cries Lady Kew, losing her temper.

"Is that *gracieuseté* for me? How much goodness! This good Monsieur de Blackball is not very well bred; but, for an Englishman, he is not too bad. I have met with people who are more ill-bred than Englishmen in my travels."

"And they are?" said Lady Ann, who had been in vain endeavouring to put an end to this colloquy.

"English women, Madam! I speak not for you. You are kind; you—you are too soft, dear Lady Ann, for a persecutor."

The counsels of the worldly woman who governed and directed that branch of the Newcome family of whom it is our business to speak now for a little while, bore other results than those which the elderly lady desired, and foresaw. Who can foresee everything and always? Not the wisest among us. When his Majesty, Louis XIV., jockeyed his grandson on to the throne of Spain (founding thereby the present revered dynasty of that country), did he expect to peril his own, and bring all Europe about his royal ears? Could a late king of France, eager for the advantageous establishment of one of his darling sons, and anxious to procure a beautiful Spanish princess, with a crown and kingdom in reversion, for the simple and obedient youth, ever suppose that the welfare of his whole august race and reign would be upset by that smart speculation? We take only the most noble examples to illustrate the conduct of such a noble old personage as her ladyship of Kew, who brought a prodigious deal of trouble upon some of the innocent members of her family, whom no doubt she thought to better in life by her experienced guidance, and undoubted worldly wisdom. We may be as deep as Jesuits, know the world ever so well, lay the best ordered plans, and the profoundest combinations, and by a certain not unnatural turn of fate, we, and our plans and combinations, are sent flying before the wind. We may be as wise as Louis Philippe, that many-counselled Ulysses whom the respectable world admired so; and after years of patient scheming, and prodigies of skill, after coaxing, wheedling, doubling, bullying, wisdom, behold yet stronger powers interpose: and schemes, and skill and violence, are nought.

Frank and Ethel, Lady Kew's grandchildren, were both the obedient subjects of this ancient despot: this imperious old Louis XIV. in a black front and a cap and ribbon, this scheming old Louis Philippe in tabinet; but their blood was good and their tempers high; and for all her bitting and driving, and the training of her *manège*, the generous young colts were hard to break. Ethel, at this time, was especially stubborn in training, rebellious to the whip, and wild under harness; and the way in which Lady Kew managed her won the admiration of her family: for it was a maxim among these folks that no one could manage Ethel but Lady Kew. Barnes said no one could manage his sister but his grandmother. He couldn't, that was certain. Mamma never tried, and indeed was so good-natured, that rather than ride the filly, she would put the saddle on her own back and let the filly ride her; no, there was no one but her ladyship capable of managing that girl, Barnes owned, who held Lady Kew in much respect and awe. "If the tightest hand were not kept on her, there's no knowing what she mightn't do," said her brother. "Ethel Newcome, by Jove, is capable of running away with the writing-master."

After poor Jack Belsize's mishap and departure, Barnes's own bride showed no spirit at all, save one of placid contentment. She came at call and instantly, and went through whatever paces her owner demanded of her. She laughed whenever need was, simpered and smiled when spoken to, danced whenever she was asked; drove out at Barnes's side in Kew's phaeton, and received him certainly not with warmth, but with politeness and welcome. It is difficult to describe the scorn with which her sister-in-law regarded her. The sight of the patient timid little thing chafed Ethel, who was always more haughty and flighty, and bold when in Clara's presence than at any other time. Her ladyship's brother, Captain Lord Viscount Rooster, before mentioned, joined the family party at this interesting juncture. My Lord Rooster found himself surprised, delighted, subjugated by Miss Newcome, her wit and spirit. "By Jove, she is a plucky one," his lordship exclaimed. "To dance with her is the best fun in life. How she pulls all the other girls to pieces, by Jove, and how splendidly she chaffs everybody! But," he added with the shrewdness and sense of humour which distinguished the young officer, "I'd rather dance with her than marry her—by a doosid long score—I don't envy you that part of the business Kew, my boy." Lord Kew did not set himself up as a person to be envied. He thought his cousin beautiful: and with his grandmother, that she would make a very handsome countess, and he thought the money which Lady Kew would give or leave to the young couple a very welcome addition to his means.

On the next night, when there was a ball at the room, Miss Ethel who was ordinarily exceedingly simple in her attire, and dressed below the mark of the rest of the world, chose to appear in a toilette the very grandest and finest which she had ever assumed.[1] Her clustering ringlets, her shining white shoulders, her splendid raiment (I believe indeed it was her court-dress which the young lady assumed) astonished all beholders. She *écraséd* all other beauties by her appearance; so much so that Madame d'Ivry's court could not but look, the men in admiration, the women in dislike, at this dazzling young creature. None of the countesses, duchesses, princesses, Russ, Spanish, Italian, were so fine or so handsome. There were some New York ladies at Baden as there are everywhere else in Europe now. Not even these were more magnificent than Miss Ethel. General Jeremiah J. Bung's lady owned that Miss Newcome was fit to appear in any party in Fifth Avenue.[2] She was the only well-dressed English girl Mrs. Bung had seen in Europe. A young German Durchlaucht deigned to explain to his aide-de-camp how very handsome he thought Miss Newcome. All our acquaintances were of one mind. Mr. Jones of England pronounced her stunning; the admirable Captain Blackball examined her points with the skill of an *amateur,* and described them with agreeable frankness. Lord Rooster was charmed as he surveyed her, and complimented his late companion in arms on the possession of such a paragon. Only Lord Kew was not delighted—nor did Miss Ethel mean that he should be. She looked as splendid as Cinderella in the prince's palace. But what need for all this splendour? this wonderful toilette? this dazzling neck and shoulders, whereof the brightness and beauty blinded the eyes of lookers on? She was dressed as gaudily as an actress of the Variétés going to a supper at the Trois Frères. "It was Mademoiselle Mabille *en habit de cour,*" Madame d'Ivry remarked to Madame Schlangenbad. Barnes who with his bride-elect for a partner made a vis-à-vis for his sister and the admiring Lord Rooster, was puzzled likewise by Ethel's countenance and appearance. Little Lady Clara looked like a little school-girl dancing before her.

One, two, three, of the attendants of her Majesty the Queen of Scots were carried off in the course of the evening by the victorious young beauty, whose triumph had the effect, which the headstrong girl perhaps herself anticipated, of mortifying the Duchesse d'Ivry, of exasperating old Lady Kew, and of annoying the young nobleman to whom Miss Ethel was engaged. The girl seemed to take a pleasure in defying all three, a something embittered her, alike against her friends and her enemies. The old dowager chafed and vented her wrath upon Lady Ann and Barnes. Ethel kept the ball alive by herself almost. She refused to go home, declining hints and commands alike. She was engaged for ever so many dances more. Not dance with Count Punter? it would be rude to leave him after promising him. Not waltz with Captain Blackball? He was not a proper partner

[1] chose to appear in a toilette the very grandest and finest which she had ever assumed. *R*] [placed before "who was ordinarily"] *E1*
[2] Fifth Avenue. *HM NY*] Fifth avenue *R*] Fourth avenue *E1*

for her. Why then did Kew know him? Lord Kew walked and talked with
Captain Blackball every day. Was she to be so proud as not to know Lord
Kew's friends? She greeted the Captain with a most fascinating smile as
he came up whilst the controversy was pending, and ended it by whirling
round the room in his arms.

Madame d'Ivry viewed with such pleasure as might be expected the
defection of her adherents, and the triumph of her youthful rival, who
seemed to grow more beautiful with each waltz, so that the other dancers
paused to look at her, the men breaking out in enthusiasm, the reluctant
women being forced to join in the applause. Angry as she was, and knowing
how Ethel's conduct angered her grandson, old Lady Kew could not help
admiring the rebellious beauty, whose girlish spirit was more than a match
for the imperious dowager's tough old resolution. As for Mr. Barnes's displeasure, the girl tossed her saucy head, shrugged her fair shoulders, and
passed on with a scornful laugh. In a word, Miss Ethel conducted herself
as a most reckless and intrepid young flirt, using her eyes with the most
consummate effect, chattering with astounding gaiety, prodigal of smiles,
gracious thanks and killing glances. What wicked spirit moved her? Perhaps had she known the mischief she was doing, she would have continued
it still.

The sight of this wilfulness and levity smote poor Lord Kew's honest[3]
heart with cruel pangs of mortification. The easy young nobleman had
passed many a year of his life in all sorts of wild company. The chaumière
knew him, and the balls of Parisian actresses, the coulisses of the opera
at home and abroad. Those pretty heads of ladies whom nobody knows,
used to nod their shining ringlets at Kew, from private boxes at theatres,
or dubious Park-broughams. He had run the career of young men of pleasure, and laughed and feasted with jolly prodigals and their company. He
was tired of it: perhaps he remembered an earlier and purer life, and was
sighing to return to it. Living as he had done amongst the outcasts, his
ideal[4] of domestic virtue was high and pure. He chose to believe that good
women were entirely good. Duplicity he could not understand; ill temper
shocked him: wilfulness he seemed to fancy belonged only to the profane
and wicked, not to good girls, with good mothers, in honest homes. Their
nature was to love their families; to obey their parents; to tend their poor;
to honour their husbands; to cherish their children. Ethel's laugh woke
him up from one of these simple reveries very likely, and then she swept
round the ball-room rapidly, to the brazen notes of the orchestra. He never
offered to dance with her more than once in the evening; went away to
play, and returned to find her still whirling to the music. Madame d'Ivry
remarked his tribulation and gloomy face, though she took no pleasure at
his discomfiture, knowing that Ethel's behaviour caused it.

In plays and novels, and I daresay in real life too sometimes, when the
wanton heroine chooses to exert her powers of fascination, and to flirt with
Sir Harry, or the Captain, the hero, in a pique, goes off and makes love to
somebody else: both acknowledge their folly after a while, shake hands and

[3] honest *E1*] [omitted] *R*
[4] ideal *E1*] idea *R*

are reconciled, and the curtain drops, or the volume ends. But there are some people too noble and simple for these amorous scenes and smirking artifices. When Kew was pleased he laughed, when he was grieved he was silent. He did not deign to hide his grief or pleasure under disguises. His error, perhaps, was in forgetting that Ethel was very young; that her conduct was not design so much as girlish mischief and high spirits; and that if young men have their frolics, sow their wild oats, and enjoy their pleasure, young women may be permitted sometimes their more harmless vagaries of gaiety, and sportive outbreaks of wilful humour.

When she consented to go home at length, Lord Kew brought Miss Newcome's little white cloak for her (under the hood of which her glossy curls, her blushing cheeks, and bright eyes looked provokingly handsome), and encased her in this pretty garment without uttering one single word. She made him a saucy curtsey in return for this act of politeness, which salutation he received with a grave bow; and then he proceeded to cover up old Lady Kew, and to conduct her ladyship to her chariot. Miss Ethel chose to be displeased at her cousin's displeasure. What were balls made for but that people should dance? She a flirt? She displease[5] Lord Kew? If she chose to dance, she would dance; she had no idea of his giving himself airs, besides it was such fun taking away the gentlemen of Mary Queen of Scots' court from her: such capital fun! So she went to bed, singing and performing wonderful roulades as she lighted her candle, and retired to her room. She had had such a jolly evening! such famous fun, and, I daresay, (but how shall a novelist penetrate these mysteries?) when her chamber door was closed, she scolded her maid and was as cross as two sticks. You see there come moments of sorrow after the most brilliant victories; and you conquer and rout the enemy utterly, and then you[6] regret that you fought.

---

[5] displease *E1*] displeased *R*
[6] you *E1*] [omitted] *R*

Chapter XXXIV.

ENTION has been made of an elderly young person from Ireland, engaged by Madame la Duchesse d'Ivry, as companion and teacher of English for her little daughter. When Miss O'Grady, as she did some time afterwards, quitted Madame d'Ivry's family, she spoke with great freedom regarding the behaviour of that duchess, and recounted horrors which she, the latter, had committed. A number of the most terrific anecdotes issued from the lips of the indignant Miss, whose volubility Lord Kew was obliged to check, not choosing that his countess, with whom he was paying a bridal visit to Paris, should hear such dreadful legends. It was there that Miss O'Grady, finding herself in misfortune, and reading of Lord Kew's arrival at the Hôtel Bristol, waited upon his lordship and the Countess of Kew, begging them to take tickets in a raffle for an invaluable ivory writing-desk, sole relic of her former prosperity, which she proposed to give her friends the chance of acquiring: in fact, Miss O'Grady lived for some years on the produce of repeated raffles for this beautiful desk: many religious ladies of the Faubourg St. Germain, taking an interest in her misfortunes, and alleviating them by the simple lottery system. Protestants as well as Catholics were permitted to take shares in Miss O'Grady's raffles; and Lord Kew, good-natured then as always, purchased so many tickets, that the contrite O'Grady informed him of a transaction which had nearly affected his happiness, and in which she took a not very creditable share. "Had I known your lordship's real character," Miss O'G. was pleased to say, "no tortures would have induced me to do an act for which I have undergone penance. It was that blackhearted woman, my lord, who maligned your lordship to me: that woman whom I called friend once, but who is the most false, depraved, and dangerous of her sex." In this way do ladies' companions sometimes speak of ladies when quarrels separate them, when confidential attendants are dismissed, bearing away family secrets in their minds, and revenge in their hearts.

The day after Miss Ethel's feats at the assembly, old Lady Kew went over to advise her granddaughter, and to give her a little timely warning about the impropriety of flirtations; above all, with such men as are to be found at watering-places, persons who are never seen elsewhere in society. "Remark the peculiarities of Kew's temper, who never flies into a passion like you and me, my dear," said the old lady, (being determined to be particularly gracious and cautious); "when once angry he remains so, and is so obstinate that it is almost impossible to coax him into good humour. It is much better, my love, to be like us," continued the old lady, "to fly out in a rage and have it over, but *que voulez-vous?* such is Frank's temper, and we must manage him." So she went on, backing her advice by a crowd of examples drawn from the family history; showing how Kew was like his grandfather, her own poor husband; still more like his late father, Lord Walham, between whom and his mother there had been differences, chiefly brought on by my Lady Walham of course, which had ended in the almost total estrangement of mother and son. Lady Kew then administered her advice, and told her stories with Ethel alone for a listener; and in a most edifying manner, she besought Miss Newcome to *ménager* Lord Kew's susceptibilities, as she valued her own future comfort in life, as well as the happiness of a most amiable man, of whom, if properly managed, Ethel might make what she pleased. We have said Lady Kew managed everybody, and that most of the members of her family allowed themselves to be managed by her ladyship.

Ethel, who had permitted her grandmother to continue her sententious advice, while she herself sat tapping her feet on the floor, and performing the most rapid variations of that air which is called the Devil's Tattoo, burst out, at length, to the elder lady's surprise, with an outbreak of indignation, a flushing face, and a voice quivering with anger.

"This most amiable man," she cried out, "that you design for me, I know everything about this most amiable man, and thank you and my family for the present you make me! For the past year, what have you been doing? Everyone of you! my father, my brother, and you yourself, have been filling my ears with cruel reports against a poor boy, whom you choose[1] to depict as everything that was dissolute and wicked, when there was nothing against him; nothing, but that he was poor. Yes, you yourself, Grandmamma, have told me many and many a time, that Clive Newcome was not a fit companion for us; warned me against his bad courses, and painted him as extravagant, unprincipled, I don't know how bad. How bad! I know how good he is; how upright, generous, and truth-telling: though there was not a day until lately, that Barnes did not make some wicked story against him,—Barnes, who, I believe, is bad himself, like—like other young men. Yes, I am sure, there was something about Barnes in that newspaper which my father took away from me. And you come, and you lift up your hands, and shake your head, because I dance with one gentleman or another. You tell me I am wrong; Mamma has told me so this morning.

[1] choose *E1*] chose *R*

Barnes, of course, has told me so, and you bring me Frank as a pattern, and tell me to love and honour and obey *him!* Look here," and she drew out a paper and put it into Lady Kew's hands. "Here is Kew's history, and I believe it is true; yes, I am sure it is true."

The old dowager lifted her eyeglass to her black eyebrow, and read a paper written in English, and bearing no signature, in which many circumstances of Lord Kew's life were narrated for poor Ethel's benefit. It was not a worse life than that of a thousand young men of pleasure, but there were Kew's many misdeeds set down in order: such a catalogue as we laugh at when Leporello trolls it, and sings his master's victories in France, Italy, and Spain. Madame d'Ivry's name was not mentioned in this list, and Lady Kew felt sure that the outrage came from her.

With real ardour Lady Kew sought to defend her grandson from some of the attacks here made against him; and showed Ethel that the person who could use such means of calumniating him, would not scruple to resort to falsehood in order to effect her purpose.

"Her purpose," cries Ethel. "How do you know it is a woman?" Lady Kew lapsed into generalities. She thought the handwriting was a woman's—at least it was not likely that a man should think of addressing an anonymous letter to a young lady, and so wreaking his hatred upon Lord Kew. "Besides Frank has had no rivals—except—except one young gentleman who has carried his paint-boxes to Italy," says Lady Kew. "You don't think your dear Colonel's son would leave such a piece of mischief behind him? You must act, my dear," continued her ladyship, "as if this letter had never been written at all, the person who wrote it no doubt will watch you. Of course we are too proud to allow him to see that we are wounded; and pray, pray do not think of letting poor Frank know a word about this horrid transaction."

"Then the letter is true!" burst out Ethel. "You know it is true, Grandmamma, and that is why you would have me keep it a secret from my cousin; besides," she added with a little hesitation, "your caution comes too late, Lord Kew has seen the letter."

"You fool," screamed the old lady, "you were not so mad as to show it to him?"

"I am sure the letter is true," Ethel said, rising up very haughtily. "It is not by calling me bad names that your ladyship will disprove it. Keep them, if you please, for my Aunt Julia, she is sick and weak, and can't defend herself. I do not choose to bear abuse from you, or lectures from Lord Kew. He happened to be here a short while since, when the letter arrived. He had been good enough to come to preach me a sermon on his own account. He to find fault with my actions!" cried Miss Ethel, quivering with wrath and clenching the luckless paper in her hand. "He to accuse me of levity, and to warn me against making improper acquaintances! He began his lectures too soon. I am not a lawful slave yet, and prefer to remain unmolested, at least as long as I am free."

"And you told Frank all this, Miss Newcome, and you showed him that letter," said the old lady.

"The letter was actually brought to me whilst his lordship was in the midst of his sermon," Ethel replied. "I read it as he was making his speech," she continued, gathering anger and scorn as she recalled the circumstances of the interview. "He was perfectly polite in his language. He did not call me a fool or use a single other bad name. He was good enough to advise me and to make such virtuous pretty speeches, that if he had been a bishop he could not have spoke better, and as I thought the letter was a nice commentary on his lordship's sermon I gave it to him. I gave it to him," cried the young woman, "and much good may it do him. I don't think my Lord Kew will preach to me again for some time."

"I don't think he will indeed," said Lady Kew, in a hard dry voice. "You don't know what you may have done. Will you be pleased to ring the bell and order my carriage? I congratulate you on having performed a most charming morning's work."

Ethel made her grandmother a very stately curtsey. I pity Lady Julia's condition when her mother reached home.

All who know Lord Kew may be pretty sure that in that unlucky interview with Ethel, to which the young lady has just alluded, he said no single word to her that was not kind, and just, and gentle. Considering the relation between them he thought himself justified in remonstrating with her as to the conduct which she chose to pursue, and in warning her against acquaintances of whom his own experience had taught him the dangerous character. He knew Madame d'Ivry and her friends so well that he would not have his wife elect a member of their circle. He could not tell Ethel what he knew of those women and their history. She chose not to understand his hints—did not, very likely, comprehend them. She was quite young, and the stories of such lives as theirs had never been told before her. She was indignant at the surveillance which Lord Kew exerted over her, and the authority which he began to assume. At another moment and in a better frame of mind she would have been thankful for his care, and very soon and ever after she did justice to his many admirable qualities—his frankness, honesty, and sweet temper. Only her high spirit was in perpetual revolt at this time against the bondage in which her family strove to keep her. The very worldly advantages of the position which they offered her served but to chafe her the more. Had her proposed husband been a young prince with a crown to lay at her feet, she had been yet more indignant very likely, and more rebellious. Had Kew's younger brother been her suitor, or Kew in his place, she had been not unwilling to follow her parents' wishes. Hence the revolt in which she was engaged—the wayward freaks and outbreaks her haughty temper indulged in. No doubt she saw the justice of Lord Kew's reproofs. That self-consciousness was not likely to add to her good humour. No doubt she was sorry for having shown Lord Kew the letter the moment after she had done that act, of which the poor young lady could not calculate the consequences that were now to ensue.

Lord Kew on glancing over the letter, at once divined the quarter whence it came. The portrait drawn of him was not unlike, as our characters described by those who hate us are not unlike. He had passed a reckless youth, indeed he was sad and ashamed of that past life, longed like the poor prodigal to return to better courses, and had embraced eagerly the chance afforded him of a union with a woman young, virtuous, and beautiful, against whom and against Heaven he hoped to sin no more. If we have told or hinted at more of his story than will please the ear of modern conventionalism, I beseech the reader to believe that the writer's purpose at least is not dishonest, nor unkindly. The young gentleman hung his head with sorrow over that sad detail of his life and its follies. What would he have given to be able to say to Ethel, "This is not true!"

His reproaches to Miss Newcome of course were at once stopped by this terrible assault on himself. The letter had been put in the Baden post-box, and so had come to its destination. It was in a disguised handwriting. Lord Kew could form no idea even of the sex of the scribe. He put the envelope in his pocket, when Ethel's back was turned. He examined the paper when he left her. He could make little of the superscription or of the wafer which had served to close the note. He did not choose to caution Ethel as to whether she should burn the letter or divulge it to her friends. He took his share of the pain, as a boy at school takes his flogging, stoutly and in silence.

When he saw Ethel again, which he did in an hour's time, the generous young gentleman held his hand out to her. "My dear," he said, "if you had loved me you never would have shown me that letter." It was his only reproof. After that he never again reproved or advised her.

Ethel blushed. "You are very brave and generous, Frank," she said, bending her head, "and I am captious and wicked." He felt the hot tear blotting on his hand from his cousin's downcast eyes.

He kissed her little hand. Lady Ann, who was in the room with her children when these few words passed between the two in a very low tone—thought it was a reconciliation. Ethel knew it was a renunciation on Kew's part—she never liked him so much as at that moment. The young man was too modest and simple to guess himself what the girl's feelings were. Could he have told them, his fate and hers might have been changed.

"You must not allow our kind letter-writing friend," Lord Kew continued, "to fancy we are hurt. We must walk out this afternoon, and we must appear very good friends."

"Yes, always, Kew," said Ethel, holding out her hand again. The next minute her cousin was at the table carving roast fowls and distributing the portions to the hungry children.

The assembly of the previous evening had been one of those which the *fermier des jeux* at Baden beneficently provides for the frequenters of the place, and now was to come off a much more brilliant entertainment, in which poor Clive, who is far into Switzerland by this time, was to have taken a share. The Bachelors had agreed to give a ball, one of the last entertainments of the season, a dozen or more of them had subscribed the funds, and we may be sure Lord Kew's name was at the head of the list, as it was of any list, of any scheme, whether of charity or fun. The English were invited, and the Russians were invited; the Spaniards and Italians, Poles, Prussians, and Hebrews; all the motley frequenters of the place, and the warriors in the Duke of Baden's army. Unlimited supper was set in the restaurant. The dancing-room glittered with extra lights, and a profusion of cut paper flowers decorated the festive scene. Everybody was present, those crowds with whom our story has nothing to do, and those two or three groups of persons who enact minor or greater parts in it. Madame d'Ivry came in a dress of stupendous splendour, even more brilliant than that in which Miss Ethel had figured at the last assembly. If the Duchess intended to *écraser* Miss Newcome by the superior magnificence of her toilet, she was disappointed. Miss Newcome wore a plain white frock on the occasion, and resumed, Madame d'Ivry said, her *rôle* of *ingénue* for that night.

During the brief season in which gentlemen enjoyed the favour of Mary Queen of Scots, that wandering sovereign led them through all the paces and vagaries of a regular passion. As in a fair, where time is short and pleasures numerous, the master of the theatrical booth shows you a tragedy, a farce, and a pantomime, all in a quarter of an hour, having a dozen new audiences to witness his entertainments in the course of the forenoon; so this lady with her platonic lovers went through the complete dramatic course,—tragedies of jealousy, pantomimes of rapture, and farces of parting. There were billets on one side and the other; hints of a fatal destiny, and a ruthless lynx-eyed tyrant, who held a demoniac grasp over the Duchess by means of certain secrets which he knew: there were regrets that we had not known each other sooner: why were we brought out of our convent and sacrificed to Monsieur le Duc? There were frolic interchanges of fancy and poesy: pretty *bouderies;* sweet reconciliations; yawns finally—and separation. Adolphe went out and Alphonse came in. It was the new audience; for which the bell rang, the band played, and the curtain rose; and the tragedy, comedy and farce were repeated.

Those Greenwich performers who appear in the theatrical pieces above mentioned, make a great deal more noise than your stationary tragedians; and if they have to denounce a villain, to declare a passion, or to threaten an enemy, they roar, stamp, shake their fists, and brandish their sabres, so that every man who sees the play has surely a full pennyworth for his penny. Thus Madame la Duchesse d'Ivry perhaps a little exaggerated her heroines' parts; liking to strike her audiences quickly, and also to change them often. Like good performers, she flung herself heart and soul into the business of the stage, and *was* what she acted. She was Phèdre, and if in the first part of the play she was uncommonly tender to Hippolyte, in the second she hated him furiously. She was Medea, and if Jason was *volage,* woe to Creusa! Perhaps our poor Lord Kew had taken the first character in a performance with Madame d'Ivry; for his behaviour in which part, it was difficult enough to forgive him; but when he appeared at Baden the affianced husband of one of the most beautiful young creatures in Europe,— when his relatives scorned Madame d'Ivry,—no wonder she was maddened and enraged, and would have recourse to revenge, steel, poison.

There was in the Duchess's Court a young fellow from the South of France, whose friends had sent him to *faire son droit* at Paris, where he had gone through the usual course of pleasures and studies of the young inhabitants of the Latin Quarter. He had at one time exalted republican opinions, and had fired his shot with distinction at St. Méri. He was a poet of some little note—a book of his lyrics—*Les Râles d'un Asphyxié*—having made a sensation at the time of their appearance. He drank great quantities of absinthe of a morning; smoked incessantly; played roulette whenever he could get a few pieces; contributed to a small journal, and was especially great in his hatred of *l'infâme Angleterre. Delenda est Carthago* was tatooed beneath his shirt-sleeve. Fifine and Clarisse, young milliners of the Students' district, had punctured this terrible motto on his manly right arm. *Le léopard*, emblem of England, was his aversion; he shook his fist at the caged monster in the Garden of Plants. He desired to have "Here lies an enemy of England" engraved upon his early tomb. He was skilled at billiards and dominos; adroit in the use of arms; of unquestionable courage and fierceness. Mr. Jones of England was afraid of M. de Castillonnes, and cowered before his scowls and sarcasms. Captain Blackball, the other English aid-de-camp of the Duchesse d'Ivry, a warrior of undoubted courage, who had been "on the ground" more than once, gave him a wide berth, and wondered what the little beggar meant when he used to say, "Since the days of the Prince Noir, Monsieur! my family has been at feud with l'Angleterre!" His family were grocers at Bordeaux, and his father's name was M. Cabasse. He[2] had married a noble in the revolutionary times; and the son at Paris called himself Victor Cabasse de Castillonnes; then Victor C. de Castillonnes; then M. de Castillonnes. One of the followers of the Black Prince had insulted a lady of the house of Castillonnes, when the English were lords of Guienne; hence our friend's wrath against the Leopard. He had written, and afterwards dramatised a terrific legend describing the circumstance[3] and the punishment of the Briton by a knight of the Castillonnes family. A more awful coward never existed in a melodrama than that felon English knight. His *blanche-fille*, of course, died of hopeless love for the conquering Frenchman, her father's murderer. The paper in which the feuilleton appeared died at the sixth number of the story. The theatre of the Boulevard refused the drama; so the author's rage against *l'infâme Albion* was yet unappeased. On beholding Miss Newcome, Victor had fancied the resemblance between her and Agnes de Calverley, the blanche Miss of his novel and drama, and cast an eye of favour upon the young creature. He even composed verses in her honour (for I presume that the "Miss Betti" and the Princess Crimhilde of the poems which he subsequently published, were no other than Miss Newcome, and the Duchess, her rival). He had been one of the lucky gentlemen who had danced with Ethel on the previous evening. On the occasion of the ball he came to her with a high-flown compliment, and a request to be once more allowed to waltz with her—a request to which he expected a favourable answer, thinking, no doubt, that his wit, his powers of conversation, and the *amour qui flambait dans son regard* had had their effect upon the charming Meess. Perhaps he had a copy of the very verses in his breast pocket, with which he intended to complete his work of fascination. For her sake alone, he had been heard to say, that he would enter into a truce with England, and forget the hereditary wrongs of his race.

But the blanche Miss on this evening declined to waltz with him. His compliments were not of the least avail. He retired with them and his unuttered verses in his crumpled bosom. Miss Newcome only danced in one quadrille with Lord Kew, and left the party quite early to the despair of many of the bachelors, who lost the fairest ornament of their ball.

[2] He *E1*] Cabasse *R*
[3] circumstance *E1*] circumstances *R*

Lord Kew, however, had been seen walking with her in public, and particularly attentive to her during her brief appearance in the ball-room; and the old dowager, who regularly attended all places of amusement, and was at twenty parties and six dinners the week before she died, thought fit to be particularly gracious to Madame d'Ivry upon this evening, and, far from shunning the Duchesse's presence, or being rude to her, as on former occasions, was entirely smiling and good-humoured. Lady Kew, too, thought there had been a reconciliation between Ethel and her cousin. Lady Ann had given her mother some account of the handshaking. Kew's walk with Ethel, the quadrille which she had danced with him alone, induced the elder lady to believe that matters had been made up between the young people.

So by way of showing the Duchesse that her little shot of the morning had failed in its effect, as Frank left the room with his cousin, Lady Kew gaily hinted, "that the young earl was *aux petits soins* with Miss Ethel; that she was sure her old friend, the Duc d'Ivry, would be glad to hear that his godson was about to range himself. He would settle down on his estates. He would attend to his duties as an English peer and a country gentleman. We shall go home," says the benevolent Countess, "and kill the *veau gras,* and you shall see our dear prodigal will become a very quiet gentleman."

The Duchesse said, "my Lady Kew's plan was most edifying. She was charmed to hear that Lord Kew loved veal; there were some who thought that meat rather insipid." A waltzer came to claim her hand at this moment; and as she twirled round the room upon that gentleman's arm, wafting odours as she moved, her pink silks, pink feathers, pink ribands, making a mighty rustling, the Countess of Kew had the satisfaction of thinking, that she had planted an arrow in that shrivelled little waist, which Count Punter's arms embraced, and had returned the stab which Madame d'Ivry had delivered in the morning.

Mr. Barnes, and his elect bride, had also appeared, danced, and disappeared. Lady Kew soon followed her young ones; and the ball went on very gaily, in spite of the absence of these respectable personages.

Being one of the managers of the entertainment, Lord Kew returned to it after conducting Lady Ann and her daughter to their carriage, and now danced with great vigour and with his usual kindness, selecting those ladies whom other waltzers rejected because they were too old, or too plain, or too stout, or what not. But he did not ask Madame d'Ivry to dance. He could condescend to dissemble so far as to hide the pain which he felt; but did not care to engage in that more advanced hypocrisy of friendship, which, for her part, his old grandmother had not shown the least scruple in assuming.

Amongst other partners, my lord selected that intrepid waltzer, the Gräfinn von Gumpelheim, who, in spite of her age, size, and large family, never lost a chance of enjoying her favourite recreation. "Look with what a camel my lord waltzes," said M. Victor to Madame d'Ivry, whose slim waist he had the honour of embracing to the same music. "What man but an Englishman would ever select such a dromedary!"

"Avant de se marier," said Madame d'Ivry, "il faut avouer que my lord se permet d'énormes distractions."

"My lord marries himself! And when and whom," cries the Duchesse's partner.

"Miss Newcome. Do not you approve of his choice? I thought the eyes of Stenio (the duchess called M. Victor, Stenio,) looked with some favour upon that little person. She is handsome, even very handsome. Is it not so often in life, Stenio? Are not youth and innocence (I give Miss Ethel the compliment of her innocence, now surtout that the little painter is dismissed)—are we not cast into the arms of jaded roués? Tender young flowers, are we not torn from our convent gardens, and flung into a world of which the air poisons our pure life, and withers the sainted buds of hope and love and faith? Faith! The mocking world tramples on it, n'est-ce pas? Love! The brutal world strangles the Heaven-born infant at its birth. Hope! It smiled at me in my little convent chamber, played among the flowers which I cherished, warbled with the birds that I loved. But it quitted me at the door of the world, Stenio. It folded its white wings and veiled its radiant face! In return for my young love, they gave me—sixty years, the dregs of a selfish heart, egotism cowering over its fire, and cold for all its mantle of ermine! In place of the sweet flowers of my young years, they gave me these, Stenio!" and she pointed to her feathers and her artificial roses. "O, I should like to crush them under my feet!" and she put out the neatest little slipper. The Duchesse was great upon her wrongs, and paraded her blighted innocence to every one who would feel interested by that piteous spectacle. The music here burst out more swiftly and melodiously than before; the pretty little feet forgot their desire to trample upon the world. She shrugged the lean little shoulders—"Eh!" said the Queen of Scots, "dansons et oublions;" and Stenio's arm once more surrounded her fairy waist (she called herself a fairy; other ladies called her a skeleton), and they whirled away in the waltz again: and presently she and Stenio came bumping up against the stalwart Lord Kew and the ponderous Madame de Gumpelheim, as a wherry dashes against the oaken ribs of a steamer.

The little couple did not fall; they were struck on to a neighbouring bench, luckily: but there was a laugh at the expense of Stenio and the Queen of Scots—and Lord Kew settling his panting partner on to a seat, came up to make excuses for his awkwardness to the lady, who had been its victim. At the laugh produced by the catastrophe, the Duchesse's eyes gleamed with anger.

"M. de Castillonnes," she said, to her partner, "have you had any quarrel with that Englishman?"

"With ce Milor? But no," said Stenio.

"He did it on purpose. There has been no day but his family has insulted me!" hissed out the Duchesse, and at this moment Lord Kew came up to make his apologies. He asked a thousand pardons of Madame la Duchesse for being so maladroit.

"Maladroit! et très maladroit, Monsieur," says Stenio, curling his moustache; "C'est bien le mot, Monsieur."

"Also, I make my excuses to Madame la Duchesse, which I hope she will receive," said Lord Kew. The Duchesse shrugged her shoulders and sunk her head.

"When one does not know how to dance, one ought not to dance," continued the Duchesse's knight.

"Monsieur is very good to give me lessons in dancing," said Lord Kew.

"Any lessons which you please, Milor!" cries Stenio; "and everywhere where you will them."

Lord Kew looked at the little man with surprise. He could not understand so much anger for so trifling an accident, which happens a dozen times in every crowded ball. He again bowed to the Duchesse, and walked away.

"This is your Englishman—your Kew, whom you vaunt everywhere," said Stenio, to M. de Florac, who was standing by and witnessed the scene. "Is he simply bête, or is he poltron as well? I believe him to be both."

"Silence, Victor!" cried Florac, seizing his arm, and drawing him away. "You know me, and that I am neither one nor the other. Believe my word, that my Lord Kew wants neither courage nor wit!"

"Will you be my witness, Florac?" continues the other.

"To take him your excuses? yes. It is you who have insulted—"

"Yes, parbleu, I have insulted!" says the Gascon.

"A man who never willingly offended soul alive. A man full of heart: the most frank: the most loyal. I have seen him put to the proof, and believe me he is all I say."

"Eh! so much the better for me!" cried the Southern. "I shall have the honour of meeting a gallant man: and there will be two on the field."

"They are making a tool of you, my poor Gascon," said M. de Florac, who saw Madame d'Ivry's eyes watching the couple. She presently took the arm of the noble Count de Punter, and went for fresh air into the adjoining apartment, where play was going on as usual; and Lord Kew and his friend Lord Rooster were pacing the room apart from the gamblers.

My Lord Rooster, at something which Kew said, looked puzzled, and said, "Pooh, stuff, damned little Frenchman! Confounded nonsense!"

"I was searching you, Milor!" said Madame d'Ivry, in a most winning tone, tripping behind him with her noiseless little feet. "Allow me a little word. Your arm! You used to give it me once, mon filleul! I hope you think nothing of the rudeness of M. de Castillonnes: he is a foolish Gascon: he must have been too often to the buffet this evening."

Lord Kew said, No, indeed he thought nothing of M. de Castillonnes' rudeness.

"I am so glad! These heroes of the *salle d'armes* have not the commonest manners. These Gascons are always *flamberge au vent*. What would the charming Miss Ethel say, if she heard of the dispute?"

"Indeed there is no reason why she should hear of it," said Lord Kew, "unless some obliging friend should communicate it to her."

"Communicate it to her—the poor dear! who would be so cruel as to give her pain?" asked the innocent Duchesse. "Why do you look at me so, Frank?"

"Because I admire you," said her interlocutor, with a bow. "I have never seen Madame la Duchesse to such advantage as to-day."

"You speak in enigmas! Come back with me to the ball-room. Come and dance with me once more. You used to dance with me. Let us have one waltz more, Kew. And then, and then, in a day or two I shall go back to Monsieur le Duc, and tell him that his filleul is going to marry the fairest of all Englishwomen: and to turn hermit in the country, and orator in the Chamber of Peers. You have wit! ah si—you have wit!" And she led back Lord Kew, rather amazed himself at what he was doing, into the ball-room; so that the good-natured people who were there, and who beheld them dancing, could not refrain from clapping their hands at the sight of this couple.

The Duchess danced as if she was bitten by that Neapolitan spider, which, according to the legend, is such a wonderful dance incentor. She would have the music quicker and quicker. She sank on Kew's arm, and clung on his support. She poured out all the light of her languishing eyes into his face. Their glances rather confused than charmed him. But the bystanders were pleased; they thought it so good-hearted of the Duchesse, after the little quarrel, to make a public avowal of reconciliation!

Lord Rooster looking on, at the entrance of the dancing-room, over Monsieur de Florac's shoulder, said, "It's all right! She's a clipper to dance, the little Duchess."

"The viper!" said Florac, "how she writhes!"

"I suppose that business with the Frenchman is all over," says Lord Rooster. "Confounded piece of nonsense."

"You believe it finished? We shall see!" said Florac, who perhaps knew his fair cousin better. When the waltz was over, Kew led his partner to a seat, and bowed to her; but though she made room for him at her side, pointing to it, and gathering up her rustling robes, so that he might sit down, he moved away, his face full of gloom. He never wished to be near her again. There was something more odious to him in her friendship, than her hatred. He knew hers was the hand that had dealt that stab at him and Ethel in the morning. He went back and talked with his two friends in the doorway. "Couch yourself, my little Kiou," said Florac. "You are all pale. You were best in bed, mon garçon!"

"She has made me promise to take her in to supper," Kew said, with a sigh.

"She will poison you," said the other. "Why have they abolished the roue chez nous? My word of honour they should rétabliche it for this woman."

"There is one in the next room," said Kew, with a laugh. "Come Vicomte, let us try our fortune," and he walked back into the play-room.

That was the last night on which Lord Kew ever played a gambling game. He won constantly. The double zero seemed to obey him; so that the croupiers wondered at his fortune. Florac backed it; saying with the superstition of a gambler, "I am sure something goes to arrive to this boy." From time to time M. de Florac went back to the dancing-room, leaving his *mise* under Kew's charge. He always found his heaps increased; indeed the worthy Vicomte wanted a turn of luck in his favour. On one occasion he returned with a grave face, saying to Lord Rooster, "She has the other one in hand. We are going to see." "Trente-six encor! et rouge gagne," cried the croupier with his nasal tone. Monsieur de Florac's pockets overflowed with double Napoleons, and he stopped his play, luckily, for Kew putting down his winnings, once, twice, thrice, lost them all.

When Lord Kew had left the dancing-room, Madame d'Ivry saw Stenio following him with fierce looks, and called back that bearded bard. "You were going to pursue M. de Kew," she said, "I knew you were. Sit down here, Sir," and she patted him down on her seat with her fan.

"Do you wish that I should call him back, Madame?" said the poet, with the deepest tragic accents.

"I can bring him when I want him, Victor," said the lady.

"Let us hope others will be equally fortunate," the Gascon said, with one hand in his breast, the other stroking his moustache.

"Fi, Monsieur, que vous sentez le tabac! je vous le défends, entendez-vous, Monsieur?"

"Pourtant, I have seen the day when Madame la Duchesse did not disdain a cigar," said Victor. "If the odour incommodes, permit that I retire."

"And you also would quit me, Stenio. Do you think I did not mark your eyes towards Miss Newcome? your anger when she refused you to dance? Ah! we see all. A woman does not deceive herself, do you see? You send me beautiful verses, Poet. You can write as well of a statue or a picture, of a rose or a sunset, as of the heart of a woman. You were angry just now because I danced with M. de Kew. Do you think in a woman's eyes jealousy is unpardonable?"

"You know how to provoke it, Madame," continued the tragedian.

"Monsieur," replied the lady, with dignity. "Am I to render you an account of all my actions, and ask your permission for a walk?"

"In fact, I am but the slave, Madame," groaned the Gascon, "I am not the master."

"You are a very rebellious slave, Monsieur," continues the lady, with a pretty *moue*, and a glance of the large eyes artfully brightened by her rouge. "Suppose—suppose I danced with M. de Kew, not for his sake—Heaven knows to dance with him is not a pleasure—but for yours. Suppose I do not want a foolish quarrel to proceed. Suppose I know that he is ni sot ni poltron as you pretend. I overheard you, Sir, talking with one of the basest of men, my good cousin, M. de Florac: but it is not of him I speak. Suppose I know the Comte de Kew to be a man, cold and insolent, ill-bred, and grossier, as the men of his nation are—but one who lacks no courage—one who is terrible when roused; might I have no occasion to fear, not for him, but—"

"But for me! Ah Marie! Ah Madame! Believe you that a man of my blood will yield a foot to any Englishman? Do you know the story of my race? do you know that since my childhood I have vowed hatred to that nation? Tenez, Madame, this M. Jones who frequents your salon, it was but respect for you that has enabled me to keep my patience with this stupid islander. This Captain Blackball, whom you distinguish, who certainly shoots well, who mounts well to horse, I have always thought his manners were those of the marker of a billiard. But I respect him because he has made war with Don Carlos against the English. But this young M. de Kew, his laugh crisps me the nerves; his insolent air makes me bound; in beholding him I said to myself, I hate you; think whether I love him better after having seen him as I did but now, Madame!" Also, but this Victor did not say, he thought Kew had laughed at him at the be-

LAYING A TRAIN

THE EXPLOSION

ginning of the evening, when the blanche Miss had refused to dance with him.

"Ah, Victor, it is not him, but you that I would save," said the Duchess. And the people round about, and the Duchess herself afterwards said, yes, certainly, she had a good heart. She entreated Lord Kew; she implored M. Victor; she did everything in her power to appease the quarrel between him and the Frenchman.

After the ball came the supper, which was laid at separate little tables, where parties of half-a-dozen enjoyed themselves. Lord Kew was of the Duchess's party, where our Gascon friend had not a seat. But being one of the managers of the entertainment, his lordship went about from table to table, seeing that the guests at each lacked nothing. He supposed too that the dispute with the Gascon had possibly come to an end; at any rate, disagreeable as the other's speech had been, he had resolved to put up with it, not having the least inclination to drink the Frenchman's blood, or to part with his own on so absurd a quarrel. He asked people in his good-natured way to drink wine with him; and catching M. Victor's eye scowling at him from a distant table, he sent a waiter with a champagne bottle to his late opponent, and lifted his glass as a friendly challenge. The waiter carried the message to M. Victor, who, when he heard it, turned up his glass, and folded his arms in a stately manner. "M. de Castillonnes dit qu'il refuse, Milor," said the waiter, rather scared. "He charged me to bring that message to Milor." Florac ran across to the angry Gascon. It was not while at Madame d'Ivry's table that Lord Kew sent his challenge and received his reply; his duties as steward had carried him away from that pretty early.

Meanwhile the glimmering dawn peered into the windows of the refreshment-room, and behold, the sun broke in and scared all the revellers. The ladies scurried away like so many ghosts at cock-crow, some of them not caring to face that detective luminary. Cigars had been lighted ere this; the men remained smoking them with those sleepless German waiters still bringing fresh supplies of drink. Lord Kew gave the Duchesse d'Ivry his arm, and was leading her out; M. de Castillonnes stood scowling directly in their way, upon which, with rather an abrupt turn of the shoulder, and a "Pardon, Monsieur," Lord Kew pushed by, and conducted the Duchess to her carriage. She did not in the least see what had happened between the two gentlemen in the passage; she ogled, and nodded, and kissed her hands quite affectionately to Kew as the fly drove away.

Florac in the meanwhile had seized his compatriot, who had drunk champagne copiously with others, if not with Kew, and was in vain endeavouring to make him hear reason. The Gascon was furious; he vowed that Lord Kew had struck him. "By the tomb of my mother," he bellowed, "I swear I will have his blood!" Lord Rooster was bawling out—"D— him; carry him to bed, and shut him up;" which remarks Victor did not understand, or two victims would doubtless have been sacrificed on his mamma's mausoleum.

When Kew came back (as he was only too sure to do), the little Gascon rushed forward with a glove in his hand, and having an audience of smokers round about him, made a furious speech about England, leopards, cowardice, insolent islanders, and Napoleon at St. Helena; and demanded reason for Kew's conduct during the night. As he spoke, he advanced towards Lord Kew, glove in hand, and lifted it as if he was actually going to strike.

"There is no need for further words," said Lord Kew, taking his cigar out of his mouth. "If you don't drop that glove, upon my word I will pitch you out of the window. Ha! . . . Pick the man up, somebody. You'll bear witness, gentlemen, I couldn't help myself. If he wants me in the morning, he knows where to find me."

"I declare that my Lord Kew has acted with great forbearance, and under the most brutal provocation—the most brutal provocation entendez-vous, M. Cabasse," cried out M. de Florac, rushing forward to the Gascon, who had now risen; "Monsieur's conduct has been unworthy of a Frenchman and a galant homme."

"D— it; he has had it on his nob, though," said Lord Viscount Rooster, laconically.

"Ah Roosterre! ceci n'est pas pour rire," Florac cried sadly, as they both walked away with Lord Kew; "I wish that first blood was all that was to be shed in this quarrel."

"Gaw! how he did go down!" cried Rooster, convulsed with laughter.

"I am very sorry for it," said Kew, quite seriously; "I couldn't help it. God forgive me." And he hung down his head. He thought of the past, and its levities, and punishment coming after him *pede claudo*. It was with all his heart the contrite young man said "God forgive me." He would take what was to follow as the penalty of what had gone before.

"*Pallas te hoc vulnere, Pallas immolat,* mon pauvre Kiou," said his French friend. And Lord Rooster, whose classical education had been much neglected, turned round, and said, "Hullo, mate, what ship's that?"

Viscount Rooster had not been two hours in bed, when the Count de Punter (formerly of the Black Jägers), waited upon him upon the part of M. de Castillonnes and the Earl of Kew, who had referred him to the Viscount to arrange matters for a meeting between them. As the meeting must take place out of the Baden territory, and they ought to move before the police prevented them, the Count proposed that they should at once make for France; where, as it was an affair of honneur,[4] they would assuredly be let to enter without passports.

Lady Ann and Lady Kew heard that the gentlemen after the ball had all gone out on a hunting party, and were not alarmed for four-and-twenty hours at least. On the next day none of them returned; and on the day after, the family heard that Lord Kew had met with rather a dangerous accident; but all the town knew he had been shot by M. de Castillonnes on one of the islands on the Rhine, opposite Kehl, where he was now lying.

---

[4] honneur, *E1*] honour, *R*

Chapter XXXV.

UR discursive muse must now take her place in the little britzka in which Clive Newcome and his companions are travelling, and cross the Alps in that vehicle, beholding the snows on St. Gothard, and the beautiful region through which the Ticino rushes on its way to the Lombard lakes, and the great corn-covered plains of the Milanese; and that royal city, with the cathedral for its glittering crown, only less magnificent than the imperial dome of Rome. I have some long letters from Mr. Clive, written during this youthful tour, every step of which, from the departure at Baden, to the gate of[1] Milan, he describes as beautiful; and doubtless, the delightful scenes through which the young man went, had their effect in soothing any private annoyances with which his jour‧ ney commenced. The aspect of nature, in that fortunate route which he took, is so noble and cheering, that our private affairs and troubles shrink away abashed before that serene splendour. O, sweet peaceful scene of azure lake, and snow-crowned mountain, so wonderfully lovely is your aspect, that it seems like Heaven almost, and as if grief and care could not enter it! What young Clive's private cares were I knew not as yet in those days; and he kept them out of

[1] of *E1*] at *R*

his letters; it was only in the intimacy of future life that some of these pains were revealed to me.

Some three months after taking leave of Miss Ethel, our young gentleman found himself at Rome, with his friend Ridley still for a companion. Many of us, young or middle-aged, have felt that delightful shock which the first sight of the great city inspires. There is one other place of which the view strikes one with an emotion even greater than that with which we look at Rome, where Augustus was reigning when He saw the day, whose birthplace is separated but by a hill or two from the awful gates of Jerusalem. Who that has beheld both can forget that first aspect of either. At the end of years the emotion occasioned by the sight still thrills in your memory, and it smites you as at the moment when you first viewed it.

The business of the present novel however, lies neither with priest nor pagan, but with Mr. Clive Newcome, and his affairs and his companions at this period of his life. Nor, if the gracious reader expects to hear of cardinals in scarlet, and noble Roman princes and princesses, will he find such in this history. The only noble Roman into whose mansion our friend got admission, was the Prince Polonia, whose footmen wear the liveries of the English Royal family, who gives gentlemen and even painters cash upon good letters of credit; and, once or twice in a season, opens his transtiberine palace and treats his customers to a ball. Our friend Clive used jocularly to say, he believed there were no Romans. There were priests in portentous hats; there were friars with shaven crowns; there were the sham peasantry, who dressed themselves out in masquerade costumes, with bagpipe and goat-skin, with crossed leggings and scarlet petticoats, who let themselves out to artists at so many pauls per sitting; but he never passed a Roman's door except to buy a cigar or to purchase a handkerchief. Thither, as elsewhere, we carry our insular habits with us. We have a little England at Paris, a little England at Munich, Dresden, everywhere. Our friend is an Englishman, and did at Rome as the English do.

There was the polite English society, the society that flocks to see the Colosseum lighted up with blue fire, that flocks to the Vatican to behold the statues by torchlight, that hustles into the churches on public festivals in black veils and deputy-lieutenants' uniforms, and stares, and talks, and uses opera-glasses while the pontiffs of the Roman church are performing its ancient rites, and the crowds of faithful are kneeling round the altars; the society which gives its balls and dinners, has its scandal and bickerings, its aristocrats, parvenues, toadies imported from Belgravia; has its club, its hunt, and its Hyde Park on the Pincio: and there is the other little English world, the broad-hatted, long-bearded, velvet-jacketted, jovial colony of the artists, who have their own feasts, haunts, and amusements by the side of their aristocratic compatriots, with whom but few of them have the honour to mingle.

J.J. and Clive engaged pleasant lofty apartments in the Via Gregoriana. Generations of painters had occupied these chambers and gone their way. The windows of their painting-room looked into a quaint old garden, where there were ancient statues of the Imperial time, a babbling fountain and noble orange-trees, with broad clustering leaves and golden balls of fruit, glorious to look upon. Their walks abroad were endlessly pleasant and delightful. In every street there were scores of pictures of the graceful characteristic Italian life, which our painters seem one and all to reject, preferring to depict their quack brigands, Contadini, Pifferari, and the like, because Thompson painted them before Jones, and Jones before Thompson, and so on, backwards into time. There were the children at play, the women huddled round the steps of the open doorways, in the kindly Roman winter; grim portentous old hags, such as Michael Angelo painted, draped in majestic raggery; mothers and swarming bambins; slouching countrymen, dark of beard and noble of countenance, posed in superb attitudes, lazy, tattered, and majestic. There came the red troops, the black troops, the blue troops of the army of priests; the snuffy regiments of Capuchins, grave and grotesque; the trim French abbés; my lord the bishop, with his footman (those wonderful footmen); my lord the cardinal, in his ramshackle coach and his two, nay three, footmen behind him;—flunkeys that look as if they had been dressed by the costumier of a British pantomime;—coach with prodigious emblazonments of hats and coats of arms, that seems as if it came out of the pantomime too, and was about to turn into something else. So it is, that what is grand to some persons' eyes appears grotesque to others; and for certain sceptical persons, that step, which we have heard of, between the sublime and the ridiculous, is not visible.

"I wish it were not so," writes Clive, in one of the letters wherein he used to pour his full heart out in those days. "I see these people at their devotions, and envy them their rapture. A friend, who belongs to the old religion, took me, last week, into a church where the Virgin lately appeared in person to a Jewish gentleman, flashed down upon him from Heaven in light and splendour celestial, and, of course, straightway converted him. My friend bade me look at the picture, and, kneeling down beside me, I know prayed with all his honest heart that the truth might shine down upon me too; but I saw no glimpse of Heaven at all, I saw but a poor picture, an altar with blinking candles, a church hung with tawdry strips of red and white calico. The good, kind W— went away, humbly saying, 'that such might have happened again if Heaven so willed it.' I could not but feel a kindness and admiration for the good man. I know his works are made to square with his faith, that he dines on a crust, lives as chastely as a hermit, and gives his all to the poor.

"Our friend J.J., very different to myself in so many respects, so superior in all, is immensely touched by these ceremonies. They seem to answer to some spiritual want of his nature, and he comes away satisfied as from a feast, where I have only found vacancy. Of course our first pilgrimage was to St. Peter's. What a walk! Under what noble shadows does one pass; how great and liberal the houses are, with generous casements and courts, and great grey portals which giants might get through and keep their turbans on. Why, the houses are twice as tall as Lamb Court itself; and over them hangs a noble dinge, a venerable mouldy splendour. Over the solemn portals are ancient mystic escutcheons—vast shields of princes and cardinals, such as Ariosto's knights might take down; and every figure about them is a picture by himself. At every turn there is a temple: in every court a brawling fountain. Besides the people of the streets and houses, and the army of priests black and brown, there's a great silent population of marble. There are battered gods tumbled out of Olympus and broken in the fall, and set up under niches and over fountains; there are senators namelessly, noselessly, noiselessly seated under archways, or lurking in courts and gardens. And then, besides these defunct ones, of whom these old figures may be said to be the corpses; there is the reigning family, a countless carved hierarchy of angels, saints, confessors, of the latter dynasty which has conquered the court of Jove. I say, Pen, I wish Warrington would write the history of the Last of the Pagans. Did you never have a sympathy for them as the monks came rushing into their temples, kicking down their poor altars, smashing the fair calm faces of their gods, and sending their vestals a-flying? They are always preaching here about the persecution of the Christians. Are not the churches full of martyrs with choppers in their meek heads; virgins on gridirons; riddled St. Sebastians, and the like? But have they never persecuted in their turn? Oh, me! You and I know better, who were bred up near to the pens of Smithfield, where Protestants and Catholics have taken their turn to be roasted.

"You pass through an avenue of angels and saints on the bridge across Tiber, all in action; their great wings seem clanking, their marble garments clapping; St. Michael, descending upon the Fiend, has been caught and bronzified just as he lighted on the Castle of St. Angelo, his enemy doubtless fell crushing through the roof and so downwards. He is as natural as blank verse—that bronze angel—set, rhythmic, grandiose. You'll see, some day or other, he's a great sonnet, Sir, I'm sure of that. Milton wrote in bronze; I am sure Virgil polished off his Georgics in marble—sweet calm shapes! exquisite harmonies of line! As for the Æneid; that, Sir, I consider to be so many bas-reliefs, mural ornaments which affect me not much.

"I think I have lost sight of St. Peter's, haven't I? Yet it is big enough. How it makes your heart beat when you first see it! Ours did as we came in at night from Civita Vecchia, and saw a great ghostly darkling dome rising solemnly up into the gray night, and keeping us company ever so long as we drove, as if it had been an orb fallen out of heaven with its light put out. As you look at it from the Pincio, and the sun sets behind it, surely that aspect of earth and sky is one of the grandest in the world. I don't like to say that the façade of the church is ugly and obtrusive. As long as the dome overawes, that façade is supportable. You advance towards it—through, O, such a noble court! with fountains flashing up to meet the sunbeams; and right and left of you two sweeping half-crescents of great columns; but you pass by the courtiers and up to the steps of the throne, and the dome seems to disappear behind it. It is as if the throne was upset, and the king had toppled over.

"There must be moments, in Rome especially, when every man of friendly heart, who writes himself English and Protestant, must feel a pang at thinking that he and his countrymen are insulated from European Christendom. An ocean separates us. From one shore or the other one can see the neighbour cliffs on clear days: one must wish sometimes that there were no stormy gulf between us; and from Canterbury to Rome a pilgrim could pass, and not drown beyond Dover. Of the beautiful parts of the great Mother Church I believe among us many people have no idea: we think of lazy friars, of pining cloistered virgins, of ignorant peasants worshipping wood and stones, bought and sold indulgences, absolutions, and the like common-places of Protestant satire. Lo! yonder inscription, which blazes round the dome of the temple, so great and glorious it looks like Heaven almost, and as if the words were written in stars, it proclaims to all the world, that this is Peter, and on this rock the Church shall be built, against which Hell shall not prevail. Under the bronze canopy his throne is lit with lights that have been burning before it for ages. Round this stupendous chamber are ranged the grandees of his court. Faith seems to be realised in their marble figures. Some of them were alive but yesterday: others, to be as blessed as they, walk the world even now doubtless; and the commissioners of Heaven, here holding their court a hundred years hence, shall authoritatively announce their beatification. The signs of their power shall not be wanting. They heal the sick, open the eyes of the blind, cause the lame to walk to-day as they did eighteen centuries ago. Are there not crowds ready to bear witness to their wonders? Isn't[2] there a tribunal appointed to try their claims; advocates to plead for and against; prelates and clergy and multitudes of faithful to back and believe them? Thus you shall kiss the hand of a priest to-day, who has given his to a friar whose bones are already beginning to work miracles, who has been the disciple of another whom the Church has just proclaimed a saint,—hand in hand they hold by one another till the line is lost up in Heaven. Come, friend, let us acknowledge this, and go and kiss the toe of St. Peter. Alas! there's the Channel always between us; and we no more believe in the miracles of St. Thomas of Canterbury, than that the bones of His Grace, John Bird, who sits in St. Thomas's chair presently, will work wondrous cures in the year 2000: that his statue will speak, or his portrait by Sir Thomas Lawrence will wink.

"So, you see, at those grand ceremonies which the Roman church exhibits at Christmas, I looked on as a Protestant. Holy Father on his throne or in his palanquin, cardinals with their tails and their train-bearers, mitred bishops and abbots, regiments of friars and clergy, relics exposed for adoration, columns draped, altars illuminated, incense smoking, organs pealing, and boxes of piping soprani, Swiss guards with slashed breeches and fringed halberts;—between us and all this splendour of old-world ceremony, there's an ocean flowing: and yonder old statue of Peter might have been Jupiter again, surrounded by a procession of flamens and augurs, and Augustus as Pontifex Maximus, to inspect the sacrifices,—and my feelings at the spectacle had been, doubtless, pretty much the same.

"Shall I utter any more heresies? I am an unbeliever in Raphael's Transfiguration—the scream of that devil-possessed boy, in the lower part of the figure of eight (a stolen boy too), jars the whole music of the composition. On Michael Angelo's great wall, the grotesque and terrible are not out of place. What an awful achievement! Fancy the state of mind of the man who worked it—as alone, day after day, he devised and drew those dreadful figures! Suppose in the days of the Olympian dynasty, the subdued Titan rebels had been set to ornament a palace for Jove, they would have brought

2 Isn't *E1*] Is not *R*

in some such tremendous work: or suppose that Michael descended to the Shades, and brought up this picture out of the halls of Limbo. I like a thousand and a thousand times better to think of Raphael's loving spirit. As he looked at women and children, his beautiful face must have shone like sunshine; his kind hand must have caressed the sweet figures as he formed them. If I protest against the Transfiguration, and refuse to worship at that altar before which so many generations have knelt; there are hundreds of others which I salute thankfully. It is not so much in the set harangues (to take another metaphor), as in the daily tones and talk that his voice is so delicious. Sweet poetry, and music, and tender hymns drop from him: he lifts his pencil, and something gracious falls from it on the paper. How noble his mind must have been! it seems but to receive, and his eye seems only to rest on, what is great, and generous, and lovely. You walk through crowded galleries, where are pictures ever so large and pretentious; and come upon a grey paper, or a little fresco, bearing his mark—and over all the brawl and the throng you recognise his sweet presence. 'I would like to have been Giulio Romano,' J.J. says (who does not care for Giulio's pictures), 'because then I would have been Raphael's favourite pupil.' We agreed that we would rather have seen him and William Shakspeare, than all the men we ever read of. Fancy poisoning a fellow out of envy—as Spagnoletto did! There are some men whose admiration takes that bilious shape. There's a fellow in our mess at the Lepre, a clever enough fellow too—and not a bad fellow to the poor. He was a Gandishite. He is a genre and portrait painter by the name of Haggard. He hates J.J. because Lord Fareham, who is here, has given J.J. an order; and he hates me, because I wear a clean shirt, and ride a cock-horse.

"I wish you could come to our mess at the Lepre. It's such a dinner! such a table-cloth: such a waiter: such a company! Every man has a beard and a sombrero: and you would fancy we were a band of brigands. We are regaled with woodcocks, snipes, wild swans, ducks, robins, and owls and οἰωνοῖσί τε πᾶσι for dinner: and with three pauls worth of wines and victuals, the hungriest has enough, even Claypole the sculptor. Did you ever know him? He used to come to the Haunt. He looks like the Saracen's head with his beard now. There is a French table still more hairy than ours, a German table, an American table. After dinner we go and have coffee and mezzo-caldo at the Café Greco over the way. Mezzo-caldo is not a bad drink—a little rum—a slice of fresh citron—lots of pounded sugar, and boiling water for the rest. Here in various parts of the cavern (it is a vaulted low place), the various nations have their assigned quarters, and we drink our coffee and strong waters, and abuse Guido, or Rubens, or Bernini, selon les gouts, and blow such a cloud of smoke as would make Warrington's lungs dilate with pleasure. We get very good cigars for a bajoccho and half—that is very good for us, cheap tobaccanalians; and capital when you have got no others. M'Collop is here: he made a great figure at a cardinal's reception in the tartan of the M'Collop. He is splendid at the tomb of the Stuarts, and wanted to cleave Haggard down to the chine with his claymore for saying that Charles Edward was often drunk.

"Some of us have our breakfasts at the Café Greco at dawn. The birds are very early birds here: and you'll see the great sculptors—the old Dons you know who look down on us young fellows, at their coffee here when it is yet twilight. As I am a swell, and have a servant, J.J. and I breakfast at our lodgings. I wish you could see Terribile our attendant, and Ottavia our old woman! You will see both of them on the canvas one day. When he *hasn't* blacked our boots and has got our breakfast, Terribile the valet-de-chambre becomes Terribile the model. He has figured on a hundred canvases ere this, and almost ever since he was born. All his family were models. His mother having been a Venus, is now a Witch of Endor. His father is in the patriarchal line: he has himself done the cherubs, the shepherd-boys, and now is a grown man, and ready as a warrior, a pifferaro, a Capuchin, or what you will.

"After the coffee and the Café Greco we all go to the Life Academy. After the Life Academy, those who belong to the world dress and go out to tea-parties just as if we were in London. Those who are not in society have plenty of fun of their own—and better fun than the tea-party fun too. Jack Screwby has a night once a week, sardines and ham for supper, and a cask of Marsala in the corner. Your humble servant entertains on Thursdays: which is Lady Fitch's night too; and I flatter myself some of the London dandies who are passing the winter here, prefer the cigars and humble liquors which we dispense, to tea and Miss Fitch's performance on the pianoforte.

"What is that I read in Galignani about Lord K— and an affair of honour at Baden? Is it my dear kind jolly Kew with whom some one has quarrelled? I know those who will be even more grieved than I am, should anything happen to the best of good fellows. A great friend of Lord Kew's, Jack Belsize commonly called, came with us from Baden through Switzerland, and we left him at Milan. I see by the paper that his elder brother is dead, and so poor Jack will be a great man some day. I wish the chance had happened sooner if it was to befal at all. So my amiable cousin, Barnes Newcome Newcome, Esq., has married my lady Clara Pulleyn; I wish her joy of her bridegroom. All I have heard of that family is from the newspaper. If you meet them, tell me anything about them. We had a very pleasant time altogether at Baden. I suppose the accident to Kew will put off his marriage with Miss Newcome. They have been engaged you know ever so long—And—do, do write to me and tell me something about London. It's best I should stay here and work this winter and the next. J.J. has done a famous picture, and if I send a couple home, you'll give them a notice in the 'Pall Mall Gazette,' won't you? for the sake of old times, and yours affectionately,

"CLIVE NEWCOME."

Chapter XXXVI.

IN WHICH M. DE FLORAC IS PROMOTED.

OWEVER much Madame la Duchesse d'Ivry was disposed to admire and praise her own conduct in the affair which ended so unfortunately for poor Lord Kew, between whom and the Gascon her grace vowed that she had done everything in her power to prevent a battle, the old Duke, her lord, was, it appeared, by no means delighted with his wife's behaviour, nay, visited her with his very sternest displeasure. Miss O'Grady, the Duchesse's companion, and her little girl's instructress, at this time resigned her functions in the Ivry family; it is possible that in the recriminations consequent upon the governess's dismissal, the Miss Irlandaise, in whom the family had put so much confidence, divulged stories unfavourable to her patroness, and caused the indignation of the Duke, her husband. Between Florac and the Duchesse there was also open war and rupture. He had been one of Kew's seconds in the latter's affair with the Vicomte's countryman. He had even cried out for fresh pistols and proposed to engage Castillonnes when his gallant principal fell; and though a second duel was luckily averted as murderous and needless, M. de Florac never hesitated afterwards and in all companies to denounce with the utmost virulence the instigator and the champion of the odious original quarrel. He vowed that the Duchesse had shot *le petit Kiou* as effectually as if she had herself fired the pistol at his breast. Murderer, poisoner, Brinvilliers, a hundred more such epithets he used against his kinswoman, regretting that the good old times were past—that there was no Chambre Ardente to try her, and no rack and wheel to give her her due.

The biographer of the Newcomes has no need (although he possesses the fullest information) to touch upon the Duchesse's doings, farther than as they relate to that most respectable English family. When the Duke took his wife into the country, Florac never hesitated to say that to live with her was dangerous for the old man, and to cry out to his friends of the Boulevards or the Jockey Club, "Ma parole d'honneur, cette femme le tuera!"

Do you know, O gentle and unsuspicious readers, or have you ever reckoned as you have made your calculation of society, how many most respectable husbands help to kill their wives—how many respectable wives aid in sending their husbands to Hades? The wife of a chimney-sweep or a journeyman butcher comes shuddering before a police magistrate—her head bound up—her body scarred and bleeding with wounds, which the drunken ruffian, her lord, has administered: a poor shopkeeper or mechanic is driven out of his home by the furious ill temper of the shrill virago his wife—takes to the public-house—to evil courses—to neglecting his business—to the gin-bottle—to delirium tremens—to perdition. Bow Street, and policemen, and the newspaper reporters, have cognisance and a certain jurisdiction over these vulgar matrimonial crimes; but in politer company how many murderous assaults are there by husband or wife—where the woman is not felled by the actual fist, though she staggers and sinks under blows quite as cruel and effectual; where, with old wounds yet unhealed, which she strives to hide under a smiling face from the world, she has to bear up and to be stricken down and to rise to her feet again, under fresh daily strokes of torture; where the husband, fond and faithful, has to suffer slights, coldness, insult, desertion, his children sneered away from their love for him, his friends driven from his door by jealousy, his happiness strangled, his whole life embittered, poisoned, destroyed! If you were acquainted with the history of every family in your street, don't you know that in two or three of the houses there such tragedies have been playing? Is not the young mistress of number 20 already pining at her husband's desertion? The kind master of number 30 racking his fevered brains and toiling through sleepless nights to pay for the jewels on his wife's neck, and the carriage out of which she ogles Lothario in the park? The fate under which man or woman falls, blow of brutal tyranny, heartless desertion, weight of domestic care too heavy to bear—are not blows such as these constantly striking people down? In this long parenthesis we are wandering ever so far away from M. le Duc and Madame la Duchesse d'Ivry, and from the vivacious Florac's statement regarding his kinsman, that that woman will kill him.

There is this at least to be said, that if the Duc d'Ivry did die he was a very old gentleman, and had been a great *viveur* for at least three-score years of his life. As Prince de Montcontour in his father's time before the Revolution, during the Emigration, even after the Restoration M. le Duc had *vécu* with an extraordinary vitality. He had gone through good and bad fortune; extreme poverty, display and splendour, affairs of love—affairs of honour,—and of one disease or another a man must die at the end. After the Baden business—and he had dragged off his wife to Champagne—the Duke became greatly broken; he brought his little daughter to a convent at Paris, putting the child under the special guardianship of Madame de Florac, with whom and with whose family in these latter days the old chief of the house effected a complete reconciliation. The Duke was now for ever coming to Madame de Florac; he poured all his wrongs and griefs into her ear with garrulous senile eagerness. "That little Duchesse is a Médée, a monstre, a femme d'Eugène Sue," the Vicomte used to say; "the poor old Duke he cry—ma parole d'honneur, he cry and I cry too when he comes to recount to my poor mother, whose sainted heart is the *asile* of all griefs, a real Hôtel Dieu, my word the most sacred, with beds for all the afflicted, with sweet words, like Sisters of Charity, to minister to them:—I cry, mon bon Pendennis, when this *vieillard* tells his stories about his wife and tears his white hairs to the feet of my mother."

When the little Antoinette was separated by her father from her mother, the Duchesse d'Ivry, it might have been expected that that poetess would have dashed off a few more *cris de l'âme*, shrieking according to her wont, and baring and beating that shrivelled maternal bosom of hers, from which her child had been just torn. The child skipped and laughed to go away to the convent. It was only when she left Madame de Florac that she used to cry; and when urged by that good lady to exhibit a little decorous sentiment in writing to her mamma, Antoinette would ask, in her artless way, "Pourquoi? Mamma used never to speak to me except sometimes before the world, before ladies that understands itself. When her gentleman came, she put me to the door; she gave me tapes, *o oui*, she gave me tapes! I cry no more; she has so much made to cry M. le Duc, that it is quite enough of one in a family." So Madame la Duchesse d'Ivry did not weep, even in print, for the loss of her pretty little Antoinette; besides, she was engaged, at that time, by other sentimental occupations. A young grazier of their neighbouring town, of an aspiring mind and remarkable poetic talents, engrossed the Duchesse's platonic affections at this juncture. When he had sold his beasts at market, he would ride over and read Rousseau and Schiller with Madame la Duchesse, who formed him. His pretty young wife was rendered miserable by all these readings, but what could the poor little ignorant countrywoman know of Platonism? Faugh! there is more than one woman we see in society smiling about from house to house, pleasant and sentimental and *formosa supernè* enough; but I fancy a fish's tail is flapping under her fine flounces, and a forked fin at the end of it!

Finer flounces, finer bonnets, more lovely wreaths, more beautiful lace, smarter carriages, bigger white bows, larger footmen, were not seen, during all the season of 18—, than appeared round about St. George's, Hanover Square, in the beautiful month of June succeeding that September when so many of our friends, the Newcomes, were assembled at Baden. Those flaunting carriages, powdered and favoured footmen, were in attendance upon members of the Newcome family and their connexions, who were celebrating what is called a marriage in high life in the temple within. Shall we set down a catalogue of the dukes, marquises, earls, who were present; cousins of the lovely bride? Are they not already in the *Morning Herald,* and *Court Journal,* as well as in the *Newcome Chronicle* and *Independent,* and the *Dorking Intelligencer and Chanticlere Weekly Gazette?* There they are, all printed at full length sure enough; the name of the bride, Lady Clara Pulleyn, the lovely and accomplished daughter of the Earl and Countess of Dorking; of the beautiful bridesmaids, the Ladies Henrietta Belinda Adelaide Pulleyn, Miss Newcome, Miss Alice Newcome, Miss Maude Newcome, Miss Anna Maria (Hobson) Newcome; and all the other

persons engaged in the ceremony. It was performed by the Right Honourable[1] Viscount Gallowglass, Bishop of Ballyshannon, brother-in-law to
the bride, assisted by the Honourable and Reverend Hercules O'Grady,
his lordship's Chaplain, and the Reverend John Bulders, Rector of St.
Mary's, Newcome. Then follow the names of all the nobility who were
present, and of the noble and distinguished personages who signed the
book. Then comes an account of the principal dresses, chefs-d'œuvre of
Madame Crinoline; of the bride's coronal of brilliants, supplied by Messrs.
Morr and Stortimer; of the veil of priceless Chantilly lace, the gift of the
Dowager Countess of Kew. Then there is a description of the wedding
breakfast at the house of the bride's noble parents, and of the cake, decorated by Messrs. Gunter with the most delicious taste and the sweetest
hymeneal allusions.

No mention was made by the fashionable chronicler, of a slight disturbance which occurred at St. George's, and which indeed was out of the
province of such a genteel purveyor of news. Before the marriage service
began, a woman of vulgar appearance, and disorderly aspect, accompanied by two scared children who took no part in the disorder occasioned
by their mother's proceeding,[2] except by their tears and outcries to augment the disquiet, made her appearance in one of the pews of the church,
was noted there by persons in the vestry, was requested to retire by a beadle, and was finally induced to quit the sacred precincts of the building by
the very strongest persuasion of a couple of policemen; X and Y laughed at
one another, and nodded their heads knowingly as the poor wretch with
her whimpering boys was led away. They understood very well who the
personage was who had come to disturb the matrimonial ceremony; it did
not commence until Mrs. De Lacy (as this lady chose to be called), had quitted this temple of Hymen. She slunk through the throng of emblazoned
carriages, and the press of footmen arrayed as splendidly as Solomon in
his glory. John jeered at Thomas, William turned his powdered head,
and signalled Jeames, who answered with a corresponding grin, as the
woman with sobs, and wild imprecations, and frantic appeals, made her
way through the splendid crowd, escorted by her aides-de-camp in blue. I
dare say her little history was discussed at many a dinner-table that day in
the basement story of several fashionable houses. I know that at clubs in St.
James's, the facetious little anecdote was narrated. A young fellow came to
Bays's after the marriage breakfast and mentioned the circumstance with
funny comments; although the *Morning Post,* in describing this affair in
high life, naturally omitted all mention of such low people as Mrs. De Lacy
and her children.

Those people who knew the noble families whose union had been celebrated by such a profusion of grandees, fine equipages, and footmen, brass
bands, brilliant toilets, and wedding favours, asked how it was that Lord
Kew did not assist at Barnes Newcome's marriage: other persons in society inquired waggishly why Jack Belsize was not present to give Lady Clara
away.

---

[1] Right Honourable *E1*] Right Honourable and Right Reverend *R*
[2] proceeding, *E1*] proceedings, *R*

As for Jack Belsize, his clubs had not been ornamented by his presence for a year past. It was said he had broken the bank at Hombourg last autumn; had been heard of during the winter at Milan, Venice, and Vienna; and when a few months after the marriage of Barnes Newcome and Lady Clara, Jack's elder brother died, and he himself became the next in succession to the title and estates of Highgate, many folks said it was a pity little Barney's marriage had taken place so soon. Lord Kew was not present, because Kew was still abroad; he had had a gambling duel with a Frenchman, and a narrow squeak for his life. He had turned Roman Catholic, some men said; others vowed that he had joined the Methodist persuasion. At all events Kew had given up his wild courses, broken with the turf, and sold his stud off; he was delicate yet, and his mother was taking care of him; between whom and the old dowager of Kew, who had made up Barney's marriage, as everybody knew, there was no love lost.

Then who was the Prince de Montcontour, who, with his princess, figured at this noble marriage? There was a Montcontour, the Duc d'Ivry's son, but he died at Paris before the revolution of '30: one or two of the oldsters at Bays's, Major Pendennis, General Tufto, old Cackleby—the old fogies in a word—remembered the Duke of Ivry when he was here during the Emigration, and when he was called Prince de Montcontour, the title of the eldest son of the family. Ivry was dead, having buried his son before him, and having left only a daughter by that young woman whom he married, and who led him such a life. Who was this present Montcontour?

He was a gentleman to whom the reader has already been presented, though when we lately saw him at Baden, he did not enjoy so magnificent a title. Early in the year of Barnes Newcome's marriage, there came to England, and to our modest apartment in the Temple, a gentleman bringing a letter of recommendation from our dear young Clive, who said that the bearer, the Vicomte de Florac, was a great friend of his, and of the Colonel's, who had known his family from boyhood. A friend of our Clive and our Colonel was sure of a welcome in Lamb Court; we gave him the hand of hospitality, the best cigar in the box, the easy chair with only one broken leg; the dinner in chambers and at the club, the banquet at Greenwich (where, ma foi, the little *whites baits* elicited his profound satisfaction); in a word, did our best to honour that bill which our young Clive had drawn upon us. We considered the young one in the light of a nephew of our own; we took a pride in him, and were fond of him; and as for the Colonel, did we not love and honour him; would we not do our utmost in behalf of any stranger who came recommended to us by Thomas Newcome's good word? So Florac was straightway admitted to our companionship. We showed him the town, and some of the modest pleasures thereof; we introduced him to the Haunt, and astonished him by the company which he met there. Between Brent's "Deserter," and Mark Wilder's "Garryowen," Florac sang—

> Tiens voici ma pipe, voila mon bri—quet;
> Et quand la Tulipe fait le noir tra—jet
> Que tu sois la seule dans le régi—ment
> Avec la brûle-gueule, de ton cher z'a—mant;

to the delight of Tom Sarjent, who, though he only partially comprehended the words of the song, pronounced the singer to be a rare gentleman, full of most excellent differences. We took our Florac to the Derby; we presented him in Fitzroy Square, whither we still occasionally went, for Clive's and our dear Colonel's sake.

The Vicomte pronounced himself strongly in favour of the blanche misse, little Rosy Mackenzie, of whom we have lost sight for some few chapters. Mrs. Mack he considered, my faith, to be a woman superb. He used to kiss the tips of his own fingers, in token of his admiration for the lovely widow; he pronounced her again more pretty than her daughter; and paid her a thousand compliments which she received with exceeding good humour. If the Vicomte gave us to understand presently, that Rosy and her mother were both in love with him, but that for all the world he would not meddle with the happiness of his dear little Clive, nothing unfavourable to the character or constancy of the before-mentioned ladies must be inferred from M. de Florac's speech; his firm conviction being, that no woman could pass many hours in his society without danger to her subsequent peace of mind.

For some little time we had no reason to suspect that our French friend was not particularly well furnished with the current coin of the realm. Without making any show of wealth, he would, at first, cheerfully engage in our little parties: his lodgings in the neighbourhood of Leicester Square, though dingy, were such as many noble foreign exiles have inhabited. It was not until he refused to join some pleasure trip which we of Lamb Court proposed, honestly confessing his poverty, that we were made aware of the Vicomte's little temporary calamity; and, as we became more intimate with him, he acquainted us, with great openness, with the history of all his fortunes. He described energetically, that splendid run of luck which had set in at Baden with Clive's loan: his winnings, at that fortunate period, had carried him through the winter with considerable brilliancy, but Bouillotte and Mademoiselle Atala, of the Variétés, (*une ogresse, mon cher!* who devours thirty of our young men every year in her cavern, in the Rue de Bréda), had declared against him, and the poor Vicomte's pockets were almost empty when he came to London.

He was amiably communicative regarding himself, and told us his virtues and his faults, (if indeed a passion for play and for women could be considered as faults in a gay young fellow of two or three-and-forty), with a like engaging frankness. He would weep in describing his angel mother: he would fly off again into tirades respecting the wickedness, the wit, the extravagance, the charms of the young lady of the Variétés. He would then (in conversation) introduce us to Madame de Florac, née Higg, of Manchesterre. His prattle was incessant, and to my friend Mr. Warrington especially, he was an object of endless delight and amusement and wonder. He would roll and smoke countless paper cigars, talking unrestrainedly when we were not busy, silent when we were engaged: he would only rarely partake of our meals, and altogether refused all offers of pecuniary aid. He disappeared at dinner-time into the mysterious purlieus of Leicester Square, and dark ordinaries only frequented by Frenchmen. As we walked with him in the Regent Street precincts, he would exchange marks of recognition with many dusky personages, smoking bravos, and whiskered refugees of his nation. "That gentleman," he would say, "who has done me the honour to salute me, is a coiffeur of the most celebrated; he forms the *délices* of our table d'hôte. 'Bon jour, mon cher Monsieur!' We are friends, though not of the same opinion. Monsieur is a republican of the most distinguished; conspirator of profession, and at this time engaged in constructing an infernal machine to the address of His Majesty, Louis Philippe, King of the French." "Who is my friend with the scarlet beard and the white paletôt?" "My good Warrington! you do not move in the world: you make yourself a hermit, my dear! Not know Monsieur!— Monsieur is secretary to Mademoiselle Caracoline, the lovely rider at the circus of Astley; I shall be charmed to introduce you to this amiable society some day at our table d'hôte."

Warrington vowed that the company of Florac's friends would be infinitely more amusing than the noblest society ever chronicled in the *Morning Post;* but we were neither sufficiently familiar with the French language to make conversation in that tongue as pleasant to us as talking in our own; and so were content with Florac's description of his compatriots, which the Vicomte delivered in that charming French-English of which he was a master.

However threadbare in his garments, poor in purse, and eccentric in morals our friend was, his manners were always perfectly gentlemanlike, and he draped himself in his poverty with the grace of a Spanish grandee. It must be confessed, that the grandee loved the estaminet where he could play billiards with the first comer; that he had a passion for the gambling house; that he was a loose and disorderly nobleman: but, in whatever company he found himself, a certain kindness, simplicity, and politeness distinguished him always. He bowed to the damsel who sold him a penny cigar, as graciously as to a duchess; he crushed a *manant's* impertinence or familiarity, as haughtily as his noble ancestors ever did at the Louvre, at Marli, or Versailles. He declined to *obtempérer* to his landlady's request to pay his rent; but he refused with a dignity which struck the woman with awe: and King Alfred, over the celebrated muffin, (on which Gandish and other painters have exercised their genius,) could not have looked more noble than Florac in a robe-de-chambre, once gorgeous, but shady now as became its owner's clouded fortunes; toasting his bit of bacon at his lodgings, when the fare even of his table d'hôte had grown too dear for him.

As we know from Gandish's work, that better times were in store for the wandering monarch, and that the officers came acquainting him that his people demanded his presence, *à grands cris*, when of course King Alfred laid down the toast[3] and resumed the sceptre; so in the case of Florac, two humble gentlemen, inhabitants of Lamb Court, and members of the Upper Temple, had the good luck to be the heralds as it were, nay indeed the occasion of the rising fortunes of the Prince de Montcontour. Florac had informed us of the death of his cousin the Duc d'Ivry, by whose demise the Vicomte's father, the old Count de Florac, became the representative of the house of Ivry, and possessor, through his relative's bequest, of an

[3] toast *E1*] toasting fork *R*

old chateau still more gloomy and spacious than the Count's own house in the Faubourg St. Germain—a chateau, of which the woods, domains, and appurtenances, had been lopped off by the Revolution. "Monsieur le Comte," Florac says, "has not wished to change his name at his age; he has shrugged his old shoulder, and said it was not the trouble to make to engrave a new card; and for me," the philosophical Vicomte added, "of what good shall be a title of prince in the position where I find myself?" It is wonderful for us who inhabit a country where rank is worshipped with so admirable a reverence, to think that there are many gentlemen in France who actually have authentic titles and do not choose to bear them.

Mr. George Warrington was hugely amused with this notion of Florac's ranks and dignities. The idea of the Prince purchasing penny cigars; of the Prince mildly expostulating with his landlady regarding the rent; of his punting for half-crowns at a neighbouring hall[4] in Air Street, whither the poor gentleman desperately ran when he had money in his pocket, tickled George's sense of humour. It was Warrington who gravely saluted the Vicomte, and compared him to King Alfred, on that afternoon when we happened to call upon him and found him engaged in cooking his modest dinner.

We were bent upon an excursion to Greenwich, and on having our friend's company on that voyage, and we induced the Vicomte to forego his bacon, and be our guest for once. George Warrington chose to indulge in a great deal of ironical pleasantry in the course of the afternoon's excursion. As we went down the river, he pointed out to Florac the very window in the Tower where the captive Duke of Orleans used to sit when he was an inhabitant of that fortress. At Greenwich, which palace Florac informed us was built by Queen Elizabeth, George showed the very spot where Raleigh laid his cloak down to enable her Majesty to step over a puddle. In a word he mystified M. de Florac: such was Mr. Warrington's reprehensible spirit.

It happened that Mr. Barnes Newcome came to dine at Greenwich on the same day when our little party took place. He had come down to meet Rooster and one or two other noble friends whose names he took care to give us, cursing them at the same time for having thrown him over. Having missed his own company, Mr. Barnes condescended to join ours, Warrington gravely thanking him for the great honour which he conferred upon us by volunteering to take a place at our table. Barnes drank freely and was good enough to resume his acquaintance with Monsieur de Florac whom he perfectly well recollected at Baden, but had thought proper to forget on the one or two occasions when they had met in public since the Vicomte's arrival in this country. There are few men who can drop and resume an acquaintance with such admirable self-possession as Barnes Newcome. When, over our dessert, by which time all tongues were unloosed and each man talked gaily, George Warrington feelingly thanked Barnes, in a little mock speech, for his great kindness in noticing us, presenting him at the same time to Florac as the ornament of the city, the greatest banker of his age, the beloved kinsman of their friend Clive who was always writing about him; Barnes said, with one of his accustomed curses,

[4] hall *E1*] hell *R*

he did not know whether Mr. Warrington was "chaffing" him or not, and indeed could never make him out. Warrington replied that he never could make himself out: and if ever Mr. Barnes could, George would thank him for information on that subject.

Florac, like most Frenchmen, very sober in his potations, left us for a while over ours, which were conducted after the more liberal English manner, and retired to smoke his cigar on the terrace. Barnes then freely uttered his sentiments regarding him, which were not more favourable than those which the young gentleman generally emitted respecting gentlemen whose backs were turned. He had known a little of Florac the year before, at Baden: he had been mixed up with Kew in that confounded row in which Kew was hit: he was an adventurer, a pauper, a blackleg, a regular Greek; he had heard Florac was of old family, that was true: but what of that? He was only one of those d—— French counts; every body was a count in France, confound 'em! The claret was beastly—not fit for a gentleman to drink!—He swigged off a great bumper as he was making the remark: for Barnes Newcome abuses the men and things which he uses, and perhaps is better served than more grateful persons.

"Count!" cries Warrington, "what do you mean by talking about beggarly counts? Florac's family is one of the noblest and most ancient in Europe. It is more ancient than your illustrious friend, the barber-surgeon; it was illustrious before the house, aye, or the pagoda of Kew was in existence." And he went on to describe how Florac, by the demise of his kinsman, was now actually Prince de Montcontour, though he did not choose to assume that title. Very likely the noble Gascon drink in which George had been indulging, imparted a certain warmth and eloquence to his descriptions of Florac's good qualities, high birth, and considerable patrimony; Barnes looked quite amazed and scared at these announcements, then laughed and declared once more that Warrington was chaffing him.

"As sure as the Black Prince was lord of Acquitaine—as sure as the English were masters of Bordeaux—and why did we ever lose the country?" cries George, filling himself a bumper, "every word I have said about Florac is true;" and Florac coming in at this juncture, having just finished his cigar, George turned round and made him a fine speech in the French language, in which he lauded his constancy and good humour under evil fortune, paid him two or three more cordial compliments, and finished by drinking another great bumper to his good health.

Florac took a little wine, replied "with effusion" to the toast which his excellent, his noble friend had just carried. We rapped our glasses at the end of the speech. The landlord himself seemed deeply touched by it as he stood by with a fresh bottle. "It is good wine—it is honest wine—it is capital wine," says George, "and honni soit qui mal y pense! What business have you, you little beggar, to abuse it? my ancestor drank the wine and wore the motto round his leg long before a Newcome ever showed his pale face in Lombard Street." George Warrington never bragged about his pedigree except under certain influences. I am inclined to think that on this occasion he really did find the claret very good.

"You don't mean to say," says Barnes, addressing Florac in French, on which he piqued himself, "que vous avez un tel manche à votre nom, et que vous ne l'usez pas?"

Florac shrugged his shoulders; he at first did not understand that familiar figure of English speech, or what was meant by 'having a handle to your name.' "Montcontour cannot dine better than Florac," he said. "Florac has two louis in his pocket, and Montcontour exactly forty shillings. Florac's proprietor will ask Montcontour to-morrow for five weeks' rent; and as for Florac's friends, my dear, they will burst out laughing to Montcontour's nose!" "How droll you English are!" this acute French observer afterwards said, laughing, and recalling the incident. "Did you not see how that little Barnes, as soon as he knew my title of Prince, changed his manner and became all respect towards me?" This, indeed, Monsieur de Florac's two friends remarked with no little amusement. Barnes began quite well to remember their pleasant days at Baden, and talked of their acquaintance there: Barnes offered the Prince the vacant seat in his brougham, and was ready to set him down anywhere that he wished in town.

"Bah!" says Florac; "we came by the steamer, and I prefer the *péniboat*." But the hospitable Barnes, nevertheless, called upon Florac the next day. And now having partially explained how the Prince de Montcontour was present at Mr. Barnes Newcome's wedding, let us show how it was that Barnes's first cousin, the Earl of Kew, did not attend that ceremony.

Chapter XXXVII.

E do not propose to describe at length or with precision the circumstances of the duel which ended so unfortunately for young Lord Kew. The meeting was inevitable: after the public acts and insult of the morning, the maddened Frenchman went to it convinced that his antagonist had wilfully outraged him, eager to show his bravery upon the body of an Englishman, and as proud as if he had been going into actual war. That commandment, the sixth in our decalogue, which forbids the doing of murder, and the injunction which directly follows on the same table, have been repealed by a very great number of Frenchmen for many years past; and to take the neighbour's wife, and his life subsequently, has not been an uncommon practice with the politest people in the world. Castillonnes had no idea but that he was going to the field of honour; stood with an undaunted scowl before his enemy's pistol; and discharged his own, and brought down his opponent with a grim satisfaction, and a comfortable conviction afterwards that he had acted *en galant homme.* "It was well for this Milor that he fell at the first shot, my dear," the exemplary young Frenchman remarked, "a second might have been yet more fatal to him; ordinarily I am sure of my *coup*, and you conceive that in an affair so grave it was absolutely necessary that one or other should remain on the ground." Nay, should M. de Kew recover from his wound, it was M. de Castillonnes' intention to propose a second encounter between himself and that nobleman. It had been Lord Kew's determination never to fire upon his opponent, a confession which he made not to his second, poor scared Lord Rooster, who bore the young Earl to Kehl; but to some of his nearest relatives, who happened fortunately to be not far from him when he received his wound, and who came with all the eagerness of love to watch by his bed-side.

We have said that Lord Kew's mother, Lady Walham, and her second son were staying at Hombourg, when the Earl's disaster occurred. They had proposed to come to Baden to see Kew's new bride, and to welcome her; but the presence of her mother-in-law deterred Lady Walham, who gave up her heart's wish in bitterness of spirit, knowing very well that a meeting between the old Countess and herself could only produce the wrath, pain, and humiliation which their coming together always occasioned. It was Lord Kew who bade Rooster send for his mother, and not for Lady Kew; and as soon as she received those sad tidings, you may be sure the poor lady hastened to the bed where her wounded boy lay.

The fever had declared itself, and the young man had been delirious more than once. His wan face lighted up with joy when he saw his mother; he put his little feverish hand out of the bed to her; "I knew you would come, dear," he said, "and you know I never would have fired upon the poor Frenchman." The fond mother allowed no sign of terror or grief to appear upon her face, so as to disturb her first-born and darling; but no doubt she prayed by his side as such loving hearts know how to pray, for the forgiveness of his trespass, who had forgiven those who sinned against him. "I knew I should be hit, George," said Kew to his brother when they were alone; "I always expected some such end as this. My life has been very wild and reckless; and you, George, have always been faithful to our mother. You will make a better Lord Kew than I have been, George. God bless you." George flung himself down with sobs by his brother's bed-side, and swore Frank had always been the best fellow, the best brother, the kindest heart, the warmest friend in the world. Love—prayer—repentance, thus met over the young man's bed. Anxious and humble hearts, his own the least anxious and the most humble, awaited the dread award of life or death; and the world, and its ambition and vanities, were shut out from the darkened chamber where the awful issue was being tried.

Our history has had little to do with characters resembling this lady. It is of the world, and things pertaining to it. Things beyond it, as the writer imagines, scarcely belong to the novelist's province. Who is he, that he should assume the divine's office; or turn his desk into a preacher's pulpit? In that career of pleasure, of idleness, of crime we might call it (but that the chronicler of worldly matters had best be chary of applying hard names to acts which young men are doing in the world every day), the gentle widowed lady, mother of Lord Kew, could but keep aloof, deploring the course upon which her dear young prodigal had entered; and praying with that saintly love, those pure supplications, with which good mothers follow their children, for her boy's repentance and return. Very likely her mind was narrow; very likely the precautions which she had used in the lad's early days, the tutors and directors she had set about him, the religious studies and practices to which she would have subjected him, had served only to vex and weary the young pupil, and to drive his high spirit into revolt. It is hard to convince a woman perfectly pure in her life and intentions, ready to die if need were for her own faith, having absolute confidence in the instruction of her teachers, that she and they (with all their sermons) may be doing harm. When the young catechist yawns over his reverence's discourse, who knows but it is the doctor's vanity which is enraged, and not Heaven which is offended? It may have been, in the differences which took place between her son and her, the good Lady Walham never could comprehend the lad's side of the argument; or how his protestantism against her doctrines should exhibit itself on the turf, the gaming-table, or the stage of the opera-house; and thus but for the misfortune under which poor Kew now lay bleeding, these two loving hearts might have remained through life asunder. But by the boy's bedside;—in the paroxysms of his fever; in the wild talk of his delirium; in the sweet patience and kindness with which he received his dear nurse's attentions; the gratefulness with which he thanked the servants who waited on him; the fortitude with which he suffered the surgeon's dealings with his wound;—the widowed woman had an opportunity to admire with an exquisite thankfulness the generous goodness of her son; and in those hours, those sacred hours passed in her own chamber, of prayers, fears, hopes, recollections, and passionate maternal love, wrestling with fate for her darling's life;—no doubt the humbled creature came to acknowledge that her own course regarding him had been wrong; and, even more for herself than for him, implored forgiveness.

For some time George Barnes had to send but doubtful and melancholy bulletins to Lady Kew and the Newcome family at Baden, who were all greatly moved and affected by the accident which had befallen poor Kew. Lady Kew broke out in wrath and indignation. We may be sure the Duchesse d'Ivry offered to condole with her upon Kew's mishap the day after the news arrived at Baden; and, indeed, came to visit her. The old lady had just received other disquieting intelligence. She was just going out, but she bade her servant to inform the Duchess that she was never more at home to the Duchesse d'Ivry. The message was not delivered properly, or the person for whom it was intended did not choose to understand it, for presently as the Countess was hobbling across the walk on her way to her daughter's residence, she met the Duchesse d'Ivry, who saluted her with a demure curtsey and a commonplace expression of condolence. The Queen of Scots was surrounded by the chief part of her court, saving of course M.M. Castillonnes and Punter absent on service. "We were speaking of this deplorable affair," said Madame d'Ivry (which indeed was the truth, although she said it). "How we pity you, Madame!" Blackball and Loder, Cruchecassée and Schlangenbad, assumed sympathetic countenances.

Trembling on her cane, the old Countess glared out upon Madame d'Ivry, "I pray you, Madame," she said in French, "never again to address me the word. If I had, like you, assassins in my pay, I would have you killed; do you hear me?" and she hobbled on her way. The household to which she went was in terrible agitation; the kind Lady Ann frightened beyond measure, poor Ethel full of dread, and feeling guilty almost as if she had been the cause, as indeed she was the occasion, of Kew's misfortune. And the family had further cause of alarm from the shock which the news had given to Sir Brian. It has been said, that he had had illnesses of late which caused his friends much anxiety. He had passed two months at Aix-la-Chapelle, his physicians dreading a paralytic attack; and Madame d'Ivry's party still sauntering on the walk, the men smoking their cigars, the women breathing their scandal, now beheld Doctor Finck issuing from Lady Ann's apartments, and wearing such a face of anxiety, that the Duchesse asked, with some emotion, "Had there been a fresh bulletin from Kehl?"

FRENCH CONDOLENCE

"No, there had been no fresh bulletin from Kehl; but two hours since Sir Brian Newcome had had a paralytic seizure."

"Is he very bad?"

"No," says Dr. Finck, "he is not very bad."

"How inconsolable M. Barnes will be!" said the Duchesse, shrugging her haggard shoulders. Whereas the fact was that Mr. Barnes retained perfect presence of mind under both of the misfortunes which had befallen his family. Two days afterwards the Duchesse's husband arrived himself, when we may presume that exemplary woman was too much engaged with her own affairs, to be able to be interested about the doings of other people. With the Duke's arrival the court of Mary Queen of Scots was broken up. Her majesty was conducted to Loch Leven, where her tyrant soon dismissed her very last lady-in-waiting, the confidential Irish secretary, whose performance had produced such a fine effect amongst the Newcomes.

Had poor Sir Brian Newcome's seizure occurred at an earlier period of the autumn, his illness no doubt would have kept him for some months confined at Baden; but as he was pretty nearly the last of Dr. Von Finck's bath patients, and that eminent physician longed to be off to the Residenz, he was pronounced in a fit condition for easy travelling in rather a brief period after his attack, and it was determined to transport him to Manheim, and thence by water to London and Newcome.

During all this period of their father's misfortune no sister of charity could have been more tender, active, cheerful, and watchful, than Miss Ethel. She had to wear a kind face and exhibit no anxiety when occasionally the feeble invalid made inquiries regarding poor Kew at Baden; to catch the phrases as they came from him; to acquiesce, or not to deny, when Sir Brian talked of the marriages—both marriages—taking place at Christmas. Sir Brian was especially eager for his daughter's, and repeatedly, with his broken words, and smiles, and caresses, which were now quite senile, declared that his Ethel would make the prettiest countess in England. There came a letter or two from Clive, no doubt, to the young nurse in her sick-room. Manly and generous, full of tenderness and affection, as those letters surely were, they could give but little pleasure to the young lady, indeed, only add to her doubts and pain.

She had told none of her friends as yet of those last words of Kew's, which she interpreted as a farewell on the young nobleman's part. Had she told them they very likely would not have understood Kew's meaning as she did, and persisted in thinking that the two were reconciled. At any rate, whilst he and her father were still lying stricken by the blows which had prostrated them both, all questions of love and marriage had been put aside. Did she love him? She felt such a kind pity for his misfortune, such an admiration for his generous gallantry, such a remorse for her own wayward conduct and cruel behaviour towards this most honest, and kindly, and affectionate gentleman, that the sum of regard which she could bestow upon him might surely be said to amount to love. For such a union as that contemplated between them, perhaps for any marriage, no greater degree of attachment was necessary as the common cement. Warm friendship and thorough esteem and confidence (I do not say that our young lady calculated in this matter-of-fact way) are safe properties invested in the prudent marriage stock, multiplying and bearing an increasing value with every year. Many a young couple of spendthrifts get through their capital of passion in the first twelvemonths, and have no love left for the daily demands of after life. O me! for the day when the bank account is closed, and the cupboard is empty, and the firm of Damon and Phyllis insolvent!

Miss Newcome, we say, without doubt, did not make her calculations in this debtor and creditor fashion; it was only the gentlemen of that family who went to Lombard Street. But suppose she thought that regard, and esteem, and affection, being sufficient, she could joyfully and with almost all her heart bring such a portion to Lord Kew; that her harshness towards him as contrasted with his own generosity, and above all with his present pain, infinitely touched her; and suppose she fancied that there was another person in the world to whom, did fates permit, she could offer not esteem, affection, pity only, but something ten thousand times more precious? We are not in the young lady's secrets, but if she has some as she sits by her father's chair and bed, who day or night will have no other attendant; and, as she busies herself to interpret his wants, silently moves on his errands, administers his potions, and watches his sleep, thinks of Clive absent and unhappy, of Kew wounded and in danger, she must have subject enough of thought and pain. Little wonder that her cheeks are pale and her eyes look red; she has her cares to endure now in the world, and her burden to bear in it, and somehow she feels she is alone, since that day when poor Clive's carriage drove away.

In a mood of more than ordinary depression and weakness Lady Kew must have found her granddaughter upon one of the few occasions after the double mishap when Ethel and her elder were together. Sir Brian's illness, as it may be imagined, affected a lady very slightly, who was of an age when these calamities occasion but small disquiet, and who having survived her own father, her husband, her son, and witnessed their lordships' respective demises with perfect composure, could not reasonably be called upon to feel any particular dismay at the probable departure from this life of a Lombard Street banker, who happened to be her daughter's husband. In fact not Barnes Newcome himself could await that event more philosophically. So finding Ethel in this melancholy mood, Lady Kew thought a drive in the fresh air would be of service to her, and Sir Brian happening to be asleep, carried the young girl away in her barouche.

They talked about Lord Kew, of whom the accounts were encouraging, and who is mending in spite of his silly mother and her medicines, and as soon as he is able to move we must go and fetch him, my dear, Lady Kew graciously said, before that foolish woman has made a methodist of him. He is always led by the woman who is nearest him, and I know one who will make of him just the best little husband in England. Before they had come to this delicate point the lady and her grandchild had talked Kew's character over, the girl, you may be sure, having spoken feelingly and eloquently about his kindness and courage, and many admirable qualities. She kindled when she heard the report of his behaviour at the commencement of the fracas with M. de Castillonnes, his great forbearance and good-nature, and his resolution and magnanimity, when the moment of collision came.

But when Lady Kew arrived at that period of her discourse, in which she stated that Kew would make the best little husband in England, poor Ethel's eyes filled with tears; we must remember that her high spirit was worn down by watching and much varied anxiety, and then she confessed that there had been no reconciliation, as all the family fancied, between Frank and herself—on the contrary, a parting, which she understood to be final; and she owned that her conduct towards her cousin had been most captious and cruel, and that she could not expect they should ever again come together. Lady Kew, who hated sick-beds and surgeons, except for herself, who hated her daughter-in-law above all, was greatly annoyed at the news which Ethel gave her; made light of it, however, and was quite confident that a very few words from her would place matters on their old footing, and determined on forthwith setting out for Kehl. She would have carried Ethel with her, but that the poor Baronet with cries and moans insisted on retaining his nurse, and Ethel's grandmother was left to undertake this mission by herself, the girl remaining behind acquiescent, not unwilling, owning openly a great regard and esteem for Kew, and the wrong which she had done him, feeling secretly a sentiment which she had best smother. She had received a letter from that other person, and answered it with her mother's cognisance, but about this little affair neither Lady Ann nor her daughter happened to say a word to the manager of the whole family.

Chapter XXXVIII.

MMEDIATELY after Lord Kew's wound, and as it was necessary to apprise the Newcome family of the accident which had occurred, the good-natured young Kew had himself written a brief note to acquaint his relatives with his mishap, and had even taken the precaution to antedate a couple of billets to be dispatched on future days; kindly forgeries, which told the Newcome family and the Countess of Kew, that Lord Kew was progressing very favourably, and that his hurt was trifling. The fever had set in, and the young patient was lying in great danger, as most of the laggards at Baden knew, when his friends there were set at ease by this fallacious bulletin. On the third day after the accident, Lady Walham arrived with her younger son, to find Lord Kew in the fever which ensued after the wound. As the terrible anxiety during the illness had been Lady Walham's, so was hers the delight of the recovery. The commander-in-chief of the family, the old lady at Baden, showed her sympathy by sending couriers, and repeatedly issuing orders to have news of Kew. Sick-beds scared her away invariably. When illness befel a member of her family she hastily retreated from before the sufferer, showing her agitation of mind, however, by excessive ill-humour to all the others within her reach.

A fortnight passed, a ball had been found and extracted, the fever was over, the wound was progressing favourably, the patient advancing towards convalescence, and the mother, with her child once more under her wing, happier than she had been for seven years past, during which her young prodigal had been running the thoughtless career of which he himself was weary, and which had occasioned the fond lady such anguish. Those doubts which perplex many a thinking man, and when formed and uttered, give many a fond and faithful woman pain so exquisite, had most fortunately never crossed Kew's mind. His early impressions were such as his mother had left them, and he came back to her as she would have him, as a little child, owning his faults with a hearty humble repentance, and with a thousand simple confessions lamenting the errors of his past days. We have seen him tired and ashamed of the pleasures which he was pursuing, of the companions who surrounded him, of the brawls and dissipations which amused him no more; in those hours of danger and doubt, when he had lain, with death perhaps before him, making up his account of the vain life which probably he would be called upon to surrender, no wonder this simple, kindly, modest, and courageous soul, thought seriously of the past, and of the future; and prayed, and resolved, if a future were awarded to him, it should make amends for the days gone by; and surely as the mother and son read together the beloved assurance of the divine forgiveness, and of that joy which angels feel in Heaven for a sinner repentant, we may fancy in the happy mother's breast a feeling somewhat akin to that angelic felicity, a gratitude and joy of all others the loftiest, the purest, the keenest. Lady Walham might shrink with terror at the Frenchman's name, but her son could forgive him, with all his heart, and kiss his mother's hand, and thank him as the best friend of his life.

During all the days of his illness, Kew had never once mentioned Ethel's name, and once or twice as his recovery progressed, when with doubt and tremor his mother alluded to it, he turned from the subject as one that was disagreeable and painful. Had she thought seriously on certain things? Lady Walham asked. Kew thought not, "but those who are bred up as you would have them, Mother, are often none the better," the humble young fellow said. "I believe she is a very good girl. She is very clever, she is exceedingly handsome, she is very good to her parents and her brothers and sisters; but—" he did not finish the sentence. Perhaps he thought, as he told Ethel afterwards, that she would have agreed with Lady Walham even worse than with her imperious old grandmother.

Lady Walham then fell to deplore Sir Brian's condition, accounts of whose seizure of course had been despatched to the Kehl party, and to lament that a worldly man as he was should have such an affliction, so near the grave and so little prepared for it. Here honest Kew, however, held out. "Every man for himself, Mother," says he. "Sir Brian was bred up very strictly, perhaps too strictly as a young man. Don't you know that that good Colonel, his elder brother, who seems to me about the most honest and good old gentleman I ever met in my life, was driven into rebellion and all sorts of wild courses by old Mrs. Newcome's tyranny over him? As for Sir Brian, he goes to church every Sunday: has prayers in the family every day: I'm sure has led a hundred times better life than I have, poor old Sir Brian. I often have thought, Mother, that though our side was wrong, yours could not be altogether right, because I remember how my tutor, and Mr. Bonner and Dr. Laud, when they used to come down to us at Kewbury, used to make themselves so unhappy about other people." So the widow withdrew her unhappiness about Sir Brian; she was quite glad to hope for the best regarding that invalid.

With some fears yet regarding her son,—for many of the books with which the good lady travelled could not be got to interest him; at some he would laugh outright,—with fear mixed with the maternal joy that he was returned to her, and had quitted his old ways; with keen feminine triumph, perhaps, that she had won him back, and happiness at his daily mending health, all Lady Walham's hours were passed in thankful and delighted occupation. George Barnes kept the Newcomes acquainted with the state of his brother's health. The skilful surgeon from Strasbourg reported daily better and better of him, and the little family were living in great peace and contentment, with one subject of dread, however, hanging over the mother of the two young men, the arrival of Lady Kew, as she was foreboding,[1] the fierce old mother-in-law who had worsted Lady Walham in many a previous battle.

It was what they call the summer of St. Martin, and the weather was luckily very fine; Kew could presently be wheeled into the garden of the hotel, whence he could see the broad turbid current of the swollen Rhine: the French bank fringed with alders, the vast yellow fields behind them, the great avenue of poplars stretching away to the Alsatian city, and its purple minster yonder. Good Lady Walham was for improving the shining hour by reading amusing extracts from her favourite volumes, gentle anecdotes of Chinese and Hottentot converts, and incidents from missionary travel. George Barnes, a wily young diplomatist, insinuated "Galignani," and hinted that Kew might like a novel; and a profane work called "Oliver Twist" having appeared about this time, which George read out to his family with admirable emphasis, it is a fact that Lady Walham became so interested in the parish boy's progress, that she took his history into her bed-room (where it was discovered, under Blatherwick's "Voice from Mesopotamia," by her ladyship's maid), and that Kew laughed so immensely at Mr. Bumble, the Beadle, as to endanger the reopening of his wound.

While, one day, they were so harmlessly and pleasantly occupied, a great whacking of whips, blowing of horns, and whirring of wheels was heard in the street without. The wheels stopped at their hotel gate; Lady Walham started up; ran through the garden door, closing it behind her; and divined justly who had arrived. The landlord was bowing; the courier pushing about; waiters in attendance; one of them, coming up to pale-faced Lady Walham, said, "Her Excellency the Frau Gräfinn von Kew is even now absteiging."

"Will you be good enough to walk into our salon, Lady Kew?" said the daughter-in-law, stepping forward and opening the door of that apartment. The Countess, leaning on her staff, entered that darkened chamber. She ran up towards an easy-chair, where she supposed Lord Kew was. "My dear Frank!" cries the old lady; "my dear boy, what a pretty fright you have given us all! They don't keep you in this horrid noisy room facing the — Ho—what is this?" cries the Countess, closing her sentence abruptly.

"It is not Frank. It is only a bolster, Lady Kew: and I don't keep him in a noisy room towards the street," said Lady Walham.

"Ho! how do you do? This is the way to him, I suppose;" and she went to another door—it was a cupboard full of the relics of Frank's illness, from which Lady Walham's mother-in-law shrunk back aghast. "Will you please to see that I have a comfortable room, Maria; and one for my maid, next me? I will thank you to see yourself," the Empress of Kew said, pointing with her stick, before which many a time the younger lady had trembled.

---

[1] as she was foreboding *E1*] [omitted] *R*

This time Lady Walham only rang the bell. "I don't speak German; and have never been on any floor of the house but this. Your servant had better see to your room, Lady Kew. That next is mine; and I keep the door, which you are trying, locked on the other side."

"And I suppose Frank is locked up there!" cried the old lady, "with a basin of gruel and a book of Watts's hymns." A servant entered at this moment, answering Lady Walham's summons. "Peacock, the Countess of Kew says that she proposes to stay here this evening. Please to ask the landlord to show her ladyship rooms," said Lady Walham; and by this time she had thought of a reply to Lady Kew's last kind speech.

"If my son were locked up in my room, Madam, his mother is surely the best nurse for him. Why did you not come to him three weeks sooner, when there was nobody with him?"

Lady Kew said nothing, but glared and showed her teeth—those pearls set in gold.

"And my company may not amuse Lord Kew—"

"He—e—e!" grinned the elder, savagely.

"But at least it is better than some to which you introduced my son," continued Lady Kew's daughter-in-law, gathering force and wrath as she spoke. "Your ladyship may think lightly of me, but you can hardly think so ill of me as of the Duchesse d'Ivry, I should suppose, to whom you sent my boy, to form him, you said; about whom, when I remonstrated—for though I live out of the world I hear of it sometimes—you were pleased to tell me that I was a prude and a fool. It is you I thank for separating my child from me—yes, you—for so many years of my life; and for bringing me to him when he was bleeding and almost a corpse, but that God preserved him to the widow's prayers;—and you, you were by, and never came near him."

"I—I did not come to see you—or—or—for this kind of scene, Lady Walham," muttered the other. Lady Kew was accustomed to triumph, by attacking in masses, like Napoleon. Those who faced her routed her.

"No; you did not come for me, I know very well," the daughter went on. "You loved me no better than you loved your son, whose life, as long as you meddled with it, you made wretched. You came here for my boy. Haven't you done him evil enough? And now God has mercifully preserved him, you want to lead him back again into ruin and crime. It shall not be so, wicked woman! bad mother! cruel, heartless parent!—George!" (Here her younger son entered the room, and she ran towards him with fluttering robes and seized his hands.) "Here is your grandmother; here is the Countess of Kew, come from Baden at last; and she wants—she wants to take Frank from us, my dear, and to—give—him—back to the—Frenchwoman again. No, no! O, my God! Never! never!" And she flung herself into George Barnes's arms, fainting with an hysteric burst of tears.

"You had best get a strait-waistcoat for your mother, George Barnes," Lady Kew said, scorn and hatred in her face. (If she had been Iago's daughter, with a strong likeness to her sire, Lord Steyne's sister could not have looked more diabolical.) "Have you had advice for her? Has nursing poor Kew turned her head? I came to see *him*. Why have I been left alone for half-an-hour with this mad-woman? You ought not to trust her to give Frank medicine. It is positively—"

"Excuse me," said George, with a bow; "I don't think the complaint has as yet exhibited itself in my mother's branch of the family. (She always hated me," thought George; "but if she had by chance left me a legacy, there it goes.) You would like, Ma'am, to see the rooms up-stairs? Here is the landlord to conduct your ladyship. Frank will be quite ready to receive you when you come down. I am sure I need not beg of your kindness that nothing may be said to agitate him. It is barely three weeks since M. de Castillonnes' ball was extracted; and the doctors wish he should be kept as quiet as possible."

Be sure that the landlord, the courier, and the persons engaged in showing the Countess of Kew the apartments above spent an agreeable time with her Excellency the Frau Gräfinn von Kew. She must have had better luck in her encounter with these than in her previous passages with her grandson and his mother; for when she issued from her apartment in a new dress and fresh cap, Lady Kew's face wore an expression of perfect serenity. Her attendant may have shook her fist behind her, and her man's eyes and face looked Blitz and Donnerwetter; but their mistress's features wore that pleased look which they assumed when she had been satisfactorily punishing somebody. Lord Kew had by this time got back from the garden to his own room, where he awaited Grandmamma. If the mother and her two sons had in the interval of Lady Kew's toilette tried to resume the history of Bumble the Beadle, I fear they could not have found it very comical.

"Bless me, my dear child! How well you look! Many a girl would give the world to have such a complexion. There is nothing like a mother for a nurse! Ah, no! Maria, you deserve to be the Mother Superior of a House of Sisters of Charity, you do. The landlord has given me a delightful apartment, thank you. He is an extortionate wretch; but I have no doubt I shall be very comfortable. The Dodsburys stopped here, I see, by the travellers' book—quite right, instead of sleeping at that odious buggy Strasbourg. We have had a sad, sad time, my dears, at Baden. Between anxiety about poor Sir Brian, and about you, you naughty boy, I am sure I wonder how I have got through it all. Doctor Finck would not let me come away to-day; but I would come."

"I am sure it was uncommonly kind, Ma'am," says poor Kew, with a rueful face.

"That horrible woman against whom I always warned you—but young men will not take the advice of old grandmammas—has gone away these ten days. Monsieur le Duc fetched her; and if he locked her up at Montcontour, and kept her on bread and water for the rest of her life, I am sure he would serve her right. When a woman once forgets religious principles, Kew, she is sure to go wrong. The Conversation Room is shut up. The Dorkings go on Tuesday. Clara is really a dear little artless creature; one that you will like, Maria—and as for Ethel, I really think she is an angel. To see her nursing her poor father is the most beautiful sight; night after night she has sate up with him. I know where she would like to be, the dear child. And if Frank falls ill again, Maria, he won't need a mother or useless old grandmother to nurse him. I have got some pretty messages to deliver from her; but they are for your private ears, my lord; not even mammas and brothers may hear them."

"Do not go, Mother! Pray stay, George!" cried the sick man (and again Lord Steyne's sister looked uncommonly like that lamented marquis). "My cousin is a noble young creature," he went on. "She has admirable good qualities, which I appreciate with all my heart; and her beauty, you know how I admire it. I have thought of her a great deal as I was lying on the bed yonder (the family look was not so visible in Lady Kew's face), and— and—I wrote to her this very morning; she will have the letter by this time, probably."

"Bien! Frank!" Lady Kew smiled (in her supernatural way) almost as much as her portrait, by Harlowe, as you may see it at Kewbury to this very day. She is represented seated before an easel, painting a miniature of her son, Lord Walham.

"I wrote to her on the subject of the last conversation we had together," Frank resumed, in rather a timid voice, "the day before my accident. Perhaps she did not tell you, Ma'am, of what passed between us. We had had a quarrel; one of many. Some cowardly hand, which we both of us can guess at, had written to her an account of my past life, and she showed me the letter. Then I told her, that if she loved me she never would have showed it me: without any other words of reproof I bade her farewell. It was not much, the showing that letter; but it was enough. In twenty differences we have had together; she had been unjust and captious, cruel towards me, and too eager, as I thought, for other people's admiration. Had she loved me, it seemed to me Ethel would have shown less vanity and better temper. What was I to expect in life afterwards from a girl who before her marriage used me so? Neither she nor I could be happy. She could be gentle enough, and kind, and anxious to please any man whom she loves, God bless her! As for me, I suppose, I'm not worthy of so much talent and beauty, so we both understood that that was a friendly farewell; and as I have been lying on my bed yonder, thinking, perhaps, I never might leave it, or if I did, that I should like to lead a different sort of life to that which ended in sending me there, my resolve of last month was only confirmed. God forbid that she and I should lead the lives of some folks we know; that Ethel should marry without love, perhaps to fall into it afterwards; and that I, after this awful warning I have had, should be tempted back into that dreary life I was leading. It was wicked, Ma'am, I knew it was; many and many a day I used to say so to myself, and longed to get rid of it. I am a poor weak devil, I know, I am only too easily led into temptation, and I should only make matters worse if I married a woman who cares for the world more than for me, and would not make me happy at home."

"Ethel care for the world!" gasped out Lady Kew; "a most artless, simple, affectionate creature; my dear Frank, she——"

He interrupted her, as a blush came rushing over his pale face. "Ah!" said he, "if I had been the painter, and young Clive had been Lord Kew, which of us do you think she would have chosen? And she was right. He is a brave, handsome, honest young fellow, and is a thousand times cleverer and better than I am."

"Not better, dear, thank God," cried his mother, coming round to the other side of his sofa, and seizing her son's hand.

"No, I don't think he is better, Frank," said the diplomatist, walking away to the window. And as for Grandmamma at the end of this little speech and scene, her ladyship's likeness to her brother, the late revered Lord Steyne, was more frightful than ever.

After a minute's pause, she rose up on her crooked stick, and said, "I really feel I am unworthy to keep company with so much exquisite virtue. It will be enhanced, my lord, by the thought of the pecuniary sacrifice which you are making, for I suppose you know that I have been hoarding—yes, and saving, and pinching,—denying myself the necessities of life, in order that my grandson might one day have enough to support his rank. Go and live and starve in your dreary old house, and marry a parson's daughter, and sing psalms with your precious mother; and I have no doubt you and she—she who has thwarted me all through life, and whom I hated,—yes, I hated from the moment she took my son from me and brought misery into my family, will be all the happier when she thinks that she has made a poor, fond, lonely old woman more lonely and miserable. If you please, George Barnes, be good enough to tell my people that I shall go back to Baden;" and waving her children away from her, the old woman tottered out of the room on her crutch.

So the wicked Fairy drove away disappointed in her chariot with the very dragons which had brought her away in the morning, and just had time to get their feed of black bread. I wonder whether they were the horses Clive and J.J. and Jack Belsize had used when they passed on their road to Switzerland? Black Care sits behind all sorts of horses, and gives a trinkgelt to postillions all over the map. A thrill of triumph may be permitted to Lady Walham after her victory over her mother-in-law. What Christian woman does not like to conquer another; and if that other were a mother-in-law, would the victory be less sweet? Husbands and wives both will be pleased that Lady Walham has had the better of this bout: and you, young boys and virgins, when your turn comes to be married, you will understand the hidden meaning of this passage. George Barnes got "Oliver Twist" out, and began to read therein. Miss Nancy and Fanny again were summoned before this little company to frighten and delight them. I daresay even Fagin and Miss Nancy failed with the widow, so absorbed was she with the thoughts of the victory which she had just won. For the evening service, in which her sons rejoiced her fond heart by joining, she lighted on a psalm which was as a *te deum* after the battle—the battle of Kehl by Rhine, where Kew's soul, as his mother thought, was the object of contention between the enemies. I have said, this book is all about the world and a respectable family dwelling in it. It is not a sermon, except where it cannot help itself, and the speaker pursuing the destiny of his narrative finds such a homily before him. O friend, in your life and mine, don't we light upon such sermons daily?—don't we see at home as well as amongst our neighbours that battle betwixt Evil and Good? Here on one side is Self and Ambition and Advancement; and Right and Love on the other. Which shall we let to triumph for ourselves—which for our children?

The young men were sitting smoking the Vesper cigar. (Frank would do it, and his mother actually lighted his cigar for him now, enjoining him straightway after to go to bed.) Kew smoked and looked at a star shining above in the heaven. Which is that star? he asked: and the accomplished young diplomatist answered it was Jupiter.

"What a lot of things you know, George!" cries the senior, delighted; "You ought to have been the elder, you ought, by Jupiter. But you have lost your chance this time."

"Yes, thank God!" says George.

"And I am going to be all right—and to turn over a new leaf, old boy— and paste down the old ones, eh? I wrote to Martins this morning to have all my horses sold; and I'll never bet again—so help me—so help me, Jupiter. I made a vow—a promise to myself, you see, that I wouldn't if I recovered. And I wrote to cousin Ethel this morning.—As I thought over the matter yonder, I felt quite certain I was right, and that we could never, never pull together. Now the Countess is gone, I wonder whether I was right—to give up sixty thousand pounds, and the prettiest girl in London?"

"Shall I take horses and go after her? My mother's gone to bed, she won't know," asked George. "Sixty thousand is a lot of money to lose."

Kew laughed. "If you were to go and tell our grandmother that I could not live the night through; and that you would be Lord Kew in the morning, and your son, Viscount Walham, I think the Countess would make up a match between you and the sixty thousand pounds, and the prettiest girl in England: she would by—by Jupiter. I intend only to swear by the heathen gods now, Georgy.—No, I am not sorry I wrote to Ethel. What a fine girl she is!—I don't mean her beauty merely, but such a noble bred one! And to think that there she is in the market to be knocked down to.—I say, I was going to call that three-year-old, Ethelinda.—We must christen her over again for Tattersall's, Georgy."

A knock is heard through an adjoining door, and a maternal voice cries, "It is time to go to bed." So the brothers part, and, let us hope, sleep soundly.

The Countess of Kew, meanwhile, has returned to Baden; where, though it is midnight when she arrives, and the old lady has had two long bootless journeys, you will be grieved to hear that she does not sleep a single wink. In the morning she hobbles over to the Newcome quarters; and Ethel comes down to her pale and calm. How is her father? He has had a good night: he is a little better, speaks more clearly, has a little more the use of his limbs.

"I wish *I* had had a good night!" groans out the Countess.

"I thought you were going to Lord Kew, at Kehl," remarked her granddaughter.

"I did go, and returned with wretches who would not bring me more than five miles an hour! I dismissed that brutal grinning courier; and I have given warning to that fiend of a maid."

"And Frank is pretty well, Grandmamma?"

"Well! He looks as pink as a girl in her first season! I found him, and his brother George, and their mamma. I think Maria was hearing them their catechism," cries the old lady.

"N. and M. together! Very pretty," says Ethel, gravely. "George has always been a good boy, and it is quite time for my Lord Kew to begin."

The elder lady looked at her descendant, but Miss Ethel's glance was impenetrable. "I suppose you can fancy, my dear, why I came back?" said Lady Kew.

"Because you quarrelled with Lady Walham, Grandmamma. I think I have heard that there used to be differences between you." Miss Newcome was armed for defence and attack; in which cases we have said Lady Kew did not care to assault her. "My grandson told me that he had written to you," the Countess said.

"Yes: and had you waited but half an hour yesterday, you might have spared me the humiliation of that journey."

"*You*—the humiliation—Ethel!"

"Yes, *me*," Ethel flashed out. "Do you suppose it is none to have me bandied about from bidder to bidder, and offered for sale to a gentleman who will not buy me? Why have you and all my family been so eager to get rid of me? Why should you suppose or desire that Lord Kew should like me? Hasn't he the Opera; and such friends as Madame la Duchesse d'Ivry, to whom your ladyship introduced him in early life? He told me so: and she was good enough to inform me of the rest. What attractions have I in comparison with such women? And to this man from whom I am parted by good fortune; to this man who writes to remind me that we are separated—your ladyship must absolutely go and entreat him to give me another trial! It is too much, Grandmamma. Do please to let me stay where I am; and worry me with no more schemes for my establishment in life. Be contented with the happiness which you have secured for Clara Pulleyn and Barnes; and leave me to take care of my poor father. Here I know I am doing right. Here, at least, there is no such sorrow, and doubt, and shame, for me, as my friends have tried to make me endure. There is my father's bell. He likes me to be with him at breakfast and to read his paper to him."

"Stay a little, Ethel," cried the Countess, with a trembling voice. "I am older than your father, and you owe me a little obedience, that is, if children *do* owe any obedience to their parents now-a-days. I don't know. I am an old woman—the world perhaps has changed since my time; and it is you who ought to command, I dare say, and we to follow. Perhaps I have been wrong all through life, and in trying to teach my children to do as I was made to do. God knows I have had very little comfort from them: whether they did or whether they didn't. You and Frank I had set my heart on; I loved you out of all my grandchildren—was it very unnatural that I should wish to see you together? For that boy I have been saving money these years past. He flies back to the arms of his mother, who has been pleased to hate me as only such virtuous people can; who took away my own son from me; and now his son—towards whom the only fault I ever committed was to spoil him and be too fond of him. Don't leave me too, my child. Let me have something that I can like at my years. And I like your pride, Ethel, and your beauty, my dear; and I am not angry with your hard words; and if I wish to see you in the place in life which becomes you—do I do wrong? No. Silly girl! There—give me the little hand. How hot it is! Mine is as cold as a stone—and shakes, doesn't it?—Eh! it was a pretty hand once! What did Ann—what did your mother say to Frank's letter?"

"I did not show it to her," Ethel answered.

"Let me see it, my dear," whispered Lady Kew, in a coaxing way.

"There it is," said Ethel, pointing to the fireplace, where there[2] lay some torn fragments and ashes of paper. It was the same fireplace at which Clive's sketches had been burned.

END OF VOL. I.

2 there *E1*] [omitted] *R*

CHRISTMAS AT ROSEBURY

THE

NEWCOMES

A HISTORY of

A MOST RESPECTABLE FAMILY

by

A PENDENNIS Esqre

VOL 2

LONDON.

BRADBURY & EVANS. WHITEFRIARS.

CONTENTS.

———◇———

iv CONTENTS

LIST OF PLATES.

———◇———

vi LIST OF PLATES

THE NEWCOMES.

Chapter I.

AMONGST THE PAINTERS.

HEN Clive New-come comes to be old, no doubt he will remem-ber his Roman days as amongst the happiest which fate ever awarded him. The simplicity of the student's life there, the great-ness and friendly splendour of the scenes surrounding him, the delightful nature of the oc-cupation in which he is engaged, the pleasant company of comrades, in-spired by a like pleasure over a similar calling, the labour, the medita-tion, the holiday and the kindly feast afterwards, should make the Art-students the happiest of youth, did they but know their good fortune. Their work is for the most part delightfully easy. It does not exercise the brain too much, but gently occupies it, and with a subject most agree-able to the scholar. The mere poetic flame, or jet of invention, needs to be lighted up but very seldom, namely, when the young painter is devising his subject, or settling the composition thereof. The posing of figures and drapery; the dexterous copying of the line; the artful pro-cesses of cross-hatching, of stumping, of laying on lights, and what not; the arrangement of colour, and the pleasing operations of glazing and the like, are labours for the most part merely manual. These, with the smoking of a proper number of pipes, carry the student through his day's work. If you pass his door you will very probably hear him singing at his easel. I should like to know what young lawyer, mathematician, or di-vinity scholar, can sing over his volumes, and at the same time advance with his labour? In every city where Art is practised there are old gen-tlemen who never touched a pencil in their lives, but find the occupation and company of artists so agreeable that they are never out of the stu-dios; follow one generation of painters after another; sit by with perfect contentment while Jack is drawing his pifferaro, or Tom designing his car-toon, and years afterwards when Jack is established in Newman Street, and Tom a Royal Academician, shall still be found in their rooms, occupied now by fresh painters and pictures, telling the youngsters, their successors, what glorious fellows Jack and Tom were. A poet must retire to privy places and meditate his rhymes in secret; a painter can practise his trade in the company of friends. Your splendid *chef d'école*, a Rubens or a Horace Vernet, may sit with a secretary reading to him; a troop of admiring scholars watching the master's hand; or a company of court ladies and gentlemen, (to whom he addresses a few kind words now and again,) looking on admiringly; whilst the humblest painter, be he ever so poor, may have a friend watching at his easel, or a gentle wife sitting by with her work in her lap, and with fond smiles or talk or silence, cheering his labour.

Amongst all ranks and degrees of painters assembled at Rome, Mr. Clive found companions and friends. The cleverest man was not the best artist very often: the ablest artist not the best critic nor the best companion. Many a man could give no account of the faculty within him, but achieved success because he could not help it; and did, in an hour and without effort, that which another could not effect with half a life's labour. There were young sculptors who had never read a line of Homer, who took on themselves nevertheless to interpret and continue the heroic Greek art. There were young painters with the strongest natural taste for low humour, comic singing, and Cyder-Cellar jollifications, who would imitate nothing under Michael Angelo, and whose canvases teemed with tremendous allegories of fates, furies, genii of death and battle. There were long-haired lads who fancied the sublime lay in the Peruginesque manner, and depicted saintly personages with crisp draperies, crude colours, and haloes of gold-leaf. Our friend marked all these practitioners of Art with their various oddities and tastes, and was welcomed in the ateliers of all of them, from the grave dons and seniors, the senators of the French and English Academy, down to the jovial students who railed at the elders over their cheap cups at the Lepre. What a gallant, starving, generous, kindly life, many of them led! What fun in their grotesque airs, what friendship and gentleness in their poverty! How splendidly Carlo talked of the marquis his cousin, and the duke his intimate friend! How great Federigo was on the subject of his wrongs, from the Academy at home, a pack of tradesmen who could not understand high art, and who had never seen a good picture! With what haughtiness Augusto swaggered about at Sir John's soirées, though he was known to have borrowed Fernando's coat, and Luigi's dress-boots! If one or the other was ill, how nobly and generously his companions flocked to comfort him, took turns to nurse the sick man through nights of fever, contributed out of their slender means to help him through his difficulty. Max, who loves fine dresses and the carnival so, gave up a costume and a carriage so as to help Paul. Paul, when he sold his picture (through the agency of Pietro, with whom he had quarrelled, and who recommended him to a patron) gave a third of the money back to Max, and took another third portion to Lazaro, with his poor wife and children, who had not got a single order all that winter—and so the story went on. I have heard Clive tell of two noble young Americans who came to Europe to study their art; of whom the one fell sick whilst the other supported his penniless comrade, and out of sixpence a day absolutely kept but a penny for himself, giving the rest to his sick companion. "I should like to have known that good Samaritan, Sir," our Colonel said, twirling his mustachios, when we saw him again, and his son told him that story.

J.J., in his steady silent way, worked on every day, and for many hours every day. When Clive entered their studio of a morning, he found J.J. there, and there he left him. When the Life Academy was over, at night, and Clive went out to his soirées, J.J. lighted his lamp and continued his happy labour. He did not care for the brawling supper-parties of his comrades; liked better to stay at home than to go into the world, and was seldom abroad of a night except during the illness of Luigi before mentioned, when J.J. spent constant evenings at the other's bed-side. J.J. was fortunate as well as skilful: people in the world took a liking to the modest young man, and he had more than one order for pictures. The Artists' Club, at the Lepre, set him down as close with his money; but a year after he left Rome, Lazaro and his wife, who still remained there, told a different tale. Clive Newcome, when he heard of their distress, gave them something— as much as he could spare; but J.J. gave more, and Clive was as eager in acknowledging and admiring his friend's generosity as he was in speaking of his genius. His was a fortunate organisation indeed. Study was his chief amusement. Self-denial came easily to him. Pleasure, or what is generally called so, had little charm for him. His ordinary companions were pure and sweet thoughts; his out-door enjoyment the contemplation of natural beauty; for recreation, the hundred pleasant dexterities and manipulations of his craft were ceaselessly interesting to him: he would draw every knot in an oak panel, or every leaf in an orange-tree, smiling, and taking a gay delight over the simple feats of skill: whenever you found him he seemed watchful and serene, his modest virgin-lamp always lighted and trim. No gusts of passion extinguished it; no hopeless wandering in the darkness afterwards led him astray. Wayfarers through the world, we meet now and again with such purity; and salute it, and hush whilst it passes on.

We have it under Clive Newcome's own signature, that he intended to pass a couple of years in Italy, devoting himself exclusively to the study of his profession. Other besides professional reasons were working secretly in the young man's mind, causing him to think that absence from England was the best cure for a malady under which he secretly laboured. But change of air may cure some sick people more speedily than the sufferers ever hoped; and also it is on record, that young men with the very best intentions respecting study, do not fulfil them, and are led away from their scheme by accident, or pleasure, or necessity, or some good cause. Young Clive worked sedulously two or three months at his vocation at Rome, secretly devouring, no doubt, the pangs of sentimental disappointment under which he laboured; and he drew from his models, and he sketched round about everything that suited his pencil on both sides of Tiber; and he laboured at the Life Academy of nights—a model himself to other young students. The symptoms of his sentimental malady began to abate. He took an interest in the affairs of Jack, and Tom, and Harry round about him: Art exercised its great healing influence on his wounded spirit, which to be sure had never given in. The meeting of the painters at the Café Greco, and at their private houses, was very jovial, pleasant, and lively. Clive smoked his pipe, drank his glass of Marsala, sang his song, and took part in the general chorus as gaily as the jolliest of the boys. He was the cock of the whole painting school, the favourite of all; and to be liked by the people, you may be pretty sure that we for our parts must like them.

Then, besides the painters, he had, as he has informed us, the other society of Rome. Every winter there is a gay and pleasant English colony in that capital, of course more or less remarkable for rank, fashion, and agreeability with every varying year. In Clive's year some very pleasant folks set up their winter quarters in the usual foreigners' resort round about the Piazza di Spagna. I was amused to find, lately, on looking over the travels of the respectable M. de Pöllnitz, that, a hundred and twenty years ago, the same quarter, the same streets and palaces, scarce changed from those days, were even then polite foreigners' resort. Of one or two of the gentlemen, Clive had made the acquaintance in the hunting-field; others he had met during his brief appearance in the London world. Being a youth of great personal agility, fitted thereby to the graceful performance of polkas, &c.; having good manners, and good looks, and good credit with Prince Polonia, or some other banker, Mr. Newcome was thus made very welcome to the Anglo-Roman society; and as kindly received in genteel houses, where they drank tea and danced the galop, as in those dusky taverns and retired lodgings where his bearded comrades, the painters, held their meetings.

Thrown together every day, and night after night; flocking to the same picture-galleries, statue-galleries, Pincian drives, and church functions, the English colonists at Rome perforce become intimate, and in many cases friendly. They have an English library where the various meets for the week are placarded: on such a day the Vatican galleries are open: the next is the feast of Saint so and so: on Wednesday there will be music and Vespers at the Sistine chapel: on Thursday, the Pope will bless the animals—sheep, horses, and what-not: and flocks of English accordingly rush to witness the benediction of droves of donkeys. In a word, the ancient city of the Cæsars, the august fanes of the Popes, with their splendour and ceremony, are all mapped out and arranged for English diversion; and we run in a crowd to high mass at St. Peter's, or to the illumination on Easter-day, as we run when the bell rings to the Bosjesmen at Cremorne, or the fireworks at Vauxhall.

Running to see fireworks alone, rushing off to examine Bosjesmen by one's self, is a dreary work: I should think very few men would have the courage to do it unattended, and personally would not prefer a pipe in their own rooms. Hence if Clive went to see all these sights, as he did, it is to be concluded that he went in company, and if he went in company and sought it, we may suppose that little affair which annoyed him at Baden no longer tended to hurt his peace of mind very seriously. The truth is, our countrymen are pleasanter abroad than at home; most hospitable, kindly, and eager to be pleased and to please. You see a family half a dozen times in a week in the little Roman circle, whom you shall not meet twice in a season afterwards in the enormous London round. When Easter is over and everybody is going away at Rome, you and your neighbour shake hands, sincerely sorry to part: in London we are obliged to dilute our kindness so that there is hardly any smack of the original milk. As one by one the pleasant families dropped off with whom Clive had spent his happy winter; as Admiral Freeman's carriage drove away, whose pretty girls he had caught at St. Peter's kissing St. Peter's toe; as Dick Denby's family ark appeared with all Denby's sweet young children kissing farewells to him out of window; as those three charming Miss Baliols with whom he had that glorious day in the Catacombs; as friend after friend quitted the great city with kind greetings, warm pressures of the hand, and hopes of meeting in a yet greater city on the banks of the Thames, young Clive felt a depression of spirit. Rome was Rome, but it was pleasanter to see it in company; our painters are smoking still at the Café Greco, but a society all smoke and all painters did not suit him. If Mr. Clive is not a Michael Angelo or a Beethoven, if his genius is not gloomy, solitary, gigantic, shining alone, like a lighthouse, a storm round about him, and breakers dashing at his feet, I cannot help myself; he is as Heaven made him, brave, honest, gay, and friendly, and persons of a gloomy turn must not look to him as a hero.

So Clive and his companion worked away with all their hearts from November until far into April when Easter came, and the glorious gala with which the Roman church celebrates that holy season. By this time Clive's books were full of sketches. Ruins, imperial and mediæval; peasants and bagpipemen; Passionists with shaven polls; Capuchins and the equally hairy frequenters of the Café Greco; painters of all nations who resort there; Cardinals and their queer equipages and attendants; the Holy Father himself (it was Gregory sixteenth of the name); the dandified English on the Pincio and the wonderful Roman members of the hunt—were not all these designed by the young man and admired by his friends in after-days? J.J.'s sketches were few, but he had painted two beautiful little pictures, and sold them for so good a price that Prince Polonia's people were quite civil to him. He had orders for yet more pictures, and having worked very hard, thought himself authorised to accompany Mr. Clive upon a pleasure trip to Naples, which the latter deemed necessary after his own tremendous labours. He for his part had painted no pictures, though he had commenced a dozen and turned them to the wall; but he had sketched, and dined, and smoked, and danced, as we have seen. So the little britzska was put behind horses again, and our two friends set out on their tour, having quite a crowd of brother artists to cheer them, who had assembled and had a breakfast for the purpose at that comfortable osteria, near the Lateran Gate. How the fellows flung their hats up, and shouted, "Lebe wohl," and "Adieu," and "God bless you, old boy," in many languages! Clive was the young swell of the artists of that year, and adored by the whole of the jolly company. His sketches were pronounced on all hands to be admirable: it was agreed that if he chose he might do anything.

So with promises of a speedy return they left behind them the noble city, which all love who once have seen it, and of which we think afterwards ever with the kindness and the regard of home. They dashed across the Campagna and over the beautiful hills of Albano, and sped through the solemn Pontine Marshes, and stopped to roost at Terracina (which was not at all like Fra Diavolo's Terracina at Covent Garden, as J.J. was distressed to remark), and so, galloping onwards through a hundred ancient cities that crumble on the shores of the beautiful Mediterranean, behold, on the second day as they ascended a hill about noon, Vesuvius came in view, its great shape shimmering blue in the distant haze, its banner of smoke in the cloudless sky. And about five o'clock in the evening (as everybody will who starts from Terracina early and pays the post-boy well), the travellers came to an ancient city walled and fortified, with drawbridges over the shining moats.

"Here is CAPUA," says J.J. and Clive burst out laughing: thinking of *his* Capua which he had left—how many months—years it seemed ago. From Capua to Naples is a fine straight road, and our travellers were landed at the latter place at supper-time; where, if they had quarters at the Vittoria Hotel, they were as comfortable as any gentlemen painters need wish to be in this world.

The aspect of the place was so charming and delightful to Clive:—the beautiful sea stretched before his eyes when waking, Capri a fairy island in the distance, in the amethyst rocks of which Syrens might be playing,—that fair line of cities skirting the shore glittering white along the purple water,—over the whole brilliant scene Vesuvius rising with cloudlets playing round its summit, and the country bursting out into that glorious vegetation with which sumptuous nature decorates every spring—this city and scene of Naples were so much to Clive's liking that I have a letter from him dated a couple of days after the young man's arrival, in which he announces his intention of staying there for ever, and gives me an invitation to some fine lodgings in a certain palazzo, on which he has cast his eye. He is so enraptured with the place, that he says to die and be buried there even would be quite a treat, so charming is the cemetery where the Neapolitan dead repose.

The Fates did not, however, ordain that Clive Newcome should pass all his life at Naples. His Roman banker presently forwarded a few letters to his address; some which had arrived after his departure, others which had been lying at the Poste Restante, with his name written in perfectly legible characters, but which the authorities of the post, according to their custom, would not see when Clive sent for them.

It was one of these letters which Clive clutched the most eagerly. It had been lying since October, actually, at the Roman post, though Clive had asked for letters there a hundred times. It was that little letter from Ethel, in reply to his own, whereof we have made mention in a previous chapter. There was not much in the little letter. Nothing, of course, that Virtue or Grandmamma might not read over the young writer's shoulder. It was affectionate, simple, rather melancholy; described in a few words Sir Brian's seizure and present condition; spoke of Lord Kew, who was mending rapidly, as if Clive, of course, was aware of his accident; of the children; of Clive's father; and ended with a hearty "God bless you," to Clive, from his sincere Ethel.

"You boast of its being over. You see it is not over," says Clive's monitor and companion. "Else, why should you have dashed at that letter before all the others, Clive?" J.J. had been watching, not without interest, Clive's blank face as he read the young lady's note.

"How do you know who wrote the letter?" asks Clive.

LETTERS FROM ENGLAND

"I can read the signature in your face," says the other; "and I could almost tell the contents of the note. Why have you such a tell-tale face, Clive?"

"It is over; but when a man has once, you know, gone through an affair like that," says Clive, looking very grave, "he—he's anxious to hear of Alice Gray, and how she's getting on, you see, my good friend." And he began to shout out as of old—

"Her heart it is another's, she—never—can—be—mine."

and to laugh at the end of the song. "Well, well," says he; "it is a very kind note, a very proper little note; the expressions is elegant, J.J., the sentiments is most correct. All the little t's is most properly crossed, and all the little i's have dots over their little heads. It's a sort of a prize note, don't you see; and one such, as is[1] in the old spelling-book story, the good boy received a plum-cake for writing. Perhaps you weren't educated on the old spelling-book, J.J.? My good old father taught me to read out of his—I say, I think it was a shame to keep the old boy waiting whilst I have been giving an audience to this young lady. Dear old Father!" and he apostrophised the letter. "I beg your pardon, Sir; Miss Newcome requested five minutes' conversation, and I was obliged, from politeness, you know, to receive. There's nothing between us; nothing but what's most correct, upon my honour and conscience." And he kissed his father's letter, and calling out again "Dear old Father!" proceeded to read as follows:—

" 'Your letters, my dearest Clive, have been the greatest comfort to me. I seem to hear you as I read them. I can't but think that this, the *modern and natural style*, is a great progress upon the *old-fashioned* manner of my day, when we used to begin to our fathers, "Honoured Father," or even "Honoured Sir" some *precisians* use to write still from Mr. Lord's Academy, at Tooting, where I went before Grey Friars'—though I suspect parents

[1] such, as is *E1*] such, as *R*] such as, *HM NY*

were no more *honoured* in those days than now-a-days. I know one who had rather be trusted than honoured; and you may call me what you please, so as you do that.

" 'It is not only to me your letters give pleasure. Last week I took yours from Baden Baden, No. 3, September 15, into Calcutta, and could not help showing it at Government House, where I dined. Your sketch of the old Russian Princess and her little boy, gambling, was *capital*. Colonel Buckmaster, Lord Bagwig's private secretary, knew her, and says it is to a *T.* And I read out to some of my young fellows what you said about play, and how you had given it over. I very much fear some of the young rogues are at dice and brandy-pawnee before tiffin. What you say of young Ridley, I take *cum grano*. His sketches I thought very agreeable; but to compare them to *a certain gentleman's*— Never mind, I shall not try to make him think too well of himself. I kissed dear Ethel's hand in your letter. I write her a long letter by this mail.

" 'If Paul de Florac in any way resembles his mother, between you and him there ought to be a very warm regard. I knew her when I was a boy, long before you were born or thought of; and in wandering forty years through the world since, I have seen no woman in my eyes so good or so beautiful. Your cousin Ethel reminded me of her; as handsome, but not so *lovely*. Yes, it was that pale lady you saw at Paris, with eyes full of care, and hair streaked with grey. So it will be the turn of you young folks, come eight more *lustres*, and your heads will be bald like mine, or grey like Madame de Florac's, and bending over the ground where we are lying in quiet. I understand from you that young Paul is not in very flourishing circumstances. If he still is in need, mind and be his banker, and *I will be yours*. Any child of hers must never want when I have a spare guinea. I do not mind telling you, Sir, that I cared for her more than millions of guineas once; and half broke my heart about her when I went to India, as a young chap. So, if any such misfortunes happen to *you*, consider, my boy, you are not the *only* one.

" 'Binnie writes me word that he has been ailing. I hope you are a good correspondent with him. What made me turn to him just after speaking of unlucky love affairs? Could I be thinking about little Rosey Mackenzie? She is a sweet little lass, and James will leave her a pretty piece of money. *Verbum sap.* I should like you to marry; but God forbid you should marry for a million of gold mohurs.

" 'And gold mohurs bring me to another subject. Do you know, I narrowly missed losing half a lakh of rupees which I had at an agent's here? And who do you think warned me about him? Our friend Rummun Lall, who has lately been in England, and with whom I made the voyage from Southampton. He is a man of wonderful tact and observation. I used to think meanly of the honesty of natives, and treat them haughtily, as I recollect doing this very gentleman at your Uncle Newcome's in Brianstone Square. He heaped coals of fire on my head by saving my money for me; and I have placed it at interest in his house. If I would but listen to him, my capital might be trebled in a year, he says, and the interest immensely increased. He enjoys the greatest esteem among the monied men here; keeps a splendid establishment and house here, in Barrackpore; is princely in his benefactions. He talks to me about the establishment of a bank, of which the profits are so enormous and the scheme so (seemingly) clear, that I don't know whether I mayn't be tempted to take a few shares. *Nous verrons.* Several of my friends are longing to have a finger in it; but be sure of this, I shall do nothing rashly and without the very *best advice.*

"'I have not been frightened yet by your draughts upon me. Draw as many of these as you please. You know I don't half like the other kind of drawing, except as a *délassement:* but if you chose to be a weaver, like my grandfather, I should not say you nay. Don't stint yourself of money or of honest pleasure. Of what good is money, unless we can make those we love happy with it? There would be no need for me to save, if you were to save too. So, and as you know as well as I what our means are, in every honest way use them. I should like you not to pass the whole of next year in Italy, but to come home and pay a visit to honest James Binnie. I wonder how the old barrack in Fitzroy Square looks without me? Try and go round by Paris on your way home, and pay your visit, and carry your father's fond remembrances to Madame la Comtesse de Florac. I don't say remember me to my brother, as I write Brian by this mail. Adieu mon fils! je t'embrasse!—and am always my Clive's affectionate father. T.N.'

"Isn't he a noble old trump?" That point had been settled by the young men any time these three years. And now Mr. J.J. remarked that when Clive had read his father's letter once, then he read Ethel's over again, and put it in his breast-pocket, and was very disturbed in mind that day, pishing and pshawing at the statue gallery which they went to see at the Museo.

"After all," says Clive, "what rubbish these second-rate statues are! what a great hulking abortion is this brute of a Farnese Hercules! There's only one bit in the whole gallery that is worth a twopenny piece."

It was the beautiful fragment called Psyche. J.J. smiled as his comrade spoke in admiration of this statue—in the slim shape, in the delicate formation of the neck, in the haughty virginal expression, the Psyche is not unlike the Diana of the Louvre—and the Diana of the Louvre we have said was like a certain young lady.

"After all," continues Clive, looking up at the great knotted legs of that clumsy caricatured porter which Glykon the Athenian sculptured in bad times of art surely,—"She could not write otherwise than she did—don't you see? Her letter is quite kind and affectionate. You see she says she shall always hear of me with pleasure: hopes I'll come back soon, and bring some good pictures with me, since pictures I will do. She thinks small beer of painters, J.J.—well, we don't think small beer of ourselves, my noble friend. I—I suppose it must be over by this time, and I may write to her as the Countess of Kew." The custode of the apartment had seen admiration and wonder expressed by hundreds of visitors to his marble Giant: but he had never known Hercules occasion emotion before, as in the case of the young stranger, who, after staring a while at the statue, dashed his hand across his forehead with a groan, and walked away from before the graven image of the huge Strongman, who had himself been made such a fool by women.

"My father wants me to go and see James and Madame de Florac," says

Clive, as they stride down the street to the Toledo.

J.J. puts his arm through his companion's, which is deep in the pocket of his velvet paletot. "You must not go home till you hear it is over, Clive," whispers J.J.

"Of course not, old boy," says the other, blowing tobacco out of his shaking head.

Not very long after their arrival, we may be sure they went to Pompeii, of which place, as this is not an Italian tour, but a history of Clive Newcome, Esquire, and his most respectable family, we shall offer to give no description. The young man had read Sir Bulwer Lytton's delightful story, which has become the history of Pompeii, before they came thither, and Pliny's description, *apud* the Guide Book. Admiring the wonderful ingenuity with which the English writer had illustrated the place by his text, as if the houses were so many pictures to which he had appended a story, Clive, the wag, who was always indulging his vein for caricature, was proposing that they should take the same place, names, people, and make a burlesque story: "What would be a better figure," says he, "than Pliny's mother, whom the historian describes as exceedingly corpulent, and walking away from the catastrophe with slaves holding cushions behind her, to shield her plump person from the cinders! Yes, old Mrs. Pliny shall be my heroine!" says Clive. A picture of her on a dark grey paper, and touched up with red at the extremities, exists in Clive's album to the present day.

As they were laughing, rattling, wondering, mimicking, the cicerone attending them with his nasal twaddle, anon pausing and silent, yielding to the melancholy pity and wonder which the aspect of that strange sad smiling lonely place inspires; behold they come upon another party of English, two young men accompanying a lady.

"What, Clive!" cries one.

"My dear, dear Lord Kew!" shouts the other; and as each young man rushes up and grasps the two hands of the other, they both begin to blush. . . .

Lord Kew and his family resided in a neighbouring hotel on the Chiafa at Naples, and that very evening on returning from the Pompeian excursion, the two painters were invited to take tea by those friendly persons. J.J. excused himself, and sate at home drawing all night. Clive went, and passed a pleasant evening; in which all sorts of future tours and pleasure-parties were projected by the young men. They were to visit Pæstum, Capri, Sicily; why not Malta and the east? asked Lord Kew.

Lady Walham was alarmed. Had not Kew been in the east already? Clive was surprised and agitated too. Could Kew think of going to the east, and making long journeys when he had—he had other engagements that would necessitate his return home? No, he must not go to the east; Lord Kew's mother avowed, Kew had promised to stay with her during the summer at Castellammare, and Mr. Newcome must come and paint their portraits there—all their portraits. She would like to have an entire picture-gallery of Kews, if her son would remain at home during the sittings.

At an early hour Lady Walham retired to rest, exacting Clive's promise to come to Castellammare: and George Barnes disappeared to array himself in an evening costume, and to pay his round of visits as became a young diplomatist. This part of diplomatic duty does not commence until after the opera at Naples; and society begins when the rest of the world has gone to bed.

Kew and Clive sate till one o'clock in the morning when the latter returned to his hotel. Not one of those fine parties at Pæstum, Sicily, &c., was[2] carried out. Clive did not go to the east at all, and it was J.J. who painted Lord Kew's portrait that summer, at Castellammare. The next day Clive went for his passport to the embassy; and a steamer departing direct for Marseilles on that very afternoon, behold Mr. Newcome was on board of her; Lord Kew and his brother and J.J. waving their hats to him as the vessel left the shore.

Away went the ship, cleaving swiftly through the azure waters; but not swiftly enough for Clive. J.J. went back with a sigh to his sketch-book and easels. I suppose the other young disciple of Art had heard something which caused him to forsake his sublime mistress, for one who was much more capricious and earthly.

[2] was *R*] were *E1*

Chapter II.

NE morning in the month of July, when there was actually sunshine in Lamb Court, and the two gentlemen who occupied the third floor chambers there in partnership, were engaged, as their custom was, over their pipes, their manuscripts, and their *Times* newspaper, behold a fresh sunshine burst into their room in the person of young Clive, with a bronzed face, and a yellow beard and mustachios, and those bright cheerful eyes, the sight of which was always so welcome to both of us. "What, Clive! What, the young one! What, Benjamin!" shout Pendennis and Warrington. Clive had obtained a very high place indeed in the latter's affections, so much so, that if I could have found it in my heart to be jealous of such a generous brave fellow, I might have grudged him his share of Warrington's regard. He blushed up with pleasure to see us again. Pidgeon, our boy, introduced him with a jubilant countenance; and Flanagan, the laundress, came smirking out of the bed-room, eager to get a nod of recognition from him, and bestow a smile of welcome upon everybody's favourite, Clive.

In two minutes an arm-chair full of magazines, slips of copy, and books for review, was emptied over the neighbouring coal scuttle, and Clive was in the seat, a cigar in his mouth, as comfortable as if he had never been away. When did he come? Last night. He was back in Charlotte Street, at his old lodgings: he had been to breakfast in Fitzroy Square that morning; James Binnie chirped for joy at seeing him. His father had written to him desiring him to come back and see James Binnie; pretty Miss Rosey was very well thank you: and Mrs. Mack? Wasn't Mrs. Mackenzie delighted to behold him? "Come Sir, on your honour and conscience, didn't the widow give you a kiss on your return?" Clive sends an uncut number of the *Pall Mall Gazette* flying across the room at the head of the inquirer; but blushes so sweetly, that I have very little doubt some such pretty meeting had taken place.

What a pity it is he had not been here a short while since for a marriage in high life, to give away his dear Barnes, and sign the book, along with the other dignitaries! We described that ceremony to him, and announced the promotion of his friend, Florac, now our friend also, Director of the Great Anglo-Gallic Railway, the Prince de Montcontour. Then Clive told us of his deeds during the winter; of the good fun he had had at Rome, and the jolly fellows he had met there. Was he going to astonish the world by some grand pictures? He was not. The more he worked, the more discontented he was with his performances somehow: but J.J. was coming out very strong, J.J. was going to be a stunner. We turned with pride and satisfaction to that very number of the *Pall Mall Gazette*, which the youth had flung at us, and showed him a fine article by F. Bayham, Esq., in which the picture sent home by J.J. was enthusiastically lauded by the great critic.

So he was back amongst us, and it seemed but yesterday he had quitted us. To Londoners everything seems to have happened but yesterday; nobody has time to miss his neighbour who goes away. People go to the Cape, or on a campaign, or on a tour round the world, or to India, and return with a wife and two or three children, and we fancy it was only the other day they left us, so engaged is every man in his individual speculations, studies, struggles; so selfish does our life make us:—selfish but not ill-natured. We are glad to see an old friend, though we do not weep when he leaves us. We humbly acknowledge, if fate calls us away likewise, that we are no more missed than any other atom.

After talking for a while, Mr. Clive must needs go into the City, whither I accompanied him. His interview with Messrs. Jolly and Baines, at the house in Fog Court, must have been very satisfactory; Clive came out of the parlour with a radiant countenance. "Do you want any money, old boy?" says he; "the dear old governor has placed a jolly sum to my account, and Mr. Baines has told me how delighted Mrs. Baines and the girls will be to see me at dinner. He says my father has made a lucky escape out of one house in India, and a famous investment in another. Nothing could be more civil; how uncommonly kind and friendly everybody is in London. Everybody!" Then bestowing ourselves in a Hansom cab, which had probably just deposited some other capitalist in the City, we made for the West End of the town, where Mr. Clive had some important business to transact with his tailors. He discharged his outstanding little account with easy liberality, blushing as he pulled out of his pocket a new cheque book, page one of which he bestowed on the delighted artist. From Mr. B.'s shop to Mr. Truefitt's is but a step. Our young friend was induced to enter the hair-dresser's, and leave behind him a great portion of the flowing locks and the yellow beard, which he had brought with him from Rome. With his mustachios he could not be induced to part; painters and cavalry officers having a right to those decorations. And why should not this young fellow wear smart clothes, and a smart mustache, and look handsome, and take his pleasure, and bask in his sun when it shone? Time enough for flannel and a fire when the winter comes; and for grey hair and cork-soled boots in the natural decline of years.

Then we went to pay a visit at a hotel in Jermyn Street to our friend Florac, who was now magnificently lodged there. A powdered giant lolling in the hall, his buttons emblazoned with prodigious coronets, took our cards up to the Prince. As the door of an apartment on the first floor opened, we heard a cry as of joy; and that nobleman, in a magnificent Persian dressing-gown, rushing from the room, plunged down the stairs and began kissing Clive to the respectful astonishment of the Titan in livery.

"Come that I present you, my friends," our good little Frenchman exclaimed, "to Madame la—to my wife!" We entered the drawing-room; a demure little lady, of near sixty years of age, was seated there, and we were presented in form to Madame la Princesse de Montcontour née Higg, of Manchester. She made us a stiff little curtsey, but looked not ill-natured; indeed, few women could look at Clive Newcome's gallant figure and brave smiling countenance and keep a frown on their own very long.

"I have eard of you from somebodys else besides the Prince," said the lady, with rather a blush. "Your uncle has spoke to me hoften about you, Mr. Clive, and about your good father."

"C'est son Directeur," whispers Florac to me. I wondered which of the firm of Newcome had taken that office upon him.

"Now you are come to England," the lady continued (whose Lancashire pronunciation being once indicated, we shall henceforth, out of respect to the Princess's rank, generally pretermit),—"now you are come to England, we hope to see you often. Not here in this noisy hotel, which I can't bear, but in the country. Our house is only three miles from Newcome—not such a grand place as your uncle's; but I hope we shall see you there a great deal, and your friend, Mr. Pendennis, if he is passing that way." The invitation to Mr. Pendennis, I am bound to say, was given in terms by no means so warm as those in which the Princess's hospitality to Clive were professed.

"Shall we meet you at your Huncle Obson's?" the lady continued, to Clive; "his wife is a most charming, well-informed woman, has been most kind and civil, and we dine there to-day. Barnes and his wife is gone to spend the honeymoon at Newcome. Lady Clara is a sweet dear thing, and her pa and ma most affable, I am sure. What a pity Sir Brian couldn't attend the marriage! There was every body there in London, a'most. Sir Harvey Diggs says he is mending very slowly. In life we are in death, Mr. Newcome! Isn't it sad to think of him, in the midst of all his splendour and prosperity, and he so infirm and unable to enjoy them! But let us hope for the best, and that his health will soon come round!"

With these and similar remarks, in which poor Florac took but a very small share (for he seemed dumb and melancholy in the company of the Princess, his elderly spouse), the visit sped on. Mr. Pendennis, to whom very little was said, having leisure to make his silent observations upon the person to whom he had been just presented.

As there lay on the table two neat little packages, addressed "The Princess de Montcontour"—an envelope to the same address, with "The Prescription, No. 9396" farther inscribed on the paper, and a sheet of note-paper, bearing cabalistic characters, and the signature of that most fashionable physician, Sir Harvey Diggs, I was led to believe that the lady of Montcontour was, or fancied herself, in a delicate state of health. By the side of the physic for the body was medicine for the soul—a number of pretty little books in middle age bindings, in antique type many of them, adorned with pictures of the German School, representing demure ecclesiastics, with their heads on one side, children in long starched nightgowns, virgins bearing lilies, and so forth, from which it was to be concluded that the owner of the volumes was not so hostile to Rome as she had been at an earlier period of her religious life; and that she had migrated (in spirit) from Clapham to Knightsbridge, as so many wealthy mercantile families have likewise done in the body.   A

long strip of embroidery, of the Gothic pattern, furthermore betrayed her present inclinations; and the person observing these things, whilst nobody was taking any notice of him, was amused when the accuracy of his conjectures was confirmed by the re-appearance of the gigantic footman, calling out "Mr. Oneyman," in a loud voice, and preceding that divine into the room.

"C'est le Directeur. Venez fumer dans ma chambre, Pen," growled Florac, as Honeyman came sliding over the carpet, his elegant smile changing to a blush when he beheld Clive, his nephew, seated by the Princess's side. This, then, was the uncle who had spoken about Clive and his father to Madame de Florac. Charles seemed in the best condition. He held out two bran-new lavender-coloured kid gloves to shake hands with his dear Clive; Florac and Mr. Pendennis vanished out of the room as he appeared, so that no precise account can be given of this affecting interview.

When I quitted the hotel, a brown brougham, with a pair of beautiful horses, the harness and panels emblazoned with the neatest little ducal coronets you ever saw, and a cypher under each crown as easy to read as the arrow-headed inscriptions on one of Mr. Layard's Assyrian chariots, was in waiting, and I presumed that Madame la Princesse was about to take an airing.

Clive had passed the avuncular banking-house in the City, without caring to face his relatives there. Mr. Newcome was now in sole command, Mr. Barnes being absent at Newcome, the Baronet little likely ever to enter bank parlour again. But his bounden duty was to wait on the ladies; and of course, only from duty's sake, he went the very first day and called in Park Lane.

"The family was habsent ever since the marriage simminery last week," the footman, who had accompanied the party to Baden, informed Clive, when he opened the door and recognised that gentleman. "Sir Brian pretty well, thank you, Sir. The family was at Brighting. That is, Miss Newcome is in London staying with her grandmammar in Queen Street, May Fear, Sir." The varnished doors closed upon Jeames within; the brazen knockers grinned their familiar grin at Clive; and he went down the blank steps discomfited. Must it be owned that he went to a Club, and looked in the Directory for the number of Lady Kew's house in Queen Street? Her ladyship had a furnished house for the season. No such noble name was to be found among the inhabitants of Queen Street.

Mrs. Hobson was from home; that is, Thomas had orders not to admit strangers on certain days, or before certain hours; so that Aunt Hobson saw Clive without being seen by the young man. I cannot say how much he regretted that mischance. His visits of propriety were thus all paid; and he went off to dine dutifully with James Binnie, after which meal he came to a certain rendezvous given to him by some bachelor friends for the evening.

James Binnie's eyes lightened up with pleasure on beholding his young Clive; the youth, obedient to his father's injunction, had hastened to Fitzroy Square immediately after taking possession of his old lodgings—his, during the time of his absence. The old properties and carved cabinets, the picture of his father looking melancholy out of the canvas, greeted Clive strangely on the afternoon of his arrival. No wonder he was glad to get away from a solitude peopled with a number of dismal recollections, to the near hospitality of Fitzroy Square and his guardian and friend there.

James had not improved in health during Clive's ten months absence. He had never been able to walk well, or take his accustomed exercise, after his fall. He was no more used to riding than the late Mr. Gibbon, whose person James's somewhat resembled, and of whose philosophy our Scottish friend was an admiring scholar. The Colonel gone, James would have arguments with Mr. Honeyman over their claret, bring down the famous XVth and XVIth chapters of the Decline and Fall upon him, and quite get the better of the clergyman. James, like many other sceptics, was very obstinate, and for his part believed that almost all parsons had as much belief as the Roman augurs in their ceremonies. Certainly, poor Honeyman, in their controversies, gave up one article after another, flying from James's assault; but the battle over, Charles Honeyman would pick up these accoutrements which he had flung away in his retreat, wipe them dry, and put them on again.

Lamed by his fall, and obliged to remain much within doors, where certain society did not always amuse him, James Binnie sought excitement in the pleasures of the table, partaking of them the more freely now that his health could afford them the less. Clive, the sly rogue, observed a great improvement in the commissariat since his good father's time, ate his dinner with thankfulness, and made no remarks. Nor did he confide to us for awhile his opinion that Mrs. Mack bored the good gentleman most severely; that he pined away under her kindnesses; sneaked off to his study-chair and his nap; was only too glad when some of the widow's friends came, or she went out; seeming to breathe more freely when she was gone, and drink his wine more cheerily when rid of the intolerable weight of her presence.

I protest the great ills of life are nothing—the loss of your fortune is a mere flea-bite; the loss of your wife—how many men have supported it and married comfortably afterwards? It is not what you lose, but what you have daily to bear that is hard. I can fancy nothing more cruel, after a long easy life of bachelorhood, than to have to sit day after day with a dull handsome woman opposite; to have to answer her speeches about the weather, housekeeping, and what not; to smile appropriately when she is disposed to be lively (that laughing at the jokes is the hardest part), and to model your conversation so as to suit her intelligence, knowing that a word used out of its downright signification will not be understood by your fair breakfast-maker. Women go through this simpering and smiling life, and bear it quite easily. Theirs is a life of hypocrisy. What good woman does not laugh at her husband's or father's jokes and stories time after time, and would not laugh at breakfast, lunch, and dinner, if he told them? Flattery is their nature—to coax, flatter, and sweetly befool some one is every woman's business. She is none if she declines this office. But men are not provided with such powers of humbug or endurance—they perish and pine away miserably when bored—or they shrink off to the club or public-house for comfort. I want to say as delicately as I can, and never liking to use rough terms regarding a handsome woman, that Mrs. Mackenzie, herself being in the highest spirits and the best humour, extinguished her half-brother, James Binnie, Esq.; that she was as a malaria to him, poisoning his atmosphere, numbing his limbs, destroying his sleep—that day after day as he sate down at breakfast, and she levelled common-places at her dearest James, her dearest James became more wretched under her. And no one could see what his complaint was. He called in the old physicians at the club. He dosed himself with poppy, and mandragora, and blue pill—lower and lower went poor James's mercury. If he wanted to move to Brighton or Cheltenham, well and good. Whatever were her engagements, or whatever pleasures darling Rosey might have in store, dear thing!—at her age, my dear Mrs. Newcome, would not one do all to make a young creature happy?—under *no* circumstances could I *think* of leaving my poor brother.

Mrs. Mackenzie thought herself a most highly principled woman, Mrs. Newcome had also a great opinion of her. These two ladies had formed a considerable friendship in the past months, the captain's widow having an unaffected reverence for the banker's lady, and thinking her one of the best informed and most superior women in the world. When she had a high opinion of a person Mrs. Mack always wisely told it. Mrs. Newcome in her turn thought Mrs. Mackenzie a very clever, agreeable, lady-like woman— not accomplished, but one could not have everything. "No, no, my dear," says simple Hobson, "never would do to have every woman as clever as *you* are, Maria. Women would have it all their own way then."

Maria, as her custom was, thanked God for being so virtuous and clever, and graciously admitted Mrs. and Miss Mackenzie into the circle of adorers of that supreme virtue and talent. Mr. Newcome took little Rosey and her mother to some parties. When any took place in Brianstone Square, they were generally allowed to come to tea.

When on the second day of his arrival the dutiful Clive went to dine with Mr. James, the ladies, in spite of their raptures at his return and delight at seeing him, were going in the evening to his aunt. Their talk was about the Princess all dinner time. The Prince and Princess were to dine in Brianstone Square. The Princess had ordered such and such things at the jeweller's—the Princess would take rank over an English Earl's daughter—over Lady Ann Newcome for instance. "O dear! I wish the Prince and Princess were smothered in the tower," growled James Binnie, "since you have got acquainted with 'em I have never heard of anything else."

Clive, like a wise man, kept his counsel about the Prince and Princess, with whom we have seen that he had had the honour of an interview that very day. But after dinner Rosey came round and whispered to her mamma, and after Rosey's whisper Mamma flung her arms round Rosey's neck and kissed her, and called her a thoughtful darling. "What do you think this creature says, Clive?" says Mrs. Mack, still holding her darling's little hand, "I wonder I had not thought of it myself."

"What is it, Mrs. Mackenzie?" asks Clive, laughing.

"She says why should not you come to your aunt's with us? We are sure Mrs. Newcome would be most happy to see you."

Rosey, with a little hand put to Mamma's mouth, said, "Why did you tell—you naughty Mamma! Isn't she a naughty Mamma, Uncle James?" More kisses follow after this sally, of which Uncle James receives one with perfect complacency: Mamma crying out as Rosey retires to dress, "That darling child is *always* thinking of others—always!"

Clive says, "he will sit and smoke a cheroot with Mr. Binnie, if they please." James's countenance falls. "We have left off *that* sort of thing here, my dear Clive, a long time," cries Mrs. Mackenzie, departing from the dining-room.

"But we have improved the claret, Clive, my boy!" whispers Uncle James. "Let us have another bottle, and we will drink to the dear Colonel's good health and speedy return—God bless him! I say, Clive, Tom seems to have had a most fortunate escape out of Winter's house—thanks to our friend Rummun Lall, and to have got into a capital good thing with this Bundelcund bank. They speak famously of it at Hanover Square, and I see the Hurkara quotes the shares at a premium already."

Clive did not know anything about the Bundelcund bank, except a few words in a letter from his father, which he had found in the City this morning, "And an uncommonly liberal remittance the governor has sent me home, Sir;" upon which they fill another bumper to the Colonel's health.

Mamma and Rosey come and show their pretty pink dresses before going to Mrs. Newcome's, and Clive lights a cigar in the hall—and isn't there a jubilation at the Haunt when the young fellow's face appears above the smoke-clouds there?

Chapter III.

ANY of Clive's Roman friends were by this time come to London, and the young man renewed his acquaintance with them, and had speedily a considerable circle of his own. He thought fit to allow himself a good horse or two, and appeared in the Park among other young dandies. He and Monsieur de Montcontour were sworn allies. Lord Fareham, who had purchased J.J.'s picture, was Clive's very good friend: Major Pendennis himself pronounced him to be a young fellow of agreeable manners, and very favourably *vu* (as the Major happened to know) in some very good quarters.

Ere many days Clive had been to Brighton to see Lady Ann and Sir Brian, and good Aunt Honeyman, in whose house the Baronet was lodged: and I suppose he found out, by some means or other, where Lady Kew lived in May Fair.

But her ladyship was not at home, nor was she at home on the second day, nor did there come any note from Ethel to her cousin. She did not ride in the Park as of old. Clive, *bien vu* as he was, did not belong to that great world as yet, in which he would be pretty sure to meet her every night at one of those parties where everybody goes. He read her name in the paper morning after morning, as having been present at Lady This's entertainment and Lady That's ministerial *réunion*. At first he was too shy to tell what the state of the case was, and took nobody into his confidence regarding his little *tendre*.

There he was riding through Queen Street, May Fair, attired in splendid raiment: never missing the Park; actually going to places of worship in the neighbourhood; and frequenting the opera—a waste of time which one would never have expected in a youth of his nurture. At length a certain observer of human nature remarking his state: rightly conjectured that he must be in love, and taxed him with the soft impeachment—on which the young man, no doubt anxious to open his heart to some one, poured out all that story which has before been narrated; and told how he thought his passion cured, and how it was cured; but when he heard from Kew at Naples that the engagement was over between him and Miss Newcome, Clive found his own flame kindle again with new ardour. He was wild to see her. He dashed off from Naples instantly on receiving the news that she was free. He had been ten days in London without getting a glimpse of her. "That Mrs. Mackenzie bothers me so I hardly know where to turn," said poor Clive, "and poor little Rosey is made to write me a note about something twice a day. She's a good dear little thing—little Rosey—and I really had thought once of—of—O never mind that! O Pen! I'm up another tree now! and a poor miserable young beggar I am!" In fact Mr. Pendennis was installed as confidant *vice* J.J.—absent on leave.

This is a part, which, especially for a few days, the present biographer has always liked well enough. For a while at least, I think almost every man or woman is interesting when in love. If you know of two or three such affairs going on in any soirée to which you may be invited—is not the party straightway amusing? Yonder goes Augustus Tomkins, working his way through the rooms to that far corner where demure Miss Hopkins is seated, to whom the stupid grinning Bumpkins thinks he is making himself agreeable. Yonder sits Miss Fanny *distraite*, and yet trying to smile as the captain is talking his folly, the parson his glib compliments. And see, her face lights up all of a sudden: her eyes beam with delight at the captain's stories, and at that delightful young clergyman likewise. It is because Augustus has appeared; their eyes only meet for one semi-second, but that is enough for Miss Fanny. Go on, Captain, with your twaddle!—Proceed, my reverend friend, with your smirking common-places! In the last two minutes the world has changed for Miss Fanny. That moment has come for which she has been fidgetting and longing and scheming all day! How different an interest, I say, has a meeting of people for a philosopher who knows of a few such little secrets, to that which your vulgar looker-on feels, who comes but to eat the ices, and stare at the ladies' dresses and beauty! There are two frames of mind under which London society is bearable to a man—to be an actor in one of those sentimental performances above hinted at: or to be a spectator and watch it. But as for the mere *dessus de cartes*—would not an arm-chair and the dullest of books be better than that dull game?

So, I not only became Clive's confidant in this affair, but took a pleasure in extracting the young fellow's secrets from him, or rather in encouraging him to pour them forth. Thus was the great part of the previous tale revealed to me: thus Jack Belsize's misadventures, of the first part of which we had only heard in London (and whither he returned presently to be reconciled to his father, after his elder brother's death). Thus my Lord Kew's secret history came into my possession; let us hope for the public's future delectation, and the chronicler's private advantage. And many a night until daylight did appear, has poor Clive stamped his chamber or my own, pouring his story out to me, his griefs and raptures; recalling, in his wild young way, recollections of Ethel's sayings and doings; uttering descriptions of her beauty: and raging against the cruelty which she exhibited towards him.

As soon as the new confidant heard the name of the young lover's charmer, to do Mr. Pendennis justice, he endeavoured to fling as much cold water upon Clive's flame, as a small private engine could be brought to[1] pour on such a conflagration. "Miss Newcome! my dear Clive," says the confidant, "do you know to what you are aspiring? For the last three months Miss Newcome has been the greatest lioness in London: the reigning beauty: the winning horse: the first favourite out of the whole Belgravian harem. No young woman of this year has come near her: those of past seasons she has distanced, and utterly put to shame. Miss Blackcap, Lady Blanch Blackcap's daughter was (as perhaps you are not aware) considered by her mamma the great beauty of last season; and it was considered rather shabby of the young Marquis of Farintosh, to leave town without offering to change Miss Blackcap's name. Heaven bless you! this year Farintosh will not look at Miss Blackcap! *He* finds people at home when (ha! I see you wince, my suffering innocent!)—when he calls in Queen Street; yes, and Lady Kew, who is one of the cleverest women in England, will listen for hours to Lord Farintosh's conversation; than whom, the Rotten Row of Hyde Park cannot show a greater booby. Miss Blackcap may retire, like Jephthah's daughter, for all Farintosh will relieve her. Then, my dear fellow, there were, as possibly you do not know, Lady Hermengilde and Lady Yseult, Lady Rackstraw's lovely twins, whose appearance created such a sensation at Lady Hautbois' first—was it her first or was it her second?—yes, it was her second—breakfast. Whom weren't they going to marry? Crackthorpe was mad they said about both.—Bustington, Sir John Fobsby, the young Baronet with the immense Northern property—the Bishop of Windsor was actually said to be smitten with one of them, but did not like to offer, as her present M——y, like Qu—n El—z—b—th, of gracious memory, is said to object to bishops, as bishops, marrying. Where is Bustington? Where is Crackthorpe? Where is Fobsby, the young Baronet of the North? My dear fellow, when those two girls come into a room now, they make no more sensation than you or I. Miss Newcome has carried their admirers away from them: Fobsby has actually, it is said, proposed for her: and the *real* reason of that affair between Lord Bustington and Captain Crackthorpe of the Royal Horse Guards Green, was a speech of Bustington's, hinting that Miss Newcome had not behaved well in throwing Lord Kew over. Don't you know what old Lady Kew will do with this girl, Clive? She will marry Miss Newcome to the best man. If a richer and better parti than Lord Farintosh presents himself—then it will be Farintosh's

[1] be brought to *E1*] [omitted] *R*

turn to find that Lady Kew is not at home. Is there any young man in the Peerage unmarried and richer than Farintosh? I forget. Why does not some one publish a list of the young male nobility and baronetage, their names, weights, and probable fortunes? I don't mean for the matrons of May Fair—they have the list by heart and study it in secret—but for young men in the world; so that they may know what their chances are, and who naturally has the pull over them. Let me see—there is young Lord Gaunt, who will have a great fortune, and is desirable because you know his father is locked up—but he is only ten years old—no—they can scarcely bring him forward as Farintosh's rival.

"You look astonished, my poor boy? You think it is wicked in me to talk in this brutal way about bargain and sale; and say that your heart's darling is, at this minute, being paced up and down the May Fair market to be taken away by the best bidder. Can you count purses with Sultan Farintosh? Can you compete even with Sir John Fobsby of the North? What I say is wicked and worldly, is it? So it is: but it is true, as true as Tattersall's—as true as Circassia or Virginia. Don't you know that the Circassian girls are proud of their bringing up, and take rank according to the prices which they fetch? And you go and buy yourself some new clothes, and a fifty pound horse, and put a penny rose in your button hole, and ride past her window, and think to win this prize? O, you idiot! A penny rosebud! Put money in your purse. A fifty pound hack when a butcher rides as good a one!—Put money in your purse. A brave young heart, all courage and love and honour! Put money in thy purse—t'other coin don't pass in the market—at least where old Lady Kew has the stall."

By these remonstrances, playful though serious, Clive's adviser sought to teach him wisdom about his love affair; and the advice was received as advice upon those occasions usually is.

After calling thrice, and writing to Miss Newcome, there came a little note from that young lady, saying, "Dear Clive. We were so sorry we were out when you called. We shall be at home to-morrow at lunch, when Lady Kew hopes you will come, and see, yours ever, E. N."

Clive went—poor Clive. He had the satisfaction of shaking Ethel's hand, and a finger of Lady Kew; of eating a mutton chop in Ethel's presence; of conversing about the state of art at Rome with Lady Kew, and describing the last works of Gibson and Macdonald. The visit lasted but for half an hour. Not for one minute was Clive allowed to see Ethel alone. At three o'clock Lady Kew's carriage was announced and our young gentleman rose to take his leave, and had the pleasure of seeing the most noble Peer, Marquis of Farintosh and Earl of Rossmont, descend from his lordship's brougham and enter at Lady Kew's door, followed by a domestic bearing a small stack of flowers from Covent Garden.

It befel that the good-natured Lady Fareham had a ball in these days; and meeting Clive in the Park, her lord invited him to the entertainment. Mr. Pendennis had also the honour of a card. Accordingly Clive took me up at Bays's, and we proceeded to the ball together.

The lady of the house, smiling upon all her guests, welcomed with particular kindness her young friend from Rome. "Are you related to *the* Miss

Newcome, Lady Ann Newcome's daughter? Her cousin? She will be here to-night." Very likely Lady Fareham did not see Clive wince and blush at this announcement, her ladyship having to occupy herself with a thousand other people. Clive found a dozen of his Roman friends in the room, ladies young and middle aged, plain and handsome, all glad to see his kind face. The house was splendid; the ladies magnificently dressed; the ball beautiful, though it appeared a little dull until that event took place whereof we treated two pages back (in the allegory of Mr. Tomkins and Miss Hopkins), and Lady Kew and her granddaughter made their appearance.

That old woman, who began to look more and more like the wicked fairy of the stories, who is not invited to the Princess's Christening Feast, had this advantage over her likeness, that she was invited everywhere; though how she, at her age, could fly about to so many parties, unless she was a fairy, no one could say. Behind the fairy, up the marble stairs, came the most noble Farintosh, with that vacuous leer which distinguishes his lordship. Ethel seemed to be carrying the stack of flowers which the marquis had sent to her. The noble Bustington (Viscount Bustington, I need scarcely tell the reader, is the heir of the house of Podbury), the Baronet of the North, the gallant Crackthorpe, the first men in town, in a word, gathered round the young beauty forming her court; and little Dick Hitchin, who goes everywhere, you may be sure was near her with a compliment and a smile. Ere this arrival, the twins had been giving themselves great airs in the room—the poor twins! when Ethel appeared they sank into shuddering insignificance, and had to put up with the conversation and attentions of second-rate men, belonging to second-rate clubs, in heavy dragoon regiments. One of them actually walked with a dancing barrister; but he was related to a duke, and it was expected the Lord Chancellor would give him something very good.

Before he saw Ethel, Clive vowed he was aware of her. Indeed, had not Lady Fareham told him Miss Newcome was coming? Ethel, on the contrary, not expecting him, or not having the prescience of love, exhibited signs of surprise when she beheld him, her eyebrows arching, her eyes darting looks of pleasure. When Grandmamma happened to be in another room, she beckoned Clive to her, dismissing Crackthorpe and Fobsby, Farintosh and Bustington, the amorous youth who around her bowed, and summoning Mr. Clive up to an audience with the air of a young princess.

And so she was a princess; and this the region of her special dominion. The wittiest and handsomest, she deserved to reign in such a place, by right of merit and by general election. Clive felt her superiority, and his own shortcomings; he came up to her as to a superior person. Perhaps she was not sorry to let him see how she ordered away grandees and splendid Bustingtons, informing them, with a superb manner, that she wished to speak to her cousin—that handsome young man with the light mustache yonder.

"Do you know many people? This is your first appearance in society? Shall I introduce you to some nice girls to dance with? What very pretty buttons!"

"Is that what you wanted to say?" asked Clive, rather bewildered.

"What does one say at a ball? One talks conversation suited to the place. If I were to say to Captain Crackthorpe, 'What pretty buttons!' he would be delighted. But you—you have a soul above buttons, I suppose."

"Being, as you say, a stranger in this sort of society, you see I am not accustomed to—to the exceeding brilliancy of its conversation," said Clive.

"What! you want to go away, and we haven't seen each other for near a year," cries Ethel, in quite a natural voice. "Sir John Fobsby, I'm very sorry—but do let me off this dance. I have just met my cousin, whom I have not seen for a whole year, and I want to talk to him."

"It was not my fault that you did not see me sooner. I wrote to you that I only got your letter a month ago. You never answered the second I wrote you from Rome. Your letter lay there at the post ever so long, and was forwarded to me at Naples."

"Where?" asked Ethel.

"I saw Lord Kew there." Ethel was smiling with all her might, and kissing her hand to the twins, who passed at this moment with their mamma. "O, indeed, you saw—how do you do?—Lord Kew."

"And, having seen him, I came over to England," said Clive.

Ethel looked at him, gravely. "What am I to understand by that, Clive?— You came over because it was very hot at Naples, and because you wanted to see your friends here, n'est-ce pas? How glad Mamma was to see you! You know she loves you as if you were her own son."

"What, as much as that angel, Barnes!" cries Clive, bitterly; "impossible."

Ethel looked once more. Her present mood and desire was to treat Clive as a chit, as a young fellow without consequence—a thirteenth younger brother. But in his looks and behaviour there was that which seemed to say not too many liberties were to be taken with him.

"Why weren't you here a month sooner, and you might have seen the marriage? It was a very pretty thing. Everybody was there. Clara, and so did Barnes really, looked quite handsome."

"It must have been beautiful," continued Clive; "quite a touching sight, I am sure. Poor Charles Belsize could not be present because his brother was dead; and ——"

"And what else, pray, Mr. Newcome!" cries Miss, in great wrath, her pink nostrils beginning to quiver. "I did not think, really, that when we met after so many months, I was to be—insulted; yes, insulted, by the mention of that name."

"I most humbly ask pardon," said Clive, with a grave bow. "Heaven forbid that I should wound your sensibility, Ethel! It is, as you say, my first appearance in society. I talk about things or persons that I should not mention. I should talk about buttons, should I? which you were good enough to tell me was the proper subject of conversation. Mayn't I even speak of connexions of the family? Mr. Belsize, through this marriage, has the honour of being connected with you; and even I, in a remote degree, may boast of a sort of an ever-so-distant cousinship with him. What an honour for me!"

"Pray what is the meaning of all this?" cries Miss Ethel, surprised, and perhaps alarmed. Indeed, Clive scarcely knew. He had been chafing all the while he talked with her; smothering anger as he saw the young men round about her; revolting against himself for the very humility of his obedience, and angry at the eagerness and delight with which he had come at her call.

"The meaning is, Ethel"—he broke out, seizing the opportunity—"that when a man comes a thousand miles to see you, and shake your hand, you should give it him a little more cordially than you choose to do to me; that when a kinsman knocks at your door, time after time, you should try and admit him; and that when you meet him you should treat him like an old friend: not as you treated me when my Lady Kew vouchsafed to give me admittance: not as you treat these fools that are fribbling round about you," cries Mr. Clive, in a great rage, folding his arms, and glaring round on a number of the most innocent young swells; and he continued looking as if he would like to knock a dozen of their heads together. "Am I keeping Miss Newcome's admirers from her?"

"That is not for me to say," she said, quite gently. He was; but to see him angry did not displease Miss Newcome.

"That young man who came for you just now," Clive went on—"that Sir John ——"

"Are you angry with me because I sent him away?" said Ethel, putting out a hand. "Hark! there is the music. Take me in and waltz with me. Don't you know it is not *my* door at which you knocked?" she said, looking up into his face as simply and kindly as of old. She whirled round the dancing-room with him in triumph, the other beauties dwindling before her; she looked more and more beautiful with each rapid move of the waltz, her colour heightening and her eyes seeming to brighten. Not till the music stopped did she sink down on a seat, panting, and smiling radiant—as many many hundred years ago I remember to have seen Taglioni, after a conquering *pas seul*. She nodded a thank you to Clive. It seemed that there was a perfect reconciliation. Lady Kew came in just at the end of the dance, scowling when she beheld Ethel's partner; but in reply to her remonstrances Ethel shrugged her fair shoulders; with a look which seemed to say *je le veux*, gave an arm to her grandmother, and walked off, saucily protecting her.

Clive's friend had been looking on observingly and curiously as the scene between them had taken place, and at the dance with which the reconciliation had been celebrated. I must tell you that this arch young creature had formed the object of my observation for some months past, and that I watched her as I have watched a beautiful panther at the Zoological Gardens, so bright of eye, so sleek of coat, so slim in form, so swift and agile in her spring.

A more brilliant young coquette than Miss Newcome, in her second season, these eyes never looked upon, that is the truth. In her first year, being engaged to Lord Kew, she was perhaps a little more reserved and quiet. Besides, her mother went out with her that first season, to whom Miss Newcome, except for a little occasional flightiness, was invariably obedient and ready to come to call. But when Lady Kew appeared as her Duenna, the girl's delight seemed to be to plague the old lady, and she would dance with the very youngest sons merely to put Grandmamma in a passion. In this way poor young Cubley (who has two hundred a year of allowance, besides eighty, and an annual rise of five in the Treasury) actually thought that Ethel was in love with him, and consulted with the young men in his room in Downing Street, whether two hundred and eighty a year, with five pound more next year, would be enough for them to keep house on? Young Tandy of the Temple, Lord Skibbereen's younger son, who sate in the House for some time on the Irish Catholic side, was also deeply smitten, and many a night in our walks home from the parties at the other end of the town, would entertain me with his admiration and passion for her.

"If you have such a passion for her, why not propose?" it was asked of Mr. Tandy.

"Propose! propose to a Russian Archduchess," cries young Tandy. "She's beautiful, she's delightful, she's witty. I have never seen anything like her eyes; they send me wild—wild," says Tandy—(slapping his waistcoat under Temple Bar)—but a more audacious little flirt never existed since the days of Cleopatra."

With this opinion likewise in my mind, I had been looking on during Clive's proceedings with Miss Ethel—not I say without admiration of the young lady who was leading him such a dance. The waltz over, I congratulated him on his own performance. His continental practice had greatly improved him. "And as for your partner, it is delightful to see her," I went on. "I always like to be by when Miss Newcome dances. I had sooner see her than anybody since Taglioni. Look at her now, with her neck up, and her little foot out, just as she is preparing to start! Happy Lord Bustington!"

"You are angry with her because she cut you," growls Clive, "You know you said she cut you, or forgot you; and your vanity's wounded, that is why you are so satirical."

"How can Miss Newcome remember all the men who are presented to her?" says the other. "Last year she talked to me because she wanted to know about you. This year she doesn't talk: because I suppose she does not want to know about you any more."

"Hang it. Do—on't, Pen," cries Clive, as a schoolboy cries out to another not to hit him.

"She does not pretend to observe: and is in full conversation with the amiable Bustington. Delicious interchange of noble thoughts! But she is observing us talking, and knows that we are talking about her. If ever you marry her, Clive, which is absurd, I shall lose you for a friend. You will infallibly tell her what I think of her: and she will order you to give me up." Clive had gone off in a brown study, as his interlocutor continued. "Yes, she is a flirt. She can't help her nature. She tries to vanquish every one who comes near her. She is a little out of breath from waltzing, and so she pretends to be listening to poor Bustington, who is out of breath too, but puffs out his best in order to make himself agreeable. With what a pretty air she appears to listen! Her eyes actually seem to brighten."

"*What?*" says Clive, with a start.

I could not comprehend the meaning of the start: nor did I care much to know: supposing that the young man was waking up from some lover's

CLIVE IN TROUBLE

reverie: and the evening sped away, Clive not quitting the ball until Miss Newcome and the Countess of Kew had departed. No further communication appeared to take place between the cousins that evening. I think it was Captain Crackthorpe who gave the young lady an arm into her carriage; Sir John Fobsby having the happiness to conduct the old Countess, and carrying the pink bag for the shawls, wrappers, &c., on which her ladyship's coronet and initials are emblazoned. Clive may have made a movement as if to step forward, but a single finger from Miss Newcome warned him back.

Clive and his two friends in Lamb Court had made an engagement for the next Saturday to dine at Greenwich; but on the morning of that day there came a note from him to say that he thought of going down to see his aunt, Miss Honeyman, and begged to recal his promise to us. Saturday is a holiday with gentlemen of our profession. We had invited F. Bayham, Esquire, and promised ourselves a merry evening, and were unwilling to balk ourselves of the pleasure on account of the absence of our young Roman. So we three went to London Bridge Station at an early hour, proposing to breathe the fresh air of Greenwich Park before dinner. And, at London Bridge, by the most singular coincidence, Lady Kew's carriage drove up to the Brighton entrance, and Miss Ethel and her maid stepped out of the brougham.

When Miss Newcome and her maid entered the Brighton station, did Mr. Clive, by another singular coincidence, happen also to be there? What more natural and dutiful than that he should go and see his aunt Miss Honeyman? What more proper than that Miss Ethel should pass the Saturday and Sunday with her sick father; and take a couple of wholesome nights' rest after those five weary past evenings, for each of which we may reckon a couple of soirées and a ball? And that relations should travel together, the young lady being protected by her *femme-de-chambre;* that surely, as every one must allow, was perfectly right and proper.

That a biographer should profess to know everything which passes, even in a confidential talk in a first-class carriage between two lovers, seems perfectly absurd; not that grave historians do not pretend to the same wonderful degree of knowledge—reporting meetings the most occult of conspirators; private interviews between monarchs and their ministers, even the secret thoughts and motives of those personages, which possibly the persons themselves did not know—all for which the present writer will pledge his known character for veracity is, that on a certain day certain parties had a conversation of which the upshot was so and so. He guesses, of course, at a great deal of what took place; knowing the characters, and being informed at some time of their meeting. You do not suppose that I bribed the *femme-de-chambre,* or that those two city gents, who sate in the same carriage with our young friends, and could not hear a word they said, reported their talk to me? If Clive and Ethel had had a coupé to themselves, I would yet boldly tell what took place, but the coupé was taken by other three young city gents who smoked the whole way.

"Well, then," the bonnet begins close up to the hat, "tell me, Sir, is it true that you were so very much *épris* of the Miss Freemans at Rome; and that

afterwards you were so wonderfully attentive to the third Miss Balliol? Did
you draw her portrait? You know you drew her portrait. You painters always pretend to admire girls with auburn hair, because Titian and Raphael
painted it. Has the Fornarina red hair? Why we are at Croydon, I declare!"

"The Fornarina"—the hat replies to the bonnet, "if that picture at the
Borghese palace be an original, or a likeness of her—is not a handsome
woman, with vulgar eyes and mouth, and altogether a most mahogany-
coloured person. She is so plain, in fact, I think that very likely it *is* the real
woman; for it is with their own fancies that men fall in love,—or rather
every woman is handsome to the lover. You know how old Helen must
have been."

"I don't know any such thing, or anything about her. Who was Helen?"
asks the bonnet; and indeed she did not know.

"It's a long story, and such an old scandal now, that there is no use in
repeating it," says Clive.

"You only talk about Helen because you wish to turn away the conversation from Miss Freeman," cries the young lady—"from Miss Balliol, I
mean."

"We will talk about whichever you please. Which shall we begin to pull
to pieces?" says Clive. You see, to be in this carriage—to be actually with
her—to be looking into those wonderful lucid eyes—to see her sweet mouth
dimpling, and hear her sweet voice ringing with its delicious laughter—
to have that hour and a half his own, in spite of all the world-dragons,
grandmothers, *convenances*, the future—made the young fellow so happy,
filled his whole frame and spirit with a delight so keen, that no wonder he
was gay, and brisk, and lively.

"And so you knew of my goings on?" he asked. O me! they were at
Reigate by this time; there was Gatton Park flying before them on the wings
of the wind.

"I know of a number of things," says the bonnet, nodding with ambrosial
curls.

"And you would not answer the second letter I wrote to you?"

"We were in great perplexity. One cannot be always answering young
gentlemen's letters. I had considerable doubt about answering a note I got
from Charlotte Street, Fitzroy Square," says the lady's chapeau. "No, Clive,
we must not write to one another," she continued more gravely, "or only
very, very seldom. Nay, my meeting you here to-day is by the merest chance
I am sure; for when I mentioned at Lady Fareham's the other evening that
I was going to see Papa at Brighton to-day, I never for *one moment* thought
of seeing *you* in the train. But as you are here, it can't be helped; and I may
as well tell you that there are obstacles."

"What, *other* obstacles?" Clive gasped out.

"Nonsense—you silly boy! No other obstacles but those which always
have existed, and must. When we parted—that is, when you left us at
Baden, you knew it was for the best. You had your profession to follow, and
could not go on idling about—about a family of sick people and children.
Every man has his profession, and you yours, as you would have it. We are
so nearly allied that we may—we may like each other like brother and sister

almost. I don't know what Barnes would say if he heard me? Wherever you and your father are, how can I ever think of you but—but you know how? I always shall, always. There are certain feelings we have which I hope never can change; though, if you please, about them I intend never to speak any more. Neither you nor I can alter our conditions, but must make the best of them. You shall be a fine clever painter; and I,—who knows what will happen to me? I know what is going to happen to-day; I am going to see Papa and Mamma, and be as happy as I can till Monday morning."

"I know what I wish would happen now," said Clive,—they were going screaming through a tunnel.

"What?" said the bonnet in the darkness; and the engine was roaring so loudly, that he was obliged to put his head quite close to say—

"I wish the tunnel would fall in and close upon us, or that we might travel on for ever and ever."

Here there was a great jar of the carriage, and the lady's maid, and I think Miss Ethel, gave a shriek. The lamp above was so dim that the carriage was almost totally dark. No wonder the lady's maid was frightened! but the daylight came streaming in, and all poor Clive's wishes of rolling and rolling on for ever were put an end to by the implacable sun in a minute.

Ah, why was it the quick train? Suppose it had been the parliamentary train?—even that too would have come to an end. They came and said, "Tickets, please," and Clive held out the three of their party—his, and Ethel's, and her maid's. I think for such a ride as that he was right to give up Greenwich. Mr. Kuhn was in waiting with a carriage for Miss Ethel. She shook hands with Clive, returning his pressure.

"I may come and see you?" he said.

"You may come and see Mamma—yes."

"And where are you staying?"

"Bless my soul—they were staying at Miss Honeyman's!" Clive burst into a laugh. Why he was going there too! Of course Aunt Honeyman had no room for him, her house being quite full with the other Newcomes.

It was a most curious coincidence their meeting; but altogether Lady Ann thought it was best to say nothing about the circumstance to Grandmamma. I myself am puzzled to say which would have been the better course to pursue under the circumstances; there were so many courses open. As they had gone so far, should they go on farther together? Suppose they were going to the same house at Brighton, oughtn't they to have gone in the same carriage, with Kuhn and the maid of course? Suppose they met by chance at the station, ought they to have travelled in separate carriages? I ask any gentleman and father of a family, when he was immensely smitten with his present wife, Mrs. Brown, if he had met her travelling with her maid, in the mail, when there was a vacant place, what would he himself have done?

Chapter IV.

INJURED INNOCENCE.

FROM CLIVE NEWCOME, ESQ., TO LIEUT.-COL. NEWCOME, C.B.

"BRIGHTON, *June* 12. 18—

Y DEAREST FATHER,—
As the weather was growing very hot at Naples and you wished I should come to England to see Mr. Binnie, I came accordingly: and have been here three weeks and write to you from Aunt Honeyman's parlour at Brighton, where you ate your last dinner before embarking for India. I found your splendid remittance on calling in Fog Court: and have invested a part of the sum in a good horse to ride, upon which I take my diversion with other young dandies in the Park. Florac is in England, but he has no need of your kindness— Only think! he is Prince de Montcontour now, the second title of the Duc d'Ivry's family: and M. le Comte de Florac is Duc d'Ivry in consequence of the demise of t'other old gentleman. I believe the late Duke's wife shortened his life. O what a woman! She caused a duel between Lord Kew and a Frenchman, which has in its turn occasioned all sorts of evil and division in families as you shall hear.

"In the first place, in consequence of the duel and of incompatibility of temper, the match between Kew and E. N. has been broken off. I met Lord Kew at Naples with his mother and brother, nice quiet people as you would like them. Kew's wound and subsequent illness have altered him a good deal. He has become much *more serious* than he used to be: not ludicrously so at all, but he says he thinks his past life has been useless and even criminal and he wishes to change it. He has sold his horses and sown his wild oats. He has turned quite a sober quiet gentleman.

"At our meeting he told me of what had happened between him and

Ethel, of whom he spoke *most kindly and generously,* but avowing his opinion that they never could have been happy in married life. And now I think my dear old father will see that there may be another reason besides my desire to see Mr. Binnie which has brought me tumbling back to England again. If need be to speak, I never shall have, I hope, any secrets from you. I have not said much about one which has given me the deuce's disquiet for ten months past: because there was no good in talking about it, or vexing you needlessly with reports of my griefs and woes.

"Well, when we were at Baden' in September last, and E. and I wrote those letters in common to you, I daresay you can fancy what my feelings might have been towards such a beautiful young creature who has a hundred faults for which I love her just as much as for the good that is in her. I became dreadfully smitten indeed, and knowing that she was engaged to Lord Kew, I did as you told me you did once when the enemy was too strong for you, *I ran away.*—I had a bad time of it for two or three months. At Rome, however, I[1] began to take matters more easily, my naturally fine appetite returned, and at the end of the season[2] I found myself uncommonly happy in the society of the Miss Balliols and the Miss Freemans—but when Kew told me at Naples of what had happened; there was straightway *a fresh eruption* in my heart, and I was fool enough to come almost without sleep to London in order to catch a glimpse of the bright eyes of E. N.

"She is now in this very house up-stairs with one aunt whilst the other lets lodgings to her. I have seen her but very seldom indeed since I came to London, where Sir Brian and Lady Ann do not pass the season and Ethel goes about to a dozen parties every week with old Lady Kew, who neither loves you nor me. Hearing E. say she was coming down to her parents at Brighton, I made so bold as to waylay her at the train (though I didn't tell her that I passed three hours in the waiting-room); and we made the journey together, and she was very very kind and beautiful, and though I suppose I might just as well ask the[3] Royal Princess to have me, I can't help hoping and longing and hankering after her—And Aunt Honeyman must have found out that I am fond of her, for the old lady has received me with a scolding. Uncle[4] Charles seems to be in very good condition again. I saw him in full clerical feather at Madame de Montcontour's, a good-natured body who drops her h's, though Florac is not aware of their absence. Pendennis and Warrington I know would send you their best regards. Pen is conceited but much kinder in reality than he has the air of being. Fred Bayham is doing well and prospering in his mysterious way.

"Mr. Binnie is not looking at all well: and Mrs. Mack—well, as I know you never attack a lady behind her lovely back, I won't say a word of Mrs. Mack—but she has taken possession of Uncle James: and seems to me to

[1] months. At Rome, however, I *E1*] months—it so happened there was another fellow running away for the same reason, Captain Belsize whom you may remember—We groaned and moaned together for a month and consoled each other as best we might. Then we parted, and I and J.J. went to Rome; then I *Ms*
[2] season *E1*] Roman season *Ms*
[3] the *E1*] a *Ms*
[4] scolding. Uncle *E1*] scolding on my return from abroad and is as sulky and angry and as proud as old Lady Kew. ¶"Uncle *Ms*

weigh upon him somehow. Rosey is as pretty and good-natured as ever and has learned two new songs; but you see with my sentiments in another quarter, I feel as it were guilty and awkward in company of Rosey and her mamma. They have become the very greatest friends with Brianstone Square and Mrs. Mack is always citing Aunt Hobson as the most superior of women—in which opinion I daresay Aunt Hobson concurs.

"Good bye, my dearest Father: my sheet is full. I wish I could put my arm in yours and pace up and down the pier with you and tell you more and more. But you know enough now and that I am your affectionate Son always,   "C. N."

In fact when Mr. Clive appeared at Steyne Gardens stepping out of the fly, and handing Miss Ethel thence, Miss Honeyman of course was very glad to see her nephew, and saluted him with a little embrace to show her sense of pleasure at his visit. But the next day being Sunday, when Clive with a most engaging smile on his countenance walked over to breakfast from his hotel: Miss Honeyman would scarcely speak to him during the meal, looked out at him very haughtily from under her Sunday cap[5] in the most haughty manner, and received his stories about Italy with oh, ah, indeed,— in a very unkind manner. And when breakfast was over and she had done washing her china,[6] she fluttered up to Clive, with such an agitation of plumage, redness of craw, and anger[7] of manner as a maternal hen shows if she has reason to think you menace her chickens—She fluttered up to Clive I say, and cried out—"Not in *this*[8] house, Clive. Not in this house I beg you to understand *that*."

Clive looking amazed said, "Certainly not, Ma'am. I never did do it in the house as I know you don't like it. I was going into the Square." The young man meaning that he was about to smoke,[9] and conjecturing that his aunt's anger applied to that practice.

"*You* know very well what I mean, Sir! Don't try to turn *me* off in that highty-tighty way. My dinner to-day is at half-past one. You can[1] dine or not as you like"—and the old lady flounced out of the room.

Poor Clive stood rolling his cigar in sad perplexity of spirit: until Mrs. Honeyman's servant Hannah entered, who for her part grinned and looked particularly sly. "In the name of goodness, Hannah, what is the row about?" cries Mr. Clive. "What is my aunt scolding at? what are you grinning at,[2] you old Cheshire Cat?"

"Git long,[3] Master Clive," says Hannah patting the cloth.[4]

---

[5] him very haughtily ... cap *E1*] him from under her Sunday cap in the most haughty manner, *Ms*
[6] her china, *E1*] up her chayny *Ms*
[7] anger *E1*] furiousness *Ms*
[8] [Italics added in *E1*]
[9] smoke, *E1*] smoke his cigar in the Square, *Ms*
[1] can *E1*] are welcome to *Ms*
[2] grinning at, *E1*] grinning it, *Ms*
[3] long, *Ms E1*] along, *R*
[4] patting the cloth. *E1*] patting and folding the table cloth. *Ms*

"Git along! why git along and where[5] am I to git along to?"[6]

"Did ee do ut really now? Master Clive," cries Mrs. Honeyman's attendant grinning with the utmost good humour. "Well! she be as pretty a young lady as ever I saw. And as I told my Missis, 'Miss Martha,' says I, 'there's a pair on 'em.' Though Missis was mortal angry to be sure. She never could bear it."[7]

"Bear *what?* you old goose!" cries Clive who by these playful[8] names had been wont to designate Hannah these twenty years past.

"A young gentleman and a young lady a kissing of each other in[9] the railway coach," says Hannah jerking up with her finger to the cieling—as much as to say, "There[1] she is! Lar, she be a pretty young creature, that she be! and so I told Miss Martha." Thus differently had the news which had come to them on the previous night affected the old lady and her maid.

The news was, that Miss Newcome's maid (a giddy thing from the country, who had not even learned as yet to hold her tongue) had announced with giggling delight to Lady Ann's maid, who was taking tea with Mrs. Hicks, that Mr. Clive had given Miss Ethel a kiss in the tunnel, and she supposed it was a match. This intelligence Hannah Hicks took to her mistress, of whose angry behaviour to Clive the next morning you may now understand the cause.

Clive did not know whether to laugh or to be in a rage. He swore that he was as innocent of all intention of kissing Miss Ethel as of embracing Queen Elizabeth. He was shocked to think of his cousin, walking above, fancy-free in maiden meditation, whilst this conversation regarding her was carried on below. How could he face her, or her mother, or even her maid, now he had cognisance of this naughty calumny? "Of course Hannah had contradicted it?" "Of course I have a done no such a thing indeed," replied Master Clive's old friend; "of course I have set 'em down a bit; for when little Trimmer said it, and she supposed it was all settled between you, seeing how it had been a going on in foreign parts last year, Mrs. Pincott says, 'Hold your silly tongue, Trimmer,' she says; 'Miss Ethel marry a painter, indeed, Trimmer!' says she, 'while she has refused to be a Countess,' she says; 'and can be a Marchioness any day, and will be a Marchioness. Marry a painter, indeed!' Mrs. Pincott says; 'Trimmer I'm surprised at your impidence.' So, my dear, I got angry at that," Clive's champion continued, "and says I, if my young Master ain't good enough for any young lady in this world, says I, I'd like you to show her to me: and if his dear father, the Colonel, says I, ain't as good as your old gentleman up-stairs, says I, who has gruel and dines upon doctor's stuff, then, Mrs. Pincott, says I, my name isn't what it is, says I. Those were my very words, Master Clive, my dear;

---

[5] and where *E1*] and confound it where *Ms*

[6] [*Ms* adds: exclaims the youth.]

[7] could bear it." *E1*] could abide it—Lar, Master Clive! Down tu Borhambury one day in the shrobberee when one of the young gentlemen was a courting your poor mother, Miss Ann—Lar bless us you should ha seen Miss Martha and how she came on! She never cude bear it and never wude." *Ms*

[8] playful *E1*] playful but imperious *Ms*

[9] other in *E1*] other as you did yesterday in *Ms*

[1] [Page 4 of the *Ms* is missing. Text from "she is!" through "innocent as you are." (34.13) is supplied from the first edition.]

and then Mrs. Pincott says, Mrs. Hicks, she says, you don't understand society, she says; you don't understand society, he! he!" and the country lady, with considerable humour, gave an imitation of the town lady's manner.

At this juncture Miss Honeyman re-entered the parlour, arrayed in her Sunday bonnet, her stiff and spotless collar, her Cashmere shawl, and Agra brooch, and carrying her Bible and Prayer-book, each stitched in its neat cover of brown silk. "Don't stay chattering here, you idle woman," she cried to her attendant with extreme asperity. "And you, Sir, if you wish to smoke your cigars, you had best walk down to the cliff where the Cockneys are!" she added, glowering at Clive.

"Now I understand it all," Clive said, trying to deprecate her anger, "My dear good aunt, it's a most absurd mistake; upon my honour Miss Ethel is as innocent as you are."

"Innocent or not—this house is not intended for assignations, Clive! As long as Sir Brian Newcome lodges here, you will be pleased to keep away from it, Sir: and though I don't approve of Sunday travelling I think the very best thing you can do is to put yourself into[2] the train and go back to London."

And now young people who read my moral pages, you will see how highly imprudent it is to sit with your cousins in railway-carriages; and how, though you may not mean the slightest harm in the world, a great deal may be attributed to you; and how, when you think you are managing your little absurd love-affairs ever so quietly, Jeames and Betsy in the servants' hall are very likely talking about them, and you are putting yourself in the power of those[3] menials. If the perusal of these lines has rendered one single young couple uncomfortable, surely my amiable end is answered, and I have written not altogether in vain.

Clive was going away, innocent though he was, yet quivering under his aunt's reproof: and so put out of countenance that he had not even thought of lighting the great cigar which he stuck into his foolish mouth; when a shout of "Clive Clive!" from half-a-dozen little voices roused him and presently as many little Newcomes came toddling down the stairs, and this one clung round his knees, and that at the skirts of his coat, and another took his hand and said he must come and walk with them on the beach.

So away went Clive to walk with his cousins, and then[4] to see his old friend Miss Cann with whom and the elder children he walked to Church,

[2] into *Ms*] in *E1*
[3] those *Ms E1*] these *R*
[4] beach ... and then *E1*] beach; and their attendants made him a bow, among them little Trimmer who acknowledged him quite respectfully, and looked as demure and innocent as if she had not caused all this disturbance we have been narrating. With Sir Brian ill and Lady Ann and Ethel up-stairs of course requiring apartments for themselves, how could all these little folks get room in Miss Honeyman's house and would they not interrupt their papa by their noise? I think it is most possible that they and their Governess were at Thompson's the lodgings next door, from the bow-windows of which they could crow and sing and make the signs to their elders in the neighbouring house—Thompson's lodgings very clean and nice now, how different from the same apartments when the careless Bugsby rented them! So away went Clive to walk with his cousins—who told him all their news and how they had got a new Governess, such a funny little kind old Governess, much nicer than Miss Quigley who knew Clive too, and her name was Miss Cann—And they all went forth on to the Chain Pier, and there some of them went below among the great pier-beams with

and issuing thence greeted Lady Ann and Ethel, who had also attended the service, in the most natural way in the world.

While engaged in talking with these, Miss Honeyman came out of the sacred edifice, crisp and stately in the famous Agra brooch and Cashmere shawl. The good-natured Lady Ann had a smile and a kind word for her as for everybody. Clive went up to his maternal aunt to offer his arm. "You must give him up to us for dinner, Miss Honeyman, if you please to be so very kind. He was so good-natured in escorting Ethel down," Lady Ann said.

"Hm! my lady," says Miss Honeyman perking her head up in her collar. Clive did not know whether to laugh or not, but a fine blush illuminated his countenance. As for Ethel, she was and looked perfectly unconscious. So, rustling in her stiff black silk, Martha Honeyman walked with her nephew silent by the shore of the much sounding sea. The idea of Courtship, of osculatory processes, of marrying and giving in marriage made this elderly virgin chafe and fume—she never having at any period of her life indulged in any such ideas or practices, and being angry against them, as childless wives will sometimes be angry and testy against matrons with their prattle about their nurseries. Now Miss Cann was a different sort of Spinster; and loved a bit of sentiment with all her heart—from which I am led to conclude—but, pray, is this the history of Miss Cann or of the Newcomes?

All these Newcomes then entered into Miss Honeyman's house, where a number[5] of little knives and forks were laid in waiting for them.[6] Ethel was cold and thoughtful. Lady Ann was perfectly good-natured as her wont was. Sir Brian came in on the arm of his valet presently; wearing that look of extra neatness which invalids have who have just been shaved and combed and made ready by their attendants to receive company. He was voluble: though there was[7] a perceptible change in his voice: he talked chiefly of matters which had occurred forty years ago, and especially of Clive's own father when he was a boy—in a manner which interested the young man and Ethel. "He threw me down in a chaise, sad chap,[8] always reading Orme's History of India wanted marry French'oman. He wondered Mrs. Newcome didn't leave Tom anything—'pon my word quite s'prize." The events of to-day, the House of Commons, the City, had little interest for him. All the children went up and shook him by the hand with awe in their looks, and he patted their yellow heads vacantly and kindly. He asked Clive (several times) where he had been? and said he himself had had a slight 'tack—vay slight—was getting well ev'y day—strong as a horse—go back to Parliament d'rectly. And then he became a little peevish with Parker, his man, about his broth. The man retired, and came back presently with profound bows and gravity to tell Sir Brian dinner was ready, and he went away quite briskly at this news, giving a couple of fingers

---

the green waters tossing and shimmering below—a sight of pleasure and wonderment—and there Clive smoked that cigar which has been waiting all this while—and then he went *Ms*

[5] number *E1*] great number *Ms*

[6] them. *E1*] them, and a leg of mutton was roasting for them in the kitchen. *Ms*

[7] though there was *E1*] there was scarcely *Ms*

[8] chaise, sad chap, *E1*] chaise, sad, wild chap, *Ms*

to Clive before he disappeared into the upper apartments. Good-natured Lady Ann was as easy about this as about the other events of this world. In later days with what a strange feeling we remember that last sight we have of the old friend; that nod of farewell or shake of the hand, that last look of the face and figure as the door closes on him, or the coach drives away! So the roast mutton was ready and all the children dined very heartily.

The infantile meal had not been long concluded, when servants announced "the Marquis of Farintosh," and that nobleman made his appearance to pay his respects to Miss Newcome and Lady Ann. He brought the very last news of the very last party in London, where "Really upon my honour now it was quite a stupid party because Miss Newcome wasn't there. It was now, really."

Miss Newcome remarked, if he said so upon his honour, of course she was satisfied.

"As you weren't there," the young nobleman continued, "the Miss Rackstraws[9] came out quite strong: really they did now, upon my honour. It was quite a quiet thing. Lady Merriborough hadn't even got a new gown on. Lady Ann, you shirk London society this year and we miss you: we expected you to give us two or three things this season; we did now, really. I said to Tufthunt only yesterday, why hasn't Lady Ann Newcome given anything? You know Tufthunt?—They say he's a clever fellow and that, but he's a low little beast and I hate him!"

Lady Ann said Sir Brian's bad state of health prevented her from going out or receiving at home this season.

"It don't prevent your mother from going out though," continued my lord. "Upon my honour, I think unless she got two or three things every night I think she'd die. Lady Kew's like one of those horses, you know, that unless they go they drop."

"Thank you for my mother," said Lady Ann.

"She is, upon my honour. Last night, I know she was at ever so many places. She dined at the Bloxam's, for I was there. Then she said she was going to sit with old Mrs. Crackthorpe who has broke her collar bone (that Crackthorpe in the Life Guards, her grandson, is a brute, and I hope she won't leave him a shillin') and then she came on to Lady Hawkstone's where I heard her say she had been at the—at the Flowerdales' too. People begin to go to those Flowerdales. Hanged if I know where they won't go next. Cotton spinner, wasn't he?"

"So were we, my lord," says Miss Newcome.

"O yes, I forgot! But you're of an old family—very old family."

"We can't help it," said Miss Ethel archly. Indeed, she thought she was.

"Do you believe in the Barber-Surgeon?" asked Clive. And my lord looked at him with a noble curiosity, as much as to say, "Who the deuce was the Barber-Surgeon? And who the devil are you?"

"Why should we disown our family?" Miss Ethel said simply. "In those early days I suppose people did—did all sorts of things and it was not considered at all out of the way to be Surgeon to William the Conqueror."

9 Rackstraws *E1*] [blank space] *Ms*

THE MOST NOBLE THE MARQUIS OF FARINTOSH

"Edward the Confessor," interposed Clive. "And it must be true because I have seen a picture of the Barber-Surgeon—a friend of mine, M'Collop, did the picture and I daresay it is for sale still."

Lady Ann said she should be delighted to see it. Lord Farintosh remembered that the M'Collop had the moor next to his in Argyleshire: but did not choose to commit himself with the stranger, and preferred looking at his own handsome face and admiring it in the glass until the last speaker had concluded his remarks.

As Clive did not offer any farther conversation, but went back to a table where he began to draw the Barber-Surgeon, Lord Farintosh resumed the delightful talk. "What infernal bad glasses these are in these Brighton lodging-houses! They make a man look quite green, really they do—and there's nothing green in me is there, Lady Ann?"

"But you look very unwell—Lord Farintosh: indeed you do," Miss Newcome said gravely. "I think late hours, and smoking, and going to that horrid Platt's where I daresay you go—"

"Go? don't I—But don't call it horrid: really now, don't call it horrid!" cried the noble Marquis.

"Well—something has made you look far from well. You know how very well Lord Farintosh used to look, Mamma—and to see him now—in only his second season, O it is melancholy!"

"God bless my soul, Miss Newcome! what do you mean? I think I look pretty well," and the noble youth passed his hand through his hair. "It *is* a hard life, I know; that tearin' about night after night and sittin' up till ever so much o'clock; and then all these races, you know, comin' one after another—it's enough to knock up any fellow. I'll tell you what I'll do, Miss Newcome. I'll go down to Codlington to my mother; I will upon my honour: and lie quiet[1] all July and then I'll go to Scotland—and you shall see whether I don't look better next Season."

"Do, Lord Farintosh!" said Ethel greatly amused, as much perhaps at the young Marquis, as at her cousin Clive, who sate whilst the other was speaking, fuming with rage at his table. "What are you doing, Clive?" she asks.

"I was trying to draw Lord knows who—Lord Newcome who was killed at the battle of Bosworth," said the Artist, and the girl ran to look at the picture.

"Why, you have made him like Punch!" cries the young lady.

"It's a shame caricaturing one's own flesh and blood, isn't it?" asked Clive gravely.

"What a droll funny picture!" exclaims Lady Ann. "Isn't it capital? Lord Farintosh."

"I daresay—I confess I don't understand that sort of thing," says his lordship. "Don't, upon my honour. There's Odo Carton, always making those caricatures—*I* don't understand 'em. You'll come up to town to-morrow, won't you? and you're goin' to Lady Hm's and to Hm and Hmm, ain't you?" (The names of these aristocratic places of resort were quite inaudible.) "You mustn't let Miss Blackcap[2] have it all her own way you know,

---

[1] lie quiet *E1*] live quiet quiet *Ms*
[2] Blackcap *E1*] [blank space] *Ms*

that you mustn't."

"She won't have it all her own way," says Miss Ethel. "Lord Farintosh, will you do me a favour? Lady Innishowan is your aunt."

"Of course she is my aunt."

"Will you be so very good as to get a card for her party on Tuesday for my cousin, Mr. Clive Newcome? Clive, please be introduced to the Marquis of Farintosh."

The young Marquis perfectly well recollected those mustachios and their wearer on a former night, though he had not thought fit to make any sign of recognition. "Anything you wish, Miss Newcome," he said; "delighted I'm sure"—and turning to Clive—"In the army I suppose?"

"I am an artist," says Clive turning very red.

"O really, I didn't know!" cries the nobleman; and, my lord bursting out laughing presently as he was engaged in conversation with Miss Ethel on the balcony, Clive thought, very likely with justice, "He is making fun of my mustachios, confound him! I should like to pitch him over into the street." But this was only a kind wish on Mr. Newcome's part: not followed out by any immediate fulfilment.

As the Marquis of Farintosh seemed inclined to prolong his visit, and his company was exceedingly disagreeable to Clive, the latter took his departure for an afternoon walk, consoled to think that he should have Ethel to himself at the evening's dinner, when Lady Ann would be occupied[3] about Sir Brian and would be sure to be putting the children to bed, and in a word would give him a quarter of an hour of delightful tête-à-tête with the beautiful Ethel.[4]

Clive's disgust was considerable when he came to dinner at length, and found Lord Farintosh likewise invited, and[5] sprawling in the drawing-room. His hopes of a[6] tête-a-tête were over. Ethel and Lady Ann and my lord talked, as all people will, about their mutual acquaintance; what parties were coming off, who was going to marry whom, and so forth. And as the persons about whom they conversed were in their own station in life, and belonged to the fashionable world of which Clive had but a slight knowledge, he chose to fancy that his cousin was giving herself airs, and to feel sulky and uneasy during their conversation.[7]

[3] be occupied *E1*] have to occupy herself *Ms*
[4] Ethel. *E1*] Ethel. So Clive amused himself as best he might in the interim. He wrote that letter to his father. He sketched boats along the sea-shore; he walked to Hove and made a drawing of the Church there. He strove to pacify his aunt, Mrs. Honeyman, by jokes, conversation about his travels, talk about old times and a contrite and affectionate demeanour. Mrs. Honeyman received the poor lad's flatteries very gruffly and curtly: as she sate in her little back parlour: she perfectly understood that the young man's heart was on the first floor whilst his person encumbered her room down below. ¶The splendid menials arrayed in powder and plush who adorned Sir Brian's London house, were not brought down to the Brighton lodgings. Mrs. Honeyman said with reason that her house was too small to accommodate those big men. Her cook must provide Lady Ann's meals, if her ladyship took the lodgings; and Mrs. Honeyman herself made the currant tarts ~~and~~ prepared the custards with which she treated the inmates of her house. Mr. Kuhn waited at table, and Lady Ann's women-servants being much too fine ladies to do any such work; Hannah gave a helping hand at the dinner. *Ms*
[5] Farintosh likewise invited, and *E1*] Farintosh *who* had likewise been invited, *Ms*
[6] a *E1*] [omitted] *Ms*
[7] conversation ↑dialogue↓. *Ms* [insertion not in Thackeray's hand]

Miss Newcome had faults of her own and was worldly enough, as perhaps the reader has begun to perceive: but in this instance no harm, sure, was to be attributed to her. If two gossips in Aunt Honeyman's parlour had talked over the affairs of Mr. Jones and Mr. Brown, Clive would not have been angry: but a young man of spirit not unfrequently mistakes his vanity for independence: and it is certain that nothing is more offensive to us of the middle class than to hear the names of great folks constantly introduced into conversation.

So Clive was silent and ate no dinner, to the alarm of Hannah[8] who had put him to bed many a time and always had a maternal eye over him. When he actually refused currant and raspberry tart, and custard, the chef-d'œuvre of Mrs. Honeyman, for which she had seen him absolutely cry in his childhood, the good Hannah[9] was alarmed—"Law, Master Clive," she said, "do'ee eat some. Missis made it, you know she did," and she insisted on bringing back the tart to him.

Lady Ann and Ethel laughed at this eagerness on the worthy old woman's part. "Do'ee eat some, Clive," says Ethel imitating honest Mrs. Hicks who had left the room.

"It's doosid good," remarked Lord Farintosh.

"Then do'ee eat some more," said Miss Newcome—on which the young nobleman holding out his plate observed with much affability that the cook of the lodgings was really a stunner for tarts.

"The cook, dear me, it's not the *cook!*" cries Miss Ethel. "Don't you remember the Princess in the Arabian Nights who was such a stunner for tarts, Lord Farintosh?"

Lord Farintosh couldn't say that he did.

"Well, I thought not; but there was a Princess in Arabia or China or somewhere who made such delicious tarts and custards that nobody's could compare with them, and there is an old lady in Brighton who has the same wonderful talent. She is the mistress of this house."

"And she is my aunt, at your lordship's service," said Mr. Clive with great dignity.

"Upon my honour, *did* you make 'em? Lady Ann!" asked my lord.

"The Queen of Hearts made tarts!" cried out Miss Newcome rather eagerly and blushing somewhat.

"My good old aunt Miss Honeyman made this one," Clive would go on to say—

"Mr. Honeyman's sister, the preacher, you know where we go on Sunday," Miss Ethel interposed.[1]

"The Honeyman pedigree is not a matter of very great importance," Lady Ann remarked gently. "Kuhn, will you have the goodness to take away these things? When did you hear of Colonel Newcome, Clive—"

An air of deep bewilderment and perplexity had spread over Lord Farintosh's fine countenance, whilst this talk about pastry had been going on. The Arabian Princess, the Queen of Hearts making tarts, Miss

---

[8] Hannah] Martha *Ms E1*

[9] Hannah] Martha *Ms E1*

[1] interposed. *E1*] breaks out. *Ms*

Honeyman?—who the deuce were all these? Such may have been his lordship's doubts and queries. Whatever his cogitations were he did not give utterance to them but remained in silence for some time as did the rest of the little party. Clive tried to think he had asserted his independence by showing that he[2] was not ashamed of his old aunt; but the doubt may be whether there was any necessity for presenting her in this company, and whether Mr. Clive had not much better have left the tart-question alone.

Ethel evidently thought so: for she talked and rattled in the most lively manner with Lord Farintosh for the rest of the evening, and scarcely chose to say a word to her cousin. Lady Ann was absent with Sir Brian and her children for the most part of the time: and thus Clive had the pleasure of listening to Miss Newcome making fun of her friends,[3] uttering all sorts of odd little paradoxes, firing the while sly shots[4] at Mr. Clive, and indeed exhibiting herself in not the most agreeable light. Her talk only served the more to bewilder Lord Farintosh who did not understand a tithe of her allusions: for Heaven which had endowed the young Marquis with personal charms, a large estate, an ancient title and the pride belonging to it, had not supplied his lordship with a great quantity of brains, or a very feeling heart.

Lady Ann came back from the upper-regions presently with rather a grave face, and saying that Sir Brian was not so well that evening upon which the young men rose to depart. My lord said he had[5] a most delightful dinner and a most delightful tart, 'pon his honour, and was the only one of the little company who laughed at his own remark. Miss Ethel's eyes flashed scorn at Mr. Clive when that unfortunate subject was introduced again.

My lord was going back to London next morning[6]—was Miss Newcome going back? wouldn't he like to go back in the train with her!—another unlucky observation. Lady Ann said it would depend on the state of Sir Brian's health the next morning whether Ethel would return; and "both of you gentlemen are too young to be her escort," added the kind lady. Then she shook hands with Clive, as thinking she had said something too severe for[7] him.

Farintosh in the meantime was taking leave of Miss Newcome. "Pray, pray," said his lordship, "don't throw me over at Lady Innishowan's. You know I hate balls and never go to 'em except when you go. I hate dancing, I do, 'pon my honour."

"Thank you," said Miss Newcome with a curtsey.

"Except with one person—only one person—upon my honour. I'll remember and get the invitation for your friend.[8] And if you would but try

[2] that he E1] he Ms
[3] The phrase "making fun of her friends," an insertion in the manuscript, is misplaced after "indeed" in E1.
[4] shots E1] side shots Ms
[5] had Ms E1] had had R
[6] next morning Ms] tomorrow E1] "next morning" is not cancelled, but "tomorrow" is inserted in a hand other than Thackeray's.
[7] for E1] to Ms
[8] remember and get the invitation for your friend. E1] remember your commission

that mare, I give you my honour I bred her at Codlington—she's a beauty
to look at and as quiet as a lamb."

"I don't want a horse like a lamb," replied the young lady.

"Well—she'll go like blazes now: and over timber she's splendid now.
She is upon my honour."

"When I come to London perhaps you may trot her out," said Miss Ethel
giving him her hand and a fine smile.

Clive came up biting his lips. "I suppose you don't condescend to ride
Bhurtpore any more now?" he said.

"Poor old Bhurtpore! The children ride him now," said Miss Ethel—
giving Clive at the same time a dangerous look of her eyes as though to see
if her shot had[9] hit. Then she added, "No—he has not been brought up
to town this year: he is at Newcome, and I like him very much"—perhaps
she thought the shot had struck too deep.

But if Clive was hurt he did not show his wound. "You have had him
these four years—yes, it's four years since my father broke him for you.
And you still continue to like him? What a miracle of Constancy! You
use him sometimes in the country—when you've no better horse—what a
compliment to Bhurtpore—"

"Nonsense!" Miss Ethel here made Clive a sign in her most imperious
manner to stay a moment when Lord Farintosh had departed.

But he did not choose to obey this order. "Good-night," he said, "before
I go I must shake hands with my aunt down-stairs." And he was gone following close upon Lord Farintosh who I daresay thought, "Why the doose
can't he shake hands with his aunt up here?": and when Clive entered
Miss Honeyman's back parlour making a bow to the young nobleman, my
lord went away more perplexed than ever: and the next day told friends
at White's what uncommonly queer people those Newcomes were. "I give
you my honour there was a fellow at Lady Ann's whom they call Clive, who
is a painter by trade, his uncle is a preacher, his father is a horse-dealer, and
his aunt lets lodgings and cooks the dinner!"

(Peule! says Ethel with a shrug of her shoulder. ↑an askance look at Clive.↓) *Ms*
[9] had *E1*] at *Ms*

Chapter V.

RETURNS TO SOME OLD FRIENDS.

HE haggard youth burst into my chambers in the Temple on the very next morning and confided to me the story which has been just here narrated. "I saw her, Sir," he added when he had concluded it with many ejaculations regarding the heroine of the little tale,[1] "walking with the children and Miss Cann as I drove round in the fly to the station—and didn't even bow to her."

"Why did you go round by the cliff?" asked Clive's friend. "That is not the way from[2] the Steyne Arms to the railroad."

"Hang it," says Clive turning very red, "I wanted to pass just under her windows and if I saw her, *not* to see her: and that's what I did."

"Why did she walk on the cliff?" mused Clive's friend, "at that early hour? Not to meet Lord Farintosh I should think. He never gets up before twelve. It must have been to see you. Didn't you tell her you were going away in the morning?"

"I tell you what she does with me," continues Mr. Clive. "Sometimes she seems to like me, and then she leaves me. Sometimes she is quite kind—kind she always is—I mean you know, Pen—*you* know what I mean; and then up comes the old Countess, or a young Marquis, or some fellow with a handle to his name, and she whistles me off till the next convenient opportunity."

[1] "I saw her, . . . little tale, *Ms*] When he had concluded it, with many ejaculations regarding the heroine of the tale, "I saw her, sir," he added, *E1* [Compositor's misplacement of *Ms* insertion.]
[2] from *E1*] to *Ms*

"Women are like that, my ingenuous youth," says Clive's Counsellor.

"*I* won't stand it. *I* won't be made a fool of!" he continues. "She seems to expect every body to bow to her, and moves through the world with her imperious airs—O how confoundedly handsome she is with them! I tell you what—I feel inclined to tumble down and put[3] one of her pretty little feet on my neck and say, There! Trample my life out. Make a slave of me. Let me get a silver collar and mark 'Ethel' on it and go through the world with my badge."

"And a blue ribbon for a footman to hold you by; and a muzzle to wear in the dog-days. Bow wow!" says Mr. Pendennis.

(At this noise Mr. Warrington puts his head in from the neighbouring bed-chamber and shows a beard just lathered for shaving. "We are talking Sentiment! Go back till you are wanted!" says Mr. Pendennis. Exit he of the soap-suds.)

"Don't make fun of a fellow," Clive continues laughing ruefully. "You see I *must* talk about it to somebody. I shall die if I don't. Sometimes, Sir, I rise up in my might and I defy her lightning. The sarcastic dodge is the best: I have borrowed that from you, Pen old boy. That puzzles her: that would beat her if I could but go on with it. But there comes a tone of her sweet voice, a look out of those killing grey eyes, and all my frame is in a thrill and a tremble. When she was engaged to Lord Kew I did battle with the confounded passion—and I ran away from it like an honest man, and the gods rewarded me with ease of mind after a while. But now the thing rages worse than ever. Last night, I give you my honour, I heard every one of the confounded hours toll, except the last when I was dreaming of my father and the chamber-maid woke[4] me with a hot water jug."

"Did she scald you? What a cruel chamber-maid! I see you have shaven the mustachios off."

"Farintosh asked me whether I was going in[5] the army," said Clive, "and[6] she laughed. I thought I had best dock them.[7] O I would like to cut my head off as well as my hair!"[8]

"Have you—ever—asked her to marry you?" asked Clive's friend.[9]

"I have seen her but five times since my return from abroad," the lad went on. "There has been always somebody by. Who am I? a painter with five hundred a year for an allowance. Isn't she used to walk upon velvet and dine upon silver, and hasn't she got Marquises and Barons and all sorts of swells in her train? I daren't ask her—"

---

[3] put *Ms*] feel *E1*

[4] woke *E1*] came and woke *Ms*

[5] was going in *E1*] was in *Ms*

[6] Clive, "and *E1*] Clive with another ingenuous blush; "and *Ms*

[7] dock them. *E1*] dock off the facial ornaments. Do you know old Gandish called upon me three days ago with a pair of mustachios, and yesterday I saw a little fellow by the name of Moss swaggering about Brighton pier with another pair? You remember Moss? *Ms*

[8] hair!" *E1*] hair! I'm mad about this woman—mad about her!" And he bit the backs of his hands, fired off twenty vollies of cigar-smoke: dashed the cigar into the fireplace, drank off tumbler after tumbler of water and gave other marks of distraction. *Ms*

[9] friend. *E1*] friend, coming to the point. *Ms*

Here his friend hummed Montrose's lines—"He either fears his fate too much or his desert is small who dares not put it to the touch and win or lose it all."

"I[1] own I dare not ask her. If she were to refuse me, I know I should never ask again. This isn't the moment, when all Swelldom is at her feet—for me to come forward and say, 'Maiden, I have watched thee daily and I think thou lovest me well.' I read that ballad to her at Baden, Sir. I drew a picture of the Lord of Burleigh wooing the maiden and asked what she would have done?"

"O you *did?* I thought when we were at Baden we were so modest that we did not even whisper our condition?"

"A fellow can't help letting it be seen and hinting it," says Clive with another blush. "They can read it in our looks fast enough: and what is going on in our minds, hang them! I recollect she said, in her grave cool way, that after all the Lord and Lady of Burleigh did not seem to have made a very good marriage and that the lady would have been much happier in marrying one of her own degree."

"That was a very prudent saying for a young lady of eighteen," remarks Clive's friend.[2]

"Yes—but it wasn't an unkind one. Say Ethel thought—thought what was the case: and being engaged herself, and knowing how friends of mine had provided a very pretty little partner for me—she is a dear good little girl, little Rosey: and twice as good, Pen, when her mother is away—knowing this and that, I say, suppose Ethel wanted to give me a hint to keep quiet? was she not right in the counsel she gave me? She is not fit to be a poor man's wife. Fancy Ethel Newcome going into the kitchen and making pies like Aunt Honeyman!"

"The Circassian beauties don't sell under so many thousand purses," remarked Mr. Pendennis. "If there's a beauty in a well-regulated Georgian family, they fatten her; they feed her with the best *Racahout des Arabes.* They give her silk robes, and perfumed baths; have her taught to play on the dulcimer and dance and sing: and, when she is quite perfect, send her down to Constantinople for the Sultan's inspection. The rest of the family never think of grumbling, but eat coarse meat and[3] bathe in the river, wear old clothes, and praise Allah for their Sister's Elevation. Bah! Do you suppose the Turkish system doesn't obtain all the world over? My poor Clive, this article in the May Fair Market is beyond your worship's price. Some things in this world are made for our betters, young man. Let Dives say grace for his dinner and the dogs and Lazarus be thankful for the crumbs. Here comes Warrington shaven and smart as if he was going out a courting."

Thus it will be seen that in his communications with certain friends who approached nearer to his own time of life, Clive was much more eloquent and rhapsodical than in the letters which he wrote to his father, regarding his passion for Miss Ethel. He celebrated her with pencil and pen.

---

1 "I *E1*] "Well I *Ms*
2 Clive's friend. *E1*] the friend. *Ms*
3 and *Ms*] [omitted] *E1*

He was for ever drawing the outline of her head, the solemn eyebrow, the nose (that wondrous little nose) descending from the straight forehead, the short upper-lip, and chin sweeping in a full curve to the neck—&c. &c. &c. A frequenter of his studio might see a whole gallery of Ethels there represented: when Mrs. Mackenzie visited that place and remarked one face and figure repeated on a hundred canvases and papers, grey, white, and brown, I believe she was told that the original was a famous[4] Roman model from whom Clive had studied a great deal during his residence in Italy; on which Mrs. Mack gave it as her opinion that Clive was a sad wicked young fellow. The widow thought rather the better of him for being a sad wicked young fellow; and as for Miss Rosey, she,[5] of course was of Mamma's way of thinking. Rosey went through the world constantly smiling at whatever occurred. She was good-humoured through the dreariest long evenings at the most stupid parties; sate good-humouredly for hours at Shoolbred's whilst Mamma was making purchases: heard good-humouredly those old old stories of her mother's day after day; bore an hour's joking or an hour's scolding with equal good humour, and whatever had been the occurrences of her simple day, whether there was sunshine or cloudy weather or flashes of lightning and bursts of rain, I fancy Miss Mackenzie slept after them quite undisturbedly and was sure to greet the morrow's dawn with a smile.

Had Clive become more knowing in his travels, had Love or Experience opened his eyes, that they looked so differently now upon objects which before used well enough to please them?[6] It is a fact that until he went abroad, he thought Widow Mackenzie a dashing lively agreeable woman: he used to receive her stories—about Cheltenham, the Colonies, the balls at Government House, the observations which the Bishop made and the peculiar attentions of the Chief-Justice to Mrs. Major McShane with the Major's uneasy behaviour—all these to hear at one time did Clive not ungraciously incline. "Our friend Mrs. Mack," the good old Colonel used to say, "is a clever woman of the world, and has seen a great deal of company."[7] That story of Sir Thomas Sadman dropping a pocket-handkerchief in his Court at Colombo: which the Queen's Advocate O'Goggarty picked up, and on which Laura Mac S. was embroidered—whilst the Major was absolutely in the witness box giving evidence against a native servant who had stolen one of his cocked-hats—that story always made good Thomas Newcome laugh, and Clive used to enjoy it too, and the widow's mischievous fun in narrating it—and now, behold, one day when Mrs. Mackenzie recounted the anecdote in her best manner to Messrs. Pendennis, Warrington, and Frederick Bayham who had been invited to meet Mr. Clive in Fitzroy Square—when Mr. Binnie chuckled, when Rosey as in duty bound looked discomposed and said, "Law Mamma!"—not one sign of good humour—not one ghost of a smile made its apparition on Clive's dreary face. He painted imaginary portraits with a strawberry stalk: he looked into his water-glass, as though he would plunge and drown there; and Bayham

[4] famous *E1*] certain famous *Ms*
[5] she, *E1*] she, the dear innocent, *Ms*
[6] them? *E1*] these? *Ms*
[7] company." *E1*] good company." *Ms*

had to remind him that the claret-jug was anxious to have another embrace from its constant friend F.B. When Mrs.[8] Mack went away distributing smiles, Clive[9] groaned out, "Good Heavens how that story does bore me," and lapsed into his former moodiness; not giving so much as a glance to Rosey whose sweet face looked[1] at him kindly for a moment, as she followed in[2] the wake of her mamma.[3]

"The mother's the woman for my money," I heard F.B. whisper to Warrington. "Splendid figure-head, Sir—magnificent build, Sir—from bows to stern—I like 'em of that sort. Thank[4] you, Mr. Binnie, I *will* take a backhander, as Clive don't seem to drink. The youth, Sir, has grown melancholy with his travels; I'm inclined to think some noble Roman has stolen the young man's heart. Why did *you* not send us over a picture of the Charmer, Clive? Young Ridley, Mr. Binnie, you will be a happy[5] to hear, is bidding fair to take a distinguished place in the world of arts. His picture has been greatly admired, and my good friend Mrs. Ridley tells me that Lord Todmorden has sent him over an order to paint him a couple of pictures at a hundred guineas a-piece."

"I should think so. J.J.'s pictures will be worth five times a hundred guineas ere five years are over," says Clive.

"In that case it wouldn't be a bad speculation for our friend Sherrick," remarked F.B., "to purchase a few of the young man's works. I would—only I haven't the capital to spare.[6] Mine has been vested in an Odessa venture, Sir—in a large amount of wild oats which up to the present moment make me no return. But it will always be a consolation to me to think that I have been the means—the humble means of furthering that deserving young man's prospects in life."

"You, F.B.! and how?" we asked.

"By certain humble contributions of mine to the press," answered Bayham majestically. "Mr. Warrington, the claret happens to stand with you; and exercise does it good, Sir. Yes—the articles, trifling as they may appear, have attracted notice," continued F.B. sipping his wine with great gusto. "They are noticed, Pendennis, give me leave to say, by parties who don't value so much the literary or even the political part of the *Pall Mall Gazette*, though both, I am told by those who read them, are conducted with considerable—consummate ability. John Ridley sent a hundred[7] pounds over to his father the other day, who funded[8] it in his son's name. And Ridley told the story to Lord Todmorden when the venerable nobleman congratulated him on having such a child. I wish F.B. had one of the same sort, Sir." In which sweet prayer we all of us joined with a laugh.

[8] Mrs. *E1*] the radiant Mrs. *Ms*
[9] smiles, Clive *E1*] smiles to us, Clive who sate next me *Ms*
[1] looked *E1*] I thought, looked *Ms*
[2] followed in *E1*] followed out of the room in *Ms*
[3] mamma. *E1*] bustling mamma. *Ms*
[4] sort. Thank *E1*] sort. F.B. owns to a partiality for—thank *Ms*
[5] a happy *Ms*] happy *E1*
[6] capital to spare. *E1*] capital at present to spare. *Ms*
[7] a hundred *E1*] an order for a hundred *Ms*
[8] who funded *E1*] who banked it, Sir—funded *Ms*

One of us had told Mrs. Mackenzie (let the criminal blush to own that quizzing his fellow-creatures used at one time to form part of his youthful amusement) that F.B. was the son of a gentleman of most ancient family and vast landed possessions, and as Bayham was particularly attentive to the widow, and grandiloquent in his remarks, she was greatly pleased by his politeness, and pronounced him a most distangy man—reminding her indeed of General Hopkirk who commanded in Canada. And she bade Rosey sing for Mr. Bayham who was in a rapture at the young lady's performances, and said no wonder such an accomplished daughter came from such a mother—though how such a mother could have a daughter of such an age he, F.B., was at a loss to understand. O Sir! Mrs. Mackenzie was charmed and overcome at this novel compliment. Meanwhile the little artless Rosey warbled on her pretty ditties.

"It *is* a wonder," growled out Mr. Warrington, "that that sweet girl can belong to such a woman. I don't understand much about women: but that one appears to me to be—hum!"

"What, George?" asked Warrington's friend.

"Well, an ogling leering scheming artful old campaigner," grumbled the misogynist. "As for the little girl I should like to have her to sing to me all night long. Depend upon it she would make a much better wife for Clive than that fashionable cousin of his he is hankering after. I heard him bellowing about her the other day in chambers, as I was dressing. What the deuce does the boy want with a wife at all?" And Rosey's song being by this time finished, Warrington went up with a blushing face and absolutely paid a compliment to Miss Mackenzie—an almost unheard of effort on George's part.

"I wonder whether it is every young fellow's lot," quoth George as we trudged home together, "to pawn his heart away to some girl that's not worth the winning? Psha! It's all mad rubbish this sentiment. The women ought not to be allowed to interfere with us: married if a man must be, a suitable wife should be portioned out to him, and there an end of it. Why doesn't the young man marry this girl,[9] and get back to his business and paint his pictures? Because his father wishes it—and the old Nabob yonder, who seems a kindly-disposed easy-going old Heathen philosopher. Here's a pretty little girl: money I suppose in sufficiency—everything satisfactory except, I grant you, the Campaigner. The lad might daub his canvases: christen a child a year: and be as happy as any young donkey that browses on this common of our's—but he must go and heehaw after a zebra forsooth! a *lusus naturæ* is she?—I never spoke to a woman of fashion, thank my stars—I don't know the nature of the beast; and since I went to our race-balls as a boy, scarcely ever saw one, as I don't frequent operas[1] and parties in London like you young flunkies of the aristocracy. I heard you talking about this one. I couldn't help it as my door was open and the young one was shouting like a madman. What! does he choose to hang on on sufferance and hope to be taken, provided Miss can get no better? Do you mean to say that is the genteel custom, and that women in your

---

9 young man marry this girl, *E1*] young one marry this little girl, *Ms*
1 frequent operas *E1*] go to operas *Ms*

confounded society do such things every day? Rather than have such a creature I would take a savage woman who should nurse my dusky brood: and rather than have a daughter brought up to the trade I would bring her down from the woods and sell her in Virginia." With which burst of indignation our friend's anger ended for that night.

Though Mr. Clive had the felicity to meet his cousin Ethel at a party or two in the ensuing weeks of the season, every time he perused the features of Lady Kew's brass knocker in Queen Street, no result came of the visit. At one[2] of their meetings in the world Ethel fairly told him that her grandmother would not receive him. "You know, Clive, I can't help myself: nor would it be proper to make you signs out of the window. But you must call for all that: Grandmamma may become more good-humoured: or if you don't come she may suspect I told you not to come: and to battle with her day after day, is no pleasure, Sir, I assure you. Here is Lord Farintosh coming to take me to dance. You must not speak to me[3] all the evening. Mind that. Sir!" and away goes the young lady in a waltz[4] with the Marquis.[5]

On the same evening—as he was biting his nails or cursing his fate or wishing to invite Lord Farintosh into the neighbouring garden of Berkeley Square; whence the policeman might carry to the station-house the corpse of the survivor—Lady Kew would bow to him with perfect graciousness; on other[6] nights her ladyship would pass and no more recognise him than the servant who opened the door.

If she was not to see him at her grandmother's house, and was not particularly unhappy at his exclusion, why did Miss Newcome encourage Mr. Clive so that he should try and see her? If Clive could not get into the little house in Queen Street: why was Lord Farintosh's enormous cab-horse looking daily into the first floor windows of that street?[7] Why were little quiet dinners made for him, before the opera, before going to the play, upon a half-dozen occasions, when some of the old old Kew port was brought out of the cellar where cobwebs had gathered round it ere Farintosh was born? The dining-room was so tiny that not more than five people could sit at the little round table—that is, not more than Lady Kew and her granddaughter, one of the Miss Toadins, Miss Crochit the late vicar's daughter at Kewbury,[8] and Captain Walleye or Tommy Henchman, Farintosh's kinsmen and admirers who were of no consequence, or old Fred. Tiddler whose wife was an invalid and who was always ready at a moment's notice? Crackthorpe once went to one of these dinners but that young soldier being a frank and high-spirited youth abused the entertainment and

---

[2] visit. At one *E1*] visit—a footman as brazen and implacable as the knocker itself announcing that her ladyship and Miss Newcome were just gone out. At one *Ms*

[3] me *E1*] me again *Ms*

[4] lady in a waltz *E1*] lady to caper in a waltz *Ms*

[5] Marquis. *E1*] noble Marquis. *Ms*

[6] graciousness; on other *E1*] graciousness, smile and ask him how his studies were going on, and if he had heard from his father and regret that she was not at home when he called once. On other *Ms*

[7] street? *E1*] street as though he would crop the roses and geraniums in the balconies? *Ms*

[8] The words "Miss Crochit ... Kewbury," a manuscript insertion, were erroneously placed after "granddaughter" in *E1*.

declined more of them. "I tell you what I was wanted for," the Captain told his mess and Clive at the Regent's Park Barracks afterwards. "I was expected to go as Farintosh's Groom of the Stole, don't you know, to stand, or sit if I could,[9] in the back seat of the box whilst His Royal Highness made talk with the Beauty, to go out and fetch the carriage, and walk down-stairs with that d— crooked old dowager that looks as if she usually rode on a broomstick, by Jove, or else with that bony old painted sheep-faced companion, who's raddled like an old bell-weather. I think, Newcome, you seem to be rather hit by the Belle Cousine—so was I last season, so were ever so many of the fellows. By Jove, Sir! there's nothing I know more comfortable or inspiritin' than a younger son's position, when a Marquis cuts in with fifteen thousand a year. We fancy we've been making runnings[1] and suddenly we find ourselves nowhere. Miss Mary or Miss Lucy or Miss Ethel, saving your presence, will no more look at us than my dog will look at a bit of bread when I offer her this cutlet. Will you? old woman?— no, you old slut, that you won't!" (to Mag, an Isle of Skye terrier who in fact prefers the cutlet, having snuffed disdainfully at the bread)—"that you won't, no more will[2] any of your sex. Why, do you suppose if Jack's eldest brother had been dead—Barebones Belsize they used to call him (I don't believe he was a bad fellow though he was fond of psalm-singin')—do you suppose that Lady Clara would have looked at that cock-tail Barney Newcome? Beg your pardon if he's your cousin—but a more odious little snob I never saw."

"I give you up Barnes," says Clive laughing, "anybody may shy at *him* and I sha'n't interfere."

"I understand, but at nobody else of the family. Well, what I mean is that that old woman is enough to spoil any young girl she takes in hand. She dries 'em up and poisons 'em, Sir; and I was never more glad than when I heard that Kew had got out of her old clutches. Frank's a fellow that will always be led by some woman or another; and I'm only glad it should be a good one. They say his mother's serious and that; but why shouldn't she be?" continues honest Crackthorpe puffing his cigar with great energy. "They say that[3] old dowager doesn't believe in God nor devil: but that she's in such a funk to be left in the dark that she howls and raises the doose's own delight if her candle goes out. Toppleton slept next room to her at Groningham and heard her: didn't you, Top?"

"Heard her howling like an old cat on the tiles," says Toppleton, "—thought she was at first. My man told me that she used to fling all sorts of things—bootjacks and things, give you my honour—at her maid—and that the woman was all over black and blue."

"Capital head that is Newcome has done of Jack Belsize!" says Crackthorpe from out of his cigar.

"And Kew's too—famous likeness! I say, Newcome, if you have 'em printed the whole brigade'll subscribe—make your fortune, see if you won't," cries Toppleton.

[9] sit if I could *Ms*] if I could sit *E1* [compositor's misplacement of manuscript insertion]
[1] runnings *Ms*] running *E1*
[2] will *Ms*] than *E1*
[3] that *Ms*] the *E1*

"He's such a heavy swell: he don't want to make his fortune," ejaculates Butts.

"Butts, old boy, he'll paint you for nothing—and send you to the Exhibition where some widow will fall in love with you; and you shall be put as frontispiece for the Book of Beauty, by Jove," cries another military satirist—to whom Butts:

"You hold your tongue, you old Saracen's Head! They're going to have you done on the bear's grease pots. I say, I suppose Jack's all right now. When did he write to you last, Cracky?"

"He wrote from Palermo—a most jolly letter from him and Kew. He hasn't touched a card for nine months; is going to give up play—so is Frank too, grown quite a good boy. So will you too, Butts, you old miscreant, repent of your sins, pay your debts, and do something handsome for that poor deluded milliner in Albany Street. Jack says Kew's mother has written over to Lord Highgate—a beautiful letter—and the[4] old boy's relenting, and they'll[5] come together again—Jack's[6] eldest son now, you know—— bore for Lady Susan, only having girls."

"Not a bore for Jack, though," cries another. And what a good fellow Jack was, and what a trump Kew is; and how famously he stuck by him— went to see him in prison and paid him out—and what good fellows we all are, in general became the subject of the conversation, the latter part of which took place in the smoking-room of the Regent's Park Barracks then occupied by that regiment of Life Guards of which Lord Kew and Mr. Belsize had been members. Both were still fondly remembered by their companions, and it was because Belsize had spoken very warmly of Clive's friendliness to him that Jack's[7] friend the gallant Crackthorpe had been interested in our hero and found an opportunity of making his acquaintance.

With these frank and pleasant young men Clive soon formed a considerable intimacy: and if any of his older and peaceful friends chanced to take their afternoon airing in the Park, and survey the horsemen there, we might have the pleasure of beholding Mr. Newcome in Rotten Row, riding side by side with other dandies, who had mustachios blonde or jet, who wore flowers in their buttons (themselves being flowers of spring), who rode magnificent thoroughbred horses, scarcely touching their stirrups with the tips of their varnished boots and who kissed the most beautiful primrose-coloured kid-gloves to lovely ladies passing them in the Ride. Clive drew portraits of half the officers of the Life Guards Green; and was appointed painter in ordinary to that distinguished corps. His likeness of the Colonel would make you die with laughing: his picture of the Surgeon was voted a masterpiece. He drew the men in the saddle, in the stable, in their flannel dresses, sweeping their flashing swords about, receiving lancers, repelling infantry,—nay, cutting a sheep in two as some of the warriors are known to be able to do at one stroke. Detachments of Life Guardsmen made their appearance in Charlotte Street which was not very

[4] and the *E1*] and that the *Ms*
[5] and they'll *E1*] and that they'll *Ms*
[6] again—Jack's *E1*] again—especially as Jack's *Ms*
[7] Jack's *E1*] his *Ms*

distant from their barracks; the most splendid cabs were seen prancing before his door: and curly-whiskered youths of aristocratic appearance smoking cigars out of his painting-room window. How many times did Clive's next door neighbour, little Mr. Finch,[8] the miniature painter, run to peep through his parlour-blinds hoping that a sitter was coming and "a carriage-party" driving up! What wrath Mr. Scowler, A.R.A., was in, because a young hopomythumb dandy who wore gold-chains and his collars turned down, should spoil the trade and draw portraits for nothing. Why did none of the young men come to Scowler?[9] Scowler was obliged to own that Mr. Newcome had considerable talent and a good knack at catching a likeness. He could not paint a bit, to be sure: but his heads in black and white were really tolerable: his sketches of horses very vigorous and life-like. Mr. Gandish said if Clive would come for three or four years into his Academy he could make something of him. Mr. Smee shook his head, and said he was afraid that kind of loose desultory study, that keeping of aristocratic company, was anything but favourable to a young artist—Smee, who would walk five miles to attend an evening party of ever so little a great man!

[8] Finch, *E1*] Runt Finch, *Ms*
[9] Scowler? *E1*] Mr. Scowler? *Ms*

Chapter VI.

R. FREDERICK BAYHAM waited at Fitzroy Square while Clive was yet talking with his friends there, and favoured that gentleman with his company home to the usual smoky refreshment. Clive always rejoiced in F.B.'s society,[1] whether he was in a sportive mood, or, as now, in a solemn and didactic vein. F.B. had been more than ordinarily majestic all the evening. "I daresay you find me a good deal altered, Clive," he remarked. "I *am* a good deal altered. Since that good Samaritan, your kind[2] father, had compassion on a poor fellow fallen among thieves (though I don't say, mind you, he was much better than his company), F.B. has mended some of his ways. I am trying a course of industry, Sir. Powers, perhaps naturally great, have been neglected over the wine cup and the die—I am beginning to feel my way; and my chiefs yonder, who have just walked home with their cigars in their mouths and without as much as saying 'F.B., my boy, shall we go to the Haunt and have a cool lobster and a glass of table beer,'—which they certainly do not consider themselves to be,—I say, Sir, the *Politician* and the *Literary Critic* (there was a most sarcastic emphasis laid on these phrases characterising Messrs. Warrington and Pendennis)—may find that there is a humble Contributor to the *Pall Mall Gazette*, whose name may be the amateur shall[3] one day reckon even higher than their own. Mr. Warrington I do not say so much—he is an able man, Sir, an able man—but there is that about your exceedingly self-satisfied friend, Mr. Arthur Pendennis, which—well, well—let time show. You did not—get the—hem—paper at Rome and Naples I

[1] society, *E1*] company, *Ms*
[2] kind *E1*] precious *Ms*
[3] shall *E1*] may *Ms*

suppose?"

"Forbidden by the Inquisition," says Clive delighted; "and at Naples the king furious against it."

"I *don't wonder* they don't like it at Rome, Sir. There's serious matter in it which may set the prelates of a certain church rather in a tremor. You haven't read—the—ahem—the Pulpit Pencillings in the P.M.G.? Slight sketches, mental and corporeal, of our chief divines now in London—and signed Laud Latimer?"

"I don't do much in that way," said Clive.

"So much the worse for you, my young friend. Not that I mean to judge any other fellow harshly—I mean any other fellow[4] *Sinner* harshly—or that I mean that those Pulpit Pencillings would be likely to do you any great good. But such as they are, they have been productive of benefit. Thank you, Mary my dear, the tap is uncommonly good and I drink to your future husband's good health. A glass of good sound beer refreshes after all that claret. Well, Sir, to return to the Pencillings, pardon my vanity in saying that, though Mr. Pendennis laughs at them, they have been of essential service to the paper. They give it a character, they rally round it the respectable classes. They create correspondence. I have received many interesting letters, chiefly from females, about the Pencillings. Some complain that their favourite preachers are slighted, others applaud because the clergymen they sit under are supported by F.B. *I* am Laud Latimer, Sir—though I have heard the letters attributed to the Revd. Dr.[5] Bunker and to a Member of Parliament eminent in the religious world."

"So you are the famous Laud Latimer?" cries Clive who had in fact seen letters signed by those right reverend names in our paper.

"Famous is hardly the word. One who scoffs at everything—I need not say I allude to Mr. Arthur Pendennis—would have had the letters signed— the Beadle of the Parish. He calls me the Venerable Beadle sometimes— it being, I grieve to say, his way to deride grave subjects. You wouldn't suppose now, my young Clive, that the same hand which pens the Art Criticisms, occasionally when his Highness Pendennis is lazy, takes a minor theatre, or turns the sportive epigram, or the ephemeral paragraph, should adopt a graver[6] theme on a Sunday, and chronicle the sermons of British Divines? For eighteen consecutive Sunday evenings, Clive, in Mrs. Ridley's front parlour which I now occupy, vice Miss Cann promoted, I have written the Pencillings—scarcely allowing a drop of refreshment, except under extreme exhaustion, to pass my lips. Pendennis laughs at the Pencillings. He wants to stop them; and says they bore the public—I don't want to *think* a man is jealous, who was himself the cause of my engagement at the P.M.G.—perhaps my powers were not developed then."

"Pen thinks he writes better now than when he began," remarked Clive, "I have heard him say so."

"His opinion of his own writings *is* high whatever their date. Mine, Sir, are only just coming into notice. They begin to know F.B., Sir, in the sacred

---

[4] other fellow *E1*] fellow *Ms*
[5] Dr. *Ms*] Mr. *E1*
[6] graver *Ms*] grave *E1*

edifices of this[7] metropolitan city. I saw the Bishop of London looking at me last Sunday week, and am sure his Chaplain whispered him, 'It's Mr. Bayham, my lord, nephew of your lordship's right reverend brother, the Lord Bishop of Bullocksmithy.' And last Sunday being at church—at Saint Mungo the Martyr's, Revd. S. Sawders—by Wednesday I got in a female hand—Mrs. Sawders's no doubt—the biography of the Incumbent of St. Mungo; an account of his early virtues; a copy of his poems; and a hint that he was the gentleman destined for the vacant Deanery.

"Ridley is not the only man I have helped in this world," F.B. continued. "Perhaps I should blush to own it—I *do* blush: but I feel the ties of early acquaintance and I own that I have puffed your uncle, Charles Honeyman, most tremendously. It was partly for the sake of the Ridleys and the tick he owes 'em; partly for old times' sake. Sir, are you aware that things are greatly changed with Charles Honeyman, and that the poor F.B. has very likely made his fortune?"

"I am delighted to hear it," cried Clive, "and how, F.B., have you wrought this miracle?"

"By common sense and enterprise, lad—by a knowledge of the world and a benevolent disposition. You'll see Lady Whittlesea's chapel bears a very different aspect now. That miscreant Sherrick owns that he owes me a turn[8] and has sent me a few dozen of wine—without any stamped paper on my part in return as an acknowledgment of my service. It chanced, Sir, soon after your departure for Italy, that going to his private residence respecting a little bill to which a heedless friend had put his hand, Sherrick invited me to partake of tea in the bosom of his family. I was thirsty—having

walked in from Jack Straw's Castle at Hampstead, where poor Kiteley and I had been taking a chop—and accepted the proffered entertainment. The ladies of the family gave us music after the domestic muffin—and then, Sir, a great idea occurred to me. You know how magnificently Miss Sherrick

7 this *NY*] his *Ms E1 R*
8 a turn *E1*] the turn *Ms*

and her[9] mother sing. They sang Mozart, Sir. 'Why,' I asked of Sherrick, 'should those ladies who sing Mozart to a piano, not sing Handel to an organ?'

" 'D— it, you don't mean a hurdy-gurdy?'[1]

" 'Sherrick,' says I, 'you are no better than a Heathen ignoramus. I mean why shouldn't they sing Handel's church music, and church music in general in Lady Whittlesea's chapel? Behind the screens[2] up in the organ-loft, what's to prevent 'em? by Jingo! Your singing boys have gone to the Cave of Harmony; you and your choir have split[3]—why should not these ladies lead it?' He caught at the idea. You never heard the chaunts more[4] finely given—and they would be better still if the congregation would but hold their confounded tongues. It was an excellent though a harmless dodge, Sir: and drew immensely, to speak profanely. They dress the part, Sir, to admiration—a sort of nun-like costume they come in: Mrs. Sherrick has the soul of an artist still—by Jove, Sir, when they have once smelt the lamps, the love of the trade never leaves 'em. The ladies actually practised by moonlight in the chapel and came over to Honeyman's to an oyster afterwards. The thing took, Sir. People began to take box—seats I mean, again:—and Charles Honeyman, easy in his mind through your noble father's generosity, perhaps inspired by returning good fortune, has been preaching more eloquently than ever. He took some lessons of Husler of the Haymarket, Sir—His sermons are old, I believe, but so to speak he has got them up with new scenery, dresses, and effects, Sir. They have flowers, Sir, about the buildin'. Pious ladies are supposed to provide 'em, but *entre nous* Sherrick contracts for them with Nathan or some one in Covent Garden. And—don't tell this now, upon your honour!"

"Tell what, F.B.?" asks Clive.

"I got up a persecution against your uncle[5] for Popish practices: summoned a meetin' at the Running Footman in Bolingbroke Street. Billings the butterman, Sharwood the turner and blacking-maker, and the Honourable Phelim O'Curraghs,[6] Lord Scullabogue's son, made speeches. Two or three respectable families (your aunt, Mrs. Whaddyoucallem Newcome among the number) quitted the chapel in disgust—I wrote an article of controversial biography in the P.M.G., set the business going in the daily press; and the thing was done, Sir. That property is a paying one to the incumbent and to Sherrick over him. Charles's affairs are getting all right, Sir. He never had the pluck to owe much, and if it be a sin to have wiped his slate clean, satisfied his creditors, and made Charles easy—upon my conscience I must confess that F.B. has done it. I hope I may never do anything worse in this life, Clive. It ain't bad to see him doing the martyr, Sir: Se-

9 her *Ms*] the *E1*
1 hurdy-gurdy?'] hurdy-gurdy?" *E1*] hurdy-gurdy?' says he, for he still swears in a very reckless manner. *Ms*
2 screens *Ms*] screen *E1*
3 Harmony; you and ... split *E1*] Harmony; and your choir have struck *Ms*
4 more *E1*] so *Ms*
5 your uncle *E1*] him *Ms*
6 O'Curraghs, *Ms*] O'Curragh *E1*

bastian[7] riddled with paper pellets; Bartholomew on a cold gridiron. Here comes the lobster. Upon my word, Mary, a finer fish I've seldom seen."

Now surely this account of his uncle's affairs and prosperity was enough to send Clive to Lady Whittlesea's chapel, and it was not because Miss Ethel had said that she and Lady Kew went there, that Clive was induced to go there too? He attended punctually on the next Sunday, and in the Incumbent's pew, whither the pew woman conducted him, sate Mr. Sherrick in great gravity with large gold pins, who handed him at the Anthem, a large, new, gilt hymn-book.

An odour of *mille fleurs* rustled by them as Charles Honeyman accompanied by his ecclesiastical valet passed the pew from the vestry; and took his place at the desk. Formerly he used to wear a flaunting scarf over his surplice which was very wide and full, and Clive remembered when as a boy he entered the sacred robing-room, how his uncle used to pat and puff out the scarf and the sleeves of his vestment, arrange the natty curl on his forehead, and take his place, a fine example of florid church decoration. Now the scarf was trimmed down to be as narrow as your neckcloth, and hung loose and straight over the back; the ephod was cut straight and as close and short as might be,—I believe there was a little trimming of lace to the narrow sleeves, and a slight arabesque of tape or other substance round the edge of the surplice. As for the curl on the forehead, it was no more visible than the Maypole in the Strand or the Cross at Charing. Honeyman's hair was parted down the middle, short in front, and curling delicately round his ears and the back of his head. He read the service in a swift manner and with a gentle twang. When the music began he stood with head on one side and two slim fingers on the book as composed as a statue in a mediæval niche. It was fine to hear Sherrick who had an uncommonly good voice join in the musical parts of the service. The produce of the market-gardener decorated the church here and there: and the Impresario of the Establishment having picked up a Flemish painted window from[8] old Moss in Wardour Street, had placed it in his chapel. Labels of faint green[9] and gold with long Gothic letters painted thereon meandered over the organ-loft and galleries and strove to give as mediæval a look to Lady Whittlesea's as the place was capable of assuming.

In the sermon Charles dropped the twang with the surplice, and the priest gave way to the preacher. He preached short stirring discourses on the subjects of the day. It happened that a noble young Prince, the hope of a nation, and heir of a royal house had just then died by a sudden accident. Absolon, the son of David,[1] furnished Honeyman with a parallel. He drew a picture of the two deaths, of the grief of kings, of the fate that is superior to them. It was indeed a stirring discourse, and caused thrills through the crowd to whom Charles imparted it. "Famous ain't it?" says Sherrick, giving Clive a hand when the rite was over. "How he's come out, hasn't he? Didn't think he had it in him." Sherrick seemed to have become of late impressed with the splendour of Charles's talents, and spoke of him—was

[7] Sir: Sebastian *E1*] Sir, and Sebastian *Ms*
[8] window from *E1*] window, a bargain from *Ms*
[9] faint green *E1*] pink, green *Ms*
[1] David, *E1*] Saul *Ms*

Lady Whittlesea's Chapel—Lady Kew's Carriage stops the Way

it not disrespectful?—as a manager would of a successful tragedian. Let us pardon Sherrick: he *had* been in the theatrical way. "That Irishman was no go at all," he whispered to[2] Mr. Newcome, "got rid of him—let's see, at Michaelmas."

On account of Clive's tender years and natural levity, a little inattention may be allowed to the youth, who certainly looked about him very eagerly during the service. The house was filled by the ornamental classes, the bonnets of the newest Parisian fashion. Away in a darkling corner under the organ sate a squad of footmen. Surely that powdered one in livery wore Lady Kew's colours?[3] So Clive looked under all the bonnets, and presently spied old Lady Kew's face, as grim and yellow as her brass knocker, and by it Ethel's beauteous countenance. He dashed out of church when the congregation rose to depart. "Stop and see Honeyman, won't yer?" asked Sherrick surprised. "Yes yes: come back again," said Clive, and was gone.

He kept his word, and returned presently. The young Marquis and an elderly lady were in Lady Kew's company. Clive had passed close under Lady Kew's venerable Roman nose without causing that organ to bow in ever so slight a degree towards the ground. Ethel had recognised him with a smile and a nod. My lord was whispering one of his noble pleasantries in her ear. She laughed at the speech or the speaker. The steps of a fine belozenged[4] carriage were let down with a bang. The Yellow One had jumped up behind it, by the side of his brother Giant Canary, Lady Kew's equipage had disappeared, and Mrs. Canterton's was stopping the way.

Clive returned to the chapel by the little door near to the Vestiarium. All the congregation had poured out by this time. Only two ladies were standing near the pulpit; and Sherrick with his hands rattling[5] his money in his pockets was pacing up and down the aisle.

"Capital house, Mr. Newcome, wasn't it? I counted no less than fourteen nobs. The Princess of Montcontour and her husband, I suppose, that chap with the beard, who yawned[6] so during the sermon, I'm blessed if I didn't think he'd have yawned his head off—Countess of Kew and her daughter, Countess of Canterton and the Honourable Miss Fetlock—no, Lady Fetlock—a countess's daughter is a lady, I'm dashed if she ain't. Lady Glenlivat and her sons, the most noble the Marquis of Farintosh and Lord Enry Roy, that makes seven—no, nine—with the Prince and Princess.— Julia my dear, you came out like a good un to-day. Never heard you in finer voice. Remember Mr. Clive Newcome?"

Mr. Clive made bows to the ladies, who acknowledged him by graceful curtsies. Miss Sherrick was always looking to the vestry door.

"How's the old Colonel? the best fellow[7]—excuse my calling him a feller—but he is, and a good one too. I went to see Mr. Binnie, my other tenant. He looks a little yellow about the gills Mr. Binnie. Very proud woman that is who lives with him—uncommon haughty. When will you

---

[2] whispered to *E1*] whispered *Ms*
[3] livery . . . colours? *E1*] yellow . . . livery? *Ms*
[4] belozenged *E1*] bepainted *Ms*
[5] rattling *E1*] jingling *Ms*
[6] yawned *Ms*] yawns *E1*
[7] fellow *Ms*] feller *E1*

come down and take your mutton in the Regent's Park, Mr. Clive. There's some tolerable good wine down there. Our reverend gent drops in and takes a glass, don't he, Missis?"

"We shall be most 'appy to see Mr. Newcome, I'm sure," says the handsome and good-natured Mrs. Sherrick; "Won't we, Julia?"

"O certainly," says Julia who seems rather absent. And behold at this moment the reverend gent enters from the vestry. Both the ladies run towards him holding forth their hands.

"O Mr. Honeyman! What a sermon. Me and Julia cried so up in the orgin-loft, we thought you would have heard us! didn't we, Julia?"

"O yes!" says Julia whose hand the pastor is now pressing.

"When you described the young man, I thought of my poor boy, didn't I, Julia," cries the mother, with tears streaming down her face.[8]

"We had a loss more than ten years ago," whispers Sherrick to Clive gravely. "And she's always thinking of it. Women are so."

Clive was touched and pleased by this exhibition of kind feeling. "You know his mother was an Absolon," the good wife continues, pointing to her husband. "Most respectable diamond-merchants in ——"

"Hold your tongue, Betsy, and leave my poor old mother alone; do now," says Mr. Sherrick darkly. Clive is in his uncle's fond embrace by this time, who rebukes him for not having called[9] in Walpole Street.

"Now, when will you two gents come up to my shop to 'ave a family dinner?" asks Sherrick.

"Ah, Mr. Newcome, do come!" says Julia in her deep rich voice looking

---

[8] face. *E1*] handsome face. *Ms*
[9] having called *E1*] having sooner called *Ms*

up to him with her great black eyes. And if Clive had been a vain fellow like some folks, who knows but he might have thought he had made an impression on the handsome Julia?

"Thursday, now make it Thursday, if Mr. H. is disengaged. Come along, girls, for the flies bites the ponies when they're a standin' still and makes 'em mad this weather. Any thing you like for[1] dinner? Cut of salmon and cucumber?—no, pickled salmon's best this weather."

"Whatever you give me, you know I'm thankful!"[2] says Honeyman in a sweet sad voice to the two ladies who are standing looking at him, the mother's hand clasped in the daughter's.

"Should you like that Mendelssohn for the Sunday after next? Julia sings it splendid!"

"No I don't, Ma."

"You do, dear! She's a good, good *dear,* Mr. H., that's what she is."

"You must not call—a—him—in that way. *Don't* say 'Mr. H.,' Ma," says Julia.

"Call me what you please!" says Charles with the most heart-rending simplicity—and Mrs. Sherrick straightway kisses her daughter. Sherrick meanwhile has been pointing out the improvements of the chapel to Clive (which now has indeed a look of the Gothic Hall at Rosherville), and has confided to him the sum for which he screwed the painted window out of old Moss. "When he came to see it up in this place, Sir, the old man was mad, I give you my word! His son ain't no good: says he knows you: he's such a screw that chap that he'll overreach himself, mark my words. At least, he'll never die rich. Did you ever hear of *me* screwing? No, I spend my money like a man. How those girls are a goin' on about[3] their music with Honeyman! I don't let 'em sing in the evening, or him do duty more than once a day—and you can calc'late how the music draws because in the evenin' there ain't half the number of people here. Revd. Mr. Jurnyman does the duty now—quiet Hoxford man—ill, I suppose, this morning. H. sits in his pew, where we[4] was; and coughs—that's to say I told him to cough. The women like a consumptive parson, Sir. Come, gals!"

Clive went to his uncle's lodgings and was received by Mr. and Mrs. Ridley with great glee and kindness. Both of those good people had made it a point to pay their duty to Mr. Clive immediately on his return to England and thank him over and over again for his kindness to John James. Never never would they forget his goodness and the Colonel's, they were sure. A cake, a heap of biscuits, a pyramid of jams, six frizzling hot mutton chops and four kinds of wine came bustling up to Mr. Honeyman's room twenty minutes after Clive had entered it,—as a token of the Ridleys' affection for him.

Clive remarked with a smile the *Pall Mall Gazette* upon a side-table and in the chimney-glass almost as many cards as in the time of Honeyman's early prosperity. That he and his uncle should be very intimate together was impossible from the nature of the two men; Clive being frank clear-

---

[1] like for *E1*] like particklar for *Ms*
[2] I'm thankful!" *E1*] I am—a—thankful!" *Ms*
[3] goin' on about *E1*] goin' about *Ms*
[4] we *Ms E1*] he *R HM NY*

sighted and imperious, Charles, timid, vain and double-faced, conscious that he was a humbug and that most people found him out: so that he would quiver and turn away and be more afraid of young Clive and his direct straightforward way than of many older men. Then there was the sense of the money-transactions between him and the Colonel, which made Charles Honeyman doubly uneasy. In fine, they did not like each other: but as he is a connection of the most respectable Newcome family, surely he is entitled to a page or two in these their memoirs.

Thursday came and with it Mr. Sherrick's entertainment, to which also Mr. Binnie and his party had been invited to meet Colonel Newcome's son. Uncle James and Rosey brought Clive in their carriage; Mrs. Mackenzie sent a headache as an apology. She chose to treat Uncle James's landlord with a great deal of hauteur and to be angry with her brother for visiting such a person. "In fact you see how fond I must be of dear little Rosey, Clive, that I put up with all Mamma's tantrums for her sake," remarks Mr. Binnie.[5]

"O Uncle," says little Rosey, and the old gentleman stopped her remonstrances with a kiss.

"Yes," says he, "your mother *does* have tantrums, Miss, and though you never complain, there's no reason why I shouldn't. You will not tell on me (it was "O Uncle!" again)—and Clive won't, I am sure. This little thing, Sir," James went on, holding Rosey's pretty little hand and looking fondly in her pretty little face: "is her old uncle's only comfort in life. I wish I had had her out to India to me, and never come back to this great dreary town of yours. But I was tempted home by Tom Newcome: and I'm too old to go back, Sir. Where the stick falls let it lie. Rosey would have been whisked out of my house in India, in a month after I had her there. Some young fellow would have taken her away from me, and now she has promised never to leave her old[6] Uncle James, hasn't she?"

"No never, Uncle," said Rosey.

"*We* don't want to fall in love: do we, child? We don't want to be breaking our hearts like some young folks, and dancing attendance at balls night after[7] night and capering about in the Park to see if we can get a glimpse of the beloved object, eh Rosey?"

Rosey blushed. It was evident that she and Uncle James both knew of Clive's love affair. In fact the front seat and back[8] seat of the carriage both blushed. And as for the secret, why, Mrs. Mackenzie and Mrs. Hobson had talked it a hundred[9] times over.

"This little Rosey, Sir, has promised to take care of me on this side of Styx," continued Uncle James, "and if she could but be left alone, and to do it without Mamaw,—There—I won't say a word more against her—we should get on none the worse."

"Uncle James, I must make a picture of you for Rosey," said Clive, good-humouredly. And Rosey said, "O, thank you, Clive," and held out that

[5] sake," ... Binnie. *E1*] sake." *Ms*
[6] her old *E1*] old *Ms*
[7] after *E1*] and after *Ms*
[8] back *E1*] the back *Ms*
[9] talked it a hundred *E1*] talked Master Clive's absurd infatuation a hundred *Ms*

pretty little hand and looked so sweet and kind and happy, that Clive could not but be charmed at the sight of so much innocence and candour.

"Quasty peecoly, Rosiny," says James in a fine Scotch Italian,[1] "e la piu balla, la piu cara, ragazza ma[2] la mawdry e il diav—"

"Don't, Uncle!" cried Rosey again—and Clive laughed at Uncle James's wonderful outbreak in a foreign tongue.

"Eh—I thought ye didn't know a word of the sweet language, Rosey! It's just the Lengy[3] Toscawny in Bocky Romawny that I thought to try in comepliment[4] to this young monkey who has seen the world." And by this time Saint John's Wood was reached; and Mr. Sherrick's handsome villa, at the door of which the three beheld the Reverend Charles Honeyman stepping out of a neat brougham.

The drawing-room contained several pictures of Mrs. Sherrick when she was in the theatrical line, Smee's portrait of her which was never half handsome enough for my Betsy, Sherrick said indignantly, the print of her in *Artaxerxes* with her signature as Elizabeth Folthorpe (not in truth a fine specimen of calligraphy), the testimonial presented to her "on the conclusion of the Triumphal Season of 18— at Drury Lane by her ever grateful friend Adolphus Smacker, Lessee" (who of course went to law with her next year) and other Thespian emblems. But Clive remarked with not a little amusement that the drawing-room tables were now covered with a number of those books which he had seen at Madame de Montcontour's and many French and German ecclesiastical gimcracks such as are familiar to numberless readers of mine. There were the Lives of Saint Botibol of Islington and Saint Willibald of Bareacres—with pictures of those confessors. Then there was The Legend of Margery Dawe, Virgin and Martyr—with a sweet double-frontispiece representing (1) the sainted woman selling her featherbed for the benefit of the[5] poor; and (2) reclining upon straw, the leanest of invalids. There was Old Daddy Longlegs, and how he was brought to say his Prayers; a Tale for Children by a Lady, with a preface dated Saint Chad's Eve—and signed, C.H. The Reverend Charles Honeyman's Sermons delivered at Lady Whittlesea's chapel. Poems of Early Days by Charles Honeyman, A.M. The Life of good Dame Whittlesea by Do Do. Yes, Charles had come out in the literary line—and there in a basket was a strip of Berlin work of the very same Gothic pattern which Madame de Montcontour was weaving, and which you afterwards saw round the pulpit of Charles's chapel. Rosey was welcomed most kindly by the kind ladies; and as the gentlemen sate over their wine after dinner in the summer evening, Clive beheld Rosey and Julia pacing up and down the lawn, Miss Julia's arm round her little friend's waist: he thought they would make a pretty little picture.

"My girl ain't a bad one to look at. Is she?" said the pleased father. "A fellow might look far enough and see not prettier than them[6] two."

---

[1] in a fine Scotch Italian, *E1*] in an Italian with a fine Edinburgh accent, *Ms*
[2] ragazza ma *E1*] ma *Ms*
[3] Lengy *Ms*] Lenguy *E1*
[4] comepliment *Ms*] compliment *E1*
[5] for the benefit of the *E1*] for †benefit↓ the *Ms*
[6] not prettier than them *E1*] not many prettier girls than either of them *Ms*

Charles sighed out that there was a German print—the Two Leonoras, which put him in mind of their various styles of beauty.

"I wish I could paint them," said Clive.

"And why not, Sir?" asks his host. "Let me give you your first commission now, Mr. Clive; I wouldn't mind paying a good bit for a picture of my Julia. I forget how much Old Smee got for Betsy's, the old humbug!"

Clive said it was not the will but the power that was deficient. He succeeded with men,[7] but the ladies were too much for him as yet.

"Those you've done up at Albany Street Barracks are famous. I've seen 'em," said Mr. Sherrick; and remarking that his guest looked rather surprised at the idea of his being in such company—Sherrick said, "What, you think they are too great swells for me? Law bless you. I often go there. I've business with several of 'em—had with Captain Belsize, with the Earl of Kew, who's every inch the gentleman—one of nature's aristocracy and paid up like a man. The Earl and me has had many dealings together."

Honeyman smiled faintly—and nobody complying with Mr. Sherrick's boisterous entreaties to drink more—the gentlemen quitted the dinner-table which had been served in a style of prodigious splendour, and went to the drawing-room for a little music.

This was all of the gravest and best kind—so grave indeed that James Binnie might be heard in a corner giving an accompaniment of little snores to the singers and the piano. But Rosey was delighted with the performance[8] and Sherrick remarked to Clive, "That's a good gal, that is; I like that gal. She ain't jealous of Julia cutting her out in the music: but listens as pleased as any one. She's a sweet little pipe of her own too. Miss Mackenzie, if ever you like to go to the opera, send a word either to my West End or my City office. I've boxes every week, and you're welcome to anything I can give you."

So all agreed that the evening had been a very pleasant one; and they of Fitzroy Square returned home talking in a most comfortable friendly way— that is, two of them, for Uncle James fell asleep again taking possession of the back seat; and Clive and Rosey prattled together. He had offered to try and take all the young ladies'[9] likenesses. "You know what a failure the last was, Rosey?"—he had very nearly said "dear Rosey."

"Yes, but Miss Sherrick is so handsome, that[1] you will succeed better with her than with my round face—Mr. Newcome."

"Mr. *What?*" cries Clive.

"Well, Clive, then," says Rosey in a little voice.

He sought for a little hand which was not very far away. "You know we are like brother and sister, dear Rosey," he said this time.

"Yes," said she and gave a little pressure of the hand. And then Uncle James woke up: and it seemed as if the whole drive didn't occupy a minute and they shook hands very very kindly at the door of Fitzroy Square.

Clive made a famous likeness of Miss Sherrick, with which Mr. Sherrick was delighted and so was Mr. Honeyman who happened to call upon his

---

[7] men, *E1*] men pretty well: *Ms*
[8] performance *E1*] -'formance *Ms*
[9] young ladies' *E1*] ladies' *Ms*
[1] handsome, that *E1*] handsome and has such decided features, that *Ms*

nephew once or twice when the ladies happened to be sitting. Then Clive proposed to the Reverend Charles Honeyman to take *his* head off—and made an excellent likeness in chalk of his uncle—that one in fact from which the print was taken, which you may see any day at Hogarth's in the Haymarket—along with a whole regiment of British Divines. Charles became so friendly,[2] that he was constantly[3] coming to Charlotte Street—once or twice a week.

Mr. and Mrs. Sherrick came to look at the drawing,—and were charmed with it; and when Rosey was sitting, they came to see *her* portrait, which again was not quite so successful. One Monday, the Sherricks and Honeyman too happened to call to see the picture of Rosey who trotted over with her uncle to Clive's studio, and they all had a great laugh at a paragraph in the *Pall Mall Gazette*, evidently from F.B.'s hand to the following effect.

"CONVERSION IN HIGH LIFE. A foreign nobleman of princely rank who has married an English lady and has resided among us for some time is likely, we hear and trust, to join the English Church. The Prince de M—ntc—nt—r has been a constant attendant at Lady Whittlesea's chapel, of which the Revd. C. Honeyman is the eloquent incumbent—and it is said this sound and talented Divine has been the means of awakening the Prince to a sense of the erroneous doctrines in which he has been bred. His ancestors were Protestant and fought by the side of Henry IV at *Ivry*. In Louis XIV's time they adopted the religion of that persecuting monarch. We sincerely trust that the present heir of the house of Ivry will see fit to return to the creed which his forefathers so unfortunately abjured."

The ladies received this news with perfect gravity: and Charles uttered a meek wish that it might prove true. As they went away they offered more hospitalities to Clive and Mr. Binnie and his niece. They[4] liked the music, would they not come and hear it again?

When they had departed with Mr. Honeyman, Clive could not help saying to Uncle James, "Why are those people always coming here; praising me; and asking[5] me to dinner? Do you know, I can't help thinking that they rather want me as a *prétendu* for Miss Sherrick?"

Binnie burst into a loud guffaw and cried out, "O Vanitas Vanitawtum!" Rosey laughed too.

"I don't think it[6] any joke at all," said Clive.

"Why, you stupid lad, don't you see it is Charles Honeyman the girl's in love with?" cried Uncle James. "Rosey saw it in the very first instant we entered their drawing-room three weeks ago."

"Indeed, and how?" asked Clive.

"By—by the way she looked at him," said little Rosey.

---

[2] friendly, *E1*] friendly and was so pleased with this drawing *Ms*
[3] constantly *E1*] now constantly *Ms*
[4] niece. They *E1*] niece: as they *Ms*
[5] praising me; and asking *E1*] always praising me; and always asking *Ms*
[6] it *E1*] it is *Ms*

Chapter VII.

A STAG OF TEN.

HE London season was very nearly come to an end, and Lord Farintosh had danced I don't know how many times with Miss Newcome, had drunk several bottles of the old Kew port, had been seen at numerous breakfasts, operas, races, and public places by the young lady's side, and had not as yet made any such proposal as Lady Kew expected for her granddaughter. Clive going to see his military friends in the Regent's Park once, and finish Captain Butts's portrait in barracks, heard two or three young men talking, and one[1] say to another, "I bet you three to two Farintosh don't marry her and I bet you even

that he don't ask her." Then as he entered Mr. Butts's room where these

[1] talking, and one *E1*] heard one *Ms*

gentlemen were conversing, there was a silence and an awkwardness. The young fellows were making an "event" out of Ethel's marriage and sporting their money freely on it.

To have an old Countess hunting a young Marquis so resolutely that all the world should be able to look on and speculate whether her game would be run down by that staunch toothless old pursuer—that is an amusing sport, isn't it? and affords plenty of fun and satisfaction to those who follow the hunt. But for a heroine of a story, be she ever so clever, handsome and sarcastic, I don't think for my part at this present stage of the tale, Miss Ethel Newcome occupies a very dignified position. To break her heart in silence for Tomkins who is in love with another, to suffer no end of poverty, starvation, capture by ruffians, ill treatment by a bullying husband, loss of beauty by the small-pox, death even at the end of the volume—all these mishaps a young heroine may endure (and has endured in romances over and over again) without losing the least dignity, or suffering any diminution of the sentimental reader's esteem. But a girl of great beauty, high temper, and strong natural intellect, who submits to be dragged hither and thither in an old grandmother's leash, and in pursuit of a husband who will run away from the couple—such a person, I say, is in a very awkward position as a heroine—and I declare if I had another ready to my hand (and unless there were[2] extenuating circumstances), Ethel should be deposed at this very sentence.

But, a novelist must go on with his heroine, as a man with his wife, for better or worse, and to the end. For how many years have the Spaniards borne with their gracious Queen, not because she was faultless but because she was there. So Chambers and grandees cried, God save her. Alabarderos turned out, drums beat, cannons fired and people saluted Isabella Segunda, who was no better than the humblest washerwoman of her subjects. Are *we* much better than our neighbours? Do we never yield to our peculiar temptation, our pride, or our avarice, or our vanity or what not? Ethel is very wrong certainly. But, recollect, she is very young. She is in other people's hands. She has been bred up and governed by a very worldly family: and taught their traditions. We would hardly for instance, the stanchest Protestant in England would hardly be angry with poor little Isabella Segunda for being a Catholic. So if Ethel worships at a certain Image which a great number of good folks in England bow to, let us not be too angry with her idolatry and bear with our Queen a little longer before we make our Pronunciamento.

No, Miss Newcome, yours is not a dignified position in life, however you may argue that hundreds of people in the world are doing like you. O me! what a confession it is, in the very outset of life and blushing brightness of youth's morning, to own that the aim with which a young girl sets out and the object of her existence is to marry a rich man—that she was endowed with beauty so that she might buy wealth and a title with it—that as sure as she has a soul to be saved, her business here on earth is to try

[2] were *E1*] are *Ms*

and get a rich husband. That is the career for which many a woman is bred and trained. A young man begins the world with some aspirations at least; he will try to be good and follow the truth: he will strive to win honour for himself and never do a base action: he will pass nights over his books and forego ease and pleasure so that he may atchieve a name. Many a poor wretch who is worn out now and old and bankrupt of fame and money too, has commenced life at any rate with noble views, and generous schemes, from which weakness, idleness, passion or overpowering hostile fortune have turned him away. But a girl of the world, *bon Dieu!* the doctrine with which she begins is that she is to have a wealthy husband: the article of Faith in her Catechism is, "I believe in Elder Sons, and a house in town and a house in the country." They are mercenary as they step fresh and blooming into the world out of the nursery. They have been schooled there to keep their bright eyes to look only on the Prince and the Duke, Crœsus and Dives. By long cramping and careful process their little natural hearts have been squeezed up, like the feet of their fashionable little sisters in China. As you see a pauper's child with an awful premature knowledge of the pawn-shop, able to haggle at market with her wretched halfpence, and battle bargains at huxter's stalls; you shall find a young Beauty, who was a child in the school-room a year since, as wise and knowing as the old practitioners on that Exchange; as economical of her smiles; as dexterous in keeping back or producing her beautiful wares; as skilful in setting one bidder against another; as keen as the smartest merchant in Vanity Fair.

If the young gentlemen of the Life Guards Green who were talking about Miss Newcome and her suitors were silent when Clive appeared amongst them, it was because they were aware not only of his relationship to the young lady, but his unhappy condition regarding her. Certain men there are who never tell their love, but let concealment like a worm in the bud feed on their damask cheeks: others again must be not always thinking but talking about the darling object. So it was not very long before Captain Crackthorpe was taken into Clive's confidence and through Crackthorpe very likely the whole mess became acquainted with his passion. These young fellows who had been early introduced into the world, gave Clive small hopes of success, putting to him in their downright phraseology the point of which he was already aware, that Miss Newcome was intended for his superiors and that he had best not make his mind uneasy by sighing for those beautiful grapes which were beyond his reach.

But the good-natured Crackthorpe, who had a pity for the young painter's condition, helped him so far (and gained Clive's warmest thanks for his good offices), by asking admission for Clive to certain evening parties of the *beau monde,* where he had the gratification of meeting his charmer. Ethel was surprised and pleased and Lady Kew surprised and angry at meeting Clive Newcome at these fashionable houses—the girl herself was touched very likely at his pertinacity in following her. As there was no actual feud between them, she could not refuse now and again to dance with her cousin; and thus he picked up such small crumbs of consolation as a youth in his state can get; lived upon six words vouchsafed to him in a quadrille, or brought home a glance of the eyes which she had presented to him in a waltz, or the remembrance of a squeeze of the hand on parting or meeting. How eager he was to get a card to this party or that! how attentive to the givers of such entertainments! Some friends of his accused him of being a tuft-hunter and flatterer of the aristocracy on account of his politeness to certain people; the truth was he wanted to go wherever Miss Ethel was; and the ball was blank to him which she did not attend.

This business occupied not only one season but two. By the time of the second season Mr. Newcome had made so many acquaintances that he needed few more introductions into society. He was very well known as a good-natured handsome young man and a very good waltzer, the only son of an Indian officer of large wealth, who chose to devote himself to painting, and who was supposed to entertain an unhappy fondness for his cousin, the beautiful Miss Newcome. Kind folks who heard of this little *tendre* and were sufficiently interested in Mr. Clive, asked him to their houses in consequence: I daresay those people who were good to him may have been themselves at one time unlucky in their own love affairs.

When the first season ended without a declaration from my lord, Lady Kew carried off her young lady to Scotland, where it also so happened that Lord Farintosh was going to shoot; and people made what surmises they chose upon this coincidence. Surmises! why not? You who know the world, know very well that if you see Mrs. Soandso's name in the list of people at an entertainment; on looking down the list, you will presently be sure to come on Mr. Whatdyoucallem's. If Lord and Lady Blank of Suchandsuch Castle received a distinguished circle (including Lady Dash) for Christmas or Easter, without reading farther the names of the guests, you may venture on any wager that Captain Asterisk is one of the company. These coincidences happen every day: and some people are so anxious to meet other people, and so irresistible is the magnetic sympathy I suppose, that they will travel hundreds of miles in the worst of weather to see their friends, and break your door open almost, provided the friend is inside it.

I am obliged to own the fact that for many months Lady Kew hunted after Lord Farintosh. This rheumatic old woman went to Scotland where, as he was pursuing the deer, she stalked his lordship: from Scotland she went to Paris where he was taking lessons in dancing at the Chaumière; from Paris to an English country house for Christmas where he was expected but didn't come—not being, his professors said, quite complete in the Polka and so on. If Ethel were privy to these manœuvres, or anything more than unwittingly a[3] consenting party, I say we would depose her from her place of heroine at once. But she was acting under her grandmother's orders, a most imperious, irresistible, managing old woman who exacted every body's obedience and managed every body's business in her family; Lady Ann Newcome being in attendance on her sick husband, Ethel was consigned to the Countess of Kew, her grandmother, who hinted that she should leave Ethel her property when dead; and whilst alive expected the girl should go about with her. She had and wrote as many letters as a Secretary of State almost. She was accustomed to set off without taking any

[3] unwittingly a *Ms*] an unwittingly *E1* [misplaced manuscript insertion]

body's advice or announcing her departure until within an hour or two of the event. In her train moved Ethel against her own wish[4] which would have led her to stay at home with her father, but at the special wish and order of her parents. Was such a sum as that of which Lady Kew had the disposal (Hobson Brothers knew the amount of it quite well) to be left out of the family? Forbid it all ye powers! Barnes—who would have liked the money himself and said truly that *he* would live with his grandmother anywhere she liked if he could get it—Barnes joined most energetically with Sir Brian and Lady Ann in ordering Ethel's obedience to Lady Kew—you know how difficult it is for one young woman not to acquiesce when the family Council strongly orders. In fine I hope there[5] was a good excuse for the Queen of this history and that it was her wicked domineering old prime minister who led her wrong. Otherwise I say we would have another dynasty. O, to think of a generous nature and the world and nothing but the world to occupy it!—of a brave intellect and the milliner's bandboxes, and the scandal of the coteries, and the fiddle-faddle etiquette of the Court for its sole exercise! of the rush and hurry from entertainment to entertainment; of the constant smiles and cares of representation; of the prayerless rest at night, and the awaking to a Godless morrow! This was the course of life to which Fate, and not her own fault altogether, had for a while handed over Ethel Newcome. Let those pity her who can feel their own weakness and misgoing; let those punish her who are without fault themselves.

Clive did not offer to follow her to Scotland. He knew quite well[6] that the encouragement he had had was only of the smallest; that as a relation she received him frankly and kindly enough, but checked him when he would have adopted another character. But it chanced that they met in Paris, whither he went in the Easter of the ensuing year, having worked to some good purpose through the winter and dispatched as on a former occasion his three or four pictures to take their chance at the Exhibition.

Of these it is our pleasing duty to be able to corroborate to some extent Mr. F. Bayham's favourable report. Fancy sketches and historical pieces our young man had eschewed; having convinced himself either that he had not an epic genius, or that to draw portraits of his friends was a much easier task than that which he had set himself formerly. Whilst all the world was crowding round a pair of J.J.'s little pictures; a couple of chalk[7] heads were admitted into the Exhibition (his great picture of Captain Crackthorpe[8] on horseback in full uniform I must own was ignominiously rejected) and the friends of the parties had the pleasure of recognising in the miniature room, no. 1246, Portrait of an Officer—viz., Augustus Butts,[9] Esqr., of the Life Guards Green; and Portrait of the Revd. Charles Honeyman, no. 1272. Miss Sherrick the

4 <will>↑wish↓ *Ms*] will *E1*
5 there *E1*] that there *Ms*
6 knew quite well *E1*] felt well enough *Ms*
7 of chalk *E1*] of Clive's chalk *Ms*
8 Crackthorpe *E1*] Butts *Ms*
9 Augustus Butts *E1*] Frederick Crackthorpe, *Ms*

hangers refused; Mr. Binnie, Clive had spoiled as usual in the painting; the chalk heads, however, before named were voted to be faithful likenesses and executed in a very agreeable and spirited manner. F. Bayham's criticism on these performances, it need not be said, was tremendous. Since the days of Michael Angelo you would have thought there never had been such drawings. In fact F.B., as some other critics do, clapped his friends so boisterously on the back and trumpeted their merits with such prodigious energy as to make his friends themselves sometimes uneasy.

Mr. Clive, whose good father was writing home more and more wonderful accounts of the Bundelcund Bank in which he had engaged, and who was always pressing his son to draw for more money, treated himself to comfortable rooms at Paris, in the very same hotel where the young Marquis of Farintosh occupied lodgings much more splendid, and where he lived no doubt so as to be near the professor who was still teaching his lordship the Polka. Indeed it must be said that Lord Farintosh made great progress under this Artist and that he danced very much better in his third season than in the first and second years after he had come upon the town. From the same instructor the Marquis learned the latest novelties in French conversation, the choicest oaths and phrases (for which he[1] was famous), so that although his French grammar was naturally defective, he was enabled to order a dinner at Philippe's, and to bully a waiter or curse a hackney coachman with extreme volubility. A young nobleman of his rank was received with the distinction which was his due by the French sovereign of that period; and at the Tuileries, and the houses of the French nobility which he visited, Monsieur le Marquis de Farintosh excited considerable remark by the use of some of the phrases which his young professor had taught to him. People even went so far as to say that the Marquis was an awkward and dull young man of the very worst manners.

Whereas the young Clive Newcome—and it comforted the poor fellow's heart somewhat, and be sure pleased Ethel who was looking on at his triumphs—was voted the most charming young Englishman who had been seen for a long time in our salons. Madame de Florac, who loved him as a son of her own, actually went once or twice into the world in order to see his *début*. Madame de Montcontour inhabited a part of the Hôtel de Florac and received society there. The French people did not understand what bad English she talked, though they comprehended Lord Farintosh's French blunders. "Monsieur Newcome is an artist! What a noble career!" cries a great French lady, the wife of a Marshal, to the astonished Miss Newcome. "This young man is the cousin of the charming Meess? You must be proud to possess such a nephew, Madame!" says another French lady to the Countess of Kew (who you may be sure is delighted to have such a relative). And the French lady invites Clive to her receptions expressly in order to make herself agreeable to the old Comtesse. Before the cousins have been three minutes together in Madame de Florac's salon, she sees that Clive is in love with Ethel Newcome. She takes

---

[1] he *HM NY*] she *Ms E1 R*

the boy's hand and says *"J'ai votre secret, mon ami;"* and her eyes regard him for a moment as fondly, as tenderly, as ever they looked at his father. O what tears have they shed, gentle eyes—O what faith has it kept, tender heart! If Love lives through all life and survives through all sorrows;[2] and remains steadfast with us through all changes; and in all darkness of spirit burns brightly, and if we die, deplores us for ever and loves still equally; and exists with the very last gasp and throb of the faithful bosom—whence it passes with the pure soul, beyond death; surely it shall be Immortal? Though we who remain are separated from it, is it not our's in Heaven? If we love still those we lose, can we altogether lose those we love? Forty years have passed away. Youth and dearest memories revisit her and Hope almost wakes up again out of its grave, as the constant lady holds the young man's hand, and looks at the son of Thomas Newcome.

2 sorrows *Ms*] sorrow *E1*

Chapter VIII.

SINCE the death of the Duc d'Ivry, the husband of Mary Queen of
Scots, the Comte de Florac who is now the legitimate owner of the ducal
title, does not choose to bear it: but continues to be known in the world by
his old name. The old Count's world is very small. His doctor, and his director who comes daily to play his game of picquet; his daughter's children
who amuse him by their laughter and play round his chair in the garden
of his hotel; his faithful wife; and one or two friends as old as himself form
his society. His son the Abbé is with them but seldom. The austerity of
his manners frightens his old father, who can little comprehend the reli-
gionism of the new school. After going to hear his son preach through
Lent at Notre Dame where the Abbé de Florac gathered a great congregation, the old Count came away quite puzzled at his son's declamations.
"I do not understand your new priests," he says, "I knew my son had become a Cordélier, I went to hear him and found he was a Jacobin. Let me
make my salut in quiet, my good Léonore. My director answers for me
and plays a game at trictrac into the bargain with me." Our history has but
little to do with this venerable nobleman. He has his chamber looking out
into the garden of his hotel; his faithful old domestic to wait upon him, his
House of Peers to attend when he is well enough, his few acquaintances
to help him to pass the evening. The rest of the hotel he gives up to his
son, the Vicomte de Florac, and Madame la Princesse de Montcontour, his
daughter-in-law.

When Florac has told his friends of the Club why it is he has assumed
a new title—as a means of reconciliation (a reconciliation all philosophical, my friends,—) with his wife *née* Higg of Manchester, who adores titles
like all Anglaises, and has recently made a great succession; every body
allows that the measure was dictated by prudence, and there is no more
laughter at his change of name. The Princess takes the first floor of the
hotel at the price paid for it by the American General, who has returned
to his original pigs at Cincinnati. Had not Cincinnatus himself pigs on his
farm, and was he not a general and member of Congress too? The honest
Princess has a bed-chamber, which to her terror, she is obliged to open of
reception-evenings, when gentlemen and ladies play cards there. It is fitted up in the style of Louis XVI. In her bed is an immense looking-glass
surmounted by stucco cupids: it is an alcove which some powdered Venus

before the Revolution might have reposed in. Opposite that looking glass, between the tall windows at some forty feet distance is another huge mirror, so that when the poor Princess is in bed in her prim old curl-papers she sees a vista of elderly princesses twinkling away into the dark perspective; and is so frightened that she and Betsy, her Lancashire maid, pin up the jonquil silk curtains over the bed-mirror after the first night; though the Princess never can get it out of her head that her image is still there, behind the jonquil hangings, turning as she turns, waking as she wakes &c. The chamber is so vast and lonely that she has a bed made for Betsy in the room. It is of course whisked away into a closet on reception-evenings. A boudoir, rose-tendre with more Cupids and Nymphs by Boucher sporting over the door-pannels—nymphs who may well shock old Betsy and her old mistress—is the Princess's morning-room. "Ah Mum, what would Mr. Jowls to Newcome, Mr. Humper at Manchester,[1] (the minister whom in early days Miss Higg used to sit under) say[2] if they was browt into this room!" But there is no question of Mr. Jowls and Mr. Humper, excellent Dissenting Divines who preached to Miss Higg, being brought into the Princesse de Montcontour's boudoir.

That paragraph respecting a "Conversion in High Life" which F.B. in his enthusiasm inserted in the *Pall Mall Gazette,* caused no small excitement in the Florac family. The Florac family read the *Pall Mall Gazette,* knowing[3] that Clive's friends were engaged in that periodical.[4] When Madame de Florac who did not often read newspapers happened to cast her eye upon that poetic paragraph of F.B.'s, you may fancy with what a panic it filled the good and pious lady. Her son become a Protestant! After all the grief and trouble his wildness had occasioned to her, Paul forsake his religion! But that her husband was so ill and aged as not to be able to bear her absence; she would have hastened to London to rescue her son out of that perdition. She sent for her younger son, who undertook the embassy; and the Prince and Princesse de Montcontour in their hotel at London were one day surprised[5] by the visit of the Abbé de Florac.

As Paul was quite innocent of any intention of abandoning his religion; the mother's kind heart was very speedily set at rest by her envoy. Far from Paul's conversion to Protestantism, the Abbé wrote home the most encouraging accounts of his sister-in-law's precious dispositions. He had communications with Madame de Montcontour's Anglican director, a man

---

[1] *E1* mistakenly reversed the order; Miss Higg is from Manchester, so Mr. Humper was her early minister.

[2] say *E1*] [omitted] *Ms*

[3] *Gazette,* knowing *E1*] *Gazette.* Knowing *Ms*

[4] periodical. When *E1*] periodical, Thomas Newcome had ordered Messrs. Smith and Elder, his booksellers, to send half a dozen copies weekly [to] friends of his whom he pointed out—(and "twelve copies of any book which Mr. Pendennis publishes, you will be sure to send out to me in India," said the good Colonel on going away.) so that honest Jack Seedham living on little more than his lieutenant's half-pay at Culhampton, Tom Skinner in the same station of life at Bury St. Edmunds: Miss Featherstone, Laurel House Academy, Taunton Dean, Somersetshire (where Charley Bayford's poor girls were, who was killed in Burleigh): and Madame la Comtesse de Florac, *à son hôtel, Rue St. Dominique, St. Germain à Paris,* became readers of our paper for many years without any expense to themselves. ¶When *Ms*

[5] surprised *E1*] surprised there *Ms*

of not powerful mind, wrote M. l'Abbé, though of considerable repute for eloquence in his sect. The good dispositions of his sister-in-law were improved by the French clergyman who could be most captivating and agreeable when a work of conversion was in hand. The visit reconciled the family to their English relative, in whom good nature and many other good qualities were to be seen now that there were hopes of reclaiming her. It was agreed that Madame de Montcontour should come and inhabit the Hôtel de Florac at Paris; perhaps the Abbé tempted the worthy lady by pictures of the many pleasures and advantages she would enjoy in that capital. She was presented at her own Court by the French Ambassadress of that day: and was received at the Tuileries with a cordiality which flattered and pleased her.

Having been presented herself, Madame la Princesse in turn presented to her august sovereign Mrs. T. Higg and Miss Higg of Manchester, Mrs. Samuel Higg of Newcome, the husbands of those ladies (the Princess's brothers) also sporting a court dress for the first time.[6] Sam Higg's neighbour, the Member for Newcome, Sir Brian Newcome, Bart., was too ill to act as Higg's sponsor before majesty; but Barnes Newcome was uncommonly civil to the two Lancashire gentlemen; though their politics were different to his and Sam had voted against Sir Brian at his last election. Barnes took them to dine at a club: recommended his tailor: sent Lady Clara Pulleyn to call on Mrs. Higg: who pronounced her to be a pretty young woman and most haffable. The Countess of Dorking would have been delighted to present these ladies had the Princess not luckily been in London to do that office. The Hobson Newcomes were very civil to the Lancashire party and entertained them splendidly at dinner. I believe Mrs. and Mr. Hobson themselves went to Court this year, the latter in a deputy lieutenant's uniform.[7]

If Barnes Newcome was so very civil to the Higg family we may suppose he had good reason. The Higgs were very strong in Newcome and it was advisable to conciliate them. They were very rich and their account would not be disagreeable at the Bank. Madame de Montcontour's—a large easy private account—would be more pleasant still. And, Hobson Brothers having entered largely into the Anglo-Continental Railway whereof mention has been made; it was a bright thought of Barnes to place the Prince of Montcontour, &c. &c., on the French Direction of the Railway: and to take the princely prodigal down to Newcome with his new title and reconcile him to his wife and the Higg family. Barnes we may say invented the Principality: rescued the Vicomte de Florac out of his dirty lodgings in Leicester Square and sent the Prince of Montcontour back to his worthy middle-aged wife again. The disagreeable dissenting days were over. A brilliant young curate of Doctor Bulders who also wore long hair, straight waistcoats and no shirt collars had already reconciled the Vicomtesse de Florac

---

[6] time. *E1*] time or, I cannot be certain of this fact, a Deputy Lieutenant's uniform. *Ms*

[7] uniform. *E1*] uniform; Mrs. Mackenzie I know was wild for going and to present Rosey; and that James Binnie, Esqr., of the Bengal Civil Service should appear at St. James's "on his return from India." But James declined to wear tights and a sword and bag; he said that his gracious Queen could live very comfortably without seeing him dressed up like a Tom-noddy. Such were James's disrespectful notions about Court dresses and ceremonies. *Ms*

to the persuasion whereof the ministers are clad in that queer uniform. The landlord of their hotel in Saint James's got his wine from Sherrick and sent his "families" to Lady Whittlesea's chapel. The Revd. Charles Honeyman's eloquence and amiability were appreciated by his new disciple—thus the historian has traced here step by step how all these people became acquainted.

Sam Higg, whose name was very good on 'Change in Manchester and London, joined the direction of the Anglo-Continental. His sister,[8] a brother had died lately leaving his money amongst them and his wealth had added considerably to Madame de Florac's means, invested a portion of her capital in the Railway in her husband's name. The shares were at a premium and gave a good dividend. The Prince de Montcontour took his place with great gravity at the Paris board, whither Barnes made frequent flying visits. The sense of Capitalism sobered and dignified Paul de Florac: at the age of five-and-forty he was actually giving up being a young man, was[9] not ill-pleased at having to enlarge his waistcoats and to show a little grey in his mustache. His errors were forgotten: he was *bien vu* by the government. He might have had the Embassy Extraordinary to Queen Pomaré: but the health of Madame la Princesse was delicate. He paid his wife visits every morning: appeared at her parties and her opera box and was seen constantly with her in public. He gave quiet little dinners still, at which Clive was present sometimes; and had a private door and key to his apartments which were separated by all the dreary length of the reception-rooms from the mirrored chamber and jonquil couch where the Princess and Betsy reposed. When some of his London friends visited Paris he showed us these rooms and introduced us duly to Madame la Princesse. He was as simple and as much at home in the midst of these splendours, as in the dirty little lodgings in Leicester Square where he painted his own boots, and cooked his herring over the tongs. As for Clive, he was the infant of the house. Madame la Princesse could not resist his kind face; and Paul was as fond of him in his way, as Paul's mother in her's. Would he live at the Hôtel de Florac? There was an excellent atélier in the pavillion, with a chamber for his servant. "No. Thou wilt be most at ease in apartments of your own. You will have here but the society of women. I do not rise till late: and my affairs, my board, call me away for the greater part of the day. Thou wilt but be ennuyé to play trictrac with my old father. My mother waits on him. My sister, au second, is given up entirely to her children who always have the *pituite*. Madame la Princesse is not amusing for a young man. Come and go when thou wilt, Clive, my garçon, my son: thy cover is laid. Wilt thou take the portraits of all the family? Hast thou want of money? I had at thy age and almost ever since, *mon ami:* but now we swim in gold, and when there is a louis in my purse, there are ten francs for thee." To show his mother that he did not think of the Reformed Religion, he did not miss going to mass with her on Sunday. Sometimes Madame Paul went too, between whom and her mother-in-law there could not be any liking, but there was now great civility. They saw each other once a day: Madame

Paul always paid her visit to the Comte de Florac: and Betsy, her maid, made the old gentleman laugh by her briskness and talk. She brought back to her mistress the most wonderful stories which the old man told her about his doings during the emigration—before he married Madame la Comtesse—when he gave lessons in dancing, parbleu! There was his fiddle still, a trophy of those old times. He chirped and coughed and sang in his cracked old voice as he talked about them. "Law[1] bless you, Mum," says Betsy, "he must have been a terrible old man!" He remembered the times well enough, but the stories he sometimes told over twice or thrice in an hour. I am afraid he had not repented sufficiently of those wicked old times: else why did he laugh and giggle so when he recalled them? He would laugh and giggle till he was choked with his old cough: and old St. Jean, his man, came and beat M. le Comte on the back; and made M. le Comte take a spoonful of his syrup.

Between two such women as Madame de Florac and Lady Kew of course there could be little liking or sympathy. Religion, love, duty, the family were the French lady's constant occupations—duty and the family, perhaps, Lady Kew's aim too—only the notions of duty were different in either person—Lady Kew's idea of duty to her relatives being to push them on in the world; Madame de Florac's to soothe,[2] to pray, to attend them with constant watchfulness, to strive to mend them with pious counsel. I don't know that one lady was happier than the other. Madame de Florac's eldest son was a kindly prodigal: her second had given his whole heart to the Church: her daughter had centered her's on her own children, and was jealous if their grandmother laid a finger on them. So Léonore de Florac was quite alone. It seemed as if Heaven had turned away all her children's hearts from her. Her daily business in life was to nurse a selfish old man, into whose service she had been forced in early youth, by a paternal decree which she never questioned; giving him obedience, striving to give him respect,—everything but her heart which had gone out of her keeping. Many a good woman's life is no more cheerful: a spring of beauty, a little warmth and sunshine of love, a bitter disappointment, followed by pangs and frantic tears, then a long monotonous story of submission. "Not here, my daughter, is to be your happiness," says the priest. "Whom Heaven loves it afflicts." And he points out to her the agonies of suffering saints of her sex; assures her of their present beatitudes and glories; exhorts her to bear her pains with a faith like their's; and is empowered to promise her a like reward.

The other matron is not less alone. Her husband and son are dead without a tear for either—to weep was not in Lady Kew's nature—her grandson whom she had loved perhaps more than any human being is rebellious and estranged from her; her children separated from her save one whose sickness and bodily infirmity the mother resents as disgraces to herself; her darling schemes fail somehow, she moves from town to town and ball to ball and hall to castle for ever uneasy and always alone. She sees people scared at her coming, is received by sufferance and fear rather than by

---

[1] Law *Ms*] Lor! *E1*
[2] soothe, *E1*] watch, *Ms*

welcome; likes perhaps the terror which she inspires and to enter over the breach rather than[3] through the hospitable gate. She will try and command wherever she goes: and trample over dependants and society, with a grim consciousness that it dislikes her, a rage at its cowardice, and an unbending will to domineer. To be old, proud, lonely and not have a friend in the[4] world, that is her lot in it. As the French lady may be said to resemble the bird which the fables say feeds her young with her blood; this one, if she has a little natural liking for her brood, goes hunting hither and thither and robs meat for them. And so I suppose to make the simile good we must compare the Marquis of Farintosh to a lamb for the nonce, and Miss Ethel Newcome to a young eaglet. Is it not a rare provision of nature (or fiction of poets who have their own natural history) that the strong-winged bird can soar to the sun and gaze at it; and then come down from heaven to[5] pounce on a piece of carrion?

After she became acquainted with certain circumstances, Madame de Florac was very interested about Ethel Newcome and strove in her modest way to become intimate with her. Miss Newcome and Lady Kew attended Madame de Montcontour's Wednesday-evenings. "It is as well, my dear, for the interests of the family that we should be particularly civil to these people," Lady Kew said, and accordingly she came[6] to the Hôtel de Florac and was perfectly insolent to Madame la Princesse every Thursday evening. Towards Madame de Florac even Lady Kew could not be rude. She was so gentle as to give no excuse for assault: Lady Kew vouchsafed to pronounce that Madame de Florac was "très grande-dame—of the sort which is almost impossible to find nowadays," Lady Kew said who thought she possessed this dignity in her own person. When Madame de Florac, blushing, asked Ethel to come and see her: Ethel's grandmother consented with the utmost willingness. "She is very *dévote* I have heard and will try and convert you. Of course you will hold your own about that sort of thing; and have the good sense to keep off theology. There is no Roman Catholic *parti* in England or Scotland that is to be thought of for a moment. You will see they will marry young Lord Derwentwater to an Italian Princess but he is only seventeen and his directors never lose sight of him: Sir Bartholomew Fawkes will have a fine property when Lord Campion dies, unless Lord Campion leaves the money to the convent where his daughter is[7]—and of the other families who is there? I made every enquiry purposely—that is of course one is anxious to know about the Catholics as about one's own people: and little Mr. Rood, who was one of my poor brother Steyne's lawyers, told me there is not one young man of that party at this moment who can be called a desirable person. Be very civil to Madame de Florac, she sees some of the old Legitimists, and you know I am *brouillée* with that party of late years."

"There is the Marquis de Montluc who has a large fortune for France," said Ethel gravely. "He has a hump-back but he is very *spirituel*. Mon-

---

[3] rather than *E1*] than *Ms*
[4] in the *E1*] in all the *Ms*
[5] to *Ms*] and *E1*
[6] she came *E1*] came *Ms*
[7] daughter is *E1*] daughter *Ms*

The Marquis "en Montangnard"

sieur de Cadillan paid me some compliments the other night and even asked George Barnes what my *dot* was. He is a widower, and has a wig and two daughters. Which do you think would be the greatest encumbrance, Grandmamma, a hump-back, or a wig and two daughters? I like Madame de Florac—for the sake of the borough I must try and like poor Madame de Montcontour, and I will go and see them whenever you please."

So Ethel went to see Madame de Florac. She was very kind to Madame de Préville's children, Madame de Florac's grandchildren; she was gay and gracious with Madame de Montcontour. She went again and again to the Hôtel de Florac, not[8] caring for Lady Kew's own circle of statesmen and diplomatists, Russian and Spanish and French, whose talk about the Courts of Europe,—who was in favour at St.[9] Petersburg and who was in disgrace at Schoenbrunn,—naturally did not amuse the lively young person. The goodness of Madame de Florac's life, the tranquil grace and melancholy kindness with which the French lady received her, soothed and pleased Miss Ethel. She came and reposed in Madame de Florac's quiet chamber or sate in the shade in the sober old garden of her hotel; away from all the trouble and chatter of the salons, the gossip of the embassies, the fluttering ceremonial of the Parisian ladies' visits in their fine toilettes; the *fadaises* of the dancing dandies; and the pompous mysteries of the old statesmen who frequented her grandmother's apartment. The world began for her at night; when she went in the train of the old Countess from hotel to hotel and danced waltz after waltz with Prussian and Neapolitan secretaries, with Princes' Officers of Ordonnance—with personages even more lofty very likely; for the Court of the Citizen King was then in its splendour; and there must surely have been a number of nimble young Royal Highnesses who would like to dance with such a beauty as Miss Newcome. The Marquis of Farintosh had a share in these polite amusements. His English conversation was not brilliant as yet although his French was eccentric. But at the Court balls, whether he appeared in his uniform of the Scotch Archers, or in his native Glenlivat tartan, there certainly was not in his own or the public estimation a handsomer young nobleman in Paris that season. It has been said that he was greatly improved in dancing; and, for a young man of his age, his whiskers were really extraordinarily large and curly.

Miss Newcome, out of consideration for her grandmother's strange antipathy to him, did not inform Lady Kew, that a young gentleman by the name of Clive, occasionally came to visit the Hôtel de Florac. At first, with her French education, Madame de Florac never would have thought of allowing the cousins to meet in her house. But with the English it was different. Paul assured her that in the English chateaux, *les Meess* walked for entire hours with the young men, made parties of the fish, mounted to horse with them, the whole with the permission of the mothers. "When I was at Newcome Miss Ethel rode with me several times," Paul said; "*à preuve* that we went to visit an old relation of the family, who adores Clive and his father." When Madame de Florac questioned her son about the young

---

[8] not *E1*] whilst not *Ms*
[9] St. *E1*] [omitted] *Ms*

Marquis to whom it was said Ethel was engaged, Florac flouted the idea. "Engaged! This young Marquis is engaged to the Théâtre des Variétés, my mother. He laughs at the notion of an engagement. When one charged him with it of late at the club: and asked how Mademoiselle Louqsor— she is so tall that they call her the Louqsor—she is an *Odalisque-Obélisque,* ma mère—When one asked how the Louqsor would pardon his pursuit of Miss Newcome—my Écossois permitted himself to say in full club that it was Miss Newcome pursued him,—that nymph, that Diane, that charming and peerless young creature! on which, as the others laughed and his friend Monsieur Walleye applauded, I dared to say in my turn, 'Monsieur le Marquis, as a young man, not familiar with our language, you have said what is not true, Milor, and therefore luckily not mischievous. I have the honour to count of my friends the parents of the young lady of whom you have spoken. You never could have intended to say that a young Miss who lives under the guardianship of her parents and is obedient to them, whom you meet in society all the nights, and at whose door your carriage is to be seen every day—is capable of that with which you charge her so gaily. These things say themselves, Monsieur, in the *coulisses* of the theatre:—of women from whom you learn our language; not of young persons pure and chaste, Monsieur de Farintosh! Learn to respect your compatriots, to honour youth and innocence everywhere, Monsieur!—and when you forget yourself, permit one who might be your father to point where you are wrong.'"

"And what did he answer?" asked the Countess.

"I attended myself to a *soufflet,"* replied Florac; "but his reply was much more agreeable. The young insulary with many blushes and a *gros juron* as his polite way is—said he had not wished to say a word against that person—'Of whom the name,' cried I, 'ought never to be spoken in these places;' and herewith[1] our little dispute ended."

So occasionally Mr. Clive had the good luck to meet with his cousin at the Hôtel de Florac; where I daresay all the inhabitants wished he should have his desire regarding this young lady. The Colonel had talked early to Madame de Florac about this wish of his heart, impossible then to gratify, because Ethel was engaged to Lord Kew: Clive in the fulness of his had[2] imparted his passion to Florac, and in answer to Paul's offer to himself, had shown the Frenchman that kind letter in which his father bade him carry aid to "Léonore de Florac's son," in case he should need it. The case was all clear to the lively Paul. "Between my mother and your good Colonel there must have been an affair of the heart in the early days during the emigration." Clive owned his father had told him as much, at least that he himself had been attached to Mademoiselle de Blois. "It is for that that her heart yearns towards thee—that I have felt myself entrained towards thee since I saw thee"—Clive momentarily expected to be kissed again. "Tell thy father that I feel—am touched by his goodness with an eternal gratitude, and love every one that loves my mother." As far as wishes went these two were eager promoters of Clive's little love-affair; and Madame la Princesse

---

[1] places;' and herewith *Ms*] places.' Herewith *E1*
[2] his had *Ms*] his heart *E1*

became an ally[3] not less willing, Clive's good looks and good nature had had their effects upon that good-natured woman, and he was as great a favourite with her, as with her husband. And thus it happened that when Miss Ethel came to pay her visit and sate with Madame de Florac and her grandchildren in the garden, Mr. Newcome would sometimes walk up the avenue there and salute the ladies.[4]

If Ethel had not wanted to see him, would she have come?[5] Yes—she used to say she was going to Madame de Préville's—not to Madame de Florac's—and would insist, I have no doubt, that it *was* Madame de Préville whom she went to see (whose husband was a member of the Chamber of Deputies, a Conseiller d'État or other French big wig) and that she had no idea of going to meet Clive, or that he was more than a casual acquaintance at the Hôtel de Florac. There was no part of her conduct in all her life which when it was impugned[6] this lady would defend more strongly than this intimacy at the Hôtel de Florac. It is not with this I quarrel especially. My fair young readers, who have seen a half-dozen of seasons—can you call to mind the time when you had such a friendship for Emma Tomkins that you were always at the Tomkins's, and notes were constantly passing between your house and her's? When her brother, Paget Tomkins, returned to India, did not your intimacy with Emma fall off? If your younger sister is not in the room, I know you will own as much to me. I think you are always deceiving yourselves and other people. I think the motive you put forward is very often not the real one; though you will confess, neither to yourself nor to any human being what the real motive is. I think that which[7] you desire you pursue, and are as selfish in your way as your bearded fellow creatures are. And as for the truth being in you: of all the women in a great acquaintance, I protest there are but—never mind. A perfectly honest woman—a woman who never flatters, who never manages, who never cajoles, who never conceals, who never uses her eyes, who never speculates on the effect which she produces, who never is conscious of unspoken admiration—what a monster, I say, would such a female be! Miss Hopkins, you have been a coquette since you were a year old; you worked on your papa's friends in the nurse's arms by the fascinations[8] of your lace frock and pretty new sash and shoes: when you could just toddle, you practised your arts upon other children in the square, poor little lambkins sporting among the daisies—and *nunc in ovilia, mox in reluctantes dracones*, proceeding from the lambs to reluctant dragoons—you tried your arts upon Captain Paget

---

[3] an ally *Ms*] equally *E1* [Compositor's misreading.]

[4] and salute the ladies. *E1*] and pay his respects to those ladies. *Ms*

[5] come? *E1*] come? When Madame de Florac in her first talk with the young lady spoke to her with such special tenderness and kindness, told her how her uncle Thomas Newcome had spoken of her, and offered her friendship to the young girl; it may be that Miss Newcome half divined what was in her new friend's heart, and that something respecting Clive was lurking there. She embraced this proffered friendship with such uncommon eagerness: she found that quiet old house and garden so exceedingly pleasant; that she was always going to see Madame de Préville. *Ms*

[6] The phrase "when it was impugned" is interlined in the manuscript and misplaced after "this lady" in *E1*.

[7] wh. *Ms*] what *E1*

[8] fascinations *Ms*] fascination *E1*

Tomkins, who behaved so ill and went to India without—without making those proposals which of course you never expected.[9] Your intimacy was with Emma. It has cooled. Your sets are different. The Tomkins's are not *quite* &c. &c.—You believe Captain Tomkins married a Miss O'Grady &c. &c. Ah, my pretty, my sprightly Miss Hopkins: be gentle in your judgment of your neighbours!

[9] expected. *E1*] expected, or had the least idea of. *Ms*

Chapter IX.

CONTAINS TWO OR THREE ACTS OF A LITTLE COMEDY.

LL this story is told by one, who if he was not actually present at the circumstances here narrated, yet had information concerning them, and could supply such a narrative of facts and conversations as is, indeed, not less authentic than the details we have of other histories. How can I tell the feelings in a young lady's mind, the thoughts in a young gentleman's bosom?—as Professor Owen or Professor Agassiz takes a fragment of a bone and builds an enormous forgotten monster out of it, wallowing in primæval quagmires, tearing down leaves and branches of plants that flourished thousands of years ago and perhaps[1] may be coal by this time—so the novelist puts this and that together: from the footprint finds the foot; from the foot the brute who trod on it, from the brute the plant he browsed on, the marsh in which he swam—and thus in[2] his humble way a physiologist, too, depicts[3] the habits, size, appearance of the beings whereof he has to treat—traces this slimy reptile through the mud and describes his habits filthy and rapacious; prods down this butterfly with a pin and depicts his beautiful coat and embroidered waistcoat; points out the singular structure of yonder more important animal, the megatherium of his history.

Suppose then in the quaint old garden of the Hôtel de Florac, two young people are walking up and down in an avenue of lime trees which are still permitted to grow in that ancient place. In the centre of that[4] avenue is a fountain surmounted by a Triton so grey and moss-eaten that though he holds his conch to his swelling lips, curling his tail in the arid basin, his instrument has had a sinecure for at least fifty years; and did not think

1 perhaps *E1*] parts *Ms*
2 thus in *E1*] thus, the romancer, in *Ms*
3 depicts *E1*] traces *Ms*
4 that *E1*] the *Ms*

fit even to play when the Bourbons in whose time he was erected came back from their exile. At the end of the lime-tree avenue is a broken-nosed damp Faun with a marble panpipe who pipes to the spirit ditties which I believe never had any tune. The *perron* of the hotel is at the other end of the avenue, a couple of Cæsars on either side of the door-window, from which the inhabitants of the hotel issue into the garden—Caracalla frowning over his mouldy shoulder at Nerva on to whose clipped hair the roofs of the grey chateau have been dribbling for ever so many long years. There are more statues gracing this noble place. There is Cupid who has been at[5] the point of kissing Psyche this half-century at least, though the delicious event has never come off through all those blazing summers and dreary winters: there is Venus and her boy under the damp little dome of a cracked old temple. Through the *allées* of this old garden in which their ancestors have disported in hoops and powder, Monsieur de Florac's chair is wheeled by St. Jean his attendant, Madame de Préville's children trot about, and skip, and play at cache-cache. The R.P. de Florac (when at home) paces up and down and meditates his sermons; Madame de Florac sadly walks sometimes to look at her roses; and Clive and Ethel Newcome are marching up and down, the children and their bonne of course being there jumping to and fro and Madame de Florac having just been called away to Monsieur le Comte whose physician has come to see him.

Ethel says, "How charming and odd this solitude is: and how pleasant to hear the voices of the children playing in the neighbouring Convent-garden," of which they can see the new chapel rising over the trees.

Clive remarks that the neighbouring hotel has curiously changed its destination. One of the members of the Directory had it, and no doubt in the groves of its garden, Madame Tallien, and Madame Récamier and Madame Beauharnais have danced under the lamps. Then a Marshal of the Empire inhabited it. Then it was restored to its legitimate owner, Monsieur le Marquis de Bricquabracque, whose descendants having a lawsuit about the Bricquabracque succession,[6] sold the hotel to the Convent.

After some talk about nuns, Ethel says there were convents in England. She often thinks she would like to retire to one, and she sighs as if her heart were in that scheme.

Clive with a laugh says Yes—if you could retire after the season when you were very weary of the balls, a convent would be very nice. At Rome he had seen San Pietro in Montorio and Sant Onofrio,[7] that delightful old place where Tasso died: people go and make a retreat there. In the ladies' convents the ladies do the same thing—and he doubts whether they are much more or less wicked after their retreat than gentlemen and ladies in England or France.

Ethel. Why do you sneer at all faith? Why should not a retreat do people good? Do you suppose the world is so satisfactory that those who are in it never wish for a while to leave it? (*She heaves a sigh and looks down towards a beautiful new dress of many flounces which Madame Flouncival the great milliner has sent her home that very day.*)

5 at *E1*] on *Ms*
6 succession, *E1*] [omitted]
7 Sant Onofrio *E1*] [blank space] *Ms*

At the Hotel de Florac

Clive. I do not know what the world is except from afar off. I am like the Peri who looks into Paradise and sees angels within it. I live in Charlotte Street, Fitzroy Square: which is not within the gates of Paradise. I take the gate to be somewhere in Davies Street leading out of Oxford Street into Grosvenor Square. There's another gate in Hay Hill: and another in Bruton Street, Bond—

Ethel. Don't be a Goose.

Clive. Why not? It is as good to be a goose, as to be a lady—no, a gentleman of fashion. Suppose I were a Viscount, an Earl, a Marquis, a Duke, would you say Goose? No, you would say Swan.

Ethel. Unkind and unjust!—ungenerous to make taunts which common people make: and to repeat to me those silly sarcasms which your low *Radical literary* friends are always putting in their books! Have I ever made any difference to *you?* Would I not sooner see you than the fine people? Would I talk with you or with the young dandies most willingly? Are we not of the same blood, Clive; and of all the grandees I see about, can there be a grander gentleman than your dear old father?—You need not squeeze my hand so.—Those little imps are look—that has nothing to do with the question. Viens Léonore! Tu connois bien Monsieur, n'est-ce pas? qui te fait de si jolis dessins?[8]

Léonore. Ah oui!—Vous m'en ferez toujours n'est-ce pas, Monsieur Clive? des chevaux, et puis des petites filles avec leurs gouvernantes, et puis des maisons—et puis—et puis des maisons encore—où est bonne Maman?

[*Exit little* LÉONORE *down an alley.*

Ethel. Do you remember when we were children and you used to make drawings for us? I have some now that you did—in my geography book which I used to read and read with Miss Quigley.

Clive. I remember all about our youth, Ethel.

Ethel. Tell me what you remember?

Clive. I remember one of the days when I first saw you, I had been reading the "Arabian Nights" at school—and you came in in a bright dress of shot silk, amber and blue—and I thought you were like that fairy or princess[9] who came out of the crystal box—because——

Ethel. Because why?

Clive. Because I always thought that fairy somehow must be the most beautiful creature in all the world—that is 'Why and because.' Do not make me May Fair curtsies. You know whether you are good-looking or not: and how long I have thought you so. I remember when I thought I would like to be Ethel's knight and that if there was anything she would have me do, I would try and atchieve it in order to please her. I remember when I was so ignorant I did not know there was any difference in rank between us.

Ethel. Ah Clive!

Clive. Now it is altered. Now I know the difference between a poor painter and a young lady of the world. Why haven't I a title and a great fortune? Why did I ever see you, Ethel; or, knowing the distance which it seems fate has placed between us, why have I seen you again?

[8] dessins? *E1*] desseins *Ms*
[9] fairy or princess] fairy or Princess *Ms*] fairy-princess *E1*

Ethel (innocently). Have I ever made any difference between us? Whenever I may see you, am I not too glad? Don't I see you sometimes when I should not—no—I do not say when I should not—but when others whom I am bound to obey forbid me? What harm is there in my remembering old days? Why should I be ashamed of our relationship—no, not ashamed—why should I forget it?—Don't do that, Sir, we have shaken hands twice already. Léonore! Xavier!

Clive. At one moment you like me: and at the next you seem to repent it. One day you seem happy when I come, and another day, you are ashamed of me. Last Tuesday, when you came with those fine ladies to the Louvre, you seemed to blush when you saw me copying at my picture and that stupid young lord looked quite alarmed because you spoke to me. My lot in life is not very brilliant but I would not change it against that young man's—no, not with all his chances.

Ethel. What do you mean with all his chances?

Clive. You know very well. I mean I would not be as selfish or as dull or as ill-educated—I won't say worse of him—not to be as handsome or as wealthy or as noble as he is. I swear I would not now change my place against his or give up being Clive Newcome to be my Lord Marquis of Farintosh with all his acres and titles of nobility.

Ethel. Why are you for ever harping about Lord Farintosh and his titles? I thought it was only women who were jealous—you gentlemen say so— (*Hurriedly.*) I am going to-night with Grandmamma to the Minister of the Interior and then to the Russian ball; and to-morrow to the Tuileries, we dine at the Embassy first; and on Sunday I suppose we shall go to the Rue d'Aguesseau. I can hardly come here before Mon—Madame de Florac! Little Léonore is very like you—resembles you very much. My cousin says he longs to make a drawing of her.

Madame de Florac. My husband always likes that I should be present at his dinner. Pardon me, young people, that I have been away from you for a moment.

[*Exeunt* CLIVE, ETHEL *and* Madame DE F. *into the house.*

CONVERSATION II.—*Scene* 1.

Miss Newcome arrives in Lady Kew's carriage, which enters the court of the Hôtel de Florac.[1]

Saint Jean. Mademoiselle—Madame la Comtesse is gone out: but Madame has charged me to say that she will be at home to the dinner of M. le Comte, as to the ordinary.

Miss Newcome. Madame de Préville is at home?

Saint Jean. Pardon me, Madame is gone out with M. le Baron and M. Xavier and Mademoiselle de Préville. They are gone, Miss, I believe to visit the parents of Monsieur le Baron: of whom it is probably to-day the fête: for Mademoiselle Léonore carried a bouquet—no doubt for her grandpapa. Will it please Mademoiselle to enter? I think Monsieur the Count sounds me. (*Bell rings.*)

---

[1] This stage direction added in *E1*.

Miss Newcome. Madame la Prince—Madame la Vicomtesse is at home? Monsieur St. Jean!

Saint Jean. I go to call the people of Madame la Vicomtesse.

[*Exit old* SAINT JEAN *to the carriage: a* Lackey *comes presently in a gorgeous livery with buttons like little cheeseplates.*

The Lackey. The Princess is at home, Miss, and will be most 'appy to see you, Miss. (MISS *trips up the great stair: a gentleman out of livery has come forth to the landing and introduces her to the apartments of* Madame la Princesse.)

The Lackey (to the Servants on the box). Good morning, Thomas. How dy' do, old Backystopper!

Backystopper. How de do, Jim. I say, you couldn't give a feller a drink

of beer could yer, Muncontour? It was precious *wet* last night, I can tell you. 'Ad to stop for three hours at the Napolitum Embassy where we was a dancing. Me and some chaps went into Bob Parsom's and had a drain. Old cat came out and couldn't find her carriage, not by no means, could she, Tommy? Blest if I didn't nearly drive her into a wegetable cart. I was so uncommon scruy! Who's this a hentering at your pot-coshare? Billy, my fine feller!

Clive Newcome (by the most singular coincidence). Madame la Princesse?

Lackey. We, Munseer. (*He rings a bell, the gentleman in black appears as before on the landing-place.*)[2]

[*Exit* CLIVE *up the stair.*

Backystopper. I say, Billy:[3] is that young chap often a coming about here? They'd run pretty in a curricle, wouldn't they? Miss N. and Master N.

[2] *landing-place. Ms*] *landing-place up the stair. E1* [Manuscript insertion misplaced in *E1*; see next line.]
[3] Billy: *Ms*] Bill: *E1*

Quiet old woman! Jest look to that mare's 'ead will you, Billy?[4] He's a fine young feller, that is. He gave me a sovering the other night. Whenever I sor him in the park, he was always riding an 'ansum hanimal. What is he? They said in our 'all he was a Hartis. I can 'ardly think that. Why, there used to be a[5] Hartis come to our club, and painted two or three of my 'osses, and my old woman too.

Lackey. There's Hartises and Hartises, Backystopper. Why there's some on 'em comes here with more stars on their coats than Dukes has got. Have you never 'eard of Mossyer Verny or Mossyer Gudang?

Backysto. They say this young gent is sweet on Miss N. Which I guess I wish he may git it.

Tommy. He He He!

Backysto. Brayvo, Tommy. Tom ain't much of a man for conversation but he's a precious one to drink. *Do* you think the young gent is sweet on her? Tommy. I sor him often prowling about our 'ouse in Queen Street when we was in London.

Tommy. I guess he wasn't let in in Queen Street. I guess hour little Buttons was very near turned away for saying we was at home to him. I guess a footman's place is to keep his mouth hopen—no, his *heyes* hopen—and his mouth shut. (*He lapses into silence.*)

Lackey. I think Thomis is in love, Thomis is. Who was that young woman I saw you a dancing of at the Showmier, Thomis? How the young Marquis was a cuttin' of it about there! The pleace was obliged to come up and stop him dancing. His man told old Buzfuz up-stairs that the Marquis's goings on is hawful. Up till four or five[6] every morning—blind hookey, shampaign, the dooce's own delight. That party have had I don't know how much in diamonds—and they quarrel and swear at each other and fling plates: it's tremendous.

Tommy. Why doesn't the Marquis's man mind his own affairs? He's a supersellious beast: and will no more speak to a man except he's outalivery than he would to a chimbly swip. He! Cuss him, I'd fight 'im for 'alf a crownd.

Lackey. And we'd back you, Tommy. Buzfuz up-stairs ain't supersellious, nor is the Prince's walet nether. That old Sangjang's a rum old guvnor. He was in Hengland with the Count fifty years ago—in the Hemigration—in Queen Hann's time, you know. He used to support the old Count. He says he remembers a young Musseer Newcome then that used to take lessons from the Shevallier, the Countess's father—there's my bell. [*Exit Lackey.*[7]

Backystopper. Not a bad chap that. Sports his money very free—sings an uncommon good song.

Thomas. Pretty woice but no cultiwation.

Lackey (*who re-enters*). Be here at two o'clock for Miss N. Take any thing? Come round the corner. There's a capital shop round the corner.

[*Exeunt Servants.*

---

[4] Billy? *E1*] Billy, and give her a link or two more curb. *Ms*
[5] to be a *E1*] to a *Ms*
[6] five *E1*] five o'clock *Ms*
[7] This stage direction added in *E1*.

SCENE 2.

Ethel. I can't think where Madame de Montcontour has gone. How very odd it was that you should come here—that we should both come here to-day! How surprised I was to see you at the Minister's! Grandmamma was so angry! That boy pursues us wherever we go, she said. I am sure I don't know why we shouldn't meet, Clive. It seems to be wrong even my seeing you by chance here. Do you know, Sir, what a scolding I had about—about going to Brighton with you? My grandmother did not hear of it till we were in Scotland when that foolish maid of mine talked of it to her maid and there was O such a tempest! If there were a Bastille here she would like to lock you into it. She says that you are always upon our way—I don't know how, I am sure. She says, but for you I should have been—you know what I should have been: but I am thankful[8] that I wasn't, and Kew has got a much nicer wife in Henrietta Pulleyn than I could ever have been to him. She will be happier than Clara, Clive. Kew is one of the kindest creatures in the world—not very wise: not very strong: but he is just such a kind easy generous little man as will make a girl like Henrietta quite happy.

Clive. But not you? Ethel.

Ethel. No, nor I him. My temper is difficult, Clive, and I fear few men would bear with me. I feel somehow always very lonely. How old am I? twenty—I feel sometimes as if I was a hundred; and in the midst of all these admirations and fêtes and flatteries, so tired, O so tired! And yet if I don't have them, I miss them. How I wish I was religious like Madame de Florac. There is no day that she does not go to church. She is for ever busy with charities, clergymen, conversions; I think the Princess will be brought over ere long—that dear old Madame de Florac! And yet she is no happier than the rest of us. Hortense is an empty little thing who thinks of her prosy fat Camille with spectacles and of her two children and of nothing else in the world besides. Who is happy? Clive!

Clive. You say Barnes's wife is not.

Ethel. We are like brother and sister, so I may talk to you. Barnes is very cruel to her. At Newcome last winter poor Clara used to come into my room with tears in her eyes morning after morning. He calls her a fool; and seems to take a pride in humiliating her before company. My poor father has luckily taken a great liking to her: and before him, for he has grown very very hot-tempered since his illness, Barnes leaves poor Clara alone. We were in hopes that the baby might make matters better, but as it is a little girl, Barnes chooses to be very much disappointed. He wants Papa to give up his seat in Parliament, but he clings to that more than any thing. O dear me, who is happy in the world? What a pity Lord Highgate's father[9] had not died sooner! He and Barnes have been reconciled. I wonder my brother's spirit did not revolt against it. The old lord used to keep a great sum of money at the bank, I believe: and the present one does so still: he has paid all his debts[1] off: and Barnes is actually friends with him. He is always abusing the Dorkings who want to borrow money from the bank,

---

[8] I am thankful *E1*] I am sure I am thankful *Ms*
[9] Highgate's father *E1*] Highgate *Ms*
[1] debts *E1*] old debts *Ms*

he says. This eagerness for money is horrible. If I had been Barnes I would never have been reconciled with Mr. Belsize, never, never! And yet they say he was quite right: and Grandmamma is even pleased that Lord Highgate should be asked to dine in Park Lane. Poor Papa is there: come to attend his parliamentary duties as he thinks. He went to a division the other night; and was actually lifted out of his carriage and wheeled into the lobby in a chair. The Ministers thanked him for coming. I believe he thinks he will have his peerage yet. O what a life of vanity our's is!

Enter Madame de Montcontour. What are you young folks a talkin' about— Balls and operas? When first I was took to the opera I did not like it—and fell asleep. But now O, it's 'eavenly to hear Grisi sing!

The Clock. Ting Ting!

Ethel. Two o'clock already! I must run back to Grandmamma; Good bye, Madame de Montcontour; I am so sorry I have not been able to see dear Madame de Florac—I will try and come to her on Thursday— please tell her. Shall we meet you at the American Minister's to-night or at Madame de Brie's to-morrow? Friday is your own night—I hope Grand- mamma will bring me. How charming your last music was! Good bye, mon cousin. You shall *not* come down-stairs with me, I insist upon it, Sir: and had much best remain here and finish your drawing of Madame de Montcontour.

Princess. I've put on the velvet, you see, Clive—though it's very 'ot in May. Good bye, my dear.   [*Exit* ETHEL.

As far as we can judge from the above conversation, which we need not prolong—as the talk between Madame de Montcontour and Monsieur Clive, after a few complimentary remarks about Ethel, had nothing to do with the history of the Newcomes—as far as we can judge, the above lit- tle colloquy took place on Monday: and about Wednesday Madame la Comtesse de Florac received a little note from Clive in which he said that one day when she came to the Louvre, where he was copying, she had ad- mired a picture of a Virgin and Child by Sasso Ferrato, since when he had been occupied in making a water-colour drawing after the picture, and hoped she would be pleased to accept the copy from her affectionate and grateful servant, Clive Newcome. The drawing would be done the next day when he would call with it in his hand. Of course Madame de Florac received this announcement very kindly; and sent back by Clive's servant a note of thanks to that young gentleman.

Now on Thursday morning about one o'clock, by one of those singular coincidences which &c. &c.—who should come to the Hôtel de Florac but Miss Ethel Newcome? Madame la Comtesse was at home waiting to receive Clive and his picture: but Miss Ethel's appearance frightened the good lady, so much so that she felt quite guilty at seeing the girl whose parents might think—I don't know what they might not think—that Madame de Florac was trying to make a match between the young people. Hence arose the words uttered by the Countess after a while in

CONVERSATION III.

Madame de Florac (at work). And so you like to quit the world, and to come to our *triste* old hotel. After to-day you will find it still more melancholy, my poor child.

Ethel. And why?

Madame de F. Some one who has been here to *égayer* our little meetings will come no more.

Ethel. Is the Abbé de Florac going to quit Paris, Madame?

Madame de F. It is not of him that I speak, thou knowest it very well, my daughter. Thou hast seen my poor Clive twice here. He will come once again and then no more. My conscience reproaches me that I have admitted him at all. But he is like a son to me and was so confided to me by his father. Five years ago, when we met after an absence of how many years!—Colonel Newcome told me what hopes he had cherished[2] for his boy. You know well, my daughter, with whom those hopes were connected. Then he wrote me that family arrangements rendered his plans impossible—that the hand of Miss Newcome was promised elsewhere. When I heard from my son Paul how those[3] negotiations were broken—my heart rejoiced, Ethel, for my friend's sake. I am an old woman now who have seen the world and all sorts of men. Men more brilliant no doubt I have known. But such a heart as his, such a faith as his, such a generosity and simplicity as Thomas Newcome's, never.

Ethel (smiling). Indeed, dear lady, I think with you.

Madame de F. I understand thy smile, my daughter. I can say to thee, that when we were children almost, I knew thy good uncle. My poor father took the pride of his family into exile with him. Our poverty only made his pride the greater. Even before the emigration a contract had been passed between our family and the Count de Florac: I could not be wanting to the word given by my father. For how many long years have I kept it! But when I see a young girl who may be made the victim—the subject of a marriage of convenience as I was—my heart pities her. And if I love her as I love you, I tell her my thoughts. Better poverty, Ethel: better a cell in a convent: than a union without love. Is it written eternally that men are to make slaves of us? Here in France above all, our fathers sell us every day. And what a society our's is! Thou wilt know this when thou art married. There are some laws so cruel that Nature revolts against them, and breaks them—or we die in keeping them. You smile. I have been nearly fifty years dying—*n'est-ce pas*—and am here an old woman complaining to a young girl. It is because our recollections of youth are always young: and because I have suffered so, that I would spare those I love a like grief. Do you know that the children of those who do not love in[4] marriage seem to bear an[5] hereditary coldness: and do not love their parents as other children do? They witness our differences and our indifference, hear our recriminations, take one side or the other in our disputes, and are partisans for father or mother. We force ourselves to be hypocrites and hide our wrongs from them; we speak of a bad father with false praises; we wear feint smiles over our tears and deceive our children—deceive them, do we? Even from the exercise of that pious deceit there is no woman but suffers in

---

2 had cherished *E1*] cherished *Ms*
3 those *Ms*] these *E1*
4 love in *E1*] love each other in *Ms*
5 an *E1*] the *Ms*

the estimation of her sons. They may shield her as champions against their father's selfishness or cruelty. In this case what a war! What a home, where the son sees a tyrant in the father and in the mother but a trembling victim! I speak not for myself—whatever may have been the course of our long wedded life, I have not to complain of these ignoble storms. But when the family Chief neglects his wife, or prefers another to her, the children too, courtiers as we are, will desert her. You look incredulous about domestic love. Tenez, my child, if I may so surmise, I think you cannot have seen it.

Ethel (blushing and thinking, perhaps, how she esteems her father, how her mother, and how much they esteem each other). My father and mother have been most kind to all their children, Madame: and no one can say that their marriage has been otherwise than happy. My mother is the kindest and most affectionate mother, and—(*Here a vision of Sir Brian alone in his room, and nobody really caring for him so much as his valet who loves him to the extent of fifty pounds a year and perquisites, or perhaps Miss Cann who reads to him and plays a good deal of evenings, much to Sir Brian's liking—here this vision, we say, comes, and stops Miss Ethel's sentence.*)

Madame de F. Your father, in his infirmity—and yet he is five years younger than Colonel Newcome—is happy to have such a wife and such children. They comfort his age: they cheer his sickness: they confide their griefs and pleasures to him, is it not so? His closing days are soothed by their affection.

Ethel. Oh, no no! And yet it is not his fault or our's that he is a stranger to us. He used to be all day at the bank or at night in the House of Commons, or he and Mamma went to parties and we young ones remained with the governess. Mamma is very[6] kind. I have never, almost, known her angry: never with us: about us, sometimes with the servants. As children we used to see Papa and Mamma at breakfast and then when she was dressing to go out. Since he has been ill: she has given up all parties. I wanted to do so too. I feel ashamed in the world sometimes when I think of my poor father at home alone. I wanted to stay but my mother and my grandmother forbade me. Grandmamma has a fortune which she says I am to have; since then they have insisted on my being with her. She is very clever, you know: she is kind too in her way: but she cannot live out of Society. And I who pretend to revolt, I like it too; and I who rail and scorn flatterers—O, I like admiration! I am pleased when the women hate me, and the young men leave them for me. Though I despise many of these, yet I can't help drawing them towards me. One or two of them I have seen unhappy about me and I like it: and if they are indifferent I am angry, and never tire till they come back. I love beautiful dresses; I love fine jewels; I love a great name and a fine house—O, I despise myself when I think of these things! When I lie in bed and say I have been heartless and a coquette, I cry with humiliation: and then rebel and say, Why not?—and to-night—yes, to-night after leaving you, I shall be wicked, I know I shall.

Madame de F. (sadly). One will pray for thee, my child.

Ethel (sadly). I thought I might be good once. I used to say my own prayers then. Now I speak them but by rote, and feel ashamed—yes,

---

6 very *E1*] very very *Ms*

ashamed to speak them. Is it not horrid to say them, and next morning to be no better than you were last night? Often I revolt at these as at other things and am dumb. The Vicar comes to see us at Newcome, and eats so much dinner; and pays us such court and "Sir Brian's" Papa and "Your ladyship's" Mamma. With Grandmamma I go to hear a fashionable preacher—Clive's uncle, whose sister lets us the lodgings at Brighton; such a queer bustling pompous honest old lady. Do you know that Clive's aunt lets lodgings at Brighton?

Madame de F. My father was an usher in a school. Monsieur de Florac gave lessons in the emigration. Do you know in what.

Ethel. O, the old Nobility! that is different, you know. That Mr. Honeyman is so affected that I have no patience with him!

Madame de F. (with a sigh). I wish you could attend the services of a better church. And when was it that[7] you thought you might be good? Ethel!

Ethel. When I was a girl. Before I came out. When I used to take long rides with my dear Uncle Newcome; and he used to talk to me in his sweet simple way: and he said I reminded him of some one he once knew.

Madame de F. Who—who was that, Ethel.

Ethel (looking up at Gerard's picture of the Countess de Florac). What odd dresses you wore in the time of the Empire, Madame de Florac! How could you ever have such high waists, and such wonderful *fraises*! (MADAME DE FLORAC *kisses* ETHEL. *Tableau. Enter* SAINT JEAN *preceding a gentleman with a drawing-board under his arm.*)

Saint Jean. Monsieur Claive!   [*Exit* SAINT JEAN.

Clive. How do you do, Madame la Comtesse. Mademoiselle, j'ai l'honneur de vous souhaiter le bon jour.

Madame de F. Do you come from the Louvre? Have you finished that beautiful copy, mon ami!

Clive. I have brought it for you. It is not very good. There are always so many *petites demoiselles* copying that Sasso Ferrato; and they chatter about it so and hop from one easel to another; and the young artists are always coming to give them advice—so that there is no getting a good look at the picture. But I have brought you the sketch; and am so pleased that you asked[8] for it.

Madame de F. (surveying the sketch). It is charming! charming! What shall we give to our painter for his chef-d'œuvre?

Clive (kisses her hand). There is my pay! And you will be glad to hear that two of my portraits have been received at the Exhibition. My uncle, the clergyman, and Mr. Butts of the Life-Guards.

Ethel. Mr. Butts—quel nom! Je ne connois aucun M. Butts!

Clive. He has a[9] famous head to draw. They refused Crackthorpe and—and one or two other heads I sent in.

Ethel (tossing up her's). Miss Mackenzie's, I suppose!

Clive. Yes Miss Mackenzie's. It is a sweet little face, too delicate for my hand though.

---

[7] that *Ms*] [omitted] *E1*
[8] asked *E1*] asked me *Ms*
[9] He has a *E1*] Hm! He is the Surgeon—a *Ms*

Ethel. So is a wax-doll's a pretty face. Pink cheeks; china-blue eyes; and hair the colour of old Madame Hempenfeld's—not her last hair—her last but one. (*She goes to a window that looks into the court.*)

Clive (*to the* COUNTESS). Miss Mackenzie speaks more respectfully of other people's eyes and hair. She thinks there is nobody in the world to compare to[1] Miss Newcome.

Madame de F.[2] (*aside*). And you, mon ami? This is the[3] last time, entendez-vous? You must never come here again. If M. le Comte knew it, he never would pardon me. Encore! (*He kisses her ladyship's hand again.*)

Clive. A good action gains to be repeated. Miss Newcome, does the view of the court-yard please you? The old trees and the garden are better. That dear old Faun without a nose! I must have a sketch of him: the creepers round the base are beautiful.

Miss N. I was looking to see if the carriage was[4] come for me. It is time that I return home.

Clive. That is my Brougham. May I carry you anywhere? I hire him by the hour: and I will carry you to the end of the world.

Miss N. Where are you going, Madame de Florac!—to show that sketch to M. le Comte? Dear me! I don't fancy that M. de Florac can care for such things! I am sure I have seen many as pretty on the quays for twenty-five sous. I wonder the carriage is not come for me.

Clive. You can take mine without my company as that seems not to please you.

Miss N. Your company is sometimes very pleasant: when you please. Sometimes, as last night, for instance, you are not particularly lively.

Clive. Last night, after moving Heaven and Earth to get an invitation to Madame de Brie—I say, Heaven and Earth—that is a French phrase; I arrive there; I find Miss Newcome engaged for almost every dance, waltzing with M. de Klingenspohr: gallopping with Count de Capri, gallopping and waltzing with the most noble the Marquis of Farintosh; she will scarce speak to me during the evening; and when I wait till midnight, her grandmamma whisks her home, and I am left alone for my pains. Lady Kew is in one of her high moods and the only words she condescends to say to me are, "O, I thought you had returned to London," with which she turns her venerable back upon me.

Miss N. A fortnight ago, you said you were going to London. You said the copies you were about here would not take you another week, and that was three weeks since.

Clive. It were best I had gone.

Miss N. If you think so, I cannot but think so.

Clive. Why do I stay and hover about you, and follow you—you know I follow you. Can I live on a smile vouchsafed twice a week, and no brighter than you[5] give to all the world? What do I get but to hear your beauty praised and to see you, night after night, happy and smiling and

---

[1] to *E1*] with *Ms*
[2] *Madame de F. E1*] *The Countess Ms*
[3] is the *E1*] is for the *Ms*
[4] was *Ms*] had *E1*
[5] than you *E1*] than that you *Ms*

triumphant, the partner of other men? Does it add zest to your triumph, to think that I behold it? I believe you would like a crowd of us to pursue you.

Miss N. To pursue me and if they find me alone by chance to compliment me with such speeches as you make? That would be pleasure indeed! Answer me here in return, Clive: Have I ever disguised from any of my friends the regard I have for you? Why should I? Have I not[6] taken your part when you were maligned? In former days when—when Lord Kew asked me, as he had a right to do then—I said it was as a brother I held you: and always would: If I have been wrong—it has been for[7] two or three times in seeing you at all—or seeing you thus; in letting you speak to me as you do:—injure me as you do. Do you think I have not had hard enough words said to me about you; but that you must attack me too in turn?[8] Last night only, because you were at the[9] ball. It was very, very wrong of me to tell you I was going there; as we went home, Lady Kew—Go, Sir—I never thought you would have seen in me this[1] humiliation.

Clive. Is it possible that I should have made Ethel Newcome shed tears? O, dry them, dry them. Forgive me, Ethel, forgive me! I have no right to jealousy: or to reproach you. I know that. If others admire you, surely I ought to know that they—they do but as I do: I should be proud, not angry, that they admire my Ethel—my sister, if you can be no more.

Ethel. I will be that always whatever harsh things you think or say of me. There, Sir, I am not going to be so foolish as to cry again. Have you been studying very hard? are your pictures good at the Exhibition? I like you with your mustachios best and order you not to cut them off again; the young men here wear them. I hardly knew Charles Beardmore when he arrived from Berlin the other day, like a sapper and miner. His little sisters cried out and were quite frightened by his apparition. Why are you not in diplomacy? That day at Brighton when Lord Farintosh asked whether you were in the army? I thought to myself, why is he not?

Clive. A man in the army may pretend to anything, *n'est-ce pas?* He wears a lovely uniform. He may be a General, a K.C.B., a Viscount, an Earl. He may be valiant in arms and wanting a leg, like the lover in the song. It is peace-time, you say? So much the worse career for a soldier. My father would not have me, he said, for ever dangling in barracks or smoking in country billiard-rooms. I have no taste for law: and as for diplomacy, I have no relations in the Cabinet, and no uncles in the House of Peers. Could my uncle who is in Parliament help me much, do you think; or would he, if he could?—or Barnes, his noble son and heir, after him?

Ethel (musing). Barnes would not, perhaps, but Papa might even still, and you have friends who are fond of you.

Clive. No—no one can help me. And my Art, Ethel, is not only my choice and my love but my honour too. I shall never distinguish myself in it. I may take smart likenesses but that is all. I am not fit to grind my

6 I not *Ms*] not I *E1*
7 been for *E1*] been now for *Ms*
8 in turn? *E1*] in your turn? *Ms*
9 the *E1*] that *Ms*
1 in me this *E1*] in me in this *Ms*

friend Ridley's colours for him. Nor would my father who loves his own profession so, make a good general probably. He always says so. I thought better of myself when I began as a boy; and was a conceited youngster expecting to carry it[2] all before me. But as I walked the Vatican and looked at Raphael and at the great Michael—I knew I was but a poor little creature and in contemplating his genius shrunk up till I felt myself as small as a man looks under the dome of Saint Peter's. Why should I wish to have a great genius?—Yes, there is one reason why I should like to have it.

Ethel. And that is?

Clive. To give it you, if it pleased you, Ethel. But I might wish for the Roc's egg. There's no way of robbing the bird. I must take a humble place and you want a brilliant one. A brilliant one! O, Ethel, what a Standard we folks measure fame by! To have your name in the *Morning Post* and to go to three balls every night. To have your dress described at the Drawing-Room; and your arrival, from a round of visits in the country, at your town house: and the entertainment of the Marchioness of Farin——

Ethel. Sir, if you please, no calling names.

Clive. I wonder at it. For you are in the world, and you love the world, whatever you may say. And I wonder that one of your strength of mind should so care for it. I think my simple old father is much finer than all your grandees: his single-mindedness more lofty than all their bowing and haughtiness and scheming—What are you thinking of as you stand in that pretty attitude like Mnemosyne—with your finger to[3] your chin?

Ethel. Mnemosyne, who was she?—I think I like you best when you are quiet and gentle and not when you are flaming out and sarcastic, Sir. And so you think you will never be a famous painter? They are quite in society here. I was so pleased because two of them dined at the Tuileries when Grandmamma was there; and she mistook one who was covered all over with crosses for an Ambassador, I believe, till the Queen called him Monsieur Delaroche. She says there is no knowing people in this country. And do you think you will never be able to paint as well as M. Delaroche?

Clive. No. Never.

Ethel. And—and—you will never give up painting?

Clive. No. Never. That would be like leaving your friend who was poor; or deserting your mistress because you were disappointed about her money. They do those things in the great world, Ethel.

Ethel (with a sigh). Yes.

Clive. If it is so false and base and hollow this great world: if its aims are so mean; its successes so paltry; the sacrifices it asks of you so degrading; the pleasures it gives you so wearisome, shameful even, why does Ethel Newcome cling to it? Will you be fairer, dear, with any other name than your own? Will you be happier after a month at bearing a great title, with a man whom you can't esteem tied for ever to you to be the father of Ethel's children and the lord and Master of her life and actions? The proudest woman in the world consents to bend herself to this ignominy, and owns that a coronet is a bribe sufficient for her honour! What is the end of a

[2] it *Ms E1*] [omitted] *R*
[3] to *Ms*] on *E1*

Christian life, Ethel; of a[4] girl's pure nurture—it can't be this. Last week as we walked in the garden here and heard the nuns singing in their chapel, you said how hard it was that poor women should be imprisoned so, and were thankful that in England we had abolished that slavery. Then you cast your eyes to the ground; and mused as you paced the walk; and thought, I know, that perhaps their lot was better than some others'.

Ethel. Yes, I did. I was thinking that almost all women are made slaves one way or other: and that these poor nuns perhaps were better off than we are.

Clive. I never will quarrel with nun or matron for following her vocation. But for our women, who are free, why should they rebel against Nature: shut their hearts up: sell their lives for rank and money: and forego the most precious right of their liberty? Look, Ethel dear, I love you so, that if I thought another had your heart, an honest man, a loyal gentleman, like—like him of last year even—I think I could go back with a God bless you, and take to my pictures again and work on in my own way.[5] You seem like a queen to me somehow; and I am but a poor humble fellow, who might be happy, I think, if you were. In those balls where I have seen you surrounded by those brilliant young men, noble and wealthy, admirers like me, I have often thought, "How could I aspire to such a creature, and ask her to forego a palace to share the crust of a poor painter?"

Ethel. You spoke quite scornfully of palaces just now, Clive. I won't say a word about the—the regard which you express for me—I think you have it. Indeed I do. But it were best not said, Clive; best for me, perhaps, not to own that I know it. In your speeches, my poor boy—and you will please not to make any more, or I never can see you or speak to you again, never— you forget one part of a girl's duty: obedience to her parents. They would never agree to my marrying any one below—any one whose union would not be advantageous in a worldly point of view. I never would give such pain to the poor father or to the kind soul who never said a harsh word to me since I was born. My grandmother[6] is kind, too, in her way. I came to her of my own free will. When she said she would leave me her fortune; do you think it was for myself alone that I was glad? My father's passion is to make an estate and all my brothers and sisters will be but slenderly[7] portioned. Lady Kew said she would help them if I came to her—and— it is the welfare of those little people that depends upon me, Clive. Now do you see, *brother,* why you must speak to me so no more? There is the carriage. God bless you, dear Clive.

(CLIVE *sees the carriage drive away after Miss* NEWCOME *has entered it without once looking up to the window where he stands. When it is gone: he goes to the opposite windows of the salon, which are open towards the garden. The chapel music begins to play from the Convent next door. As he hears it, he sinks down, his head in his hands.*)

Enter Madame de Florac. (*She goes to him with anxious looks.*) What hast thou, my child? Hast thou spoken?

[4] of a *Ms*] a *E1*
[5] <humble> way. *Ms*] humble way. *E1*
[6] grandmother *Ms*] grandmamma *E1*
[7] slenderly *E1*] very slenderly *Ms*

Clive (very steadily). Yes.

Madame de F. And she loves thee? I know she loves thee.

Clive. You hear the organ[8] of the Convent?

Madame de F. Qu'as tu?

Clive. I might as well hope to marry one of the sisters of yonder Convent, dear lady. (*He sinks down again and she kisses him.*)

Clive. I never had a mother: but you seem like one.

Madame de F. Mon fils, O mon fils!

[8] organ *E1*] music <of yonder> organs *Ms*

Chapter X.

IN WHICH BENEDICK IS A MARRIED MAN.

E have all heard of the dying French Duchess, who viewed her coming dissolution and subsequent fate so easily, because she said she was sure that Heaven must deal politely with a person of her quality;—I suppose Lady Kew had some such notions regarding people of rank: her long-suffering towards them was extreme; in fact, there were vices which the old lady thought pardonable, and even natural, in a young nobleman of high station, which she never would have excused in persons of vulgar condition.

Her ladyship's little knot of associates and scandal-bearers — elderly roués and ladies of the world, whose business it was to know all sorts of noble intrigues and exalted tittle-tattle; what was happening among the devotees of the exiled court at Frohsdorf; what among the citizen princes of the Tuileries; who was the reigning favourite of the Queen Mother at Aranjuez; who was smitten with whom at Vienna or Naples; and the last particulars of the *chroniques scandaleuses* of Paris and London;—Lady Kew, I say, must have been perfectly aware of my Lord Farintosh's amusements, associates, and manner of life, and yet she never, for one moment, exhibited any anger or dislike towards that nobleman. Her amiable heart was so full of kindness and forgiveness towards the young prodigal, that, even without any repentance on his part, she was ready to take him to her old arms, and give him her venerable benediction. Pathetic sweetness of nature! Charming tenderness of disposition! With all his faults and wickednesses, his follies and his selfishness, there was no moment when Lady Kew would not have received the young lord, and endowed him with the hand of her darling Ethel.

But the hopes which this fond forgiving creature had nurtured for one season, and carried on so resolutely to the next, were destined to be disappointed yet a second time, by a most provoking event, which occurred in the Newcome family. Ethel was called away suddenly from Paris by her father's third and last paralytic seizure. When she reached her home, Sir Brian could not recognise her. A few hours after her arrival, all the vanities of the world were over for him: and Sir Barnes Newcome, Baronet, reigned in his stead. The day after Sir Brian was laid in his vault at Newcome—a letter appeared in the local papers addressed to the Independent Electors of that Borough, in which his orphaned son, feelingly alluding to the virtue, the services, and the political principles of the deceased, offered himself as a candidate for the seat in Parliament now vacant. Sir Barnes announced, that he should speedily pay his respects in person to the friends and supporters of his lamented father. That he was a staunch friend of our admirable constitution, need not be said. That he was a firm, but conscientious, upholder of our Protestant religion, all who knew Barnes Newcome must be aware. That he would do his utmost to advance the interests of this great agricultural, this great manufacturing county and borough, we may be sure he avowed; as that he would be (if returned to represent Newcome in Parliament) the advocate of every rational reform, the unhesitating opponent of every reckless innovation. In fine, Barnes Newcome's manifesto to the Electors of Newcome was as authentic a document, and gave him credit for as many public virtues, as that slab over poor Sir Brian's bones in the chancel of Newcome church; which commemorated the good qualities of the defunct, and the grief of his heir.

In spite of the virtues, personal and inherited, of Barnes, his seat for Newcome was not got without a contest. The dissenting interest and the respectable liberals of the borough wished to set up Samuel Higg, Esq., against Sir Barnes Newcome: and now it was that Barnes's civilities of the previous year, aided by Madame de Montcontour's influence over her brother, bore their fruit. Mr. Higg declined to stand against Sir Barnes Newcome, although Higg's political principles were by no means those of the honourable Baronet; and the candidate from London, whom the Newcome extreme radicals set up against Barnes, was nowhere on the poll when the day of election came. So Barnes had the desire of his heart; and, within two months after his father's demise,[1] he sate in Parliament as Member for Newcome.

The bulk of the late Baronet's property descended, of course, to his elder son: who grumbled, nevertheless, at the provision made for his brothers and sisters, and that the town-house should have been left to Lady Ann, who was too poor to inhabit it. But Park Lane is the best situation in London, and Lady Ann's means were greatly improved by the annual produce

---

[1] demise, *E1*] decease *R*

of the house in Park Lane: which, as we all know, was occupied by a foreign minister for several subsequent seasons. Strange mutations of fortune; old places; new faces; what Londoner does not see and speculate upon them every day? Cœlia's boudoir, who is dead with the daisies over her at Kensal Green, is now the chamber where Delia is consulting Dr. Locock, or Julia's children are romping: Florio's dining-tables have now Pollio's wine upon them: Calista, being a widow, and (to the surprise of everybody who knew Trimalchio, and enjoyed his famous dinners) left but very poorly off, lets the house and the rich, chaste, and appropriate planned furniture, by Dowbiggin, and the proceeds go to keep her little boys at Eton. The next year, as Mr. Clive Newcome rode by the once familiar mansion (whence the hatchment had been removed, announcing that there was *in Cœlo Quies* for the late Sir Brian Newcome, Bart.) alien faces looked from over the flowers in the balconies. He got a card for an entertainment from the occupant of the mansion, H. E. the Bulgarian minister; and there was the same crowd in the reception-room and on the stairs, the same grave men from Gunter's distributing the refreshments in the dining-room, the same old Smee, R.A., (always in the room where the edibles were) cringing and flattering to the new occupants; and the same effigy of poor Sir Brian, in his deputy-lieutenant's uniform, looking blankly down from over the sideboard, at the feast which his successors were giving. A dreamy old ghost of a picture. Have you ever looked at those round George IV.'s banquetting hall at Windsor? Their frames still hold them, but they smile ghostly smiles, and swagger in robes and velvets which are quite faint and faded: their crimson coats have a twilight tinge: the lustre of their stars has twinkled out: they look as if they were about to flicker off the wall and retire to join their originals in limbo.

Nearly three years had elapsed since the good Colonel's departure for India, and during this time certain changes had occurred in the lives of the principal actors and the writer of this history. As regards the latter, it must be stated that the dear old firm of Lamb Court had been dissolved, the junior member having contracted another partnership. The chronicler of these memoirs was a bachelor no longer. My wife and I had spent the winter at Rome, (favourite resort of young married couples); and had heard from the artists there Clive's name affectionately repeated; and many accounts of his sayings and doings, his merry supper-parties, and the talents of young Ridley, his friend. When we came to London in the spring, almost our first visit was to Clive's apartments in Charlotte Street, whither my wife delightedly went to give her hand to the young painter.

But Clive no longer inhabited that quiet region. On driving to the house, we found a bright brass plate, with the name of Mr. J.J. Ridley on the door, and it was J.J.'s hand which I shook (his other being engaged with a great palette, and a sheaf of painting-brushes), when we entered the well-known quarters. Clive's picture hung over the mantel-piece, where his father's head used to hang in our time—a careful and beautifully executed portrait of the lad in a velvet coat, and a Roman hat, with that golden beard which was sacrificed to the exigencies of London fashion. I showed Laura the likeness until she could become acquainted with the original. On her expressing her delight at the picture, the painter was pleased to say, in his modest blushing way, that he would be glad to execute my wife's portrait too, nor as I think, could any artist find a subject more pleasing.

After admiring others of Mr. Ridley's works, our talk naturally reverted to his predecessor. Clive had migrated to much more splendid quarters. Had we not heard? he had become a rich man, a man of fashion. "I fear he is very lazy about the arts," J.J. said, with regret on his countenance; "though I begged and prayed him to be faithful to his profession. He would have done very well in it, in portrait-painting especially. Look here, and here, and here!" said Ridley, producing fine vigorous sketches of Clive's. "He had the art of seizing the likeness, and of making all his people look like gentlemen, too. He was improving every day, when this abominable bank came in the way, and stopped him."

What bank? I did not know the new Indian bank of which the Colonel was a director? Then of course I was aware that the mercantile affair in question was the Bundelcund Bank, about which the Colonel had written to me from India more than a year since, announcing that fortunes were to be made by it, and that he had reserved shares for me in the company. Laura admired all Clive's sketches, which his affectionate brother artist showed to her, with the exception of one representing the reader's humble servant; which, Mrs. Pendennis considered, by no means did justice to the original.

Bidding adieu to the kind J.J., and leaving him to pursue his art, in that silent serious way in which he daily laboured at it, we drove to Fitzroy Square hard by, where I was not displeased to show the good old hospitable James Binnie the young lady who bore my name. But here too we were disappointed. Placards wafered in the windows announced that the old house was to let. The woman who kept it, brought a card in Mrs. Mackenzie's frank hand-writing, announcing Mr. James Binnie's address was "Poste restante Pau in the Pyrenees," and that his London Agents were Messrs. So-and-so. The woman said she believed the gentleman had been unwell. The house, too, looked very pale, dismal, and disordered; we drove away from the door, grieving to think that ill-health, or any other misfortunes, had befallen good old James.

Mrs. Pendennis drove back to our lodgings, Brixham's, in Jermyn Street, while I sped to the City, having business in that quarter. It has been said that I kept a small account with Hobson Brothers, to whose bank I went, and entered the parlour with that trepidation which most poor men feel on presenting themselves before City magnates and capitalists. Mr. Hobson Newcome shook hands most jovially and good-naturedly, congratulated me on my marriage, and so forth, and presently Sir Barnes Newcome made his appearance, still wearing his mourning for his deceased father.

Nothing could be more kind, pleasant, and cordial than Sir Barnes's manner. He seemed to know well about my affairs; complimented me on every kind of good fortune; had heard that I had canvassed the borough in which I lived; hoped sincerely to see me in parliament and on the right side; was most anxious to become acquainted with Mrs. Pendennis, of whom Lady Rockminster said all sorts of kind things; and asked for our address, in order that Lady Clara Newcome might have the pleasure of calling on my wife. This ceremony was performed soon afterwards; and an invitation to dinner from Sir Barnes and Lady Clara Newcome speedily followed it.

Sir Barnes Newcome, Bart., M.P., I need not say, no longer inhabited the small house which he had occupied immediately after his marriage; but dwelt in a much more spacious mansion in Belgravia, where he entertained his friends. Now that he had come into his kingdom, I must say that Barnes was by no means so insufferable as in the days of his bachelorhood. He had sown his wild oats, and spoke with regret and reserve of that season of his moral culture. He was grave, sarcastic, statesmanlike; did not try to conceal his baldness (as he used before his father's death, by bringing lean wisps of hair over his forehead from the back of his head); talked a great deal about the House; was assiduous in his attendance there and in the City; and conciliating with all the world. It seemed as if we were all his constituents, and though his efforts to make himself agreeable were rather apparent, the effect succeeded pretty well. We met Mr. and Mrs. Hobson Newcome, and Clive, and Miss Ethel looking beautiful in her black robes. It was a family party, Sir Barnes said, giving us to understand, with a decorous solemnity in face and voice, that no *large* parties as yet could be received in that house of mourning.

To this party was added, rather to my surprise, my Lord Highgate, who under the sobriquet of Jack Belsize has been presented to the reader of this history. Lord Highgate gave Lady Clara his arm to dinner, but went and took a place next Miss Newcome, on the other side of her; that immediately by Lady Clara being reserved for a guest who had not as yet made his appearance.

Lord Highgate's attentions to his neighbour, his laughing and talking, were incessant; so much so that Clive, from his end of the table, scowled in wrath at Jack Belsize's assiduities: it was evident that the youth, though hopeless, was still jealous and in love with his charming cousin.

Barnes Newcome was most kind to all his guests: from Aunt Hobson to your humble servant there was not one, but the master of the house had an agreeable word for him. Even for his cousin Samuel Newcome, a gawky youth with an eruptive countenance, Barnes had appropriate words of conversation, and talked about King's College, of which the lad was an ornament, with the utmost affability. He complimented that institution and young Samuel, and by that shot knocked not only over Sam but his mamma too. He talked to Uncle Hobson about his crops; to Clive about his pictures; to me about the great effect which a certain article in the *Pall Mall Gazette* had produced in the House, where the Chancellor of the Exchequer was perfectly livid with fury, and Lord John bursting out laughing at the attack: in fact, nothing could be more amiable than our host on this day. Lady Clara was very pretty; grown a little stouter since her marriage, the change only became her. She was a little silent, but then she had Uncle Hobson on her left-hand side, between whom and her ladyship there could not be much in common, and the place at the right hand was still vacant. The person with whom she talked most freely was Clive, who had made a beautiful drawing of her and her little girl, for which the mother and the father too, as it appeared, were very grateful.

What had caused this change in Barnes's behaviour? Our particular merits or his own private reform? In the two years over which this narrative has had to run in the course of as many chapters, the writer had[2] inherited a property so small that it could not occasion a banker's civility; and I put down Sir Barnes Newcome's politeness to a sheer desire to be well with me. But with Lord Highgate and Clive the case was different, as you must now hear.

Lord Highgate, having succeeded to his father's title and fortune, had paid every shilling of his debts, and had sowed his wild oats to the very last corn. His lordship's account at Hobson Brothers was very large. Painful events of three years' date, let us hope, were forgotten—gentlemen cannot go on being in love and despairing, and quarreling for ever. When he came into his funds, Highgate behaved with uncommon kindness to Rooster, who was always straitened for money: and when the late Lord Dorking died and Rooster succeeded to him, there was a meeting at Chanticlere between Highgate and Barnes Newcome and his wife, which went off very comfortably. At Chanticlere, the Dowager Lady Kew and Miss Newcome were also staying, when Lord Highgate announced his prodigious admiration for the young lady; and, it was said, corrected Farintosh, as a low-minded foul-tongued young cub for daring to speak disrespectfully of her. Nevertheless, *vous concevez*, when a man of the Marquis's rank was supposed to look with the eyes of admiration upon a young lady, Lord Highgate would not think of spoiling sport, and he left Chanticlere declaring that he was always destined to be unlucky in love. When old Lady Kew was obliged to go to Vichy for her lumbago, Highgate said to Barnes, "Do ask your charming sister to come to you in London; she will bore herself to death with the old woman at Vichy, or with her mother at Rugby" (whither Lady Ann had gone to get her boys educated), and accordingly Miss Newcome came on a visit to her brother and sister, at whose house we have just had the honour of seeing her.

When Rooster took his seat in the House of Lords, he was introduced by Highgate and Kew, as Highgate had been introduced by Kew previously. Thus these three gentlemen all rode in gold coaches; had all got coronets on their heads; as you will, my respected young friend, if you are the eldest son of a peer who dies before you. And now they were rich, they were all going to be very good boys, let us hope. Kew, we know, married one of the Dorking family, that second Lady Henrietta Pulleyn, whom we described as frisking about at Baden, and not in the least afraid of him. How little the reader knew, to whom we introduced the girl in that chatty off-hand way, that one day the young creature would be a countess! But *we* knew it all the while—and, when she was walking about with the governess, or romping with her sisters; and when she had dinner at one o'clock; and when she wore a pinafore very likely—we secretly respected her as the future Countess of Kew, and mother of the Viscount Walham.

Lord Kew was very happy with his bride, and very good to her. He took Lady Kew to Paris, for a marriage trip; but they lived almost altogether

[2] had *E1*] has *R*

at Kewbury afterwards, where his lordship sowed tame oats now after his
wild ones, and became one of the most active farmers of his county. He and
the Newcomes were not very intimate friends; for Lord Kew was heard
to say that he disliked Barnes more after his marriage than before. And
the two sisters, Lady Clara and Lady Kew, had a quarrel on one occasion,
when the latter visited London just before the dinner at which we have just
assisted, nay, at which we are just assisting, took place—a quarrel about
Highgate's attentions to Ethel very likely. Kew was dragged into it—and
hot words passed between him and Jack Belsize; and Jack did not go down
to Kewbury afterwards, though Kew's little boy was christened after him.
All these interesting details, about people of the very highest rank, we are
supposed to whisper in the reader's ear as we are sitting at a Belgravian
dinner-table. My dear Barmecide friend: isn't it pleasant to be in such fine
company?

And now we must tell how it is that Clive Newcome, Esq., whose eyes are
flashing fire across the flowers of the table at Lord Highgate who is making
himself so agreeable to Miss Ethel—now we must tell how it is, that Clive
and his Cousin Barnes are[3] grown to be friends again.

The Bundelcund Bank, which had been established for four years had
now grown to be one of the most flourishing Commercial Institutions
in Bengal. Founded, as the prospectus announced, at a time when all
private credit was shaken by the failure of the great Agency Houses, of
which the downfal had carried dismay and ruin throughout the Presidency; the B.B. had been established on the *only* sound principle of commercial prosperity—that of Association. The native capitalists headed by
the great Firm of Rummun Lall & Co. of Calcutta had largely embarked
in the B.B.: and the officers of the two Services and the European mercantile body of Calcutta had been invited to take Shares in an Institution
which to merchants native and English, civilians and military men, was
alike advantageous and indispensable. How many young men of the latter
services had been crippled for life by the ruinous cost of agencies, of which
the profits to the agents themselves were so enormous! The shareholders
of the B.B. were their own agents, and the greatest Capitalist in India as
well as the youngest Ensign in the service might invest at the largest and
safest premium, and borrow at the smallest interest, by becoming according to his means a Shareholder in the B.B. Their correspondents were
established in each Presidency and in every chief city of India as well as at
Sydney, Singapore, Canton and, of course, London. With China they did
an immense opium trade of which the profits were so great that it was only
in private sittings of the B.B. managing committee that the details and accounts of these operations could be brought forward. Otherwise the books
of the bank were open to every Shareholder and the Ensign or the young
civil servant was at liberty at any time to inspect his own private account as
well as the common ledger. With New South Wales they carried on a vast
trade in wool, supplying that great colony with goods which their London
agents enabled them to purchase in such a way as to give them the command of the Market. As if to add to their prosperity, copper-mines were

3 are *Ms E1*] have *R*

discovered on lands in the occupation of the B. Banking Company which gave the most astonishing returns. And throughout the vast territories of British India, through the great native firm of Rummun Lall & Co., the Bundelcund Banking Company had possession of the native markets— The order from Birmingham for Idols alone (made with their copper and paid in their wool) was enough to make the low Church party in England cry out; and a debate upon this subject actually took place in the House of Commons, of which the effect was to send up the shares of the Bundelcund Banking Company very considerably upon the London Exchange.

The fifth half-yearly dividend was announced at twelve and a quarter per cent of the paid up capital: the accounts from the copper mine sent the dividends up to a still greater height and carried the shares to an extraordinary premium. In the third year of the concern the house of Hobson Brothers of London became the agents of the Bundelcund Banking Company of India: and amongst our friends, James Binnie who had prudently held out for some time,[4] and Clive Newcome, Esq., became shareholders, Clive's good father having paid the lad's first instalments of[5] shares up in Calcutta; and invested every rupee he could himself command in this enterprise. When Hobson Brothers joined it, no wonder James Binnie was convinced; Clive's friend, the Frenchman, and through that connection the house of Higg of Newcome and Manchester entered into the affair, and amongst the minor contributors in England we may mention Miss Cann who took a little fifty pound note share,[6] and dear old Miss Honeyman; and J.J. and his father Ridley who brought a small bag of savings—all knowing that their Colonel who was eager that his friends should participate in his good fortune would never lead them wrong. To Clive's surprise Mrs. Mackenzie between whom and himself there was a considerable coolness came to his chambers,[7] and with a solemn injunction that the matter between them should be quite private, requested him to purchase 1500£ worth of Bundelcund Shares for her and her darling girls which he did, astonished to find the thrifty widow in possession of so much money. Had Mr. Pendennis's mind not been bent at this moment on quite other subjects, he might have increased his own fortune by the Bundelcund Bank speculation: but in these two years I was engaged in matrimonial affairs (having Clive Newcome, Esq., as my groomsman on a certain interesting occasion). When we returned[8] from our tour abroad, the India Bank shares were so very high that I did not care to purchase; though I found an affectionate letter from our good Colonel (enjoining me to make my fortune) awaiting me at the Agent's; and my wife received a pair of beautiful Cashmere shawls from the same kind friend.

---

[4] time, *E1*] time; and Samuel Sherrick, Esq.; *Ms*
[5] *E1* misplaced the insertion "first instalments of" after "paid".
[6] pound note share, *E1*] pound share *Ms*
[7] chambers, *E1*] Chambers in the Albany, *Ms*
[8] returned *E1*] came back *Ms*

Chapter XI.

CONTAINS AT LEAST SIX MORE COURSES AND TWO DESSERTS.

HE banker's dinner party over, we returned to our apartments, having dropped Major Pendennis at his lodgings and there, as the custom is amongst most friendly married couples, talked over the company and the dinner. I thought my wife would naturally have liked Sir Barnes[1] Newcome who was very attentive to her took her to dinner[2] as the bride and talked ceaselessly to her during the whole entertainment.

Laura said No—she did not know why, could there be any better reason? There was a tone about Sir Barnes[3] Newcome she did not like—especially in his manner to women.

I remarked that he spoke sharply and in a sneering manner to his wife, and treated one or two remarks which she made as if she was an idiot.

Mrs. Pendennis flung up her head as much as to say, and so she is.

Mr. Pendennis. What the wife too; my dear Laura? I should have thought such a pretty, simple, innocent young woman with just enough good looks to make her pass muster, who is very well bred and not brilliant at all—I should have thought such a one might have secured a sister's approbation.

Mrs. Pendennis. You fancy we are all jealous of one another—No protests of our's can take that notion out of your heads—my dear Pen, I do not intend to try. We are not jealous of mediocrity: we are not patient of it. (I daresay we are angry because we see men admire it so—you gentlemen who pretend to be our betters give yourselves such airs of protection; pro-

---

[1] Barnes *E1*] Bryan *Ms*
[2] to dinner *E1*] dinner *Ms*
[3] Barnes *E1*] Bryan *Ms*

fess such a lofty superiority over us, and[4] prove it by quitting the cleverest woman in the room for the first pair of bright eyes and dimpled cheeks that enter. It was those charms which attracted you in Lady Clara, Sir.

Pendennis. I think she is very pretty and very innocent and artless.

Mrs. P. Not very pretty—and perhaps not so very artless.

Pendennis. How can you tell, you wicked woman? Are you such a profound deceiver yourself that you can instantly detect artifice in others? O Laura!

Mrs. P. We can detect all sorts of things. The inferior animals have instincts you know. (I must say my wife is always very satirical upon this point of the relative rank of the sexes). One thing I am sure of is that she is not happy—and O Pen! that she does not care much for her little girl.

Pendennis. How do you know that, my dear?

Mrs. P. We went up-stairs to see the child after dinner. It was at my wish. The mother did not offer to go. The child was awake and crying. Lady Clara did not offer to take it. Ethel—Miss Newcome took it rather to my surprise for she seems very haughty—and the nurse who I suppose was at supper came running up at the noise—and then the poor little thing was quiet.

Pendennis. I remember we heard the music as the dining-room door was open: and Newcome said "That is what you will have to expect, Pendennis."

Mrs. P. Hush, Sir! If my baby cries I think you must expect me to run out of the room. I liked Miss Newcome after seeing her with that[5] poor little thing. She looked so handsome as she walked with it! I longed to have it myself.

Pendennis. Tout vient a fin, a qui sait ...[6]

Mrs. P. Don't be silly. What a dreadful dreadful place this great world of yours is, Arthur—where husbands do not seem to care for their wives: where mothers do not love their children: where children love their nurses the[7] best: where men talk what they call gallantry!

Pendennis. What?

Mrs. P. Yes, such as that dreary, languid, pale, bald, cadaverous, leering man whispered to me—O, how I dislike him! I am sure he is unkind to his wife, I am sure he has a bad temper, and if there is any excuse for——

Pendennis. For what?

Mrs. P. For nothing. But you heard yourself that he had a bad temper, and spoke sneeringly[8] to his wife. What could make her marry him?

Pendennis. Money and the desire of Papa and Mamma. For the same reason Clive's flame, poor Miss Newcome, was brought out to-day; that vacant seat at her side was for Lord Farintosh who did not come. And the Marquis not being present, the Baron took his innings. Did you not see how tender he was to her and how fierce poor Clive looked?

Mrs. P. Lord Highgate was very attentive to Miss Newcome, was he?

[4] and *Ms*] [omitted] *E1*
[5] that *Ms*] the *E1*
[6] *sait ... E1*] *sait*↑.↓ ~~attendre~~. *Ms*
[7] the *Ms*] [omitted] *E1*
[8] sneeringly *E1*] roughly *Ms*

Pendennis. And four years ago, Lord Highgate was breaking his heart about whom do you think—about Lady Clara Pulleyn—our hostess of last night. He was Jack Belsize then, a younger son, plunged over head and ears in debt; and of course there could be no marriage. Clive was present at Baden when a terrific[9] scene took place, and carried off poor Jack to Switzerland and Italy, where he remained till his father died and he came into the title in which he rejoices. And now he is off with the old love, Laura, and on with the new. Why do you look at me so? Are you thinking that other people have been in love two or three times too?

Mrs. P. I am thinking that I should not like to live in London, Arthur.

And this was all that Mrs. Laura could be brought to say. When this young woman chooses to be silent, there is no power that can extract a word from her. It is true that she is generally in the right; but that is only the more aggravating. Indeed what can be more provoking after a dispute with your wife than to find it is you and not she who has been in the wrong?

Sir Barnes Newcome politely caused us to understand that the entertainment of which we had just partaken was given in honour of the bride. Clive must needs not be outdone in hospitality; and invited us and others to a fine feast at the Star and Garter at Richmond, where Mrs. Pendennis was placed at his right hand. I smile as I think how much dining has been already commemorated in these veracious pages; but the story is an everyday record; and does not dining form a certain part of the pleasure and business of every day? It is at that pleasant hour that our sex has the privilege of meeting the other. The morning man and woman alike devote to business; or pass mainly in the company of their own kind. John has his office; Jane her household, her nursery, her milliner, her daughters, and their masters. In the country he has his hunting, his fishing, his farming, his letters; she her schools, her poor, her garden, or what not. Parted through the shining hours, and improving them let us trust, we come together towards sunset only, we make merry and amuse ourselves. We chat with our pretty neighbour, or survey the young ones sporting; we make love and are jealous; we dance, or obsequiously turn over the leaves of Cecilia's music-book; we play whist, or go to sleep in the arm-chair, according to our ages and conditions. Snooze gently in thy arm-chair, thou easy baldhead! play your whist, or read your novel, or talk scandal over your work, ye worthy dowagers and fogies! Meanwhile the young ones frisk about, or dance, or sing, or laugh; or whisper behind curtains in moonlit-windows; or shirk away into the garden, and come back smelling of cigars; nature having made them so to do.

Nature at this time irresistibly impelled Clive Newcome towards love-making. It was pairing-season with him. Mr. Clive was now some three-and-twenty years old: enough has been said about his good looks, which were in truth sufficient to make him a match for the young lady on whom he had set his heart, and from whom, during this entertainment which he gave to my wife, he could never keep his eyes away for three minutes. Laura's did not need to be so keen as they were in order to see what poor Clive's condition was. She did not in the least grudge the young fellow's

---

[9] terrific *Ms*] terrible *E1*

inattention to herself; or feel hurt that he did not seem to listen when she spoke; she conversed with J.J., her neighbour, who was very modest and agreeable; while her husband, not so well pleased, had Mrs. Hobson Newcome for his partner during the chief part of the entertainment. Mrs. Hobson and Lady Clara were the matrons who gave the sanction of their presence to this bachelor-party. Neither of their husbands could come to Clive's little fête; had they not the City and the House of Commons to attend? My uncle, Major Pendennis, was another of the guests; who for his part found the party was what you young fellows call very slow. Dreading Mrs. Hobson and her powers of conversation, the old gentleman nimbly skipped out of her neighbourhood, and fell by the side of Lord Highgate, to whom the Major was inclined to make himself very pleasant. But Lord Highgate's broad back was turned upon his neighbour, who was forced to tell stories to Captain Crackthorpe which had amused dukes and marquises in former days and were surely quite good enough for any baron in this realm. "Lord Highgate sweet upon *la belle* Newcome, is he?" said the testy Major afterwards. "He seemed to me to talk to Lady Clara the whole time. When I awoke in the garden after dinner as Mrs. Hobson was telling one of her confounded long stories: I found her audience was diminished to one. Crackthorpe, Lord Highgate, and Lady Clara, we had all been sitting there when the bankeress cut in (in the midst of a very good story I was telling them which entertained them very much) and never ceased talking till I fell off into a doze. When I roused myself, begad, she was still going on. Crackthorpe was off smoking a cigar on the terrace: my lord and Lady Clara were nowhere; and you four with the little painter were chatting cozily in another arbour. Behaved himself very well, the little painter. Doosid good dinner Ellis gave us. But as for Highgate being *aux soins* with *la belle Banquière*.—Upon my word, my dear, it seemed to me his thoughts went quite another way. To be sure Lady Clara is a *belle Banquière* too now. He He He! How could he say he had no carriage to go home in? He came down in Crackthorpe's cab; who passed us just now driving back young Whatdyecall the painter."

Thus did the Major discourse as we returned towards the City. I could see in the open carriage which followed us (Lady Clara Newcome's) Lord Highgate's white hat, by Clive's on the back seat.

Laura looked at her husband. The same thought may have crossed their minds though neither uttered it; but although Sir Barnes and Lady Clara Newcome offered us other civilities during our stay in London: no inducements could induce Laura to accept the proffered friendship of that lady. When Lady Clara called, my wife was not at home: when she invited us, Laura pleaded engagements. At first she bestowed on Miss Newcome too a share of this haughty dislike; and rejected the advances which that young lady, who professed to like my wife very much, made towards an intimacy. When I appealed to her (for Newcome's house was after all a very pleasant one—and you met the best people there) my wife looked at me with an expression of something like scorn—and said, "Why don't I like Miss Newcome? of course because I am jealous of her. All women, you know Arthur, are jealous of such beauties."

I could get for a long while no better explanation than these sneers, for my wife's antipathy towards this branch of the Newcome family. An event came presently which silenced my remonstrances; and showed to me that Laura had judged Barnes and his wife only too well.

Poor Mrs. Hobson Newcome had reason to be sulky at the neglect which all the Richmond party showed her, for nobody, not even Major Pendennis, as we have seen, would listen to her intellectual conversation; nobody, not even Lord Highgate, would drive back to town in her carriage, though the vehicle was large and empty, and Lady Clara's barouche, in which his Lordship chose to take a place, had already three occupants within it:—but in spite of these rebuffs and disappointments the virtuous lady of Brianstone Square, was bent upon being good-natured and hospitable; and I have to record, in the present chapter, yet one more feast of which Mr. and Mrs. Pendennis partook at the expense of the most respectable Newcome family.

Although Mrs. Laura here also appeared, and had the place of honour in her character of bride, I am bound to own my opinion that Mrs. Hobson only made us the pretext of her party, and that in reality it was given to persons of a much more exalted rank. We were the first to arrive, our good old Major, the most punctual of men, bearing us company. Our hostess was arrayed in unusual state and splendour; her fat neck was ornamented with jewels, rich bracelets decorated her arms, and this Brianstone Square Cornelia had likewise her family jewels distributed round her, priceless male and female Newcome gems, from the King's College youth with whom we have made a brief acquaintance, and his elder sister, now entering into the world, down to the last little ornament of the nursery, in a prodigious new sash, with ringlets hot and crisp from the tongs of a Marylebone hairdresser. We had seen the cherub faces of some of these darlings pressed against the drawing-room windows as our carriage drove up to the door; when, after a few minutes' conversation, another vehicle arrived, away they dashed to the windows again, the innocent little dears crying out "Here's the Marquis;" and in sadder tones, "No, it isn't the Marquis," by which artless expressions they showed how eager they were to behold an expected guest of a rank only inferior to Dukes in this great empire.

Putting two and two together, as the saying is, it was not difficult for me to guess who the expected Marquis was—and indeed, the King's College youth set that question at once to rest, by wagging his head at me, and winking his eye, and saying, "We expect Farintosh."

"Why, my dearest children," Matronly Virtue exclaimed, "this anxiety to behold the young Marquis of Farintosh, whom we expect at our modest table, Mrs. Pendennis, to-day? Twice you have been at the window in your eagerness to look for him. Louisa, you silly child, do you imagine that his lordship will appear in his robes and coronet? Rodolf, you absurd boy, do you think that a Marquis is other than a man? I have never admired aught but intellect, Mrs. Pendennis; *that,* let us be thankful, is the only true title to distinction in our country now-a-days."

"Begad, Sir," whispers the old Major to me, "intellect may be a doosid fine thing, but in my opinion, a Marquisate and eighteen or twenty thousand a year; I should say the Farintosh property, with the Glenlivat estate, and the Roy property in England, must be worth nineteen thousand a year at the very lowest figure; and I remember when this young man's father was only Tom Roy, of the 42nd, with no hope of succeeding to the title, and doosidly out at elbows too ... I say what does the bankeress mean by chattering about intellect? Hang me, a Marquis is a Marquis; and Mrs. Newcome knows it as well as I do." My good Major was growing old, and was not unnaturally a little testy at the manner in which his hostess received him. Truth to tell, she hardly took any notice of him; and cut down a couple of the old gentleman's stories before he had been five minutes in the room.

To our party presently comes the host in a flurried countenance, with a white waistcoat, holding in his hand an open letter, towards which his wife looks with some alarm. "How dy' doo, Lady Clara; how dy' doo, Ethel?" he says, saluting those ladies whom the second carriage had brought to us. "Sir Barnes is not coming, that's one place vacant; that Lady Clara you won't mind, you see him at home: but here's a disappointment for you, Miss Newcome, Lord Farintosh can't come."

At this, two of the children cry out "O! O!" with such a melancholy accent, that Miss Newcome and Lady Clara burst out laughing.

"Got a dreadful tooth-ache!" said Mr. Hobson; "here's his letter."

"Hang it, what a bore!" cries artless young King's College.

"Why a bore, Samuel? A bore, as you call it, for Lord Farintosh I grant; but do you suppose that the high in station are exempt from the ills of mortality? I know nothing more painful than a tooth-ache," exclaims a virtuous matron, using the words of philosophy but showing the countenance of anger.

"Hang it, why didn't he have it out?" says Samuel.

Miss Ethel laughed. "Lord Farintosh would not have that tooth out for the world, Samuel," she cried, gaily. "He keeps it in on purpose, and it always aches when he does not want to go out to dinner."

"I know *one* humble family who will never ask him again," Mrs. Hobson exclaims, rustling in all her silks, and tapping her fan and her foot. The eclipse, however, passes off her countenance and light is restored; when at this moment, a cab having driven up during the period of darkness, the door is flung open, and Lord Highgate is announced by a loud-voiced butler.

My wife being still the bride on this occasion, had the honour of being led to the dinner-table by our banker and host. Lord Highgate was reserved for Mrs. Hobson, who, in an engaging manner, requested poor Clive to conduct his cousin Maria to dinner, handing over Miss Ethel to another guest. Our Major gave his arm to Lady Clara, and I perceived that my wife looked very grave as he passed the place where she sat, and seated Lady Clara in the next chair to that which Lord Highgate chanced to occupy. Feeling himself *en veine*, and the company being otherwise rather mum and silent, my uncle told a number of delightful anecdotes about the beau monde of his time, about the Peninsular war, the Regent, Brummell, Lord Steyne, Pea Green Payne, and so forth. He said the evening was very pleasant, though some others of the party, as it appeared to me, scarcely seemed to think so. Clive had not a word for his cousin Maria, but looked across the table at Ethel all dinner time. What could Ethel have to say to her partner, old Colonel Sir Donald M'Craw, who gobbled and drank as his wont is, and if he had a remark to make, imparted it to Mrs. Hobson, at whose right hand he was sitting, and to whom, during the whole course, or courses, of the dinner, my Lord Highgate scarcely uttered one single word.

His lordship was whispering all the while into the ringlets of Lady Clara; they were talking a jargon which their hostess scarcely understood, of people only known to her by her study of the peerage. When we joined the ladies after dinner, Lord Highgate again made way towards Lady Clara, and at an order from her as I thought, left her ladyship, and strove hard to engage in a conversation with Mrs. Newcome. I hope he succeeded in smoothing the frowns in that round little face. Mrs. Laura, I own, was as grave as a judge all the evening; very grave and even[1] reserved with my uncle, when the hour for parting came, and we took him home.

"He, he!" said the old man, coughing, and nodding his old head and laughing in his senile manner, when I saw him on the next day. "That was a pleasant evening we had yesterday; doosid pleasant, and I think my two neighbours seemed to be uncommonly pleased with each other; not an amusing fellow, that young painter of yours, though he is good-looking enough, but there's no conversation in him. Do you think of giving a little dinner, Arthur, in return for these hospitalities? Greenwich, hey, or something of that sort? I'll go you halves, Sir, and we'll ask the young banker and bankeress—not yesterday's Amphitryon nor his wife; no, no, hang it! but Barnes Newcome is a devilish clever, rising man, and moves in about as good society as any in London. We'll ask him and Lady Clara and Highgate, and one or two more, and have a pleasant party."

But to this proposal when the old man communicated it to her, in a very quiet, simple, artful[2] way, Laura, with a flushing face said NO quite abruptly, and quitted the room, rustling in her silks, and showing at once dignity and indignation.

Not many more feasts was Arthur Pendennis, senior, to have in this world. Not many more great men was he to flatter, nor schemes to wink at, nor earthly pleasures to enjoy. His long days were well nigh ended: on his last couch,—which Laura tended so affectionately, with his last breath almost, he faltered out to me, "I had other views for you, my boy, and once hoped to see you in a higher position in life; but I begin to think now, Arthur, that I was wrong; and as for that girl, Sir, I am sure she is an angel."

May I not inscribe the words with a grateful heart? Blessed he,—blessed though maybe undeserving, who has the love of a good woman.

[1] and even *NY*] even and *E1 R*
[2] artful *E1*] artless *R*

Chapter XII.

Y wife was much better pleased with Clive than[1] with some of his relatives to whom I had presented her. His face carried a recommendation with it that few honest people could resist. He was always a welcome friend in our lodgings, and even our uncle the Major signified his approval of the lad as a young fellow of very good manners and feeling,[2] who if he chose to throw himself away and be a painter ma foi, was rich enough no doubt to follow his own caprices. Clive executed a capital head of Major Pendennis which now hangs in our drawing-room at Fairoaks; and reminds me[3] of that friend of my youth. Clive occupied ancient lofty chambers in Hanover Square now. He had furnished them in an antique manner, with hangings, cabinets, carved work, Venice glasses, fine prints and water-colour sketches of good pictures by his own and other hands. He had horses to ride and a liberal purse full of paternal money. Many fine equipages drew up opposite to his chambers: few artists had such luck as young Mr. Clive. And above his own chambers were other three which the young gentleman had hired, and where says he, "I hope ere very long my dear old father will be lodging with me. In another year he says he thinks he will be able to come home: when the affairs of the Bank are quite settled. You shake your head!

[1] My wife . . . pleased with Clive than *E1*] With Clive my fair critic was much better pleased than *Ms*
[2] feeling *Ms*] feelings *E1*
[3] me *E1*] us *Ms*

Why! the Shares are worth four times what we gave for them. We are men of fortune, Pen, I give you my word. You should see how much they make of me at Baynes and Jolly's and how civil they are to me at Hobson Brothers! I go into the City now and then and see our Manager, Mr. Blackmore. He tells me such stories about indigo and wool and copper and sicca rupees and Company's rupees:—I don't know anything about the business, but my father likes me to go and see Mr. Blackmore.[4] Dear Cousin Barnes is for ever asking me to dinner: I might call Lady Clara Clara if I liked, as Sam Newcome does in Brianstone Square. You can't think how kind they are to me there. My aunt reproaches me tenderly for not going there oftener—it's not very good fun dining in Brianstone Square, is it? And she praises my Cousin Maria to me—you should hear my aunt praise her! I have to take Maria down to dinner; to sit by the piano and listen to her songs in all languages. Do you know Maria can sing Hungarian and Polish, besides your common German, Spanish, and Italian. Those I have at our *other* agents, Baynes and Jolly's—Baynes's that is in the Regent's Park, where the girls are prettier and just as civil to me as at Aunt Hobson's." And here Clive would amuse us by the accounts which he gave us of the snares which the Misses Baynes, those young syrens of Regent's Park, set for him; of the songs which they sang to enchant him, the albums in which they besought him to draw—the thousand winning ways which they employed to bring him into their cave in York Terrace. But neither Circe's smiles nor Calypso's blandishments had any effect on him; his ears were stopped to their music, and his eyes rendered dull to their charms by those of the flighty young enchantress with whom my wife had of late made acquaintance.

Capitalist though he was, our young fellow was still very[5] affable. He forgot no old friends in his prosperity: and the lofty antique chambers would not unfrequently be lighted up of[6] nights to receive F.B. and some of the old cronies of the Haunt, and some of the Gandishites, who if Clive had been of a nature that was to be spoiled by flattery had certainly done mischief to the young man. Gandish[7] himself, when Clive paid a visit to that illustrious artist's Academy, received his former pupil as if the young fellow had been a sovereign prince almost, accompanied him to his horse, and would have held his stirrup as he mounted, whilst the beautiful daughters of the house waved adieus to him from the parlour-window. To the young men assembled in his studio, Gandish was never tired of talking about Clive. The Professor would take occasion to inform them that he had been to visit his distinguished young friend, Mr. Newcome, son of Colonel Newcome; that last evening he had been present at an elegant entertainment at Mr. Newcome's new apartments. Clive's drawings were hung up in Gandish's gallery, and pointed out to visitors by the worthy Professor. On one or two occasions I was

---

4 [The rest of this paragraph was added at proof stage.]
5 ¶Capitalist though he was, our young fellow was still very *E1*] Howbeit our young fellow, Capitalist though he was, was very *Ms*
6 of *Ms*] at *E1*
7 [From "Gandish" to the next note was added in proof stage.]

allowed to become a bachelor again, and participate in these jovial meetings. How guilty my coat was on my return home; how haughty the looks of the mistress of my house, as she bade Martha carry away the obnoxious garment! How grand F.B. used to be as president of Clive's smoking party, where he laid down the law, talked the most talk, sang the jolliest

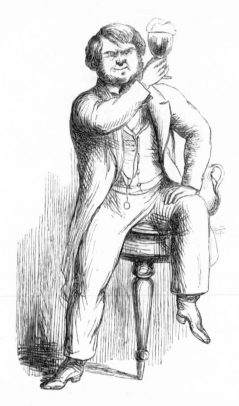

song, and consumed the most drink of all the jolly talkers and drinkers! Clive's popularity rose prodigiously; not only youngsters, but old practitioners of the fine arts, lauded his talents.[8] What a shame that his pictures were all refused this year at the Academy! Alfred Smee, Esq.,[9] R.A., was indignant at their rejection: but J.J. confessed with a sigh, and Clive owned good-naturedly that he had been neglecting his business, and that his pictures were not so good as those of two years before. I am afraid Mr. Clive went to too many balls and parties, to clubs and jovial entertainments, besides losing yet more time in that other pursuit we wot of—Meanwhile J.J. went steadily on with his work, no day passed without a line; and Fame was not very far off though this he heeded but little; and Art his sole mistress rewarded him for his steady and fond pursuit of her.

"Look at him," Clive would say with a sigh. "Isn't he the mortal of all

[8] [The manuscript resumes with "What a shame"; see previous note.]
[9] Alfred Smee, Esq., *Ms E1*] Mr. Smee, *R*

A Meditation

others the most to be envied? He is so fond of his art that in all the world there is no attraction like it for him. He runs to his easel[1] at sun-rise, and sits before it caressing his picture all day till night-fall. He takes leave of it sadly when dark comes: spends the night in a Life Academy, and begins next morning *da capo*. Of all the pieces of good fortune which can befal a man, is not this the greatest: to have your desire and then never tire of it? I have been in such a rage with my own short-comings that I have dashed my foot through the canvases; and vowed I would smash my palette and easel. Sometimes I succeed a little better in my work, and then it will happen for half an hour that I am pleased: but pleased of[2] what? pleased at drawing Mr. Muggins's head rather like Mr. Muggins. Why, a thousand fellows can do better and when one day I reach my very best, yet[3] thousands will be able to do better still. Our's is a trade for which nowadays there's no excuse unless one can be great in it: and I feel I have not the stuff for that. No. 666. Portrait of Joseph Muggins, Esq., Newcome, Great George Street.[4] No. 979. Portrait of Mrs. Muggins on her grey poney, Newcome. No. 579. Portrait of Joseph Muggins, Esq.'s, dog Toby, Newcome—this is what I'm fit for. These are the victories I have set myself on atchieving. O Mrs. Pendennis! Isn't it humiliating? Why isn't there a war? Why can't I go and distinguish myself somewhere and be a general? Why haven't I a genius? I say, Pen, Sir, why haven't I a genius? There is a painter who lives hard by and who sends sometimes to beg me to come and look at his work. He is in the Muggins line too. He gets his canvases with a good light upon them: excludes the contemplation of all other objects, stands beside his pictures in an attitude himself and thinks that he and they are Masterpieces. Masterpieces! O me, what drivelling wretches we are. Fame!—except that of just the one or two—what's the use of it? I say, Pen, would you feel particularly proud now if you had written Hayley's poems—and as for a second place in painting—who would care to be Caravaggio or Caracci? I wouldn't give a straw to be Caracci or Caravaggio—I would just as soon be yonder artist who is painting up Foker's Entire over the public house at the corner. He will have his payment afterwards, five shillings a day and a pot of beer.—Your head a little more to the light, Mrs. Pendennis, if you please. I am tiring you, I daresay, but then, O I am doing it so badly!"

I, for my part, thought Clive was making a very pretty drawing of my wife, and having affairs of my own to attend to would often leave her at his chambers as a sitter, or find him at our lodgings visiting her. They became the very greatest friends. I knew the young fellow could have no better friend than Laura: and not being ignorant of the malady under which he was labouring, concluded naturally and justly that Clive grew so fond of my wife not for her sake entirely, but for his own, because he could pour his heart out to her, and her sweet kindness and compassion would soothe him in his unhappy condition.

Miss Ethel, I have said, also professed a great fondness for Mrs. Pendennis: and there was that charm in the young lady's manner which speedily

---

[1] easel *E1*] card *Ms*
[2] of *E1 HM NY*] at *Ms*
[3] yet *Ms E1*] [omitted] *R*
[4] Great George Street. *E1*] Great George St. *Ms*] George St. *R*

could overcome even female jealousy. Perhaps Laura determined magnanimously to conquer it: perhaps she hid it so as to vex me and prove the injustice of my suspicions: perhaps honestly she was conquered by the young beauty and gave her a regard and admiration which the other knew she could inspire whenever she had the will. My wife was fairly captivated by her at length. The untameable young creature was docile and gentle in Laura's presence: modest, natural, amiable, full of laughter and spirit,[5] delightful to see and to hear, her presence cheered our quiet little household: her charm fascinated my wife as it had subjugated poor Clive. Even the reluctant Farintosh was compelled to own her power, and confidentially told his male friends that hang it she was so handsome and so clever and so confoundedly pleasant and fascinating and that—that he had been on the point of popping the fatal question ever so many times, by Jove—"And hang it, you know," his lordship would say, "I don't want to marry until I have had my fling, you know."—As for Clive, Ethel treated him like a boy; like a big brother. She was jocular, kind, pert, pleasant with him, ordered him on her errands, accepted his bouquets and compliments, admired his drawings, liked to hear him praised and took his part in all companies; laughed at his sighs; and frankly owned to Laura her liking for him and her pleasure in seeing him. "Why," said she, "should not I be happy as long as the sunshine lasts? To-morrow I know will be glum and dreary enough. When Grandmamma comes back I shall scarcely be able to come and see you. When I am settled in life—eh!—I shall be settled in life! Do not grudge me my holyday, Laura. O, if you knew how stupid it is to be in the world: and how much pleasanter to come and talk and laugh and sing and be happy with you, than to sit in that dreary Eaton Place with poor Clara!"

"Why do you stay in Eaton Place?" asks Laura.

"Why? because I must go out with somebody. What an unsophisticated little country creature you are! Grandmamma is away, and I cannot go about to parties by myself."

"But why should you go to parties, and why not go back to your mother?" says Mrs. Pendennis gently.

"To the nursery and my little sisters and Miss Cann?—I like being in London best, thank you. You look grave? You think a girl should like to be with her mother and sisters best? My dear, Mamma wishes me to be here and I stay with Barnes and Clara by Grandmamma's orders. Don't you know that I have been made over to Lady Kew, who has adopted me? Do you think a young lady of my pretensions can stop at home in a damp house in Warwickshire and cut bread and butter for little boys at school? Don't look so very grave and shake your head so, Mrs. Pendennis! If you had been bred as I have: you would be as I am—I know what you are thinking, Madam."

"I am thinking," said Laura blushing and bowing her head, "I am thinking, if it pleases God to give me children, I should like to live at home at Fairoaks." My wife's thoughts, though she did not utter them, and a certain modesty and habitual awe kept her silent upon subjects so very sacred,

[5] spirit, *Ms*] spirits, *E1*

went deeper yet. She had been bred to measure her actions by a standard, which the world may nominally admit but which it leaves for the most part unheeded. Worship; Love; Duty; as taught her by the devout study of the Sacred Law which interprets and defines it,—if these formed the outward practice of her life, they were also its constant and secret endeavour[6] and occupation. She spoke but very seldom of her religion though it filled her heart and influenced all her behaviour. Whenever she came to that sacred subject, her demeanour appeared to her husband so awful, that he scarcely dared to approach it in her company: and stood without as this pure creature entered into the Holy of Holies. What must the world appear to such a person? Its ambitions, rewards,[7] disappointments, pleasures, worth how much? Compared to the possession of that priceless treasure and happiness unspeakable, a perfect faith, what has Life to offer?[8] I see before me now her sweet grave face as she looks out from the balcony of the little Richmond villa we occupied during the first happy year after our marriage, following Ethel Newcome, who rides away with a staid groom behind her, to her brother's summer-residence not far distant.[9] Clive had been with us in the morning; and had brought us stirring news. The Colonel[1] was by this time on his way home. "If Clive could tear himself away from London," the good man[2] wrote (and we thus saw he was acquainted with the state of the young man's mind), "why should not Clive go and meet his father at Malta?" He was feverish and eager to go: and his two friends strongly counselled him to take the journey. In the midst of our talk Miss Ethel came among us. She arrived flushed and in high spirits: she rallied Clive upon his gloomy looks: she turned rather pale, as it seemed to us, when she heard the[3] news. Then she coldly told him she thought the voyage must be a pleasant one and would do him good: it was[4] pleasanter than that journey she was going to take herself with her grandmother, to those dreary German springs which the old Countess frequented year after year. Mr. Pendennis having business retired to his study, whither presently Mrs. Laura followed,—having to look for her scissors or a book she wanted—or[5] upon some pretext or other. She sate down in the conjugal study: not one word did either of us say for a while about the young people left alone in the drawing-room yonder. Laura[6] talked about our own home at Fairoaks, which our tenants were about to vacate. She vowed and declared that we must live at Fairoaks: that Clavering, with all its tittle-tattle and stupid inhabitants, was better than this wicked London. Besides there were some new and very pleasant families settled in the neighbourhood. Clavering

---

[6] endeavour *Ms*] endeavours *E1*

[7] ambitions, rewards] ambitions rewards *Ms*] ambitious rewards, *E1*

[8] offer? *E1*] offer her? *Ms*

[9] not far distant. *E1*] not very far away. *Ms*

[1] <good> Colonel *Ms*] good Colonel *E1*

[2] the good man *E1*] his good father *Ms*

[3] the *E1*] his *Ms*

[4] him good: it was *E1*] him—much *Ms*

[5] a book she wanted—or] a book she wanted, or *E1*] a book she wanted or for a book she wanted—or *Ms*

[6] Laura *E1*] She *Ms*

Park was taken by some delightful people—"and you know, Pen, you were always very fond of fly-fishing, and may fish the Brawl, as you used in old days, when——" The lips of the pretty satirist who alluded to these unpleasant bygones were silenced as they deserved to be by Mr. Pendennis. "Do you think, Sir, I did not know," says the sweetest voice in the world, "when you went out on your fishing excursions with Miss Amory?" Again the flow of words is checked by the styptic previously applied.

"I wonder," says Mr. Pendennis, archly, bending over his wife's fair hand—"I wonder whether this kind of thing is taking place in the drawing-room?"

"Nonsense, Arthur. It is time to go back to them. Why, I declare, I have been three quarters of an hour away!"

"I don't think they will much miss you, my dear," says the gentleman.

"She is certainly very fond of him. She is always coming here. I am sure it is not to hear you read Shakspeare, Arthur; or your new novel, though it is very pretty. I wish Lady Kew and her sixty thousand pounds were at the bottom of the sea."

"But she says she is going to portion her younger brothers with a part of it; she told Clive so," remarks Mr. Pendennis.

"For shame! Why does not Barnes Newcome portion his younger brothers? I have no patience with that—— Why! Goodness! There is Clive going away, actually! Clive! Mr. Newcome!" But though my wife ran to the study-window and beckoned our friend, he only shook his head, jumped on his horse, and rode away gloomily.

"Ethel had been crying when I went into the room," Laura afterwards told me. I knew she had; but she looked up from some flowers over which she was bending, began to laugh and rattle, would talk about nothing but Lady Hautboi's[7] great breakfast the day before, and the most insufferable May-Fair jargon; and then declared it was time to go home and[8] dress for Mrs. Booth's *déjeuner,* which was to take place that afternoon.

And so Miss Newcome rode away—back amongst the roses and the rouges—back amongst the fiddling, flirting, flattery, falseness—and Laura's sweet serene face looked after her departing. Mrs. Booth's was a very grand *déjeuner.* We read in the newspapers a list of the greatest names there. A Royal Duke and Duchess; a German Highness, a Hindoo Nabob, &c.; and, amongst the Marquises, Farintosh; and, amongst the Lords, Highgate; and Lady Clara Newcome, and Miss Newcome, who looked killing, our acquaintance Captain Crackthorpe informs us, and who was in perfectly stunning spirits. "His Imperial Highness the Grand Duke of Farintosh is wild about her," the Captain said, "and our poor young friend Clive may just go and hang himself. Dine with us at the Gar and Starter? Jolly party. O, I forgot! married man now!" So saying, the Captain entered the hostelry near which I met him, leaving this present chronicler to return to his own home.

---

7 Hautboi's *E1*] Hautbois' *R*
8 and *E1*] to *R*

Chapter XIII.

MIGHT open the present chapter, as a cotemporary[1] writer of Romance is occasionally in the habit of commencing his tales of Chivalry, by a description of a November afternoon, with falling leaves, tawny forests, gathering storms, and other autumnal phenomena; and two horsemen winding up the romantic road which leads from—from Richmond Bridge to the Star and Garter. The one rider is youthful, and has a blonde moustache: the cheek of the other has been browned by foreign suns; it is easy to see by the manner in which he bestrides his powerful charger that he has followed the profession of arms. He looks as if he had faced his country's enemies on many a field of Eastern battle. The cavaliers alight before the gate of a cottage on Richmond Hill, where a gentleman receives them with eager welcome. Their steeds are accommodated at a neighbouring hostelry,—I pause in the midst of the description, for the reader has made the acquaintance of our two horsemen long since. It is Clive returned from Malta, from Gibraltar, from Seville, from Cadiz, and with him our dear old friend the Colonel. His campaigns are over, his sword is hung up, he leaves Eastern suns and battles to warm younger[2] blood. Welcome back to England, dear Colonel and kind friend! How quickly the years have passed since he has been gone! There is a streak or two more silver in his hair. The wrinkles about his honest eyes are somewhat deeper, but their look is as steadfast and kind as in the early, almost boyish days when first we[3] knew them.

---

[1] cotemporary *E1*] contemporary *R*
[2] younger *E1*] young *R*
[3] first we *E1*] we first *R*

We talk awhile about the Colonel's voyage home, the pleasures of the Spanish journey, the handsome new quarters in which Clive has installed his father and himself, my own altered condition in life, and what not. During the conversation a little querulous voice makes itself audible above stairs, at which noise Mr. Clive begins to laugh, and the Colonel to smile. It is for the first time in his life Mr. Clive listens to the little voice; indeed, it is only since about six weeks that that small organ has been heard in the world at all. Laura Pendennis believes its tunes[4] to be the sweetest, the most interesting, the most mirth-inspiring, the most pitiful and pathetic, that ever baby uttered; which opinions, of course, are backed by Mrs. Hokey, the confidential nurse. Laura's husband is not so rapturous; but, let us trust, behaves in a way becoming a man and a father. We forego the description of his feelings as not pertaining to the history at present under consideration. A little while before the dinner is served, the lady of the cottage comes down to greet her husband's old friends.

And here I am sorely tempted to a third description, which has nothing to do with the story to be sure, but which, if properly hit off, might fill half a page very prettily. For is not a young mother one of the sweetest sights which life shows us? If she has been beautiful before, does not her present pure joy give a character of refinement and sacredness almost to her beauty, touch her sweet cheeks with fairer blushes, and impart I know not what serene brightness to her eyes? I give warning to the artist who designs the pictures for this veracious story, to make no attempt at this subject. I never would be satisfied with it were his drawing ever so good.

When Sir Charles Grandison stepped up and made his very beautifullest bow to Miss Byron, I am sure his gracious dignity never exceeded that of Colonel Newcome's first greeting to Mrs. Pendennis. Of course from the very moment they beheld one another they became friends. Are not most of our likings thus instantaneous? Before she came down to see him, Laura had put on one of the Colonel's shawls—the crimson one, with the red palm leaves and the border of many colours. As for the white one, the priceless, the gossamer, the fairy web, which might pass through a ring, *that*, every lady must be aware, was already appropriated to cover the cradle, or what I believe is called the bassinet of Master Pendennis.

So we all became the very best of friends; and during the winter months whilst we still resided at Richmond, the Colonel was my wife's constant visitor. He often came without Clive. He did not care for the world which the young gentleman frequented, and was more pleased and at home by my wife's fireside than at more noisy and splendid entertainments. And, Laura being a sentimental person interested in pathetic novels and all unhappy attachments, of course she and the Colonel talked a great deal about Mr. Clive's little affair, over which they would have such deep confabulations that even when the master of the house appeared, Pater Familias, the man whom, in the presence of the Revd. Dr. Portman, Mrs. Laura had sworn to love, honour, &c., these two guilty ones would be silent, or change the subject of conversation, not caring to admit such an unsympathising person as myself into their conspiracy.

4 tunes *E1*] tones *R*

From many a talk which they have had together since the Colonel and his son embraced at Malta, Clive's father had been led to see how strongly the passion which our friend had once fought and mastered, had now taken possession of the young man. The unsatisfied longing left him indifferent to all other objects of previous desire or ambition. The misfortune darkened the sunshine of his spirit, and clouded the world before his eyes. He passed hours in his painting-room, though he tore up what he did there. He forsook his usual haunts, or appeared amongst his old comrades moody and silent. From cigar smoking, which I own to be a reprehensible practice, he plunged into still deeper and darker dissipation; for I am sorry to say, he took to pipes and the strongest tobacco, for which there is *no* excuse. Our young man was changed. During the last fifteen or twenty months, the malady had been increasing on him, of which we have not chosen to describe at length the stages; knowing very well that the reader (the male reader at least) does not care a fig about other people's sentimental perplexities, and is not wrapped up heart and soul in Clive's affairs like his father, whose rest was disturbed if the boy had a headache, or who would have stripped the coat off his back to keep his darling's feet warm.

The object of this hopeless passion had, meantime, returned to the custody of the dark old duenna, from which she had been liberated for a while. Lady Kew had got her health again, by means of the prescriptions of some doctors, or by the efficacy of some baths; and was again on foot and in the world, tramping about in her grim pursuit of pleasure. Lady Julia, we are led to believe, had retired upon half-pay, and into an inglorious exile at Brussels, with her sister, the outlaw's wife, by whose bankrupt fireside she was perfectly happy. Miss Newcome was now her grandmother's companion, and they had been on a tour of visits in Scotland, and were journeying from country-house to country-house about the time when our good Colonel returned to his native shores.

The Colonel loved his nephew Barnes no better than before perhaps, though we must say, that since his return from India the young Baronet's conduct had been particularly friendly. "No doubt marriage had improved him; Lady Clara seemed a good-natured young woman enough; besides," says the Colonel, wagging his good old head knowingly, "Tom Newcome, of the Bundelcund Bank, is a personage to be conciliated; whereas Tom Newcome, of the Bengal Cavalry, was not worth Master Barnes's attention. He has been very good and kind on the whole; so have his friends been uncommonly civil. There was Clive's acquaintance, Mr. Belsize that was, Lord Highgate who is now, entertained our whole family sumptuously last week—wants us and Barnes and his wife to go to his country-house at Christmas—is as hospitable, my dear Mrs. Pendennis, as man can be. He met you at Barnes's, and as soon as we are[5] alone," says the Colonel, turning round to Laura's husband, "I will tell you in what terms Lady Clara speaks of your wife. Yes. She is a good-natured kind little woman, that Lady Clara." Here Laura's face assumed that gravity and severeness, which it always wore when Lady Clara's name was mentioned, and the conversation took another turn.

[5] are *HM NY*] were *E1*

Returning home from London one afternoon, I met the Colonel who hailed me on the omnibus, and rode on his way towards the City. I knew, of course, that he had been colloguing with my wife; and taxed that young woman with these continued flirtations. "Two or three times a week, Mrs. Laura, you dare to receive a Colonel of Dragoons. You sit for hours closetted with the young fellow of sixty; you change the conversation when your own injured husband enters the room, and pretend to talk about the weather, or the baby. You little arch hypocrite, you know you do.—Don't try to humbug *me*, Miss; what will Richmond, what will society, what will Mrs. Grundy in general say to such atrocious behaviour?"

"O! Pen," says my wife, closing my mouth in a way which I do not choose farther to particularise; "that man is the best, the dearest, the kindest creature. I never knew such a good man; you ought to put him into a book. Do you know, Sir, that I felt the very greatest desire to give him a kiss when he went away; and that one which you had just now, was intended for him."

"Take back thy gift, false girl!" says Mr. Pendennis; and then, finally, we come to the particular circumstance which had occasioned so much enthusiasm on Mrs. Laura's part.

Colonel Newcome had summoned heart of grace, and in Clive's behalf had regularly proposed him to Barnes, as a suitor to Ethel; taking an artful advantage of his nephew Barnes Newcome, and inviting that Baronet to a private meeting, where they were to talk about the affairs of the Bundelcund Banking Company.

Now this Bundelcund Banking Company, in the Colonel's eyes, was in reality his son Clive. But for Clive there might have been a hundred banking companies established, yielding a hundred per cent. in as many districts of India, and Thomas Newcome, who had plenty of money for his own wants, would never have thought of speculation. His desire was to see his boy endowed with all the possible gifts of fortune. Had he built a palace for Clive, and been informed that a roc's egg was required to complete the decoration of the edifice, Tom Newcome would have travelled to the world's end in search of the wanting article. To see Prince Clive ride in a gold coach with a princess beside him, was the kind old Colonel's ambition; that done, he would be content to retire to a garret in the prince's castle, and smoke his cheroot there in peace. So the world is made. The strong and eager covet honour and enjoyment for themselves; the gentle and disappointed (once, they may have been strong and eager, too,) desire these gifts for their children. I think Clive's father never liked or understood the lad's choice of a profession. He acquiesced in it, as he would in any of his son's wishes. But, not being a poet himself, he could not see the nobility of that calling; and felt secretly that his son was demeaning himself by pursuing the art of painting. "Had he been a soldier, now," thought Thomas Newcome, "(though I prevented that), had he been richer than he is, he might have married Ethel, instead of being unhappy as he now is, God help him! I remember my own time of grief well enough: and what years it took before my wound was scarred over."

So with these things occupying his brain, Thomas Newcome artfully invited Barnes, his nephew, to dinner, under pretence of talking of the affairs of the great B.B.C. With the first glass of wine at dessert, and according to the Colonel's good old-fashioned custom of proposing toasts, they drank the health of the B.B.C. Barnes drank the toast with all his generous heart. The B.B.C. sent to Hobson Brothers and Newcome a great deal of business, was in a most prosperous condition, kept a great balance at the bank,—a balance that would not be overdrawn as Sir Barnes Newcome very well knew. Barnes was for having more of these bills, provided there were remittances to meet the same. Barnes was ready to do any amount of business with the Indian bank, or with any bank, or with any individual, Christian or heathen, white or black, who could do good to the firm of Hobson Brothers and Newcome. He spoke upon this subject with great archness and candour: of course as a City man he would be glad to do a profitable business any where, and the B.B.C.'s business *was* profitable. But the interested motive which he admitted frankly as a man of the world, did not prevent other sentiments more agreeable. "My dear Colonel," says Barnes, "I am happy, most happy, to think that our house and our name should have been useful, as I know they have been, in the establishment of a concern in which one of our family is interested; one whom we all so sincerely respect and regard." And he touched his glass with his lips and blushed a little, as he bowed towards his uncle. He found himself making a little speech, indeed; and to do so before one single person seems rather odd. Had there been a large company present Barnes would not have blushed at all, but have tossed off his glass, struck his waistcoat possibly, and looked straight in the face of his uncle as the chairman; well, he *did* very likely believe that he respected and regarded the Colonel.

The Colonel said—"Thank you, Barnes, with all my heart. It is always good for men to be friends, much more for blood relations, as we are."

"A relationship which honours me, I'm sure!" says Barnes, with a tone of infinite affability. You see he believed that Heaven had made him the Colonel's superior.

"And I am very glad," the elder went on, "that you and my boy are good friends."

"Friends! of course. It would be unnatural if such near relatives were otherwise than good friends."

"You have been hospitable to him, and Lady Clara very kind, and he wrote to me telling me of your kindness. Ahem! this is tolerable claret. I wonder where Clive gets it?"

"You were speaking about that indigo, Colonel!" here Barnes interposes. "Our house has done very little in that way to be sure: but I suppose that our credit is *about* as good as Battie's and Jolly's, and if——" but the Colonel is in a brown study.

"Clive will have a good bit of money when I die," resumes Clive's father.

"Why, you are a hale man—upon my word, quite a young man, and may marry again, Colonel," replies the nephew fascinatingly.

"I shall never do that," replies the other. "Ere many years are gone, I shall be seventy years old, Barnes."

"Nothing in this country, my dear Sir! positively nothing. Why, there was Titus, my neighbour in the country—when will you come down to Newcome?—who married a devilish pretty girl, of very good family, too, Miss Burgeon, one of the Devonshire Burgeons. He looks, I am sure, twenty years older than you do. Why should not you do likewise?"

"Because I like to remain single, and want to leave Clive a rich man. Look here, Barnes, you know the value of our bank shares, now?"

"Indeed I do; rather speculative; but of course I know what some sold for last week," says Barnes.

"Suppose I realise now. I think I am worth six lakhs. I had nearly two from my poor father. I saved some before and since I invested in this affair; and could sell out to-morrow with sixty thousand pounds."

"A very pretty sum of money, Colonel," says Barnes.

"I have a pension of a thousand a year."

"My dear Colonel, you are a capitalist! we know it very well," remarks Sir Barnes.

"And two hundred a year is as much as I want for myself," continues the capitalist, looking into the fire, and jingling his money in his pockets. "A hundred a year for a horse; a hundred a year for pocket-money, for I calculate you know that Clive will give me a bed-room and my dinner."

"He—He! If your son won't, your *nephew* will, my dear Colonel!" says[6] the affable Barnes, smiling sweetly.

"I can give the boy a handsome allowance, you see," resumes Thomas Newcome.

"You can make him a handsome allowance now, and leave him a good fortune when you die!" says the nephew, in a noble and courageous manner,—and as if he said Twelve times twelve are a hundred and forty-four, and you have Sir Barnes Newcome's authority—Sir Barnes Newcome's, mind you—to say so.

"Not when I die, Barnes," the uncle goes on. "I will give him every shilling I am worth to-morrow morning, if he marries as I wish him."

"*Tant mieux pour lui!*" cries the nephew; and thought to himself, "Lady Clara must ask Clive to dinner instantly. Confound the fellow! I hate him—always have; but what luck he has."

"A man with that property may pretend to a good wife, as the French say; hey, Barnes?" asks the Colonel, rather eagerly looking up in his nephew's face.

That countenance was lighted up with a generous enthusiasm. "To any woman, in any rank—to a nobleman's daughter, my dear Sir!" exclaims Sir Barnes.

"I want your sister; I want my dear Ethel for him, Barnes," cries Thomas Newcome, with a trembling voice, and a twinkle in his eyes. "That was the hope I always had till my talk with your poor father stopped it. Your sister was engaged to my Lord Kew then; and my wishes of course were impossible. The poor boy is very much cut up, and his whole heart is bent upon possessing her. She is not, she can't be, indifferent to him. I am sure she would not be, if her family in the least encouraged him. Can either of these young folks have a better chance of happiness again offered to them in life? There's youth, there's mutual liking, there's wealth for them almost—only saddled with the incumbrance of an old dragoon, who won't be much in their way. Give us your good word, Barnes, and let them come

---

[6] says *E1*] said *R*

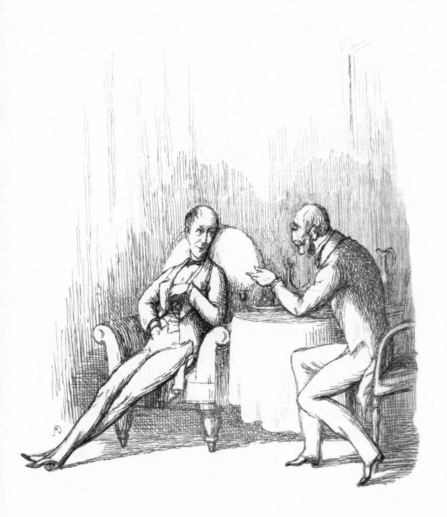

A Proposal

together; and upon my word the rest of my days will be made happy if I can eat my meal at their table."

Whilst the poor Colonel was making his appeal, Barnes had time to collect his answer; which, since in our character of historians we take leave to explain gentlemen's motives as well as record their speeches and actions, we may thus interpret. "Confound the young beggar!" thinks Barnes, then. "He will have three or four thousand a-year, will he? Hang him, but it's a good sum of money. What a fool his father is to give it away! Is he joking? No, he was always half crazy—the Colonel. Highgate seemed uncommonly sweet on her, and was always hanging about our house. Farintosh has not been brought to book yet; and perhaps neither of them will propose for her. My grandmother, I should think, won't hear of her making a low marriage, as this certainly is: but it's a pity to throw away four thousand a-year, ain't it?" All these natural calculations passed briskly through Barnes Newcome's mind, as his uncle, from the opposite side of the fireplace, implored him in the above little speech.

"My dear Colonel," said Barnes; "my dear, kind Colonel! I needn't tell you that your proposal flatters us, as much as your extraordinary generosity surprises me. I never heard anything like it—never. Could I consult my own wishes—I would at once. I would, permit me to say, from sheer admiration of your noble character, say yes, with all my heart, to your proposal. But, alas, I haven't that power."

"Is—is she engaged?" asks the Colonel, looking as blank and sad as Clive himself when Ethel had conversed with him.

"No—I cannot say engaged—though a person of the very highest rank has paid her the most marked attention. But my sister has, in a way, gone from our family, and from my influence as the head of it—an influence which I, I am sure, had most gladly exercised in your favour. My grandmother, Lady Kew, has adopted her; purposes, I believe, to leave Ethel the greater part of her fortune, upon certain conditions; and, of course, expects the—the obedience, and so forth, which is customary in such cases. By the way, Colonel, is our young *soupirant* aware that papa is pleading his cause for him?"

The Colonel said no; and Barnes lauded the caution which his uncle had displayed. It was quite as well for the young man's interests (which Sir Barnes had most tenderly at heart) that Clive Newcome should not himself move in the affair, or present himself to Lady Kew. Barnes would take the matter in hand at the proper season; the Colonel might be sure it would be most eagerly, most ardently pressed. Clive came home at this juncture, whom Barnes saluted affectionately. He and the Colonel had talked over their money business; their conversation had been most satisfactory, thank you. "Has it not, Colonel?" The three parted the very best of friends.

As Barnes Newcome professed that extreme interest for his cousin and uncle, it is odd he did not tell them that Lady Kew and Miss Ethel Newcome were at that moment within a mile of them, at her ladyship's house in Queen Street, May Fair. In the hearing of Clive's servant, Barnes did not order his brougham to drive to Queen Street, but waited until he was in Bond Street before he gave the order.

And, of course, when he entered Lady Kew's house, he straightway asked for his sister, and communicated to her the generous offer which the good Colonel had made.

You see Lady Kew was in town, and not in town. Her ladyship was but passing through, on her way from a tour of visits in the north, to another tour of visits somewhere else. The newspapers were not even off the blinds. The proprietor of the house cowered over a bed-candle and a furtive tea-pot in the back drawing-room. Lady Kew's *gens* were not here. The tall canary ones with white polls, only showed their plumage and sang in spring. The solitary wretch who takes charge of London houses, and the two servants specially affected to Lady Kew's person, were the only people in attendance. In fact her ladyship was *not* in town. And that is why, no doubt, Barnes Newcome said nothing about her being there.

Chapter XIV.

FAMILY SECRETS.

HE figure cowering over the furtive tea-pot glowered grimly at Barnes as he entered: and an old voice said, "Ho it's you!"

"I have brought you the notes, Ma'am," says Barnes—taking a packet of those documents from his pocket-book. "I could not come sooner. I have been engaged upon bank business until now."

"I daresay. You smell of smoke like a courier."

"A foreign capitalist: he would smoke. They will, Ma'am. *I* didn't smoke, upon my word."

"I don't see why you shouldn't if you like it. You will never get anything out of me whether you do or don't. How is Clara? Is she gone to the country with the children? Newcome is the best place for her."

"Doctor Bambury thinks she can move in a fortnight. The boy has had a little——"

"A little fiddlestick! I tell you it is she who likes to stay, and makes that fool, Bambury, advise her not going away. I tell you to send her to Newcome. The air is good for her."

"By that confounded smoky town, my dear Lady Kew?"

"And invite your mother and little brothers and sisters to stay Christmas there. The way in which you neglect them is shameful, it is, Barnes."

"Upon my word, Ma'am, I propose to manage my own affairs without your ladyship's assistance," cries[1] Barnes starting up; "and did not come

---

[1] cries *Ms E 1*] cried *R*

at this time of night to hear this kind of——"

"Of good advice—I sent for you to give it you. When I wrote to you to bring me the money I wanted, it was but a pretext—Barkins might have fetched it from the City in the morning. I want you to send Clara and the children to Newcome. They ought to go, Sir. That is why I sent for you; to tell you that. Have you been quarreling as much as usual?"

"Pretty much as usual," says Barnes drumming on his hat.

"Don't beat that devil's tattoo—you *agaçez* my poor old nerves. When Clara was given to you she was as well broke a girl as any in London."

Sir Barnes responded by a groan.

"She was as gentle, as amenable to reason, as good-natured a girl as could be—a little vacant and silly but you men like dolls for your wives—and now in three years you have utterly spoiled her. She's restive, she's artful, she flies into rages, she fights you and beats you. He! He! and that comes of your beating her!"

"I didn't come to hear this, Ma'am," says Barnes livid with rage.

"You struck her, you know you did, Sir Barnes Newcome. She rushed over to me last year on the night you did it—you know she did . . . ."

"Great God, Ma'am! You know the provocation!" screams Barnes.

"Provocation or not, I don't say. But from that moment she has beat you. You fool, to write her a letter and ask her pardon! If I had been a man I would rather have strangled my wife, than have humiliated myself so before her. She will never forgive that blow."

"I was mad when I did it: and she drove me mad," says Barnes. "She has the temper of a fiend and the ingenuity of the devil. In two years an entire change has come over her. If I had used a knife to her I should not have been surprised. But it is not with you to reproach me about Clara. Your ladyship found her for me."

"And you spoilt her after she was found, Sir. She told me part of her story that night she came to me. I know it is true, Barnes. You have treated her dreadfully, Sir."

"I know that she makes my life miserable and there is no help for it," says Barnes grinding a curse between his teeth. "Well, well, no more about this. How is Ethel. Gone to sleep after her journey? What do you think, Ma'am, I have brought for her?—A proposal."

"*Bon Dieu!* You don't mean to say Charles Belsize was in earnest!" cries the Dowager. "I always thought it was a—"

"It is not from Lord Highgate, Ma'am," Sir Barnes said gloomily. "It is some time since I have known that he was not in earnest—and he knows that I am, now."

"Gracious goodness! You have not come to blows with him too?[2] That would be the very thing to make the world talk," says the Dowager with some anxiety.

"No,[3] answers Barnes. "He knows well enough that there can be no open rupture. We had some words the other day at a dinner he gave at

---

[2] You have not . . . too? *Ms*] come to blows with him, too? You have not? *E1* [misplaced manuscript insertion]

[3] "No," *E1*] "No —— him," *Ms*

his own house—Colonel Newcome and that young beggar, Clive, and that fool, Mr. Hobson, were there. Lord Highgate was confoundedly insolent. He told me that I did not dare to quarrel with him because of the account he kept at our house. I should like to have massacred him! She has told him that I struck her—the insolent brute!—he says he will tell it at my clubs; and threatens personal violence to me there if I do it again. Lady Kew, I'm not safe from that man and that woman," cries poor Barnes in an agony of terror.

"Fighting is Jack Belsize's business. Barnes Newcome, banking is your's luckily," said the Dowager. "As old Lord Highgate was to die, and his eldest son too, it is a pity certainly they had not died a year or two earlier, and left poor Clara and Charles to come together. You should have married some woman in the serious way: my daughter Walham could have found you one. Frank, I am told, and his wife go on very sweetly together; her mother-in-law governs the whole family. They have turned the theatre back into a chapel again: they have six little ploughboys dressed in surplices to sing the service: and Frank and the Vicar of Kewbury play at cricket with them on holydays.—Stay—why should not Clara go to Kewbury?"

"She and her sister have quarreled about this very affair with Lord Highgate. Some time ago it appears they had words about it. And when I told Kew that bygones had best be bygones, that Highgate was very sweet upon Ethel now and that I did not choose to lose such a good account as his— Kew was very insolent to me; his conduct was blackguardly, Ma'am—quite blackguardedly, and you may be sure but for our relationship I would have called him to—"

Here the talk between Barnes and his ancestress was interrupted by the appearance of Miss Ethel Newcome, taper in hand, who descended from the upper-regions envelloped in a shawl.

"How do you do, Barnes! How is Clara? I long to see my little nephew. Is he like his pretty papa?" cries the young lady giving her fair cheek to her brother.

"Scotland has agreed with our Newcome rose," says Barnes gallantly. "My dear Ethel, I never saw you in greater beauty."

"By the light of one bed-room candle! What should I be if the whole room were lighted? You would see my face then was covered all over with wrinkles and quite pale and wobegone with the dreariness of the Scotch journey. O, what a time we have spent!—Haven't we? Grandmamma! I never wish to go to a great Castle again; above all I never wish to go to a[4] little shooting-box. Scotland may be very well for men—but for women— allow me to go to Paris when next there is talk of a Scotch expedition. I had rather be in a boarding-school in the Champs Elysées than in the finest castle in the Highlands. If it had not been for a blessed quarrel with Fanny Follington, I think I should have died at Glen Shorthorn. Have you seen my dear dear uncle, the Colonel? When did he arrive?"

"Is he come? Why is he come?" asks Lady Kew.

---

[4] go to a *E1*] go a *Ms*

"Is he come? Look here, Grandmamma! did you ever see such a darling shawl! I found it in a packet in my room."

"Well it is beautiful—" cries the Dowager bending her ancient nose over the web. "Your Colonel is a *galant homme.* That must be said of him; and in this does not quite take after the rest of the family, hum hum. Is he going away again soon?"

"He has made a fortune—a very considerable fortune for a man in that rank of[5] life," says Sir Barnes. "He cannot have less than sixty thousand pounds."

"Is that much?" asks Ethel.

"Not in England at our rate of interest—but his money is in India where he gets a great per centage. His income must be five or six thousand pounds, Ma'am," says Barnes, turning to Lady Kew.

"A few of the Indians were in society in my time, my dear," says Lady Kew musingly. "My father has often talked to me about Barwell of Stanstead and his house in St. Jeames's Square—the man who ordered 'more curricles' when there were not carriages enough for his guests. I was taken to Mr. Hastings's trial. It was very stupid and long. The young man, the painter, I suppose will leave his paint-pots now and set up as a gentleman. I suppose they were very poor; or his father would not have put him to such a profession. Barnes, why did you not make him a clerk in the bank and save him from the humiliation?"

"Humiliation! Why he is proud of it. My uncle is as proud as a Plantagenet; though he is as humble as—as what? Give me a simile, Barnes. Do you know what my quarrel with Fanny Follington was about? She said we were not descended from the Barber-Surgeon and laughed at the Battle of Bosworth. She says our great-grandfather was a weaver. *Was* he a weaver?"

"How should I know? and what on earth does it matter, my child. Except the Gaunts, the Howards, and one or two more—there is scarcely any good blood in England. You are lucky in sharing some of mine. My poor Lord Kew's grandfather was an apothecary at Hampton Court: and founded the family by giving a dose of rhubarb to Queen Caroline. As a rule, nobody is of good[6] family. Didn't that young man—that son of the Colonel's—go about last year? How did he get in society? Where did we meet him? Oh!— at Baden—yes!—when Barnes was courting and my grandson—yes, my grandson acted so wickedly—" Here she began to cough: and to tremble so, that her old stick shook under her hand. "Ring the bell for Ross. Ross, I will go to bed. Go you too, Ethel. You have been travelling enough to-day."

"Her memory seems to fail her a little," Ethel whispered to her brother— "or she will only remember what she wishes—Don't you see that she has grown very much older?"

"I will be with her in the morning. I have business with her," said Barnes.

"Good night. Give my love to Clara and kiss the little ones for me. Have you done what you promised me, Barnes?"

"What?"

---

[5] of *Ms*] in *E1*

[6] of good *Ms*] of a good *E1*

"To be—to be kind to Clara. Don't say cruel things to her. She has a high spirit and she feels them though she says nothing."

"*Doesn't* she?" said Barnes grimly.

"Ah, Barnes. Be gentle with her! Seldom as I saw you together when I lived with you in the Spring, I could see that you were harsh though she affected to laugh when she spoke of your conduct to her. Be kind. I am sure it is the best, Barnes, better than all the wit in the world. Look at Grandmamma, how witty she was and is, what a reputation she had, how people were afraid of her—and see her now—quite alone."

"I'll see her in the morning quite alone, my dear," says Barnes waving a little gloved hand. "Bye Bye!" And his brougham drove away. While Ethel Newcome had been under her brother's roof, where I and friend Clive and scores of others had been smartly entertained, there had been quarrels and recriminations, misery and heart-burning, cruel words and shameful struggles, the wretched combatants in which appeared before the world with smiling faces; resuming their battles[7] when the feast was concluded and the company gone.

On the next morning when Barnes came to visit his grandmother, Miss Newcome was gone away to see her sister-in-law, Lady Kew said, with whom she was going to pass the morning; so Barnes and Lady Kew had an uninterrupted *tête-à-tête* in which the former acquainted the old lady with the proposal which Colonel Newcome had made to him on the previous night.

Lady Kew wondered what the Impudence of the world would come to. An artist propose for Ethel! One of her footmen might propose next and she supposed Barnes would bring the message. "The father came and proposed for this young painter, and you didn't order him out of the room!"

Barnes laughed—"The Colonel is one of my constituents. I can't afford to order the[8] Bundelcund Banking Company out of its[9] own room."

"You did not tell Ethel this pretty news, I suppose?"

"Of course I didn't tell Ethel—Nor did I tell the Colonel that Ethel was in London. He fancies her in Scotland with your ladyship at this moment."

"I wish the Colonel were at Calcutta and his son with him. I wish he was in the Ganges. I wish he was under Juggernaut's car," cried the old lady. "How much money has the wretch really got? If he is of importance to the bank of course you must keep well with him. Five thousand a year and he says he will settle it all on his son? He must be crazy. There is nothing some of these people will not do, no sacrifice they will not make, to ally themselves with good families. Certainly you must remain on good terms with him and his bank. And we must say nothing of the business to Ethel, and trot out of town as quickly as we can. Let me see. We go to Drummington on Saturday. This is Tuesday. Barkins, you will keep

7 battles *Ms*] battle *E1*
8 the *Ms E1*] one of the *R*
9 of its *E1*] its *Ms*

the front drawing-room shutters shut and remember we are not in town, unless Lady Glenlivat or Lord Farintosh should call."

"Do you think Farintosh will—will call, Ma'am?" asks[1] Sir Barnes demurely.

"He will be going through to Newmarket. He has been where we have been at two or three places in Scotland," replies the lady with equal gravity. "His poor mother wishes him to give up his bachelor's life—as well she may—for you young men are terribly dissipated. Rossmont is quite a regal place. His Norfolk house is not inferior. A young man of that station ought to marry, and live at his places; and be an example to his people instead of frittering away his time at Paris and Vienna amongst the most odious company."

"Is he going to Drummington?" asks the grandson.

"I believe he has been invited. We shall go to Paris for November, he probably will be there," answers[2] the Dowager casually: "and tired of the dissipated life he has been leading, let us hope he will mend his ways and find a virtuous well-bred young woman to keep him right." With this her ladyship's apothecary is announced, and her banker and grandson takes his leave.

Sir Barnes walked into the City with his umbrella, read his letters, conferred with his partners and confidential clerks; and[3] was for a while not the exasperated husband or the affectionate brother or the amiable grandson, but the shrewd brisk banker engaged entirely with his business. Presently he has occasion to go on 'Change or elsewhere to confer with brother Capitalists, and in Cornhill behold he meets his uncle, Colonel Newcome, riding towards the India House, a groom behind him.

The Colonel springs off his horse; and Barnes greets him in the blandest manner. "Have you any news for me, Barnes?" cries the officer.

"The accounts from Calcutta are remarkably good. That cotton is of[4] admirable quality really. Mr. Briggs of our house who knows cotton as well as any man in England says—"

"It's not the cotton, my dear Sir Barnes," cries the other.

"The bills are perfectly good—there's no sort of difficulty about them. Our house will take half a million of 'em if—"

"You are talking of bills and I am thinking of poor Clive," the Colonel interposes. "I wish you could give me good[5] news for him, Barnes."

"I wish I could! I heartily trust I[6] may some day. My good wishes you know are enlisted in your son's behalf," cries Barnes gallantly. "Droll place to talk sentiment in—Cornhill, isn't it? But Ethel as I told you is in the hands of higher powers, and we must conciliate Lady Kew if we can. She has always spoken very highly of Clive—very."

"Had I not best go to her?" asks the Colonel.

[1] asks *Ms E1*] asked *R*
[2] answers *Ms*] answered *E1*
[3] and *Ms*] [omitted] *E1*
[4] is of *E1*] is *Ms*
[5] good *E1*] any good *Ms*
[6] I *Ms*] that I *E1*

"Into the north? my good Sir. She is—ah—she is travelling about. I think you had best depend upon me. Good morning. In the City we have no hearts you know, Colonel. Be sure you shall hear from me as soon as Lady Kew and Ethel come to town."

And the Banker hurried away shaking his finger-tips to his uncle, and leaving the good Colonel utterly surprized at his statements. For the fact is the Colonel knew that Lady Kew was in London, having been apprised of the circumstance in the simplest manner in the world, namely by a note from Miss Ethel which billet he had in his pocket whilst he was talking with the head of the house of Hobson Brothers.

"My dear Uncle" (the note said) "How glad I shall be to see you! How shall I thank you for the beautiful Shawl, and the kind, kind remembrance of me? I found your present yesterday evening on our arrival from the North. We are only here *en passant* and see *nobody* in Queen Street but Barnes, who has just been about business and he does not count, you know. I shall go and see Clara to-morrow and make her take me to see your pretty friend, Mrs. Pendennis. How glad I should be if you *happened* to pay Mrs. P. a visit *about two*! Good night. I thank you a thousand times and am always your affectionate—   E.

"Queen Street. Tuesday night. *Twelve o'clock.*"

This note came to Colonel Newcome's breakfast-table, and he smothered the exclamation of wonder which was rising to his lips, not choosing to provoke the questions of Clive who sate opposite to him. Clive's father was in a woful perplexity all that forenoon. Tuesday night, twelve o'clock! thought he. Why, Barnes must have gone to his grandmother from my dinner-table: and he told me she was out of town and said so again just now when we met in the City. (The Colonel was riding towards Richmond at this time.) What cause had the young man to tell me these lies? Lady Kew may not wish to be at home for me but need Barnes Newcome say what is untrue to mislead me? The fellow actually went away simpering and kissing his hand to me with a falsehood on his lips! What a pretty villain! A fellow would deserve and has got a horse-whipping for less. And to think of a Newcome doing this to his own flesh and blood;—a young Judas! Very sad and bewildered, the Colonel rode towards Richmond where he was to happen to call on Mrs. Pendennis.

It was not much of a fib that Barnes had told. Lady Kew announcing that she was out of town, her grandson no doubt thought himself justified in saying so, as any other of her servants would have done. But if he had recollected how Ethel came down with the Colonel's shawl on her shoulders, how it was possible she might have written to thank her uncle, surely Barnes Newcome would not have pulled that unlucky long bow. The Banker had other things to think of than Ethel and her shawl.

When Thomas Newcome dismounted at the door of Honeymoon Cottage, Richmond, the temporary residence of A. Pendennis, Esq.,—one of the handsomest young women in England ran into the passage with outstretched arms, called him her dear old uncle, and gave him two kisses that I daresay brought blushes on his lean sun-burnt cheeks. Ethel clung always to his affection. She wanted that man rather than any other in the whole world to think well of her. When she was with him, she was the amiable and simple, the loving impetuous creature of old times. She chose to think of no other. Worldliness, heartlessness, eager scheming, cold flirtations, Marquis-hunting and the like disappeared for a while—and were not, as she sate at that honest man's side. Oh me! that we should have to record such charges against Ethel Newcome!

He was come home for good now? He would never leave that boy he spoiled so who was a good boy too: she wished she could see him oftener. At Paris at Madame de Florac's—"I found out all about Madame de Florac, Sir!" says Miss Ethel with a laugh: "we[7] used often to meet there.[8] And here sometimes in London. But in London it was different. You know what peculiar notions some people have; and as I live with Grandmamma who is most kind to me and my brothers—of course I must obey her and see her friends rather than my own. She likes going out into the world and I am bound in duty to go with her," &c. &c. Thus the young lady went on talking, defending herself whom nobody attacked, protesting her dislike to gaiety and dissipation—you would have fancied her an[9] artless young country lass only longing to trip back to her village, milk her cows at sunrise and sit spinning of winter evenings by the fire.

"Why do you come and spoil my tête-à-tête with my uncle, Mr. Pendennis!" cries the young lady to the master of the house who happens to enter. "Of all the men in the world the one I like best to talk to! Does he not[1] look younger than when he went to India? When Clive marries that pretty little Miss Mackenzie, you will marry again, Uncle—and I will be jealous of your wife."

"Did Barnes tell you that we had met last night, my dear?" asks the Colonel.

"Not one word. Your shawl and your dear kind note told me you were come. Why did not Barnes tell us? Why do you look so grave?"

"He has not told her that I was here and would have me believe her absent," thought Newcome as his countenance fell. "Shall I give her my own message; and plead my poor boy's cause with her?" I know not whether he was about to lay his suit before her: he said himself subsequently that his mind was not made up, but at this juncture, a procession of nurses and babies made their appearance, followed by[2] the two mothers who had been comparing their mutual prodigies (each lady having her own private opinion)—Lady Clara and my wife—the latter for once gracious to Lady Clara Newcome in consideration of the infantine company with which she came to visit Mrs. Pendennis.

Luncheon was served presently. The carriage of the Newcomes drove away, my wife smilingly pardoning Ethel for the assignation which the young person had made at our house. And when those ladies were gone, our good Colonel held a council of war with us, his two friends; and told

7 we *E1*] they *Ms*
8 meet there. *E1*] meet. *Ms*
9 fancied her an *E1*] fancied an *Ms*
1 world the one . . . he not *E1*] world I like to talk best to! Does not he *Ms*
2 followed by *E1*] and *Ms*

us what had happened between him and Barnes on that morning, and the previous night. His offer to sacrifice every shilling of his fortune to young Clive seemed to him to be perfectly simple (though the recital of the circumstance brought tears into my wife's eyes)—he mentioned it by the way, and as a matter that was scarcely to call for comment, much less praise.

Barnes's extraordinary statements respecting Lady Kew's absence puzzled the elder Newcome; and he spoke of his nephew's conduct with much indignation. In vain I urged that her ladyship desiring to be considered absent from London, her grandson was bound to keep her secret. "Keep her secret, yes. Tell me lies, No!" cries out the Colonel. Sir Barnes's conduct was in fact indefensible though not altogether unusual—the worst deduction to be drawn from it, in my opinion, was, that Clive's chance with the young lady was but a poor one, and that Sir Barnes Newcome, inclined to keep his uncle in good humour, would therefore give him no disagreeable refusal.

Now this gentleman could no more pardon a lie than he could utter one. He would believe all and everything a man told him until deceived once, after which he never forgave. And wrath being once roused in his simple mind, and distrust firmly fixed there; his anger and prejudices gathered daily. He could see no single good quality in his opponent; and hated him with a daily increasing bitterness.

As ill luck would have it, that[3] very same evening, at his return to town, Thomas Newcome entered Bays's Club, of which at our request he had become a member during his last visit to England, and there was Sir Barnes as usual on his way homeward from the City. Barnes was writing at a table, and sealing and closing a letter as he saw the Colonel enter: he thought he had been a little inattentive and curt with his uncle in the morning; had remarked perhaps the expression of disapproval on the Colonel's countenance. He simpered up to his uncle as the latter entered the Club-room and apologised for his haste when they met in the City in the morning—all City men were so busy! "And I—I[4] have been writing about that[5] little affair, just as you came in," he said—"quite a moving letter to Lady Kew, I assure you—and I do hope and trust we shall have a favourable answer in a day or two."

"You said her ladyship was in the North, I think?" said the Colonel, drily.

"O yes—in the North—at—at Lord Wallsend's—great coal-proprietor you know."

"And your sister is with her?"

"Ethel is always with her."

"I hope you'll send her my very best remembrances," said the Colonel.

"I'll open the letter, and add 'em in a postscript," said Barnes.

"Confounded Liar!" cried the Colonel mentioning the circumstance to me afterwards. "Why does not somebody pitch him out of the bow-window."

[3] that *E1*] on that *Ms*
[4] I—I] I [new page] I *Ms*] I *E1*
[5] that *Ms E1*] this *R*

If we were in the secret of Sir Barnes Newcome's correspondence and could but peep into that particular letter to his grandmother, I daresay we should read that he had seen the Colonel who was very anxious about his darling youth's suit, but pursuant to Lady Kew's desire, Barnes had stoutly maintained that her ladyship was still in the North enjoying the genial hospitality of Lord Wallsend. That of course he should say nothing to Ethel except with Lady Kew's full permission: that he wished her a pleasant trip to ——, and was &c., &c.

Then if we could follow him, we might see him reach his Belgravian mansion and fling an angry word to his wife as she sits alone in the darkling drawing-room poring over the embers. He will ask her, probably with an oath, why the —— she is not dressed; and if she always intends to keep her company waiting? An hour hence each with a smirk, and the lady in smart raiment with flowers in her hair, will be greeting their guests as they arrive. Then will come dinner and such conversation as it brings. Then at night Sir Barnes will issue forth, cigar in mouth; to return to his own chamber at his own hour: to breakfast by himself: to go City-wards, money-getting. He will see his children once a[6] fortnight: and exchange a dozen sharp words with his wife twice in[7] that time.

More and more sad does the Lady[8] Clara become from day to day; likely[9] more to sit lonely over the fire; careless about the sarcasms of her husband; the prattle of her children. She cries sometimes over the cradle of the young heir. She is aweary, aweary. You understand, the man to whom her parents sold her does not make her happy, though she has been bought with diamonds, two carriages, several large footmen, a fine country-house with delightful gardens and conservatories, and with all this she is miserable—is it possible?

[6] once a *E1*] once in a *Ms*
[7] twice in *E1*] twice or thrice in *Ms*
[8] the Lady *E1*] Lady *Ms*
[9] likely *Ms*] liking *E1*

Chapter XV.

OT the least difficult part of Thomas Newcome's present business was to keep from his son all knowledge of the negotiation in which he was engaged on Clive's behalf. If my gentle reader has had sentimental disappointments,[1] he or she is aware that the friends who have given him most sympathy under these calamities have been persons who have had dismal histories of their own at some time of their lives, and I conclude Colonel Newcome in his early days must have suffered very cruelly in that affair of which we have a slight cognisance, or he would not have felt so very much anxiety about Clive's condition.

A few chapters back and we described the first attack and Clive's manful cure: then we had to indicate the young gentleman's relapse, and the noisy exclamations of the youth under this second outbreak of fever.[2] Why did the girl encourage him, as she certainly did? calling him back after she had dismissed him and finding pretext after pretext to see him.[3] I allow with Mrs. Grundy and most moralists that Miss Newcome's conduct in this matter was highly reprehensible: that if she did not intend to marry Clive she should have broken with him altogether; that a virtuous young woman of high principle &c. &c. having once determined to reject a suitor should separate from him utterly then and there, never give him again the least chance of a hope, or re-illume the extinguished fire in the wretch's bosom.

But coquetry, but kindness, but family affection, and a strong, very strong partiality for the rejected lover—are these not to be taken in account, and to plead as excuses for her behaviour to her cousin? The least

---

1 disappointments, *E1*] disappoints *Ms*
2 fever. *Ms*] fever—calling him back after she had dismissed him, and finding pretext after pretext to see him. *E1* [manuscript insertion misplaced]
3 did? calling ... see him. *Ms*] did? *E1*

unworthy part of her conduct some critics will say was that desire to see Clive and be well with him: as she felt the greatest regard for him the showing it was not blameable; and every flutter which she made to escape out of the meshes which the world had cast about her, was but the natural effort at liberty. It was her prudence which was wrong; and her submission wherein she was most culpable. In the early church story, do we not read how young martyrs constantly had to disobey worldly papas and mammas, who would have had them silent, and not utter their dangerous opinions? how their parents locked them up, kept them on bread and water, whipped and tortured them in order to enforce obedience?— nevertheless they would declare the truth: they would defy the gods by law established, and deliver themselves up to the lions or the tormentors. Are not there Heathen Idols enshrined among us still? Does not the world worship them and persecute those who refuse to kneel? Do not many timid souls sacrifice to them; and other bolder spirits rebel and, with rage at their hearts, bend down their stubborn knees at their Altars? See! I began by siding with Mrs. Grundy and the world, and at the next turn of the seesaw have lighted down on Ethel's side, and am disposed to think that the very best part of her conduct has been those escapades which—which right-minded persons most justly condemn. At least that a young beauty should torture a man with alternate liking and indifference; allure, dismiss, and call him back out of banishment; practise arts to please upon him, and ignore them when rebuked for her coquetry—these are surely occurrences so common in young women's history as to call for no special censure: and, if on these charges Miss Newcome is guilty; is she, of all her sex, alone in her criminality?

So Ethel and her duenna went away upon their tour of visits to mansions so splendid and among hosts and guests so polite that the present modest historian does not dare to follow them. Suffice it to say that Duke This and Earl That were according to their hospitable custom entertaining a brilliant circle of friends at their respective castles, all whose names the *Morning Post* gave, and among them those of Dow'r. Countess of Kew and Miss Newcome.

During her absence Thomas Newcome grimly awaited the result of his application to Barnes. That Baronet showed his uncle a letter or rather a postscript from Lady Kew which had probably been dictated by Barnes himself, in which the Dowager said she was greatly touched by Colonel Newcome's noble offer: that though she owned she had very different views for her granddaughter, Miss Newcome's choice of course lay with herself. Meanwhile, Lady K. and Ethel were engaged in a round of visits to the country, and there would be plenty of time to resume this subject when they came to London for the season. And lest dear Ethel's feelings should be needlessly agitated by a discussion of the subject, and the Colonel should take a fancy to write to her privately, Lady Kew gave orders that all letters from London should be dispatched under cover to her ladyship, and carefully examined the contents of the packet before Ethel received her share of the correspondence.

To write to her personally on the subject of the marriage, Thomas Newcome had determined, was not a proper course for him to pursue. "They consider themselves," says he, "above us, forsooth, in their rank of life (O mercy! what pigmies we are! and don't angels weep at the brief authority in which we dress ourselves up!—) And of course the approaches on our side must be made in regular form, and the parents of the young people must act for them. Clive is too honourable a man to wish to conduct the affair in any other way. He might try the influence of his *beaux yeux* and run off to Gretna with a girl who had nothing: but—but[4] the young lady being wealthy and his relation, Sir, we must be on the point of honour; and all the Kews in Christendom sha'n't have more pride than we in this matter."

All this time we are keeping Mr. Clive purposely in the background. His face is so wo-begone that we do not care to bring it forward in the family picture. His case is so common that surely its lugubrious symptoms need not be described at length. He works away fiercely at his pictures, and in spite of himself improves in his art. He sent "a Combat of Cavalry" and a picture of "Sir Brian the Templar carrying off Rebecca," to the British Institution this year: both of which pieces were praised in other journals besides the *Pall Mall Gazette*. He did not care for the newspaper praises. He was rather surprised when a dealer purchased his "Sir Brian the Templar." He came and went from our house a melancholy swain. He was thankful for Laura's kindness and pity. J.J.'s studio was his principal resort; and I daresay, as he set up his own easel there and worked by his friend's side; he bemoaned his lot to his sympathising friend.

Sir Barnes Newcome's family was absent from London during the winter. His mother and his brothers and sisters, his wife and his two children were gone to Newcome for Christmas. Some six weeks after seeing him, Ethel wrote her uncle a kind merry letter. They had been performing private theatricals at the Country House where she and Lady Kew were staying. "Captain Crackthorpe made an admirable Jeremy Diddler in 'Raising the Wind'—Lord Farintosh broke down lamentably as Fusbos in 'Bombastes Furioso.'" Miss Ethel had distinguished herself in both of these facetious little comedies. "I should like Clive to paint me as Miss Plainways,"[5] she wrote. "I wore a powdered front: painted my face all over wrinkles, imitated old Lady Griffin as well as I could and looked sixty at least."

Thomas Newcome wrote an answer to his fair niece's pleasant letter. Clive, he said, would be happy to bargain to paint her and nobody else but her all the days of his life; and the Colonel was sure, would admire her at sixty as much as he did now when she was forty years younger. But, determined on maintaining his appointed line of conduct respecting Miss Newcome, he carried his letter to Sir Barnes, and desired him to forward it to his sister. Sir Barnes took the note, and promised to dispatch it. The communications between him and his uncle had been very brief and cold, since the telling of those little fibs concerning old Lady Kew's visits to London, which the Baronet dismissed from his mind as soon as they were spoken, and which the good Colonel never could forgive. Barnes asked his uncle to dinner once or twice, but the Colonel was engaged. How was Barnes to know the reasons[6] of the elder's refusal? A London man, a banker, and a

---

4 but—but] but but *Ms*] but *E1*
5 Plainways," *E1*] [blank] *Ms*
6 reasons *Ms*] reason *E1*

member of Parliament has a thousand things to think of; and no time to wonder that friends refuse his invitations to dinner. Barnes continued to grin and smile most affectionately when he met the Colonel, to press his hand, to congratulate him on the last accounts from India, unconscious of the scorn and distrust with which his Senior mentally regarded him. "Old boy is doubtful about the young Cub's love affair," the Baronet may have thought. "We'll ease his old mind on that point some time hence." No doubt Barnes thought he was conducting the business very smartly and diplomatically.

I heard myself news at this period from the gallant Crackthorpe, which, being interested in my young friend's happiness, filled me with some dismay. "Our friend the painter and glazier has been hankering about our barracks at Knightsbridge" (the noble Life Guards Green had now pitched their tents in that suburb), "and pumping me about *la belle Cousine*. I don't like to break it to him—I don't really now. But it's all up with his chance I think. Those private theatricals at Fallowfield have done Farintosh's business. He used to rave about the Newcome to me, as we were riding home from hunting. He gave Bob Henchman[7] the lie who told a story which Bob got from his man, who had it from Miss Newcome's lady's maid—about—about some journey to Brighton which the cousins took—" Here Mr. Crackthorpe grinned most facetiously—"Farintosh swore he'd knock Henchman[8] down; and vows he will be the death of—will murder our friend Clive when he comes to town. As for Henchman, he was in a desperate way. He lives on the Marquis, you know; and Farintosh's anger or his marriage will be the loss of free quarters and ever so many good dinners a year to him." I did not deem it necessary to impart Crackthorpe's story to Clive, or explain to him the reason why Lord Farintosh scowled most fiercely upon the young painter, and passed him without any other sign of recognition one day as Clive and I were walking together in Pall Mall. If my lord wanted a quarrel, young Clive was not a man to baulk him; and would have been a very fierce customer to deal with, in his actual state of mind.

A pauper child in London at seven years old knows how to go to market, to fetch the beer, to pawn father's coat, to choose the largest fried fish or the nicest ham-bone, to nurse Mary Jane of three,—to conduct a hundred operations of trade or housekeeping, which a little Belgravian does not perhaps acquire in all the days of her life. Poverty and necessity force this precociousness on the poor little brat. There are children who are accomplished shop-lifters and liars almost as soon as they can toddle and speak. I daresay little Princes know the laws of etiquette as regards themselves, and the respect due to their rank at a very early period of their royal existence. Every one of us according to his degree can point to Princekins[9] of private life who are flattered and worshipped, and whose little shoes grown men kiss as soon almost as they walk upon ground.

---

[7] <Hardyman>†Henchman↓ *Ms*

[8] Henchman] Hardyman *Ms*] Honeyman *E1 R*

[9] Princekins *Ms*] the Princekins *E1*

It is a wonder what human nature will support: and that considering the amount of flattery some people are crammed with from their cradles they do not grow worse and more selfish than they are. Our poor little pauper just mentioned is dosed with Daffy's Elixir, and somehow survives the drug. Princekin or Lordkin from his earliest days has nurses, dependents, governesses, little friends, school-fellows, schoolmasters, fellow-collegians, college tutors, stewards and valets, led-captains of his suite, and women innumerable flattering him and doing him honour. The tradesman's manner which to you and me is decently respectful becomes straightway frantically servile before Princekin. Honest folks[1] at Railway Stations whisper to their families, "That's the Marquis of Farintosh," and look hard at him as he passes. Landlords cry, "This way my lord, this room for your lordship." They say at public schools Princekin is taught the beauties of equality, and thrashed into some kind of subordination. Psha! Toadeaters in pinafores surround Princekin. Do not respectable people send their children so as to be at the same school with him; don't they follow him to college: and eat his toads through life?

And as for women—O my dear friends and brethren in this vale of tears—did you ever see anything so curious, monstrous and amazing as the way in which women court Princekin when he is marriageable and pursue him with their daughters? Who was the British nobleman in old old days who brought his three daughters to the King of Mercia, that His Majesty might choose one after inspection? Mercia was but a petty province and its King in fact a Princekin. Ever since those extremely ancient and venerable times the custom exists not only in Mercia, but in all the rest of the provinces inhabited by the Angles, and before Princekins the daughters of our nobles are trotted out.

There was no day of his life which our young acquaintance the Marquis of Farintosh could remember, on which he had not been flattered; and no society which did not pay him court. At a private school he could recollect the master's wife stroking his pretty curls and treating him furtively to goodies: at college he had the tutor simpering and bowing as he swaggered over the grass-plat: old men at clubs would make way for him and fawn on him—not your mere *pique assiettes* and penniless parasites, but most respectable toad-eaters, fathers of honest families, gentlemen themselves of good station: who respected this young gentleman as one of the institutions of their country and admired the wisdom of the nation that set him to legislate over us. When Lord Farintosh walked the streets at night he felt himself like Haroun Alraschid (that is, he would have felt so had he ever heard of the Arabian potentate)—a monarch in disguise affably observing and promenading the city. And let us be sure there was a Mesrour in his train to knock at the doors for him and run the errands of this young Caliph. Of course he met with scores of men in life who neither flattered him nor would suffer his airs: but he did not like the company of such, or for the sake of truth to undergo the ordeal of being laughed at: he preferred toadies generally speaking. "I like," says he, "you know, those fellows who are always saying pleasant things, you know, and who would

---

[1] Honest folks *Ms E1*] Folks *R*

run from here to Hammersmith if I asked 'em—much better than those fellows who are always making fun of me you know." A man of his station who likes flatterers need not shut himself up: he can get plenty of society.

As for women it was his lordship's opinion that every daughter of Eve was bent upon[2] marrying him. A Scotch Marquis, an English Earl, of the best blood in the Empire, with a handsome[3] person, and a fortune of fifteen thousand a year; how could the poor creatures do otherwise than long for him? He blandly received their caresses: took their coaxing and cajolery as matters of course: and surveyed the beauties of his time as the Caliph the moonfaces of his harem. My lord intended to marry certainly. He did not care for money, nor for rank: he expected consummate beauty and talent, and some day would fling his handkerchief to the possessor of these; and place her by his side upon the Farintosh throne.

At this time there were but two or three young ladies in society endowed with the necessary qualifications or who found favour in his eyes. His lordship hesitated in his selection from these beauties. He was not in a hurry, he was not angry at the notion that Lady Kew (and Miss Newcome with her) hunted him. What else should they do but pursue an object so charming? Everybody hunted him. The other young ladies, whom we need not mention, languished after him still more longingly. He had little notes from these: presents of purses worked by them and cigar-cases embroidered with his coronet. They sang to him in cozy boudoirs—Mamma went out of the room and sister Ann forgot something in the drawing-room. They ogled him as they sang. Trembling they gave him a little foot to mount them, that they might ride on horseback with him. They tripped along by his side from the Hall to the pretty country church on Sundays. They warbled hymns; sweetly looking at him the while. Mamma whispered confidentially to him, "What an angel Cecilia is!" And so forth and so forth—with which chaff our noble bird was by no means to be caught. When he had made up his great mind, that the time was come and the woman: he was ready to give a Marchioness of Farintosh to the English nation.

Miss Newcome has been compared ere this to the statue of Huntress Diana at the Louvre, whose haughty figure and beauty, the young lady indeed somewhat resembled. I was not present when Diana—and Diana's grandmother—hunted the noble Scottish stag of whom we have just been writing; nor care to know how many times Lord Farintosh escaped, and how at last he was brought to bay and taken by his resolute pursuers. Paris, it appears, was the scene of his fall and capture. The news was no doubt well known amongst Lord Farintosh's brother dandies, among exasperated matrons and virgins in May Fair, and in polite society generally, before it came to simple Tom Newcome and his son. Not a word on the subject had Sir Barnes mentioned to the Colonel: perhaps not choosing to speak till the intelligence was authenticated, perhaps not wishing to be the bearer of tidings so painful.

Though the Colonel may have read in his *Pall Mall Gazette* a paragraph which announced an approaching MARRIAGE IN HIGH LIFE, "between a noble

---

[2] upon *Ms*] on
[3] handsome *E1*] beautiful *Ms*

young marquis and an accomplished and beautiful young lady, daughter and sister of a northern baronet," he did not know who were the fashionable persons about to be made happy nor until he received a letter from an old friend who lived at Paris was the fact conveyed to him. Here is the letter preserved by him along with all that he ever received from the same hand.

"Rue St. Dominique, St. Germain. Paris, 10 Fev.

"So behold you of return my friend! you quit for ever the sword and those arid plains where you have passed so many years of your life separated from those to whom at the commencement you held very nearly. Did it not seem once as if two hands never could unlock, so closely were they enlaced together? Ah, mine are old and feeble now; forty years have passed since the time when you used to say they were young and fair. How well I remember me of every one of those days though there is a death between me and them and it is as across a grave I review them. Yet another parting, and regrets and tears[4] are finished. *Tenez*, I do not believe them when they say there is no meeting for us afterwards there above. To what good to have seen you, friend, if we are to part here and in Heaven too? I have not altogether forgotten your language, is it not so? I remember it because it was yours and that of my happy days. I radote like an old woman as I am. M. de Florac has known my history from the commencement. May I not say after so many of years that[5] I have been faithful to him and to all my promises? When the End comes with its great absolution I shall not be sorry. One supports the combats of life, but they are long and one comes from them very wounded; ah, when shall they be over?

"You return and I salute you with wishes for parting. How much egoism![6] I have another project which I please myself to arrange. You know how I am arrived to love Clive as my own child. I very quick surprised his secret, the poor boy, when he was here it is twenty months. He looked so like you as I repeal me of you in the old time! He told me he had no hope of his beautiful cousin. I have heard of the fine marriage that one makes her. Paul, my son, has been at the English Ambassade last night and has made his congratulations to M. de Farintosh. Paul says him handsome, young, not too spiritual, rich and haughty like all, all[7] noble Montagnards.

"But it is not of M. de Farintosh I write, whose marriage without doubt has to you been announced.[8] I have a little project, very foolish, very *pet*.[9] You know Mr. the Duke of Ivry has left me guardian of his little daughter Antoinette whose *affreuse* mother no one sees more. Antoinette is pretty and good and soft and with an affectionate heart. I love her already as my Infant. I wish to bring her up and that Clive should marry her. They say you are returned very rich. What follies are these I write! In the long

---

[4] regrets and tears *Ms*] tears and regrets *E1*
[5] after . . . years that *Ms*] that after . . . years *E1* [misplaces manuscript insertion]
[6] egoism! *Ms*] egotism! *E1*
[7] all, all *Ms E1*] all *R*
[8] to you been announced. *Ms*] been announced to you. *E1*
[9] foolish, very *pet*. *Ms*] foolish, perhaps. *E1*

evenings of winter, the children escaped it is a long time from the maternal nest,—a silent old man my only company,—I live but of the past; and play with its souvenirs as the detained caress little birds, little flowers in their prisons. I was born for the happiness; my God! I have learned it in knowing you. In losing you I have lost it. It is not against the will of Heaven I oppose myself. It is man who makes himself so much of this evil and misery, this slavery, these tears, these crimes, perhaps.

"This marriage of the young Scotch marquis and the fair Ethel (I love her in spite of all and shall see her soon and congratulate her, for, do you see, I might have stopped this fine marriage and did[1] my best and more than my duty for our poor Clive) shall make itself in London next Spring, I hear. You shall assist scarcely at the ceremony: he, poor boy, shall not care to be there. Bring him to Paris to make the court to my little Antoinette: bring him to Paris to his good friend, Comtesse de Florac.[2]

"I read marvels of his works in an English journal which one sends me."

Clive was not by when this letter reached his father. Clive was in his painting-room, and lest he should meet his son, and in order to devise the best means of breaking the news to the lad, Thomas Newcome retreated out of doors; and from the Oriental he crossed Oxford Street, and from Oxford Street he stalked over the roomy pavements of Gloster[3] Place, and there he bethought him how he had neglected Mrs. Hobson Newcome of late and the interesting family of Brianstone Square. So he went to leave his card at Maria's door: her daughters, as we have said,[4] are quite grown girls.[5] If they have been lectured and learning and back-boarded and practising and using the globes and laying in a store of ologies ever since, what a deal they must know! Colonel Newcome was admitted to see his nieces and Consummate Virtue, their parent. Maria was charmed to see her brother-in-law; she greeted him with reproachful tenderness: "Why why," her fine eyes seemed to say, "have you neglected us so long?[6] Do you think because I am Wise and Gifted and good, and you are, it must be confessed, a poor creature with no education, I am not also affable? Come, let the prodigal be welcomed by his Virtuous relatives—come and lunch with us, Colonel!" He sate down accordingly to the family tiffin.

When the meal[7] was over, the mother who had matter *of importance to impart to him* besought him to go to the drawing-room, and[8] there poured out such a eulogy upon her children's qualities as fond mothers know how to utter. They knew this and they knew that. They were instructed by the most eminent professors—that wretched French woman whom you may remember here—Mademoiselle Lenoir, Maria remarked parenthetically— turned out O frightfully! She taught the girls the *worst* accent, it appears.

---

[1] did *E1*] did I did *Ms* [faulty manuscript insertion]
[2] Comtesse de Florac.] COMTESSE DE FLORAC. *E1*] Comtesse E. de Florac. *Ms*
[3] Gloster *Ms*] Gloucester *E1*
[4] daughters, as we have said, *E1*] daughters *Ms*
[5] girls. *E1*] girls since last we saw them. *Ms*
[6] neglected us so long? *Ms*] so long neglected us? *E1*
[7] the meal *E1*] <the girls retired their mother> meal *Ms*
[8] and *E1*] whither and *Ms*

Her father was *not* a Colonel. He was—O never mind! It is a mercy I got rid of that *fiendish woman* and before my precious ones knew *what* she was! And then followed details of the perfections of the two girls with occasional side-shots at Lady Ann's family just as in the old time. "Why don't you bring your boy whom I have always loved as a son, and who avoids me? Why does not Clive know his cousins? They are very different from others of his kinswomen who think but[9] of the *heartless world!*"

"I fear, Maria, there is too much truth in what you say," sighs the Colonel drumming on a book on the drawing-room table, and looking down sees it is a great, large, square, gilt peerage, open at FARINTOSH, MARQUIS OF. Fergus Angus Malcolm Mungo Roy. Marquis of Farintosh. Earl of Glenlivat in the Peerage of Scotland; also Earl of Rossmont, in that of the United Kingdom. Son of Angus Fergus Malcolm, Earl of Glenlivat, and grandson and heir of Malcolm Mungo Angus, first Marquis of Farintosh and Twenty-Fifth Earl, &c. &c.

"You have heard the news regarding Ethel?" remarks Mrs. Hobson.

"I have just heard," says the poor Colonel.

"I have a letter from Ann this morning," Maria continues—"They are of course delighted with the match. Lord Farintosh is wealthy, handsome,— has been a little wild I hear—is not such a husband as I would choose for *my* darlings but poor Brian's family have been educated to love the world: and Ethel no doubt is flattered by the prospects before her. I *have* heard that some one else was a little *épris* in that quarter. How does Clive bear the news, my dear Colonel?"

"He has long expected it," says the Colonel rising; "and I left him very cheerful at breakfast this morning."

"Send him to see us—the naughty boy!" cries Maria. "*We* don't change; we remember old times, to us he will ever be welcome!" And with this confirmation of Madame de Florac's news, Thomas Newcome walked sadly homewards.

And now Thomas Newcome had to break the news to his son; who received the shot in such a way as caused his friends and confidants to admire his high spirit. He said he had long been expecting some such announcement:—it was many months since Ethel had prepared him for it. Under her peculiar circumstances he did not see how she could act otherwise than she had done. And he narrated to the Colonel the substance of the conversation which the two young people had had together several months before in Madame de Florac's garden.

Clive's father did not tell his son of his own bootless negociation with Barnes Newcome. There was no need to recal that now; but the Colonel's wrath against his nephew exploded in conversation with me, who was the confidant of father and son in this business. Ever since that luckless day when Barnes thought proper to—to give a wrong address for Lady Kew, Thomas Newcome's anger had been growing. He smothered it yet for a while, sent a letter to Lady Ann Newcome briefly congratulating her on the choice which he had heard Miss Newcome had made: and in acknowledgment of Madame de Florac's more sentimental epistle he wrote a reply

[9] but *Ms R*] best *E1*

which has not been preserved, but in which he bade her rebuke Miss New-come for not having answered him when he wrote to her and not having acquainted her old uncle with her projected Union.

To this message Ethel wrote back a brief, hurried reply. It said:—

"I saw Madame de Florac last night at her daughter's reception; and she gave me my dear uncle's messages. *Yes, the news is true* which you have heard from Madame de Florac and in Brianstone Square. I did not like to write it to you because I know one whom I regard as a brother (and a great, great deal better), and to whom I know it will give pain. He knows that I have done *my duty;* and *why* I have acted as I have done. God bless him and his dear father.

"What is this about a letter which[1] I never answered? Grandmamma knows nothing about a letter. Mamma has enclosed to me that which you wrote to her but there has been *no letter* from T. N. to his sincere and affec-tionate   E.N.

"Rue de Rivoli. Friday."

This was too much, and the cup of Thomas Newcome's wrath over-flowed. Barnes had lied about Ethel's visit to London: Barnes had lied in saying that he delivered the message with which his uncle charged him: Barnes had lied about the letter which he had received and never sent! With these accusations firmly proven in his mind, against his nephew, the Colonel went down to confront that sinner.

Wherever he should find Barnes, Thomas Newcome was determined to tell him his mind. Should they meet on the steps of a church, on the flags of 'Change, or in the newspaper-room at Bays's at evening-paper time, when men most do congregate, Thomas the Colonel was determined upon exposing and chastising his father's grandson. With Ethel's letter in his pocket he took his way into the City—penetrated into the unsuspecting back parlour of Hobson's bank and was disappointed at first at only finding his half-brother Hobson there engaged over his newspaper. The Colonel signified his wish to see Sir Barnes Newcome: Sir Barnes was not come in yet. "You've heard about the marriage?" says Hobson. "Great news for the Barnes's, ain't it? The head of the house is as proud as a peacock about it—Said he was going out to Samuels, the diamond-merchants—going to make his sister some uncommon fine present. Jolly to be uncle to a marquis, ain't it, Colonel? I'll have nothing under a duke for my girls. I say, I know whose nose is out of joint. But young fellows get over these things and Clive won't die this time, I daresay."

While Hobson Newcome made these satiric and facetious remarks, his half-brother paced up and down the glass[2] parlour scowling over the panes into the bank where the busy young clerks sate before their ledgers. At last he gave an "Ah" as of satisfaction. Indeed he had seen Sir Barnes Newcome enter into the bank.

The Baronet stopped and spoke with a clerk, and presently entered, followed by that young gentleman into his private parlour. Barnes tried to grin when he saw his uncle and held out his hand to greet the Colonel but

---

[1] which *E1*] that *Ms*
[2] glass *Ms E1*] dark *R*

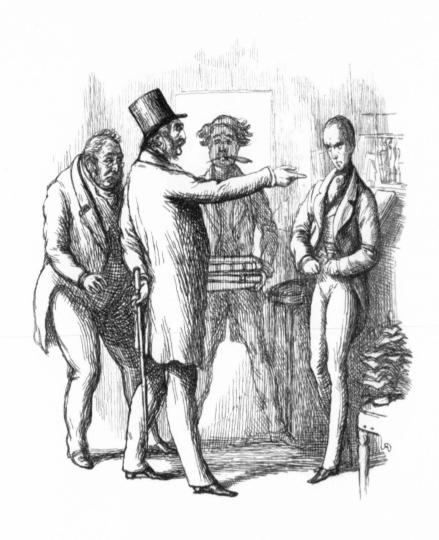

THE COLONEL TELLS SIR BARNES A BIT OF HIS MIND

the Colonel put both his behind his back; that which carried his faithful bamboo cane shook nervously. Barnes was aware that the Colonel had the news. "I was going to—to write to you this morning with—with some intelligence that I am—very—very sorry to give—"

"This young gentleman is one of your clerks?" asked[3] Thomas Newcome blandly.

"Yes—Mr. Boltby who has your private account. This is Colonel Newcome, Mr. Boltby;" says Sir Barnes in some wonder.

"Mr. Boltby, brother Hobson, you heard what Sir Barnes Newcome said just now respecting certain intelligence which he grieved to give me?"

At this the three other gentlemen respectively wore looks of amazement.[4]

"Allow me to say in your presence that I don't believe one single word Sir Barnes Newcome says. When[5] he tells me that he is very sorry for some intelligence he has to communicate, he[6] lies, Mr. Boltby, he is very glad. I made up my mind that in whatsoever company I met him and on the very first day I found him—Hold your tongue, Sir—you shall speak afterwards and tell more lies when I have done—I made up my mind, I say, that on the very first occasion I would tell Sir Barnes Newcome that he was a liar and a cheat. He takes charge of letters and keeps them back. Did you break the seal, Sir? There was nothing to steal in my letter to Miss Newcome;—He tells me people are out of town whom he goes to see in the next street after leaving my table, and whom I see myself half an hour before he lies to me about their absence."

"D— you, go out and don't stand staring there, you booby!" screams out Sir Barnes to the clerk—"Stop, Boltby—Colonel Newcome,—unless you leave this room I shall—I shall."

"You shall call a policeman—send for the gentleman and I will tell the Lord Mayor what I think of Sir Barnes Newcome, Baronet—Mr. Boltby! shall we have the constable in?"

"Sir—you are an old man, and my father's brother or you know very well I would . . ."

"You would what, Sir! Upon my word, Barnes Newcome (here the Colonel's two hands and the bamboo cane came from the rear and formed in front), but that you are my father's grandson—after a menace like that—I would take you out and cane you in the presence of your clerks. I repeat, Sir, I[7] consider you guilty of treachery, falsehood and knavery. And if ever I see you at Bays's Club, I will make the same statement to your acquaintance at the west end of the town. A man of your baseness ought to be known, Sir; and it shall be my business to make men of honour aware of your character. Mr. Boltby, will you have the kindness to make out my account? Sir Barnes Newcome, for fear of consequences that I should deplore, I recommend you to keep a wide berth of me, Sir." And the Colonel twirled his

[3] asked *E1*] ask *Ms*] asks *R*
[4] amazement *E1*] amusement. *Ms*
[5] says. When *Ms*] says, when *E1*
[6] communicate, he *Ms*] communicate. He *E1*
[7] I *Ms*] that I *E1*

mustachios and waved his cane in an ominous manner, as[8] Barnes started back spontaneously out of its dangerous circle.

What Mr. Boltby's sentiments may have been regarding this extraordinary scene in which his principal cut so sorry a figure—whether he narrated the conversation to other gentlemen connected with the establishment of Hobson Brothers or prudently kept it to himself, I cannot say: having no means of pursuing Mr. B.'s subsequent career. He speedily quitted his desk at Hobson Brothers and let us presume that Barnes *thought* Mr. B. had told all the other clerks of the avuncular quarrel. That conviction will make us imagine Barnes still more comfortable. Hobson Newcome no doubt was rejoiced at Barnes's discomfiture; he had been insolent and domineering beyond measure of late to his vulgar good-natured uncle, whereas after the above interview with the Colonel, he became very humble and quiet in his demeanour; and for a long, long time never said a rude word. Nay, I fear Hobson must have carried an account of the transaction to Mrs. Hobson and the circle in Brianstone Square: for Sam Newcome, now entered at Cambridge, called the Baronet "Barnes" quite familiarly, asked after Clara and Ethel: and requested a small loan of Barnes.

Of[9] course the story did not get wind at Bays's: of course Tom Eaves did not know all about it and say that Sir Barnes had been beaten black and blue. Having been treated very ill by the committee in a complaint which he made about the Club-cookery, Sir[1] Barnes Newcome never came to Bays's: and at the end of the year took off his name from the lists of the club.

Sir Barnes though a little taken aback in the morning, and not ready with an impromptu reply to the Colonel and his cane, could not allow the occurrence to pass without a protest and indited a letter which Thomas Newcome kept along with some others previously quoted by the compiler of the present Memoirs. It is as follows.

"Colonel Newcome, C.B. Private.

Belgrave St., Feb. 15, 18—

"Sir.

"The incredible insolence and violence of your behaviour to-day (inspired by whatever causes or mistakes of your own)—cannot be passed without some comment on my part. I laid before a friend of your own profession a statement of the words which you applied to me in the presence of my partner and one of my clerks this morning, and my adviser is of opinion that considering the relationship unhappily subsisting between us, I can take no notice of insults, for which you knew when you uttered them I could not call you to account.

("There is some truth in that," said the Colonel. "He couldn't fight, you know: but then he was such a liar that I could not help speaking my mind.")

[8] as *Ms*] and *E1*
[9] Barnes. ¶Of *E1*] Barnes having had the devil's own ill luck at blind hookey. Of *Ms*
[1] Having … Sir *E1*] Sir *Ms*

"I gathered from the brutal language which you thought fit to employ towards a disarmed man,[2] the ground of one of your monstrous accusations against me, that I deceived you in stating that my relative, Lady Kew, was in the country when in fact she was at her house in London.

"To this absurd charge I at once plead guilty. The venerable lady in question was passing through London[3] where she desired to be free from intrusion. At her ladyship's wish I stated that she was out of town; and *would* under the same circumstances unhesitatingly make the same statement. Your slight acquaintance with the person in question did not warrant that you should force yourself on her privacy, as you would doubtless know were you more familiar with the customs of the society in which she moves.

"I declare upon my honour as a gentleman that I gave her the message which I promised to deliver from you, and also that I transmitted a letter with which you entrusted me; and repel with scorn and indignation the charges which you were pleased to bring against me; as I treat with contempt the language and the threats which you thought fit to employ.

"Our books show the amount of x£ xs xd to your credit which you will be good enough to withdraw at your earliest convenience; as of course all intercourse must cease henceforth between you and

"Yours, &c.,

"*B. Newcome. Newcome.*"

"I think, Sir, he doesn't make out a bad case," Mr. Pendennis remarked to the Colonel who showed him this majestic letter.

"It would be a good case if I believed a single word of it, Arthur," replied my friend placidly twirling the old grey moustache. "If you were to say so and so, and say that I had brought false charges against you, I should cry *mea culpa* and apologise with all my heart. But as I have a perfect conviction that every word this fellow says is a lie: what is the use of arguing any more about the matter? I would not believe him if he brought twenty other liars as witnesses, and if he lied till he was black in the face. Give me the walnuts. I wonder who Sir Barnes's military friend was."

Barnes's military friend was our gallant acquaintance General Sir George Tufto, K.C.B.; who a short while afterwards talked over the quarrel with the Colonel; and manfully told him that (in Sir George's opinion,) he was wrong. "The little beggar behaved very well I thought in the first business. You bullied him so—and in the front of his regiment, too—that it was almost past bearing and when he deplored with tears in his eyes, almost—the little humbug!—that his relationship prevented him calling you out, ecod, I believed him! It was in the second affair that poor little Barney showed he was a cocktail."

"What second affair?" asked Thomas Newcome.

"Don't you know? Ho ho this is famous!" cries Sir George. "Why, Sir, two days after your business, he comes to me with another letter and a face as long as my mare's, by Jove. And that letter, Newcome, was from your young 'un. Stop, here it is!" and from his padded bosom General Sir George Tufto drew a pocket-book, and from the pocket-book a copy of a

[2] man, *E1*] man: that *Ms*
[3] London *E1*] to London *Ms*

letter inscribed, Clive Newcome, Esq., to Sir B. N. Newcome—"There's no mistake about *your* fellow—Colonel—no, —— him:" and the man of war fired a volley of oaths as a salute to Clive. And[4] the Colonel, on horseback, riding by the other cavalry officer's side, read as follows:—

"George[5] St., Hanover Square. February 16.

"Sir.

"Colonel Newcome this morning showed me a letter bearing your signature in which you state 1. that Colonel Newcome has uttered calumnious and insolent charges against you. 2. That Colonel Newcome so spoke knowing that you could take no notice of his charges of falsehood and[6] treachery on account of the relationship subsisting between you.

"Your statements would evidently imply that Colonel Newcome has been guilty of ungentlemanlike conduct and of cowardice towards you.

"As there can be no reason why *we* should not meet in any manner that you desire, I here beg leave to state on my own part that I fully coincide with Colonel Newcome in his opinion that you have been guilty of falsehood and treachery; and that the charge of cowardice which you dare to make against a gentleman of his tried honour and courage, is another wilful and cowardly falsehood on your part.

"And I hope you will refer the bearer of this note, my friend, Mr. George Warrington of the Upper Temple, to the military gentleman whom you consulted in respect to the just charges of Colonel Newcome. Waiting a prompt reply,

"Believe me, Sir,
"Your obedient Servant
"Clive Newcome.

"Sir Barnes Newcome Newcome, Bart., M.P. &c., &c."

"What a blunderhead I am!" cries the Colonel with delight on his countenance, spite of his professed repentance. "It never once entered my head that the youngster would take any part in the affair. I showed him his cousin's letter casually just to amuse him, I think, for he has been deuced low lately about—about a young man's scrape that he has got into. And he must have gone off and dispatched his challenge straightway. I recollect he appeared uncommonly brisk at breakfast the next morning. And so you say, General, the Baronet did not like the *poulet?*"[7]

"By no means—never saw a fellow show such a confounded whitefeather. At first I congratulated him, thinking your boy's offer must please him, as it would have pleased any fellow in our time to have a shot. Dammy!—but I was mistaken in my man. He entered into some confounded long-winded story about a marriage you wanted to make with that infernal pretty sister of his who is going to marry young Farintosh, and how you were in a rage because the scheme fell to the ground, and how a family

[4] And *Ms*] ¶And *E1*
[5] "George *E1*] "Clive Newcome, Esq., to Sir Barnes Newcome Newcome Bart. ¶"George *Ms*
[6] and *E1*] [omitted] *Ms*
[7] *poulet?*" *E1*] *froulet?*" *Ms*

duel might occasion unpleasantries to Miss Newcome—though I showed
him how this could be most easily avoided and that the lady's name need
never appear in the transaction. 'Confound it, Sir Barnes,' says I, 'I recollect this boy when he was a youngster throwing a glass of wine in your face!
We'll put it upon that, and say it's an old feud between you.' He turned
quite pale, and he said your fellow had apologised for the glass of wine."

"Yes," said the Colonel sadly, "my boy apologised for the glass of wine.
It is curious how we have disliked that Barnes ever since we set eyes on
him."

"Well, Newcome!" Sir George resumed as his mettled charger suddenly
jumped and curvetted displaying the padded warrior's cavalry-seat to
perfection—"quiet, old lady! easy, my dear!—Well, Sir, when I found the
little beggar turning tail in this way I said to him, 'Dash me, Sir, if you
don't want me, why the dash do you send for me,[8] dash me? Yesterday
you talked as if you would bite the Colonel's head off, and to-day when his
son offers you every accommodation, by dash, Sir, you're afraid to meet
him. It's my belief you had better send for a policeman. A 22 is your man,
Sir Barnes Newcome.' And with that I turned on my heel and left him.
And the fellow went off to Newcome that very night."

"A poor devil can't command courage, General," said the Colonel quite
peaceably, "any more than he can make himself six feet high."

"Then why the dash did the beggar send for *me*?" called out General Sir
George Tufto in a loud and resolute voice and presently the two officers
parted company.

When the Colonel reached home, Mr. Warrington and Mr. Pendennis
happened to be on a visit to Clive and all three were in the young fellow's
painting-room. We knew our lad was unhappy and did our little best to
amuse and console him. The Colonel came in. It was in the dark February
days: we had lighted gas in the Studio—Clive had made a sketch from some
favourite verses of mine and George's, those charming lines of Scott's:—

> "He turned his charger as he spake
> Beside the river-shore;
> He gave his bridle-rein a shake
> With adieu for ever more,
> My dear!
> Adieu for ever more."

Thomas Newcome held up a finger at Warrington, and he came up to
the picture and looked at it and George and I trolled out[9]

> "Adieu for ever more,
> My dear!
> Adieu for ever more!"

From the picture the brave old Colonel turned to the painter, regarding
his son with a look of beautiful inexpressible affection. And he laid his hand

[8] for me, *E1*] for, *Ms*
[9] out *E1*] out the Chorus *Ms*

on his son's shoulder; and smiled, and stroked Clive's yellow moustache.

"And—and did Barnes send no answer to—that letter you wrote him?" he said slowly.

Clive broke out into a laugh that was almost a sob. He took both his father's hands. "My dear, dear old father!" says he, "what a—what an—old—trump you are!" My eyes were so dim I could hardly see the two men as they embraced.

Chapter XVI.

LIVE presently answered the question which his father put to him in the last chapter, by producing from the ledge of his easel a crumpled paper, full of Cavendish now, but on which was written Sir Barnes Newcome's reply to his cousin's polite invitation.

Sir Barnes Newcome wrote that he thought a reference to a friend was quite unnecessary in the most disagreeable and painful dispute in which Mr. Clive desired to interfere as a principal; that the reasons which prevented Sir Barnes from taking notice of Colonel Newcome's shameful and ungentlemanlike conduct applied equally, as Mr. Clive Newcome very well knew, to himself; that if farther insult was offered or outrage attempted, Sir Barnes should resort to the police for protection: that he was about to quit London and certainly should not delay his departure on account of Mr. Clive Newcome's monstrous proceedings; and that he desired to take leave of an odious subject, as of an individual whom he had striven to treat with kindness; but from whom from youth upwards Sir Barnes Newcome had received nothing but insolence, enmity and ill-will.

"He is an ill man to offend," remarked Mr. Pendennis. "I don't think he has ever forgiven that claret, Clive."

"Pooh! the feud dates from long before that," said Clive, "Barnes wanted to lick me when I was a boy and I declined: in fact, I think he had rather the worst of it. But then I operated freely on his shins and that wasn't fair in war, you know."

"Heaven forgive me," cries the Colonel, "I have always felt the fellow was my enemy: and my mind is relieved now war is declared. It has been a kind of hypocrisy with me to shake his hand and eat his dinner. When I trusted him it was against my better instinct; and I have been struggling against it these ten years thinking it was a wicked prejudice and ought to be overcome."

"Why should we overcome such instincts?" asks Mr. Warrington. "Why shouldn't we hate what is hateful in people and scorn what is mean? From what friend Pen has described to me, and from some other accounts which have come to my ears, your respectable nephew is about as loathsome a little villain as crawls on the earth. Good seems to be out of his sphere: and away from his contemplation. He ill treats every one he comes near; or, if gentle to them, it is that they may serve some base purpose. Since my attention has been drawn to the creature, I have been contemplating his ways with wonder and curiosity. How much superior Nature's rogues are, Pen, to the villains you novelists put into your books! This man goes about his life-business with a natural propensity to darkness and evil—as a bug crawls and stings and stinks. I don't suppose the fellow feels any more remorse than a cat that runs away with a mutton chop—I recognise the Evil Spirit, Sir, and do honour to Ahrimanes, in taking off my hat to this young man. He seduced a poor girl in his father's country town—is it not natural? deserted her and her children—don't you recognise the beast? married for rank—could you expect otherwise from him? invites my Lord Highgate to his house in consideration of his balance at the bank;—Sir, unless somebody's heel shall crunch him on the way, there is no height to which this aspiring vermin mayn't crawl. I look to see Sir Barnes Newcome prosper more and more: I make no doubt he will die an immense capitalist and an exalted Peer of this realm. He will have a marble monument and a pathetic funeral sermon. There is a Divine in your family, Clive, that shall preach it. I will weep respectful tears over the grave of Baron Newcome, Viscount Newcome, Earl Newcome; and the children whom he has deserted and who, in the course of time, will be sent by a grateful nation to New South Wales, will proudly say to their brother convicts—yes the Earl was our honoured father!"

"I fear he is no better than he should be, Mr. Warrington," says the Colonel shaking his head. "I never heard the[1] story about the deserted children."

"How should you? O you guileless man!" cries Warrington. "I am not in the ways of scandal-hearing myself much: but this tale I had from Sir Barnes Newcome's own country. Mr. Batters,[2] of the *Newcome Independent* is my esteemed client. I write leading articles for his newspaper, and when he was in town last spring he[3] favoured me with the anecdote; and proposed to amuse the member for Newcome by publishing it in his journal. This kind of writing is not much in my line: and,—out of respect to you and your young one, I believe—I strove with Mr. Batters,[4] and entreated him, and prevailed with him, not to publish the story. That[5] is how I came to know it."

I sate with the Colonel in the evening, when he commented on Warrington's story and Sir Barnes's adventures in his simple way. He said his

---

[1] the *E1*] this *Ms*
[2] Mr. Batters, *E1*] Mr. I [blank] *Ms*
[3] he *E1*] Mr. [blank] *Ms*
[4] Mr. Batters, *E1*] Mr. [blank], *Ms*
[5] That *Ms E1*] This *R*

brother Hobson had been with him the morning after the dispute, reiterating Barnes's defence of his conduct: and professing on his own part nothing but good will towards his brother. " 'Between ourselves the young Baronet carries matters with rather a high-hand sometimes and I am not sorry that you gave him a little dressing. But you were too hard upon him, Colonel, really you were'—Had I known that child-deserting story I would have given it harder still, Sir," says Thomas Newcome twirling the mustachios: "but my brother had nothing to do with the quarrel, and very rightly did not wish to engage in it. He has an eye to business has Master Hobson too," my[6] friend continued: "for he brought me a cheque for my private account which of-course, he said, could not remain after my quarrel with Barnes. But the Indian bank account which is pretty large, he supposed need not be taken away? and indeed why should it? So that which is little business of mine remains where it was; and brother Hobson and I remain perfectly good friends.

"I think Clive is much[7] better since he has been quite put out of his suspense. He speaks with a great deal more kindness and good-nature about the marriage than I am disposed to feel regarding it: and, depend on it, has too high a spirit to show that he is beaten. But I know he is a good deal cut up, though he says nothing; and he agreed willingly enough to take a little journey, Arthur, and be out of the way when this business takes place. We shall go to Paris: I don't know where else besides. These misfortunes do good in one way, hard as they are to bear: they unite people who love each other. It seems to me my boy has been nearer to me, and likes his old father better than he has done of late." And very soon after this talk our friends departed.

The Crimean Minister having been recalled, and Lady Ann Newcome's house in Park Lane being vacant, her ladyship and her family came to occupy the mansion for this eventful season, and sate once more in the dismal dining-room under the picture of the defunct Sir Brian. A little of the splendour and hospitality of old days was revived in the house: entertainments were given by Lady Ann: and amongst other festivities a fine ball took place, where pretty Miss Alice, Miss Ethel's younger[8] sister, made her first appearance in the world to which she was afterwards to be presented by the Marchioness of Farintosh. All the little sisters were charmed, no doubt, that the beautiful Ethel was to become a beautiful Marchioness, who as they came up to womanhood one after another, would introduce them severally to amiable young Earls, Dukes and Marquises, when they would be married off and wear Coronets and diamonds of their own right. At Lady Ann's ball I saw my acquaintance, young Mumford, who was going to Oxford next October, and about to leave Rugby where he was at the head of the School, looking very dismal as Miss Alice whirled round the room dancing in Viscount Bustington's arms—Miss Alice with whose mamma he used to take tea at Rugby, and for whose pretty sake Mumford did Alfred Newcome's verses for him and let him off his thrashings. Poor

[6] my *E1*] thy *Ms*
[7] much *E1*] very much *Ms*
[8] younger *Ms R*] youngest *E1*

Mumford! he dismally went about under the protection of young Alfred, a fourth form boy—not one soul did he know in that rattling London ball-room: his young face was as white as the large white-tie, donned two hours since at the Tavistock with such nervousness and beating of heart!

With these lads, and decorated with a tie equally splendid, moved about young Sam Newcome, who was shirking from his sister and his mamma— Mrs. Hobson had actually assumed clean gloves for this festive occasion. Sam stared at all the "Nobs": and insisted upon being introduced to "Farintosh" and congratulated his lordship with much graceful ease: and then pushed about the rooms perseveringly hanging on to Alfred's jacket. "I say I wish you wouldn't call me Al," I heard Master Alfred say to his cousin. Seeing my face Mr. Samuel ran up to claim acquaintance. He was good enough to say he thought Farintosh seemed devlish haughty. Even my wife could not help saying that Mr. Sam was an odious little creature.

So it was to[9] young Alfred and his brothers and sisters who would want protection and help[1] in the world, that Ethel was about to give up her independence, her inclination perhaps, and to bestow her life on yonder young nobleman. Looking at her as a girl devoting herself to her family, her sacrifice gave her a melancholy interest in our eyes. My wife and I watched her, grave and beautiful, moving through the rooms receiving and returning a hundred greetings, bending to compliments, talking with this friend and that, with my lord's lordly relations, with himself to whom she listened deferentially; faintly smiling as he spoke now and again, doing the honours of her mother's house. Lady after lady of his lordship's clan and kinsfolk complimented the girl and her pleased mother. Old Lady Kew was radiant (if one can call radiance the glances of those darkling old eyes). She sate in a little room apart and thither people went to pay their Court to her. Unwittingly[2] I came in on this levee, with my wife on my arm: Lady Kew scowled at me over her crutch, but without a sign of recognition. What an awful countenance that old woman has! Laura whispered as we retreated out of that gloomy presence.

And Doubt (as its wont is) whispered too a question in my ear. "Is it for her brothers and sisters only that Miss Ethel is sacrificing herself? Is it not for the coronet and the triumph and the fine houses?" "When two motives may actuate a friend, we surely may try and believe in the good one," says Laura. "But, but I am glad Clive does not marry her—poor fellow—he would not have been happy with her. She belongs to this great world: she has spent all her life in it: Clive would have entered into it very likely in her train; and you know, Sir, it is not good that we should be our husbands' superiors," adds Mrs. Laura with a curtsey.

She presently pronounced that the air was very hot in the rooms and in fact wanted to go home to see her child. As we passed out we saw Sir Barnes Newcome eagerly smiling, smirking, bowing and in the fondest conversation with his sister and Lord Farintosh. By Sir Barnes presently brushed Lieutenant General Sir George Tufto, K.C.B., who, when he saw

9 <for the sake +of+> ↑to↓ Ms] for E1
1 protection and help Ms] help and protection E1
2 Unwittingly R] Unwillingly Ms E1

THE OLD LOVE AGAIN

on whose foot he had trodden, grunted out, "Hm, beg your pardon," and turning his back on Barnes forthwith began complimenting Ethel and the Marquis. "Served with your lordship's father in Spain—Glad to make your lordship's acquaintance," says Sir George. Ethel bows to us as we pass out of the rooms and we hear no more of Sir George's conversation.

In the cloak-room sits Lady Clara Newcome with a gentleman bending over her—just in such an attitude as the bride is in Hogarth's Marriage à la Mode as the Counsellor talks to her. Lady Clara starts up as a crowd of blushes come into her wan face, and tries to smile and rises to greet my wife and says something about its being so dreadfully hot in the upper rooms and so very tedious waiting for the carriages. The gentleman advances towards me with a military stride and says, "How do you do, Mr. Pendennis! How's our young friend the painter?" I answer Lord Highgate civilly enough whereas my wife will scarce speak a word in reply to Lady Clara Newcome.

Lady Clara asked us to her ball: which my wife declined altogether to attend. Sir Barnes published a series of quite splendid entertainments on the happy occasion of his sister's betrothal. We read the names of all the Clan Farintosh in the *Morning Post* as attending these banquets. Mr. and Mrs. Hobson Newcome in Brianstone Square gave also signs of rejoicing at their niece's marriage. They had a grand banquet followed by a tea to which latter amusement the present biographer was invited. Lady Ann and Lady Kew and her granddaughter and the Baronet and his wife, and my Lord Highgate and Sir George Tufto attended the dinner: but it was rather a damp entertainment. "Farintosh," whispers Sam Newcome, "sent word just before dinner that he had a sore throat and Barnes was as sulky as possible—Sir George wouldn't speak to him and the Dowager wouldn't speak to Lord Highgate. Scarcely anything was drank," concluded Mr. Sam with a slight hiccup. "I say, Pendennis—how sold Clive will be!" And the amiable youth went off to commune with others of his parents' guests.

Thus the Newcomes entertained the Farintoshes and the Farintoshes entertained the Newcomes. And the Dowager Countess of Kew went from assembly to assembly every evening: and to jewellers and upholsterers and dress makers every morning: and Lord Farintosh's town house was splendidly redecorated in the newest fashion: and he[3] seemed to grow more and more attentive as the happy day approached; and he gave away all his cigars to his brother Rob: and his sisters were delighted with Ethel and constantly in her company, and his mother was pleased with her, and thought a girl of her spirit and resolution would make a good wife for her son: and select crowds flocked to see the service of plate at Handyman's, and the diamonds which were being set for the lady: and Smee, R.A., painted her portrait as a souvenir for Mamma when Miss Newcome should be Miss Newcome no more; and Lady Kew made a will leaving all she could leave to her beloved granddaughter, Ethel, daughter of the late Sir Brian Newcome, Baronet; and Lord Kew wrote an affectionate letter to his cousin, congratulating her, and wishing her happiness with all his heart; and I was

---

[3] Farintosh's town house was splendidly redecorated in the newest fashion: and he *Ms E1*] Farintosh *R*

glancing over the *Times* newspaper at breakfast one morning, when I laid it down with an exclamation which caused my wife to start with surprise.

"What is it?" cries Laura—and I read as follows.

"DEATH OF THE COUNTESS DOWAGER OF KEW. We regret to have to announce the awfully sudden death of this venerable lady. Her ladyship who had been at several parties of the nobility the night before last, seemingly in perfect health; was seized with a fit, as she was waiting for her carriage, and about to quit Lady Pallgrave's assembly. Immediate medical assistance was procured and her ladyship was carried to her own house in Queen Street, May Fair. But she never rallied or, we believe spoke, after the first fatal seizure and sank at eleven o'clock last evening. The deceased, Louisa Joanna Gaunt, widow of Frederick, first Earl of Kew, was daughter of Charles, Earl of Gaunt, and sister of the late, and aunt of the present, Marquis of Steyne. The present Earl of Kew is her ladyship's grandson, his lordship's father, Lord Walham having died before his own father, the first Earl.

"Many noble families are placed in mourning by this sad event. Society has to deplore the death of a lady who has been its ornament for more than half a century: and who was known, we may say throughout Europe, for her remarkable sense, extraordinary memory and brilliant wit."

Chapter XVII.

BARNES'S SKELETON CLOSET.

HE demise of Lady Kew of course put a stop for a while to the matrimonial projects so interesting to the house of Newcome. Hymen blew his torch out; put it into the cup-board for use on a future day; and exchanged his garish saffron-coloured robe for decent temporary mourning. Charles Honeyman improved the occasion at Lady Whittlesea's chapel hard by; and "Death at the Festival" was one of his most thrilling sermons reprinted at the request of some of the congregation. There were those of his flock, especially a pair whose quarter of the fold was the organ-loft, who were always charmed with the piping of that melodious pastor.

Shall we too, while the coffin yet rests on the outer earth's surface, enter the chapel whither these void remains of our dear sister departed are borne by the smug undertaker's gentlemen, and pronounce an elegy over that bedizened box of corruption? When the young are stricken down and their roses nipped in an hour by the destroying blight, even the stranger can sympathise, who counts the scant years on the gravestone, or reads the notice in the newspaper corner. The contrast forces itself on you. A fair young creature bright and blooming yesterday, distributing smiles, levying homage, inspiring desire, conscious of her power to charm, and gay with the natural enjoyment of her conquests,[1]—who in his walk through the world has not looked on many such a one; and, at the notion of her sudden call away from beauty, triumph, pleasure; her helpless outcries during her short pain; her vain pleas for a little respite, her sentence and its

---

[1] conquests, *E1*] triumphs, *Ms*

execution—has not felt a shock of pity? When the days of a long life come to its close, and a white head sinks to rise no more: we bow our own with respect as the mourning train passes and salute the heraldry and devices of yonder pomp, as symbols of age, wisdom, deserved respect and merited honour, long experience of suffering and action—the wealth he may have atchieved is the harvest which he sowed; the titles on his hearse, fruits of the field he bravely and laboriously wrought in. But to live to fourscore years, and be—found dancing among the idle virgins! To have had near a century of allotted time and then be called away from the giddy notes of a May Fair fiddle! to have to yield your roses too, and then drop out of the bony clutch of your old fingers a wreath that came from a Parisian band-box! One fancies round some graves unseen troops of mourners waiting: many and many a poor pensioner trooping to the place: many weeping charities: many kind actions: many dear friends beloved and deplored rising up at the toll of that bell to follow the honoured hearse: dead parents waiting above and calling "Come daughter!" lost children (Heaven's foundlings) hovering round like cherubim and whispering "Welcome mother!" Here is one who reposes after a long feast where no love has been; after girlhood without kindly maternal nurture: marriage without affection: matronhood without its precious griefs and joys: after fourscore years of lonely vanity—let us take off our hats to that procession too as it passes; admiring the different lots awarded to the children of men, and the various usages to which Heaven puts its Creatures.

Leave we yonder velvet-palled box, spangled with fantastic heraldry and containing within the aged slough and envelope of a soul gone to render its account. Look rather at the living audience standing round the shell;—the[2] deep grief on Barnes Newcome's fine countenance; the sadness depicted in the face of the most noble the Marquis of Farintosh; the sympathy of her ladyship's medical man (who came in the third mourning carriage); better than these the awe and reverence and emotion exhibited in the kind face of one of the witnesses of this scene as he listens to those words, which the priest rehearses over our dead. What magnificent words! what a burning faith, what a glorious triumph, what a heroic life, death, hope, they record!—They are read over all of us alike—as the sun shines on just and unjust. We have all of us heard them; and I have fancied for my part, that they fell and smote like the sods on the coffin.

The ceremony over, the undertaker's gentlemen clamber on the roof of the vacant hearse, into which palls, trestles, trays of feathers are inserted, and the horses break out into a trot, and the empty carriages expressing the deep grief of the deceased lady's friends depart homewards. It is remarked that Lord Kew hardly has any communication with his cousin, Sir Barnes Newcome. His lordship jumps into a cab and goes to the railroad. Issuing from the cemetery the Marquis of Farintosh hastily orders that thing to be taken off his hat, and returns to town in his brougham smoking a cigar. Sir Barnes Newcome rides in the brougham beside Lord Farintosh, as far as Oxford Street where he gets a cab and goes to the City. For Business is Business, and must be attended to though Grief be ever so severe.

---

[2] the shell;—the *E1*] yonder shell. The *Ms*

A very short time previous to her demise, Mr. Rood (that was Mr. Rood—that other little gentleman in black who shared the third mourning coach along with her ladyship's medical man) had executed a will by which almost all the Countess's property was devised to her granddaughter, Ethel Newcome. Lady Kew's decease of course delayed the marriage projects for a while. The young heiress returned to her mother's house in Park Lane. I daresay the deep mourning habiliments in which the domestics of that establishment appeared were purchased out of the funds left in his hands, which Ethel's banker and brother had at her disposal.

Sir Barnes Newcome who was one of the trustees of his sister's property grumbled no doubt because his grandmother had bequeathed to him but a paltry recompense of five hundred pounds for his pains and trouble of trusteeship; but his manner to Ethel was extremely bland and respectful: an heiress now, and to be Marchioness in a few months, Sir Barnes treated her with a very different regard to that which he was accustomed to show to other members of his family. For while this worthy Baronet would contradict his mother at every word she uttered and take no pains to disguise his opinion that Lady Ann's intellect was of the very poorest order, he would listen deferentially to Ethel's smallest observations, exert himself to amuse her under her grief, which he chose to take for granted was very severe, visit her constantly and show the most charming solicitude for her general comfort and welfare.

During this time my wife received constant[3] notes from Ethel Newcome and the intimacy between the two ladies much increased. Laura was so unlike the women of Ethel's circle, the young lady was pleased to say, that to be with her was Ethel's greatest comfort. Miss Newcome was now her own mistress, had her carriage, and would drive day after day to our cottage at Richmond. The frigid society of Lord Farintosh's sisters, the conversation of his mother, did not amuse Ethel and she escaped from both with her usual impatience of control. She was at home every day dutifully to receive my lord's visits, but though she did not open her mind to Laura as freely regarding the young gentleman as she did when the character and disposition of her future mother and sisters-in-law was the subject of their talk, I could see from the grave look of commiseration which my wife's face bore after her young friend's visits, that Mrs. Pendennis augured rather ill of the future happiness of this betrothed pair. Once at Miss Newcome's special request I took my wife to see her in Park Lane, where the Marquis of Farintosh found us. His lordship and I had already a half acquaintance which was not however improved after my regular presentation to him by Miss Newcome: he scowled at me with a countenance indicative of anything but welcome and did not seem in the least more pleased when Ethel entreated her friend Laura not to take her bonnet, not to think of going away so soon. She came to see us the very next day, stayed much longer with us than usual and returned to town quite late in the evening, in spite of the entreaties of the inhospitable Laura, who would have had her leave us, long before. "I am sure," says clear-sighted Mrs. Laura, "she is come

---

[3] constant *Ms E1*] frequent *R*

out of bravado, and after we went away yesterday that there were words between her and Lord Farintosh on our account."

"Confound the young man," breaks out Mr. Pendennis in a fume; "what does he mean by his insolent airs?"

"He may think we are partisans *de l'autre*," says Mrs. Pendennis, with a smile first and a sigh afterwards, as she said, "poor Clive."

"Do you ever talk about Clive?" asks the husband.

"Never. Once, twice perhaps, in the most natural manner in the world, we mentioned where he is; but nothing farther passes. The subject is a sealed one between us. She often looks at his drawings in my album (Clive had drawn our baby there and its mother in a great variety of attitudes) and gazes at his sketch of his dear old father, but of him she never says a word."

"So it is best," says Mr. Pendennis.

"Yes—best," echoes Laura with a sigh.

"You think, Laura," continues the husband—"You think she—"

"She what?" What did Mr. Pendennis mean? Laura his wife certainly understood him, though upon my conscience the sentence went no farther—for she answered at once,

"Yes—I think she certainly did, poor boy. But that of course is over now: and Ethel, though she can not help being a worldly woman, has such firmness and resolution of character, that if she has once determined to conquer any inclination of that sort I am sure she will master it, and make Lord Farintosh a very good wife."

"Since the Colonel's quarrel with Sir Barnes," cries Mr. Pendennis adverting by a natural transition from Ethel to her amiable brother, "our banking-friend doesn't invite us any more: Lady Clara sends you no cards. I have a great mind to withdraw my account."

Laura who understands nothing about accounts did not perceive the fine irony of this remark: but her face straightway put on the severe expression which it chose to assume whenever Sir Barnes's family was mentioned, and she said, "My dear Arthur, I am very glad indeed that Lady Clara sends us no more of her invitations. You know very well why I dislike—a—*them*."[4]

"Why?"

"I hear baby crying," says Laura—O Laura, Laura! how could you tell your husband such a fib?—and she quits the room without deigning to give any answer to that "Why."

Let us pay a brief visit to Newcome in the North of England, and there we may get some answer to the question of which Mr. Pendennis had just in vain asked a reply from his wife. My design does not include a description of that great and flourishing town of Newcome, and of the manufactures which caused its prosperity; but only admits of the introduction of those Newcomites who are concerned in the affairs of the family which has given its respectable name to these volumes.

Thus in previous pages we have said nothing about the Mayor and Corporation of Newcome, the magnificent bankers and manufacturers who

---

[4] dislike—a—*them*." *Ms*] dislike them." *E1*

had their places of business in the town and their splendid villas outside its smoky precincts; people who would give their thousand guineas for a picture or a statue and write you off a cheque for ten times the amount any day: people who if there was talk of a statue to the Queen or the Duke would come down to the Town All and subscribe their one two three undred apiece (especially if in the neighbouring city of SLOWCOME they were putting up a statue to the Duke or the Queen)—not of such men have I spoken, the magnates of the place; but of the humble Sarah Mason in Jubilee Row—of the Reverend Dr. Bulders the Vicar, Mr. Vidler the apothecary, Mr. Duff the baker—of Tom Potts the jolly reporter of the *Newcome Independent* and — Batters, Esq., the proprietor of that journal—persons with whom our friends have had already or will be found presently to have, some connection.

And it is from these[5] that we shall[6] arrive at some particulars regarding the Newcome family, which will show us that they have a skeleton or two in *their* closets, as well as their neighbours.

Now, how will you have the story? Worthy mammas of families—if you do not like to have your daughters told that bad husbands will make bad wives: that marriages begun in indifference make homes unhappy: that men, whom girls are brought to swear to love and honour, are sometimes false, selfish and cruel, and that women forget the oaths which they have been made to swear—if you will not hear of this, ladies, close the book and send for some other. Banish the newspaper out of your houses; and shut your eyes to the truth, the awful truth of life and sin. Is the world made of Jennies and Jessamies; and passion the play of school-boys and school-girls, scribbling valentines and interchanging lollipops? Is life all over when Jenny and Jessamy are married; and are there no subsequent trials, griefs, wars, bitter heart-pangs, dreadful temptations, defeats, remorses, sufferings to bear and dangers to overcome? As you and I, friend, kneel with our children round about us, prostrate before the Father of us all, and asking mercy for miserable sinners; are the young ones to suppose the words are mere form, and don't apply to us?—to some outcasts in the free seats probably, or those naughty boys playing in[7] the Church yard? Are they not to know that we err too and pray with all our hearts to be rescued from temptation? If such a knowledge is wrong for them, send them to church apart; go you and worship in private—or if not too proud, kneel humbly in the midst of them owning your wrong, and praying Heaven to be merciful to you a sinner.

When Barnes Newcome became the reigning Prince of the Newcome family, and after the first agonies of grief for his father's death had subsided, he made strong attempts to conciliate the principal persons in the neighbourhood and to render himself popular in the borough. He gave handsome entertainments to the townsfolk and to the country gentry; he tried even to bring those two warring classes together. He endeavoured

---

5 these *E1*] persons even more humble than these *Ms*
6 shall *E1*] must get the meaning of that "Why?" which Mrs. Laura did not choose to interpret. We must suborn kitchen-maids forsooth. We must converse with Ladies' maids: we must interrogate Doctor's boys: and then we shall *Ms*
7 playing in *E1*] playing at marbles in *Ms*

to be civil to the *Newcome Independent,* the Opposition paper, as well as to the *Newcome Sentinel,* that true old Uncompromising Blue. He asked the Dissenting Clergyman to dinner, and the Low Church Clergyman as well as the orthodox Doctor Bulders and his curates. He gave a lecture at the Newcome Athenæum, which everybody said was very amusing, and which *Sentinel* and *Independent* both agreed in praising. Of course he subscribed to that statue which the Newcomites were raising; to the philanthropic missions which the Reverend Low Church gentlemen were engaged in; to the races (for the young Newcomite manufacturers are as sporting gents as any in the North), to the Hospital, the People's Library, the restoration of the Rood Screen and the great painted window in Newcome Old Church (Revd. J. Bulders)—and he had to pay in fine a most awful price for his privilege of sitting in Parliament as Representative of his native place as he called it in his speeches[8] "the cradle of his forefathers, the home of his race" &c.—though Barnes was in fact born at Clapham.

Lady Clara could not in the least help this young Statesman in his designs upon Newcome and the Newcomites. After she came into Barnes's hands a dreadful weight fell upon her. She would smile and simper and talk kindly and gaily enough at first during Sir Brian's life; and among women, when Barnes was not present. But as soon as he joined the company, it was remarked that his wife became silent, and[9] looked eagerly towards him whenever she ventured to speak. She blundered; her eyes filled with tears; the little wit she had left her in her husband's presence: he grew angry, and[1] tried to hide his anger with a sneer, or broke out with a jibe and an oath, when he lost patience, and Clara whimpering would leave the room. Everybody at Newcome knew that Barnes bullied his wife.

People had worse charges against Barnes than wife-bullying. Do you suppose that little interruption which occurred at Barnes's marriage was not known in Newcome? His victim had been a Newcome girl—the man to whom she was betrothed was in a Newcome factory. When Barnes was a young man and, in his occasional visits to Newcome, lived along with those dashing young blades Sam Jollyman (Jollyman Brothers and Bowdres), Bob Homer, Cross Country Bill, Al. Rucker (for whom his father had to pay eighteen thousand pound after the Leger, the year Toggery won it) and that wild lot, all sorts of stories were told of them, and of Barnes especially. Most of them were settled, and steady business men by this time. Al., it was known, had become very serious besides making his fortune in cotton. Bob Homer managed the Bank and as for S. Jollyman, Mrs. S. J. took uncommon good care that *he* didn't break out of bounds any more; why, he was not even allowed to play a game at billiards or to dine out without her ...I could go on giving you interesting particulars of a hundred members of the Newcome aristocracy, were not our attention especially directed to one respectable family.

All Barnes's endeavours at popularity were vain, partly from his own fault and partly from the nature of mankind, and of the Newcome folks

---

[8] speeches *E1*] official speeches *Ms*
[9] and *E1*] or *Ms*
[1] and *E1*] or *Ms*

especially whom no single person could possibly conciliate. Thus, suppose he gave the advertisements to the *Independent*; the old Blue paper, the *Sentinel*, was very angry: suppose he asked Mr. Hunch, the dissenting minister, to bless the table-cloth after dinner, as he had begged Doctor Bulders to utter a benediction on the first course? Hunch and Bulders were both angry.—He subscribed to the races, what heathenism! to the missionaries, what sanctimonious humbug! And the worst was that Barnes being young at that time and not able to keep his tongue in order could not help saying not to but of such and such a man that he was an infernal Ass or a confounded old idiot and so forth—peevish phrases which undid in a moment the work of a dozen dinners, countless compliments and months of grinning good humour.

Now he is wiser. He is very proud of being Newcome of Newcome and quite believes that the place is his hereditary principality—But still he says his father was a fool for ever representing the borough, "Dammy, Sir," cries Sir Barnes, "never sit for a place that lies at your park-gates—and above all never try to conciliate 'em. Curse em! Hate 'em well, Sir. Take a line, and flog the fellows on the other side. Since I have sate in Parliament for another place; I have saved myself I don't know how much a year. I never go to High Church or Low: don't give a shillin' to the confounded races, or the infernal soup-tickets, or to the miserable missionaries; and at last live in quiet."

So in spite of all his subscriptions and his coaxing of the various orders of Newcomites Sir Barnes Newcome was not popular among them: and while he had enemies on all sides, had sturdy friends not even on his own. Scarce a man but felt Barnes was laughing at him; Bulders in his pulpit, Holder who seconded him in his election, the Newcome Society, and the ladies even more than the men were uneasy under his ominous familiarity; and recovered their good humour when he left them. People felt as if it was a truce only, and not an alliance with him and always speculated on the possibility of war. When he turned his back on them in the market, men felt relieved, and as they passed his gate, looked with no friendly glances over his park-wall.

What happened within was perfectly familiar to many persons. Our friend was insolent to all his servants: and of course very well served, but very much disliked in consequence. The housekeeper had a friend at Newcome, Mrs. Taplow in fact of the King's Arms—the butler was familiar with Taplow—one[2] of the grooms at Newcome Park kept company with Mrs. Bulders' maid: the incomings and outgoings, the quarrels and tears, the company from London, and all the doings of the folks at[3] Newcome Park were thus known to the neighbourhood round about. The apothecary brought an awful story back from Newcome. He had been called to Lady Clara in strong hysterical fits—He found her ladyship with a bruise on her face. When Sir Barnes approached her—he would not allow the medical

---

[2] consequence. The housekeeper had a friend at Newcome, Mrs. Taplow in fact of the King's Arms—the butler was familiar with Taplow—one *Ms*] consequence. The butler was familiar with Taplow—the housekeeper had a friend at Newcome, Mrs. Taplow in fact of the King's Arms—one *E1*

[3] at *E1*] of *Ms*

man to see her except in his presence—she screamed and bade him not come near her. These things did Mr. Vidler weakly impart to Mrs. Vidler: these under solemn vows of secresy Mrs. Vidler told to one or two friends. Sir Barnes and Lady Clara were seen shopping together very graciously in Newcome a short time afterwards; persons who dined at the Park said the Baronet and his wife seemed on very good terms;—but—but that story of the bruised cheek remained in the minds of certain people, and lay by at compound interest as such stories will.

Now, say people quarrel and make it up; or don't make it up but wear a smirking face to society and call each other my dear and my love, and smoothe over their countenances before John who enters with the coals as they are barking and biting, or who announces the dinner as they are tearing each other's eyes out? Suppose a woman is ever so miserable and yet smiles and doesn't show her grief? Quite right say her prudent friends and her husband's relations above all. "My dear, you have too much propriety to exhibit your grief before the world, or above all before the darling children." So to lie is your duty—to lie to your friends, to yourself if you can, to your children.

Does this discipline of hypocrisy improve any mortal woman? Say she learns to smile after a blow, do you suppose in this matter alone she will be a hypocrite? Poor Lady Clara! I fancy a better lot for you than that to which Fate handed you over—I fancy there need have been no deceit in your fond simple little heart could it but have been given into other keeping. But you were consigned to a master whose scorn and cruelty terrified you: under whose sardonic glances your scared eyes were afraid to look up and before whose gloomy coldness you dared not be happy. Suppose a little plant very frail and delicate from the first, but that might have bloomed sweetly and borne fair flowers had it received warm shelter and kindly nurture; suppose a young creature taken out of her home and given over to a hard master whose caresses are as insulting as his neglect, consigned to cruel usage, to weary loneliness, to bitter bitter recollections of the past; suppose her schooled into hypocrisy by tyranny—and then quick, let us hire an advocate to roar out to a British jury the wrongs of her injured husband, to paint the agonies of his bleeding heart (if Mr. Advocate gets plaintiff's brief in time, and before defendant's attorney has retained him) and to show Society injured through him—let us console that martyr, I say, with thumping damages; and as for the woman—the guilty wretch! let us lead her out and stone her.

Chapter XVIII.

ROSA QUO LOCORUM SERA MORATUR.

LIVE NEWCOME bore his defeat with such a courage and resolution, as those who knew the young fellow's character were sure he would display. It was whilst he had a little lingering hope still that the poor lad was in the worst condition; as a gambler is restless and unhappy whilst his last few guineas remain with him, and he is venturing them against the overpowering chances of the bank. His last piece however gone, our friend rises up from that unlucky table, beaten at the contest but not broken in spirit. He goes back into the world again and withdraws from that dangerous excitement; sometimes when he is alone, or wakeful tossing in his bed of[1] nights, he may recal the fatal game and think how he might have won it,—think what a fool he was ever to have played it at all—but these cogitations Clive kept for himself. He was magnanimous enough not even to blame Ethel much, and to take her side against his father, who it must be confessed now exhibited a violent hostility against that young lady and her belongings. Slow to anger and utterly beyond deceit himself, when Thomas Newcome was once roused or at length believed that he was cheated, wo to the offender! From that day forth, Thomas believed no good of him. Every thought or action of his enemy's life seemed treason to the worthy Colonel. If Barnes gave a dinner-party his uncle was ready to fancy that the banker wanted to poison somebody; if he made a little speech in the House of Commons (Barnes did make little speeches in the House of Commons), the Colonel was sure some infernal conspiracy lay under the villain's words.—The whole of that branch of the Newcomes fared little better at their kinsman's hands—they were all deceitful, sordid, heartless, worldly;—Ethel herself no better now than the people who had bred her

---

[1] of Ms] at E1

up. People hate, as they love, unreasonably: whether is it the more[2] mortifying to us, to feel that we are disliked or liked undeservedly?

Clive was not easy until he had the sea between him and his misfortune: and now Thomas Newcome had the chance of making that tour with his son, which in early days had been such a favourite project with the good man. They travelled Rhineland and Switzerland together—they crossed into Italy—went[3] from Milan to Venice (where Clive saluted the greatest painting in the world—the glorious "Assumption" of Titian), they went to Trieste and over the beautiful Styrian Alps to Vienna—they beheld the[4] Danube and the plain where the Turk and Sobieski fought. They travelled at a prodigious fast pace. They did not speak much to one another. They were a pattern pair of English travellers. I daresay many persons whom they met smiled to observe them; and shrugged their shoulders at the aspect of *ces Anglais*. They did not know the care in the young traveller's mind; and the deep tenderness and solicitude of the elder. Clive wrote to say it was a very pleasant tour but I think I should not have liked to join[5] it. Let us dismiss it in this single sentence. Other gentlemen have taken the same journey, and with Sorrow perhaps as their silent fellow traveller.[6] How you remember the places afterwards and the thoughts which pursued you! If in after days when your Grief is dead and buried, you revisit the scenes in which it was your companion, how its Ghost rises, and shows itself again! Suppose this part of Mr. Clive's life were to be described at length in several chapters, and not in a single brief sentence—what dreary pages they would be! In two or three months our friends saw a number of men, cities, mountains, rivers and what not. It was yet early Autumn when they were back in France again, and September found them at Brussels, where James Binnie, Esq., and his family were established in comfortable quarters and where we may be sure Clive and his father were very welcome.

Dragged abroad at first sorely against his will, James Binnie had found the Continental life pretty much to his liking. He had passed a winter at Pau; a summer at Vichy where the waters had done him good. His ladies had made several charming foreign acquaintances. Mrs. Mackenzie had quite a list of Counts and Marchionesses among her friends. The excellent Captain Goby wandered about the country with them. Was it to Rosey, was it to her mother the Captain was most attached? Rosey received him as a god-papa, Mrs. Mackenzie as a wicked odious good-for-nothing dangerous delightful creature. Is it humiliating, is it consolatory, to remark with what small wit some of our friends are amused? The jovial sallies of Goby appeared exquisite to Rosey's mother, and to the girl probably; though that young Bahawder of a Clive Newcome chose to wear a grave face (confound his insolent airs!) at the very best of the Goby jokes.

In Goby's train was his fervent admirer and inseparable young friend, Clarence Hoby. Captain Hoby and Captain Goby travelled the world together, visited Hombourg and Baden, Cheltenham and Leamington, Paris

---

[2] more *E1*] most *Ms*
[3] Italy—went *E1*] Italy they went *Ms*
[4] the *HM NY*] [absent] *Ms E1 R*
[5] not have . . . join *E1*] not like to have joined *Ms*
[6] fellow traveller *E1*] companion. *Ms*

and Brussels in company, belonged to the same club in London—the centre of all pleasure, fashion and joy for the young officer and the older campaigner. The jokes at the Flag, the dinners at the Flag, the committee of the Flag, were the theme of their constant conversation. Goby fifty years old, unattached, and with dyed mustachios was the affable comrade of the youngest member of his club: when absent, a friend wrote him the last riddle from the smoking-room: when present, his knowledge of horses, of cookery wines and cigars and military history rendered him a most acceptable companion. He knew the history and atchievements of every regiment in the army; of every general and commanding officer. He was known to have been 'out' more than once himself, and had made up a hundred quarrels. He was certainly not a man of an ascetic life or a profound intellectual culture: but though poor he was known to be most honourable; though more than middle-aged he was cheerful, busy and kindly; and though the youngsters called him old Goby, he bore his years very gaily and handsomely and I daresay numbers of ladies besides Mrs. Mackenzie thought him delightful. Goby's talk and rattle perhaps somewhat bored James Binnie, but Thomas Newcome found the Captain excellent company: and Goby did justice to the good qualities of the Colonel.

Clive's father liked Brussels very well. He and his son occupied very handsome quarters, near the spacious apartments in the Park which James Binnie's family inhabited. Waterloo was not far off, to which the Indian officer paid several visits with Captain Goby for a guide: and many of Marlborough's battle-fields were near, in which Goby certainly took but a minor interest—but on the other hand Clive beheld these with the greatest pleasure, and painted more than one dashing piece in which Churchill and Eugene, Cutts and Cadogan were the heroes: whose flowing periwigs huge boots and thundering Flemish chargers were, he thought, more novel and picturesque than the Duke's surtout, and the French Grenadiers' hairy caps, which so many English and French artists have portrayed.

Mr. and Mrs. Pendennis were invited by our kind Colonel to pass a month—six months if they chose—at Brussels, and were most splendidly entertained by our friends in that city. A suite of handsome rooms was set apart for us—My study communicated with Clive's atélier. Many an hour did we pass, and many a ride and walk did we take together. I observed that Clive never mentioned Miss Newcome's name; and Laura and I agreed that it was as well not to recal it. Only once when we read the death of Lady Glenlivat, Lord Farintosh's mother, in the newspaper, I remember to have said, "I suppose that marriage will be put off again."

"*Qu'est ce que cela me fait?*" says Mr. Clive gloomily over his picture—a cheerful piece representing Count Egmont going to Execution; in which I have the honour to figure as a halberdier, Captain Hoby as the Count; and Captain Goby as the Duke of Alva looking out of window.

Mrs. Mackenzie was in a state of great happiness and glory during this winter. She had a carriage and worked that vehicle most indefatigably. She knew a great deal of good company at Brussels. She had an evening for receiving. She herself went to countless evening-parties: and had the joy of being invited to a couple of Court balls, at which I am bound to say her daughter and herself both looked very handsome. The Colonel brushed up his old uniform and attended these entertainments. M. Newcome fils, as I should judge, was not the worst-looking man in the room; and, as these young people waltzed together (in which accomplishment Clive was very much more skilful than Captain Goby),[7] I daresay many people thought he and Rosey made a pretty couple.

Most persons, my wife included, difficult as that lady is to please, were pleased with the pretty little Rosey. She sang charmingly now and looked so while singing. If her mother would but have omitted that chorus, which she cackled perseveringly behind her daughter's pretty back: about Rosey's angelic temper; about the compliments Signor Polonini paid her; about Sir Horace Dash, our minister, *insisting* upon her singing Batti Batti over again, and the Archduke clapping his hands and saying O yes! about Count Vanderslaapen's attentions to her, &c., &c.—but for these constant remarks of Mrs. Mack's I am sure no one would have been better pleased with Miss Rosey's singing and behaviour than myself. As for Captain Hoby, it was easy to see how *he* was affected towards Miss Rosalind's music and person.

And indeed few things could be pleasanter than to watch the behaviour of this pretty little maid with her Uncle James and his old chum the Colonel. The latter was soon as fond of her as James Binnie himself, whose face used to lighten with pleasure whenever it turned towards her's. She seemed to divine his wants, as she would trip across the room to fulfil them. She skipped into the carriage and covered his feet with a shawl. James was lazy and chilly now, when he took his drive. She sate opposite to him and smiled on him: and if he dozed, quick another handkerchief was round his neck. I do not know whether she understood his jokes but she saluted them always with a sweet kind smile. How she kissed him and how delighted she was if he bought her a bouquet for her ball that night! One day, upon occasion of one of these balls, James and Thomas, those two old boys, absolutely came into Mrs. Mackenzie's drawing-room with a bouquet apiece for Miss Rosey; and there was a fine laughing!

"O you little Susanna!" says James, after taking his usual payment; "now go and pay t'other elder." Rosey did not quite understand at first, being, you see, more ready to laugh at jokes than to comprehend them, but when she did, I promise you she looked uncommonly pretty as she advanced to Colonel Newcome and put that pretty fresh cheek of her's up to his grizzled mustache.

"I protest I don't know which of you blushes the most," chuckles James Binnie—and the truth is the old man and the young girl had both hung out those signals of amiable distress.

On this day and as Miss Rosey was to be overpowered by flowers—who should come presently to dinner but Captain Hoby with another bouquet? on which Uncle James said Rosey should go to the ball like an American Indian with her scalps at her belt.

"Scalps!" cries Mrs. Mackenzie.

"Scalps—O law, Uncle!" exclaims Miss Rosey, "what can you mean by anything so horrid?"

[7] Goby), *Ms E1*] Hoby), *R*

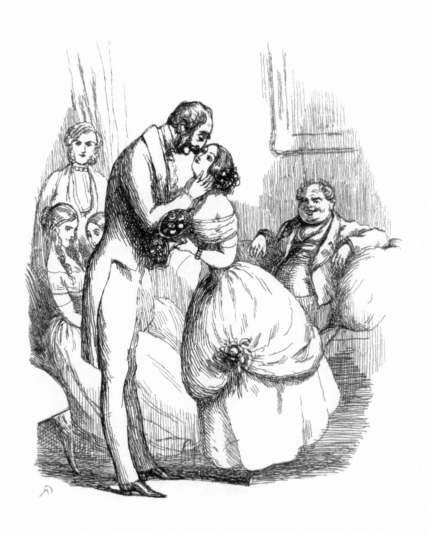

ROSA RETURNS THANKS

Goby recals to Mrs. Mack—Hook-ee-ma-goosh—the Indian Chief whom she must have seen when the Hundred and Fiftieth were at Quebec; and who had his lodge full of them: and who used to lie about the barracks so drunk, and who used to beat his poor little European wife—: and presently Mr. Clive Newcome joins this company, when the chirping, tittering, joking, laughing, cease somehow.

Has Clive brought a bouquet too? No—He has never thought about a bouquet. He is dressed in black, with long hair, a long mustache and melancholy imperial. He looks very handsome: but as glum as an undertaker. And James Binnie says, "Egad, Tom. They used to call you the knight of the woful countenance—and Clive has just inherited the paternal mug." Then James calls out in a cheery voice, "Dinner, dinner!" and trots off with Mrs. Pendennis under his arm; Rosey nestles up against the Colonel; Goby and Mrs. Mack walk away arm in arm very contentedly; and I don't know with which of her three nosegays pretty Rosey appears at the ball.

Our stay with our friends at Brussels could not be prolonged beyond a month, for at the end of that period we were under an engagement to other friends in England, who were good enough to desire the presence of Mrs. Pendennis and her suite of baby, nurse and husband. So we presently took leave of Rosey and the Campaigner, of the two stout elders and our melancholy young Clive, who bore us company to Antwerp and who won Laura's heart by the neat way in which he took her child on board ship. Poor fellow! how sad he looked as he bowed to us and took off his hat. His eyes did not seem to be looking at us though: they and his thoughts were turned another way. He moved off immediately, with his head down, puffing his eternal cigar, and lost in his own meditations; our going or our staying was of very little importance to the lugubrious youth.

"I think it was a great pity they came to Brussels," says Laura as we sate on the deck while her unconscious infant was cheerful; and while the water of the lazy Scheldt as yet was smooth.

"Who? the Colonel and Clive?—they are very handsomely lodged. They have a good maître-d'hôtel. Their dinners I am sure are excellent; and your child, Madam, is as healthy as it possibly can be."

"Blessed darling! Yes! (Blessed darling crows, moos, jumps in his nurse's arms, and holds out a little mottled hand for a biscuit of Savoy, which Mamma supplies)—I can't help thinking, Arthur, that Rosey would have been much happier as Mrs. Hoby, than she will be as Mrs. Newcome."

"Who thinks of her being Mrs. Newcome?"

"Her mother, her uncle and Clive's father. Since the Colonel has been so rich, I think Mrs. Mackenzie sees a great deal of merit in Clive. Rosey will do anything her mother bids her. If Clive can be brought to the same obedience, Uncle James and the Colonel will be delighted. Uncle James has set his heart on this marriage. (He and his sister agree upon this point.) He told me last night that he would sing 'Nunc dimittis' could he but see the two children happy; and that he should lie easier in purgatory if that could be brought about."

"And what did you say, Laura!"

"I laughed and told Uncle James I was of the Hoby faction. He is very good-natured, frank, honest and gentlemanlike, Mr. Hoby. But Uncle James said he thought Mr. Hoby was so—well, so stupid—that his Rosey would be thrown away upon the poor Captain. So I did not tell Uncle James that before Clive's arrival Rosey had found Captain Hoby far from stupid. He used to sing duets with her: he used to ride with her before Clive came. Last winter when they were at Pau, I feel certain Miss Rosey thought Captain Hoby very pleasant indeed. She thinks she was attached to Clive formerly, and now she admires him, and is dreadfully afraid of him. He is taller and handsomer and richer and cleverer than Captain Hoby certainly."

"I should think so, indeed," breaks out Mr. Pendennis—"Why, my dear, Clive is as fine a fellow as one can see on a summer's day. It does one good to look at him. What a pair of frank bright blue eyes he has, or used to have till this mishap overclouded them! What a pleasant laugh he has! What a well-built agile figure it is—what pluck and spirit and honour there is about my young chap! I don't say he is a genius of the highest order—but he is the stanchest, the bravest, the cheeriest, the most truth-telling, the kindest heart—Compare him and Hoby! Why Clive is an eagle, and yonder little creature a mousing owl!"

"I like to hear you speak so," cries Mrs. Laura very tenderly. "People say that you are always sneering, Arthur—but I know my husband better. We know Papa better, don't we? baby! (Here my wife kisses the infant Pendennis with great effusion who has come up dancing on his nurse's arms)—But," says she coming back and snuggling by her husband's side again—"But suppose your favourite Clive is an eagle, Arthur, don't you think he had better have an eagle for a mate? If he were to marry little Rosey, I daresay he would be very good to her; but I think neither he nor she would be very happy. My dear, she does not care for his pursuits: she does not understand him when he talks. The two Captains, and Rosey and I and the Campaigner as you call her laugh and talk and prattle and have the merriest little jokes with one another and we all are as quiet as mice when you and Clive come in."

"What, am I an eagle too? I have no aquiline pretensions at all, Mrs. Pendennis."

"No. Well we are not afraid of *you*—We are not afraid of Papa, are we, darling?"—this young woman now calls out to the other member of her family, who if you will calculate has just had time to be walked twice up and down the deck of the steamer whilst Laura has been making her speech about eagles—and soon the mother, child and attendant descend into the lower cabins; and then dinner is announced and Captain Jackson treats us to champagne from his end of the table and yet a short while and we are at sea and conversation becomes impossible; and morning sees us under the grey London sky, and amid the million of masts in the Thames.

Chapter XIX.

HE friends to whom we were engaged in England were Florac and his wife, Madame la Princesse de Montcontour, who were determined to spend the Christmas holydays at the Princess's country seat. It was for the first time since their reconciliation that the Prince and Princess dispensed their hospitalities at the latter's chateau. It is situated as the reader has already been informed at some five miles from the town of Newcome: away from the chimneys and smoky atmosphere of that place, in a sweet country of rural woodlands, over which quiet villages, grey church spires, and ancient gabled farmhouses are scattered still wearing the peaceful aspect which belonged to them, when Newcome was as yet but an antiquated country-town, before mills were erected on its river banks, and dies and cinders blackened its stream. Twenty years since Newcome Park was the only great house in that district. Now scores of fine villas have sprung up in the suburb lying between the town and Park. Newcome New Town, as everybody knows, has grown round the Park gates, and the New Town Hotel (where the railway station is) is a splendid structure in the Tudor style more ancient in appearance than the Park itself—surrounded by little antique villas with spiked gables, stacks of crooked chimnies, and plate-glass windows looking upon trim lawns, with glistening hedges of evergreens, spotless gravel-walks and Elizabethan gig-houses. Under the great railway viaduct of the New Town goes the old tranquil winding London high-road; once busy with a score of gay coaches and ground by innumerable wheels but at a few miles from the New Town station, the road has become so mouldy that the grass actually grows on it; and Rosebury, Madame de Montcontour's house, stands at one end of a village green which is even more quiet now than it was a hundred years ago.

When first Madame de Florac bought the place it scarcely ranked amongst the county houses; and she, the sister of manufacturers at Newcome and Manchester, did not of course visit the county families. A homely little body, married to a Frenchman from whom she was separated, may or may not have done a great deal of good in her village, have had pretty gardens and won prizes at the Newcome flower and fruit-shows but of course was nobody in such an aristocratic county as we all know ——shire is. She had her friends and relations[1] from Newcome. Many of them were Quakers—many were retail shopkeepers. She even frequented the little branch Ebenezer on Rosebury Green; and it was only by her charities and kindness at Christmas time, that the Revd. Dr. Potter, the Rector at Rosebury, knew her. The old clergy, you see, live with the county families. Good little Madame de Florac was pitied and patronised by the Doctor and treated with no little superciliousness by Mrs. Potter and the young ladies, who only kept the first society. Even when her rich brother died and she got her share of all that money Mrs. Potter said poor Madame de Florac did well in not trying to move out of her natural sphere (Mrs. P. was the daughter of a bankrupt hatter in London and had herself been governess in a noble family, out of which she married Mr. P. who was private tutor) that Madame[2] de Florac did well, we say, not to endeavour to leave her natural sphere, and that the county never would receive her. Tom Potter, the rector's son, with whom I had the good fortune to be a fellow student at Saint Boniface College, Oxbridge, a rattling forward and it must be owned vulgar youth—asked me whether Florac was not a billiard-marker by profession? and was even so kind as to caution his sisters not to speak of billiards before the lady of Rosebury. Tom was surprised to learn that Monsieur Paul de Florac was a gentleman of lineage incomparably better than that of any except two or three families in England—(including your own my dear and respected reader of course, if you hold to your pedigree).— But the truth is, heraldically speaking, that that union with the Higgs of Manchester was the first misalliance which the Florac family had made for long long years. Not that I would wish for a moment to insinuate that any nobleman is equal to an English nobleman; nay, that an English Snob with a coat of arms bought yesterday or stolen out of Edmonstone,[3] or a pedigree purchased from a peerage-maker, has not a right to look down upon any of your paltry foreign nobility.

One day the carriage-and-four with the well-known chaste liveries of the Newcomes[4] came in state from Newcome Park, and drove up Rosebury

[1] relations *Ms*] relatives *E1*
[2] tutor) that Madame] tutor) so †'that↓ Madame *Ms*] tutor). Madame *E1*
[3] Edmonstone *Ms*] Edmonton *E1*] Edmonston *R*
[4] with ... Newcomes *Ms*] [manuscript insertion misplaced after "Newcome Park,"] *E1*

Green; towards the parsonage-gate where Mrs. and the Miss Potters happened to be standing cheapening fish from a donkey-man with whom they

were in the habit of dealing. The ladies were in their pokiest old headgear[5] and most dingy gowns, when they perceived the carriage approaching; and considering of course that the visit of the Park-people was intended for them, dashed into the Rectory to change their clothes, leaving Rowkins the costermonger in the very midst of the negotiation about the three mackarel. Mamma got that new bonnet out of the band-box. Lizzy and Liddy skipped up to their bed-room and brought out those dresses which they wore at the *déjeuner* at the Newcome Athenæum when Lord Leveret came down to lecture, into which they no sooner had hooked their lovely shoulders than they reflected with terror that Mamma had been altering one of Papa's flannel-waistcoats and had left it in the drawing-room[6] when they were called out by the song of Rowkins and the appearance of his donkey's ears over the green gate of the Rectory. To think of the Park-people coming, and the drawing-room in that dreadful state!

But when they came down-stairs—the Park-people were not in the room—the woollen garment was still on the table (How they plunged it into the chiffonier!) and the only visitor was Rowkins the costermonger grinning at the open French windows with the three mackarel and crying, "Make it sixpence, Miss. Don't say fippens, Ma'am, to a pore feller[7] that has a wife and famly." So that the young ladies had to cry—"Impudence!" "Get away you vulgar insolent creature!" "Go round Sir to the back door." "How dare you!" and the like—fearing lest[8] Lady Ann Newcome and young Ethel and Barnes should[9] enter in the midst of this ignoble controversy.

They never came at all—those Park-people. How very odd! They

---

5 head-gear *E1*] bonnets *Ms*
6 in the drawing-room *E1*] on the drawing-room table *Ms*
7 feller *Ms*] fellow *E1*
8 lest *E1*] [omitted] *Ms*
9 should *E1*] would *Ms*

passed the Rectory gate: they drove on to Madame de Florac's lodge. They went in. They staid for half an hour: the horses driving round and round the gravel road before the house; and Mrs. Potter and the girls speedily going to the upper chambers and looking out of the room where the maids slept, saw Lady Ann, Ethel and Barnes walking with Madame de Florac, going into the conservatories, issuing thence with MacWhirter, the gardener, bearing huge bunches of grapes and large fasces of flowers—they saw Barnes talking in the most respectful manner to Madame de Florac— and when they went down-stairs and had their work before them—Liddy her gilt music-book, Lizzy her embroidered altar-cloth, Mamma her scarlet cloak for one of the old women—they had the agony of seeing the barouche over the railings whisk by with the Park-people inside and Barnes driving the four horses.

It was on that day when Barnes had determined to take up Madame de Florac; when he was bent upon reconciling her to her husband. In spite of all Mrs. Potter's predictions the County families did come and visit the manufacturer's daughter. And when Madame de Florac became Madame la Princesse de Montcontour, when it was announced that she was coming to stay at Rosebury for Christmas, I leave you to imagine whether the circumstance was or was not mentioned in the *Newcome Sentinel* and the *Newcome Independent*, and whether Revd. G. Potter, D.D., and Mrs. Potter did or did not call on the Prince and Princess. I leave you to imagine whether the lady did or did not inspect all the alterations which Vineer's people from Newcome were making at Rosebury House—the chaste yellow satin and gold of the drawing-room—the carved oak for the dining-room—the chintz for the bed-rooms—the Princess's apartment— the Prince's apartment—the guests' apartments—the smoking-room gracious goodness!—the[1] stables (these were under Tom Potter's superintendence) "and I'm dashed," says he one day, "if here doesn't come a billiard-table!"

The house was most comfortably and snugly appointed from top to bottom; and thus it will be seen that Mr. and Mrs. Pendennis were likely to be in very good quarters for their Christmas of 184—.

Tom Potter was so kind as to call on me two days after our arrival—and to greet me in the Princess's pew at Church on the previous day. Before desiring to be introduced to my wife: he requested me to present him to "my friend the Prince." He called him your Highness. His Highness (who had behaved with exemplary gravity save once when he shrieked an ah! as Miss Liddy led off the children in the organ-loft in a hymn and the whole pack went wofully out of tune) complimented Monsieur Tom on the sermon of Monsieur his father. Tom walked back with us to Rosebury Lodge gate. "Will you not come in, and make a party of billiard with me?" says his Highness—"Ah pardon! I forgot. You do not play the billiard the Sunday!" *"Any other day*, Prince, I shall be delighted," says Tom: and squeezed his Highness's hand tenderly at parting. "Your comrade of college was he?" asks Florac. "My dear, what men are these comrades of college! What

[1] the *Ms E1*] these *R*

men are you English! My word of honour there are some of them here—
if I were to say to them wax my boots, they would take them and wax
them! Did'st thou see how the Révérend eyed us during the sermon? He
regarded us over his book, my word of honour!"

Madame de Florac said simply, she wished the Prince would go and hear
Mr. Jowls[2] at the Ebenezer. Mr. Potter was not a good preacher certainly.

"Savez-vous qu'elle est furieusement belle la fille du Révérend?" whispered his Highness to me. "I have made eyes at her during the sermon.
They will be of pretty neighbours these Meess!"—and Paul looked unutterably roguish and victorious as he spoke. To my wife I am bound to say,
Monsieur de Montcontour showed a courtesy, a respect and kindness, that
could not be exceeded. He admired her. He payed her compliments innumerable, and gave me I am sure sincere congratulations at possessing
such a treasure. I do not think he doubted about his power of conquering
her, or any other of the daughters of women. But I was the friend of his
misfortunes: his guest;—and he spared me.

I have seen nothing more amusing, odd and pleasant than Florac at this
time of his prosperity. We arrived, as this veracious chronicle has already
asserted, on a Saturday evening. We were conducted to our most comfortable apartments,—with crackling fires blazing on the hearths and every
warmth of welcome. Florac expanded and beamed with good-nature. He
shook me many times by the hand: he patted me: he called me his good, his
brave:—he cried to his maître-d'hôtel—"Frédéric! Remember Monsieur is
master here! Run before his orders—Prostrate thyself to him. He was
good to me in the days of my misfortune. Hearest thou, Frédéric. See that
everything be done for Monsieur Pendennis—for Madame sa charmante
lady—for her angelic infant and the bonne. None of thy garrison tricks
with that young person, Frédéric! vieux scélérat. Garde toi de la, Frédéric,
si non je t'envoie à Botani Bay, je te traduis devant le Lord Maire!

"En Angleterre je me fais Anglais, vois tu, mon ami," continued the
Prince. "Demain c'est Sunday—et tu vas voir! I hear the bell: dress thyself for the dinner—my fürend!"—here there was another squeeze of both
hands from the good-natured fellow. "It do good to my art to ave you in
my ouse! Heuh!"—he hugged his guest: he had tears in his eyes as he
performed this droll, this kind embrace. Not less kind in her way, though
less expansive and *embracive*, was Madame de Montcontour to my wife as I
found on comparing notes with that young woman, when the day's hospitalities were ended. The little Princess trotted from bed-chamber to nursery to see that everything was made comfortable for her guests. She sate
and saw the child washed and put to bed. She had never beheld such a
little angel. She brought it a fine toy to play with. She and her grim old
maid frightened the little creature at first; but it was very speedily reconciled to their countenances. She was in the nursery almost[3] as early as the
child's mother. "Ah," sighed the poor little woman, "how happy you must
be to have one!" In fine my wife was quite overcome by her goodness and
welcome.

[2] Jowls *Ms*] Jacobs *E1*
[3] almost *Ms E1*] [omitted] *R*

Sunday morning arrived in the course of time; and then Florac[4] appeared as a most wonderful Briton indeed! He wore top-boots and buckskins; and after breakfast when we[5] went to Church a white great coat with a little cape, in which garment he felt that his similarity to an English gentleman was perfect. In conversation with his grooms and servants he swore freely—not that he was accustomed to employ oaths in his own private talk; but he thought the employment of these expletives necessary as an English country-gentleman. He never dined without a roast beef: and insisted that the piece of meat should be bleeding "as you love it, you others." He got up boxing-matches; and kept birds for combats of cock. He assumed the sporting language with admirable enthusiasm, drove over to covere[6] with a steppère, rode

across countri like a good one, was splendid in the hunting-field in his velvet cap and Napoleon-boots; and made the —— Hunt welcome at Rosebury, where his good-natured little wife was as kind to the gentlemen in scarlet, as she used to be of old to the stout dissenting gentlemen in black who sang hymns and spake sermons on her lawn. These folks, scared

4 Florac *E1*] indeed Florac *Ms*
5 we *Ms E1*] he *R*
6 covere *Ms*] cover *E1*

at the change which had taken place in the little Princess's habits of life, lamented her falling away: but in the county she and her husband got a great popularity, and in Newcome-town itself they were not less liked, for her benefactions were unceasing, and Paul's affability the theme of all praise. The *Newcome Independent*[7] and the *Newcome Sentinel* both paid him compliments; the former journal contrasting his behaviour with that of Sir Barnes, their member. Florac's pleasure was to drive his Princess with four horses into Newcome. He called his carriage his "trappe," his "drague"— the street boys cheered and hurrayed the Prince as he passed through the town. One haberdasher had a yellow stock called "The Montcontour" displayed in his windows: another had a pink one marked "the Princely"; and as such recommended it to the young Newcome gents.

The drague conveyed us once to the neighbouring house of Newcome whither my wife accompanied Madame de Montcontour at that lady's own request, to whom Laura very properly did not think fit to confide her antipathy for Lady Clara Newcome. Coming away from a great house, how often she and I, egotistical philosophers, thanked our fates that our own home was a small one! How long will great houses last in this world? Do not their owners now prefer a lodging at Brighton, or a little entresol on the Boulevard, to the solitary ancestral palace in a park barred round with snow? We were as glad to get out of Newcome as out of a prison—my wife and our hostess skipped into the carriage and began to talk freely as the lodge gates closed after us. Would we be lords of such a place under the penalty of living in it?[8] We agreed that the little angle of earth called Fairoaks was dearer to us than the clumsy Newcome pile of Tudor Masonry. The house had been fitted up in the time of George IV and the quasi-Gothic revival. We were made to pass through Gothic dining-rooms where there was now no hospitality; Gothic drawing-rooms shrouded in brown hollands, to one little room at the end of the dusky suite where Lady Clara sate alone,[9] or in the company of the nurses and children. The blank gloom of the place had fallen upon the poor lady. Even when my wife talked about children (good-natured Madame de Montcontour vaunting our's as a prodigy) Lady Clara did not brighten up. Her pair of young ones was exhibited and withdrawn. A something weighed upon the woman. We talked about Ethel's marriage. She said it was fixed for the New Year, she believed. She did not know whether Glenlivat had been very handsomely fitted up. She had not seen Lord Farintosh's house in London.— Sir Barnes came down once twice—of a Saturday sometimes—for three or four days to hunt—to amuse himself—as all men do she supposed—she did not know when he was coming again. She rang languidly when we rose to take leave—and sank back on her sofa where lay a heap of French novels. "She has chosen some pretty books," says Paul as we drove through the sombre avenues, through the grey park, mists lying about the melancholy ornamental waters, dingy herds of huddled sheep speckling the grass here and there—no smoke rising up from the great stacks of chimnies of the

---

[7] *Independent E1*] *Examiner Ms*
[8] living in it? *E1*] living it? *Ms*
[9] alone, *E1*] alone and alone, *Ms*

building we were leaving behind us; save one little feeble thread of white which we knew came from the fire by which the lonely Mistress of Newcome was seated. "Ouf!" cries Florac, playing his whip, as the lodge-gates closed on us and his team of horses rattled merrily along the road—"What a blessing it is to be out of that vault of place! There is something of fatal in this house in this woman—one smells misfortune there."

The Hotel which our friend Florac patronised on occasion of his visits to Newcome was the King's Arms, and it happened one day as we entered that place of entertainment in company, that a visitor of the house was issuing through the hall, to whom Florac seemed as if he would administer one of his customary embraces, and to whom the Prince called out "Jack" with great warmth and kindness as he ran towards the stranger.

Jack did not appear to be particularly well pleased on beholding us; he rather retreated from before the Frenchman's advances.

"My dear Jack, my good, my brave Ighgate! I am delighted to see you!" Florac continues regardless of the stranger's reception, or of the landlord's looks towards us, who was bowing the Prince into his very best room.

"How do you do, Monsieur de Florac," growls the new comer surlily; and was for moving on after this brief salutation; but, having a second thought seemingly, turned back and followed Florac into the apartment whither our host conducted us. *À la bonne heure!* Florac renewed his cordial greetings to Lord Highgate. "I knew[1] not, mon bon, what fly had stung you," says he to my lord. The landlord rubbing his hands smirking and bowing was anxious to know whether the Prince would take anything after his drive. As the Prince's attendant and friend, the lustre of his reception partially illuminated me. When the chief was not by, I was treated with great attention (mingled with a certain degree of familiarity) by my landlord.

Lord Highgate waited until Mr. Taplow[2] was out of the room; and then said to Florac, "Don't call me by my name here please, Florac. I am here incog."

"*Plait-il?*" asks Florac, "where is incog?" He laughed when the word was interpreted to him. Lord Highgate had turned to me: "There was no rudeness you understand intended, Mr. Pendennis:—but I am down here on some business, and don't care to wear the handle to my name. Fellows work it so, don't you understand—never leave you at rest in a country town—that sort of thing. Heard of our friend Clive lately?"

"Whether you ave andle or no andle, Jack, you are always the *bien venu* to me. What is thy affair? Old monster! I gage—"[3]

"No—no—no such nonsense," says Jack rather eagerly. "I give you my honour. I—I want to—to raise a sum of money—that is, to invest some in a speculation down here—deuced good the speculations down here—and—by the way—if the landlord asks you, I'm Mr. Harris.[4] I'm a Civil Engineer.

[1] knew *Ms E1*] know *R*
[2] Taplow *E1*] [blank] *Ms*
[3] gage—. *Ms*] wager ..." *E1*
[4] Harris *E1*] Hampton. *Ms* [changed throughout]

I'm waiting for the arrival of the 'Canada' at Liverpool from America, and very uneasy about my brother who is on board."

"What does he recount to us there? Keep these stories for the landlord, Jack. To us 'tis not the pain to lie. My good Mr. Harris, why have we not seen you at Rosebury? The Princess will scold me if you do not come: and you must bring your dear brother when he arrive too. Do you hear?" The last part of this sentence was uttered for Mr. Taplow's[5] benefit who had re-entered the George bearing a tray of wine and biscuit.

The Master of Rosebury and Mr. Harris went out presently to look at a horse which was waiting the former's inspection in the stable-yard of the hotel. The landlord took advantage of his business, to hear a bell which never was rung; and to ask me questions about the guest who had been staying at his house for a week past. Did I know that party? Mr. Pendennis said, "Yes, he knew that party."

"Most respectable party I have no doubt," continues Boniface. "Do you suppose the Prince of Montcontour knows *any* but respectable parties?" asks Mr. Pendennis—a query of which the force was so great as to discomfit and silence our landlord; who retreated to ask questions concerning Mr. Harris, of Florac's grooms.

What was Highgate's business here? Was it mine to know? I might have suspicions but should I entertain them, or communicate them, and had I not best keep them to myself? I exchanged not a word on the subject of Highgate with Florac as we drove home: though from the way in which we looked at one another—each saw that the other was acquainted with that unhappy gentleman's secret. We[6] fell to talking about Madame la Duchesse d'Ivry as we trotted on; and then of English manners by way of contrast, of intrigues, elopements, Gretna-Grin, &c., &c. "You are a droll nation!" says Florac.[7] "To make love well, you must absolutely have a chaise-de-poste, and a scandal afterwards. If our affairs of this kind made themselves on the grand'route—what armies of postillions we should need!"

I held my peace. In that vision of Jack Belsize I saw misery, guilt, children dishonoured, homes deserted,—ruin for all the actors and victims of the wretched conspiracy. Laura marked my disturbance when we reached home. She even divined the cause of it and charged me with it at night when we sate alone by our dressing-room fire, and had taken leave of our kind entertainers. Then under her cross-examination, I own that I told what I had seen—Lord Highgate under a feigned name staying at Newcome. It might be nothing. Nothing! Gracious Heavens! Could not this crime and misery be stopped? "It might be too late," Laura's husband said sadly bending down his head into the fire.

She was silent too for a while. I could see she was engaged where pious women ever will betake themselves in moments of doubt, of grief, of pain, of separation, of joy even, or whatsoever other trial. They have but to will, and as it were an invisible temple rises round them; their hearts can kneel down there; and they have an audience of the Great, the Merciful,

Untiring, Counsellor and Consoler. She would not have been frightened at Death near at hand—I have known her to tend the poor round about us, or to bear pain—not her own merely but even her children's or[8] mine with a surprising outward constancy and calm. But the idea of this crime being enacted close at hand and no help for it—quite overcame her. I believe she lay awake all that night; and rose quite haggard and pale after the bitter thoughts which had deprived her of rest.

She embraced her own child with extraordinary tenderness that morning, and even wept over it, calling it by a thousand fond names of maternal endearment. "Would I leave you, my darling—Could I ever ever ever quit you, my blessing and treasure!" The unconscious little thing hugged to his[9] mother's bosom and scared at her tones and tragic face clung frightened and weeping round Laura's neck. Would you ask what the husband's feelings were as he looked at that sweet love, that sublime tenderness, that pure Saint blessing the life of him unworthy?[1] Of all the gifts of Heaven to us below, that felicity is the sum and the chief. I tremble as I hold it lest I should lose it, and be left alone in the blank world without it: again, I feel humiliated to think that I possess it; as hastening home to a warm fireside and a plentiful table, I feel ashamed sometimes before the poor outcast beggar shivering in the street.[2]

Breakfast was scarcely over when Laura asked for a poney-carriage, and said she was bent on a private visit. She took her baby and nurse with her. She refused our company, and would not even say whither she was bound, until she had passed the lodge-gate. I may have suspected what the object was of her journey. Florac and I did not talk of it. We rode out to meet the hounds of a cheery winter morning: on another day I might have been amused with my host—the splendour of his raiment; the neatness of his velvet cap, the gloss of his hunting-boots; the cheers, shouts, salutations to dog and man, the oaths and outcries of this Nimrod who shouted louder than the whole field and the whole pack too—but on this morning I was thinking of the tragedy yonder enacting, and came away early from the hunting-field, and found my wife already returned to Rosebury.

Laura had[3] been as I suspected to Lady Clara. She did not know why, indeed. She scarce knew what she should say when she arrived—how she could say what she had in her mind. "I hoped, Arthur, that I should have something—something told me to say," whispered Laura with her head on my shoulder; "and as I lay awake last night thinking of her, prayed—that is hoped—I might find a word of consolation for that poor lady. Do you know I think she has hardly ever heard a kind word? She said so: she was very much affected after we had talked together a little.

"At first she was very indifferent; cold and haughty in her manner; asked what had caused the pleasure of this visit, for I would go in, though at the

[8] or *Ms*] and *E1*
[9] his *E1*] her *Ms*
[1] the life of him unworthy? *Ms E1*] his life? *R*
[2] it: again, I feel humiliated to think that I possess it; as hastening home to a warm fireside and a plentiful table, I feel ashamed sometimes before the poor outcast beggar shivering in the street. *Ms E1*] it. *R*
[3] Laura had *E1*] Eh bien? She had *Ms*

lodge they told me her ladyship was unwell, and they thought received no company—I said I wanted to show our boy to her—that the children[4] ought to be acquainted—I don't know what I said. She seemed more and more surprised—then all of a sudden—I don't know how—I said, 'Lady Clara, I have had a dream about you and your children and I was so frightened that I came over to you to speak about it.' And I *had* the dream, Pen; it came to me absolutely as I was speaking to her.

"She looked a little scared and I went on telling her the dream. 'My dear,' I said, 'I dreamed that I saw you happy with those children.'

"'Happy!' says she—the three were playing in the conservatory into which her sitting-room opens.

"'And that a bad spirit came and tore them from you: and drove you out into the darkness: and I saw you wandering about quite lonely and wretched and looking back into the garden where the children were playing. And you asked and implored to see them: and the Keeper at the gate said No, never—and then—then I thought they passed by you, and they did not know you—'

"'Ah,' said Lady Clara.

"'And then I thought, as we do in dreams, you know, that it was *my* child who was separated from me and who would not know me; and O, what a pang that was! Fancy that. Let us pray God it was only a dream. And worse than that, when you, when I implored to come to the child and the man said no never, I thought there came a Spirit—an angel that fetched the child to Heaven—and you said, let me come too—O let me come too—I am so miserable—And the angel said, No never never.'

"By this time Lady Clara was looking very pale. 'What do you mean?' she asked of me," Laura continued.

"'O dear lady, for the sake of the little ones, and Him who calls them to Him—go you with them—never never part from them! Cling to His knees, and take shelter there.' I took her hands, and I said more to her in this way, Arthur, that I need not—that I ought not to speak again. But she was touched at length when I kissed her—and she said I was very kind to her and no one had ever been so: and that she was quite alone in the world and had no friend to fly to: and would I go and stay with her? and I said, 'Yes'—and we must go, my dear. And I think you should see that person at Newcome—see him, and warn him," cried Laura warming as she spoke, "and pray God to enlighten and strengthen him, and to keep him from this temptation, and implore him to leave this poor weak frightened trembling creature—if he has the heart of a gentleman and the courage of a man, he will: I know he will."

"I think he would, my dearest," I said, "if he but heard the petitioner." Laura's cheeks were blushing, her eyes brightened, her voice rang with a sweet pathos of love, that vibrates through my whole being sometimes. It seems to me as if evil must give way, and bad thoughts retire before that pure[5] creature.

---

4 our boy ... children *E1*] our Helen to her little girl, that the two children *Ms*
5 pure *Ms*] purest *E1*

"Why has she not some of her family with her, poor thing!" my wife continued. "She perishes in that solitude. Her husband prevents her, I think—and—O—I know enough of *him* to know what his life is. I shudder, Arthur, to see you take the hand of that wicked selfish man. You must break with him, do you hear, Sir?"

"Before or after going to stay at his house? my love!" asks Mr. Pendennis.

"Poor thing! she lighted up at the idea of any one coming. She ran and showed me the rooms we were to have. It will be very stupid: and you don't like that. But you can write your book and still hunt and shoot with our friends here. And Lady Ann Newcome must be made to come back again. Sir Barnes quarrelled with his mother and drove her out of the house on her last visit—think of that! The servants here know it. Martha brought me the whole story from the housekeeper's room. This Sir Barnes Newcome is a dreadful creature, Arthur—I am so glad I loathed him from the very first moment I saw him."

"And into this ogre's den you propose to put me and my family, Madam!" says the husband. "Indeed, where won't I go if you order me. O who will pack my portmanteau?"

Florac and the Princess were both in desolation when at dinner we announced our resolution to go away—and to our neighbours at Newcome! that was more extraordinary. "Que diable goest thou to do in this galley?" asks our host as we sate alone over our wine.

But Laura's intended visit to Lady Clara was never to have a fulfilment, for on this same evening as we sate at our dessert, comes a messenger from Newcome with a note for my wife from the lady there.

"*Dearest, kindest* Mrs. Pendennis," Lady Clara wrote with many italics, and evidently in much distress of mind. "Your visit *is not to be.* I spoke about it to Sir B., who *arrived this afternoon*: and who has already begun to treat me *in his usual way.* O, I am so unhappy! Pray pray Do not be angry at this rudeness—though indeed it is only a kindness to keep you from this wretched place! I feel as *if I cannot bear this much longer.* But whatever happens, I shall always remember your goodness, your beautiful goodness and kindness: and shall worship you as *an angel* deserves to be worshipped. O why had I not such a friend *earlier!* But alas! I have none—only *this*[6] *odious family* thrust upon me for companions to the *wretched, lonely*

C.N.

"P.S. He does not know of my writing—Do not be surprised if you get another note from me in the morning, written in a *ceremonious style,* and regretting that we *cannot have the pleasure* of receiving Mr. and Mrs. Pendennis for the present at Newcome.

"P.S. The hypocrite!"

This letter was handed to my wife at dinner-time, and she gave it to me as she passed out of the room with the other ladies.

I told Florac that the Newcomes could not receive us, and that we would remain, if he willed it, his guests for a little longer. The kind fellow was

[6] *this Ms E1] his R*

only too glad to keep us. "My wife would die without *Bébi*;" he said—"she becomes, she becomes quite dangerous about Bébi." It was gratifying that the good old lady was not to be parted as yet from the innocent object of her love.

My host knew as well as I, the terms upon which Sir Barnes and his wife were living. Their quarrels were the talk of the whole county; one side brought forward his treatment of her; and his conduct elsewhere, and said that he was so bad that honest people should not know him. The other party laid the blame upon her and declared that Lady Clara was a languid silly weak frivolous creature; always crying out of season—who had notoriously taken Sir Barnes for his money, and who as certainly had had an attachment elsewhere. Yes, the accusations were true on both sides. A bad selfish husband had married a woman for her rank: a weak thoughtless girl had been sold to a man for his money; and the union, which might have ended in a comfortable indifference, had taken an ill turn and resulted in misery, cruelty, fierce mutual recriminations, bitter tears shed in private, husband's curses and maledictions, and open scenes of wrath and violence for servants to witness, and the world to sneer at. We arrange such matches every day, we sell or buy beauty or rank or wealth, we inaugurate the bargain in churches with sacramental services in which the parties engaged call upon Heaven to witness their vows—we know them to be lies, and we seal them with God's name. "I, Barnes, promise to take you, Clara, to love and honour till death do us part." "I, Clara, promise to take you, Barnes"—&c. &c. Who has not heard the ancient words, how many of us have uttered them knowing them to be untrue; and is there a Bishop[7] on the Bench that has not amen'd the Humbug in his lawn-sleeves and called a blessing over the kneeling pair of perjurers?

"Does Mr. Hariss know of Newcome's return?" Florac asked when I acquainted him with this intelligence. "Ce scélérat de Highgate—Va!"

"Does Newcome know that Lord Highgate is here?" I thought within myself, admiring my wife's faithfulness and simplicity, and trying to believe with that pure and guileless creature that it was not yet too late to save the unhappy Lady Clara.

"Mr. Harris had best be warned," I said to Florac: "Will you write him a word? and let us send a messenger to Newcome."

At first Florac said, "Parbleu! No;" the affair was none of his, he attended himself always to this result of Lady Clara's marriage. He had even complimented Jack upon it years before, at Baden when scenes enough tragic, enough comical, ma foi, had taken place à-propos of this affair. Why should he meddle with it now?

"Children dishonoured," said I, "honest families made miserable; for Heaven's sake, Florac, let us stay this catastrophe if we can." I spoke with much warmth, eagerly desirous to avert this calamity if possible and very strongly moved by the tale which I had heard only just before dinner from that noble and[8] innocent creature whose pure heart had already prompted

---

[7] Bishop] bishop *E1*] smug Bishop *Ms*
[8] noble and *Ms E1*] [omitted] *R*

her to plead the cause of right and truth, and to try and rescue an unhappy desperate sister trembling on the verge of ruin.

"If you will not write to him," said I in some heat. "If your grooms don't like to go out of a night (this was one of the objections which Florac had raised), I will walk." We were talking over the affair rather late in the evening, the ladies having retreated to their sleeping apartments and some guests having taken leave, whom our hospitable host and hostess had entertained that night, and before whom I naturally did not care to speak upon a subject so dangerous.

"Parbleu, what virtue, my friend! what a Joseph!" cries Florac puffing his cigar. "One sees well that your wife has made you the sermon, my poor Pendennis. You are hen-pecked, my pauvre bon! You become the husband model. It is true my mother writes that thy wife is an angel!"

"I do not object to obey such a woman when she bids me do right," I said; and would indeed at that woman's request have gone out upon the errand, but that we here found another messenger. On days when dinner parties were held at Rosebury, certain auxiliary waiters used to attend from Newcome whom the landlord of the King's Arms was accustomed to supply; indeed, it was to secure these and make other necessary arrangements respecting fish, game, &c., that the Prince de Montcontour had ridden over to Newcome on the day when we met Lord Highgate, alias Mr. Harris, before the bar of the hotel. Whilst we were engaged in the above conversation a servant enters and says, "My lord, Jenkins and the other man is going back to Newcome in their cart and is there anything wanted?"

"It is the Heaven which sends him," says Florac turning round to me with a laugh, "Make Jenkins to wait five minutes, Robert; I have to write to a gentleman at the King's Arms." And so saying Florac wrote a line which he showed me and having sealed the note, directed it to Mr. Harris at the King's Arms. The cart, the note and the assistant waiters departed on their way to Newcome. Florac bade me go to rest with a clear conscience. In truth, the warning was better given in that way than any other, and a word from Florac was more likely to be effectual[9] than an expostulation from me. I had never thought of making it, perhaps: except at the expressed desire of a lady whose counsel in all the difficult circumstances of life I own I am disposed to take.

Mr. Jenkins's horse no doubt trotted at a very brisk pace as gentlemen's horses will of a frosty night after their masters have been regaled with plentiful supplies of wine and ale. I remember in my bachelor days that my horses always trotted quicker after I had had a good dinner, the champagne used to communicate itself to them somehow, and the claret get into their heels. Before midnight the letter for Mr. Harris was in Mr. Harris's hands in the King's Arms.

It has been said that in the Boscawen Room at the Arms some of the jolly fellows of Newcome had a club of which Parrot the auctioneer, Tom Potts the talented reporter now editor of the *Independent*, Vidler the apothecary and other gentlemen were members.

---

[9] effectual *E1*] more effectual *Ms*

The Letter

When we first had occasion to mention that society it was at an early stage of this history, long before Clive Newcome's fine moustache had grown. If Vidler the apothecary was old and infirm then, he is near ten years older now; he has had various assistants, of course, and one of them of late years had become his partner though the firm continues to be known by Vidler's ancient and respectable name. A jovial fellow was this partner—a capital convivial member of the Jolly Britons, where he used to sit very late, so as to be in readiness for any nightwork that might come in.

So the Britons were all sitting smoking drinking and making merry in the Boscawen Room, when Jenkins enters with a note which he straightway delivers to Mr. Vidler's partner. "From Rosebury? The Princess ill again I suppose," says the surgeon not sorry to let the company know that he attends her. "I wish the old girl would be ill in the day-time. Confound it," says he, "what's this—" and he reads out, "'Sir Newcome est de retour, Bon voyage, mon ami. F.' What does this mean?"

"I thought you knew French, Jack Harris," says Tom Potts, "you're always bothering us with your French songs."

"Of course I know French," says the other, "but what's the meaning of this?"

"Screwcome came back by the five o'clock train. I was in it and his royal highness would scarcely speak to me. Took Brown's fly from the station. Brown won't enrich his family much by the operation," says Mr. Potts.

"But what do *I* care?" cries Jack Harris. "We don't attend him, and we don't lose much by that. Howell attends him ever since Vidler and he had that row."

"Hulloh! I say it's a mistake," cries Mr. Taplow, smoking in his chair. "This letter is for the party in the Benbow. The gent which the Prince spoke to him and called him Jack the other day when he was here. Here's a nice business and the seal broke and all. Is the Benbow party gone to bed, John. You must carry him in this here note." John, quite innocent of the note and its contents, for he that moment had entered the club-room with Mr. Potts's supper, took the note to the Benbow from which he presently returned to his master with a very scared countenance. He said the gent in the Benbow was a most Harbitraty gent. He had amost choked John after reading the letter and John wouldn't stand it, and when John said he supposed that Mr. Harris in the Boscawen, that Mr. Jack Harris, had opened the letter, the other gent cursed and swore awful.

"Potts," said Taplow who was only too communicative on some occasions after he had imbibed too much of his own brandy-and-water, "it's my belief that that party's name is no more Harris than mine is. Mrs. T. have[1] sent his linen to the wash and there was two white pocket-handkerchiefs with H and a coronet."[2]

On the next day we drove over to Newcome hoping perhaps to find that Lord Highgate had taken the warning sent to him and quitted the place. But we were disappointed. He was walking in front of the hotel where a thousand persons might see him as well as ourselves.

---

[1] Mrs. T. have *Ms*] I have *E1*
[2] coronet." *E1*] coronet, & Potts" *Ms*

We entered into his private apartment with him, and there expostulated upon his appearance in the public street where Barnes Newcome or any passer-by might recognise him. He then told us of the mishap which had befallen Florac's letter on the previous night.

"I can't go away now, whatever might have happened previously: by this time that villain knows that I am here. If I go, he will say I was afraid of him and ran away. O! how I wish he would come and find me." He broke out with a savage laugh.

"It is best to run away," one of us interposed sadly.

"Pendennis," he said with a tone of great softness; "your wife is a good woman. God bless her. God bless her for all she has said and done—would have done if that villain had let her. Do you know the poor thing hasn't a single friend in the world—not one—one—except me; and that girl they are selling to Farintosh and who does not count for much. He has driven away all her friends from her. One and all turn upon her. Her relations of course: when did *they* ever fail to hit a poor fellow or a poor girl when she was down? The poor Angel! The mother who sold her comes and preaches at her: Kew's wife turns up her little cursed nose and scorns her: Rooster, forsooth, must ride the high-horse now he is married and lives at Chanticlere, and give her warning to avoid my company or his. Do you know the only friend she ever had was that old woman with the stick— old Kew—the old witch whom they buried four months ago after nobbling her money for the beauty of the family? She used to protect her—that old woman—Heaven bless her for it,[3] wherever she is now, the old hag— a good word won't do her any harm. Ha-Ha!" His laughter was cruel to hear.

"Why did I come down?" he continued in reply to our sad queries. "Why did I come down do you ask? Because she was wretched and sent for me. Because if I was at the end of the world and she was to say, 'Jack, come!' I'd come."

"And if she bade you go?" asked his friends.

"I would go: and I *have* gone. If she told me to jump into the sea, do you think I would not do it? But I go: and when she is alone with him, do you know what he does? He strikes her:—strikes *that* poor little thing! He has owned to it. She fled from him and sheltered with the old woman who's dead. He may be doing it now. Why did I ever shake hands with him?—that's humiliation sufficient, isn't it? But she wished it: and I'd black his boots, curse him, if she told me. And because he wanted to keep my money in his confounded bank; and because he knew he might rely upon my honour and her's, poor dear child, he chooses to shake hands with me—me whom he hates worse than a thousand devils—and quite right too. Why isn't there a place where we can go and[4] meet like man to man and have it over?—If I had a ball through my brains—I shouldn't mind, I tell you—I've a mind to do it for myself, Pendennis—You don't understand me, Viscount."

[3] it, *E1*] it now, *Ms*
[4] go and *E1*] go out and *Ms*

"Il est vrai," said Florac with a shrug, "I comprehend neither the suicide nor the chaise-de-poste. What will you? I am not yet enough English, my friend. We make marriages of convenance in our country, que diable— and what follows follows—but no scandal afterwards. Do not adopt our institutions a demi, my friend. Vous ne me comprenez pas non plus, mon pauvre Jack!"

"There is one way still, I think," said the third of the speakers in this scene. "Let Lord Highgate come to Rosebury in his own name, leaving that of Mr. Harris behind him. If Sir Barnes Newcome wants you, he can seek you there. If you will go, as go you should and God speed you; you can go and in your own name too."

"Parbleu c'est ça," cries Florac; "he speaks like a book, the Romancier!" I confess for my part I thought that a good woman might plead with him, and touch that manly not disloyal heart now trembling on the awful balance between Evil and Good.

"Allons! let us make to come the drague!" cries Florac. "Jack, thou returnest with us, my friend! Madame Pendennis, an angel my friend, a *quakre* the most charming, shall roucoule to thee the sweetest sermons. My wife shall tend thee like a mother—a grandmother. Go make thy packet!"

Lord Highgate was very much pleased and relieved seemingly. He shook our hands: he said he should never forget our kindness, never! In truth the didactic part of our conversation was carried on at much greater length than as here noted down—And he would come that evening—but not with us, thank you—he had a particular engagement—some letters he must write. Those done he would not fail us and would be at Rosebury by dinner-time.

Chapter XX.

"ONE MORE UNFORTUNATE."

HE Fates did not ordain that the plan should succeed which Lord Highgate's friends had devised for Lady Clara's rescue or respite. He was bent upon one more interview with the unfortunate lady; and in that meeting the future destiny of their luckless lives was decided. On the morning of[1] his return home Barnes Newcome had information that Lord Highgate, under a feigned name, had been staying in the neighbourhood of his house; and had repeatedly been seen in the company of Lady Clara. She may have gone out to meet him but for one hour more. She had taken no leave of her children on the day when she left her home, and far from making preparations for her own departure, had been engaged in getting the house ready for the reception of members of the family whose arrival her husband announced as speedily to follow his own. Ethel and Lady Ann and some of the children were coming. Lord Farintosh's mother and sisters were to follow. It was to be a réunion previous to the marriage which was closer to unite the two families. Lady Clara said Yes to her husband's orders; rose mechanically to obey his wishes and arrange for the reception of the guests; and spoke tremblingly to[2] the housekeeper, as her husband gibed at her. The little ones had been consigned to bed early and before Sir Barnes's arrival. He did not think fit to see them in their sleep: nor did their mother. She did not know, as[3] the poor little

---

[1] of *E1*] after *Ms*
[2] to *E1*] with *Ms*
[3] know, as *E1*] know that as *Ms*

creatures left her room in charge of their nurses, that she looked on them for the last time. Perhaps had she gone to their bedsides that evening, had the wretched panic-stricken soul been allowed leisure to pause and to think and to pray; the fate of the morrow might have been otherwise, and the trembling balance of the scale have inclined to right's side. But the pause was not allowed her. Her husband came, and saluted her with his accustomed greetings of scorn and sarcasm and brutal insult. On a future day he never dared to call a servant of his household to testify to his treatment of her; though many were ready to attend[4] to prove his cruelty and her terror. On that very last night, Lady Clara's maid, a country-girl from her father's house at Chanticlere, told Sir Barnes in the midst of a conjugal dispute that her lady might bear his conduct but she could not: and that she would no longer live under the roof of such a brute. The girl's interference was not likely to benefit her mistress much: the wretched Lady Clara passed the[5] last night under the roof of her husband and children, unattended save by this poor domestic who was about to leave her, in tears and hysterical outcries, and then in moaning stupor. Lady Clara put to sleep with laudanum, her maid carried down the story of her wrongs to the servants' quarters: and half a dozen of them took in their resignation to Sir Barnes as he sate over his breakfast the next morning—in his ancestral hall—surrounded by the portraits of his august forefathers—in his happy home.

Their mutiny of course did not add to their master's good humour: and his letters brought him news which increased Barnes's fury. A messenger arrived with[6] a letter from his man of business at Newcome, upon the receipt of which he started up with such an execration as frightened the servant waiting on him, and letter[7] in hand he ran to Lady Clara's sitting-room. Her ladyship was up: Sir Barnes breakfasted rather late on the first morning after an arrival at Newcome. He had to look over the Bailiff's books, and to look about him round the park and grounds: to curse the gardeners: to damn the stable and kennel grooms: to yell at the woodman for clearing not enough or too much: to rail at the poor old work-people brooming away the fallen leaves, &c.—so Lady Clara was up and dressed when her husband went to her room which lay at the end of the house as we have said, the last of a suite of ancestral halls.

The mutinous servant heard high voice and curses within: then Lady Clara's screams: then Sir Barnes Newcome burst out of the room locking the door and taking the key with him and saluting with more curses James the mutineer over whom his master ran.

"Curse your wife, and don't curse *me*, Sir Barnes Newcome!" said James the mutineer; and knocked down a hand which the infuriated Baronet raised against him with an arm that was thrice as strong as Barnes's own. This man and maid followed their mistress in the[8] sad journey upon which she was bent. They treated her with unalterable respect. They never could

---

[4] many were ready to attend *E1*] twenty were in attendance *Ms HM NY*
[5] the *E1*] her *Ms*
[6] arrived with *E1*] brought him *Ms HM NY*
[7] letter *E1*] this letter *Ms*
[8] the *E1*] that *Ms HM NY*

be got to see that her conduct was wrong. When Barnes's counsel subsequently tried to impugn their testimony, they dared him; and hurt the plaintiff's case very much. For the balance had weighed over; and it was Barnes himself who caused what now ensued: and what we learned in a very few hours afterwards from Newcome where it was the talk of the whole neighbourhood.

Florac and I, as yet ignorant of all that was occurring, met Barnes near his own lodge-gate riding in the direction of Newcome, as we were ourselves returning to Rosebury. The Prince de Montcontour who was driving, affably saluted the Baronet who gave us a scowling recognition, and rode on, his groom behind him. "The figure of this garçon," says Florac as our acquaintance passed, "is not agreeable. Of pale, he has become livid. I hope these two men will not meet: or evil will come." Evil to Barnes there might be, Florac's companion thought, who knew the previous little affairs between Barnes and his uncle and cousin; and that Lord Highgate was quite able to take care of himself.

In half an hour after Florac spoke that meeting between Barnes and Highgate actually had taken place—in the open square of Newcome; within four doors of the King's Arms Inn, close to which lives Sir Barnes Newcome's man of business; and before which, Mr. Harris, as he was called, was walking, and waiting till a carriage which he had ordered came round from the Inn yard. As Sir Barnes Newcome rode into the place many people touched their hats to him however little they loved him. He was bowing and smirking to one of these, when he suddenly saw Belsize.

He started back causing his horse to back with him on to the pavement, and it may have been rage and fury, or accident and nervousness merely, but at this instant Barnes Newcome looking towards Lord Highgate shook his whip.

"You cowardly villain!" said the other springing forward—"I was going to your house."

"How dare you, Sir," cries Sir Barnes, still holding up that unlucky cane, "how dare you to—to—"

"Dare! you scoundrel!" said Belsize. "Is that the cane you strike your wife with, you ruffian!" Belsize[9] seized and tore him out of the saddle, flinging him screaming down on the pavement. The horse, rearing and making a way for himself, galloped down the clattering street; a hundred people were round Sir Barnes in a moment.

The carriage which Belsize had ordered came round at this very juncture. Amidst the crowd shrieking,[1] bustling, expostulating, threatening, who pressed about him, he shouldered his way. Mr. Taplow, aghast, was one of the hundred spectators of the scene.

"I am Lord Highgate," said Barnes's adversary. "If Sir Barnes Newcome wants me, tell him I will send him word where he may hear of me." And getting into the carriage he told the driver to go "to the usual place."

Imagine the hubbub in the town, the conclaves at the inns, the talks in the counting-houses, the commotion amongst the factory people; the

9 Belsize *E1*] And before Barnes could answer, Belsize *Ms*
1 shrieking, *Ms*] shrinking *E1*

Sir Barnes Newcome in Trouble

paragraphs in the Newcome papers, the bustle of surgeons and lawyers after this event. Crowds gathered at the King's Arms and waited round Mr. Speers[2] the lawyer's house into which Sir Barnes was carried. In vain policemen told them to move on: fresh groups gathered after the seceders. On the next day,[3] when Barnes Newcome who was not much hurt had a fly to go home—a factory man shook his fist in at the carriage window, and with a curse said, "Serve you right, you villain!" It was the man whose sweetheart this Don Juan had seduced and deserted years before; whose wrongs were well-known amongst his mates, a leader in the chorus of hatred which growled round Barnes Newcome.

Barnes's mother and sister Ethel had reached Newcome shortly[4] before the return of the master of the house. The people there were in disturbance. Lady Ann and Miss Newcome came out with pallid looks to greet him. He laughed and re-assured them about his accident: indeed his hurt had been trifling: he had been bled by the surgeon, a little jarred by the fall from his horse; but there was no sort of danger. Still their pale and doubtful looks continued. What caused them? In the open day, with a servant attending her, Lady Clara Newcome had left her husband's house: and a letter was forwarded to him that same evening from my Lord Highgate informing Sir Barnes Newcome, that Lady Clara Pulleyn could bear his tyranny no longer and had left his roof: that Lord Highgate proposed to leave England almost immediately, but would remain long enough to afford Sir Barnes Newcome the opportunity for an interview in case he should be disposed to demand one: and a friend (of Lord Highgate's late regiment) was named who would receive letters and act in any way necessary for his lordship.

The debates of the House of Lords must tell what followed afterwards in the dreary history of Lady Clara Pulleyn. The proceedings in the Newcome Divorce Bill filled the usual number of columns in the papers;— especially the Sunday papers. The witnesses were examined by learned peers whose business—nay, pleasure—it seems to be to enter into such matters; and for the ends of justice and morality doubtless, the whole story of Barnes Newcome's household was told to the British public. In the previous trial in the Court of Queen's Bench, how grandly Serjeant Rowland stood up for the rights of British husbands! with what pathos he depicted the conjugal paradise, the innocent children prattling round their happy parents, the serpent, the destroyer entering into that Belgravian Eden; the wretched and deserted husband alone by his desecrated hearth, and calling for redress on his country! Rowland wept freely during his noble harangue. At not a shilling under twenty thousand pounds would he estimate the cost of his client's injuries. The jury was very much affected: the evening papers gave Rowland's address *in extenso* with some pretty sharp raps at the aristocracy in general. The *Day*, the principal morning journal of that period came out with a leading article the next morning, in which every party concerned and every institution was knocked about. The disgrace of the peerage, the ruin of the monarchy (with a retrospective view

<hr>

[2] Speers *E1*] [blank] *Ms*
[3] On the next day, *E1*] In the evening, *Ms*
[4] shortly *E1*] an hour *Ms HM NY*

of the well-known case of Gyges and Candaules), the monstrosity of the crime and the absurdity of the tribunal and the punishment[5] were all set forth in the terrible leading article of the *Day*.

But when on the next day Serjeant Rowland was requested to call witnesses to prove that connubial happiness which he had depicted so pathetically, he had none at hand.

Oliver, Q.C., now had his innings—a man, a husband and a father, Mr. Oliver could not attempt to defend the conduct of his unfortunate client—but if there could be any excuse for such conduct, that excuse he was free to confess the plaintiff had afforded—whose cruelty and neglect twenty[6] witnesses in court were ready to prove—neglect so outrageous, cruelty so systematic that he wondered the plaintiff had not been better advised than to bring this trial with all its degrading particulars to a public issue. On the very day when the ill-omened marriage took place, another victim of cruelty had interposed as vainly—as vainly as Serjeant Rowland himself interposed in Court to prevent this case being made known—and with piteous outcries, in the name of outraged neglected woman—of castaway children pleading in vain for bread, had besought the bride to pause, and the bridegroom to look upon the wretched beings who owed him life. Why had not Lady Clara Pulleyn's friends listened to that appeal? and so on—and so on—between[7] Rowland and Oliver the battle waged fiercely that day—Many witnesses were mauled and slain——out of that combat scarce any body came well, except the two principal champions, Rowland, Serjeant, and Oliver, Q.C. The whole country looked on and heard the wretched story—not only of Barnes's fault and Highgate's fault—but of the private peccadilloes of their suborned footmen and conspiring housemaids. Mr. Justice C. Sawyer charged the Jury at great length—those men were respectable men and fathers of families themselves—of course they dealt full measure to Lord Highgate for his delinquencies; consoled the injured husband with immense damages and left him free to pursue the farther steps for releasing himself altogether from the tie—which had been bound with affecting Episcopal benedictions[8] at St. George's, Hanover Square.

So Lady Clara flies from the custody of her tyrant, but to what a rescue? The very man who loves her and gives her asylum, pities and deplores her. She scarce dares to look out of the windows of her new home upon the world, lest it should know and reproach her. All the sisterhood of friendship is cut off from her. If she dares to go abroad she feels the sneer of the world as she goes[9] through it; and knows that Malice and Scorn whisper behind her. People, as criminal but undiscovered, make room for her as if her touch were pollution. She knows she has darkened the lot and made wretched the home of the man whom she loves best; that his friends who see her, treat her with but a doubtful respect; and the domestics who attend her with a suspicious obedience. In the country lanes or the streets of the county town, neighbours look aside as the carriage

---

5 and the punishment *E1*] [interlined ambiguously after "absurdity"] *Ms*
6 twenty *E1*] fifty living *Ms*
7 between *E1*] So between *Ms*
8 benedictions *Ms*] benediction *E1*
9 goes *E1*] passes *Ms*

passes in which she sits splendid and lonely. Rough hunting companions of her husband's come to her table: he is driven perforce to the company of flatterers and men of inferior sort; his equals, at least in his own home, will not live with him. She would be kind, perhaps and charitable to the cottagers round about her, but she fears to visit them lest they too should scorn her. The clergyman who distributes her charities, blushes and looks awkward on passing her in the village, if he should be walking with his wife or one of his children. Shall they go to the Continent, and set up a grand house at Paris or at Florence? There they can get Society, but of what a sort! Our acquaintances of Baden, Madame Schlangenbad and Madame de Cruchecassée and Madame d'Ivry, and Messrs. Loder and Punter and Blackball and Deuceace will come—and dance and flirt and quarrel and gamble and feast round about her—but what in common with such wild people has this poor timid shrinking Soul? Even these scorn her. The leers and laughter on those painted faces are quite unlike her own sad countenance. She has no reply to their wit. Their infernal gaiety scares her more than the solitude at home. No wonder that her husband does not like home—except for a short while in the hunting season—no wonder that he is away all day—how can he like a home which she has made so wretched? In the midst of her sorrow and doubt and misery a child comes to her: how she clings to it! How her whole being and hope and passion centres itself on this feeble infant! . . but she no more belongs to our story: with the new name she[1] has taken, the poor lady passes out of the history of the Newcomes.

If Barnes Newcome's children meet yonder solitary lady do they know her? If her once-husband thinks upon the unhappy young creature whom his cruelty drove from him, does his conscience affect his sleep at nights?[2] Why should Sir Barnes Newcome's conscience be more squeamish than his country's which has put money in his pocket for having trampled on the poor weak young thing, and scorned her and driven her to ruin? When the whole of the accounts of that wretched bankruptcy are brought up for final Audit which of the unhappy partners shall be shown to be most guilty? Does the Right Reverend Prelate who did the benedictory business for Barnes and Clara his wife repent in secret? Do the parents who pressed the marriage, and the fine folks who signed the book, and ate the breakfast and applauded the bridegroom's speech feel a little ashamed? O Hymen Hymenæe! The bishops, beadles, clergy, pew-openers and other officers of the temple dedicated to Heaven under the invocation of St. George will officiate in the same place at scores and scores more of such marriages. And St. George of England may behold virgin after virgin offered up to the devouring monster Mammon—(with many most respectable female-dragons looking on)—may see virgin after virgin given away, just as in the Soldan of Babylon's time—but with never a Champion to come to the rescue!

---

[1] she *E1*] which she *Ms*
[2] nights? *Ms*] night? *E1*

Chapter XXI.

IN WHICH ACHILLES LOSES BRISEIS.

LTHOUGH the years of the Marquis of Farintosh were few, he had spent most of them in the habit of command; and from his childhood upwards had been obeyed by all persons round about him. As an infant he had but to roar, and his mother and nurses were as much frightened as though he had been a Libyan lion. What he willed and ordered was law amongst his clan and family. During the period of his London and Parisian dissipations his poor mother did not venture to remonstrate with her young prodigal, but shut her eyes, not daring to open them on his wild courses. As for the friends of his person and house, many of whom were portly elderly gentlemen, their affection for the young Marquis was so extreme that there was no company into which their fidelity would not lead them to follow him; and you might see him dancing at Mabille with veteran aides-de-camp looking on, or disporting with opera dancers at a Trois-Frères banquet, which some old gentleman of his father's age had taken the pains to order. If his lordship Count Almaviva wants a friend to carry the lanthorn or to hold the ladder; do you suppose there are not many most respectable men in society who will act Figaro? When Farintosh thought[1] fit, in the fullness of time, and the blooming pride of manhood, to select a spouse, and to elevate a marchioness to his throne, no one dared gainsay him. When he called upon his mother and sisters and their ladyships' hangers on and[2] attendants, upon his own particular kinsmen, led captains and toadies to bow the knee and do homage to the woman whom he delighted to honour, those duteous subjects trembled and obeyed. In

[1] family. During the period ... When Farintosh thought *E1*] family. When he thought *Ms HM NY*
[2] hangers on and *E1*] hangers and *Ms*

fact he thought that the position of a Marchioness of Farintosh was, under Heaven and before men, so splendid that had he elevated a beggar-maid to that sublime rank, the inferior world was bound to worship her.

So my lord's lady-mother and my lord's sisters and his captains and his players of billiards and the toadies of his august person all performed obeisance to his bride elect and never questioned the will of the young chieftain. What were the private comments[3] of the ladies of the family we have[4] no means of knowing; but it may naturally be supposed that his lordship's gentlemen in waiting, Captain Henchman, Jack Todhunter and the rest, had many misgivings of their own respecting their patron's change in life and could not view without anxiety the advent of a mistress who might reign over him and them, who might possibly not like their company and might exert her influence over her husband to oust these honest fellows from places in which they were very comfortable. The jovial rogues had the run of my lord's kitchen, stables, cellars, and cigar-boxes. A new marchioness might hate hunting, smoking, jolly parties and toad-eaters in general, or might bring into the house favourites of her own. I am sure any kind-hearted man of the world must feel for the position of these faithful, doubtful, disconsolate vassals and have a sympathy for their rueful looks and demeanour as they eye the splendid preparations for the ensuing marriage, the grand furnitures sent to my lord's castles and houses, the magnificent plate provided for his tables—tables at which they may never have a knife and fork; castles and houses of which the poor rogues may never be allowed to pass the doors.

When then "the Elopement in High Life" which has been described in the previous pages burst upon the town in the morning papers, I can fancy the agitation which the news occasioned in the faithful bosoms of the generous Todhunter, and the attached Henchman. My lord was not in his own house as yet. He and his friends still lingered on in the little house in May Fair, the dear little bachelor's quarters, where they had enjoyed such good dinners, such good suppers, such rare doings, such a jolly time. I fancy Hench coming down to breakfast and reading the *Morning Post*. I imagine Tod dropping in from his bed-room over the way, and Hench handing the paper over to Tod, and the conversation which ensued between those worthy men. Elopement in high life—excitement in N—come, flight[5] of Lady Cl— N—come, daughter of the late and sister of the present Earl of D— rking, with Lord H—gate; personal rencontre between Lord H—gate and Sir B—nes N—come. Extraordinary disclosures. I say, I can fancy Hench and Tod over this awful piece of news.

"Pretty news, ain't it, Toddy," says Henchman looking up from a Perigord pie, which the faithful creature is discussing.

"Always expected it," remarks the other. "Any body who saw them together last season must have known it.[6] The Chief himself spoke of it to me."

[3] comments *E1*] sentiments *Ms*
[4] have *Ms*] had *E1*
[5] flight *Ms*] and flight *E1*
[6] it. *E1*] of it. *Ms*

"It'll cut him up awfully when he reads it. Is it in the *Morning Post?* He has the *Post* in his bed-room. I know he has rung his bell: I heard it. Bowman, has his lordship read his paper yet?"

Bowman the valet said, "I believe you he *have* read his paper. When he read it; he jumped out of bed and swore most awful. I cut as soon as I could," continued Mr. Bowman, who was on familiar nay contemptuous terms with the other two gentlemen.

"Enough to make any man swear," says Toddy to Henchman; and both were alarmed in their noble souls, reflecting that their Chieftain was now actually getting up and dressing himself; that he would, speedily and in the course of nature, come down-stairs; and then most probably would begin swearing at *them.*

The most noble Mungo Malcolm Angus was in an awful state of mind when at length he appeared in his[7] breakfast-room. "Why the dash do you make a tap-room of this," he cries—the trembling Henchman who has begun to smoke as he has done a hundred times before in this bachelor's hall, flings his cigar into the fire.

"There you go! Nothing like it! Why don't you fling some more in?[8] You can get 'em at Hudson's for five guineas a pound;" bursts out the youthful Peer.

"I can understand why you are out of sorts, old boy," says Henchman stretching out his manly hand. A tear of compassion twinkled in his eyelid, and coursed down his mottled cheek. "Cut away at old Frank, Farintosh,— a fellow who has been attached to you since before you could speak. It's not when a fellow's down and cut up, and riled—naturally riled as you are— I know you are, Marquis—it's not then that I'm going to be angry with him.[9] Pitch in to old Frank Henchman—hit away, my young one"—and Frank put himself into an attitude as of one prepared to receive a pugilistic assault. He bared his breast as it were and showed his scars and said, "Strike." Frank Henchman was a florid toady—my uncle, Major Pendennis, has often laughed with me about the fellow's pompous flatteries and ebullient fidelity.

"You have read this confounded paragraph?" says the Marquis.

"We *have* read it: and were deucedly cut up too," says Henchman, "for your sake, my dear boy."

"I remembered what you said last year, Marquis," cries Todhunter (not unadroitly). "You yourself pointed out—in this very room, I recollect, at this very table—that night Coralie and the little Spanish dancer and her mother supped here, and there was a talk about Highgate—you yourself pointed out what was likely to happen. I doubted it: for I have dined at the Newcomes' and seen Highgate and her together in society often. But though you are a younger bird you have better eyes than I have—and you saw the thing at once—at once, don't you remember? and Coralie said how glad she was, because Sir Barnes ill-treated her friend—what was the name of Coralie's friend, Hench."

[7] his *Ms*] the *E1*
[8] in? *E1*] cigars in? *Ms*
[9] him. *Ms*] you. *E1*

"How should *I* know her confounded name?" Henchman briskly answers. "What do I care for Sir Barnes Newcome and his private affairs? He is no friend of mine. I never said he was a friend of mine. I never said I liked him. Out of respect for the Chief here, I held my tongue about him and shall hold my tongue. Have some of this pâté, Chief! No? Poor old boy. I know you haven't got an appetite. I know this news cuts you up. I say nothing and make no pretence of condolence: though I feel for you—and you know you can count on old Frank Henchman—don't you, Malcolm?" And again he turns away to conceal his gallant sensibility and generous emotion.

"What does it matter to me?" bursts out the Marquis, garnishing his conversation with the usual expletives which adorned his eloquence when he was strongly moved, "What do I care for Barnes Newcome and his confounded affairs and family? I never want to see him again but in the light of a banker, when I go to the City where he keeps my account. I say I have nothing to do with him or all the Newcomes under the sun. Why, one of them is a painter, and will paint my dog Ratcatcher, by Jove, or my horse, or my groom if I give him the order. Do you think I care for any one of the pack? It's not the fault of the Marchioness of Farintosh that her family is not equal to mine. Besides two others in England and Scotland I should like to know what family is? I tell you what, Hench—I bet you five to two, that before an hour is over, my mother will be here, and down on her knees to me begging me to break off this engagement."

"And what will you do, Farintosh," asks Henchman slowly, "Will you break it off?"

"No!" shouts the Marquis. "Why shall I break off with the finest girl in England,—and the best-plucked one, and the cleverest and wittiest, and the most beautiful creature, by Jove, that ever stepped, for no fault of hers, and because her sister-in-law leaves her brother who I know treated her infernally? We have talked this matter over at home before. I wouldn't dine with the fellow; though he was always asking me; nor meet, except just out of civility, any of his confounded family—Lady Ann is different— she is a lady, she is. She is a good woman: and Kew is a most respectable man, though he is only a peer of George III's creation, and you should hear how *he* speaks of Miss Newcome, though she refused him. I should like to know who is to prevent me marrying Lady Ann Newcome's daughter?"

"By Jove you are a good-plucked fellow, Farintosh—give me your hand, old boy!" says Henchman.

"Hm! am I? You would have said, give me your hand, old boy, whichever way I determined, Hench. I tell you I ain't intellectual and that sort of thing. But I know my rank, and I know my place; and when a man of my station gives his word, he sticks to it, Sir; and my lady and my sisters may go on their knees all round, and by Jove I won't flinch."

The justice of Lord Farintosh's views was speedily proved by the appearance of his lordship's mother Lady Glenlivat whose arrival put a stop to a conversation which Captain Francis Henchman has often subsequently narrated. She besought to see her son in terms so urgent that the young nobleman could not be denied to his parent: and no doubt a long and interesting interview took place in which Lord Farintosh's mother passionately implored him to break off a match upon which he was as resolutely bent.

Was it a sense of honour, a longing desire to possess this young beauty and call her his own, or a fierce and profound dislike to being balked in any object of his wishes, which actuated the young lord? Certainly he had borne very philosophically delay after delay which had taken place in the devised union; and being quite sure of his mistress, had not cared to press on the marriage but lingered over the dregs of his bachelor cup complacently still. We all know in what an affecting farewell he took leave of the associates of his *vie de garçon*: the speeches made (in both languages), the presents distributed, the tears and hysterics of some of the guests assembled; the cigar boxes given over to this friend, the *écrin* of diamonds to that, et cetera, et cetera, et cetera. Don't we know?—if we don't it is not Henchman's fault who has told the story of Farintosh's *sposalizie*[1] a thousand and one times at his clubs, at the houses where he is asked to dine on account of his intimacy with the nobility, among the young men of fashion or no fashion whom this two-bottle Mentor and burly admirer of youth has since taken upon himself to form. The farewell at Greenwich was so affecting that all[2] "traversed the cart" and took another farewell at Richmond, where there was crying too, but it was Eucharis cried because fair Calypso wanted to tear her eyes out; and where not only Telemachus (as was natural to his age) but Mentor likewise[3] quaffed the wine cup too freely. You are virtuous, O reader, but there are still cakes and ale. Ask Henchman if there be not. You will find him in the park any afternoon; he will dine with you if no better man ask him in the interval. He will tell you story upon story regarding young Lord Farintosh, and his marriage, and what happened before his marriage, and afterwards; and he will sigh, weep almost at some moments, as he narrates their subsequent quarrel and Farintosh's unworthy conduct, and tells you how he formed that young man. My uncle and Captain Henchman disliked each other very much I am sorry to say—sorry too to[4] add that it was very amusing to hear either one of them speak of the other.

Lady Glenlivat, according to the Captain then, had no success in the[5] interview with her son; who, unmoved by the maternal tears, commands and entreaties swore he would marry Miss Newcome, and that no power on earth should prevent him. "As if trying to thwart that man—*could* ever prevent his having his way!" ejaculated his quondam friend.

But on the next day after ten thousand men in clubs and coteries had talked the news over; after the evening had repeated and improved the delightful theme of our "morning contemporaries"; after Calypso and Eucharis driving together in the park and reconciled now had kissed their hands to Lord Farintosh, and made him their compliments—after a night

---

[1] *sposalizie Ms*] betrothals *E1*
[2] all *E1*] they all *Ms*
[3] likewise *E1*] too *Ms*
[4] too to *Ms*] to *E1*
[5] the *E1*] her *Ms*

of natural disturbance, doubt,[6] defiance, fury—as men whispered to each other at the club where his lordship dined and at the theatre where he took his recreation—after an awful time at breakfast in which Messrs. Bowman, valet, and Todhunter and Henchman, captains of the Farintosh bodyguard, all got their share of kicks and growling—behold Lady Glenlivat came back to the charge again; and this time with such force that poor Lord Farintosh was shaken indeed.

Her ladyship's ally was no other than Miss Newcome herself; from whom Lord Farintosh's mother received by that day's post a letter which she was commissioned to read to her son.

"DEAR MADAM (wrote the young lady in her firmest hand-writing), Mamma is at this moment in a state of such *grief and dismay* at the *cruel* misfortune and *humiliation* which has just befallen our family; that she is really not able to write to you as she *ought*, and this task, painful as it is, must be *mine*. Dear Lady Glenlivat, the kindness and confidence which I have ever received from you and *yours*, merit truth and most grateful respect and regard from *me*. And I feel after the late fatal occurrence, what I have often and often owned to myself though I did not *dare* to acknowledge it, that I ought to release Lord F. *at once and for ever,* from an engagement *which he could never think* of maintaining with a family *so unfortunate as our's*. I thank him with all my heart for his goodness in bearing with my humours so long; if I have given him pain as I *know* I have sometimes I beg his pardon and would do so *on my knees*. I hope and pray he may be happy, as I feared he never could be with me. He has many good and noble qualities; and, in bidding him farewell, I trust I may retain his friendship, and that he will believe in the esteem and gratitude of your most sincere

"ETHEL NEWCOME."

A copy of this farewell letter was seen by a lady who happened to be a neighbour of Miss Newcome's when the family misfortune occurred: and to whom in her natural dismay and grief the young lady fled for comfort and consolation. "Dearest Mrs. Pendennis," wrote Miss Ethel to my wife, "I hear you are at Rosebury; do, do come to your affectionate E. N."—The next day, it was "Dearest Laura. If you can, pray, pray come to Newcome this morning. I want very much to speak to you about the poor children, to consult[7] you about something most *important*." Madame de Montcontour's poney-carriage was trotting constantly between Rosebury and Newcome in these days of calamity.

And my wife as in duty bound gave me full reports of all that happened in that house of mourning. On the very day of[8] the flight, Lady Ann, her daughter, and some others of her family arrived at Newcome. The deserted little girl, Barnes's eldest child, ran with tears and cries of joy to her Aunt Ethel whom she had always loved better than her mother; and clung to her and embraced her; and in her artless little words told her

---

[6] disturbance, doubt, *Ms*] doubt, disturbance, *E1*
[7] to consult *E1*] consult *Ms*
[8] very day of *E1*] day after *Ms HM NY*

that Mamma had gone away, and that Ethel should be her mamma now. Very strongly moved by the misfortune as by the caresses and affection of the poor orphaned creature, Ethel took the little girl to her heart, and promised to be a mother to her, and that she would not leave her; in which pious resolve I scarcely need say Laura strengthened her, when, at her young friend's urgent summons, my wife came to her.

The household at Newcome was in a state of disorganisation after the catastrophe. Two of Lady Clara's servants, it has been stated already, went away with her. The luckless master of the house was lying wounded in the neighbouring town. Lady Ann Newcome, his mother, was terribly agitated by the news which was abruptly broken to her of the flight of her daughter-in-law and her son's danger. Now she thought of flying[9] to Newcome to nurse him; and then feared lest she should be ill received by[1] the invalid— indeed ordered by Sir Barnes to go home and not to bother him. So at home Lady Ann remained, where[2] the thoughts of the sufferings she had already undergone in that house, of Sir Barnes's cruel behaviour to her at[3] her last visit which he had abruptly requested her to shorten—of the happy days which she had passed as mistress of that house and wife of the defunct Sir Brian—the sight of that departed angel's picture in the dining-room and wheel-chair in the gallery; the recollection of little Barnes as a cherub of a child in that very gallery and pulled out of the fire by a nurse in the second year of his age when he was all that a fond mother could[4] wish—these incidents and reminiscences so agitated Lady Ann Newcome, that she for her part went off in a series of hysterical fits and acted as one distraught: her second daughter screamed in sympathy with her: and Miss[5] Newcome had to take the command of the whole of this demented household, hysterical mamma and sister, mutineering servants, and shrieking abandoned nursery; and bring young people and old to peace and quiet.

On the morrow[6] after his little concussion Sir Barnes Newcome came home, not much hurt in body but wofully afflicted in temper, and venting his wrath upon every body round about him in that strong language which he employed when displeased; and under which his valet, his housekeeper, his butler, his farm-bailiff, his lawyer, his doctor, his dishevelled mother herself—who rose from her couch and her sal-volatile to fling herself round her dear boy's knees—all had to suffer. Ethel Newcome, the Baronet's sister, was the only person in his house to whom Sir Barnes did not utter oaths or proffer rude speeches. He was afraid of offending her or encountering that resolute spirit, and lapsed into a surly silence in her presence. Indistinct maledictions growled about Sir Barnes's[7] chair, when

---

[9] Now ... flying *E1*] She insisted on flying *Ms*
[1] and then ... received by *E1*] and being received not very graciously by *Ms*
[2] him. So ... remained, where *E1*] him—home Lady Ann returned where *Ms*
[3] at *E1*] on *Ms*
[4] could *Ms E1*] would *R*
[5] her: and Miss *E1*] her so that Miss *Ms*
[6] morrow *E1*] third day *Ms*
[7] maledictions growled about Sir Barnes's *E1*] maledictory expressions growled about his *Ms HM NY*

he beheld my wife's poney-carriage drive up; and he asked what brought *her*[8] here? But Ethel sternly told her brother that Mrs. Pendennis came at her particular request; and asked him whether he supposed any body could come into that house for pleasure now, or for any other motive but kindness? upon which Sir Barnes fairly burst out into tears intermingled with execrations against his enemies and his own fate and assertions that he was the most miserable beggar alive. He would not see his children: but with more tears he would implore Ethel never to leave them, and anon would ask what he should do when she married, and he was left alone in that infernal house?

T. Potts, Esquire, of the *Newcome Independent* used to say afterwards that the Baronet was in the direst terror of another meeting with Lord Highgate, and kept a policeman at the lodge gate and a second in the kitchen, to interpose in event of a collision. But Mr. Potts made this statement in after days when the quarrel between his party and paper and Sir Barnes Newcome was flagrant. Five or six days after the meeting of the two rivals in Newcome market-place, Sir Barnes received a letter from a[9] friend of Lord Highgate informing him that his lordship having waited for him according to promise, had now left England and presumed that the differences between them were to be settled by their respective lawyers—infamous behaviour on a par with the rest of Lord Highgate's villainy, the Baronet said—"When the scoundrel knew I could lift my pistol-arm," Barnes said, "Lord Highgate fled the country"—thus hinting that death and not damages were what he intended to seek from his enemy.

After that interview in which Ethel communicated to Laura her farewell-letter to Lord Farintosh, my wife returned to Rosebury with an extraordinary brightness and gaiety in her face and her demeanour. She pressed Madame de Montcontour's hands with such warmth, she blushed and looked so handsome, she sang and talked so gaily, that our host was struck by her behaviour, and paid her husband more compliments regarding her beauty, amiability and other good qualities, than need be set down here. It may be that I like Paul de Florac so much (in spite of certain undeniable faults of character) because of his admiration for my wife. She was in such a hurry to talk to me that night that Paul's game and Nicotian amusements were cut short by her visit to the billiard-room; and when we were alone by the cozy dressing-room fire she told me what had happened during the day. Why should Ethel's refusal of Lord Farintosh have so much elated my wife?

"Ah," cries Mrs. Pendennis, "she has a generous nature, and the world has not had time to spoil it. Do you know there are many points that she never has thought of—I would say problems that she has to work out for herself, only you, Pen, do not like us poor ignorant women to use such a learned word as problems. Life and experience force things upon her mind, which others learn from their parents or those who educate them, but for which she has never had any teachers. Nobody has ever told her,

[8] *her E1*] her *Ms*
[9] a *Ms*] the *E1*

Arthur, that it was wrong to marry without love, or pronounce lightly those awful vows which we utter before God at the altar. I believe, if she knew that her life was futile, it is but of late she has thought it could be otherwise and that she might mend it. I have read (besides that poem of Goethe of which you are so fond), in books of Indian travels, of Bayaderes, dancing girls brought up by troops round about the temples; whose calling is to dance and wear jewels and look beautiful—They perform before the priests in the pagodas;—I believe they are quite respected in—in Pagoda-land— and the Brahmins and the Indian princes marry them. Can we cry out against these poor creatures, or against the custom of their country?—It seems to me that young women in our world are bred up in a way not very different. What they do they scarcely know to be wrong. They are educated for the world and taught to display: their mothers will give them to the richest suitor, as they themselves were given before. How can these think seriously, Arthur, of souls to be saved, weak hearts to be kept out of temptation, prayers to be uttered, and a better world to be held always in view, when the vanities of this one are all their thought and scheme? Ethel's simple talk made me smile sometimes do you know and her *strenuous* way of imparting her discoveries. I thought of the shepherd boy who made a watch and found on taking it into the town how very many watches there were, and how much better than his. But the poor child has had to make her's for herself, such as it is; and indeed is employed now in working on it. She told me very artlessly her little history, Arthur: it affected me to hear her simple talk; and—and I blessed God for our mother, my dear, and that my early days had had a better guide.

"You know that for[1] a long time it was settled that she was to marry her cousin Lord Kew. She was bred to that notion from her earliest youth; about which she spoke as we all can about our early days. They were spent, she said, in the nursery and schoolroom for the most part. She was allowed to come to her mother's dressing-room, and sometimes to see more of her during the winter at Newcome. She describes her mother as always the kindest of the kind: but from very early times the daughter must have felt her own superiority, I think, though she does not speak of it. You should see her at home now in their dreadful calamity. She seems the only person of the house who keeps her head.

"She told very nicely and modestly how it was Lord Kew who parted from her, not she who had dismissed him, as you know the Newcomes used to say—I have heard that—oh—that *man* Sir Barnes say so myself. She says humbly that her cousin Kew was a great deal too good for her—and so is everyone almost, she adds, poor thing!"

"Poor everyone! Did you ask about him? Laura," said Mr. Pendennis.

"No I did not venture. She looked at me out of her downright eyes and went on with her little tale. 'I was scarcely more than a child then,' she continued. 'And though I liked Kew very much—who would not like such a generous honest creature?—I felt somehow that I was *taller* than my cousin and as if I ought not to marry him or should make him unhappy if

[1] that for *E1*] for *Ms*

I did. When poor Papa used to talk, we children remarked that Mamma hardly listened to him: and so we did not respect him as we should and Barnes especially was[2] scoffing and odious with him. Why, when he was a boy he used to sneer at Papa openly before us younger ones—now Harriet admires everything that Kew says and that makes her a great deal happier at being with him.' And then," added Mrs. Pendennis, "Ethel said, 'I hope you respect *your* husband, Laura: depend on it you will be happier if you do.' Was not that a fine discovery of Ethel's? Mr. Pen!

" 'Clara's terror of Barnes frightened me when I staid in the house,'[3] Ethel went on. 'I am sure *I* would not tremble before any man in the world as she did—I saw early that she used to deceive him and tell him lies, Laura—I do not mean lies of words alone—but lies of looks, and actions. O, I do not wonder at her flying from him! He was dreadful to be with: cruel and selfish[4] and cold. He was made worse by marrying a woman he did not love, as she was by that unfortunate union with him. Suppose he had found a clever woman who could have controlled him, and amused him, and whom he and his friends could have admired, instead of poor Clara who made his home wearisome and trembled when he entered it? Suppose she could have married that unhappy man to whom she was attached early? I was frightened, Laura, to think how ill this worldly marriage had prospered.

" 'My poor grandmother, whenever I spoke upon such a subject, would break out into a thousand gibes and sarcasms and point to many of our friends who had made love-matches and were quarreling now as fiercely as though they had never loved each other. You remember that dreadful case in France of the Duc de —— who murdered his Duchess? That was a love-match and I can remember the sort of *screech* with which Lady Kew used to speak about it; and of the journal which the poor Duchess kept and in which she noted down all her husband's ill behaviours.' "

"Hush, Laura! Do you remember where we are? If the Princess were to put down all Florac's culpabilities in an Album—what a ledger it would be—as big as Dr. Portman's Chrysostoms." But this was parenthetical, and after a smile, and a little respite, the young woman proceeded in her narration of her friend's history.

" 'I was willing enough to listen,' Ethel said, 'to Grandmamma then: for we are glad of an excuse to do what we like; and I liked admiration and rank and great wealth, Laura; and Lord Farintosh offered me these. I liked to surpass my companions and I saw *them* so eager in pursuing him! You can not think, Laura, what meannesses women in the world will commit—mothers and daughters too, in the pursuit[5] of a person of his great rank. Those Miss Burrs,[6] you should have seen them at the country-houses where we visited together and how they followed him—how they would meet him in the parks and shrubberies: how they liked smoking

---

[2] especially was *Ms*] was especially *E1*
[3] house,' *E1*] with them,' *Ms*
[4] cruel and selfish *Ms*] cruel, and selfish, *E1*
[5] the pursuit *E1*] pursuit *Ms*
[6] Burrs, *E1*] [blank] *Ms*

though I knew it made them ill—how they were always finding pretexts for getting near him. O it was odious.'"

I would not willingly interrupt the narrative, but let[7] the reporter be allowed here to state that at this point of Miss Newcome's story (which my wife gave with a very pretty imitation of the girl's manner), we both burst out laughing so loud that little Madame de Montcontour put her head into the drawing-room[8] and asked what we was a laughing at?[9] We did not tell our hostess that poor Ethel and her grandmother had been accused of doing the very same thing, for which she found fault with the Misses Burr. Miss Newcome thought *herself* quite innocent, or how should she have cried out at the naughty behaviour of other people?[1]

" 'Wherever we went, however,' resumed my wife's young penitent, 'it[2] was easy to see, I think I may say so without vanity, who was the object of Lord Farintosh's attention. He followed us everywhere; and we could not go upon any visit in England or Scotland but he was in the same house. Grandmamma's whole heart was bent upon that marriage, and when he proposed for me I do not disown that I was very pleased and vain.

" 'It is in these last months that I have heard about him more and learned to know him better—him and myself too, Laura. Some one, some one you know and whom I shall always love as a brother reproached me in former days for a worldliness about which you talk too sometimes. But it is not worldly to give yourself up for your family, is it? One cannot help the rank in which one is born, and surely it is but natural and proper to marry in it— not that Lord Farintosh thinks me or any one of his rank. (Here Miss Ethel laughed.)[3] He is the Sultan and we—every unmarried girl in society—is his humblest slave. His Majesty's opinions upon this subject did not suit me I can assure you!—I have no notion of such pride!

" 'But I do not disguise from you, dear Laura, that after accepting him, as I came to know him better and heard him and heard of him and talked with him daily and understood Lord Farintosh's character, I looked forward with more and more doubt to the day when I was to become his wife. I have not learned to respect him in these months that I have known him and during which there has been mourning in our families. I will not talk to you about him; I have no right, have I? to hear him speak out his heart, and tell it to any friend. He said he liked me because I did not flatter him. Poor Malcolm! They all do. What was my acceptance of him, Laura, but flattery? yes flattery, and servility to rank, and a desire to possess it. Would I have accepted plain Malcolm Roy? I sent away a better than him, Laura.

" 'These things have been brooding in my mind, for some months past— I must have been but an ill companion for him, and indeed he bore with my

7 I would not willingly interrupt the narrative, but let *E1 R*] [footnote] In order not to interrupt the narrative let *Ms*
8 drawing-room *E1*] dressing-room *Ms*
9 I would not willingly ... a laughing at? *E1 R*] [In a footnote] *Ms HM NY*
1 We did not ... other people? *E1*] [absent] *Ms HM NY*
2 however,' ... penitent, 'it *E1 R*] however, it *Ms HM NY*
3 (Here Miss Ethel laughed.) *E1 R*] [parenthetical interruption placed after "marry in it" above and reads: marry in it—not (here Miss Ethel laughed)—not that Lord Farintosh] *Ms HM NY*

waywardness much more kindly than I ever thought possible; and when four days since we came to this sad house, where he was to have joined us, and I found only dismay and wretchedness and these poor children deprived of a mother whom I pity, God help her, for she has been made so miserable—and is now and must be to the end of her days;—as I lay awake, thinking of my own future life, and that I was going to marry as poor Clara had married but for an establishment and a position in life—I, my own mistress, and not obedient by[4] nature or a slave to others as that poor creature was—I thought to myself, why shall I do this? Now Clara has left us, and is, as it were, dead to us who made her so unhappy, let me be the mother to her orphans. I love the little girl and she has always loved me and came crying to me that day when we arrived and put her dear little arms round my neck, and said, *You* won't go away, will you, Aunt Ethel? in her sweet voice. And I will stay with her: and will try and learn myself that I may teach her: and learn to be good too—better than I have been. Will praying help me, Laura? I did. I[5] am sure I was right, and that it is my duty to stay here.'"

Laura was greatly moved as she told her friend's confessions; and when the next day at church the clergyman read the opening words of the service I thought a peculiar radiance and happiness beamed from her bright face.

Some subsequent occurrences in the history of this branch of the New-come family I am enabled to report from the testimony of the same infor-mant who has just given us an account of her own feelings and life. Miss Ethel and my wife were now in daily communication, and "my-dearesting" each other with that female fervour, which, cold men of the world as we are,—not only chary of warm expressions of friendship but averse to en-tertaining warm feelings at all,—we surely must admire in persons of the inferior sex, whose loves grow up and reach the skies in a night; who kiss, embrace, console, call each other by Christian names, in that sweet kindly sisterhood of Misfortune and Compassion who are always entering into partnership here in life. I say the world is full of Miss Nightingales; and we, sick and wounded in our private Scutaris, have countless nurse-tenders. I did not see my wife, ministering to the afflicted family at Newcome Park; but I can fancy her there amongst the women and children, her prudent counsel, her thousand gentle offices, her apt pity and cheerfulness, the love and truth glowing in her face, and inspiring her words, movements, demeanour. Mrs. Pendennis's husband for his part did not attempt to con-sole Sir Barnes Newcome Newcome, Baronet. I never professed to have a halfpennyworth of pity at that gentleman's command. Florac who owed Barnes his principality and his present comforts in life did make some futile efforts at condolence, but was received by the Baronet with such fierceness and evident ill-humour that he did not care to repeat his visits, and allowed him to vent his curses and peevishness on his own immediate dependents. We used to ask Laura on her return to Rosebury from her charity-visits to Newcome, about the poor suffering master of the house.

---

[4] by *E1*] of my *Ms*
[5] I *E1*] And I *Ms*

She faltered and stammered in describing him and what she heard of him: she smiled, I grieve to say, for this unfortunate lady cannot help having a sense of humour; and we could not help laughing outright sometimes at the idea of that discomfited wretch, that overbearing creature overborne in his turn—which laughter Mrs. Laura used to chide as very naughty and unfeeling. When we went into Newcome the landlord of the King's Arms looked knowing and quizzical: Tom Potts grinned at me and rubbed his hands. "This business serves the paper better than Mr. Warrington's articles," says Mr. Potts. "We have sold no end of Independents: and if you polled the whole borough, I bet that five to one would say Sir Screwcome Screwcome was served right. By the way what's up about the Marquis of Farintosh, Mr. Pendennis? He arrived at the Arms last night; went over to the Park this morning and is gone back to town by the afternoon train."

What had happened between the Marquis of Farintosh and Miss Newcome I am enabled to know from the report of Miss Newcome's confidante. On the receipt of that letter of *congé* which has been mentioned in a former chapter, his lordship must have been very much excited, for he left town straightway by that evening's mail and on the next morning, after a few hours of rest at his inn, was at Newcome lodge gate demanding to see the Baronet.

On that morning it chanced that Sir Barnes had left home with Mr. Speers,[6] his legal adviser: and hereupon the Marquis asked to see Miss Newcome; nor could the lodge-keeper venture to exclude so distinguished a person from the Park. His lordship drove up to the house, and his name was taken to Miss Ethel: she turned very pale when she heard it; and my wife divined at once who was her visitor. Lady Ann had not left her room as yet. Laura Pendennis remained in command of the little conclave of children with whom the two ladies were sitting when Lord Farintosh arrived. Little Clara wanted to go with her aunt as she rose to leave the room—the child could scarcely be got to part from her now.

At the end of an hour the carriage was seen driving away, and Ethel returned looking as pale as before, and red about the eyes. Miss Clara's mutton chop for dinner coming in at the same time, the child was not so presently eager for her aunt's company. Aunt Ethel cut up the mutton chop very neatly, and then having seen the child comfortably seated at her meal, went with her friend into a neighbouring apartment (of course with some pretext of showing Laura a picture, or a piece of china, or a new child's frock, or with some other hypocritical pretence by which the ingenuous female attendants pretended to be utterly blinded) and there, I have no doubt, before beginning her story, dearest Laura embraced dearest Ethel and *vice versâ*.

"He is gone!" at length gasps dearest Ethel.

"*Pour toujours?* poor young man!" sighs dearest Laura. "Was he very unhappy, Ethel?"

"He was more angry," Ethel answers. "He had a right to be hurt but not to speak as he did. He lost his temper quite at last, and broke out in

6 Speers, *E1*] [blank] *Ms*

the most frantic reproaches. He forgot all respect and even gentlemanlike behaviour. Do you know he used words—words such as Barnes uses sometimes when he is angry?—and dared this language to me? I was sorry till then, very sorry and very much moved: but I know more than ever now that I was right in refusing Lord Farintosh."

Dearest Laura now pressed for an account of all that had happened, which may be briefly told as follows. Feeling very deeply upon the subject which brought him to Miss Newcome, it was no wonder that Lord Farintosh spoke at first in a way which moved her. He said he thought her letter to his mother was very rightly written under the circumstances and thanked her for her generosity in offering to release him from his engagement. But the affair—the painful circumstance of Highgate and that—which had happened in the Newcome family was no fault of Miss Newcome's, and Lord Farintosh could not think of holding her accountable. His friends had long urged him to marry, and it was by his mother's own wish that the engagement was formed which he was determined to maintain. In his course through the world (of which he was getting very tired) he had never seen a woman, a lady who was so—so, you[7] understand, Ethel—whom he admired so much, who was likely to make so good a wife for him as you are. "You allude," he continued, "to differences we have had: and we *have* had them: but many of them, I own, have been from my fault. I have been bred up in a way different to most young men. I cannot help it if I have had temptations to which other men are not exposed; and have been placed by—by Providence—in a high rank of life; I am sure if you share it with me you will adorn it, and be in every way worthy of it, and make me much better than I have been. If you knew what a night of agony I passed after my mother read that letter to me—I know you'd pity me, Ethel—I know you would. The idea of losing you makes me wild. My mother was dreadfully alarmed when she saw the state I was in; so was the Doctor:—I assure you he was. And I had no rest at all and no peace of mind until I determined to come down to you; and say that I adored you and you only; and that I would hold to my engagement in spite of everything—and prove to you that—that no man in the world could love you more sincerely than I do." Here the young gentleman was so overcome that he paused in his speech, and gave way to an emotion for which surely no man who has been in the same condition with Lord Farintosh, will blame him.

Miss Newcome was also much touched by this exhibition of natural feeling; and, I daresay, it was at this time that her eyes showed the first symptoms of that malady of which the traces were visible an hour after.

"You are very generous and kind to me, Lord Farintosh," she said. "Your constancy honours me very much and proves how good and loyal you are: but, but do not think hardly of me for saying that the more I have thought of what has happened here, of the wretched consequences of interested marriages, the long union growing each day so miserable that at last it becomes intolerable and is burst asunder as in poor Clara's case, the more I am resolved not to commit that first fatal step of entering into a

---

[7] so—so, you *Ms*] so—you *E1*

marriage without—without the degree of affection which people who take
that vow ought to feel for one another."

"Affection! Can you doubt it? Gracious Heavens I adore you. Isn't my
being here a proof that I do?" cries the young lady's lover.

"But I?" answered the girl. "I have asked my own heart that question
before now.[8] I have thought to myself; if he comes after all, if his affection
for me survives this disgrace of our family, as it has, and every one of us
should be thankful to you—ought I not to show at least gratitude for so
much kindness and honour, and devote myself to one who makes such
sacrifices for me? But before all things I owe you the truth, Lord Farintosh.
I never could make you happy, I know I could not: nor obey you as you
are accustomed to be obeyed; nor give you such a devotion as you have a
right to expect from your wife. I thought I might once; I can't now. I know
that I took you because you were rich and had a great name: not because
you were honest and attached to me as you show yourself to be. I ask your
pardon for the deceit I practised on you—Look at Clara, poor child, and
her misery! My pride I know would never have let me fall as far as she has
done: but, O! I am humiliated to think that I could have been made to say
I would take the first step in that awful career."

"What career, in God's name!" cries the astonished suitor—"Humiliated,
Ethel! Who's going to humiliate you? I suppose there is no woman in
England who[9] need be humiliated by becoming my wife. I should like to
see the one that I can't pretend to—or to royal blood if I like: it's not better
than mine. Humiliated indeed! That *is* news. Ha ha! You don't suppose
that your pedigree which I know all about and the Newcome family, with
your barber surgeon to Edward the Confessor, are equal to . . ."

"To your's? No. It is not very long that I have learned to disbelieve in
that story altogether. I fancy it was an odd whim of my poor father's and
that our family were quite poor people."

"I knew it," said Lord Farintosh: "Do you suppose there were not plenty
of women to tell it me?"

"It was not because we were poor that I am ashamed,"[1] Ethel went on.
"That can not be our fault though some of us seem to think it is, as they
hide the truth so. One of my uncles used to tell me that my grandfather's
father was a labourer in Newcome: but I was a child then, and liked to
believe the prettiest story best."

"As if it matters!" cries Lord Farintosh.

"As if it matters in your wife? *n'est-ce pas?* I never thought that it would.
I should have told you as it was my duty to tell you all. It was not my
ancestors you cared for; and it is you yourself that your wife must swear
before Heaven to love."

"Of course it's me," answers the young man not quite understanding the
train of ideas in his companion's mind. "And I've given up every thing—
everything—and have broken off with my old habits and—and things you
know—and intend to lead a regular life—and will never go to Tattersall's

8 now. *E1*] this *Ms HM NY*
9 who *E1*] that *Ms*
1 am ashamed," *E1*] was humiliated," *Ms HM NY*

again; nor bet a shilling; nor touch another cigar if you like—that is, if you don't like; for I love you so, Ethel—I do, with all my heart I do!"

"You are very generous and kind, Lord Farintosh," Ethel said. "It is myself, not you, I doubt. O! I am humiliated to make such a confession!"

"How humiliated?" Ethel withdrew the hand which the young nobleman endeavoured to seize.

"If," she continued, "if[2] I found it was your birth and your name and your wealth that I coveted, and had nearly taken, ought I not to feel humiliated, and ask pardon of you and—and[3] of God? O what perjuries poor Clara was made to speak,—and see what has befallen her! We stood by and heard her without being shocked. We applauded even. And to what shame and misery we brought her! Why did her parents and mine consign her to such ruin? She might have lived pure and happy but for us. With her example before me—not her flight, poor child, I am not afraid of *that* happening to me—but her long solitude, the misery of her wasted years, my brother's own wretchedness and faults[4] aggravated a hundred-fold by his unhappy union with her—I must pause while it is yet time, and recal a promise which I know I should make you unhappy if I fulfilled. I ask your pardon that I deceived you, Lord Farintosh, and feel ashamed for myself[5] that I could have consented to do so."[6]

"Do you mean," cried the young Marquis, "that after my conduct to you—after my loving you so that even this—this disgrace in your family don't prevent my going on—after my mother has been down on her knees to me to break off and I wouldn't—no I wouldn't—after all White's sneering at me and laughing at me—and all my friends, friends of my family, who would go to—go anywhere for me, advising me and saying, 'Farintosh, what a fool you are: break off this match'—and I wouldn't back out— because I loved you so, by Heaven—and because as a man and a gentleman when I give my word I keep it—do you mean that *you* throw me over? It's a shame—it's a shame!" And again there were tears of rage and anguish in Farintosh's eyes.

"What I did was a shame, my lord," Ethel said humbly, "and again I ask your pardon for it. What I do now is only to tell you the truth: and to grieve with all my soul for the falsehood—yes the falsehood which I told you,—and which has given your kind heart such cruel pain."

"Yes it *was* a falsehood!" the poor lad cried out—"You follow a fellow and you make a fool of him and you make him frantic in love with you and then you fling him over. I wonder you can look me in the face after such an infernal treason. You've done it to twenty fellows before—I know you have—Every body said so, and warned me. You draw them on; and get them to be in love; and then you fling them away. Am I to go back to

---

[2] mind. "And I've given up every thing—everything … ¶"If," she continued, "if *E1*] mind. ¶"But if *Ms NY*

[3] and—and *Ms*] and *E1*

[4] faults *E1*] fault *Ms*

[5] ashamed for myself *E1*] ashamed <of> †and humiliated for↓ myself *Ms*] ashamed and humiliated for myself *NY*

[6] so." *E1*] it." *Ms HM NY*

London, and be made the laughing-stock of the whole town—I who might marry any woman in Europe, and who am at the head of the nobility of England?"

"Upon my word—if you will believe me after deceiving you once"— Ethel interposed still very humbly: "I will never say that it was I who withdrew from you: and that it was not you who refused me. What has happened here fully authorises you. Let the rupture of the engagement come from you, my lord. Indeed, indeed, I would spare you all the pain I can. I have done you wrong enough already, Lord Farintosh."

And now the Marquis burst forth[7] with tears and imprecations, wild cries of anger, love and disappointment, so fierce and incoherent that the lady to whom they were addressed did not repeat them to her confidante: only she generously charged Laura to remember, if ever she heard the matter talked of in the world, that it was Lord Farintosh's family which broke off the marriage, but that his lordship had acted most kindly and generously throughout the whole affair.

He went back to London in such a state of fury; and raved so wildly amongst his friends against the whole Newcome family that many men knew what the case really was. But all women averred that that intriguing worldly Ethel Newcome, the apt pupil of her wicked old grandmother, had met with a deserved rebuff: that after doing every thing in her power to catch the great *parti*, Lord Farintosh who had long been tired of her, flung her over, not liking the connection; and that she was living out of the world now at Newcome under the pretence of taking care of that unfortunate Lady Clara's children: but really because she was pining away for Lord Farintosh who as we all know married six months afterwards.

---

[7] burst forth *E1*] broke out *Ms HM NY*

SENTENCE IN THE CASE OF THE MARQUIS OF FARINTOSH

Chapter XXII.

 EEMING that her brother Barnes had cares enough of his own presently on hand, Ethel did not think fit to confide to him the particulars of her interview with Lord Farintosh: nor, even, was poor Lady Ann informed that she had lost a noble son-in-law. The news would come to both of them soon enough Ethel thought; and indeed before many hours were over it reached Sir Barnes Newcome in a very abrupt and unpleasant way. He had dismal occasion now to see his lawyers every day: and on the day after Lord Farintosh's abrupt visit and departure, Sir Barnes, going into Newcome upon his own unfortunate affairs, was told by his attorney, Mr. Speers,[1] how the Marquis of Farintosh had slept for a few hours at the King's Arms, and returned to town the[2] same evening by the train. We may add, that his lordship had occupied the very room in which Lord Highgate had previously slept; and Mr. Taplow recommends the bed accordingly and shows it with pride to this very day.

Much disturbed by this intelligence, Sir Barnes was making his way to his cheerless home in the evening, when near his own gate he overtook another messenger. This was the railway porter who daily brought telegraphic messages from his uncle and the bank in London. The message of that day was "Consols so and so. French Rentes so much. *Highgate's and Farintosh's accounts withdrawn.*" The wretched keeper of the lodge owned with trembling, in reply to the curses and queries of his employer, that a gentleman calling himself the Marquis[3] of Farintosh had gone up to the house the day before and come away an hour afterwards—did not like to speak to Sir Barnes when he came home—Sir Barnes looked so bad like.

[1] Speers *E1*] [blank] *Ms*
[2] the *E1*] that *Ms*
[3] the Marquis *E1*] Marquis *Ms*

Now of course there could be no concealment from her brother, and Ethel and Barnes had a conversation in which the latter expressed himself with that freedom of language which characterised the head of the house of Newcome. Madame de Montcontour's poney-chaise was in waiting at the hall door when the owner of the house entered it; and my wife was just taking leave of Ethel and her little people when Sir Barnes Newcome entered the lady's sitting-room.

The livid scowl with which Barnes greeted my wife surprised that lady though it did not induce her to prolong her visit to her friend. As Laura took leave, she heard Sir Barnes screaming to the nurses to "take those little beggars away," and she rightly conjectured that some more unpleasantries had occurred to disturb this luckless gentleman's temper.

On the morrow dearest Ethel's usual courier, one of the boys from the lodge, trotted over on his donkey to dearest Laura at Rosebury, with one of those missives which were daily passing between the ladies. This letter said:—

"Barnes m'a fait une scène terrible hier. I was obliged to tell him every-thing about Lord F.; and *to use the plainest language.* At first he forbade you the house. He thinks that you have been the cause of F.'s dismissal and charged me *most unjustly* with a desire to bring back poor C.N. I replied *as became me,* and told him fairly I would leave the house if *odious insulting charges* were made against me, if my friends were not received. He stormed, he cried, he employed *his usual language,*—he was in a dreadful state. He relented and asked pardon. He goes to town to-night by the mail-train. *Of course* you come as usual, dear dear Laura. I am miserable without you: and you know I cannot leave poor Mamma. Clarykin sends a *thousand kisses* to little Arty; and I am *his mother's* always affectionate,—E. N.

"Will the gentlemen like to shoot our pheasants? Please ask the Prince to let Warren know when. I sent a brace to poor dear old Mrs. Mason: and had such a nice letter from her!"

"And Who is poor dear Mrs. Mason?" asks Mr. Pendennis, as yet but imperfectly acquainted with the history of the Newcomes.

And Laura told me—perhaps I had heard before and forgotten—that Mrs. Mason was an old nurse and pensioner of the Colonel's, and how he had been to see her for the sake of old times: and how she was a great favourite with Ethel—and Laura kissed her little son and was exceedingly bright, cheerful and hilarious that evening; in spite of the affliction under which her dear friends at Newcome were labouring.

People in country-houses should be exceedingly careful about their blotting-paper. They should bring their own portfolios with them. If my kind readers[4] will bear this simple little hint in mind, how much mischief may they save themselves,—nay, enjoy possibly, by looking at the pages of the next portfolio in the next friend's bed-room in which they sleep. From such a book I once cut out, in Charles Slyboots's well-known and perfectly clear[5] handwriting, the words "Miss Emily Hartington, James St., Buck-

---

[4] my kind readers *Ms*] any kind readers *E1*
[5] perfectly clear *E1*] perfectly ~~legible~~ ↑clearly↓ *Ms*

ingham Gate, London" and produced as legibly on the blotting paper as on the envelope which the postman delivered. After showing the paper round to the company I enclosed it in a note sent to[6] Mr. Slyboots: who married Miss Hartington three months afterwards. In such a book at the club I read as plainly as you may read this page, a holograph page of the Right Honourable the Earl of Bareacres, which informed the whole club of a painful and private circumstance, and said, "My dear Green. I am truly sorry that I shall not be able to take up the bill for eight hundred and fifty-six pounds which becomes due next Tu . . ."—and upon such a book going to write a note in Madame de Montcontour's drawing-room at Rosebury, what should I find but proofs that my own wife was engaged in a clandestine correspondence with a gentleman residing abroad!

"Colonel Newcome, C.B., Montagne de la Cour, Brussels," I read in this young woman's handwriting, and asked turning round upon Laura who entered the room just as I discovered her guilt: "What *have* you been writing to Colonel Newcome about? Miss!"

"I wanted him to get me some lace," she said.

"To lace some nightcaps for me, didn't you, my dear? He is such a fine judge of lace! If I had known you had been writing I would have asked you to send him a message—I want something from Brussels—Is the letter—ahem—gone?" (In this artful way, you see, I just hinted that I should like to *see* the letter.)

"The letter is—ahem—gone," says Laura. "What do you want from Brussels, Pen?"

"I want some Brussels sprouts, my love—they are so fine in their native country."

"Shall I write to him to send the letter back?" palpitates poor little Laura for she thought her husband was offended by using the ironic method.

"No, you dear little woman! You need not send for the letter back: and you need not tell me what was in it: and I will bet you a hundred yards of lace to a cotton nightcap—and you know whether *I*, Madam, am a man *à bonnet-de-coton*—I will bet you that I know what you have been writing about, under pretence of a message about lace to our Colonel."

"He promised to send it me. He really did. Lady Rockminster gave me twenty pounds . . ." gasps Laura.

"Under pretence of lace you have been sending over a love-message. You want to see whether Clive is still of his old mind. You think the coast is now clear, and that dearest Ethel may like him. You think Mrs. Mason is growing very old and infirm, and the sight of her dear boy would . . ."

"Pen! Pen! *did you open my letter?*" cries Laura—and a laugh which could afford to be good-humoured (followed by yet another expression of the lips) ended this colloquy. No; Mr. Pendennis did not see the letter—but he knew the writer;—flattered himself that he knew women in general.

"Where did you get your experience of them, Sir?" asks Mrs. Laura. Question answered in the same manner as the previous demand.

"Well, my dear, and why should not the poor boy be made happy?" Laura continues standing very close up to her husband. "It is evident to

6 note sent to *Ms*] note and sent it to *E1*

me that Ethel is fond of him. I would rather see her married to a good young man whom she loves, than the mistress of a thousand palaces and coronets. Suppose—suppose you had married Miss Amory, Sir, what a wretched worldly creature you would have been by this time; whereas now——"

"Now that I am the humble slave of a good woman there is some chance for me," cries this model of husbands. "And all good women are match-makers as we know very well, and you have had this match in your heart ever since you saw the two young people together. Now, Madam, since I did not see your letter to the Colonel—though I have guessed part of it—tell me what have you said in it? Have you by any chance told the Colonel that the Farintosh alliance was broken off?"

Laura owned that she had hinted as much.

"You have not ventured to say that Ethel is well inclined to Clive?"

"O no—O *dear* no!" But after much cross-examining and a little blushing on Laura's part she is brought to confess that she has asked the Colonel whether he will not come and see Mrs. Mason, who is pining to see him and is growing very old. And I find out that she has been to see this Mrs. Mason; that she and Miss Newcome visited the old lady the day before yesterday: and Laura thought from the manner in which Ethel looked at Clive's picture, hanging up in the parlour of his father's old friend, that she really *was* very much &c. &c. So, the letter being gone, Mrs. Pendennis is most eager about the answer to it, and day after day examines the bag, and is provoked that it brings no letter bearing the Brussels post-mark.

Madame de Montcontour seems perfectly well to know what Mrs. Laura has been doing and is hoping. "What no letters again to-day? Ain't it pro-voking?" she cries. She is in the conspiracy, too; and presently Florac is one of the initiated. "The[7] women wish to *bâcler* a marriage between the belle Meess and *le petit* Claive," Florac announces to me. He pays the highest compliments to Miss Newcome's person, as he speaks regarding the mar-riage. "I continue to adore your Anglaises," he is pleased to say. "What of freshness, what of beauty, what roses! and then they are so adorably good. Go, Pendennis, thou art a happy *coquin!*" Mr. Pendennis does not say No. He has won the twenty thousand pound prize; and we know there are worse than blanks in that lottery.

---

7 "The *Ms*] "These *E1*

Chapter XXIII.

O answer came to Mrs. Pendennis's letter to Colonel Newcome at Brussels, for the Colonel was absent from that city, and at the time when Laura wrote was actually in London whither affairs of his own had called him. A note from George Warrington acquainted me with this circumstance; he mentioned that he and the Colonel had dined together at Bays's on the day previous, and that the Colonel seemed to be in the highest spirits. High spirits about what?[1] This news put Laura in a sad perplexity. Should she write and tell him to get his letters from Brussels? She would in five minutes have found some other pretext for writing to Colonel Newcome; had not her husband sternly cautioned the young woman to leave the matter alone.

The more readily perhaps because he had quarrelled with his nephew Sir Barnes, Thomas Newcome went to visit his brother Hobson and his sister-in-law; bent on showing that there was no division between him and this branch of his family. And you may suppose that the admirable woman just named had a fine occasion for her virtuous conversational powers in discoursing upon the painful event which had just happened to Sir Barnes. When we fall, how our friends cry out for us! Mrs. Hobson's homilies must have been awful. How that outraged virtue must have groaned and lamented, gathered its children about its knees, wept over them and warned[2] them; gone into sackcloth and ashes and tied up the knocker; confabulated with its spiritual adviser; uttered commonplaces to its husband; and bored the whole house! The punishment of worldliness and vanity, the evil of marrying out of one's station, how these points must have been explained and enlarged on. Surely the *Peerage* was taken off the drawing-room table and removed to Papa's study, where it could not open, as it used naturally once, to Highgate, Baron or Farintosh, Marquis of, being shut behind wires and closely jammed in on an upper shelf between

---

[1] previous, ... what? *E1*] previous. *Ms HM NY*
[2] warned *Ms*] washed *E1*

Blackstone's Commentaries and the Farmer's Magazine! The breaking of the engagement with the Marquis of Farintosh was known in Brianstone Square; and you may be sure interpreted by Mrs. Hobson in the light the most disadvantageous to Ethel Newcome. A young nobleman, with grief and pain Ethel's aunt must own the fact—a young man of notoriously dissipated habits but of great wealth and rank, had been pursued by the unhappy Lady Kew—Mrs. Hobson would *not* say by her *niece*, that were *too* dreadful—had been pursued and followed and hunted down in the most notorious manner and finally made to propose! Let Ethel's *conduct* and *punishment* be a warning to my dearest girls, and let them bless *Heaven* they have parents who are not worldly! After all the trouble and pains, Mrs. Hobson did[3] not say *disgrace*, the Marquis takes *the very first pretext* to break off the match, and leaves the unfortunate girl for ever!

And now we have to tell of the hardest blow which fell upon poor Ethel, and this was that her good Uncle Thomas Newcome believed the charges against her. He was willing enough to listen now to any thing which was said against that branch of the[4] family. With such a traitor, double-dealer, dastard as Barnes at its head, what could the rest of the race be? When the Colonel offered to endow Ethel and Clive with every shilling he had in the world, had not Barnes, the arch-traitor, temporised and told him falsehoods, and hesitated about throwing him off until the Marquis had declared himself? Yes. The girl he and poor Clive loved so was ruined by her artful relatives, was unworthy of his affection and his boy's, was to be banished like her worthless brother out of his regard for ever. And the man she had chosen in preference to his Clive! a roué, a libertine, whose extravagances and dissipations were the talk of every club; who had no wit, nor talents, not even constancy (for had he not taken the first opportunity to throw her off?) to recommend him—only a great title and a fortune wherewith to bribe her! For shame, for shame! Her engagement to this man was a blot upon her—the rupture only a just punishment and humiliation. Poor unhappy girl! let her take care of her wretched brother's abandoned children, give up the world and amend her life.

This was the sentence Thomas Newcome delivered: a righteous and tender-hearted man, as we know, but judging in this case wrongly, and bearing much too hardly, as we who knew her better must think, upon one who had her faults certainly; but whose errors were not all of her own making. Who set her on the path she walked in? It was her parents' hands which led her, and her parents' voices which commanded her to accept the temptation set before her. What did she know of the character of the man selected to be her husband? Those who should have known better brought him to her, and vouched for him. Noble unhappy young creature! Are you the first of your sisterhood who has been bidden to traffic your beauty; to crush and slay your honest natural affections; to sell your truth and your life for rank and title? But, the Judge who sees not the outward acts merely, but their causes; and views not the wrong alone, but

[3] did *E1*] will *Ms*
[4] the *E1*] his *Ms*

the temptations, struggles, ignorance of erring creatures, we know has a different Code to our's—to our's who fall upon the fallen, who fawn upon the prosperous so; who administer our praises and punishments so prematurely; who now strike so hard, and anon spare so shamelessly.

Our stay with our hospitable friends at Rosebury was perforce coming to a close, for indeed weeks after weeks had passed since we had been under their pleasant roof; and in spite of dearest Ethel's remonstrances it was clear that dearest Laura must take her farewell. In these last days, besides the visits which daily took place between one and other, the young messenger was put in ceaseless requisition, and his donkey must have been worn off his little legs with trotting to and fro between the two houses. Laura was quite anxious and hurt at not hearing from the Colonel: it was a shame that he did not have over his letters from Belgium and answer that one which she had honoured him by writing. By some information, received who knows how? our host was aware of the intrigue which Mrs. Pendennis was carrying on; and his little wife almost as much interested in it as my own. She whispered to me in her kind way that she would give a guinea, that she would, to see a certain couple made happy together; that they were born for one another, that they were; she was for having me go off to fetch Clive: but who was I to act as Hymen's messenger; or to interpose in such delicate family affairs?

All this while Sir Barnes Newcome, Bart., remained[5] absent in London, attending to his banking duties there and pursuing the dismal enquiries which ended, in the ensuing Michaelmas Term, in the famous suit of Newcome v. Ld. Highgate. Ethel pursuing the plan which she had laid down for herself from the first, took entire charge of his children and house: Lady Ann returned to her own family; never indeed having been of much use in her son's dismal household. My wife talked to me of course about her pursuits and amusements at Newcome—in the ancestral hall which we have mentioned. The children played and ate their dinner (mine often partook of his infantine mutton in company with little[6] Clara and the poor young heir of Newcome) in the room which had been called my lady's own, and in[7] which her husband had locked her, forgetting that the conservatories were open through which the hapless woman had fled. Next to this was the baronial library, a side of which was fitted with the gloomy books from Clapham which old Mrs. Newcome had amassed; rows of tracts, and missionary magazines, and dingy quarto volumes of worldly travel and history which that lady had admitted into her collection.

Almost on the last day of our stay at Rosebury, the two young ladies bethought them of paying a visit to the neighbouring town of Newcome, to that old Mrs. Mason who has been mentioned in a foregoing page and in some yet earlier chapters[8] of our history. She was very old now, very faithful to the recollections of her own early time, and oblivious of yester-

[5] my own. She whispered to me ... Newcome, Bart., remained *E1*] my own. Barnes meanwhile remained *Ms NY*
[6] little *E1*] the little *Ms*
[7] in *E1*] into *Ms*
[8] page and in ... chapters *Ms*] page in ... chapter *E1*

day. Thanks to Colonel Newcome's bounty she had lived in comfort for many a long year past; and he was as much her boy now as in those early days of which we have given but an outline. There were Clive's pictures of himself and his father over her little mantel-piece near which she sate in comfort and warmth by the winter-fire which his bounty supplied.

Mrs. Mason remembered Miss Newcome, prompted thereto by the hints of her little maid, who was much younger and had a more faithful memory than her mistress. Why, Sarah Mason would have forgotten the pheasants whose very tails decorated the chimney-glass; had not Keziah the maid reminded her that the young lady was the donor. Then she recollected her benefactor, and asked after her father, the Baronet; and wondered, for her part, why *her* boy, the Colonel, was not made baronet and why his brother had the property? Her father was a very good man; though Mrs. Mason had heard he was not *much* liked in those parts. "Dead and gone was he, poor man?" (this came in reply to a hint from Keziah, the attendant, bawled in the old lady's ears, who was very deaf) "Well, well, we must all go: and if we were all good, like the Colonel, what was the use of staying? I hope his wife will be good, I am sure such a good man deserves one," added Mrs. Mason.

The ladies thought the old woman doting, led thereto by the remark of Keziah the maid that Mrs. Mason have a lost her memory. And she asked who the other bonny lady was, and Ethel told her that Mrs. Pendennis was a friend of the Colonel's and Clive's.

"O, Clive's friend! Well, she was a pretty lady and he was a dear pretty boy. He drew those pictures; and he took off me in my cap, with my old cat and all—my poor old cat that's buried this ever so long ago."

"She has had a letter from the Colonel, Miss," cries out Keziah. "Haven't you had a letter from the Colonel, Mum?—It came only yesterday." And Keziah takes out the letter and shows it to the ladies. They read as follows.

"London, Feb. 12, 184—

"MY DEAR OLD MASON.

"I have just heard from a friend of mine who has been staying in your neighbourhood, that you are well and happy, and that you have been making enquires[9] after *your young scagegrace*, Tom Newcome, who is well and happy too, and who proposes to be *happier still* before any very long time is over.[1]

"The letter which was written to me about you was sent to me *in Belgium*, at Brussels where I have been living—a town near the place where the famous *Battle of Waterloo* was fought: and as I had run away from Waterloo *it followed me to England*.

"I cannot come to Newcome just now to shake my dear old friend and nurse *by the hand*. I have business in London: and there are those of my name *living in Newcome* who would not be very happy to see me and mine.

"But I promise you a visit before very long and Clive will come with me: and when we come I shall introduce a new friend to you, a very pretty little

---

9 enquires *Ms*] inquiries *E1*
1 too, ... over. *E1*] too. *Ms HM NY*

daughter-in-law, whom you must promise to love very much. She is a *Scotch lassie,* niece of my oldest friend, James Binnie, Esquire, of the Bengal Civil Service, who will give her *a pretty bit of siller,* and her present name is Miss Rosa Mackenzie.

"We shall send you a *wedding cake* soon, and a new gown for Keziah (to whom remember me) and when I am gone, my grandchildren after me will hear what a dear friend you were to

"Your affectionate
"Thomas Newcome."

Keziah must have thought that there was something between Clive and my wife, for when Laura had read the letter she laid it down on the table; and, sitting down by it, and hiding her face in her hands, burst into tears.

Ethel looked steadily at the two pictures of Clive and his father. Then she put her hand on her friend's shoulder. "Come, my dear," she said. "It is growing late: and I must go back to my children." And she saluted Mrs. Mason and her maid in a very stately manner and left them, leading my wife away who was still exceedingly overcome.

We could not stay long at Rosebury after that. When Madame de Mont-contour heard the news, the good lady cried too. Mrs. Pendennis's emotion was renewed as we passed the gates of Newcome Park on our way to the Railroad.

Chapter XXIV.

MR. AND MRS. CLIVE NEWCOME.

HE friendship between Ethel and Laura which the last narrated sentimental occurrences had so much increased, subsists very little impaired up to the present day. A lady with many domestic interests and increasing family &c. &c. cannot be supposed to cultivate female intimacies out of doors, with that ardour and eagerness which young spinsters exhibit in their intercourse, but Laura whose kind heart first led her to sympathise with her young friend in the latter's days of distress and misfortune, has professed ever since a growing esteem for Ethel Newcome and says that the trials and perhaps grief which the young lady now had to undergo, have brought out the noblest qualities of her disposition. She is a very different person from the giddy and worldly girl who compelled our admiration of late in the days of her triumphant youthful beauty, of her wayward generous humour, of her frivolities and her flirtations.

Did Ethel shed tears in secret over the marriage which had caused Laura's gentle eyes to overflow. We might divine the girl's grief but we respected it. The subject was never mentioned by the ladies between themselves and even in her most intimate communications with her husband that gentleman is bound to say his wife maintained a tender reserve upon the point, nor cared to speculate upon a subject which her friend held sacred. I could not for my part but acquiesce in[1] this reticence; and, if Ethel felt regret and remorse, admire the dignity of her silence and the sweet composure of her now changed and saddened demeanour.

The interchange of letters between the two friends was constant, and in these the younger lady described at length the duties, occupations and pleasures of her new life. She had quite broken with the world and devoted

---

[1] acquiesce in *E1*] ~~admire~~ ↑acquiesce↓ *Ms*

herself entirely to the nurture and education of her brother's orphan children. She educated herself in order to teach them. Her letters contain droll yet touching confessions of her own ignorance and her determination to overcome it. There was no lack of masters of all kinds in Newcome. She set herself to work like a school-girl—the piano in the little room near the conservatory was thumped by Aunt Ethel until it became quite obedient to her and yielded the sweetest music under her fingers. When she came to pay us a visit at Fairoaks some two years afterwards and she[2] played for our dancing children (our third is named Ethel, our second Helen after one still more dear), we were in admiration of her skill—there must have been the labour of many lonely nights when her little charges were at rest, and she and her sad thoughts sat up together, before she overcame the difficulties of the instrument so as to be able to soothe herself and to charm and delight her children.

When the divorce was pronounced which came in due form, though we know that Lady Highgate was not much happier than the luckless Lady Clara Newcome had been, Ethel's dread was lest Sir Barnes should marry again, and by introducing a new mistress into his house should deprive her of the care of her children.

Miss Newcome judged her brother rightly in that he would try to marry, but a noble young lady to whom he offered himself rejected him, to his surprise and indignation, for a beggarly clergyman with a small living on which she elected to starve; and the wealthy daughter of a neighbouring manufacturer whom he next proposed to honour with his gracious hand, fled from him with horror into the arms of her father, wondering how such a man as that should ever dare to propose marriage to an honest girl. Sir Barnes Newcome was much surprised at this outbreak of anger, he thought himself a very ill-used and unfortunate man, a victim of most cruel persecutions, which we may be sure did not improve his temper or tend to the happiness of his circle at home. Peevishness, and selfish rage, quarrels with servants and governesses, and other domestic disquiet, Ethel had of course to bear from her brother but not actual personal ill-usage. The fiery temper of former days was subdued in her, but the haughty resolution remained, which was more than a match for her brother's cowardly tyranny: besides, she was the mistress of sixty thousand pounds, and by many wily hints and piteous appeals to his sister Sir Barnes sought to secure this desirable sum of money for his poor dear unfortunate children.

He professed to think that she was ruining herself for her younger brothers whose expenses the young lady was defraying, this one at college, that in the army, and whose maintenance he now[3] thought might be amply defrayed out of their own little fortunes and his mother's jointure; and by ingeniously proving that a vast number of his household expenses were personal to Miss Newcome and would never have been incurred but for her residence in his house, he subtracted for his own benefit no inconsiderable portion of her income. Thus the carriage horses were hers, for what need had he, a miserable bachelor of anything more than a riding

[2] and she *Ms*] she *E1*
[3] now *Ms*] [omitted] *E1*

horse and a brougham? A certain number of the domestics were hers, and as he could get no scoundrel of his own to stay with him, he took Miss Newcome's servants. He would have had her pay the coals which burnt in his grate and the taxes due to our Sovereign Lady the Queen; but in truth at the end of the year, with her domestic bounties and her charities round about Newcome, which daily increased as she became acquainted with her indigent neighbours, Miss Ethel the heiress was as poor as many poorer persons.

Her charities increased daily with her means of knowing the people round about her. She gave much time to them and thought; visited from house to house, without ostentation; was awe-stricken by that spectacle of the poverty which we have with us always, of which the sight rebukes our selfish griefs into silence, the thought compels us to charity, humility, devotion.[4] The priests of our various creeds, who elsewhere are doing battle together continually, lay down their arms in its presence and kneel before it, subjugated by that overpowring master. Death never dying out, hunger always crying and children born to it day after day,—our young London lady, flying from the splendours and follies in which her life had been past, found herself in the presence of these—threading darkling alleys which swarmed with wretched life, sitting by naked beds, whither by God's blessing she was sometimes enabled to carry a little comfort and consolation, or whence she came heart-stricken by the overpowering misery or touched by the patient resignation of the new friends to whom fate had directed her. And here she met the priest upon his shrift, the homely missionary bearing his words of consolation, the quiet curate pacing his round, and was known to[5] all these and enabled now and again to help their people in trouble. "O what good there is in this woman," my wife would say to me, as she laid one of Miss Ethel's[6] letters aside, "who would have thought this was the girl of your glaring London ball-room? If she has had grief to bear, how it has chastened and improved her."

And now I have to confess that all this time, whilst Ethel Newcome has been growing in grace with my wife, poor Clive has been lapsing[7] sadly out of favour. She has no patience with Clive. She drubs her little foot when his name is mentioned and turns the subject. Whither are all the tears and pities fled now? Mrs. Laura has transferred all her regard to Ethel, and when that lady's ex-suitor writes to his old friend, or other news is had of him, Laura flies out in her usual tirades against the world, the horrid wicked selfish world which spoils every body who comes near it. What has Clive done, in vain his apologist asks, that an old friend should be so angry with him?

She is not angry with him, not she—she only does not care about him. She wishes him no manner of harm—not the least, only she has lost all interest in him. And the Colonel too, the poor good old Colonel, was actually in Mrs. Pendennis's black books and when he sent her the Brussels veil

4 <&> devotion. *Ms*] and devotion. *E1*
5 to *E1*] by *Ms*
6 Miss Ethel's *E1*] Ethel's *Ms*
7 been lapsing *E1*] been going *Ms*

which we have heard of, she did not think it was a bargain at all, not particularly pretty, in fact rather dear at the money. When we met Mr. and Mrs. Clive Newcome in London whither they came a few months after their marriage and where Rosey appeared as pretty happy good-humoured a little blushing bride as eyes need behold—Mrs. Pendennis's reception of her was quite a curiosity of decorum. "I not receive her well!" cries[8] Laura, "How on earth would you have me receive her? I talked to her about every thing, and she only answered yes or no. I showed her the children, and she did not seem to care. Her only conversation was about millinery and Brussels' balls and about her dress at the Drawing-room. The Drawing-room! What business has she with such follies."

The fact is that the Drawing-room was Tom Newcome's affair—not his son's who was heartily ashamed of the figure he cut in that astounding costume which English private gentlemen are made to sport when they bend the knee before their Gracious Sovereign.

Warrington toasted[9] poor Clive upon the occasion and complimented him with his usual gravity until the young fellow blushed and his father somewhat testily signified to our friend that his irony was not agreeable. "I suppose," says the Colonel with great hauteur, "that there is nothing ridiculous in an English gentleman entertaining feelings of loyalty and testifying his respect to his Queen, and I presume that Her Majesty knows best and has a right to order in what dress her subjects shall appear before her and I don't think it's kind of you, George, I say I don't think it's kind of you to quiz my boy for doing his duty to his Queen and to his father too, Sir—for it was at my request that Clive went—and we went together, Sir—to the Levee and then to the Drawing-room afterwards with Rosey, who was presented by the lady of my old friend, Sir George Tufto, a lady of rank herself and the wife of as brave an officer as ever drew a sword."

Warrington stammered an apology for his levity, but no explanations were satisfactory and it was clear George had wounded the feelings of our dear simple old friend.

After Clive's marriage which was performed at Brussels, Uncle James and the lady his sister, whom we have sometimes flippantly ventured to call the Campaigner, went off to perform that journey to Scotland which James had meditated[1] for ten years past and now little Rosey was made happy for life to renew acquaintance with little Josey. The Colonel and his son and daughter-in-law came to London, not to the bachelor quarters where we have seen them, but to an hotel which they occupied until their new house could be provided for them, a sumptuous mansion in the Tyburnian district, and one which became people of their station.

We have been informed already what the Colonel's income was, and have the gratification of knowing that it was very considerable. The simple gentleman who would dine off a crust and wear a coat for ten years, desired that his children should have the best of every thing, ordered about upholsterers, painters, carriage-makers in his splendid Indian way, presented pretty Rosey with brilliant jewels for her introduction at Court, and

[8] cries *Ms*] cried *E1*
[9] toasted *Ms*] roasted *E1*
[1] which James had meditated *E1*] James had been meditating *Ms*

was made happy by the sight of the blooming young creature decked in these magnificencies and admired by all his little circle. The old boys, the old generals, the old colonels, the old qui-his from the club, came and paid her their homage; the directors' ladies and the generals' ladies called upon her and feasted her at vast banquets served on sumptuous plate. Newcome purchased plate and gave banquets in return for these hospitalities. Mrs. Clive had a neat close carriage for evenings and a splendid barouche to drive in the Park. It was pleasant to see this equipage at four o'clock of an afternoon driving up to Bays's with Rosey most gorgeously attired reclining within and to behold the stately grace of the old gentleman as he stepped out to welcome his daughter-in-law, and the bow he made before he entered her carriage. Then they would drive round the Park; round and round and round; and the old generals and the old colonels and old fogies and their ladies and daughters would nod and smile out of their carriages as they crossed each other upon this charming career of pleasure.

I confess that a dinner at the Colonel's—now he appeared in all his magnificence—was awfully slow. No peaches could look fresher than Rosey's cheeks—no damask was fairer than her pretty little shoulder—no one, I am sure, could be happier[2] than she, but she did not impart her happiness to her friends and replied chiefly by smiles to the conversation of the gentlemen at her side. It is true that these were for the most part elderly dignitaries, distinguished military officers with blue-black whiskers, retired old Indian judges, and the like, occupied with their victuals and generally careless to please. But that solemn happiness of the Colonel, who shall depict it—that look of affection with which he greeted his daughter as she entered, flounced to the waist, twinkling with innumerable jewels, holding a dainty[3] pocket-handkerchief with smiling eyes, dimpled cheeks and golden ringlets. He would take her hand and follow her about from group to group exchanging precious observations about the weather, the Park, the Exhibition, nay, the Opera, for the old man actually went to the Opera with his little girl and solemnly snoozed by her side in a white waistcoat.

Very likely this was the happiest period of Thomas Newcome's life. No woman (save one perhaps fifty years ago) had ever seemed[4] so fond of him as that little girl. What pride he had in her and what care he took of her— If she was a little ailing, what anxiety and hurrying for doctors. What droll letters came from James Binnie and how they laughed over them: with what respectful attention he acquainted Mrs. Mack with every thing that took place: with what enthusiasm that Campaigner replied. Josey's husband called a special blessing upon his head in the church at Musselburgh[5] and little Jo herself sent a tinful of Scotch bun to her darling sister with a request from her husband that he might have a few shares in the famous Indian Company.

The Company was in a highly flourishing condition, as you may suppose, when one of its directors, who at the same time was one of the hon-

---

[2] be happier *E1*] be entirely happier *Ms*
[3] a dainty *E1*] dainty *Ms*
[4] seemed *E1*] been *Ms HM NY*
[5] head in the church at Musselburgh *E1*] head tin the church† at Musselbourough *Ms*

estest men alive, thought it was his duty to live in the splendour in which we now behold him. Many wealthy City men did homage to him. His brother Hobson, though the Colonel had quarrelled with the chief of the firm, yet remained on amicable terms with Thomas Newcome and shared and returned his banquets for a while. Charles Honeyman we may be sure was present at many of them, and smirked a blessing over the plenteous meal. The Colonel's influence was such with[6] Mr. Sherrick that he pleaded Charles's cause with that gentleman and actually brought to a successful termination that little love affair in which we have seen Miss Sherrick and Charles engaged. Mr. Sherrick was not disposed to part with much money during his lifetime—indeed he proved to Colonel Newcome that he was not so rich as the world supposed him—but by the Colonel's interest, the chaplaincy of Boggly Wollah was procured for the Revd. C. Honeyman, who now forms the delight of that flourishing station.

All this while we have said little about Clive who in truth was somehow in the background in this flourishing Newcome group. To please the best father in the world, the kindest old friend who endowed his niece with the best part of his savings to settle that question about marriage and have an end of it, Clive Newcome had taken a pretty and fond young girl who respected and admired him beyond all men, and who heartily desired to make him happy. To do as much would not his father have stripped his coat from his back, have put his head under Juggernaut's chariot wheel, have sacrificed any ease, comfort or pleasure for the youngster's benefit. One great passion he had had and closed the account of it—a worldly ambitious girl—how foolishly worshipped and passionately beloved no matter—had played with him for years, had flung him away when a dissolute suitor with a great fortune and title had offered himself. Was he to whine and despair because a jilt had fooled him?—He had too much pride and courage for any such submission; he would accept the lot in life which was offered to him, no undesirable one surely; he would fulfil the wish of his father's heart, and cheer his kind declining years. In this way the marriage was brought about. It was but a whisper to Rosey in the drawing-room, a start and a blush from the little girl as he took the little willing hand, a kiss for her from her delighted old father-in-law, a twinkle in good old James's eyes and double embrace from the Campaigner as she stood over them in a benedictory attitude expressing her surprise at an event for which she had been jockeying ever since she set eyes on young Newcome—and calling upon Heaven to bless her children. So as a good thing when it is to be done had best be done quickly, these worthy folks went off almost straightway to a clergyman, and were married out of hand—to the astonishment of Captains Hoby and Goby when they came to hear of the event. Well, my gallant young painter and friend of my boyhood—if my wife chooses to be angry at your marriage, shall her husband not wish you happy? suppose we had married our first loves, others of us, were we the happier now? Ask Mr. Pendennis, who sulked in his tents when his Costigan, his Briseis, was ravished from him. Ask poor George Warrington, who had his own way, Heaven help him. There was no need why Clive should turn monk because

---

6 was such with *E1*] with *Ms*

number one refused him—and that charmer removed, why he should not take to his heart number two. I am bound to say that when I expressed these opinions to Mrs. Laura, she was more angry and provoked than ever.

It is in the nature of such a simple soul as Thomas Newcome to see but one side of a question and having once fixed Ethel's worldliness in his mind, and her brother's treason—to allow no argument of advocates of the other side to shake his displeasure. Hence the one or two appeals which Laura ventured to make on behalf[7] of her friend were checked by the good Colonel with a stern negation. If Ethel[8] was not guiltless, she could not make him see at least that she was not guilty. He dashed away all excuses and palliations, exasperated as he was and persisted in regarding the poor girl's conduct in its most unfavourable light. "She was rejected, and deservedly rejected, by the Marquis of Farintosh," he broke out to me once—who was not indeed authorised to tell all I knew regarding the story. "The whole town knows it, all the clubs ring with it—I blush, Sir, to think that my brother's child should have brought such a stain upon our name." In vain I told him that my wife who knew all the circumstances much better, judged Miss Newcome far more favourably and indeed greatly esteemed and loved her. "Pshaw, Sir," breaks out the indignant Colonel, "your wife is an innocent creature who does not know the world as we men of experience do—as I do, Sir," and would have no more of the discussion. There is no doubt about it, there was a coolness between my old friend's father and us.

As for Barnes Newcome we gave up that worthy, and the Colonel shewed him no mercy. He recalled words used by Warrington which I have recorded in a former page—and vowed that he only watched[9] for an opportunity to crush the miserable reptile. He hated Barnes as a loathsome traitor, coward and criminal—he made no secret of his opinion; and Clive—with the remembrance of former injuries, of dreadful heartpangs the inheritor of his father's blood, his honesty of nature and his impetuous enmity against wrong—shared to the full his sire's antipathy against his cousin and publicly expressed his scorn and contempt for him. About Ethel he would not speak. "Perhaps what you say, Pen, is true," he said. "I hope it is. Pray God it is." But his quivering lips and fierce countenance, when her name was mentioned or her defence attempted, showed that he too had come to think ill of her. "As for her brother—as for that scoundrel," he would say clinching his fist, "if ever I can punish him I will. I shouldn't have the soul of a dog,[1] if ever I forgot the wrongs that have been done me by that vagabond. Forgiveness? Pshaw! Are you dangling to sermons, Pen, at your wife's leading-strings? Are you preaching that cant? There are some injuries that no honest man should forgive and I shall be a rogue on the day I shake hands with that villain."

"Clive has adopted the Iroquois ethics," says George Warrington smoking his pipe sententiously, "rather than those which are at present received

[7] on behalf *E1*] in behalf *Ms*
[8] Ethel *E1*] she *Ms*
[9] watched *E1*] waited *Ms*
[1] a dog, *E1*] dog, *Ms*

among us. I am not sure that something is not to be said as against the Eastern upon the Western or Tomahawk or Ojibbeway side of the question. I should not like," he added, "to be in a vendetta or feud and to have you, Clive, and the old Colonel engaged against me."

"I would rather," I said, "for my part, have half-a-dozen such enemies as Clive and the Colonel than one like Barnes. You never know where or when that villain may hit you." And before a very short period was over, Sir Barnes Newcome, Bart., hit his two hostile kinsmen—such a blow as one might expect from such a quarter.

Chapter XXV.

CLIVE and his father did not think fit to conceal their opinions regarding their kinsman Barnes Newcome, and uttered them in many public places when Sir Barnes's conduct was brought into question, we may be sure that their talk came to the Baronet's ears and did not improve his already angry feeling towards those gentlemen. For a while they had the best of the attack. The Colonel routed Barnes out of his accustomed club at Bays's where also the gallant Sir George Tufto expressed himself pretty openly with respect to the poor Baronet's want of courage. The Colonel had bullied and browbeaten Barnes in the parlour of his own bank and the story was naturally well known in the City, where it certainly was not pleasant for Sir Barnes as he walked to 'Change to meet sometimes the scowls of the angry man of war, his uncle, striding down to the offices of the Bundelcund Bank, and armed with that terrible bamboo cane.

But though his wife had undeniably run away after notorious ill treatment from her husband, though he had shown two white feathers in those unpleasant little affairs with his uncle and cousin, though Sir Barnes Newcome was certainly neither amiable nor popular in the City of London, his reputation as a most intelligent man of business still stood, the credit of his house was deservedly high, and people banked with him and traded with him in spite of faithless wives and hostile Colonels.

When the outbreak between Colonel Newcome and his nephew took place, it may be remembered that Mr. Hobson Newcome, the other partner of the firm of Hobson Brothers, waited upon Colonel Newcome as one of the principal English directors of the B.B.C. and hoped that although private differences would of course oblige Thomas Newcome to cease all personal dealings with the bank of Hobson, the affairs of the Company in which he was interested ought not to suffer on this account and that the Indian firm should continue dealing with Hobsons on the same footing as before. Mr. Hobson Newcome represented to the Colonel, in his jolly frank way, that whatever happened between the latter and his nephew Barnes, Thomas Newcome had still one friend in the house; that the transactions between it and the Indian Company were mutually advantageous; finally that the manager of the Indian bank might continue to do business with Hobsons as before. So the B.B.C. sent its consignments to Hobson Brothers[1] and drew its bills which were duly honoured by that firm.

More than one of Colonel Newcome's City acquaintances, among them his agent Mr. Jolly and his ingenuous friend Mr. Sherrick especially, hinted to Thomas Newcome to be very cautious in his dealings with Hobson Brothers, and keep a special care lest that house should play him an evil turn. They both told him that Barnes Newcome had said more than once in answer to reports of the Colonel's own speeches against Barnes, "I know that hotheaded blundering Indian uncle of mine is furious against me, on account of an absurd private affair and misunderstanding which he is too obstinate to see in the proper light. What is my return for the abuse and rant which he lavishes against me? I cannot forget that he is my grandfather's son, an old man utterly ignorant both of society and business here, and as he is interested in this Indian Banking company, which must be preciously conducted when it appointed him as the guardian and overseer of its affairs in England, I do my very best to serve the company and I can tell you, its blundering muddle-headed managers, black and white, owe no little to the assistance which they have had from our house. If they don't like us, why do they go on dealing with us? We don't want them and their bills. We were a leading house fifty[2] years before they were born, and shall continue to be so long after they come[3] to an end." Such was Barnes's case as stated by himself. It was not a very bad one, or very unfairly stated considering the advocate. I believe he has always persisted in thinking that he never did his uncle any wrong.

Mr. Jolly and Mr. Sherrick then both entreated Thomas Newcome to use his best endeavours, and bring the connection of the B.B.C. and Hobson Brothers to a speedy end. But Jolly was an interested party; he and his friends would have had the agency of the B.B.C. and the profits thereof which Hobsons had taken from them. Mr. Sherrick was an outside practitioner, a guerilla amongst regular merchants. The opinions of one and the other, though submitted by Thomas Newcome duly to his co-partners, the managers and London Board of Directors of the Bundelcund Banking Company, were overruled by that assembly.

They had their establishment and apartments in the City; they had their clerks and messengers, their managers' room and board-room, their meet-

---

[1] Brothers *E1*] and Brothers *Ms HM NY*
[2] fifty *E1*] in the city fifty *Ms*
[3] they come *E1*] they have come *Ms*

ings where no doubt great quantities of letters were read, vast ledgers produced, where Tom Newcome was voted into the chair and voted out with thanks, where speeches were made, and the affairs of the B.B.C. properly discussed. These subjects are mysterious, terrifying, unknown to me. I cannot pretend to describe them. Fred Bayham, I remember, used to be great in his knowledge of the affairs of the Bundelcund Banking Company. He talked of cotton, wool, copper, opium, indigo, Singapore, Manilla, China, Calcutta, Australia, with prodigious eloquence and fluency. His conversation was about millions. The most astounding paragraphs used to appear in the *Pall Mall Gazette* regarding the annual dinner at Blackwall which the directors gave and to which he and George and I as friends of the court were invited. What orations were uttered, what flowing bumpers emptied in the praise of this great Company—what quantities of turtle and punch did Fred devour at its expense. Colonel Newcome was the kindly old chairman at these banquets; the Prince his son, taking[4] but a modest part in these[5] ceremonies and sitting with us, his old cronies.

All the gentlemen connected with the board, all those with whom the B.B.C. traded in London, paid Thomas Newcome extraordinary respect. His character for wealth was deservedly great, and of course multiplied by the tongue of Rumour: F.B. knew to a few millions of rupees more or less, what the Colonel possessed and what Clive would inherit. Thomas Newcome's distinguished military services, his high bearing, lofty courtesy, simple but touching garrulity;—for the honest man talked much more now than he had been accustomed to do in former days, and was not insensible to the flattery which his wealth brought him;—his reputation as a keen man of business who had made his own fortune by operations equally prudent and spirited, and who might make the fortunes of hundreds of other people, brought the worthy Colonel a number of friends, and I promise you that the loudest huzzahs greeted his health when it was proposed at the Blackwall dinners. At the second annual dinner after Clive's marriage some friends presented[6] Mrs. Clive Newcome with a fine testimonial. There was a superb silver cocoa-nut tree, whereof the leaves were dexterously arranged for holding candles and pickles, under the cocoa-nut was an Indian prince on a camel giving his hand to a cavalry officer on horse back—a howitzer, a plough, a loom, a bale of cotton, on which were the East India Company's arms, a brahmin, Britannia, and Commerce with a cornucopia were grouped round the principal figures: and if you would see a noble account of this chaste and elegant specimen of British Art, you are referred to the pages of the *Pall Mall Gazette* of that year,[7] as well as to Fred. Bayham's noble speech in the course of the evening, when it was exhibited. The East and its wars, and its heroes, Assaye and Seringapatam ('and Lord Lake and Laswaree too,' calls out the Colonel greatly elated) tiger-hunting palanquins, Juggernaut, elephants, the burning of widows— all passed before us in F.B.'s splendid oration. He spoke of the product of the Indian forest, the palm-tree, the cocoa-nut tree, the banyan tree. Palms

4 taking *E1*] though a director too, taking *Ms HM NY*
5 these *E1 Ms*] the *R*
6 presented *E1*] of Colonel Thomas Newcome C.B. presented *Ms*
7 [Text from here to next note added to *E1* at proof stage.]

the Colonel had already brought back with him, the palms of valour, won in the field of war (cheers). Cocoa-nut trees he had never seen, though he had heard wonders related regarding the milky contents of their fruit. Here at any rate was one tree of the kind, under the branches of which he humbly trusted often to repose—and, if he might be so bold as to carry on the Eastern metaphor, he would say, knowing the excellence of the Colonel's claret and the splendour of his hospitality, that he would prefer a cocoa-nut day at the Colonel's to a banyan day anywhere else. Whilst F.B.'s speech went on, I remember[8] J.J. eyeing the trophy and the queer expression of his shrewd face. The health of British Artists was drunk apropos of this splendid specimen of their skills[9] and poor J.J. Ridley, Esq., A.R.A., had scarce a word to say in return. He and Clive sat by one another, the latter very silent and gloomy. When J.J. and I met in the world, we talked about our friend and it was easy for both of us to see that neither was satisfied with Clive's condition.

The fine house in Tyburnia was completed by this time as gorgeous as money could make it. How different it was from the old Fitzroy Square mansion with its ramshackle furniture, and spoils of brokers' shops, and Tottenham-court Road odds and ends! An Oxford Street upholsterer had been let loose in the yet virgin chambers; and that inventive genius had decorated them with all the wonders his fancy could devise. Roses and Cupids quivered on the ceilings, up to which golden arabesques crawled from the walls; your face (handsome or otherwise) was reflected by countless looking-glasses, so multiplied and arranged as, as it were, to carry you into the next street. You trod on velvet, pausing with respect in the centre of the carpet, where Rosey's cypher was worked in the sweet flowers which bear her name. What delightful crooked legs the chairs had! What corner-cupboards there were filled with Dresden gimcracks, which it was a part of this little woman's business in life to purchase! What étagères, and bon-bonnières, and chiffonnières! What awfully bad pastels there were on the walls! What frightful Boucher and Lancret shepherds and shepherdesses leered over the portières! What velvet-bound volumes, mother-of-pearl albums, inkstands representing beasts of the field, prie-dieux chairs, and wonderful nick-nacks I can recollect! There was the most magnificent piano, though Rosey seldom sang any of her six songs now; and when she kept her couch at a certain most interesting period, the good Colonel, ever anxious to procure amusement for his darling, asked whether she would not like a barrel-organ grinding fifty or sixty favourite pieces, which a bearer could turn? And he mentioned how Windus, of their regiment, who loved music exceedingly, had a very fine instrument of this kind out to Barrackpore in the year 1810, and relays of barrels by each ship with all the new tunes from Europe. The testimonial[1] took its place in the centre of Mrs. Clive's table surrounded by satellites of plate. The delectable parties were constantly gathered together, the grand barouche rolling in the Park or stopping at the principal shops. Little Rosey bloomed in millinery

---

[8] year, as well ... I remember *E1*] year. I remember *Ms HM NY* [See previous note.]
[9] skills *Ms*] skill *E1*
[1] could make it. ... testimonial *E1*] could make it—The testimonial *Ms HM NY*

and was still the smiling little pet of her father-in-law, and poor Clive in the midst of all these splendours was gaunt and sad and silent; listless at most times, bitter and savage at others, pleased only when he was out of the society which bored him, and in the company of George and J.J., the simple friends of his youth.

His careworn look and altered appearance mollified my wife towards him—who had almost taken him again into favour. But she did not care for Mrs. Clive, and the Colonel somehow grew cool towards us and to look askance upon the little band of Clive's friends. It seemed as if there were two parties in the house. There was Clive's set—J.J., the[2] shrewd silent little painter; Warrington, the cynic; and the author of the present biography who was I believe supposed to give himself contemptuous airs, and to have become very high and mighty since his marriage. Then there was the great, numerous and eminently respectable set, whose names were all registered in little Rosey's little visiting-book and to whose houses she drove round, duly delivering the cards of Mr. and Mrs. Clive Newcome, and[3] Colonel Newcome;—the Generals, and the[4] Colonels, the Judges, and the Fogeys. The only man who kept well with both sides of the house was F. Bayham, Esq., who having got into clover, remained in the enjoyment of that welcome pasture, who really loved Clive and the Colonel too, and had a hundred pleasant things and funny stories (the droll odd creature) to tell to the little lady for whom we others could scarcely find a word. The old friends of the student-days were not forgotten but they did not seem to get on in[5] the new house. The Miss Gandishes came to one of Mrs. Clive's balls, still in blue crape, still with ringlets on their wizened old foreheads, accompanying Papa with his shirt collars turned down—who gazed in mute wonder on the splendid scene. Warrington actually asked Miss Gandish to dance, making woful blunders, however, in the Quadrille while Clive with some thing like one of his old smiles on his face took out Miss Zoe Gandish, her sister. We made Gandish overeat and overdrink himself in the supper-room and Clive cheered him by ordering a full length of Mrs. Clive Newcome from his distinguished pencil. Never was seen a grander exhibition of white satin and jewels. Smee, R.A., was furious at the preference shown to his rival.

We had Sandy M'Collop too at the party, who had returned from Rome with his red beard, and his picture of the murder of the Red Comyn which made but a dim effect in the Octagon Room of the Royal Academy where the bleeding agonies of the dying warrior were veiled in an unkind twilight. On Sandy and his brethren little Rosey looked rather coldly. She tossed up her little head in conversation with me, and gave me to understand that this party was only an *omnium gatherum*, not one of the select parties, from which Heaven defend us. "We are Poins and Nym and Pistol," growled out George Warrington as he strode away—to finish the evening in Clive's painting and smoking-room. Now Prince Hal is married and shares the paternal throne, his Princess is ashamed of his brigand associates of former

2 the *E1*] a *Ms*
3 and *E1*] [omitted] *Ms*
4 the *Ms*] [omitted] *E1*
5 get on in *E1*] fit into *Ms*

days. She came and looked at us with a feeble little smile as we sat smoking and let the daylight in on us from the open door and hinted to Mr. Clive that it was time to go to bed.

So Clive Newcome lay in a bed of down and tossed and tumbled there. He went to fine dinners and sat silent over them. Rode fine horses and black Care jumped up behind the moody horseman—was[6] cut off in a great measure from the friends of his youth—or saw them by a kind of stealth and sufferance; was a very lonely poor fellow, I am afraid, now that people were testimonialising his wife, and many an old comrade growling at his haughtiness and prosperity.

In former days, when his good father recognised the difference which fate and time and temper had set between him and his son, we have seen with what a gentle acquiescence the old man submitted to his inevitable fortune—and how humbly he bore that stroke of separation which afflicted the boy lightly[7] enough but caused the loving sire so much pain.

Then there was no bitterness between them, in spite of the fatal division; but now it seemed as if there was anger on Thomas Newcome's part because, though come together again, they were not united, though with every outward appliance of happiness Clive was not happy. What young man on earth could look for more—A sweet young wife, a handsome[8] home of which the only encumbrance was an old father, who would give his last drop of blood in his son's behalf. And it was to bring about this end that Thomas Newcome had toiled and had amassed a[9] fortune. Could not Clive, with his talents and education, go down once or twice a week to the City and take a decent part in the business by which his wealth was secured?—He appeared at the various board-rooms and City conclaves, yawned at the meetings and drew figures on the blotting-paper of the Company; had no interest in its transactions, no heart in its affairs; went away and galloped his horse alone or returned to his painting-room, put on his old velvet jacket and worked with his palettes and brushes. Palettes and brushes! could he not give up these toys when he was called to a much higher station in the world? Could he not go talk with Rosey? Drive with Rosey, that[1] kind little soul whose whole desire was to make him happy? Such thoughts as these no doubt darkened the Colonel's mind, and deepened the furrows round his old eyes. So it is we judge men by our own standards, judge our nearest and dearest often wrong.

Many and many a time did Clive try and talk with the little Rosey who chirped and prattled so gaily to his father. Many a time would she come and sit by his easel and try her little powers to charm him, bring him little tales about their acquaintances, stories about this ball and that concert, practise artless smiles upon him, gentle little bouderies, tears perhaps, followed by caresses and reconciliation. At the end of which he would return to his cigar and she, with a sigh and a heavy heart, to the good old man who had bidden her to go and talk with him. He used to feel that his father had sent

[6] horseman—was] horseman—Was *Ms*] horseman. He was *E1*
[7] lightly *E1*] likely *Ms*
[8] handsome *E1*] splendid *Ms*
[9] amassed a *E1*] a master *Ms*
[1] that *Ms*] [omitted] *E1*

her; the thought came[2] across him in their conversations and straight-way his heart would shut up and his face grow gloomy. They were not made to mate with one another—that was the truth; the shoe was a[3] very pretty little shoe but Clive's foot was too big for it.[4]

Just before the testimonial Mr. Clive was in constant attendance at home and very careful and kind and happy with his wife, and the whole family party went very agreeably. Doctors were in constant attendance at Mrs. Clive Newcome's door; prodigious care was taken by the good Colonel in wrapping her and in putting her little feet on sofas and in leading her to her carriage. The Campaigner came over in immense flurry from Edinburgh (where Uncle James was now very comfortably lodged in Picardy Place with the most agreeable society round about him) and all this circle was in a word very close and happy and intimate; but woe is me, Thomas Newcome's fondest hopes were disappointed this time: his little grandson lived but to see the light and leave it, and sadly sadly those preparations were put away, those poor little robes and caps, those delicate muslins and cambrics over which many a care had been forgotten, many a fond prayer thought if not uttered. Poor little Rosey! she felt the grief very keenly but she rallied from it very soon—in a very few months her cheeks were blooming and dimpling with smiles again and she was telling us how her party was an *omnium gatherum.*

The Campaigner had ere this returned to the scene of her northern exploits; not I believe entirely of the worthy woman's own free will. Assuming the command of the household, whilst her daughter kept her sofa, Mrs. Mackenzie had set that establishment into uproar and mutiny. She had offended the butler, outraged the housekeeper, wounded the sensibilities of the footmen, insulted the doctor and trampled on the inmost corns of the nurse. It was surprising what a change appeared in the Campaigner's conduct and how little in former days, Colonel Newcome had known her. What the Emperor Napoleon the First said respecting our Russian enemies, might be applied to this lady, Grattez la and she appeared a Tartar. Clive and his father had a little comfort and conversation in conspiring against her. The old man never dared to try but was pleased with the younger's spirit and gallantry in the series of final actions which, commencing over poor little Rosey's prostrate body in the dressing-room, were continued in the drawing-room, resumed with terrible vigour on the enemy's part in the dining-room and ended, to the triumph of the whole establishment, at the outside of the hall door.

When the routed Tartar force had fled back to its native north, Rosey made a confession which Clive told me afterwards, bursting with bitter laughter. "You and Papa seem to be very much agitated," she said. (Rosey called the Colonel Papa in the absence of the Campaigner.) "I do not mind it a bit except just at first when it made me a little nervous—Mamma used always to be so—she used to scold and scold all day, both me and Josey in Scotland, till Grandmamma sent her away and then in Fitzroy Square and

2 came *E1*] would come *Ms*
3 shoe was a *E1*] shoe—a *Ms*
4 The shoe . . . big for it. *Ms E1*] [omitted] *R*

then in Brussels, she used to box my ears and go into such tantrums and I think," adds Rosey with one of her sweetest smiles, "she had quarrelled with Uncle James before she came to us."

"She used to box Rosey's ears," roars out poor Clive, "and go into such tantrums in[5] Fitzroy Square and Brussels[6] afterwards and the pair would come down with their arms round each other's waists, smirking and smiling as if they had done nothing but kiss each other all their mortal lives. This is what we know about women—this is what we get, and find years afterwards when we think we have married a smiling artless young creature. Are you all such hypocrites, Mrs. Pendennis," and he pulled his moustachios in his wrath.

"Poor Clive," says Laura very kindly. "You would not have had her tell tales of her mother, would you?"

"O, of course not," breaks out Clive—"that is what you all say and so you are hypocrites out of sheer virtue."

It was the first time Laura had called him Clive for many a day.[7] She was becoming reconciled to him. We had our own opinion about the young fellow's marriage.

And to sum up all, upon a casual rencontre with the young gentleman[8] in question, whom we saw descending from a hansom at the steps of the Flag, Pall Mall, I opined that dark thoughts of Goby[9] had entered into Clive Newcome's mind. Othello-like he scowled after that unconscious Cassio[1] as the other passed into the club on[2] his laquered boots.

[5] in *E1*] and in *Ms*
[6] Brussels *E1*] at Brussels *Ms*
[7] day. *E1*] long day. *Ms*
[8] young gentleman *E1*] gentleman *Ms*
[9] Goby *Ms*] Hoby *E1*
[1] Cassio *E1*] cashier *Ms*
[2] on *Ms*] in *E1*

Chapter XXVI.

ABSIT OMEN.[1]

T the first of the Blackwall festivals Hobson Newcome was present in spite of the quarrel which had taken place between his elder brother and the chief of the firm of Hobson Brothers and Newcome. But it was the individual Barnes and the individual Thomas who had had a difference together; the Bundelcund Bank was not at variance with its chief house of commission in London, no man drank prosperity to the B.B.C. upon occasion of this festival, with greater fervour than Hobson Newcome, and the manner in which he just slightly alluded in his own little speech of thanks to the notorious differences between Colonel Newcome and his nephew, praying that these might cease some day and meanwhile that the confidence between the great Indian establishment and its London agents might never diminish, was appreciated and admired by six-and-thirty gentlemen, all brimfull of claret and enthusiasm and in that happy state of mind in which men appreciate and admire everything.

At the second dinner when the testimonial was presented, Hobson was not present. Nor did his name figure amongst those engraven on the trunk of Mrs. Newcome's allegorical silver cocoa-nut tree. As we travelled homewards in the omnibus, Fred Bayham noticed the circumstance to me. "I have looked over the list of names," says he, "not merely that on the trunk, Sir, but the printed list; it was rolled up, and placed in one of the nests on the top of the tree. Why is Hobson's name not there—Ha! it mislikes me, Pendennis."

F.B., who was[2] now very great about City affairs, discoursed about stocks and companies with immense learning and gave me to understand that he

---

MR. FREDERICK BAYHAM

had transacted one or two little operations in Capel Court on his own account with great present and still larger prospective advantages to himself. It is a fact that Mr. Ridley was paid, and that F.B.'s costume though still excentric was comfortable, cleanly and variegated. He occupied the apartments once tenanted by the amiable Honeyman. He lived in ease and comfort there. "You don't suppose," says he, "that the wretched stipend I draw from the *Pall Mall Gazette* enables me to maintain this kind of thing? F.B., Sir, has a station in the world; F.B. moves among moneyers, and City nobs, and eats cabobs with wealthy nabobs. He may marry, Sir, and settle in life." We cordially wished every worldly prosperity to the brave F.B.

Happening to descry him one day in the Park, I remarked that his countenance wore an ominous and tragic appearance which seemed to deepen as he neared me. I thought he had been toying affably with a nursery maid the[3] moment before, who stood with some of her little charges watching the yachts upon the Serpentine. Howbeit, espying my approach, F.B. strode away from the maiden and her innocent companions and advanced to greet his old acquaintance, enveloping his face with shades of funereal gloom.

"Yon were the children of my good friend Colonel Huckaback of the Bombay Marines. Alas unconscious of their doom, the little infants play. I was watching them at their sports. There is a pleasing young woman in attendance upon the poor children. They were sailing their little boats upon the Serpentine—racing and laughing and making merry; and as I looked on, Master Hastings Huckaback's boat went down. *Absit omen*, Pendennis. I was moved by the circumstance. F.B. hopes that the child's father's argosy may not meet with shipwreck."

"You mean the little yellow-faced man whom we met at Colonel Newcome's," says Mr. Pendennis.

"I do, Sir," growled F.B. "You know that he is a brother director with our Colonel, in the Bundelcund Bank."

"Gracious Heavens," I cried in sincere anxiety, "nothing has happened I hope to the Bundelcund Bank."

"No," answers the other, "nothing has happened, the good ship is safe, Sir, as yet. But she has narrowly escaped a great danger. Pendennis," cries F.B. gripping my arm with great energy, "there was a traitor in her crew—she has weathered the storm nobly—who[4] would have sent her on the rocks, Sir—who would have scuttled her at midnight."

"Pray drop your nautical metaphors and tell me what you mean," cries F.B.'s companion, and Bayham continued his narration.

"Were you in the least conversant with City affairs," he said, "or did you deign to visit the spot where merchants mostly congregate, you would have heard the story, which was over the whole City yesterday and spread dismay from Threadneedle Street to Leadenhall.—The story is, that the firm of Hobson Brothers and Newcome, yesterday refused acceptance of thirty thousand pounds worth of bills of the Bundelcund Banking Company of India.

[3] the *E1*] in the *Ms*
[4] nobly—who *E1*] nobly, and *Ms*

"The news came like a thunderclap upon the London Board of Directors, who had received no notice of the intentions of Hobson Brothers, and caused a dreadful panic amongst the shareholders of the concern. The board-room was besieged by Colonels and Captains, widows and orphans, within an hour after protest the bills were taken up and you will see, in the City article of the *Globe* this very evening, an announcement that henceforward, the house of Baines and Jolly of Fog[5] Court will meet engagements of the Bundelcund Banking Company of India, being provided with ample funds to do honour to[6] every possible liability of that company. But the shares fell, Sir, in consequence of the panic. I hope they will rally. I trust and believe they will rally. For our good Colonel's sake, and that of his friends, for the sake of the innocent children sporting by the Serpentine yonder.

"I had my suspicions when they gave that testimonial," said F.B. "In my experience of life, Sir, I always feel rather shy about testimonials, and when a party gets one—somehow look out to hear of his smashing the next month. *Absit omen.* I will say again. I like not the going down of yonder little yacht."

The *Globe* sure enough contained a paragraph that evening announcing the occurrence which Mr. Bayham had described and the temporary panic which it had occasioned, and containing an advertisement stating that Messrs. Baines and Jolly would henceforth act as agents of the Indian Company. Legal proceedings were presently threatened by the Solicitors of the Company against the banking firm which had caused so much mischief. Mr. Hobson Newcome was absent abroad when the circumstance took place and it was known that the protest of the bills was solely attributable to his nephew and partner. But after the break between the two firms, there was a rupture between Hobson's family and Colonel Newcome. The exasperated Colonel vowed that his brother and his nephew were traitors alike and would have no further dealings with one or the other. Even poor innocent Sam Newcome coming up to London from Oxford where he had been plucked and offering a hand to Clive, was frowned away by our Colonel who spoke in terms of great displeasure to his son[7] for taking the least notice of the young traitor.

Our Colonel was changed, changed in his heart, changed in his whole demeanour[8] towards the world and above all towards his son for whom he had made so many kind sacrifices in his old[9] days. We have said how, ever since Clive's marriage, a tacit strife had been growing up between father and son. The boy's evident unhappiness was like a reproach to his father. His very silence angered the old man. His want of confidence daily chafed and annoyed him. At the head of a large fortune, which he rightly persisted in spending, he felt angry with himself because he could not enjoy it, angry with his son who should have helped him in the administration of his new estate, and who was but a listless useless member of the little confederacy,

[5] Fog *R*] Fob *Ms*] Job *E1*
[6] do honour to *E1*] meet *Ms*
[7] son *E1*] own son *Ms*
[8] whole demeanour *E1*] demeanour *Ms*
[9] his old *E1*] old *Ms*

a living protest against all the schemes of the good man's past life. The catastrophe in the City again brought father and son together somewhat, and the vindictiveness of both was roused by Barnes's treason. Time was when the Colonel himself would have viewed his kinsman[1] more charitably, but fate and circumstance had angered[2] that originally friendly and gentle disposition; hate and suspicion had mastered him, and if it cannot be said that his new life had changed him, at least it had brought out faults for which there had hitherto been no occasion, and qualities latent before. Do we know ourselves, or what good or evil circumstance may bring from us?[3] Did Cain know as he and his younger brother played round their mother's knee that the little hand which caressed Abel should one day grow large[4] and seize a brand to slay him? Thrice fortunate he, to whom circumstance is made easy: whom fate visits with gentle trial, and kindly Heaven keeps out of temptation.

In the stage which the family feud now reached and which the biographer of the Newcomes is bound to describe, there is one gentle moralist who gives her sentence decidedly against Clive's father;[5] whilst on the other hand a rough philosopher and friend of mine, whose opinions used to have some weight with me, stoutly declares that he was[6] right. "War and Justice are good things," says George Warrington rattling his clenched fist on the table, "I maintain them, and the common-sense of the world maintains them against the preaching of all the Honeymans that ever puled from a[7] pulpit. I have not the least objection in life to a rogue being hanged: when[8] a scoundrel is whipped I am pleased, and say, serve him right. If any gentleman will horsewhip Sir Barnes Newcome, Baronet; I shall not be shocked but on the contrary go home and order an extra mutton chop for dinner."

"Ah! Revenge is wrong, Pen," pleads the other counsellor. "Let alone that the wisest and best of all Judges has condemned it. It blackens the hearts of men. It distorts their views of right. It sets them to devise evil. It causes them to think unjustly of others. It is not the noblest return for injury, not even the bravest way of meeting it. The greatest courage is to bear persecution, not to answer when you are reviled, and when a wrong has been done you to forgive. I am sorry for what you call the Colonel's[9] triumph and his enemy's[1] humiliation. Let Barnes be as odious as you will, he[2] ought never to have humiliated Ethel's brother, but he is weak. Other gentlemen as well are weak, Mr. Pen, although you are so much cleverer than women. I[3] have no patience with the Colonel, and I beg you to tell

[1] kinsman *E1*] kinsmen *Ms*
[2] angered *E1*] changed *Ms*
[3] us? *E1*] ourselves *Ms*
[4] large *Ms*] larger *E1*
[5] Clive's father; *E1*] Clive and his father. *Ms*] Clive and his father; *HM NY*
[6] he was] they were *Ms E1*
[7] a *Ms*] the *E1*
[8] hanged: when *Ms*] hung. When *E1*
[9] the Colonel's *E1*] Clive's *Ms HM NY*
[1] enemy's *E1*] enemies' *Ms HM NY*
[2] he *E1*] Clive *Ms HM NY*
[3] I *E1*] He has been led in this affair by his father—I *Ms HM NY*

him whether he asks you or not that he has lost my good graces, and that I for one will not huzzah at what his friends and flatterers call his triumphs and that I don't think in this instance he has acted like the dear Colonel and the good Colonel and the good Christian that I once thought him."

We must now tell what the Colonel and Clive had been doing and what caused two such different opinions respecting their conduct from the two critics just named. The refusal of the London Banking House to accept the bills of the great Indian Company of course affected very much the credit of that Company in this country. Sedative announcements were issued by the Directors in London, brilliant accounts of the Company's affairs abroad were published; proof incontrovertible was given that the B.B.C. was never in so flourishing a state as at that time when Hobson Brothers had refused its drafts; there[4] could be no question that the Company had received a severe wound and was deeply if not vitally injured by the conduct of the London firm.

The propensity to sell out became quite epidemic amongst the share-holders. Every body was anxious to realise—Why out of the thirty names inscribed on poor Mrs. Clive's cocoa-nut tree no less than twenty deserters might be mentioned, or at least who would desert could they find an op-portunity of doing so with arms and baggage. Wrathfully the good Colonel scratched the names of those faithless ones out of his daughter's visiting book: haughtily he met them in the street: to desert the B.B.C. at the hour of peril was, in his idea, like applying for leave of absence on the eve of an action. He would not see that the question was not one of sentiment at all, but of chances and arithmetic, he would not hear with patience of men quitting the ship as he called it. "They may go, Sir," says he, "but let them never more be officers of mine." With scorn and indignation he paid off one or two timid friends, who were anxious to fly, and purchased their shares out of his own pocket. But his purse was not long enough for this kind of amusement. What money he had was invested in the Company already and his name further pledged for meeting the engagements from which their late London Bankers had withdrawn.

Those gentlemen in the meanwhile, spoke of their differences with the Indian Bank as quite natural, and laughed at the absurd charges of per-sonal hostility which poor Thomas Newcome publicly preferred. "Here is a hot-headed old Indian Dragoon," says Sir Barnes, "who knows no more about business than I do about cavalry tactics or Hindostanee—who gets into a partnership along with other dragoons and Indian wiseacres with some uncommonly wily old native practitioners and they pay great Divi-dends, and they set up a bank. Of course, we will do these people's busi-ness as long as we are covered, but I have always told their manager that we would run no risks whatever and close the account the very moment it did not suit us to keep it, and so we parted company six weeks ago, since when there has been a panic in the Company, a panic which has been in-creased by Colonel Newcome's absurd swagger and folly. He says I am his enemy, enemy indeed. So I am in private life but what has that to do with

---

[4] had refused its drafts; there *E1*] refused its draughts, but there *Ms*

business. In business, begad, there are no friends and no enemies at all. I leave all my sentiments on t'other[5] side of Temple Bar."

So Thomas Newcome and Clive the son of Thomas had wrath in their hearts against Barnes their kinsman and desired to be revenged upon him and were eager after his undoing, and longed for an opportunity when they might meet him and overcome him and put him to shame.

When men are in this frame of mind, a certain personage is said always to be at hand to help them and give[6] them occasion for indulging in their pretty little passion. What is sheer hate seems to the individual entertaining the sentiment so like indignant virtue, that he often indulges in the propensity to the full, nay, lauds himself for the exercise of it. I am sure if Thomas Newcome in his present desire for retaliation against Barnes had known the real nature of his sentiments towards that worthy, his conduct would have been different and we should have heard of no such active hostilities as ensued.

---

[5] sentiments on t'other *Ms*] sentiment on the other *E1*
[6] give *E1*] to give *Ms*

Chapter XXVII.

IN WHICH MRS. CLIVE COMES INTO HER FORTUNE.

SPEAKING of the affairs of the B.B.C. Sir Barnes Newcome always took care to maintain his candid surprise relating to the proceedings of that Company. He set about evil reports against it! He endeavour to do it a wrong—Absurd! If a friend were to ask him (and it was quite curious what a number did manage to ask him), whether he thought the Company was an advantageous investment of course he would give an answer. He could not say conscientiously he thought so—never once had said so—in the time of their connection which had been formed solely[1] with a view of obliging his amiable uncle. It was a quarrelsome Company, a dragoon Company, a Company of gentlemen accustomed to gunpowder and fed on mulligatawny. He, forsooth, be hostile to it! There were some Companies that required no enemies at all and would be pretty sure to go to the deuce their own way.

Thus and with this amiable candour spake Barnes, about a commercial speculation, the merits of which he had a right to canvass as well as any other citizen. As for Uncle Hobson, his conduct was characterised by a timidity which one would scarcely have expected from a gentleman of his florid jolly countenance, active habits and generally manly demeanour. He kept away from the cocoa-nut feast as we have seen, he protested privily to the Colonel that his private good-will continued undiminished, but

---

[1] been formed solely *E1*] solely been formed *Ms*

he was deeply grieved at the B.B.C. affair which took place while he was[2] on the Continent—confound the Continent, my wife would go, and which was entirely without his cognisance. The Colonel received his brother's excuses, first with awful bows and ceremony, and finally with laughter. "My good Hobson," says he with the most insufferable kindness, "of course you intended to be friendly—of course the affair was done without your knowledge. We understand that sort[3] of thing—London Bankers have no hearts—for these last fifty[4] years past that I have known you and your brother and my amiable nephew, the present commanding officer, has there been anything in your conduct that has led me to suppose you had?" and herewith Colonel Newcome burst out into a laugh. It was not a pleasant laugh to hear. Worthy Hobson took his hat and walked away brushing it round and round and looking very confused. The Colonel strode after him down-stairs and made him an awful bow at the hall door. Never again did Hobson Newcome set foot in that Tyburnian mansion.

During the whole of that season of the testimonial—the cocoa-nut figured in[5] an extraordinary number of banquets—the Colonel's hospitalities were more profuse than ever and Mrs. Clive's toilettes more brilliant. Clive in his confidential conversations with his friends was very dismal and gloomy. When I asked City news of our well informed friend F.B., I am sorry to say his countenance became funereal. The B.B.C. shares which had been at an immense premium twelve months since were now slowly falling, falling.

"I wish," says Mr. Sherrick to me, "the Colonel would realise even now, like that[6] Mr. Ratray who has just come out of the ship and brought a hundred thousand pounds with him."

"Come out of the ship! You little know the Colonel, Mr. Sherrick, if you think he will ever do that."

Mr. Ratray, though he had returned to Europe, gave the most cheering accounts of the B.B.C. It was in the most flourishing state. Shares[7] sure to get up again. He had sold out entirely on account of his liver. Must come home—the doctor said so.

Some months afterwards another director,[8] Mr. Hedges, came home. Both of these gentlemen, as we know, entertained the fashionable world, got seats in Parliament, purchased places in the country, and were greatly respected. Mr. Hedges came out, but his wealthy partner, Mr. McGaspey, entered into the B.B.C. The entry of Mr. McGaspey into the affairs of the Company did not seem to produce very great excitement in England. The shares slowly fell. However there was a prodigious indigo crop. The London Manager was in perfect good-humour. In spite of this and that, of defections, of unpleasantries, of unfavourable whispers and doubtful friends—Thomas Newcome kept his head high, and his face was always

---

2 while he was *E1*] during his absence *Ms*
3 sort *E1*] kind *Ms*
4 last fifty *E1*] fifty *Ms*
5 in *E1*] with *Ms*
6 like that *E1*] that *Ms*
7 Shares *E1*] Share *Ms*
8 director, *E1*] of the Indian directors, *Ms*

kind and smiling except when certain family enemies were mentioned and he frowned like Jove in anger.

We have seen how very fond little Rosey was of her Mamma, of her uncle, James Binnie, and now of her Papa as she affectionately styled Thomas Newcome. This affection I am sure the two gentlemen returned with all their hearts and but that they were much too generous and simple-minded to entertain such a feeling, it may be wondered that the two good old boys were not a little jealous of one another. Howbeit it does not appear that they entertained such a feeling, at least it never interrupted the kindly friendship between them, and Clive was regarded in the light of a son by both of them, and each contented himself with his moiety of the smiling little girl's affection.

As long as they were with her, the truth is, little Mrs. Clive was very fond of people, very docile, obedient, easily pleased, brisk, kind and good-humoured. She charmed her two old friends with little songs, little smiles, little kind offices, little caresses; and having administered Thomas Newcome's cigar to him in the daintiest prettiest way, she would trip off to drive with James Binnie or sit at his dinner if he was indisposed and be as gay, neat-handed, watchful and attentive a child as any old gentleman could desire.

She did not seem to be very sorry to part with Mamma, a want of feeling which that lady bitterly deplored in her subsequent conversation with her friends about Mrs. Clive Newcome. Possibly there were reasons why Rosey should not be very much vexed at quitting Mamma, but surely, she might have dropped a little tear as she took leave of kind good old James Binnie. Not she. The gentleman's voice faltered but hers did not in the least. She kissed him on the face, all smiles, blushes and happiness and tripped into the railway carriage with her husband and father-in-law at Brussels, leaving the poor old uncle very sad. Our women said, I know not why, that little Rosey had no heart at all. Women are accustomed to give such opinions respecting the wives of their newly married friends. I am bound to add, when they do so during Mr. Clive Newcome's absence from England (otherwise I should not like to venture upon the statement),[9] that some men concur with the ladies' opinions of Mrs. Clive. For instance Captains Goby and Hoby declare that her treatment of the latter, her encouragement, and desertion of him when Clive made his proposals, were shameful.

At this time Rosey was in a pupillary state. A good obedient little girl, her duty was to obey the wishes of her dear mamma—how show her sense of virtue and obedience better than by promptly and cheerfully obeying Mamma and, at the orders of that experienced Campaigner, trading[1] up Bobby Hoby, and going to England to a fine house, to be presented at Court, to have all sorts of pleasure with a handsome young husband and a kind father-in-law by her side? No wonder Rosey was not in a very active state of grief at parting from Uncle James. He strove to console himself with these considerations when he had returned to the empty house, where

---

[9] add, when they do ... England (otherwise ... statement),] add when they do ... England otherwise ... statement, *Ms*] add, (and I do ... England, otherwise ... statement,) *E1*

[1] trading *Ms*] giving *E1*

she had danced and smiled and warbled; and he looked[2] at the chair she sat in; and at the[3] great mirror which had so often reflected her fresh pretty face;—the great callous mirror which now only framed upon its shining sheet the turban and the ringlets and the plump person and the resolute smile of the old Campaigner.

After that parting with her uncle at the Brussels' railway, Rosey never again beheld him. He passed into the Campaigner's keeping, from which alone he was rescued by the summons of pallid Death. He met that summons like a philosopher; rejected rather testily all the mortuary consolations which his nephew-in-law, Josey's husband, thought proper to bring to his bedside; and uttered opinions which scandalised that divine. But as he left Mrs. M'Craw only 500£, thrice[4] that sum to his sister and the remainder of his property to his beloved niece, Rosa MacKenzie, now Rosa Newcome, let us trust that Mr. M'Craw, hurt and angry at the ill-favour shown to his wife, his third young wife, his best beloved Josey, at the impatience with which the deceased had always received his, Mr. M'Craw's, own sermons;—let us hope I say, that the reverend gentleman was mistaken in his views respecting the present position of Mr. James Binnie's soul, and that Heaven may have some regions yet accessible to James which Mr. M'Craw's intellect has not yet explored. Look, gentlemen, does a week pass without the announcement of the discovery of a new comet in the sky, a new star in the heaven twinkling dimly out of a yet farther distance, and only now becoming visible to human ken though existent for ever and ever?[5] So let us hope divine truths may be shining and regions of light and love extant which Geneva glasses cannot yet perceive[6] and are beyond the focus of Roman telescopes.

I think Clive and the Colonel were more affected by the news of James's death than Rosey, concerning whose wonderful strength of mind good Thomas Newcome discoursed to my Laura and me, when, fancying that[7] my friend's wife needed comfort and consolation, Mrs. Pendennis went to visit her. "Of course we shall have no more parties this year," sighed Rosey. She looked very pretty in her black dress. Clive, in his hearty way, said a hundred kind feeling things about the departed friend. Thomas Newcome's recollections of him and regret were no less tender and sincere. "See," says he, "how that dear child's sense of duty makes her hide her feelings—Her grief is most deep but she wears a calm countenance. I see her looking sad in private but I no sooner speak than she smiles." "I think," said Laura as we came away, "that Colonel Newcome performs all the courtship part of the marriage and Clive, poor Clive, though he spoke very nobly and generously about Mr. Binnie, I am sure it is not his old friend's death merely which makes him so unhappy."

[2] and he looked *E1*] looked *Ms*
[3] and at the *E1*] the *Ms*
[4] thrice *E1*] double *Ms HM NY*
[5] distance, and . . . ever and ever? *E1*] only now their existence for ever and ever becoming visible to human ken *Ms*
[6] yet perceive] yet perceive, *E1*] perceive *Ms*
[7] me, when, fancying that *E1*] me. When fancying *Ms*

Poor Clive, by right of his wife, was now rich Clive; the little lady having inherited from her kind relative no inconsiderable sum of money. In a very early part of this story mention has been made of a small sum producing one hundred pounds a-year which Clive's father had made over to the lad when he sent him from India. This little sum Mr. Clive had settled upon his wife before marriage, being indeed all he had of his own; for the famous bank shares which his father presented to him were only made over formally[8] when the young man came to London after his marriage and at the paternal request and order appeared as a most inefficient director of the B.B.C. Now Mrs. Newcome, of her own inheritance, possessed not only B.B.C. shares but monies in bank and shares in East India stock, so that Clive in the right of his wife had a seat in the assembly of East India shareholders and a voice in the election of directors of that famous company. I promise you Mrs. Clive was a personage of no little importance. She carried her little head with an aplomb and gravity which amused some of us. F.B. bent his most respectfully down before her; she sent him on messages and deigned to ask him to dinner. He once more wore a cheerful countenance; the clouds which gathered o'er the sun of Newcome were in the bosom of the ocean buried, Bayham said, by James Binnie's brilliant behaviour to his niece.

Clive was a proprietor of East India stock and had a vote in electing the directors of that company, and who so fit to be a director of his[9] affairs as Thomas Newcome, Esq., Companion of the Bath and so long a distinguished officer in its army. To hold this position of director used, up to very late days, to be the natural ambition of many East Indian gentlemen. Colonel Newcome had often thought of offering himself as a candidate and now openly placed himself on the lists and publicly announced his intention. His interest was rather powerful through the Indian bank, of which he was a director, and many of the shareholders of which were proprietors of the East India Company. To have a director of the B.B.C. also a member of the parliament in Leadenhall Street would naturally be beneficial to the former institution. Thomas Newcome's prospectuses were issued accordingly and his canvass received with tolerable favour.

Within a very short time another candidate appeared in the field, a retired Bombay lawyer of considerable repute and large means, and at the head of this gentleman's committee appeared the names of Hobson Brothers and Newcome, very formidable personages at the East India House with which the bank of Hobson Brothers have had dealings for half a century past and where the old lady who founded or consolidated that family had had three stars before her own venerable name which had descended upon her son Sir Brian, and her grandson Sir Barnes.

War was thus openly declared between Thomas Newcome and his nephew. The canvass on both sides was very hot and eager. The number of promises was pretty equal. The election was not to come off yet for a while, for aspirants to the honourable Office of Director used to announce their wishes years before they could be fulfilled and returned again

---

[8] formally *E1*] formerly *Ms*
[9] his *Ms E1*] its *R*

and again to the contest before they finally won it. Howbeit the Colonel's prospects were very fair and, a prodigious Indigo Crop come[1] in to favour the B.B.C. with the most brilliant report from the board at Calcutta, the shares still somewhat sluggish rose again, the Colonel's hopes with them and the courage of gentlemen at home who had invested their money in the transaction.

We were sitting one day round the Colonel's dinner-table. It was not one of the cocoa-nut tree days, that emblem was locked up in the butler's pantry and only beheld the lamps on occasions of state. It was a snug family party in the early part of the year, when scarcely anybody was in town; only George Warrington and F.B. and Mr. and Mrs. Pendennis, and the ladies having retired we were having such a talk as we used to enjoy in quite old days before marriages and cares and divisions had separated us.

F.B. led the conversation. The Colonel received his remarks with great gravity and thought him an instructive personage. Others considered him rather as amusing than instructive, and so his eloquency[2] was generally welcome. The canvass for the directorship was talked over. The improved affairs of a certain great banking company which shall be nameless but one which F.B. would take the liberty to state would in his opinion unite for ever the mother country to our great Indian possessions;—the prosperity of this great company was enthusiastically drunk by Mr. Bayham in some of the very best claret. The conduct of the enemies of that company was characterised in terms of bitter but not undeserved satire. F.B. rather liked to air his oratory and neglected few opportunities for making speeches after dinner.

The Colonel admired his voice and sentiments not the less perhaps because the latter were highly laudatory of the good man. And not from interest, at least as far as he himself knew, not from any mean or selfish motives did F.B. speak. He called Colonel Newcome his friend, his benefactor— kissed the hem of his garment. He wished fervently that he could have been the Colonel's son: he expressed repeatedly a desire that some one would speak ill of the Colonel so that he, F.B., might have the opportunity of polishing that individual off in about two seconds. He revered the Colonel with all his heart, nor is any gentleman proof altogether against this constant regard and devotion from another.

The Colonel used to wag his head wisely, and say Mr. Bayham's suggestions were often exceedingly valuable, as indeed the fact was—though his conduct was no more of a piece with his opinions than those of some other folks occasionally are.

"What the Colonel ought to do, Sir, to help him in the direction," says F.B., "is to get into Parliament. The House of Commons would aid him into the Court of Directors and the Court of Directors would help him in the House of Commons."

"Most wisely said," says Warrington.

The Colonel declined. "I have long had the House of Commons in my eye," he said, "but not for me. I wanted my boy to go there. It would be a proud day for me if I could see him there."

[1] come *Ms*] came *E1*
[2] eloquency *Ms*] eloquence *E1*

"I can't speak," says Clive from his end of the table. "I don't understand about parties like F.B. here."

"I believe I do know a thing or two," Mr. Bayham here politely interposes.

"And politics do not interest me in the least," Clive sighs out, drawing pictures with his fork on his napkin and not heeding the other's interruptions.

"I wish I knew what would interest him," his father whispers to me who happened to be at his[3] side. "He never cares to be out of his painting-room—and he doesn't seem to be very happy even in there. I wish to God, Pen, I knew what had come over the boy." I thought I knew but what was the use of telling now there was no remedy.

"A dissolution is expected every day," continued F.B. "The papers are full of it. Ministers cannot go on with this majority—cannot possibly go on, Sir. I have it on the best authority, and men who are anxious about their seats are writing to their constituents or are subscribing at missionary meetings or are gone down to lecturing at Athenæums and that sort of thing."

Here Warrington burst out into a laughter, much louder than the occasion or the speech of F.B. seemed to warrant, and the Colonel turning round with some dignity asked the cause of George's amusement.

"What do you think your darling, Sir Barnes Newcome Newcome, has been doing during the recess," cries Warrington. "I had a letter this morning from my liberal and punctual employer, Thomas Potts, Esquire, of the *Newcome Independent*, who states in language scarcely respectful that Sir Barnes Newcome Newcome is trying to come the religious dodge, as Mr. Potts calls it. He professes to be stricken down by grief on account of late family circumstances; wears black and puts on the most piteous aspect, and asks ministers of various denominations to tea with him. And the last announcement is the most stupendous of all—stop I have it in my great coat"—and ringing the bell George orders a servant to bring him a newspaper from his great-coat pocket. "Here it is actually in print," Warrington continues and reads to us—" 'Newcome Athenæum. 1. for the[4] benefit of the Newcome Orphan Children's Home, and 2. for the benefit of the Newcome Soup Association, without distinction of denomination, Sir Barnes Newcome Newcome, Bart.,[5] proposes to give two lectures on Friday the 23rd and Friday the 30th instant. No. 1, The Poetry of Childhood: Doctor Watts, Mrs. Barbauld, Jane Taylor. No. 2, The Poetry of Womanhood and the Affections: Mrs. Hemans, L.E.L. Threepence will be charged at the doors which will go to the use of the above two admirable societies.' Potts wants me to go down and hear him. He has an eye to business. He has had a quarrel with Sir Barnes and wants me to go down and hear him and smash him, he kindly says. Let us go down, Clive. You shall draw your cousin as you have drawn his villainous little mug a hundred times before—and I will do the smashing part, and we will have some fun out of the transaction."

[3] his *E1*] my *Ms*
[4] 1. for the *E1*] The *Ms*
[5] Newcome Newcome, Bart., *E1*] Newcome, Newcome Park, *Ms*

"Besides Florac will be in the country; going to Rosebury is a journey worth the taking I can tell you, and we have[6] old Mrs. Mason to go and see, who sighs after you, Colonel. My wife went to see her," remarks Mr. Pendennis, "and—"

"And Miss Newcome I know," says the Colonel.

"She is away at Brighton with her little charges for sea air. My wife heard from her to-day."

"O indeed. Mrs. Pendennis corresponds with her?"—says our host darkling under his eyebrows; and at this moment my neighbour, F.B., is kind enough to scrunch my foot under the table with the weight of his heel as much as to warn me by an appeal to my own corns to avoid treading on so delicate a subject in that house. "Yes," said I in spite—perhaps in consequence of this interruption. "My wife does correspond with Miss Ethel who is a noble creature and whom those who know her know how to love and admire. She is very much changed since you knew her, Colonel Newcome; since the misfortunes in Sir Barnes' family and the differences between you and him. Very much changed and very much improved. Ask my wife about her who knows her most intimately and hears from her constantly."

"Very likely, very likely," cried the Colonel hurridly. "I hope she is improved with all my heart. I am sure there was room for it. Gentlemen, shall we go up to the ladies and have some coffee?" And herewith the colloquy ended and the party ascended to the drawing-room.

The party ascended to the drawing-room, where no doubt both the ladies were pleased by the invasion which ended their talk. My wife and the Colonel talked apart, and I saw the latter looking gloomy, and the former pleading very eagerly, and using a great deal of action as the little hands are wont to do when the mistress's heart is very much moved. I was sure she was pleading Ethel's cause with her uncle.

So indeed she was: and Mr. George too knew what her thoughts were. "Look at her!" he said to me, "Don't you see what she is doing? She believes in that girl whom you all said Clive took a fancy to—before he married his present little placid wife,—a nice little simple creature who is worth a dozen Ethels."

"Simple certainly," says Mr. P. with a shrug of the shoulder.

"A simpleton of twenty is better than a roué of twenty. It is better not to have thought at all than to have thought such things as must go through a girl's mind whose life is passed in jilting and being jilted; whose eyes as soon as they are opened are turned to the main chance and are taught to leer at an earl, to languish at a marquis, and to grow blind before a commoner. I don't know much about fashionable life, Heaven help us! (You young Brummell! I see the reproach in your face!)—Why, Sir, it absolutely appears to me as if this little hop-o-my-thumb of a creature has begun to give herself airs since her marriage and her carriage. Do you know I rather thought she patronised me? Are all women spoiled by their contact with the world, and their bloom rubbed off in the market? I know *one* who seems to me to remain pure—to be sure I only know her and this little person and Mrs. Flanagan, our laundress, and my sisters at home who don't count.

[6] we have *E1*] have *Ms*

But that Miss Newcome to whom once you introduced me? O the cocka-trice! Only that poisons don't affect your wife, the other would kill her. I hope the Colonel will not believe a word which Laura says." And my wife's *tête-à-tête* with our host coming to an end about this time, Mr. Warrington in high spirits goes up to the ladies, recapitulates the news of Barnes's lecture, recites "How doth the little busy bee," and gives a quasi-satirical[7] comment upon that well-known poem, which bewilders Mrs. Clive, until, set on by the laughter of the rest of the audience, she laughs very freely at that odd man, and calls him "You droll satirical creature you!" and says she never was so much amused in her life—"Were you, Mrs. Pendennis."

Meanwhile Clive, who has been sitting apart moody,[8] biting his nails, not listening to F.B.'s remarks—has broken into a laugh once or twice and gone to a writing-book, on which, whilst George is still disserting, Clive is drawing.

At the end of the other's speech, F.B. goes up to the draughtsman, looks over his shoulder, makes one or two violent efforts as of inward convulsion, and finally explodes in an enormous guffaw. "It's capital! By Jove, it's capital! Sir Barnes would never dare to face his constituents with that picture of him hung up in Newcome!"

And F.B. holds up the drawing, at which we all laugh except Laura. As for the Colonel he paces up and down the room, holding the sketch close to his eyes, holding it away from him, patting it, clapping his son delightedly[9] on the shoulder. "Capital! Capital! We'll have the picture printed by Jove, Sir; show vice its own images,[1] and shame the Viper in his own nest, Sir. That's what we will!—"

Mrs. Pendennis came away with rather a heavy heart from this party. She chose to interest herself about the right or wrong of her friends; and her mind was disturbed by the Colonel's vindictive spirit. On the subsequent day we had occasion to visit our friend J.J., (who was completing the sweetest little picture, No. 263 in the Exhibition, 'Portrait of a Lady and Child,') and we found that Clive had been with the painter that morning likewise; and that J.J. was acquainted with his scheme. That he did not approve of it we could read in the artist's grave countenance. "Nor does Clive approve of it either!" cried Ridley, with greater eagerness than he usually displayed, and more openness than he was accustomed to exhibit in judging unfavourably of his friends.

"Among them they have taken him away from his art," Ridley said. "They don't understand him when he talks about it; they despise him for pursuing it. Why should I wonder at that? my parents despised it too, and my father was not a grand gentleman like the Colonel, Mrs. Pendennis. Ah! why did the Colonel ever grow rich? Why had not Clive to work for his bread as I have? He would have done something that was worthy of him then; now his time must be spent in dancing attendance at balls and operas, and yawning at City board-rooms. They call that business: they

---

[7] quasi-satirical *E1*] quasi sanctified satirical *Ms*
[8] moody, *Ms*] moodily *E1*
[9] son delightedly *E1*] son delighted *Ms*
[1] images, *Ms*] image; *E1*

think he is idling when he comes here, poor fellow! As if life was long enough for our art; and the best labour we can give, good enough for it! He went away groaning this morning, and quite saddened in spirits. The Colonel wants to set up himself for Parliament, or to set Clive up; but he says he won't. I hope he won't; do not you, Mrs. Pendennis?"

The painter turned as he spoke; and the bright northern light which fell upon the sitter's head was intercepted, and lighted up his own as he addressed us. Out of that bright light looked his pale thoughtful face, and long locks and eager brown eyes. The palette on his arm was a great shield painted of many colours: he carried his maul-stick and a sheaf of brushes along with it, the weapons of his glorious but harmless war. With these he achieves conquests, wherein none are wounded save the envious: with that he shelters him against how much idleness, ambition, temptation! Occupied over that consoling work, idle thoughts cannot gain the mastery over him: selfish wishes or desires are kept at bay. Art is truth: and truth is religion: and its study and practice a daily work of pious duty. What are the world's struggles, brawls, successes, to that calm recluse pursuing his calling? See, twinkling in the darkness round his chamber, numberless beautiful trophies of the graceful victories which he has won:—sweet flowers of fancy reared by him:—kind shapes of beauty which he has devised and moulded. The world enters into the artist's studio, and scornfully bids him a price for his genius, or makes dull pretence to admire it. What know you of his art? You cannot read the alphabet of that sacred book, good old Thomas Newcome! What can you tell of its glories, joys, secrets, consolations? Between his two best beloved mistresses, poor Clive's luckless father somehow interposes; and with sorrowful, even angry protests. In place of Art the Colonel brings him a ledger; and in lieu of first love, shows him Rosey.

No wonder that Clive hangs his head; rebels sometimes, desponds always: he has positively determined to refuse to stand for Newcome, Ridley says. Laura is glad of his refusal, and begins to think of him once more as of the Clive of old days.

Chapter XXVIII.

IN WHICH THE COLONEL AND THE NEWCOME ATHENÆUM ARE BOTH
LECTURED.

T breakfast with his family, on the
morning after the little entertainment to which we were bidden, in
the last chapter, Colonel Newcome
was full of the projected invasion of
Barnes's territories, and delighted to
think that there was an opportunity
of at last humiliating that rascal.

"Clive does not think he is a rascal at all, Papa," cries Rosey, from
behind her tea-urn; "that is, you
said you thought Papa judged him
too harshly; you know you did, this
morning!" And from her husband's
angry glances, she flies to his father's for protection. Those were
even fiercer than Clive's. Revenge
flashed from beneath Thomas New-
come's grizzled eyebrows, and glanced in the direction where Clive sat.
Then the Colonel's face flushed up, and he cast his eyes down towards his
tea-cup, which he lifted with a trembling hand. The father and son loved
each other so, that each was afraid of the other. A war between two such
men is dreadful; pretty little pink-faced Rosey, in a sweet little morning cap
and ribbons, her pretty little fingers twinkling with a score of rings, sat simpering before her silver tea-urn, which reflected her pretty little pink baby
face. Little artless creature! what did she know of the dreadful wounds
which her little words inflicted in the one generous breast and the other?

"My boy's heart is gone from me," thinks poor Thomas Newcome; "our
family is insulted, our enterprises ruined, by that traitor, and my son is
not even angry! he does not care for the success of our plans—for the
honour of our name even; I make him a position of which any young man
in England might be proud, and Clive scarcely deigns to accept it."

"My wife appeals to my father," thinks poor Clive; "it is from him she
asks counsel, and not from me. Be it about the ribbon in her cap, or any
other transaction in our lives, she takes her colour from his opinion, and

goes to him for advice, and I have to wait till it is given, and conform myself to it. If I differ from the dear old father, I wound him; if I yield up my opinion, as I do always, it is with a bad grace, and I wound him still. With the best intentions in the world, what a slave's life it is that he has made for me!"

"How interested you are in your papers," resumes the sprightly Rosey. "What can you find in those horrid politics?" Both gentlemen are looking at their papers with all their might, and no doubt cannot see one single word which those brilliant and witty leading articles contain.

"Clive is like you, Rosey," says the Colonel, laying his paper down, "and does not care for politics."

"He only cares for pictures, Papa," says Mrs. Clive. "He would not drive with me yesterday in the park, but spent hours in his room, while you were toiling in the city, poor Papa!—spent hours painting a horrid beggar-man dressed up as a monk. And this morning, he got up quite early, quite early, and has been out ever so long, and only came in for breakfast just now! just before the bell rung."

"I like a ride before breakfast," says Clive.

"A ride! I know where you have been, Sir! He goes away morning after morning, to that little Mr. Ridley's—his chum, Papa, and he comes back with his hands all over horrid paint. He did this morning; you know you did, Clive."

"I did not keep anyone waiting, Rosa," says Clive. "I like to have two or three hours at my painting when I can spare them."[1] Indeed, the poor fellow used so to run away of summer mornings for Ridley's instructions, and gallop home again, so as to be in time for the family meal.

"Yes," cries Rosey, tossing up the cap and ribbons, "he gets up so early in the morning, that at night he falls asleep after dinner; very pleasant and polite, isn't he, Papa?"

"I am up betimes too, my dear," says the Colonel (many and many a time he must have heard Clive as he left the house); I have a great many letters to write, affairs of the greatest importance to examine and conduct. Mr. Betts from the city is often with me for hours before I come down to your breakfast-table. A man who has the affairs of such a great bank as ours to look to, must be up with the lark. We are all early risers in India."

"You dear kind Papa!" says little Rosey, with unfeigned admiration; and she puts out one of the plump white little jewelled hands, and pats the lean brown paw of the Colonel which is nearest to her.

"Is Ridley's picture getting on well, Clive?" asks the Colonel, trying to interest himself about Ridley and his picture.

"Very well; it is beautiful; he has sold it for a great price; they must make him an academician next year," replies Clive.

"A most industrious and meritorious young man; he deserves every honour that may happen to him," says the old soldier. "Rosa, my dear, it is time that you should ask Mr. Ridley to dinner, and Mr. Smee, and some of those gentlemen. We will drive this afternoon and see your portrait."

---

[1] them." *HM NY*] them?" *E1*] them!" *R*

"Clive does not go to sleep after dinner when Mr. Ridley comes here," cries Rosa.

"No; I think it is my turn then," says the Colonel, with a glance of kindness. The anger has disappeared from under his brows; at that moment the menaced battle is postponed.

"And yet I know that it must come," says poor Clive, telling me the story as he hangs on my arm, and we pace through the Park. "The Colonel and I are walking on a mine, and that poor little wife of mine is perpetually flinging little shells to fire it. I sometimes wish it were blown up, and I were done for, Pen. I don't think my widow would break her heart about me. No; I have no right to say that; it's a shame to say that; she tries her very best to please me, poor little dear. It's the fault of my temper, perhaps, that she can't. But they neither understand me, don't you see; the Colonel can't help thinking I am a degraded being, because I am fond of painting. Still, dear old boy, he patronises Ridley; a man of genius, whom those sentries ought to salute by Jove, Sir, when he passes. Ridley patronised by an old officer of Indian dragoons, a little bit of a Rosey, and a fellow who is not fit to lay his palette for him! I want sometimes to ask J.J.'s pardon, after the Colonel has been talking to him in his confounded condescending way, uttering some awful bosh about the fine arts. Rosey follows him, and trips round J.J.'s studio, and pretends to admire, and says, 'how soft; how sweet;' recalling some of Mamma-in-law's dreadful expressions, which make me shudder when I hear them. If my poor old father had a confidant into whose arm he could hook his own, and whom he could pester with his family griefs as I do you, the dear old boy would have his dreary story to tell too. I hate banks, bankers, Bundelcund, indigo, cotton, and the whole business. I go to that confounded board, and never hear one syllable that the fellows are talking about. I sit there because he wishes me to sit there; don't you think he sees that my heart is out of the business; that I would rather be at home in my painting-room? We don't understand each other, but we feel each other as it were by instinct. Each thinks in his own way, but knows what the other is thinking. We fight mute battles, don't you see, and our thoughts, though we don't express them, are perceptible to one another, and come out from our eyes, or pass out from us somehow, and meet, and fight, and strike, and wound."

Of course Clive's confidant saw how sore and unhappy the poor fellow was, and commiserated his fatal but natural condition. The little ills of life are the hardest to bear, as we all very well know. What would the possession of a hundred thousand a-year, or fame, and the applause of one's countrymen, or the loveliest and best-beloved woman,—of any glory, and happiness, or good-fortune, avail to a gentleman, for instance, who was allowed to enjoy them only with the condition of wearing a shoe with a couple of nails or sharp pebbles inside it? All fame and happiness would disappear, and plunge down that shoe. All life would rankle round those little nails. I strove, by such philosophic sedatives as confidants are wont to apply on these occasions, to soothe my poor friend's anger and pain; and I daresay the little nails hurt the patient just as much as before.

Clive pursued his lugubrious talk through the Park, and continued it as far as the modest-furnished house which we then occupied in the Pimlico region. It so happened that the Colonel and Mrs. Clive also called upon us that day, and found this culprit in Laura's drawing-room, when they entered it, descending out of that splendid barouche in which we have already shown Mrs. Clive to the public.

"He has not been here for months before; nor have you Rosa; nor have you, Colonel; though we have smothered our indignation, and been to dine with you, and to call, *ever* so many times!" cries Laura.

The Colonel pleaded his business engagements; Rosa, that little woman of the world, had a thousand calls to make, and who knows how much to do? since she came out. She had been to fetch Papa at Bays's, and the porter had told the Colonel that Mr. Clive and Mr. Pendennis had just left the club together.

"Clive scarcely ever drives with me," says Rosa; "Papa almost always does."

"Rosey's is such a swell carriage, that I feel ashamed," says Clive.

"I don't understand you young men. I don't see why you need be ashamed to go on the course with your wife in her carriage, Clive," remarks the Colonel.

"The Course! the Course is at Calcutta, Papa!" cries Rosey. "*We* drive in the Park."

"We have a park at Barrackpore too, my dear," says Papa.

"And he calls his grooms *saices!* He said he was going to send away a *saice* for being tipsy, and I did not know in the least what he could mean, Laura!"

"Mr. Newcome! you must go and drive on the course with Rosa, now; and the Colonel must sit and talk with me, whom he has not been to see for such a long time." Clive presently went off in state by Rosey's side, and then Laura showed Colonel Newcome his beautiful white Cashmere shawl round a successor of that little person who had first been wrapped in that web, now a stout young gentleman whose noise could be clearly heard in the upper regions.

"I wish you could come down with us, Arthur, upon our electioneering visit."

"That of which you were talking last night? Are you bent upon it?"

"Yes, I am determined on it."

Laura heard a child's cry at this moment, and left the room with a parting glance at her husband, who in fact had talked over the matter with Mrs. Pendennis, and agreed with her in opinion.

As the Colonel had opened the question, I ventured to make a respectful remonstrance against the scheme. Vindictiveness on the part of a man so simple and generous, so fair and noble in all his dealings as Thomas Newcome, appeared in my mind unworthy of him. Surely his kinsman had sorrow and humiliation enough already at home. Barnes's further punishment we thought, might be left to time, to remorse, to the Judge of right and wrong; Who better understands than we can do, our causes and temptations towards evil actions, Who reserves the sentence for His own tribunal. But when angered, the best of us mistake our own motives, as we do those of the enemy who inflames us. What may be private revenge, we take to be indignant virtue, and just revolt against wrong. The Colonel would not hear of counsels of moderation, such as I bore him from a sweet Christian pleader. "Remorse!" he cried out with a laugh, "that villain will never feel it until he is tied up and whipped at the cart's tail! Time change that rogue! Unless he is wholesomely punished, he will grow a greater scoundrel every year. I am inclined to think, Sir," says he, his honest brows darkling as he looked towards me, "that you too are spoiled by this wicked world, and these heartless, fashionable, fine people. You wish to live well with the enemy, and with us too, Pendennis. It can't be. He who is not with us is against us. I very much fear, Sir, that the women, the women, you understand, have been talking you over. Do not let us speak any more about this subject, for I don't wish that my son, and my son's old friend, should have a quarrel." His face became red, his voice quivered with agitation, and he looked with glances which I was pained to behold in those kind old eyes: not because his wrath and suspicion visited myself, but because an impartial witness, nay, a friend to Thomas Newcome in that family quarrel, I grieved to think that a generous heart was led astray, and to see a good man do wrong. So with no more thanks for his interference than a man usually gets who meddles in domestic strifes, the present luckless advocate ceased pleading.

To be sure, the Colonel and Clive had other advisers, who did not take the peaceful side. George Warrington was one of these; he was for war *à l'outrance* with Barnes Newcome; for keeping no terms with such a villain. He found a pleasure in hunting him and whipping him. "Barnes ought to be punished," George said, "for his poor wife's misfortune; it was Barnes's infernal cruelty, wickedness, selfishness, which had driven her into misery and wrong." Mr. Warrington went down to Newcome, and was present at that lecture whereof mention has been made in a preceding chapter. I am afraid his behavior was very indecorous; he laughed at the pathetic allusions of the respected member for Newcome; he sneered at the sublime passages; he wrote an awful critique in the *Newcome Independent* two days after, whereof the irony was so subtle, that half the readers of the paper mistook his grave scorn for respect, and his gibes for praise.

Clive, his father, and Frederick Bayham, their faithful aide-de-camp, were at Newcome likewise when Sir Barnes's oration was delivered. At first it was given out at Newcome that the Colonel visited the place for the purpose of seeing his dear old friend and pensioner, Mrs. Mason, who was now not long to enjoy his bounty, and so old, as scarcely to know her benefactor. Only after her sleep, or when the sun warmed her and the old wine with which he supplied her, was the good old woman able to recognise her Colonel. She mingled father and son together in her mind. A lady who now often came in to her, thought she was wandering in her talk, when the poor old woman spoke of a visit she had had from her boy; and then the attendant told Miss Newcome that such a visit had actually taken place, and that but yesterday Clive and his father had been in that room, and occupied the chair where she sat,—"The young lady was taken quite ill, and seemed ready to faint almost," Mrs. Mason's servant and spokeswoman told Colonel Newcome when that gentleman arrived shortly after Ethel's departure, to see his old nurse. "Indeed! he was very sorry." The maid told many stories about Miss Newcome's goodness and charity; how she

"Sir Barnes Newcome on the Affections"

was constantly visiting the poor now; how she was for ever engaged in good works for the young, the sick, and the aged. She had had a dreadful misfortune in love; she was going to be married to a young marquis; richer even than Prince de Montcontour down at Rosebury; but it was all broke off on account of that dreadful affair at the Hall.

"Was she very good to the poor? did she come often to see her grandfather's old friend? it was no more than she ought to do," Colonel Newcome said; without, however, thinking fit to tell his informant that he had himself met his niece Ethel, five minutes before he had entered Mrs. Mason's door.

The poor thing was in discourse with Mr. Harris, the surgeon, and talking (as best she might, for no doubt the news which she had just heard, had agitated her), talking about blankets, and arrowroot, wine, and medicaments for her poor, when she saw her uncle coming towards her. She tottered a step or two forwards to meet him; held both her hands out, and called his name; but he looked her sternly in the face, took off his hat and bowed, and passed on. He did not think fit to mention the meeting even to his son, Clive; but we may be sure Mr. Harris, the surgeon, spoke of the circumstance that night after the lecture, at the club, where a crowd of gentlemen were gathered together, smoking their cigars, and enjoying themselves according to their custom, and discussing Sir Barnes Newcome's performance.

According to established usage in such cases, our esteemed representative was received by the committee of the Newcome Athenæum, assembled in their committee-room, and thence marshalled by the chairman and vice-chairman, to his rostrum in the lecture hall, round about which the magnates of the institution, and the notabilities of the town were rallied on this public occasion. The Baronet came in some state from his own house, arriving at Newcome in his carriage with four horses, accompanied by my lady, his mother, and Miss Ethel, his beautiful sister, who now was mistress at the Hall. His little girl was brought—five years old now; she sate on her aunt's knee, and slept during a greater part of the performance. A fine bustle, we may be sure, was made on the introduction of these personages to their reserved seats on the platform, where they sate encompassed by others of the great ladies of Newcome, to whom they and the lecturer were especially gracious at this season. Was not Parliament about to be dissolved, and were not the folks at Newcome Park particularly civil at that interesting period? So Barnes Newcome mounts his pulpit, bows round to the crowded assembly in acknowledgment of their buzz of applause or recognition, passes his lily-white pocket handkerchief across his thin lips, and dashes off into his lecture about Mrs. Hemans, and the poetry of the affections. A public man, a commercial man as we well know, yet his heart is in his home, and his joy in his affections; the presence of this immense assembly here this evening; of the industrious capitalists; of the intelligent middle class; of the pride and mainstay of England, the operatives of Newcome; these surrounded by their wives and their children (a graceful bow to the bonnets to the right of the platform), show that they too have hearts to feel, and homes to cherish; that they too, feel the love of women, the innocence of children, the love of song! Our lecturer then makes a distinction between man's poetry, and woman's poetry, charging considerably in favour of the latter. We show that to appeal to the affections is after all the true office of the bard; to decorate the homely threshold, to wreathe flowers round the domestic hearth, the delightful duty of the Christian singer. We glance at Mrs. Hemans's biography, and state where she was born, and under what circumstances she must have at first, &c., &c. Is this a correct account of Sir Barnes Newcome's lecture? I was not present, and did not read the report. Very likely the above may be a reminiscence of that mock lecture which Warrington delivered in anticipation of the Baronet's oration.

After he had read for about five minutes, it was remarked the Baronet suddenly stopped and became exceedingly confused over his manuscript; betaking himself to his auxiliary glass of water before he resumed his discourse, which for a long time was languid, low, and disturbed in tone. This period of disturbance, no doubt, must have occurred when Sir Barnes saw before him F. Bayham and Warrington seated in the amphitheatre; and, by the side of those fierce scornful countenances, Clive Newcome's pale face.

Clive Newcome was not looking at Barnes. His eyes were fixed upon the lady seated not far from the lecturer—upon Ethel, with her arm round her little niece's shoulder, and her thick black ringlets drooping down over a face paler than Clive's own.

Of course she knew that Clive was present. She was aware of him as she entered the Hall; saw him at the very first moment; saw nothing but him I daresay, though her eyes were shut and her head was turned now towards her mother, and now bent down on the little niece's golden curls. And the past and its dear histories, and youth and its hopes and passions, and tones and looks for ever echoing in the heart, and present in the memory— these, no doubt, poor Clive saw and heard as he looked across the great gulf of time, and parting, and grief, and beheld the woman he had loved for many years. There she sits; the same, but changed: as gone from him as if she were dead; departed indeed into another sphere, and entered into a kind of death. If there is no love more in yonder heart, it is but a corpse unburied. Strew round it the flowers of youth. Wash it with tears of passion. Wrap it and envelop it with fond devotion. Break heart, and fling yourself on the bier, and kiss her cold lips and press her hand! It falls back dead on the cold breast again. The beautiful lips have never a blush or a smile. Cover them and lay them in the ground, and so take thy hat-band off, good friend, and go to thy business. Do you suppose you are the only man who has had to attend such a funeral? You will find some men smiling and at work the day after. Some come to the grave now and again out of the world, and say a brief prayer, and a "God bless her!" With some men, she gone, and her viduous mansion your heart to let, her successor, the new occupant, poking in all the drawers, and corners, and cupboards of the tenement, finds her miniature and some of her dusty old letters hidden away somewhere, and says—Was this the face he admired so? Why, allowing even for the painter's flattery, it is quite ordinary, and the eyes certainly do not look straight. Are these the letters you thought so charming? Well, upon my word, I never read anything more common-place in my life. See, here's a line half blotted out. O, I suppose she was crying then—some of her tears, idle tears. . . Hark, there is Barnes Newcome's eloquence still plapping on like water from a cistern—and our thoughts, where have they wandered? far away from the lecture—as far away as Clive's almost. And now the fountain ceases to trickle; the mouth from which issued that cool and limpid flux ceases to smile; the figure is seen to bow and retire; a buzz, a hum, a whisper, a scuffle, a meeting of bonnets and wagging of feathers and rustling of silks ensues. Thank you! delightful I am sure! I really was quite overcome; Excellent; *So* much obliged, are rapid phrases heard amongst the polite on the platform. While down below, yaw! quite enough of *that*. Mary Jane cover your throat up, and don't kitch cold, and don't push *me*, please Sir. Arry! Coom along and av a pint a ale, &c., are the remarks heard, or perhaps not heard, by Clive Newcome, as he watches at the private entrance of the Athenæum, where Sir Barnes's carriage is waiting with its flaming lamps, and domestics in state liveries. One of them comes out of the building bearing the little girl in his arms, and lays her in the carriage. Then Sir Barnes, and Lady Ann, and the Mayor; then Ethel issues forth, and as she passes under the lamps, beholds Clive's face as pale and sad as her own.

Shall we go visit the lodge-gates of Newcome Park with the moon shining on their carving? Is there any pleasure in walking by miles of grey paling, and endless palisades of firs? O you fool, what do you hope to see behind that curtain? Absurd fugitive, whither would you run? Can you burst the tether of fate: and is not poor dear little Rosey Mackenzie sitting yonder waiting for you by the stake? Go home, Sir; and don't catch cold. So Mr. Clive returns to the King's Arms, and up to his bed-room, and he hears Mr. F. Bayham's deep voice as he passes by the Boscawen Room, where the jolly Britons are as usual assembled.

Chapter XXIX.

NEWCOME AND LIBERTY.

E have said that the Baronet's lecture was discussed in the midnight senate assembled at the King's Arms: where Mr. Tom Potts showed the orator no mercy. The senate of the King's Arms was hostile to Sir Barnes Newcome. Many other Newcomites besides were savage and inclined to revolt against the representative of their borough. As these patriots met over their cups, and over the bumper of friendship uttered the sentiments of freedom, they had often asked of one another, where should a man be found to rid Newcome of its dictator. Generous hearts writhed under the oppression; patriotic eyes scowled when Barnes Newcome went by: with fine satire Tom Potts—at Brown the hatter's shop who made the hats for Sir Barnes Newcome's domestics—proposed to take one of the beavers—a gold-laced one with a cockade and a cord—and set it up in the market-place and bid all Newcome come bow to it, as to the hat of Gessler. "Don't you think, Potts," says F. Bayham who of course was admitted into the King's Arms Club and ornamented that assembly by his presence and discourse—"Don't you think the Colonel would make a good William Tell to combat against that Gessler?" Ha! Proposal received with acclamation—eagerly adopted by Charles Tucker, Esq., Attorney-at-Law, who would not have the slightest objection to conduct Colonel Newcome's, or any other gentleman's electioneering business in Newcome or elsewhere.

Like those three gentlemen in the plays and pictures of William Tell who conspire under the moon, calling upon liberty and resolving to elect Tell as their especial champion—like Arnold, Melchthal and Werner—Tom

A Deputation

Potts, F. Bayham, and Charles Tucker, Esquires, conspired round a punch bowl and determined that Thomas Newcome should be requested to free his country. A deputation from the electors of Newcome—that is to say— these very gentlemen, waited on the Colonel in his apartment the very next morning; and set before him the state of the borough; Barnes Newcome's tyranny under which it groaned; and the yearning of all honest men to be free from that usurpation. Thomas Newcome received the Deputation with great solemnity and politeness—crossed his legs, folded his arms, smoked his cheroot, and listened most decorously, as now Potts, now Tucker, expounded to him—Bayham giving the benefit of his emphatic "hear hears" to their statements; and explaining dubious phrases to the Colonel in the most affable manner.

Whatever the conspirators had to say against poor Barnes, Colonel Newcome was only too ready to believe. He had made up his mind that that criminal ought to be punished and exposed. The lawyer's covert inuendoes who was ready to insinuate any amount of evil against Barnes which could safely be uttered, were by no means strong enough for Thomas Newcome. " 'Sharp practice! exceedingly alive to his own interests—reported violence of temper and tenacity of money'—say swindling at once, Sir—say falsehood and rapacity; say cruelty and avarice," cries the Colonel, "I believe upon my honour and conscience, that unfortunate young man to be guilty of every one of those crimes."

Mr. Bayham remarks to Mr. Potts that our friend the Colonel when he does utter an opinion takes care that there shall be no mistake about it.

"And I took care there should be no mistake before I uttered it at all, Bayham!" cries F.B.'s patron. "As long as I was in any doubt about this young man, I gave the criminal the benefit of it, as a man who admires 'our glorious constitution' should do, and kept my own counsel, Sir."

"At least," remarks[1] Mr. Tucker, "enough is proven to show that Sir Barnes Newcome Newcome Baronet is scarce a fit person to represent this great borough in parliament!"

"Represent Newcome in parliament! It is a disgrace to that noble Institution the English House of Commons that Barnes Newcome should sit in it! A man whose word you cannot trust—a man stained with every private crime, what right has he to sit in the assembly of the legislators of the land, Sir?" cries the Colonel waving his hand as if addressing a Chamber of Deputies.

"You are for upholding the House of Commons?" inquires the lawyer.

"Of course, Sir, of course."

"And for increasing the franchise, Colonel Newcome, I should hope?" continues Mr. Tucker.

"Every man who can read and write ought to have a vote, Sir, that is my opinion!" cries the Colonel.

"He's a liberal to the back bone," says Potts to Tucker.

"To the back bone!" responds Tucker to Potts—"The Colonel will do for us, Potts."

"We want such a man, Tucker—the *Independent* has been crying out for such a man for years past. We ought to have a liberal as second representa-

---

[1] remarks *E1*] insinuates *Ms*

tive of this great town—not a sneaking half-and-half ministerialist like Sir Barnes—a fellow with one leg in the Carlton and the other in Brookes's. Old Mr. Bunce we can't touch. His place is safe—he is a good man of business—we can't meddle with Mr. Bunce—I know that, who know the feeling of the country pretty well."

"Pretty well!—better than any man in Newcome, Potts!" cries Mr. Tucker.

"But a good man like the Colonel—a good liberal like the Colonel—a man who goes in for household suffrage."

"Certainly, gentlemen."

"And the general great liberal principles—*we* know, of course—such a man would assuredly have a chance against Sir Barnes Newcome at the coming election! could we find such a man! a real friend of the people!"

"I[2] know a friend of the people if ever there was one," F. Bayham interposes.

"A man of wealth, station, experience; a man who has fought for his country; a man who is beloved in this place as *you* are, Colonel Newcome; for your goodness is known, Sir—*You* are not ashamed of your origin, and there is not a Newcomite old or young but knows how admirably good you have been to your old friend, Mrs.—Mrs. Whatdyoucallem."

"Mrs. Mason," from F.B.

"Mrs. Mason. If such a man as you, Sir, would consent to put himself in nomination at the next election; every true liberal in this place would rush to support you; and crush the oligarch who rides over the liberties of this borough!"

"Something of this sort, gentlemen, I own to you had crossed my mind," Thomas Newcome remarked. "When I saw that disgrace to my name, and the name of my father's birth-place, representing the borough in parliament, I thought for the credit of the town and the family, the member for Newcome at least might be an honest man. I am an old soldier; have passed all my life in India; and am little conversant with affairs at home (cries of You are, you are). I hoped that my son, Mr. Clive Newcome, might have been found qualified to contest this borough against his unworthy cousin, and possibly to sit as your representative in Parliament. The wealth I have had the good fortune to amass will descend to him naturally, and at no very distant period of time, for I am nearly seventy years of age, gentlemen."

The gentlemen are astonished at this statement.

"But," resumed the Colonel; "my son Clive, as friend Bayham knows, and to my own regret and mortification, as I don't care to confess to you, declares he has no interest in politics, or desire for public distinction— prefers his own pursuits—and even these I fear do not absorb him— declines the offer which I made him, to present himself in opposition to Sir Barnes Newcome. It becomes men in a certain station, as I think, to assert that station; and though a few years back I never should have thought of public life at all, and proposed to end my days in quiet as a retired dragoon officer, since—since it has pleased Heaven to increase very greatly my pecuniary means, to place me as a director and manager of an important banking-company, in a station of great public responsibility, I and my brother directors have thought it but right that one of us should sit in par-

2 people!" ¶"I *R*] people! I *E l*

liament, if possible, and I am not a man to shirk from that or from any other duty."

"Colonel, will you attend a meeting of electors which we will call, and say as much to them and as well?" cries Mr. Potts. "Shall I put an announcement in my paper to the effect that you are ready to come forward?"

"I am prepared to do so, my good Sir."

And presently this solemn palaver ended.

Besides the critical article upon the Baronet's lecture, of which Mr. Warrington was the author, there appeared in the leading columns of the ensuing number of Mr. Potts's *Independent,* some remarks of a very smashing or hostile nature, against the member for Newcome. "This gentleman has shown such talent in the lecturing business," the *Independent* said, "that it is a great pity he should not withdraw himself from politics, and cultivate what all Newcome knows are the arts which he understands best; namely, poetry and the domestic affections. The performance of our talented representative last night was so pathetic as to bring tears into the eyes of several of our fair friends. We have heard but never believed until now that Sir Barnes Newcome possessed such a genius *for making women cry.* Last week we had the talented Miss Noakes from Slowcome, reading Milton to us; how far superior was the eloquence of Sir Barnes Newcome Newcome, Bart., even to that of the celebrated actress! Bets were freely offered in the room last night that Sir Barnes would *beat any woman.* Bets, which were not taken as we scarcely need say, so well do our citizens appreciate the character of our excellent, our admirable representative. Let the Baronet stick to his lectures, and let Newcome relieve him of his political occupations. He is not fit for them, he is too sentimental a man for us; the men of Newcome want a sound practical person; the liberals of Newcome have a desire to be represented. When we elected Sir Barnes, he talked liberally enough, and we thought he would do, but you see the honourable Baronet is so poetical! we ought to have known that and not to have believed him. Let us have a straight forward gentleman. If not a man of words, at least let us have a practical man. If not a man of eloquence, one at any rate whose word we can trust, and we can't trust Sir Barnes Newcome's; we have tried him and we can't really. Last night when the ladies were crying, we could not for the souls of us help laughing. We hope we know how to conduct ourselves as gentlemen. We trust we did not interrupt the harmony of the evening, but Sir Barnes Newcome, prating about children and virtue, and affection and poetry, this is really too strong.

"The *Independent,* faithful to its name, and ever actuated by principles of honour, has been, as our thousands of readers know, disposed to give Sir Barnes Newcome Newcome, Bart., a fair trial. When he came forward after his father's death, we believed in his pledges and promises, as a retrencher and reformer, and we stuck by him. Is there any man in Newcome, except, perhaps, our twaddling old cotemporary the *Sentinel,* who believes in Sir B. N. any more? We say no, and we now give the readers of the *Independent,* and the electors of this borough fair notice, that when the dissolution of Parliament takes place, a good man, a true man, a man of experience, no dangerous radical, or brawling tap orator—Mr. Hicks' friends well understand whom we mean—but a gentleman of liberal principles, well-won wealth, and deserved station and honour, will ask the electors of Newcome whether they are or are not discontented with their present unworthy member. The *Independent,* for one, says we know good men of your family, we know in it men who would do honour to any name; but you, Sir Barnes Newcome Newcome, Bart., we trust no more."

In[3] the electioneering matter which had occasioned my unlucky interference and that subsequent little coolness upon the good Colonel's part, Clive Newcome had himself shown that the scheme was not to his liking; had then submitted as his custom was: and doing so with a bad grace, as also was to be expected, had got little thanks for his obedience. Thomas Newcome was hurt at his son's faint-heartedness, and of course little Rosey was displeased at his hanging back. He set off in his father's train a silent unwilling partisan. Thomas Newcome had the leisure to survey Clive's glum face opposite to him during the whole of their journey, and to chew his mustachios, and brood upon his wrath and wrongs. His life had been a sacrifice for that boy?[4] What darling schemes had he not formed in his behalf, and how superciliously did Clive meet his projects! The Colonel could not see the harm of which he had himself been[5] the author. Had he not done everything in mortal's power for his son's happiness and how many young men in England were there with such advantages as this moody discontented spoiled boy? As Clive backed out of the contest of course his father urged it only the more vehemently. Clive slunk away from committees and canvassing and lounged about the Newcome manufactories, whilst his father with anger and bitterness in his heart, remained at the post of honour as he called it, bent upon overcoming his enemy and carrying his point against Barnes Newcome. "If Paris will not fight, Sir," the Colonel said with a sad look[6] following his son, "Priam must." Good old Priam believed his cause to be a perfectly just one and that duty and his honour called upon him to draw the sword. So there was difference between Thomas Newcome and Clive his son. I protest it is with pain and reluctance I have to write that the good old man was in error:—that there was a wrong-doer, and that Atticus was he.

Atticus be it remembered, thought himself compelled by the very best motives. Thomas Newcome, the Indian banker, was at war with Barnes, the English banker. The latter had commenced the hostilities, by a sudden and cowardly act of treason. There were private wrongs, to envenom the contest, but it was the mercantile quarrel, on which the Colonel chose to set his declaration of war. Barnes' first dastardly blow had occasioned it, and his uncle was determined to carry it through. This I have said was also George Warrington's judgment, who in the ensuing struggle between Sir Barnes and his uncle, acted as a very warm and efficient partisan of the latter. "Kinsmanship!" says George, "what has old Tom Newcome ever had from his kinsman but cowardice and treachery? If Barnes had held up his finger the young one might have been happy; if he could have effected it, the Colonel and his bank would have been ruined. I am for war, and for

3 [In the manuscript this passage began a new unnumbered chapter.]
4 boy? *Ms*] boy! *E1*
5 himself been *E1*] been *Ms*
6 a sad look *E1*] sad looks *Ms*

seeing the old boy in parliament. He knows no more about politics than I do about dancing the polka; but there are five hundred wiseacres in that assembly who know no more than he does, and an honest man taking his seat there, in place of a confounded little rogue, at least makes a change for the better."

I daresay, Thomas Newcome, Esq., would by no means have concurred, in the above estimate of his political knowledge, and thought himself as well informed as another. He used to speak with the greatest gravity about our constitution as the pride and envy of the world, though he surprised you as much by the latitudinarian reforms, which he was eager to press forward, as by the most singular old Tory opinions which he advocated on other occasions. He was for having every man to vote; every poor man to labour short time and get high wages; every poor curate to be paid double or treble; every bishop to be docked of his salary, and dismissed from the House of Lords. But he was a staunch admirer of that assembly, and a supporter of the rights of the crown. He was for sweeping off taxes from the poor, and as money must be raised to carry on government, he opined that the rich should pay. He uttered all these opinions with the greatest gravity and emphasis, before a large assembly of electors and others convened in the Newcome Town Hall, amid the roars of applause of the non-electors, and the bewilderment and consternation of Mr. Potts, of the *Independent*, who had represented the Colonel in his paper, as a safe and steady reformer. Of course the *Sentinel* showed him up as a most dangerous radical, a sepoy republican, and so forth, to the wrath and indignation of Colonel Newcome. He a republican, he scorned the name! He would die as he had bled many a time for his sovereign. He an enemy of our beloved church! He esteemed and honoured it, as he hated and abhorred the superstitions of Rome. (Yells, from the Irish in the crowd.) He an enemy of the House of Lords! He held it to be the safeguard of the constitution and the legitimate prize of our most illustrious naval, military, and—and—legal heroes (ironical cheers). He repelled with scorn the dastard attacks of the Journal which had assailed him; he asked, laying his hands on his heart, if as a gentleman, an officer bearing her Majesty's commission, he could be guilty of a desire to subvert her empire and to insult the dignity of her crown?

After this second speech at the Town Hall, it was asserted by a considerable party in Newcome, that Old Tom (as the mob familiarly called him) was a Tory, while an equal number averred that he was a Radical. Mr. Potts tried to reconcile his statements, a work in which I should think the talented editor of the *Independent* had no little difficulty. "He knows nothing about it," poor Clive said with a sigh; "his politics are all sentiment and kindness, he will have the poor man paid double wages, and does not remember that the employer would be ruined: you have heard him, Pen, talking in this way at his own table, but when he comes out armed *cap-à-pied*, and careers against windmills in public, don't you see that as Don Quixote's son I had rather the dear brave old gentleman was at home?"

So this *fainéant* took but little part in the electioneering doings, holding moodily aloof from the meetings, and councils, and public-houses, where his father's partisans were assembled.

Chapter XXX.

Miss Ethel Newcome to Mrs. Pendennis.

ᴅEAREST LAURA. I have not written to you for many weeks past. There have been some things too trivial and some too sad to write about—some things I know I shall write of if I begin, and yet that I know I had best leave—for of what good is looking to the past now? why vex you or myself by reverting to it? Does not every day bring its own duty and task and are these not enough to occupy one? What a fright you must have had with my little god-daughter! Thank Heaven she is well now and restored to you. You and your husband I know do not think it essential, but I do, *most essential* and am very[1] grateful that she was taken to church before her illness.

"Is Mr. Pendennis proceeding with[2] his canvass? I try and avoid a certain subject, but it *will* come. You know who is canvassing against us here. My poor uncle has met with very considerable success amongst the lower classes. He makes them rambling speeches, at which my brother and his friends laugh, but which the people applaud. I saw him only yesterday, on the balcony of the King's Arms, speaking to a great mob, who were cheering vociferously below. I had met him before. He would not even stop and give his Ethel of old days his hand. I would have given him[3] I don't know what, for one kiss, for one kind word; but he passed on and would not answer me. He thinks me—what the world thinks me, worldly and heartless—what I *was*. But at least, dear Laura, you know that I always truly loved *him* and do now although[4] he is our enemy, though he believes and utters the most cruel things against Barnes, though he says that Barnes Newcome, my father's son, my brother, Laura! is not an honest man. Hard,

[1] very *E1*] very very *Ms*
[2] with *E1*] well with *Ms*
[3] given him *E1*] given *Ms*
[4] although *E1*] though *Ms*

selfish, worldly, I own my poor brother to be and pray Heaven to amend him; but[5] dishonest! and to be so maligned by the person one loves best in the world! This is a hard trial. I pray a proud heart may be bettered by it.

"And I have seen my cousin: once at a lecture which poor Barnes gave and who seemed very much disturbed on perceiving Clive: once afterwards at good old Mrs. Mason's whom I have always continued to visit for Uncle's sake. The poor old woman whose wits are very nearly gone held both our hands and asked when we were going to be married?—and laughed, poor old thing! I cried out to her that Mr. Clive had a wife at .home—'a dear young wife,' I said. He gave a dreadful sort of laugh and turned away into the window.—He looks terribly ill, pale, and oldened.

"I asked him a great deal about his wife—whom I remember a very pretty sweet-looking girl indeed at my Aunt Hobson's, but with a not agreeable mother as I thought then. He answered me by monosyllables, appeared as though he would speak, and then became silent. I am pained and yet glad that I saw him. I said not very distinctly I daresay, that I hoped the difference between Barnes and Uncle would not extinguish his regard for Mamma and me, who have always loved him—when I said loved him, he gave one of his bitter laughs again: and so he did when I said I hoped his wife was well. You never would tell me much about Mrs. Newcome, and I fear she does not make my cousin happy. And yet this marriage was of my uncle's making—another of the unfortunate marriages in our family! I am glad that I paused in time before the commission of that sin: I strive my best, and to amend my temper, my inexperience, my short-comings, and try to be the mother of my poor brother's children. But Barnes has never forgiven me my refusal of Lord Farintosh. He is of the world still, Laura—nor must we deal too hardly[6] with people of his nature, who cannot perhaps comprehend a world beyond. I remember in old days when we were travelling on the Rhine—in the happiest days of my whole life—I used to hear Clive and his friend Mr. Ridley talk of Art and of Nature in a way that I could not understand at first but came to comprehend better as my cousin taught me; and since then I see pictures and landscapes and flowers with quite different eyes—and beautiful secrets as it were, of which I had no idea before. The secret of all Secrets, the Secret of the Other Life and the Better World beyond ours—may not this be unrevealed to some? I pray for them all, dearest Laura—for those nearest and dearest to me, that the truth may lighten their darkness; and Heaven's great Mercy defend them in the perils and dangers of their night.

"My boy at Sandhurst has done very well indeed: and Egbert, I am happy to say, thinks of taking orders; he has been *very* moderate at College—not so Alfred, but the Guards are a sadly dangerous school for a young man—I have promised to pay his debts and he is to exchange into the line. Mamma is coming to us at Christmas with Alice;[7] my sister is very pretty indeed, I think, and I *am* rejoiced she is to marry young Mr. Mum-

---

[5] amend him; but *E1*] amend—but *Ms*
[6] hardly *Ms*] harshly *E1*
[7] Alice; *E1*] [blank]; *Ms*

ford,[8] who has a tolerable living: and who has been attached to her ever since he was a boy at Rugby School.[9]

"Little[1] Barnes comes on bravely with his Latin; and Mr. Whitestock, *a most excellent and valuable* person in this place, where there is so much Romanism and Dissent, speaks highly of him. Little Clara is so like her unhappy mother in a thousand ways and actions, that I am shocked often; and see my brother starting back and turning his head away, as if suddenly wounded. I have heard the most deplorable accounts of Lord and Lady Highgate. O, dearest friend and sister!—save you, I think I scarce know any one that is happy in the world: I trust you may continue so—you who impart your goodness and kindness to all who come near you—you in whose sweet serene happiness, I am thankful to be allowed to repose sometimes. You are the island in the desert, Laura! and the birds sing there, and the fountain flows; and we[2] come and repose by you for a little while, and to-morrow the march begins again and the toil and the struggle and the desert. Good bye Fountain! Whisper kisses to my dearest little ones for their affectionate

"AUNT ETHEL.

"A friend of his, a Mr. Warrington, has spoken against us several times with extraordinary ability as Barnes owns. Do you know Mr. W.? He wrote a dreadful article in the *Independent* about the last poor lecture which was indeed sad, sentimental, commonplace: and the critique is terribly comical. I could not help laughing remembering some passages in it, when Barnes mentioned it: and my brother became so angry! They have put up a dreadful caricature of B. in Newcome: and my brother says he did it, but I hope not. It is very droll though: he used to make them very funnily. I am glad he has spirits for it. Good bye again.—E.N."

"He says he did it!" cries Mr. Pendennis laying the letter down. "Barnes Newcome would scarcely caricature himself, my dear!"

" 'He' often means—means Clive—I think," says Mrs. Pendennis in an off-hand manner.

"O! he means Clive, does He? Laura!"

"Yes—and You mean Goose, Mr. Pendennis," that saucy lady replies.

It must have been about the very time when this letter was written that a critical conversation occurred between Clive and his father, of which the lad did not inform me until much later days, as was the case—the reader has been more than once begged to believe—with many other portions of this biography.

One night the Colonel having come home from a round of electioneering visits, not half-satisfied with himself, exceedingly annoyed (much more than he cared to own) with the impudence of some rude fellows at the public-houses, who had interrupted his fine speeches with odious hiccups and familiar jeers, was seated brooding over his cheroot by his

---

[8] Mumford, *E1*] [blank], *Ms*
[9] *Ms* page ends with uncancelled but unfinished start: Mr [blank] Curate
[1] [This paragraph through "flows; and we" is taken from *E1* because the manuscript appears to have been torn away.]
[2] [The paragraph to this point is not in the manuscript.]

chimney-fire, friend F.B. (of whose companionship his patron was occasionally tired) finding much better amusement with the Jolly Britons in the Boscawen Room below. The Colonel, as an electioneering business, had made his appearance in the Club. But that ancient Roman Warrior had frightened those simple Britons. His manners were too awful for them: so were Clive's who visited them also under Mr. Potts's introduction; but the two gentlemen—each being full of care and personal annoyance at the time, acted like wet-blankets upon the Britons—whereas F.B. warmed them and cheered them, affably partook of their meals with them, and graciously shared their cups.—So the Colonel was alone listening to the far-off roar of the Britons' choruses by an expiring fire, as he sate by a glass of cold negus, and the ashes of his cigar.

I daresay he may have been thinking that his fire was well nigh out, his cup at the dregs, his pipe little more now than dust and ashes—when Clive, candle in hand, came into their sitting-room.

As each saw the other's face it was so very sad and worn and pale, that the young man started back, and the elder with quite the tenderness of old days cried, "God bless me, my boy, how ill you look!—Come and warm yourself—look, the fire's out! Have something, Clivy!"

For months past they had not had a really kind word. The tender old voice smote upon Clive and he burst into sudden tears. They rained upon his father's trembling old brown hand as he stooped down and kissed it.

"You look very ill too, Father," says Clive.

"Ill? not I!" cries the father still keeping the boy's hand under both his own on the mantel-piece. "Such a battered old fellow as I am, has a right to look the worse for wear—but you, boy, why do *you* look so pale?"

"I have seen a ghost, Father," Clive answered. Thomas Newcome[3] looked alarmed and inquisitive, as though the boy was wandering in his mind.

"The ghost of my youth, Father—the ghost of my happiness—and the best days of my life," groaned out the young man. "I saw Ethel to-day. I went to see Sarah Mason and she was there."

"I had seen her—but I did not speak of her," said the father. "I thought it was best not to mention her to you, my poor boy. And are—are you fond of her still? Clive!"

"Still!—once means always in those things, Father—doesn't it? Once means to-day and yesterday, and for ever and ever."

"Nay my boy. You mustn't talk to me so—or even[4] to yourself so. You have the dearest little wife at home—a dear little wife and child."

"You had a son and have been kind enough to him, God knows. *You* had a wife: but that doesn't prevent other—other thoughts. Do you know you never spoke twice in your life about my mother? You didn't care for her."

"I—I—did my duty by her: I denied her nothing. I scarcely ever had a word with her and I did my best to make her happy," interposed the Colonel.

"I know: but your heart was with the other. So is mine. It's fatal: it runs in the family, Father."

---

[3] Thomas Newcome *Ms*] Thomas, however, *E1*
[4] even *E1*] think ever *Ms*

The boy looked so ineffably wretched, that the father's heart melted still more. "I did my best, Clive," the Colonel gasped out. "I went to that villain Barnes and offered him to settle every shilling I was worth on you—I did— you didn't know that—I'd kill myself for your sake, Clivy. What's an old fellow worth living for? I can live upon a crust and a cigar—*I* don't care about a carriage and only go in one[5] to please Rosey. I wanted to give up all for you—but he played me false—that scoundrel cheated us both—he did, and[6] so did Ethel."

"No Sir. I may have thought so in my rage once: but I know better now. She was the victim and *not* the agent. Did Madame de Florac play *you* false when she married her husband? It was her Fate, and she underwent it. We all bow to it. We are in the track and the car passes over us. You know it does, Father." The Colonel was a Fatalist: he had often advanced this oriental creed in his simple discourses with his son and Clive's friends.

"Besides," Clive went on, "Ethel does not care for me. She received me to-day quite coldly and held her hand out as if we had only parted last year—I suppose she likes that marquis who jilted her—God bless her! How shall we know what wins the hearts of women? She has mine. There was my Fate. Praise be to Allah. It is over."

"But there's that villain who injured you—His isn't over yet," cried the Colonel clenching his trembling hand.

"Ah, Father! Let us leave him to Allah too! Suppose Madame de Florac had had[7] a brother who insulted you. You know you wouldn't have revenged yourself. You would have[8] wounded her in striking him."

"You called out Barnes yourself, boy," cried the father—

"That was for another cause—and, not for my quarrel. And how do you know I intended to fire? By Jove, I was so miserable then that an ounce of lead would have done me little harm."

The father saw the son's mind more clearly than he had ever done hitherto. They had scarcely ever talked upon that subject which the Colonel found was so deeply fixed in Clive's heart. He thought of his own early days and how he had[9] suffered, and beheld his son before him racked with the same cruel pangs of enduring grief. And he began to own that he had pressed him too hastily in his marriage; and to make an allowance for an unhappiness of which he had in part been the cause.

"Mashallah!—Clive, my boy," said the old man, "what is done is done."

"Let us break up our camp before this place and not go to war with Barnes, Father," said Clive. "Let us have peace—and forgive him if we can."

"And retreat before this scoundrel? Clive."

"What is a victory over such a fellow? One gives a chimney-sweep the wall, Father."

"I say again—What is done is done. I have promised to meet him at the hustings and I will. I think it is best: and you are right: and you act like a

---

[5] <it> ↑tone↓ *Ms*] it *E1*
[6] he did, and *E1*] he and *Ms*
[7] had had *Ms*] had *E1*
[8] would have *E1*] have *Ms*
[9] how he had *E1*] how had *Ms*

high-minded gentleman—and my dear—dear old boy—not to meddle in the quarrel—though I didn't think so—and the difference gave me a great deal of pain—and so did what Pendennis said—and I'm wrong—and thank God I am wrong—and God bless you, my own boy," the Colonel cried out in a burst[1] of emotion—and the two went to their bed-rooms together, and were happier as they shook hands at the doors of their adjoining chambers than they had been for many a long day and year.

[1] burst *E1*] great burst *Ms*

Chapter XXXI.

AVING thus given his challenge, reconnoitered the enemy, and pledged himself to do battle at the ensuing election, our Colonel took leave of the Town of Newcome, and returned to his banking affairs in London. His departure was as that of a great public personage; the gentlemen of the Committee followed him obsequiously down to the train. "Quick," bawls out Mr. Potts to Mr. Brown, the station-master, "Quick, Mr. Brown, a carriage for Colonel Newcome!" Half-a-dozen hats are taken off as he enters into the carriage, F. Bayham and his servant after him, with portfolios, umbrellas, shawls, despatch-boxes. Clive was not there to act as his father's aide-de-camp. After their conversation together, the young man had returned to Mrs. Clive and his other duties in life.

It has been said that Mr. Pendennis was in the country, engaged in a pursuit exactly similar to that which occupied Colonel Newcome. The menaced dissolution of parliament did not take place so soon as we expected. The ministry still hung together, and by consequence, Sir Barnes Newcome kept the[1] seat in the House of Commons, from which his elder kinsman was eager to oust him. Away from London, and having but few correspondents, save on affairs of business, I heard little of Clive and the Colonel, save an occasional puff of one of Colonel Newcome's entertainments in the *Pall Mall Gazette*, to which journal F. Bayham still condescended to contribute; and a satisfactory announcement in a certain part of that paper, that on such a day, in Hyde Park Gardens, Mrs. Clive Newcome had presented her husband with a son. Clive wrote to me presently, to inform me

[1] the *E 1*] his *R*

of the circumstance, stating at the same time, with but moderate gratification on his own part, that the Campaigner, Mrs. Newcome's mamma, had upon this second occasion, made a second lodgment in her daughter's house and bed-chamber, and showed herself affably disposed to forget the little unpleasantries which had clouded over the sunshine of her former visit.

Laura with a smile of some humour, said she thought now would be the time when if Clive could be spared from his bank, he might pay us that visit at Fairoaks which had been due so long, and hinted that change of air and a temporary absence from Mrs. Mackenzie, might be agreeable to my old friend.

It was on the contrary Mr. Pendennis's opinion that his wife artfully chose that period of time when little Rosey was, per force, kept at home and occupied with her delightful maternal duties to invite Clive to see us. Mrs. Laura frankly owned that she liked our Clive better without his wife than with her, and never ceased to regret that pretty Rosey had not bestowed her little hand upon Captain Hoby, as she had been very well disposed at one time to do. Against all marriages of interest this sentimental Laura never failed to utter indignant protests; and Clive's had been a marriage of interest, a marriage made up by the old people, a marriage to which the young man had only yielded out of good-nature and obedience. She would apostrophise her unconscious young ones, and inform those innocent babies that *they* should never be made to marry except for love, never—an announcement which was received with perfect indifference by little Arthur on his rocking-horse, and little Helen smiling and crowing in her mother's lap.

So Clive came down to us careworn in appearance, but very pleased and happy, he said, to stay for a while with the friends of his youth. We showed him our modest rural lions; we got him such sport and company as our quiet neighbourhood afforded, we gave him fishing in the Brawl, and Laura in her pony-chaise drove him to Baymouth, and to Clavering Park, and town, and to visit the famous cathedral at Chatteris, where she was pleased to recount certain incidents of her husband's youth.

Clive laughed at my wife's stories, he pleased himself in our home; he played with our children with whom he became a great favourite; he was happier he told me with a sigh than he had been for many a day. His gentle hostess echoed the sigh of the poor young fellow. She was sure that his pleasure was only transitory, and was convinced that many deep cares weighed upon his mind.

Ere long my old school-fellow made me sundry confessions, which showed that Laura's surmises were correct. About his domestic affairs he did not treat much, the little boy was said to be a very fine little boy, the ladies had taken entire possession of him. "I can't stand Mrs. Mackenzie any longer, I own," says Clive; "but how resist a wife at such a moment? Rosa was sure she would die, unless her mother came to her, and of course we invited Mrs. Mack. This time she is all smiles and politeness with the Colonel: the last quarrel is laid upon me, and in so far I am easy, as the old folks get on pretty well together." To me, considering these things, it was clear that Mr. Clive Newcome was but a very secondary personage indeed in his father's new fine house which he inhabited, and in which the poor Colonel had hoped they were to live such a happy family.

But it was about Clive Newcome's pecuniary affairs that I felt the most disquiet when he came to explain these to me. The Colonel's capital and that considerable sum which Mrs. Clive had inherited from her good old uncle, were all involved in a common stock, of which Colonel Newcome took the management. "The governor understands business so well you see," says Clive, "is a most remarkable head for accounts, he must have inherited that from my grandfather, you know, who made his own fortune: all the Newcomes are good at accounts except me, a poor useless devil who knows nothing but to paint a picture, and who can't even do that." He cuts off the head of a thistle as he speaks, bites his tawny mustachios, plunges his hands into his pockets and his soul into reverie.

"You don't mean to say?" asks Mr. Pendennis, "that your wife's fortune has not been settled upon herself?"

"Of course it has been settled upon herself, that is, it is entirely her own—you know the Colonel has managed all the business, he understands it better than we do."

"Do you say that your wife's money is not vested in the hands of trustees, and for her benefit?"

"My father is one of the trustees. I tell you he manages the whole thing. What is his property is mine and ever has been: and I might draw upon him as much as I liked: and you know it's five times as great as my wife's. What is his is ours, and what is ours is his, of course; for instance, the India Stock, which poor Uncle James left, that now stands in the Colonel's name. He wants to be a Director: he will be at the next election—he must have a certain quantity of India Stock, don't you see?"

"My dear fellow, is there then no settlement made upon your wife at all?"

"You needn't look so frightened," says Clive. "I made a settlement on her: with all my worldly goods I did her endow—three thousand three hundred and thirty-three pounds six and eight pence, which my father sent over from India to my uncle, years ago, when I came home."

I might well indeed be aghast at this news, and had yet further intelligence from Clive, which by no means contributed to lessen my anxiety. This worthy old Colonel, who fancied himself to be so clever a man of business, chose to conduct it in utter ignorance and defiance of law. If anything happened to the Bundelcund Bank it was clear that not only every shilling of his own property but every farthing bequeathed to Rosa Mackenzie would be lost, only his retiring pension which was luckily considerable, and the hundred pounds a year which Clive had settled on his wife, would be saved out of the ruin.

And now Clive confided to me his own serious doubts and misgivings regarding the prosperity of the Bank itself. He did not know why, but he could not help fancying that things were going wrong. Those partners who had come home—having sold out of the Bank, and living in England so splendidly—Why had they quitted it? The Colonel said it was a proof of the prosperity of the Company, that so many gentlemen were enriched who had taken shares in it. "But when I asked my father," Clive continued, "why he did not himself withdraw? the dear old boy's countenance fell: he told me such things were not to be done every day; and ended, as usual, by saying that I do not understand any thing about business. No more I do: that is the truth. I hate the whole concern, Pen! I hate that great tawdry house in which we live; and those fearfully stupid parties:—O, how I wish we were back in Fitzroy Square! But who can recal bygones, Arthur; or wrong steps in life? We must make the best of to-day and to-morrow must take care of itself. Poor little child! I could not help thinking, as I took it crying in my arms the other day, 'What has life in store for you, my poor weeping baby?' My mother-in-law cried out that I should drop the baby, and that only the Colonel knew how to hold it. My wife called from her bed: the nurse dashed up, and scolded me: and they drove me out of the room amongst them. By Jove, Pen, I laugh when some of my friends congratulate me on my good fortune! I am not quite the father of my own child, nor the husband of my own wife, nor even the master of my own easel. I am managed for, don't you see? boarded, lodged, and done for. And here is the man they call happy! Happy! O J.J.![2] why had I not your strength of mind; and why did I ever leave my Art, my Mistress?"

And herewith the poor lad fell to chopping thistles again; and quitted Fairoaks shortly; leaving his friends there very much disquieted about his prospects, actual and future.[3]

The expected Dissolution of Parliament came at length. All the county-papers[4] in England teemed with electioneering addresses; and the country was in a flutter with party-coloured ribbons. Colonel Thomas Newcome pursuant to his promise offered himself to the independent Electors of Newcome in the liberal journal of the family town, whilst Sir Barnes Newcome Newcome, Bart.,[5] addressed himself to his old and tried friends, and called upon the friends of the Constitution to rally round him in the Conservative print. The addresses of our friend were sent to us at Fairoaks, by the Colonel's indefatigable aide-de-camp, Mr. Frederick Bayham. During the period which had elapsed since the Colonel's last canvassing visit, and the issuing of the writs now daily expected for the new Parliament; many things of great importance had occurred in Thomas Newcome's family,— events which were kept secret from his biographer, who was, at this period also, pretty entirely occupied with his own affairs. These, however, are not the present subject[6] of this history, which has Newcome for its business, and the parties engaged in the family quarrel there.

There were four candidates in the field for the representation of that borough. That old and tried member of Parliament, Mr. Bunce, was considered to be secure: and the Baronet's seat was thought to be pretty safe on account of his influence in the place. Nevertheless Thomas Newcome's supporters were confident for their champion, and that when the parties came to the poll; the extreme liberals of the borough would divide their

<hr>

[2] O J.J.! *Ms*] O!!! *E1*
[3] [The *Ms* indicates a chapter break at this point.]
[4] county-papers *Ms*] country papers *E1*
[5] Newcome Newcome, Bart., *Ms*] Newcome, Bart., *E1*
[6] present subject *E1*] subject *Ms*

votes between him and the Fourth Candidate, the Uncompromising Radical, Mr. Barker.

In due time the Colonel and his staff arrived at Newcome, and resumed the active canvass which they had commenced some months previously. Clive was not in his father's suite this time, nor Mr. Warrington, whose engagements took him elsewhere. The lawyer, the editor of the *Independent*, and F.B., were the Colonel's chief men. His head-quarters (which F.B. liked very well), were at the hotel where we last saw him, and whence issuing with his aide-de-camp at his heels, the Colonel went round, to canvass personally, according to his promise, every free and independent elector of the Borough. Barnes too was canvassing eagerly on his side, and was most affable and active; the two parties would often meet nose to nose in the same street, and their retainers exchange looks of defiance. With Mr. Potts of the *Independent* a big man, on his left; with Mr. Frederick, a still bigger man, on his right; his own trusty bamboo cane in his hand, before which poor Barnes had shrunk abashed ere now, Colonel Newcome had commonly the best of these street encounters, and frowned his nephew, Barnes, and Barnes's staff off the pavement. With the non-electors, the Colonel was a decided favourite; the boys invariably hurrayed him; whereas they jeered and uttered ironical cries after poor Barnes, asking, "Who beat his wife? Who drove his children to the workhouse?" and other unkind personal questions. The man upon whom the libertine Barnes had inflicted so cruel an injury in his early days, was now the Baronet's bitterest enemy. He assailed him with curses and threats when they met, and leagued his brother workmen against him. The wretched Sir Barnes owned with contrition, that the sins of his youth pursued him: his enemy scoffed at the idea of Barnes's repentance; he was not moved at the grief, the punishment in his own family; the humiliation and remorse which the repentant prodigal piteously pleaded. No man was louder in his cries of *mea culpa* than Barnes: no man professed a more edifying repentance. He was hat in hand to every black coat, established, or dissenting. Repentance was to his interest, to be sure, but yet let us hope it was sincere. There is some hypocrisy, of which one does not like even to entertain the thought; especially that awful falsehood which trades with divine truth, and takes the name of Heaven in vain.

The Roebuck Inn, at Newcome, stands in the market-place directly facing the King's Arms, where as we know, Colonel Newcome, and uncompromising toleration held their head quarters. Immense banners of blue and yellow floated from every window of the King's Arms, and decorated the balcony from which the Colonel and the assistants were in the habit of addressing the multitude. Fiddlers and trumpeters arrayed in his colours paraded the town and enlivened it with their melodious strains. Other trumpeters and fiddlers bearing the true blue cockades and colours of Sir Barnes Newcome, Bart., would encounter the Colonel's musicians, on which occasions of meeting it is to be feared small harmony was produced. They banged each other with their brazen instruments. The warlike drummers thumped each other's heads in lieu of the professional sheepskin. The town-boys and street blackguards rejoiced in these combats, and exhibited their valour on one side or the other. The Colonel had to pay a

Newcome versus Newcome

long bill for broken brass when he settled the little accounts of the election.

In after times, F.B. was pleased to describe the circumstances of a contest in which he bore a most distinguished part. It was F.B.'s opinion that his private eloquence brought over many waverers to the Colonel's side, and converted numbers of the benighted followers of Sir Barnes Newcome. Bayham's voice was indeed magnificent, and could be heard from the King's Arms balcony above the shout and roar of the multitude, the gongs and bugles of the opposition bands. He was untiring in his oratory—undaunted in the presence of the crowds[7] below. He was immensely popular, F.B. Whether he laid his hand upon his broad chest, took off his hat and waved it, or pressed his blue and yellow ribbons to his bosom, the crowd shouted, "Hurra! silence! bravo! Bayham for ever!" "They would have carried me in triumph," said F.B.; "if I had but the necessary qualification I might be member for Newcome this day or any other I chose."

I am afraid in this conduct of the Colonel's election Mr. Bayham resorted to acts of which his principal certainly would disapprove, and engaged auxiliaries whose alliance was scarcely creditable—Whose was the hand which flung the potato which struck Sir Barnes Newcome, Bart., on the nose as he was haranguing the people from the Roebuck? How came it that whenever Sir Barnes and his friends essayed to speak, such an awful yelling and groaning took place in the crowd below, that the words of those feeble orators were inaudible? Who smashed all the front windows of the Roebuck? Colonel Newcome had not words to express his indignation at proceedings so unfair. When Sir Barnes and his staff were hustled in the market-place and most outrageously shoved, jeered, and jolted, the Colonel from the King's Arms organised a rapid sally, which he himself headed with his bamboo cane; cut out Sir Barnes and his followers from the hands of the mob and addressed those ruffians in a noble speech, of which the bamboo cane—Englishman—shame—fair-play, were the most emphatic expressions. The mob cheered Old Tom as they called him—they made way for Sir Barnes, who shrunk pale and shuddering back into his hotel again—who always persisted in saying that that old villain of a dragoon had planned both the assault and the rescue.

"When the dregs of the people—the scum of the rabble, Sir, banded together by the myrmidons of Sir Barnes Newcome, attacked us at the King's Arms, and smashed ninety-six pounds' worth of glass at one volley, besides knocking off the gold unicorn's head and the tail of the British lion; it was fine, Sir," F.B. said, "to see how the Colonel came forward, and the coolness of the old boy in the midst of the action. He stood there in front, Sir, with his old hat off, never so much as once bobbing his old head, and I think he spoke rather better under fire than he did when there was no danger. Between ourselves, he ain't much of a speaker, the old Colonel; he hems and hahs, and repeats himself a good deal. He hasn't the gift of natural eloquence which some men have, Pendennis. You should have heard my speech, Sir, on the Thursday in the Town Hall—that was something like a speech. Potts was jealous of it, and always reported me most shamefully."

7 crowds *E1*] crowd *R*

In spite of his respectful behaviour to the gentlemen in black coats, his soup tickets and his flannel tickets, his own pathetic lectures and his sedulous attendance at other folk's sermons, poor Barnes could not keep up his credit with the serious interest at Newcome, and the meeting-houses and their respective[8] pastors and frequenters turned their backs upon him. The case against him was too flagrant: his enemy, the factory-man, worked it with an extraordinary skill, malice, and pertinacity. Not a single man, woman, or child in Newcome but was made acquainted with Sir Barnes's early peccadillo. Ribald ballads were howled through the streets describing his sin, and his deserved punishment. For very shame, the reverend dissenting gentlemen were obliged to refrain from voting for him; such as ventured, believing in the sincerity of his repentance, to give him their voices, were yelled away from the polling-places. A very great number who would have been his friends, were compelled to bow to decency and public opinion, and supported the Colonel.

Hooted away from the hustings, and the public places whence the rival candidates addressed the free and independent electors, this wretched and persecuted Sir Barnes invited his friends and supporters to meet him at the Athenæum Room—scene of his previous eloquent performances. But, though this apartment was defended by tickets, the people burst into it; and Nemesis in the shape of the persevering factory-man appeared, before the scared Sir Barnes and his puzzled committee. The man stood up and bearded the pale Baronet. He had a good cause, and was in truth a far better master of debate than our banking friend, being a great speaker amongst his brother operatives, by whom political questions are discussed, and the conduct of political men examined, with a ceaseless interest and with an ardour and eloquence which are often unknown in what is called superior society. This man and his friends round about him fiercely silenced the clamour of "turn him out," with which his first appearance was assailed by Sir Barnes's hangers-on. He said, in the name of justice he would speak up; if they were fathers of families and loved their wives and daughters he dared them to refuse him a hearing. Did they love their wives and their children? it was a shame that they should take such a man as that yonder for their representative in parliament. But the greatest sensation he made was when in the middle of his speech after inveighing against Barnes's cruelty and parental ingratitude, he asked, "Where were Barnes's children," and actually thrust forward two, to the amazement of the committee and the ghastly astonishment of the guilty Baronet himself.

"Look at them," says the man: "they are almost in rags, they have to put up with scanty and hard food; contrast them with his other children, whom you see lording it[9] in gilt carriages, robed in purple and fine linen, and scattering mud from their wheels over us humble people as we walk the streets; ignorance and starvation is good enough for these, for those others nothing can be too fine or too dear. What can a factory girl expect from such a fine high-bred white-handed aristocratic gentleman as Sir Barnes Newcome, Baronet, but to be cajoled, and seduced, and deserted, and left

[8] respective *E1*] respected *R*
[9] lording it *R*] lording *E1*

to starve. When she has served my lord's pleasure, her natural fate is to be turned into the street; let her go and rot there, and her children beg in the gutter."

"This is the most shameful imposture," gasps out Sir Barnes; "these children are not—are not"—

The man interrupted him with a bitter laugh. "No," says he, "they are not his; that's true enough, friends. It's Tom Martin's girl and boy, a precious pair of lazy little scamps. But, at first he *thought* they were his children. See how much he knows about them! He hasn't seen his children for years; he would have left them, and their mother, to starve, and did, but for shame and fear. The old man, his father, pensioned them, and he hasn't the heart to stop their wages now. Men of Newcome, will you have this man to represent you in Parliament?" And the crowd roared out, no; and Barnes and his shame-faced committee slunk out of the place, and no wonder the dissenting clerical gentlemen were shy of voting for him.

A brilliant and picturesque diversion in Colonel Newcome's favour was due to the inventive genius of his faithful aide-de-camp, F.B. On the polling-day, as the carriages full of voters came up to the market-place, there appeared nigh to the booths an open barouche, covered all over with ribbon, and containing Frederick Bayham, Esq., profusely decorated with the Colonel's colours, and a very old woman and her female attendant, who were similarly ornamented. It was good old Mrs. Mason, who was pleased with the drive and the sunshine, though she scarcely understood the meaning of the turmoil, with her maid by her side, delighted to wear such ribbons, and sit in such a post of honour. Rising up in the carriage, F.B. took off his hat, bade his men of brass be silent, who were accustomed to bray "See the Conquering Hero comes," whenever the Colonel, or Mr. Bayham, his brilliant aide-de-camp, made their appearance;—bidding, we say, the musicians and the universe to be silent, F.B. rose, and made the citizens of Newcome a splendid speech. Good old unconscious Mrs. Mason was the theme of it, and the Colonel's virtues and faithful gratitude in tending her. She was his father's old friend. She was Sir Barnes Newcome's grandfather's old friend. She had lived for more than forty years at Sir Barnes Newcome's door, and how often had he been to see her? Did he go every week? No. Every month? No. Every year? No. Never in the whole course of his life, had he set his foot into her doors! (Loud yells, and cries of shame.) Never had he done her one single act of kindness. Whereas for years and years past, when he was away in India, heroically fighting the battles of his country, when he was distinguishing himself at Assaye, and—and—Mulligatawny, and Seringapatam, in the hottest of the fight, and the fiercest of the danger, in the most terrible moment of the conflict, and the crowning glory of the victory, the good, the brave, the kind old Colonel,—why should he say Colonel? why should he not say Old Tom at once? (immense roars of applause) always remembered his dear old nurse and friend. Look at that shawl, boys, which she has got on! My belief is that Colonel Newcome took that shawl in single combat, and on horseback, from the prime minister of Tippoo Saib. Immense cheers and cries of "Bravo Bayham!" Look at that brooch the dear old thing wears! (he kissed her hand whilst so apostrophising her); Tom Newcome never brags about his military achievements, he is the most modest as well as the bravest man in the world; what if I were to tell you that he cut that brooch from the throat of an Indian rajah? He's man enough to do it (He is; he is; from all parts of the crowd). What, you want to take the horses out, do you? (to the crowd, who were removing those quadrupeds); I ain't a going to prevent you; I expected as much of you: Men of Newcome, I expected as much of you, for I know you! Sit still, old lady; don't be frightened, Ma'am, they are only going to pull you to the King's Arms, and show you to the Colonel.

This, indeed, was the direction in which the mob (whether inflamed by spontaneous enthusiasm, or excited by cunning agents placed amongst the populace by F.B., I cannot say,) now took the barouche and its three occupants. With a myriad roar and shout the carriage was dragged up in front of the King's Arms, from the balconies of which a most satisfactory account of the polling was already placarded. The extra noise and shouting brought out the Colonel, who looked at first with curiosity at the advancing procession, and then, as he caught sight of Sarah Mason, with a blush and a bow of his kind old head.

"Look at him, boys!" cried the enraptured F.B., pointing up to the old man. "Look at him; the dear old boy! Isn't he an old trump? which will you have for your member, Barnes Newcome or Old Tom?"

And as might be supposed, an immense shout of "Old Tom!" arose from the multitude; in the midst of which, blushing and bowing still, the Colonel went back to his committee-room: and the bands played "See the Conquering Hero" louder than ever: and poor Barnes in the course of his duty having to come out upon his balcony at the Roebuck opposite, was saluted with a yell as vociferous as the cheer for the Colonel had been: and old Mrs. Mason asked what the noise was about: and after making several vain efforts, in dumb show, to the crowd, Barnes slunk back into his hole again as pale as the turnip which was flung at his head: and the horses were brought; and Mrs. Mason driven home; and the day of election came to an end.

Reasons of personal gratitude as we have stated already, prevented his Highness the Prince de Montcontour from taking a part in this family contest. His brethren of the House of Higg, however, very much to Florac's gratification gave their second votes to Colonel Newcome, carrying with them a very great number of electors: we know that in the present parliament, Mr. Higg and Mr. Bunce sit for the Borough of Newcome. Having had monetary transactions with Sir Barnes Newcome, and entered largely into Railway speculations with him, the Messrs. Higg had found reason to quarrel with the Baronet; accuse him of sharp practices to the present day, and have long stories to tell which do not concern us about Sir Barnes's stratagems—grasping and extortion. They and their following, deserting Sir Barnes, whom they had supported in previous elections, voted[1] for the Colonel, although some of the opinions of that gentleman were rather too extreme for such sober persons.

---

[1] voted *R*] and voted *E1*

Not exactly knowing what his politics were when he commenced the canvass, I can't say to what opinions the poor Colonel did not find himself committed by the time when the election was over. The worthy gentleman felt himself not a little humiliated by what he had to say and to unsay, by having to answer questions, to submit to familiarities, to shake hands, which to say truth he did not care for grasping at all. His habits were aristocratic; his education had been military; the kindest and simplest soul alive, he yet disliked all familiarity, and expected from common people the sort of deference which he had received from his men in the regiment. The contest saddened and mortified him; he felt that he was using wrong means to obtain an end that perhaps was not right (for so his secret conscience must have told him); he was derogating from his own honour in tampering with political opinions, submitting to familiarities, condescending to stand by whilst his agents solicited vulgar suffrages or uttered clap-traps about retrenchment and reform. "I felt I was wrong," he said to me in after days, "though *I* was too proud to own my error in those times, and you and your good wife and my boy were right in protesting against that mad election." Indeed, though we little knew what events were speedily to happen, Laura and I felt very little satisfaction when the result of the Newcome election was made known to us, and we found Sir Barnes Newcome third, and Colonel Thomas Newcome second upon the poll.

Ethel was absent with her children at Brighton. She was glad, she wrote, not to have been at home during the election. Mr. and Mrs. C. were at Brighton, too. Ethel had seen Mrs. C. and her child once or twice. It was a very fine child. "My brother came down to us," she wrote, "after all was over. He is furious against M. de Montcontour, who, he says, persuaded the Whigs to vote against him, and turned the election."

Chapter XXXII.

CHILTERN HUNDREDS.

E shall say no more regarding Thomas Newcome's political doings; his speeches against Barnes, and the Baronet's replies. The nephew was beaten by his stout old uncle.

In due time the *Gazette* announced that Thomas Newcome, Esq., was returned as one of the Members of Parliament for the borough of Newcome; and, after triumphant dinners, speeches, and rejoicings, the member came back to his family in London, and to his affairs in that city.

The good Colonel appeared to be by no means elated by his victory. He would not allow that he was wrong in engaging in that family war, of which we have just seen the issue; though it may be that his secret remorse on this account in part occasioned his disquiet. But there were other reasons which his family not long afterwards came to understand, for the gloom and low spirits which now oppressed the head of their home.

It was observed (that is, if simple little Rosey took the trouble to observe) that the entertainments at the Colonel's mansion were more frequent and splendid even than before; the silver cocoa-nut tree was constantly in requisition, and around it were assembled many new guests, who had not formerly been used to sit under those branches. Mr. Sherrick and his wife appeared at those parties, at which the proprietor of Lady Whittlesea's chapel made himself perfectly familiar. Sherrick cut jokes with the master of the house, which the latter received with a very grave acquiescence; he ordered the servants about, addressing the butler as "Old Corkscrew," and bidding the footman, whom he loved to call by his Christian name, to "look alive." He called the Colonel "Newcome" sometimes, and facetiously speculated upon the degree of relationship subsisting between them now that his daughter was married to Clive's uncle, the Colonel's brother-in-law. Though I daresay Clive did not much relish receiving news of his aunt,

Sherrick was sure to bring such intelligence when it reached him; and announced, in due time, the birth of a little cousin at Bogglywallah, whom the fond parents designed to name "Thomas Newcome Honeyman."

A dreadful panic and ghastly terror seized poor Clive on an occasion which he described to me afterwards. Going out from home one day with his father, he beheld a wine-merchant's cart, from which hampers were carried down the area gate into the lower regions of Colonel Newcome's house. "Sherrick and Co., Wine Merchants, Walpole Street," was painted upon the vehicle.

"Good Heavens! Sir; do you get your wine from *him?*" Clive cried out to his father, remembering Honeyman's provisions in early times. The Colonel, looking very gloomy and turning red, said, "Yes, he bought wine from Sherrick, who had been very good-natured and serviceable; and who—and who, you know, is our connection now." When informed of the circumstance by Clive, I too, as I confess, thought the incident alarming.

Then Clive, with a laugh, told me of a grand battle which had taken place in consequence of Mrs. Mackenzie's behavior to the wine-merchant's wife. The Campaigner had treated this very kind and harmless, but vulgar woman, with extreme *hauteur*—had talked loud during her singing—the beauty of which, to say truth, time had considerably impaired—had made contemptuous observations regarding her upon more than one occasion. At length the Colonel broke out in great wrath against Mrs. Mackenzie—bade her to respect that lady as one of his guests—and if she did not like the company which assembled at his house, hinted to her that there were many thousand other houses in London where she could find a lodging. For the sake of her child and her adored grandchild, the Campaigner took no notice of this hint; and declined to remove from the quarters which she had occupied ever since she had become a grandmamma.

I myself dined once or twice with my old friends under the shadow of the picklebearing cocoa-nut tree; and could not but remark a change of personages in the society assembled. The manager of the City branch of the B.B.C. was always present—an ominous-looking man whose whispers and compliments seemed to make poor Clive at his end of the table very melancholy. With[1] the City manager came the City manager's friends, whose jokes passed gaily round, and who kept the conversation to themselves. Once I had the happiness to meet Mr. Ratray, who had returned, filled with rupees from the Indian bank; who told us many anecdotes of the splendour of Rummun Lall at Calcutta, who complimented the Colonel on his fine house and grand dinners with sinister good humour. Those compliments did not seem to please our poor friend, that familiarity choked him.[2] A brisk little chattering attorney, very intimate with Sherrick, with a wife of dubious gentility, was another constant guest. He enlivened the table by his jokes, and recounted choice stories about the aristocracy, with certain members of whom the little man seemed very familiar. He knew to a shilling how much this lord owed—and how much the creditors allowed to that marquis. He had been concerned for[3] such and such a nobleman,

[1] [The passage from here to the next note was added at proof stage.]
[2] With the City ... choked him. [Added at proof stage.]
[3] ~~with~~ ↑for↓ *Ms*] with *E1*

who was now in the Queen's Bench. He spoke of their lordships affably and without their titles—calling upon "Louisa, my dear," his wife, to testify to the day when Viscount Tagrag dined with them, and Earl Bareacres sent them the pheasants. F.B., as sombre and downcast as his hosts now seemed to be, informed me demurely that this[4] attorney was a member of one of the most eminent firms in the City—that he had been engaged in procuring the Colonel's parliamentary title for him—and in various important matters appertaining to the B.B.C.; but my knowledge of the world and the law was sufficient to make me aware that this gentleman belonged to a well-known firm of money-lending solicitors, and I trembled to see such a person in the house[5] of our good Colonel. Where were the Generals and the Judges?—Where were the Fogies and their respectable ladies?—Stupid they were, and dull their company, but better a stalled ox in their society, than Mr. Campion's jokes over Mr. Sherrick's wine.[6]

After the little rebuke administered by Colonel Newcome, Mrs. Mackenzie abstained from overt hostilities against any guest[7] of her daughter's father-in-law; and contented herself by assuming grand and princess-like airs in the company of the new ladies. They flattered her, and poor little Rosey intensely. The latter liked their company no doubt. To a man of the world looking on, who has seen the men and morals of many cities, it was curious; almost pathetic to watch that poor little innocent creature fresh and smiling, attired in bright colours and a thousand gewgaws, simpering in the midst of these darkling people—practising her little arts, and coquetries, with such a court round about her. An unconscious little maid with rich and rare gems sparkling on all her fingers, and bright gold rings as many as belonged to the late Old Woman of Banbury Cross—still she smiled and prattled innocently before those banditti,—I thought of Zerlina and the Brigands in *Fra-Diavolo*.

Walking away with F.B. from one of these parties of the Colonel's and seriously alarmed at what I had observed there, I demanded of Bayham whether my conjectures were not correct that some misfortune overhung our old friend's house? At first Bayham denied stoutly or pretended ignorance,—but at length having reached the Haunt together, which I had not visited since I was a married man—we entered that place of entertainment and were greeted by its old landlady and waitress—and accommodated with a quiet parlour. And here F.B., after groaning—after sighing—after solacing himself with a prodigious quantity of bitter beer—fairly burst out, and, with tears in his eyes, made a full and sad confession respecting this unlucky Bundelcund Banking Company. The shares had been going lower and lower so that there was no sale now for them at all. To meet the liabilities the directors must have undergone the greatest sacrifices. He did not know—he did not like to think what the Colonel's personal losses were. The respectable solicitors of the Company had retired long since, after having secured payment of a most respectable bill, and had given place to the firm of dubious law-agents of whom I had that evening seen a

[4] this *Ms*] the *E1*
[5] house *Ms*] home *E1*
[6] wine. *Ms*] wines. *E1*
[7] guest *Ms*] guests *E1*

partner. How the retiring partners from India had been allowed to withdraw, and to bring fortunes along with them, was a mystery to Mr. Frederick Bayham. The great Indian *millionnaire* was in his, F.B.'s, eyes "a confounded old mahogany-coloured heathen humbug." These parties which the Colonel was giving and that fine carriage which was always flaunting about the Park with poor Mrs. Clive and the Campaigner and the nurse and the baby—were in F.B.'s opinion all decoys and shams. He did not mean to say that the meals were not paid, and that the Colonel had to plunder for his horses' corn; but he knew that Sherrick and the attorney—and the manager—insisted upon the necessity of giving these parties, and keeping up this state and grandeur, and opined that it was at the special instance of these advisers that the Colonel had contested the borough for which he was now returned. "Do you know how much that contest cost?" asked F.B. "The sum, Sir, was awful! and we have ever so much of it to pay. I came up twice from Newcome myself to Campion and Sherrick about it. I betray no secrets—F.B., Sir, would die a thousand deaths before he would tell the secrets of his benefactor![8] But, Pendennis, you understand a thing or two. You know what o'clock it is, and so does yours truly, F.B. who drinks your health. *I*[9] know the taste of Sherrick's wine well enough. F.B., Sir, fears the Greeks and all the gifts they bring. Confound his Amontillado! I had rather drink this honest malt and hops all my life than ever see a drop of his abominable golden sherry. Golden?—F.B. believes it *is* golden—and a precious deal dearer than gold too"—and herewith, ringing the bell, my friend asked for a second pint of the first named[1] and cheaper fluid.

I have of late had to recount portions of my dear old friend's history which much[2] needs be told and over which the writer does not like to dwell. If Thomas Newcome's opulence was unpleasant to describe and to contrast with the bright goodness and simplicity I remembered in former days, how much more painful is that part of his story to which we are now come perforce, and which the acute reader of novels has no doubt long foreseen? Yes, Sir or Madam, you are quite right in the opinion which you have held all along regarding that Bundelcund Banking Company in which our Colonel has invested every rupee he possesses, *Solvuntur rupees* &c. I disdain for the most part the tricks and surprises of the novelist's art knowing from the very beginning of our story what was the issue of this Bundelcund Banking Concern. I have scarce had patience to keep my counsel about it and whenever I have had occasion to mention the Company have scarcely been able to refrain from breaking out into fierce diatribes against that complicated enormous outrageous swindle. It was one of many similar cheats which have been successfully practised upon the simple folks, civilian and military, who toil and struggle—who fight with sun and enemy—who pass years of long exile and gallant endurance in the service of our empire in India. Agency houses after agency houses have been established and have flourished in splendour and magnificence and have paid fabulous dividends—and have enormously enriched two

---

[8] benefactor!] benefactor!— *E1*] benefactors! *Ms*
[9] *I E1*] I *Ms*
[1] first named *Ms*] just-named *E1*
[2] much *Ms*] must *E1*

or three wary speculators—and then have burst in bankruptcy involving widows, orphans, and countless simple people who trusted their all to the keeping of these unworthy treasurers. The[3] failure of the Bundelcund Bank which we now have to record was one only of many similar schemes[4] ending in ruin. About the time when Thomas Newcome was chaired as Member of Parliament for the borough of which he bore the name, the great Indian Merchant who was at the head of the Bundelcund Banking Company's affairs at Calcutta suddenly died of cholera at his palace at Barrackpore.[5] He had been giving of late a series of the most splendid banquets with which Indian prince ever entertained a Calcutta society. The greatest and proudest personages of that aristocratic city had attended his feasts. The fairest Calcutta beauties had danced in his halls.—Did not poor F.B. transfer from the columns of the *Bengal Hŭrkarŭ* to the *Pall Mall Gazette* the most astounding descriptions of those Asiatic Nights Entertainments of which the very grandest was to come off on the night when cholera seized Rummun Lall in its grip. There was to have been a masquerade outvying all European masquerades in splendour. The two rival queens of the Calcutta society were to have appeared each with her court around her. Young civilians at the college and young ensigns fresh landed had gone into awful expenses and borrowed money at fearful interest from the B.B.C. and other banking companies in order to appear with befitting splendour as knights and noblemen of Henrietta Maria's Court (Henrietta Maria, wife of Hastings Hicks, Esq., Sudder Dewanee Adawlut) or as princes and warriors surrounding the palanquin of Lalla Rookh (the lovely wife of Hon. Cornwallis Bobus, Member of Council): all[6] these splendours were there. As[7] carriage after carriage[8] drove up from Calcutta they were met[9] at Rummun Lall's gates[1] by ghastly weeping servants who announced their master's demise.[2]

On the next day the Bank at Calcutta was closed—and the day after when heavy bills were presented which must be paid, although by this time Rummun Lall was not only dead but buried and his widows howling over his grave, it was announced throughout Calcutta that but 800 rupees were left in the treasury of the B.B.C. to meet engagements to the amount of four lakhs then immediately due and sixty days afterwards the shutters were closed at No. 175 Lothbury, the London offices of the B.B.C. of India, and £35000 worth of their bills refused by their agents, Messrs. Baines, Jolly & Co. of Fog Court.

When the accounts of that ghastly bankruptcy arrived from Calcutta, it was found of course that the merchant prince Rummun Lall owed the

---

[3] The *Ms*] ¶The *E1*
[4] similar schemes *E1*] schemes *Ms*
[5] Barrackpore. *R*] Bharapore *Ms*] Barackpore. *E1*
[6] Council): all *E1*] Council. All *Ms*
[7] there. As *E1*] then as *Ms*
[8] carriage after carriage *E1*] carriages after carriages *Ms*
[9] they were met *E1*] they met *Ms*
[1] gates *Ms*] gate *E1*
[2] demise. *E1*] decease. *R*

B.B.C. twenty-five lakhs of rupees the value of which was scarcely even represented by his respectable signature. It was found that one of the auditors of the Bank, the generally esteemed Charley Condor[3] (a capital fellow— famous for his good dinners and for playing low comedy characters at the Chowringhee[4] Theatre), was indebted to the Bank in £90,000; and also it was discovered that the revered Baptist Bellman, Chief Registrar of the Calcutta Tape and Sealing Wax Office (a most valuable and powerful amateur preacher who had converted two natives and whose serious soirees were thronged at Calcutta), had helped himself to £73,000 more, for which he settled in the Bankruptcy Court before he resumed his duties in his own. In justice to Mr. Bellman it must be said that he could have had[5] no idea of the catastrophe impending over the B.B.C., for only three weeks before that great Bank closed its doors, Mr. Bellman, as guardian of the children of his widowed sister Mrs. Colonel Green, had sold the whole of the late Colonel's property out of Company's paper and invested it in the Bank which gave a high interest and with bills of which, drawn upon their London correspondents, he had accommodated Mrs. Colonel Green when she took her departure for Europe with her numerous little family on board the Burrumpooter.[6]

And now you have the explanation of the title of this chapter and know wherefore Thomas Newcome never sat in Parliament. Where are our dear old friends now? Where are Rose's chariots and horses? Where her[7] jewels and gewgaws? Bills are up in the fine new house. Swarms of Hebrew gentlemen with their hats on are walking about the drawing-rooms, peering into the bed-rooms—weighing and poising the poor old silver cocoa-nut tree—eying the plate and crystal—thumbing the damask of the curtains and inspecting ottomans, mirrors, and a hundred articles of splendid trumpery. There is Rose's boudoir which her father-in-law loved to ornament—there is Clive's studio with a hundred sketches—there is the Colonel's bare room at the top of the house with his little iron bedstead[8] and ship's drawers—and a camel trunk or two which have[9] accompanied him on many an Indian march—and his old regulation sword and that one which the native officers of his regiment gave him when he bade them farewell. I can fancy the brokers' faces as they look over this camp wardrobe and that the uniforms will not fetch much in Holywell Street. There is the old one still and that new one which he ordered and wore when poor little Rosey was presented at Court. I had not the heart to examine their plunder and go amongst those wreckers. F.B. used to attend[1] the sale regularly and report its proceedings to us with eyes full of tears. "A fellow laughed at me," says F.B., "because when I came into the dear

---

3 Condor *E1*] Condons *Ms*
4 Chowringhee *E1*] Chowrugher *Ms*
5 had *E1*] [omitted] *R*
6 Burrumpooter. *E1*] Burrumpoota. *Ms*
7 her *E1*] are *Ms*
8 bedstead *E1*] bed *Ms*
9 have *E1*] has *Ms*
1 attend *E1*] go to *Ms*

old drawing-room I took my hat off. I told him that if[2] he dared say another word I would knock him down." I think F.B. may be pardoned in this instance for emulating the office of auctioneer. "Where are you, pretty Rosey and poor little helpless baby?[3] Where are you, dear Clive—gallant young friend of my youth? Ah! it is a sad story—a melancholy page to pen! Let us pass it over quickly—I love not to think of any[4] friend in pain.

[2] that if *E1*] if *Ms*
[3] baby? *Ms E1 R*] Baby? *P1*
[4] any *Ms*] my *E1*

Chapter XXXIII.

LL the friends of the Newcome family of course knew the disaster which had befallen the good Colonel, and I was aware for my part that not only his own but almost the whole of Rosa Newcome's property was involved in the common ruin. Some proposals of temporary relief were made to our friends from more quarters than one but were thankfully rejected—and we were led to hope that the Colonel having still his pension secured to him, which the law could not touch, might live comfortably enough in the retirement to which of course he would betake himself[1] when the melancholy proceedings consequent on the bankruptcy were brought to an end. It was shewn that he had been egregiously duped in the transaction—that his credulity had cost him and his family a large fortune—that he had given up every penny which belonged to him—that there could not be any sort of stain upon his honest reputation. The judge before whom he appeared spoke with feeling and regard of the unhappy gentleman—the lawyers[2] who examined him respected the grief and fall of that simple old man. Thomas Newcome[3] took a little room near the Court where his affairs and the affairs of the Company were adjudged— lived with a frugality which never was difficult to him—avoided me—and once perchance I met him in the City with a bow[4] and courtesy that was quite humble though proud and somehow inexpressibly touching to me. Fred Bayham was the only person[5] whom he admitted. Fred always faithfully insisted upon attending him in and out of Court. J.J. came to me immediately after he heard of the disaster, eager to place all his savings at

[1] betake himself *E1*] be taken *Ms*
[2] lawyers *Ms*] lawyer *E1*
[3] Thomas Newcome *E1*] He *Ms*
[4] him—avoided me—and once perchance I met him in the City with a bow *Ms*] him—and once when perchance I met him in the City, avoided me, with a bow *E1*
[5] person *E1*] one *Ms*

the service of his friends. Laura and I came to London, and were urgent with similar[6] offers. Our good friend declined to see any of us. F.B., again with tears trickly[7] on his rough cheeks and a break in his voice, told me he feared that affairs must be very bad indeed, for the Colonel absolutely denied himself a cheroot to smoke. Laura drove to his lodgings and took him a box which was held up to him as he came to open the door to my wife's knock by our smiling little boy. He patted the child on his golden head and kissed him. My wife wished he would have done as much for her—but he would not—though she owned she kissed his hand. He drew it across his eyes and thanked her in a very calm and stately[8] manner—but he did not invite her within the threshold of his door, saying simply that such a room was not a fit place to receive a lady "as you ought to know very well, Mrs. Smith," he said to the landlady who had accompanied my wife up the stairs. "He will eat scarcely anything," the woman told us, "his meals come down untouched; his candles are burning all night almost, as he sits poring over his papers." "He was bent—he who used to walk so uprightly," Laura said. "He seemed to have grown many years older and was indeed quite a decrepid old man."

"I am glad they have left Clive out of the bankruptcy," the Colonel said to Bayham; it was almost the only time when his voice exhibited any emotion. "It was very kind of them to leave out Clive, poor boy,—and I have thanked the lawyers in Court." Those gentlemen and the judge himself were very much moved at this act of gratitude. The judge made a very feeling speech to the Colonel when he came up for his certificate. He passed very different comments on the conduct of the Manager of the Bank when that person appeared for examination. He wished that the law had power to deal with those gentlemen, who had come home with large fortunes from India realised but a few years before the bankruptcy. Those gentlemen had known how to take care of themselves very well, and as for the Manager, is not his wife[9] giving elegant balls at her elegant house at Cheltenham at this very day?

What weighed most upon the Colonel's mind, F.B. imagined, was the thought that he had been the means of inducing many poor friends to embark their money in this luckless speculation. Take J.J.'s money after he had persuaded old Ridley to place £200 in Indian shares! Good God, he and his family should rather perish than he would touch a farthing of it! Many fierce words were uttered to him by Mrs. Mackenzie, for instance— by her angry son-in-law[1] at Musselburgh—Josey's husband—by Mr. Smee, R.A.,[2] and two or three Indian officers, friends of his own who had entered into the speculation on his recommendation. These rebukes Thomas Newcome bore with an affecting meekness as his faithful F.B. described to me, striving with many oaths and much loudness to carry off his own emo-

---

6 Laura and I came to London, and were urgent with similar *E1*] Laura drove from Rosebury and came to London with similar *Ms*

7 trickly *Ms*] trickling *E1*

8 and stately *E1*] stately *Ms*

9 his wife *E1*] Mrs. —— *Ms*

1 son-in-law *R*] daughter *Ms E1*

2 Mr. Smee, R.A., *E1*] Mrs. R.A. *Ms*

tion[3]—but what moved the Colonel most of all was a letter which came at this time from Honeyman in India saying that he was doing well—that of course he knew of his benefactor's misfortune and that he sent a remittance which D.V. should be annual in payment of his debt to the Colonel and his good sister at Brighton. "On receipt of this letter," said F.B., "the old man was fairly beat—the letter with the bill in it dropt out of his hands. He clasped them both together shaking in every limb and his head dropped down on his breast as he said, "I thank my God Almighty for this!" and he sent the cheque off to Mrs. Honeyman by the post that night, Sir, every shilling of it; and he passed his old arm under mine—and we went out to Tom's Coffee House and he ate some dinner for the first time for ever so long and drank a couple of glasses of port wine, and F.B. stood it, Sir, and would stand his heart's blood for that dear old boy.""

It was on a Monday morning that those melancholy shutters were seen over the offices of the Bundelcund Bank in Lothbury which were not to come down until the rooms were handed over to some other, and let us trust, more fortunate speculators. The Indian bills had arrived and been protested in the City on the previous Saturday. The Campaigner and Mrs. Rosey had arranged a little party to the theatre that evening and the gallant Captain Goby had agreed to quit the delights of the Flag Club in order to accompany the ladies. Neither of them knew what was happening in the City or could account otherwise than by the common domestic causes for Clive's gloomy despondency and his father's sad reserve. Clive had not been in the City on this day. He had spent it as usual in his studio, *boudé* by his wife, and not disturbed by the mess-room raillery of the Campaigner. They dined early in order to be in time for the theatre. Goby entertained them with the latest jokes from the smoking-room at the Flag, and was in his turn amused by the brilliant plans for the season which Rosey and her Mamma sketched out. The entertainments which Mrs. Clive proposed to give—the ball—she was dying for a masked ball—just such a one as that described in the *Pall Mall Gazette* of last week, out of that paper with the droll title the *Bengal Hŭrkarŭ* which the merchant prince, the head of the Bank you know in India, had given at Calcutta. "We must have a ball, too," says Mrs. Mackenzie, "society demands it of you." "Of course it does," echoes Captain Goby, and he bethought him of a brilliant circle of young fellows from the Flag, whom he would bring in splendid uniform to dance with the pretty Mrs. Clive Newcome.

After the dinner, they little knew it was to be their last in that fine house, the ladies retired to give a parting kiss to baby—a parting look to the toilettes, with which they proposed to fascinate the inhabitants of the pit and public boxes at the Olympic. Goby made vigorous play with the claret bottle during the brief interval of potation allowed to him; he, too, little deeming that he should never drink bumper there again; Clive looking on with the melancholy and silent acquiescence which had, of late, been his part in the household. The carriage was announced—the ladies came down—pretty capotes on—the lovely Campaigner, Goby vowed, looking as

[3] own emotion *E1*] only notion *Ms*

young and as handsome as her daughter, by Jove,—and the hall door was opened to admit the two gentlemen and ladies to their carriage, when, as they were about to step in, a Hansom cab drove up rapidly in which was perceived Thomas Newcome's anxious face. He got out of the vehicle— his own carriage making way for him—the ladies still on the steps. "O, the play! I forgot:" said the Colonel.

"Of course we are going to the play, Papa," cries little Rosey with a[4] gay little tap of her hand.

"I think you had best not," Colonel Newcome said gravely.

"Indeed my darling child has set her heart upon it and I would not have her disappointed for the world in her situation," cries the Campaigner tossing up her head.

The Colonel for reply bade his coachman drive to the stables and come for further orders, and turning to his daughter's guest expressed to Captain Goby his regret that the proposed party could not take place on that evening as he had matter of very great importance to communicate to his family. On hearing these news,[5] and understanding that his further company was not desirable, the Captain, a man of great presence of mind, arrested the Hansom cabman who was about to take his departure and who blithely, knowing the Club and its inmates full well, carried off the jolly Captain to finish his evening at the Flag.

"Has it come, Father," said Clive with a sure prescience looking in his father's face.

The father took and grasped the hand which his son held out. "Let us go back into the dining-room," he said. They entered it and he filled himself a glass of wine out of the bottles[6] still standing amidst the dessert. He bade the butler retire,[7] who was lingering about the room and sideboard and only wanted to know whether his master would have dinner—that was all. And this gentleman having withdrawn Colonel Newcome finished his glass of sherry and broke a biscuit; the Campaigner assuming an attitude of surprise and indignation whilst Rosey had leisure to remark, that Papa looked very ill, and that something must have happened.

The Colonel took both her hands and drew her towards him and kissed her, whilst Rosey's mamma flouncing down on a chair beat a tattoo upon the table-cloth with her fan. "Something has happened, my love," the Colonel said very sadly; "you must show all your strength of mind, for a great misfortune has befallen us."

"Good Heavens, Colonel, what is it? don't frighten my beloved child," cries the Campaigner, rushing towards her darling, and enveloping her in her robust arms, "What can have happened? don't agitate this darling child, Sir," and she looked indignantly towards the poor Colonel.

"We have received the very worst news from Calcutta—a confirmation of the news by the last mail, Clivey, my boy."

"It is no news to me. I have always been expecting it, Father," says Clive, holding down his head.

[4] a *E1*] the *Ms*
[5] family. On hearing these news, *E1*] family; on hearing which, *Ms*
[6] bottles *Ms*] bottle *E1*
[7] retire *E1*] to retire, *Ms*

"Expecting what? What have you been keeping back from us? In what have you been deceiving us, Colonel Newcome?" shrieks the Campaigner, and Rosa crying out, "O, Mamma, Mamma!" begins to whimper.

"The chief of the bank in India is dead," the Colonel went on. "He has left its affairs in worse than disorder. We are, I fear, ruined, Mrs. Mackenzie," and the Colonel went on to tell how the bank could not open on Monday morning, and its bills to a great amount had already been protested in the City that day.

Rosey did not understand half these news, or comprehend the calamity which was to follow; but Mrs. Mackenzie, rustling in great wrath, made a speech, of which the anger gathered as she proceeded; in which she vowed and protested that her money which the Colonel, she did not know from *what motives*, had induced her to subscribe, should *not* be sacrificed, and that have it she would, the Bank shut or not, the next Monday morning— that her daughter had a fortune of her own which her poor dear brother James should have divided and would have divided much more fairly, had he not been wrongly influenced—she would not say by *whom*, and she commanded Colonel Newcome upon that *instant* if he was as he always pretended to be, an *honourable* man, to give an account of her blessed Darling's property, and to pay back her own, every sixpence of it—she would not lend it for an hour longer and to see that that dear blessed child now sleeping unconsciously up-stairs and his dear brothers and sisters who might follow, for Rosey was a young woman—a poor innocent creature too young to be married—and never would have been married had she listened to her mamma's advice. She demanded that baby and all succeeding babies should have their *rights* and should be looked to by their grandmother if their father's father was so *unkind* and so *wicked* and so *unnatural* as to give their money to rogues and deprive them of their just bread.

Rosey began to cry more loudly than ever during the utterance of Mamma's sermon—so loudly that Clive peevishly cried out, "Hold your toungue"—on which the Campaigner, clutching her daughter to her breast again, turned on her son-in-law—and abused him as she had abused his father before him—calling out that they were both in a conspiracy to defraud her child and the little darling up-stairs of its bread—and she would speak—yes she would—and no power should prevent her—and her money she would have on Monday as sure as her poor dear husband Captain Mackenzie was dead—and she never would have been *cheated* so—yes *cheated*—if he had been alive.

At the word "cheated" Clive broke out with an execration—the poor Colonel with a groan of despair—the widow's[8] storm continued—and above that howling tempest of words rose Mrs. Clive's piping screams[9] who went off into downright hysterics at last in which she was encouraged by her mother, and in which she gasped out frantic ejaculations regarding baby-dear; darling, ruined baby and so forth.

The sorrow-stricken Colonel had to quell the women's tongues and shrill anger—and his son's wrothful replies who could not bear the weight of

---

[8] widow's *E1*] widow whose *Ms*

[9] screams *Ms*] scream *E1*

Mrs. Mackenzie upon him, and it was not until these three were allayed that Thomas Newcome was able to continue his sad story—to explain what had happened and what the actual state of the case was—and to oblige the terror-stricken women at length to hear something like reason.

He then had to tell them, to their dismay, that he would inevitably be declared a bankrupt in the ensuing week—that the whole of his property in that house, as elsewhere, would be seized and sold for the creditors' benefit—and that his daughter had best immediately leave a home where she would be certainly subject to humiliation and annoyance. "I would have Clive, my boy, take you out of the Country, and—and return to me when I have need of him and shall send for him," the father said fondly in reply to a rebellious look in his son's face. "I would have you quit this house as soon as possible. Why not to-night? The law bloodhounds may be upon us ere an hour is over—at this moment for what I know."

At that moment the door bell was heard to ring and the women gave a scream a-piece as if the bailiffs were actually coming to take possession. Rosey went off in quite a series of screams, peevishly repressed by her husband and always encouraged by Mamma who called her son-in-law an unfeeling wretch. It must be confessed that Mrs. Clive Newcome did not exhibit much strength of mind or comfort her husband much at a moment when he needed consolation.

From angry rebellion and fierce remonstrance this pair of women now passed to an extreme terror and desire for instantaneous flight. They would go that moment—they would wrap that blessed child up in its shawls—and nurse should take it anywhere—anywhere—poor neglected thing. "My trunks," cries Mrs. Mackenzie, "you know are ready packed—I am sure it is not the treatment which I have received—it is nothing but my *duty* and my *religion*—and the protection which I owe to this blessed unprotected—yes *unprotected* and *robbed* and *cheated* darling child—which have made me stay a *single day* in this house. I never thought I should have been *robbed* in it, or my darlings with their fine fortunes flung naked on the world. If my Mack was here you never had dared to have done this, Colonel Newcome—no never. He had his faults—Mackenzie had—but he would never have robbed his own children. Come away, Rosey, my blessed love—come let us pack your things—and let us go and *hide* our *heads* in sorrow somewhere. Ah! didn't I tell you to beware of all *painters* and that Clarence was a true gentleman and loved you with all his heart—and would never have cheated you out of your money—for which I will have justice as sure as there is justice in England."

During this outburst the Colonel sat utterly scared and silent—supporting his poor head between his hands. When the harem had departed he turned sadly to his son. Clive did not believe that his father was a cheat and a rogue. No, thank God! The two men embraced with tender cordiality and almost happy emotion on the one side and the other. Never for one moment could Clive think his dear old father went[1] wrong—though the speculations were unfortunate in which he had engaged—though Clive had not liked them—it was a relief to his mind that they were now come

[1] went *Ms*] meant *E1*

to an end—they should all be happier now, thank God! those clouds of distrust being removed. Clive felt not one moment's doubt but that they should be able to meet fortune with a brave face,—and that happier—much happier days were in store for him than ever they had known since the period of this confounded prosperity.

"Here's a good end to it," says Clive with flashing eyes and a flushed face, "and here's a good health till to-morrow, Father"—and he filled into two glasses the wine still remaining in the flask. "Good bye to our fortunes— and bad luck go with her—I puff the prostitute away—*si celeres quatit pennas,* you remember what we used to say at Grey Friars *resigno quæ dedit et mea virtute me involvo, probamque pauperiem sine dote quæro.*" And he pledged his father who drank his wine, his hand shaking as he raised the glass to his lips and his kind voice trembly as he uttered the well-known old school words with an emotion that was as sacred as a prayer. Once more and with hearts full of love, the two men embraced. Clive's voice would tremble now if he told the story as it did when he spoke it to me in happier times one calm summer evening when we sat together and talked of dear old days.

Thomas Newcome explained to his son the plan which to his mind, as he came away from the City after the day's misfortunes, he thought it was best to pursue. The women and the child were clearly best out of the way. "And you too, my boy, must be on duty with them until I send for you which I will do if your presence can be of the least service to me, or is called for by—by—our honour," said the old man with a drop in his voice. "You must obey me in this, dear Clive, as you have done in everything and been a good and dear and obedient son to me. God pardon me for having trusted to my own simple old brains too much and not to you who know so much better. You will obey me this once more, my boy—you will promise me this," and the old man as he spoke took Clive's hand in both his and fondly caressed it.

Then with a shaking hand he took out of his pocket his old purse with the steel rings which he had worn for many and many a long year. Clive remembered it and his father's face how it would[2] beam with delight when he used to take that very purse out in Clive's boyish days and tip him just after he left school. "Here are some notes and some gold," he said. "It is Rosey's, honestly, Clive dear,—her half year's dividend for which you will give an order, please, to Sherrick. He has been very kind and good, Sherrick. All the servants were providentially paid last week—there are only the outstanding week's bills out—we shall manage to meet those I daresay. And you will see that Rosey only takes away such clothes for herself and her baby as are actually necessary—won't you, dear? the plain things you know—none of the fineries—they may be packed in a petara[3] or two— and you will take them with you—but the pomps and vanities, you know, we will leave behind—the pearls and bracelets and the plate and all that rubbish—and I will make an inventory of them to-morrow when you are gone and give them up, every rupee's worth, Sir, every anna, by Jove, to the creditors."

[2] would *E1*] used to *Ms*
[3] a petara *E1*] [blank space] *Ms*

The darkness had fallen by this time and the obsequious butler entered to light the dining-room lamps. "You have been a very good and kind servant to us, Martin," says the Colonel making him a low bow, "I should like to shake you by the hand. We must part company now and I have no doubt you and your fellow-servants will find good places, all of you, as you merit, Martin—as you merit. Great losses have fallen upon our family— we are ruined, Sir,—we are ruined. The great Bundelcund Banking Company has stopped payment in India and our branch here must stop on Monday. Thank my friends down-stairs for their kindness to me and my family." Martin bowed in silence with great respect. He and his comrades in the servants' hall had been expecting this catastrophe quite as long as the Colonel himself—who thought he had kept his affairs so profoundly secret.

Clive went up into his women's apartments,[4] looking with but little regret, I daresay, round those cheerless nuptial chambers with all their gaudy fittings; the fine looking-glasses, in which poor Rosey's little person had been reflected; the silken curtains under which he had lain by the poor child's side, wakeful and lonely. Here[5] he found his child's nurse and his wife and his wife's mother busily engaged with a multiplicity of boxes with flounces feathers fal-lals and finery which they were stowing away in this trunk and that; while the baby lay on its little pink pillow breathing softly, a little pearly fist placed close to its mouth. The aspect of the tawdry vanities scattered here and there chafed and annoyed the young man. He kicked the robes over with his foot. When Mrs. Mackenzie interposed with loud ejaculations, he sternly bade her to be silent and not wake the child. His words were not to be questioned when he spoke in that manner. "You will take nothing with you, Rosey, but what is strictly necessary—only two or three of your plainest dresses and what is required for the boy. What is in the trunk?"

Mrs. Mackenzie stepped forward and declared and the nurse vowed upon her honour and the lady's maid asserted really now upon her honour too, that there was nothing but what was most strictly necessary in that trunk to which affidavits, when Clive applied to his wife, she gave a rather timid assent.

"Where are the keys of that trunk?" Upon Mrs. Mackenzie's exclamation of "what nonsense!" Clive, putting his foot upon the flimsy oil covered box vowed he would kick the lid off unless it was instantly opened. Obeying this grim summons, the fluttering women produced the keys, and the black box was opened before him.

The box was found to contain a number of objects which Clive pronounced to be by no means necessary to his wife's and child's existence. Trinket[6] boxes and favourite little gim-cracks—chains—rings—and pearl necklaces—the tiara poor Rosey had worn at Court—the feathers and the gorgeous train which had decorated the little person—all these were found packed away in this one receptacle; and in another box, I am sorry to

[4] [Passage from here to next note added at proof stage.]
[5] apartments, looking . . . lonely. Here *E1*] apartments where *Ms*
[6] opened. Obeying . . . existence. Trinket *E1*] opened. Trinket *Ms*

say, were silver forks and spoons (the butler wisely judging that the rich and splendid electrotype ware might as well be left behind)—all the silver forks spoons and ladles and our poor old friend the cocoa-nut tree which these female robbers would have carried out of the premises. Clive[7] burst out into fierce laughter[8] when he saw the cocoa-nut tree—he laughed so loud that baby woke[9] and his mother-in-law called him a 'brute'—and the nurse ran to give its accustomed quietus to the little screaming infant. Rosey's eyes poured forth a torrent of little protests and she would have cried yet more loudly than the other baby—had not her husband, again fiercely checking her, sworn with a dreadful oath that unless she told him the whole truth, "By Heavens she should leave the house with nothing but what covered her." Even[1] the Campaigner could not make head against Clive's stern resolution; and the incipient insurrection of the maids and the mistresses was quelled by his spirit. The lady's maid, a flighty creature, received her wages and took her leave: but the nurse could not find it in her heart to quit her little nursling so suddenly, and accompanied Clive's household in the journey upon which those poor folks were bound. What[2] stolen goods were finally discovered when the family reached foreign parts were found in Mrs. Mackenzie's trunks—not in her daughter's; a silver filligree basket—a few tea-spoons—baby's gold coral and a costly crimson velvet-bound copy of the Hon. Miss Grimstone's Church Service to which articles, having thus appropriated them, Mrs. Mackenzie henceforward laid claim as her own.

So when the packing was done a cab was called to receive the modest trunks of this fugitive family—the coachman was bidden to put his horses to again and for the last time poor Rosey Newcome sat in her own carriage to which the Colonel conducted her with his courtly old bow, kissing the baby as it slept once more unconscious in its nurse's embrace—and bestowing a very grave and polite parting salute upon the Campaigner.

Then Clive and his father entered a cab on which the trunks were borne and they drove to the Tower Stairs where the ship lay which was to convey them out of England—and during that journey, no doubt, they talked over their altered prospects and I am sure Clive's father blessed his son fondly and committed him and his family to a good God's gracious keeping—and thought of him with sacred love when they had parted—and Thomas Newcome had returned to his lonely house to watch and to think of his ruined fortunes and to pray that he might have courage under them—that he might bear his own fate honourably—and that a gentle one might be dealt to those beloved beings for whom his life had been sacrificed in vain.

---

7 Clive *Ms*] Mr. Clive Newcome *E1*
8 into fierce laughter *E1*] laughing *Ms*
9 woke *Ms E1*] awoke *R*
1 [Passage from here to next note added at proof stage.]
2 her." Even ... bound. What *E1*] her." What *Ms*

Chapter XXXIV.

HEN the sale of Colonel Newcome's effects took place, a friend of the family bought in for a few shillings those two swords which had hung as we have said in the good man's chamber— and for which no single broker pres- ent had the heart to bid. The head of Clive's father painted by himself which had always kept its place in the young man's studio—together with a lot of his oil sketchings, easels and painting apparatus were purchased by the faithful J.J. who kept them until his friend should return to London and reclaim them and who shewed the most generous solicitude in Clive's behalf. J.J. was elected of the Royal Academy this year and Clive it was evident was working hard at the profession which he had always loved; for he sent over three pictures to the Academy—and I never knew man more mortified than the affectionate J.J. when two of these unlucky pieces were rejected by the committee for the year. One pretty little piece called "The Stranded Boat"[1] got a fair place on the Exhibition walls and you may be sure was loudly praised by a certain critic in the *Pall Mall Gazette*. The picture was sold on the first day of the Exhibition at the price of £25 which the artist demanded; and, when the kind J.J. wrote to inform his friend of this satisfactory circumstance and to say that he held the money at Clive's disposal, the latter replied with many expressions of sincere gratitude, at the same time begging him directly to forward the money with our old friend Thomas Newcome's love to Mrs. Sarah Mason at Newcome. But J.J. never informed his friend that he himself was the purchaser of the picture—nor was Clive made acquainted with the

---

[1] *Ms* indicates a space for an illustration here, but none appeared in *E1*.

"To be Sold"

fact until sometime[2] afterwards when he found it hanging in Ridley's studio.

I have said that we none of us were aware at this time what was the real state of Colonel Newcome's finances—and hoped that after giving up every shilling of his property which was confiscated to the creditors of the Bank—he had still from his retiring pension and military allowances at least enough reputably to maintain him. On one[3] occasion, having business in the City, I there met Mr. Sherrick. Affairs had been going ill with that gentleman—he had been let in terribly, he informed me, by Lord Levant's insolvency—having had large money transactions with his lordship. "There's none of them so good as old Newcome," Mr. Sherrick said with a sigh; "that was a good one—that was an honest man if ever I saw one—with no more guile and no more idea of business than a baby. Why didn't he take my advice, poor old cove—he might be comfortable now. Why did he sell away that annuity, Mr. Pendennis? I got it done for him when nobody else perhaps could have got it done for him—for the security ain't worth twopence if Newcome wasn't an honest man;—but I know he is and would rather starve and eat the nails off his fingers than not keep to his word—the old trump. And when he came to me a good two months before the smash of the Bank, which I knew it, Sir, and saw that it must come—when he came and raised three thousand pounds to meet them d—d electioneering bills, having to pay lawyers, commission, premium, life-insurance,—you know the whole game, Mr. P.—I as good as went down on my knees to him—I did—at the North and South American Coffee House where he was to meet the party about the money and said, 'Colonel, don't raise it—I tell you let it stand over—let it go in along with the bankruptcy that's a-coming,—but he wouldn't, Sir—he went on like an old Bengal tiger roaring about his honour—he paid the bills every shilling—infernal long bills they were— and it's my belief that at this minute he ain't got £50 a year of his own to spend. I would send him back my commission—I would by Jove—only times is so bad—and that rascal[4] Levant has let me in. It went to my heart to take the old cock's money—but it's gone—that and ever so much more— and Lady Whittlesea's chapel[5] too, Mr. P. Hang[6] that young Levant."

Squeezing my hand after this speech, Sherrick ran across the street after some other capitalist who was entering the Diddlesex Insurance Office and left me very much grieved and dismayed at finding that my worst fears in regard to Thomas Newcome were confirmed. Should we confer with his wealthy family respecting the Colonel's impoverished condition? Was his brother Hobson[7] Newcome aware of it? as for Sir Barnes, the quarrel between him and his uncle had been too fierce to admit of hopes of relief from that quarter. Barnes had been put to very heavy expenses in the first contested election—had come forward again immediately on his un-

[2] sometime *Ms*] some time *E1*
[3] one *E1*] some *Ms*
[4] rascal *E1*] d—d *Ms*
[5] chapel *E1*] trapple *Ms*
[6] Hang *E1*] D—n *Ms*
[7] Hobson *E1*] H[blank] *Ms*

cle's resignation but again had been beaten by a more liberal candidate, his quondam former friend, Mr. Higg—who formally declared against Sir Barnes—and who drove him finally out of the representation of Newcome. From this gentleman it was vain of course for Colonel Newcome's friends to expect relief.

How to aid him—he was proud—past work—nearly seventy years old. "Ah[8] why did those cruel academicians refuse Clive's pictures?" cries Laura. "I have no patience with them—had the pictures been exhibited I know who might have bought them—but that is vain now. He would suspect at once and send her money away. Oh, Pen! Why, why didn't he come when I wrote that letter to Brussels?"

From persons so poorly endowed with money as ourselves, any help but of the merest temporary nature was out of the question. We knew our friends too well not to know that they would disdain to receive it. It was agreed between me and Laura that at any rate I should go and see Clive. Our friends indeed were at a very short distance from us—and having exiled themselves from England could yet see its coasts from their windows upon any clear day. Boulogne was their present abiding place—refuge of how many thousands of other unfortunate Britons—and to this friendly port I betook myself speedily, having the address of Colonel Newcome. His quarters were in a quiet grass-grown old street of the old town. None of the family were at home when I called. There was indeed no servant to answer the bell but the good-natured French domestic of a neighbouring lodger told me that the young Monsieur went out every day to make his designs and that I should probably find the elder gentleman upon the rampart where he was in the custom of going every day. I strolled[9] along by those pretty old walls[1] and bastions, under the pleasant trees which shadow them, and the grey old gabled houses from which you look down upon the gay new city, and the busy port, and the piers stretching into the shining sea dotted with a hundred white sails or black smoking steamers—and bounded by the friendly lines of the bright English shore. There are few prospects more charming than the familiar view from those old French walls—few places where young children may play and ruminating[2] old age repose more pleasantly than on those peaceful rampart gardens.

I found our dear old friend seated on one of the benches—a newspaper on his knees—and by his side a red-cheeked little French lass upon whose lap Thomas Newcome the younger lay sleeping. The Colonel's face flushed up when he saw me. As he advanced a step or two towards me I could see that he trembled in his walk. His hair had grown almost quite white. He looked now to be more than his age—he whose carriage last year had been so erect—whose figure had been so[3] straight and manly. I was very much moved at meeting him and at seeing the sad traces which pain and grief had left in the countenance of the dear old man.

[8] "Ah *Ms*] "Oh, *E1*
[9] strolled *E1*] walked *Ms*
[1] walls *Ms*] walks *E1*
[2] ruminating *E1*] rankling *Ms*
[3] had been so *E1*] so *Ms*

A Friend in Need

"So you are come to see me, my good young friend," cried the Colonel with a trembling voice. "It is very very kind of you. Is not this a pretty drawing-room to receive our friends in? We have not many of them now— Boy and I come and sit here for hours every day. Hasn't he grown a fine boy. He can say several words now, Sir, and can walk surprisingly well— soon he will be able to walk with his grandfather—and then Marie will not have the trouble to wait upon either of us." He repeated this sentiment in his pretty old French and turning with a bow to Marie. The girl said[4] Monsieur knew very well that she did not desire better than to come out with baby—that it was better than staying at home, pardieu—and the clock striking at this moment, she rose up with her child crying out that it was time to return or Madame would scold.

"Mrs. Mackenzie has rather a short temper," the Colonel said with a gentle smile. "Poor thing, she has had a great deal to bear in consequence, Pen, of my imprudence. I am glad you never took shares in our banks. I should not be so glad to see you as I am now if I had brought losses upon you as I have upon so many of my friends." I, for my part, trembled to hear that the good old man was under the domination of the Campaigner.

"Bayham sends me the paper regularly—he is a very kind faithful creature. How glad I am that he has got a snug berth in the City. His company really prospers, I am happy to think, unlike some companies you know of, Pen. I have read your two speeches, Sir, and Clive and I liked them very much. The poor boy works all day at his pictures. You know he has sold one at the Exhibition, which has given us a great deal of heart—and he has completed two or three more—and I am sitting to him now for—what do you think, Sir? for Belisarius. Will you give *Belisarius and Obolus* an offer?"[5]

"My dear, dear old friend," I said in great emotion, "if you will do me the kindness[6] to take my Obolus or to use my services in any way, you will give me more pleasure than ever I had from your generous bounties in old days. Look, Sir, I wear the watch which you gave me when you went to India. Did you not tell me then to look over Clive and serve him if I could? Can't I serve him now?" and I went on further in this strain asseverating with great warmth and truth that my wife's affection and my own were[7] most sincere for both of them and that our pride would be to be able to help such dear friends.

The Colonel said I had a good heart, and my wife had though— though—he did not finish this sentence, but I could interpret it without need of its completion. My wife and the two ladies of Colonel Newcome's family never could be friends, however much my poor Laura tried to be intimate with these women. Her very efforts at intimacy caused a frigidity and hauteur which Laura could not overcome. Little Rosey and her mother set us down as but[8] aristocratic personages, nor for our parts

---

[4] said *E1*] said that *Ms*

[5] *Belisarius and Obolus* an offer?"] Belisarius and Obolus an offer? *Ms*] Belisarius and the Obolus kind word? *E1*] Belisarius and the Obolus a kind word?" *R*

[6] kindness *E1*] great kindness *Ms*

[7] were *E1*] was *Ms*

[8] but *Ms*] two *E1*

were we very much disturbed at this opinion of the Campaigner and little Rosey.

I talked with the Colonel for half an hour or more about his affairs which indeed were very gloomy and Clive's prospects, of which he strove to present as cheering a view as possible. He was obliged to confirm the news which Sherrick had given me and to own, in fact, that all his pension was swallowed up by a payment of interest and life insurance for sums which he had been compelled to borrow. How could he do otherwise than meet his engagements? Thank God, he had Clive's full approval for what he had done—had communicated the circumstance to his son almost immediately after it took place—and that was a comfort to him—an immense comfort. "For the women are very angry," said the poor Colonel, "you see they do not understand the laws of honour, at least as we understand them, and perhaps I was wrong in hiding the truth as I certainly did from Mrs. Mackenzie—but I acted for the best—I hoped against hope that some chance might turn in our favour. God knows—I had a hard task enough in wearing a cheerful face for months and in following my little Rosey about to her parties and balls—but poor Mrs. Mackenzie has a right to be angry—only I wish my little girl did not side with her mother so entirely—for the loss of her affection gives me great[9] pain."

So it was as I suspected. The Campaigner ruled over this family and added to all their distresses by her intolerable presence and tyranny. "Why, Sir," I ventured to ask, "if as I gather from you—and I remember," I added with a laugh, "certain battles royal which Clive described to me in old days—if you and the Campai—Mrs.[1] Mackenzie—do not agree—why should she continue to live with you, when you would all be so much happier apart?"

"She has a right to live in the house," says the Colonel, "it is I who have no right in it. I am a poor old pensioner, don't you see, subsisting on Rosey's bounty. We live on the hundred a-year secured to her at her marriage—and Mrs. Mackenzie has her forty pounds of pension which she adds to the common stock. It is I who have made away with every shilling of Rosey's £17000, God help me,—and with £1500 of her mother's. They put their little means together and they keep us—me and Clive. What can we do for a living? Great God! What can we do? Why, I am so useless that even when my poor boy earned £25 for his picture, I felt we were bound to send it to Sarah Mason, and you may fancy when this came to Mrs. Mackenzie's ears what a life my boy and I led. I have never spoken of these things to any mortal soul—I even don't speak of them with Clive—but seeing your kind honest face has made me talk—you must pardon my garrulity—I am growing old, Arthur.[2] This poverty and these quarrels have beaten my spirit down——there, I shall talk on this subject no more. I wish, Sir, I could ask you to dine with us—but"—and here he smiled—"we must get the leave of the higher powers."

[9] great *Ms E1*] [omitted] *R*
[1] Campai—Mrs. *E1*] Camp—and Mrs. *Ms*
[2] Arthur. *E1*] Author. *Ms*

I was determined in spite of prohibitions and Campaigners to see my old friend[3] Clive—and insisted on walking back with the Colonel to his lodgings, at the door of which we met Mrs. Mackenzie and her daughter. Rosey blushed up a little—looked at her Mamma—and then greeted me with a hand and a curtsey. The Campaigner also saluted me in a majestic but amicable manner—made no objection even to my entering her apartments and seeing the condition to which they were *reduced:*[4] this phrase was uttered with particular emphasis and a significant look towards the Colonel who bowed his meek head and preceded me into the lodgings which were in truth very homely, pretty and comfortable. The Campaigner was an excellent manager—restless—bustling[5]—brushing—perpetually. Such fugitive gim-cracks as they had brought away with them decorated the little salon.[6] Mrs. Mackenzie who took the entire command, even pressed me to dine and partake—if so fashionable a gentleman would *condescend* to partake of a humble exile's fare. No fare was perhaps very pleasant to me in company with that woman—but I wanted to see my dear old Clive and gladly accepted his voluble mother-in-law's not disinterested hospitality. She beckoned the Colonel aside—whispered to him putting something into his hand—on which he took his hat and went away. Then Rosey was dismissed upon some other pretext and I had the felicity to be left alone with Mrs. Captain Mackenzie.

She instantly improved the occasion—and with great eagerness and volubility entered into her statement of the present affairs and position of this unfortunate family. She described darling Rosey's delicate state, poor thing—nursed with tenderness and in the lap of luxury—brought up with every delicacy and the fondest mother—never knowing in the least how to take care of herself—and likely to fall down and perish unless the[7] kind Campaigner were by to prop and protect her. She was in delicate health—very delicate—ordered cod liver oil by the doctor. Heaven knows how he could be paid, or those expensive medicines,[8] out of the pittance which the *imprudence*—the most culpable and designing[9] *imprudence*—and *extravagance*—and *folly* of Colonel Newcome had reduced them! Looking out from the window as she spoke I saw—we both saw—the dear old gentleman sadly advancing towards the house, a parcel in his hand. Seeing his near approach and that our interview was likely to come to an end, Mrs. Mackenzie rapidly whispered to me that she knew I had a good heart—that I had been blest by Providence with a fine fortune which I knew how to keep better than *some* folks—and that if as no doubt was my intention—for with what other but a charitable view could I have come to see them, "and most generous and noble was it of you to come—and I always thought it of

3 old friend *E1*] friend *Ms*
4 the condition to which they were *reduced:* [the whole phrase is underlined and then underlining is cancelled except for *reduced:*] *Ms*] *the condition to which they were reduced: E1*
5 bustling *Ms*] bothering *E1*
6 salon. *E1*] [omitted] *Ms*
7 the *E1*] her *Ms*
8 paid, or ... medicines,] paid or ... medicines *Ms*] paid for ... medicines *E1*
9 designing *E1*] disingenuous *Ms*

you, Mr. Pendennis—whatever *other* people said to the contrary"—if I proposed to give them relief which was most needful—and for which a *mother's blessings* would follow me—let it be to her, the Campaigner, that my loan should be confided—for as for the Colonel, he is not fit to be trusted with a shilling and has already flung away *immense sums* upon some old woman he keeps in the country, leaving his darling Rosey without the actual necessaries of life.

The woman's greed and rapacity—the flattery with which she chose to belabour me at dinner so choked and disgusted me that I could hardly swallow the meal—though my poor old friend had been sent out to purchase a paté from the pastry-cook's for my special[1] refection. Clive was not at the dinner. He seldom returned till late at night on sketching days.—Neither his wife nor his mother-in-law seemed much to miss him, and seeing that the Campaigner engrossed the entire share of the conversation and proposed not to leave me for five minutes alone with the Colonel, I took leave rather speedily of my entertainers leaving a message for Clive and a prayer that he would come and see me at my hotel.

---

[1] for my special] for my especial *E1*] from my special *Ms*

Chapter XXXV.

WAS sitting in the dusk in my room at the Hôtel des Bains when the visitor for whom I hoped made his appearance in the person of Clive with his broad shoulders and broad hat and a shaggy beard, which he had thought fit in his quality of painter to assume. Our greeting it need not be said was warm and our talk which extended far into the night very friendly and confidential. If I make my readers confidants[1] in Mr. Clive's private affairs, I ask my friend's pardon for narrating his history in their behoof. The world had gone very ill with my poor Clive, and I do not think that the pecuniary losses which had visited him and his father afflicted him near so sorely as the state of his home. In a pique with the woman he loved and from that generous weakness which formed part of his character and which led him to acquiesce in most wishes of his good father, the young man had gratified the darling desire of the Colonel's heart and taken the wife whom his two old friends brought to him. Rosey, who was also as we have shewn of a very obedient and ductile nature, had acquiesced gladly enough in her mamma's opinion that she was in love with the rich and handsome young Clive and accepted him for better or worse. So undoubtedly would this good child have accepted Captain Hoby her previous adorer—have smilingly promised fidelity to the Captain at Church and have made a very good, happy and sufficient little wife for that officer—had not Mamma commanded her to jilt him. What wonder that these elders should wish to see their two dear young ones united. They began with suitable age, money, good temper, and parents' blessings. It is not the first time that with all these excellent helps to prosperity and happiness, a marriage has turned out unfortunately—a pretty tight ship gone to wreck that set forth on its voyage with cheers from the shore and every prospect of fair wind and fine weather.

[1] confidants *E1*] a confidantes *Ms*

We have before quoted poor Clive's simile of the shoes with which his good old father provided him—as pretty a little pair of shoes as need be—only they did not fit the wearer. If they pinched him at first—how they blistered and tortured him now![2] If Clive was gloomy and discontented even when the honeymoon had scarce waned—and he and his family sat at home in state and splendour under the boughs of the famous silver cocoa-nut tree—what was the young man's condition now in poverty when they had no love along with a scant dinner of herbs—when his mother-in-law grudged each morsel which his poor old father ate—when a vulgar coarse-minded woman pursued with brutal sarcasm and deadly rancour one of the tenderest and noblest gentlemen in the world—when an ailing wife always under some one's domination received him with helpless hysterical cries and reproaches—when a coarse female tyrant, stupid, obstinate, utterly unable to comprehend the son's kindly genius or the father's gentle spirit, bullied over both using the intolerable undeniable advantage which her actual wrongs gave her to tyrannise over these two wretched men. He had never heard the last of that money which they had sent to Mrs. Mason, Clive said;—when the knowledge of the fact came to the Campaigner's ears, she raised such a storm as almost killed the poor Colonel and drove his son half mad. She seized the howling infant, vowing that its unnatural father and grandfather were bent upon starving it. She consoled and blest[3] Rosey into hysterics. She took the outlawed parson to whose church they went and the choice society of bankrupt captains, captains' ladies, fugitive stock-brokers' wives and dingy frequenters of billiard-rooms and refugees from the Bench into her councils—and in her daily visits amongst these person-ages and her walks on the pier whither she trudged with poor Rosey in her train—Mrs. Mackenzie made known her own wrongs and her daughter's—shewed how the Colonel, having robbed and cheated them previously, was now living upon them in so much that Mrs. Bolter, the levanting[4] auction-eer's wife, would not make the poor old man a bow when she met him—that Mrs. Captain Kitely whose husband had lain for seven years past in Boulogne jail[5] ordered her son to cut Clive; and when, the child being sick, the poor old Colonel went for arrowroot to the Chemist's, young Snooks the apothecary's assistant refused to allow him to take the powder away without[6] previously depositing the money.

He had no money, Thomas Newcome,—he gave up every farthing. After having impoverished all around him, he had no right, he said, to touch a sixpence of the wretched pittance remaining to them—he had even given up his cigar, the poor old man, the companion and comforter of forty years—he was "not fit to be trusted with money," Mrs. Mackenzie said, and the good man owned, as he cut[7] his scanty crust and bowed his noble old head in silence under that cowardly persecution.

[2] We have before . . . tortured him now! *Ms E1*] [omitted] *R*
[3] blest] blst *Ms*] sent *E1*
[4] levanting *E1*] Levantine *Ms*
[5] jail *Ms*] gaol *E1*
[6] without *E1*] with *Ms*
[7] cut *Ms*] ate *E1*

And this at the end of three score and seven or eight years was to be the close of a life which had been spent in freedom and splendour and kindness and honour—this the reward of the noblest heart that ever beat—the[8] tomb and prison of a gallant warrior who had ridden in twenty battles— whose course through life had been a bounty wherever it had passed— whose name had been followed by blessings and whose career was to end here—here—in a mean room, in a mean alley of a foreign town—a low furious woman standing over him and stabbing the kind defenceless heart[9] with killing insult and daily outrage!

As we sat together in the dark Clive told me this wretched story which was wrung from him with a passionate emotion that[1] I could not but keenly share. He wondered the old man lived, Clive said. Some of the woman's taunts and jibes, as he could see, struck his father so that he gasped and started back as if some one had lashed him with a whip. "He would make away with himself," said poor Clive, "but he deems this is his punishment and that he must bear it as long as it pleases God. He does not care for his own losses as far as they concern himself: but these reproaches of Mrs. Mackenzie and some things which were said to him in the Bankruptcy Court by one or two widows of old friends who were induced through his representations to take shares in that infernal Bank, have affected him dreadfully. I hear him lying awake and groaning at night, God bless him. Great God! what can I do—what can I do!" burst out the young man in a dreadful paroxysm of grief. "I have tried to get lessons—I went to London on the deck of a steamer and took a lot of drawings with me—tried picture dealers—pawnbrokers—Jews—Moss whom you may remember at Gandish's and who gave me, for forty-two drawings, £18. I brought the money back to Boulogne. It was enough to pay the doctor and bury our last poor little dead baby. *Tenez*, Pen, you must give me some supper. I have had nothing all day but a *pain de deux sous*, I can't stand it at home— my heart's almost broken—you must give me some money Pen, old boy. I know you will. I thought of writing to you, but I wanted to support myself, you see. When I went to London with the drawings[2] I tried George's chambers but he was in the country. I saw Crackthorpe on the street—in Oxford Street—but I could not face him and bolted down Hangmanyard.[3] I tried and I could not ask him—and I got the £18 from Moss that day and came home with it."

Give him money! of course I would[4] give him money—my dear old friend—and as an alterative[5] and a wholesome shock to check that burst of passion and grief in which the poor fellow indulged, I thought fit to break into[6] a very fierce and angry invective on my own part (which served to disguise the extreme feeling of pain and pity that I did not somehow choose

---

8 the noblest heart that ever beat—the *Ms E1*] a noble heart—the *R*
9 heart *Ms E1*] breast *R*
1 emotion that *E1*] emotion—but *Ms*
2 drawings *E1*] drawing *Ms*
3 Hangmanyard *Ms*] Hanway-yard *E1*
4 would *Ms E1*] will *R*
5 alterative *Ms E1*] alternative *R*
6 into *E1*] out in *Ms*

to exhibit).[7] I rated Clive soundly—and taxed him with unfriendliness and ingratitude for not having sooner applied to friends who would think shame of themselves whilst he was in need. Whatever he wanted was his as much as mine. I could not understand how the necessity of the family should in truth be so extreme as he described it—for after all many a poor family lived upon very much less—but I uttered none of these objections—checking them with the thought that Clive on his first arrival at Boulogne, entirely ignorant of the practice of economy, might have imprudently engaged in expenses which had reduced him to this present destitution.*

I took the liberty of asking about debts and of these Clive gave me to understand there were none—at least none of his or his father's contracting. "If we were too proud to borrow and I think we were wrong, Pen, my dear old boy—I think we were wrong now—at least we were too proud to owe. My colourman takes his bill out in drawings—and I think owes me a trifle. He got me some lessons at fifty sous a ticket—a pound the ten—from an economical Swell who has taken a chateau here—and has two flunkies in livery. He has four daughters who take advantage of the lessons,[8] and screws ten per cent upon the poor colourman's pencils and drawing paper. It's pleasant work to give the lessons to the children—and to be patronised by the swell—and not expensive to him—is it, Pen? Bah—I don't mind that, if I could but get lessons enough—for you see besides our expenses here, we must have some more money—and the dear old governor would die outright if poor old Sarah Mason did not get her £50 a-year."

And now there arrived a plentiful supper and a bottle of good wine of which the giver[9] was not sorry to partake after the meagre dinner at three o'clock—to which I had been invited by the Campaigner—and it was midnight when I walked back with my friend to his house in the upper town—and all the stars of heaven were shining cheerily—and my dear Clive's face wore an expression of happiness such as I remembered in old days as we shook hands and parted with a "God bless you."

To Clive's friend, revolving these things in his mind as he lay in one of those most snug and comfortable beds at the excellent Hôtel des Bains, it appeared[1] that this town of Boulogne was a very bad market for the artist's talents and that he had best bring them to London where a score of old friends would assuredly be ready to help him.—And if the Colonel, too, could be got away from the domination of the Campaigner, I felt certain that the dear old gentleman could but profit by his leave of absence. My wife and I at this time inhabited a spacious old house in Queen's Square, Westminister, where there was plenty of room for father and son. I knew that Laura would be delighted to welcome these guests—may the wife of every worthy gentleman who reads these pages be as ready to receive her husband's friends.—It was the state of Rosey's health and the Campaigner's

---

[7] *E1* omits the parentheses.
* I did not know at the time that Mrs. Mackenzie had taken entire superintendence of the family treasury—and that this exemplary woman was putting away, as she had done previously, sundry little sums to meet rainy days.
[8] the lessons, *E1*] lessons, *Ms*
[9] giver *E1*] giver himself *Ms*
[1] appeared *E1*] appeared clearly *Ms*

authority and permission about which I was in doubt and whether this lady's two slaves would be allowed to go away.

These cogitations kept the present biographer long awake, and he did not breakfast next[2] day until an hour before noon. I had the coffee-room to myself by chance and my meal was not yet ended when the waiter announced a lady to visit Mr. Pendennis and Mrs. Mackenzie made her appearance.[3] No signs of care or poverty were visible in the attire or countenance of the buxom widow. A handsome bonnet decorated within with a profusion of poppies, blue-bells, and ears of corn—a jewel on her forehead, not costly but splendid in appearance and glittering artfully over that central spot from which her wavy chestnut hair parted to cluster in ringlets round her ample cheeks—a handsome India shawl—smart gloves—a rich silk dress—a neat parasol of blue with pale yellow lining—a multiplicity of glittering rings and a very splendid gold watch and chain which I remembered in former days as hanging round poor Rosey's white neck—all these adornments set off the widow's person so that you might have thought her a wealthy capitalist's lady—and never could have supposed that she was a poor cheated ruined robbed unfortunate Campaigner.—

Nothing could be more gracious than the *accueil* of this lady. She paid me many handsome compliments about my literary works—asked most affectionately for dear Mrs. Pendennis and the dear children—and then, as I expected, coming to business, contrasted the happiness and genteel position of my wife and family with the misery and wrongs of her own blessed child and grandson. She never could call that child by the odious name which he received at his baptism. *I* knew what bitter reasons she had to dislike the name of Thomas Newcome.

She again rapidly enumerated the wrongs she had received at the hands of that gentleman; mentioned the vast sums of money out of which she and her soul's darling had been tricked by that poor muddle-headed creature, to say no worse of him—and described finally their present pressing need. The doctor's—the burial—Rosey's delicate condition—the cost of sweetbreads calf's-foot jelly and cods-liver[4] oil were again passed in a rapid calculation before me—and she ended her speech by expressing her gratification that I had attended to her advice of the previous day and not given Clive Newcome a direct loan—that the family wanted it, the Campaigner called upon Heaven to witness—that Clive and his absurd poor father would fling guineas out of the window was a fact equally certain,—the rest of the argument was obvious—namely—that Mr. Pendennis should administer a donation[5] to herself.

I had brought but a small sum of money[6] in my pocket-book, though Mrs. Mackenzie intimate with bankers, and having thank Heaven, in spite of all her misfortunes the utmost confidence of *all* her tradesmen, hinted a

---

2 next *E1*] on the next *Ms*
3 Originally the *Ms* started a new paragraph at this point, but a long dash cancelled the paragraphing.
4 cods-liver] cods liver *Ms*] cod-liver *E1*
5 donation *E1*] sum of money *Ms*
6 sum of money *E1*] sum *Ms*

perfect willingness on her part to accept an order upon her friends Hobson Brothers of London.

This direct thrust I gently and smilingly parried by asking Mrs. Mackenzie whether she supposed a gentleman who had just paid an electioneering bill and had at the best of times but a very small income might sometimes not be in a condition to draw satisfactorily upon Messrs. Hobson or any other bankers? Her countenance fell at this remark, nor was her cheerfulness much improved by the tender of one of the two bank notes which then happened to be in my possession. I said that I had a use for the remaining note and that it would not be more than sufficient to pay my hotel bill and the expenses of my party back to London.

My party? I had here to divulge[7] with some little trepidation the plan which I had been making[8] over night—to explain how I thought that Clive's great talents were wasted at Boulogne—now could only find a proper market in London—how I was pretty certain through my connection with booksellers[9] to find some advantageous employment for him and would have done so months ago had I known the state of the case—but I had believed until within a very few days since that the Colonel, in spite of his bankruptcy, was still in the enjoyment of considerable military pensions.

This statement, of course, elicited from the widow a number of remarks not complimentary to my dear old Colonel. He might have kept his pensions had he not been a fool—he was a baby about money matters—misled himself and everybody—was a log in the house &c. &c. &c.

I suggested that his annuities might possibly be put into some more satisfactory shape—that I had trustworthy lawyers with whom I would put him in communication—that he had best come to London to see to these matters—and that my wife had a large house where she would most gladly entertain the two gentlemen.

This I said with some reasonable dread—fearing in the first place her refusal—in the second, her acceptance of the invitation with a proposal, as our house was large, to come herself and inhabit it for a while. Had[1] I not seen that Campaigner arrive for a month at poor James Binnie's house in Fitzroy Square and stay there for many years? Was I not aware that when she once set her foot in a gentleman's establishment, terrific battles must ensue before she could be dislodged? Had she not once been routed by Clive? and was she not now in command and possession? Do I not, finally, know something of the world? and have I not a weak easy temper? I protest it was with terror that I awaited the widow's possible answer to my proposal.

To my great relief she expressed the utmost approval of both my plans. I was uncommonly kind, she was sure, to interest myself about the two gentlemen and for her blessed Rose's sake—a fond mother thanked me. It was most advisable that Clive should earn some money by that horrid profession which he had chosen to adopt—*trade, she* called it. She was clearly

---

[7] here to divulge *E1*] hereto divulged *Ms*
[8] making *E1*] maturing *Ms*
[9] booksellers *E1*] booksellers to be able *Ms*
[1] Had *E1*] Have *Ms*

anxious to get rid both of father and son—and agreed that the sooner they went the better.

We walked back arm in arm to the Colonel's quarters in the old town, Mrs. Mackenzie in the course of our walk doing me the honour to introduce me by name to several dingy acquaintances whom we met sauntering up the street—and imparting to me, as each moved away, the pecuniary cause of his temporary residence in Boulogne. Spite of Rosey's delicate state of health—Mrs. Mackenzie did not hesitate to break the news to her of the gentlemen's probable departure, abruptly and eagerly, as if the intelligence was likely to please her—and[2] it did rather than otherwise. The young woman being in the habit of letting Mamma judge for her—continued it in this instance—and whether her husband stayed or went seemed to be equally content or apathetic. "And is it not most kind and generous of dear Mr. and Mrs. Pendennis to propose to receive Mr. Newcome and the Colonel?" This opportunity for gratitude being pointed out to Rosey, she acquiesced in it straightway—it was very kind of me, Rosey was sure. "And don't you ask after dear Mrs. Pendennis and the dear children—you poor dear suffering darling child?" Rosey who had neglected this inquiry immediately hoped Mrs. Pendennis and the children were well. The overpowering mother had taken utter possession of this poor little thing. Rosey's eyes followed the Campaigner about and appealed to her at all moments. She sat under Mrs. Mackenzie as a bird before a boa-constrictor, doomed—fluttering—fascinated—scared and pavid[3] as a whipt spaniel before a keeper.

The Colonel was on his accustomed bench on the rampart at this sunny hour. I repaired thither and found the old gentleman seated by his grandson, who lay, as yesterday, on the little bonne's lap, one of his little purple hands closed round the grandfather's finger. "Hush!" says the good man, lifting up his other finger to his moustache, as I approached, "Boy's asleep. Il est bien joli quand il dort—le Boy, n'est ce pas, Marie?" The maid believed Monsieur well—the boy was a little angel. "This maid is a most trustworthy, valuable person, Pendennis," the Colonel said, with much gravity.

The boa-constrictor had fascinated him, too—the lash of that woman at home had cowed that helpless, gentle, noble spirit. As I looked at the head so upright and manly, now so beautiful and resigned—the year of his past life seemed to pass before me somehow in a flash of thought. I could fancy the accursed tyranny—the dumb acquiescence—the brutal jeer—the helpless remorse—the sleepless nights of pain and recollection—the gentle heart lacerated with deadly stabs—and the impotent hope. I own I burst into a sob at the sight, and thought of the noble suffering creature, and hid my face, and turned away.

He sprang up, releasing his hand from the child's, and placing it, the kind, shaking hand, on my shoulder. "What is it, Arthur—my dear boy?" he said, looking wistfully in my face. "No bad news from home, my dear? Laura and the children well?"

[2] and *E1*] and so *Ms*
[3] pavid] pavied *Ms*] fawning *E1*

The emotion was mastered in a moment, I put his arm under mine, and as we slowly sauntered up and down the sunny walk of the old rampart, I told him how I had come with special commands from Laura to bring him for awhile to stay with us, and to settle his business, which I was sure had been wofully mismanaged, and to see whether we could not find the means of getting some little out of the wreck of the property for the boy yonder.

At first Colonel Newcome would not hear of quitting Boulogne where Rosey would miss him—he was sure she would want him—but before the ladies of his family, to whom we[4] presently returned, Thomas Newcome's resolution was quickly recalled. He agreed to go, and Clive coming in at this time was put in possession of our plan and gladly acquiesced in it. On that very evening I came with a carriage to conduct my two friends to the steam-boat. Their little packets were made and ready. There was no pretence of grief at parting on the women's side, but Marie, the little maid, with Boy in her arms, cried sadly; and Clive heartily embraced the child; and the Colonel going back to give it one more kiss, drew out of his neckcloth a little gold brooch which he wore, and which, trembling, he put into Marie's hand, bidding her take good care of Boy till his return.

"She is a good girl—a most faithful, attached girl, Arthur, do you see," the kind old gentleman said; "and I had no money to give her—no, not one single rupee."

---

[4] we *E1*] he *R*

Chapter XXXVI.

IN WHICH CLIVE BEGINS THE WORLD.

E are ending our history, and yet poor Clive is but beginning the world. He has to earn the bread which he eats henceforth; and, as I saw his labours, his trials, and his disappointments, I could not but compare his calling with my own.

The drawbacks and penalties attendant upon our profession are taken into full account, as we well know, by literary men, and their friends. Our poverty, hardships, and disappointments are set forth with great emphasis, and often with too great truth by those who speak of us; but there are advantages belonging to our trade which are passed over, I think, by some of those who exercise it and describe it, and for which, in striking the balance of our accounts, we are not always duly thankful. We have no patron, so to speak—we sit in antechambers no more, waiting the present of a few guineas from my lord; in return for a fulsome dedication. We sell our wares to the book purveyor, between whom and us there is no greater obligation than between him and his paper-maker or printer. In the great towns in our country, immense stores of books are provided for us, with librarians to class them, kind attendants to wait upon us, and comfortable appliances for study. We require scarce any capital wherewith to exercise our trade. What other so called learned profession is equally fortunate? A doctor, for example, after carefully and expensively educating himself, must invest in house and furniture, horses, carriage, and men-servants, before the public patient will think of calling him in. I am told that such gentlemen have to coax and wheedle dowagers, to humour hypochondriacs, to practise a score of little subsidiary arts in order to make that of healing profitable. How many many hundreds of pounds has a barrister to sink upon his stock in trade before his returns are available? There are the costly charges of university education—the costly chambers in the Inn of Court—the clerk and his maintenance—the inevitable travels on circuit—certain expenses all to be defrayed before the possible client makes his appearance, and the chance of fame or competency arrives. The prizes are great, to be sure, in the law, but what a prodigious sum the lottery ticket costs! If a man of letters cannot win, neither does he risk so much. Let us speak of our trade as we find it, and not be too eager in calling out for public compassion.

The artists, for the most part, do not cry out their woes as loudly as some gentlemen of the literary fraternity, and yet I think the life of many of them is harder; their chances even more precarious, and the conditions of their profession less independent and agreeable than ours. I have watched Alfred Smee,[1] Esq., R.A., flattering and fawning, and at the same time boasting and swaggering, poor fellow, in order to secure a sitter. I have listened to a Manchester magnate talking about fine arts before one of J.J.'s pictures, assuming the airs of a painter, and laying down the most absurd laws respecting the art. I have seen poor Tomkins bowing a rich amateur through a private view, and noted the eager smiles on Tomkins' face at the amateur's slightest joke, the sickly twinkle of hope in his eyes as Amateur stopped before his own picture. I have been ushered by Chipstone's black servant through hall after hall peopled with plaster gods and heroes, into Chipstone's own magnificent studio, where he sat longing vainly for an order, and justly dreading his landlord's call for the rent. And, seeing how severely these gentlemen were taxed in their profession, I have been grateful for my own more fortunate one, which necessitates cringing to no patron; which calls for no keeping up of appearances; and which requires no stock in trade save the workman's industry; his best ability; and a dozen sheets of paper.

Having to turn with all his might to his new profession, Clive Newcome, one of the proudest men alive, chose to revolt and to be restive at almost every stage of his training. He had a natural genius for his art, and had acquired in his desultory way a very considerable skill. His drawing was better than his painting (an opinion which, were my friend present, he of course would utterly contradict); his designs and sketches were far superior to his finished compositions. His friends presuming to judge of this artist's qualifications, ventured to counsel him accordingly, and were thanked for their pains in the usual manner. We had in the first place to bully and browbeat Clive most fiercely, before he would take fitting lodgings for the execution of those designs which we had in view for him. "Why should I take expensive lodgings?" says Clive slapping his fist on the table, "I am a pauper, and can scarcely afford to live in a garret. Why should you pay me for drawing your portrait and Laura's and the children? What the deuce does Warrington want with the effigy of his grim old mug? You don't want them a bit—you only want to give me money. It would be much more honest of me to take the money at once and own that I am a beggar; and I tell you what, Pen, the only money which I feel I come honestly by, is that which is paid me by a little printseller in Long Acre who buys my drawings,

---

[1] watched Alfred Smee] watched — Smee *El R*

one with another, at fourteen shillings a piece, and out of whom I can earn pretty nearly two hundred a-year. I am doing Mail Coaches for him, Sir, and charges of Cavalry; the public like the Mail Coaches best—on a dark paper—the horses and milestones picked out white—yellow dust—cobalt distance, and the guard and coachman of course in vermilion. That's what a gentleman can get his bread by—Portraits, pooh! it's disguised beggary. Crackthorpe, and a half-dozen men of his regiment came, like good fellows as they are, and sent me five pounds a-piece for their heads, but I tell you I am ashamed to take the money." Such used to be the tenor of Clive Newcome's conversation as he strode up and down our room after dinner, pulling his moustache and dashing his long yellow hair off his gaunt face.

When Clive was inducted into the new lodgings at which his friends counselled him to hang up his ensign, the dear old Colonel accompanied his son, parting with a sincere regret from our little ones at home, to whom he became greatly endeared during his visit to us, and who always hailed him when he came to see us with smiles and caresses and sweet infantile welcome. On that day when he went away, Laura went up and kissed him with tears in her eyes. "You know how long I have been wanting to do it," this lady said to her husband. Indeed I cannot describe the behaviour of the old man during his stay with us, his gentle gratitude, his sweet simplicity and kindness, his thoughtful courtesy. There was not a servant in our little household but was eager to wait upon him. Laura's maid was as tender-hearted at his departure as her mistress. He was ailing for a short time, when our cook performed prodigies of puddings and jellies to suit his palate. The youth who held the offices of butler and valet in our establishment—a lazy and greedy youth whom Martha scolded in vain—would jump up and leave his supper to carry a message to our Colonel. My heart is full as I remember the kind words which he said to me at parting, and as I think that we were the means of giving a little comfort to that stricken and gentle soul.

Whilst the Colonel and his son stayed with us, letters of course passed between Clive and his family at Boulogne, but my wife remarked that the receipt of those letters appeared to give our friend but little pleasure. They were read in a minute, and he would toss them over to his father, or thrust them into his pocket with a gloomy face. "Don't you see," groans out Clive to me one evening, "that Rosa scarcely writes the letters, or if she does, that her mother is standing over her? That woman is the Nemesis of our life, Pen. How can I pay her off? Great God! how can I pay her off?" And so having spoken, his head fell between his hands, and as I watched him I saw a ghastly domestic picture before me of helpless pain, humiliating discord, stupid tyranny.

What, I say again, are the so called great ills of life compared to these small ones?

The Colonel accompanied Clive to the lodgings which we had found for the young artist, in a quarter not far removed from the old house in Fitzroy Square, where some happy years of his youth had been spent. When sitters came to Clive—as at first they did in some numbers, many of his early friends being anxious to do him a service—the old gentleman was extraordinarily cheered and comforted. We could see by his face that affairs were going on well at the studio. He showed us the rooms which Rosey and the boy were to occupy. He prattled to our children and their mother, who was never tired of hearing him, about his grandson. He filled up the future nursery with a hundred little knicknacks of his own contriving; and with wonderful cheap bargains, which he bought in his walks about Tottenham Court Road. He pasted a most elaborate book of prints and sketches for Boy. It was astonishing what notice Boy already took of pictures. He would have all the genius of his father. Would he had had a better grandfather than the foolish old man, who had ruined all belonging to him!

However much they like each other, men in the London world see their friends but seldom. The place is so vast[2] that even next door is distant; the calls of business, society, pleasure, so multifarious that mere friendship can get or give but an occasional shake of the hand in the hurried moments of passage. Men must live their lives; and are per force selfish, but not un-friendly. At a great need you know where to look for your friend, and he that he is secure of you. So I went very little to Howland Street, where Clive now lived; very seldom to Lamb Court, where my dear old friend Warring-ton still sate in his old chambers, though our meetings were none the less cordial when they occurred, and our trust in one another always the same. Some folks say the world is heartless: he who says so either prates common-places, (the most likely and charitable suggestion) or is heartless himself, or is most singular and unfortunate in having made no friends. Many such a reasonable mortal cannot have: our nature, I think, not sufficing for that sort of polygamy. How many persons would you have to deplore your death; or whose death would you wish to deplore? Could our hearts let in such a harem of dear friendships, the mere changes and recurrences of grief and mourning would be intolerable, and tax our lives beyond their value. In a word we carry our own burthen in the world; push and struggle along on our own affairs: are pinched by our own shoes—though Heaven forbid we should not stop and forget ourselves sometimes, when a friend cries out in his distress, or we can help a poor stricken wanderer in his way.[3]

As for good women—these, my worthy reader, are different from us—the nature of these is to love, and to do kind offices, and devise untiring charities:—so, I would have you to know, that, though Mr. Pendennis was *parcus suorum cultor et infrequens,* Mrs. Laura found plenty of time to go from Westminster to Bloomsbury: and to pay visits to her Colonel and her Clive, both of whom she had got to love with all her heart again, now misfortune was on them; and both of whom returned her kindness with an affection blessing the bestower and the receiver; and making the husband proud and thankful, whose wife had earned such a noble regard. What is the dearest praise of all to a man? his own—or that you should love those whom he loves?—I see Laura Pendennis ever constant and tender and pure; ever ministering in her sacred office of kindness—bestowing[4] love and followed by blessings:—which would I have, think you; that priceless crown hymeneal; or the glory of a Tenth Edition?

---

[2] vast *E1*] fast *R*
[3] [*E1* and *R* continue without a paragraph break.]
[4] bestowing *E1 R*] taking *Ms*

Clive and his father had found not only a model friend in the lady above mentioned, but a perfect prize landlady in their happy lodgings. In her house, besides those apartments which Mr. Newcome had originally engaged, were rooms just sufficient to accommodate his wife, child, and servant, when they should come to him, with a very snug little upper-chamber for the Colonel, close by Boy's nursery, where he liked best to be. "And if there is not room for the Campaigner, as you call her," says Mrs. Laura, with a shrug of her shoulders, "why I am very sorry, but Clive must try and bear her absence as well as possible. After all, my dear Pen, you know he is married to Rosa and not to her mamma; and so—and so I think it will be quite best that they shall have their *ménage* as before."

The cheapness of the lodgings which the prize-landlady let, the quantity of neat new furniture which she put in, the consultations which she had with my wife regarding these supplies, were quite singular to me. "Have you pawned your diamonds, you reckless little person, in order to supply all this upholstery?" "No, Sir, I have not pawned my diamonds," Mrs. Laura answers—and I was left to think (if I thought on the matter at all) that the landlady's own benevolence had provided these good things for Clive, for the wife of Laura's husband was perforce poor; and she asked me for no more money at this time than at any other.

At first, in spite of his grumbling, Clive's affairs looked so prosperous, and so many sitters came to him from amongst his old friends that I was half inclined to believe with the Colonel and my wife that he was a prodigious genius, and that his good fortune would go on increasing. Laura was for having Rosey return to her husband. Every wife ought to be with her husband. J.J. shook his head about the prosperity. "Let us see whether the Academy will have his pictures this year, and what a place they will give him," said Ridley. To do him justice, Clive thought far more humbly of his compositions[5] than Ridley did. Not a little touching was it to us who had known the young men in former days, to see them in their changed positions. It was Ridley whose genius and industry had put him in the rank of a patron[6]—Ridley, the good industrious apprentice, who had won the prize of his Art: and not one of his many admirers saluted his talent and success with such a hearty recognition;[7] whose generous soul knew no envy, and who always fired and kindled at the successes[8] of his friends.

When Mr. Clive used to go over to Boulogne from time to time to pay his dutiful visits to his wife, the Colonel did not accompany his son, but during the latter's absence would dine with Mrs. Pendennis.

Though the preparations were complete in Howland Street, and Clive dutifully went over to Boulogne, Mrs. Pendennis remarked that he seemed still to hesitate about bringing his wife to London.

Upon this Mr. Pendennis observed that some gentlemen were not particularly anxious about the society of their wives and that this pair were perhaps better apart.[9]

---

5 compositions *E1 R*] own compositions *Ms*
6 a patron *E1*] patron *Ms*
7 recognition; *Ms*] recognition as Clive, *E1 R*
8 successes *Ms*] success *E1 R*
9 [Paragraph break] *Ms*] [omitted] *E1 R*

Upon which Mrs. Pendennis, drubbing on the ground with a little foot, said "Nonsense for shame, Arthur! How can you speak so flippantly? Did he not swear before Heaven to love and cherish her, never to leave her, Sir? Is not his *duty* his *duty*, Sir? (a most emphatic stamp of the foot). Is she not his for better or for worse?"

"Including the Campaigner, my dear?" says Mr. P.

"Don't laugh, Sir! She *must* come to him. There is no room in Howland Street for Mrs. Mackenzie."

"You artful scheming creature! We have some spare rooms. Suppose we ask Mrs. Mackenzie to come and live with us, my dear; and we could then have the benefit of the garrison anecdotes, and mess jocularities of your favourite, Captain Goby."

"I could never bear the horrid man!" cried Mrs. Pendennis. And how can I tell why she disliked him?

Everything being now ready for the reception of Clive's little family, we counselled our friend to go over to Boulogne, and bring back his wife and child, and then to make some final stipulation with the Campaigner. He saw, as well as we, that the presence and tyranny of that fatal woman destroyed his father's health and spirits—that the old man knew no peace or comfort in her neighbourhood, and was actually hastening to his grave under that dreadful and unremitting persecution. Mrs. Mackenzie made Clive scarcely less wretched than his father—she governed his household—took away his weak wife's allegiance and affection from him—and caused the wretchedness of every single person round about her. They ought to live apart. If she was too poor to subsist upon her widow's pension, which, in truth, was but a very small pittance, let Clive give up to her say the half of his wife's income of 100*l.* a-year. His prospects and present means of earning money were such that he might afford to do without that portion of his income: at any rate, he and his father would be cheaply ransomed at that price, from their imprisonment to this intolerable person. "Go, Clive," said his counsellors, "and bring back your wife and child, and let us all be happy together." For, you see, those advisers opined that if we had written over to Mrs. Clive Newcome—"Come"—she would have come with the Campaigner in her suite.

Vowing that he would behave like a man of courage; and we know that Clive had shown himself to be such in two or three previous battles; Clive crossed the water to bring back his little Rosey. Our good Colonel agreed to dine at our house during the days of his son's absence. I have said how beloved he was by young and old there—and he was kind enough to say afterwards, that no woman had made him so happy as Laura. We did not tell him—I know not from what reticence—that we had advised Clive to offer a bribe of 50*l.* a-year to Mrs. Mackenzie; until about a fortnight after Clive's absence, and a week after his return, when news came that poor old Mrs. Mason was dead at Newcome, whereupon we informed the Colonel that he had another pensioner now in the Campaigner.

Colonel Newcome was thankful that his dear old friend had gone out of the world in comfort and without pain. She had made a will long since, leaving all her goods and chattels to Thomas Newcome—but having no money to give, the Colonel handed over these to the old lady's faithful attendant Keziah.

Although many of the Colonel's old friends had parted from him or quarrelled with him in consequence of the ill-success of the B.B.C., there were two old ladies who yet remained faithful to him—Miss Cann namely, and honest little Miss Honeyman of Brighton, who, when she heard of the return to London of her nephew and brother-in-law, made a railway journey to the Metropolis (being the first time she ever engaged in that kind of travelling), rustled into Clive's apartments in Howland Street in her neatest silks, and looking not a day older than on that when we last beheld her; and after briskly scolding the young man for permitting his father to enter into money affairs—of which the poor dear Colonel was as ignorant as a baby—she gave them both to understand that she had a little sum at her bankers at their disposal—and besought the Colonel to remember that her house was his, and that she should be proud and happy to receive him as soon and as often and for as long a time as he would honour her with his company. "Is not my house full of your presents"—cried the stout little old lady—"have I not reason to be grateful to all the Newcomes—yes, to all the Newcomes;—for Miss Ethel and her family have come to me every year for months, and I don't quarrel with them, and I won't, although you do, Sir. Is not this shawl—are not these jewels that I wear," she continued, pointing to those well-known ornaments, "my dear Colonel's gift? Did you not relieve my brother Charles in this country and procure for him his place in India? Yes, my dear friend—and though you have been imprudent in money matters, my obligations towards you, and my gratitude, and my affection are always the same." Thus Miss Honeyman spoke, with somewhat of a quivering voice at the end of her little oration, but with exceeding state and dignity—for she believed that her investment of two hundred pounds in that unlucky B.B.C., which failed for half a million, was a sum of considerable importance, and gave her a right to express her opinion to the Managers.

Clive came back from Boulogne in a week as we have said—but he came back without his wife, much to our alarm, and looked so exceedingly fierce and glum when we demanded the reason of his return without his family, that we saw wars and battles had taken place, and thought that in this last continental campaign, the Campaigner had been too much for her friend.

The Colonel, to whom Clive communicated, though with us the poor lad held his tongue, told my wife what had happened:—not all the battles; which no doubt raged at breakfast, dinner, supper, during the week of Clive's visit to Boulogne,—but the upshot of these engagements. Rosey, not unwilling in her first private talk with her husband to come to England with him and the boy, showed herself irresolute on the second day at breakfast when the fire was opened on both sides—cried at dinner when fierce assaults took place, in which Clive had the advantage—slept soundly, but besought him to be very firm, and met the enemy at breakfast with a quaking heart—cried all that day, during which, pretty well without cease, the engagement lasted—and when Clive might have conquered and brought her off; but the weather was windy and the sea was rough, and he was pronounced a brute to venture on it with a wife in Rosey's situation.

Behind that "situation" the widow shielded herself. She clung to her adored child, and from that bulwark discharged abuse and satire at Clive and his father. He could not rout her out of her position. Having had the advantage on the first two or three days, on the four last he was beaten, and lost ground in each action. Rosey found that in her situation she could not part from her darling mamma. The Campaigner for her part averred that she might be reduced to beggary—that she might be robbed of her last farthing and swindled and cheated—that she might see her daughter's fortune flung away by unprincipled adventurers, and her blessed child left without even the comforts of life—but desert her in such a situation, she never would—no, never! Was not dear Rosa's health already impaired by the various shocks which she had undergone? Did she not require every comfort, every attendance? Monster! ask the doctor! She would stay with her darling child in spite of insult and rudeness and vulgarity. (Rosa's father was a king's officer, not a company's officer, thank God!) She would stay as long at least as Rosa's situation continued, at Boulogne, if not in London, but with her child. They might refuse to send her money, having robbed her of all her own, but she would pawn her gown off her back for her child. Whimpers from Rosey—cries of "Mamma, Mamma, compose yourself,"—convulsive sobs—clenched knuckles—flashing eyes—embraces rapidly clutched—laughs—stamps—snorts—from the dishevelled Campaigner—grinding teeth—livid fury and repeated breakages of the third commandment by Clive—I can fancy the whole scene. He returned to London without his wife, and when she came she brought Mrs. Mackenzie with her.

Chapter XXXVII.

OSEY came, bringing discord and wretchedness with her to her husband, and the sentence of death or exile to his dear old father, all of which we foresaw—all of which Clive's friends would have longed to prevent—all of which were inevitable under the circumstances. Clive's domestic affairs were often talked over by our little set. Warrington and F.B. knew of his unhappiness. We three had strongly opined that the women being together at Boulogne, should stay there and live there, Clive sending them over pecuniary aid as his means permitted. "They must hate each other pretty well by this time," growls George Warrington. "Why on earth should they not part?" "What a woman that Mrs. Mackenzie is," cries F.B. "What an infernal tartar and catamaran! She who was so uncommonly smiling and soft spoken, and such a fine woman, by jingo! What puzzles all women are." F.B. sighed and drowned further reflection in beer.

On the other side, and most strongly advocating Rosa's return to Clive was Mrs. Laura Pendennis; with certain arguments for which she had chapter and verse, and against which we of the separatist party had no appeal. "Did he marry her only for the days of her prosperity?" asked Laura. "Is it right, is it manly, that he should leave her now she is unhappy—poor little creature—no woman had ever more need of protection; and who should be her natural guardian save her husband? Surely, Arthur, you forget—have you forgotten them yourself, Sir?—the solemn vows which Clive made at the altar. Is he not bound to his wife to keep only unto her so long as they both shall live, to love her, comfort her, honour her, and keep her in sickness and health?"

"To keep her, yes—but not to keep the Campaigner," cries Mr. Pendennis. "It is a moral bigamy, Laura, which you advocate, you wicked, immoral young woman!"

But Laura, though she smiled at this notion, would not be put off from her first proposition. Turning to Clive, who was with us, talking over his doleful family circumstances, she took his hand and pleaded the cause of right and religion with sweet artless fervour. She agreed with us that it was a hard lot for Clive to bear. So much the nobler the task, and the fulfilment of duty in enduring it. A few months too would put an end to his trials. When his child was born Mrs. Mackenzie would take her departure. It would even be Clive's duty to separate from her then, as it now was to humour his wife in her delicate condition, and to soothe the poor soul who had had a great deal of ill health, of misfortune, and of domestic calamity to wear and shatter her. Clive acquiesced with a groan, but with a touching and generous resignation as we both thought. "She is right, Pen," he said, "I think your wife is always right. I will try, Laura, and bear my part, God help me! I will do my duty and strive my best to soothe and gratify my poor dear little woman. They will be making caps and things, and will not interrupt me in my studio. Of nights I can go to Clipstone Street and work at the Life. There's nothing like the Life, Pen. So you see I shan't be much at home except at meal times, when by nature I shall have my mouth full, and no opportunity of quarreling with poor Mrs. Mack." So he went home, followed and cheered by the love and pity of my dear wife, and determined stoutly to bear this heavy yoke which fate had put on him.

To do Mrs. Mackenzie justice, that lady backed up with all her might the statement which my wife had put forward, with a view of soothing poor Clive, viz., that the residence of his mother-in-law in his house was only to be temporary. "Temporary!" cries Mrs. Mack (who was kind enough to make a call on Mrs. Pendennis, and treat that lady to a piece of her mind). "Do you suppose, Madam, that it could be otherwise? Do you suppose that worlds would induce me to stay in a house where I have received such *treatment;* where, after I and my daughter had been robbed of every shilling of our fortune, where we are daily insulted by Colonel Newcome and his son? Do you suppose, Ma'am, that I do not know that Clive's friends hate me, and give themselves airs and look down upon my darling child, and try and make differences between my sweet Rosa and me—Rosa who might have been dead, or might have been starving, but that her dear mother came to her rescue? No, I would never stay. I loathe every day that I remain in the house—I would rather beg my bread—I would rather sweep the streets and starve—though, thank God, I have my pension as the widow of an officer in Her Majesty's Service, and I can live upon that—and of *that* Colonel Newcome *cannot* rob me; and when my darling love needs a mother's care no longer, I will leave her. I will shake the dust off my feet and leave that house, I will—And Mr. Newcome's friends may then sneer at me and abuse me, and blacken my darling child's heart towards me if they choose. And I thank you, Mrs. Pendennis, for all your *kindness* towards my daughter's family, and for the furniture which you have sent into the house, and for the *trouble* you have taken about our family arrangements. It was for this I took the liberty of calling upon you, and I wish you a very good morning." So speaking, the Campaigner left my wife; and Mrs. Pendennis enacted the pleasing scene with great spirit to her husband afterwards, concluding the whole with a splendid curtsey and toss of the head, such as Mrs. Mackenzie performed as her parting salute.

Our dear Colonel had fled before. He had acquiesced humbly with the decree of fate; and, lonely, old and beaten, marched honestly on the path of duty. It was a great blessing, he wrote to us, to him to think that in happier days and during many years he had been enabled to benefit his kind and excellent relative Miss Honeyman. He could thankfully receive her hospitality now, and claim the kindness and shelter which this old friend gave him. No one could be more anxious to make him comfortable. The air of Brighton did him the greatest good; he had found some old friends, some old Bengalees there, with whom he enjoyed himself greatly, &c. How much did we, who knew his noble spirit, believe of this story? To us Heaven had awarded health, happiness, competence, loving children, united hearts, and modest prosperity. To yonder good man, whose long life shone with benefactions, and whose career was but kindness and honour, fate decreed poverty, disappointment, separation, a lonely old age. We bowed our heads, humiliated at the contrast of his lot and ours; and prayed Heaven to enable us to bear our present good fortune meekly, and our evil days, if they should come, with such a resignation as this good Christian showed.

I forgot to say that our attempts to better Thomas Newcome's money affairs were quite in vain, the Colonel insisting upon paying over every shilling of his military allowances and retiring pension to the parties from whom he had borrowed money previous to his bankruptcy. "Ah! what a good man that is," says Mr. Sherrick with tears in his eyes, "what a noble fellow, Sir. He would die rather than not pay every farthing over. He'd starve, Sir, that he would. The money ain't mine, Sir, or if it was do you think I'd take it from the poor old boy? No, Sir; by Jove I honour and reverence him more now he ain't got a shilling in his pocket, than ever I did when we thought he was a rolling in money."

My wife made one or two efforts at Samaritan visits in Howland Street, but was received by Mrs. Clive with such a faint welcome, and by the Campaigner with so grim a countenance, so many sneers, innuendoes, insults almost, that Laura's charity was beaten back, and she ceased to press good offices thus thanklessly received. If Clive came to visit us, as he very rarely did, after an official question or two regarding the health of his wife and child, no farther mention was made of his family affairs. His painting, he said, was getting on tolerably well; he had work, scantily paid it is true, but work sufficient. He was reserved, uncommunicative, unlike the frank Clive of former times, and oppressed by his circumstances, as it was easy to see. I did not press the confidence which he was unwilling to offer, and thought best to respect his silence. I had a thousand affairs of my own; who has not in London? If you die to-morrow, your dearest friend will feel for you a hearty pang of sorrow, and go to his business as usual. I could divine, but would not care to describe, the life which my poor Clive was now leading; the vulgar misery, the sordid home, the cheerless toil, and lack of friendly companionship which darkened his kind soul. I was glad Clive's father was away. The Colonel wrote to us twice or thrice; could it be three months ago? bless me, how time flies! He was happy, he wrote, with Miss Honeyman, who took the best care of him.

Mention has been made once or twice in the course of this history of the Grey Friars school,—where the Colonel and Clive and I had been brought up,—an ancient foundation of the time of James I., still subsisting in the heart of London city. The death-day of the founder of the place is still kept solemnly by Cistercians. In their chapel, where assemble the boys of the school, and the fourscore old men of the Hospital; the founder's tomb stands, a huge edifice, emblazoned with heraldic decorations and clumsy, carved allegories. There is an old Hall, a beautiful specimen of the architecture of James's time; an old Hall? many old halls; old staircases, old passages, old chambers decorated with old portraits, walking in the midst of which, we walk as it were in the early seventeenth century. To others than Cistercians, Grey Friars is a dreary place possibly. Nevertheless, the pupils educated there love to revisit it; and the oldest of us grow young again for an hour or two as we come back into those scenes of childhood.

The custom of the school is, that on the 12th of December, the Founder's Day, the head gown-boy shall recite a Latin oration, in praise *Fundatoris Nostri*, and upon other subjects; and a goodly company of old Cistercians is generally brought together to attend this oration: after which we go to chapel and hear a sermon; after which we adjourn to a great dinner, where old condisciples meet, old toasts are given, and speeches are made. Before marching from the oration-hall to chapel, the stewards of the day's dinner, according to old-fashioned rite, have wands put into their hands, walk to church at the head of the procession, and sit there in places of honour. The boys are already in their seats, with smug fresh faces, and shining white collars; the old black-gowned pensioners are on their benches; the chapel is lighted, and Founder's Tomb, with its grotesque carvings, monsters, heraldries, darkles and shines with the most wonderful shadows and lights. There he lies, Fundator Noster, in his ruff and gown, awaiting the great Examination Day. We oldsters, be we ever so old, become boys again as we look at that familiar old tomb, and think how the seats are altered since we were here, and how the doctor—not the present doctor, the doctor of *our* time—used to sit yonder, and his awful eye used to frighten us shuddering boys, on whom it lighted; and how the boy next us *would* kick our shins during service time, and how the monitor would cane us afterwards because our shins were kicked. Yonder sit forty cherry-cheeked boys, thinking about home and holidays to-morrow. Yonder sit some threescore old gentlemen pensioners of the Hospital, listening to the prayers and the psalms. You hear them coughing feebly in the twilight,— the old reverend blackgowns. Is Codd Ajax alive, you wonder?—the Cistercian lads called these old gentlemen Codds, I know not wherefore—I know not wherefore—but is old Codd Ajax alive, I wonder? or Codd Soldier? or kind old Codd Gentleman, or has the grave closed over them? A plenty of candles lights up this chapel, and this scene of age and youth, and early memories, and pompous death. How solemn the well-remembered prayers are, here uttered again in the place where in childhood we used to hear them! How beautiful and decorous the rite; how noble the ancient

words of the supplications which the priest utters, and to which generations of fresh children, and troops of bygone seniors have cried Amen!
under those arches! The service for Founder's Day is a special one; one of
the psalms selected being the thirty-seventh, and we hear—

> 23. The steps of a good man are ordered by the Lord, and he delighteth in
> his way.
> 24. Though he fall, he shall not be utterly cast down, for the Lord upholdeth
> him with his hand.
> 25. I have been young, and now am old, yet have I not seen the righteous
> forsaken, nor his seed begging their bread.

As we came to this verse, I chanced to look up from my book towards the
swarm of black-coated pensioners: and amongst them—amongst them—
sate Thomas Newcome.

His dear old head was bent down over his prayer-book; there was no
mistaking him. He wore the black gown of the pensioners of the Hospital
of Grey Friars. His order of the Bath was on his breast. He stood there
amongst the poor brethren, uttering the responses to the psalm. The steps
of this good man had been ordered hither by Heaven's decree: to this Alms-
House! Here it was ordained that a life all love, and kindness, and honour,
should end! I heard no more of prayers, and psalms, and sermon, after
that. How dared I to be in a place of mark, and he, he yonder among
the poor? O pardon, you noble soul! I ask forgiveness of you for being
of a world that has so treated you—you my better, you the honest, and
gentle, and good! I thought the service would never end, or the organist's
voluntaries, or the preacher's homily.

The organ played us out of chapel at length, and I waited in the ante-
chapel until the pensioners took their turn to quit it. My dear, dear old
friend! I ran to him with a warmth and eagerness of recognition which no
doubt showed themselves in my face and accents as my heart was moved
at the sight of him. His own wan face flushed up when he saw me, and
his hand shook in mine. "I have found a home, Arthur," said he. "Don't
you remember, before I went to India, when we came to see the old Grey
Friars, and visited Captain Scarsdale in his room?—a poor brother like
me—an old Peninsular man; Scarsdale is gone now, Sir, and is where the
wicked cease from troubling and the weary are at rest; and I thought then,
when we saw him,—here would be a place for an old fellow when his career
was over, to hang his sword up; to humble his soul, and to wait thankfully
for the end, Arthur. My good friend, Lord H., who is a Cistercian like
ourselves, and has just been appointed a governor, gave me his first nomination. Don't be agitated, Arthur, my boy, I am very happy. I have good
quarters, good food, good light and fire, and good friends; blessed be God!
my dear kind young friend—my boy's friend; you have always been so, Sir;
and I take it uncommonly kind of you, and I thank God for you, Sir. Why,
Sir, I am as happy as the day is long." He uttered words to this effect as we
walked through the courts of the building towards his room, which in truth
I found neat and comfortable, with a brisk fire crackling on the hearth; a
little tea-table laid out, a Bible and spectacles by the side of it, and over the
mantel-piece a drawing of his grandson by Clive.

"You may come and see me here, Sir, whenever you like, and so may
your dear wife and little ones, tell Laura, with my love;—but you must not

stay now. You must go back to your dinner." In vain I pleaded that I had no stomach for it. He gave me a look, which seemed to say he desired to be alone, and I had to respect that order and leave him.

Of course I came to him on the very next day; though not with my wife and children, who were in truth absent in the country at Rosebury, where they were to pass the Christmas holidays; and where, this school-dinner over, I was to join them. On my second visit to Grey Friars my good friend entered more at length into the reasons why he had assumed the Poor Brother's gown: and I cannot say but that I acquiesced in his reasons, and admired that noble humility and contentedness of which he gave me an example.

"That which had caused him most grief and pain," he said, "in the issue of that unfortunate bank, was the thought that poor friends of his had been induced by his representations to invest their little capital in that speculation. Good Miss Honeyman for instance, meaning no harm, and in all respects a most honest and kindly-disposed old lady, had nevertheless alluded more than once to the fact that her money had been thrown away; and these allusions, Sir, made her hospitality somewhat hard to bear," said the Colonel. "At home—at poor Clivey's, I mean—it was even worse," he continued; "Mrs. Mackenzie for months past, by her complaints, and—and her conduct, has made my son and me so miserable—that flight before her, and into any refuge, was the best course. She too does not mean ill, Pen. Do not waste any of your oaths upon that poor woman" (he added, holding up his finger, and smiling sadly). "She thinks I deceived her, though Heaven knows it was myself I deceived. She has great influence over Rosa. Very few persons can resist that violent and head-strong woman, Sir. I could not bear her reproaches, or my poor sick daughter, whom her mother leads almost entirely now, and, it was with all this grief on my mind, that, as I was walking one day upon Brighton cliff, I met my schoolfellow, my Lord H.—who has ever been a good friend of mine—and who told me how he had just been appointed a governor of Grey Friars. He asked me to dine with him on the next day, and would take no refusal. He knew of my pecuniary misfortunes, of course—and showed himself most noble and liberal in his offers of help. I was very much touched by his goodness, Pen,—and made a clean breast of it to his lordship; who at first would not hear of my coming to this place—and offered me out of the purse of an old brother schoolfellow and an old brother soldier as much—as much as should last me my time. Wasn't it noble of him, Arthur? God bless him! There are good men in the world, Sir, there are true friends, as I have found, in these later days. Do you know, Sir," here the old man's eyes twinkled, "that Fred Bayham fixed up that bookcase yonder—and brought me my little boy's picture to hang up? Boy and Clive will come and see me soon."

"Do you mean they do not come?" I cried.

"They don't know I am here, Sir," said the Colonel, with a sweet, kind smile. "They think I am visiting his lordship in Scotland. Ah! they are good people! When we had had our talk down-stairs over our bottle of claret— where my old commander-in-chief would not hear of my plan: we went up-stairs to her ladyship, who saw that her husband was disturbed, and asked the reason. I daresay it was the good claret that made me speak, Sir;

for I told her that I and her husband had had a dispute, and that I would take her ladyship for umpire. And then I told her the story over, that I had paid away every rupee to the creditors, and mortgaged my pensions and retiring allowances for the same end, that I was a burden upon Clivey, who had work enough, poor boy, to keep his own family and his wife's mother, whom my imprudence had impoverished,—that here was an honourable asylum which my friend could procure for me, and was not that better than to drain his purse? She was very much moved, Sir—she is a very kind lady, though she passed for being very proud and haughty in India—so wrongly are people judged. And Lord H. said, in his rough way, 'that, by Jove, if Tom Newcome took a thing into his obstinate old head no one could drive it out.' And so," said the Colonel, with his sad smile, "I *had* my own way. Lady H. was good enough to come and see me the very next day—and do you know, Pen, she invited me to go and live with them for the rest of my life—made me the most generous, the most delicate offers. But I knew I was right, and held my own. I am too old to work, Arthur: and better here, whilst I am to stay, than elsewhere. Look! all this furniture came from H. House—and that wardrobe is full of linen, which she sent me. She has been twice to see me, and every officer in this hospital is as courteous to me as if I had my fine house."

I thought of the psalm we had heard on the previous evening, and turned to it in the opened Bible, and pointed to the verse, "Though he fall, he shall not be utterly cast down, for the Lord upholdeth him." Thomas Newcome seeing my occupation, laid a kind, trembling hand on my shoulder; and then, putting on his glasses, with a smile, bent over the volume. And who that saw him then, and knew him and loved him as I did—who would not have humbled his own heart, and breathed his inward prayer, confessing and adoring the Divine Will, which ordains these trials, these triumphs, these humiliations, these blest griefs, this crowning Love?

I had the happiness of bringing Clive and his little boy to Thomas Newcome that evening; and heard the child's cry of recognition and surprise, and the old man calling the boy's name, as I closed the door upon that meeting; and by the night's mail I went down to Newcome, to the friends with whom my own family was already staying.

Of course, my conscience-keeper at Rosebury was anxious to know about the school-dinner, and all the speeches made, and the guests assembled there; but she soon ceased to enquire about these when I came to give her the news of the discovery of our dear old friend in the habit of a Poor Brother of Grey Friars. She was very glad to hear that Clive and his little son had been reunited to the Colonel; and appeared to imagine at first, that there was some wonderful merit upon my part in bringing the three together.

"Well—no great merit, Pen, as you *will* put it," says the Confessor; "but it was kindly thought, Sir—and I like my husband when he is kind best; and don't wonder at your having made a stupid speech at the dinner, as you say you did, when you had this other subject to think of. That is a beautiful psalm, Pen, and those verses which you were reading when you saw him, especially beautiful."

"But in the presence of eighty old gentlemen, who have all come to decay, and have all had to beg their bread in a manner, don't you think the clergyman might choose some other psalm?" asks Mr. Pendennis.

"They were not forsaken *utterly*, Arthur," says Mrs. Laura, gravely: but rather declines to argue the point raised by me; namely, that the selection of that especial thirty-seventh psalm was not complimentary to those decayed old gentlemen.

"*All* the psalms are good, Sir," she says, "and this one, of course, is included," and thus the discussion closed.

I then fell to a description of Howland Street, and poor Clive, whom I had found there over his work. A dubious maid scanned my appearance rather eagerly when I asked to see him. I found a picture-dealer chaffering with him over a bundle of sketches, and his little boy, already pencil in hand, lying in one corner of the room, the sun playing about his yellow hair. The child looked languid and pale, the father worn and ill. When the dealer at length took his bargains away, I gradually broke my errand to Clive, and told him from whence I had just come.

He had thought his father in Scotland with Lord H.: and was immensely moved with the news which I brought.

"I haven't written to him for a month. It's not pleasant letters I have to write, Pen, and I can't make them pleasant. Up, Tommykin, and put on your cap." Tommykin jumps up. "Put on your cap, and tell them to take off your pinafore, and tell Grandmamma" * *

At that name Tommykin begins to cry.

"Look at that!" says Clive, commencing to speak in the French language, which the child interrupts by calling out in that tongue, "I speak also French, Papa."

"Well, my child! You will like to come out with Papa, and Betsy can dress you." He flings off his own paint-stained shooting-jacket as he talks, takes a frock-coat out of a carved wardrobe, and a hat from a helmet on the shelf. He is no longer the handsome splendid boy of old times. Can that be Clive, with that haggard face and slouched handkerchief? "I am not the dandy I was, Pen," he says bitterly.

A little voice is heard crying over-head—and giving a kind of gasp, the wretched father stops in some indifferent speech he was trying to make— "I can't help myself," he groans out; "my poor wife is so ill, she can't attend to the child. Mrs. Mackenzie manages the house for me—and—here! Tommy, Tommy! Papa's coming!" Tommy has been crying again, and flinging open the studio door, Clive calls out, and dashes up-stairs.

I hear scuffling, stamping, loud voices, poor Tommy's scared little pipe—Clive's fierce objurgations, and the Campaigner's voice barking out—"Do, Sir, do! with my child suffering in the next room. Behave like a brute to me, do. He shall not go out. He shall not have the hat"—"He shall"—"Ah—ah!" A scream is heard. It is Clive tearing a child's hat out of the Campaigner's hands, with which, and a flushed face, he presently rushes down-stairs, bearing little Tommy on his shoulder.

"You see what I am come to, Pen," he says with a heart-broken voice, trying, with hands all of a tremble, to tie the hat on the boy's head. He laughs bitterly at the ill-success of his endeavours. "Oh, you silly Papa!" laughs Tommy, too.

The door is flung open, and the red-faced Campaigner appears. Her face is mottled with wrath, her bandeaux of hair are disarranged upon her forehead, the ornaments of her cap, cheap, and dirty, and numerous, only give her a wilder appearance. She is in a large and dingy wrapper, very different from the lady who had presented herself a few months back to my wife—how different from the smiling Mrs. Mackenzie of old days!

"He shall *not* go out of a winter day, Sir," she breaks out. "I have his mother's orders, whom you are *killing*. Mr. Pendennis!" She starts, perceiving me for the first time, and her breast heaves, and she prepares for combat, and looks at me over her shoulder.

"You and his father are the best judges upon this point, Ma'am," says Mr. Pendennis, with a bow.

"The child is delicate, Sir," cries Mrs. Mackenzie; "and this winter—" "Enough of this," says Clive with a stamp, and passes through her guard with Tommy, and we descend the stairs, and at length are in the free street. Was it not best not to describe at full length this portion of poor Clive's history?

Chapter XXXVIII.

E have known our friend Florac under two aristocratic names, and might now salute him by a third, to which he was entitled, although neither he nor his wife ever chose to assume it. His father was lately dead, and M. Paul de Florac might sign himself Duc d'Ivry if he chose, but he was indifferent as to the matter, and his wife's friends indignant at the idea that their kinswoman, after having been a Princess, should descend to the rank of a mere Duchess. So Prince and Princess these good folks remained, being exceptions to that order, inasmuch as their friends could certainly put their trust in them.

On his father's death Florac went to Paris, to settle the affairs of the paternal succession; and, having been for some time absent in his native country, returned to Rosebury for the winter, to resume that sport of which he was a distinguished amateur. He hunted in black during the ensuing season; and, indeed, henceforth laid aside his splendid attire and his *allures* as a young man. His waist expanded, or was no longer confined by the cestus which had given it a shape. When he laid aside his black, his whiskers, too, went into a sort of half-mourning, and appeared in grey. "I make myself old, my friend," he said, pathetically; "I have no more neither twenty years nor forty." He went to Rosebury Church no more; but, with great order and sobriety, drove every Sunday to the neighbouring Catholic chapel at C—— Castle. We had an ecclesiastic or two to dine with us at Rosebury, one of whom I am inclined to think was Florac's Director.

A reason, perhaps, for Paul's altered demeanour, was the presence of his mother at Rosebury. No politeness or respect could be greater than Paul's towards the Countess. Had she been a sovereign princess, Madame de Florac could not have been treated with more profound courtesy than she now received from her son. I think the humble-minded lady could have dispensed with some of his attentions; but Paul was a personage who demonstrated all his sentiments, and performed his various parts in life with the greatest vigour. As a man of pleasure, for instance, what more active roué than he? As a *jeune homme*, who could be younger, and for a longer time? As a country gentleman, or an *homme d'affaires*, he insisted upon dressing each character with the most rigid accuracy, and an exactitude that reminded one somewhat of Bouffé, or Ferville, at the play. I wonder whether, when he is quite old, he will think proper to wear a pig-tail, like his old father? At any rate, that was a good part which the kind fellow was now acting, of reverence towards his widowed mother, and af-fectionate respect for her declining days. He not only felt these amiable sentiments, but he imparted them to his friends freely, as his wont was. He used to weep freely,—quite unrestrained by the presence of the domestics, as English sentiment would be;—and when Madame de Florac quitted the room after dinner, would squeeze my hand and tell me with streaming eyes, that his mother was an angel. "Her life has been but a long trial, my friend," he would say. "Shall not I, who have caused her to shed so many tears, endeavour to dry some?" Of course all the friends who liked him best encouraged him in an intention so pious.

The reader has already been made acquainted with this lady by letters of hers, which came into my possession some time after the events which I am at present narrating: my wife, through our kind friend, Colonel Newcome, had also had the honour of an introduction to Madame de Florac at Paris; and, on coming to Rosebury for the Christmas holidays, I found Laura and the children greatly in favour with the good Countess. She treated her son's wife with a perfect though distant courtesy. She was thankful to Madame de Montcontour for the latter's great goodness to her son. Fa-miliar with but very few persons, she could scarcely be intimate with her homely daughter-in-law. Madame de Montcontour stood in the greatest awe of her; and, to do that good lady justice, admired and reverenced Paul's mother with all her simple heart. In truth, I think almost every one had a certain awe of Madame de Florac, except children, who came to her trustingly, and, as it were, by instinct. The habitual melancholy of her eyes vanished as they lighted upon young faces and infantile smiles. A sweet love beamed out of her countenance: an angelic smile shone over her face, as she bent towards them and caressed them. Her demeanour, then, nay, her looks and ways at other times;—a certain gracious sadness, a sympathy with all grief, and pity for all pain; a gentle heart, yearning towards all chil-dren; and, for her own especially, feeling a love that was almost an anguish; in the affairs of the common world only a dignified acquiescence, as if her place was not in it, and her thoughts were in her Home elsewhere;—these qualities, which we had seen exemplified in another life, Laura and her husband watched in Madame de Florac, and we loved her because she was like our mother. I see in such women the good and pure, the patient and faithful, the tried and meek, the followers of Him whose earthly life was divinely sad and tender.

But, good as she was to us and to all, Ethel Newcome was the French lady's greatest favourite. A bond of extreme tenderness and affection united these two. The elder friend made constant visits to the younger at Newcome; and when Miss Newcome, as she frequently did, came to Rosebury, we used to see that they preferred to be alone; divining and re-specting the sympathy which brought those two faithful hearts together. I can imagine now the two tall forms slowly pacing the garden walks, or turn-ing, as they lighted on the young ones in their play. What was their talk? I never asked it. Perhaps Ethel never said what was in her heart, though, be sure, the other knew it. Though the grief of those they love is untold, women hear it; as they soothe it with unspoken consolations. To see the elder lady embrace her friend as they parted, was something holy—a sort of saint-like salutation.

Consulting the person from whom I had no secrets, we had thought best at first not to mention to our friends the place and position in which we had found our dear Colonel; at least to wait for a fitting opportunity on which we might break the news to those who held him in such affection. I told how Clive was hard at work, and hoped the best for him. Good-natured Madame de Montcontour was easily satisfied with my replies to her questions concerning our friend. Ethel only asked, if he and her uncle were well, and once or twice made enquiries respecting Rosa and her child. And now it was that my wife told me, what I need no longer keep secret, of Ethel's extreme anxiety to serve her distressed relatives, and how she, Laura, had already acted as Miss Newcome's almoner in furnishing and hiring those apartments which Ethel believed were occupied by Clive and his father, and wife and child. And my wife farther informed me, with what deep grief Ethel had heard of her uncle's misfortune, and how, but that she feared to offend his pride, she longed to give him assistance. She had even ventured to offer to send him pecuniary help; but the Colonel (who never mentioned the circumstance to me or any other of his friends), in a kind but very cold letter, had declined to be beholden to his niece for help.

So I may have remained some days at Rosebury, and the real position of the two Newcomes was unknown to our friends there. Christmas Eve was come, and, according to a long-standing promise, Ethel Newcome and her two children had arrived from the Park, which dreary mansion, since his double defeat, Sir Barnes scarcely ever visited. Christmas was come, and Rosebury Hall was decorated with holly. Florac did his best to welcome his friends, and strove to make the meeting gay, though in truth it was rather melancholy. The children, however, were happy: they had pleasure enough, in the school festival, in the distribution of cloaks and blankets to the poor, and in Madame de Montcontour's gardens, delightful and beautiful though winter was there.

It was only a family meeting, Madame de Florac's widowhood not permitting her presence in large companies. Paul sate at his table between his mother and Mrs. Pendennis; Mr. Pendennis opposite to him with Ethel and Madame de Montcontour on each side. The four children were placed between these personages, on whom Madame de Florac looked with her tender glances, and to whose little wants the kindest of hosts ministered with uncommon good-nature and affection. He was very soft-hearted about children. "Pourquoi n'en avons-nous pas, Jeanne? He! pourquoi n'en avons-nous pas?" he said, addressing his wife by her Christian name. The poor little lady looked kindly at her husband, and then gave a sigh, and turned and heaped cake upon the plate of the child next to her. No mamma or Aunt Ethel could interpose. It was a very light wholesome cake. Brown made it on purpose for the children, "the little darlings!" cries the Princess.

The children were very happy at being allowed to sit up so late to dinner, at all the kindly amusements of the day, at the holly and misletoe clustering round the lamps—the misletoe, under which the gallant Florac, skilled in all British usages, vowed he would have his privilege. But the misletoe was clustered round the lamp, the lamp was over the centre of the great round table—the innocent gratification which he proposed to himself was denied to M. Paul.

In the greatest excitement and good-humour, our host at the dessert made us *des speech*. He carried a toast to the charming Ethel, another to the charming Mistriss Laura, another to his good fren', his brave frren', his 'appy fren', Pendennis—'appy as possessor of such a wife, 'appy as writer of works destined to the immortality, &c., &c. The little children round about clapped their happy little hands, and laughed and crowed in chorus. And now the nursery and its guardians were about to retreat, when Florac said he had yet a speech, yet a toast—and he bade the butler pour wine into every one's glass—yet a toast—and he carried it to the health of our dear friends, of Clive and his father,—the good, the brave Colonel! "We who are happy," says he, "shall we not think of those who are good? We who love each other, shall we not remember those whom we all love?" He spoke with very great tenderness and feeling. *"Ma bonne mère*, thou too shalt drink this toast!" he said, taking his mother's hand, and kissing it. She returned his caress gently, and tasted the wine with her pale lips. Ethel's head bent in silence over her glass; and, as for Laura, need I say what happened to her? When the ladies went away my heart was opened to my friend Florac, and I told him where and how I had left my dear Clive's father.

The Frenchman's emotion on hearing this tale was such that I have loved him ever since. Clive in want! Why had he not sent to his friend? *Grands Dieux!* Clive who had helped him in his greatest distress. Clive's father, *ce preux chevalier, ce parfait gentilhomme!* In a hundred rapid exclamations Florac exhibited his sympathy, asking of Fate, why such men as he and I were sitting surrounded by splendours—before golden vases—crowned with flowers—with valets to kiss our feet—(these were merely figures of speech in which Paul expressed his prosperity)—whilst our friend the Colonel, so much better than we, spent his last days in poverty, and alone.

I liked Florac[1] none the less, I own, because that one of the conditions of the Colonel's present life, which appeared the hardest to most people, affected Florac but little. To be a Pensioner of an Ancient Institution? Why not? Might not any officer retire without shame to the Invalides at the close of his campaigns, and had not Fortune conquered our old friend, and age and disaster overcome him? It never once entered Thomas Newcome's head, nor Clive's, nor Florac's, nor his mother's, that the Colonel demeaned himself at all by accepting that bounty; and I recollect Warrington sharing our sentiment and trowling out those noble lines of the old poet:—

"His golden locks time hath to silver turned;
    O time too swift, O swiftness never ceasing!
His youth 'gainst time and age hath ever spurned,
    But spurned in vain; youth waneth by encreasing.
Beauty, strength, youth, are flowers but fading seen.

[1] Florac *E 1*] my host *R*

Duty, faith, love, are roots, and ever green.

His helmet now shall make a hive for bees,
  And lovers' songs be turned to holy psalms;
A man at arms must now serve on his knees,
  And feed on prayers, which are old age's alms."

*   *   *   *   *   *   *

These, I say, respected our friend, whatever was the coat he wore; whereas, among the Colonel's own kinsfolk, dire was the dismay, and indignation even, which they expressed, when they came to hear of this, what they were pleased to call degradation to their family. Clive's dear mother-in-law made outcries over the good old man as over a pauper, and inquired of Heaven, what she had done that her blessed child should have a mendicant for a father? And Mrs. Hobson,[2] in subsequent confidential communication with the writer of these memoirs, improved the occasion religiously as her wont was; referred the matter to Heaven too, and thought fit to assume that the celestial powers had decreed this *humiliation*, this *dreadful trial* for the Newcome family, as a warning to them all that they should not be too much puffed up with prosperity, nor set their affections too much upon things of this earth. Had they not already received *one* chastisement in Barnes's punishment, and Lady Clara's awful falling away? They had taught *her* a lesson, which the Colonel's *lamentable errors* had *confirmed*,—the vanity of trusting in all earthly grandeurs! Thus it was this worthy woman plumed herself, as it were, on her relative's misfortunes; and was pleased to think the latter were designed for the special warning and advantage of her private family. But Mrs. Hobson's philosophy is only mentioned by the way. Our story, which is drawing to its close, has to busy itself with other members of the house of The Newcomes.

My talk with Florac lasted for some time: at its close, when we went to join the ladies in the drawing-room we found Ethel cloaked and shawled, and prepared for her departure with her young ones, who were already asleep. The little festival was over, and had ended in melancholy—even in weeping. Our hostess sate in her accustomed seat by her lamp and her work-table; but, neglecting her needle, she was having perpetual recourse to her pocket-handkerchief, and uttering ejaculations of pity between the intervals of her gushes of tears. Madame de Florac was in her usual place, her head cast downwards, and her hands folded. My wife was at her side, a grave commiseration showing itself[3] in Laura's countenance whilst I read a yet deeper sadness in Ethel's pale face. Miss Newcome's carriage had been announced; the attendants had already carried the young ones asleep to the vehicle; and she was in the act of taking leave. We looked round at this disturbed party, guessing very likely what the subject of their talk had been, to which, however, Miss Ethel did not allude: but, announcing that she had intended to depart without disturbing the two gentlemen, she bade us farewell and good-night. "I wish I could say merry Christmas," she added

---

[2] Clive's dear mother-in-law...father? And Mrs. Hobson, *E1*] Mrs. Hobson Newcome, *R*

[3] itself *HM NY*] herself *E1 R*

gravely, "but none of us, I fear, can hope for that." It was evident that Laura had told the last chapter of the Colonel's story.

Madame de Florac rose up and embraced Miss Newcome; and, that farewell over, she sank back on the sofa exhausted, and with such an expression of affliction in her countenance, that my wife ran eagerly towards her. "It is nothing, my dear," she said, giving a cold hand to the younger lady, and sate silent for a few moments, during which we heard Florac's voice without, crying Adieu! and the wheels of Miss Newcome's carriage as it drove away.

Our host entered a moment afterwards; and, remarking as Laura had done, his mother's pallor, and look of anguish, went up and spoke to her with the utmost tenderness and anxiety.

She gave her hand to her son, and a faint blush rose up out of the past as it were, and trembled upon her wan cheek. "He was the first friend I ever had in the world, Paul," she said; "the first and the best. He shall not want, shall he, my son?"

No signs of that emotion in which her daughter-in-law had been indulging were as yet visible in Madame de Florac's eyes; but, as she spoke, holding her son's hand in hers, the tears at length overflowed; and, with a sob, her head fell forwards. The impetuous Frenchman flung himself on his knees before his mother, uttered a hundred words of love and respect for her, and with tears and sobs of his own called God to witness that their friend should never want. And so this mother and son embraced each other, and clung together in a sacred union of love; before which, we, who had been admitted as spectators of that scene, stood hushed and respectful.

That night Laura told me, how, when the ladies left us, their talk had been entirely about the Colonel and Clive. Madame de Florac had spoken especially, and much more freely than was her wont. She had told many reminiscences of Thomas Newcome and his early days; how her father taught him mathematics when they were quite poor, and living in their dear little cottage at Blackheath; how handsome he was then, with bright eyes, and long black hair flowing over his shoulders; how military glory was his boyish passion, and he was for ever talking of India, and the famous deeds of Clive and Lawrence. His favourite book was a history of India—the history of Orme. "He read it, and I read it also, my daughter," the French lady said, turning to Ethel; "ah! I may say so after so many years."

Ethel remembered the book as belonging to her grandmother, and now in the library at Newcome. Doubtless the same sympathy which caused me to speak about Thomas Newcome that evening, impelled my wife likewise. She told her friends, as I had told Florac, all the Colonel's story; and it was while these good women were under the impression of the melancholy history, that Florac and his guest found them.

Retired to our rooms, Laura and I talked on the same subject until the clock tolled Christmas, and the neighbouring church bells rang out a jubilation. And, looking out into the quiet night, where the stars were keenly shining, we committed ourselves to rest with humbled hearts; praying, for all those we loved, a blessing of peace and good-will.

Chapter XXXIX.

N the ensuing Christmas morning, I chanced to rise betimes, and entering my dressing-room, opened the windows, and looked out on the soft landscape, over which mists were still lying; whilst the serene sky above, and the lawns and leafless woods in the foreground near, were still pink with sunrise. The grey had not even left the west yet, and I could see a star or two twinkling there, to vanish with that twilight.

As I looked out, I saw the not very distant lodge-gate open after a brief parley, and a lady on horseback, followed by a servant, rode rapidly up to the house.

This early visitor was no other than Miss Ethel Newcome. The young lady espied me immediately. "Come down; come down to me this moment, Mr. Pendennis," she cried out. I hastened down to her, supposing rightly, that news of importance had brought her to Rosebury so early.

The news were of importance indeed. "Look here!" she said, "read this;" and she took a paper from the pocket of her habit. "When I went home last night, after Madame de Florac had been talking to us about Orme's India, I took the volumes from the bookcase and found this paper. It is in my grandmother's—Mrs. Newcome's—hand-writing; I know it quite well; it is dated on the very day of her death. She had been writing and reading in her study on that very night; I have often heard Papa speak of the circumstance. Look and read. You are a lawyer, Mr. Pendennis; tell me about this paper."

I seized it eagerly, and cast my eyes over it; but having read it, my countenance fell.

"My dear Miss Newcome, it is not worth a penny," I was obliged to own.

"Yes it is, Sir, to honest people!" she cried out, "My brother and uncle will respect it as Mrs. Newcome's dying wish. They *must* respect it."

The paper in question was a letter in ink that had grown yellow from time, and was addressed by the late Mrs. Newcome, to "my dear Mr. Luce."

A Friend in Need

"That was her solicitor, my solicitor still," interposes Miss Ethel.

"The Hermitage, *March* 14, 182—.

"My dear Mr. Luce" (the defunct lady wrote). "My late husband's grand-son has been staying with me lately, and is a most pleasing, handsome, and engaging little boy. He bears a strong likeness to his grandfather, I think; and though he has no claims upon *me*, and I know is sufficiently provided for by his father, Lieutenant-Colonel Newcome, C.B., of the East India Company's Service, I am sure my late dear husband will be pleased that I should leave his grandson, Clive Newcome, a token of *peace and good-will;* and I can do so with the more readiness, as it has pleased Heaven greatly to increase my means since my husband was called away hence.

"I desire to bequeath a sum equal to that which Mr. Newcome willed to my eldest son, Brian Newcome, Esq., to Mr. Newcome's grandson, Clive Newcome; and furthermore, that a token of my esteem and affection, a ring, or a piece of plate, of the value of £100, be given to Lieutenant-Colonel Thomas Newcome, my step-son, whose excellent conduct *for many years,* and whose repeated acts of gallantry in the *service of his sovereign,* have long obliterated the just feelings of displeasure with which I could not but view his early *disobedience and misbehavior,* before he quitted England against my will, and entered the military service.

"I beg you to prepare immediately a codicil to my will, providing for the above bequests; and desire that the amount of these legacies should be taken from the property bequeathed to my eldest son. You will be so good as to prepare the necessary document, and bring it with you when you come on Saturday, to

"Yours very truly,

"Tuesday night.   SOPHIA ALETHEA NEWCOME."

I gave back the paper with a sigh to the finder. "It is but a wish of Mrs. Newcome, my dear Miss Ethel," I said. "Pardon me, if I say, I think I know your elder brother too well to suppose that he will fulfil it."

"He *will* fulfil it, Sir, I am sure he will," Miss Newcome said, in a haughty manner. "He would do as much without being asked, I am certain he would, did he know the depth of my dear uncle's misfortune. Barnes is in London now, and—"

"And you will write to him? I know what the answer will be."

"I will go to him this very day, Mr. Pendennis! I will go to my dear, dear uncle. I cannot bear to think of him in that place," cried the young lady, the tears starting into her honest[1] eyes. "It was the will of Heaven. O God be thanked for it! Had we found my grandmamma's letter earlier, Barnes would have paid the legacy immediately, and the money would have gone in that dreadful bankruptcy. I will go to Barnes to-day. Will you come with me? Won't you come to your old friends. We may be at his,—at Clive's house this evening; and O, praise be to God! there need be no more want in his family."

"My dear friend, I will go with you round the world on such an errand," I said, kissing her hand. How beautiful she looked! the generous colour

---

[1] honest *E 1*] [omitted] *R*

rose in her face, her voice thrilled with happiness. The music of Christmas church bells leaped up at this moment with joyful gratulations; the face of the old house, before which we stood talking, shone out in the morning sun.

"You will come? thank you! I must run and tell Madame de Florac," cried the happy young lady, and we entered the house together. "How came you to be kissing Ethel's hand, Sir; and what is the meaning of this early visit," asks Mrs. Laura, as soon as I had returned to my own apartments.

"Martha, get me a carpet bag! I am going to London in an hour," cries Mr. Pendennis. If I had kissed Ethel's hand just now, delighted at the news which she brought to me, was not one a thousand times dearer to me, as happy as her friend? I know who prayed with a thankful heart that day as we sped, in the almost solitary train, towards London.

Chapter XL.

EFORE I parted with Miss Newcome at the station, she made me promise to see her on the morrow at an early hour at her brother's house; and having bidden her farewell and repaired to my own solitary residence which presented but a dreary aspect on that festive day I thought I would pay Howland Street a visit; and, if invited, eat my Christmas dinner with Clive.

I found my friend at home, and at work still in spite of the day. He had promised a pair of pictures to a dealer for the morrow. "He pays me pretty well, and I want all the money he will give me, Pen," the painter said—rubbing on at his canvas. "I am pretty easy in my mind since I have become acquainted with a virtuous dealer. I sell myself to him body and soul for some half-dozen pounds a week. I know I can get my money and he is regularly supplied with his pictures. But for Rosey's illness we might carry on well enough."

Rosey's illness? I was sorry to hear of that: and poor Clive entering into particulars told me how he had spent upon doctors rather more than a fourth of his year's earnings—"There is a solemn fellow to whom the women have taken a fancy, who lives but a few doors off in Gower Street; and who for his last sixteen visits has taken sixteen pounds sixteen shillings out of my pocket with the most admirable gravity and as if guineas grew there. He talks the fashions to my mother-in-law. My poor wife hangs on every word he says—Look! There is his carriage coming up now! and there is his fee, confound him!" says Clive casting a rueful look towards a little packet lying upon the mantel-piece, by the side of that skinned figure in plaister of Paris which we have seen in most studios.

I looked out of window and saw a certain Fashionable Doctor[1] tripping out of his chariot; that[2] Ladies' Delight who has subsequently migrated from Bloomsbury to Belgravia; and who has his polite foot now in a thousand nurseries and boudoirs. What Confessors were in old times, Quackenboss and his like are in our Protestant country. What secrets they know! into what mystic chambers do they not enter! I suppose the Campaigner made a special toilette to receive her fashionable friend, for that lady, attired in considerable splendour, and with the precious jewel on her head which I remembered at Boulogne, came into the studio two minutes after the Doctor's visit was announced; and made him a low curtsey. I cannot describe the overpowering civilities of that woman.

Clive was very gracious and humble to her. He adopted a lively air in addressing her—"Must work you know, Christmas day and all—for the owner of the pictures will call for them in the morning. Bring me a good report about Rosey, Mrs. Mackenzie, please—and if you will have the kindness to look by the *Écorché* there you will see that little packet, which I have left for you." Mrs. Mack advancing, took the money. I thought that plaister of Paris figure was not the only *Écorché* in the room.

"I want you to stay to dinner. You must stay, Pen, please," cried Clive; "and be civil to her, will you? My dear old father is coming to dine here. They fancy that he has lodgings at the other end of the town, and that his brothers do something for him. Not a word about Grey Friars. It might agitate Rosa, you know. Ah. Isn't he noble, the dear old boy! and isn't it fine to see him in that place?" Clive worked on as he talked: using up the last remnant of the light of Christmas day, and was cleaning his palette and brushes when Mrs. Mackenzie returned to us.

Darling Rosey was very delicate, but Doctor Quackenboss was going to give her the very same medicine which had done the charming young Duchess of Clackmannanshire so much good, and he was not in the least disquiet.

On this I cut into the conversation with anecdotes concerning the family of the Duchess of Clackmannanshire remembering early days when it used to be my sport to entertain the Campaigner with anecdotes of the aristocracy, about whose proceedings she still maintained a laudable curiosity. Indeed one of the few books escaped out of the wreck of Tyburn Gardens was a Peerage, now a well-worn volume, much read by Rosa and her mother.

The anecdotes were very politely received—perhaps it was the season which made Mrs. Mack and her son-in-law on more than ordinarily good terms. When, turning to the Campaigner, Clive said he wished that she could persuade me to stay to dinner, she acquiesced graciously and at once in that proposal—and vowed that her daughter would be delighted if I could condescend to eat their *humble* fare. "It is not such a dinner as you *have* seen at her house, with six side dishes, two flanks, that splen-

[1] Doctor *E1*] Doctor, Doctor Quackenboss, *Ms*
[2] that *E1*] of that *Ms*

did epergne, and the silver dishes top and bottom—but such as my Rosa *has* she offers with a willing *heart*," cries the Campaigner.

"And Tom may sit to dinner, mayn't he? Grandmamma?" asks Clive in a humble voice.

"O if you wish it, Sir."

"His grandfather will like to sit by him," said Clive—"I will go out and meet him; he comes through Guilford Street and Russell Square," says Clive. "Will you walk, Pen?"

"O pray don't let *us* detain you," says Mrs. Mackenzie with a toss of her head: and when she retreated Clive whispered that she would not want me; for she looked to the roasting of the beef and the making of the pudding and the mince-pie.

"I thought she might have a finger in it," I said, and we set forth to meet the dear old father who presently came walking very slowly, along the line by which we expected him. His stick trembled as it fell on the pavement: so did his voice as he called out Clive's name; so did his hand as he stretched it to me. His body was bent and feeble. Twenty years had not weakened him so much as the last score of months. I walked by the side of my two friends as they went onwards linked lovingly together. How I longed for the morrow and hoped they might be united once more! Thomas Newcome's voice once so grave went up to a treble and became almost childish as he asked after Boy. His white hair hung over his collar—I could see it by the gas under which we walked—and Clive's great back and arm as his father leaned on it, and his brave face turned towards the old man. O Barnes Newcome, Barnes Newcome! Be an honest man for once, and help your kinsfolk! thought I.

The Christmas meal went off in a friendly manner enough. The Campaigner's eyes were every where; it was evident that the little maid who served the dinner and had cooked a portion of it under their keen supervision cowered under them as well as other folks. Mrs. Mack did not make more than ten allusions to former splendours during the entertainment, or half as many apologies to me for sitting down to a table very different from that to which I was *accustomed*. Good faithful F. Bayham was the only other guest. He complimented the mince-pies, so that Mrs. Mackenzie owned she had made them. The Colonel was very silent, but he tried to feed Boy, and was only once or twice[3] sternly corrected by the Campaigner. Boy in the best little words he[4] could muster asked why Grandpapa wore a black cloak?—Clive nudged my foot under the table: the secret of the Poor Brothership was very nearly out. The Colonel blushed—and with great presence of mind said he wore a cloak to keep him warm in winter. Rosey did not say much. She had grown lean and languid: the light of her eyes had gone out: all her pretty freshness had faded.[5] She ate scarce anything, though her mother pressed her eagerly; and whispered loudly that a woman in her situation ought to strengthen herself. Poor Rosey was always in a situation.

---

[3] once or twice *E1*] once twice *Ms*
[4] he *E1*] which he *Ms*
[5] had faded. *E1*] was gone †had faded.↓ *Ms*

When the cloth was withdrawn; the Colonel bending his head said, "Thank God for what we have received," so reverently[6] and with an accent so touching that Fred Bayham's big eyes as he turned towards the old man filled up with tears. When his mother and grandmother rose to go away, poor little Boy cried to stay longer, and the Colonel would have meekly interposed, but the domineering Campaigner cried, "Nonsense, let him go to bed!" and flounced him out of the room: and nobody appealed against that sentence. Then we three remained and strove to talk as cheerfully as we might, speaking now of old times, and presently of new. Without the slightest affectation, Thomas Newcome told us that his life was comfortable and that he was happy in it. He wished that many others of the old gentlemen, he said, were as contented as himself, but some of them grumbled sadly, he owned, and—and[7] quarrelled with their bread and butter. He for his part had everything he could desire: all the officers of the Establishment were most kind to him; an excellent physician came to him when wanted: a most attentive woman waited on him. "And if I wear a black gown," said he, "is not that uniform as good as another—and if we have to go to church every day, at which some of the Poor Brothers grumble—I think an old fellow can't do better; and I can say my prayers with a thankful heart, Clivey my boy—and should be quite happy but for my—for my past imprudence, God forgive me. Think of Bayham here coming to our chapel to-day! he often comes—that was very right, Sir—very right."

Clive, filling a glass of wine, looked at F.B. with eyes that said God bless you: F.B. gulped down another bumper. "It is almost a merry Christmas," said I, "and O I hope it will be a happy New Year!"

Shortly after nine o'clock the Colonel rose to depart saying he must be "in barracks" by ten: and Clive and F.B. went a part of the way with him. I would have followed them, but Clive whispered me to stay—and talk to Mrs. Mack for Heaven's sake, and that he would be back ere long. So I went and took tea with the two ladies; and as we drank it Mrs. Mackenzie took occasion to tell me she did not know what amount of income the Colonel had from his *wealthy brother*,[8] but that *they* never received any benefit from it; and again she computed to me all the sums, principal and interest, which ought at that moment to belong to her darling Rosey. Rosey now and again made a feeble remark. She did not seem pleased or sorry when her husband came in; and, presently, dropping me a little curtsey, went to bed under charge of the Campaigner. So Bayham and I and Clive retired to the studio, where smoking was allowed, and where we brought that Christmas day to an end.

At the appointed time on the next forenoon I called upon Miss Newcome at her brother's house. Sir Barnes Newcome was quitting his own door as I entered it, and he eyed me with such a severe countenance, as made me augur but ill of the business upon which I came. The expression of Ethel's face was scarcely more cheering: she was standing at the window sternly looking at Sir Barnes, who yet lingered at his own threshold having some

[6] so reverently *E1*] so very reverently *Ms*
[7] and—and *Ms*] and *E1*
[8] *brother,* *E1*] *brothers,* *Ms*

altercation with his cab-boy ere he mounted his vehicle to drive into the City.

Miss Newcome was very[9] pale when she advanced and gave me her hand—I looked with some alarm into her face, and enquired what news?

"It is as you expected, Mr. Pendennis," she said—"not as I did. My brother is averse to making restitution. He just now parted from me in some anger. But it does not matter, the restitution must be made, if not by Barnes, by one of our family, must it not?"

"God bless you for a noble creature, my dear dear Miss Newcome!" was all I could say.

"For doing what is right? Ought I not to do it? I am the eldest of our family after Barnes: I am the richest, after him. Our father left all his younger children the very sum of money which Mrs. Newcome here devises to Clive—and you know besides, I have all my grandmother's, Lady Kew's, property. Why, I don't think I could sleep if this act of justice were not done. Will you come with me to my lawyer's? He and my brother Barnes are trustees of my property: and I have been thinking—dear Mr. Pendennis—and you are very good to be so kind, and to express so kind an opinion of me, and you and Laura have always always been the best friends to me—(she says this, taking one of my hands and placing her other hand over it)—I have been thinking, you know, that this transfer had better be made through Mr. Luce, you understand—and as coming from the *family*, and then I need not appear in it at[1] all, you see—and—and my dear good uncle's pride need not be wounded." She fairly gave way to tears as she spoke—and for me, I longed to kiss the hem of her robe or—or[2] anything else she would let me embrace, I was so happy, and so touched by the simple demeanour and affection of the noble young lady.

"Dear Ethel," I said, "Did I not say I would go to the end of the world with[3] you—and won't I go to Lincoln's Inn?"

A cab was straightway sent for, and in another half hour we were in the presence of the courtly little old Mr. Luce, in his chambers in Lincoln's Inn Fields.

He knew the late Mrs. Newcome's hand-writing at once. He remembered having seen the little boy at the Hermitage, had talked with Mr. Newcome regarding his son in India, and had even encouraged Mrs. Newcome in her idea of leaving some token of good will to the latter—"I *was* to have dined with your grandmamma on the Saturday, with my poor wife. Why, bless my soul! I remember the circumstance perfectly well, my dear young lady. There can't be a doubt about the letter—but of course the bequest is no bequest at all—and Colonel Newcome has behaved so ill to your brother that I suppose Sir Barnes will not go out of his way to benefit the Colonel."

"What would *you* do? Mr. Luce," asks the young lady.

"Hm! And pray why should I tell you what I should do under the circumstances?" replied the little lawyer. "Upon my word, Miss Newcome, I

[9] very *E1*] looking very *Ms*
[1] at *E1*] [omitted] *Ms*
[2] or—or *Ms*] or *E1*
[3] with *E1*] for *Ms*

think I should leave matters as they stand. Sir Barnes and I, you are aware, are not the very best of friends—as your father's, your grandmother's, old friend and adviser—and your own too, my dear young lady, I and Sir Barnes Newcome remain on civil terms. But neither is over much pleased with the other, to say the truth, and at any rate I cannot be accused—nor can any one else that I know of—of being a very warm partisan of your brother's. But, candidly, were his case mine, had I a relation who had called me unpleasant names, and threatened me I don't know with what, with sword and pistol—who had put me to five or six thousand pounds' expense in contesting an election which I had lost;—I should give him, I think, no more than the law obliged me to give him—and that, my dear Miss Newcome, is not one farthing."

"I am very glad you say so," said Miss Newcome, rather to my astonishment.

"Of course, my dear young lady—and so you need not be alarmed at showing your brother this document. Is not that the point about which you came to consult me? You wished that I should prepare him for the awful disclosure, did you not? You know perhaps that he does not like to part with his money, and thought the appearance of this note to me might agitate him? It has been a long time coming to its address—but nothing can be done, don't you see?—and, be sure, Sir Barnes Newcome will not be the least agitated when I tell him its contents."

"I mean I am very glad you think my brother is not called upon to obey Mrs. Newcome's wishes—because I need not think so hardly of him as I was disposed to do," Miss Newcome said. "I showed him the paper this morning and he repelled it with scorn—and not kind words passed between us, Mr. Luce—and unkind thoughts remained in my mind. But if he you think is justified, it is I who have been in the wrong for saying that he was self—for upbraiding him as I own I did."

"You called him selfish!—You had words with him! Such things have happened before, my dear Miss Newcome, in the best regulated families."

"But if he is not wrong, Sir, holding his opinions—surely I should be wrong, Sir, with mine, not to do as my conscience tells me; and having found this paper only yesterday at Newcome in the library there in one of my grandmother's books—I consulted with this gentleman, the husband of my dearest friend, Mrs. Pendennis—the most intimate friend of my uncle and cousin Clive; and I wish and I desire and insist that my share of what my poor father left us girls should be given to my cousin, Mr. Clive Newcome, in accordance with my grandmother's dying wishes."

"My dear—you gave away your portion to your brothers and sisters ever so long ago!" cried the lawyer.

"I desire, Sir, that six thousand pounds may be given to my cousin," Miss Newcome said blushing deeply. "My dear uncle, the best man in the world, whom I love with all my heart, Sir, is in the most dreadful poverty. Do you know where he is, Sir? my dear kind generous uncle!"—and kindling as she spoke and with eyes beaming a bright kindness, and flushing cheeks, and a voice that thrilled to the heart of those two who heard her, Miss Newcome went on to tell of her uncle's and cousin's misfortunes and of her wish, under God, to relieve them. I see before me now the figure of the noble girl as she speaks; the pleased little old lawyer, bobbing his white head looking up at her with his twinkling eyes—patting his knees, patting his snuff-box—as he sits before his tapes and his deeds, surrounded by a great background of tin boxes.

"And I understand you want this money paid as coming from the family, and not from Miss Newcome?" says Mr. Luce.

"Coming from the family—exactly"—answers Miss Newcome.

Mr. Luce rose up from his old chair—his worn-out[4] old horsehair chair—where he had sate for half a century and listened to many a speaker very different from this one. "Mr. Pendennis," he said, "I envy you your journey along with this young lady. I envy you the good news you are going to carry to your friends—and, Miss Newcome, as I am an old old gentleman who have known your family these sixty years, and saw your father in his long-clothes—may I tell you how heartily and sincerely I—I love and respect you, my dear? When should you wish Mr. Clive Newcome to have his legacy?"

"I think I should like Mr. Pendennis to have it this instant, Mr. Luce, please," said the young lady—and her veil dropped over her face as she bent her head down, and clasped her hands together for a moment as if she was praying.

Mr. Luce laughed at her impetuosity; but said that if she was bent upon having the money, it was at her instant service; and before we left the room, Mr. Luce prepared a letter addressed to Clive Newcome, Esquire, in which he stated that amongst the books of the late Mrs. Newcome a paper had only just been found of which a copy[5] was enclosed, and that the family of the late Sir Brian Newcome, desirous to do honour to the wishes of the late Mrs. Newcome, had placed the sum of £6,000 at the bank of Messrs. Hob——[6] at the disposal of Mr. Clive Newcome, of whom Mr. Luce had the honour to sign himself the most obedient servant &c.—And, the letter approved and copied, Mr. Luce said Mr. Pendennis might be the postman thereof if Miss Newcome so willed it: and with this document in my pocket, I quitted the lawyer's chambers with my good and beautiful young companion.

Our cab had been waiting several hours in Lincoln's Inn Fields, and I asked Miss Ethel whither I now should conduct her?

"Where is Grey Friars?" she said. "Mayn't I go to see my uncle?"

[4] his worn-out *E1*] worn-out *Ms*
[5] a copy *E1*] copy *Ms*
[6] Hob—— *Ms*] H. W—— *E1*

Chapter XLI.

E made the descent of Snowhill, we passed by the miry pens of Smithfield, we travel through the street of St. John, and presently reach the ancient gateway, in Cistercian Square, where lies the old Hospital of Grey Friars. I passed through the gate, my fair young companion on my arm, and made my way to the rooms occupied by Brother Newcome.

As we traversed the court the Poor Brothers were coming from dinner. A couple of score or more of old gentlemen in black gowns, issued from the door of their refectory, and separated over the court, betaking themselves to their chambers. Ethel's arm trembled under mine as she looked at one and another, expecting to behold her dear uncle's familiar features. But he was not among the brethren. We went to his chamber, of which the door was open: a female attendant was arranging the room; she told us Colonel Newcome was out for the day, and thus our journey had been made in vain.

Ethel went round the apartment, and surveyed its simple decorations; she looked at the pictures of Clive and his boy; the two sabres crossed over the mantel-piece: the Bible laid on the table by the old latticed window. She walked slowly up to the humble bed, and sat down on a chair near it. No doubt her heart prayed for him who slept there; she turned round where his black Pensioner's cloak was hanging on the wall, and lifted up the homely garment, and kissed it. The servant looked on admiring, I should think, her melancholy and her gracious beauty—I whispered to the woman that the young lady was the Colonel's niece; "He has a son who comes here, and is very handsome, too," said the attendant.

The two women spoke together for a while. "O Miss!" cried the elder and humbler, evidently astonished at some gratuity which Miss Newcome bestowed upon her, "I didn't want this to be good to him. Every body here loves him for himself; and I would sit up for him for weeks—that I would."

[7] IN WHICH ... TOGETHER. E1] IN WHICH THE READER IS INVITED TO TWO DINNERS. Ms

My companion took a pencil from her bag, and wrote "Ethel" on a piece of paper, and laid the paper on the Bible. Darkness had again fallen by this time; feeble lights were twinkling in the chamber-windows of the Poor Brethren, as we issued into the courts;—feeble lights illumining a dim, grey, melancholy, old scene. Many a career, once bright, was flickering out here in the darkness; many a night was closing in. We went away silently from that quiet place; and in another minute were in the flare and din and tumult of London.

"The Colonel is most likely gone to Clive's," I said. Would not Miss Newcome follow him thither? We consulted whether she should go. She took heart and said yes. "Drive, cabman, to Howland Street!" The horse was no doubt tired for the journey seemed extraordinarily long: I think neither of us spoke a word on the way.

I ran upstairs to prepare our friends for the visit. Clive, his wife, his father, and his mother-in-law were seated by a dim light in Mrs. Clive's sitting-room. Rosey on the sofa as usual; the little boy on his grandfather's knees.

I hardly made a bow to the ladies, so eager was I to communicate with Colonel Newcome. "I have just been to your quarters at Grey Friars, Sir," said I. "That is—"

"You have been to the Hospital, Sir! You need not be ashamed to mention it, as Colonel Newcome is not ashamed *to go there,*" cried out the Campaigner—"Pray speak in your own language, Clive, unless there is something *not fit* for ladies to hear." Clive was growling out to me in German that there had just been a terrible scene, his father having, a quarter of an hour previously, let slip the secret about Grey Friars.

"Say at once, Clive!" the Campaigner cried rising in her might, and extending a great strong arm over her helpless child, "that Colonel Newcome owns that he has gone to live as a pauper in a hospital! He who has squandered his own money:—he who has squandered my money: he who has squandered the money of that darling helpless child—Compose yourself, Rosey my love!—has completed the disgrace of the family, by his present mean and unworthy, yes I say *mean* and *unworthy* and *degraded* conduct. O my child, my blessed child! to think that your husband's father should have come to a *work-house!*" Whilst this maternal agony bursts over her, Rosa, on the sofa,[1] bleats and whimpers amongst the faded chintz cushions.

I took Clive's hand, which was cast up to his head; striking his forehead with mad impotent rage, whilst this fiend of a woman lashed his good father. The veins of his great fist were swollen; his whole body was throbbing and trembling with the helpless pain under which he writhed. "Colonel Newcome's friends, Ma'am," I said, "think very differently from you and that he is a better judge than you or any one else, of his own honour. We all, who loved him in his prosperity, love and respect him more than ever for the manner in which he bears his misfortune. Do you suppose that his noble friend the Earl of H—— would have counselled him to a step unworthy of a gentleman; that the Prince de Montcontour would applaud his

---

[1] Rosa, ... sofa, *E1*] Rosa on the sopha below *Ms*

conduct as he does, if he did not think it admirable?" I can hardly say with what scorn I used this argument, or what a depth[2] of contempt I felt for the woman whom I knew it would influence. "And at this minute," I added, "I have come from visiting the Grey Friars with one of the Colonel's relatives whose love and respect for him is boundless, who longs to be reconciled to him, and who is waiting below eager to shake his hand and embrace Clive's wife."

"Who is that?" says the Colonel looking gently up, as he pats Boy's head. "Who is it, Pen!" says Clive. I said in a low voice, "Ethel;" and starting up and crying "Ethel! Ethel!" he ran from the room.

Little Mrs. Rosa started up too on her sofa, clutching hold of the table-cover with her lean hand, and the two red spots on her cheeks burned[3] more fiercely than ever. I could see what passion was beating in that poor little heart, Heaven help us! what a resting place had friends and parents prepared for it!

"Miss Newcome, is it? My darling Rosa, get on your shawl!" cried the Campaigner, a grim smile lighting her face.

"It is Ethel. Ethel is my niece. I used to love her when she was quite a little girl," says the Colonel patting Boy on the head; "and she is a very good beautiful little child—a very good child." The torture had been too much for that kind old heart—there were times when Thomas Newcome passed beyond it. What still maddened Clive, excited his father no more. The pain yonder woman inflicted, only felled and stupified him.

As the door opened, the little whiteheaded child trotted forward towards the visitor, and Ethel entered on Clive's arm who was as haggard and pale as death. Little Boy, looking up at the stately lady, still followed beside her, as she approached her uncle who remained sitting, his head bent to the ground. His thoughts were elsewhere. Indeed he was following the child and about to caress it again.

"Here is a friend, Father!" says Clive laying a hand on the old man's shoulder. "It is I. Ethel, Uncle!" the young lady said taking his hand and kneeling down between his knees she flung her arms round him, and kissed him and wept on his shoulder. His consciousness had quite returned ere an instant was over. He embraced her, with the warmth of his old affection, uttering many brief words of love, kindness, tenderness,[4] such as men speak when strongly moved.

The little boy had come wondering up to the chair whilst this embrace took place and Clive's tall figure bent over the three. Rosa's eyes were not good to look at, as she stared at the group with a ghastly smile. Mrs. Mackenzie surveyed the scene in haughty state, from behind the sofa cushions. She tried to take one of Rosa's lean hot hands. The poor child tore it away, leaving her rings behind her; lifted her hands to her face; and cried—cried as if her little heart would break. Ah me! what a story was there, what an outburst of pent-up feeling! what a passion of pain! The ring had fallen to the ground; the little boy crept towards it and picked it

---

[2] a depth *Ms*] depth *E1*
[3] burn[ed over ing] *Ms*] burning *E1*
[4] tenderness, *Ms*] and tenderness *E1*

up, and came towards his mother, fixing on her his large wondering eyes. "Mamma crying. Mamma's ring!" he said holding up the circle of gold. With more feeling than I had ever seen her exhibit, she clasped the boy in her wasted arms. Great Heaven! what passion, jealousy, grief, despair were tearing and trying all these hearts, that but for fate might have been happy?

Clive went round and with the utmost sweetness and tenderness hanging round his child and wife soothed her with words of consolation that in truth I scarce heard, being ashamed almost of being present at this sudden scene. No one however took notice of the witnesses; and even Mrs. Mackenzie's voice was silent for the moment. I daresay Clive's words were incoherent; but women have more presence of mind; and now Ethel with a noble grace which I cannot attempt to describe, going up to Rosa, seated herself by her, spoke of her long grief at the differences between her dearest uncle and herself; of her early days when he had been as a father to her; of her wish, her hope that Rosa should love her as her sister, and of her belief that better days and happiness were in store for them all. And she spoke to the mother, about her boy so beautiful and intelligent, and told her[5] how she had brought up her brother's children, and hoped that this one too, would call her Aunt Ethel. She would not stay now, might she come again? Would Rosa come to her with her little boy? Would he kiss her? He did so with a very good grace, but when Ethel at parting embraced the child's mother, Rosa's face wore a smile ghastly to look at, and the lips that touched Ethel's cheek were quite white.

"I shall come and see you again to-morrow, Uncle, may I not? I saw your room to-day, Sir, and your housekeeper, such a nice old lady, and your black-gown. And you shall put it on to-morrow and walk with me and show me the beautiful old buildings of the old Hospital. And I shall come and make tea for you. The housekeeper says I may. Will you come down with me to my carriage? No, Mr. Pendennis must come," and she quitted the room beckoning me after her.

"You will speak to Clive now, won't you?" she said, "and come to me this evening, and tell me all before you go to bed?" I went back, anxious in truth to be the messenger of good tidings to my dear old friends.

Brief as my absence had been, Mrs. Mackenzie had taken advantage of that moment again to outrage Clive and his father, and to announce that Rosa might go to see this Miss Newcome whom people respected because she was rich but whom *she* would never visit; no never! 'An insolent proud impertinent thing! Does she take me for a housemaid?" Mrs. Mackenzie had inquired, "Am I dust to be trampled beneath her feet? Am I a dog that she can't throw me a word?" Her arms were stretched out, and she was making this inquiry as to her own canine qualities as I re-entered the rooms,[6] and remembered that Ethel had never once addressed a single word to Mrs. Mackenzie in the course of her visit.

---

[5] her *E1*] [omitted] *Ms*
[6] rooms, *Ms*] room, *E1*

I affected not to perceive the incident and presently said that I wanted to speak to Clive in his Studio. Knowing that I had brought my Friend one or two commissions for drawings, Mrs. Mackenzie was civil to me and did not object to our colloquies.

"Will you come too and smoke a pipe, Father?" says Clive.

"*Of course* your father intends to stay to *dinner!*" says the Campaigner with a scornful toss of her head; Clive groaned out as we were on the stair, that he could not bear this much longer, by Heavens he could not.

"Give the Colonel his pipe, Clive," said I. "Now, Sir, down with you in the Sitter's Chair, and smoke the sweetest cheroot you ever smoked in your life! My dear dear old Clive! you need not bear with the Campaigner any longer—you may go to bed without this night mare to-night if you like; you may have your father back under your roof again ..."

"My dear Arthur! I must be back at ten, Sir, back at ten military time, drum beats, no—bell tolls at ten, and gates close!" and he laughed and shook his old head. "Besides, I am to see a young lady, Sir, and she is coming to make tea for me, and I must speak to Mrs. Jones to have all things ready—all things ready."—and again the old man laughed as he spoke.

His son looked at him and then at me with eyes full of sad meaning, "How do you mean, Arthur," Clive said, "that he *can* come and stay with me, and that that woman can go?"

Then feeling in my pocket for Mr. Luce's letter, I grasped my dear Clive by the hand and bade him prepare for good news. I told him how Providentially two days since, Ethel in the Library at Newcome, looking into Orme's History of India, a book which old Mrs. Newcome had been reading on the night of her death, had discovered a paper of which the accompanying letter enclosed a copy, and I gave my friend the letter.

He opened it and read it through. I cannot say that I saw any particular expression of wonder in his countenance, for somehow, all the while Clive perused this document, I was looking at the Colonel's sweet kind face. "It—it is Ethel's doing"—said Clive, in a hurried voice. "There was no such letter!"

"Upon my honour," I answered, "there was. We came up to London with it last night, a few hours after she had found it. We showed it to Sir Barnes Newcome, who—who could not disown it. We took it to Mr. Luce who recognised it at once, who was old Mrs. Newcome's man of business and continues to be the family lawyer, and the family recognises the legacy and has paid it, and you may draw for it to-morrow as you see. What a piece of good luck it is that it did not come before the B.B.C. time. That confounded Bundelcund Bank, would have swallowed up this, like all the rest."

"Father, Father, do you remember Orme's History of India?" cries Clive.

"Orme's history! of course I do, I could repeat whole pages of it when I was a boy," says the old man, and began forthwith, " 'The two battalions advanced against each other cannonading, until the French, coming to a hollow way, imagined that the English would not venture to pass it. But Major Lawrence ordered the sepoys and artillery—the sepoys and artillery to halt and defend the convoy against the Morattoes'—Morattoes Orme calls 'em. Ho! Ho! I could repeat whole pages, Sir!"

"It is the best book that ever was written!" calls out Clive. The Colonel said he had not read it, but he was informed Mr. Mill's was a very learned history, he intended to read it, "Eh! there is plenty of time now," said the good Colonel, "I have all day long at Grey Friars,—after chapel, you know. Do you know, Sir, when I was a boy I used what they call to tib out and run down to a public-house in Cistercian Lane—The Red Cow, Sir—and buy rum there? I was a terrible wild boy, Clivey. You weren't so, Sir, thank Heaven. A terrible wild boy, and my poor father flogged me, though I think it was very hard on me. It wasn't the pain you know, it wasn't the pain, but . . . ." here tears came into his eyes and he dropped his head on his hand, and the cigar from it fell on to the floor, burnt almost out, and scattering white ashes.

Clive looked sadly at me, "He was often so at Boulogne, Arthur," he whispered; "After a scene with that—that woman yonder, his head would go: he never replied to her taunts: he bore her infernal cruelty without an unkind word—O! I can pay her back, thank God I can pay her! But who shall pay her," he said trembling in every limb, "for what she has made that good man suffer?"

He turned to his father who still sate, lost in his meditations, "You need never go back to Grey Friars, Father!" he cried out.

"Not go back, Clivey? must go back, boy, to say *Adsum* when my name is called—Newcome! Adsum! Hey! that is what we used to say—we used to say!"

"You need not go back except to pack your things, and return and live with me and Boy," Clive continued, and he told Colonel Newcome rapidly the story of the legacy. The old man seemed hardly to comprehend it. When he did, the news scarcely elated him; when Clive said they could now pay Mrs. Mackenzie, the Colonel replied, "Quite right, quite right;" and added up the sum, principal and interest; in which they were indebted to her—he knew it well enough, the good old man. "Of course we shall pay her, Clivey, when we can!" But in spite of what Clive had said he did not appear to understand the fact, that the debt to Mrs. Mackenzie was now actually to be paid.

As we were talking, a knock came to the studio door, and that summons was followed by the entrance of the maid who said to Clive, "If you please, Sir, Mrs. Mackenzie says how long are you agoing to keep the dinner waiting?"

"Come, Father, come to dinner!" cries Clive, "and, Pen, you will come too, won't you?" he added, "It may be the last time you dine in such pleasant company. Come along," he whispered hurriedly. "I should like you to be there. It will keep her tongue quiet." As we proceeded to the dining-room, I gave the Colonel my arm; and the good man prattled to me something about Mrs. Mackenzie having taken shares in the Bundelcund Banking Company, and about her not being a woman of business, and fancying we had spent her money. "And I have always felt a wish that Clivey should pay her and he will pay her I know he will," says the Colonel, "and then we shall lead a quiet life, Arthur; for, between ourselves, some women are the deuce when they are angry, Sir." And again he laughed, as he told me this sly news, and he bowed meekly his gentle old head as we entered the dining-room.

That apartment was occupied by little Boy already seated in his high chair, and by the Campaigner only, who stood at the mantel-piece in a majestic attitude. On parting with her, before we adjourned to Clive's studio, I had made my bow and taken my leave in form, not supposing that I was about to enjoy her hospitality yet once again. My return did not seem to please her. "Does Mr. Pendennis favour us with his company to[7] dinner again, Clive?" she said turning to her son-in-law. Clive curtly said, Yes, he had asked Mr. Pendennis to stay.

"You might at least have been *so kind* as to give me notice," says the Campaigner, still majestic but ironical. "You will have but a poor meal, Mr. Pendennis; and one such as I am not accustomed to give my guests."

"Cold beef! what the deuce does it matter?" says Clive beginning to carve the[8] joint which, hot, had served our yesterday's Christmas table.

"It *does* matter, Sir! I am not accustomed to treat my guests in this way. Maria! who has been cutting that beef? Three pounds of that beef have been cut away since one o'clock to-day," and with flashing eyes, and a finger twinkling all over with rings, she pointed towards the guilty joint.

Whether Maria had been dispensing secret charities, or kept company with an occult policeman partial to roast beef, I do not know; but she looked very much alarmed, and said, Indeed and indeed, Mum, she had not touched a morsel of it:—not she.

"Confound the beef!" says Clive carving on.

"She *has* been cutting it!" cries the Campaigner, bringing her fist down with a thump upon the table. "Mr. Pendennis! You saw the beef yesterday; eighteen pounds it weighed, and this is what comes up of it! As if there was not already ruin enough in the house!"

"D—n the beef!" cries out Clive.

"No no! Thank God for our good dinner, Benedicti Benedicamus, Clivey my boy!" says the Colonel in a tremulous voice.

"Swear on, Sir! let the child hear your oaths! let my blessed child, who is too ill to sit at table and picks her bit of sweetbread on her sofa,—which her poor mother *prepares* for her, Mr. Pendennis,—which I cooked it—and gave it to her with *these hands*,—let *her* hear your curses, and blasphemies, Clive Newcome! They are loud enough."

"Do let us have a quiet life," groans out Clive,[9] and for me, I confess I kept my eyes steadily down upon my plate, nor dared to lift them, until my portion of cold beef had vanished.

No farther outbreak took place until the appearance of the second course; which consisted, as the ingenious reader may suppose, of the plum-pudding, now in a grilled state, and the remanent mince-pies from yesterday's meal. Maria, I thought, looked particularly guilty, as these delicacies

---

[7] to *E1*] at *Ms*
[8] carve the *E1*] carve upon the *Ms*
[9] Clive, *E1*] poor Clive, *Ms*

were placed on the table: she set them down hastily, and was for operating an instant retreat.

But the Campaigner shrieked after her, "Who has eaten that pudding? I insist upon knowing who has eaten it. I saw it at two o'clock when I went down to the kitchen and fried a bit for my darling child, and there's pounds of it gone since then! There were five mince-pies, Mr. Pendennis— you saw yourself there were five went away from table yesterday,—where's the other two, Maria? You leave the house this night, you thieving wicked wretch—and I'll thank you to come back to me afterwards for a character. Thirteen servants have we had in nine months, Mr. Pendennis, and this girl is the worst of them all and the greatest liar and the greatest thief."

At this charge the outraged Maria stood up in arms and as the phrase is, gave the Campaigner as good as she got. Go! wouldn't she go? Pay her her wages and let her[1] go out of that Ell upon hearth was Maria's prayer. "It isn't you, Sir," she said turning to Clive. "*You* are good enough, and works hard enough to git the guineas which you give out to pay that Doctor; and she *don't* pay him—and I see five of them in her purse wrapped up in paper, myself I did—and she abuses you to him,—and I heard her and Jane Black who was here before told me she heard her. Go! won't I just go, I despises your puddens and pies!" and with a laugh of scorn this rude Maria snapped her black fingers in the immediate vicinity of the Campaigner's nose.

"I will pay her her wages and she shall go this instant!" says Mrs. Mackenzie taking her purse out.

"Pay me with them suvverings that you have got in it, wrapped up in paper—see if she haven't, Mr. Newcome," the refractory waiting-woman cried out, and again she laughed a strident laugh.

Mrs. Mackenzie briskly shut her porte-monnaie, and rose up from table, quivering with indignant virtue. "Go!" she exclaimed, "Go and pack your trunks this instant! you quit the house this night, and a policeman shall see to your boxes before you leave it!"

Whilst uttering this sentence against the guilty Maria, the Campaigner had intended, no doubt, to replace her purse in her pocket;—a handsome fillagree gimcrack of poor Rosa's, one of the relics of former splendours: but, agitated by Maria's insolence, the trembling hand missed the mark and the purse fell to[2] the ground.

Maria dashed at the purse in a moment, with a scream of laughter shook its contents upon the table, and sure enough, five little packets wrapped in paper rolled out upon the cloth, besides bank notes and silver and golden[3] coin. "I'm to go? am I? I'm a thief am I?" screamed the girl clapping her hands, "*I* sor em yesterday when I was a lacing of her: and thought of that pore young man working night and day, to get the money;—me a thief indeed! I despise you and *I* give you warning."

"Do you wish to see me any longer insulted by this woman? Clive! Mr. Pendennis! I am shocked that you should witness such horrible vulgarity!" cries the Campaigner turning to her guest, "Does the wretched creature

---

[1] let her *E1*] her *Ms*
[2] fell to *E1*] fell down to *Ms*
[3] golden *Ms E1*] gold *HM NY R*

suppose that I, I who have given *thousands*, I who have denied myself *everything*, I who have spent my *all* in support of this house; and Colonel Newcome *knows* whether I have given thousands or not, and *who* has spent them and *who* has been robbed, I say, and . . ."

"Here! You! Maria! go about your business," shouted out Clive Newcome starting up, "Go and pack your trunks if you like and pack this woman's trunks too. Mrs. Mackenzie! I can bear you no more; go in peace and if you wish to see your daughter she shall come to you, but I will never, so help me God! sleep under the same roof with you, or break the same crust with you, or bear your infernal cruelty; or sit to hear my father insulted; or listen to your wicked pride and folly more. There has not been a day, since you thrust your cursed foot into our wretched house, but you have tortured one and all of us. Look here:—at the best gentleman, and the kindest heart in all the world, you fiend! and see to what a condition you have brought him! Dearest Father! She is going, do you hear? She leaves us, and you will come back to me, won't you? Great God, woman," he gasped out, "Do you know what you have made me suffer—what you have done to this good man. Pardon, Father, pardon," and he sank down by his father's side sobbing with passionate emotion. The old man even now did not seem to comprehend the scene. When he heard that woman's voice, in anger, a sort of stupor came over him.

"I am a *fiend*, am I?" cries the lady. "You hear, Mr. Pendennis, this is the language to which I am accustomed, I am a widow and I trusted my child and my all to that old man; he robbed me and my darling of almost every farthing we had, and what has been my return, for such baseness? I have lived in this house and toiled like a *slave*: I have acted as servant to my blessed child. Night after night I have sat with her; and month after month when *her husband* has been away, I have nursed that poor innocent, and the father having robbed me, the son turns me out of doors!"

A sad thing it was to witness and a painful proof how frequent these battles;—that,[4] as this one raged, the poor little boy sat almost careless whilst his bewildered grandfather stroked his golden head. "It is quite clear to me, Madam," I said, turning to Mrs. Mackenzie, "that you and your son-in-law are better apart, and I came to tell him to-day, of a most fortunate legacy which has just been left to him, and which will enable him to pay you to-morrow morning, every shilling—every shilling which he does NOT owe you."

"I will not leave this house until I am paid every shilling of which I have been robbed," hissed out Mrs. Mackenzie and she sat down folding her arms across her chest.

"I am sorry," groaned out Clive, wiping the sweat off his brow. "I used a harsh word; I will never sleep under the same roof with you. To-morrow I will pay you what you claim; and the best chance I have, of forgiving you the evil which you have done me, is that we never should meet again. Will you give me a bed at your house, Arthur? Father, will you come out and walk? Good night, Mrs. Mackenzie, Pendennis will settle with you in the

---

[4] these battles;—that, *Ms*] were these battles, that, *E 1*

How 'Boy said Our Father'

morning. You will not be here, if you please, when I return; and so God forgive you and farewell."

Mrs. Mackenzie in a tragic manner dashed aside the hand which poor Clive held out to her and disappeared from the scene of this dismal dinner. Boy presently fell a crying: in spite of all the battle and fury, there was sleep in his eyes.

"Maria is too busy, I suppose, to put him to bed," said Clive with a sad smile; "shall we do it, Father? Come, Tommy, my son!" and he folded his arms round the child and walked with him to the upper regions. The old man's eyes lighted up; his scared thoughts returned to him: he followed his two children up the stairs, and saw his grandson in[5] his little bed; and, as we walked home with him, he told me how sweetly Boy said Our Father, and prayed God bless all those who loved him, as they laid him to rest.

So these three generations had joined in that supplication:—the strong man, humbled by trial and grief, whose loyal heart was yet full of love;—the child, of the sweet age of those little ones whom the Blessed Speaker of the prayer first bade to come unto Him;—and the old man, whose heart was well nigh as tender and as innocent; and whose day was approaching, when he should be drawn to the Bosom of the Eternal Pity.

---

[5] in *E1*] laid in *Ms*

Chapter XLII.

HE vow which Clive had uttered, never[1] to share bread with his mother-in-law or sleep under the same roof with her, was broken on the very next day. A stronger Will than the young man's intervened, and he had to confess the impotence of his wrath before that superior Power. In the forenoon of the day following that unlucky dinner, I went with my friend to the banking-house: whither Mr. Luce's letter directed us, and carried away with me the principal sum, in which the Campaigner said Colonel Newcome was indebted to her, with the interest accurately computed and reimbursed. Clive went off with a pocket full of money to the dear old Poor Brother of Grey Friars; and he promised to return with his father, and dine with my wife in Queen's Square. I had received a letter from Laura by the morning's post; announcing her return by the express-train from Newcome, and desiring that a spare bed-room should be got ready for a friend who accompanied her.

On reaching Howland Street, Clive's door was opened, rather to my surprise, by the rebellious maid-servant who had received her dismissal on the previous night; and the Doctor's carriage drove up as she was still speaking to me. The polite practitioner sped up-stairs to Mrs. Newcome's apartment. Mrs. Mackenzie in a robe-de-chambre and cap very different from yesterday's came out eagerly to meet the physician on the landing.

---

[1] never *E1*] never more *Ms*

Ere they had been a quarter of an hour together, arrived a cab which discharged an elderly person with her band-box and bundles; I had no difficulty in recognising a professional nurse in the new comer. She too disappeared into the sick-room and left me sitting in the neighbouring chamber, the scene of the last night's quarrel.

Hither presently came to me Maria, the maid. She said she had not the heart to go away now she was wanted: that they had passed a sad night and that no one had been to bed. Master Tommy was below and the landlady taking care of him: the landlord had gone out for the nurse. Mrs. Clive had been taken bad after Mr. Clive went away the night before. Mrs. Mackenzie had gone in to² the poor young thing and there she had went³ on crying and screaming and stamping as she used to do in her tantrums, which was most cruel of her, and made Mrs. Clive so ill. And presently the young lady began: my informant told me. She came screaming into the sitting-room, her hair over her shoulders, calling out she was deserted, deserted, and would like to die. She was like a mad woman for some time. She had fit after fit of hysterics: and there was her mother, kneeling, and crying, and calling out to her darling child to calm herself;—which it was all her⁴ doing, and she had much best⁵ have held her own tongue, remarked the resolute Maria. I understood only too well from the girl's account, what had happened; and that Clive, if resolved to part with his mother-in-law, should not have left her, even for twelve hours, in possession of his house. The wretched woman, whose Self was always predominant, and who, though she loved her daughter after her own fashion, never forgot her own vanity or passion, had improved the occasion of Clive's absence; worked upon her child's weakness, jealousy, ill-health, and driven her, no doubt, into the fever, which yonder physician was called to quell.

The Doctor presently enters to write a prescription, followed by Clive's mother-in-law who had cast Rosa's fine Cashmere shawl over her shoulders to hide her disarray. "You here still, Mr. Pendennis!" she exclaims. She knew I was there. Had not she changed her dress in order to receive me?

"I have to speak to you for two minutes on important business, and then I shall go," I replied gravely.

"O Sir! to what a Scene you have come! to what a state has Clive's conduct last night driven my darling child!"

As the odious woman spoke so, the Doctor's keen eyes, looking up from the prescription, caught mine. "I declare before Heaven, Madam," I said hotly, "I believe you yourself are the cause of your daughter's present illness, as you have been of the misery of my friends."

"Is this, Sir!" she was breaking out, "Is this language to be used to . . ."

"Madam,⁶ will you be silent?" I said, "I am come to bid you farewell on the part of those whom your temper has driven into infernal torture. I am come to pay you every halfpenny of the sum which my friends do not owe you, but which they restore. Here is the account: and here is the money to

---

² in to *Ms*] to *E1*
³ had went *Ms*] went *E1*
⁴ her *Ms*] her own *E1*
⁵ best *Ms*] better *E1*
⁶ "Madam, *E1*] "Woman, *Ms*

settle it. And I take this gentleman to witness to whom, no doubt, you have imparted what you call your wrongs, (the Doctor smiled and shrugged his shoulders[7])—that now you are paid."

"A widow—a poor lonely insulted widow!" cries the Campaigner with trembling hands taking possession of the notes.

"And I wish to know," I continued, "when my friend's house will be free to him, and he can return in peace."

Here Rosa's voice was heard from the inner-apartment screaming, "Mamma, Mamma!"

"I go to my child, Sir!" she said. "If Captain Mackenzie had been alive, you would not have *dared*[8] to insult me so." And, carrying off her money, she left us.

"Cannot she be got out of the house?" I said to the Doctor. "My friend will never return until she leaves it. It is my belief she is the cause of her daughter's present illness."

"Not altogether, my dear Sir. Mrs. Newcome was in a very, very delicate state of health. Her mother is a lady of impetuous temper who expresses herself very strongly—too strongly, I own. In consequence of unpleasant family discussions, which no physician can prevent—Mrs. Newcome has been wrought up to a state of—of agitation. Her fever is in fact at present very high. You know her condition. I am apprehensive of ulterior consequences. I have recommended an excellent and experienced nurse to her. Mr. Smith, the medical man at the corner, is a most able practitioner—I shall myself call again in a few hours and I trust that, after the event which I apprehend, every thing will go well."

"Cannot Mrs. Mackenzie leave the house, Sir?" I asked.

"Her daughter cries out for her at every moment. Mrs. Mackenzie is certainly not a judicious nurse but in Mrs. Newcome's present state I cannot take upon myself to separate them. Mr. Newcome may return and I do think and believe that his presence may tend to impose silence and restore tranquility."

I had to go back to Clive with these gloomy tidings. The poor fellow must put up a bed in his studio, and there await the issue of his wife's illness. I saw Thomas Newcome could not sleep under his son's roof that night. That dear meeting which both so desired was delayed, who could say for how long?

"The Colonel may come to us," I thought, "our old house is big enough." I guessed who was the friend coming in my wife's company; and pleased myself by thinking that two friends so dear should meet in our home. Bent upon these plans I repaired to Grey Friars and to Thomas Newcome's chamber there.

Bayham opened the door when I knocked; and came towards me with a finger on his lip, and a sad sad countenance. He closed the door gently behind him and led me into the court. "Clive is with him, and Miss Newcome. He is very ill—he does not know them," said Bayham with a sob. "He calls out for both of them: they are sitting there and he does not know them."

7 shoulders *E1*] shoulder *Ms*
8 *dared E1*] [no italics] *Ms*

In a brief narrative, broken by more honest tears, Fred Bayham as we paced up and down the court told me what had happened. The old man must have passed a sleepless night, for on going to his chamber in the morning, his attendant found him dressed in his chair, and his bed undisturbed. He must have sat all through the bitter night without a fire: but his hands were burning hot, and he rambled in his talk. He spoke of some one coming to drink tea with him, and[9] pointed to the fire and asked why it was not made? He would not go to bed, though the nurse pressed him. The bell began[1] to ring for morning chapel, he got up and went towards his gown, groping towards it as though he could hardly see, and put it over his shoulders and would go out, but he would have fallen in the court if the good nurse had not given him her arm, and the Physician of the Hospital passing fortunately at this moment, who had always been a great friend of Colonel Newcome's, insisted upon leading him back to his room again and got him to bed. "When the bell stopped he wanted to rise once more; he fancied he was a boy at school again," said the nurse, "and that he was going in to Dr. Raine who was schoolmaster here ever so many years ago." So it was that when happier days seemed to be dawning for the good man, that reprieve came too late. Grief and years and humiliation and care and cruelty had been too strong for him, and Thomas Newcome was stricken down.

Bayham's story told, I entered the room over which the twilight was falling, and saw the figures of Clive and Ethel seated at each end of the bed. The poor old man within it was calling incoherent sentences. I had to call Clive from the present grief before him, with intelligence of further sickness awaiting him at home. Our poor patient did not heed what I said to his son. "You must go home to Rosa," Ethel said. "She will be sure to ask for her husband, and forgiveness is best, dear Clive. I will stay with Uncle. I will never leave him. Please God he will be better in the morning when you come back." So Clive's duty called him to his own sad home; and, the bearer of dismal tidings, I returned to mine. The fires were lit there, and the table spread, and kind hearts were waiting to welcome the friend who never more was to enter my door.

It may be imagined, that the intelligence which I brought alarmed and afflicted my wife and Madame de Florac our guest. Laura immediately went away to Rosa's house to offer her services if needed. The accounts which she brought thence were very bad: Clive came to her for a minute or two, but Mrs. Mackenzie could not see her. Should she not bring the little boy home to her children? Laura asked and Clive thankfully accepted that offer. The little man slept in our nursery that night; and was at play with our young ones on the morrow, happy and unconscious of the fate impending over his home.

Yet two more days passed, and I had to take two advertisements to the *Times* newspaper on the part of poor Clive. Among the announcements of Births was printed, "On the 28th. in Howland Street, Mrs. Clive Newcome of a son still-born." And, a little lower, in the third division of the same

---

[9] and *Ms*] [omitted] *E1*
[1] began *E1*] beginning *Ms*

column appeared the words, "On the 29th. in Howland Street, aged 26, Rosa, wife of Clive Newcome, Esquire."—So, one day shall the names of all of us be written there; to be deplored by how many? to be remembered how long? to occasion what tears, praises, sympathy, censure—yet for a day or two while the busy world has time to recollect us who have passed beyond it. So this poor little flower had bloomed for its little day, and pined, and withered, and perished. There was only one friend by Clive's side following the humble procession which laid poor Rosa and her child out of sight of a world that had been but unkind to her. Not many tears were there, to water her lonely little grave. A grief that was akin to shame and remorse humbled him[2] as he knelt over her. Poor little harmless lady! no more childish triumphs and vanities, no more hidden griefs are you to enjoy or suffer; and earth closes over your simple pleasures and tears! The snow was falling and whitening the coffin, as they lowered it into the ground. It was at the same cemetery in which Lady Kew was buried. I daresay the same clergyman read the same service over the two graves—as he will read it for you or any of us to-morrow, and until his own turn comes. Come away from the place, poor Clive! Come sit with your orphan little boy; and bear him on your knee and hug him to your heart. He seems yours now, and all a father's love may pour out upon him. Until this hour Fate uncontrollable and homely tyranny had separated him from you.

It was touching to see the eagerness and tenderness with which the great strong man now assumed the guardianship of the child, and endowed him with his entire wealth of affection. The little boy now ran to Clive whenever he came in, and sate for hours prattling to him. He would take the boy out to walk, and from our windows we could see Clive's tall[3] black figure striding over the snow in St. James's Park, the little man trotting beside him or perched on his father's shoulder. My wife and I looked at them one morning as they were making their way towards the City. "He has inherited that loving heart from his father," Laura said, "and is paying over the whole property to his son."

Clive, and the boy sometimes with him, used to go daily to Grey Friars, where the Colonel still lay ill. After some days, the fever, which had attacked him, left him; but left him so weak and enfeebled that he could only go from his bed to the chair by his fire-side. The season was exceedingly bitter, the chamber which he inhabited was warm and spacious; it was considered unadvisable to move him until he had attained greater strength, and till warmer weather. The medical men of the House hoped he might rally in spring. My friend, Dr. Goodenough, came to him: he hoped too; but not with a hopeful face. A chamber, luckily vacant, hard by the Colonel's, was assigned to his friends, where we sate when we were too many for him. Besides his customary attendant, he had two dear and watchful nurses, who were almost always with him—Ethel, and Madame de Florac, who had passed many a faithful year by an old man's bedside, who would have come, as to a work of religion, to any sick couch, much

---

[2] him *E1*] [omitted] *Ms*
[3] tall *Ms*] [omitted] *E1*

more to this one, where he lay for whose life she would once gladly have given her own.

But our Colonel, we all were obliged to acknowledge, was no more our friend of old days. He knew us again and was good to every one round him as his wont was. Especially when Boy came, his old eyes lighted up with simple happiness, and, with eager trembling hands, he would seek under his bed-clothes or the pockets of his dressing-gown for toys or cakes which he had caused to be purchased for his grandson. There was a little laughing, red-cheeked, white-headed gown-boy of the school, to whom the old man had taken a great fancy. One of the symptoms of his returning consciousness and recovery as we hoped, was his calling for this child, who pleased our friend by his archness and merry ways; and who, to the old gentleman's unfailing delight, used to call him "Codd Colonel." "Tell little F— that Codd Colonel wants to see him!" and[4] the little gown-boy was brought to him; and the Colonel would listen to him for hours; and hear all about his lessons and his play; and prattle almost as childishly about Dr. Raine and his own early school-days. The boys of the school, it must be said, had heard the noble old gentleman's touching history and had all got to know and love him. They came every day to hear news of him; sent him in books and papers to amuse him; and some benevolent young souls, God's blessing on all honest boys, say I, painted theatrical characters, and sent them in to Codd Colonel's grandson. The little fellow was made free of gown-boys and once came thence to his grandfather in a little gown which delighted the old man hugely. Boy said he would like to be a little gown-boy; and I make no doubt, when he is old enough, his father will get him that post, and put him under the tuition of my friend Dr. Senior.

So, weeks passed away during which our dear old friend still remained with us. His mind was gone at intervals; but would rally feebly; and, with his consciousness, returned his love, his simplicity, his sweetness. He would talk French with Madame de Florac, at which time, his memory appeared to awaken with surprising vividness, his cheek flushed, and he was a youth again—a youth all love and hope—a stricken old man with a beard as white as snow, covering the noble care-worn face. At such times he called her by her Christian name of Léonore:[5] he addressed courtly old words of regard and kindness to the aged lady: anon he wandered in his talk and spoke to her as if they still were young. Now, as in those early days, his heart was pure; no anger remained in it; no guile tainted it; only peace and good will dwelt in it.

Rosa's death had seemed to shock him for a while when the unconscious little boy spoke of it. Before that circumstance Clive had even forborne[6] to wear mourning lest the news should agitate his father. The Colonel remained silent and was very much disturbed all that day; but he never appeared to comprehend the fact quite; and, once or twice afterwards, asked why she did not come to see him? "She was *prevented*," he supposed— "she was prevented," he said with a look of terror: he never once otherwise

4 him!" and *E1*] him—that Codd Colonel wants to see him!": and *Ms*
5 Léonore *E1*] Eleanore *Ms*
6 forborne *Ms*] forebore *E1*

alluded to that unlucky tyrant of his household who had made his last years so unhappy.

The circumstance of Clive's legacy he never understood; but more than once spoke of Barnes to Ethel, and sent his compliments to him, and said he should like to shake him by the hand. Barnes Newcome never once offered to touch that honoured hand though his sister bore her uncle's message to him. They came often from Brianstone Square: Mrs. Hobson even offered to sit with the Colonel, and read to him and brought him books for his improvement. But her presence disturbed him: he cared not for her books; the two nurses whom he loved faithfully watched him; and my wife and I were admitted to him sometimes, both of whom he honoured with regard and recognition. As for F.B., in order to be near his Colonel, did not that good fellow take up his lodging in Cistercian Lane at the Red Cow? He is one whose errors, let us hope, shall be pardoned, *quia multum amavit.* I am sure he felt ten times more joy at hearing of Clive's legacy, than if thousands had been bequeathed to himself. May good health and good fortune speed him!

The days went on, and our hopes, raised sometimes, began to flicker and fail. One evening the Colonel left his chair for his bed in pretty good spirits; but passed a disturbed night and the next morning was too weak to rise. Then he remained in his bed, and his friends visited him there. One afternoon he asked for his little gown-boy and the child was brought to him, and sate by the bed with a very awe-stricken face; and then gathered courage and tried to amuse him by telling him, how it was a half-holiday and they were having a cricket match with the St. Peter's boys in the green, and Grey Friars was in and winning. The Colonel quite understood about it; he would like to see the game: he had played many a game on that green when he was a boy. He grew excited—Clive dismissed his father's little friend and put a sovereign into his hand; and away he ran to say that Codd Colonel had come into a fortune, and to buy tarts, and to see the match out. *I, curre,* little white-haired gown-boy! Heaven speed you, little friend.

After the child had gone, Thomas Newcome began to wander more and more. He talked louder: he gave the word of command, spoke Hindostanee as if to his men. Then[7] he spoke words in French rapidly, seizing a hand that was near him and crying *Toujours Toujours!* But it was Ethel's hand which he took. Ethel and Clive and the nurse were in the room with him: the latter came to us who were sitting in the adjoining apartment— Madame de Florac was there, with my wife and Bayham.

At the look in the woman's countenance, Madame de Florac started up. "He is very bad, he wanders a great deal," the nurse whispered. The French lady fell instantly on her knees, and remained rigid in prayer.

Some time afterwards Ethel came in with a scared face to our pale group. "He is calling for you again, dear lady," she said going up to Madame de Florac who was still kneeling—"And just now he said he wanted Pendennis to take care of his boy. He will not know you." She hid her tears as she spoke.

---

7 command, . . . Then *E1*] command and murmured Threes about and Charge—then *Ms*

We[8] went into the room where Clive was at the bed's foot—the old man within it talked on rapidly for awhile—then again would[9] sigh and be still—once more I heard him say hurriedly—"Take care of him when I'm in India," and then with a heart-rending voice he called out "Léonore, Léonore!"[1] She was kneeling by his side now. The patient's voice sank into faint murmurs; only a moan now and then announced that he was not asleep.

At the usual evening hour the chapel bell began to toll, and Thomas Newcome's hands outside the bed feebly beat a time. And just as the last bell struck—a peculiar sweet smile shone over his face, and he lifted up his head a little, and quickly said "Adsum!" and fell back. It was the word we used at school when names were called; and lo, he, whose heart was as that of a little child, had answered to his name, and stood in the presence of The Master.

———

Two years ago, walking with my children in some pleasant fields, near to Berne in Switzerland, I strayed from them into a little wood; and, coming out of it presently, told them how the story had been revealed to me somehow, which for three-and-twenty months the reader has been pleased to follow. As I write the last line with rather a[2] sad heart, Pendennis and Laura, and Ethel and Clive fade away into fable-land. I hardly know whether they are not true: whether they do not live near us somewhere. They were alive, and I heard their voices but five minutes since, was touched by their grief: and have we parted with them here on a sudden and without so much as a shake of the hand? Is yonder line (————) which I drew with my own pen a barrier between me and Hades as it were—across which I can see those figures retreating and only dimly glimmering? Before taking leave of Mr. Arthur Pendennis, might he not have told us whether Miss Ethel married anybody finally? It was provoking that he should retire to the Shades without answering that sentimental question.

But though he has disappeared as irrevocably as Eurydice, these minor questions may settle the major[3] one above mentioned—how could Pendennis have got all that information about Ethel's goings on at Baden and with Lord Kew, unless she had told somebody—her husband for instance who, having made Pendennis an early confidant in his amour, gave him the whole story? Clive, Pendennis writes expressly, is travelling abroad with his wife. Who *is* that wife? By a most monstrous blunder Mr. Pendennis kills Lady Glenlivat,[4] at one page[5] and brings[6] her to life again at another[7]—

---

[8] We *Ms*] She *E1*

[9] would *Ms*] he would *E1*

[1] "Léonore, Léonore!" *E1*] "Eleanore Eleanore!" *Ms*

[2] rather a *Ms*] a rather *E1* ["rather" is inserted without a caret ambiguously]

[3] See textual note for II.365.31. From this point until 367.2, below, the text of *E1* is based on an uncancelled but superseded manuscript, indicated in the notes as *Ms1*. The present edition is based on the new manuscript indicated as *Ms2*.

[4] Glenlivat, *Ms2*] Farintosh's mother *Ms1 E1*

[5] at one page *E1*] at page ([blank]) *Ms2*

[6] brings *Ms2*] brought *Ms1 E1*

[7] again at another *E1*] again page ([blank]) *Ms2*

but Rosey, who is so lately consigned to Kensal Green, it is surely not[8] with *her* that Clive is travelling, for then Mrs. Mackenzie would be[9] with them to a live certainty, and the tour would be by no means pleasant. Again, how[1] could Pendennis have got all those private letters, &c., unless the Colonel had[2] kept them in a teak-box which Clive inherited and handed[3] over to his friend? My belief is then, that Clive and Ethel[4] are living most comfortably together; that she is immensely fond of his little boy; and a great deal happier now than they would have been had they married at first when they took a liking to each other as young people, and when she was a mere young lady of fashion.[5] That picture by J.J., of "Mrs. Clive Newcome" in the Crystal Palace Exhibition in fable-land, is certainly not in the least like Rosey who we read was fair: but it represents a tall handsome dark lady, who must be Mrs. Ethel.

Again, why did Pendennis introduce[6] J.J. with such a flourish? giving us as it were an overture and no piece to follow it. J.J.'s history let me confidentially state has been revealed to me likewise, and may be told some of these fine summer months or Christmas evenings when the kind reader has leisure to hear.

What about Barnes[7] Newcome ultimately? My impression is that he is married again and my hope[8] that his present wife bullies him. Mrs. Mackenzie cannot have the face to keep that money which Clive paid over to her, beyond her lifetime; and will certainly leave it and her savings to little Tommy. I should not be surprised if Madame de Montcontour left a smart legacy to the Pendennis' children, and Lord Kew stood godfather in case—in case Mr. and Mrs. Clive wanted such an article. But have they any children? I for my part should like her best without, and entirely devoted to little Tommy. But for you, dear friend, it is as you like. You may settle your fable-land in your own fashion. Any thing you like happens in fable-land. Wicked folks die apropos (for instance that death of Lady Kew was most artful, for if she had not died, don't you see that Ethel would have married Lord Farintosh the next week?)—annoying folks are got out of the way; the poor are rewarded (O those legacies! why do not some people die and leave Somebody some?) the upstarts[9] are set down—in fable-land—

---

[8] surely not *Ms2*] not surely *Ms1 E1*

[9] would be *Ms2*] would probably be *Ms1 E1*

[1] Again, how *Ms2*] How *Ms1 E1*

[2] unless the Colonel had *Ms2*] but that the Colonel *Ms1 E1*

[3] handed *Ms2*] made *Ms1 E1*

[4] belief ... Ethel *Ms2*] belief then is that in Fable-land somewhere Ethel and Clive *Ms1 E1*

[5] people, ... fasion. *Ms2*] people. *Ms1 E1*

[6] Ethel. ¶Again, ... introduce *E1*] Ethel. Nor can we judge much of her likeness by Mr. Doyle's etchings in the present volumes, for where the Heroine has been introduced, our provoking English Timanthes has turned her face away, and only shown the public a head of hair. ¶Some would like to know from Mr. Pendennis why he introduced *Ms2*] Ethel— You cannot judge of the likeness by Mr. Doyle's etchings to the present volumes, for then this heroine is introduced; our provoking English Timanthes has generally turned her face away, and only whown the reader a head of hair. ¶Again why did Pendennis introduce *Ms1*

[7] Barnes *Ms2*] Sir Barnes *Ms1 E1*

[8] my hope *Ms2*] it is my fervent hope *Ms1 E1*

[9] rewarded ... upstarts *Ms2*] rewarded—the upstarts *Ms1 E1*

the frog bursts with wicked rage, the fox is caught in his trap, the lamb is rescued from the wolf, and so forth, just in the nick of time. And the poet of fable-land rewards and punishes absolutely. He splendidly deals out bags of sovereigns which won't buy any thing; belabours wicked backs with awful blows which do not hurt; endows heroines with preternatural beauty and creates heroes who if ugly sometimes yet possess a thousand good qualities and usually end by being immensely rich; makes the hero and heroine happy at last, and happy ever after. Ah happy harmless fable-land, where these things are! Friendly Reader! may you and the Author meet there on some future day! He hopes so; as he yet[1] keeps a lingering hold of your hand, and bids you farewell with a kind heart.

PARIS, 28 JUNE, 1855.

THE END

---

[1] hopes so; as he *E1*] hopes ~~as~~ ↑so↓ he yet ~~lingers has hold of their hand,~~ ↑keeps a lingering hold of your hand,↓ *Ms*

Editorial Apparatus

Composition, Publication, and Reception

R. D. McMaster

"I can't jump further than I did in *The Newcomes*," said Thackeray.[1] Both critically and financially, his judgement was borne out by the book's success. It earned him £4,561.3.9, more than any other of his novels.[2] And the reviewers considered it his greatest work, one of the great masterpieces of English fiction. That opinion prevailed throughout the Victorian period. Though *The Newcomes* has fared less well in the twentieth century, for a literate reader it still has high claims to attention. Gordon Ray, referring to its densely allusive texture, calls it "in some respects the richest, not only of Thackeray's books but of all Victorian fictions," a work beside which the novels of Edwardian novelists such as Bennett and Galsworthy, for all their specificity, "seem the work of frivolous impressionists."[3] To Thackeray's contemporaries caught up in the fashion of realism, *The Newcomes* with its copious personal and social reference seemed evidence of his uncanny power of literal representation. They were less easy about his concomitant reflexivity, his constantly reminding us of the work's fictionality and of our own thirst for fictional constructs in our everyday lives. In an age of metafiction and appreciation of polyphonic discourse, while still appreciating the richness of his social representation, we can perhaps see new dimensions to his artistry and appreciate afresh what a remarkable achievement *The Newcomes* is.

The Newcomes and Thackeray's experience run together. Thackeray wrote most of the novel while travelling with his daughters on the continent, re-experiencing the scenes of his youth and his early interest in art, matching present and past, anticipating the adventures of his youthful artist-hero, Clive. In Rome, he writes: "There are only about 6 pictures and statues of all I have seen here that I care to see again. Eh! where are the joyful eyes and bright perceptions of youth? ... What *will* happen when Mr. Clive Newcome comes here?"[4] He has Clive visit Paris and go on a version of the grand tour through the places a younger Thackeray had lived in and written about. Baden recalls "the days of my youth to me— I'm obliged to go back into those well-remembered regions to get materials for the Commencement of the new story."[5] In many of its other characters and incidents the novel artistically recapitulates Thackeray's life. His stepfather, Henry Carmichael-Smyth, is a model (among others) for Colonel Newcome; the Bundelcund Bank crash that ruins the Colonel reiterates the crash that practically eliminated Thackeray's patrimony, and he is very conscious of writing *The Newcomes* to restore that financial reserve for his

---

[1] Whitwell Elwin, *Some Eighteenth Century Men of Letters*, 2 vols. (1902. Port Washington: Kennikat Press, 1970), I, 156.

[2] See Peter L. Shillingsburg, *Pegasus in Harness: Victorian Publishing and W. M. Thackeray.* (Charlottesville: University Press of Virginia, 1992), 75.

[3] Gordon N. Ray, *Thackeray: The Age of Wisdom* (New York: McGraw-Hill, 1958), 237.

[4] To Mrs. Carmichael-Smyth, 25–28 January 1854, *The Letters and Private Papers of William Makepeace Thackeray*, ed. Gordon N. Ray, 4 vols. (Cambridge, Mass.: Harvard University Press, 1946), III, 337. This collection of letters is hereafter referred to as *Letters*.

[5] To Mrs. Carmichael-Smyth, 18 Jul 1853, *Letters*, III, 288.

daughters. The novel's heroine, Ethel, is a compound of his young American friend, Sally Baxter, and Mrs. Brookfield, for whom he still felt a lingering attachment, and Blanche Stanley, for whom his illustrator Richard Doyle had a hopeless passion, as Clive has for Ethel. The ferocious virago, Mrs. Mackenzie, the Campaigner, is a version, said Thackeray, of "my she-devil of a mother-in-law, you know, whom I have the good-luck to possess still."[6] Within the novel itself, the Colonel imposes on his son Clive a recycling of his own misfortunes in love. And the aged Colonel, coming full circle, dies with the schoolboy's answer to roll-call on his lips: "Adsum." Thackeray seems to be seeing both life and art according to the paradigm he repeatedly appealed to from Ecclesiastes: "The thing that hath been, it is that which shall be ... and there is no new thing under the sun," but "all is vanity and vexation of spirit." Formally, repetition is the principle of the novel's plan, stressed in the opening chapter's proposition that all stories are essentially the same story. Reiteration, and the comparisons therefore constantly involved, nourish the work's remarkably reflexive and meditative manner. Things not only repeat: we are called upon to reflect upon the principles of repetition, parody and construction both in art and in life, as one mode or vision aspires to, mocks, or destroys another. *The Newcomes* is largely about the shaping impulse.

As for vexation of spirit, Thackeray had enough to preoccupy him as he started shaping *The Newcomes*. Overshadowing the whole enterprise was his anxiety to provide for his daughters. To his American friends, the Baxters, he writes, "I have signed and sealed with Bradbury and Evans for a new book in 24 numbers like Pendennis—Price 3600£ + 500£ from Harper and Tauchnitz. It's coining money isn't it? and if I can make another expedition to a certain country as remunerative as the last, why, 2 years hence will see my girls snugly provided for. Thank God."[7] And again: "if I can get 3000£ for my darters, I mean 3000 *to put away* besides living, I will go backwards or forwards or any way."[8]

No doubt his anxiety about his daughters was compounded by premature feelings of age and by the ill health that dogged him through his travels and the writing of the book, particularly at Rome and Naples. In December 1853, while working on Number 6 at Rome, he writes, "I can't write the fever won't admit of it ... and the daily walks we must take and so forth and so forth prevent the work from proceeding and cloud my noble brow with melancholy."[9] In February 1854 he says, "I 'aven't 'ad my 'ealth at all here that is the fact: but for the last month have been in constant work, and am now in the middle of No VIII I'm pleased to say."[1] In Naples the

---

[6] Quoted by James Russell Lowell, letter to Charles Eliot Norton, 11 August 1855, *Letters of James Russell Lowell*, ed. Charles Eliot Norton, 2 vols. (New York, 1894), I, 239.

[7] Letter to the Baxters, 25–30 June 1853, *Letters*, III, 280.

[8] Letter to Sarah Baxter, 4 July 1853, *Letters*, III, 283. For a thorough and detailed account of the commercial success of *The Newcomes*, see Peter L. Shillingsburg, *Pegasus in Harness*.

[9] Letter to Mrs. Carmichael-Smyth, 31 December 1853, *Letters*, III, 332–33. Thackeray's itinerary and record of when he was working on individual numbers can be seen for the most part in his diaries for 1853 and 1854, printed in Appendices XIV and XV of *Letters*, III, 664–77.

[1] Letter to Mrs. Procter, January—4 February 1854, *Letters*, III, 341.

illness became general, both girls going down with scarlatina:

> Luckily we had a fortnights hard work just before these attacks during wʰ 2 numbers were polished off. Before them I had a week of illness myself—old stomach complaint brought on without rhyme or reason by the beautiful air of this country. No 3 in three months. If I get the Scarlets from the girls won't it be a good spell.²

He experienced another attack of "bowowels," so that

> we were all three ... stretched on our backs looking out at the Mediterranean yonder—so provokingly bright and blue.... 3 months of ill health & gloom in this charming climate have made me about 70.... 'Come' says the cheerful monitor, rouse yourself. Finish Newcomes. Get a few thousand pounds more, my man, for those daughters of your's. For your time is short, and the sexton wants you.³

In mid-August he writes, "I have been 2 months away from England during wʰ I have done 5 numbers of Newcomes and had 4 smart attacks of illness."⁴ And in November, "I am to day just out of bed with the dozenth severe fit of spasms which I have had this year. My book would have been written but for them...."⁵ Further attacks of "disorganized liver" and "defective water-works" continued through the winter of 1854–55.

A third source of vexation in this nomadic life-style was the problem of communicating serial parts to the publisher. "If I were to lose a number of the Newcomes I don't know what I should do. I never could write it over again: the idea of the calamity frightens me; and when we were abroad I never used to let the MS out of my sight."⁶ But every writer's fear of outright loss was only part of the problem. If he miscalculated the amount of copy, he was not at hand to cut or add. He arranged with Percival Leigh in London to oversee the printing of each number and make minor corrections, cuts or additions. But a crisis occurred with Number 6, due to be published on March 1. He sent most of it from Rome at the end of December, and three additional sheets of manuscript during January. Proofs reached him on February 21, and Number 6 had little more than 25 of the requisite 32 pages. On February 25 he wrote to Leigh, "There's no time to communicate now about it: and the mischief whatever it is is done. I might have had the proofs months ago. But what's the use of talking now?"⁷ On March 8 he adds,

> You see now I cant tell what has happened to VI how the Lacune has been filled up ... nor will there be time for me this month to get your reply, and send back copy if need be.
> ... If you can see how to fill up 3 pages of your own noble invention—just going goose-step as it were and making the story pretend to march (wʰ indeed it has been doing for some time) pray do write them....
> Confound those 3 pages! wʰ I got up trembling in a fever to supply in January!⁸

---

² Letter to Mrs. Carmichael-Smyth, 7–8 March 1854, *Letters*, III, 352.
³ Letter to Mrs. Baxter, 17–28 March 1854, *Letters*, III, 356–59.
⁴ Letter to Willard S. Felt, 18 August 1854, *Letters*, III, 382.
⁵ Letter to William Bradford Reed, 8 November, 1854, *Letters*, III, 401.
⁶ Letter to Mrs. Procter, 24–25 October 1854, *Letters*, III, 394.
⁷ Letter to Percival Leigh, 25 February 1854, *Letters*, III, 350.
⁸ Letter to Percival Leigh, 8 March 1854, *Letters*, III, 354–55.

In the end all was well, though not for subsequent editors of the work. Presumably (one doesn't know—see the Textual Introduction), Leigh and the printer set to work, the printer depressing the chapter heading and reducing the number of lines per page on nine pages, Leigh adding a description of the Colonel's house previously cut from Number 5, and Doyle, the illustrator, contributing extra pictures and an unusually large initial letter to fill space. Moreover, there were over three hundred changes from manuscript to text, many of them *deletions*. The time constraints of getting revisions from Italy and setting them suggest it was virtually impossible for Thackeray to have made them and that, therefore, they must have been made by Leigh, forced into greater responsibility than he could have anticipated.

A final vexation, not new to Thackeray, was the sense that he was not writing up to the mark. Before even starting the novel, he gloomily wrote Sally Baxter that "It won't be a good one—not a step forwards as some ambitious young American folks would have it."[9] To his mother he confessed, "I can't but see it as a repetition of past performances, and think that vein is pretty nigh worked out in me."[1] Three days later he at least had some doubt: "I am about a new story but don't know as yet whether it will be any good. It seems to me I am too old for story-telling."[2] And again to Sally, in a terminology students of Thackeray get used to when he is in the throes of creation: "I'm in low spirits about the Newcomes. It's not good. It's stupid. It haunts me like a great stupid ghost. I think it says why do you go on writing this rubbish? You are old, you have no more invention &c. Write sober books, books of history leave novels to younger folks." But he adds perceptively, "You see half of my life is grumbling; and lecturing or novel-writing or sentimentalizing I am never content."[3] As Edgar Harden has shown, such apparent disgust with his work was fairly characteristic of Thackeray and has to be taken with a grain of salt:

> A portion of *Pendennis* is "stupid ... and yet how well written"; a part of *Esmond* "is clever but it is also stupid and no mistake"; *The Newcomes*, so far as it is written, is "not good. It's stupid"; *The Virginians*, as one can now easily predict, is "clever but stupid that's the fact," "most admirable" but also "devilish stupid."[4]

As Anne Ritchie recalled, "My father was always diffident about his work, especially at the starting of it."[5] Beside these dismal comments, one must put his more satisfied remark to Whitwell Elwin when the novel was finished, that he couldn't jump further than he had done in *The Newcomes*.[6]

---

[9] Letter to Sarah Baxter, 4–5 July 1853, *Letters*, III, 283.

[1] Letter to Mrs. Carmichael-Smyth, 18 July 1853, *Letters*, III, 287.

[2] Letter to William Bradford Reed, 21 July 1853, *Letters*, III, 293–94.

[3] Letter to Sarah Baxter, 7 August 1853, *Letters*, III, 299.

[4] Edgar F. Harden, *The Emergence of Thackeray's Serial Fiction* (Athens: University of Georgia Press, 1979), 6, quoting *Letters*, II, 685; III, 69, 299; IV, 80, 85n. Harden's point is that these are responses to minor inconsistencies and show rather that he is "compulsively troubled by minor imperfections" than that his work is indeed careless or "stupid."

[5] *The Works of William Makepeace Thackeray, With Biographical Introductions by his Daughter, Anne Ritchie*, 13 vols (London: Smith Elder, 1898), VIII, xxiv.

[6] Whitwell Elwin, *Some Eighteenth Century Men of Letters*, I, 156. Thackeray's comment is not necessarily absolute. He told James T. Fields in 1852 that *Esmond* was "the *very* best I can do.... and [I] am willing to leave it, when I go, as my card" (James T. Fields,

25 COMPOSITION, PUBLICATION, AND RECEPTION

All of these complaints about composition seem to stem from something fundamental in Thackeray's creativity, a characteristic doubleness in his appreciation of himself, the world and fiction. He typically represents himself as a fogey, aged, past it—but in 1853 he was only forty-two. At forty-seven he declares, "at 47 Venus may rise from the sea, and I for one should hardly put on my spectacles to have a look," and so with all pleasures: "What that we have tried is so very much worth repetition or endurance?"[7] So of stories, he asks, "What stories are new? All types of all characters march through all fables." What makes the repetition endurable? "There may be nothing new under and including the sun; but it looks fresh every morning" (ch. 1). His art is intensely intertextual, or in other words, repetitive— on his theory all art is repetitive, new only in perspective and conjunction, now seen as comedy, now as tragedy, more likely both together. That tension, constantly oscillating between a romance mode and an ironic mode, is essential to Thackeray, as is his self-mockery and reflexivity, his presentation of himself as both preacher and harlequin, his prompting the reader to recognize fictionality not only on the page but in our everyday constructions of experience. Nearly all criticism of Thackeray worries over this question, consciously or unconsciously. The figure that represents Thackeray's double consciousness best is perhaps that sketch of himself as a fool with a mask at the end of *Vanity Fair*, Chapter 9. James Fitzjames Stephen said of it:

> He is removing a laughing mask attached to a cap and bells, and underneath appear the author's own features, wearing a look of half-bewildered sadness—the face of a man who has hardly shaken off an unpleasant dream. Again and again, in various parts of his books, the impression under which this little figure was drawn is conveyed to the reader by casual allusions, by turns of expression, by a thousand subtle intimations to the effect that the actor was rather tired of his part, and never heartily liked it.[8]

The trouble that has dogged much Thackeray criticism in his own time and later has been a desire to essentialize his outlook, *either* romantic, 'sentimental,' *or* ironic, 'cynical.' More characteristically he is both, or both possibilities are held in suspension in his work. His instinct was parodic in the widest sense, not only in echoing texts for the sake of ridicule, as in *Punch's Prize Novelists*, but in making repetition and inversion a means of ironic reflection.[9] Ecclesiastes, with its emphasis on repetition and weariness is the great Thackerayan intertext. The various characters of *The Newcomes* obsessively conform to inherited imaginative patterns, and a cyclical

Yesterdays with Authors, [Boston, 1872], 17), and his daughter recalled his saying late in life that "*Vanity Fair* is undoubtedly the best of my books. It has the best story . . . ." (Anne Thackeray Ritchie, Introduction to *Vanity Fair*, Vol. 1 of *The Works of William Makepeace Thackeray*, [London: Smith Elder, 1899], xxx).

[7] Letter to Dr. John Brown, 4–10 November 1858, *Letters*, IV, 115.

[8] James Fitzjames Stephen, Obituary article in *Fraser's Magazine*, 69 (April 1864), 404. Similarly the *North British Review*, 40 (February 1864), 261, notices the mask's reflection of the "deep steady melancholy of his nature."

[9] I am thinking of Linda Hutcheon's discussion of parody as "repetition, but repetition that includes difference . . . it is imitation with critical ironic distance, whose irony can cut both ways," in *A Theory of Parody: The Teachings of Twentieth-Century Art Forms*, (New York and London: Methuen, 1985), 37.

repetitive view of experience shapes the whole design of *The Newcomes*.[1]

The immediate topics that fed in to this design were many, but one can isolate a few major ones. In the postscript, Thackeray tells us "the story had been revealed to me somehow" while walking in a wood near Berne in the summer of 1853. In September he wrote,

> I read Don Quixote nearly through when I was away. What a vitality in those two characters! What gentlemen they both are! I wish Don Quixote was not thrashed so very often. There are sweet pastoralities through the book, and that piping of shepherds and pretty sylvan ballet which dances always round the principal figures is delightfully pleasant to me . . . .[2]

Both the Don and the pastoralities feed into *The Newcomes*. Colonel Newcome, "the finest single character in English fiction" according to Trollope,[3] is repeatedly associated with Don Quixote both in the text and in Doyle's illustrations.[4] The Colonel himself makes the connection (compounded with a number of others) when he says of his reading: "I like to be in the company of gentlemen; and Sir Roger de Coverley, and Sir Charles Grandison, and Don Quixote are the finest gentlemen in the world" (ch. 4). Robert Colby notes that Thackeray meant "this old soldier to exemplify the aristocratic ideal of chivalry in a modern bourgeois setting" and quotes J. H. Stocqueler's *The British Officer: His Positions, Duties, Emoluments and Privileges* (1851) for the type.[5] In concert with his social-climbing family, the Colonel is a contribution to the general Victorian debate about what now constitutes a gentleman. Pastoralities (the Cave of Harmony, Mrs. Newcome's villa at Clapham, where the Calvinist gardener occupies himself with the melons and pines only "provisionally, and until the end of the world" [ch. 2], Madame de Florac's garden) provide an ironic contrast for the bourgeois world. Ethel persuades herself that she would like to have been a simple shepherdess or a nun. And Doyle provides Watteau-like pastoral figures in the headletter sketches. In the multifariously allusive texture of *The Newcomes*, the echo of *Don Quixote* sounds the essential Thackerayan note of parody and double-sidedness.

The title, *The Newcomes*, announces that this is a social novel, one that addresses the Victorian phenomenon of unprecedented social mobility, of the newly arrived in class, status and wealth. The elder Thomas Newcome, a cloth merchant from the north, follows the pattern of Dick Whittington and Hogarth's Industrious 'Prentice, marrying into prosperity and respectability. As G. M. Young points out at the beginning of his magisterial *Victorian England: Portrait of an Age*, as Carlyle had observed in *Past and Present*, and as Dickens in *Little Dorrit* and Arnold in *Culture and Anarchy* would emphasize, Victorian society saw a profound coalescence of mercantile and religious values. Thackeray develops this alliance in the Newcome

---

[1] I talk about this phenomenon in "The Pygmalion Motif in *The Newcomes*," *Nineteenth-Century Fiction*, 29 (June 1974), 22–39.

[2] Letter to Bryan Waller Procter, September 1853, *Letters*, III, 304.

[3] "W. M. Thackeray," *Cornhill Magazine*, February 1864, 137.

[4] See my *Thackeray's Cultural Frame of Reference: Allusion in* The Newcomes (London: Macmillan, 1991), 53–54, and Alexander Welsh, *Reflections on the Hero as Quixote* (Princeton: Princeton UP, 1981), passim.

[5] Robert A. Colby, *Thackeray's Canvass of Humanity: An Author and his Public* (Columbus: Ohio State University Press, 1979), 365–66.

family, the zeal of Clapham[6] combining with the mercenary power of the banking district—rising in the case of Sir Brian and Lady Ann Newcome into a further alliance of middle class and aristocracy. Class distinctions in this society, as Young observes, also imply moral distinctions, the two being comprehended in the portmanteau term, "respectability." The subtitle of *The Newcomes* is "Memoirs of a Most Respectable Family."

In its presentation of marriage as a market adjusting the tensions and accommodations between aristocracy and middle class, *The Newcomes* presents an elaborate fictional case study of society as Thackeray's habitual butt of satire, Bulwer, described it in *England and the English* (1832):

> In most other countries the middle classes rarely possessing the riches of the no-bility, have offered to the latter no incentive for seeking their alliance. But wealth is the greatest of all levellers, and the highest of the English nobles willingly repair the fortunes of hereditary extravagance by intermarriage with the families of the banker, the lawyer, and the merchant: this, be it observed, tends to extend the roots of their influence among the middle classes, who, in other countries are the natural barrier of the aristocracy. It is the ambition of the rich trader to obtain the alliance of nobles; and he loves, as well as respects, those honours to which he himself or his children may aspire.[7]

The Newcomes construct their descent from the "surgeon-barber to King Edward the Confessor" (ch. 2). The girls of this society have as their credo: "I believe in elder sons, and a house in town, and a house in the country," and are "as keen as the smartest merchant in Vanity Fair" (ch. 45). Their principal social activity, and a central theme of *The Newcomes*, is selling themselves in the marriage market. As Bulwer says:

> A notorious characteristic of English society is the universal marketing of our unmarried women;—a marketing peculiar to ourselves in Europe, and only ri-valled by the slave-merchants of the East. We are a matchmaking nation; the lively novels of Mrs. Gore give a just and unexaggerated picture of the intrigues, the manouvres, the plotting and the counterplotting that make the staple of ma-tronly ambition.... in good society, the heart is remarkably prudent, and seldom falls violently in love without a sufficient settlement: where the heart is, *there* will the *treasure* be also![8]

Lady Kew puts Ethel on display before various aristocratic and wealthy bachelors, while Clive, a mere artist, languishes for her in vain. "We are as much sold as Turkish women," says Ethel, "the only difference being that our masters may have but one Circassian at a time" (ch. 32). Ethel's partici-pation in this auction is complicated by her spirit and intellect. "The rich young man," Bulwer continues, "is to be flattered in order that he may be won; ...you talk to him of balls and races; you fear to alarm him by appearing his intellectual superior; ...and you harmonize *your* mind into 'gentle dulness,' that it may not jar upon his own."[9] Even Ethel's talk of so elementary a topic as nursery rhymes bewilders poor Lord Farintosh (ch.

---

[6] Clapham was famous for the activities of the Clapham sect, a group of wealthy evan-gelicals (Thackeray makes them dissenters) who were moving forces in the abolition of slavery, in missionary work, assistance to the poor, and prison reform. They flourished from about 1790 to 1832.

[7] Edward Lytton Bulwer, *England and the English*, (1832. Chicago: University of Chicago Press, 1970), 30.

[8] *Ibid.*, 85–86.

[9] *Ibid.*, 86–87.

42). Major Pendennis puts the prevailing point of view about intelligence with his usual vehemence:

"Begad, sir, ...intellect may be a doosid fine thing, but in my opinion, a marquisate and eighteen or twenty thousand a year—I should say the Farintosh property, with the Glenlivat estate, and the Roy property in England, must be worth nineteen thousand a year at the very lowest figure ... I say, what does the bankeress [Maria] mean by chattering about intellect? Hang me, a marquis is a marquis ...." (ch. 49)

Few social novels are so richly nuanced as *The Newcomes*, a penetrating guide to "the most polite, and most intelligent, and best informed, and best dressed, and most selfish people in the world" (ch. 25). No wonder Henry James, also a great artist of manners and accommodation, admired and imitated it.[1]

As an artist, Clive has no claim to either respectability or status in the marriage market. Major Pendennis, puts the issue squarely: "I don't know what the dooce the world is coming to. An artist! By gad, in my time a fellow would as soon have thought of making his son a hair-dresser, or a pastry-cook, by gad" (ch. 24). In his depiction of the art world, its divisions and attitudes, Thackeray draws on his own experience, interests and acquaintances as an art student and later, refreshing his memory in his travels as we have seen. For the vicissitudes of Clive and Ethel in the marriage market, though his characters tend to be composites, he had some immediate models. His illustrator, Richard Doyle, seems to have been infatuated with Blanche Stanley of Alderley Park, Cheshire, a young woman noted for spirit, intelligence and independence. However, she married a rich young Scot, Lord Airlie, and became Countess of Airlie. Rodney Engen, in his biography of Richard Doyle, notes that in Doyle's illustrations to *The Newcomes* "Ethel is drawn with the wide-eyed dark-haired beauty of Dick's beloved Blanche; Lord Farintosh, her unfortunate suitor, is made to look ridiculous in his kilt and sporran suggestive of Blanche's Scottish husband, Lord Airlee; and the inventive young fantasy artist, J. J. Ridley, is given many of Dick's own features."[2] Blanche evidently found her husband dull: "in a fit of frustration she told Jane Carlyle she believed Lord Airlie was in-

---

[1] See my " 'An honourable emulation of the author of *The Newcomes*': James and Thackeray," *Nineteenth-Century Fiction* 32 (March 1978), 399–419.

[2] Rodney Engen, *Richard Doyle* (Stroud, Glos.: Catalpa Press, 1983), 104. Engen also frequently refers to an unpublished biography of Doyle in the Bibliothèque Cantonale et Universitaire, Lausanne. J. R. Harvey (in *Victorian Novelists and their Illustrators* [London: Sidgewick and Jackson, 1970], 65–6) also observes that Doyle used his own face for the illustration of J. J. Ridley. Margaret Stetz ("*The Newcomes* and the Artist's World," *Pre-Raphaelite Studies* [1983], 80–95) makes a case for Ridley being modelled also on William Henry Hunt, Ridley being "a sickly and almost deformed child," son of a butler, and Hunt deformed in his legs, son of a tinman.

Maunsell B. Field, (in *Memories of Many Men* [New York, 1874], 132–33) says Thackeray identified John Alexander Thynne (1831–1896), fourth Marquess of Bath, as Farintosh. A principal model for Ethel was Sarah Baxter whom he met in America in November 1852. He was forty-one, she not yet twenty. The Baxters became regular correspondents. Thackeray liked to indulge in playful amatory talk to her: "Miss Sally, I shall never fall in love any more. There's a pretty girl with whom I could do it though" (Letter to the Baxters, 25–30 June 1853, *Letters*, III, 280). Lucy Baxter says he reproduces some impressions of Sally in the accounts of Ethel holding court at one of the great London balls (*Thackeray's Letters to an American Family* [New York, 1904], 6–7). Julia Ward Howe says Sally claimed to recognize "bits of her own conversation in some of the sayings of

tellectually inferior to her.... Whenever possible she returned to London and stayed in her husband's Campden Hill house, where she re-established old acquaintances with Thackeray and inevitably Dick Doyle."[3] Lord Stanley evidently forbad his daughters to read Thackeray "on the ground that the picture of London society in his novels was too accurate to be good for young girls."[4] It doesn't seem that Thackeray had anything to tell them that they did not know already.

To readers of the novel as it emerged in 1853–55, the whole marriage theme, particularly the part concerning Clara Pulleyn and Barnes Newcome, who gives lectures on "The Poetry of Childhood" and "The Poetry of Womanhood and the Affections," and who tyrannizes over and beats his wife, would have had an immediate topical resonance. Caroline Norton's monstrous husband, whose legal persecution of his wife had been notorious public lore for almost two decades, was pursuing her in the courts again in 1853, determined to claim her money and her copyrights. In 1854 she published her *English Laws for Women*, which influenced the passing of the 1857 Divorce Bill and the Married Women's Property Bills. She was a friend of Thackeray's, and he had her lot in mind while writing of Barnes and Clara. For their divorce he "read the trial of Norton v. Melbourne having a crim-con affair coming on in the Newcomes."[5] Readers could hardly fail to notice the relevance of the Barnes and Clara plot to current legal debates about the status of women in marriage.

The serial had hardly begun (the first number appeared on 1 October 1853) before Thackeray had a further, unexpected cause for anxiety. The first reviews were generally favourable, with inevitable comparisons to *Vanity Fair*, *Pendennis*, and *Esmond*. *The Leader* (8 Oct. 1853) thought it had "all Thackeray's excellences, and gives better promise than either *Vanity Fair* or *Pendennis* gave at starting" (976). The *Spectator* (1 Oct. 1853) agreed. *The Athenaeum* (1 Oct. 1853) could not guess a direction, and the *New Quarterly*

Ethel Newcome" (*Reminiscence, 1819–1899* [Boston and New York, 1918], 131). Another of the associations attached to Ethel is Thackeray's lingering attachment to Mrs. Brookfield. Gordon Ray cites a letter from an American lady, Mrs. George B. Jones, in which she describes how Thackeray "told me a great deal about the Newcomes and whence he drew his characters.... He loves another, but seeks in the rigid discharge of his duty to his family, to shut out the dangerous contemplation of what might be his happiness" (Manuscript letter, 8 July 1855, quoted in Ray's *The Buried Life: A Study of the Relation Between Thackeray's Fiction and his Personal History* [London: Oxford University Press, 1952], 98).

[3] *Ibid.*, 111.

[4] Quoted in Ray, *Thackeray: The Age of Wisdom*, 243.

[5] Letter to Mrs. Carmichael-Smyth, 6–7 March 1855, *Letters*, III, 428. Caroline Norton could neither divorce her husband (since she had returned after leaving him and thus 'condoned' his behaviour) nor get custody of their children. Her *A Plain Letter* influenced the passing of the Infant Custody Bill in 1839, but her husband spirited the children away to Scotland. For an account of Caroline Norton and the law as it affected women, see Lee Holcombe, *Wives and Property: Reform of the Married Women's Property Law in Nineteenth-Century England* (Toronto: University of Toronto Press, 1983), 55–58. For an account of *The Newcomes* as rendering sympathetic support for Caroline Norton's views on the status of women in marriage, see Micael Clarke, "William Makepeace Thackeray's Fiction and Caroline Norton's Biography: Narrative Matrix of Feminist Legal Reform," *Dickens Studies Annual*, 18 (1989), 337–51. The 1836 case of Norton v. Melbourne was reported by Dickens and partly used for Bardell v. Pickwick in *Pickwick Papers*. The Norton story was taken up also by George Eliot and George Meredith.

Review (Jan. 1853) stated flatly that "the genealogies of the Newcomes are tiresome" (5). But with an eye on American profits, Thackeray was appalled by a sudden flap over George Washington. In Chapter 2, setting the late eighteenth-century background, Thackeray harked back humorously to a time when among other events "Mr. Washington was heading the American rebels with a courage, it must be confessed, worthy of a better cause." The *New York Evening Post* (5 Nov. 1853) responded with no humour at all: "We had hoped Mr. Thackeray had been long enough in this country to learn better than to indulge in such a sneer at the authors and conductors of the successful revolution of 1776. If he did not, he should at least have had prudence enough to suppress a sentiment which is scarcely more acceptable to his own countrymen that [sic] ours" (2). Then the American correspondent to *The Times* (22 Nov. 1853) reported the comment, adding, "It was hoped that a man of so much perception and sagacity as Mr. Thackeray has had credit for would have avoided any of those offensive flings which have too often appeared in the works of foreign writers when speaking of the United States" (7). Thackeray at once wrote a letter to *The Times* (23 November 1853), defending himself and insisting that he thought "the cause for which Washington fought entirely just and right, and the Champion the very noblest, purest, bravest, best of God's men." The American correspondent had ominously reminded Thackeray that "the majority of his readers are found on this side of the Atlantic," and he saw the pecuniary point: "I fear that confounded line about 'Mr Washington' has done me a world of mischief in the States—for though English and French laugh when they read it,—there's no use explaining & apologizing to an angry half-educated man—and, ah me! the other 10000 dollars I counted upon are I fear knocked into nothing by that unlucky blunder."[6] "As the author may possibly take another trip across the Atlantic," wrote the *New Quarterly Review* (Jan. 1854), "the misunderstanding was a serious affair" (5–6). More waggishly, reviewing the last number nearly two years later, the *Spectator* (18 August 1855) remarked on Thackeray's anticipated visit to America: "may no Loafer, unable to understand irony, take him for a loathsome aristocrat, and challenge him to gin-sling and bowie-knives" (861). He would probably not have been amused.

Whatever Thackeray's habitual misgivings about its calibre, as the novel reached its conclusion its status among critics and reviewers became clear— it was an outstanding success. *Harper's* (July, 1854) perhaps looking to its impending sales in book form called Thackeray "the great novelist of the present age" (385) and *The Newcomes* "the most unexceptionable and finished production of Thackeray's pen" (391). Mrs. Oliphant in *Blackwood's* (Jan. 1855) thought no other work of Thackeray's "so worthy of a great reputation" (93). Coventry Patmore (*North British Review*, Nov. 1855) considered *The Newcomes* was certain to become a classic (202). The *New Quarterly Review* (Oct. 1855) congratulated Thackeray "upon the completion of his greatest work," adding, "He now ranks among the first writers of his age. His triumph is signal" (423). The *Examiner* (1 Sept. 1855) judged *The Newcomes* "Mr. Thackeray's best work" (548). Malcolm Elwin, in the

---

[6] Letter to the Baxters, 17 December 1853, *Letters*, III, 327–28.

Quarterly Review (Sept. 1855) said, "This is Mr. Thackeray's masterpiece, as it is undoubtedly one of the masterpieces of English fiction" (350). And the youthful painter Burne-Jones, in the *Oxford and Cambridge Magazine* (Jan. 1856), went one further, declaring this "last and greatest work of Mr. Thackeray" the "masterpiece of all novel writing" (50–51). Its reputation as arguably Thackeray's greatest work lasted throughout the nineteenth century, as, for example, in George Smith's review of the Popular Edition of Thackeray's works (*Edinburgh Review*, Jan. 1873). Considering Thackeray's career as a whole, Smith writes that he "rose to the perfection of his art in fiction in 'The Newcomes.' ... It is the *chef d'oeuvre* in our opinion, of its author.... Having written 'The Newcomes' Thackeray may be said to have shaken hands as an equal with the two or three great masters of fiction" (106–7).

While pondering the question of Thackeray's alleged cynicism once again, critics found a gentler quality in *The Newcomes*. *Harper's* (May 1854) found it "mellow and exquisite in tone" (840)—with "a steady, tragical persistence," it "makes its impression, like life, silently and unsuspectedly" (July 1854, 259). James Hannay, in the *Leader* (8 Sept. 1855), found "a quieter and more decent kind of life" in *The Newcomes* than in *Vanity Fair* (870–71). *Putnam's* (Sept. 1855), rather mawkishly, detected "gushes of tenderer feelings, gleams of heavenlier light, a deeper pity and a more tearful love. Not that the work has any sentimentalism in it" (287). Elwin (*Quarterly Review*, Sept. 1855) dismissed the charge of cynicism, saying it "is now become an anachronism" (354). A harsher critic, William Roscoe (*National Review*, Jan. 1856) addressed the question at large, arguing that "*Vanity Fair* is the name, not of one, but of all Mr Thackeray's books" (192). Concluding that "the impression left by his books is that of weariness" and that his "philosophy might be called a religious stoicism rooted in fatalism" (193), Roscoe nevertheless allows that in *The Newcomes* "the life is more pleasantly selected, and the baser ingredients not scattered with so lavish a hand" (212). The *London and Quarterly Review* (July 1861), though coming down heavily on Thackeray's cynicism ("we grope with him through the black mist of worldliness, which, like a sooty London fog, hangs over all his pictures of life" [296]), conceded that "There is a better and brighter tone in 'The Newcomes'" (294), due perhaps to the helpful guidance offered by critics. The American *Christian Examiner*, which in January and May 1856 had taken a very harsh line towards Thackeray morally and artistically, reversed itself in September 1860, suggesting that "His peculiarities of style must be softened to us by familiarity, before we can detect the great humanity under the surface cynicism, and fully recognize the artistic grace of his life-like creations" (167). Anticipating Geoffrey Tillotson's argument that Thackeray's novels cannot be properly appreciated by the young ("His writings ought to be denied them, as wines should, and the latest music of Mozart and Beethoven"[7]), *The Times* (29 Aug. 1855) remarked that "Happily, Mr. Thackeray's novels are of that rich and ripe flavour which commends itself to persons of age and experience" (5). And *The Newcomes* es-

---

[7] Geoffrey Tillotson, *Thackeray the Novelist* (Cambridge: Cambridge University Press, 1954), 269.

pecially seems to have evoked such a response as a work of seasoned and mellow artistry.

Critics believed that *The Newcomes*, like Thackeray's other novels, was deficient in plot—"he obviously does not attempt it," said the *Dublin Review* (June 1856, 300). The *North British Review* (Feb. 1864) agreed: "It is not so much that he is a bad constructor of a plot as that his stories have no plot at all" (230). James Hannay in the *Leader* (Sept. 1855) distinguished between Romance and the philosophical novel, which he pronounced *The Newcomes* to be, then insisted: "Be it distinctly understood that PLOT is not required by the philosophical novel. What is the *plot* of *Don Quixote?*" (870). Open-ended though it is, *The Newcomes* obviously does have a plot in that its shape is determined by the cycle of the Colonel's life, ending in his famous "Adsum," a cycle ironically repeated in the amatory pattern of Clive's life as the Colonel partly imposes it on him. What we have to remember is the Victorian understanding of plot (and character) as implied in the distinction the *Leader* was making. Trollope puts it quite clearly in *An Autobiography*:

> Among English novels of the present day, and among English novelists, a great division is made. There are sensational novels and anti-sensational; sensational novelists and anti-sensational; sensational readers and anti-sensational. The novelists who are considered to be anti-sensational are generally called realistic. ... The readers who prefer the one are supposed to take delight in the elucidation of character. They who hold by the other are charmed by the construction and gradual development of a plot.[8]

Trollope's explanation and examples suggest that he thinks of plot as a matter of sensational, highly dramatic incident. And he approves—though for himself he says: "I have never troubled myself much about the construction of plots .... But the novelist has other aims than the elucidation of his plot. He desires to make his readers so intimately acquainted with his characters that the creations of his brain should be to them speaking, moving, living, human creatures."[9] Trollope's distinctions are clearly born out in the reception of *The Newcomes*. Plot, especially as Trollope has described it, is seen as secondary to character in Thackeray's accomplishment, and the emphasis of those who approve is on his 'realism.'

Whether in praise or blame, nearly all readers agreed on what they took to be Thackeray's representational power. *Harper's* (May 1854) purported to quote him on it: "'I have no head above my eyes,' he is reported to have said to a friend; meaning that he wrote from observation, and not from theory, nor what is called imagination. His new work, *The Newcomes*, is, in every way, worthy of him" (840). Elwin (*Quarterly Review*, Sept. 1855) doubted "if fiction is the proper term to apply to the most minute and faithful transcript of actual life which is anywhere to be found" (350). The *Spectator* (18 Aug. 1855), too, asserted that "Mr. Thackeray never draws upon his imagination solely: the world he paints is the world he has seen and lived in—the world of Belgravia, Pall Mall, the Inns of Court, the regions haunted by men and women of fashion with lions from the outer districts,

---

[8] Anthony Trollope, *An Autobiography*, introd. P. D. Edwards, World's Classics (1883. London: Oxford University Press, 1980), 226–27.
[9] *Ibid.*, 211.

by working men of letters, barristers, and artists" (860). William Roscoe (*National Review*, Jan. 1856), noting that his figures are "exact figures from modern life" (182), attributed his creative power to "his way of knitting his narrative on at every point to some link of our every-day experience," and concluded: "There is no reason why he should begin where he does, no reason why he should end at all. He cuts a square out of life, just as much as he wants, and sends it to Bradbury and Evans" (183). Francis Palgrave (*Westminster Review*, Oct. 1860), in an article entitled "W. M. Thackeray as Novelist and Photographer," seized upon the new technology of photography to underscore the point, finding a similarity between "the photography of Mr. Thackeray and the photography of Mr. Talbot" (502). (Roscoe had called Thackeray "a daguerreotypist of the world about us," [182].) Though Thackeray's early novels are minutely accurate but without an encompassing vision, in these later novels (*Esmond, Newcomes, Virginians*) "Mr. Thackeray shows himself a creative artist in the full force of the term; preserving his minute accuracy, and yet rising above it to larger truth" (521). Like Roscoe, who had moral and religious objections about Thackeray's social realism ("He never penetrates into the interior, secret, *real* life that every man leads in isolation from his fellows" [179],) *The Times* (29 Aug. 1855) tempered its praise with a "chief and important defect, which is, that he fails on the side of imagination. He is always restricted to the domain of pure facts. He has no dreams, no superstitions, no tentative aspirations to the unseen" (5).

This preoccupation with the real is no doubt as much a matter of dominant fashion in critical discourse as it is of Thackeray's practice. As we have seen, he is characteristically reflexive, double, polyphonic, constantly drawing our attention to the fictionality of his representation, examining the constructive imagination at work, reminding us that what we see as unique to our experience is merely a recurrence of familiar patterns in literature and life. Some readers responded to this subversion, or at least complication, of realism. Mrs. Oliphant, for example (*Blackwood's*, Jan. 1855), though seeing the book as "worthy of a great reputation" (93), complained that "it is not good taste of Mr. Pendennis to appear so frequently before the curtain, and remind us unpleasantly that it is fiction we are attending to, and not reality" (94–95). Thackeray, on the other hand, was much relieved by having thought of the device of making Pendennis the narrator: " ... the story advancing very pleasantly. I am not to be the author of it. Mr. Pendennis is to be the writer of his friend's memoirs and by the help of this little mask (wh I borrowed from Pisistratus Bulwer I suppose) I shall be able to talk more at ease than in my own person. I only thought of the plan last night and am immensely relieved by adopting it."[1] *The Examiner* (1 Sept. 1855), too, had reservations about the degree of reflexivity: "there is generally too large an amount of reflection scattered through it not to damage the story now and then, though these reflective passages are always in a light, satirical, attractive form, and written in very pure English" (548). Though Whitwell Elwin (*Quarterly Review*, Sept. 1855)

---

[1] Letter to Sarah Baxter, 26 July 1853, *Letters*, III, 297–98. Bulwer-Lytton's '*My Novel*' by *Pisistratus Caxton, or Varieties of English Life* (1853) is ostensibly by the hero of *The Caxtons* (1850).

also considered Pendennis "an excrescence" as narrator and wished him away (360), he nevertheless perceptively observed that Thackeray's reflective quality was fundamental to his art: "Mr. Thackeray, beyond all other novelists, loves to comment upon his own text—to stop in his story, indulge in reflections, analyze the motives of his characters, and cross-examine his readers upon their individual propensities" (356).

Only one review focussed on Thackeray's frequency of allusion, through which his parodic concern with eternal recurrence and imaginative design makes itself felt (as in the multiplied fairy tales of the opening). The American *Christian Examiner* (May 1856) despised everything about *The Newcomes*, including its intertextuality: "We do not like the style of 'The Newcomes' much better than we like its contents. It is diffuse and wearisome, abounding with scraps of all sorts of plundered prose and verse. It is a mishmash of all languages, and of no language that is in use among gentlemen. It is positively deformed with the easy pedantry of classical quotation, hackneyed phrases in French and Italian, and cant words of which we are unwilling to write down the true title" (443).

Perhaps the outstanding success of *The Newcomes*, as seen by reviewers, was the character of Colonel Newcome.[2] For Elwin, he was "the principal object of interest throughout" (*Quarterly Review*, Sept. 1855, 362). *The Times* (29 Aug. 1855) pronounced the Colonel "a noble creation, worthy of any age, or of any reputation, present or past.... Upon the creation of this character, Mr. Thackeray may rest his fame" (5). The *Spectator* (18 Aug. 1855) compared the Colonel with Sterne's Le Fever, since whose death "more generous tears have not been wept over a book than have fallen for you" (859–60). The *Weekly Dispatch* (12 Aug. 1855) knew "of no instance ...of the tragedy of pathos being carried to so majestic a height as the *euthenasia* of Colonel Thomas Newcome" (6). George Smith, reviewing an edition of the works, said that, "within the whole scope of fiction there is

[2] The Colonel naturally aroused considerable speculation about his original. The leading model seems to have been Thackeray's step-father, Henry Carmichael-Smyth. Thackeray's daughter, Anne Ritchie, said, "I never heard my father say that, when he wrote Colonel Newcome, any special person was in his mind, but it was always an understood thing that my step-grandfather had many of Colonel Newcome's characteristics, and there was also a brother of the Major's, General Charles Carmichael, who was very like Colonel Newcome in looks; a third family Colonel Newcome was Sir Richmond Shakspear, and how many more are there not, present, and yet to come?" (Introduction to *The Newcomes*, Vol VIII of *The Works of William Makepeace Thackeray*, [London: Smith Elder, 1898], xxxviii). Ray notes that "Mrs. Bayne (*Memorials*, pp. 310–11) suggests that [John Dowdeswell] Shakespear [d. 1866] was one of Thackeray's several Anglo-Indian models for Colonel Newcome" (*Letters*, III, 334n). Doyle's pictures of Colonel Newcome, which according to *The Month* (March 1884), were "by common consent ... acknowledged as the masterpiece of his illustrations of Thackeray" (313), are said to be "a portrait of the aging John Doyle" (Rodney Engen, *Richard Doyle*, 107), though the sketch of the Colonel with his cane raised in the Cave of Harmony is based on a similar sketch of Thackeray's (see Viola Hopkins Winner, "Thackeray and Richard Doyle, the 'wayward artist' of *The Newcomes*," *Harvard Library Bulletin*, 26 [April 1978], 193–211).
   Since much of *The Newcomes* explores the obsessive drive towards imaginative design in 'real life,' Thackeray might have been amused by the way his characters became the moulds for actual people. Among his friends at *Punch*, John Tenniel was nick-named 'Colonel Newcome,' "an apt expression for the dignified presence Tenniel brought to the *Punch* table, which was modelled after Thackeray's supreme gentleman character in *The Newcomes*" (Rodney Engen, *Sir John Tenniel, Alice's White Knight* [Aldershot: Scolar Press, 1991], 51).

no single character which stands out more nobly" (*Edinburgh Review*, Jan. 1873, 106). And Anthony Trollope bore the same testimony in his obituary for Thackeray (*Cornhill Magazine*, Feb. 1864), saying, "*The Newcomes* stands conspicuous for the character of the Colonel, who as an English gentleman has no equal in English fiction" (136). In fact "Colonel Newcome is the finest single character in English fiction" (137).

Inasmuch as the novel addresses the marriage market and the possibilities women face in marriage, it touched on the increasingly contentious issue of women's roles and natures. And the women of the novel aroused considerable comment. A repeating pattern in the work (perhaps reflecting Thackeray's continued brooding over Mrs. Brookfield) is that of the lover (the Colonel and Clive) who longs for a more intelligent and spirited woman but marries a pretty, anemic, young thing. "It's fatal, it runs in the family, father," says Clive (ch. 68). Marriage in the novel is frequently dismal. Rosey, the domestic, sweet young lady of the Victorian sentimental ideal, is stupid. Or as the *Christian Examiner* said in an article on "The Women of Thackeray" (Sept. 1860): "She is one of those harmless, negative characters, endowed with amiability and gentleness, if not with intelligent capacity" (188). Barnes tyrannizes over a similarly mindless Clara—"a little vacant and silly," says Lady Kew, "but you men like dolls for your wives" (ch. 52). Clara melodramatically runs away to a life of ostracism with Lord Belsize. The Newcome brothers, the d'Ivrys, the Floracs all have marriages that survive largely through mutual indifference between husband and wife. Laura, continued from *Pendennis*, is cloyingly moral and sentimental. Ethel, on the other hand, is full of spirit, intelligence, and enterprise, identified with Diana the virgin huntress, and to Victorian males both frightening and attractive: "I'd rather dance with her than marry her—by a doosid long score," exclaims Lord Rooster (ch. 33). Like Madame de Florac, she is restive in the domestic sphere: "almost all women," she says, "are made slaves one way or other" (ch. 47).

Reviewers responded variously according to their participations in the various Victorian constructions of women. Conventry Patmore (*North British Review*, Nov. 1855), author of *The Angel in the House*, as one might expect, professed "an unbounded esteem and affection" for Mrs. Laura, finding Ethel "vastly less attractive" though "neither stupid nor bad" (202). Elwin, who showed Thackeray a proof copy of his defence of Thackeray in the *Quarterly Review* (Sept. 1855), assuming Thackeray intended Laura as a domestic ideal, objected to her "air of prudery and self-conceit" and to "the strings by which she leads her pliant husband," adding "we are by no means reconciled to this exhibition of uxorious weakness" (360). Thackeray replied, "Pendennis's uxoriousness and admiration for Laura I take to show that he is a weak character & led by women. I hope no offence."[3] The *Rambler* (Oct. 1855) expressed its distaste for Laura with brisk concision: "a soft heart and brains to match." Seeing Laura as Thackeray's "*beau-ideal* of a young mother," it found her "absolutely a nuisance; offensively perfect; and, as a specimen of good-breeding, decidedly second-rate" (279). On behalf of women Mrs. Oliphant in *Blackwood's* (Jan. 1855) begged Thackeray

---

[3] Letter to Whitwell Elwin, 12 September 1855, *Letters*, III, 469.

"to add a little common-sense to his feminine goodness. When these tender pretty fools are rational creatures, the world of Mr. Thackeray's imagination will have a better atmosphere" (95). Sir James Fitzjames Stephen,
bracingly patriarchal and conservative as usual, characteristically asserted
that Laura was "much the kind of wife that Pendennis deserved, and that
every man deserves who cannot take the place of prophet, priest, and king
in his own household" (*Fraser's Magazine*, April 1864, 414). These judge-
ments are ideologically driven, proceeding as much from the critics' *parti
pris* as from any evidence in the text, and assuming too easily where Thackeray stands. The *North British Review* (Feb. 1864) saw Thackeray's women
in general as varying "between the extremes of pure goodness and pure
intellect" (238), but it had high praise for his delineation of women: "It
seems to us that Thackeray has drawn women more carefully and more
truly than any novelist in the language, except Miss Austen; and it is small
reproach to any writer, that he has drawn no female character so evenly
good as Anne Elliot or Elizabeth Bennet" (239).

Ethel was a problematic character, as the *Spectator* (Aug. 1855) recog-
nized: "and Ethel herself, '*la prèmiere demoiselle amoureuse*'—how we have
heard her part abused, how angry she makes everybody interested in
her!... she perpetually excites our fears lest she should irretrievably commit herself to either character [woman of the world or *ingénue*] and repent with unsatisfied heart and composed smile ever after" (860). Mrs.
Oliphant, too, had reservations about Ethel, finding her rejection of Lord
Kew too capricious: "Ethel is very attractive, very brilliant; but we would
rather not have our daughters resemble this young lady, it must be confessed" (*Blackwood's*, Jan. 1855, 95). Smith considered Thackeray's Ethel
"the best female character which has proceeded from his fertile brain" (*Edinburgh Review*, Jan. 1873, 107). W. D. Howells, who in 1900 wrote three
pieces on Thackeray's women for *Harper's Bazar: A Weekly Magazine for
Women*,[4] also liked her, saying: "He has not pretended that she was at once,
or ever, perfect, ... [but] He is admirably successful in making us feel her
growth.... Ethel sums up... the virtues and defects of the highest type of
Thackeray women ...." (Dec. 15, 2094).

Another topic that gained attention in the reviews was Thackeray's style.
With his instinct for parody and linguistic register, Thackeray shows a lively
interest in the way a linguistic manner evokes a background of place, age,
class, community, etc. Tough old aristocratic Lady Kew, nostalgic for the
Regency, appreciates the racy style of her grandchildren and their friends,
and savours their terminology: "Ethel is a brick, and Alfred is a trump, I
think you say, ... and Barnes is a snob. This is very satisfactory to know"
(ch. 10). Critics, however, were of two minds about his language. As K. C.
Phillipps observes, early Victorians often associated slang with the low and
disreputable.[5] Sir James Fitzjames Stephen noted in his obituary (*Fraser's*

---

[4] Under the general heading "Heroines of Nineteenth-Century Fiction" the articles are:
"Thackeray's Bad Heroines," (November 17, 1900), 1799–1804; "Thackeray's Good
Heroines," (December 1, 1900), 1945–1950; and "Thackeray's Ethel Newcome and
Charlotte Bronte's Jane Eyre," December 15, 1900), 2094–2100. Reprinted in Howells's
Heroines of Fiction, 2 vols. (New York: Harper, 1901), I, 190–227.

[5] K. C. Phillipps, *The Language of Thackeray* (London: Deutsch, 1978), chapter 3,

Magazine, April 1864) that "Mr. Thackeray was aware of all the refinements of what might be described as his native slang, and he reproduced it with marvellous fidelity" (407). But Mrs. Oliphant remarked sniffily (*Blackwood's*, Jan. 1855), "it is very doubtful if it will be an advantage to make these Islands no better than a broad margin for the witticisms and the dialect of Cockaigne" (96). The *Christian Examiner* (May 1856), extreme on this as on other aspects of *The Newcomes*, judged Thackeray's tendency "to describe the coarse and base, the imbecile and wicked, and this in terms too low for polite use and too fast for the dictionaries" as exceeded only by his sceptical spirit (441). The Reverend Whitwell Elwin, though charitably disposed (*Quarterly Review*, Sept. 1855), also had moral qualms about the range of Thackeray's style: "It is with reluctance we confess that he has turned language to good account which in all other hands has hitherto revolted every person of cultivated mind, for we fear the evil effects of his example, and are sorry the black patches should heighten the beauty" (358). Roscoe in the *National Review* (Jan. 1856), noting that "irony is the essence of his wit" (187), observed with discrimination: "He has an art peculiarly his own of reproducing every-day language with just enough additional sparkle or humour or pathos of his own to make it piquant and entertaining without losing *vraisemblance*" (182). The *Times* (29 August 1855) confessed itself won over by the delight of Florac's Frenchified English: "a page of Florac's English atones for all Mr. Thackeray's abuse of his mother tongue" (5). In many of these comments on Thackeray's raciness, along with the predilection for a manner that is perfectly proper pleasant and placid goes a relief that Thackeray's isn't. Once again, it is refreshing to hear Henry James on the subject of Thackeray's style (*Nation*, 9 Dec. 1875): "There is no writer of whom one bears better being reminded, none from whom any chance quotation, to whom any chance allusion or reference, is more unfailingly delectable. Pick out something at hazard from Thackeray, and ten to one it is a prize" (376).

A few reviewers commented on Doyle's illustration of *The Newcomes*.[6] As an artifact, *The Newcomes* was a piece of collaborative artistry, Thackeray providing the text, Richard Doyle the title illustrations, principal sketches, and pictorial initial letters at the beginnings of chapters. There are two title-pages (the finished work appearing in two volumes), forty-four plates, forty-three inset sketches, and seventy-five initial letters (five chapters lack them), altogether a considerable outpouring of creativity by a prominent artist. Thackeray had several reasons for having Doyle do the illustrations. In part it was a friendly act since Doyle had recently felt obliged to resign from *Punch* over its virulent anti-Catholicism. Having someone to make

---

"Slang." The word slang itself had extended application. Phillipps quotes Queen Victoria writing to the Prince of Wales about dress: "we do expect that you will never wear anything extravagant or slang, not because we don't like it, but because it would prove a want of self-respect and be an offence against decency, leading—as it has often done in others—to an indifference to what is morally wrong" (60).

[6] For Doyle's collaboration with Thackeray, see Viola Winner Hopkins, "Thackeray and Richard Doyle, the 'wayward artist' of *The Newcomes*," *Harvard Library Bulletin*, 26 (April 1978). 193–211; John C. Olmsted, "Richard Doyle's Illustrations to *The Newcomes*," *Studies in the Novel*, XIII (Spring-Summer 1981), 93–108; and Rodney Engen, *Richard Doyle*, (Stroud, Glos.: Catalpa Press, 1983), Chapter 14.

the illustrations also left Thackeray free to travel. He felt "almost sorry I am not to do them myself: but it will be a great weight off my mind and I can now move about Withersumever I will."[7] His inspection of the engravings for Number I left him grumbling: "Doyle has been 3 weeks doing the engravings and they are not as good as mine now they are done."[8] On the whole, however, he grew to appreciate them: "He does beautifully and easily what I wanted to do and can't. There are capital bits in almost all the etchings."[9] On the other hand, Doyle was frequently dilatory, to Thackeray's great exasperation. In June 1854, he threatens, "if as I expect Doyle has not done the Newcomes plates I shall take them in hand and do them henceforth myself."[1] In August, he pleads for a title page for the completed first volume: "If you have not sent in an engraved title can you do one by tomorrow night .... *If not I can and will*."[2] The stress was not all on Thackeray's side. Doyle complained that Thackeray hardly ever described a character all at once or gave sufficient notice of what he intended.[3] And occasionally they had differences about how characters should look, differences that reached the text of the novel, as in the narrator's comment on Clive: "he is a much handsomer fellow than our designer has represented" (ch. 24). Whatever the tensions and frustrations, however, critics consider Doyle's drawings for *The Newcomes* among the best he created.[4]

As the novel began its run, the *Spectator* (1 Oct. 1853) was "inclined to regret that Mr. Thackeray ceases here to be his own illustrator—even though in favour of such a substitute as Richard Doyle" (949). The *Art Journal* (1 Nov. 1853) anticipated one of Doyle's problems in providing illustrations for Thackeray: "He is the most difficult of all modern writers to anticipate or to calculate upon" (300). Getting at the substance, the *Examiner* (1 Sept. 1855), certainly much aided by both Doyle and Thackeray, asserted that "What Hogarth meant by his pictures entitled Marriage *à la mode* Mr. Thackeray means by his novel of *The Newcomes*" (548). Thackeray invokes *Marriage à la Mode* several times in the novel and in Chapter 54 comments on Doyle's illustration of Lady Clara and Belsize, "The Old Love Again": "In the cloak-room sits Lady Clara Newcome, with a gentleman bending over her, just in such an attitude as the bride is in Hogarth's 'Marriage-à-la-mode' as the counsellor talks to her." The elder Thomas Newcome is introduced to the novel as a Hogarthian virtuous apprentice, and Doyle obliges with a headletter for Chapter 2, showing a weaving apprentice who recalls Hogarth's *Industry and Idleness*. This sort of pictorial cross-referencing was, of course, something that Victorian readers were used to analyzing.[5]

---

7 Letter to Mrs. Carmichael-Smyth, 1 September 1853, *Letters*, III, 302.
8 Letter to Mrs. Carmichael-Smyth, 23 September 1853, *Letters*, III, 305.
9 Letter to Percival Leigh, 12 April 1854, *Letters*, III, 362.
1 Letter to Mrs. Carmichael-Smyth, 12? June 1854, *Letters*, III, 375.
2 Letter to Richard Doyle, 20 August 1854, *Letters*, III, 384.
3 See Rodney Engen, *Richard Doyle*, 106. Engen gives a full account of Doyle's and Thackeray's working relationship on *The Newcomes*.
4 Rodney Engen, *Richard Doyle*, 108.
5 See John Harvey, *Victorian Novelists and their Illustrators* and J. Hillis Miller, *The Fiction of Realism: Sketches by Boz, Oliver Twist, and Cruikshank's Illustrations* (Los Angeles: Wm. Andrews Clark Memorial Library, University of California, 1971).

By far the most interesting review of the illustrations was an "Essay on The Newcomes" by the young Edward Burne-Jones in the *Oxford and Cambridge Magazine* (Jan. 1856). The review is full of brash enthusiasm for *The Newcomes* as a masterpiece, and also complimentary to Doyle: "from such a happy combination of author and artist as so rarely occurs much was to be expected, and has accordingly been fulfilled" (60). In assessing Doyle's contribution, he is discriminating: "The main illustrations, however, seem to me far less successful than the rest ... but in the symbolical drawings, which form round the initial letters of chapters, it is very different; here he is wonderfully successful, and, as an artist should ever be, no faint echo of other men's thoughts, but a voice concurrent or prophetical, full of meaning; they are little sketches apt to be passed over in carelessness, but on examination found to be full of real art and poetical comprehension" (60–1). Burne-Jones remained a particularly sympathetic reader of *The Newcomes*. Years later, as reader-aloud in his studio, his daughter Margaret read through the whole of Thackeray twice.[6] In 1895 he interrupts a discussion of *The Newcomes* with praise of its illustrations: "Ethel beautifully riding on a donkey as Dicky Doyle drew her. He did it so well. To read *The Newcomes* with Doyle's pictures is the only way—Ethel, Colonel Newcome, Clive, and all of them done beautifully. It's a treasure of a book."[7] The illustrations of *The Newcomes* still invite close examination, and Burne-Jones's emphasis on the quality of the initial letters seems to me an accurate assessment.

Readers characteristically have some trouble with self-reflexive works. In his ending Thackeray tells the reader, "You may settle your fable-land in your own fashion. Anything you like happens in fable-land." By blurring the conventional boundaries of life and art in his conclusion, refusing to summarize his characters' subsequent careers, and telling readers to finish the story as they like, Thackeray induced a degree of frustration in the tidy reader. Noting this, Hain Friswell, in "A Missing Chapter from *The Newcomes*," for *Sharpe's London Magazine* (Sept. 1855), set out, fairly successfully, to wrap things up in a comic vein. On behalf of readers who have shared in the reality of Clive's and Ethel's sorrows, he vigorously protests that Thackeray "comes before the public to claim the guerdon of his labours, and to cheat us with a kind of apologue about 'Dream-land.' *Dream-land*, forsooth!" (167). Invoking the precedent of *Rebecca and Rowena*, in which Thackeray has "taken the liberty of carrying further the history of Rowena, in Scott's masterpiece of 'Ivanhoe,'" *Sharpe's* author intends to do the same in "CHAPTER XLI—(VOLUME II) IN WHICH CLIVE AND ETHEL PERFORM A DUTY THEY OWE TO THEMSELVES, AND TO SOCIETY" (168). He has "black care" (Thackeray's favourite allusion) recall memories of his dead wife to Clive, and remarks appropriately enough that he "expected every devotion from his wife, and yet had given her so little warmth himself" (169). In the breathless parodic manner of *Rebecca and Rowena*, he has Clive reflect on Ethel: "Yes, it had been for her, through her, that he had paid this lip devotion to his dead wife" (169). Laura arranges a meeting of Clive and Ethel eighteen months later. Clive, "throwing himself into the attitude of the écorché

[6] Georgiana Burne-Jones, *Memorials of Edward Burne-Jones*, 2 vols. (1904. New York: Blom, 1971), II, 160.
[7] *Ibid.*, II, 266.

of Michael Angelo, which stood upon his mantel" (recalling Thackeray's avatar, Michael Angelo Titmarsh, as well as the puppetry of *Vanity Fair*), he exclaims: "Oh, Ethel, Ethel, without you I die: and yet how can I, dare I, hope, Ethel, dear Ethel?" and a low, clear voice answers him, "I am here, Clive; here" (170).

The Newcomes held on to its high favour throughout the nineteenth century, and was part of the public consciousness. As Ray notes, "As late as 1908 Saintsbury could contend that it had been on the whole 'Thackeray's most popular book.'"[8] In *The Decay of Lying*, arguing his paradoxical case that "a great artist invents a type, and Life tries to copy it," Oscar Wilde assures us that the noble gentleman from whom Thackeray drew Colonel Newcome "died, a few months after *The Newcomes* had reached a fourth edition, with the word 'Adsum' on his lips."[9] A Canadian writer of short stories, Duncan Campbell Scott, could rely on his readership's understanding the context when he appropriated characters from *The Newcomes* in his short story, "An Adventure of Mrs. Mackenzie's," which he starts with an extract from Chapter 23 where the Campaigner reminisces about her life in Montreal—the story recounts how her flirtation provokes Mackenzie into a duel.[1] Colonel Newcome played his part in World War I as well. The actor-manager Herbert Beerbohm Tree had achieved one of his great successes in Michael Morton's dramatization of *The Newcomes*, entitled *Colonel Newcome*, in 1906. The *Daily Mail*, under the headline, "Should Mr. Tree be *allowed* to play Colonel Newcome?," argued that an actor who had developed renown and a gutteral accent in playing Fagin and Svengali should not be permitted (as Hesketh Pearson summarizes it) "to appear as the *beau idéal* of an English gentleman and to murmur that heart-searching last word *Adsum*." The first night's performance ended with great applause and cries for a speech from Tree, who concisely declared, "Ladies and Gentlemen—I think we win."[2] In the winter of 1916–17, Tree toured Canada and the United States, including *Colonel Newcome* in his performances. In New York, he opened with it at the New Amsterdam Theatre on 10 April 1917. Interpolating a toast to the British navy to great applause, he added "And let us not forget our friends across the Seas!" to even greater applause.[3] Pearson notes that "for a charity in aid of mutilated soldiers at the Metropolitan Opera House he appeared as Colonel Newcome, closing the performance with 'Colonel Newcome begs respectfully to salute the Star Spangled Banner', which raised the roof."[4] Always a gentleman, the Colonel perhaps made up for those American sensibilities offended by Thackeray's ironic comment on George Washington. Photographs from

8 Gordon N. Ray, *Thackeray: The Age of Wisdom*, 248.

9 Oscar Wilde, "The Decay of Lying," *Intentions, The First Collected Edition of the Works of Oscar Wilde, 1908-22*, ed. Robert Ross, 15 vols (London: Dawsons, 1969), VI, 37.

1 Duncan Campbell Scott, "An Adventure of Mrs. Mackenzie's: Being a Variation on a Theme of Thackeray's," *Ainslee's Magazine*, 8 (1901), 49–58; reprinted in *The Witching of Elspie: A Book of Stories* (Toronto: McClelland and Stewart, 1923), 198–222.

2 Hesketh Pearson, *Beerbohm Tree: His Life and Laughter* (New York: Harper, 1956), 155. See Also Madeleine Bingham, *The Great Lover: the Life and Art of Herbert Beerbohm Tree* (London: Hamish Hamilton, 1978), 164.

3 Bingham, *The Great Lover*, 262.

4 Pearson, *Beerbohm Tree*, 231.

Tree's staging of the play appeared in the Collins Illustrated Pocket Classics edition.

The novel has not fared so well in the mid-twentieth century. More Jamesian than James, Percy Lubbock in *The Craft of Fiction* set off James's 'scenic' method against Thackeray's 'panoramic' method to Thackeray's disadvantage,[5] and subsequently, for a time, it became almost a nervous tick in criticism to praise James by deflating Thackeray. James himself took a less partisan view, and it may be salutary to conclude by recalling his poetic evocation of the great Victorian serials as "strokes of the great Victorian clock," and of *The Newcomes*, in *Notes of a Son and Brother*:

> For these appearances, these strong time-marks in such stretches of production as that of Dickens, that of Thackeray, that of George Eliot, had in the first place simply a genial weight and force, a direct importance, and in the second a command of the permeable air and the collective sensibility, with which nothing since has begun to deserve comparison .... I witnessed, for that matter, with all my senses, young as I was, the never-to-be-equalled degree of difference made, for what may really be called the world-consciousness happily exposed to it, by the prolonged "coming out" of The Newcomes, yellow number by number, and could take the general civilised participation in the process for a sort of basking in the light of distinction.[6]

5 Percy Lubbock, *The Craft of Fiction* (London: Jonathan Cape, 1921). Geoffrey Tillotson in *Thackeray the Novelist*, pp. 71 ff. and 82 ff., corrects Lubbock's extreme emphasis.

6 Henry James, *Notes of a Son and Brother* (London: Macmillan, 1914), 20–21. It is unfortunate that James's offhand remark about *The Newcomes* along with *War and Peace* and *The Three Musketeers* as "loose, baggy monsters" has such currency. For his more considered judgement and emulation, see my " 'An honourable emulation of the author of *The Newcomes*': James and Thackeray," *Nineteenth-Century Fiction*, 32 (1978), 399–419.

Textual History and Editorial Methods

P. L. Shillingsburg

Composition

Thackeray must already have planned to write *The Newcomes* as early as June, 1853, when he responded to an offer for it from his friend George Smith, the publisher of his two most recent books (*Henry Esmond*, 1852, and *The English Humourists*, 1853), expressing some sorrow that his next serial novel was already committed to the firm of Bradbury and Evans, which had published *Vanity Fair*, 1847–48, and *Pendennis*, 1848–50. The writing itself did not begin in a serious way, however, until July, while Thackeray was on the Continent.[1] By the end of August, when he returned to London, Thackeray had produced enough manuscript for four installments. He arranged with his friend and former colleague on *Punch*, Richard Doyle, to illustrate the novel; and he arranged with another *Punch* colleague, Percival Leigh, to help handle any textual problems arising during production.

Near the end of September, he read proof for the first installment, published on 1 October 1853. In October, back in Paris, Thackeray wrote installment 5 and read proof for installment 2. In November he returned to London for about a week, during which he read proofs for installment 3 and wrote portions of installment 6, which however he did not complete until January. At the end of November he returned to Paris, gathered his daughters, and headed for Rome, where he planned to spend the winter. Installment 6, not quite completed, was sent to London from Rome sometime in December, and three additional pages for that number were sent in January. Those three pages seem never to have reached their destination.[2]

Although an attempt was made to have proofs sent to Thackeray for correction, and although he was far enough ahead in the writing to make that plan work, it appears that all did not run smoothly. Installment 5 was too long, and it may be that Thackeray was able to make the changes required to shorten it, either at the end of November before he left London or by receiving proofs for that installment and returning them by post.[3] Installment 6, published on 1 March 1854, appears to have been seen through the press entirely by Percival Leigh; but, as will be shown in more detail in the discussion of editorial principles and decisions below, the evidence is not conclusive about who made the changes occasioned by the loss of three pages of manuscript.[4]

---

[1] The details in this brief summary are drawn for the most part from Edgar F. Harden's thorough examination of Thackeray's movements and practice in *The Emergence of Thackeray's Serial Fiction* (Athens: U Georgia P, 1979), chapters 4 and 5.

[2] Professor Harden opines that the three pages arrived and were mistakenly inserted in installment 5 (pp. 76–77), but all of the manuscript for the installment survives and there is not a three-page section with sufficient integrity to be considered the pages sent from Rome in January.

[3] It is possible that proof-stage changes introduced in installment 5 were made by Percival Leigh, most of them being cuts designed to make the number fit the 32-page installment format.

[4] Professor Harden, analyzing the same evidence, concludes that the nature of variance between the manuscript and printed versions of installment 6 indicate that Thackeray

By the end of February, Thackeray had completed the manuscript for installment 9; but he had become confused about what parts of the story were included in each installment, for he did not know what had been done for installment 6. He had directed that Leigh send additional proofs and mail to him in Florence, where he intended to go next, but his daughters falling ill, he was forced to remain in Naples through most of March. By 12 April he was back in Paris, happy to be away from "the confounded Italian Malaria" (*Letters*, III, 362), and happy, too, to see that installment 7 had come out so well. If Leigh had sent anything to Florence, it was still there. Forced to rely on Leigh's good judgment in handling installment 6, Thackeray was relieved to find so little was affected.

By the end of April, Thackeray was again in London, seeing to the proofing and final adjustments himself, never leaving for very long and not going further than Paris or Brussels until the novel was completed.

The following fragmentary plans are all that is known to survive of Thackeray's working outlines for the work. The first is from a loose sheet in the Robert H. Taylor Collection, Princeton University. Writing begins at the top of the page as if this page were a continutaion from a now misplaced sheet.

XVI.	The Colonel comes back, and proposes to Barnes for Ethel for Clive.
	[squeezed in] Rupture between the Colonel & Barnes—
XVII.	Announcement of her engagement to Lord Farintosh. death of Lady Kew.
XVIII.	Clives marriage. Binnies Nunc Dimittis.
XIX	Elopement of Lady Clara. Ethel's revolt.
XX	The Election. Height of Clives prosperity. Bitterness at home.
XXI.	Failure of the B.B. Mrs Mack comes to live with the young people.
XXII.	Retreat of the Colonel before her. His resolve and its execution.
XXIII-IV.	Orme's History of India. Too late. The Colonels Euthanasia.

The second is a brief schedule of events in Thackeray's handwriting found on the back of the manuscript page on which begins Chapter XI, Volume II (for installment 16, published in January 1855). That manuscript portion is in the Berg Collection, New York Public Library.

The Colonel goes away	August	41.
Clive goes to ~~Baden~~ ↑Rome↓.	October	41.
return to England	June	42—
↑Lord Highgate & Lord Dorking die	—	42↓
meets Ethel at Paris	May	43.
Sir Bryan dies	June	—
Pendennis marries	September	43.
meets the company	May	44.

made most if not all the proof-stage changes. He believes there was just enough time between Thackeray's reception of the proofs in Naples on 21 February and publication on the evening of the 28th for Thackeray to have corrected and returned the proofs.

Virtually complete manuscripts survive for installments numbers 4–6, 10, 14–15, 17–20, and 22–24. Partial manuscripts survive for numbers 2 (2 leaves), 16 (3 leaves), and 21 (10 leaves). There are some 530 surviving manuscript leaves and fragments. Thackeray dictated substantial portions of the novel, so that of the surviving leaves 54 are in George Hodder's handwriting and about 240 are in Anne Thackeray's handwriting. The remaining 236 leaves are in Thackeray's hand. Anne's handwriting is very large, so though her page count is high she produced only about 33% of the surviving manuscript text. George's hand was also larger than Thackeray's, though not as large as Anne's; his 54 pages account for about 4% of the surviving manuscript text. The largest portion of manuscript (456 pages) is at the Charterhouse School. The Berg Collection houses 65 pages. There are two pages each at the Taylor Collection (Princeton), the University Texas (Humanities Center), and the British Library. The Huntington Library has one page.

The First Edition

The Newcomes was printed and issued in monthly installments from 1 October 1853, through 1 August 1855: twenty-four numbers issued in 23 parts, numbers 23 and 24 making up the last part together. Each installment except the last contained 32 pages of text and two full-page steel-engraved plate illustrations. Embedded in the text pages were a variety of wood-cut illustrations. Each 32-page installment was made up of two sheets or gatherings of eight leaves each. The steel-engraved plates were printed on heavier stock and tipped into the two gatherings at appropriate points.

The serial-edition and the first book-edition, though different in their methods of issue and binding (and thus different in outward appearance), are the same in their typesetting and printing. Many original purchasers of the serially issued parts had their copies bound to order, so that many bound copies now extant have individualized, rather than standard, bindings. However, since left-over sheets from the serial issue were bound up and issued as whole books along with newly printed sheets from stereotyped plates cast from the original type-setting, many copies in the publisher's standard binding contain sheets originally slated for parts-issue. Inconclusive evidence suggests that installments could also be purchased separately long after the book was available bound as a whole; for example, some copies of books in made-to-order bindings have gatherings originally issued as installments along with other gatherings that were never so issued.[5] In addition, the publishers' records indicate that throughout the publishing history of the book, reprint orders were given by installment number.

---

[5] For any copy of the book, this fact about the method of issue can be deduced from the presence or absence of "stab-holes" in the inner margins. The serial installments were sewn by the "stabbing" method rather than through the back of the fold as is normal in book bindings. Gatherings sewn for installment issue and subsequently disassembled and rebound into a book, of course, retain the "stab-holes" near the inner margins.

According to the publisher's records,[6] each installment was composed, corrected, printed, and cast for stereotypes in a continuous operation. The records show that production proceeded according to the following schedule:

Date:	Number:	Copies:
Oct/Nov 53	1 and 2	15,000
Dec–Aug 54	3–11	14,000
Sept–Aug 55	12–23/24	13,000
Reprints		
Nov. 1855	2, 4, 12	1000
Jan. 1856	1, 3, 8, 9, 14–24	1000
Feb. 1856	2, 4	750
	10, 11	1000
July 1857	21	500
June 1858	5	500
Feb. 1859	6, 13, 14	500
Sept. 1860	23/24	500
Oct. 1862	15	250
Jan. 1864	1, 16, 19, 20–22	250

In summary, from the original issue of part one in January 1847 until 1865 when Bradbury and Evans sold all back stock and stereotyped plates to Smith, Elder, the number of copies printed for each part range from a grand total of 16,250 copies of number 1 down to 14,500 of numbers 23/24, all printed from the original typesetting (in standing type for the initial printing and then in stereotyped form for subsequent printings).

Though it is unclear from the publishers' records whether the stereotypes were cast before or after the first printing, it appears from the evidence of variants in copies of the first edition that stereotyping came after the first printing was completed. Indeed, the logistics of production almost dictated that the first printing should be done from standing type and that stereotyped plates be made afterward: there was simply not enough time to produce stereotypes between the correction of final proofs, sometimes as late as the 27th or 28th of the month, and the distribution of printed and bound installments to booksellers on the evening of the last day of the month.[7]

That being the case, 15,000 copies of number 1 would have been printed from standing type and only 1,250 from stereotyped plates. Likewise, for

[6] Bradbury and Evans Archive, formerly with Bradbury, Agnew Publishers, London, most recently owned by Amalgamated Newspapers. My work with the archive was in what was known as the Punch Office. See also P. Shillingsburg, *Pegasus in Harness*, for further descriptions of the archive and of Bradbury and Evans production processes.

[7] It may also have been thought that a slight delay in casting stereotypes might allow for the discovery of errors through the services of reviewers or that the author might be able to make changes or corrections before the book version; however, the principle that drove the use of stereotypes was opposed to any delay, for the printers would not wish to delay the recycling of type for other jobs. It is most likely that stereotyped plates were cast as soon as the type was cleaned at completion of the first printing. Note that in the case of Thackeray's serial books the printers did not use the special low-bodied type developed for works whose first printing would be from stereotyped plates.

the double number 23/24, 13,000 would be from standing type and only 1,500 from the stereotypes. Therefore the odds greatly favor the likelihood that surviving copies of the first edition of the novel would represent the first printing.

I have examined eight copies of the first edition. One of them was bound and issued in 1866 by Smith, Elder, and it probably represents one of the last printings from the plates. (It is possible that number 23/24 in that copy is from the first printing, however; for its measurements and its texts correspond to printings from standing type. That could have happened; for, as stock for any number dwindled in the bindery, new printed sheets were probably stacked on top of the few remaining old ones. Thus, a few copies of first printing sheets might have survived unbound until the 1866 re-issue by Smith, Elder.)

Of the other seven copies, one is obviously made up from some sheets printed from standing type and other sheets printed from stereotypes: some of its gatherings have the stab-holes of serial issue, some do not; some of its variants agree with the 1866 text, some do not; those gatherings that agree with the 1866 text do not have the stab-holes; and, finally, some of its pages have the narrower type-page measurement characteristic of sheets printed from stereotypes.[8]

The most plausible conclusion appears to be that, the first printing from standing type having been completed, a few corrections were made in the type and then stereotyped plates were cast. The stereotypes would have been used to produce all subsequent printings, beginning with the 1000 copies each of numbers 2, 4, and 12 in November, 1855. A glance at the chart above, however, confirms the fact that a majority of copies printed (and therefore probably a majority of copies extant) belonged to the first printing, from standing type. The following chart lists the corrections and adjustments made in preparation for stereotyping. One change (in vol. II, page 279) was apparently inadvertent.

Volume I

6.13	honest days,]	merry days,
7.16-22	[6 *lines reset with new line breaks but no text changes*]	
	just / come]	come in), / began
	after / the]	the manner / of
	pocket-handkerchief / in]	in the most / ludicrous
	ribaldry by / sternly]	looking / towards
	called upon / the gents]	to give / their
	room, and / (Mr. Bellow]	to sing / a song.
8.25-26	the / honest warrior's]	the / warrior's

[8] For a full discussion of this phenomenon see P. Shillingsburg's "The First Edition of *Pendennis,*" *PBSA*, 66 (1972), 35–49. Plaster-of-Paris molds used for stereotyping shrank slightly during drying and heating required before the molten lead could be poured into them, causing the stereotyped plate to be slightly smaller than the standing type. Some variation in dimensions is also caused by paper shrinkage; for the novel was printed on damp paper.

13.2	Newcome, does not]	Newcome, could not
18.30	the present Baronet's]	the Baronet's
18.30	this very day); / —by]	his dying day);—by /
160.35	morning, and the ride	
	with father over, this]	morning, this
160.36	Gandishe's]	Gandish's
.36–38	[*3 lines reset with new line breaks but no text changes*]	
	Gandishe's / Drawing]	Academy, / where
	hours at / work]	his art, / before
	be spared / from]	his books / to
380.	END OF VOLUME I]	[omitted]
380.	[Bradbury and Evans imprint]]	[Smith, Elder imprint]

Volume II

13.35	well thank you:]	well, thank you;
233.30	fromher]	from her
279.34	satisfactory]	satisfactry
295.9	Rosey]	Rosey,
295.9	baby?]	Baby?
375.	[Bradbury and Evans imprint]]	[Smith, Elder imprint added p. [376]]

In addition to these deliberate changes, there is a slight amount of type-damage that shows up in copies printed from plates: tails lost from a few commas, missing periods at the ends of lines, dropped-out or otherwise damaged apostrophes and quotation marks, a few missing hyphens, a few dots missing from i's and an i missing from its dot.

The research undertaken for this edition does not include examination of numbers 23/24 in a printing from stereotyped plates. If a copy of the book with such sheets exists, I have not found it.[9]

Subsequent Editions

American Editions

The Newcomes appeared serially in *Harper's New Monthly Magazine* from November 1853 through October 1855, with the exception of March 1854. Thus, it began publication one month after serialization commenced in London, fell another month behind by missing the March 1854 issue (postponing installment number 5), and so finished two months after the completion of the London issue. The first four numbers were published without illustrations.

---

[9] It is common for bibliographers of nineteenth-century serialized fiction to note that they have collated a number of copies in serial form with a number of copies in book form and to report their findings in that way. One should note that variants are produced not by the differences in binding but by the differences in printing. Most copies of *The Newcomes* in both serial and book form were the result of a single initial printing. Only a diligent search for a copy printed late, with the characteristic measurements of pages printed from stereotyped plates, is likely to produce any additional variant readings.

At the completion of serialization, Harper and Brothers published the novel in two volumes, adding the illustrations for the first four numbers. It is probable that the American text commanded a larger readership than the British editions, for *Harper's Magazine* had a circulation of about 125,000 during the period when *The Newcomes* appeared. We do not have a record of how many copies were printed of the book issue, but it was reprinted in 1856, 1859, 1865, and 1868.

Harper and Brothers had stipulated in its negotiations with Thackeray and with Bradbury and Evans that it would pay £10 per number for *The Newcomes*, but only if it received setting copy "6 weeks before it was printed" in London.[1] Because Thackeray was out of town when Harper's offer was made, because Bradbury and Evans failed at every turn to respond to Harper and Brothers or to Sampson Low (Harper's London agent), the Harper company did not receive advance sheets of number 1 six weeks before it appeared in London. In the end Thackeray was paid a total of £150, not the £240 of the original offer (Harpers' records, cited in Shillingsburg, 134).

Full collation of *Harper's Magazine* and the book edition of *The Newcomes* against the London serial indicates that the magazine text for numbers 1-4, 16, and 19–20 were set from advance proofsheets not containing the final corrections, and that the rest of the work was set either from *finally* corrected proofsheets for the London serial issue or from the printed installments. Furthermore, the Harper book edition was printed from the same type used for the magazine except in the case of numbers 1–4, which were entirely reset using the London serial text, not *Harper's Magazine* text, as setting copy. It is clear, however, that the London firm continued to send advance proofsheets to New York, even though for the most part the New Edition was set from final copy, because in number 9 (chap. 29), both New York texts contain a woodcut omitted from the first English edition, in which chap. 29 ends at the bottom of the last page of the installment. The illustration shows Lord Kew and Barnes, the latter with his hand in his pocket. One can surmise that when it appeared there was no room for the illustration in the London installment, the phrase "dropped his hand from my arm" was extended to say "into his pocket"—an addition that did not get into the more fully illustrated New York texts.[2] (See Textual Notes for I.275.33.)

We can only speculate about why the American issue of the novel, already one month late getting started, fell two months behind by missing the March issue with the fifth number. Elizabeth James notes that the American serial had no illustrations through its first four installments and that their addition, beginning with number 5, might have delayed production.[3]

[1] P. Shillingsburg, *Pegasus in Harness* (Charlottesville, Va.: Univ. of Virginia Press, 1992), p. 133.

[2] The London publisher's print records identify payments to Richard Doyle for his illustrations, numbering each illustration consecutively from 1 to 124 and indicating the installment in which they were used. However, there are nine illustration numbers missing from the records (and not used in the novel), including three that might have fallen in installment number 9. Presumably, this extra New York illustration is one of them.

[3] Elizabeth James, "William Makepeace Thackeray's *The Newcomes* in America," *Proof*, 5 (1977), 45–56.

There were also difficulties in the London production of number 5—for which there was too much manuscript and upon which Thackeray worked very late in the month as he was about to leave on his extended trip to the Continent—but since the American serial was already a whole month behind, the London problem with that number was probably not a factor.

In spite of lagging one month behind the London serial publication for the first four numbers, *Harper's Magazine* setting copy for those four numbers was advanced proof-sheets, not incorporating Thackeray's final corrections for the London serial. Since the manuscript for those four numbers no longer survives, the *Harper's Magazine* version of these installments is the closest approach we have to the corresponding manuscript substantives. However, because the *Harper's* compositors heavily copy-edited the spelling, punctuation and capitaization, as is clear from their practice in portions for which the manuscript survives, these early *Harper's* numbers cannot serve as a guide to accidentals underlying the London serial. Perhaps the most remarkable substantive variant occurs when the American magazine text refers to Whittlesea's chapel several times as Hickathrift's chapel in number 2. Because the *Harper's* substantives in numbers 1–4 *do* reflect manuscript readings otherwise lost, they are recorded in the footnotes as indications of passages revised by Thackeray in his final proofing.

Collation of the *Harper's Magazine*, the Harper's book text, and the London serial text indicates that the American book edition represents a complete resetting of type for the first four numbers, using the London serial as setting copy. It was in this resetting that the illustrations were first added to the Harper's text for numbers 1–4. From number 5 forwards, following the one month publication haitus in March, the *Harper's Magazine* text is set from the finally published London serial–except for numbers 16 and 19–20.[4] Furthermore, from number 5 forward the type use to produce the magazine was cleaned, and arranged in new formes, without recomposition, to produce the book text. Therefore, from number 5 onward both Harper's texts agree closely in substantives with the published London serial–except numbers 16 and 19–20. Of course, a scattering of substantive differences appear throughout the novel, most of which can be explained as attempts by the American compositors to emend the text. Except in numbers 1–4, 16, and 19–20 (based on proof-sheets), the New York editions are deemed to have no independent authority. Therefore, New York readings from numbers based on the London serial publication are reported only selectively in Notes on the Text and theEmendations rather than in the footnotes.

Unlike 1–4, numbers 16 and 19–20 reflect the London serial's proof-state for both *Harper's Magazine* and the book text, since the book text was not reset but used the type from the magazine.[5] In number 16, an

---

[4] I have noted one substantive difference between the magazine and volume texts, in vol. II.111.13 (in this text) grave and even *NY*, grave even and *HM*—in which the magazine agrees with the English editions, but the book text seems to me the correction of an error.
[5] James notes this fact for numbers 19 and 20 (p. 49), but she mistakenly lists a change in number 5, as well, which she thought suggested that it, too, was based on uncorrected proofs. James reports a phrase in the New York text that she thought was missing from the first edition (number 5–at 160.35 in the London edition), but unfortunately she was

eleven line passage added in proof to the London serial is missing from the New York editions. In numbers 19–20, likewise, several passages added in proof to the London serial are missing from the New York edition but, in addition, an unusually large number of rephrasings occur in the London serial where the New York edition and the manuscript agree. All substantive *agreements* between the manuscript and the New York editions for these numbers are indicated at the foot of the text page in the present edition. Instances in which the New York editions *differ substantively* from the manuscript and the London serial are indicated, as throughout the novel, selectively in the textual notes; for they are without authority. It remains a mystery why numbers 16 and 19–20 were set from uncorrected proofs when the London serial had been printed a full two months before the New York appearance of these numbers.

We do not know why the *Harper's Magazine* issue was unillustrated for the first four installments, but the effect on the text of the Harper's book edition is clear. Both the magazine and the book edition were printed in double column formats of identical width (160 points). Both were set in six-point type on a seven-point base. The illustrations usually are a full column or a full two columns wide in the book, but occasionally they are narrower or wider than a single column, causing type to be "wrapped" around the illustrations. In addition, unless an initial vignette is used for the first letter of the chapter, every initial in the American book is two lines high. In the magazine only the first letter of the whole installment is two lines high. These differences were apparently sufficient to induce the compositors of the Harper book edition, when they added the illustrations, to reset type rather than try to rearrange type for the first four numbers. For the rest of the novel, the chapter initials remained a problem, causing the resetting of the first line or two or three in order to accomodate the taller chapter intial used in the book issue. None of these casual and limited resettings resulted in verbal variants.

In resetting the first four numbers, using the London serial rather than *Harper's Magazine* as setting copy, the compositors of the New York book issue introduced a number of variants in punctuation, inserting commas, changing commas to semicolons and question marks to exclamation points. These many changes are of a kind with those introduced in the remainder of the book—the result of differing house styling in punctuation and spelling, of compositorial slips, or of independent efforts to correct errors in the English copy.[6] None of these changes has any authority. In a very few instances, however, the New York compositors correct errors in the London serialization. These corrections are adopted in the present text and recorded in the list of emendations.

---

using a copy of the first edition printed from stereotyped plates as her source, and the phrase in question was removed for that late printing of the first edition. See the chart of variants within the first edition, above.

6 What are sometimes called American spellings, such as "ize" and "or" endings instead of "ise" or "our," are not American at all at mid-century. Thackeray frequently uses "ize" and "or" in his manuscripts, and other American publishers routinely used the so-called English spellings. Eighteenth century spelling practice in America and England included both.

The fact that the manuscript survives for numbers 16 and 19–20 of the book,[7] proves beyond doubt that the New York editions' pattern of agreement with the manuscript resulted from the American text having been set from uncorrected, unrevised, proofs. It seems clear also that was the case for numbers 1-4 where no manuscript survives. In no other part of the book are the differences between the American text and the London serial substantial enough to suggest that the American edition incorporates manuscript readings. In other words, from number 5 forward, the (relatively few) substantive variants between the American text and the London serial text cannot be taken to indicate manuscript readings that were altered in the last stage of London production.

It is unfortunate that more of the American text was not set from advance sheets. That it was not, renders the American edition irrelevant as a source of information about the composition of the novel–except for number 1–4. The information the Harper text supplies in numbers 16 and 19–20 we already know from the differences between the extant manuscript and London serial. And where the manuscript is missing, the American edition is clearly based on the printed London text. Whenever a variant in the American editions suggested an appropriate emendation adopted for the present edition, it is noted in the list of emendations; otherwise, Harper variants are recorded only selectively as indicated above.

Tauchnitz Edition

Although the contract between Thackeray and Baron Bernhard Tauchnitz for *The Newcomes* does not survive, a written agreement of sort survives in a letter Thackeray wrote to the German publisher: "I don't think I ever sent you the sealed paper investing you with the right over *The Newcomes*—I fear I have lost it: but you need not fear that I shall shrink from my bargain."[8] Agreement or no, the baron had no legal right to *The Newcomes* or any other British work, for there was no international copyright agreement under which such a right could be claimed. Tauchnitz was concerned, however, that Thackeray might encourage continental competition by entering into publishing agreements with one or two other continental publishers with lists of British works in English: Charles Jugell of Frankfurt am Main and Baudry in Paris. Neither publisher produced *The Newcomes*, though each published other works by Thackeray.

It is evident that the Tauchnitz *Newcomes* was published from sheets of the first English edition. Not only does the German edition contain no significant alterations in text, it is without independent authority. None of its variants is recorded in this edition.

Revised Edition

On 1 July 1859, according to Bradbury and Evans' ledgers, the publisher issued "2 vols for cheap edn. to WMT." The clear implication is that Thackeray would review and revise setting copy for the cheap edition: one volume, without illustrations, to be sold for six shillings (as opposed

---

[7] All the manuscript of numbers 19 and 20 survives; eleven pages of number 16 survives in manuscript, including the one place where the New York editions differ substantively from the English edition.

[8] Quoted in P. Shillingsburg, *Pegasus in Harness* (U Virginia P, 1992), p. 139.

to twenty-three shillings for the first edition in two volumes). That copy for revision is not known to exist. There is no way to know exactly what Thackeray did in the copy. We can only infer from our notions of "normal practice" and from occasional indications in the publishers' ledgers what processes resulted in the publication late in December 1859 when an initial printing of 4000 copies sold just over 2000 copies by the time the books were closed for that year.

Thackeray probably reread the novel and marked his revisions, most of them cuts removing references to the illustrations or matters he now considered redundant or unnecessary. Although it stands to reason that the "Cheap Edition" would be cheaper if shorter, it is not very likely that Thackeray was under an order to shorten the novel. When revising *Pendennis* for the same reasons in 1855, he had cut the equivalent of eighteen pages of text, in addition to the illustrations. In revising *The Newcomes* he cut less than a page and a half, most of it in small snips of four lines or less from the first volume, and no more than a total of ten or twelve lines from the second volume.

But one cannot attribute to Thackeray all the changes made, for most of the differences between the first edition and the revision are of the same sort imposed in the first edition by the compositors. It is very likely that the frequent omission of the word "honest" as an adjective in combination with "poor," "old," "simple," or "little" was done by Thackeray. And he may have identified for excision the references to the illustrations, though a compositor would have been on the lookout for them and could have removed them independently—though no one caught the remark at I.54.17 (in this text) about the artist doing justice to Clive's portrait. There are occasional grammatical lapses, corrected in the revision, sometimes more felicitously than others. That aspect of change, too, could have been the shared responsibility of author and compositor, for in a number of cases, new grammatical lapses are introduced in what appear to be attempts to improve grammar.

After the initial 1859 printing of 4000 copies, 1000 more copies of the cheap edition were printed in 1863, for by July there were only 124 copies left in stock. Thackeray died in December, 1863, a shock that created a demand for all his books, and 1000 more copies were printed in April 1864. A final printing of 500 in June of 1865 closed the books on this edition. No intentional revisions were introduced after the first printing of the cheap edition; the reprints were made from stereotyped plates.

When the revised edition corrects grammatical and factual errors in the first edition, these corrections are also incorporated in the present text, unless the manuscript exists to provide original readings. Such corrections are recorded as emendations.

When the revised edition offers an alternative to an already viable reading from the manuscript or first editions, the revision is recorded at the foot of the text. Such readings are "alter-texts" and should not be thought of as "rejected"—they represent the text as it became in 1859.

Hundreds of other changes are recorded in the historical collation, and a full list of differences between the first edition, the revised edition, and the present text is recorded and available in electronic form from the editor.

Editorial Principles

General Considerations

Inevitably, when one prepares a critical edition such as this one in a paper format (as opposed, say, to a variorum edition, an archive of documents, or an electronic hypertext edition), one must edit the text in one way and relegate alternatives to footnotes or textual apparatuses at the end of the volume. There are a number of legitimate goals one could pursue in editing this text; consequently, persons who wish a text to have been edited in one certain way will be disappointed when it is edited in a different way. Disappointments of this sort are unavoidable, for there is no universally subscribed way to edit.

This condition is especially important to note, for the traditional desire of editors and users of scholarly editions has been for a definitive edition, one that was done right. The present text was done right—according to one of several possible ways of defining right. I survey here some of the other possible ways to have proceeded.

First, persons who equate the work of literary art with the documents that contain them would not want a new edition that mixed readings from more than one document. Editing from this perspective consists, first, of selecting one document because for some reason it seems the best for the editor's purposes and, second of identifying and correcting or noting its typographical errors. The manuscript, if one exists, is the manuscript version of the work; the serial text is the serial version; the revised edition text provides the revised version, and so on, with text and version coinciding in the documents. Editors convinced of the importance and desirability of this view would provide the text (possibly corrected) of a carefully selected document, and they would list the variants from the other documents or provide facsimiles of some sort, perhaps in an electronic archive. (In preparing the present edition, I did, in fact, collect all of the available documents, and I prepared electronic transcriptions of them, and I collated them. But I did not choose to edit the text according to this view.)

Second, persons who equate the work of literary art with the complex of social and economic forces that made its production necessary or even possible would value the work of compositors and editors on a par with the work of authors. According to this view, if an author enters a working relationship with a publisher to produce and market a work, then the work that the publisher marketed must be the result we should be interested in studying. An editor convinced of this view would very likely prefer a printed, over a manuscript, base text. Such an editor would choose the serial or first edition, or the revised edition and reprint it. Depending on how faithful such editors are to the "social contract," they might emend typographical errors in the text or note them in the apparatus. Like the documentary editor above, the social editor would provide lists of variants or facsimile reproductions of other versions. (In preparing the present edition, I have violated the dictates of this view by choosing the manuscript for copy-text, thus negating a great deal of the textural [sic] effect of the production team's work.)

Third, persons who equate the work of literary art with its best potential embodiment might posit an ideal towards which the author and publisher aimed. An editor pursuing this ideal might rely on a variety of aesthetic and historical principles to select a base text and emend it to approximate this ideal final product, which it is hoped the newly edited text should embody more nearly than any previous edition had. Such an editor might feel obliged to list all the emendations made and list many or all the alternative readings that were rejected from documents deemed authoritative sources. It is probably that all authoritative documents would be seen as representing in faulty form the ultimate text towards which the author was striving. (In preparing the present edition I have rejected the notion that the ideal text toward which one can imagine the author and/or production crews to have been striving is also the goal of the scholarly edition.)

Very good arguments can be mounted on behalf of these alternatives, but no edition can fulfill the dictates of all of them simultaneously. The present edition was prepared according to yet a different course, for which the general considerations follow. From the point of view developed here, a specific analysis of *The Newcomes*'s textual situation is provided. It is important to note that textual situations are analyzed and described from particular points of view, and, consequently, textual evidence will appear to signify different conclusions to different people according to the notions about the "real" relationship between "the work" and "the documents" that are brought to the task. I do not think this "problem" can be avoided, but it can be noticed rather than ignored.

The present edition is based on the notion that the work of art is so complex that no single text will capture or convey its full character. A definitive text is not possible. A single-text edition of a literary work is like a snapshot of an event; it does not show what went before or after; it is limited by its inability to show the direction of the event. A scholarly edition is, in part, like an album of photographs of a complex event. Every edition is hopelessly still and physical, while a literary work is constantly in motion both as a physical event and as a conceptual effect. Consequently, this scholarly edition seeks to present the author's achievement and intention for the work at a given stage in its development and to chronicle not only the documentary history of that and· other stages of development but to distinguish as far as possible the agents of that development. There are limits to how much of that history can be provided. I have limited myself to those documents over which Thackeray exercised direct effects and those documents which contain indirect evidence of his work when the direct evidence is missing.

We can imagine, though we cannot prove or palpably experience, the work of art as a developing idea in the mind of an author. We can also imagine but cannot firmly identify the complex of desires, allegiances, and social and economic factors that helped to shape what the author wrote. We can see the manuscript and its drafts as attempts by an author to capture in a conventional sign system the ideas that were developing in the mind. We can see those manuscripts and the other physical documents bearing the linguistic signs of the text as the results of attempts to solidify, standardize, and make permanent a text representing the mentally conceived and intended text. If we do so, we can also see that the physical texts might not fully capture or accurately represent that mental conception of the work.[9]

However, as practical persons, we must accept that the physical representation of the text is the basis upon which editors and readers interact with the work of art. A physical text is what the compositor had as a basis for the published work, which is also a physical text. Compositors of *The Newcomes* made thousands of changes. The most pervasive change is from manuscript to print, adding legibility, elegance, multiplicity of copies, and permanence; but this transformation from handwriting to print also altered punctuation, spelling and sometimes wording and word order. Compositors are hired and retained for their professional skills in transforming authors' manuscripts into printed texts. And in the nineteenth century they were paid by the amount of letterpress they produced; they were required to make corrections in their work on their own time. Inevitably, compositors were simultaneously deliberate and hasty in "improving" the text. Thus, compositors (and editors) added their voice(s) to the voice of the author. Thus, they occasionally misrepresented the author's voice, perhaps through well-intentioned but bad, hasty, or over-bold judgment, or, perhaps, through errors of their own.

As readers and editors we approach *the work of art*, or, more accurately, we approach *a document* (covered not with words but with inked symbols), and we "read"—that is, we transform the inert text on the page into a dynamic conceptualization of the text. We do this with varying degrees of skill and under a variety of circumstances which impinge on the conception of the text which we produce by reading. But it is the "read text" to which we respond, not the inked signs; and if we have "misread it" or if we begin with a document with textual forms about which we do not know the origins or authorizing agents, we will conceptualize a "false" text or one that depends on contextual "facts" and assumptions about facts which we may have constructed from whole cloth.

The aim striven for in editing the text of the present volume was to produce a text that represented what the author actually wrote, altered to fulfill the author's known desire to have the work appear in a conventionally published form of 32-page installments with illustrations. In order to achieve that text, the existing documents were examined to see what the author wrote (as opposed to what was altered by other agents of the text) and to see what alterations were required by the stated intent to publish the novel serially. The resulting text is one that has never before appeared in print as a single unit. It represents a critically derived text and therefore cannot be vouched for in every detail.

This procedure is based on two abstract principles: first, the principle of limited authorial achievement, and, second, the principle of limited delegated authority. To embody the first principle, I posit an author who took responsibility for creating a novel, which he did in a manuscript that he knew from experience would only be the *basis* of the published book, for he knew the conventional forms (italics, punctuation, capitalization) would be "attended to" by the production crew. So the author *limited his achievement*

---

[9] One is tempted to say that the physical texts *will* not fully capture or accurately represent the mental conception, but I am not speaking of absolutes here, merely of possibilities both for failure and for improvement.

to words, word order and the modicum of punctuation and indication of italics and capitalization that reflected his habitual and deliberate practice and intention for the work. But he did not worry over the details because they would be taken care of by the compositors. To embody the second principle, I posit a crew of compositors (their names in the margins of the setting copy were Snowsill, Brown, Porter, Spence, Dampier, Knick—or Kinch—Dunman, and Carroll), who with varying degrees of skill undertook the *limited delegated authority* involved in making a printed book from the manuscript in hand. Since that delegation of authority is not explicitly defined in any extant document, readers and editors have no choice but to accept the responsibility to define the limits for themselves. The role of the modern editor is to adjudicate the fulfillment of achievement, using the work of the compositor to finish the work of the author.

The easiest ways to adjudicate that fulfillment is either to grant full authority to the compositors and accept their work as the contracted achievement of the novel, or to deny the compositors any authority whatsoever and print a transcription of the manuscript as an accurate representation of what the author wrote. Any middle ground requires that the critical judgment of the editor be exercised at every point in the text. This edition strives for middle ground.

So the first aim of this edition is to produce a reading text representing what the author wrote but altered to fulfill certain conventions: a 32-page per month installment and a necessary but not interfering conventionalization of punctuation, spelling, capitalization, and italicization. The dual nature of this first aim is slightly contradictory: on the one hand, to enable readers to encounter the text as Thackeray wrote it; on the other hand, to fulfill the limited delegated authority which, in my opinion, the original publishers overstepped. No text of *The Newcomes* can be both "what the author wrote" and "what the author wanted." But an equally important second aim of this edition may mitigate this conflict. It is to make it possible for students of Thackeray's work to "watch" as Thackeray altered the text during the process of composition and during the processes of proof-correction and to watch as his original editors and I worked to transform an incompletely polished manuscript into a publishable book. In order to show the range of authoritative texts that have existed and to identify as fully as possible the agents who created those alternatives, variant readings are reported in footnotes, in tables at the end of the volume, and in electronic form available from the publisher or editor.

That Thackeray obviously "intended" to have some assistance in developing the published work complicates the editorial task but does not make it impossible. The fact that his assistants in these processes undertook more responsibility than was required also complicates the task. Thackeray sometimes complained and sometimes did not complain about his assistants. He is famously on record as being unhappy about the editorial interventions in the publications of the second and third volumes of *The Miscellanies*—where unacceptable changes were made in *The Luck of Barry Lyndon* and *Rebecca and Rowena* and where "Epistles to the Literati" reappeared unpleasantly. He was especially angry and disappointed over the editorial work on *The English Humourists*.[1] And he was upset and frustrated by the handling of parts of *The Newcomes*, as is detailed below. On the other hand, he was explicitly grateful for his publishers' assistance on other occasions.

Critical judgment is inevitably and obviously involved in any attempt to sort intentional from inadvertent readings, or to distinguish the contributions of the author from those of other agents of textual change, or to adjudicate between levels of authorization for textual variation. Editors who object to the exercise of critical judgment for these purposes advocate editorial principles different from those followed in this edition.

Choice of Copy-Text

In keeping with the general principles of this edition of Thackeray's works, the copy-text is the manuscript except where it does not survive. Thus, for installments 1–3, 7–9, 11–13, most of 16, and parts of 21 the copy-text is the first edition.[2] Virtually complete manuscripts for the other installments are extant. One page of manuscript from number 2 survives.

The crucial factor in the choice of copy-text was the desire to produce a text reflecting the author's practice in punctuation. It is the editor's belief that, although Thackeray's manuscripts are inadequately punctuated (the principle of limited achievement), the punctuation contained in the manuscript fulfills the demands of what is known as "rhetorical punctuation"—a system which appears to some modern eyes as somewhat erratic but which indicates oratorical cadences. Rhetorical punctuation as described in a printer's manual of the period[3] indicates pauses of different lengths intended to show how the sentence should be read aloud: commas indicate short pauses, semicolons indicate slightly longer pauses, colons longer yet, and periods indicate full stops. The dash is a frequent interrupter or indication of significant rhetorical pauses and can appear in combination with any other punctuation mark.

By contrast, the compositors of the first edition were following more or less well what is known as "syntactical punctuation"—a system that follows rules designating syntactical units and indicating relative coordination and subordination of grammatical elements in the sentence. Syntactical punctuation is far more orderly than rhetorical, because rhetorical punctuation indicates how the sentence "sounds" to the writer and changes to suit mood and pace. Syntactical punctuation is what most modern readers are familiar with, for some form of it is taught in most modern English-language schools. Although there is a great deal of overlap between the two systems, the compositors of the first edition smoothed out and suppressed many of the rhetorical nuances of the manuscript version.

---

[1] On *The Miscellanies*, see *Pegasus in Harness*, p. 119–23; on *The English Humourists*, see *Pegasus*, pp. 94–96, and Edgar F. Harden, "The Writing and Publication of Thackeray's *English Humourists*," *PBSA* 76 (1982), 197–207.

[2] It has been shown above that for numbers 1–4, the *Harper's New Monthly Magazine* text is based on proofsheets, not finally corrected, and that therefore its substantives are closer to the manuscript than those of the first English edition. However, the accidentals of the American magazine version are derived from the London type-setting and are therefore further removed from the manuscript than are the accidentals of the London serial.

[3] C. H. Timperly, *The Printer's Manual* (London: H. Johnson, 1838).

Principles of Emendation

The present text relies primarily for its accidental forms (spelling, punctuation, capitalization, italicization) on the copy-text, which is the manuscript where it survives and the first edition where the manuscript is lost. For its substantive forms, the present edition relies primarily on the first edition. This general policy is modified as explained below, for the manuscript is inadequate in its accidental forms and the first edition is both flawed and mixed in its authority for substantive forms.

A. Accidentals

A crucial part of the foundation for the emendation policy is the decision to produce a reading text representing the author's intentions for a conventionally published text. The compositors were essential in producing such a text, but they did not content themselves with supplying a necessary augmentation of Thackeray's punctuation; rather, they liberally changed and added punctuation as befitted the demands of their syntactical system and their sometimes (in my opinion) erroneous notion of the meaning of the text. No one has ever argued or could argue that Thackeray fully punctuated his manuscripts; he did not. However, the punctuation he did supply is expressive rhetorically.

1. For this edition, punctuation was added to the manuscript copy-text as needed to mitigate its inadequacies. The majority of this added punctuation is done silently because the occasions for adding it are utterly routine. (See the account of silent emendations, below.) All punctuation substitutions and deletions are itemized as emendations; there are very few of these. Punctuation additions, unless they fall into the limited categories described in the explanation of silent emendations, are also listed individually in the Table of Emendations. When adding needed punctuation, first consideration was always given to the punctuation supplied in the first edition. Thus virtually all of the punctuation in the present edition derives either from the manuscript or the first edition.

2. Spelling of names is regularized as indicated in the explanation of silent emendations. Spelling corrections in the portions of the manuscript in Thackeray's hand are listed individually as emendations. Anne Thackeray's numerous misspellings are corrected but listed collectively with the silent emendations rather than reported in each instance. When her misspellings are indicative of misunderstandings of dictated words, they are listed separately, for though these are usually merely humorous and not of interpretive significance, they do demonstrate that Anne was writing from dictation, not copying from a previous draft. Perhaps the most notable instances have Anne's manuscript reading "a master fortune" "descended from a handsome" and "cashier" where the first edition reads "amassed a fortune" "descended from a hansom" and "Cassio". A similarly startling indication of dictation woes occurs in portions of the manuscript in George Hodder's handwriting, where we find F.B. striving with loudness to carry off his "only notion" which is corrected in the first edition to his "own emotion."

3. Capitalization is frequently left as in the manuscript because it appears to be expressive; it may, however, strike some readers as erratic. Some regularization of capitalization has been undertaken as indicated in

the explanation of silent emendations. Anne Thackeray's practice, which is highly erratic, has been heavily regularized but noted.

B. Substantives

Another crucial factor at the foundation of emendation policy for this edition is the decision to produce a reading text representing the author's intentions for installment publication. Serial publication entailed the production of 32 pages per installment, which was achieved by adding or subtracting manuscript text, by adding or subtracting woodcuts embedded in the text (or by producing large or small woodcuts), and by minor adjustments to the number of lines printed on each page.

1. In general, the substantive alterations introduced by the first edition are accepted into the present text as Thackeray's choices, particularly when these changes affected the length of the installment. It seems clear, however, that some changes resulted from compositorial misreadings of the manuscript and that others resulted from memory lapses by the compositors. The editor has rejected first-edition readings when, in his judgment, they resulted from accidental or inept compositorial misrepresentations of the manuscript. All such judgments are to some degree speculative; therefore, both substantive emendations and substantives from the first edition that have been rejected are listed at the foot of the text pages where they can easily be assessed by readers of this edition.

2. Corrections of apparent errors in the copy-text (whether manuscript or first edition) are made by giving first consideration to other early printed sources, but in all instances are made by the editor on the basis of his judgment that the copy-text is in error. Corrections of manuscript readings reflect the first edition reading unless, in the editor's judgment, it did not provide a viable solution to the textual crux.

A Comment on "Copy-Text"

Most editors facing the textual situation of *The Newcomes* would be at least partially torn between choosing the first edition or the manuscript as copy-text: the text upon which the new edition will be based and to which the editor resorts for readings wherever the variant texts offer "indifferent" choices (those for which a conclusive argument either way cannot be made. The term "copy-text" and its practical use in resolving textual cruxes derives from Renaissance editorial practice where much of the textual evidence was no longer extant. Given enough evidence, no copy-text is needed, since the editor would have sufficient evidence to make a judgment in every case.[4] That is not quite the situation with *The Newcomes*, but the two main candidates for copy-text are each inadequate in some serious way.

Having chosen the manuscript for copy-text, I will appear to users of the present edition to have accepted some first-edition readings as emendations and rejected others. Had I chosen the first edition for copy-text and striven to create a text according to the same principles I have chosen, the resulting text would be the same as the one I have produced, but

---

[4] The classic text on copy-text is W. W. Greg's "The Rationale of Copy-Text," *Studies in Bibliography*, 1950. Much provocative discussion of Greg's formulation has transpired since, but the clearest exposition of the issues involved has been by G. Thomas Tanselle, particularly in "Editing Without a Copy-Text," *Studies in Bibliography*, 1994.

it would appear to users that I was accepting and rejecting manuscript readings as emendations. It might be more useful to think that there are two copy-texts: one relied upon mostly for accidentals and the other relied upon mostly for substantives, but each having some authority for both. In each case there is frequently sufficient evidence to make an informed judgment about what reading best fulfills the author's intention. Looked at in that way, it seems a bit clearer that what the editor "has done to the text" is to adjudicate the author's limited achievement with the compositors' limited authority to fulfill the expectations for a published novel. In adjudicating that fulfillment, I probably have been more sympathetic to authorial practice than to compositorial practice.

Editorial Problems

For installments 1–5, Thackeray was in and out of London—available for proofreading. The manuscript was "ahead" of print by three or four months, but the printers continued to set type in the month immediately preceding the installment date. As a result, while Thackeray was writing installments 5 and 6, he was reading proof for installments 3 and 4. This was a new procedure for Thackeray, whose other books were written installment by installment in the month due. Typically for his previous serials, about three-fourths of the manuscript for an installment was sent to the printer by the 22nd or so of the month; proofs of that part went back to Thackeray by the 24th or 25th; corrected proofs and the additional fourth of the installment in manuscript went back to the printer by the 26th or 27th. Thackeray is frequently on record in his letters as reading final proofs at the printer's premises. Printing from standing type, binding in parts, and distribution out the back door of the printery to the line of booksellers' carts was regularly achieved by the evening of the last day of the month, so that the installment could be sold in bookstores everywhere on the first day of the month. Under the altered circumstances of composing and printing *The Newcomes*, Thackeray read proof for number 4 while writing number 6; the lapse of time between initial writing and proof correction was much greater than had been the case in his other books. The aim of the present edition is to produce a text that reflects Thackeray's efforts to produce an installment novel. But a serious problem arose with number 6.

Thackeray wanted to spend the winter in Italy. He was three months ahead in the writing, he had Richard Doyle in London doing the illustrations, and he appointed Percival Leigh, a regular contributor to *Punch Magazine*, as his on-the-spot crisis manager and "editor." Thackeray left in early December 1853 for Italy, having just made the final adjustments to number 4 (for January) and possibly to number 5. He sent the manuscript of number 6 to London in two batches. The first batch, sent in December, arrived safely, but the second, three pages of text sent in January, apparently did not. Whether proofs of number 6 were held up, waiting for those three pages or for some other reason, we do not know. In any case, proof for number 6 amounting to "only 25 pages and a bit" along with proof for number 7 was mailed by Bradbury and Evans on February 11, 1854, to Thackeray in Rome. February 11 was an unusually late date for an installment that had to be on the streets on the first of March. The proofs arrived in Rome after Thackeray had left for Naples, where he finally received them on February 21.

On February 25, Thackeray wrote to Percival Leigh: "Four days ago I got a letter from B & E. dated 11 February and come round by Rome: containing proofs of VI & VII—the former having only 25 pages and a bit. It was for VI I sent the additions 2 months ago from Rome. There is no time to communicate now about it: and the mischief whatever it is is done. I might have had the proofs months ago. But what's the use of talking now? I hope you have eked out the number somehow: and trust in the Lord."[5] February in 1854 had only 28 days, and in the best of circumstances mail from Rome to London took five days, and Thackeray was in Naples. So *if* Thackeray did what he had to do to augment the length of the proofs, and *if* he got them back in the mail by the next day, and *if* the mail moved as fast as it ever did, *then* the London publisher had one day to correct type, print 14,000 copies of two sheets, bind them in their yellow wrappers, and deliver them out the back door to the waiting booksellers' vans on the evening of February 28. The publisher's records indicate only £3 of "night work" were required on number 6, compared with over £9 for number 4.[6] That is, there is no indication of rushed work at the end.

What Thackeray's specific instructions to Leigh were when he left for Rome, we do not know, but six months later, in reference to number 11, Thackeray wrote: "There will be a little too much letter press in No XI. for August. Will you kindly snip off the extra sentence or two in case I should not be here?"[7] Unfortunately, the manuscript for number 11 is no longer extant, so one cannot check to see if Leigh's snipping skills were required. It may be that when Thackeray embarked for Italy general instructions to Percival Leigh were of the same sort, though it is equally possible that when the instructions for number 11 were issued they were meant to prevent Leigh from indulging in the sort of revisions, which, by my interpretation of the evidence, he had undertaken in February.

Because the evidence is inconclusive, adjudication of the textual problem here depends on individual judgment that, more than usually, is open to question. I do not believe that Thackeray corrected or augmented the proofs of number 6. The key phrases in his letter to Leigh are "There is no time to communicate now about it: and the mischief whatever it is is done." Later in the same letter Thackeray adds: "D. Roberts the artist takes No VIII with him to London today. Where he'll be soon after this letter reaches you. In the ride *on* Bhurtpore not *at* Bhurtpore is an awful error in VI. In VII. I have corrected one or 2 blunders, and am once more my dear Leigh, yours very thankfully."[8] I take this to mean that Roberts was carrying the manuscript of number 8 to London, and that corrected proofs for number 7 were carried in the same way or were included in Thackeray's letter of February 25. The remark about the error in number VI (*at* instead of *on* Bhurtpore) I take as an indication that Thackeray

---

[5] *Letters*, III, 349–50.
[6] Bradbury and Evans archive, Punch Office.
[7] *Letters*, III, 378.
[8] *Letters*, III, 351. For the passage in question see I.185.8.

had thrown up his hands and trusted the Lord for number 6, lamenting in this way the fact that he had had no opportunity to correct its errors. Furthermore, if he is being accurate when he said, "I have corrected one or 2 blunders," and if he meant he had done so in number 6, then he cannot have been responsible for the hundreds of proof-stage alterations that in fact appeared in that installment.

The fact that the published edition has the correct *on Bhurtpore* does not mean Thackeray succeeded in getting the correction in; it may only mean that Leigh caught the error as well. The manuscript says *on* and the context makes it perfectly obvious that Bhurtpore is the name of the little horse Colonel Newcome gave Ethel, not the location in India for which it is obviously named. There were plenty of other errors that nobody found: the omission of Clive's name at 157; *turns* for *tones* at 158; misplacing of *he sat* at 159; *numerous* for *numberless* at 159; *Pa!* for *Pen* at 159; *Had* for *It ad* at 160; *those* for *these* at 166; *bought* for *brought* at 167; *Vordor* for *Vorder* at 168; *life academy and costume;* for *Life and Costume Academy* at 168; *Jones's* for *Tom's* at 171; *angels* for *Angeli* at 175; *Mrs. Gandish* for *Mr. Gandish* at 177; *glittering* for *glistering* at 177; *spirited* for *spoiled* at 178; misplacing the phrase *Who can be more respectable than a butler?* before *"A man* instead of after *somebody's son:* at 178; *the* for *this* at 178; *prejudice* for *prejudices* at 179; *Tommy* for *Fanny* at 182; *whole pages* for *pages* at 187. Many of these make perfectly good sense either way, but all of them are departures from the manuscript, and I can defend none of them as an improvement or necessary correction.

It cannot of course be proven that these are compositors' errors, but the manuscript at each of these points could, in haste, be read to say what the compositor wrote. Careful examination of the manuscript reveals the readings chosen for the present edition.

And yet, one cannot be absolutely sure who made the changes. Professor Edgar Harden examined all this evidence and concluded there was just enough time for Thackeray to have corrected and mailed the proofs, and that all the changes in number 6 were made by Thackeray.[9] All that survives are the manuscript, the printed book, and the letter to Percival Leigh. So we do not know from external evidence who made the changes in number 6, which successfully appeared on March 1 with 32 pages. There are extra pictures in the number, one in particular of three men standing looking like El Greco saints at a cocktail party—very tall and elongated, taking up most of the page. One third of the pages are printed one or two lines shorter than normal. One chapter begins one half inch lower down the page than usual. A chapter break not indicated in the manuscript was added. And one and one half pages that had been cut from number 5, because it was too long, were added back into number 6.

If that were all that was done in order to make number 6 a 32-page installment, no strain would be felt by the editorial procedures of the present edition. The problem arises when one looks at the other changes in the number: several phrases are cut (including two references to Guy Fawkes and several unflattering descriptions of characters), a number of phrases are added (almost always with the effect of extending a paragraph by one

---

[9] Edgar F. Harden, *The Emergence of Thackeray's Serial Fiction*, pp. 86–90.

more line), and a myriad of phrases substitute one way of saying a thing to another way of saying more or less the same thing without materially affecting length. Of these three, the last is the most surprising. First, Thackeray never did that kind of revising in those numbers where we know for sure he worked on the proofs—not in this novel, not in any novel. We know that if Thackeray made any changes in this number that he made them at break-neck speed. That in itself is not unusual, however, for he was frequently proofreading against the clock late in the month.

Although the extant evidence is inconclusive, I take what does survive to mean that there is a high likelihood all the changes in number 6 were effected by Percival Leigh.

The editorial options are:

A. to accept the changes as Thackeray's;

B. to accept the changes as Percival Leigh's with the transmitted authority given him by Thackeray;

C. to accept those changes that adjust the length of the text mechanically (i.e. shorter pages, more pictures, the chapter divided into two chapters, the transferred passage cut from number 5) because we know Thackeray wanted a 32-page installment. But to reject the few cuts, minor additions, and myriad revisions as unnecessary intervention by Percival Leigh, who probably in good faith overstepped the charge given him by Thackeray.

One might question why Leigh, under pressure to lengthen the number, would cut any passages at all, and it might be argued that neither Percival Leigh nor anyone other than the author would have had the temerity to make nearly 300 verbal changes in the 32-page number. If, as I believe, the corrections from Thackeray never arrived, then Percival Leigh is the only one who could have made them. His boldness may have derived from unclear or misunderstood directions about the role he was to play in shepherding the number through press. The fact that Bradbury and Evans did not send proof until February 11, suggests that they were waiting for more manuscript and waited till the last minute. Had Thackeray received proofs in Rome on the 16th, there would have been little if any problem in his returning corrections and additions on time. But after the 11th and before finally giving up on receiving anything from Italy, Leigh had plenty of time to start worrying and deciding that the number really would depend upon his work. I find it plausible to believe that, under those conditions, Leigh was capable of making all the changes that appeared in the printed number 6. I believe, however, he was authorized to make the changes required to produce a 32-page number and no more.

The argument so far has been based entirely on the logistics of time and space and on the general character of the changes in number 6 relative to those in other numbers known to have been proofread by Thackeray. In addition, I believe that a large number of the changes are of a linguistic and literary quality inferior to Thackeray's norm. That in itself does not prove that Thackeray did not make them, but it does tend to diminish the attractiveness of the first edition as a guide to emendations in this particular number. Other changes in this number demonstrate a fussiness about grammar and sentence structure that Thackeray does not exhibit elsewhere. That is no proof that Leigh made the revisions, but the character of the changes helped to persuade me that they were not Thackeray's.

It has been suggested that when an editor is in doubt about the evidence, there should be a prudent fall-back position, a document that can be turned to, in desperation, so to speak. That is the whole reasoning behind choosing a copy-text for an edition on the basis of accidentals, for it is usually about accidentals that one is in doubt. For this edition of *The Newcomes* it can be said that in general the default document for accidentals has been the manuscript and the default document for substantives has been the first edition. However, the evidence that normally leads one to rely on the first edition for substantive readings is absent, or very ambiguous, for number 6. The first edition for number 6 has no presumptive authority.[1] The only document about whose authority we have no doubt is the manuscript. So, one could argue that in this case the manuscript should be the default document for both accidentals and substantives. However, just as I have not slavishly followed the accidentals of the manuscript, I do not slavishly follow the substantives of that document, for we have a general understanding of Thackeray's choice to be published by a professional publisher in a conventional 32-page format. This general expression of textual intent is what I appeal to when making changes in accidentals and substantives for number 6. Changes made by the first edition which were not required by this understanding of general intent to be published in a conventional manner are not accepted into this newly edited text.

Edgar Harden, the only creditable scholar to address this question previously, accepts all of the changes as Thackeray's (alternative A, above). The near miracle of postal delivery required by that theory, the sharp difference in style of revisions that it requires one to attribute to Thackeray, and the letter of lament from Thackeray to Leigh mailed on February 27 (discussed above) prevent me from believing the changes were made by Thackeray.

Alternative B is attractive to editors who see the author as one of a group of authoring figures in the social contingencies of book production. This choice would also simplify the editor's task, for it encourages the acceptance of all first-edition readings into the newly edited text. To accept such a policy would also prevent an editor from "contaminating the documentary purity" of either the first edition or the manuscript, forcing the choice of one or the other as the determiner of readings in the present edition. That line of reasoning, taken very far, would render a photocopy machine the quintessential editorial tool.

In practice, alternatives A and B have the same effect: adopting all of the substantive changes introduced in the first edition.

Alternative C requires the belief that Thackeray was unable to revise the proofs for number 6 in time. It requires one to believe that the movement of text originally intended for number 5 to number 6 had to have

---

[1] "Authority" is defined here to mean reliable guide to authorial readings, either actually produced by Thackeray or produced in response to an explicit desire by the author for change. An elaboration of the rationale for emendations that fulfill "authorial expectations" is provided in P. Shillingsburg, *Scholarly Editing in the Computer Age* (Athens: U Georgia P, 1986), pp. 56–74.

been done by Leigh. It further requires one to believe that Leigh understood his job to be that of a very active editor, a surrogate author, standing in for Thackeray, particularly for this number for which there were no corrected proofs from Italy. Finally, it requires that one believe Leigh's editorial function was misunderstood by him, thus allowing him to make changes not necessitated by the 32-page format or by any other standard for publishing the novel.

Alternative C was chosen for the present edition in order to produce a reading text reflecting Thackeray's choices and Thackeray's composition. The present edition incorporates changes required to make the text fit the 32-page format, for that reflects Thackeray's choice to produce such a book. Manuscript readings are retained wherever someone other than Thackeray is suspected of introducing changes not *required* by format, grammar, plot, characterization or style; for that fulfills the aim of producing Thackeray's text.

This position is arguable on various grounds, as I have indicated in general ways in other writings on textual criticism.[2] The two most important points to argue are, however, first the fact that my editorial policy frankly involves the exercise of editorial judgment in distinguishing authorial from non-authorial readings where the evidence is inconclusive, and second, the fact that the resulting text is "non-documentary"—that is, one that never before existed in a document; my aim is therefore to produce an "ideal text," though of course not a "definitive" one.

Some scholars abhor the exercise of editorial judgment, preferring policies that follow blanket rules and which preserve the integrity of the physical, historical documents. But all editorial methods rely on critical judgment; for a decision not to do something is as critical as a decision to do it. In the absence of an "industry standard," single correct method of editing, the best one can hope is that the method chosen and its consequences are clearly declared. I hope the method I have chosen will please those who prefer a text approximating *The Newcomes* as Thackeray wrote it rather than as it was rewritten by production personnel when they exceeded the requirements of their real business to help produce Thackeray's writing in a 32-page format.

This is not to say that other editorial methods are inferior or wrong. Readers will continue to be interested in reading and studying the raw manuscript, the London serial edition, the first edition, and the revised edition; and they may be interested in other historical texts beginning with the Harper editions and Tauchnitz, and extending through all editions to the present time. But readers interested in *Thackeray's* text will not find it in any other edition as purely as it can be found in the present edition. The purpose of the textual apparatus in this edition is to provide readers with a clear sense of the range of viable texts that indicate the voices of the author, of the work's original publishers and editors, and of the present editor.

---

[2] See in particular *Scholarly Editing in the Computer Age* and "Text as Matter, Concept, and Action," *Studies in Bibliography*, 44 (1991), 31–82.

Conclusion to the Problem of Number 6

Because the problem with number 6 is unique, because there are two equally viable solutions that fall within the general editorial principles for the edition, I have edited the number in two ways. Following alternative (A) or alternative (B) (accepting virtually all the verbal changes in the first edition), would result in the same editorial emendations, so they constitute in practice only one alternative. Following plan (C) (accepting length adjustments but rejecting verbal changes) results in a very different text.

The reading text *in* the novel can be only one or the other and will become the de facto standard text for my edition. The format I have followed makes it possible for the reader to reconstruct the substantive alternatives from the notes at the foot of the page. In addition, an edited text of this number, representing the first edition substantives, is included as an appendix, complete with footnotes showing the manuscript readings. Readers persuaded by Edgar Harden's interpretation of the surviving evidence should substitute No. 6 as it appears in the appendix for the number as printed in the main text.

An Anomaly in the Final Chapter

A textually important anomaly crops up in the last four pages of manuscript for the novel.[3] In brief, Thackeray finished writing the novel on a manuscript page that should have been, but was not, numbered 6. He then decided first to revise and then to expand the portion beginning on page 5. Page 5 itself is heavily revised, and then on a new sheet numbered 6, Thackeray recopied from the top of page 5, making further revisions and additions. The new page 6 did not hold as much text as page 5, for it contains added passages. Thackeray then crossed out the original ending on the final (unnumbered) page of manuscript, turned it top-to-bottom, and finished copying from the original page 5 and recomposed (rather than simply recopying) the final passage. However, he then forgot to cancel page 5.

The compositor of the first edition, seeing no indication that it had been superceded, set type from the heavily marked up, but uncancelled, page 5, only discovering when he had finished that page 6 was a repetition of page 5 with revisions. The compositor must have scanned page 6 quickly, finding two passages that were expanded in the new manuscript, incorporating them into his already set type. The compositor then finished setting type from the new page 7.

Copy-text for the present edition is page 6, rather than page 5 (which served as basic copy for the first edition). The substantive readings of the first edition, reflecting the earlier version (page 5), are rejected in favor of those in the revised manuscript version (pages 6–7). The usual reliance on the first edition for substantive readings is interrupted by this procedure because first edition readings reflecting the earlier manuscript are not introduced. However, the first edition did introduce one major revision, obviously made in proof. A five-line humorous complaint about Richard

---

[3] The details are clearly and accurately recounted in Edgar Harden's *The Emergence of Thackeray's Serial Fiction*, pp. 127–30.

Doyle's depictions of Ethel in the novel's illustrations was deleted, probably because its claim that Doyle only showed the back of her head was not true. Both manuscripts contain the passage. The deletion is accepted as a revision.

Summary of Textual Presentation

The plan for the whole novel in this edition is

a. to print for reading a text that relies primarily on the manuscript for accidental forms and relies primarily on the serial edition for substantives;

b. to put revisions (including those from the 1860 "Cheap Edition") and major MS alterations at the foot of the page;

c. to print a list of emendations (summarizing those we call silent) at the end of the book (emendations involving acceptance of substantive changes from the first edition or revised edition are also reported at the foot of the text);

d. to supply, in electronic computer-readable form:

1. a full collation of Fair Copy MS with the new text (providing in this way a list of all emendations, including the so-called silent ones);

2. a full collation of the new text with the first edition and the revised edition (providing in this way a list of all rejected readings, including accidentals, from authoritative editions);

3. a diplomatic transcription of the manuscript.

Silent Emendations

The following categories of regularizations have been imposed on the copy-text, particularly but not exclusively on the manuscript portions of the copy-text. A separate, itemized list of these changes, keyed to page and line number, has been compiled and is available in computer-readable form.

Having chosen the manuscript as copy-text, the editor has imposed the following routine regularizations in the belief that the author expected regularization but got, in the serialization, more than was required. This editor judges the manuscript to be demonstrably deficient in form; that is, a straight transcription of the manuscript would not be easily read, nor would it fulfill the expectations for the work attributable to the author or to any of the book's original producers. On the other hand, the serialization and first edition, which did fulfill the expectations of the book's producers and which could be argued to have fulfilled those of the author as well, both misrepresent, in this editor's judgment, the author's practice and did not fulfill his expectations in ways that are important to modern readers, though they may not have been important enough to the author to have prompted an objection from him.

For the most part, these regularizations reflect the practice of the serialization and first edition. In addition to the separate computer-readable listing of the regularizations described here, a separate computer-readable listing has been compiled of all instances in which the present edition does NOT adopt first edition readings.

Abbreviations, Spelling, Contractions, and Possessives

1. Abbreviations regularized and expanded: &-and (except in names of firms and in the form &c.), ordinals (1st-first, 2nd-second and so on, except in names of kings and regiments), affte.-affectionate, Col. and Coll.-Colonel, Esqr. and Esqre.-Esq. or Esquire, fm.-from, honble.-honourable, shd.-should, Sq.-Square, St.-Street, Q.-Queen (except when Q stands for Kew), wh. and whh.-which, yr.-your.

2. Arabic numerals up to 99 have been spelled out (except in hours, dates, and addresses). However, variations in forms like £1500 and 1500£ and fifteen hundred pounds are not regularized.

3. Spelling of names have been regularized to the spelling most frequently used in Thackeray's portions of the manuscript: **Ann Newcome** from Anne Newcome; **Binnie** from Bennie; **Boigne** from Biogne; **Brian** from Bryan; **Brianstone** from Bryanstone and Bryanston; **Brussels** from Brussells; **Bundelcund** from Bundlecund; **Clivey** from Clivy; **Crackthorpe** from Crackthorp; **Duke and Duchess d'Ivry** from Prince and Princess de Montaign;[4] **la Duchesse** from le Duchesse; **Frederick Bayham** from Frederic Bayham; **F.B. Bayham** from F B and F.B Bayhams; **Hannah** from

---

[4] Leonore de Blois, daughter of a French émegré to England, and in love with Thomas Newcome, marries Florac, another émegré, who in England is a fiddlemaster, but in France was a vicomte. Florac, considerably older than Leonore, was a cousin to the Duc d'Ivry. The Duc D'Ivry was also Prince de Moncontour; he had two sons and grandsons who all pre-deceased him. So he married again to a wife of sixteen who bore him only a daughter. Florac and Leonore gave birth to a boy also named Florac, who figures as an acquaintance of Clive. Florac the elder, vicomte and fiddlemaster, inherited the titles

Martha (Hannah Hicks is Martha Honeyman's housekeeper; Pendennis has a housekeeper named Martha); **Hobson** from Hodson; **Hobson Brothers** from Hobson brothers; **Hôtel de Florac** from Hotel de Florac; **J.J. Ridley** from JJ J.J Ridley Rigby; **Jenny and Jessamy** from Jinney and Jessamy; **Kean** from Keane; **Kew** from Key; **Kitt's** from Kitts; **M'Collop** from McOllop, Mc. Collop, and McCollop; **Mackenzie** from M'Kenzie; **Mack** from Mac; **M'Mull** from M'Mull; **Marble Head** from Marblehead, Marble-head, and Marble Hill; **Montcontour** from Moncontour; **Rosey** from Rosie; **Rummun Lall** from Rummun Loll and Ram-un-Lal; **Vidler** from Viddler; **Jock** (of Hazeldean) from Jack.

4. Spelling of certain words ending in *ize* is regularized to *ise* (equalise, patronise, patronising, recognise, etc.); certain words ending in *ise* are regularized to *ice* (*practice* is a noun, *practise* is a verb); words ending in *ase* are regularized to *aze* (glaze); words ending in *or* regularized to *our*, (favour, favourable, honour, honourable, humour—but humorous); and words ending in *ick* regularized to *ic* (music, frolics).

5. The following words appear inconsistently as single words, hyphenated compounds, or separate words in the copy-text. (Note: all end-of-line hypens in this paragraph are intended as hyphens.) The inconsistencies are regularized: names of numbers (**four-and-twenty, twenty-five**); **daresay** from dare say; **bed-room, bed-chamber, billiard-room, board-room, breakfast-room, dining-room, drawing-room, mess-room, painting-room, sitting-room, smoking-room, waiting-room** from one word and two words; **breakfast-table, cuddy-table, gambling-table, library-table, tea-table** from two words; **brother-in-law, father-in-law, mother-in-law, sister-in-law** from three words or partial hyphenation; **deputy-lieutenant** from two words; **down-stairs, up-stairs** from two words or one word; **fable-land** from Fable-land, fableland, Fableland; **fireplace** from two words or hyphenated; **good bye** from good-bye, goodbye; **good-natured, good-humoured, ill-natured, ill-humoured, ill-treatment, ill-pleased, kind-hearted** from two words; **granddaughter, grandson** from two words and hyphenated combinations; **half-dozen, half-and-half, half-yearly** from two or three words; **man-servant, woman-servant, maid-servant, chamber-maid** from 2 words; **major-domo** from two words; **May Fair** from May-fair and Mayfair; **meantime, meanwhile** from two words;

---

of his son-less cousin, the Duc d'Ivry and Prince de Moncontour. Young Florac, an ordinance officer in the French army, was often called vicomte or viscount, a title he held by the right of his father even before the death of the Duc d'Ivry. When his father died, young Florac added the titles of Duc d'Ivry and Prince de Moncontour.

When writing chapter 31, Thackeray briefly employed characters named the Prince and Princess de Montaign. In a revising pass through the manuscript, reviewing a portion in Anne Thackeray's hand, but extending over manuscript in his own hand, Thackeray changed most of the references to Prince and Princess Montaigne to Duc and Duchesse or Duke and Duchess d'Ivry. Whether the name Montaign was a mistake for d'Ivry or whether Thackeray latter decided to conflate the roles of Montaign and d'Ivry, I cannot tell. In correcting such references to d'Ivry, Thackeray also occasionally changed the generic reference of Prince to Duc or Duke. Likewise, references to the Princess or Princesse are occasionally changed to Duchess or Duchesse even when Montaign is not present. As often happens with such revisions, a number of references to the Prince and Princess are left unaltered. They may have been overlooked, but Prince and Princess remain appropriate titles for the Duke and Duchess of Ivry, for they are also the Prince and Princess of Moncontour.

nowhere from two words; **post-chaise** from postchase; **to-night, to-day, to-morrow** from tonight, to night, today, to day, tomorrow; **scapegrace** from scape grace.

In some instances words rendered inconsistently as one word, two words, or hyphenated compounds sound to modern ears like dead metaphors. But they were not so in the mid-nineteenth century where the two-word combinations listed here were frequently used to mean what the single compound word means today: **any body, some body, every body, any thing, some thing**. These forms are left as in the copy-text.

6. Spelling of words in secretarial hands (Anne Thackeray and George Hodder) and where *E1* is the copy-text has been regularized to the following forms: attachment (from attachement), canvas (from painting surface or sails), canvass (from survey or electioneering), eccentric (from excentric), envelop, holiday (from holliday), homage (from hommage), quarrel, quarreling, and quarreled (from double-l forms), gallop (from single-l form), making, mustachios, Newmarket (from Newmaket), retiring, shaking, taking (from makeing, retireing, shakeing, takeing), post-chaising (from post-chaseing), sepoy (from seapoy).

7. Contractions were frequently written without apostrophes or with them misplaced. The following forms have been made standard: don't, it's (for *it is*), sha'n't, wha's (for *what is* in slurred speech), s'prize.

8. Possessives were frequently written without apostrophes, which have been added silently. Occasionally an apostrophe was added to words that were merely plural; these have been removed. Occasionally apostrophes for plural possessives were misplaced; these have been corrected.

9. Possessive forms of pronouns occasionally maintain an obsolete form, as in *her's, their's, our's*; these forms have been maintained as evidence that they had not yet died out in the mid-1850s.

10. Words inadvertently repeated, usually a word at the end of a line repeated at the beginning of the next line, are rendered as one.

Capitalization

1. Titles of nobility are capitalized when referring to a specific person: King Stephen, the Earl, the Duke, her Majesty, his Royal Highness.

2. The words *Lord, Lady* and their derivatives are capitalized when they are parts of a proper name: my lady, my lord, his lordship; my Lord Marquis of Farintosh; but Milady and Milor.

3. The words *Ma'am, Madam, Miss, Monsieur, Mesdemoiselles, Sir,* and *Dowager* are capitalized when used as nouns of address or parts of proper names.

4. Common nouns that are part of proper nouns have been capitalized: Albemarle Street, Morning Post, Cave of Harmony, House of Commons, Park Lane, Court of Directors.

5. Words signaling family relationships are lower case unless the word is used as a person's name: my brother, Brother, my father, Father, my aunt, the mother, Mother, Uncle Newcome, my son.

6. Thackeray's scribes, Anne Thackeray and George Hodder, writing from dictation, were erratic capitalizers. In their parts of the manuscript, non-nouns and common nouns have been rendered in lower-case unless they begin sentences or appear to be personifications. Words like the fol-

lowing have been minisculized: austere, breakfast, brougham (meaning a coach), coachmen, court (unless referring to a royal Court or a place name), duenna, education, ethics, hotel, indigo, jelly, lawyer, major-domo, porters, punch, rogue, rope, scapegrace, sentinels, taverns, turtle, tutor.

7. Frequently used personifications and nicknames have been capitalized according to most frequent practice: the Yellow One, Pincushion, the Campaigner.

8. Generic names occasionally have the force of proper nouns and are capitalized: Battle (meaning a specific one, such as Battle of Waterloo), Church (meaning the Church of England), City (meaning the old walled City of London, and more specifically the financial district); Drawing-room (meaning the king's drawing-room in St. James's; Park (meaning a specifically named park and used as a short form of the name), Heaven, Heavens (meaning the deity or abode of the dead, but not when referring to the sky), and Hospital (meaning Grey Friars). But chapel is in lower case even when referring to Lady Whittlesea's chapel, according to the prevailing usage, though both the manuscript and the first edition are inconsistent. Parliament is inconsistently rendered in both the manuscript (where it is mostly capitalized) and the first edition (where it is mostly lower-cased); consistency has not been imposed in the present edition.

Italics

1. Isolated and infrequent foreign words and phrases appear in italics. When French is spoken intermittently, it is left in roman, as in the first edition, in order to alow italics in these passages to stand for emphasis or for interspersed Latin.

2. Titles of newspapers, magazines, books, operas, plays, and paintings are in italics or quotation marks. Both the manusccript and the first edition are inconsistent. Silent emendations impose italics where the copy-text lacks any indication, but quotation marks, when present in the copy-text, are allowed to stand.

Punctuation

Punctuation in the edited text that does *not* conform to the following policies and is not listed as an emendation is punctuation found in the copy-text and deemed unobtrusive or even subtly expressive.

1. Quotation marks have been regularized silently. The manuscript often omits quotation marks altogether or indicates only the opening or closing marks, or substitutes a dash to indicate opening or closing marks. When the manuscript does have quotation marks, they are usually single, not double, marks. Occasionally, when moving from indirect speech to direct speech it is impossible to tell where the transition comes. In general, it can be assumed that quotation marks and the punctuation accompanying them have been added by the editor. Usually the practice of the first edition has been adopted.

2. Commas have been inserted to set off nouns of direct address.

3. Periods have been added to abbreviations: Mr., Mrs., Revd., Esq.

4. Periods are added at the ends of paragraphs unless the following paragraph is an interruption. End-of-sentence periods are added silently within paragraphs when the sentence ends at the end of a manuscript line

and there is no ambiguity about the capital letter beginning the next sentence on a new line.

5. Extraneous periods following exclamation points and question marks are removed.

6. Appositives are set off by commas unless they are very short and unconfusing (i.e., her cousin Clive).

7. Items in a series are set off by commas when their omission causes temporary confusion. Frequently, series of single-word adjectives are left without commas. Commas have not been inserted before coordinating conjunctions.

8. Dashes are used quite liberally in the MS to signal interruptions, closely linked thoughts, and opening or closing of quotations. Dashes that can be read ambiguously as either a quotation or a pause are kept to indicate the pause and quotation marks added. When they are merely the indication of beginning or ending quotations, quotation marks and other punctuation are substituted in the form used in the first edition.

9. All dashes found in the edited text are in the copy-text unless listed separately in the emendations.

10. Occasionally it is not possible to distinguish between a period and a dash in the manuscript. Any decision in these cases is arbitrary. Usually the practice of the first edition was followed.

11. Commas are inserted in street addresses.

12. Punctuation in signatures for letters is regularized.

13. In volume II, chapter IX, Thackeray adopted the conventions of drama to present dialogue. Speakers' names and stage directions have been silently conventionalized, as in the first edition, to be in italics, with names within stage directions given in small caps. Manuscript practice in that section was very irregular, but not subtly or expressively so.

14. The forms "&c" and "&ca" have been rendered "&c."

Notes on the Text

The following notes explain editorial decisions reported in the footnotes for which the rationale may not be self-evident. Also given here is a selection of substantive readings from those parts of *Harper's Magazine* (*HM*) and New York edition (*NY*) that have no independent authority. (See discussion of these editions on pages 397–401.) Finally, some notes given here explain why substantive variants in the first edition (*E1*) or revised edition (*R*) are errors. Such items, of course, do not appear in the footnotes, which are devoted to reporting variants for which Thackeray was or may have been responsible.

I.7.39 did you good: *NY* omits "you".

I.17.17 expression, which *E1 R*] expression, that *NY*

I.44.24 both Mr. Hobson and Mr. Brian,] Mr. Hobson and Mr. Brian both, *E1*: The copy-text reading seems obviously faulty. One can imagine the manuscript having read: "and between ourselves, both the present Baronet …" after which an unmarked insertion was squeezed between the lines, which was erroneously rendered by the compositor. But all such matters are speculation in the absence of the manuscript.

I.47.28 Mrs. Martha Honeyman: Martha Honeyman is a spinster, but the appelation "Mrs." as a common abbreviation of "Mistress" is appropriate. *HM* and *NY* frequently changed it to "Miss".

I.54.4 which were *E1 R*] as were *NY*

I.55.16 lowering *E1*] louring *R* : The OED distinguishes between these two words as verbs (descending / threatening) but concedes that in reference to the sky it is "not always possible to discover which vb. was in the mind of the writer."

I.55.39 ill of the measles *E1 R*] ill with the measles *NY*

I.58.40 forgot about *E1 R*] forgot all about *NY*

I.66.34 native country *E1 R*] country *NY*

I.72.32 ungenerous, *E1 R*] ill-natured, *HM NY*

I.73.5 bland *E1*] blind *HM* Although the base text for the *HM* reprint was uncorrected proofs, *HM* in all probability introduced errors of its own. *HM* readings that might reflect Thackeray's manuscript prose are reported at the foot of the text pages.

I.73.44 and 76.24 Whittlesea's chapel *E1 R*] Hickathrift's chapel *HM NY*

I.78.9 "for young Scapegrace": the term is a name in this construction and is capitalized, as elsewhere when so used. The change to "for your Scapegrace" in *R* renders it generic, which should be in lower case. *R* however left the capital in this instance and raised it anomalously to capital at 78.31.

I.78.19 imaginative: R, probably erroneously, changed this reading to "imagination".

I.88.16 Brazen Nose *E1*] Brazenose *R* "Brazen Nose" is the child's error; correction, as in *R*, removes the pretext for the joke to follow.

I.88.31 Cibber Wright *E1*] Downy *R* Cibber Wright: (i.e., sybarite).

I.90.44 bread *E1 R* bed *NY*

I.96.6 people has never *E1 R*] people have never *NY*

I.101.11 I drove 'em *E1*: The *Ms* is ambiguous, reading as I believe "em" without an apostrophe, or, possibly, "on".

I.104.1, 106.7, 106.10 Pedro *Ms E1 R*] Peter *NY*

I.106.33 scared functionary *Ms E1 R*] sacred functionary *NY*: Because the deferential guide has shown no fear, the alteration does seem almost plausible.

I.107.21 Beatrice *E1*] Emily *Ms NY*: *HM* agrees with *Ms* here as it does in many places in numbers 1-4. That *NY* also agrees with *Ms*, although when the first four numbers were reset for *NY*, its setting copy was the first edition, suggests that from time to time the *NY* compositors restored readings from the *HM* text or that parts of the *NY* book text were set from *HM*. See also I.108.12: were gentlefolks *E1 R*] was gentlefolks *Ms HM NY*

I.109.20 kneeling *Ms E1*] [absent] *HM* Here is a clear case of the *HM* text departing from the text it was set from. There is no way to know, for numbers 1–2, which of the readings from *HM* represent the now lost *Ms* or proofs and which represent similar departures from the setting copy text. See I.115.41, etc.

I.109.29 Babylon *Ms E1 R*] Bagdad *HM NY*

I.112.38 hall *Ms E1*] [absent] *HM*

I.113.29 guggling *Ms E1 NY R*] gurgling *HM*

I.115.title EVERYBODY *E1 R*] EVERY ONE *HM NY*

I.116.10 who *E1*] whom *R*: Although the revised "whom" is standard, "who" is idiomatic.

I.117.21 so *Ms E1 NY R*] and so *HM*

I.119.9 that room *Ms E1*] the room *HM NY* Here might be evidence that parts of the *NY* text of numbers 2–4 were set from *HM*. See also the note at 119.16. However, see the conflicting evidence of 121.6 and 121.13.

I.119.16 any should *Ms E1*] any one should *HM NY*

I.121.6 for receiving *Ms E1 NY*] of receiving *HM*

I.121.13 o'Hazeldean *Ms E1*] o'Hozeldean *HM NY*

I.126.24 applaud *NY*] applauded *Ms E1 R*

I.141.24 He can spare but that evening,: *E1* has a sentence fragment here.

I.154.23 on foot, on horseback *Ms E1*] on foot, or horseback *HM NY*

I.154.27 Father] father *Ms E1*] his father *HM NY*

I.157.25 Alfred *E1*] Frederick *Ms*] Andrew *R* : Smee is named in the manuscript only three times: first as Frederick, then twice as Alfred. *E1* rationalizes it as Alfred. But, perhaps, because of Ethel's little brother Alfred and Smee's painting of King Alfred, someone seems to have thought Smee should have a different name. The revised edition offers Andrew here and at 182.13. Thackeray left a dash for Smee's first name in the manuscript at II.322.16, which was repeated in all editions.

I.161.18 "When the British warrior queen, / Bleeding from the Roman rods— ¶"Jolly verses! Haven't I translated them into Alcaics?" says Clive, with a merry laugh, and resumes his history. *E1*] When the [blank] ~~Roman~~ ↑British↓ Queen. [blank] / Trochaic Tetrameter— *Ms*: Thackeray remembered accurately that it was trochaic tetrameter, but left blanks in the manuscript to indicate that his memory failed about the exact wording. It is possible he meant to indicate that Clive's memory had failed, but it is more likely that he expected Percival Leigh to supply the missing verses from a copy of Cowper's poems.

I.161.23 exhibited 1816 *Ms E1 R*] in exhibited 1816 *HM NY*

I.163.32 deformed; the other adorned ... Horses used actually *E1*] deformed. He was the butt ... Horses actually used *Ms* : I believe the added prose here is by Percival Leigh; it and the accompanying portrait of Gandish (moved to the first line of the paragraph from the middle in order to accomodate the page of this edition) seem designed to extend the length of this number. See textual introduction for a discussion of the problems in producing number 6.

I.171.24 Tom's *Ms*] Jones's *E1* [Compositor's misreading; cf seven lines below]

I.171.36 a bric-a-brac *Ms E1 R*] the bric-a-brac *HM NY*

I.172.1 Our good Colonel's house: Begins interpolated material from number 6. See note at 173.18.

I.173.18 He, who *E1*] Our good Colonel who *Ms*: note that the *Ms* phrasing was preserved at the beginning of the chapter where the interpolation of material left over from number 5 began.

I.175.21 180– : The year might be 1805, when Nelson died; it is not clear if Thackeray forgot the date or intended to be vague.

I.179.31 entertainment. ¶Newcome's behaviour : This paragraph break is indicated in the *Ms* by a blank space, a device often used in Thackeray's letters but not usually in his novel manuscripts.

I.180.11 may *Ms E1 R*] might *HM NY*

I.202.31 smell *E1 R*] smelt *HM NY*

I.208.36 his best *E1 R*] Brown's best *HM NY*

I.213.23 Rosey doesn't remember Montreal. *E1 R*] [omitted] *NY*

I.214.5: Binnie *E1*] Honeyman *R* : Binnie could be referring to himself in the third person, or it could be Honeyman.

I.221.24 awaits *E1 R*] await *NY*: The *NY* reading is grammatically correct but seems unidiomatic.

I.228.11 than she became when after years of suffering had softened her nature: This somewhat awkward locution could be "fixed" by dropping the word "when" or by hyphenating "after-years" as *HM NY* do.

I.237.21 Bellew *E1 R*] [omitted] *NY*

I.238.20 foot *E1 R*] feet *NY*

I.238.27 alycompaine *E1 R*] elecempane *NY*

I.241.1 hour early *E1 R*] early hour *HM NY*

I.243.1 and let people, who know the world better, deal with him. : The commas after "people" and "better" seem wrong, or there should perhaps be another dash after the word "creditors" instead of a comma.

I.248.25 have a treated *E1 R*] had treated *NY*

I.248.32 should *E1 R*] shall *HM NY*

I.250.9 a year," he thought, "more, added *E1 R*] a year more," he thought, "added *HM NY*

I.252.24 or entering *E1 R*] on entering *HM NY*

I.259.47, 48 Balderstone / Balderstoun : Florac's reference to Caleb Balderston in Scott's *Bride of Lammermoor* is wrong in both spellings but may represent his pronunciation, which is frequently rendered phonetically.

I.262.23 where their *E1 R*] and where their *HM NY*

I.266.38 wherein we lately indulged, *E1*] wherewith this chapter commences, *HM NY*

I.268.23 mortgaged up to *E1 R*] unto *HM NY*

I.271.4 de Newcomyn, *E1 R*] Newcomyn, *HM NY*

I.271.43 beard, a *E1 R*] beard, and a *HM NY*

I.273.13 promenade; of *E1 R*] promenade; and of *HM NY*

I.275.33 into his pocket, *E1 R*] [omitted] *HM NY*

I.275.35 Dorking's apartment. : HM and NY contain a woodcut illustration, omitted from E1, of Lord Kew and Barnes with his hand in his pocket. See facing page.

I.278.45 What do you mean, Viscount?" says Jack Belsize once more,] Do you mean, Viscount?" says Belsize, Jack Belsize once more, *E1* : Neither the apparently truncated phrase "Do you mean, Viscount?" nor the repeated name "Belsize, Jack Belsize," seem right and could represent a misapplied correction.

I.284.6 bran new : The Oxford English Dictionary does not specifically illustrate "bran" or "brand" in this construction, but both spellings carry the meaning of sort or type.

I.289.38 Newcome Newcome, *Ms E1 R*] Newcome, *NY*

I.294.32 Putiphar *Ms E1 R*] Potiphar *NY*. Pharaoh's captain's name is Potiphar in King James' Bible.

I.297.5 weary weary *Ms E1 R*] weary *NY*

I.297.30 opening her saloons to Art : in the nineteenth century saloon/salon was a mere spelling variant.

I.297.39 sowed Ms] sewed E1 : Not an uncommon spelling for the act of sewing with a needle.

I.298.17 august *Ms E1 R*] the august *NY*

I.304.5 Baron Punter : Punter is a Count in other references to him.

I.316.39 elderly *E1 R*] elder *HM NY*

I.325.9 even *E1 R*] [omitted] *HM NY*

I.344.43 *Chanticlere*] *Chanticleer* E1 : All other references to the Dorking Chanticleres use this spelling; but Chanticleer appears in the fable opening chapter I.

I.347.10 again *E1 R*] again and again *HM NY*

I.362.10 Be sure *E1 R*] You may be sure *HM NY*

Vol. II

II.16.41 parsons *E1 R*] persons *HM NY*

II.18.20 says *E1 R*] said *HM NY*

II.18.39 Bundelcund] Bumdlecund *E1*: Binnie makes no other pronunciation errors, so it seems more likely a compositor's error. *E1 R NY* all spell it Bundlecund in the surrounding instances, but the prevailing spelling in *Ms* is Bundelcund.

II.27.7 are *E1 R*] were *NY*

II.40.40 remember and get the invitation for your friend. *E1*] remember your commission (Peule! says Ethel with a shrug of her shoulder. ↑an askance look at Clive.↓) *Ms* : The final inserted phrase seems to replace the last original phrase which is not cancelled. But the insertion is in a hand other than Thackeray's, and both phrases were replaced in proof-stage by the reading adopted for this text.

II.48.13 to battle *Ms E1 R*] to do battle *HM NY*

II.49.33 that she's *Ms E1 R*] she is *HM NY*. The word "that" appears three times in this sentence in the *Ms*; every printed version reduced that number to two.

II.53.10 young friend *Ms E1 R*] friend *HM NY*

II.56.39 Absolon, the son of David, *E1* Absolon, the son of Saul *Ms* : Originally spelled "Absalom" in the *Ms* but written over to form "Absolon"; he was the son of King David, not Saul. 2 Samuel 18–19. Cf. II.58.17 where the *Ms* has "Absolon" with no changes.

II.62.22 performance *E1*] -'formance *Ms* : It is conceivable that the truncated form " 'formance" represents Rosey's comment, which is otherwise rendered indirectly.

II.82.44 *a sigh Ms E1 R*] *a deep sigh HM NY*

II.85.1 at home? Monsieur St. Jean!: This form of punctuating questions, with the noun of address after the question mark, is common in the manuscript, and frequently, as in this case, survives in the first edition. It has been accepted as an effective, if not very conventional, way to indicate the intonation of questions.

II.87.36 very very *Ms E1 R*] very *HM NY*

II.105.24 What *Ms E1 R*] What! *HM NY*

II.105.28 protests *Ms E1 R*] protest *HM NY*

II.106.20 door *Ms E1 R*] [omitted] *HM NY*

II.109.22 round her, *E1 R*] around her, *HM NY*

II.110.46 Payne *E1 R*] Hayne *HM NY* This is the only mention of Payne in the novel.

II.111.13 grave and even reserved *NY*] grave even and reserved *E1 R* : It is possible that Thackeray meant for this to be a series: grave, even, and reserved—or that he meant it to be: grave even, and reserved. However, the fact that he had just said Laura was as "grave as a judge" makes the latter possibility unlikely.

II.111.34 tended *E1 R*] attended *HM NY*

II.113.7–26 Dear Cousin Barnes ... made acquaintance. [Although this passage was added in proof and, therefore, is not in the manuscript, this passage appears in *HM NY*, and must have been added to the proofs at an earlier stage than the subsequent addition lower on the page (113.32–114.8).]

II.113.32–114.8 Gandish himself, ... lauded his talents. [This passage is absent from the *Ms*, for it was added in proof stage. Its absence from the *HM NY* edition indicates, therefore, that this portion of the *HM NY* text probably was set from early proofs even though the New York publication lagged two months behind the London appearance of each number.

II.114.9 Alfred Smee: see note at I.157.25.

II.115.15 Great George St. : The manuscript's abbreviation of *Street* creates the slight ambiguity that it might not be the end of the sentence, so that that next picture might seem to be one of Great George Street itself (numbered 979), rather than the address for Joseph Muggins. But each picture's number seems to precede each title; thus, the period is taken to indicate the end of the previous title.

II.116.10 confidentially *Ms E1 R*] confidently *HM NY*

II.118.13 much miss you *E1 R*] miss you *HM NY*

II.118.41 Gar and Starter? *E1 R*] Star and Garter? *HM NY*

II.121.3 cotemporary: Thackeray uses this word twice in the novel.

II.125.4 our character of historians : "historian" might be more appropriate than the narrator's apparent reference to himself in the plural; but occasionally the narrator refers to himself as a member of a fraternity of novelists who have privileges and responsibilities.

II.139.1 says he *Ms E1 R*] said he *NY*

II.140.22 Henchman] Hardyman *Ms*] Honeyman *E1 HM NY R* Note the *Ms* alteration from Hardyman to Henchman a few lines before. In *Ms* the second instance is on the verso of the leaf where it was probably overlooked when the first change was made.

II.147.35 in front), *Ms E1*] in the front), *HM NY*

II.148.9 That conviction will make us imagine Barnes still more comfortable. : Literal sense would demand *un*comfortable here; but the statement, as is, strikes a heavily ironic note.

II.153.title ENDING *Ms E1 HM R*] END *NY*

II.155.33 Ethel's younger *Ms R*] Ethel's youngest *E1* : Ethel has two younger sisters; Maud is younger than Alice.

II.157.28 drank," *Ms E1 R*] drunk," *HM NY*

II.163.11 — Batters : The proprietor of *The Newcome Independent* is mentioned several times in volume I and three times in volume II, but never with a first name.

II.164.3a Clergyman *E1*] Clergymen *R* : the revised edition plural "clergymen" seems an error, for each type of clergyman seems to be represented by one person.

II.164.7 statue *E1*] state *R* : the revised edition "state" is probably an error.

II.165.38 consequence. The housekeeper had a friend at Newcome, Mrs. Taplow in fact of the King's Arms—the butler was familiar with Taplow—one *Ms*] consequence. The butler was familiar with Taplow—the housekeeper had a friend at Newcome, Mrs. Taplow in fact of the King's Arms—one *E1* [The phrase: "the butler ... with Taplow" is ambiguously inserted in *Ms*.]

II.174.39 Edmonstone: It should be Joseph Edmondson, author of *Complete Book of Heraldry*.

II.178.2 as a most *Ms E1 R*] as the most *HM NY*

II.178.12 covere *Ms*] cover *E1* : This is the last word on the *Ms* line, squeezed slightly, but clear on close examination. The compositor probably saw "cover", but it seems a likely Gallicism matching the others in this sentence.

II.184.32 your goodness, *Ms E1 R*] [omitted] *HM NY*

II.206.3–11 I would not willingly interrupt ... was a laughin at? We did not tell ... behaviour of other people? *E1 R*] [footnote] In order not to interrupt ... was a laughing at? [rest absent] *Ms NY* The fact that *NY* agrees with *Ms* against *E1* by having this passage in a footnote suggests, but does not prove, that the English proofs originally had the material in a footnote, which was cancelled when the final passage was added.

II.206.24 (Here Miss Ethel laughed): The placement of this interruption is unambiguous in *Ms*. The fact that *NY* agrees with *Ms* indicates that the proofs originally followed *Ms*. Therefore, its present position in *E1* represents a deliberate revision at proof stage.

II.210.43 "And I've given up ... continued, "if *E1*] ¶"But if *Ms NY*: Three paragraphs added at proof stage.

II.211.19 ashamed for myself: The fact that *NY* agrees with *Ms* indicates that the proofs originally followed *Ms* copy. Therefore, the omission was a deliberate proof stage revision.

II.218.10 they *Ms E1 R*] that they *HM NY*

II.227.31 kind declining *Ms E1 R*] declining *HM NY*

II.228.16 our name." *Ms E1 R*] his name." *HM NY*

II.234.15 little Rosey's little *Ms E1 R*] Rosey's little *NY*

II.240.7 Fog Court: Anne's "Fob" is ambiguously written—hence *E1*'s "Job" is probably a misreading by the compositor; at II.294.7 in George Hodder's hand it is "Fog"—as also in *E1* and *R*.

II.241.10 their *Ms E1 R*] his *HM NY*

II.241.19 he was] they were [The change at 244.19 focuses the passage on Clive's father rather than on both father and son, and thus requires this change. Other changes in *E1* systematically exclude Clive from Laura's censure.]

II.254.8 that rascal *E1 R*] the rascal *HM NY*

II.257.16 young men. *E1 R*] young man. *HM NY*

II.259.14 to meet him; *E1 R*] to meet; *HM NY*

II.260.47 in my life. *E1 R*] in all my life. *HM NY*

II.264.12 people!" ¶"I *R*] people! I *E1* : *R* correctly indicated "I know" as the beginning of Bayham's interruptions, but incorrectly assigns the following paragraph to him also. Potts' speech is interrupted occasionally by F.B., not taken over by him.

II.265.44 cotemporary *Ms E1 R*] contemporary *HM NY*

II.272.34 in his marriage *Ms E1 R*] into his marriage *HM NY*

II.277.7 make the best *Ms E1 R*] make the most *HM NY*

II.282.43 deserting Sir Barnes, ... voted: There is no *Ms* for this passage; *E1*'s reading is obviously erroneous. *R* corrected by removing the word "and"; *HM NY* corrected by changing "deserting" to "deserted".

II.287.29 his story *Ms E1 R*] the story *HM NY*

II.287.32 that Bundelcund *Ms E1 R*] the Bundelcund *HM NY*

II.290.4 little helpless *Ms E1 R*] helpless *HM NY*

II.292.33 "embark" is not clearly written and could be "embank"— meaning both to run aground and to put in a bank.

II.294.39 cries the Campaigner, *E1 R*] [omitted] *HM NY*

II.297.26 know *E1*] knew *HM NY*

II.301.22 The *Ms* as usual lacks commas or apostrophes in this series, leading to the possiblity that it consists of "lawyer's commission, premium life-insurance"—two things instead of four.

II.301.33 *Ms* "trapple" for "chapel" is mysterious but may be the result of dictation: Hodder, who did not inscribe any of the earlier references to Whittlesea chapel, may have written what he thought he heard.

II.302.21 old street *Ms E1 R*] street *NY*

II.305.31 paid, or ... medicines,: either reading makes sense, though the *Ms* with the added commas suggests that the doctor prescibed medicines for a fee and the medicines purchased elsewhere cost extra, while the first edition reading suggests that the doctor made his fee by charging for medicines deemed to be expensive. The practice of charging fees was not common at the time; so *E1*'s reading may be correct.

II.308.29 Both "Levantine" and "levanting" mean one from the east and one who absconds; cf Bolter.

II.309.38 alterative: a medical term for a catalyst, not a mistake for "alternative."

II.310.38 See note at II.358.25.

II.313.23 pavid] pavied *Ms*] fawning *E1* : although the manuscript is misspelled (pavied), it could not be mistaken as the word "fawning"; but it is sufficiently unclear for a compositor unfamiliar with the word "pavid" to seek a substitution.

II.316.12 Alfred Smee] — Smee *E1* : The dash in *E1* represents an omitted word, not punctuation. Thackeray apparently had trouble remembering Smee's name. See note at I.157.25.

II.319.33 recognition; *Ms*] recognition as Clive *E1 R* : Although the *Ms* passage is ambiguous, it seems more likely that Ridley was unenvious of Clive's successess, on which the paragraph is focused, than Clive unenvious of Ridley. A better emendation than those offered in *E1* and *R* might be: "and not one of Clive's many admirers saluted his talent and success with such a hearty recognition;". The following clause then parallels the "whose" phrasing which to this point has referred to Ridley.

II.327.10 their bread *E1 R*] bread *HM NY*

II.327.36 we saw *E1*] I saw *HM NY*

II.329.22 pointed *E1 R*] pointing *HM NY*

II.330.29 takes *E1 R*] and takes *HM NY*

II.332.14 for some time *E1 R*] some time *HM NY*

II.333.50 be sure *E1 R*] to be sure *HM NY*

II.338.21 news were *E1 R*] news was *HM NY*

II.339.15 £100, be given: "£100, to be given" (*R*) is an obvious error.

II.344.8 we three remained: actually there are four: the Colonel, F.B. Clive, and Pendennis.

II.349.29 a hospital! *Ms E1*] an hospital! *HM NY*

II.355.36 Maria dashed at the purse in a moment with a scream of laughter shook it contents : *Ms* has no commas; *E1* places the comma after "moment." But it were placed after "laughter" instead, would be the dash and not the shaking that was marked by laughter.

II.358.25 Queen's] Queen *Ms E1* : Pendennis's address on Queen's Square is mentioned twice. In Hodder's handwriting (II.310.38) it is "Queen's Square"; in Thackeray's handwriting it is "Queen Square." Originally named "Queen Anne's Square," it had become known as "Queen's Square" by Pendennis's time.

II.359.39 of the misery *Ms E1 R*] the misery *HM NY*

II.362.38 till warmer *Ms E1 R*] still *NY*

II.365.31–367.2 A narrative account of the dual composition of this page, its typesetting from the draft manuscript, its correction by the compositor from the new manuscript, and its further revision at proof stage is given in the textual introduction, p. 416.

Alterations in the Manuscript

In order to show what Thackeray did in the process of composing and revising the text, all of the changes deemed to have originated with him are presented in footnotes to the main text or in the following list: Alterations in the Manuscript. Editorial interventions are recorded after this list.

The following list records all manuscript alterations (cancellations, additions, substitutions, illegible words or characters, false starts). Occasionally the manuscript reading, given here, has been emended for the reading text of this edition. Such changes are indicated either in the footnotes of the text, as alterations in printed texts accepted as authorial, or as Editorial Corrections in a subsequent list, unless they belong in the categories of silent emendations (see the Textual Introduction).

Parts of the manuscript are in the handwriting of Erye Crowe, Anne Thackeray, or George Hodder, each of whom took dictation. Handwriting changes are indicated in the following list. Manuscript locations are indicated at the beginning of manuscript sections. The bulk of the manuscript is at the Charterhouse School, Godalming, England.

Cancelled words are ~~crossed out~~. Insertions are enclosed ↑like this↓ in arrows. An @ sign indicates alterations made by Thackeray in manuscript sections enscribed by Anne Thackeray or George Hodder.

Vol. I.

48.33 that ~~sacred~~ fidelity
48.33 his ~~noble~~ nature,
48.33 this ~~go~~ ↑brave↓ man
48.36 sufficient (~~wh.~~↑and↓ indeed
48.36 by ~~that~~ people
48.37 their ↑future↓ lives
48.38 sent ~~tokens~~ ↑presents↓ and
48.41 Gazettes, ↑&↓ embroiders
48.42 victory; ↑wh.↓ gives
48.42ˈ moralists ~~so~~ and
48.42 enemies ~~causes~~ to
48.43 and ↑enables↓ patriots
48.43 of ↑invincible↓ British
48.45 glory, ↑the↓ crowned
48.45 ambition, ↑the↓ conquered
48.47 tears? ↑too.↓ ~~Good God what~~ ↑Besides the lives↓ of
48.47 of ↑thou↓ myriads of British ~~Soldiers who have nobly fallen from the days of~~ ↑men, conquering from↓ Plassy

[Begin Thackeray's handwriting. *Ms* in Taylor Collection, Princeton.]

49. 1 Meanee ↑&↓ bathing a hundred fields *cruore nostro*↓: think
49. 3 to ~~those~~ ↑yonder↓ shores

49. 6 them ~~[illeg.]~~: the
49. 6 must [Colonel Newcome's tender heart. 59(B)] be
49. 7 up—keep ~~them~~ ↑flowers of your home↓ beyond
49. 8 America ~~its~~ is
49. 9 wife ↑& from under the palace↓ of
49.10 pröconsul. [space] ~~[illeg.]~~ ¶Having [T over t]he experience
49.11 Newcomes ~~tender~~ ↑naturally kind↓ heart ~~naturally[?]~~ only
49.12 and ↑thence↓ he
49.13 of ↑wh↓ old
49.14 whose ↑little↓ inhabitants
49.16 children ~~[illeg.]~~ tumbling

[Begin Thackeray's handwriting. *Ms* in Charterhouse School.]

92. 2 hours ↑Lady Ann Newcome↓ was
92.20 to ~~send away~~↑part with↓ Brignol.
92.22 give ~~him~~↑Brignol↓ warning.
92.27 and ~~mut~~ Clive's—and
92.31 that ~~we~~ Dr.
93. 2 forgot ↑your Aunt↓ Louisa's
93. 3 said ↑what is this Infants name I said↓ really
93.10 am ~~sure~~↑certain↓ Mrs.

93.14 the ~~stranger~~↑visitor↓ within
93.15 them ~~the first day~~ ↑on Sunday↓, not
93.18 monsters ~~durin~~ afterwards:
93.27 and ~~the~~ little
93.28 nothing. [T over S]he place
93.29 her— ↑She could not see the sun shining on their fair flaxen heads &
93.30 pretty faces↓ the
93.31 crying ~~to~~↑the↓ answer
93.33 her bed~~[illeg]~~. Naturally
93.35 valuable ↑than ever so much arithmetic & geography.↓ ~~The sense of her ignorance humbled her heart.~~ ↑Clive has told me a story of her in her youth, wh. perhaps↓ may
93.40 lucky ~~householders~~↑dwellers↓ in
93.41 of ~~seven~~↑nine↓ or
93.45 wh. ↑may↓ account~~s~~ for
94. 2 perhaps ~~is beloved by that lady~~ ↑that a girl bestows her affections↓ on
94. 4 announced ~~at~~ his
94. 5 very morning[, over .] ↑taking his family & ~~Ethel~~ ↑↑of course↓↓ Ethel
94. 5 with him.↓ She
94. 6 inconsolable— '[W over S]hat will
94. 8 about ~~it~~↑the↓ circumstance↓. 'He
94.13 such ~~great~~↑tall↓ girl
94.15 Fancy ~~her~~ myself
94.19 Universelle ~~where~~ et
94.19 Sciences Compréhensive of
94.23 tea ↑at 6 o'clock↓, dancing,
94.24 the ~~governesses~~↑teachers↓ who
 95.6 who ↑is to↓ takes a
95. 8 But ↑of↓ this
95. 9 us: ~~nor turn aside~~↑and go on or turn aside at her bidding.↓ ¶Here
95.11 the ~~young ↑then↓~~ Earl
95.12 of ~~that~~ ↑the↓ noble
95.13 married. [Note on *Ms* verso:] Does it do better on a rough paper? Yes certainly: it runs ~~es~~ more easily, and I wish I had twenty pages or two hundred written with this very pen. Don ¶My dear Sir, I should be very glad to hear what the packet entrusted to you was safely arrived at Timbuctoo. No this is the best way. Mes Bonnes Seurs. Mes bonnes Seurs. Why do you not write a single line?

[Begin Anne Thackeray's handwriting. Thackeray's changes (marked here by @) are inserted in a slightly darker ink.]

95.14 When ~~you~~↑we↓ read
95.15 sentinels in~~mu~~↑nu↓merable in
95.18 the cantan@[ke over ca]rous humour
95.19 that not↑to↓rious old
95.20 baptismal ceremony——@~~W~~↑tw↓hen Prince
95.22 most ed[i over y]f[y over i]ing ↑educational↓ works
95.22 most ~~ver~~ venerable
95.24 the ~~stel~~ steel
95.24 & bra@[z over s]en bars
95.25 dose, ↑&↓ the
95.25 will ↑either↓ be
95.26 implacable enemies↑;↓ or
95.27 his guardians↑,↓ &
95.29 chambers empty@[; t over T]he saucy
95.29 saucy ~~heeir~~ heir
95.29 apparent flown@↑;↓ the
95.29 & Sent[i over e]nels drunk@↑;↓ the
95.30 the ancien@↑t↓ Tutor
95.30 Tutor asleep[. T over , t]hey tear
95.31 They ~~cashier~~ turn
95.33 Rope ladder@↑:↓ the
95.37 sentinels, sermon~~ised~~↑ers↓, old
95.37 old women,↑;↓ from
95.37 world without@↑;——↓& ~~are~~↑have↓ nevertheless
95.38 escaped frome all
95.40 who ro~~de~~↑bbed↓ Richard
95.41 his crown@[—t over . T]he youth
95.41 took @~~Percy's~~↑purses↓ on
95.41 on Gadshill@↑;↓ frequented
95.43 Gascoigne's ears@↑!↓ What
95.44 of mind@↑,↓ when
95.45 of @*her* beautiful [italics added by T]
95.46 horse @~~jumpers~~↑jockeys,↓ of
95.46 with Perdita@↑?↓ Besides
95.47 Royal family@↑,↓ Could
95.49 severe, ↑&↓ his

95.49 step-father ~~the~~↑a↓ most
96. 1 young gentleman@↑'↓s career
96. 1 career ~~p~~ was
96. 2 positively ~~se~~hockings He
96. 2 at taverns@↑,↓ he
96. 4 a ~~wild~~↑mad↓ prank
96. 5 the ↑lawless↓ freaks
96. 7 & spirits@↑,↓ generous
96. 7 his money@↑,↓ jovial
96. 7 his humour@↑,↓ ready
96. 8 his sword@↑,↓ frank
96. 8 frank handsome@↑,↓ prodigal
96. 8 prodigal ~~cora~~ courageous
96. 9 Young Scap@↑e↓gace Rides
96.10 seniors ~~look~~ shake
96.10 their heads@↑,↓ &
96.11 female ma↑o↓ralists are
96.12 & beauty@↑.↓ I
96.14 Newcome, @~~we~~↑most of us↓ have
96.14 a ↑sneaking↓ regard
96.15 honest Tom@↑,↓ &
96.17 ago ~~The Lady Wallom Walham~~ the
96.19 pleasures ↑for↓ wh.
96.20 cut off@↑,↓ so
96.21 we @~~seem to↑appear↓~~ grow@↑;↓ so
96.22 has ~~society~~ the
96.22 of society@↑,↓ to
96.23 must bow@↑,↓ put
96.24 amusements ↑with↓ wh.
96.24 time ~~young gentlemen of the world~~ the
96.25 many excit@~~e~~ing reports
96.25 boxing matches@¬↑.↓br Bruising
96.27 noble science@↑,↓ from
96.29 Game Chicken@↑.↓ Young
96.29 to @~~Moles«e»'s~~↑Moulsey↓ to
96.31 the ↑t↓ooting horns
96.31 horns @↑& rattling teams↓ of
96.32 Coaches, ~~& The~~ @↑(ita↓ gay
96.32 the ~~rao~~ road
96.32 days ↓before steam
96.34 Coaches ~~the~~ to
96.34 & Guards@↑,↓ to
96.35 the Road@↑,↓ to
96.36 the chin@↑,↓ were
96.38 I war↑tra↓nt did
96.38 & [A over a] Thirsty

96.40 round them@↑;↓ &@↑,↓ not
96.40 without @↑a↓ kind
96.40 kind @[C over c]onservatism, expatiated
96.41 the country@↑,↓ and
96.41 and ~~on~~ the
96.42 no more@↑:—↓D↑d↓ecay of
96.42 English spirit[— over ,]decay of
96.43 forth @↑& so forth↓. To
96.44 derogatory @to↑in↓ a
96.45 a gentleman@↑;↓ To
97. 4 Defiance? You~~r lamps~~ are
97. 4 are ~~out~~ past
97. 5 out. ~~Yon grate~~ &
97. 8 whom @~~some of us know~~↑this county knows↓—That good
97.10 of schools@[; t over T]hat writer
97.10 of ~~Kewshire~~↑@[Kew over Q-]shire↓ so
97.11 wins pri@[z over s]es at
97.13 century back@↑,↓ who
97.13 Race horses@↑;↓ patronised
97.14 patronised boxers@↑;↓ fought duel@↑;↓ thrashed
97.14 life guardsman@↑;↓ & gambled
97.15 what besides@↑?↓ ¶His
97.17 young +↑m . .↓+ gentlemans
97.18 of ~~such~~↑the most↓ careful
97.23 he ↑began to↓ distinguish~~ed~~ himself
97.24 tandems, ~~he~~ kept
97.25 Dean ~~&~~ screwed
97.28 son ~~Lord~~ the
97.32 who ~~had ma~~ in
97.33 between ~~Sir~~ Mr.
97.37 respectable ~~persons~~ of
97.41 is ~~&~~ keeps
97.42 Establishment &↑&↓ checks
[Begin Thackeray's handwriting.]
98. 3 Easter, ~~she~~↑the old lady↓ said,
98. 6 women ~~have~~ are
98. 6 the ~~balls~~ ↑half dozen parties↓ they
98. 7 their partners+.+ ↑and their toilettes.↓ Intimacy
98. 9 not ~~come to~~ ↑invaded↓ Brighton.
98.13 was ↑usually↓ amongst
98.13 the ↑Brighton↓ newspapers
98.17 at home[; over ,] and
98.19 sarcasm ~~dal~~ daily.
98.20 their ↑poor little↓ backs

98.20 shoulders ~~exposed~~↑laid bare↓, covered

98.21 wh. ~~their~~ brutal

98.23 poor ~~suf~~ patient

98.25 castigation. ↑Old↓ Lady

98.35 see ~~those~~ that

98.37 and ~~you~~↑my death↓ would

99. 4 this confession[— over :] Is

99. 5 good ~~man~~ woman

99. 6 Master ~~Arthur's~~↑Alfred's↓ health

99.12 me? ~~Send~~ When

99.15 of ~~Lord~~ the

99.16 the ~~Dowager~~↑old lady↓ delighted.

99.21 indeed wear~~in~~ a

99.24 'Before a↑n↓ ~~young~~↑unmarried↓ lady

99.25 Belsize ~~in company with~~ who

99.28 years old[; over .] and

99.28 heard ~~much~~↑a thousand times↓ worse

99.31 Pozzoprofondo ↑the famous Contralto↓ of

99.33 Doctor— ~~says~~↑interposes↓ Lady

99.34 carriage too~~a s—a~~—a-sitting behind

99.38 Steyne, ~~had~~↑possessed↓~~much~~ ↑no small share↓ of

99.42 to ~~as~~ take

99.43 Brighton ~~wer~~ where

100. 1 not ~~wish me t~~ drowned

100. 5 Your ~~&c~~ etcetera

100.13 ¶Two ~~days~~↑evenings↓ afterwards

100.16 Barnes?. Surely." my

100.18 Barnes. ~~broke in Jack Belsize.~~ I

100.18 in ~~Lady~~↑Jack↓ Belsize.

100.28 Ethel. ¶~~She~~ Ethel

100.29 say ~~say~~ remarks

100.35 cries ↑the inopportune↓ Jack

100.35 Belsize—I'm ~~alw~~ always

101. 1 we ~~came~~ were

101. 3 was ¶D[— over am]d rash

101. 5 ¶And ↑my brother↓ Frank

101.19 Kew ~~continues~~↑proceeds↓ an

101.21 ¶~~We~~This gentleman

102. 9 ¶As ~~g~~ fine

102.10 great ~~Artis~~ hand

102.13 me, ~~She is [illeg]~~ and

102.16 Lady ~~Lad~~ Key,

103. 1 Ridley's [centered and double underlined] ¶Saint

103. 1 Alcantara, ~~so~~↑as↓ I

103. 6 lay down,: his

103.17 began [the over this] regimen

103.19 the ~~devout gentleman~~↑pious individual↓ so

103.20 employed: ↑day after day, night after night,↓ on

103.23 the ↑very↓ worst

103.23 us trust) ↑with his downcast eyes)↓ under

103.24 the ↑bitter↓ snow

103.27 the ~~secon first~~↑second↓ floor

103.30 his ~~boots and~~ shower-bath

103.31 stretched ↑on boot-trees↓ and

103.31 and ~~painted~~↑daily blacked to a nicety (not varnished)↓ by

104. 2 by the~~ir boots only~~+.+ way

104. 4 the ↑white↓ hand

104. 5 passes ~~throug~~ in

104. 5 hair. ¶As sweet ~~fragrance~~↑odour↓ pervades

104. 6 his ~~ap~~ sleeping

104. 7 fragrance ↑with↓ wh.

104. 8 gratify ~~believers~~ the

104. 9 Delcrois') ~~on~~↑into↓ wh.

104.12 sermons, &↑to wh.↓ the

104.14 blue ~~satin~~silk and

104.16 in ~~par~~ anonymous

104.19 him—pen-wipers— ~~an album~~ a

104.22 ill, ↑and throat-comforters—↓ and

104.23 the ~~splen~~ rich

104.24 by ~~the~~ his

104.26 the ~~tea-~~ silver

104.30 days! ↑At one time↓ +I+if Honeyman

104.30 could ~~drink~~↑have drunk↓ tea

104.31 have ↑had↓ it.

104.32 ceremony ~~(~~of wh.

104.34 Honeyman!' ~~begins one~~↑writes Blanche,↓ what

104.35 it!' ~~Can you~~'Do, *Do*

104.39 the ~~agreeable~~↑domestic↓ accomplishments;

104.41 stories (~~with~~↑of↓ the

104.42 the ~~most~~↑utmost↓ correctness,

104.44 voice ~~to~~ better

105. 5 23 ~~a~~ Sermon↑s↓ will

105. 7 Clergyman's Grand~~x~~mother's Fund.

105. 8 in ~~behalf~~ ↑aid↓ of

105.12 Admirable ↑Institution↓ will

105.13 & declare[: over .]
~~Meanwhile every~~
~~They say that the~~ ↑though it is
said that↓ a

105.13 for preferment~~,~~: ↑His fame is
spread wide and not only women
but men come to hear him.
Members of Parliament even
Cabinet Ministers sit under him
Lord Dozeley of course is seen
in front pew: where was a public
meeting without Lord Dozeley?
The↓ men

105.17 come ~~out of~~↑away from↓ his

105.22 Besides there~~'s~~ ↑is↓ no

105.24 and that~~'s~~ ↑is↓ better

105.27 a ~~laugh~~↑solemn look↓. Dont

105.30 door ↑& a brass plate.↓. It's

105.31 over ~~val~~ vaults

105.32 Kew ~~had~~ and

105.33 ugly ~~dispute~~+.+↑row?↓ ¶What

105.34 ugly row—Its is

105.37 about money~~,~~ and

105.40 him ↑to church & brought him
thence.↓ And

105.46 as ~~dowagers~~↑ladies↓~~trot~~ ↑walk↓
home;

106. 1 as ~~little~~ children

106. 3 of ~~the—~~ ↑State↓ in

106. 5 vestry, ~~and~~↑before he↓ walks

106. 6 Alcantara ~~had~~↑could have↓ some

106.12 and ~~the~~ other

106.14 wh. ~~the~~ Colonel

106.18 some ~~chur~~ chapels

106.18 one ↑almost↓ expects

106.20 the ↑Royal Covent Garden↓
Theatre.

106.20 Theatre. [~~break a line~~] ¶The

106.22 none ~~so~~↑more↓ magnificent

106.28 Sir Thomas[; over :] of

106.28 father ↑the fifth Earl↓ by

106.31 prattle, ~~and~~ sa[ying over id] in

106.31 hollow voice[, over —] And

106.33 not ~~down~~↑inserted↓ in

106.34 for ↑their↓ half

106.34 half ~~a~~ crown. ~~M~~ Hicks's

106.45 it, ~~while~~↑when the palace is
hushed, when↓ beauties

107. 3 are ~~snoring~~↑slumbering↓: up

107. 5 the ↑secret↓ door,

107. 7 Who ~~doesn't keep~~ in

107. 9 laying ↑~~[illeg.]~~↓ down

107.10 husband ~~opposite~~+.+↑asleep
perhaps after dinner.↓ Yes,

107.10 Madam, ~~he has the closet~~+.+↑a
closet he hath: & you who pry
into everything shall never have
the key of it:↓ I

107.14 to ~~her~~↑their↓ little

107.19 with ~~his~~ smiles

107.22 has ~~a~~↑one or two skeleton↓
closett~~s~~↓ in

107.23 lodgings ~~[illeg.]~~ Queen

107.25 the ↑lodger on↓ first

107.26 bootboy ↑are at rest↓ (mind

107.28 at ~~that~~↑the↓ Ghastly

107.30 of ↑some of↓ the

107.31 Bagshot. ~~Norfolk~~ Member

107.31 Member ↑for a Norfolk
borough↓. Stout

107.35 the ↑houses of↓ great

107.36 an ~~attorney~~↑Apothecary↓:
married

107.44 always, ~~lies in bed~~↑does not rise↓
till

107.45 Bull [& over in] Bell's

108.12 inmates, ~~[illeg.]~~but in

108.14 is ~~now~~ dead,

108.15 by ~~giv~~ going

108.17 of ~~that meal~~↑the family dinner↓,
his

108.22 two [c over C]anary birds en[c
over g]aged in

108.22 window ~~having~~↑(whence is↓ a

108.23 Whittlesea's chapel[) over,] eat

108.24 singing [and over wh] chorussing

108.24 Cann ~~the lodgers being~~↑her
↑spying the occasion of the first
floor↓-lodger's absence,

108.27 Miss Cann~~,~~ it

108.32 are ↑I am given to understand↓
among

108.34 begs ~~&~~ he

108.38 what ~~he~~ a

108.40 his ~~heart~~↑soul↓, with

108.41 the ~~little~~ Artist

109. 1 listens ~~sees~~↑beholds↓ altars

109. 5 the opera~~,~~ &

109. 5 the Theatres[. A over :a]s she

109. 9 The ↑towers of the↓ great

109. 9 cathedral ~~towers~~↑rise↓ in

109.10 The ~~fountain~~↑statues↓ in

109.11 pavement: ~~and~~ but

109.12 and ↑sings and↓ wears
109.14 it a ↑the great↓ street
109.15 is ~~the street of fancy~~↑Fancy Street↓: ~~it is the street of poetry~~ ↑Poetry Street↓. Imagination
109.17 and engage[— over,] a fount↑where long↓ processions
109.20 halberts, ↑&↓ fife
109.21 and ~~will dance whether the~~ ↑bid the pifferari play↓ to
109.24 and ~~see it welcome Masaniello and Fra Diavolo~~↑see on his cream coloured charger Masaniello prances in & Fra Diavolo leaps down the balcony carabine in hand↓ and
109.26 Bordeaux ~~who «jumps out of»~~ ↑wanders in with↓ the Sultan's ↑sails up to the quay with the Sultans↓ daughter-. ↑of Babylon.↓ All
109.27 sights ↑and joys and glories, these thrills of sympathy, movements of
109.28 unknown longing, ↑↑&↓↓ visions of beauty↓ a
109.31 woman ↑is↓ playing
109.34 in ~~the~~ a
109.41 plate basket[— over .] The
109.43 sickly [& over a] dirty [& over a] timid
109.44 crying: ↑whimpering in the kitchen away from his mother who ~~of [illeg.]~~ though she loved him took Mr. Ridleys view of his character & thought him little better than an idiot↓ until
110. 1 who ~~showed~~ had
110. 5 the ~~w~~ wisest
110.16 Ridley. ↑The pore feller does no harm that I agnowledge: but↓ I
110.39 to ~~scale~~ ↑storm↓, a
110.41 cloak ~~to kneel at her feet and~~ ↑two scales the tower, who slays the tyrant & then kneels gracefully at the Princess's feet &↓ says↑s↓ 'Lady
111. 1 their ~~Sunday~~ club;—this ~~lady~~↑good soul↓ also
111. 3 upper servants↑'↓ ~~to~~ table.
111. 4 benefactor. ↓She has
111.10 his ↑long↓ lean
111.14 Robbers. ~~An~~How he
111.14 blistered ↑Thaddeus of Warsaw↓ with

111.16 him! ~~no~~ with
111.17 tight-kilt ↑&↓ with
111.27 apprenticing ~~to~~ him
111.29 and ~~the~~ terror
111.33 for ~~the~~ him:—
111.34 and ~~knew~~ no
111.40 two ~~m~~ ivory
112. 1 the [A over a]rt-cant very
112. 3 eyes ~~like~~↑such as↓ those
112. 4 to ~~common~~↑vulgar↓ sight
112. 7 familiar. ~~You~~↑One↓ read↑s↓ in
112. 8 wh. ~~an Ene~~↑the↓ wizard
112. 8 the ~~spirits~~ fairies.
112. 9 O ~~charming and~~ enchanting
112. 9 of ~~gracious~~ Nature
112. 9 the ~~gifted~~ possessor
112.10 him! ~~the gracious forms~~ spirits wh. ~~some~~+,+ the ~~most~~ strongest
112.11 master ~~them~~ +&+ compel ~~them~~ into
112.11 song. ~~It~~↑To others, it↓ is granted +to+ ~~others more~~ but to ~~see that fair art-world; or not~~ have
112.12 ambition ↑or barred by faint-heartedness,↓ or
112.13 or ~~barred~~↑driven↓ by
112.13 away ~~from it, an~~↑thence↓ to
112.16 the ~~scanty &~~ discomfortable
112.19 fairly ~~fronted~~↑coped↓ with
112.22 quality, ↑&↓ where
112.25 parlor [furnished & tenanted over tenanted & furnished] [by over as] Miss
112.28 and ~~how can you~~ the
112.33 history. ↑At night when Honeyman comes in he finds on the hall table 3 wax ↑↑bed room↓↓ candles his own, Bagshots and another. As for Miss Cann she is locked into the parlor ↑↑&↓↓ in bed long ago her stout little walking shoes being on the mat at the door.↓ At
112.37 1, ↑nay↓ at
112.38 3 ↑long after Bagshot is gone to his committees, & little Cann to her pupils↓ a
112.41 Mrs. Ridle[y over r]! &
112.42 a [passage missing] with
113. 1 Thomas ↑otherwise↓ called
113. 5 lower ↑floor↓, and

113. 9 flapping ~~the tails of his robe~~ ↑his robe tails↓ poke

113.17 fourteen stone[) over ,]. Indeed

113.18 isn't ~~Bayham~~↑Fred↓ I'm

113.32 Lordship ↑& chaplain↓ being

113.37 that ↑in boyhoods breezy hour when was the delight of his school↓ you

113.40 the ~~mante~~ chimney

114. 8 Bayham. ~~He~~ ¶O

114.10 the sofa, as

114.11 with ~~villainous~~↑murderous↓ intent? ↑& ↑↑now↓↓ he advances in an approved offensive ↑↑attitude, & then↓↓↓ Caitiff

114.13 laugh, ~~and~~↑crying↓ Ha

114.19 of ~~jaloop~~ ↑coffee↓ in

114.21 Mrs. Ridle[y over r] for

114.23 kind fellow!—A[illeg.] ¶At

115. 3 the youth's— ↑eyes;—↓no other

115.14 youthful Divinity,: when

115.14 to ~~make~~ draw

115.19 Friars [H over h]ospital (It

115.20 a [C over c]ollege for

115.21 boys) ~~who~~↑and this old man↓ would

115.21 come ~~driv~~ sometimes

115.22 from ~~that~~↑the↓ hour

115.22 until ~~the eight~~↑nine↓ o'clock

115.27 schoolboys grumble↑.↓ ~~about ↑at↓~~ It

115.29 how [he over we] would

115.31 sent ~~him~~↑Clive↓ notes

116. 7 J? ~~says~~↑cries↓ Clive

116.10 any ~~lad~~↑young man↓ of

116.11 He ~~thought~~↑considered↓ there

116.15 gentlemen ~~mak~~↑bestow↓ rather

116.17 Newcome, ↑one of↓ the

116.18 yet ↑this↓ old

116.19 familiarly. ¶[illeg.]Mr. ~~Pendennis~~↑Honeyman is↓ at

116.20 home gentlem[e over a]n the

116.31 hearing ~~my~~ a

116.40 regions. ↑He is greatly excited↓ O

116.41 Sir [he over sa] says

116.43 you know↑—only↓ in

116.46 old ~~king~~↑cove↓! You

117. 1 horses [I over &] know

117.30 stairs! ~~he~~↑Clive↓ resumes,

117.32 clothes one— holding

117.39 says ↑Clive↓ cracking

117.39 laughter— ~~[illeg.]~~ Those

117.39 words. [A over I]nd inform

117.40 he sa[id over ys] he

117.42 knew ~~of Co~~ at

118. 1 manner. +I+ ~~believe that he was~~ ↑My landlord and landlady↓ were

118. 7 was hea↑r↓d at,

118. 8 the ~~owner~~↑occupant↓ of

118. 8 lodgings ~~made his appearance~~ ↑could say come in↓ Mr.

118.12 ribbon, ↑wh.↓ allowed

118.13 frock ~~coat~~ and

118.14 hat, ~~He↑&↓~~ looked ↑somewhat↓ like a ~~preacher of~~ Dissenting

118.16 turf ↑or the driving of coaches↓ was

119. 8 Pendennis look↑ed↓↓sur surprize

119.14 was ~~continuing~~ adopting

119.15 gentleman ~~did not~~↑by no means↓ relished.

119.27 like ~~humour~~↑fun↓ even

119.30 that ↑Mr. Bayham,↓ meant

119.30 nor ~~not~~any↓ man

119.36 dining ~~at our~~ with

119.38 took ~~my~~↑some↓ little

120. 1 larboard, ~~and~~ engaged↑ing↓ in

120. 1 and walk[ing over ed] a

120. 9 India Company[? over .] ~~FB↑I↓~~ would

120.10 useful: ~~and~~ genius

120.11 rewarded. ~~Lend me~~↑Here we↓ are.

120.24 dined ~~there~~ with

120.26 Governor [G over g]eneral himself

120.31 but—well, well—(~~the~~ no

120.31 was ↑accusing himself of↓ telling

120.36 wine; ~~an~~ Mr.

120.39 the Champagne↑, Sir!↓ ¶Champagne's

120.47 and ~~he~~ examines

121.11 was ~~Jack~~↑James↓! ejaculates

121.19 to arrive[. over :] There

121.n5 a [b over g]road brown

122. 7 were Scotchmen[. T over : t]hese were,

122. 9 ¶The Southron↑s↑, with one exception,↓ were

122.18 Square ↑& the Colonel↓ had

122.28 School ~~too~~ Sir

122.29 the boy[: over ;]—succeeded his
122.30 know ↑how↓ his
122.31 be ↑Rebecca,↓ Lady
122. 1 August 18[— over illeg.], and
123.10 and ~~brite~~↓ng me
123.n5 who ~~kept~~↑had been keeping↓ as
123.21 allowed ~~me to appear~~ poor
123.n6 in ~~shin[i over g]ng~~ kerseymere
124. 1 not FB↑'s↓, but CH↑'s↓, Charles
124.15 who ~~wait upon us and d~~↑do our work in stable or household↓ should
124.16 dressed ~~too~~ like
124.18 graciously ~~gives~~↑permits↓ to
124.19 his ↑extended↓ right
124.21 of ~~th~~ two
124.28 ¶The ~~weat~~ arrival
124.33 smiles scornfully[, over —] and
124.36 Colonel. [W over T]e have
124.39 ¶The ~~grandees~~ dinner
124.44 the ~~thir~~ second
125. 3 We ~~watch~~↑mark↓ Mr.
125. 6 chap. ~~He~~ That
125. 9 keeping ~~any man~~ every
125.11 done dinner[. over —] Barnes
125.13 people, ~~thinks he ↑thinks↓to~~+,+↑whispers↓ thinks
125.19 the ↑[illeg.]↓ way
125.25 drunk ~~w~~ bumpers
125.27 filled ~~by~~ scores
125.28 drink: ~~so has that~~ but
125.30 laughing ↑loudly↓ at
125.40 but ~~Sir~~ the
125.41 and ↑at↓ its
125.45 su-ah.' ~~Ba~~ The
125.45 wh. ~~he~~ with
126. 1 cheers, ~~had~~ and
126. 3 eyes ~~flashed~~ as
126. 5 at +Bay+ ~~to~~ Pendennis
126. 6 brooding ~~when~~ unless
126.12 of ↑Major General↓ Sir
126.16 Binnie ↑now↓ proposed
126.18 his ↑twine↓ glass
126.21 hearty ~~cooperation in~~↑sympathy↓ for
126.28 the ~~Major~~↑gallant↓ General
126.29 one ~~at~~ who
126.30 partaking ↑largely of the dainties on,↓ +of+ this
126.31 hospitality ~~hand~~ administers
127. 7 of ~~the~~ it, ~~Sir~~ he,

127. 9 part ~~y~~ just
127.11 General— ~~Will~~ You
127.12 friend ~~on~~ wh.
127.14 of Cockpen[. over —] Its
127.16 Cockpen ↑I am bound to say↓ without
127.20 know ~~what~~↑how↓ a
127.22 most ~~of us~~ amused.
127.24 a ~~stunning~~ song
127.25 F. Bayham[; over —]
~~that celebrated Chant of his~~↑wh. he sang with a↓ bass
127.26 envy—and ~~then~~ of
127.26 company— ~~Then it was the Colonel's own turn~~+.+↑The cry was then for the Colonel;↓ on
127.28 with ~~an~~ Something
127.28 oath ~~and saying↓~~↑crying O↓—I can't
127.29 this. ~~was making for the door~~ ¶Then
127.30 you! ~~cried~~ said young Clive, ↑with fury in his face.↓ If
127.38 that ~~F.~~↑Fred↓ Bayham
127.42 broke down,↑.↓ He
127.44 a ~~ero~~ sort
128. 6 my table[! over —] ¶I'd
128. 9 shouted ~~out~~ his
128.10 Bayham ~~at~~↑in↓ his
128.11 deepest voice[— over ;] Come
128.13 Fred, ~~this young~~↑looking↓ round
128.14 of society[— over .]he's not
128.16 Colonel; ↑including Sir Thomas de Boots who was highly energetic and delighted with Clives spirit↓ and
128.18 Colonel ~~putting~~ puffing
129. 1 be ~~aware↑conscious~~ aware↓ of
129. 3 to ~~be aware of↑~~behold↓ his
129. 3 his bed-foot,↑—↓a reproving
129. 4 waking. ↑¶↓'You drank
129. 7 Sir, ~~Yo~~ the
129. 9 the ~~boy~~↑lad↓ hardly
129.10 him. ↑O I've got such a headache!↓ ¶Serve
129.18 ¶Clive ~~rose and~~ obeyed
129.25 father— ~~H~~See, here's
130. 2 it, ↑& he laughed because he could not help it↓ If
130. 3 salt too[, over !] and
130. 5 cries [C over c]live still

130. 9 have ↑quite↓ borne ~~such~~↑that↓—
and people

130.11 acquaintance ~~doubted~~↑sneered
at↓ my

130.17 my [word omitted] ↑if we hope
forgiveness of our own. His
voice sank down as he spoke,
and he bowed his honest head
reverently— I have heard his
son tell the simple story years
afterwards with tears in his eyes.↓

[Begin Eyre Crowe's handwriting.]

130.21 ¶~~Park Lane~~@↑~~Piccadilly~~
↑@↓Piccadilly↓ was
Hyde-Park@↑.↓
~~@when Col Newcome always
familiar with sunrise, & Clive
with a dismal head ache, had
↑with↓ as dim perception of the
events of »last« the last night
as of the Park trees & houses
now before him,~~@↑As the pair↓
walked

130.24 day. ~~Polly,~~ The

130.24 the ~~door~~ steps~~, washing the trim
feet~~ of

130.31 two ~~boys~~↑sons↓, simpering

130.32 at ~~the~~↑a↓ time

130.36 hangs opposite~~,~~ his

130.37 harp: "We are

130.38 great sovereign[. T over ; t]he
chandelier

130.42 Sir Brian@↑'s↓@ ~~Newcome's~~
blue-books [A over a]n immense

130.43 the side-board~~,~~↑.↓ [T over t]wo
people

130.44 heard ~~across~~ across

131. 1 little [s over c]herry, silent,

131. 3 a ~~brisk little~~↑snug↓ parlor,

131. 5 where ~~two or three stealthy
footmen~~ a

131. 5 Major D~~u~~omo &

131. 7 presently, ~~why does~~↑wide as↓ the

131. 8 for ~~Sir Brian~~ the

131. 8 Newcome @~~Chronicle~~↑Sentinel↓,
old

131.13 aristocrat, ~~that~~ as

131.16 Barnes. ~~B~~Punctually as

131.17 father ~~the Baronet~~ will @↑he lie↓
yet for another hour[; t over .
T]he Baronet's

131.20 a ~~blush~~ faint

131.23 are ~~you~~ come

131.24 to breakfast@↑?↓ I

131.24 said, ~~pronouncing the words~~+,+
calling it "b@↑tw↓eak[f over
w]ast", &

131.30 & said:—"[T over t]he fact

131.30 I [don't over d'ont] know

131.38 thought ↑some of↓ your

131.43 Col. @↑who had been listening
with a queer expression of
wonder & doubt on his face,↓
here

131.44 interrupted @~~him~~↑Mr. Barnes↓,
"It

131.44 Clive that@↑—that↓ spilled

132.n5 wh. ~~made the C~~ caused

132.11 coat @&↑when↓ that

132.12 or explanations+.+↑~~Of what use~~
&

132.12 his talk.—"@↑The other night↓
You

132.14 old @~~man~~↑wretch↓ had

132.14 himself. @~~The bottle~~ ↑Wine↓ has

132.18 practises, @~~& beseeches you to
beware~~ ↑& beseeches you to
beware of the bottle.↓¶ After

[Begin Thackeray's handwriting.]

132.19 Colonel ~~thought to~~ ↑farther↓
improved

132.21 the brawls, and

132.22 foolish ~~words~~ ↑speech↓ over

132.22 how ↑the had known↓ widows

132.23 orphans ~~had been~~ made

132.24 truest ~~courage~~ ↑honour↓ was

[Begin Anne's handwriting.]

132.28 effect @↑wh.↓ he

132.32 Colonel, ~~laughed smiled~~ @↑were
amused↓ often

132.32 his ~~simple~~@↑naive↓ opinions

132.33 Clive w[illeg.] had

132.34 humour ~~& this perpetually
smiled~~ ↑wh. played perpetually↓
round his fathers ~~simplicity~~
simple

132.n9 elder's ~~of~~ 50

132.n9 attained. ~~The~~ ↑Clive's with his↓
young

132.n9 began ~~to have or~~ to

132.n9 his @~~simple sire never Doubted.~~
↑artless sire never doubted the
value.↓ In truth @~~he~~ ↑Thomas
Newcome↓ was

132.n9 the @~~ways~~ ↑understanding↓ of

132.n9 you ↑rather↓ have

132.n9 trustful? [B over b]etween this

133. 1 of wit; lay,
133. 5 page, @↑may those who come after you so regard you!↓ Generous ~~youth~~ ↑Boy↓ who
133. 9 remember! [Break a line.] ¶Some ~~two or three~~ ↑four or five↓ weeks
133.11 kinsman, & ↑on↓ the
133.n1 Newcome [& over in] Park
133.11 chief ~~whole~~ ↑part of Sir Brian Newcome's↓ family
133.13 of @8 ↑eight↓:— (unless
133.14 nursery ~~was~~ ↑were↓ now
133.16 was ↑a↓ Thursday
133.17 Newcome ~~Examiner~~ ↑Independent↓ &
133.n2 the ~~family~~ ↑domestic↓ duties
133.n2 regularity. @~~The~~ ↑A↓ public
133.20 all pour~~ed~~ into
133.n3 neighbours @~~who~~ ↑whose masters↓ had
133.n3 daughter was@~~nt~~ ↑ not↓ out
133.n3 before midnight[. B over , b]ut when
133.n3 day. ↑ ¶↓I do
133.22 which, ↑at↓ that
133.22 chiming @+8+↑eight↓ o'clock
133.23 the house~~hold~~hold is
133.23 is ~~assembled~~ ↑called↓ together.
133.24 book ~~the~~ ↑for↓ three
133.25 measured cadence[: t over T]he members
133.26 in ↑an↓ attitude
133.26 decent reverence[: over ,] the
133.26 the ~~little~~ ↑younger↓ children
133.27 mothers ~~knees~~ knees:
133.30 side board@,: the
133.32 act @[at over in] wh.
133.32 are assembled[:— over ,]it is
134. 1 day @~~& ↑the↓ «e»very~~ @↑and what it brings. At the very↓ instant
134. 2 shut, @~~the~~ @↑world begins again, and for the next twenty three hours and fifty seven minutes all that ~~house are~~ ↑↑household is↓↓ given up to it. The↓ servile
134. 5 those @~~hulking menials~~ ↑tall gentlemen↓ at
134. 6 forth @~~the~~ ↑with↓ flower
134. 7 coats @↑silver lace↓ buckles
134.11 monstrous mas@[ke over

ca]rade. @~~We~~ ↑You↓ know
134.11 race ~~that~~ ↑wh.↓ inhabits
134.15 high fashion@↑ & a great establishment)↓+)+ you
134.18 course @~~see~~ ↑order↓ that
134.19 not unkind[. over:] You~~r~~ are
134.20 kitchen ~~wh~~ or
134.21 would @↑do little good and only↓ bore
134.24 know whence@+,+↑:↓ they
134.25 vice verse ↑a↓. They
134.26 coals, [f over F]or exactly
134.27 the servants↑—↓& masters↑— ↓over, the
134.28 the @~~right~~ ↑rite↓ called
134.29 who ↑warm the newspapers↓ administer
134.30 & ~~carry about~~ ↑serve out↓ the
134.32 Lady ~~Asks~~ ↑nne,↓ asks
134.33 If @~~she's~~ ↑ is↓ ill
134.34 too goodnatured—She@~~s~~ ↑ is↓ always
134.35 morning [P over p]ost &
134.36 at ~~Mrs. Bruno's~~ @↑Baroness Bosco's↓ ball
134.37 Toddle Tompkyns@↑'s↓ soirée dansante
134.37 in Belgra[v over y]e square.
134.38 there ~~Mrs~~ ↑says↓ Barnes
134.38 paper. ~~But whose~~ But @whose ↑ is↓ Mrs.
134.39 asks Mam@↑m↓a Who
134.42 really @~~devilish~~ ↑doosed↓ well
134.43 & I@~~m~~ ↑ am↓ told
135. 1 asks Ethel.~~?~~ ¶Me
135. 3 & @↑when↓ the
135. 6 Father @~~laid down~~ ↑looked up↓ his
135. 7 ungenteel.¶~~Just listen sir says Barnes & began to read from the Newcome Chronicle.~~ My
135. 9 Barnes. You[are over r] always
135.26 know ~~her~~ ↑f Clives
135.34 Brian ↑ ¶↓She was
135.40 the paper@[, over .]~~By~~ ↑ by↓ Jove. @↑And↓ Mr.
135.44 her @↑honest↓face &
135.45 Mr. Barnes—@~~His~~ ↑his↓ voice
136. 3 & ↑younger↓ "brother
136. 8 Elderly [R over r]elative who
136.10 I ~~rather~~ wish

136.13 as [he is over hes] a
136.14 of @↑the↓ people
136.15 the @~~Examiner~~ ↑Independent↓ says,
136.16 and @↑the↓ began
136.17 "Mr. @~~Examiner~~ ↑Independent↓. I
136.18 of @[Everybody & Everything over Everything & Everybody] wh.
136.19 a [B over b]riton &
136.20 native boro[ugh: over '] if
136.21 representative ~~sir~~ ↑Don↓ Pomposo
136.25 know sel@~~tled~~ ↑dom↓ favours
136.27 Our manufactur[ies over er] make
136.32 its [Fid over Vi]dler the Apothecary. [B over b]y heaven
136.33 Miss [V over F]iddlers to
136.40 names @↑cries Ethel↓ out
136.42 think it@s ↑ is↓ like
136.42 Barnes @~~willing~~ ↑perhaps willing↓ to
136.43 that @~~scoundrel~~ ↑villain↓ Duff ↑the baker↓ who
136.44 about us, at
[Begin Thackeray's handwriting.]
136.46 moment ~~has~~ favored
137. 7 N——. ¶~~Much as I~~ The
137. 7 youth ↑has↓ taken
137.14 family ~~inhabit~~ have
137.14 years ~~with~~ for
137.16 time; ↑&↓ has
137.21 Mr. ~~Sentinel~~ ↑Independent↓ Your
139. 1 above ~~extract~~ letter
[Begin Anne's handwriting.]
139. 7 Liverpool ↑Mail↓ whence
139.14 spirits [B over b]esides, had
139.15 That ↑a↓ swift
139.19 could @~~about~~ ↑gather, regarding↓ the
139.20 goodhumour @↑& interest.↓ ¶It
139.23 anyone ~~who~~ caring
139.25 traveller.¶ ~~Min~~ Mine
139.26 Kings [A over a]rms, Mr.
139.31 fashioned cordial[l]ity the
140. 1 Colonel ~~wh~~ would
140. 2 to ~~inform~~ ↑say to↓ him
140. 5 you ~~for~~ to
140. 9 visited ~~a~~ ↑&↓ alarm@↑ting↓ accounts

140.12 Mrs. ↑Sarah↓ Mason
140.16 politics? ~~Mrs.~~ Taplow's
140.17 Taplow's ~~was~~ ↑twine↓ knew
140.18 Newcome use~~d~~ the
140.19 & pass~~ed~~ numberless
140.24 the @~~sentinel~~ ↑Independent↓ form ↑@are↓@↑were↓ pretty
140.25 over ~~↑and Colonel Newcomes dinner was not over↓~~ before
140.30 jolly [B over b]ritons thought
140.35 Sir ~~Thomas's~~ ↑Brian's↓ agent
140.36 Dr. ~~Bowders~~ ↑Bulders↓ the
140.n6 card. ↑It ↓↑will be
141. 6 memory ↑had ever↓ clung
141.14 eyes, ~~that~~ ↑of↓ the
141.15 the ~~Careworn [illeg.]~~ ↑veteran↓ before
141.15 So ~~and~~ ↑for↓ near
141.17 night where~~v~~ ever
141.21 heaven ↑in↓ it
141.21 rejoice & ↑@to↓@↑in it &↓ admire
142.26 envious ~~Bugsby~~ ↑Gawler↓ scowling
142.31 than ~~Bugbys~~ ↑Gawler's↓. [W over w]hilst this
142.31 execrating ~~be~~ yet
142.38 lodged Colonels Newcome's
142.45 her ↑great↓ brooch
142.46 the @~~towers~~ ↑Taj Taj↓ of
142.46 bracelet (@↑she used to say,↓ 'I
143. 4 had achieved@↑!↓ [B over b]efore Colonel
143. 6 not ~~Betty on the look-out~~ the
143. 7 Mr. ~~Kuhm~~ ↑n↓ the
143.10 her mistress['s over es] door?
143.18 Elephants backs& George
143.n2 another ~~aged~~ ↑aging↓ woman,
143.n2 May ~~allsuch~~ ↑those↓ of
143.n2 liberally ↑be able to↓@~~count~~ ↑count↓ such
143.n2 misfortune, @& ↑or↓ a
143.n2 cruise replenished! ↑.↓¶ Miss
143.23 of coo~~e~~kery And
143.23 over ~~there~~ came
143.24 appeared ~~one~~ ↑a
143.25 little ~~tw~~trowsers long
143.29 Hannah ~~grimm~~ ↑nn↓ing acted
143.31 Ma'am" ~~&~~ ↑bobbing a↓ curtsey~~ing~~ &

143.31 & ↑giving a knowing nod to
       Master Clive as she↓ smooth[ed
       over ing] her
143.41 to illustrate ↑depict↓ the
143.42 whether ↑even↓ the
[Begin Thackeray's handwriting.]
144.n5 and loving ↑charitable;↓ the
144.n5 Love? It makes a plain face look
       beautiful+:+ it
144.n5 a feast: ↑—↓it causes
144.n5 look beautiful—if ↑as↓ our
144. 8 to shut his eyes and ↑let his
       fancy↓ paint
144. 8 for himself ↑itself↓ the
144.10 expressed in Thomas Newcomes
       ↑upon the Colonels↓ kind
144.16 brown palm[, over ;] where
146. 5 learn his ↑those↓ fine
146. 5 fine adm manners,
146. 5 manners, that ↑wh.↓ all
146. 6 him?— A ↑He had a↓ natural
146. 6 simplicity; and habitual
146. 8 and affectation—
       and no doubt+,+↑perhaps↓
       those
146. 9 had given imparted
146.11 uncle, and that
146.13 is perfectadorable. I
146.14 of your ↑my↓ grandfather,
146.17 man ↑Uncle Hod[s over [illeg]],
       & your↓ your
146.17 Papa and Uncle have
146.18 bear! I repeat Mr.
146.18 has ↑himself↓ the
146.19 is far perfect.
146.20 distinguished ↑air:↓+:+ but
146.21 are honest ↑honorable:↓ the
146.23 Papa. When we go ↑At once I
       pronounce↓ Colonel
146.23 Newcome to be a
146.26 his brothers ↑family↓ have
146.35 and they are ↑are↓ starving
146.36 of her ↑Fanny's↓ boys
146.36 the Blue↓coat School!
146.42 jaunes. seriu[?]—I could
146.43 see her ↑the child↓. I
146.46 my ↑darling!↓ Those
147. 3 Mr. [Smee over blank] saw
147. 4 some ↑in Park Lane↓ and
147. 6 to say—Good night my child.
       ↑and Doctor Belper said, my↓
       dear

147. 7 Lady Pagoda ↑Walham↓ (it
147.10 Colonel [illeg.] from
147.11 floated sky-wards+,+↑in the air,↓
       he
147.17 little ha white
147.17 is! [W over S]hen she
147.n2 must [& over .] I'll get perhaps
148.15 anything ↑or wear anything↓
       unusual.
148.20 us, ↑in↓ one
149. 1 Newcome Chr Examiner
       ↑Independent↓, and
[Begin Anne's handwriting.]
149.n1 with children[;— over ,]
       purchasing their
149.n1 by every ↑all↓ sorts
149. 5 to Astleys? but
149. 6 I think he was ↑saw↓ him
149. 9 was amas ↑z↓ed be ↑—↓amazed
       by
149.10 actor @↑to↓ the
149.15 wh. ↑belonged to↓ their
149.16 was not in
149.n3 watch ↑the↓ tenderness
149.21 & @eat ↑ate↓ an
149.21 perfect @gravity ↑satisfaction↓. I
149.n4 that Colonels Newcomes
149.n4 Ethel we well have
150.n4 have @written reams ↑covered
       quires↓ of
150.n4 She @presented ↑endowed↓ him
150.n4 She learn[ed over t] to
150.n4 make @him ↑Uncle Newcome↓ a
149.25 Clive gat↓lopped over
150. 1 over there+,+ to
150. 2 of ↑a↓ school
150. 2 is remembered ↑recalled↓ by
150. 6 very @1st ↑first↓ free
150. 8 Park Lane@[; over .] @B ↑b↓ut
       Mrs.
150.11 their holidays & & made
       ↑caused ↓them ↑to↓ @↑them
       ruefully↓ ruefully pay ↑to give↓
       back
150.12 gold soverie ↑ei↓++gn++ with
150.n7 made @them begin ↑both uncle
       and nephews↓ fine
150.n7 elder that ↑of↓ the
150.18 other households. I
150.19 beloved ones[. T over , t]hey
       want

150.20 every [comfort over elegance], with

150.20 every [elegance over comfort], with

150.22 provided? for↑?+ I

150.23 money. [M over m]ind, I

150.25 father wh &

150.25 & @sixpence ↑a shilling↓ a

150.26 rational amusements:; I

150.30 in Albermarle street.

151. 5 way. And W ¶And

151. 6 exclaimed lady ↑laying↓ a

151. 7 heart ["over [illeg.]]why did

151. 8 loco p[a over e]rentis,' because

151.22 with a her

151.n1 simplicity; continually feeling &

151.n1 & uttering the most ↑imbued with the most↓ virtuous

151.n1 benefit ↑of↓ others.

151.n1 so sel seldom

151.n1 went @there ↑thither↓ oftener

151.n1 of all almost

151.n1 the play;-of ↑—Of↓ course,

151.n1 unfortunate we weakness

151.n1 out pood ↑poor↓ dear

151.n1 him. WVery likely

151.n1 with ceremonte↓y &

151.n1 but percieve percieve

151.27 dinner @↑His Excellency the Persian Ambassador & Bucksheesh Bey↓ the

151.27 Honble. Canon ↑Cannon↓ Rowe

151.28 board o[f over n] Controle

151.28 Controle @Mrs. ↑Lady Louisa↓ Rowe,

152. 3 of makeinging. "The

152. 9 old [L over l]ady Wormly

152.11 between Profre Professor

152.11 Dr. Regis ↑Windus↓. That

152.23 that. @↑I ain't a superior man.↓ I'm a

152.24 as your are

152.33 had a[n over m] imperfect

152.36 Jove! cries exclaims

152.n2 good @Horse ↑horse↓, &

152.40 know shes is

152.41 Brian's back's is

153.n5 stone front[ed over ing], roomy,

153.n5 mansion. ¶[Compositor Snowsill] The

153. 4 Madame [Lat over la T]our's brass

153. 7 & ↑garlands &↓ the

153. 8 a carriage large

153.11 Sherrick: [t overT]hat Mr.

153.12 whose name wine

153.18 great trag[e over i]dian. I

153.19 Mr. [blank] of

153.20 St. Joh[illeg.] ↑n↓s Wood

153.n9 dinner music@↑,↓ @& the professionals «was» declared that Colonel Newcomes singing of Dibdens ballads was exquisite @↑though the Colonel steadfastly refused to sing↓. Clive

153.n9 friend [D over R]igby finding

153.28 Sherrick stopped ↑ocked↓ their

154. 2 you deat dea@t ↑lt↓ with

154. 6 in ↑the↓ inspection

Note: [A portion of manuscript originally intended to follow here in installment 5, was moved to installment 6, at pages 172–173.]

154. 9 four of fir or

154. 9 Keane ↑for↓ the

154.14 & Skidan Schidan.

154.n2 for ye those

154.n2 Newcome ↑speedily↓ ripened

154.n2 a he sincere

154.n2 regard [I over S] held

154.19 great f[ort over [illeg.]] decidedly

154.23 and plump ↑jolly↓ little

154.25 he says no

154.28 Gandishes ↑drawing↓ academy

[Begin Thackeray's handwriting.]

155. 1 ¶As if Art found ↑Amidst the faded regions of Soho, where the ↑↑British art either finds↓↓↓ its

155. 3 and love[s over d] to

155. 3 to set up ↑fix↓ its

155. 8 callings. ↑Some of ↓[t over T]he most

155. 8 dismal streets ↑quarters↓ of

155.13 when ↑ladies'↓ chair

155.16 marked ↑the artists invasion of those regions once devoted to Fashion & gaiety?↓ [C over c]entre windows

155.20 up in tothe ↑into↓ bed-rooms— bed

155.25 decadence when after

155.25 the Fashionable works Chooses

155.26 Soho ↑& Bloomsbury↓ let
156. 1 Square, ~~Doctors~~ ↑Physicians↓ come
156. 2 the ~~brass~~ ↑knockers &↓ plates
156. 5 Ladyship ~~There comes~~[A over a] boarding-house
156. 9 heart. ~~If~~Why should
156.10 and ~~an~~ a
156.12 is ~~a~~ only
156.12 He ~~cannt~~ cannot
156.13 costume ~~as~~ naturally
156.14 Dick ~~is a goo~~ under
156.15 and ~~dark~~ ↑shadowy↓ sombrero
156.17 whiskers ↑penny-velvet↓ and
156.19 wh., ~~if~~ ↑being↓ removed,
156.20 poet ~~revolving great thoughts in solitude~~ ↑avoiding mankind for the nobler company of his own great thoughts↓, but
156.21 has a↑n↓ ↓knack↑ ↑aptitude↓ for ~~copying~~ painting brocade+s+↑-gowns↓ and
156.26 merry-makings [and over f] all
156.28 yataghans, ~~and~~ toast
156.28 their ~~toledoes~~+;+~~they~~ ↑rapiers; and↓ fill
156.29 and half, ↑:↓ [I over i]f they
157. 4 different ~~faces~~ ↑phases↓, avers
157. 4 as [an over the] art student ~~abroad~~ at
157. 5 pleasantest ~~of~~ part
157. 7 the ~~report short-hand~~ ↑accurate↓ report
157.12 profession ↑wh.↓ he
157.12 follow. ↑As regarded mathematical & classical learning↓ The
157.18 all ~~hands~~ ↑eyes↓: ~~all~~ ↑were not all↓ his
157.19 draw ~~him~~ Grindley ~~with~~ instinctively
[Begin Anne's handwriting.]
157.25 that ~~great~~ ↑well known↓ portrait
157.26 recommended Gandishe ↑'↓s to
157.28 cousins; ~~&~~ he
157.32 creature, devel↑l↓op her
157.34 drew ~~Arthur~~ Alfred ~~in~~ ↑&↓ the
157.34 Blenheim Spani~~ards~~ ↑els↓ Mr. ~~Coombe~~ ↑Kuhn↓ with his Ear↑r↓↓ings, the
158. 1 the coals[c over k]uttle; the
158. 4 force ~~in~~ & ~~de~~ individual↑l↓ity there
158. 5 Jove capital[! over ,] ↑& Alfred

on his poney↓ &
158. 7 Landseer." ~~&~~ ↑And↓ the courtley artist ~~carefully~~ ↑daintily↓ envel↑l↓oped the
158.13 his hair[! over ,] such
158.13 a days!—@~~&~~ ↑And↓ the
158.14 Colonel too!—@~~If~~ ↑if↓ the
158.17 hideous vermil↑l↓ion uniforms
158.19 in ~~Kype~~ Cuyp's
158.22 flaring [D over d]eputt↑y↓↓[an over y] Lieutenants uniform ~~way-laying~~ ↑entreating↓ all
158.26 frame ~~of~~ ↑&↓ the the picture[. B over , b]ut no
158.31 eyes ~~and said~~ ↑saying↓ his
158.31 that did@~~nt~~ not
158.34 old hum~~buy~~ ↑-bugg↓ in
158.35 not al↑l↓together incorrect.
158.36 Colonel's @~~table~~ ↑house↓ were @↑also↓ somewhat
158.38 as @~~naturally as he painted~~ ↑methodically as he covered↓ his
158.39 he @~~invaded~~ ↑inveigled↓ unsuspecting
159. 2 beheld Major-Gen.↑It↓ Sir Thomas [de over B] Boots
159. 3 door ~~into~~ his
159. 4 & hurra[y over h]ed Sir
159. 5 sat @↑arrayed in gold and scarlet↓ in
159. 6 blushed ~~pup~~ purple
159. 6 beheld us@↑: no artist would have dared to imitate those ~~purple~~ ↑↑violet↓↓ tones:↓ he
159. 7 the ~~Numberless «pictures»~~ ↑victims↓ ~~of Mr. Smee. ¶How be it, T↑t↓the Colonel took Smees advice and sent his son to Gandish['over e]s whether also ↑as has been said↓ at the boys friendly suggestion his good father procured admission for young Ri«gby»↑dley↓, Clive's friend & companion~~ @↑numberless victims of Mr. Smee.↓ ¶One
[Begin Thackeray's handwriting.]
159. 8 then ↑day to be noted with a white stone,↓ Colonel
159.10 who ~~has~~ ↑was↓ perfect
159.12 the ~~queer~~ interview
159.12 that Professor[— over .]By Jove

159.14 art student[— over !]you'll find

159.14 there—Gandish ~~says~~ calls

159.16 he ~~pulled~~ ↑brought↓ out

160. 2 days; ~~You should~~ ↑and turned↓ out

160. 4 the ~~three~~ Mrs.

160.11 Gandish [(over —]wouldn't he

160.15 hit Boadish[ia over y]. ¶It

160.16 young man—~~three~~ ↑four↓ year

160.17 there's ↑good↓ pints

161. 2 own room—~~High~~Igh Art

161. 4 Art ~~says~~ ↑whispers↓ old

161. 7 right ↑of the picture,↓ very

161. 9 Art. ↑says Gandish.↓ The

161.12 Boadishia Colonel? ↑:↓ with

161.n6 the [blank] ~~Roman~~ ↑British↓ Queen.

161.n6 he ~~burst~~ ↑broke↓ into

161.22 ladies—but ~~you~~ Gandish

161.25 you. ¶~~My son, His~~not ↑Admired but↓ I

161.31 strong! ~~My~~ But

162. 2 three ↑years↓ of

162. 4 Gandish ~~cries~~ says

162.12 Gandish ~~in~~ ↑study↓ the

162.15 from ↑also↓ English

162.19 Alfred [a over h]nging up

162.25 majesty ~~&~~ ↑mingled with↓ meekness—In

162.27 are defeated[. T over , t]he daylight

163. 2 the ↑glorious↓ Venus

163.12 his name[? over —]—I told

163.13 for [illeg.] J.J.

163.16 Newcome. [illeg.] Assiduity

163.19 work ↑on wh.↓ I

163.26 rogue ↑ever↓ tell

163.26 what ~~that~~ ↑Gandish's↓ curtained

[Begin Anne's handwriting.]

163.30 his ~~seat~~ humble

163.32 almost d[e over i]fformed. He

163.34 with ~~a cock~~ ↑this father↓ &

164.n6 as aide@↑s↓ ↑de↓ camp@s on

164.n6 first day@↑;↓ Mr.

164. 7 to Gandish@↑'↓[s over e]s door

164.10 the [P over p]rofessor of

164.14 at Gandish@↑'↓[s over e]s@[. B over b]esides he

164.16 haired Scot@↑c↓h student

164.16 Sandy ~~Collops~~ ↑McCollop↓ had

165. 1 of Joh[n over es] James,

165. 1 of ~~Samuel~~ ↑Sandy↓ wh.

165. 5 Clive ~~invited~~+Mr+~~Collops~~ ↑pulled off his coat in an instant invited Mr. McCollop↓ into

165. 6 wh. ~~he required~~ ↑Clive himself had acquired↓ at

165. 8 the ~~la«y»ocoon~~ ↑[L over l]att o↓↓coon↓ wh.

165.10 Clives [b over B]rilliant opening

165.11 But [P over p]rofessor Gandish

165.13 Mr. ~~Collops~~ ↑Mc.Collop↓. The

165.16 Mr. ~~Collops @↑McOllop↓~~ @↑Mc.Collop↓ as

165.18 of [F over f]ield (painted

165.18 (painted ~~by~~ ↑for↓ Mc.Collop

165.19 of Mc~~OCO~~llop) of

165.26 the ~~Douglass dying among the Spanish Moors~~ ↑young Duke of Roths[ay over ea] starving in prison↓ ¶During

165.30 at Gandish↑'↓[s over e]s &

166. 1 jolly @↑young↓ King

[Begin Thackeray's handwriting.]

166. 9 from it↑.↓~~, that~~ The

167. 6 and ↑have↓ put

167. 8 is ↑in truth↓ as

167.12 drinks ~~in~~ ↑from↓ her

167.16 imp ~~of mischief Charley~~ ↑Harry↓ Hooker

167.20 who ~~fetched~~ ↑ran on all↓ the

167.21 and ~~ginger-beer~~ ↑walnuts.↓ ~~When~~ Clive

167.22 first ~~saw~~ ↑beheld↓ these

167.28 man ~~actu~~ (who

167.29 brought ~~a~~ cocoa-nut↑s↓, and

167.30 sold ~~it~~ ↑them↓ at

167.30 the ~~young~~ ↑lads.↓ His

168. 1 Studio, ~~both started~~ ↑seemed each disturbed↓ at

168. 6 way: ~~he said~~ ↑saying↓ 'Step

168. 7 idto ~~to~~ Vorder

168. 7 &c.') ~~This~~ This

168. 7 gentleman ~~had~~ ↑could get↓ tickets

168. 8 for ~~most~~ ↑almost all the↓ theatres,

168. 8 gave ~~brilliant~~ ↑splendid↓ accounts

168.12 midshipman. ~~When this nice young man «offered» ↑tried↓ to tempt~~ ↑Once Clive bought a half dozen of↓ theatre-tickets

168.14 the studio—[b over B]ut when

168.20 the Juniors ↑younger pupils↓, whose

168.27 by litho his

168.27 lithograph heads ↑vignettes↓ for

168.28 scanty produce ↑remuneration↓ of

168.29 the hungry ↑lonely↓ Senior

168.31 studio ↑enjoyed↓, I

168.33 compassion, ↑and he sought, and no doubt found means of feeding Chivers without offending his testy independence.↓ ¶Nigh

168.35 is an rival ↑another↓ establishment

168.36 design—Barkers; where there was [illeg.] the ↑wh. had the↓ additional

168.36 Life ↑& Costume↓ Academy;

169. 2 emulation within and

169. 2 doors. TheGandish sent

169. 4 last ↑R.A↓ Student

169.11 Barkerites had ↑were having↓ the

169.12 playing. But a very few months Fred

169.20 as ↑Prince↓ Edward

169.29 was ↑most↓ edifying

169.32 had taken their ↑entered↓ at

169.33 That ↑silent↓ young

170. 1 Clive, ↑if↓ he

170. 7 the ↑young↓ conqueror

[Begin Anne's handwriting.]

170.14 Gandish Jr.@↑Junior↓ possibly

170.17 some ↑very↓ ill

170.19 McOllop drew ↑devised↓ a

170.19 picture in wh. ↑wherein↓ the

170.22 Bean Mc@↑C↓Ollop Chief

170.22 name +&+ his astonishment at beholding for the first time descending

170.23 mountains @↑into Edinburgh↓ &

170.25 of Gandish['s over e]s studio.

170.29 Hebrew ↑artist↓ from

170.30 from Doer@↑Wardour↓ Street

170.32 hideous henhunch back

170.33 & vouvowed that

170.33 a defformity ¶Our

170.36 life @↑that↓ ↑wh.↓ he

170.37 keep ↑served to↓ increased certain ↑some↓ original

170.39 his ennemies not

170.42 he vows ↑avers↓ would

170.43 he wasnt ↑ not↓ sent

170.43 to Colle[g over d]e, where

170.43 man acquires @↑receives↓ no

170.44 he +gets+ @↑acquires↓ that

170.44 his betters ↑equals↓ in

171. 4 his Fathers ↑family's↓ rank

171. 5 who who would

171. 6 vied @↑with↓ each

171. 8 disposition led [Vertical and overwritten in margin: And imperious] him

171.12 generally not ↑only↓ venturing

171.13 sight or& of

171.15 home every ↑every↓ day

171.15 day at ↑shortly after↓ noon

171.15 when @↑his worthy Father ↑the was↓ supposed

171.16 supposed @that the lad betook ↑to betake↓ himself

171.16 to Gandish['s over e]s studio@[: over ,] but

171.17 when @supposed to be ↑his father thought he was↓ so

171.18 was @not seldom ↑sometimes↓ vacant.

171.19 the sad steady

171.20 his comrades ↑patrons↓ absen[c over s]e and

171.20 and ge no

171.23 regarding th[e over is] ↑[illeg.]↓ shortcoming↑s↓ of

171.23 the @young ↑youthful↓ s[c over k]ape grace.

[Begin Thackeray's handwriting.]

171.23 grace. The [C over c]andid reader↑s↓ may

171.24 heard To his ↑their↓ friend

171.25 her dear boy ↑darling↓ was

171.27 books ↑wh. cost such an immense sum of money↓) should

171.29 such a worldly-wise ↑acute↓ person↑s↓ a

171.29 sufficient regarding to

171.29 indicate ↑young↓ Mr.

171.32 his Son ↑boy↓ was

171.32 was a paragon of ↑the best of↓ boys.

171.34 a nice youth. ↑paragon.↓ I

171.36 Wardour Street[; over —] Two

171.37 probably ↑young↓ old

171.37 concluded ↑for the day↓ the

171.38 the bag~~for the day~~, joined
171.40 family." ¶[This deletion at
the top of a page actually
follows 166.4, above, everything
in between constituting
an extended insertion.]
~~he saw that his presence~~
~~≪acted as a≫ ↑rather↓~~
~~silenced the young men;~~
~~and left them to themselves~~
~~confiding in Clive's parole; and~~
~~went to play his honest~~
~~rubber at the Club; and~~
~~heard the young fellow≪'≫s↑'↓~~
~~steps ↑on their departure↓ many~~
~~a time tramping by his~~
~~bed-room door, as he lay within,~~
~~happy to think that his Son was~~
~~happy.~~ ¶~~The~~ ↑Our good Colonel
↑↑who↓↓ was one of the most
hospitable men alive, loved
to have his friends constantly
around him; and it must be
confessed that the↓ evening-
parties

Note Text corresponding to 172.1–
173.18 was originally intended
for installment 5 (at page 154.8).

172. 8 passages, ↑a↓ cracked
172.16 way. ~~A cart load of tables,~~ ↑One
day↓ a
172.17 a ~~cartload of tables~~ ↑waggon
waggon↓ full
172.25 soldier. ~~Mr. Binnie~~ But
172.26 as ~~bug~~ big
172.26 tent ~~&~~ a
172.26 glass ~~(whereas the~~
172.28 Stephens breeches~~)~~ and
172.29 of ~~hi~~ the
173. 2 And Clives had
173.15 not ~~coming~~ ↑invited↓ &
173.20 were ↑composed↓ of
173.22 from ~~the Club~~ Hanover
173.23 ages ~~in~~ with
173.23 costume; ↑now and again↓ a
173.26 these ~~assemblies~~
↑entertainments↓. The
174. 1 Waltzing ~~wa~~ had
174.17 of ↑artists↓ Mr.
174.17 up, ~~to the~~ with
175. 5 own insignificance[— over .]
Without I
175. 6 character, ~~I have yet~~ nay
175. 8 on ~~not~~ ↑scarce↓ one
175.10 with ~~his~~ the

175.14 Great Gandish~~?~~ ↑.↓
¶~~AnHe~~Indeed I
175.21 in 180[blank]: but
175.21 but ~~the~~ Lord
175.21 occupied th[e over at] public
175.26 in ~~light~~ sea
175.31 Gandish ↑has↓ told
175.31 told ~~in after~~ me
175.32 day ~~after~~ ↑at↓ dinner.
175.35 wicked wit[! over —]—But when
175.38 fine. ~~The W~~Mr. Pendennis
176. 1 show it's capabilities.'
[Begin Anne's handwriting.]
176. 3 Newcomes dinner↑-↓table. Mr.
176.10 a @↑court↓ ball
176.13 bidden ↑were↓ obliged
176.14 commenced ~~for~~ ↑from↓ wh.
176.14 wh. Lad[y over ey] Anne
176.22 he? (Courtley Mr.
176.25 young ~~wretch~~ wicked
176.26 as @↑s↓he admired
176.28 that cordia~~l~~lity so
176.31 so different@↑t!'↓ in
176.32 I suppose@↑?↓ Now
176.33 fan) [D over d]id I
176.36 come ¶~~My Husband~~ I
176.37 Anne ~~There~~ ↑[illeg.]↓ There↓ are
176.40 husband c[a over o]me from
177. 2 you @↑cries Mr. Hodson↓ I
177. 3 in @~~A~~ ↑the↓ hayfield
177. 9 Major M'@~~Krackin~~ ↑Cracken↓
are
177. 9 and @~~the~~ ↑then in↓ Diamonds
177.11 not ~~in his de~~ quite
177.13 the ~~seams~~ ↑seam[s over e]s↓.
Clive
177.13 wonder @↑E↓& delight
177.14 fresh ~~silks~~ brocades,
177.21 The @~~Chiné~~ ↑sheeny,↓ white
177.23 its ~~covet~~ covert? @↑That
foot light as it is crushes
Mrs. Newcome↓
@~~that foot light as it is,~~
@~~↑crushes Mrs. Newcome.↓~~
@↑No wonder she↓ winces
177.26 in ~~that~~ ↑the↓ state
177.26 sometimes +↑Mr.↓+ are
177.29 those convo@~~qued~~ ↑ked↓ to
177.31 Gandishes @~~came~~ ↑arrived↓ first,
177.37 fan ~~by~~ ↑at↓ the

178. 2 & @↑leaning↓ on
178. 5 soirée ~~Did y~~ Who
178. 6 Dinner? ~~¶Your Mot Lady Anne~~
     You
178. 6 had @~~my Ma~~ ↑my Mamma↓ &
178. 7 for they~~re~~ ↑ are↓ down
178. 8 carriage. He~~s~~ ↑ is↓ asleep
178. 8 asleep she~~s~~ ↑ is↓ as
[Begin Thackeray's handwriting.]
178.13 to ~~[illeg.]~~ me?.
178.16 of drink[— over ,]delightful boy.
178.16 boy. ~~Do you know Kew that the~~
     ↑See yonder! the young fellow is
     in conversation with his↓ most
178.17 intimate friend~~that fellow [illeg],~~
     ↑a little crooked fellow, with long
     hair. Do you know who he is?
     He↓ is
178.21 son: ↑Wh~~at~~ ↑to↓↓ can be more
     respectable than a butler?↓ When
178.22 I ↑humbly↓ hope
178.24 they would~~n't~~ ↑ not↓ look
178.24 any ↑average↓ ten
178.25 at ~~the First~~ Lord
178.27 I ~~always~~ fancy
178.27 the sideboard↑.↓ ~~or see~~ Here
     comes ~~Ga~~ that
178.29 sweetest smile—~~In~~ ↑With↓ his
     rings ↑diamond↓ shirt
178.32 would ↑ever↓ have
178.37 How ~~do~~ ↑are↓ you ~~do~~ Mr.
179. 2 reckonized ↑by your Lordship↓
     in
179. 2 house; ~~by~~ where
179. 3 pupils ~~rece~~ entertains
179. 6 Mr. Smee—~~The~~I'm not
179.14 lordship ↑will↓ think
179.14 his ↑Lordship↓ family
179.17 alone ~~Mr.~~ Smee.
179.18 addresses. ↑I wont be painted↓ I
179.20 to Phidjas—~~says~~ ↑remarks↓
     Gandish.
179.22 says ~~my~~ Lord
179.22 Kew languidly—~~I dont say~~[Y
     over y]ou are ~~not~~ ↑no doubt
     fully↓ equal
179.23 I ~~am~~ don't
179.23 resemblance ↑to—↓to the
179.24 party. I~~s~~ should
179.24 and ~~I am not handsome~~ Smee
179.30 the ~~[illeg.]~~ giver
179.30 entertainment. [blank indicating
     paragraph] ¶Newcome's

179.35 than ~~highly cor~~ cold
179.36 when ↑young Ridley &↓ his
179.36 became ~~a~~ pupils
179.40 a ↑young↓ man
179.40 father ↑may have to↓ wait
179.42 the ~~[illeg.]~~ dispute
179.42 laugh. ~~W~~First says
179.43 asked ↑and↓ then I ~~w~~ promise
180.14 been ~~passed~~ ↑spent↓; he
180.16 them ↑resolutely↓ for
180.19 that ~~of~~ in
180.21 the ~~soft~~ ↑kind↓ hand
180.24 wh. ~~had~~ ↑would have↓ received
180.26 too late+.+ ~~We who~~ ↑and
     though we↓ bring
180.26 bring ~~the~~ ↑our↓ Tribute
180.26 Tribute ~~may be~~ of
180.27 gravestone; ~~they~~ there
180.27 is ~~yet~~ an
180.27 acceptance ↑even there,↓ for
180.28 of ~~humbled~~ ↑fond ~~regrets~~
     remorse,↓ contrite
181. 3 and devised,~~ kindnesses, and ~~th~~
     gave
181. 4 made merry:~~ and~~ ↑.↓ Did
181. 7 endure ↑even↓ till
181. 9 the ~~dim~~ ↑dun-↓dreary
     November
181.12 dawn, ↑to↓ wh., for ↑so↓ many
181.18 even ~~bile~~ ↑boil↓ his
181.20 never ~~asks~~ looks
181.20 be ~~the~~ beloved
181.30 and [his over he] ↑feet↓ still
     ~~remained~~ beat
181.31 pavement. ~~¶Colonel Newcome,~~
     ↑In spite of the cold↓ reception
181.34 of ~~his~~ the
181.36 when th[eir over ese] ~~gentlemen~~
     wives
181.36 London, ~~paid~~ ↑the elder
     Newcome was for paying↓ them
     ↑at first↓ pretty
181.37 But ~~Mrs. when~~ ↑after↓ the
181.39 usual virtu[e over ous] gave
182. 4 having ~~turned him out of doors~~
     ↑so rebuked him↓. 'I
182. 6 having ~~made~~ created
182. 6 humble-minded) [W over w]hen
     Professor
182. 9 with ~~bows~~ ↑curtsies↓ and

182.12 friend's ~~door~~ ↑house↓ was
182.17 you [ve over m]ry much
182.21 see ↑too↓ much
182.23 up, ↑do↓ You
182.24 my boy↑'s society↓ is
182.24 alive. ¶~~She~~ ↑Maria↓ turned
182.27 Indian gentlem[e over a]n become
182.30 and ~~S~~ dear
182.30 will ~~enter~~ ↑go↓ into
183. 1 nephew ~~in the City.~~ He's
183. 2 He ~~flew~~ ↑went↓ off
183. 2 because ~~Maria~~ ↑your aunt↓ objected
183. 6 always ~~thought~~ ↑knew Sir↓ my
183.15 as ~~your~~ the
183.22 an [E over e]arl's daughter—no
184. 1 is ↑a↓ good
184. 3 it Barnes—~~I~~ ¶Here
184. 4 his ↑distinguished↓ friend ↑Mr↓ Pendennis,
184. 5 out '~~those~~dam ↑all↓ literary
184.14 was ~~rather~~ ↑much↓ more
184.18 associates. ↑She found no fault— who was she to find fault with *any one*? But↓ She
184.20 intimate ↑with him.↓—And so
184.27 welcome. Th[e over at] affectionate
185. 4 pretty ↑little↓ horse
185. 5 that ~~looked so~~ ↑was↓ handsomer
185.10 but ↑by↓ a
185.18 those ornaments[— over ,]~~she~~ ↑and↓ him
185.19 She ~~said~~ asked
185.26 bought ~~a fine~~ ↑on credit↓ the
185.34 on ~~his frien~~ hearsay— ↑.↓ [B over b]ut at this time ~~Mrs. Kitty Ogle was acting her favorite characters at the Haymarket~~+:+ ↑Mademoiselle Saltarelli was dancing at ~~the Opera~~ Drury Lane Theatre,↓ and ↑it certainly may be said that↓ Clives first love ~~may certainly~~ was
185.37 that ~~elderly~~ beauty,
186. 1 her ~~benefit~~ ↑'night'↓ was
186. 5 Saltarelli's mother[, over —] who
186. 7 a ↑dingy↓ vision of a ~~dirty~~ feast
186.15 laughed ~~when~~ as
186.17 you ~~beide~~ ↑behind↓ the
186.19 the Scenes?—~~On this~~Over this

~~stage~~ ↑part↓ of
186.20 harm ↑to him↓, for
186.21 others ↑been↓ behind ~~behi~~ the
186.22 old ~~fig~~ women
187. 4 about ~~Indian w~~ lovers
187.10 he ~~never~~ scarcely
187.12 knew ~~ever so~~ ever
187.14 recite ~~whole~~ pages
187.16 good man[] over ']: and
187.20 than ~~Papa~~ ↑Sir Bryan↓ in
187.24 little Egbert+,+ ↑took hold of your sword, Uncle, and↓ asked
187.25 know ~~I was thinking of the same thing~~ ↑I had the same question in my mind↓? And
187.26 I ~~hoped~~ ↑thought↓ when
187.28 Mamma's ~~Doctor~~ ↑apothecary↓ Sir Danby Jilks,↑—↓that horrid
187.29 more. ¶↑I hope↓ Egbert
187.35 directions ~~how~~ for
187.36 the Doctors'- showed
188. 1 in action[, over ;] attending
188. 1 and ~~coming~~ exposing
188. 2 Ethel ~~says he~~ ↑declares that her Uncle↓ always
188. 4 only ~~thing~~ ↑reason↓ she
188. 4 that ~~horrid~~ ↑todious↓ Sir
188. 5 Boots; ~~was~~ who
188. 6 to ~~ever~~ all ~~the~~ ladies:
188. 8 come? ~~We~~ Mamma
188.11 afterwards. '[O over I] how
188.14 the ~~time~~ ↑midst↓ of ↑her↓ splendors
188.16 season, ~~when~~ before
188.20 her ↑eh↓ little
188.20 administering ~~luncheon~~ ↑dinner↓ to
188.29 they ~~take~~ ↑drink↓ wine
188.30 (or th[eir over e] ↑before-mentioned↓ reserved
188.31 House) ~~she~~ faint
188.37 little work-~~box~~baskets, and
189.14 dear ↑told↓ lady!
189.15 that ~~offen~~hurt me.
189.16 I ~~thought~~ ↑known↓ she
189.20 condition, ~~with a few~~ who
189.20 by ~~their~~ ↑a few↓ governesses; ~~for the most part~~ and
189.25 her ↑progress,↓ from
189.26 doll, ~~now~~ ↑then↓ with

189.27 her ~~French~~ ↑German↓ lessons;

189.29 of pret[e over [illeg.]]rnatural hideousness,

189.32 to ~~the~~ Ethels

189.32 the ~~fine~~ ↑prodigious↓ new

189.34 lovely, ↑new↓ silk stockings↑.↓ ~~and white~~ ¶Lady

189.36 and ~~brought~~ ↑presented↓ her

190. 2 humour— ¶~~She~~ ↑Ethels grandmother↓ became

190. 5 daresay ~~made~~ amply

190.13 bow, [H over illeg.]er ladyship

190.15 Trembling ↑as she always did↓ before her ~~mamma~~ ↑mother↓, Lady

190.20 forward ↑presently↓ to

190.22 face—He ~~said~~ told

190.23 said ~~her Ladyship~~ ↑Lady Kew↓. I

190.27 and ~~was~~ ↑had been↓ languidly

[Begin Anne's handwriting.]

281. 3 tragedy ~~fm.~~ ↑int↓ wh.

281.20 by ~~the~~ ↑a↓ hand

281.25 tall Setl↓tza water

281.27 their @~~dead~~ ↑black↓ stu[m over illeg.]ps strewing

281.30 wont @↑when the pencil went well, and the colours arranged themselves to his satisfaction↓ over

281.33 drawing ~~board~~ ↑table↓ to the window, ↑set out his board & colo[ur over r]-box,↓ filled

282. 3 while, ~~[illeg.]~~ opened

282. 8 little strawber[ry over y] girl

282.10 & @~~something tells me~~ ↑my familiar spirit↓ came

282.15 exhibition. ~~¶Ar~~Are you

282.16 going already@↑?↓ cries

282.24 in. Ha↑n↓nibal has

282.30 & ~~in th~~ ↑with↓ the

282.34 her ~~beauty~~ ↑form↓ her

282.35 her ↑Queenly↓ grace

282.40 or th[at over e] divine

283. 5 kind confidante used

283. 7 frequently [after over illeg.] his

283.11 & Confidante would

283.12 went ↑between the 2 gentlemen↓ by

283.12 Grey ~~between the two gentlemen~~ ↑ ¶↓'Very likely

283.13 likely ~~knight~~ the

283.13 the gr[ey over ave] ~~councillor~~ ↑mentor↓ had

283.14 sad coun[s over c]il⊦: poor

283.14 the ~~despair &~~ wretchedness

283.18 indeed severe↑.↓ & [H over h]e thought

283.22 cousins, @~~He~~ ↑he↓ was

283.23 thinking ~~whether~~ ↑but of↓ the

283.26 friend ~~then~~ ↑was↓ to

283.27 could ~~exert~~ give

283.31 only s Campaign

283.32 at Asste↓erghur?— ¶'Asste↓r- What? says

283.34 wondering— ¶~~his horse had been ↑on↓ shot sir~~+,+ ~~the e«n»nemy were upon him~~+on that+↑ ¶The battle of Asse↓e↑rghur' says Clive fought on the↓ eventful

283.40 to ~~run away~~ ↑choose between death↓ and

284. 9 of Asste↓erghur. ¶And

284.12 of Assete↓rghur. I

284.12 off. [D over d]ip into

284.14 ugly, [y over l]et let

284.14 a ~~smile~~ ↑crown↓ to

284.16 labours, f Forget

284.17 so. D[e over .]..No—God bless

285. 1 any ↑generous↓ young

285. 2 a seniors co↑u↓nsel and

285.12 daylight almost[. over ,] Jack was makeing @~~deuce~~ ↑deuce↓ of

285.13 this hours I

285.14 of Laud[a over e]nu[m over illeg.] last

285.15 then ↑laughing↓ he ~~told~~ ↑gave↓ Clive

285.18 eyes. ~~If you are going to cross~~ The weather

285.19 me ~~now is~~ ↑the sooner↓ the

285.20 It's @~~devilish~~ ↑bitter↓ cold

285.23 manner— ¶H[u over l]lloh! cries

285.32 profession ~~he~~ ↑Clive↓ added

285.33 and thats is

285.33 I evere gained

285.44 you [P over p]ut the

286. 3 Barnes. [H over h]ow that poor ~~young~~ lady

286. 7 insolent ~~cock-tailed~~ coxcomb

286.14 but th[e over is] fear

286.18 year. I[t is over ts] a shame its ↑ is↓ a

286.23 have you[? over !] ¶Good
286.24 ¶Good @God ↑Heavens↓ you
286.29 those @d—d ↑confounded↓ Clubs.
286.31 angelical temper, ↑:↓ but
286.32 of course:↑—↓those factory
286.33 you know+,+↑:—↓well well
286.34 He had declared
286.36 at @Bazes ↑Bays's↓ &
286.37 Mrs. De@[L over l]acy ↑(↓Mrs. Delacy
286.38 call herself↑)↓ because
286.39 served him↑—↓as such
286.40 in Yorkshire:↑—↓rather a cheap school,↑—↓but she
286.44 was @devilishly ↑immensely↓ cut
287. 2 place. ↑They know↓ every
287. 3 do. [H over h]e is
287. 3 clever fellow↑.↓ [H over h]e is
287. 3 his way↑.↓ [W over w]hen he
287. 8 free will[: h over H]e knowing
287.14 him. In the world↑You are↓You are
287.19 hate him↑:↓ &—fancy you
287.22 is painted↑.↓ [O over o]ur friends
287.23 draw us↑:↓ &
287.23 are like↑.'↓ continued
287.30 any rate↑;↓ And
287.30 do not↑.'↓ ¶↑↓And as
287.31 of love↑,'↓ the
287.31 went on↑,↓ kindling
287.32 & colloquialisms with
287.36 sigh about↑:↓ but
287.40 supreme lot, ↑:↓ but
287.41 to Bau[ci over se]s Philemon
287.42 must compromise↑;↓ make
287.43 bad together[. A over , a]nd as
287.45 matches, [A over illeg.]]nd see
287.45 the @↑end of↓ most
288. 2 with her↑:↓ If
288. 3 world mak[e]ing money
288. 4 Why, [K over Q]ings &
288. 7 their son↑.↓; My
288. 8 Miss Deeds[: over ,] sends
288.10 and marri[es over ed] Miss
288.14 young gentlemen of
288.19 the @↑youth↓ was
288.20 'Young man[! over ,] if
288.21 an @honest ↑comely↓ face
288.21 three o[r over f] four

288.22 a year[: D over , &]o not
288.22 nature by ↑or↓ indulge
288.22 in any ↑certain↓ ambitious
288.23 Sail along down
289. 3 veteran @pleni potentiary ↑diplomatist↓ allowed
289. 7 of th two
289. 8 then the↓ went
289. 9 observing ↑& enjoying↓ his
289.10 try him Clive
289.11 a supecillious How
289.17 life ↑&↓ was
289.17 commanding stature[: over ,] @But ↑but↓ patronised
289.19 that when ge ↑a common↓ wish
289.26 beggar, stie stands
289.28 loudest oth oaths.
289.28 oaths. ¶De ↑—↓ clumsy
289.29 clumsy [Be— over O—e] screamed
289.30 women Barnes@↑: and added in a lo[ud over w]er voice. I beg your pardon. I am very clumsy.↓ ¶It
289.32 furious. ↑¶↓Mr. Clive
289.42 Clive. Though I am a ↑For our young↓ friend
289.42 friend ↑it↓ must
290. 7 go ↑out↓, &
290. 9 knew ↑to↓ what
290. 9 grandson meant ↑alluded↓ Lord
290.18 gentleness touche smote
290.19 and grati an
290.20 his honest↑yo↓ cheeks
290.22 lonely—But—But its is
290.24 the @Evil Beak ↑eagle beak↓. Baden
290.25 make acquaintainces here
290.27 French Vi@ts↓counts. We
290.31 old lad[y' over ie]s morality
290.35 transactions @↑to↓ wh.
290.36 allude: to and
290.37 eligible. ¶[My over my] good
291. 3 of the ta↓ tender
291.10 place. She never told ¶But
291.15 Anne made me very welcome ↑requested you↓ to
291.24 up between ↑amo↓@↑between↓ young
291.25 people @between whom ↑which↓ can

291.28 Jane [D over S]orkings and
291.34 Dr. Strum@f ↑pf↓ has
291.39 grandson Barnes,↑—↓in all
291.39 eligible ma union.
291.41 experienced such unhappiness & horor of another fm.
291.42 sort the ↑such↓ horrors
291.44 you. ↑ ¶↓Go ou back
291.46 windows,) Who ↑You↓ have
292. 1 And Barnes[Margn: 300] sent
292. 9 were eng[a over g]ged to
292.10 her name, ↑?↓—Miss MacPherson,
292.12 look suprp surprised.
292.14 indeed old ↑how↓ lady
292.20 of @↑wh↓ the
292.21 Newcomes ha[s over d] had
292.24 Miss Newcomeupstairs, having
292.30 was calm ↑haughty↓ almost
292.31 side to which
292.34 My Hollidays are
292.34 & Ri[gle over db]y &
292.36 but @↑ther hand↑ did
292.39 little mad Maude
292.39 was quite a toddling little ↑an impetuous little↓ thing
292.40 bye. [T over C]live sant
292.40 of @his ↑Clives↓ trowsers,
292.43 his ↑yellow↓ mustachio[s over es]. He
292.46 Claive. Es↑t↓ ce
292.48 he s[a over u]ng out.
293. 1 some catastroph[e over y] had
293. 2 than thhe had
293. 4 Baden o[f over r] the
293. 6 the cadav[e over o]urous croupiers
293. 8 how [a over [illeg.]] fair
293.24 Tiens tu p le
293.28 le Prince de Montaigne ↑Duc d'Ivry↓ is
293.28 from Ba[gn over [illeg.]]ères de
293.29 de [B over V]igo[rre over [illeg.]]. Affaires He
293.29 Affaires d'iEtat mon [accent added]
293.29 affaires d'iEtat ¶How [accent added]
293.30 the @Princesse ↑Duchess↓ will
[Begin Thackeray's handwriting.]
294. 9 Le Prince ↑Duc↓ &

294. 9 le Princesse de Montaign ↑Duchesse d'Ivry↓; the
294.12 Montaign's work ↑book of Travels, 'Footprints of the Gazelles'; by a daughter of the Crusaders.'↓ in
294.15 Arabs, who and
294.15 many ↑a↓ feats wh.
294.15 wh. would live↑s↓ in
294.16 pages. where they not forgotten. ↑for gentlemen who have the patience to peruse them.↓ He
294.16 rescued her ↑Madame la Princesse↓ from
294.18 bucksheesh, from the Princess, and
294.18 with stick[. over :] They
294.20 see ↑the↓ old
294.20 the ↑Jerusalem↓ processions
294.24 disquisitions. ↑She hesitates at nothing like other poets of her nation: not profoundly learned, she invents where she has not acquired: mingles together religion & the Opera: and performs Parisian pas-de-ballet before the gates of monasteries and the cells of Anchorites.↓ She
295. 1 suspicious ↑&↓ a
295. 2 at ↑the Circulating Library at↓ Baden;
295. 2 Madame de Montaign↓d'Ivry↑ constantly
295. 3 watering-place. The Prince de [blank] ↑M. le duc↓ was
295. 4 the book+,+↑: wh. was↓ published
295. 7 nobleman is ↑was↓ five
295. 7 France [unnumbered page] the turn of the philosophers then came—the chemists, «what know I? Last year it was the» the natural-historians, what know I? she made a laboratory in her Hotel: she spent hours in the Jardin des Plantes—Last year it was the chase and poor Kion-Kion chased the fox and she chased Kion—And, admirable thing!—there are women in the world who part from their lovers and remain friends with them; this one «quarrels with» ↑casts off↓ her friends and

~~never pardons them for leaving her. O it was a fatal wife my poor uncle took there! I believe her virtuous. Yes. She «must» ↑ought to↓ be virtuous she is so abominably wicked! «She is so jealous that I tell you she has found means to be jealous against my mother.» She has only memory for her revenges. She forgets her caprices as easily as I forget my dinner of last year.~~
France

[Begin Anne's handwriting.]
~~There were other difficulties besides the Clive perplexity & the Jack Belsize complication wh. the old plenipotentiary who has just packed our hero about his business was bent upon arranging at this Congress of Baden. ¶In our modern pictures of life, I know there are certain figures scarcely admissable. That poor wretch seated on Sir Brian Newcomes door steps and @«clamouring» ↑crying↓ for justice to her children has no doubt shocked more than one squeamish reader who would not have his or her daughters eyes offended by the «contempta» ↑sight↓ of a creature so odious, so disreputable, clamouring in foul language against her seducer. He who writes has children of his own before who«se eyes» ↑m↓ he would like to present no object that should shock their purity or sully maiden cheeks with uneasy blushes, but the purest must one day learn that the world is a sinful world [line space]~~

295. 8 institution ~~the~~ ↑of↓ marriage↑s↓ de

295. 9 folks ↑of the family↓ about

295. 9 about ~~whom~~ ↑rich↓ this

295.14 many fran[c over k]s of

295.14 dot: ~~M.~~ ↑Monsieur↓ has

295.15 certain *clientèle* bringing

295.17 much capital,↑—↓and the

295.21 light litterature of

295.26 old ~~Prince de Montaign~~ ↑Duke d'Ivry↓ of

295.29 of @~~nine-tenths~~ ↑nineteen-twentieths↓ of

295.29 the ~~Prince de Montaign~~ ↑Duc d'Ivry↓ lost

295.33 the @~~Prince~~ ↑Duke↓ was

295.34 wh. @~~fall~~ ↑the latter↓ had

295.35 and @~~at~~ ↑when he was more than↓ sixty

295.36 a ~~noble~~ young

295.36 young ~~virgin~~ ↑lady of↓ a @~~race almost as noble as his own, a virgin of sixteen was~~ ↑sufficient nobility a virgin of sixteen was↓ brought

295.41 royal @~~grace~~ ↑favours↓. Her

295.41 by [Dubuffe over Du Buffe] was

295.42 young @~~Princesse~~ ↑Duchess↓ indeed

295.43 hair ~~que~~ as

295.44 M. @~~de Montaign~~ ↑d'Ivry↓ whose

296. 2 houses, fo[t over T]he Atridæ

296. 3 the @~~Montaigns~~ ↑d'Ivrys↓ &

296. 3 so on↑—the ~~Smiths~~ ↑↑Browns↓↓ and Jones's being of no account)↓+,)+ The

296. 5 seemed @↑to be↓ so.

296. 5 so. [H over h]is hair

296. 6 the [P over p]rincesse's own,

296. 7 au Boi[s over u] with

296. 8 old [F over f]ranconi himself,

296. 8 for ~~a~~ ↑one of the↓ young

296. 9 young m[e over a]n, of

296. 9 he ~~main~~ retained

296.10 amusements, ~~A~~ ↑a↓lthough his

296.15 bachelor; [t over T]ook leave

296.15 of ~~fr~~ Phrym[e over i]i &

296.18 affreux catastroph[e over y] of

296.19 one wil[y over ey] old

296.20 & ~~takeing to his heart~~ ↑distributing↓ *poignées de*

296.21 France. @~~de Montaign~~ ↑le duc d'Ivry↓ ++who++ ↑lost his place at Court, his appointments wh. helped his income very much, and his peerage+.+ He↓ ~~had~~ ↑would↓ no

296.24 Elba. [The phrase: "lost his place . . . and his peerage" was originally inserted after "Elba", but line drawn indicates its present location.]

~~He refused the oath of~~
~~allegiance and~~@↑The ex-peer↓
retired

296.25 citizen King[, h over . H]is cousin

296.26 who @↑for his part↓ cheerfully

296.27 having @↑indeed↓ been

296.28 dynasties @~~since he and the Corsican had made matters up.~~ ↑for some years past.↓ ¶In

296.29 la @~~Princesse de Montaign~~ @↑Duchesse d'Ivry↓ gave

296.30 whom he↑r↓ noble

296.30 pleasure. @↑What the Duke desired was an heir to his rossname house—a Prince de Moncontour, to fill the place of the sons ↑↑& grandsons↓↓ gone before him to join the↑↑ir↓↓a ancestors in the tomb.↓ No

296.33 children @↑however↓ blessed

296.33 blessed @~~this~~@↑the old Duke's↓ union

296.34 Madame @~~de Montaign~~ @↑d'Ivry↓ went

296.34 watering places[: over ,] Pilgrimages

296.34 were tried[: over ,] vows

296.35 the @~~Montaign~~@↑d'Ivry↓ family,

296.36 in general[. B over , b]ut the

296.40 wh. ~~they occasionally frequented,~~ I

296.40 the @~~Prince & Princess~~@↑Duke Duchess↓ grew

296.41 into *marriage de convenance,* @~~nay~~@↑,~~sometimes~~ ↓@↑sometimes, nay as those↓ ~~who~~ ↑who light a flaming lovematch &↓ run

297. 2 Castle @↑wh. they cannot afford to fill with company↓, have

297. 3 table @↑who comes without a card, and↓ whom

297. 6 old [M over m]an of

297. 6 this ~~wakeful~~ daily

297. 7 the @~~table~~@↑board↓; this

297. 8 companion @~~that~~@↑who↓ *will*

297. 9 M. @~~de Montaign~~@↑d'Ivry↓ that

297.12 la @~~Princesse~~@↑Duchesse↓ may

297.12 general d[y over i]ed their

297.15 these mar~~r~~iages de

297.17 old ~~man ↑one↓~~@↑↑gentleman↓↓, there

297.18 at all↑:↓ [t over T]empers over

297.19 no contro~~u~~l: &

297.20 the @~~Prince~~@↑Duke↓ and

297.20 and ~~Princess~~@↑Duchess↓ quarreled

297.21 pair ~~that~~@↑who↓ ever

297.21 table. ~~They differed so fatally~~ ~~that Madame actually began~~ ~~to rally «herself with a~~ ~~bourgeoise»~~ @↑to the Bourgeoise↓ ~~dynasty at the~~ ~~Tuilleries, whilst her husband~~ ~~faithful to his family~~ ~~traditions, was conspiring~~ ~~in behalf of the elder branch.~~ ~~It is known that the~~ ~~Prince joined MADAME~~ ~~«Duch» Duchesse~~ ~~de Berri, in her attempt to~~ ~~raise the Vendu in the~~ ~~year 1834.~~ [T over t]~~he flame~~ ~~wh. was to have spread over~~ ~~all Vendú all Brittany, all~~ ~~France, was luckily put out~~ ~~in↑ ↓the↑ ↓Chimney. That~~ ~~Chimney at Rennes where a~~ ~~few grinning gens d'armes~~ ~~led by a Jewish spy.)~~ ~~trampled~~ ~~out the sparks of the~~ ~~restoration is a matter of~~ ~~history now. Monsieur le Prince~~ ~~de Montaign was in~~

[The rest of this cancellation (at the top of a new page, numbered 26) is preceded by two *Ms* leaves (numbered 23-25) in Thackeray's handwriting, from "In this unhappy state" through "by no means well pleased at that desertion."), which are an insertion.]

~~the Chimney, in company «of»~~ ~~↑of MADAME↓ the August~~ ~~Capuo«w» fugitive, & her~~ ~~squeezed adherents. 'One~~ ~~morning of his life' his wife~~ ~~said he must have passed~~ ~~without dyeing his hair.~~ ~~When we are to make~~ ~~acquaintance with the Prince, he~~ ~~has long left off @«those»~~ ~~↑this↓ youthful delusions:— he is~~ ~~quite an old man broken &~~ ~~cast down He has given up~~ ~~the battle against fate. There~~ ~~are to be no direct~~ ~~heirs to the ancient~~ ~~house of Montaign«,»↑:↓~~ ~~his kinsmen whom he does not~~

~~love will survive him &~~
~~inherit his title after him~~
~~He loves~~ ↑the family of↓
~~M. de Florac no better~~
~~«when he thinks»~~ ~~for past~~
~~disputes & future triumphs~~
[This cancelled passage is
incorporated almost verbatim in
the ensuing three-page insertion,
where it is cancelled again.]
¶(break a line) ↑In this unhappy
state of home affairs,↓ Madame

297.24 her ~~own~~ bosom, ~~she commonly~~
~~sets «such» a~~↑n enormous↓
~~value on it. Who~~ ↑of course
she sets her own price on the
article.↓ Did

[Begin Thackeray's handwriting.]

297.25 ever ~~read~~ ↑see↓ the

297.25 the ↑first↓ poems

297.26 Duchesse ~~de Montaign~~ ↑d'Ivry↓
Les

297.26 her ↑very intimate↓ friends,

297.27 back. ↑They had some success,↓
Dubufe

297.28 Scheffer ~~painted~~ ↑depicted↓ her

297.29 in ~~her~~ the

297.30 on ~~seeing~~ opening

297.33 husband ~~coming to~~ ↑entering↓
her

297.33 her ~~boudoir~~ ↑room↓ would

297.34 Basilio ~~in~~ ↑with↓ his

297.35 Sombrero ~~and Dominus~~
~~Vobiscum~~ ↑and shoe-buckles.↓
The

297.38 and ↑sanguines histories of↓
Queens

297.45 give ↑him↓ M.

297.46 de Lille—~~But~~ ↑And↓ for

297.46 school. ~~Ma foi~~+!+↑Bah!↓—these
little

298. 3 was ↑a pretty↓ constant

298. 4 might heare him

298. 5 French ↑tragedy.↓ ¶During

298. 8 first. ~~But after that deplorable~~
~~affair no~~ Of

298.10 all. ~~But after that~~
~~deplorable affair of the himney~~
~~at Rennes behind wh. MADAME~~
~~was discovered; the Duchess~~
~~gave up her~~ She

298.14 discovered afterwards—~~People~~
↑The world↓ said

298.14 that ↑our↓ silly

298.15 Duchess ↑of Paris↓ was

298.15 was ~~the~~ partly

298.15 the ~~discovery,~~ ↑.↓ Spies

298.20 Comte Tiercelin—↑le beau
Tiercelin—↓an officer

298.21 coffee ~~at th~~ in

298.21 he ↑actually↓ wounded

298.23 was ~~one of↓ his second↑s↓:~~
~~↑and↓ Florac was~~ loud

298.23 bravery. [The top of this page
was copied (and later cancelled)
by Thackeray from the end
of p. 22 which is in Anne's
hand, and which originally
formed the top of what is now
p. 26] ~~the chimney, in company~~
~~of MADAME the august~~
~~capuofugitive and her~~
~~squeezed adherents. 'One~~
~~morning of his life' Madame~~
~~la Princesse said, 'Monsieur~~
~~de Montaign«e» must have~~
~~passed without dying his~~
~~hair.' When we are to make~~
~~acquaintance with the Prince,~~
~~he has left off his youthful~~
~~delusions: he is quite an old~~
~~man, broken and cast down:~~
~~he has given up the battle~~
~~against Fate. There are to~~
~~be no direct heirs to the~~
~~ancient house of Montaign.~~
~~His kinsmen whom he does~~
~~not love will survive him~~
~~inherit his title after~~
~~him [& over :] he likes the~~
~~family of M de Florac no~~
~~better for thinking of that~~
~~«future» ↑posthumous↓~~
~~triumph↑.↓«over him.»~~ ¶That

298.25 la ~~Princess de Florac~~ ↑Duchesse
d'Ivry↓ have

298.26 l'huile ~~M~~ the

298.27 from ↑Monsieur↓ Dubufe—those

298.29 the ~~Princess~~ ↑Duchess↓ appeared

298.30 other ~~oce~~ occasions

298.36 took ↑this brother↓ the

298.42 Florac. ~~Elle~~ ↑She↓ raffoles

298.42 raffoles ~~de~~ ↑of↓ M.

298.42 she ~~keeps a fast~~ used

298.43 the ~~martyrdom~~ ↑supplice↓ of

298.44 and ↑to recall↓ the

299. 2 attend ↑the preach↓ at

299. 8 his ~~brot~~ elder:

299.11 Royalist, Philippist, Catholic,

299.11 Madame de Montaign ↑d'Ivry↓
must

299.12 Pantheism, ↑to↓ bearded

299.14 books ↑persons↓ of

299.18 par ↑Mme.↓ la

299.20 la P— de M— ↑D—— d'I↓:
Guard

299.21 from rescuing it↑!↓+↑this
Muse!↓—If you see her [illeg.]
she

299.24 London when M. de Kion came
of age, ↑once, met↓ she

299.25 costume and consulted

299.25 consulted the ↑a↓ minister

299.27 otherwise more my

299.33 taken ↑more than ever to↓ the

299.35 misfortune. ↑She calls
her lodgings Holyrood
↑↑Lochleven↓↓. Eh! I pity
the landlord of Holyrood
↑↑Lochleven↓↓!↓ She

299.39 Rizzio: and little ↑young↓ Lord

299.42 this Syren boug ↑haggard↓ Syren

299.44 cautions ↑very likely↓ would

299.45 would of course have

299.45 him ↑only the more↓ eager

300. 2 Madame de Montaign's
↑d'Ivry's↓ salon,

300. 3 He ↑had not studied Horace
Vernet for nothing: he↓ drew

300. 7 little Princess's ↑girl's↓
Governess,

300.12 Scots, the neglected

300.13 English camp ↑faction↓: so

[Begin Anne's handwriting.]

300.16 M. de Montaign ↑d'Ivry↓ and

300.17 differences A ↑—↓a long

300.18 pardon [t over T]he Vi[c over
s]omte de

300.20 The Viscomte de

300.20 been ↑allowed↓ for

300.20 space ↑to be↓ intimate

300.20 with thes chief

300.24 he remembers[: over ,] &

300.24 & @the↓ thinks

300.24 Vicomte discre[et over te]ly said

300.25 'My Uncle cousin

300.28 the number[: & over [illeg.]] that

300.31 Kew's beauty[. H over , h]ow
many

300.34 of nothing ↑few things↓ more

300.34 remarkable [or over of]
suggestive

300.35 than some of those

300.37 a gar[illeg.] jargon

[Begin Thackeray's handwriting.]

300.44 old Prince ↑Duke↓ wore

301. 5 Paris, where a

301. 7 Kiou ↑when quite a boy↓ to

301. 9 as one ↑a son↓ of

301.11 one [(over ,]and she

301.12 very ri considerably,)

301.14 donc! Kew ↑Frank↓ was

301.15 was her boy: her Lady

301.17 him. ¶ I am trying to tell this
story, not in a sermonizing tone,
wh. is a bore in society:
when the fable is acted before
us, and the observer must
point his own moral. Admit that
the novel is a «kind of»
newspaper; where the Editor
utters his «oracles» opinions
only in a small part of the
Journal, the rest being filled
up with advertisements, accidents
offences fashionable news &c,
and where Lady Brilliants last
nights party: the running at
Doncaster yesterday; Jack
Splitskulls execution and
behaviour at the Old Bailey:
the price of peas at Covent
Garden: Captain Screwby's
appearance at Bow Street for
wrenching off knockers, and so
forth are registered with a «like
impartiality.» ↑without
comment.↓ But now and
then in the newspaper
columns you must
come on a dreadful story
or two. Do your children
not see it? You take «your
children to» ↑them to↓ the
National Gallery; do they not
look at the Hogarths? Was
the painter wrong in depicting
that last awful scene of the
series—the ¶Have

301.19 exceeding his the

301.21 suffer? obtruding a rude moral,
«when he ought» or uttering
a ghastly [illeg.] ↑If this fable
were not true: if many & many
of your young men of pleasure↓
had

301.29 of you our

301.30 attendants ↑La reine↓ Marie

302. 1 luck ~~some~~ occasionally
302. 2 Majesty. ↑Her appearance used to create not a little excitement in the Saloon of Roulette the game wh. she patronized as being more 'fertile of emotions' than↓~~She used to bring in beautiful agate bonbonniere full of gold pieces.~~ [Remainder of page is sketch of man and woman.] the
302. 6 of ~~or~~ peaches
302.10 despair. ↑Madame la Baronne de la Crûche Cassée played on one side of her: Madame la Comtesse de Schlangenbad on the other↓ When
302.14 they ↑swiftly↓ pocketted
302.16 against the↑ir↓ Sovereign.
302.17 were ~~Captain~~ Count
302.30 have ~~it~~ ↑the two shields↓ painted
302.31 know [t over s]he ↑Princess↓ calls
302.32 about ↑the transmogrification of↓ our
302.34 Friars. ↑'I say Newcome!↓ The
302.36 had ~~orders,~~ ↑a bunch of orders at his button:↓ excepting,
302.36 poor ↑Jones↓ ¶Like
302.39 was ~~asto~~ enraptured
302.41 so ~~said~~ the
303. 1 de Kiou[! over ,] He
303. 5 charmante Meese and
303. 8 of Kew[(over ,]notre filleul
303.11 embarrassment. ÷ Her
303.18 Antoinette. ¥ This
303.20 Protestant ↑Governess↓ scowled
303.25 me ~~chez nous~~ at
[Begin Anne's handwriting.]
303.33 thou ~~says~~ ↑cries↓ Florac
303.44 of *calineries* and
303.44 scent bottles, to
304. 2 their pru~~dent~~dery! Can
304. 4 de Schlangen~~berg~~ ↑ad↓ [blank line] &
304. 6 & ~~honest Capt~~ ↑worthy↓ Colonel
304. 6 fancy ~~the twilight~~ ↑a moonlight↓ conclave,
304. 7 a ~~dead~~ reputation! ↑?↓ The
304. 7 The ~~laughing~~ ↑jibes↓ &
304. 8 teeth, [H over h]ow they
304. 9 the ~~qu~~ tender
305. 9 to crossprotect ↑attack↓ women
305.12 care [t over T]hought subdued

305.16 and ~~Ddid~~ not
305.19 Belsize's ~~honest~~@↑jolly↓ voice,
305.20 voice, ~~£~~ &
305.24 away ~~&~~ unceasingly
305.29 of ~~sixteen~~ ↑eventeen↓ who
305.30 Miss @~~Ethel~~ ↑Newcome↓ &
306. 2 is [jilted over guilty], is
306.12 with ↑the↓ Captains, gets
306.12 longer ~~more gracefully~~ better
306.24 very ~~heavry~~heavy &
306.30 in ~~to~~ ↑in↓ his
306.31 a bu[d over g]get of
306.32 laugh, ~~Blanche~~ ↑Henrietta↓ who
306.33 highest ~~opin~~opinion of
306.36 is ~~he~~ not
306.36 not ↑Mr. Newcome↓ always
306.37 Mayors show[; over ?] and
306.41 carriage. ~~And~~ at
306.41 he +↑r↓+ looked
307.12 in scream ↑en↓ing poor
307.17 indignation. [A over a]t the
307.19 him ↑at Baden↓ not
307.31 quitted ↑the place↓ I
307.32 chastised him, ↑.↓ [H over h]e &
307.34 especially ~~wh~~for my
308. 1 humour ~~Barnes~~ Barnes.
308. 4 my ↑man.'↓ Mr.
308. 8 parting @↑between the old lovers↓ passed
308. 8 passed ~~here~~ with
308. 9 sides. ~~Mrs~~ ↑tisses↓ Parents
308.17 Dorking ~~now~~@↑there↓ remarked
308.18 engagement ↑into↓ which
308.19 had ~~formed~~ ↑entered↓, was
308.23 feeling. '[A over @]s your
308.29 tooth ~~fa~~ was
308.29 & ~~[illeg.]~~ for
308.33 malicious, ↑&↓ the
308.37 seeing him, ↑!↓ she
309. 5 fainting ~~&~~ ↑than↓ of
309. 6 de ~~Ch~~Cruchecassée &
309. 7 curtseys, ↑persisted in↓ declaring
309.10 vous n'ete[s over t] qu'une
309.12 Kew b[u over y]t this
309.17 fancy [f over &]or turning
309.20 short ~~dr~~ makeing
310. 6 and care[. B over , b]ut she
310. 9 him ↑&↓ she
310.11 her. ↑She↓ even

310.18 It bled+,+ ~~but~~ ↑at↓ the
310.20 shocked & ↑in↓ his
310.20 feelings ~~for@↑~~by↓ his
310.22 peevishness [a over ,]nd
        remonstated
310.24 back again↑?'↓ said
310.25 be han~~d~~kering after
310.30 & ~~she~~ set
310.31 care ↑for↓ the
310.38 are ~~different~~ ↑separate↓. I
310.39 money ~~that~~ ↑it↓ would
310.41 to him↑:↓+,+ but
310.42 and @↑the↓ comes amo[n over
        g]g us
311. 1 de ~~Candia~~ ↑C——↓ my
311. 1 family ~~says~~ ↑interposed↓ Lady
311. 8 him. ~~You sold~~ your
311. 9 daughter ~~↑to Papa↓ for money,~~
        ↑was bought↓ with
311.13 she thought↑—↓of a
311.22 I ~~am of~~ ↑belong to↓ the
311.29 would ~~spo~~ spoil
311.31 and ~~I know~~@↑are no↓ better
311.32 the world↑:—↓Very goodlooking
311.33 good tempered, ↑:↓ it
311.38 temper. ~~In~~ ↑Of↓ after
311.43 her @↑grand-daughter↓ rather
312. 4 should ~~rangir~~@↑ranger↓ himself,
312. 5 in England[.' A over , a]nd the
312. 6 any ~~symptom~~ ↑igns↓ of
312. 8 truth here elder
312. 9 charming truth↑,↓ ~~of yielding~~
        ↑&↓ submitting
312.10 consious triumph[? over .] Give
312.11 of youth; of
312.11 while @↑Mr. Clives ~~papers~~
        drawings have been crackling
        in the fire place at her feet and
        the last spark of that combustion
        is twinkling out unheeded↓
        ¶[on verso: the place, I should
        certainly have chastised him]

Vol. II
[Begin Thackeray's handwriting.]
 30. 2 June ~~27~~ ↑12↓. 18—*k
 30. 8 here ~~n port~~ three
 30.15 to ride↑,↓ upon
 30.16 my ~~pleasure~~ ↑diversion↓ with
 30.24 She ~~occasioned~~ ↑caused↓ a
 30.26 of temper↑,↓ the
 30.28 at Naples, [w over [illeg.]]ith his

30.29 them. Kew↑'↓s wound
30.31 life ~~was~~ has
30.32 horses ↑and sown his wild oats↓.
        He
30.33 has ~~become~~ ↑turned↓ quite
30.33 gentleman. ¶~~After~~ ↑At↓ our
30.34 meeting ~~and we had been a week
        together at Naples;~~ he
31. 6 wh. ~~gave~~ ↑has given↓ me
31. 7 good ↑in↓ talking
31. 7 about it↑,↓ or
31. 9 we ~~are~~ ↑were↓ at
31.10 feelings ~~were~~ ↑might have been↓
        towards
31.n1 then ↓ I
31.27 train, ↑(↓though I
31.28 waiting room.↑)↓ And
31.32 lady ↑has received me with a
        scolding on my return from
        abroad &↓ is
31.33 Charles ~~is in pretty~~ ↑seems to be
        in very↓ good condition again↑.↓
        I
31.34 him ↑in full clerical feather↓ at
31.38 mysterious way. ~~Ive not seen the
        old Candishites. Candish's prate
        about Rome would be too much
        ↑for me↓ ↑Candish has been to
        see me & kindly wants me to↓~~
        ¶Mr.
31.40 never attack↑,↓ a
31.40 lovely back↑,↓ I
32. 4 friends ~~in~~ ↑with↓ Bryanstone
32.12 at [Steyne Gardens over blank]
        stepping
32.12 the ~~cab,~~ ↑fly,↓ and
32.14 of ~~joy at his return~~ ↑pleasure at
        his visit↓. But
32.16 him ~~over~~ ↑during↓ the
32.19 she ~~was~~ had
32.21 plumage ↑redness of craw↓ and
32.26 the ~~street~~ ↑Square↓. The
32.29 mean Sir[! over .] Dont
32.29 turn *me* off ~~with~~ ↑in↓ that [italics
        added]
32.30 past one↑.↓ ~~cold, so that Betty
        may go to Church.~~ You
32.31 you like'[— over illeg.]and the
32.33 Mrs. Honeyman↑'↓s servant
        [Hannah over blank] entered,
32.33 who ~~on the contrary~~ ↑for her
        part↓ grinned

32.34 sly. ↑'↓In the

32.34 Goodness [Hannah over blank]
       what

32.37 says [Hannah over blank] patting

33.n5 and whe confound

33. 1 I g ↑to↓ get

33.n6 the yo ↑youth.↓ ¶Did

33. 2 Master Clive↑,↓ cries

33. 3 humour. ↑'↓Well! she

33.n7 Clive! wh ↑Down tu
       Borhambury↓ One

33.n7 when Miss one

33. 8 designate [Hannah over blank]
       these

33.10 says [Hannah over blank] jerking

33.11 There [Ms p. 4 is missing]
       ¶Innocent

34.19 now any young

34.19 read these ↑my↓ moral

34.28 going away↑,↓ innocent

34.28 he was↑,↓ yet

34.31 of ↑arose↓ ↑'↓Clive Clive!↑'↓ from

34.31 from a half dozen ↑four half a
       dozen↓ little

34.n4 their nurses ↑attendants↓ made

34.n4 same lo apartments

34.n4 careless [Bugsby over blank]
       rented

34.n4 and saw there

34.n4 pier-beams when ↑with↓ the

35. 6 arm—You will must

35. 7 us ↑for dinner [Miss over Mrs]
       Honeyman↓ if

35. 9 said ¶Hm[illeg.]! my

35.11 or not↑,↓ but

35.13 black silk↑,↓ Martha

35.15 and dy giving

35.15 this lady ↑elderly virgin↓ chafe

35.19 was of a

35.19 different sort↑ of Spinster↓; and

35.21 is this, ↑the↓ history

35.21 or ↑of↓ the

35.25 that ↑look of↓ extra

35.26 neatness ↑wh.↓ invalids

35.29 of ↑matters wh. had occurred↓
       forty

35.30 a boy; ↑—↓in a

35.31 Ethel. ↑He threw me down in
       a chaise, sad wild f[illeg.] ↑↑ sad
       wild chap, always reading Orme's
       History of India↓↓ wanted marry

35.32 Frenchwoman.↓ He

35.37 Clive ↑(several times)↓ where

35.37 been? [a over s]nd said

35.38 evy day↑—↓strong as

35.39 a horse↑—↓go back

35.39 peevish and an ↑with Parker↓ his

35.40 man came ↑retired, and came
       back↓ presently

36. 1 into his own the

36. 2 of life.this world.

36. 4 that last look nod

36. 5 on you, and ↑him, or the↓ coach

36. 6 heartily. ¶Th[e over is] infantile

36. 7 when the servants

36. 9 to [pay over [illeg.]] his

36.13 Newcome said ↑remarked↓ if

36.15 Miss [blank] came

36.18 this year² and

36.24 out or re ↑or receiving at time or
       ↑↑home↓↓↓ this

36.29 my mamma ↑other,↓ said

36.30 know when she

36.30 was ↑at ever so many places.↓
       She

36.33 a brute,) and

36.40 archly. ↑Indeed↓ She

36.40 She believedthought she

36.41 asked Clive[. A over , a]nd my

36.43 are ↑you?↓ ¶Why

36.44 should I ↑we↓ disown

36.45 and g it

37. 2 McCollop the p did

37. 5 had a ↑the↓ moor

37. 7 his ↑own↓ handsome

37.14 very unwell—Lady ↑Lord↓
       Farintosh:

37.19 made your look

37.22 Miss Newcome↑!↓ what

37.34 Lord whknows who—Lord

37.37 like Punch↑!↓ cries

37.38 isnt ↑it↓? asked

37.40 funny picture↑!↓ exclaims

37.40 it capital↑?↓ Lord

37.43 There's ↑Odo↓ Carton

37.44 'em. You'+re+coming ↑ll come↓
       up

37.44 morrow and ↑wont↓ you?

37.46 quite inaudible.↑)↓ You

37.47 Miss [blank] have

37.47 you know↑,↓ that

38. 3 a favor↑?↓ Lady

38. 5 party ~~to~~ on
38. 8 mustachios ↑& their wearer↓ on
38. 9 make ~~the leas~~ any
38.11 suppose? ¶[verso of p. 8]
~~I'm an artist says Clive~~
~~turning very red.~~
~~¶O really I didn't know! cries~~
~~the Nobleman: and↑, my lord↓~~
~~bursting out laughing~~
~~↑presently↓ as he was engaged~~
~~in a conversation with Miss~~
~~Ethel on the balcony; Clive~~
~~thought, very likely with~~
~~justice, «that my lord was~~
~~making sport» ↑«Far»'he is~~
~~making fun↓ of «his» ↑my↓~~
~~mustachios, confound him! I~~
~~should like to pitch him over~~
~~into the street.' But this was~~
~~only a kind wish on Mr.~~
~~Newcomes part not followed out~~
~~by any fullfilment—ony a sulky~~
~~nod when he quitted his aunt's~~
~~room.~~ [pp. 9-13 are inserted] ¶'I
38.23 and ↑would be sure to be
putting↓ the
38.24 him ~~many~~ a
38.24 a ↑quarter of an hour of↓
delightful
38.n4 interim. ↑He wrote that letter to
his father.↓ He
38.n4 He ↑strove to↓ pacify
38.n4 travels, ↑talk about old times↓
and
38.n4 received ~~his~~ the
38.n4 room ~~on t~~ down
38.n4 adorned ~~M~~ Sir
38.n4 the ↑apart↓ lodgings;
38.n4 tarts ~~and~~ prepared
38.n4 work; ~~Becky~~ ↑Hannah↓ gave
38.n4 hand ~~when any such w~~ ↑at the
dinner.↓ ¶Clive's
38.26 he ↑came to dinner at length,
and↓ found
38.27 found ~~that~~ Lord
38.n5 Farintosh ~~had,~~ who
38.29 as ↑all↓ people
38.34 feel ~~rather~~ sulky
38.n7 their ~~conversation~~ ↑dialogue↓.
¶Miss
39. 3 Honeyman's ~~back~~ parlour
39. 5 been ~~offended~~ ↑angry↓: but
39. 5 spirit ~~constantly~~ ↑not
unfrequently↓ mistakes
39. 9 of ~~Becky~~ ↑Martha↓ who

39.11 refused curr[a over e]nt and
39.12 him [absolutely cry over cry
absolutely] in
39.13 good ~~Becky~~ ↑Martha↓ was
39.17 honest ~~Becky~~ ↑Mrs. Hicks↓ who
39.19 good ~~says~~ ↑remarked↓
Lord Farintosh[. over ,]
~~holding out his plate~~ ¶Then
39.21 nobleman ↑holding out his
plate↓ ~~remarked th~~ ↑observed↓
with
39.27 was ~~an~~ Princess
39.28 tarts ↑& custards↓ that
39.37 say— ¶↑Mr. Honeymans sister
the preacher you know where we
go on Sunday Miss Ethel breaks
out↓ ¶+'+I dont think its ↑'The
Honeyman pedigree is not↓ a
39.41 Ann ~~said~~ ↑remarked↓ gently.
39.43 perplexity ↑had↓ spread
39.45 on. ↑The↓ Arabian
40. 2 lordships ~~notes~~ ↑doubts↓ and
40. 2 and queries.~~such~~ ↑ Whatever↓
his
40. 5 be ~~where~~ ↑whether↓ there
40. 9 Farintosh ~~the whole~~ ↑for the rest
of the↓ evening,
40.10 Bryan ↑& her children↓ for
40.11 time: ~~so that~~ ↑& thus↓ Clive
40.12 friends, ~~and~~ ↑uttering all sorts of
~~lit~~ odd little paradoxes, firing the
while sly side shots at Mr. Clive,
and indeed↓ exhibiting
40.16 Marquis ~~ha~~ with
40.17 with ↑personal charms,↓ a
40.21 well [that over illeg.] evening
40.27 London ~~next morning~~
↑tomorrow↓—was Miss
40.29 said ~~all~~ it
40.30 and ~~y~~ both
40.31 are [too over two] young
40.31 her ~~chapero~~ ↑escort—↓added the
40.32 said ~~sometth↓ing~~ too
40.36 'em ~~[illeg.]~~ except
40.n8 shoulder. ↑an askance look at
Clive.↓) And
41. 1 I ~~wou~~ give
41. 3 dont ~~care about~~ ↑want↓ a
41. 3 horse ~~being~~ like
41. 4 blazes now+,+↑: and↓ over
41. 5 is ~~if~~ upon my
41. 5 honour ¶~~If~~ ↑When↓ I

41. 7 fine ↑smile↓ ¶Clive
41.11 time ~~one~~ ↑a↓ dangerous
41.11 eyes ↑as though↓ to
41.14 deep. ¶~~You~~But if
41.20 made ~~Mr.~~ Clive
41.20 imperious ↑~~signifying~~↓ manner
41.21 Farintosh ~~was gone away~~ ↑had
     lef↓ departed↓. ¶But ¶But
     ~~he said—Good night~~+:+ ↑he
     did not choose to obey this order.
     Good night, he said,↓ before
41.23 go ~~away~~ I
41.23 must ~~go and~~ shake
41.23 stairs.' [A over a]nd ↑the↓ was
41.23 was gone, following
41.25 Clive ~~went in to~~ ↑entered↓ Miss
41.26 back parlour+:+↑ making a bow
     to the young nobleman↓ my
41.27 and ~~told~~ the
41.27 day ~~remark~~ ↑told↓ friends
41.29 at ↓Lady Ann's
41.29 they call~~ed~~ Clive, ~~who said~~ ↑who
     is a painter by trade, his uncle is
     preacher,↓ his
41.30 father ~~was~~ ↑is↓ a
41.30 and ~~whose~~ ↑this↓ Aunt
42. 2 my ~~apart~~ chambers ~~the~~ ↑in the
     Temple on the very↓ next
42. 4 the ~~events~~ ↑story↓ wh. ha[s over
     ve] been
42. 7 Sir, ↑he added when he
     had concluded it with many
     ejaculations regarding the
     heroine of the little tale↓ walking
42.15 station—and ~~made, as if I di~~
     ↑didnt even bow↓ to
42.18 way ~~[illeg.]~~to the
42.19 the ↑Railroad↓ ¶Hang
42.20 Clive ↑turning very red↓ I
42.23 Farintosh ↑I should think ~~such~~
     +he+↓ [H over h]e never
42.24 you ~~sa~~ tell
42.27 to ~~want~~ ↑like↓ me
42.27 quite ~~tender~~kind—kind she
42.28 mean; [A over a]nd then
43. 1 Clives [C over c]oun[ci over
     se]llor. ¶I
43. 3 bow ↑to↓ her,
43. 7 a ↑silver↓ collar
43. 7 and ~~wear~~ ↑go through the world
     with↓ my
43.10 Pendennis. ¶↑(At this noise↓ Mr.
43.12 and ↑shows↓ a

43.13 wanted! ↑says Mr. Pendennis↓
     Exit
43.20 tone ~~out of~~ ↑of↓ her
43.23 and ↑the↓ Gods
43.23 after ~~a~~ ↑a ↓while. But
43.26 the ~~Boots~~ ↑Master chamber
     maid↓ came
43.26 with ~~his~~ a
43.30 in ↑the↓ Army,
43.n6 with ~~an~~ ↑another↓ ingenuous
     blush[; and over . I t] she
43.n8 about her~~.~~! And
43.n8 fired ↑off↓ twenty
43.n8 place ↑drank off tumbler after
     tumbler of water↓ and
43.35 by. ~~Besides~~ Who
43.38 of ~~swells~~ ↑swells↓ +at+ ↑in↓ her
     ~~feet~~ ↑train↓? I
44. 3 all. ¶[Well over I o] I
44.11 our ↑condition?↓ ¶ A
44.16 very ~~happy~~ ↑good↓ marriage
44.16 much happier+,+ ↑in↓ marrying
44.21 how ~~cert~~ friends
44.22 dear [g over illeg.]ood little
44.23 her mother~~'s~~ ↑ is↓ away—
     knowing
44.24 suppose ~~she~~ ↑Ethel↓ wanted
44.28 under ~~twenty~~ ↑so many↓
     thousand
44.34 coarse meat; ↑ &↓ bathe
44.34 the river~~-and~~, wear
44.37 poor ~~old~~ Clive,
44.40 was ↑going out a courting↓
     ¶~~In his communications with~~
     ~~↑certain↓~~ ↑Thus it will be seem
     that in his communications with
     certain↓ friends
44.43 life, ~~Mr.~~ Clive
44.44 regarding ~~this~~ passion
45. 1 head ~~and f~~ the
45. 3 full ~~cover~~ ↑curve↓ to
45. 3 &c &c.—~~a~~ ↑A↓ frequenter
45. 4 his ~~atelier~~ studio
45. 4 represented: ~~if~~ ↑when↓ Mrs.
45.12 whatever occurred[. over :] She
45.16 bore ~~her~~ an
45.19 of rain↑, I fancy↓ Miss
45.20 undisturbedly ~~being~~ ↑and was↓
     sure
45.20 smile. ¶~~So she was pretty~~
     ~~unconcerned about Clives~~

altered demeanour; frequent
silences when he came to
visit Fitzroy Square, and
general melancholy. Had he
↑Clive↓ become

45.22　objects that ↑wh.↓ before

45.24　dashing lively↓ agreeable

45.25　her storiest—↓(about
　　　　Cheltenham,

45.n7　good company↑'↓—That story

45.32　in ↑this↓ Court

45.34　box giv[i over e]ng evidence

45.35　stolen his one

45.35　story almost ↑always↓ made

45.38　Messrs. Pendennist,↓
　　　　Warrington,

45.39　Fitzroy Square—↑when Mr.
　　　　Binnie chuckled, when Rosey
　　　　as in duty bound looked
　　　　discomposed & said Law
　　　　Mamma!—↓not one

45.44　there; F.B ↑ & Bayham↓ had

46. 1　the Claret↑-jug↓ was

46. 2　friend Frederick Bayham: ↑F.B.↓
　　　　[W over w]hen the

46. 5　face ↑I thought,↓ looked

46. 5　him o kindly

46.n4　for [Margi: 48.] —thank

46.14　is m bidding

46.15　and ↑my good friend↓ Mrs.

46.20　Sherrick say remarked

46.21　to buy ↑purchase↓ a

46.21　works. It ↑I would—only
　　　　I haven't the capital at
　　　　present to spare. Mine has
　　　　been vested+,+↑↑ in an
　　　　[illeg.]↓↓↓O'dessa↑ ↑↑ venture
　　　　Sir—↓↓in a large amount of
　　　　wild oats wh. up to the present
　　　　moment make me no return.
　　　　But it↓ will

46.24　will be always

46.25　deserving ↑young↓ mans

46.27　'You F.B[! over ?] and

46.27　how? ↑we↓ asked

46.29　majestically. ↑Mr. Mr.↓
　　　　Warrington

46.34　both I believe are concluded ↑I
　　　　am told by those↓ who

46.34　with considerabl[e over y]—
　　　　consummate ability.

46.39　laugh. ¶We ↑One of us↓ had

47. 1　Mrs. Mackenzie, (let me ↑him↓the
　　　　criminal↓ blush

47. 2　form a-part of

47. 3　of a most

47. 4　vast p landed possessions) and

47.11　was chr ↑charmed↓ and

47.15　such an ogling ↑woman.↓ I

47.20　his you say he

47.23　a woman ↑wife↓ at

47.24　up ↑with a blushing face↓ and

47.27　lot said quoth

47.29　winning? ↑Psha!↓ Its

47.30　us: and they ↑married if a man
　　　　must be, a suitable wife↓ should

47.31　to a man him, and

47.34　kindly-disposed ↑easy going↓ old
　　　　↑Heathen↓ philosopher—

47.40　and ↑since I went to our race-
　　　　balls as a boy,↓ scarcely

47.42　parties ↑in London↓ like

47.43　as the ↑my↓ door

47.43　and you were both ↑the young
　　　　one↓ was

48. 1　a woman ↑creature↓ I

48. 6　to see meet

48. 7　ensuing months ↑weeks↓ of

48.10　him. ↑You know Clive I cant
　　　　help myself: nor would it be
　　　　proper to make you signs out
　　　　of the window.↓ But

48.16　that. S[ir over illeg.]! and

48.17　evening Lady Kew as

48.n7　balconies? A m Why were

48.33　Toadins, ↑Miss Crochit the late
　　　　Vicars daughter at Kewbury↓
　　　　and

48.34　Walleye Farintoshs cousin and
　　　　↑or Tommy Henchman
　　　　Farintoshs kinsmen and
　　　　admirers↓ who

48.36　invalid so that and

48.37　young dragoon ↑soldier↓ being

49. 1　for' I was ↑the Cap↓tain told

49. 2　mess ↑& Clive↓ at

49. 3　know and to

49. 4　sit ↑if I could↓ in

49.10　more noble ↑comfortable↓ or

49.11　a younger's Sons

49.14　Ethel [illeg.] saving

49.16　old Slut[illeg.] that

49.27　young woman that ↑girl↓ she

49.29　her ↑old↓ clutches.

49.32　be? [illeg.] ↑c↓ontinues honest

49.36 Top? ¶~~My m~~ ↑Heard↓ her
49.38 first. ~~My~~ ↑My↓ man
49.40 was ~~never without a black eye~~ ↑all over black & blue↓. ¶Capital
49.43 And ↑~~[illeg.]~~↓ Kews
50. 4 and ~~have you~~ ↑you shall be↓ put
50.13 and ~~settle that little bill at Sherrick's~~ ↑do something handsome for that poor↓ deluded
50.14 Street. ↑Jack says↓ Kew↑s↓ ~~has~~ mother
50.16 Son ↑now↓ you
50.17 for ~~his~~ Lady
50.19 Kew is[; over —] and
50.19 by him[— over :]went to
50.21 conversation ↑the latter part of↓ wh.
50.24 & ↑Mr.↓ Belsize
50.30 his ~~former~~↑older &↓ peaceful
50.31 their ~~days~~↑afternoon↓ airing
50.36 beautiful ↑primrose-coloured↓ kid-gloves
51. 2 his ~~windows~~↑door:↓ and
51. 3 his ~~win~~ painting
51. 3 did ~~his~~↑Clive's↓ next
51.n8 Runt ↑~~Finch~~ Finch↓ the
51. 9 Scowler? ~~He~~↑Scowler↓ was
51.12 really ~~very~~ tolerable:
51.17 walk ~~barefoot~~↑five miles↓ to
51.18 man! ~~The next Sunday Clive bethought him that he had not seen Uncle «at» Charles, whose revered image had not once entered his mind sin~~ ¶Mr.
52.18 you, ~~F.B~~↑the↓ was
52.24 a ↑cool↓ lobster
52.24 of ~~bitter~~↑table↓ beer—~~the~~-wh. they
52.32 did not+—+~~hem~~—get the— hem—paper
53. 6 read—the—ahem—the [P over p]ulpit Pencillings
53. 7 in London'—and signed
53.12 Pencillings ~~are of~~↑would↓ be
53.14 your ↑future↓ husband's
53.20 Pencillings. ~~They have been attributed~~↑Some complain that their favorite preachers are slighted, others applaud because the clergymen↓ they
53.24 to ~~an emine~~ Member

53.33 turns ~~at~~↑the↓ sportive
53.37 the [P over p]encillings—scarcely allowing
53.42 Clive, '~~I've~~↓ have↓ heard
53.45 into ~~play~~↑notice.↓ ~~I got Sir last nig~~↑They ~~pen~~ begin to↓ know
54.13 are ~~very much~~↑greatly↓ changed
54.22 Sir ↑soon after your departure for Italy↓ that
54.24 a ↑heedless↓ friend
54.24 hand, ~~he~~↑Sherrick↓ invited
55. 2 piano, ↑not↓ sing
55. 7 screens ↑up↓ in
55. 8 by Jingo[! over ?] Your
55.n3 Harmony; ↑and your choir↓ +Your+ ~~choir~~ have
55.14 Sherrick ~~who~~ has
55.16 'em. ~~She~~↑The ladies↓ actually
55.17 Honeyman's ~~to tea~~↑to an oyster↓ afterwards.
55.18 mean again+,+↑:—↓and Charles
55.22 are old,~~ but s~~ I
55.23 Sir. ~~Come~~They have
55.27 what, ~~Sir~~F.B.? asks
55.29 St. ↑Billings the butterman, Sharwood the turner blacking-maker, & the Honorable Phelim O'Curraghs Lord ~~[illeg.]~~ Scullabogue's son, made speeches↓ Two
55.32 three ↑respectable↓ families
55.32 Mrs. Wha[d over t]dyoucallem Newcome
55.33 among ~~t~~ the
55.33 in disgust—↑I↓ wrote an ↑article of↓ controversial ~~article in~~ bit o↓graphy in ↑the↓ P
55.40 life Clive—↑It ain't bad to see him doing the martyr Sir, Sebastian riddled with paper pellets Bartholomew on a cold gridiron↓ Here
56. 2 the lobster[. U over u]pon my
56. 5 had ~~hinted~~↑said↓ that
56. 5 Clive ~~went~~↑was induced to go↓ there
56. 6 He ~~was there~~↑attended↓~~be~~ punctually
56. 8 pins, ~~and~~↑who handed him at the Anthem↓ a
56.11 valet [p over c]assed the
56.12 the ~~lectern~~+,+ desk ~~no longer~~. ~~Before~~↑Formerly↓ he

56.13 remembered ~~how↑~~when↓ as
56.15 the ↑scarf & the↓ sleeves
~~and scarf↑[illeg.]↓~~ of
56.18 was ~~made↑~~cut↓ straight
56.20 slight ҒҒ arabesque
56.24 service ↑in a swift manner and↓
with
56.25 he ~~sate~~ stood
56.27 niche. ↑It was fine to
hear Sherrick who had an
uncommonly good voice join in
the musical parts of the service.↓
The
56.29 church ~~an~~ here
56.30 a ~~Dutch~~ Flemish
56.n8 bargain ~~at~~ ↑from old Moss in↓
+in+ Wardour
56.n9 pink ↑green↓ and
56.35 surplice, ~~and↑~~and the priest
gave way to the preacher. He↓
preached
56.38 of ~~an ancient↓~~ royal house↓ had
56.38 accident. Abs[o over a]lo[n over
m] the
56.39 furnished ~~him↑~~Honeyman↓ with
56.41 to them[— over ,]It was
56.43 giving ~~Cl~~ Clive
56.43 the ~~serv~~ rite
57. 1 manager ↑would↓ of
57. 2 Irishman ↑was↓ no
57. 6 be ~~pardoned↑~~allowed↓ to
57. 8 Away ↑in a ~~corn~~ darkling
corner↓ under
57. 9 that [P over p]owdered one
57.17 Kew's ↑venerable↓ Roman
57.22 of ~~the~~ his
57.22 Canary, ~~the↑~~Lady Kew's↓
equipage
57.36 good ~~one↑~~un↓ to
58. 1 Clive. ↑Theres some tolerable
good wine down there.↓ Our
58.10 the org[i over a]n-loft, we
58.14 loss ↑more than↓ ten
58.14 Clive ↑gravely↓. And/
58.18 in [blank]. ¶Hold
58.19 and [leave over ink blot] my
58.22 ave ~~your~~ a
58.23 Sherrick. [on verso p. 23: He
kept his word and returned
presently indeed. The young
Marquis, and an] ¶Ah
58.24 in ~~at~~her↓ deep
59. 5 ponies ~~an~~ when

59.n2 I am—~~ta~~—thankful! says
59. 9 sweet ↑sa[d over w]↓ voice
59.17 Charles ↑in↑↑with↓↓ the most
heart-rending simplicity↓— and
Mrs.
59.20 has ↑indeed↓ a
59.20 the ↑Gothic↓ Hall
59.21 the ~~cost~~ sum
59.27 him ~~preach↑~~do duty↓ more
59.28 draws ~~by the~~ because
59.29 here. ↑Revd. Mr. Jurnyman
does the duty now—quiet
Hoxford man—ill I
59.30 suppose this morning.↓ H
59.37 they ~~forgit↑~~get↓ his ~~ki~~ goodness
59.38 biscuits, ↑a pyramid of jams, &↓
six
59.40 entered ↑it,—↓as a
59.42 remarked ↑with a smile↓ the
59.42 upon ~~the~~ a
60. 3 away ~~uneasily~~ and
60. 3 of ↑young↓ Clive
60. 5 the money-~~benefits↑~~transactions↓
between
60. 8 memoirs. ¶~~When~~Thursday came
and ↑with it↓ Mr.
60. 9 entertainment,
~~Clive's uncle took him to the
wine-merchants Regents-Park
villa, whither~~ ↑to wh.↓ also
60.11 Rosey ~~came:↑~~brought Clive in
their carriage;↓ Mrs.
60.14 I ~~am↑~~must be↓ of
60.19 Miss ↑&↓ though
60.20 me [(over —]it was
60.22 Roseys ↑pretty↓ little
60.25 home ~~again~~ by
60.40 left alone↑, &↓ to
60.41 without Mamaw,—↑There—↓I
won't
60.43 Clive, ↑good humouredly.↓ And
61. 8 in com↑te↓pliment to
61.12 a ~~handsome↑~~neat↓ Brougham.
61.18 Season ↑of 18— ↑ at
61.19 who ↑of course↓ went
61.24 Botibol ↑of Islington↓ and
61.25 confessors ↑Then there was↓ The
61.26 and Martyr—↑with↓ sweet
↑~~doub~~double↓ frontispiece
representing ↑(1)↓ the
61.28 for ↑benefit↓ the

61.30 children ~~with~~ by
61.31 Sermons ~~to a~~ delivered
61.40 picture. ¶[M over S]y girl~~s not~~ aint
61.42 look far~~ther~~↓ enough↓ and
61.42 of ~~those~~↑them↓ two.
62. 1 a ↑German↓ print—~~rep~~the Two
62. 3 Clive. ↑¶↓'And why
62. 8 men ~~very~~↑pretty↓ well:
62. 8 ladies ~~defied~~ were
62.10 said ~~his host~~↑Mr. Sherrick↓; and
62.10 his ~~host~~↑guest↓ looked
62.11 of ~~his host~~ ↑this↓ being
62.12 you. ↑I often go there.↓ I've
62.14 who, ~~paid up like a m~~↑every inch the↓ gentleman—one
62.15 man. ~~Y~~The Earl
62.21 giving a[n over s] accompaniment
62.31 again ↑taking possession of the back seat↓; &
62.33 take [a over t]ll the
62.37 *What?* ~~says~~↑cries↓ Clive.
62.40 sister ↑dear↓ Rosey ↑he said this time↑ ¶Yes
63. 5 Divines. ↑Charles became so friendly and was so pleased with this drawing that he was now constantly coming to Charlotte Street—once or twice a week.↓ ¶Mr.
63. 8 to ~~see~~↑look at↓ [the over this] drawing,—and
63.12 to ~~the~~↑Clive's↓ Studio,
63.14 rank whos~~e title is taken from the~~ ↑has married an English lady↓ and
63.18 eloquent incumbent—~~who~~and it
63.26 wish ↑that↓ it
63.37 very ↑first↓ instant
63.40 Rosey. ¶The↑London↓ season
65. 3 money ↑freely↓ on
65. 4 hunting ~~an old~~ ↑young↓ Marquis
65. 5 whether ~~the~~↑her↓ game
65. 8 a ↑nov↓ story,
65.10 Miss ↑Ethel↓ Newcome ~~has~~ occupies
65.21 hand ↑(and unless, there are extenuating circumstances)↓, Ethel
65.24 man ~~does~~ with
65.32 young. Sh[e over e's] is
65.36 a Catholic—~~let us bear with Ethel~~

↑So if Ethel worships at a certain Image wh. a great number of good folks in England bow to let us not ~~quarrel~~ be too angry with her idolatry and bear with our Queen↓ a
65.38 longer ~~then and not put~~ ↑before we↓ make
65.40 dignified pos[ition over ture] in
65.42 the ↑very↓ outset
65.43 aim ~~our~~ with
65.44 rich man~~,↑~~—↓that she
66. 1 career ~~open to women~~+.+ ↑for wh. many a woman is bred & trained.↓ A
66. 2 begins ~~life~~↑the world↓ with
66. 3 good ↑& follow the truth↓: he
66. 4 base action~~,↑:↓ he
66. 7 has ~~begun life at least~~ ↑commenced ~~the~~ life at any rate↓ with
66. 7 views, ↑and generous schemes,↓ from
66. 8 overpowering ~~ill~~↑hostile↓ fortune
66.12 and ~~one~~↑a house↓ in
66.13 and ~~bright~~↑blooming↓ into
66.14 on ↑the Prince & the Duke, Crœsus and↓ Dives.
66.15 little ~~honest~~↑natural↓ hearts
66.17 child ↑with an awful premature knowledge of the pawn-shop,↓ able
66.18 market ~~and bargain~~ ↑battle bargain at stalls↓ with
66.19 shall ~~see~~ ↑find↓ a young [B over b]eauty, who
66.21 practitioners ~~there~~+;+↑on that Exchange;↓ as
66.22 or ~~placing~~↑producing↓ her
66.25 Green ↑who were talking about Miss Newcome and her suitors↓ were
66.27 it [illeg.]↑was↓ because
66.34 who ~~knew~~↑had been early introduced into↓ the
66.35 their ~~simple~~↑downright↓ phraseology
66.36 point ↑of wh.↓ he
66.40 thanks ~~by~~ for
66.44 meeting ↑Clive↓ Newcome
66.45 pertinacity [in over on] following
66.47 and ↑thus↓ he
67. 2 of ~~the~~↑a↓ squeeze

67. 8 two. ~~At the end~~ ↑By the time↓ of
67.10 needed «~~no~~» ~~not~~↑few↓ more
67.11 man ~~of~~ and
67.11 the ↑only↓ son
67.13 entertain a↑n↓ ↑unhappy↓ fond↑ness↓ ~~passion~~ for
67.22 of ~~a party~~↑people at an entertainment↓; on
67.23 the ~~names~~↑list↓, you
67.24 If ~~the~~ Lord
67.24 Lady ↑Blank↓ of
67.25 castle ~~enter~~ received
67.25 Lady ~~Thingambob↑Troisétudes↓~~ ↑Dash↓) for Christmas ~~and~~↑or↓ Easter,
67.30 weather ↑to see their friends↓, and
67.39 than ↑unwittingly↓ ~~an obedient↓~~ consenting↓ party
67.46 her. ↑She had and wrote as many letters as a Secretary of State
67.47 almost.↓ She
68. 2 own ~~will~~↑wish↓ wh.
68. 4 as ↑that of wh.↓ Lady
68. 5 (Hobson [B over b]rothers knew
68. 9 in ~~enjoining~~ ↑ordering↓ Ethel's
68. 9 to ~~her~~↑Lady↓ Kew—↑you [illeg] know how difficult it is for one young woman not to acquiesce when the family Council strongly orders↓ In
68.12 that ↑it was↓ her
68.13 minister ↑who↓ led her wrong[. O over , o]therwise I
68.19 night, ~~to~~↑& the↓ awak[ing over e] to
68.19 Godless a morrow!
68.20 and ↑but↓ not
68.20 fault ↑altogether↓, had
68.22 those ~~blame~~↑punish↓ her
68.25 was ~~but~~↑only↓ of
68.25 a relation; she
68.30 to ↑take their chance at↓ the
68.31 corroborate ↑to some extent↓ Mr.
69. 2 be ~~exe~~ faithful
69. 3 very ~~dashing~~↑agreeable↓ and
69.11 and ↑who↓ was
69.15 lived ~~so~~ no
69.15 the [P over p]rofessor who was ↑still↓ teaching
69.22 Philippe's, ↑&↓ to

69.23 volubility. ~~He~~↑A young nobleman of his rank↓ was
69.24 the [illeg.] French
69.28 the ↑Marquis↓ was
69.30 Clive Newcome↑—↓and it
69.34 own ~~went a little~~↑actually went once or twice↓ into
69.36 there. ~~They~~↑The French people↓ did
69.36 understand ~~how~~ ↑what↓ bad
69.41 another ↑French↓ lady
69.42 Kew, ~~and~~↑(who you may be sure is delighted to have such a relative) And the French lady↓~~and~~ invites Clive ↑to her receptions↓ expressly
70. 2 they ~~regarded~~ ↑looked at↓ his
70. 3 they ~~wept~~↑shed↓, gentle
70. 5 steadfast ↑with us↓ through
70. 5 all ~~four~~ changes;
70. 6 burns bright↑ly↓~~still~~, and
70. 7 and ~~does not cease till~~↑exists with↓ the
70. 7 faithful bosom—when↑ce↓ it passes ~~beyond death~~ with [↑ over p]he pure soul, ~~must it~~beyond death; surely it shall↓ +not+ be Immortal? ~~When~~↑Though↓ we
70. 9 not ~~with us~~ our's
70.10 Heaven? ~~The~~If we
70.10 lose ~~can ↑do↓ we~~ ↑can we altogether↓ lose
70.11 we love?—~~S[illeg.]~~Forty years
70.11 away. ↑Youth and dearest memories revisit her↓ and
70.12 the ~~faithful~~↑constant↓ lady ↑holds the young man's hand, and↓ looks
71. 9 his ↑lift↓ manners
71.10 School. ~~He went~~ ↑When the↓ After
71.16 me.' ~~We have~~↑Our history has↓ but
71.18 him, ↑this House of Peers to attend when he is ~~strong~~ well enough,↓ his
71.24 of reconciliation,↓ [(over —]a reconciliation all philosophical, my friends,—)↓ with
71.26 great succession;" Every
71.28 the ~~premier~~↑first floor↓ of
71.29 returned ~~like Cincinnatus~~ to his ↑original↓ pigs
71.35 cupids: ~~an~~ it

72. 1 glass, ~~at~~ between

72. 4 of ~~prim~~ elderly

72. 5 Lancashire ~~maid~~ maid

72. 7 can ~~but~~ get

72. 9 The ~~apartment~~↑chamber↓ is

72.10 reception-evenings.
As ~~for Monsieur~~↓ boudoir,
b[illeg.]~~ten~~ rose-tendre↓ with

72.14 Newcome ↑Mr. Humper at
Manchester↓ (the

72.18 Moncontour's ~~da~~ boudoir.

72.19 paragraph ↑respecting ~~the~~ a
'Conversion in High Life'↓ wh.

72.n4 ordered ↑Messrs. Smith &
Elder↓ his

72.n4 to ↑send half a dozen copies
weekly↓ friends

72.n4 on ↑little more than his his
lieutenants↓ half

72.n4 Somersetshire: ↑(where Charley
Bayfords poor girls were, who
was killed in Burleigh)↓ and

72.n4 Florac, ~~R~~ a

72.24 fancy ~~in~~↑with↓ what a ~~condition~~
↑panic it filled↓ the

72.25 lady. ~~was.~~ Her

72.25 Protestant! [A over a]fter all

72.29 perdition. ↑She sent for↓ Her

72.29 son, ↑who↓ undertook

72.32 of ~~being converted~~ ↑abandoning
his religion↓; the

72.33 her [illeg] envoy.

72.35 of ~~M~~ his

73. 1 repute ↑for eloquence↓ in

73.13 Princesse ↑in turn↓ presented

73.18 before ~~the~~ Majesty;

73.36 Railway: ↑&↓ to take ~~him~~↑the
princely prodigal↓ down

73.38 Higg family[— over :]Barnes we

73.38 the ~~Prince of Montcontour~~
↑Principality:↓ rescued

73.43 had ↑already↓ reconciled

74. 2 Saint James's~~,~~ got

74. 3 Chapel. ↑The Revd. Charles↓
Honeyman's

74. 4 new disciple—↑thus↓ the

74. 9 died ↑lately↓ leaving

74.13 great ~~dignity~~↑gravity↓ at

74.16 man ~~&~~ was

74.19 paid ~~her~~↑his wife↓ visit

74.20 parties ↑& her opera box↓ and

74.33 for ~~your~~ ↑his↓ servant. No.
~~You~~↑Thou↓ wilt

74.34 here ~~the~~ but

74.35 board ~~calls~~ me

74.36 will ~~not~~↑but↓ be
~~amused~~↑ennuyé↓ to

74.36 father. ↑My mother waits on
him.↓ My

74.39 man. ↑Come and go when thou
wilt Clive my garcon my son↓
Thy

74.43 he ~~was~~ did

74.44 Sometimes ~~the Princess~~ Madame

74.45 be ~~a~~↑any↓ liking,

74.46 day: ~~and~~ Madame

75. 8 a ~~wicked~~↑terrible↓ old

75. 8 He [Margin: slip 5] remembered

75.19 duty ↑to her relatives↓ being to
~~get on in~~ push

75.25 jealous [if over of] their

75.28 whose ~~keeping~~↑service↓ she

75.29 questioned; ~~having given away
her heart elsewhere,~~
↑giving him ~~submission~~
↑↑obedience↓↓ striving to give
him respect↓ everything keeping.
~~The long story of a womans
life is a very sad
one sometimes, a monotonous
low plaint, a long
submission, and tears~~↑Many a
good woman's life is no more
cheerful: a spring of beauty, a
little warmth and sunshine of
love, a bitter disappointment↓
followed

75.35 it ~~chastens~~↑afflicts'↓. And

75.36 assures ~~of~~ her

75.41 more ~~fondly~~ than

75.41 human being—↓ is↓ rebellious

75.44 schemes fail~~ing~~ somehow,

75.44 town ↑and ball to ball↓ and [hall
to castle over castle to hall] for

75.46 by ~~prescription~~↑sufferance,↓ and

76. 6 lady ↑may be said to↓ resembles
the

76. 9 and ~~pounces upon~~↑robs↓ meat

76. 9 good ↑we↓↓ must

76.11 nature ↑(or fiction of poets who
have their own natural history)↓
that

76.13 gaze ↑at↓ it;

76.16 Florac ~~became~~↑was very↓
interested

76.20 to ~~Madame~~ the

76.31 England ↑or Scotland↓ that

76.32 marry ↑young↓ Lord

76.32 Princess ↑but he is only seventeen and his directors never lose sight of him↓: If Sir

76.34 Fawkes has a↑will have↓a large↑ a fine↓ property

76.35 daughter died—and of

76.36 course I was↑one is↓ anxious

76.38 was ↑one of↓ my

77. 2 has ↑a wig and↓ two

77. 3 encumbrance Mam Grandmamma

77. 4 or ↑a wig and↓ two

77. 5 must ↑try and↓ like

77. 6 please.' ¶↑So↓ Ethel

77. 8 de Préville's ↑[illeg.]↓ children

77. 8 grandchildren; ↑She was↓ gay

77.n8 whilst ↑not caring for↓ Lady

77.10 Lady Kew↑'s↓ who had her own

77.13 young lady↑person↓. The

77.17 of the↑her↓ Hotel;

77.18 embassies, [illeg.]the fluttering

77.22 when on the she

77.23 and Spaniards↑Neapolitan↓ secretaries,

77.26 young Prince↑Royal Highnesses↓ who

77.28 His ↑English↓ conversation

77.29 yet but as ≪we≫ has been said he was greatly improved in dancing: ↑although his French was eccentric.↓ and at the ↑Al But at the↓ Court

77.31 in the↑his native↓ Glenlivat

77.31 not a in

77.35 curly. ¶Madame de Florac↑Miss Newcome, out↓ of

77.37 not tell↑inform↓ Lady

77.39 education, she↑Madame de Florac↓ never

77.44 me for several times—↑Paul said—↓à preuve

78. 5 so [illeg.] tall

78. 9 young creature[! over ,] on

78.13 young lad[y over ie] of

78.14 Miss living↑who lives↓ under

78.15 and ↑is↓ obedient

78.15 them, is capable↑whom you↓ meet

78.16 society every day↑all the nights↓, and

78.17 every day—you is capable

78.18 theatre: ↑—↓of women

78.22 permit your one

78.26 and ↑a↓ gros

78.27 word [illeg.] against

78.28 name said I had↑cried I↓ ought

78.28 in this [illeg.] ↑ese places↓; and

78.30 ¶So had occasionally

78.35 and ↑in answer to Paul's offer to himself had↓ shown

78.40 owned ↑said↓ his

78.40 much [a over [illeg.]]t least

78.44 feel his goo am

78.46 were ↑alto↓ eager

79.n4 those ladies.If ¶If

79. 7 come? if↑When↓ Madame

79.n5 young girlsuppose[; it over —I] ↑may be↓ that

79. 8 to ↑[illeg.]↓ Madame de Florac's—with↑and would↓ insist

79.10 she wished↑went↓ to see[(over :]whose husband

79.14 wh. ↑when it was impugned↓ this

79.14 would not defend

79.29 never [illeg.] speculates

79.31 Miss Tompkins↑Hopkins↓ you

79.32 you practised↑worked on your↓ Papas

79.33 your ↑lace frock &↓ pretty

79.34 shoes: you when

79.36 dracones you↑proceeding↓ from

80. 1 India without↑—without↓ making

80. 4 believe [C over c]aptain Tomkins

80. 5 Ah Miss my

80. 6 neighbours! [Break a line] ¶All

81.14 enormous ↑forgotten↓ monster

81.17 years of ago

81.n1 and ↑parts↓ may

81.21 habits of size

81.21 charac with wh.↑who beings whereof↓ he

81.21 to deal↑treat—↓traces this

81.22 and depicts↑describes↓ his

81.26 then the in

81.29 a triton↑nymph or naiad [illeg] triton↓ so

81.29 though ↑s↓he holds [his over her over his] conch to [his over her over his] swelling lips,

and plaps↑curling↓ [his over her
over his] tail

81.30 basin, (formos a superne
↑in marble↓ except for
the moss and the scars,
she desiuit in piscoun
the latter end of her
being lead—«She»↑As
for↓ her conch and the
water a volume wh. she once
used to pour [illeg.] from it, She
↑this instrument↓ has

82. 1 Bourbons came back in

82. 1 time she was

82. 5 avenue ↑[illeg.] a

82. 7 Nerva in↑ont to↓ whose

82. 9 There are↑is↓ Cupid

82.10 Psyche th[is over ese] fift half-

82.12 under at↑the↓ damp

82.15 his attendants, Madame

82.16 Florac pa (when

82.18 are walking marching

82.30 lawsuit ↑about the
Bricquabracque↓ sold

82.31 Convent. ¶Ethel says «it would
be» ↑she wishes↓ ↑After some
talk about nuns, Ethel says↓
there

82.37 and [blank]at↑that↓ delightful

82.38 make th a

82.40 wicked th after

83. 3 of [P over p]aradise. I

83. 6 Street ↑Bond—↓ ¶Ethel.

83. 9 were an ↑Viscount, an↓ Earl,

83.15 or ↑with↓ the

83.22 chevaux, ↑et puis des petites
filles avec leurs gouvernantes,↓
et

83.22 des maisons,et↑—et puis—et↓
puis

83.24 (exit ↑little↓ Léonore down

83.25 you mu used

83.28 Ethel. ↑¶↓Ethel. Tell

83.30 remember ↑one of the days↓
when

83.32 fairy who-e or

83.33 box—because ↑¶↓Ethel. Because

83.42 ¶ ↑¶↓Ethel. 'Ah Clive! ↑¶↓'Now
it is different.↑altered.↓ Now

84. 3 should not[— over :]but when

84. 5 our relationship?—no, not

84. 6 it?—Don't take my hand↑do
that↓ Sir, or I will go i↑.↑twe

have shaken hands twice
already.↓ Léonore!

84. 9 another ↑day, you are↓ ashamed

84.12 Lord laughed↑looked quite↓
alarmed

84.12 to me,↑.↓ My

84.14 with h all

84.17 ill educated or as—I wont

84.22 say so—↑Hurriedly.↓ I

84.27 you ↑resembles you very much↓.
My

84.28 he is goi longs

84.29 Florac. ↑I was told that
another young «lad» persons
resembled me, compliment
of wh. I was much flattered↓ My

84.31 moment. [blank space] Exeunt

84.40 & the M.

85. 1 la Vie Prince—Madame

85. 4 old [Saint over St.] Jean—to

85. 4 a groom ↑lackey↓ comes

85. 5 cheeseplates. Madame la↑ ¶The
lackey The↓ Princess

85. 7 livery ↑has come forth to the
landing &↓ introduces

85. 9 How did de

85.13 the Tur Spanish↑Napolitum↓
Embassy

85.19 Newcome Mad(by the

86.17 guess ↑hour↓ little

86.19 his ↑big↓ mouth

86.24 stairs ↑that↓ the

86.n6 o'clock ↑every morning—↓blind
Hookey

86.28 it's quite hawful tremendous.

86.30 he's ↑[?]↓ outalivery

86.37 Newcome ↑then↓ that

86.38 bell. ¶ [B over L]ackystopper Not

86.42 two el o'clock

87. 1 think why↑tere↓ Madame de
Moncontour [has over his] gone.

87.13 in Blanche↑Henrietta↓ Pulleyn

87.16 like Blanch↑Henrietta↓ quite

87.26 is a↑n↓ worldly↑flighty empty↓
little who thinks more of

87.36 but ↑as↓ it

87.38 his seat, but he in

87.40 sooner! ↑He &↓ Barnes
and Lord Highgate have

87.40 I wonder his ↑my brother's↓ spirit

87.41 not [illeg.] revolt

87.41 keep ↑a↓ great

87.42 believe: ~~and the present one~~
↑And the present one does so
still: he↓ has

88. 3 and ↑Grandmamma↓ is

88. 3 that ~~he~~ ↑Lord Highgate↓ should

88. 4 Park ~~Street~~↑Lane↓. Poor

88.26 after ~~the~~ a

88.26 Ethel, ha[d over s] nothing

88.27 little ~~talk~~↑colloquy↓ took

88.36 this ~~notifi~~ announcement

88.38 one o'clock~~who~~, by

88.40 Ethel Newcome? ~~When~~↑?↓
Madame

88.40 was ↑at home↓ waiting

88.41 picture: ↑but↓ Miss

88.41 the ~~Countess~~↑good lady↓, so

88.42 the ~~young lady~~↑girl↓ whose

88.45 countess ~~in~~ after

88.47 Florac. ~~You have seen him twice
here, Ethel.~~↑(at work) And so
you like to quit the world, and
to come to our triste old hotel.
After to day you will find it still
more ~~my~~ melancholy my poor
child.↓ ¶Ethel.

89. 2 why? ↑¶↓Mme. de

89.11 he ~~had~~ cherished ↑for↓ his

89.15 rejoiced ↑Ethel↓ for

89.17 have +seen+ ~~but~~↑known. But↓
such

89.18 simplicity ~~never~~ [a over .]s
Thomas

89.22 knew ~~Thomas Newcome.~~↑thy
good Uncle.↓ My ~~good~~↑poor↓
father

89.23 his ~~house~~↑family↓ into

89.23 him. ~~His~~↑Our↓ poverty

89.24 greater. ↑Even before
the emigration a↓ contract
~~was~~↑had been↓ passed between
~~my father~~↑our family↓ and

89.25 Florac: ~~and it was for me to~~↑I
could not be wanting↓ to

89.26 father. ~~From~~ ↑For↓ how

89.27 of ~~an interest↓~~ marriage of
convena↑tie↓↓nce↓ [Italics
removed with spelling change]

89.28 heart ~~bleeds for her.~~↑pities her.
And if↓ I

89.32 know ↑this↓ when

89.33 Nature ↑revolts against them, &↓
breaks

89.34 been f nearly

89.35 dying *n'est-ce-pas?*—and am

89.36 young girl~~e~~. It

89.38 seem ~~tainted as~~↑to bear↓ the
hereditary ~~chill~~↑coldness↓: and

89.40 our ~~differ~~ differences

89.40 our recriminations~~judge~~↑, take↓
one

89.43 wear f[e over a]int smiles

89.44 our children[— over .]deceive
them,

89.45 in ~~her~~ the

90. 2 cruelty. ~~(I speak not for myself)~~
In

90. 4 myself—whatever [illeg.] may

90. 8 child ↓ if

90.11 no ~~people~~↑one can↓ say

90.12 than ~~most~~ happy.

90.12 affectionate ~~woman~~↑mother,↓
and

90.13 nobody ↑really↓ caring

90.18 father ~~who~~ in

90.18 is ~~six~~ ↑five↓ years

90.23 yet [it over I] ~~wanted to do my
duty~~ ↑is not his fault or our's↓
that

90.24 He ~~labo~~↑used↓ to

90.25 the go↑v↓erness. She↑Mamma↓
is

90.26 never ~~scarcely~~↑almost↓ known

90.35 to revolt↑,↓ I

90.37 help ~~luring~~↑drawing↓ them

90.39 never tire~~d~~ till

90.43 to night↑—yes to night↓ after

90.45 F ~~Je prierai pour toi, ma fille~~↑
(sadly)↓. One

91.11 Nobility! ~~it~~ that

91.13 F. ↑(with a sigh)↓ I

91.18 F. Who↑—who↓ was

91.19 ¶Ethel ~~pointing to~~↑looking up
at↓ Gerards

91.21 wonderful *fraises*!—~~Ethel~~
(*Madame de*

91.22 Tableau. [blank] Enter

91.26 jour. ¶Ethel↑Madame↓ de

91.33 the sketch~~it~~; &

91.35 charming! ↑charming!↓ What

91.41 Crackthorpe and↑—and↓ one

91.42 in. ¶*Ethel*[(over .]tossing up

91.43 suppose! ↑¶↓*Clive*. Yes

91.45 though. ↑¶↓*Ethel*. So

92. 2 old ~~Monsieur~~↑Madame↓
Hempenfeld's—not

92. 3 Court— ¶[C over M]live to
92. 7 This i[s over f] for
92. 9 it, ↑he↓ never would ~~he~~ pardon
92.12 nose! ↑I must have sketch of him:↓ the
92.16 where? ↑I hire him by the hour: and↓ I
92.26 invitation ~~to get an invitation~~ to
92.29 galopping ~~and waltzing~~ with
92.30 Farintosh; ↑She will scarce speak to me during the evening↓ and
92.32 is ↑in↓ one
92.33 her ~~lady~~ high
92.33 and ~~will hardly speak to me~~+: '+↑the only words she condescends to say to me are, 'O,↓ I
92.37 you ~~a~~ ↑another↓ week,
92.43 to ~~th other men~~+?+ ↑all the world?↓ What
92.43 to ~~see~~↑hear↓ your
93. 1 add ~~pleasure~~↑zest↓ to
93. 2 to ~~follow~~↑pursue↓ you;~~and~~ ¶Miss
93.10 wrong—it ~~is~~has been↓ now
93.15 there; ↑as we went home↓ Lady
93.15 never ~~we~~ thought
93.17 have made— Ethel
93.20 they ~~they can do that they~~↑they do but as I do:↓ I
93.26 he ~~appeared~~↑arrived↓ from
93.29 day ↑at Brighton↓ when
93.33 Song. ↑It is peace↓
~~Ethel. It is peace-time Sir.~~ time, you
93.34 soldier ↑My father would not have me he said for ever dangling in barracks or smoking in country billiard-rooms.↓ I
93.40 musing. ~~Papa might~~↑Barnes would not perhaps but Papa might even still,↓ and
94. 5 & ↑at the great↓ Michael—I
94. 6 in ~~thinking of these~~ ↑contemplating his↓ genius
94. 9 is? ↑¶↓Clive. To
94.11 place an[d over y] you
94.15 from ↑a round of visits in↓ the
94.17 names. ↑¶↓Clive. I
94.22 you think↑ing↓ of
94.23 your ~~chin~~↑finger↓ to
94.26 never ~~make~~ be
94.29 Ambassador ~~for a Minister↓~~

believe, ~~till The~~↑till the↓ Queen
94.30 Delaroche. ~~[illeg.]~~ She
94.31 Delaroche? ↑¶↓Clive No. Never. ↑¶↓Ethel And—and—you
94.33 up painting.↑?↓ ↑¶↓Clive. No.
94.35 because ~~she brought~~ you
94.36 Ethel. ↑¶↓Ethel with
94.41 to ~~them~~↑it↓? Will
94.41 any ↑other↓ name
94.42 your own[? over ,] Will
94.46 the ~~meaning~~↑end↓ of
95. 1 a ~~maiden's purity~~↑girls pure nurture↓—it can't
95. 3 that ↑poor↓ women
95. 4 thankful ↑that↓ in
95. 4 you ~~closed~~↑cast↓ your
95. 7 thinking ↑that almost↓ all
95.11 But ~~if it is natural for~~↑for our women, who↓ are
95.16 own ~~humble~~ way.
95.21 her ↑to forego a palace↓ to
95.22 palaces ~~but~~↑just↓ now
95.23 about ↑the—↓↑the regard
95.26 never ~~will~~↑can↓ see
95.28 never ~~consent~~↑agree↓ to
95.29 give ↑such↓ pain
95.32 fortune; ~~who is~~ do
95.33 was glad?~~of it?~~ My
96. 1 ¶Clive. ~~Yes-very~~ steadily. Yes. [blank] Madame
96. 2 loves thee[? over —] I
96. 3 ¶Clive. ~~I never had a mother but you seem like one.~~ ↑You hear the music ~~[o over ?]If yonder~~ organs of the convent?↓ ~~yonder~~+?+ ¶Madame
[Begin Thackeray's handwriting. Ms in Berg Collection, NYPL.]
103.18 be ~~such good~~ friends
103.24 the ~~Bundelcund Bank~~ ↑B.B↓ had
103.25 of Association↑.↓~~—and~~ [T over t]he native
103.27 the ↑European↓ mercantile
103.31 of agenc[ies over y]↑, of wh. the profits to the agents themselves were so enormous!↓+!+ The
103.33 and ↑the greatest Capitalist in India as well as↓ the
103.34 at ~~a~~ ↑the↓ large[st over r] ↑&↓ safest↓ premium,
103.35 at ~~a~~ ↑the↓ smalle[st over r] interest,

103.37 every ↑chief↓ city

103.38 Singapore ~~and~~ Canton

103.43 liberty ~~to~~ at

103.45 supplying th[at over e]
~~markets there~~ ↑great Colony↓
with

103.45 goods ~~that~~ ↑wh↓ their

104. 1 the B.B.↑anking↓ Company

104. 3 great ↑native↓ firm

104. 4 Company ~~would~~ had

104. 5 order ↑[from over illeg.]
Birmingham↓ for

104. 9 upon ↑the↓ London

104.13 the ~~great~~ ↑house↓ of

104.14 London beca[me] the ~~bankers~~
↑agents↓ of

104.15 Binnie wh[o] had ↑prudently↓
held

104.17 lad's ↑first instalments of↓ shares

104.18 and ~~desiring him to forward that
little sum of 3333..6..8d
invested in the English
funds, of wh. Clive by
coming of age was that~~ ↑invested
every rupee he could himself
command in this enterprize.
When Hobson Brothers joined
it, ~~& a~~ no wonder James Binnie
was convinced; Clive↓ friend

104.20 through ~~him~~ ↑that connection↓
the

104.24 a ~~little~~ small

104.25 Colonel ↑who was eager that his
friends should participate in his
good fortune↓ would

104.34 affairs ~~and had the~~ ↑(having↓
Clive

104.38 Colonel ↑(enjoining me to make
my fortune)↓ awaiting

104.39 wife ↑received↓ a

105. 2 our ~~hotel~~ ↑apartments↓ having

105. 6 most ~~married~~ ↑friendly married
couples↓ talked

105.17 why, ~~but that was the best~~ ↑could
there be any better↓ reason?

105.32 our ~~superiors~~ ↑betters↓ give

105.32 of protection~~[illeg.]~~; profess

106. 2 and ~~rou~~ dimpled

106. 3 that ↑enter↓ enter.

106. 6 woman? ↑Are you such a
profound deceiver yourself that
you can instantly detect artifice
in others? O Laura!↓ ¶Mrs.

106.21 expect ~~Mr.~~ Pendennis.

106.23 my ~~child«ren»~~ ↑baby↓ ~~cry~~
↑cries↓ [Three levels of change:
children cry; child cries; baby
cries.]

106.27 *sait.* ~~*attendre.*~~ ¶

106.28 this ↑great↓ world

106.29 Arthur—where ~~fathers~~
↑husbands↓ do

106.33 cadaverous ↑leering↓ man

106.42 innings. ¶~~Mrs. P.~~ ↑Did you
not see how tender he was to
her and how fierce poor Clive
looked?↓ ¶[Mrs. over Pen] P.

107. 1 four ↑16↓ years

107. 2 Lady Clar[a over y] Pulleyn—our

107. 5 terrific ~~esclandre~~ ↑scene↓ took
Pendennis. ~~[illeg.]~~ I

107.10 Arthur. ~~But I knew from her
looks that my wife had
other thoughts in her head,
and of course did not
rest until I had her «[secr?]»~~
↑thoughts↓ +from+
her «w» of wh. ~~time
very soon afterwards proved
the correctness~~ ↑And this was
all that Mrs. Laura could be
brought to say.↓ When

107.14 more ~~provoking~~ ↑aggravating↓—
Indeed what

107.15 wife ↑than↓ to

[Begin Thackeray's handwriting. *Ms*
reproduced in sale catalogue.
Original location unknown.]

108.14 Crackthorpe ~~that were~~ ↑wh. had
amused Dukes Marquises in
former days and were surely↓
quite

108.16 realm ↑'Lord Highgate↓
+'+Sweet upon

108.18 I ~~fell asleep~~ ↑awoke↓ in

108.18 telling ~~me~~ one

108.24 smoking ~~a~~ ↑a↓ cigar

108.28 *belle Banquière.*—
+trust me my boy he is
think+~~ing of other things~~+.+
↑Begad Sir it seemed to me
Upon my word my dear it
seemed to me his thoughts went
quite another way.↓ To

108.31 cab; ~~who took~~ ↑who passed us
just now driving back↓ young

108.32 the painter↑.'↓ ~~back to
London~~+.+ ¶Thus

108.34 the ↑open↓ carriage ~~behind us~~
↑wh. followed↓ us—Lady

108.34   Newcome's— ~~in wh. her~~ Lord
108.35   seat. ¶~~Laura looked at her~~
         ~~husband: the same thought~~
         ↑may have↓ ~~crossed their~~
         ~~minds. «Perhaps they had~~
         ~~spoken of it» ↑ ↑He ought to have~~
         ~~gone back with↓ Mr. Hobson~~
         ~~she said. «There was plenty~~
         ~~of» ↑She sate all alone↓~~
         ~~in her carriage. Why did~~
         ~~not some gentleman «go &~~
         ~~console» ↑give her his↓~~
         ~~company? Clives aunt had~~
         ~~passed us spread out in~~
         ~~her barouche, sulky and~~
         ~~in solitude, her face~~
         ~~looking about as red~~
         ~~as the scarlet garments of~~
         ~~her Servants.~~ ¶↑Laura looked at
         her husband. The same thought
         may have crossed their minds
         though neither uttered it—but
         ↑↑although↓↓↓ Sir
108.38   London: ~~but~~ no
108.39   accept ~~further hospitalities from~~
         ~~that lady, either then or~~
         ~~in succeeding seasons+.+~~ ↑the
         proffered friendship of that
         lady.↓ When
108.41   engagements. ↑At first↓ She
         bestowed ~~at first~~ on
108.42   that ↑young↓ lady,
108.48   of ↑such↓ beauties ↑¶↓I cd.
109. 1   this ↑branch of the↓ Newcome
109. 2   wh. ~~justified her dislike~~ ↑silenced
         my ~~comp~~ remonstrances↓; and
109. 2   me ~~only too clearly~~ that ~~she~~
         ↑Laura↓ had
[Being   Thackeray's handwriting. *Ms* in
         Berg Collection, NYPL.]
112.10   lodgings, ~~where~~ ↑and↓ even
112.24   and ~~good~~ ↑water-colour↓
         sketches
112.29   hope ~~ver~~ ere
112.30   year ↑he says↓ he thinks ~~of~~ he
112.31   settled ~~He is going to leave~~
         ~~the army and has invested~~
         ~~every thing he has in~~
         ~~this great bank.~~ You
112.31   your head↑!↓ Why!
113. 4   Blackmore ~~I don't know~~ ↑He
         tells me such↓ stories
113.n5   young ~~friend~~ ↑fellow,↓ Capitalist
114.16   his ↑sole↓ mistress
115. 1   that ~~there~~ in
115. 2   at ~~day~~ ↑sun↓ ~~break~~ ↑rise↓, and

115. 3   picture ~~till~~ all
115. 9   times ↑I succeed a little better
         in my work, and↓ then it will
         happen↓ for
115.10   hour ↑that↓ I
115.15   of ~~Thomas~~ ↑Joseph↓ Muggins
115.22   lives ~~opposite me~~ ↑hard by↓ and
         ↑who↓ sends
115.22   to ↑come &↓ look
115.24   light ~~before~~ upon
115.25   stands ~~before~~ ↑beside↓ his
115.27   it? ~~Wh~~ I
115.32   afterwards [illeg] five
115.37   became ~~great~~ ↑the very greatest↓
         friends.
115.39   than ~~my wife~~ ↑Laura:↓ and
115.42   would ~~recov~~ soothe
115.43   condition. ¶~~His admiration~~
         ~~for Ethel's beauty~~
         ~~she could understand but beyond~~
         ~~this my wifes admiration for~~
         ~~the young lady did not~~
         ~~go very far—indeed she~~
         ~~asked him with a little~~
         ~~scornful surprize whether this~~
         ~~«w» beauty was all men~~
         ~~looked for in women?~~
         Compositor Gibson
         ¶~~Nor was Ethel~~
         ~~Newcome [illeg] fond of Mrs.~~
         ~~Pendennis~~ ↑Miss Ethel, I
         have said, also professed
         a great fondness for Mrs.
         Pendennis↓+.+ ~~There~~ ↑: and
         there↓ was
115.45   wh. ↑speedily↓ could
116. 9   charm ~~subjugated~~ ↑fascinated↓
         my
116.13   the ↑fatal↓ question
116.13   Jove— '[A over a]nd hang
116.14   you know↑, his lordship would
         say,↓ don't
116.16   big brother[. over :] She
116.17   his bo↑u↓quets and
116.18   and ~~bore~~ ↑took↓ his
116.19   sighs; ↑&↓ frankly
116.22   shall ~~not~~ ↑scarcely↓ be
116.25   pleasanter ~~it is~~ to come ~~and sit~~
         and
116.26   sit ~~at~~ in
116.32   you ↑go to parties, and why↓ not
116.35   think ~~you~~ a
116.37   here ↑and I stay with Barnes
         & ~~he~~ Clara by Grandmamma's
         orders↓. Dont

116.45 should ~~like to live at home at Fairoaks.~~ᵃ like
116.47 and ↑habitual↓ awe
117. 2 nominally ~~recognize~~ ↑admit↓ but
117. 3 unheeded. ~~To love; to Worship; to do her duty; to read the devout~~ [rearranged as follows] Worship; Duty; ↑as taught her by the ~~ferven[?]~~ ↑↑devout↓↓↓ study
117. 4 defines it,—↑if↓ these
117. 6 occupation. ~~As I suppose must be the privlege of other «devout»~~ ↑good↓ ~~persons, her heart being filled with love~~ She
117. 6 of ↑her↓ religion
117. 7 her behavior[. over :] Whenever
117. 8 he ~~did not~~ scarcely
117. 9 her company[: over .] and
117.11 a ~~woman~~ ↑person↓? Its
117.14 out ~~of a~~ from
117.14 little ↑Richmond↓ villa
117.17 summer-residence ~~at Wimbledon~~ ↑not very far away.↓ Clive
117.18 us ~~good~~ ↑stirring↓ news. The ~~good~~ Colonel was ↑by this time↓ on
117.19 home. ~~w~~ 'If
117.23 to [illeg] take
117.25 pale ~~we thought~~ ↑as it seemed to us↓, when
117.31 followed, ~~driven out of the~~ ↑drawing↓ room ~~by an appealing~~ —having
117.33 say ↑for a while↓ about
117.34 about ↑our own home at↓ Fairoaks,
117.35 and de[c over l]lared that
[Begin Thackeray's handwriting. *Ms* in Charterhouse School.]
127. 4 voice ↑said Ho its you!↓ ¶I
127. 8 Barnes—taking ~~bundle~~ packet
127.13 now. ↑¶I daresay.↓ You
127.17 will ↑Ma'am↓. *I*
127.25 ¶Doctor Bam~~mby~~↑bury↓ thinks
127.26 little ¶~~Pooh~~+!+↑A little fiddlestick!↓ I
127.27 who ↑likes to↓ ~~stays~~, and
127.31 and ↑little brothers↓ sisters to ~~be~~ stay
128. 2 you. ~~I w~~When I
128. 2 to ~~give~~↑bring↓ me
128. 4 morning. ~~S~~I want

128. 5 Sir. Thats ↑tis↓ why
128. 7 Barnes ~~drumming on his hat~~ ↑drumming on his hat↓. ¶Dont
128. 8 my ↑poor old↓ nerves.
128. 9 London. ¶~~Ha ha groans~~↑Sir↓ Barnes
128.10 a groan↑.↓~~implying assent~~ ¶She
128.17 Barnes Newcome—~~And~~She rushed
128.19 God Maam[! over ?] ~~do~~You know
128.19 provocation! ~~cries~~screams Barnes.
128.20 don't say↑.↓ [B over b]ut from
128.22 strangled ~~a woman~~↑my wife↓, than
128.25 has ↑the temper of a fiend and↓ the
128.25 of ~~a fiend~~ the
128.25 years a↑n entire↓ change
128.26 had ~~poi~~used knife
128.30 Barnes. ~~I kn~~You have
128.37 thought ↑it was a—↓ ¶It
128.39 time ↑since↓ I
128.40 now. ¶↑Gracious goodness!↓ You
128.41 not ~~had any~~↑open↓ ~~quarrel with him?~~ ↑come to blows with him too?↓ [T over t]hat would
128.42 talk ~~asks~~↑says↓ the
128.n3 him ↑answers Barnes↓. He
128.45 rupture. ~~Besides, hang him~~+,+ ↑We had some words↓ the
129. 1 beggar ~~on horseback~~↑Clive, and that↓ fool
129. 3 him ~~on~~because of the↓ account [he over I] kept at ~~his bank~~+.+ ↑our house.↓ +I+ ~~had very nearly~~↑I should like to have↓ massacred
129. 5 insolent brute!↑—↓he says
129. 9 Newcome, ~~not~~↑banking is↓ your's
129.13 serious ~~line~~ way:
129.14 together; ~~the~~↑her↓ mother
129.15 family. ↑They have turned the theatre back into a chapel again:↓ [t over T]hey have
129.17 and ~~they~~ Frank
129.20 Highgate. ~~Two years~~↑Some time↓ ago
129.31 Papa? ~~Barnes~~ cries
129.34 dear ↑Ethel,↓ I
129.34 beauty. ¶↑+By the light of two bed room candles!↓~~ Scotland

~~has bored me to extinction.~~
~~What should I be if «the»~~
~~I had fair play?~~ ¶By

129.37 and ~~as~~↑quite↓ pale

129.38 have ~~had of it~~↑spent!↓—Haven't we?

130. 2 my room.~~,~~ ¶Well

130. 5 hum ↑hum↓. Is

130. 8 have les[s over illeg.] than

130.17 were ↑not↓ carriages

130.18 young ~~p~~man, the

130.19 I suppose~~d~~ they

130.21 not ~~put give~~ make

130.22 the humiliation ~~[illeg.]~~? ¶Humiliation!

130.28 my ~~love~~ child.

130.29 the ~~Steynes, or~~↑Gaunts,↓ the

130.30 My ↑poor↓ lord

130.34 get in~~to~~ society?

130.35 was [c over a]ourting and

130.42 have busin~~n~~ess with her, sa[id over ys] ~~the~~ Barnes.

130.43 and ↑kiss↓ the

130.44 what ~~I~~↑you↓ promised

131.11 little ↑gloved↓ hand.

131.12 brother's roof[, over :] where

131.13 smartly entertained[, over :] there

131.34 the ↑Colonel↓ were

131.38 be ~~an old~~ crazy.

131.39 do ↑no sacrifices the will not make,↓ to ally ↑themselves↓ with

131.40 families. ~~We~~ Certainly

131.41 bank. ↑And we↓ ~~We must say~~ must

131.43 on ~~Thursday~~↑Saturday↓. This

132. 7 up ~~a~~↑this↓ bachelors

132. 8 dissipated. ~~Glenlivat~~↑Rossmont↓ is ~~really~~↑quite↓ a

132.15 the ~~dreadful~~↑dissipated↓ life

132.17 find ~~some~~↑a↓ virtuous

132.19 leave. ¶~~The Banker~~↑Sir Barnes↓ walked

132.20 the [C over c]ity with

132.22 the affectionate[illeg.] brother

132.22 the ~~agre~~↑amiable↓ grandson,

132.24 he ha[s over d] occasion

132.24 with ~~his~~ brother

132.26 riding ~~from~~ towards

132.27 horse; ~~Have you~~ and

132.31 any man~~[illeg.]~~ in

132.32 the ~~author~~other ¶The

132.36 interposes. ~~Have you~~↑I wish you could give me↓ any

133. 4 Kew ~~is in London~~↑& Ethel come to town↓. ¶And

133.13 present ~~last ni~~yesterday evening

133.17 visit ↑about 2↓! Good

133.19 your ~~↑affection↓~~ affectionate,

133.19 E. [blank] Queen

133.23 him. ~~He~~↑Clives father↓ was

133.25 have ~~been going~~↑gone to his↓ Grandmother

133.27 when ~~he~~ we

133.27 Colonel ~~had crossed the~~↑was riding towards↓ Richmond

133.28 these ↑fa↓ lies?

133.32 A ↑fellow would deserve & has got a↓ horse-whipping

133.37 grandson ~~was perhaps~~↑no doubt thought himself↓ justified

133.38 saying so~~+~~.↑+↓ as any other of her servants would have done.↓ But

133.40 to th~~i~~↑a↓nk her

133.42 of ~~besides~~↑than↓ Ethel

133.43 Cottage, ↑Richmond↓ the

133.44 Pendennis Esqr.—↓one of

133.45 young ~~creatures~~↑women↓ in

133.47 brought ~~a~~ blush↑es↓ on

133.47 sun-burnt cheek↑s↓. Ethel

134. 1 with him↑,↓ she

134. 5 to ~~recal~~↑record↓ such

134.34 of ↑nurses &↓ babies

134.36 lady ~~scornful of the other infant) &~~ ↑having her own private opinion) ~~[illeg]~~ ↓Lady Clara

134.42 young ~~lady~~↑person↓ had

134.42 house: [A over a]nd when

135. 1 happened ~~that morn~~ between

135. 2 night. ~~His~~↑His↓ offer

135. 3 simple; ~~and he~~ ↑(though↓ the

135. 5 was ~~to~~ scarcely

135.13 one, ↑&↓ that

135.13 Newcome ~~might be~~, inclined

135.14 humour, ~~and~~ would

135.16 this ~~simple~~ gentleman

135.19 there; ~~all~~ his

135.20 no ↑single↓ good ↑quality↓ in ~~the object~~ his

135.25 Barnes ↑was writing at a↓ table, & sealing & closing a letter as he saw the Colonel enter: he↓ thought

135.33 assure you—~~said~~and I

135.34 two. ¶~~Where did~~[Y over y]ou sa[id over y] her

135.35 Colonel ~~grimly~~↑drily↓. ¶O

135.38 her? ~~I hope you sent my kindest remembrances to Ethel~~ ¶Ethel

135.40 very ~~fondest~~↑best↓ remembrances,

135.41 Barnes. [blank space] Confounded

136. 1 correspondence ↑&↓ could

136. 2 letter ↑to his grandmother,↓ I

136. 8 to [blank] and

136. 9 if ~~you~~↑we↓ could

136.11 drawing-room ↑poring over the embers↓. He

136.18 dozen ↑sharp↓ words

136.20 & ~~M↑m↓ore sad

136.20 day; ~~loving~~↑lik[ely over ing]↓ more

136.21 about [the sarcasms of her husband over the prattle of her children]; [the prattle of her children over the sarcasms of her husband]. She

136.23 You ~~see~~↑understand,↓ the

136.24 not ~~treat her well~~ make

136.27 is ~~not happy~~ miserable—is

137. 5 gentle ~~public~~↑reader↓ has

137.19 the ~~bois~~ noisy

137.20 did? ↑calling him back after she had dismissed him and finding pretext after pretext to see him.↓ I

137.22 I ~~agree~~↑allow↓ with

137.22 and ~~all~~↑most↓ moralists

137.24 marry ~~him~~↑Clive↓ she

137.25 virtuous ↑and well educated young person↓ young

137.25 once ↑determined to↓ rejected a

137.27 or ~~fan t~~ reillume the ~~expiring~~↑extinguished↓ fire.

137.31 her ~~conduct~~↑behaviour↓ to

137.31 The ~~most natural~~↑least unworthy↓ part

138. 1 some ↑critics↓ will

138. 2 him: ~~the showing her~~↑as she felt the greatest↓ regard

138. 3 was ~~natural~~↑not blameable↓; ~~the~~ and every ↑flutter wh. she made to↓ escape ~~wh. she made~~ out

138. 4 the ~~worldly~~ meshes

138. 6 church stor[y over ie], do

138.12 lions ~~&~~or the ~~torturers↓.↓~~ ↑tormentors.↓ Are

138.13 not the↑re↓ Heathen ~~Gods~~↑Idols↓ enshrined

138.17 the ~~very~~ next

138.22 back ~~when~~ out

138.23 are ~~such~~↑surely↓ occurrences

138.24 young ~~ladies~~+'+↑women's↓ history

138.28 that ~~our~~↑the present↓ modest

138.29 that ~~the~~ Duke

138.30 were ↑according to their ~~custom~~ hospitable custom↓ entertaining ~~were entertaining~~ a

138.31 their ↑respective↓ castles,

138.33 Newcome. ~~Ŧ~~ ¶During

138.35 letter ~~from~~ or

138.38 she ~~herself~~ had

138.40 herself: ~~they~~ [M over m]eanwhile Lady

138.42 season.'. ~~Letters upon She had not trust to Colonel Newcome's known sense of delicacy & honour~~ And

138.48 marriage ~~Bar~~Thomas Newcome

139. 1 themselves ↑says he↓ above us↑, forsooth,↓ in life [(over ,]O mercy

139. 3 up!—) [A over a]nd of course ↑the↓ approaches

139. 5 to ↑wish to↓ conduct

139. 7 being ↑wealthy and↓ his

139.15 Templar ↑carrying of Rebecca,'↓ to

139.16 other ~~works~~ journals

139.17 the ~~public~~↑newspaper↓ praises.

139.18 Brian ~~of~~ the

139.21 he ~~sate~~ set

139.25 were ~~passing~~↑gone to↓ Newcome

139.28 made a↑n↓ ~~most admirable~~ ↑admirable↓ Jeremy

139.29 as ↑Fusbos in↓ Bombastes

139.30 in ~~the two f~~ both

139.31 me ~~in~~ as

139.31 Miss [blank] ↑she↓ wrote~~Ethel~~. 'I

139.32 wrinkles ↑imitated old Lady Griffin as well as I could↓ and

139.33 looked ~~70~~ sixty

139.33 least. ¶Th[o over e]~~Colonel~~↑mas Newcome↓ wrote

139.36 the ↑Colonel↓ was

139.38 his ↑appointed↓ line

139.42 since ~~that~~↑the telling of those↓ little

140. 2 that ~~others~~↑friends↓ refuse

140. 5 mentally ~~labored.~~↑regarded him.↓ 'Old

140.11 friends [illeg.] happiness

140.11 dismay. ~~Your~~ Our

140.17 about ~~Ethel~~ the

140.18 He ~~wanted~~ gave Bob ~~Hardyman~~↑Henchman↓ the

140.18 story ~~ab~~ wh.

140.21 facetiously—Farintosh [T.O] [On back of page: T.O.]swore he'd

140.22 and ↑vows he will be the death of↓ will

140.30 a quarrel,↑:↓ young

140.32 mind. [break a line.] ¶A

140.33 at ~~five~~↑seven↓ years

140.34 largest ↑fried↓ fish

140.37 her ~~existence~~+.+↑life.↓ Poverty

140.37 this precocity↑tousness↓ on

140.41 at ~~the~~ a

140.41 existence. ~~Princekins~~ [blank] ↑Every one of us according to his degree can point to the↓ Princekins

141. 5 Princekin ↑or Lordkin↓ from

141. 7 innumerable ↑flattering him &↓ doing

141.11 families ~~This way my~~↑Thats the Marquis↓ of

141.11 as [illeg.]he passes.

141.15 Princekin. ~~I have~~Do not

141.21 with their[illeg.] daughters?

141.21 the ~~King of Mercia~~ ↑British nobleman↓ in

141.22 the ~~King~~↑Prince~~King~~↓ of Mercia, ~~who chose~~↑that His Majesty might choose↓ one

141.25 the rest[illeg.] of

141.32 the ~~pr~~↑tutor↓ simpering

141.33 grass-plat [: over —] old

141.36 station: ~~portly conservative~~ who

141.41 the [on verso, p. 13: My dear Sir. These pens are about as good] promenading

141.41 city. [A over B]nd let

141.44 the ~~society~~ ↑companies↓ of

142. 1 run ~~fom~~ from

142. 5 Earl, ~~with~~ of

142. 6 Empire, ~~with~~↑with a beautiful person, &↓ a

142. 7 do otherwise?↓ than long for him?.↓ He

142. 9 course: ↑and↓ surveyed

142.13 side ~~under~~↑upon↓ the

142.18 else e↑sh↓ould they

142.19 we ~~shall~~↑need↓ not

142.21 these: ~~purses~~+:+↑presents of purses worked by them &↓ cigar-cases

142.22 in ~~snug~~↑cozy↓ boudoirs—mamma

142.24 foot ~~tha~~ to mount ~~and~~↑them, that they might↓ ride

142.30 his ~~noble~~↑great↓ mind,

142.30 he ~~would~~↑was ready to↓ give

142.31 nation. [break] ¶Miss

142.32 the ↑statue of↓ Huntress

142.34 when Diana↑—↓and Diana's

142.37 bay ↑& taken↓ by

142.41 Tom Newcome— and

142.45 Colonel ↑may have↓ read in ~~His~~ his

142.45 paragraph ~~announcing~~↑wh. announced↓ an [a over A]pproaching sMarriage

143. 5 with ~~others~~ ↑all that↓ he

143.10 those ~~with~~ to

143.11 if ↑two↓ hands

143.13 How ↑well↓ I

143.15 parting, ~~my friend~~+,+ and

143.18 Heaven too[? over —] I

143.19 so? ~~H~~I remember

143.21 am. ~~May I not say that for~~ ↑M. de. Florac has known my history from↓ the

143.22 say ↑after so many of years↓ that

143.27 another ~~plan~~↑project↓ wh. ~~fondly~~ please

143.27 to arrange.~~be~~ You

143.32 her. ↑Paul↓ My son ~~Paul~~ has

143.38 more. ~~She~~Antoinette is

143.40 her. ~~One~~↑They↓ says you

143.41 write! ~~My~~In ↑the↓ long ~~winter~~ evenings

144. 3 as ~~prisoners~~↑the detained↓ caress

144. 3 birds ~~wh. visit them~~↑little flowers↓ in ~~dungeons~~↑their prisons.↓ I

144. 4 born +to+ ~~be happy~~↑for the happiness↓ my

144. 4 have ~~known~~↑learned↓ it

144. 8 Ethel (↑I love her in spite of all and shall see her soon & congratulate her, for ~~I~~do you see might have stopped this fine marriage and did↓ I

144.12 You ~~will~~↑shall↓ assist

144.14 friend Co↑mtesse↓ E.

144.15 Florac. ↑I read marvels of his works in an English journal wh. one sends me.↓ ¶Clive

144.17 and ~~t~~ in

144.17 to ~~fma~~ devise

144.30 are ↑it must be confessed↓ a

144.33 down ~~to~~ accordingly

144.34 ¶When ~~the girls, retired their mother~~ ↑meal was over, the mother ~~in~~ who had matter *of importance to impart to him* besought him to go to the drawing room whither & there↓ poured

144.36 out ~~a~~ such

144.36 upon ~~their~~↑ther children's↓ qualities

144.39 Lenoir ~~obs~~ Maria

145. 1 Colonel ↑He was.↓—O never

145. 1 mind! ~~it's~~↑It is↓ a

145. 7 the ↑heartless↓ world!

145. 8 fear ~~there~~ Maria

145.12 of ~~Ross[illeg.]~~ Rossmont,

145.20 a ~~son in law~~↑husband↓ as

145.25 rising; ~~And~~and left

145.32 in ↑such↓ a way ~~that~~↑as↓ caused

145.36 had done—~~and~~↑. And↓ he

145.37 together ↑several↓ months

145.38 garden. ¶~~Clive's father did not tell hi[s over m] Son of his own bootless negociation with Barnes. What need was there to recal it, now that «the c» all chance was over for the young fellow?~~ ¶Clives

145.41 against ~~that~~ his

145.42 this business↑.↓↓~~; and his anger was not diminished by a letter from Ethel Newcome wh. he at length received ¶Sin~~Ever since

145.43 proper to↑—to↓ give

145.43 Kew, ~~the Colonel↓↑~~Thomas Newcome's↓ anger

145.45 Lady ~~The receipt of this letter only confirmed ↑the↓ suspicion under wh. Thomas Newcome had been labouring ever since the luckless day when Barnes thought proper to—to give a «long» ↑wrong↓ address for Lady Kew. He ↑sent↓ «wrote» a letter to Ethel and~~ +Lady+ Ann

145.45 congratulating ~~them~~ ↑her↓ on

146. 1 her ~~inform~~ ↑rebuke↓ Miss

146. 4 this ~~letter~~ ↑message↓ Ethel

146. 4 brief ↑hurried↓ reply+ +~~asking saying frankly Dear Uncle↑~~. It said ¶↓ 'I

146. 5 'I ~~did no~~ saw

146. 8 I ~~love~~↑regard↓ as

146. 9 I ~~think~~↑know↓ it

146.11 him +and+ ~~you~~+.+↑& his↓ dear

146.12 answered? ↑Grandmammas know↑↑s↓↓ nothing about a letter. ~~There has been none ex~~ ↑↑We hav~~ Mamma has enclosed to me that wh. you wrote to her but↓↓↓ [t over T]here has

146.14 & ↑affectionate↓ E.N.

146.21 firmly ~~fixed~~↑proven↓ in

146.32 yet. ~~I heard~~↑You've heard↓ about

146.32 the marriage[? over illeg.] says

146.32 Colonel? ~~Mr. Hobso~~ I'll

146.40 half ~~[illeg.]~~brother paced

146.43 bank. ¶~~Presently the Baronet~~ ↑The Baronet stopped↓ and

146.44 entered ~~with~~↑followed by↓ that

147. 5 clerks? ~~says~~↑ask↓ Thomas

147.11 gentlemen ~~each assumed~~ ↑respectively wore↓ looks

147.25 you ~~leave the room~~↑go out↓ and

147.26 Boltby—Colonel Newcome ~~unless you—you are an old man and my fathers brother—and and~~ unless you

147.28 a policeman—~~call him~~send for

147.29 Newcome Baronet—~~Sir, you know that if you were not my fathers grandson~~ ↑Mr. Boltby! shall we have the constable in?↓ ¶Sir—you

147.38 statement ~~at~~ to

147.43 colonel ↑twirled his mustachios and↓ waved

148. 1 ominous ~~,as~~ manner,

~~as though cautioning~~↑[as over and] Barnes started back↓ spontaneously

148. 9   quarrel. Th[at over e] conviction ~~of that~~ will

148.n9   hookey. ↑Of course the story did not get wind at Bays's: of course Tom Eaves did not know all about it & say that Sir Barnes had been beaten black & blue.↓ Sir

148.23   year ~~erased~~↑took off↓ his

148.25   morning, ~~could not~~ and

148.27   wh. +the+ ~~Colonel~~↑Thomas Newcome↓ kept

148.34   passed ~~unnoticed by me~~↑without some comment on my part↓. I

148.39   of insults↑, for↓ wh.

148.43   mind. ¶↑I gathered from the brutal language wh. you thought fit to employ towards a disarmed man: that the ground of↓ One

149. 2   of ~~the absurd~~↑your monstrous↓ accusations

149. 3   you ~~who~~ in

149. 6   question ~~desired me~~↑was passing through↓ to

149.24   replied ~~th~~ my

149.25   grey m↑to↓ustache. If

149.34   that [(i over , I]n Sir

150. 3   Clive. ¶~~Fro~~And the

150. 4   follows. ¶~~Barnes~~↑Clive↓ Newcome

150.18   is ~~a~~↑another↓ wilful

150.24   me [blank] Sir [blank] Your

150.28   Colonel ~~ha~~with delight

150.30   part [in over of] the

150.32   lately about↑↑—about↓ ~~an~~ young

150.34   so ↑you say, General,↓ the

150.35   the *froulet*↑?↓ ~~, you say, General~~+?+ ¶By

150.41   marry ↑young↓ Farintosh,

151. 4   face! ~~Put~~↑We'll put↓ it

151. 7   the ↑~~Thomas~~↓ Colonel

151.10   his ~~warlike~~ ↑mettled↓ charger

151.12   dear!—Well, ~~G~~ Sir,

151.18   I ~~left hi~~↑turned on↓ my

151.20   command ~~his~~ courage [G over g]eneral, said

151.23   loud ↑& resolute↓ voice

151.29   sketch ~~of~~↑from↓ some

151.43   his [son over soon] with

152. 5   What ↑a—↓what an—old—trump

152. 7   embraced. ~~Here's Barnes letter said Clive taking out a crumpled paper full of tobacco from the ledge of his easel. The note said.~~ ¶Clive

153. 4   of Cavendish~~, and~~ ↑now;↓ but

153. 5   written ~~the~~ Sir

153.10   most ~~odious~~↑disagreeable↓ and

153.18   should ~~apply~~↑resort↓ to

153.19   to ~~leave~~↑quit↓ London

153.21   of a↑n odious↓ subject,

153.25   is [a over i]n ~~all~~ ill

153.27   ¶Pooh ~~it~~↑the feud↓ dates

153.27   that; ↑said↓ Clive,

153.31   me, ↑cries the Colonel↓ I

153.34   I ↑have been↓ struggling

154. 3   me, ↑& from some other accounts wh. have come to my ears,↓ your

154. 7   or ~~ma~~ if ~~kind~~↑gentle↓ to them ↑it is↓ that

154. 8   the ~~reptile~~↑creature↓, I

154. 9   superior ~~natural~~↑nature's↓ rogues

154.13   mutton chop~~—a little terror of the cane perhaps—Sir~~ ↑I contemplate him with ceaseless wonder↓ I recognize

154.15   a ~~woman~~↑poor girl↓ in

154.16   the ~~best~~↑beast↓? married

154.19   unless ~~there's~~ somebodys ~~foot~~↑heel↓ shall

154.22   have ~~splendid~~↑marble↓ monument

154.26   and ~~whom~~ in

154.33   ways ↑of↓ scandal-hearing

154.33   from ~~the Cou~~ Sir

154.34   I [blank] of

154.36   Mr. [blank] favored

154.37   journal. ~~These details~~↑This kind↓ of

154.38   line: and,↑—↓out of

154.39   Mr. [blank], and

154.41   it.' ¶As ~~talked~~↑sate↓ with

154.42   evening, ~~and~~↑when↓ he

154.43   way. ~~Again I besought him to beware of «Sir» his nephew~~ ↑He said his brother Hobson had been with him the morning↓ after

155. 5   too ~~severe~~↑hard↓ upon

155. 8 quarrel, ~~you know and we remain perfectly good friends~~+.+ ↑& very rightly did not wish to engage in it.↓ He

155.11 after ~~our~~↑my↓ quarrel

155.12 supposed ~~would~~↑need↓ not

155.13 it? ↑So↓ That

155.15 friends. ↑¶↓'I think

155.17 He ~~sai~~ speaks

155.17 more ~~courage~~↑kindness↓ and

155.19 But ~~he~~ I

155.20 he ~~has~~ agreed

155.25 he ~~did~~ has

155.34 world ~~with~~↑to↓ wh.

155.43 room ↑he dancing↓ in

155.44 sake ~~he~~↑Mumford↓ did

156. 1 about ~~with lik~~ ↑under the protection of↓ young

156. 3 white-tie, ~~under wh.~~↑donned two↓ hours

156. 4 heart! ↑¶With these lads and decorated with a tie equally splendid moved about young Sam Newcome, who was shirking from his sister and his Mamma[— over ,]Mrs. Hobson had actually assumed clean gloves for this festive occasion. Sam stared at all the 'Nobs': and insisted upon being introduced to 'Farintosh' and congratulated his Lordship with much graceful ease: and then pushed about the rooms perseveringly hanging on to Alfred's jacket. I say I wish you wouldn't call me Al.' I heard Master Alfred say to his cousin—seeing my face ~~Master~~ Mr Samuel ran up to claim acquaintance~~: and~~ ↑↑He was good enough to say he thought Farintosh seemed devlish haughty↓↓ [E over e]ven my wife could not help saying that Mr. Sam was an odious little creature.↓ ¶So

156.15 was ~~for the sake~~↑to↓ +of+ young

156.15 who ~~wanted to be placed out~~ ↑would want protection and help↓ in

156.16 to ~~sacrifice~~↑give up↓ her

156.17 to ~~give up~~↑bestow↓ her life ~~to~~↑on↓ yonder

156.18 as ~~on sacrificing~~ ↑a girl devoting↓ herself ~~for~~↑to↓ her

156.23 again, ↓ doing

156.25 and kinsfolk~~,~~ complimented

156.27 apart ~~from the~~ and

156.29 crutch, ↑but↓ without

156.32 ¶And [D over d]oubt (as

156.38 has +been+ ~~educated~~↑spent↓ all

157. 8 the Coun[s over c]ellor talks

157. 8 up ~~with~~ as

157. 9 and ↑rises↓ to

157.11 gentleman ~~strides~~↑advances↓ towards me ~~in~~↑with↓ a

157.13 Highgate ~~very~~ civilly

157.17 Barnes ~~gave~~↑published↓ a

157.17 entertainments ~~bef~~ on

157.18 the [C over c]lan Farintosh

157.19 banquets. ↑Mr. & Mrs↓ Hobson

157.21 marriage. ↑They had a grand banquet followed by a tea to wh. ~~the~~ latter amusement the present biographer was invited.↓ Lady

157.24 Highgate ↑& Sir George Tufto↓ attended

157.25 entertainment. ~~for the~~ 'Farintosh

157.27 as possible~~all dinnertime—~~Sir George

157.29 be! [A over a]nd the

157.30 others ↑of his parents'↓. ¶Thus

157.34 makers ~~all the~~↑every↓ morning:

157.35 and ~~the~~ he

157.40 and ↑select↓ crowds

157.42 a ~~fa~~ souvenir

157.44 Sir ~~Barnes~~↑Bryan↓ Newcome.

157.46 I ~~took up~~↑was glancing over↓ the

158. 6 nobility ~~last night~~↑the night before last,↓ seemingly

158.10 rallied ↑or, we believe spoke,↓ after

158.15 father ↑Lord Walham↓ having

158.15 before ~~the~~ his

158.17 event. ~~And~~ Society

158.19 century: ↑&↓ who

159. 5 out; ~~and~~ put

159. 7 his ↑garish↓ saffron

159. 8 decent tempor↑ar↓y mourning.

159.16 pair who↑se↓ ~~bl[illeg.]~~ quarter

159.18 who ~~also~~ were

159.21 yet ~~remains~~↑rests↓ on th[e over is] outer

159.25 corruption? SWhen the

159.26 roses ~~suddenly blighted~~ ↑nipped in an hour↓ by

159.30 with ~~a~~↑the↓ natural

159.n1 her triumphs,↑—↓who in

159.34 her ~~plea~~ vain

160. 2 sinks ~~on the pillow~~ to

160. 3 salute ~~the lifeless emblem~~↑even
        the heraldry and devices of
        yonder pomp, as symbols↓ of

160. 7 in. ~~To do well (even
        as the commercial phrase is,
        is to do good of some sort.~~ But

160. 8 and bet—↓found ↑dancing↓
        among

160.12 fancies ~~along with~~ ↑after round↓
        some ~~funerals~~↑graves↓ unseen

160.12 mourners ~~marching~~↑waiting↓:
        many

160.13 the ~~grave~~↑place↓: many

160.14 and deplored ↑rising up at the
        toll of that bell to follow the
        honoured hearse↓: dead

160.16 daughter! ~~pretty children whisp
        ↑heavenly~~ lost children
        ~~(foundlings in~~ Heaven's
        foundlings)↓ hovering

160.17 and ~~sing~~ whispering 'Welcome
        mother'—~~but~~↑Here is one who
        reposes↓ after

160.18 been; ~~after ↑[illeg.]↓ four
        score years of lonely vanity~~+;+
        after

160.20 after ~~pride~~ four

160.23 Creatures. [On back of page:
        Sketch of Countess Gruffanuff
        (from *The Rose and the Ring*).] [At
        top of page (referring, probably
        to Gruffanuff or Glumboso from
        the same book): What became
        of G. her lover.] [Scribbled in
        pencil, probably by a former
        owner of the manuscript: Vol.
        II Chaps XIV to XVI lines 1-28
        14a 15a 16a ÷]

[Begin Anne's handwriting.]

160.24 ~~I turn away from the
        contemplation of a
        subject rather befitting
        the solemn remarks of a
        severe Divine like Charles
        Honeyman, than of the
        present writers worldly page~~
        ↑¶↓Leave ~~me~~↑we↓ yonder
        yonder vel~~p~~↑v↓et palled

160.24 spangled ↑with↓ fantastic

160.25 containing withing the
        ~~residue~~↑aged slough &
        envelope of a ~~soul~~soul↓
        ~~of near eighty years~~ gone

160.26 shell. ~~As at the Priest beside it~~
        The

160.31 the ~~performers~~ witnesses

160.32 over ~~her~~ our

[Begin Thackeray's handwriting.]

160.34 read ~~as~~ over

160.34 shines ~~over~~ on

160.35 part, ↑that↓ they

160.38 hearse, ↑into wh. palls trestles
        ~~trys~~ trays of feathers are
        inserted,↓ &

[Begin Anne's handwriting.]

161. 1 Rood @↑(That was Mr. Rood—
        ↓that other @↑little↓ gentleman

161. 3 executed ~~the~~ a

161. 3 wh. ~~al~~most all

161. 5 for while[. T over , t]he young

161.14 & ~~a~~↑to be↓ Marchioness

161.17 disguise ↑that↓ his opinion
        of↑that↓ Lady

161.19 listen defferentially to

161.19 smallest observation[s over .],
        exert

161.20 severe ~~and~~ visit

161.27 mistress ~~drove~~↑had↓ her

161.31 Laura ↑as freely↓ regarding

161.35 after ~~one~~ her

161.36 Newcomes ~~especial~~ request

162. 2 account. ↑¶"↓Confound the
        young "man↑"↓ breaks

162. 8 ¶Never. [O over o]nce, twice

[Begin Thackeray's handwriting.]

162.11 baby there, and

162.17 understood ~~the~~ him,

162.21 has ~~that~~↑such↓ firmness

162.23 any ~~resolution~~↑inclination↓ of

162.27 more ↑Lady Clara sends you no
        cards↓. I

162.29 accounts d[id over oes] not

162.30 face ~~assumed~~↑straightway put
        on↓ the

162.33 I dislike~~her~~↑—a—~~them~~↓.
        ↑¶↓Why? ↑ ↑I hear

162.36 your ~~own~~ husband

162.37 'Why'. [break.] ¶Let

162.39 we ↑may↓ get

162.39 question ↑of↓ wh.

162.42 its ~~sud~~ prosperity;

162.44 volumes. ¶↑Thus↓ In

162.45 have ~~mentioned good~~↑said
        nothing about↓ the

163. 4 Duke ~~who co~~ would
163. 6 neighbouring ~~town~~↑city↓ of
163. 9 Vicar ↑Mr. Vidler the
        Apothecary, Mr. Duff the
        baker↓—of Tom
163.12 had ↑already↓ or
163.n5 is ~~with~~↑from↓ persons
163.n6 the ~~answer to~~↑meaning of↓ that
163.18 husbands ↑will↓ make
163.19 that ~~husbands~~↑men,↓ whom
163.21 false ~~cru~~ selfish
163.22 ladies, ~~say~~↑close↓ the book
        ~~is immoral~~ and
163.23 other. ~~But, as surely as the~~
        ~~writer has children of~~
        ~~his own, whose character~~
        ~~is as dear to him, as~~
        ~~the very «charmingest»~~↑fairest
        ~~of your↓ ladyships~~
        ~~—so surely must he speak~~
        ~~the truth in his calling.~~ ↑Banish
        the newspaper out of your
        houses; and shut your eyes to
        the truth, the awful truth of life
        and sin.↓ Is
163.25 Jessamies; ↑and passion the play↓
        of
163.26 and ~~children of out~~↑schoolgirls,
        scribbling valentines and↓
        interchanging
163.27 no ↑subsequent↓ trials,
163.28 remorses, ~~danger~~ sufferings
163.29 overcome? ~~o friend~~ [A over a]s
        you & I↑, friend,↓ kneel
163.32 are ~~but~~ mere form?↑,↓ &
163.32 us?—to ~~the~~↑some↓ outcasts
163.36 to ~~worship~~ ↑church↓ apart;
163.36 kneel ~~with a~~ humbl[y over e]
        ~~heart~~ in
163.37 them ~~and pray~~↑owning your
        wrong, & praying↓ Heaven
163.40 subsided, ~~Barnes~~the↓ made
164. 3 Dissenting Clergyman↑~~minister~~↓
        to
164. 9 are ~~very~~↑as↓ sporting gents [a
        over)]s any
164.12 J. Bulders)—↑and he↓ had
164.13 place ~~as it was called~~↑as he called
        it in his official speeches 'the
        cradle of his forefather's the
        home of his race' &c.↓—though
        Barnes
164.19 first ~~when~~ during
164.27 worse ~~stories about~~↑charges
        against↓ Barnes

164.29 Newcome? ~~The~~His victim
164.31 and ~~came~~ in
164.33 Bill, ~~Al~~ Al.
164.34 pound ~~on settling day)~~↑after the
        Ledger, the year Toggery won
        it)↓ and
164.41 you ↑interesting↓ particulars
165. 8 saying ~~that~~↑not to but of↓ such
165. 9 man ↑that he↓ was
165.11 the works of ~~most~~ a
165.15 Sir ↑cries Sir Barnes↓ never
165.17 'em, [C over c]urse em!
165.20 give ~~to the~~ a
165.21 infernal soup-tickets↑,↓ or
165.26 him; ~~from~~ Bulders
165.28 men [illeg.] were
165.28 familiarity; ↑&↓ recovered
165.30 him ↑and always speculated on
        the possibility of war. When
        he turned his back on them in
        the market men felt relieved,
        & as they ~~passed~~ passed his
        gate↓+,+ ~~and looked with~~
        ~~no friendly glances over~~
        ~~his park-wall.~~, looked
165.37 King's Arms—↑the butler was
        familiar with Taplow.↓ one
165.38 the ~~maids~~↑grooms↓ at
165.38 with ~~Dr.~~ Mrs.
165.42 been ~~sent for~~ ↑called↓ to
165.43 in ↑strong↓ hysterical
165.44 Barnes ~~came near~~↑approached↓
        her—he
166. 5 said ~~they w~~ Baronet
166. 6 good terms;—↑but—↓but that
166.10 and ~~behave properly before~~
        ~~the servants~~ ↑smoothe over their
        countenances before John↓ who
166.12 are ~~tearing caps~~ ↑barking &
        biting↓, or
166.13 and ↑yet↓ smiles
166.19 she ↑learns to↓ smiles after
166.25 your ~~timid~~ scared eyes
        ~~dared not look~~↑were afraid to
        look↓ up
166.26 little ~~creature~~↑plant↓ very
166.28 it ~~had~~↑know~~ received↓ warm
166.29 and ~~consigned~~↑given over↓ to
166.30 neglect, ~~given over to~~ consigned
166.33 out ~~th~~ to
166.34 the ~~wrongs~~↑agonies↓ of
167. 1 moratur. ¶~~After his mishap~~
        ~~Clive New~~ ¶Clive

167. 2   a ~~spirit~~↑courage↓ and

167. 4   would display.~~under his~~ ↑It was whilst↓ he

167. 7   worst condition[; over :] He as

167.13   table, ~~and~~ beaten

167.14   the ~~game~~↑contest↓ but

167.18   won it,~~or~~↑—think↓ what

167.21   confessed ~~had~~ now ~~adopted~~↑exhibited↓ a

167.26   Every [thought over action] or [action over thought] of

167.26   the ~~honest~~↑worthy↓ Colonel.

167.27   Uncle ~~thought he~~↑was ready to fancy that the Banker↓ wanted

167.32   at the↑i↓r ~~Colonel's~~ ↑kinsman's↓ hands—they

168. 1   up. ~~Not~~ People

168. 1   unreasonably: ~~The fable concerns thee, o worthy reader!~~ Whether

168. 2   to ~~our vanity~~↑us,↓ to

168. 2   are [disliked over liked] or [liked over disliked] undeservedly?

168. 3   his ~~eh~~ misfortune:

168. 7   greatest ~~picture~~ painting

168. 9   the ~~weet~~ ↑beautiful↓ Styrian

168.10   fought. ~~for the liberty of~~ They

168.12   many ~~a~~ person↑s↓ whom

168.15   elder. ~~It was a pleasant tour I daresay— They~~ ↑Clive wrote to say it was a very pleasant tour↓ but

168.18   with [S over s]orrow perhaps

168.20   days ↑when↓ your

168.21   it's [G over g]host rises,

168.22   length ~~&~~ in

168.23   brief sentence[— over ,]what dreary

168.26   at ~~Dieppe~~↑Brussells↓, where

168.27   Esqr. +had+ ~~hired a little chateau~~ ↑and his family ~~had~~ were established in ~~most~~ comfortable quarters↓ and where ~~you~~we may

168.30   much ~~too~~ his

168.32   several ~~delightful~~↑charming↓ foreign

168.33   The ~~delightful~~↑excellent↓ Captain

168.35   was ↑most↓ attached?

168.37   creature. ~~It~~ Is

168.37   to ~~see~~ remark

168.39   and ↑to↓ the

168.39   probably; ~~and to~~ though

168.44   Baden, ~~[illeg.]~~ Cheltenham

169. 1   in company— belonged

169. 2   young ↑officer↓ & the ~~old~~↑older↓ campaigner.

169. 9   companion. ~~The youngsters called him old Goby. He was not a man of an ascetic life;~~ of ~~«careful»~~ ↑profound↓ ~~intellectual culture.~~ He

169. 9   every ~~man~~↑regiment↓ in

169.10   He ~~had~~↑was known to have↓ been

169.12   was ↑certainly↓ not

169.15   he ~~had to~~ bore

169.16   and ↑I daresay numbers of ladies besides↓ Mrs.

169.17   delightful. ↑Gobys talk & rattle perhaps somewhat bored James Binnie, but↓ Thomas

169.18   Thomas Newcome+,+ ~~to do him justice~~+,+ found

169.20   He ~~[illeg.]~~ and

169.22   off ~~whither~~↑to wh.↓ the

169.23   paid ~~many at~~↑several↓ visits

169.24   were ~~at hand~~↑near↓, in

169.24   wh. ~~though~~ Goby

169.28   chargers were↑, he thought,↓ more

169.30   French ~~painters~~↑artists have↓ portrayed.

169.32   and ~~found~~ were

169.33   handsome ~~apa~~ rooms

169.34   for us—[M over m]y study

169.34   'Many a↑n↓ ~~ride a~~ hour

169.35   together. ~~remarked~~↑observed↓ that

169.38   newspaper, ~~I~~↑I remember to have↓ said

169.41   Count ~~G~~ Egmont

169.41   to [E over e]xecution; ~~a~~ in

169.42   halberdier, ~~and~~ Captain

169.43   Captain ~~G~~Hoby as

169.47   went ~~into the polite~~ to

169.48   balls, ~~where~~↑at wh.↓ am

170. 1   attended ~~them~~↑these entertainments↓. M.

170. 2   the wors[t over e]-looking man

170. 4   thought, ~~they~~↑he and Rosey↓ made

170. 6   ¶Most ~~people~~↑persons↓, my

170. 6   were ~~fond~~ pleased

170. 7   sang ~~as~~ charmingly
170.11   Dash, ~~the~~ our
170.15   singing ↑& behaviour↓ than
         myself. ~~But who~~↑As for↓ Captain
170.16   affected ~~by~~↑towards↓ Miss
170.22   wants, ~~and~~↑as she would↓ trip
         across ~~their~~ room
170.26   she ~~laughed at~~↑saluted↓ them
170.27   them ↑always↓ with
170.28   a bo↑u↓quet for
170.29   balls, ~~the~~↑James & Thomas
         those↓ two
170.32   James, ↑after↓ taking
170.33   & ~~kiss~~ pay
170.35   did, ↑I promise you↓ she
170.36   and ↑put that↓ pretty
170.41   as ~~if there~~↑Miss Rosey↓ was
170.41   be ~~no end of the florals~~
         ↑overpowered↓ by
170.44   with ↑her↓ scalps
170.46   Rosey, ~~Goby «was» tries to re~~
         what
171. 3   about ↑the barracks↓ so
171. 4   his ↑poor little European↓ wife—
         [blank]: and
171. 6   laughing, ceases somehow.
171. 7   too? No—↑He has never thought
         about a bouquet↓ He
171.14   very contentedly—↑;↓ and
171.15   ball. +¶Chap.+ ¶Our
171.16   prolonged ~~much~~↑beyond↓ a
171.19   of ↑baby↓ nurse ↑&↓ husband.
171.20   two ↑goo↓ stout
         elder~~ly gentlemen~~↑s↓ and
171.21   to ~~Ostend~~↑Antwerp↓ and
171.24   us thought↑:↓ they
171.43   marriage (~~it is~~He and
171.44   dimittis ~~if those two children~~
         could ↑the but see the two
         children↓ ~~but be made~~ happy;
171.45   should ~~be~~↑lie↓ easier
171.48   faction. ↑He is very good-
         natured frank honest and
         gentlemanlike, Mr. Hoby.↓ But
172. 3   upon ~~him~~+.+↑the poor
         Captain.↓ So
172. 6   Rosey ~~found~~↑thought↓ Captain
172. 8   she ~~is~~ admires
172.11   Pendennis—Why, ↑my dear↓
         Clive
172.17   truth-telling, ~~[illeg.]~~ the
172.18   and ~~this~~ yonder

172.20   hear ~~my husband~~↑you↓ speak so
         ~~says~~↑cries↓ Mrs.
172.22   don't we↑?↓ baby!
172.24   and ~~nestling~~ snuggling
172.27   he ~~or~~↑nor↓ she
172.29   Captains, ↑&↓ Rosey ↑& I↓ &
172.36   her family[, over —] Who
172.39   soon ~~we get~~ the
172.40   cabins; ↑and then dinner is
         announced & Captain Jackson
         treats us to Champagne from his
         end of the table↓ and
173. 2   engaged ~~for~~ in
173.20   some ~~four~~↑five↓ miles
173.22   ancient ~~[illeg.]~~ gabled
173.25   banks, ↑&↓ dies ↑&↓ cinders
173.26   that ~~country~~↑district↓. Now
         ~~hundreds~~↑scores of↓ fine
173.28   the ~~tw~~ town
173.30   splendid ~~Elizabethan~~ structure
         ↑in the Tudor style↓ more
173.31   by ~~those~~ little ~~Elizabethan~~
         ↑antique↓ villas
173.33   hedges [of over on] evergreens
173.34   gig-houses. ~~where From~~ ↑&
         Under the great railway Viaduct
         of↓ the
173.35   high-road; ↑once↓ busy
174. 2   the ~~Newcome~~↑town↓ station,
174. 3   stands ~~on~~ at
174. 8   Manchester, ~~with~~ did
174.13   friends ↑& relations↓ from
174.14   were ↑retail↓ shopkeepers.
174.16   Revd ~~Mr. Hufft~~↑Dr. Potter↓ the
174.19   Mrs. ~~Hufft~~↑Potter↓ and
174.20   she ~~took~~↑got her↓ share
174.21   Mrs. ~~Hufft~~↑Potter↓ said
174.22   sphere ~~and that the~~ (Mrs.
         ~~Hufft~~↑P↓ was
174.23   of ↑bankrupt↓ hatter
174.23   London ~~who~~ and
174.24   Mr. ~~H~~↑P↓. who
174.n2   tutor) ~~so~~↑'that↓ Madame
174.25   to ~~quit~~↑leave↓ her
174.26   her. ~~Tom Hufft~~↑Tom Potter↓ the
174.29   billiard +mar+ marker
174.31   that ↑Monsieur↓ Paul
174.34   your pedigree).—[B over t]ut the
         truth is↑t, heraldically speaking,↓
         that
174.38   nobleman; ~~or~~↑nay↓ that

174.41 nobility. ¶But[O over o]ne day

174.42 four ↑with↓ the well-known chaste liveries of the Newcomes↓ came

175. 1 where ~~the Miss Huffs were ha~~ ↑Mrs.↓ & the Miss Potters happened↓ to

175. 2 donkey-man ↑with↓ whom

175. 5 & ~~taken~~ considering

175. 6 the [R over r]ectory to

175.10 wore ~~when~~↑at↓ the

175.n6 it [on over in] the

175.16 & ~~had~~ the

175.17 stairs—the [P over p]ark-people' were

175.20 and ~~saying~~ crying,

175.21 Dont ↑[illeg.]↓ say

175.24 Newcome ~~would come~~+↑&↓+ & young ~~Barnes~~↑Ethel↓ &

175.n9 would ~~come~~↑enter↓ in

176. 3 Mrs. ~~Huff~~↑Potter↓ and

176. 5 Florac, ~~looking~~↑going into↓ +at+ the

176.11 the ~~Park~~ barouche

176.16 Mrs. ~~Huff's~~↑Potters↓ predictions

176.17 visit ~~her~~↑the↓ manufacturer's daughter↓. [A over a]nd when

176.18 Princess ~~[illeg.]~~ de

176.21 G. ~~Huff~~↑Potter↓ DD

176.22 Mrs. ~~Huff~~↑Potter↓ did ↑or did↓ not

176.27 apartment—the ~~strangers~~↑guests↓ apartments— the

176.28 Tom ~~Huffs~~↑Potters↓ superintendence)

176.32 that ↑Mr↓ &

176.32 were ↑likely to↓ in

176.34 ¶Tom ~~Huff~~↑Potter↓ was

176.34 me ~~the very~~ two

176.34 our arrival[— over :]and to

176.35 day. ~~He~~Before desiring

176.37 him ↑who has beh↓ your

176.37 Highness ~~complimented him on the sermon~~ who

176.39 the ~~church & the~~↑organ-loft↓ in a↓ hymn

176.41 Monsieur [illeg.] his

176.41 Lodge ↑gate↓. Will

176.42 of bill↑i↓ard with ~~us~~↑me↓? says

176.45 his ↑Highness's↓ hand

177. 1 are ~~these~~↑you↓ English!

177. 3 them!. ~~She is~~ f Didst

177. 5 said ~~she~~ simply

177. 6 Mr. Jowls↑. ↓; ~~then the~~↑ at the Ebenezer. Mr. ~~Huff~~↑↑Potter↓↓ was not a good preacher certainly↓ ¶Savez-vous

177. 9 Meess!—and ~~the rogue~~↑Paul looked↓ unutterably

177.10 say, ~~he was oft~~↑Monsieur de Montcontour showed↓ a

177.11 courtesy ~~and~~ respect

177.13 congratulations ~~in~~↑at↓ possessing

177.19 to ~~very~~↑our most↓ comfortable

177.20 blazing [on over in] the

177.23 brave:—He ~~informed~~↑↑told cried to↓ his maitre d'hotel— Frederick,↑[! over ,]↓ ↑Remember↓ Monsieur

177.24 before hi[s over m]B orders— Prostrate

177.29 je ~~te~~↑ t'envoie

177.31 Demain ↑cest↓ Sunday—et↓ tu

177.32 dinner—My fürend!—~~an~~here there

177.32 squeeze [o over f]f both

177.35 embrace. ~~Sunday came as in the eve~~ Not

177.35 kind ↑in her way,↓ though

177.36 was ~~little~~ Madame

177.39 guests. ~~The sheets~~↑She sate↓ and

177.40 never ~~seen~~↑beheld↓ such

178. 1 morning ~~came~~↑arrived↓ in

178. 2 and buckskins[, over —] and

178. 3 and ~~in the~~after breakfast

178. 6 to ~~use~~↑employ↓ oaths

178. 7 but the↓ thought

178. 8 as a↑n English↓ country-gentleman.

178.10 others.' [H over h]e got

178.11 sporting ~~jargon~~↑language↓ with

179. 3 great popularity[, over .] ↑&↓ In

179. 6 of ~~the~~ Sir

179.10 the town—~~The~~↑One↓ haberdashers had ↑a↓ yellow stock called↓ 'The Montcontour' ~~stock in their↓ ↑displayed↓ in his↓ windows:

179.12 recommended ↑it↓ to

179.12 gents. ~~**Compositor Brewer**~~ ¶The

179.20 to ~~a~~↑the↓ solitary

179.23 under ↑the↓ penalty

179.24 little ~~of~~ angle

179.27 rooms ↑where there was now no hospitality; Gothic drawing rooms↓ shrouded

179.36 whether [G over F]lenlivat had

179.37 in ~~Berkely~~↑London.↓—Sir Barnes

179.39 to hunt—~~she did not~~↑to amuse himself↓—as all

179.40 again. ~~Her ladyships reading seemed~~ ↑She rang languidly when we↓ rose

179.43 the ↑melancholy↓ ornamental

179.45 the ↑great stacks of↓ chimnies

180. 3 Ouf! [cr over sa]ies Florac,

180.13 not ~~seem~~ appear

180.19 on ~~when~~↑after this↓ brief

180.22 not ↑mon bon~~[illeg.]~~↓ what

180.25 & friend~~?,~~ the

180.27 great ~~respect~~↑attention↓ (mingled

180.29 Mr. [blank] was

180.39 gage—. ¶~~Never mind~~↑No—no— no such. nonsense↓ says

181. 2 is [on over in] bard.

181. 4 Jack. ↑To us↓ Tis

181. 5 will ~~b~~ scold

181. 6 you ~~most~~↑ust↓ bring

181. 7 Mr. [blank] benefit

181. 9 Rosebury ↑& Mr. Hampton↓ went

181.10 waiting ~~his~~↑the former's↓ inspection

181.14 party. ↑¶↓Most respectable

181.21 entertain them↑,↓ or communicate them—~~or~~, and

181.23 though ~~it~~ from

181.26 and ↑then of↓ English

181.30 grand'route—what ~~a~~ armies

181.32 victims ~~in that dre~~↑of the wretched↓ conspiracy.

181.33 we ~~came~~↑reached↓ home.

181.38 Heavens! ~~Was~~ Could

181.41 engaged ~~as~~ where

181.42 women ~~often~~↑ever↓ will

181.43 or ↑whatsoever↓ other trial. ~~They fly out~~↑They have but↓ to

181.44 and ↑as it were↓ an

182. 2 her ↑her to tend the poor round about us, or to↓ bear

182.10 I ~~for~~ ever

182.13 round ~~the mother's~~↑Laura's↓ neck.

182.13 what ~~my~~↑the husbands↓ feelings

182.16 that ~~one~~↑felicity↓ is

182.19 poor ↑outcast↓ beggar

182.30 this ~~day~~↑morning↓ I

182.36 to say'—whisper[ed over s] Laura

183. 1 ladyship ↑was unwell, & they thought↓ received

183. 5 and ~~to tell you~~ I

183.15 asked ~~to see~~ and

183.17 know you—~~and then a~~ ¶'Ah

183.26 this ~~[illeg.]~~ Lady

183.30 I ~~spoke~~↑said↓ more

183.33 so: ↑and that she was quite alone in the world & had no friend to fly to:↓ and

183.37 enlighten ~~his wicked heart~~↑& strengthen him↓, and

183.41 petitioner. ~~Her~~↑Laura's↓ cheeks

183.45 pure ~~-minded~~↑Creature.↓ ¶Why

184. 5 Sir? ¶~~And~~↑Before↓ or

184.12 on [her over his] last

184.14 creature Arthur—↑I am so glad↓ I

184.15 first ~~&~~ moment

184.23 ¶But ~~my wife's~~↑Laura's↓ intended

184.26 Pendennis, ~~the~~ Lady

184.29 way. ↑O,↓ I

184.41 hypocrite!. ¶↑This letter was handed to my wife at dinner time, and she gave it to me as ~~of~~ she passed out of the room with the other ladies↓ I

184.44 that ~~our~~ the

185. 2 Bébi.' ↑It was gratifying that↓ + +The good

185. 4 her love.~~I told Florac of the arrival of the Baronet at Newcome, who had probably put a stop to our visit there.~~ ↑¶↓My host

185. 6 living. ¶Their quarrels

185. 6 county; ↑one side brought forward↓ his

185. 7 her; ↑&↓ his

185.14 union ~~that~~↑wh.↓ might

185.16 cruelty ↑fierce↓ mutual

185.17 and ~~publi~~↑open↓ scenes

185.20 bargain ↑in churches↓ with

185.24 words, ~~[illeg.]~~ how

185.26 not ~~blessed~~↑amen'd↓ the

185.26 and ~~said~~ called

185.27 perjurers? ~~When their friends whom Florac entertained that~~

~~day were gone I~~
~~told him of Sir Barnes's~~
~~Newcomes return~~
[Begin Anne's handwriting.]
185.28 ↑¶↓Does Mr.
185.28 Mr. Hampton↑risson↓ know
185.29 de Highgate—Vas.! ↑¶↓Does
Newcome
185.33 Clara. ↑¶↓Mr. Hampton
185.34 to Flora↑:↓ Will
185.34 him word@[? over :]
~~or stay, shall we take~~
~~yr. horses once more out~~
~~of the stable again«?»~~
~~and drive to Newcome «&»~~
~~to give him warning?~~
~~¶This plan was agreed upon.~~
~~We settled it late in~~
~~the evening for my host~~
~~had had friends to dinner~~
~~before whom I did not~~
~~care to speak about~~
~~such dangerous subject.~~ @↑and
let us ~~and~~ send a messenger to
Newcome. ~~, if I↓~~ ¶At
185.38 enough tragi~~dy~~↑c↓, enough
185.41 ¶Children dishon~~n~~oured said
185.42 this catastroph~~y~~↑e↓ if
186. 7 leave, w~~h.~~↑hom↓ our
186.11 wife ha[s over d] made
186.16 here ~~le~~ found
186.21 Mr. Ha↑r↓risson, before
186.22 the ↑in↓ hotel. Whilst
[circumflex removed from
"hotel"]
186.24 anything wanted↑?↓ ¶It
186.25 sends ~~you~~@↑his↓him↓ says
186.28 Mr. Harrison at
186.31 other, ↑And↓ ~~A~~a word fm.
~~him~~@↑Florac↓ was
186.43 that ~~at~~ in
187. 1 we ~~last~~↑first↓ had
187. 2 If Vid~~d~~ler the
187. 4 has ~~taken a partner~~+,+↑had↓
various
187. 5 by Vid~~d~~lers ancient
187. 6 A jo~~lly~~↑vial↓ fellow
187. 7 Jolly Briton↑s↓, where
187. 9 merry ~~at~~↑in the↓ Boscawen
187.11 partner ~~Jo~~From [R over
C]osebury, the
187.13 her. ~~Confound the old~~ I
187.16 french ↑Jack Harris↓ says
187.34 amost cho[k over qu]ed John

187.39 had [On back of page: sketches
of woman, crowned man,
crowns] imbibed
187.40 T. ~~[have over illeg.]~~↑have↓ sent
187.41 2 ↑white↓ pocket
187.42 coronet & [P over L]otts.
~~There's NO Lord All.~~
~~I've looked in the Peerage~~
~~& there's no such a name.~~ ¶On
187.45 the Hotel where [circumflex
removed from "Hotel"]
188. 1 private apartement with
188. 7 him @↑and ran away.↓ O!
[Begin Thackeray's handwriting.]
188.10 with ~~an air~~↑a tone↓ of great
~~kindness~~↑softness↓—Your wife
188.16 course: ~~they are always~~↑when
did *they* ever fail↓ to
188.20 company ↑or his.↓ Do
188.22 buried ~~last year after getting~~
↑four ~~six~~ months ago after
nobbling↓ her
188.27 continued ↑in reply↓ to
188.34 strikes her:↑—Strikes *that* poor
little thing!↓ [Italics removed
from "Strikes"]
188.35 woman who['s over is] dead.
189. 2 chaise-de-poste. ↑What will
you?↓ I
189. 2 not ↑yet↓ enough
189. 4 afterwards. ~~Que diable~~+!.+ Do
189. 9 can ~~sp~~ seek
189.11 can go~~, and~~ [a over I]nd in
189.14 and ~~touch his~~↑touch that ~~a~~
manly not disloyal↓ heart ↑now↓
trembling
189.17 friend! ~~My wife~~Madame
Pendennis,
189.18 sweetest sermons—
~~Madame la Prine~~↑My wife shall↓
tend
189.20 ¶ ~~But~~Lord Highgate
189.23 noted down—[A over a]nd he
190.11 meeting ~~their~~ future
190.14 decided. ↑~~Very soon~~On the
morning after his return home↓
Barnes
190.22 and ~~had made not~~↑far from
making↓ preparations for ↑her
own↓ departure,
190.24 family who[se over m] arrival
190.25 and ~~her Mother~~↑Lady Ann &↓
some

190.25 were ~~to~~ coming—~~Some of~~ Lord Farintosh's ~~family~~ ↑mother & sisters↓ were

190.26 a ~~family~~↑réunion↓ previous

190.32 their ~~poor~~ mother.

191. 1 in ~~the~~ charge

191. 2 that ~~night~~↑evening↓, had

191. 6 and ~~greeted her, as his wont was~~ ↑saluted her with his accustomed↓ greetings

191. 7 insult. ~~If~~On a

191. 8 to ~~prove his kindness~~ testify

191.10 terror. ~~and tears.~~ On

191.10 very ↑last↓ night, ~~a count~~↑Lady↓ Clara's

191.10 from ↑ther fathers house at↓ Chanticlere,

191.11 Barnes ↑in the midst of a conjugal dispute↓ that

191.15 & children,↑, unattended save by this poor domestic who was about to leave her,↓ in

191.17 in ~~abject~~↑moaning↓ stupor.

191.21 his ↑august↓ forefathers—in

191.24 news [inserted in pencil]↑wh.↓ increased

191.24 fury. ~~A boy from~~A messenger ↑brought him a letter↓ from

191.25 his ~~legal an~~ man

191.26 with ↑such↓ an execration ~~and~~ as frightened ~~his~~ the

191.27 Claras ↑sitting↓ room.

191.28 up: ~~and~~ Sir

191.29 the ~~Sh~~ Bailiff's

191.34 husband ~~vouchsafed an interview~~ ↑went to her room↓ wh.

191.43 mistress ~~upon~~ in with [illeg] unalterable

192. 7 Barnes ~~in an open carriage~~ ↑riding near his own lodge-gate; and~~ near his own lodge-gate riding in the direction of Newcome↓, as

192. 8 ourselves ~~driving~~↑returning↓ to

192.17 Florac ~~had~~ spoken that

192.20 and ~~near~~↑before↓ wh.,

192.21 a ~~gig~~↑carriage↓ wh.

192.24 Belsize. [Picture of horse in background in pencil.] [Verso p. 2: ¶~~What food for observation we all are gentlemen~~«,» ↑for ourselves & others;↓ ~~what subjects for satire; what themes for leading~~

~~articles, what morals for fables,~~ ↑what points for moralists↓ ~~what~~ «texts» ↑figures↓ ~~for caricaturists, what frequent texts for sermons! I think perforce of my own career & contrast it with yours &c~~] ¶

192.31 Sir, ~~to enter~~ cries ~~the~~ Sir Barnes, ↑still holding up that unlucky cane↓ how

192.33 scroundrel! ~~er~~ said

192.n9 answer, ~~or~~ Belsize

192.34 seized ~~him and flung him with a~~ ↑and tore him out of the saddle, flinging him↓ scream↑ing↓ down

192.36 making ↑a↓ way

192.37 moment. ¶~~When~~The carriage wh. ~~Lord High~~hg↑Belsize had↓ ordered

192.43 will ~~leave word at the Prince de Montcontour's at Rosebury,—where he may find me~~ ↑send him word where he may hear of me'↓—And getting

192.44 the ~~coach~~ driver

193. 3 Mr [blank] the lawyers ~~den~~↑house↓ into

193. 5 Newcome ↑who was not much hurt↓ had

193.15 been trifling~~, and after being~~↑: he had been↓ bled

193.17 day [w over L]ith a servant↑s↓ attending

193.20 that ~~if he~~ Lady

193.28 The ↑proceedings in the↓ Newcome

193.29 Bill ~~broug~~ filled

193.31 peers who↑se↓ ~~enter~~ business

193.32 of ~~the~~↑Barnes↓ Newcome's

193.34 Serjeant ~~Billosis st~~↑Rowland↓ stood

193.36 the ~~conj~~ conjugal

193.38 and ~~lonely~~ ↑deserted↓ husband alone ~~on~~↑by↓ his

193.39 country! ~~Billosis~~↑Rowland↓ wept

193.42 gave his↑~~Billosis's~~Rowlands↓ address

193.43 the ~~leading~~↑principal morning↓ journal

193.44 lead[ing over er]~~for a~~ article

193.45 every ~~body~~↑party concerned↓ and

193.46 the monarchy↑ (with a
retrospective view of the well
known case of

194. 1 Gyges and Candaules)↓, the
absur↑monstrosity↓ of

194. 2 absurdity ↑and the punishment↓
of

194. 4 requested ~~by~~ to

194. 7 hand. ¶Rowland↑Oliver↓ QC.
QC. ↑now↓ had his ~~retinnings~~—a
man ↑a husband↓ and

194. 7 Mr. ~~Rowland~~↑Oliver↓ could

194. 9 any ~~palliation~~↑excuse↓ for

194.12 wondered ~~Sir Bar~~ the

194.14 when th[e over is] ill-omened

194.15 Serjeant ~~Oliver~~↑Rowland↓
himself interposed ↑in Court↓
to

194.16 known—and ~~in the na~~ with

194.17 neglected wom[a over e]n—
~~with her~~of castaway

194.20 appeal? ↑and so on—and so
on↓—So between

194.26 their f suborned

194.29 delinquencies; ~~consoled~~ consoled

194.31 tie—wh. ~~affecting~~had been

194.32 affecting [E over e]piscopal
benedictions

194.32 Hanover ↑Sqre.↓. ~~—With the
new name wh. she took,
the poor lady passes out
of the history of the
Newcomes. If Barnes
children meet her, do
they know her? If her
once-husband thinks upon
the unhappy young creature
whom his cruelty «sent
to perdition, »↑drove from
him,↓ does his Conscience
affect his sleep at nights?
Why should «his» ↑Sir
Barnes Newcome's↓ conscience
be more squeamish than
his country's, wh. has put
money in his pocket for
having trampled upon the
poor weak young thing, and
scorned her, and driven
her to ruin? When the
whole «of the» accounts
of this wretched bankruptcy
are brought up for final
Audit, wh. of the unhappy
parties will be shown to
be the most guilty?
Does the Bishop who did~~

~~the benedictory business at
St. George's repent in secret?~~
[Verso p. 1: ~~My dear Sir~~¶Will
you give me the pleasure of your
company at dinner on the 1
April.] ¶~~She has fled~~↑So Lady
Clara flies↓ from

194.36 should ~~know~~ know

194.42 her ~~but~~ with

194.44 as ~~her~~ the

195. 2 come ~~home~~to her

195. 5 the ~~visitors~~ cottagers

195. 8 and ~~try~~ set

195.10 Our ~~frien~~ acquaintances

195.13 with ~~these~~↑such↓ wild

195.14 Soul? ↑Even these scorn her.↓
The

195.18 season—no ~~How can he, when~~
↑wonder that he is away all
day—how can he like a home
wh.↓ she

195.19 made ~~its~~o wretched?

195.21 being ~~wraps~~and hope

195.22 she ~~has passed out of our~~ no

195.25 ¶If Barnes'↓ Newcome's

195.33 business ~~over~~↑for↓ Barnes

195.39 scores ↑more↓ of

195.40 George ↑of England↓ ~~the
Capadocian may look down and
see~~ ↑may behold↓ virgin

195.41 respectable females-dragons
looking

[Begin Anne's handwriting.]

196. 3 of command@↑;↓ &

196. 9 Libyan @↑lion↓. What

196.31 Captains toad[ies over zs] to bow
their knee

196.31 do ho~~m~~mage to

196.32 obeyed. [I over i]n fact

197. 3 to ~~pay~~@↑worship↓ her@↑.↓
hommage ¶So

197. 7 the ↑private↓ sentiments

197. 8 of knowing@↑;↓ but

197. 9 Jack Todh~~a~~↑u↓nter &

197.13 exert ~~the~~↑ther↓ influence

197.18 man ↑of the world↓ must

197.19 their ru@↑te↓ful looks

197.22 they ~~might~~@↑may↓ never

197.23 rogues ~~might~~@↑may↓ never

197.26 the town, in

197.28 Todhunter, ~~when~~↑&↓ the

197.30 the ~~jolly~~↑dear↓ little batchelors
quarters

197.31 rare do~~e~~ings, such
197.31 jolly time@[. over :] I fancy Henchman↑tch↓ coming
197.32 the [M over m]orning [P over p]ost@&↑.↓ ↑I imagine↓ Tod
197.37 H—gate [P over p]ersonal rencontre
[Begin Thackeray's handwriting.]
197.40 a [illeg]erigord pie,
198. 2 bed-room. ~~Has my lord~~↑I know he has↓ rung
198. 8 Henchman; ~~but~~↑and↓ both
198. 9 that the↑ir↓ Chieftain
198.19 for [f over g]ive guineas
198.23 and ↑coursed↓ down
198.27 Pitch in~~to~~ to
198.29 breast ~~and~~ as
198.33 this — confounded
198.39 about Highgate— ~~whom Cora~~↑you yourself↓ pointed
198.40 dined ~~with~~ at
198.41 society often—↑.↓ But
198.43 Coralie ~~told us~~ said
199. 1 answers. ~~Sir~~What do
199. 8 on ↑told↓ Frank
199.12 the ↑usual↓ expletives wh. ↑usuall↓ adorned
199.13 strongly moved[— over ,]What do
199.19 the ~~confounded~~ pack?
199.23 in England,~~by Jove~~—and the
199.28 no [On back of page, sketch of woman and man] fault
199.31 except ↑just↓ out
199.33 a ~~good fellow and I like him~~ ↑most respectable man, though he is only a peer of George III's creation,↓ and
199.35 to ~~[illeg]~~ know
199.41 I ~~like you~~ know my rank
199.42 and ~~all~~ my sisters
199.44 Farintosh's ~~remarks~~↑views↓ was
200. 2 wh. ~~the young gentleman~~↑he was as↓ resolutely
200. 4 honour, ~~of~~ a
200. 5 own, ↑or↓ a
200. 6 had ~~accepted~~↑borne↓ very
200. 8 and ~~as~~ being
200. 9 over ↑the dregs of↓ his
200.10 of ~~his~~ the
200.14 et cetera↑—Dont we know?↓—if we

200.18 this ↑two-bottle↓ Mentor
200.20 that ~~they had~~↑they all 'traversed the cart' and took↓ another
200.21 too, ~~where~~↑but it↓ was
200.22 Telemachus ↑(as was natural to his age)↓ but
200.23 too ~~pressed~~↑quaffed↓ the
200.25 in ~~Pall Mall~~↑the park↓ any
200.28 and afterwards[; over —] &
200.32 hear ↑either↓ one
200.39 thousand ↑men in↓ clubs
201. 2 where ~~to~~ his
201. 3 wh. ↑Messrs.↓ Bowman ~~the~~ Valet,
201. 9 received ~~a letter~~ by
201.10 Son. ~~Dear M~~ ¶Dear
201.12 the ↑cruel↓ misfortune ↑& humiliation↓ wh.
201.18 often ~~al~~ owned
201.19 from ~~the~~↑an↓ engagement
201.22 pardon ~~will~~↑would↓ do
201.23 I ~~pray sincerely~~↑hope and pray↓ he
201.25 I ~~hope~~↑trust↓ I
201.25 and ↑that he will↓ believe
201.26 the ~~sincere~~ esteem
201.27 Newcome. [break a line.] ¶A
201.31 Ethel ↑~~at Rosebury~~↓ to my wife↓, I
201.34 to ↑speak to you about the poor children,↓ consult
201.39 Ann ~~and~~, her
202. 3 poor ~~little~~ orphaned
202. 6 friend's ↑urgent↓ summons,
202. 7 ¶The ~~house of~~↑household at↓ Newcome
202.10 his mother~~;~~ was
202.11 of ~~her~~ the
202.27 shrieking ↑abandoned↓ nursery;
202.30 temper, ~~wh. he vented~~↑and venting his wrath↓ upon
202.33 butler, ↑this↓ farm-bailiff, ↑this↓ lawyer, ↑this↓ doctor,
202.34 mother herself↑—↓who rose
202.36 house ~~against~~↑to↓ whom
203. 5 Barnes ↑fairly↓ burst
203. 7 see ~~the~~↑this↓ children:
203. 8 he ↑would↓ implore~~d~~ Ethel
203. 9 she ~~was~~ married,
203.10 house? [Margin: slip 5] ¶T.
203.15 between ~~him~~ his

203.17   from [a over illeg.] friend
203.19   had [illeg.] now
203.21   of his↑Lord Highgate's↓ villainy
203.23   damages where what he
         sought↑intended to seek↓ from
203.27   and eagerness↑gaiety in↓ her
203.29   sang ↑& talked↓ so
203.32   so ↑much↓ (in
203.35   and ↑when we were alone↓ by
203.36   happened that↑during the↓ day.
204. 2   I think↑believe↓, if
204. 4   it. We read↑I have read (besides
         in that poem of Goethe of wh.
         you are so fond[) over ,]↓ in
204. 8   the pagodas;↑—I believe they are
         quite respected in—in Pagoda-
         land—↓and the
204. 9   them ↑Can we cry out against
         these poor creatures, or against
         the custom of their country?↓—It
         seems
204.11   in the ↑our↓ world
204.13   their parents↑mothers↓ will
204.15   of a Souls
204.19   her th discoveries. She I
204.20   found that other on
204.24   talk; and↑—and↓ I
204.27   youth; ↑about wh.↓ She told me
         spoke
204.31   during her holydays↑the winter
         at↓ Newcome.
204.40   everyone she almost
204.44   continued. I felt somehow it
         was wrong ↑And though I liked
         Kew very much, who would not↓
         like
205. 1   When ↑poor↓ Papa
205. 4   to make↑sneer↓ at
205. 7   you do?↑.↓ Was
205.16   could ↑have↓ control↑led↓ him,
205.16   him ↑and whom he and his
         friends could have admired↓,
         instead
205.20   how ↑till↓ this
205.22   would fly↑break↓ out
205.27   wh. poor Lady
205.28   kept of ↑and in wh. she↓ noted
205.29   husbands [illeg.] ill
205.30   Laura! [D over d]o you
205.31   Florac's [illeg.] culpabilities
205.31   would be[— over !] as
205.38   *them* ↑so↓ eager to in

205.41   Miss [blank] you
205.43   the [P over p]arks and
206.n7   narrative ab let
206. 4   this juncture [illeg.] ↑point of
         Miss↓ Newcome's
206. 5   we ↑both↓ burst
206.14   and he we could scarcely↑not go
         upon↓ any
206.18   months Ethel ↑Laura↓ that
206.21   worldliness wh. about
206.25   we the every
206.26   suit my pride↑me↓ I
206.27   of the↑such↓ pride!
206.28   that ↑after accepting him↓ as
206.33   not tell↑talk to↓ you
207. 3   poor motherless children
207. 8   obedient [of over to] my
207.10   is ↑as it were↓ dead
207.19   the first↑opening↓ words
207.20   beamed round↑from↓ her
207.21   Newcome family; I
207.25   we are,↑—↓not only
207.27   at all,↑—↓we surely
207.30   sisterhood wh. m↑of M↓isfortune
         creates [C over c]ompassion who
207.30   always going partners↑entering
         into partnership↓ here
207.34   her apt↑prudent↓ counsel,
207.43   curses ↑& peevishness↓ on
207.44   her ↑charity-↓visits to
208.12   to Screw↑the Park↓ this
208.21   Mr. [blank] his
208.24   and for an hour or more was↑his
         name was taken to↓ Miss
208.26   as yet[. over :] Laura
208.28   when the Lord
208.31   hour ↑the carriage was seen
         driving away, and↓ Ethel
208.33   in then↑at the same time↓, the
208.34   aunt's company↑.↓ who↑Aunt
         Ethel↓ cut
208.36   her confid↑friend↓ into
208.42   is gone[! over ,] at
208.45   be hurt+.+↓ but not to speak as
         he did.↓ He
209. 2   used words↑—words↓ such
209.12   But ↑the affair—↓the painful
209.19   you we are.
209.20   allude ↑the continued↓ 'to
209.29   Doctor: and↑—I assure you he
         was. And↓ had

209.30 all ~~until~~ and
209.31 I ~~was~~ determined
209.33 you that↑—that↓ no
209.36 with ~~himself~~↑Lord Farintosh↓, will
209.38 eyes ~~exhibited~~ showed
209.40 very ~~good~~↑generous↓ and
209.45 case, ~~I feel that~~ the
210. 4 cries ~~Lord Farintosh~~↑the young lady's↓ lover
210. 5 I? ~~Lord Farintosh~~+?+ answered
210. 7 and ~~to the end of our~~↑every one of us↓ should
210.17 misery! ~~O I am~~My pride
210.20 suitor—Humiliated [E over !] the↓! Who's
210.24 *is* ~~a~~ news.
210.25 family, ~~and~~ with
210.28 altogether. ~~as~~↑I fancy it was↓ an
210.30 Farintosh: ~~My wife it didnt matter of what family my wife was.~~ ↑Do you suppose there were not plenty of women to tell it me?↓ ¶It
210.33 That ~~would~~↑can not↓ be
210.35 I ↑was a child then, and↓ liked
210.36 best. ~~It~~¶↓As if
210.38 *pas?* ~~The wom~~↑I never↓ thought
210.40 it ~~was~~↑is↓ you
211. 8 coveted, ~~any~~ and
211.11 even. [A over a]nd to
211.12 her! ~~Her fate makes me tremble for~~ ↑Why did her parents and mine↓ consign
211.14 child, ~~I do not think of that~~↑I am not afraid of *that* happening to me↓—but her
211.15 years, ~~B~~ my
211.16 wretchedness ↑& fault↓ aggravated
211.17 his ~~wretched~~↓ unhappy
211.18 unhappy ~~to~~↑if I↓ fulfilled.
211.19 ashamed ~~of~~↑& humiliated for↓ myself
211.21 mean, ~~said,~~↑cried↓ the
211.22 in ~~m~~ your
211.24 all ~~the men at~~ White's
211.25 me—and ↑all↓ my
211.27 are: ~~bac~~↑break off
211.30 in ~~the young~~+man's+ ↑Farintosh's↓ eyes.
211.32 lord ~~and~~ Ethel

211.34 my ~~heart~~↑soul↓ for
211.34 told you,↑—↓and wh.
211.38 and ↑then↓ you
212. 1 the laughing↑-↓stock of the ~~w~~ whole
212.16 the ↑whole↓ affair
212.18 men knew—~~how~~↑, what↓ the
212.19 women [a over i]verred that
212.19 intriguing ↑worldly↓ Ethel
212.22 Farintosh ~~had~~↑who had long been tired of her,↓ flung
212.24 under ↑the↓ pretence
212.26 married [blank] six
212.26 afterwards. ¶~~Thinking~~ ↑Deeming↓ that
213. 5 Farintosh: nor↑, even,↓ was
213.10 before ~~very~~ many
213.13 had ~~a~~ dismal
213.16 departure, ~~he~~ Sir
213.17 was ~~informed~~↑told↓ by
213.18 Mr. [blank] how
213.18 slept ↑for a few hours↓ at
213.20 train. ~~His~~↑We may add, that his↓ lordship
213.29 trembling ~~that a~~ in
213.30 gone ↑up↓ to
214.10 to ~~send~~↑'take↓ those
214.13 courier ~~brou~~ one
214.16 said. ↑¶↓'Barnes m'a
214.23 he ~~used~~↑employed↓ *his*
214.24 state. ↑He relented and asked pardon.↓ He
214.27 *mother's* ↑always↓ affectionate [Blank space] E.N.
214.30 her! ¶↑And↓ Who
214.35 her ~~in her~~↑for the sake of↓ old
214.41 this ~~court~~↑simple little hint↓ in
214.44 perfectly ~~legible~~↑clearly↓ hand
215. 3 I ~~in~~↑enclosed it in a note↓ sent
215. 5 holograph ↑page↓ of
215. 6 Bareacres, ~~so~~ wh.
215. 7 painful ↑& private↓ circumstance,
215. 9 —and ~~in this way~~ ↑upon such a book↓ going
215.12 a ~~private~~↑clandestine↓ correspondence
215.20 a message↑—I want something from Brussells↓—Is the
215.27 back? ~~so~~ palpitates
215.35 twenty pounds↓ . . .↓ gasps
215.41 by ↑yet↓ another

215.42 No ~~I~~↑Mr. Pendennis↓ did

215.47 Laura ~~asks~~↑continues↓ standing

215.47 evident ↑to me↓ that ~~th Edith~~ Ethel

216. 4 whereas now~~-I—now~~ ¶Now

216. 6 the ~~husband~~↑humble slave↓ of

216.21 picture, ~~and~~ hanging

216.23 the ~~post-~~ bag,

216.24 the ~~Newco~~ Brussells

216.28 initiated. 'They↓ women↓ wish

216.30 the marriage[— over ;]I continue

216.31 What ↑of↓ freshness

216.34 has ~~drawn~~↑won↓ the

216.34 pound prize;~~in a lottery where often men draw~~ ↑—and we know there are↓ worse

217. 1 ¶No ~~answers~~ came

217. 6 this circumstances; he

217.14 Newcome; ~~our little boy would have wanted~~ ↑had not her husband sternly cautioned↓ the

217.15 leave ↑the↓ matters alone.

218. 1 Blackstone's [C over c]ommentaries and

218.10 to [This is the second page numbered 28.] my

218.12 Marquis ~~brea~~ takes

218.13 leaves ~~that~~↑the↓ unfortunate

218.14 hardest ↑blow↓ wh.

218.16 thing ↑which was↓ said

218.18 When ↑t↓he ↑Colonel↓ offered

218.22 he ↑& poor Clive↓ loved

218.28 a ↑great↓ title

218.31 brother's ↑abandoned↓ children,

218.35 bearing ↑much too hardly↓ as

218.35 think, ↑upon one↓ who

218.36 errors ~~came~~ were

218.37 hand ↑wh.↓ led

218.42 been ~~made~~↑bidden↓ to

218.43 honest ↑natural↓ affections;

218.44 title? ~~The~~↑But, the↓ Judge who ~~weighs merely~~↑sees not↓ the

218.45 and ~~knows~~↑views↓ not

219. 1 creatures, ↑we know↓ has ↑surely,↓ a

219. 3 so; ↑who administer our ~~rewards~~ praises and punishments so prematurely;↓ who

219. 6 close, ~~w~~ for

219. 9 wh. ↑daily↓ took

219. 9 the ~~little~~↑young↓ messenger

219.10 in ~~constant~~ ↑ceaseless↓

219.11 between ~~the~~ the

219.12 the Colonel,↑:↓ it

219.24 ended ↑in the ensuing Michaelmas Term↓ in

219.26 took ↑entire↓ charge

219.27 own ~~household &~~ family;

219.28 wife ~~described~~↑talked to m↓ to

219.28 course ↑about↓ her

219.30 (mine ↑often↓ partook

219.31 with ↑the little Clara &↓ the

219.35 the ~~B~~↑b↓aronial library,

219.37 of ↑worldly↓ Travel

219.41 in ~~the~~↑a↓ foregoing chapter↑page↓ in

220. 1 she ↑had↓ lived

220. 4 mantel-piece ~~un~~↑near↓ wh.

220.11 asked [a over illeg.]fter her

220.13 father ~~th~~ was

220.22 who ~~to~~ the

220.28 Colonel Mum?—↑It came only yesterday.↓ And

220.29 takes ~~it~~ out the ~~lad~~ letter

220.45 come ~~we~~ shall

220.45 a ↑new↓ friend

221. 5 Keziah [(over ,]to whom

221.11 for ~~no sooner had~~↑when↓ Laura ↑had↓ read

221.11 letter ~~than~~ she

221.11 down ~~and burst~~ on

221.13 father. ↑Then↓ She

221.16 maid [On back of page 30:]in a

221.16 stately ~~way~~↑manner↓ and

221.21 Railroad. [End of back of page 30] [On unnumbered page:]This Volume

222. 1 that Edition.[Ends here] ¶The

222. 3 narrated sentim↑ent↓al occurrences

[Begin Anne's handwriting.]

222. 6 much ~~inflamed~~↑increased↓, subsists

222.15 first ~~gave~~↑led↓ her

222.19 disposition. "She is

222.29 but ~~admire~~↑acquiesce↓ this

223. 5 a school↑-↓girl—the piano

223. 7 her [& over —] yielded

223. 9 third ~~was~~↑is↓ named

223.17 was I[e over a]st Sir

223.17 marry again[, over .] &

223.20 rightly &↑in↓ that
223.24 to honour, with
223.32 The firey temper
223.36 to keep↑secure↓ this
223.41 amply secured↑defrayed↓ out
223.44 subtracted ↑for his own benefit↓ no
224. 6 with the↑her indigent↓ neighbouring↑s↓ poor Miss
224.11 stricken & humbled ↑awe stricken↓ by
224.12 always, ↑of wh.↓ the sight of wh. rebukes
224.13 humility & devotion.
224.14 who will swear↑else where↓ are
224.22 the overpowte↓ring misery chastened [Verso of page:] improved
224.34 subject. Where↑ither↓ are
224.35 has transferred all
224.36 that lad[y over ie]'s ex-suitor
224.37 her former↑usual↓ tirades
224.39 apologist asks? that
224.43 Colonel h↑w↓as actually
225. 2 When me we
225.16 ¶Warrington [t over r]oasted poor
225.29 but it was plain↑no↓ explanations
225.44 best off every
225.44 about upholsterers, painters
226.14 would no↑d↓ &
226.16 now her appeared
226.27 smiling cheeks eyes
226.28 He followed he would
226.29 exchanging ↑precious↓ observations
226.33 No pe woman
226.40 head ↑in the church↓ at Musselbourough
226.44 in an highly
227. 3 brother Hobson[illeg. punctuation] though
227.10 engaged. Charles accepted Mr.
227.15 little of about
227.30 him, to↑no↓ undesirable
227.34 law [a over &] twinkle
227.35 she heard the↑stood over them in a benedictory attitude expressing her↓ surprising intelligence at
228. 5 of an question & to like & dislike having

228.27 reptile. He He
228.31 full the his
228.32 & ↑publicly↓ expressed
228.39 by vag that
228.39 sermons Pens at
228.40 leading strings[? over —] Are
230. 7 & utter[ed over re] them
230. 8 places where↑n↓ Sir
230.28 shown the↑two↓ white
230.28 in that↑those↓ unpleasant
231. 1 that however↑although↓ private
231.22 he lavishe[s over illeg.] against
231.27 you, it↑s↓ owes no little blundering
231.38 would [sketch here of man's head upsidedown] have
231.40 amongst ↑regular↓ merchants
231.44 apartments &↑in↓ the
232. 4 mysterious terr[i over y]fying, unknown
232. 5 to d[e over i]scribe them.
232. 6 his knowl[e over d]dge of
232.12 were +ut- ↑ut↓terred, what
232.19 His reputation@↑character↓ for wor↑teal↓th was
232.20 Rumour: {F.B. knew
232.20 a @few↑few↓ millions
232.21 would inherit:} his@↑Thomas Newcome's↓ distinguished
232.25 his w[e over a]alth brought him;.—His@↑his character↓ reputation
232.31 presented him↑Mrs. Clive Newcome↓ with
232.32 silver palm↑cocoa nut tree↓ whereof
232.35 back—a Howat-Ser↑Howatzar↓ plough,
232.36 East lend India
233.45 or to↑stopping at↓ the
234. 4 the [s over S]ociety wh.
234.17 Colonels, [t over &]he Judges,
234.21 funny stories—([t over T]he droll
234.41 omnium gathering↑tum↓ not
234.42 & Nymm &
234.44 Painting Room &
234.44 the Paternal↑nal↓ throne,
235. 3 to [illeg.] bed.
235.24 to his business the
235.30 brushes [P over p]alettes &
236. 1 her & straight way the

236. 3 one another—[t over T]hat was

236.n3 shoe—a ~~the~~ very

236. 9 & ↑in↓ leading

223.11 in Piccar[dy over y] Place

236.26 Butler, ~~insulted~~↑outraged↓ the

236.34 the ↑series of↓ final

236.34 wh. ~~took place~~ commencing

236.36 the enem[y over ie]'s part

237. 1 Brussels ↑she used to box my
ears & go into such tantrums↓ &

237.23 his la[qu over ck]ered boots.

238.23 admire ↑mire↓ everything.

238.24 testimonial [↑~~Guthie Clames~~↓]
was

239. 2 & ↑still larger↓ prospective

239. 5 Honeyman [H over h]e lived

239. 6 says he~~r~~ that

239. 9 and ↑eats cabobs with↓ wealthy

239.11 remarked ~~on~~↑that↓ his

239.14 maid ↑in↓[?] the

239.17 funereal gloom.~~Yon~~ ¶Yon

239.19 good [Sketches of women on
back of page] friend

239.30 Cund [B over b]ank. ¶Gracious

239.35 a [Sketches of women on back of
page] traitor

239.36 & ~~her unmasted~~ would

239.37 rocks Sir—↑who↓ would

239.41 to vis~~it~~it the

240.14 F.B. ~~And~~↑In↓ my

240.20 described [& t over , T]he
temporary

240.20 was cha↑n↓ged, changed

240.37 days. @↑We have said how↓
Ever since ~~he had made~~ Clive's

240.38 between ~~them~~@↑father and
Son.↓+.+ The

240.41 he ↑rightly↓ persisted

241. 2 life. ~~Even the catastrophy
in the city did not
seem to interest Clive,
or the conduct of his
relatives to exasperate him
sufficiently.~~ @↑The catastrophe
in the City again brought father
& Son together somewhat, and
the vindictiveness of both was
roused by Barnes's treason.↓
Time

241.n2 had ~~altered~~ changed

241.13 made easy↑:↓ @↑to whom fate
~~awards~~@↑visits with↓ gentle

241.28 Pen ~~whispers~~ pleads

241.28 other coun[se over ci]llor. Let

242. 2 at ~~hi~~ what

242. 3 like ~~atthe~~↓ dear

242. 4 & ~~atthe~~↓ good

242.n4 draughts, ~~that~~↑but↓ there

242.30 was ~~engaged~~ ↑invested↓ in

242.43 weeks ↑ago↓ since

243. 1 all. ~~& a good bill is a good bill~~ I

244.11 a wrong—Absurd—↑If friend

244.19 an answere [He over It] ~~was~~
could

244.31 generally ma↑n↓ly demeanour.

244.33 Colonel of↑that↓ his

245. 4 with la↑u↓ghter. My

245.14 an a[wf over fw]ul bow

245.16 testimonial—The coc[oa over a]
nut

245.17 of ban[q over k]uets—The
Colonels

245.20 F.B. [on verso p. 58: ¶Perhaps
the reader does not remember a
letter to the shareholders of the
Bundle Cund Banking Company
wh. appeared at this time.] I

245.25 come ~~home~~ out

245.29 Europe ~~he had~~↑gave↓ the

245.36 respected. ~~When~~ Mr.

245.36 Mr. ~~Ma~~ McGaspey

246. 1 when cer~~e~~tain family

246. 3 was ~~of almost all her relatives~~ of

246.11 his moit[y over ie] of

246.21 Mamma ~~or~~ a

246.24 not ~~care~~ be

246.28 the ↑railway↓ carriage ↑(with her
husband & father in law↓ at

246.29 old ~~gentleman~~↑uncle↓ very

247. 3 great ↑callous↓ mirror

247. 5 Campaigner. ↑¶↓After that

247. 7 keeping, ~~& lived~~↑fm. wh.↓ alone

247. 8 of pa↑l↓lid Death.

247.13 niece M͏ᶜe Rosa

247.15 Josey, [a over A]t the

247.17 mistaken ~~with~~↑in his views↓
respecting

247.19 some ~~readers~~↑regions↓ yet

247.21 the ~~am~~ announcement

247.29 my ~~wife~~↑Laura↓ &

247.35 says he~~r~~ how

248. 7 Father ~~presented~~ ↑made over↑
↑presented↓ to him ↑were only
made over↓ formerly

248.10 inheritance ↑possessed↓ not
248.27 intention. H[is over e]
     ~~had tolerably large~~ ↑interest↓ was
248.39 who ~~fou~~ founded
248.40 venerable name-. wh.
248.42 ¶War ~~wasth~~↑was↓ thus
249. 2 were ~~favourable~~↑very fair↓ and
249.10 party ~~at~~↑in↓ the ~~fall~~↑early part↓ of
249.21 Bayham [in over &] some
249.28 mean ↑or selfish↓ motives
249.30 wished ~~f[illeg]er this to him~~ ↑fervently↓ that
249.44 wisely ↑said↓ says
249.45 have ↑long↓ had
250. 2 here. +I+ ¶I
250. 5 out ↑Drawing pictures with his fork on his napkin↓ &
250. 6 interruptions ↓ I
250. 9 He ~~nevers~~ cares
250.13 is e[x over v]pected every
250.19 occasion ~~of~~↑or↓ the
250.24 my ~~respected chief~~↑liberal & punctual employer↓ Thomas
250.34 and ~~two~~↑2↓ for
250.40 admirable societ[ie over y]s. Potts
250.41 Potts ~~tells~~↑wants↓ me
251.22 party a[s over ss]cended to
[Begin Thackeray's handwriting.]
251.25 latter ↑looking gloomy, & the former↓ pleading very ~~eg~~ eagerly,
251.29 her thoughts↑ were↓— Look
251.36 all than↓ to
252. 9 droll ~~amusing~~↑satirical↓ creature
252.12 remarks—has ↑broken into a laugh once or twice and↓ gone to ~~sheet of paper ↑writing↓~~ writing-book,
252.16 shoulder, ~~gives~~↑makes↓ one
252.18 Barnes ~~Newcome~~ would
252.20 ¶And ~~he~~↑F.B.↓ holds
252.25 will!— [Skip 5 screens to find next text] THE
262. 1 NEWCOMES ¶↑We have said that↓ The
262. 2 lecture ~~found no mercy in the midnight discussion of the performance wh. ensued~~ ↑was discussed↓ in
262.20 had ~~long~~ often
262.23 went by~,↑:↓ with

262.24 Newcomes domestics— ↑proposed↓ to
262.26 it ↑up↓ in
262.27 you think-~~sai~~, Potts,
262.34 elsewhere. ¶~~A deputation ↑half dozen gentlemen↓~~ Like those three ~~old~~ gentlemen ~~who~~ in
263. 2 and ~~resolved~~↑determined↓ that
263. 3 the ~~m~~ electors
263. 6 groaned; ↑&↓ the
263.10 emphatic ~~a~~ 'hear
263.11 explaining ↑dubious phrases↓ to
263.12 manner. ¶~~Any thing wh.~~ ↑Whatever↓ the
263.14 believe. ~~; and any plants↓ «to» punish↑ing↓ or crushing the Baronet sure to be welcome to his Uncle But~~ ↑He had made ~~[illeg.]~~up his ~~[illeg.]~~mind that that criminal ought to be punished and exposed↓ The
263.16 insinuate ~~quite as much~~↑any amount of↓ evil
263.17 be uttered[, over ;] were
263.20 avarice ↑cries the Colonel↓ I believe ['I be' is surmised—under ink blot] upon
263.21 that ↑unfortunate↓ young
263.24 about it.~~-A~~ ¶And
263.27 I ~~kept my cou~~ gave
263.28 'our ~~British~~↑glorious↓ constitution
263.29 least ↑insinuates Mr. Tucker↓ enough
263.34 man ~~with~~ whose
263.48 as ↑second↓ representative
264. 4 with ~~Old~~↑Mr↓ Bunce—I
264.11 would ↑assuredly↓ have
[Begin Thackeray's handwriting. Ms in the Ransom Humanities Center.]
266. 8 had ↑then↓ submitted
266. 8 grace, ~~had~~ as
266.12 survey ~~his~~ Clive's
266.14 wrongs ~~Had not~~ [H over h]is life ↑had↓ been
266.23 with ~~rage~~ ↑anger↓ and
266.25 the ~~good old man~~ ↑Colonel↓ said
266.30 was ~~wrong~~ in error:↑—↓that there
266.31 he. [(The line dont signify)-:][this page was cancelled with a line and restored with this comment] Chap.

[Begin Thackeray's hand. *Ms* in Berg Collection, NYPL.]

268. 1 Pendennis. ~~London.~~ Dearest

268. 8 past now[? over ;] why

268. 9 it? ~~Has~~ ↑Does↓ not

268. 9 day ~~get its~~ ↑bring its own↓ duty

268.10 task ~~of its own and enough~~ and

268.18 I ~~wa~~ try

268.24 I [had over have] met

268.25 give ~~Ethel~~ ↑his Ethel of old days↓ his

268.31 Newcome ~~is~~, my

269. 3 bettered ~~[illeg.]~~ by

269. 3 it. ~~I know I love my uncle still and shall~~ always ¶And

269. 5 afterwards ~~near~~ ↑at↓ good

269. 8 be married?—[a over illeg.]nd laughed

269. 9 I ~~whispered~~ ↑cried out↓ to

269.10 dreadful ~~la~~ sort

269.20 hoped [his over he] ~~was happy~~+.+ ↑wife was well.↓ You

269.21 happy. ↑And yet↓ This

269.24 I ~~will try~~ strive

269.28 nature, ~~He is what God has made him~~ who cannot ↑perhaps↓ comprehend

269.34 were ↑of↓ wh. I ~~never~~ had

269.35 Life [& over of] the [B over b]etter [W over w]orld beyond

269.38 and ↑Heaven's great Mercy↓ defend

269.44 with [blank]; my

269.45 Mr. [blank], who

270.n9 ¶ [inserted at bottom of page] Mr. [blank] Curate

270.17 affectionate [flush right AsUNT EsTHEL.] ¶A

270.19 of ~~Clives~~ ↑his↓ a

270.19 spoken ~~on the Colonels side~~ ↑against us↓ several

270.20 as ~~even~~ Barnes owns. ↑Do you know ~~him~~ ↑↑Mr. W.↓↓?↓ He

270.23 laughing ~~when~~ remembering

270.24 and ~~he~~ ↑my brother↓ became

270.25 of ~~Barnes~~ ↑B. in↓ Newcome: and ~~he~~ ↑my brother↓ says ~~Clive~~ ↑he↓ did

270.28 did it!—~~says~~ ↑cries↓ Mr.

270.33 ¶Yes—and [Y over y]ou mean

270.34 been ~~[illeg.]~~ ~~[illeg.]~~ about

270.36 reader ~~is~~ ↑has been more than once↓ begged

271. 4 appearance ~~amongst~~ in

271. 5 those ↑simple↓ Britons.

271.11 choruses ↑by an expiring fire,↓ as

271.18 how ~~pale~~ ↑till↓ you

271.21 rained ~~down~~ upon

271.22 he sto[o over p]ped down

271.24 not I[. over !]—~~but in~~ cries

271.28 alarmed ↑and inquisitive↓, as

271.30 my happiness[— over ,]and the

271.31 man. ↑I saw↓ Ethel ~~was at that place last night~~ to-

271.34 And are↑—are↓ you

271.36 means ~~for ever~~ ↑always↓ in

271.40 him [G over g]od knows.

271.43 I ~~know~~ did

271.47 Father. ¶I+I+ ~~did my best Clive~~ ↑The boy looked so ineffably wretched, that the fathers↓ heart

272. 6 in ~~it~~ ↑tone↓ to

272.19 over. ¶↑But↓ ~~And~~ there's

272.21 trembling ↑hand↓ ¶Ah

272.26 cause—and, ~~how do you~~ not

272.27 fire? ↑By Jove↓ I

272.29 father ↑Colonel↓ saw

272.29 son's ↑mind↓ ~~heart~~ more

272.29 hitherto. ~~He~~ They

272.37 break ~~our~~ up

272.43 I ~~think it~~ have

[Begin Thackeray's handwriting. *Ms* in the Ransom Humanities Center.]

276.46 the [B over b]ank, and

276.49 taken ~~a~~ share↑s↓ in

277. 1 himself withdraw[? over ,] the

277.18 my [M over m]istress?' ¶And

[Begin Thackeray's handwriting. *Ms* in Huntington Library.]

277.22 Chap. ¶[The over An] expected

277.30 indefatigable ~~ad~~ aide-de-camp,

277.31 last ~~vis~~ canvassing

277.33 family, ~~but~~ ↑—events wh. were kept secret from↓ his biographer, ↑who↓ was,

277.43 the ↑extreme↓ liberals

278. 2 Barker. ~~Whilst the Newcomites~~

[Begin Hodder's handwriting. *Ms* in Berg Collection, NYPL.]

285.30 the ~~Pickle[illeg.]~~ ↑@picklebearing↓ Cocoa

285.46 concerned ↑@for↓ ~~with~~ such
286. 3 Viscount ~~Tagrag~~ ↑@Tagrag↓ dined
286. 3 Earl B~~[illeg]~~↑@are↓acres sent
286. 4 now ~~[illeg.]~~ seemed
286. 8 the ↑@world and the↓ law
286. 9 a ~~great f~~ well
286.13 a ↑@stalled ox↓ ~~stalled ox~~ in
286.17 assuming ~~that a~~ grand
286.19 their ↑@company↓ ~~society~~ no
286.23 little ~~airs,~~ arts,
286.27 prattled ↑@innocently↓ ~~unconsciously~~ before
286.27 of ~~Cornelia~~ ↑@Zerlina↓ and
286.32 first Ba↑↓ham denied
286.34 place ↑@of entertainment↓ and
286.36 quiet parlour[. over ,] [A over a]nd here
286.38 with ~~[illeg.]~~tears in
286.40 was ~~[illeg.]~~ no
286.45 of ~~D~~ dubious
287. 2 Fredk. Ba↑↓ham. The
287. 3 his, ~~[illeg. two words]~~ F.B's
287. 6 Mrs. Clay↑tive↓ and
287.17 benefactors! [B over b]ut, Pendennis,
287.21 drink ~~a pint of~~ this
287.27 If ~~[illeg.]~~ Thomas
287.35 of ~~this~~ our
287.42 pass [y over illeg.]ears of
288.10 entertained ~~the~~ ↑a↓ Calcutta
288.12 his halls.—[D over d]id not
288.23 Esq ↑@Sudder. Dewanee Adawlut↓) or
288.32 grave, [i over I]t was
288.33 meet ~~bills~~ ↑engagements↓ to
289. 2 the [a over A]uditors of
289. 3 Bank ~~the respected~~ the
289.14 had ~~transferred~~ ↑sold↓ the
289.20 the ~~reasons I~~ explanation
289.23 are ~~jel~~ jewels
289.28 Rose's ~~B~~ boudoir
289.28 law ~~left~~ loved
289.37 at [C over c]ourt. I
289.39 to ~~me~~ us
291. 4 but ~~as~~ almost
291.21 and ~~respect~~ ↑regard↓ of
292.n6 friends. ~~Flora~~ ↑Laura↓ drove
292. 4 must ~~[illeg.]~~ be
292.19 left ~~out~~ Clive
292.27 India ~~but a f~~ realised

292.32 ¶What ~~way~~ weighed
292.41 as ~~F.B. described~~ his
293. 1 moved ~~him mo~~ the
293. 8 said ~~Thank God~~ 'I
293.10 under ~~mine~~ mine—and
293.24 studio, ~~rallied~~ ↑boude↓ ↑@boúdé↓ by
293.34 says ~~[illeg.]~~ Mrs.
[Begin Hodder's handwriting. *Ms* in Berg Collection, NYPL.]
294. 8 her hand.~~—I think you h~~ "I
294. 9 gravely. [wavy diagonal cancelled by a slash mark] "Indeed
294.17 his ~~presence~~ ↑further Company↓ was
[Begin Hodder's handwriting. *Ms* in Berg Collection, NYPL.]
295.14 morning—that ~~Her~~ her
295.22 might ~~follow~~ for
295.28 bread.—— ¶Ros[ey over ie] began
296. 7 house ~~wa~~ as
296.19 Mrs. ~~Mackenzie~~ ↑Clive Newcome↓ did
296.37 Clarence [blank] was
296.40 and silent—↑supporting↓ his
297. 5 prosperity.— [several lines scratch out the compositor's name] ¶"Here's
297. 7 filled ↑@into↓ two
297.11 virtute me↑a↓ involvo, probamque patu↓pets↓tiem sine
297.12 hand ~~trembling~~ ↑shaking↓ as
297.17 days.— ¶~~You will see that Rosey~~ ¶Thomas
297.41 in [blank] or
297.46 Creditors. ~~The~~ ¶The
298.10 bowed ~~wit~~ in
298.21 that. ~~the~~ while
298.22 little purly[?] fist
298.26 when ~~spoken~~ ↑the spoke↓ in
298.29 trunk? ¶~~Rosa declared~~ Mrs.
298.33 applied ~~She sto~~ to
299. 7 nurse ~~went~~ ↑tran↓ to
299. 8 eyes ~~called~~ poured
299.20 tea spoons—bab[y's over ies] gold
299.21 Church [S over s]ervice to
299.25 fugitive family—~~and~~ the
299.33 Clives ~~fond her bless~~ father
299.39 life ~~his~~ had
299.40 vain. [p31] [a fragment that seems detached from p31]

↑@Chap.↓

300.23 were ~~regreta~~ rejected

300.23 pretty ~~a~~ little piece ~~representing~~ called

301. 1 studio.— ¶↑I have sd. that↓ We

301. 8 Mr. Sher[rick over iff]—Affairs had

301.14 old ~~cove~~ ↑@cove↓—he might

301.19 me ~~one~~ a

301.23 P.—I ~~went~~ as

301.25 and {illeg} said

301.26 the [B over b]ankruptcy thats

301.27 his honor—~~and its~~ he

301.36 fears ~~respecting~~ ↑in regard to↓ Thomas Newcome ~~had~~ were

301.39 H [blank] Newcome

302. 2 his ↑quondam↓ former

302. 2 Higg—who ~~had~~ formally

302. 9 suspect {illeg.} at

.302.24 lodger ~~said~~ told

302.26 along {was?} ~~but~~ by

302.32 than ~~that~~ ↑the↓ familiar

302.33 where ~~repose~~ young

302.36 whose ~~left~~ lap

302.41 so {illeg.} erect—whose

302.42 and ~~had~~ at

303. 4 Hasn't ~~De~~ he

303.14 consequence ↑Pen.↓ of

303.22 Clive ↑& I↓ liked

303.n6 the ~~favor~~ great

303.29 pleasure ~~that~~ than

303.32 strain ~~by separating~~ asseverating

303.34 of ~~you~~ them

303.35 friends.— ¶"The Coll.

303.36 had though—though—" he

304. 7 for ~~somes~~ sums

304.12 "For ~~you~~ the

304.15 the best—~~God knows~~+—+I hoped

304.19 wish ~~might~~ my

304.26 with you." when

304.33 £17000, [G over g]od help

304.33 with £15000 of

305. 2 lodgings ~~with a [blank] by this time~~ at

305. 7 the condition to which they were *reduced* [Italics removed from "the condition to which they were']

305.12 little {illeg.} Mrs.

305.15 fare. [No fare over Nowhere] was

306.10 had ~~g~~ been

306.11 a ~~pastry~~ ↑pate↓ from

307. 1 sChap. [blank] ¶I

307. 5 shaggy beard[, over .] ~~He~~ ↑whh. he↓ had

307. 9 make ~~the~~ ↑my↓ readers

307.12 history ~~for~~ in their ~~benefit~~ behoof.

307.28 these ~~three~~ elders

307.29 to {illeg.} see

308. 8 of herbs?— when

308.15 intolerable {illeg.} ~~and~~ undeniable

308.22 the ↑outlawed↓ parson

308.26 poor ~~Roj~~ Rosey

308.32 Boulogne jail↑+C+↓ ordered

308.38 had ~~not~~ even

308.41 as ~~he~~ ↑@he cut↓ +get+ his

309. 2 and ~~bounty~~ +and+ kindness

309. 5 a ~~blessing~~ ↑bounty↓ wherever

309. 7 mean ~~alley~~ room,

309. 9 daily outrage!—~~As~~ ¶As

309.13 so ~~as if~~ that

309.20 infernal [B over b]ank have

309.25 may ~~rember«rember»~~ ↑remember↓ at

309.28 *Tenez* ~~pe~~ Pen,

310. 8 imprudently ~~contracted~~ ↑engaged in↓ expenses which ~~were now~~ had

310. 9 present destitution.—*[footnote mark] [line drawn across page] [from "I" to "days" in small print] ¶*I

310.f* woman ~~had~~ ↑was↓ put↑ting↓ away

310.f* days. [end of footnote]

310.10 these ~~I found~~ Clive

310.12 to ~~ask~~ borrow

310.23 year.— ¶After↑And now there arrived↓ a

310.24 and ~~some glasses~~ ↑a bottle↓ of

310.38 inhabited ~~ro~~ a ~~roomy~~ ↑spacious↓ old

310.42 was ↑@the State of Rosey's health &↓ the

311. 6 appearance. [blank, line drawn] ¶No

311.28 the ~~sum~~ vast

311.37 certain,—the ~~result~~ rest

311.42 the ~~best~~ utmost

311.42 her tradesmen̶t̶ hinted

312. 9 I s̶e̶n̶t̶ said

312.12 hereto e̶x̶p̶l̶a̶i̶n̶e̶d̶ ↑divulged↓ with

312.32 Campaigner [illeg] ↑arrive↓ for

313. 5 met s̶a̶u̶n̶t̶e̶r̶i̶n̶g̶ sauntering

313.17 Rosey t̶o̶ ̶b̶e̶ was

313.25 sunny hour—I̶ ̶h̶a̶d̶ ̶p̶r̶e̶p̶a̶r̶e̶d̶
[them?] ↑I prepaired thither↓
& found the̶m̶ ̶w̶o̶r̶n̶ ̶a̶n̶d̶ old

[Begin Thackeray's handwriting. *Ms* in
Berg Collection, NYPL.]

318.30 stop ↑& forget ourselves↓
sometimes,

318.35 that ↑, though Mr. Pendennis
was *parcus suorum cultor et
infrequens*↓, Mrs.

318.39 on them[; over —] ↑&↓ both

318.39 her r̶e̶g̶a̶r̶d̶ ↑kindness↓ with

318.41 regard. [illeg.] What

318.44 ministering ↑in↓ her

318.45 that ↑priceless↓ crown o̶n̶ ̶t̶h̶e̶
hymeneal;

318.46 a [T over t]enth Edition?—have

[Begin Thackeray's handwriting. *Ms* in
Berg Collection, NYPL.]

319.17 was ↑left to think↓ i̶n̶ ̶d̶o̶u̶b̶t̶ (if

319.22 was ↑half↓ inclined
believe [Three levels: inclined to
believe; inclined half to believe;
half inclined to believe.] with

319.27 pictures ↑this↓ n̶e̶x̶t̶ year,

319.28 thought ↑far↓ more

319.30 them n̶o̶w̶ in

319.33 saluted [his over him] ↑talent &
success↓ with

319.35 at h̶i̶s̶ ̶f̶r̶i̶e̶n̶d̶s̶' ↑the↓ success↑s of
his friends.↓ ¶↑When ↓W̶h̶e̶n̶ Mr.

319.40 he +did+ ↑seemed
still to hesitate↓
n̶o̶t̶ ̶s̶e̶e̶m̶ ̶p̶a̶r̶t̶i̶c̶u̶l̶a̶r̶l̶y̶ ̶a̶n̶x̶i̶o̶u̶s̶
about

319.43 about thei̶r̶ society

[Begin Thackeray's handwriting. *Ms* in
Charterhouse School.]

341. 1 PLEASANT D̶I̶N̶N̶E̶R̶ ERRAND.

341. 9 own ↑solitary↓ residence

341.12 aspect u̶p̶o̶n̶ ̶t̶h̶a̶t̶ ̶C̶h̶r̶i̶s̶t̶m̶a̶s̶
a̶f̶t̶e̶r̶n̶o̶o̶n̶,̶ ↑on that festive day↓
thought

341.18 found h̶i̶m̶↑my friend↓ at

341.21 a ↑pair of↓ pictures

341.22 painter said[—r over , I]ubbing
on

341.25 for a̶b̶o̶u̶t̶ ̶t̶h̶r̶e̶e̶ ̶h̶u̶n̶d̶r̶e̶d̶
a̶ ̶y̶e̶a̶r̶+,+ ↑some half dozen
pounds a week.↓ I

341.30 a ↑solemn↓ fellow

341.35 says—Look! There'̶s̶↓ is↓ his

341.35 now!—and there'̶s̶↓ is↓ his

342. 2 most studios—I̶ ̶t̶h̶o̶u̶g̶h̶t̶ ̶t̶h̶i̶s̶
écorché n̶o̶t̶ ̶u̶n̶l̶i̶k̶e̶ ̶m̶y̶ ̶p̶o̶o̶r̶ ̶f̶r̶i̶e̶n̶d̶
¶I

342. 3 saw ↑a certain Fashionable
Doctor↓ Doctor

342. 4 chariot; ↑of↓ that [L over l]adies'
[D over d]elight who

342. 8 enter! I̶ ̶«̶h̶a̶d̶»̶ ̶↑̶h̶a̶v̶e̶↓̶
h̶e̶a̶r̶d̶ ̶m̶y̶ ̶k̶i̶n̶d̶ ̶r̶o̶u̶g̶h̶
h̶e̶a̶r̶t̶y̶ ̶f̶r̶i̶e̶n̶d̶ ̶D̶r̶.̶
G̶o̶o̶d̶e̶n̶o̶u̶g̶h̶ ̶t̶a̶l̶k̶ ̶a̶b̶o̶u̶t̶
Q̶u̶a̶c̶k̶e̶n̶b̶o̶s̶s̶ ̶a̶n̶d̶ ̶l̶a̶u̶g̶h̶ ̶a̶t̶
h̶i̶s̶ ̶a̶r̶t̶s̶,̶ ̶↑̶&̶↓̶ ̶c̶l̶e̶v̶e̶r̶n̶e̶s̶s̶.̶
A̶n̶d̶ ̶I̶ ̶m̶a̶y̶ ̶h̶e̶r̶e̶
p̶a̶r̶e̶n̶t̶h̶e̶t̶i̶c̶a̶l̶l̶y̶ ̶s̶a̶y̶ ̶t̶h̶a̶t̶
w̶h̶e̶n̶ ̶G̶o̶o̶d̶e̶n̶o̶u̶g̶h̶ ̶c̶h̶a̶r̶g̶e̶d̶ ̶t̶h̶e̶
o̶t̶h̶e̶r̶ ̶w̶i̶t̶h̶ ̶t̶a̶k̶i̶n̶g̶ ̶t̶o̶o̶
s̶e̶v̶e̶r̶e̶ ̶f̶e̶e̶s̶ ̶f̶r̶o̶m̶ ̶C̶l̶i̶v̶e̶;̶
t̶h̶e̶ ̶l̶a̶d̶y̶'̶s̶ ̶D̶o̶c̶t̶o̶r̶ ̶v̶o̶w̶e̶d̶
h̶e̶ ̶o̶n̶l̶y̶ ̶t̶o̶o̶k̶ ̶a̶ ̶f̶e̶e̶
↑̶a̶t̶↓̶ ̶e̶v̶e̶r̶y̶ ̶o̶t̶h̶e̶r̶ ̶d̶a̶y̶
↑̶v̶i̶s̶i̶t̶↓̶,̶ ̶f̶r̶o̶m̶ ̶M̶r̶s̶.̶ ̶M̶a̶c̶k̶e̶n̶z̶i̶e̶
w̶h̶o̶«̶m̶ ̶h̶e̶ ̶s̶u̶p̶p̶o̶s̶e̶d̶ ̶t̶o̶ ̶b̶e̶
a̶ ̶G̶e̶n̶e̶r̶a̶l̶ ̶O̶f̶f̶i̶c̶e̶r̶s̶ ̶w̶i̶f̶e̶»̶
↑̶r̶e̶p̶r̶e̶s̶e̶n̶t̶e̶d̶ ̶h̶e̶r̶s̶e̶l̶f̶ ̶t̶o̶ ̶h̶i̶m̶
a̶s̶ ̶a̶ ̶c̶o̶m̶m̶a̶n̶d̶i̶n̶g̶-̶o̶f̶f̶i̶c̶e̶r̶'̶s̶
l̶a̶d̶y̶↓̶ ̶o̶f̶ ̶l̶a̶r̶g̶e̶ ̶m̶e̶a̶n̶s̶,̶
d̶e̶e̶p̶l̶y̶ ̶d̶i̶s̶g̶u̶s̶t̶e̶d̶ ̶a̶t̶ ̶h̶e̶r̶
d̶a̶u̶g̶h̶t̶e̶r̶'̶s̶ ̶*̶m̶é̶s̶a̶l̶l̶i̶a̶n̶c̶e̶*̶ ̶w̶i̶t̶h̶
a̶ ̶p̶a̶i̶n̶t̶e̶r̶.̶ ̶¶̶T̶h̶a̶t̶ ̶C̶a̶m̶p̶a̶i̶g̶n̶e̶r̶ ↑I
suppose the Campaigner made
a special toilette to receive her
fashionable friend, for that lady↓,
attired

342.10 with thatt̶e̶↓ precious

342.16 me the↑a good↓ report

342.19 that s̶t̶ plaister

342.23 town, i̶s̶ ̶a̶ ̶c̶l̶e̶r̶k̶ ̶t̶h̶e̶r̶e̶—̶t̶h̶a̶t̶ that

342.30 the ↑charming↓ young

342.31 and the↓ was

342.33 cut i̶n̶↑into the conversation↓
with

342.38 Peerage, a̶s̶ now

342.46 seen h̶e̶r̶ at

342.46 with s̶i̶d̶e̶ [s over f]ix side

343. 1 and ↑the↓ silver

343. 6 said Clive—W̶e̶↑I↓ will

343.10 and ↑when she retreated↓ Clive

343.13 it' o̶l̶d̶ ̶b̶o̶y̶ I

343.13 we ~~walked away~~↑set forth↓ to
343.14 came ~~tr~~ walking
343.14 slowly, ~~and on~~↑along↓ the
343.17 not ~~enfeebled~~↑weakened↓ him
343.18 last ~~twenty~~↑score of↓ months.
343.20 Newcome's ↑gr↓ voice ↑once so grave↓ went
343.21 almost ~~as~~ childish
343.24 and ~~honest~~↑his↓ brave
343.25 Newcome! [B over b]e an
343.27 Christmas ~~dinner~~↑meal↓ went
343.29 dinner ↑and had cooked ↑↑a↓↓ aportion of it under their keen supervision↓ cowered
343.32 different [from over to] that
343.33 Good ~~brave~~↑faithful↓ F.
343.34 Mackenzie ~~was~~ owned
343.37 Boy ↑in the best little words wh. he could muster↓ asked
343.38 black cloak?—↑Clive +d+ nudged my foot under the table:↓ The
343.41 languid: ↑the light of her eyes had gone out: all↓ ~~All~~ her
343.n5 gone ↑had faded↓. She
343.43 her eagerly[; over —] and
343.45 situation. ¶~~We three sate~~↑When the cloth↓ was
344. 2 received,' ↑so↓ very
344. 6 Campaigner ↑cried 'Nonsense, let him go to bed!' and↓ flounced
344.12 but some~~[illeg.]~~ of
344.21 to ~~Church~~↑our Chapel↓ to
344.26 to ~~go away~~↑depart↓ saying
344.32 his ↑wealthy↓ *brothers,*
344.33 she ~~narrated~~↑computed↓ to
344.35 feeble remark.~~or two~~+.+ She
344.43 augur ~~ill~~ but
344.43 came. ↑The expression of↓ Ethel's face ~~looked~~↑was↓ scarcely
344.45 who ~~was~~↑yet lingered at his own threshold↓ having
345. 2 City. ¶~~She~~↑Miss Newcome↓ was
345. 4 into h[er over is] face,
345. 5 she said~~curtly~~[— over .]not as
345. 9 you ↑for a noble creature↓ my
345.11 doing ~~an act of justice~~↑what is right↓? Ought
345.11 eldest ↑of our family↓ after
345.12 father ↑him↓ left ~~me himself~~↑all his younger children↓ the

345.17 and ~~I should like~~ I
345.18 kind ~~and~~ opinion
345.23 you see—and—↑Cli↓and my
345.25 robe ↑or—↓or anything
345.27 the ~~generous~~↑noble↓ young
345.28 I said—Didn't I ↑not↓ say
345.29 Inn? ¶~~We called~~[A over a] cab
345.30 in ↑the↓ presence
345.33 knew ↑the late↓ Mrs.
345.37 my ↑poor↓ wife,
346. 7 brother's. But↑, candidly,↓ were
346. 7 I ~~an~~ a
346.15 at ↑showing↓ your
346.16 this ~~awful~~ document.
346.17 wished ~~to↑~~that I should↓ prepare
346.21 you see?—and↑, be sure,↓ Sir
346.28 he ↑you think↓ is
346.30 called ~~himsel~~ selfish!—You
346.31 happened ↑before↓ my
346.37 of ↑what↓ my poor father's ~~fortu~~ left
346.38 to [m over illeg.]y Cousin
346.42 my cousin—~~cried~~-Miss Newcome
346.44 dreadful poverty— ~~My Cousin~~↑Do you know↓ where
347. 1 she speaks[; over —] the
347. 7 Newcome. ¶~~Mr. Pendennis~~↑Mr. Luce rose up from his ↑↑old chair—↓↓ worn-out old horsehair chair—where he had sate ~~and~~ for half a century and listened to many a speaker very different from this one. 'Mr. Pendennis, he said,↓ 'I
347.11 you ~~you~~ the
347.14 sincerely ~~I respect~~ I—I
347.15 my dear~~:~~? & When
347.19 and ~~looked as if she was~~ ↑clasped her hands together↓ for
347.20 praying. ¶↑Mr. Luce laughed at her impetuosity; but said that if she was bent upon having the money it was at her ~~serv~~ instant service; and↓ [b over B]efore we
347.26 Newcome ~~were disposed to~~ desirous
347.27 Messrs. ~~Hobson Brothers~~ ↑Hob——↓ at
347.29 Servant &ca—[blank space]And, the
347.31 pocket, ↑I quitted↓ the
[Begin Anne's handwriting.]

348.n7 @ ↑In Wh. the reader is invited
to two dinners. Chap.↓ [*Ms*
pp. 22-40 are in blue ink; most
changes seem to be Thackeray's
and are in brown ink.] We

348. 1 we pass@↑ed↓ by

348.10 the [P over p]oor [B over
b]rothers were

348.11 from dinner↑.↓ [A over a] couple

348.13 their refectory↑,↓ separta↓ted
over the Court↑,↓ betaking

348.15 to behold, her

348.15 features. [B over b]ut he

348.16 his chambers, of

348.18 & @↑thus↓ our

348.20 ¶Ethel walked slowly@↑went
round↓ round the apartement↑,↓
&

348.22 the mant[el over le] piece↑:↓ the

348.25 black [P over p]ensioner↑'↓s
cloak

348.26 homely garment↑,↓ &

348.26 on admiring@ her,
I should think @↑I should
think↓, her

348.28 niece; ↑'↓He has

348.29 handsome too,↑"↓ said

348.30 while, ↑↑O. Miss↓!,'↓ cried

348.31 & humbler↑,↓ evidently

348.32 her ↑'↓I didnt

349. 1 wrote ↑'↓Ethel↑'↓ on

349. 3 this time↑;↓ feeble

349. 3 the chamber↑-↓ windows

349. 4 the courts[; over ,]↑—↓feeble
lights

349. 4 a dim↑,↓ grey↑,↓ melancholy↑,↓
old

349. 6 the darkness,↑;↓ many

349. 9 to Clive↑'↓s↑'↓ I

349.11 said yes+;+[. D over d]rive↑,↓
cabman

349.11 Howland Street,↑!↓ The

349.12 extraordinarily long [: over .] I

349.17 knees. ↑¶↓I hardly

349.20 is— ¶↑'↓You have

349.21 Hospital Sir↑!↓, You

349.22 it to go there [Italics added]

349.23 own language↑,↓ Clive↑,↓ unless

349.24 *not fit* [Italics added]

349.24 to heart.↓+,+ Clive

349.26 hour previous↑ly,↓ let

349.26 Grey-Friars. ¶↑'↓Say at

349.27 once Clive↑!'↓ the

349.28 helpless-child, ↑'↓that Colonel

349.29 a Hospital+,+↑!↓ He

349.30 own money↑:—↓ He

349.30 my money↑:↓ He

349.32 my love↑!—↓ has

349.33 say *mean & unworthy & degraded*
conduct. [Italics added]

349.34 blessed child[! over ,] to

349.35 a iwork-house↑!↓ [Italics added]

349.35 Rosa ↑on the sopha↓ below

349.36 & whimper↑s↓ amongst

349.37 his head[; over ,] strinking his

349.38 this friend of

349.38 good Father↑.↓+,+ The

349.39 body @↑was↓ throbbing

349.40 trembling under↑with↓ the

349.40 writhed. ↑'↓Colonel
Newcome↑'↓s friends Ma'am↑,'↓
I said↑, '↓think very

349.42 one else↑,↓ of

349.44 his misfortune↑.↓ Do

349.46 de Montcontours wd. applatu↓d
his

350. 1 he does↑,↓ if

350. 1 it admirable↑?↓ @as he does.I
can

350. 3 influence. @['And over &] at this
minute↑,↓ I added, ↑'↓I have

350. 4 the Colonel↑'s↓ relatives

350. 5 is boundless↑,↓ who

350. 6 Clive's wife↑.↓ ¶Who is that↑?↓
says

350. 9 is it↑,↓ [P over p]en↑!↓ says

350. 9 voice ↑'↓Ethel,↑'↓ &

350.10 crying ↑'↓Ethel↑!↓ Ethel↑!'↓ he

350.11 her soph↑f↓a, clutching

350.12 cheeks burn@[ed over ing] more

350.14 help us+,+↑!↓ what

350.15 for @us.↑it↓! @↑¶↓Miss
Newcome↑,↓ is it↑?↓ @[My over
my] darling

350.16 your shawl↑!↓ cried the [C over
c]ampaigner a

350.17 face. @↑¶↓It is Ethel+,+↑.↓
Ethel

350.20 little child@↑+.+↓ ↑—a very
good child.'↓ The

350.21 old heart↑↑—↓ there

350.22 no more@,↑.↓ @[T over
t]he pain @↑yonder woman
inflicted,↓ only

350.23 stupified him↑.↓ ¶As

350.24 child tottered@↑trotted↓ fo↔↑r↓ward towards

350.26 as @[d over D]eath. Little Boy↑,↓ looking

350.26 stately lady↑,↓ still

350.27 remained sitting↑,↓ his

350.27 the gro↔↑un↓d. His

350.29 again. ¶↑'↓Here is

350.31 shoulder, ↑'↓It is

350.31 Ethel, Uncle[! over ,] the

350.31 hand an@↑d↓ keeling

350.35 of love↑,↓ kindness↑,↓ tenderness,

350.39 the group@e with a ga↔↑tha↓stly smile.

350.40 behind her the daughters sofa

350.42 behind her@[; over ,] lifted

350.42 her face↑;↓ &

350.44 of paint↑!↓ The

351. 1 eyes. ↑'↓Mamma crying.

351. 2 Mammas ring↑!'↓ he

351. 2 of gold↑.↓ With

351. 3 seen @↑her↓ @exhibited she

351. 4 wasted arms+,+↑.↓ Great Heaven↑!↓ what

351. 9 at a↑this sudden↓ scene.

351.10 the witnesses↑;↓ &

351.11 were incoherent@[; over ,] but @when he had ↑one there women have↓ more

351.13 to describe↑,↓ going

351.14 the quarrels@↑differences between↓ her

351.15 & herself↑;↓ of

351.16 her wish↑,↓ her

351.21 little Boy@↑bboy↓? Would

351.22 kiss her[? H over , h]e did

351.23 face ware wore

351.25 I not↑?↓ I

351.28 old building↑s↓ of

351.30 my carriage↑?↓ No

351.31 room bec↑k↓oning hime after @↑her↓ ¶↑'↓You will

351.32 wont you↑?'↓ she said, ↑'↓& come

351.33 to bed↑?↓ I went back↑,↓ anxious

351.34 my dears old

351.36 to insult↑outrage↓ Clive

351.38 whom *She* would [Italics added]

351.38 no never@↑!↓+,+ [A over a]n insolent

351.39 impertinent thing[! over ,] Does

351.39 a housemaid↑?↓ Mrs.

351.40 inquired, ↑'↓Am dust

351.43 remembered, poor↑that↓ Ethel

351.44 to her@↑Mrs. Mackenzie↓ in

351.44 visit. @↑¶↓I affected

352. 3 for @D↑d↓rawings Mrs.

352. 5 Clive Of c ¶*Of course* [Italics added]

352. 6 to *dinner*@[! *over ,]* says [Italics added]

352. 7 out [a over A]s we

352. 8 by [H over h]eavens he couldnt not.

352. 9 Now Sir↑,↓ down

352.10 your life+,+↑!↓ My

352.11 old Clive↑!↓ you

352.13 again... ↑¶↓My dear

352.14 at 10↑ten↓, Sir,

352.15 gates close↑!↓ he

352.18 things ready↑—↓all things ready.'@↑—& again the old man laughed as he spoke↓ ¶His

352.20 of ↑sad↓ meaning,

352.21 mean Arthur? Clive

352.23 ¶Then taking@↑feeling in my pocket for↓ Mr.

352.23 letter fm. my pocket I

352.24 news. @¶I told

352.30 his face face countenance for somehow↑,↓ all

352.31 this @D↑d↓ocument I

352.31 kind face@↑. '↓[I over i]t↑—↓it is Ethels doing↑—↓said Clive,

352.32 hurried voice@[. T over , t]here was

352.32 such letter[! over ,] ¶Upon my honour@↑, I answered,↓ there was↑.↓ [W over w]e came

352.35 showed @↑it↓ to

352.36 Newcome, who@↑—who,↓ could

352.36 disown it[. W over , w]e took

352.39 paid it↑,↓ &

352.40 before ↑the BBC time↓@[. T over t]hat confounded

352.41 up this↑,↓ like

352.43 of India↑?↓ cries

352.44 ¶Ormes history↑!↓ of

352.45 boy ↑says the old man↓, &

352.46 forthwith @↑'The two battalions advanced against each other cannonading, until the French,

coming to a hollow way,
imagined that the English would
not venture to pass it. But Major
Lawrence ordered the Seapoys &
Artillery—the seapoys & Artillery
to halt & defend the Convoy
against the Morattoes—Morattoes
Orme calls 'em. Ho! Ho! I
could repeat ~~the~~ whole pages
Sir!dn

353. 2 Sir! ↑¶'↓[I over i]t is
353. 3 was written↑!↓ calls
353. 4 Mr. Mill↑'↓s was
353. 4 learned ~~man~~@↑history↓, he
353. 5 it, ~~Ai~~@↑Eh!↓ there ~~was~~@↑is↓
         plenty
353. 5 now, @↑said the good Colonel,↓
         I
353. 6 at Grey-Friars,↑—↓after Chapel
353. 6 know ↑do↓ You
353. 8 Cistercean lane↑—↓the Red Cow
         Sir↑—↓and buy
353. 9 Rum there[? over ,] I
353. 9 boy Clivy[. Y over , y]ou wernt
353. 9 thank Heaven[— over .]A terrible
353.11 on me↑.↓ It
353.12 pain, but@;↑ . . . .↓ here
353.15 me, ↑'↓[H over h]e was
353.15 at Boulogne↑,↓ Arthur↑.↓
         he whispered↑,↓
         [A over a]fter↑—'after-~~After~~↓ a
353.16 with that↑—↓that woman
         yonder↑,↓ ~~His~~@↑this↓ head wd.
         go↑:↓ he
353.17 replied ~~an unkind word~~ to her
         taunts↑:↓+,+ he
353.18 unkind word+.+↑—↓O@↑!↓
         ~~Heaven~~↑I can↓ pay
353.18 pay her[! over .] But
353.20 man ~~Sir,~~@↑suffer?↓ ¶He
353.21 still sat↑e,↓ lost
353.22 Friars Father↑!↓ he cried
         @out.↑—↓except to
         ~~pack your things & to~~
         «come back» ↑return↓, and
         ~~live with me & Boy,~~
         ~~and he told Colonel~~
         ~~Newcome rapidly the story~~
         ~~of the Legacy. The old man~~
         ↑¶Not go back Clivey? must go
         back boy, to say *Adsum* when
         my name is called—Newcome!
         Adsum! Hey! that is what we
         used to say—we used to say!
         ↑↑¶↓↓You need not go back

except to pack your things, &
return & live with me & Boy
Clive continued, & he told
Colonel Newcome rapidly the
story of the legacy. The old
man↓ seemed

353.29 news ~~seemed~~ scarcely ~~to~~ elate↑d↓
         him,
353.30 replied @↑'↓[Q over q]uite right,
         quite right+,+↑;'↓ and
353.31 & interest[; over ,] in
353.32 to her+.+@↑—he knew it well
         enough, the good old man. '↓Of
         course
353.33 we can↑!↓ [Begin brown ink] But
353.33 not ~~seem~~@↑appear↓ to
353.37 Clive, ↑'↓If you
353.38 you ↑a↓going to
353.38 dinner waiting↑?↓ ¶Come
353.40 to dinner↑!↓ cries Clive↑,↓
         ~~looking particularly fierce~~ and
         Pen you↑!↓@↓ will↓ come
353.41 wont you↑?↓ he
353.41 added, @[I over i]t may
353.42 company. ↑'↓Come along↑'↓ he
         whispered hurri↑e↓dly I
353.43 be there↑.↓ @[I over i]t will keep
         ~~off~~++her++ ~~insolence~~@↓ tongue
         quiet.' ↓~~And~~@↑As↓ we
353.43 dining room[, over .] I
353.44 my arm↑;↓ and
353.44 good @~~old~~ man
353.46 of business↑,↓ and @~~about her~~
         fancying,
353.47 her money↑,↓+,+ &@↑And↓ I
353.47 felt ~~as~~ wish
353.48 he will↑'↓ says
353.48 Colonel, ~~on whom~~ ↑'↓& then
354. 1 Arthur; for↑,↓ between
         ourselves↑,↓ some
354. 2 are angry↑,↓ Sir.↑'↓ And
354. 3 his @↑gentle↓~~courtly~~ old
354. 6 the man↑[el over le]piece in
354. 7 with her↑,↓ before
354. 7 to Clive↑'↓s Studio,
354. 8 in form[, over .] not ~~intendin~~
         supposing
354. 9 enjoy ~~their~~↑their @her↓
         hospitality
354. 9 seem [to over f] please her.
         ↑'↓Does Mr.
354.10 favour ~~h~~us↓ with
354.10 dinner again↑,↓ Clive↑+,+?↓ she

354.13 been *so kind* [Italics added]

354.16 ¶Cold beef↑!↓ what

354.16 it matter↑?↓ says

354.17 joint wh.↑,↓ hot↑,↓ had

354.18 *does* matter↑,↓ Sir↑!↓+,+ I

354.20 finger twi~~ddling~~@↑nkling↓ all

354.22 secret charit[ies over y]↑,↓ or keept company

354.25 a morsel~~l~~ of it↑:—↓not she.

354.26 the Beef↑!↓ says

354.27 cutting it↑!↓ cries the Campaigner↑,↓ @↑again↓ bringing

354.28 Mr. Pendennis↑!↓ You

354.29 of it↑!↓ As

354.30 already, ~~fully~~↑ruin↓ enough

354.31 the beef↑!↓ cries out Clive↑.↓ [¶ over No]No no!

354.32 dinner, [B over b]enedicti [B over b]enedicamus, Clivy

354.33 my boy↑!↓ says

354.34 on Sir↑!↓ let

354.34 your oaths[! over ,] let

354.35 her sofa,↑—↓wh. her

354.36 Mother *prepares* for [Italics added]

354.36 cooked it↑—↓& gave

354.37 with *these hands,*↑—↓let *her* hear [Italics added]

354.38 Clive Newcome↑!↓ They

354.40 them, [Begin blue ink] until

354.41 vanished ↑¶↓No farther

354.42 took place; until

354.42 second course↑;↓ wh.

354.43 may suppose↑,↓ of the Plumb-pudding↑,↓ now

354.44 the ~~remainent~~@↑remanent↓ mince

354.45 meal. Maria↑,↓ thought

354.45 particularly guilty↑,↓ as

355. 1 the table↑:↓ she

355. 3 her, ↑'↓Who has

355. 3 that pudding[? over ,] I

355. 4 at [two over 2] o'clock

355. 5 theres @~~just~~ pounds

355. 6 since then↑!↓ There

355. 7 table yesterday,↑—↓wheres the

355. 8 the other@e two Maria↑?↓+,+ You

355. 8 wicked wretch+,+↑—↓& I'll

355.12 phrase i@[s over t], gave

355.13 she go↑?↓ @[P over p]ay her

355.14 hearth @↑twas Marias prayer↓. It

355.15 Clive *Your* ↑are↓ good [Italics added] enough↑,↓ &

355.16 that Doctor[; over ,] & she *dont pay* [Italics added] him+.+ ↑—↓& I

355.18 I did↑—↓ and

355.18 to him,↑—↓& I

355.19 her. Go[! over ,] wont

355.19 despises ~~that woman Mr. Clive~~ ↑yr.↓ puddens & pies↑↑!↓↓↓ &

355.21 the Campaigner↑'↓s nose.

355.22 this instant↑!↓ says

355.24 in it↑,↓ wrapped

355.25 Newcome ~~and again Maria~~@↑the ~~maid~~ refractory waiting woman cried out, and again she↓ laughed

355.27 briskly ~~popped the purse back into her pocket again~~ ↑shut her porte-monnaie↓, &

355.28 virtue. ↑'↑Go@↓! she exclaimed, 'Go↓ and

355.29 this instant[! over ,] you

355.30 leave ~~it~~@↑it↓ ¶Whilst

355.31 guilty Maria↑,↓ the

355.32 her pocket[; over ,]↑—↓a ↑handsome↓~~little~~ fillagree [g over j]imcrack of

355.33 poor Rosa↑'↓s, one

355.33 former splendours+,+~~But~~@↑: but,↓ agitated

355.35 ground @↑¶↓Maria dashed at ~~it~~@↑the purse↓ in

355.39 to go↑?↓ am I↑?↓ I'm

355.40 hands, *'I so* [Italic added]

355.41 thief indeed↑!↓ I

355.42 & *I* give [Italic added]

355.43 this woman[? over ,] Clive[! over ,] Mr. Pendennis↑!↓ I

355.44 horrible vulgarity↑!↓ cries

356. 1 given *thousands,* I [Italics added]

356. 1 myself *everything,* I [Italics added]

356. 2 my *all* in [Italics added]

356. 2 this house↑;↓ &

356. 3 Newcome *knows* [w over if]hether I [Italics added]

356. 3 & *who* has [Italics added]

356. 4 and *who* has [Italics added]

356. 5 . ¶@↑'Here!↓ You↑!↓ Maria↑!↓ go

356. 7 Mrs. MacKenzie↑!↓ I

356.10 infernal cruelty[; over ,] or listen
or

356.10 Father insulted↑;↓ or

356.12 day, wh↑since↓ you

356.13 Look here+,+↑:—↓ at

356.14 You Fiend↑!↓ see

356.15 brought him↑!↓ Dearest Father[!
over ,] She is going↑,↓ do you
hear[? over ,] She

356.16 to me↑,↓ won't you? ↑'↓Great
God woman, @↑he gasped out,↓
Do

356.21 him. ¶↑"↓I am

356.22 a *fiend* am [Italics added] I[?
over ,] @↑cries the lady↓ You

356.24 of ↑almost↓ every farthing↑ we
had↓, &

356.25 such baseness[? over ,] I have

356.26 a *slave*+,+↑:↓ I [Italics added]

356.27 after mo↑n↓th when *he*@↑r↓
@↑husband↓ has [Italics added]

356.28 poor innocent↑,↓ &

356.29 of doors↑!↓ ¶A

356.30 these battles↑;—↓that↑,↓
whilst@↑as↓ this

356.32 golden head↑. '↓It is

356.33 me Madam↑,'↓ I said↑,↓ turning

356.33 MacKenzie, ↑'↓that you

356.36 every shilling+,+↑—↓every
shilling

356.41 sorry @↑groaned out ↑↑poor↓↓
Clive, wiping the sweat off his
brow.↓ 'I

356.42 harsh word↑'↓ 'I

356.42 with you+,+↑.↓ [T over
t]omorrow I

356.43 you claim[; over ,] &

356.45 & walk↑?↓ Good

357. 1 be [end of blue ink] here,
[Begin Thackeray's handwriting.]

357.11 saw the his

357.13 bless ↑all↓ those

358. 1 wh. poor Clive

358.10 confess th[e over i]s impotence
↑of his wrath↓ before

358.34 from that of the preceding day
↑yesterday's↓ came

359. 2 elderly woman↑person↓ with

359. 6 she had↑nt↓ not↓ the

359.19 best of have

359.25 Clive's absence[; over :] worked

360. 6 house may↑will↓ be

360.11 so; [And, over &] carrying

360.22 recommended and excellent

360.23 the Apothecary↑medical man↓ at
[Begin Anne's handwriting. [begin blue
ink; T's corrections in blue also]
¶'Her daughter

360.32 fellow was fain to return to
@↑must put up a bed in↓ his

360.34 illness. ↑I saw↓ Thomas
Newcome was not to↑could not↓
sleep

360.35 both so longed for↑so desired↓
was

360.36 say @↑for↓ how long↑?↓ ¶↑'↓The
Colonel

360.37 to us↑'↓ I thought, ↑↓our old

360.39 myself +in+ @↑by↓ thinking that
[t over 2]wo friends

360.41 there The poor Brother
was in bed, ↑¶↓Bayham opened

360.42 I knocked↑;↓ and

360.43 his lip↑,↓ &

360.44 Court. ↑'↓Clive is with
him↑,+'+↓ he said ↑+'+↓& Miss

360.45 very ill↑—↓He does

360.46 of them,↑.↓ they

361. 3 sleepless night↑,↓ for

361. 4 chair, ↑&↓ his bed
unmade↑disturbed↓ He

361. 5 a fire+↑,↓+↑:↓ but

361. 7 to @↑drink↓ tea

361. 8 not made↑?↓ He

361. 8 pressed him↑—↓the bell

361. 9 morning Chapel[, over .]
He@↑he↓ got

361.11 & tried to↑would↓ go

361.11 he ↑wd.↓ wd. have

361.12 the Dr.@↑Physician↓ of

361.17 Dr. Rain@↑e who was ↑↑School-
↓↓Master here ever so many
years ago.'↓ So

361.18 days @↑were↑seemed to be↓
dawning

361.19 that sweet reprieve

361.20 for him↑,↓ and
the loyal gentleman↑Thomas
Newcome↓ was

361.25 to awaken↑call↓ Clive

361.27 son. ↑'↓You must
[Begin Thackeray's handwriting.]

361.30 him back to

361.38 Mackenzie declined could

362. 4 sympathy, censure↑,↓? Yet

362. 9 her. ~~There were~~[N over n]ot many
362.17 or ~~me~~ any
362.25 and ~~would sit~~↑sate↓ for
362.29 way ~~into~~↑towards↓ the
362.30 that lov[ing over e] ↑heart↓ from
362.30 said, ~~he~~ is
362.35 his ~~cha~~ bed
362.37 considered unadevisable to
362.37 had ~~attand~~ attained
362.38 The ~~physician~~↑medical men↓ of
363.23 came ↑thence↓ to ~~see~~ his
363.29 consciousness, ↑[illeg.]↓ returned
363.35 lady: ~~he rambled~~↑anon he wandered↓ in
364. 4 of Barnes, to
364. 5 once ~~came~~↑offered↓ ++to++ touch
364. 8 with ~~him~~↑the Colonel,↓ and
364.12 near ~~the~~ his
364.15 at ↑hearing of↓ Clive's
364.16 if ~~ten hu~~ thousands
364.19 chair ~~for his bed~~↑for his bed↓ in
364.20 spirits; ↑but passed a disturbed night↓ and
364.20 morning ~~did~~+not+~~return~~↑was too weak to↓ rise.
364.21 bed, ~~as w~~ and
364.21 friends ~~came to~~↑visited↓ him
364.23 and ~~tried~~ then
364.25 a ↑cricket-↓match with
364.25 the ~~next~~ [G over g]reen, and
364.28 excited—Clive ~~sent away~~ ↑dismissed↓ his ↑fathers↓ little
364.35 seizing ~~Eth~~ a
364.37 hand ~~and he did not know her~~+.+ ↑wh. he took.↓ Ethel
364.39 and Bayham↑.↓~~and myself.~~ ¶At↑By~~ the look in the woman's ~~face~~countenance,↓ Madame
364.40 up. ¶'He is
364.41 whispered. ~~The Chapel bell began to ring at that time.~~ The French
364.43 ¶Some ~~minutes~~↑time↓ afterwards
364.44 dear lady—↑she said↓ going
365. 5 The ↑patients↓ voice
365. 6 not ↑slee↓ asleep.
365. 8 usual ↑evening↓ hour
365. 8 and ~~his~~ ↑Thomas Newcome's↓ hands

365. 9 time. ~~to~~[A over I]nd just
365.11 and ↑quickly↓ said ~~Ads~~ ↑¶↓Adsum! and
365.12 used ~~to use~~ at
365.16 I ~~los~~ strayed
365.16 a ~~prest~~↑little↓ wood; ~~and~~ and,
365.18 somehow, ~~of the~~ wh.
365.19 with ↑rather↓ a
365.24 wh. ↑(———)↓ I
365.26 figures ↑retreating &↓ only
365.26 glimmering? [Blank space here] Before
365.29 without ~~solving~~ answering
365.30 these ↑minor↓ questions
Note: Entries from 365.34 to 367.2 refer to a draft page, referred to in the footnotes as *Ms1* and described in the textual essay (p. 416).
365.34 amour, ~~con~~ gave
365.35 story? [C over I]live~~-he~~↑, Pendennis↓ writes
365.n4 Farintosh's ↑page ( )↓ mother,
365.n7 again ↑page ( )↓: but
366. 5 a ~~teak~~↑teak↓-box, wh. Clive ↑inherited↓ made
366.n4 land ↑somewhere↓ Ethel
366. 7 deal ~~pr~~ happier
366.10 JJ's +in the+ ~~present Exhibition~~ ↑of Mrs. Cive Newcome (in the~~[illeg]~~ Crystal Palace ↑↑Exhibition↓↓ in Fableland)↓ is
366.12 but ↑it↓ represents
366.n6 introduced; ~~he~~↑our↑tour provoking↓↓ English Timanthes↓ has
366.n6 her ~~head round~~↑face away↓, and
366.14 flourish, ~~and~~ giv[ing over e] us ↑as it were↓ an
366.16 confidentially ~~tell the reader~~ ↑state↓ has
366.16 me, too↑—and may be told↓ some
366.17 Christmas ~~afternoons~~↑evenings↓ when
366.n8 and ↑it is↓ my
366.20 his ↑present↓ wife
366.23 left ~~a~~ smart
366.24 the ~~Pendennises~~ children—in
366.33 the ~~[illeg.]~~ upstarts
367. 1 caught [line omitted] in

367. 1 trap (~~≪the≫ and points a moral with his tail—~~) the

367. 2 wolf —~~just in i~~ &

367. 2 of time—~~and there poets deal about bags of sovereigns~~

[Written as a continuation of *Ms1*, the following was cancelled, and then the page was turned top to bottom and used to inscribe the revised version of the last page of the novel.]

~~and the poet rewards and punishes ≪on wil≫ ↑absolutely↓. He nobly deals out bags of sovereigns wh. will not buy anything, and ≪strike awful blows:≫ belabour[s over ed] wicked backs with awful blows wh. do not hurt, and endows heroines with preternatural beauty, and ↑creates↓ heroes who if ugly ↑possess↓ a thousand charming qualities, and makes the hero heroine happy at last and happy ever after. Ah happy ↑harmless↓ Fableland, where these things are! May the author and his reader meet there on some~~

~~future day, I hope as I bid you a kindly farewell.~~

[Cancelled Ms. ends here]

Note: Entries from 366.4 to 366.33 refer to the revised manuscript page, referred to in footnotes as *Ms2*.

366. 4 those ↑private↓ letters

366. 5 inherited ↑&↓ handed

366.16 state ~~is~~ has

366.25 article. ~~These then~~↑But have they↓ any

366.26 children? ~~I sh~~ I

366.26 best without ~~children~~, and

366.28 own ~~way~~↑fashion↓. Any

366.30 most artful),↑—↓for if

366.33 are ~~st~~ set down—[i over I]n Fable land—The f↑r↓og bursts

367. 5 heroines with ~~a~~ preternatural

367. 7 being immensely rich[; over —]makes the

367. 9 are! ~~May the~~↑Friendly Reader! may you & the↓ Author ~~and his kind readers~~ meet

367.10 day! [H over h]e hopes ~~as~~↑so↓ he yet ~~lingers has hold of their hand,~~ ↑keeps a lingering hold of your hand,↓ and bids ~~them~~↑you↓ farewell

Emendations

The first stage of emendation for this edition incorporated all the routine copy-editing described in the textual essay, above, as *silent emendations*. An electronic list of all those changes is available from the publisher.

The following list records all *additional* emendations made in the copy-text—anything not covered in the description of silent emendations. The emendation listed here are changes in the text deemed to fulfill the author's intentions for the first installment publication. The principles for determining those intentions and the limitations of any editor to fulfill them are discussed in the textual essay (see page 408).

When a *silent* emendation was made in a word that subsequently required additional emendation, this record prints the silently emended form as the base form to be emended. This stipulation affects primarily the longer entries where showing the literal reading of the copy-text and the silently emended form before showing the explicit emendation would take the space being saved by not listing silent emendations. See Silent Emendations (page 418). The present list includes all emendations (not described as silent), but it does not include other historical variations unless they were adopted as emendations.

Emendations unmarked by a symbol do not replicate exactly any of the source texts; they are made by the editor.

List of Symbols

Ms = manuscript
Ms1 = draft manuscript of penultimate page of the novel
Ms2 = revised manuscript of same page
E1 = first edition, printed from standing type
P1 = first edition, printed from stereotyped plates
HM = *Harper's Magazine* (1853–55)
NY = Harper's New York edition (1854–55)
R = revised London edition (1856)
[ ] = encloses information supplied by the editor
-/ = end-of-line hyphen.

Vol. I.

4. 9 critic's]R
critics's]E1

4.19 lions']R
lion's]E1

4.32 peacocks']R
peacock's]E1

9.17 Grey Friars]
Greyfriars]E1

9.18 served]R
serve]E1

9.22 old as,]R
old, as]E1

10. 6 anger.]R
anger]E1

14.17 right way;]R
rightway;]E1

19.33 had spoken,]R
had, spoken]E1

21. 6 lessons]HM
lesson]E1

26.41 holds]R
hold]E1

28. 6 lies]R
lie]E1

39.32 in to]
into]E1

40.20 pleasantest]HM
pleasant]E1

44.24 baronet,]R
Baronet,]E1

46.17 T.]R
J.]E1

48.38 nor]R
a]Ms

48.47 tears too?]E1
tears? ↑too.↓]Ms

48.47 on a hundred fields,]R
[omit]]Ms

[Begin Thackeray's hand]

49. 1 Meanee,]R
those of Meanee]Ms

49. 1 them]R
a hundred fields]Ms

49. 2 to]R
for]Ms

49. 3 achievements.]R
armies.]Ms

49. 7 sickening buds]R
poor wan flowers]Ms

49. 8 die. In America]R

die—In America]Ms

49.10 prŏconsul.]
prŏconsul.]Ms

49.13 laughing-stock]R
laughing stock]Ms

49.16 heathens]R
Heathens]Ms

49.45 bedchamber,]R
bed-chamber,]E1

51.39 head gown-boy]R
head-gown boy]E1

53.27 Southampton,]HM
Southampton.]E1

56.24 our]R
out]E1

58.25 Directors.]HM
Direction.]E1

64.22 you,"]
you."]E1

64.49 gentleman,]R
gentlemen,]E1

66.38 better]R
better of]E1

68.30 taking]R
taking,]E1

71.21 comer.]R
comet.]E1

75.46 children.]R
children,]E1

76.43 City]R
city]E1

78.30 question.]R
question]E1

84. 5 Brighton (believing]R
Brighton, believing]E1

84. 7 Grasse),]R
Grasse,]E1

88.12 Death]R
death]E1

[Begin Thackeray's hand]

92. 5 person and thing]E1
thing and person]Ms

92.10 veal cutlets,]E1
veal-cutlets]Ms

92.11 "Why]E1
Why]Ms

92.25 nicer?"]E1
nicer?]Ms

92.33 name—and]E1
name and]Ms

93. 1 everything,]E1
everything]Ms

93. 3 "What]E1
"what]Ms

93. 3 infant's]E1
Infant's]Ms

93. 4 "Really]E1
"really]Ms

93. 4 clergyman]E1
Clergyman]Ms

93. 8 housekeeper—what]E1
housekeeper, what]Ms

93. 8 name?—seems]E1
name? seems]Ms

93.20 she]E1
She]Ms

93.22 sun]
Sun]Ms

93.35 school]E1
School]Ms

93.35 lessons]E1
much that was]Ms

94. 5 and, of course,]
and of course]Ms

94.12 brewery]E1
Brewery]Ms

94.15 "Fancy myself," she
thought, "dressing]E1
Fancy myself she
thought dressing]Ms

94.16 Tucker!"]E1
Tucker!]Ms

94.18 stared;]E1
stared]Ms

94.19 Science]E1
Sciences]Ms

94.19 professor]E1
Professor]Ms

95. 8 she]E1
She]Ms

95. 9 she]E1
She]Ms

[Begin Anne's hand]

95.14 fairy stories]E1
Fairy stories,]Ms

95.20 to]E1
to to]Ms

95.26 passed]E1
past]Ms

95.29 heir-apparent]E1

heir apparent]Ms

95.30 anguish,]E1
anguish]Ms

95.35 mammas,]E1
mammas]Ms

95.37 women]E1
women,]Ms

95.47 Family,]E1
family,]Ms

96. 3 chronicles]E1
Chronicles]Ms

96. 9 rides]E1
Rides]Ms

96.13 be,]
be]Ms

96.19 from]E1
for]Ms

96.20 day seem,]E1
day, seem]Ms

96.30 Pet's]E1
Pit's]Ms

96.32 coaches; a]E1
coaches, (a]Ms

96.33 steam-engines]E1
steam Engines]Ms

96.33 over.]E1
over.)]Ms

96.38 "Biffin," I warrant,
]E1
Biffin I warrant]Ms

96.38 "A Thirsty Soul"]E1
A Thirsty Soul]Ms

96.39 institution.]E1
Institution.]Ms

97. 3 charioteers.]
Charioteers.]Ms

97. 4 passed]E1
past]Ms

97. 8 middle-aged]E1
middle aged]Ms

97.12 pleasant]E1
kindly]Ms

97.17 minority:]E1
minority]Ms

97.18 mischief,]E1
mischief]Ms

97.19 masters.]E1
masters]Ms

97.27 at]E1
it]Ms

97.28 retire;]E1
retire,]Ms

97.29 Christchurch]
Christ Church]Ms

97.38 well-assorted]E1

well assorted]Ms

[Begin Thackeray's hand]

98. 9 hand,]E1
hand]Ms

98.20 magistrates:]
Magistrates:]Ms

98.22 judge,]E1
Judge,]Ms

98.37 you, I know,]E1
you I know]Ms

98.42 guinea;]E1
guinea]Ms

98.45 inquire.]E1
enquire.]Ms

99. 4 use, however,]E1
use however]Ms

99.16 lady,]E1
lady]Ms

99.22 morning,]E1
morning]Ms

99.28 everything that can
be heard. Tell]E1
a thousand times
worse things than
you are going to tell
her. He He! That
she has: and I have
told them too:" cries
Lady Kew rapping
her knuckles on the
table. "Tell]Ms

99.31 contralto]E1
Contralto]Ms

99.41 mauvais]E1
Mauvais]Ms

99.43 Brighton,]E1
Brighton]Ms

100. 1 are]E1
do]Ms

100. 1 pozzo—"]E1
pozzo]Ms

100. 2 secretary— ¶"—in
a pozzoprofondo
—you]
Secretary— ¶"In
a pozzoprofondo
—You]Ms

100. 6 it,]E1
it]Ms

100.18 d——]E1
d—]Ms

100.19 "I]E1
"I]Ms

100.28 ma'am,"]E1
Ma'am,"]Ms

100.38 "Well,]E1

"Well]Ms

100.41 'No,']E1
'No,']Ms

100.44 behind—"]
behind]Ms

101. 2 wrong,]
wrong]Ms

101. 3 "D——d]E1
"D—d]Ms

101. 9 nothing,]E1
nothing]Ms

101.10 'em]E1
em]Ms

101.13 aunt, it appears,]E1
aunt it appears]Ms

101.18 fine-looking]E1
fine looking]Ms

101.19 hotel—Go]
Hotel—Go]Ms

102. 7 cub."]E1
Cub."]Ms

102. 9 "The]E1
"Lady Ann pointed it
out to us. The]Ms

102.15 spectacles. And]E1
spectacles and]Ms

102.17 grandmother:—
Ethel,]E1
grandmother. Ethel,
]Ms

103. 1 AT MRS. RIDLEY'S]E1
Ridley's]Ms

103. 7 stone wall:]E1
stone-wall:]Ms

103.11 voices,]E1
voices]Ms

103.16 Saint,]E1
Saint]Ms

103.23 trust,]E1
trust]Ms

103.27 Walpole]E1
Queen]Ms

104. 9 Delcroix's)]E1
Delcrois')]Ms

104.11 pocket-handkerchief
]E1
pocket handkerchief
]Ms

104.14 worked]E1
worked,]Ms

104.20 or,]
or]Ms

104.20 second)—yea,]

second) yea]Ms
104.32 ceremony,]
       ceremony]Ms
104.34 "what]E1
       what]Ms
104.36 do]E1
       Do]Ms
104.43 ages;]E1
       ages]Ms
105. 1 sons-in-law),]E1
       sons-in-law)]Ms
105. 3 feet. Societies]E1
       feet—Societies]Ms
105. 5 23rd,]E1
       23]Ms
105. 7 A.M.,]E1
       A.M.]Ms
105. 7 &c.,]
       &c.]Ms
105. 7 Grandmothers']E1
       Grandmother's]Ms
105. 9 Sunday, 4th May,
       ]E1
       Sunday 4 May]Ms
105.15 Parliament,]E1
       Parliament]Ms
105.15 Ministers,]E1
       Ministers]Ms
105.15 him:]E1
       him]Ms
105.22 like," says Charles.
       "They]E1
       like:" says Charles—
       "They]Ms
105.25 him.—A]E1
       him—A]Ms
105.38 row,]E1
       row]Ms
105.46 lady-dowagers]E1
       ladies]Ms
106. 2 Reverend]E1
       Revd.]Ms
106. 3 seen,]E1
       seen]Ms
106. 3 throbs,]E1
       throbs]Ms
106. 6 it?—in Walpole]E1
       it? in Queen]Ms
106.20 Theatre Royal,
       Covent Garden.]E1
       Royal Covent
       Garden Theatre.
       ]Ms
106.22 palace,]E1
       palace]Ms

106.34 half-crown.]E1
       half crown.]Ms
106.42 music—always, I say,
       ]
       music—Always I say
       ]Ms
107. 2 night,]E1
       night]Ms
107. 7 Who,]E1
       Who]Ms
107. 9 husband,]E1
       husband]Ms
107.19 Beatrice]E1
       Emily]Ms
107.23 Walpole]E1
       Queen]Ms
107.25 the]E1
       [omit]]Ms
107.26 you,]E1
       you]Ms
107.28 ghastly]E1
       Ghastly]Ms
107.36 country.]E1
       Country.]Ms
108. 2 great]E1
       Great]Ms
108. 5 family,]E1
       family]Ms
108. 8 lives]E1
       live]Ms
108. 9 company]E1
       Company]Ms
108. 9 bless you!]E1
       bless! you]Ms
108.13 Bayham's,]E1
       Bayham's]Ms
108.16 teacher.]E1
       governess.]Ms
108.19 near]E1
       near the person of
       ]Ms
108.23 chapel)]E1
       chapel]Ms
108.24 Cann,]E1
       Cann]Ms
108.25 first-floor lodger's
       ]E1
       first floor-lodger's
       ]Ms
108.26 Cann—it]E1
       Cann it]Ms
108.31 sermons (the rogue,
       ]E1
       sermons, (the rogue
       ]Ms

108.32 sure,]E1
       sure]Ms
108.32 are,]E1
       are]Ms
108.33 understand,]E1
       understand]Ms
108.34 he),]E1
       he)]Ms
108.37 is,]E1
       is:]Ms
108.42 Haydn,]E1
       Haydon,]Ms
109. 5 theatres.]E1
       Theatres.]Ms
109. 5 Don Juan,]
       Don Juan,]Ms
109.15 Rubens]E1
       Rubens,]Ms
109.20 seize]E1
       sieze]Ms
109.24 all,]
       all]Ms
109.25 Massaniello]E1
       Masaniello]Ms
109.26 balcony,]E1
       balcony]Ms
109.29 beauty,]E1
       beauty]Ms
109.36 nothink,"]E1
       nothink"]Ms
109.41 eyes,]E1
       eyes]Ms
109.41 plate-basket. The
       ]E1
       plate basket—The
       ]Ms
109.42 size. At]E1
       size—At]Ms
109.44 who,]E1
       who]Ms
109.45 him,]E1
       him]Ms
110. 2 half-witted!]E1
       half witted!]Ms
110. 3 man,]E1
       man]Ms
110. 9 gold. You]E1
       gold—You]Ms
110.16 it;]E1
       it]Ms
110.17 harm,]E1
       harm]Ms
110.18 it;]E1
       it]Ms

110.28 O]E1
    o]Ms
110.30 copy-books,]E1
    copy books,]Ms
110.33 (for]E1
    for]Ms
110.43 dressmaking]E1
    dress making]Ms
110.46 public-house,]E1
    public house,]Ms
111. 7 day-school]E1
    day school]Ms
111. 8 hours,]E1
    hours]Ms
111.13 One-handed]E1
    one-handed]Ms
111.13 Venice,]E1
    Venice]Ms
111.13 Rinaldini,]R
    Rinaldino,]Ms
111.14 *Thaddeus of Warsaw*]
    Thaddeus of Warsaw
    ]Ms
111.26 him,]E1
    him]Ms
111.30 board,]E1
    board]Ms
111.38 at]E1
    [*omit*]]Ms
111.43 foregrounds, burnt
    sienna]E1
    foregrounds burnt
    Sienna]Ms
111.43 foliage,]E1
    foliage]Ms
111.44 flesh-colour,"]E1
    flesh-colour"]Ms
112. 1 art-cant]E1
    Art-cant]Ms
112. 6 objects,]E1
    objects]Ms
112. 7 story-books]E1
    story books]Ms
112.11 masters]E1
    master]Ms
112.12 art-world;]E1
    Art-world;]Ms
112.13 faint-heartedness]
    faint-heartedness,
    ]Ms
112.17 1st.,]
    1st.]Ms
112.18 streets, to wit,]E1
    streets to wit]Ms
112.18 others,]E1

    others]Ms
112.23 night;—Walpole]E1
    night. Walpole]Ms
112.24 doctors']E1
    Doctors']Ms
112.25 No.]E1
    no.]Ms
112.27 floor,]E1
    floor]Ms
112.28 staircase]E1
    stair case]Ms
112.35 candles—his]E1
    candles his]Ms
112.35 Cann,]E1
    Cann]Ms
112.36 ago,]E1
    ago]Ms
112.38 3—long]E1
    3 long]Ms
112.39 pupils—a]E1
    pupils a]Ms
112.40 bell;]E1
    bell,]Ms
112.41 obeyed,]E1
    obeyed]Ms
112.42 pair of boots]E1
    [*omit*]]Ms
112.44 Waterloo,]E1
    Waterloo]Ms
113. 3 "Lor,]E1
    "Lor]Ms
113. 6 floor; and loosely
    enveloped in a
    ragged and]E1
    floor, and with the
    exception of a]Ms
113. 6 chambre.]E1
    chambre, and
    a slight interior
    garment in the *simple*
    appareil of an Ancient
    Briton.]Ms
113.10 reverence]E1
    Reverence]Ms
113.17 Fred Bayham]E1
    Ancient Briton]Ms
113.17 skeleton—far]
    skeleton far]Ms
113.18 "Indeed.]
    "Indeed]Ms
113.19 exaggerate,]E1
    exaggerate]Ms
113.21 glass,]E1
    glass]Ms
113.22 half-crown,]E1

    half crown]Ms
113.22 half-crown,]E1
    half crown,]Ms
113.22 pye,]E1
    pye]Ms
113.27 ill]E1
    sick]Ms
113.27 steam-packet]E1
    steam packet]Ms
113.30 Fred,]E1
    Fred]Ms
113.30 cheque]E1
    check]Ms
113.31 Harmony,]E1
    Harmony]Ms
113.31 Chaplain,]E1
    chaplain,]Ms
113.32 sea—the]E1
    Sea—the]Ms
113.35 parenthesis.]E1
    parenthesis]Ms
113.39 friend, it's]
    friend it's]Ms
113.40 chimney-glass;]
    chimney glass;]Ms
113.41 sermon—O]
    sermon—o]Ms
114. 2 true,]E1
    true]Ms
114. 5 Honeyman,]E1
    Honeyman]Ms
114. 7 manly, ay,]E1
    manly ay]Ms
114.18 half-past three?]E1
    half past one?]Ms
114.18 see,]E1
    see]Ms
114.20 bread]
    bred]Ms
115. 1 IN WHICH EVERBODY
    IS ASKED TO DINNER.
    ]E1
    [*omit*]]Ms
115.19 Hospital, (it]E1
    Hospital (It]Ms
115.21 boys,)]E1
    boys)]Ms
115.21 successor's]E1
    Successor's]Ms
115.23 Friars' gates]E1
    Friar's Gates]Ms
115.25 chapels]E1
    Chapels]Ms
116. 4 Punch.]E1

Punch—]Ms

116. 5 hunchbacked;]E1
　　　hunch backed;]Ms

116. 7 "What,]E1
　　　"What]Ms

116.14 Pendennis,]E1
　　　Pendennis]Ms

116.18 alive,]E1
　　　alive]Ms

116.18 old-fashioned]
　　　old fashioned]Ms

116.19 soldier,]E1
　　　soldier]Ms

116.20 humbly.]E1
　　　humbly—]Ms

116.28 divine seated]E1
　　　Divine sealed
　　　[uncrossed t]]Ms

116.29 along, old fellow, and
　　　show]E1
　　　along old fellow and
　　　Show]Ms

116.32 yours,]E1
　　　yours]Ms

116.35 mind.]
　　　mind]Ms

116.35 together,]E1
　　　together]Ms

116.41 "you]E1
　　　"You]Ms

116.42 Jove,]E1
　　　Jove]Ms

116.43 Nights,]E1
　　　Nights]Ms

116.44 and—what]E1
　　　and what]Ms

116.45 her?—Dinarsade
　　　]E1
　　　her? Dinarsade]Ms

117. 1 horses, I know,]E1
　　　horses I know]Ms

117. 4 table, round which
　　　]E1
　　　table while]Ms

117. 4 elders are seated.
　　　¶"I've settled it up-
　　　stairs with J.J.,"
　　　says Clive, working
　　　away with his pen.
　　　"We shall take a
　　　studio together;
　　　perhaps we will go
　　　abroad together.
　　　Won't that be fun,
　　　father?" ¶"My dear
　　　Clive," remarks

Mr. Honeyman,
with bland dignity,
"there are degrees
in society which
we must respect.
You surely cannot
think of being a
professional artist.
Such a profession is
very well for your
young protégé; but
for you—" ¶"What
for me?" cries Clive.
"We are no such
great folks that I
know of; and if
we were, I say a
painter is as good as
a lawyer, or a doctor,
or even a soldier. In
Dr. Johnson's Life,
which my father is
always reading—I
like to read about
Sir Joshua Reynolds
best: I think he is
the best gentleman
of all in the book.
My! wouldn't I like
to paint a picture
like Lord Heathfield
in the National
Gallery! *Wouldn't*
I just? I think I
would sooner have
done that, than
have fought at
Gibraltar. And those
Three Graces—
oh, aren't they
graceful! And that
Cardinal Beaufort
at Dulwich!—it
frightens me so, I
daren't look at it.
Wasn't Reynolds a
clipper, that's all!
and wasn't Rubens
a brick? He was
an ambassador and
Knight of the Bath;
so was Vandyck. And
Titian, and Raphael,
and Velasquez?—
I'll just trouble
you to show me
better gentlemen
than them, Uncle
Charles." ¶"Far be it
from me to say that

the pictorial calling is
not honourable," says
Uncle Charles;
"but as the world
goes there are
other professions in
greater repute; and I
should have thought
Colonel Newcome's
son—" ¶"He shall
follow his own bent,"
said the Colonel; "as
long as his calling
is honest it becomes
a gentleman; and
if he were to take
a fancy to play on
the fiddle—actually
on the fiddle—I
shouldn't object."
]E1
elders continue their
conversation.]Ms

117.34 figure).]E1
　　　figure.)]Ms

117.34 Harmony, he says,
　　　]E1
　　　Harmony he says
　　　]Ms

117.41 circumstances—'and
　　　]
　　　circumstances 'and
　　　]Ms

117.44 drawn,]E1
　　　drawn]Ms

118. 1 here,"]E1
　　　here:"]Ms

118. 8 "Come]E1
　　　"come]Ms

118.13 broad-brimmed]E1
　　　broad brimmed]Ms

118.15 neckcloth,]E1
　　　neck cloth]Ms

119. 6 right,]E1
　　　right]Ms

119. 7 Pendennis,]E1
　　　Pendennis]Ms

119. 7 sure,]E1
　　　sure]Ms

119.15 *persiflage*]E1
　　　persifflage]Ms

119.20 neglect, perhaps
　　　merited, perhaps
　　　undeserved,]E1
　　　neglect perhaps
　　　merited perhaps
　　　undeserved]Ms

119.21 family.]E1
family]Ms
119.22 writers]E1
writers to the]Ms
119.22 Parthenopæon,]E1
Parthenopæon.]Ms
119.23 deserts. I]E1
deserts—I]Ms
119.24 scene]E1
Scene]Ms
119.26 myself—" He]
myself—"he]Ms
119.31 me,]E1
me:]Ms
119.31 father;]E1
father]Ms
119.36 to-day,]E1
to-day]Ms
119.36 gentlemen,]E1
gentlemen]Ms
119.43 ready,]E1
ready]Ms
119.46 Berkeley]E1
Berkely]Ms
119.47 Hill,]E1
Hill]Ms
120. 2 cab,]E1
Cab,]Ms
120. 7 warrior]E1
warrior,]Ms
120. 8 he,]E1
he]Ms
120. 8 think,]E1
think]Ms
120.13 Nerot's,]E1
Nerot's]Ms
120.14 expected,"]E1
expected;"]Ms
120.16 ——]E1
—]Ms
120.26 Governor-General
]E1
Governor General
]Ms
120.29 inauguration]E1
Inauguration]Ms
120.32 school]E1
School]Ms
120.32 repentance).]E1
repentance.)]Ms
120.33 hope,]E1
hope]Ms
120.33 different.]E1
different,]Ms
120.44 Pendennis,]

Pendennis]Ms
120.44 party,]
party]Ms
121.12 "Egad,]E1
"Egad]Ms
121.12 sings."]E1
sings"]Ms
121.17 ¶And now the
carriages began to
drive up, and the
guests of Colonel
Newcome to arrive.
[new chapter] IN
WHICH THOMAS
NEWCOME SINGS HIS
LAST SONG. ¶THE
earliest comers were
the first mate and
the medical officer of
the ship]E1
One by one the
guests now began
to arrive. There was
the first mate and
the medical officer of
the Ship]Ms
122. 4 England. The]E1
England—The]Ms
122. 5 The mate was a
Scotchman:]E1
The mate was a
healthy-looking
mariner with a
broad brown face
and red whiskers
and a great pair of
hands covered with
freckles, who looked
sadly uncomfortable
in his shore-going
clothes The mate was
a Scotchman:]Ms
122. 8 were Scotchmen.
¶The Southrons,
]E1
were Scotchmen.
These were, of
course, Mr. Binnie's
guests: the South-
Britons were invited
by his chum the
Colonel. ¶The
Southrons,]Ms
122. 7 Club,]E1
Club]Ms
122.17 civil]E1
Civil]Ms
122.18 India.]E1

India; where he had
doctored himself
very freely.]Ms
122.24 Clive.]
Clive about his
school and his
doings.]Ms
122.24 India,"]E1
India:"]Ms
122.25 officer]E1
Officer]Ms
122.28 school,]E1
School,]Ms
122.29 Boys,]E1
Boys.]Ms
122.29 boy: "succeeded]
boy:—"succeeded
]Ms
122.30 Hymns, you know,
]E1
Hymns you know
]Ms
123. 1 182—,]E1
18—,]Ms
123. 3 Baronet]E1
baronet]Ms
123. 5 mate]E1
Mate]Ms
123. 6 master]
Master]Ms
123.13 brandy. ¶Here]E1
brandy ¶"I wish I
was implicated in
that transaction,"
whispers Mr.
Bayham, who
had been keeping
as close to Mr.
Pendennis as a
sheriff's officer to
a debtor. "I think
yonder weather-
beaten mariner
shows proof of his
good sense. I say—
tst! you! hi!—is
his name James?
another little glass
of" ¶Here]Ms
123.17 neckcloth,]E1
neck-cloth,]Ms
123.19 idea,]E1
idea]Ms
123.20 it, no—Hoby]E1
it no—Hely]Ms
123.22 Duke. My]E1

Duke—" and poor
F.B. here looked
down disconsolately
at his lower
extremities which
were clothed in
kerseymere shining
with old age, and in
boots whereof the
extremities curled
upwards like those of
the Turks. "My]Ms

123.22 right,]E1
right]Ms

124. 3 ¶Colonel Newcome
introduced]E1
¶"How do you
do Sir. I am very
glad to make your
acquaintance, Sir
Thomas," here
says Mr. Bayham
with a low bow and
low voice. Colonel
Newcome was
introducing]Ms

124.10 up,]E1
up]Ms

124.13 coachman,]E1
coachman]Ms

124.13 periwigged.]E1
periwigged]Ms

124.14 box, too,]E1
box too]Ms

124.16 Andrews?]
andrews?]Ms

124.17 blandly. He]
blandly he]Ms

124.18 permits]E1
permits to]Ms

124.20 charmed, of course,
]E1
charmed of course
]Ms

124.20 condescension.]E1
condescension]Ms

124.22 me,]E1
me]Ms

124.26 Street,]E1
Street]Ms

124.27 palm.]E1
palm. Of such secret
envies is the world
made.]Ms

124.29 about:]E1
about,]Ms

124.31 Boots,]E1

Boots]Ms

124.32 armholes]E1
arm-holes]Ms

124.32 engaged,]E1
engaged]Ms

124.37 seconded]E1
second]Ms

124.39 steaming,]E1
steaming]Ms

124.41 De]E1
de]Ms

125. 9 everybody]E1
every body]Ms

125.10 matter,]E1
matter]Ms

125.12 frock-coat,]E1
frock coat,]Ms

125.18 old-fashioned]E1
old fashioned]Ms

125.20 Binnie,]E1
Binnie]Ms

125.20 Brian,]E1
Brian]Ms

125.21 you,]
you]Ms

125.21 already,]E1
already]Ms

125.24 anything]E1
any thing]Ms

125.26 company:]
Company:]Ms

125.38 men. Sir]E1
men—Sir]Ms

125.43 thimble-full]E1
thimble full]Ms

125.44 heart,]E1
heart]Ms

125.45 which,]
which]Ms

125.46 drank,]E1
drank]Ms

125.47 largely,]E1
largely]Ms

126. 5 Bayham and]E1
[omit]]Ms

126.10 chief mate:]E1
Chief Mate:]Ms

126.16 effort,]E1
effort]Ms

126.26 HEAR!]E1
HEAR]Ms

126.26 applaud]NY
applauded]Ms E1 R

126.27 exalted,]E1

exalted]Ms

126.28 profession,]E1
profession]Ms

126.29 say,]E1
say]Ms

126.29 who,]E1
who]Ms

126.30 dainties]E1
dainties,]Ms

126.31 wine-cup]E1
wine cup]Ms

126.31 friend's]R
[omit]]Ms

126.33 benedictions,]E1
benedictions]Ms

126.33 it,]E1
it]Ms

126.33 say,]E1
say]Ms

126.35 childhood,]E1
childhood]Ms

126.38 child,]E1
child]Ms

126.39 man,]E1
man]Ms

126.39 told,]E1
told]Ms

126.40 but]
But]Ms

126.41 ecclesiæ]E1
ecclesia]Ms

126.43 company).]E1
company.]Ms

127. 3 ceased;]E1
ceased]Ms

127. 4 reply. Without]E1
reply—Without]Ms

127. 5 incumbent]
encumbent]Ms

127. 5 Chapel]E1
Chapel,]Ms

127.10 yet. Let]E1
yet—Let]Ms

127.11 General. You]E1
General—You]Ms

127.12 wine,"]
wine:"]Ms

127.13 song?]E1
Song?]Ms

127.16 Cockpen, without,
]E1
Cockpen]Ms

127.16 say,]E1
say without]Ms

127.22 commonty]
        Comenty]Ms
127.23 says;]E1
        says]Ms
127.23 sorry]E1
        very sorry]Ms
127.26 company. The]E1
        company—The]Ms
127.28 something]E1
        Something]Ms
127.28 oath,]E1
        oath]Ms
127.30 it,]E1
        it]Ms
127.32 "Whas]E1
        "Wha's]Ms
127.32 wine. Bayham]E1
        wine—Bayham]Ms
127.38 chorus]
        Chorus]Ms
127.41 here,]E1
        here]Ms
127.42 singers,]E1
        singers]Ms
127.42 annoyed,]E1
        annoyed]Ms
128. 8 anger.]E1
        anger—]Ms
128.12 time, mind you,]E1
        time mind you]Ms
128.18 continue; but]E1
        continue But]Ms
128.19 again."]E1
        again—"]Ms
129. 1 PARK LANE.]E1
        [omit]]Ms
129. 2 headache,]E1
        head-ache,]Ms
129. 7 said.]E1
        said,]Ms
129.10 "O,]E1
        "O]Ms
129.13 headache earned
        overnight.]E1
        head ache earned
        over night.]Ms
129.16 Make]E1
        Wide awake, and
        feeling your coppers
        hot, eh Sir? Have a
        cold-bath, make]Ms
129.18 orders;]E1
        orders]Ms
129.24 feast?]E1
        feast—the
        appearance of a

theatre when the
play is over and
the daylight comes
streaming in over
the vacant benches?
]Ms
129.28 down,]E1
        down.]Ms
130. 6 pardon.]E1
        pardon—]Ms
130.13 see,]E1
        see]Ms
130.13 after,]
        after]Ms
130.14 mouillée]E1
        mouillé]Ms
130.17 trespasses, my boy,
        ]E1
        trespasses my]Ms
[Begin Eyre Crowe's hand]
130.21 awake]
        awake,]Ms
130.23 Park, as]E1
        Park. As]Ms
130.24 housemaid,]E1
        house-maid,]Ms
130.30 harp,]E1
        harp]Ms
130.37 harp.]E1
        harp:]Ms
130.37 reign;]E1
        reign.]Ms
130.39 canvas bag;]E1
        canvass-bag;]Ms
130.43 sarcophagus,]E1
        sarcophagus]Ms
131. 5 major-domo]E1
        Major-Domo]Ms
131. 8 master]E1
        Master]Ms
131.14 Morning Herald]E1
        Morning-Herald]Ms
131.15 soirée cards]E1
        soiree-cards]Ms
131.15 Morning Post]E1
        Morning-Post]Ms
131.23 engaged,]E1
        engaged]Ms
131.24 hope,"]E1
        hope"]Ms
131.32 hall,]E1
        Hall,]Ms
131.33 two,]E1
        two]Ms
131.43 Colonel,]E1

Colonel]Ms
131.45 said;]E1
        said,]Ms
132. 8 them."]E1
        them,"—and here
        Barnes could not
        help giving a little
        look at his cousin,
        which caused
        the latter young
        gentleman to feel
        sure that Barnes was
        perfectly aware of
        the previous night's
        transaction, in spite
        of all his assertions to
        the contrary.]Ms
132. 9 gravely—"that]E1
        gravely—: "that]Ms
132.10 result.]E1
        result;" and as
        Barnes did not seem
        in the least inclined
        to press for any
        precise account of
        the transactions
        of the previous
        night, the prudent
        negociator of peace
        did not choose to
        bring them forward.
        ]Ms
132.13 you]E1
        You]Ms
132.13 "and]E1
        "And]Ms
132.17 fully]E1
        fuly]Ms
[Begin Anne's hand]
132.25 humble-minded]E1
        humble minded]Ms
132.27 reverent]E1
        reverend]Ms
132.35 comments. Between
        ]E1
        comments. Lad
        as he was he had
        a shrewdness and
        experience which the
        elder's fifty years had
        never attained. Clive
        with his young eyes
        looked more clearly
        at men and the
        world than his father
        who had seen it so

long and so little:and
the boy very soon
began to keep
his own opinion
and to question
the experience of
which his artless
sire never doubted
the value. In truth
Thomas Newcome
was but a child in
the understanding of
the world although
he fancied himself
becomingly versed
in that science;
imagining that a
man of necessity
acquired experience
by age and took
steps in knowledge,
as he did in military
rank, by seniority.
You who have
children round your
firesides would you
rather have them
humble and silent
and obedient, or
frank and trustful?
Between]Ms

133. 3 character,]E1
character]Ms

133. 7 O generous boy]E1
Generous Boy]Ms

133. 7 it,]E1
it]Ms

133.11 kinsman,]E1
kinsman, on the
morning when
the young heir of
Newcome and Park
Lane had professed
such repentance for
his excesses in wine,
]Ms

133.13 eight (unless]E1
eight:—(unless]Ms

133.14 overnight):]E1
overnight)]Ms

133.16 week,]E1
week]Ms

133.18 table.]E1
table: When
the family were
in London the
breakfast-room
naturally presented a
much more cheerful

appearance than
it wore when we
were first introduced
to it Sir Brian
discharged the
domestic duties with
stately regularity.
A public man was
separated from his
family so much and
by such constant
interruptions!He
is bound to be an
example to those
around him. Sir
Brian had a weak
but fine voice, he
thought, and an
impressive manner
of elocution.]Ms

133.21 bell. ¶I]E1
bell. ¶The Newcome
house in London
was always up
many hours before
its fashionable
neighbours whose
masters had no
banks in the city
which they were
obliged to attend.
In March Lady
Ann would rise
every morning by
candle light so as to
be at Breakfast at
eight o'clock. Her
daughter was not out
yet; and her ladyship
could get away from
her balls and parties
before midnight.
But when Ethel
should come out,
though they might
have to go to four
balls of a night and
might not get to bed
till four o'clock, Lady
Ann vowed and
declared she would
do the same thing,
she *would* be present
at her husband's
breakfast—she would
have the family
assembled at the
commencement of
the day. ¶I]Ms

133.23 urns]E1

Urns]Ms

133.30 side-board:]E1
side board:]Ms

133.30 unconscious last-born
]E1
unconsious last born
]Ms

134. 2 the]E1
[omit]]Ms

134. 5 whence,]E1
whence]Ms

134. 6 Oxford]E1
oxford]Ms

134. 7 sky-blue waistcoats,
]E1
sky blue waist coats,
]Ms

134.11 masquerade.]E1
maskerade.]Ms

134.14 streets]E1
streets,]Ms

134.15 establishment),]E1
establishment)]Ms

134.19 neighbours. Nay,
]E1
neighbours nay]Ms

134.21 hall,]E1
hall]Ms

134.25 *versâ*.]E1
versa.]Ms

134.32 ill. Lady Ann]E1
ill Lady Ann,]Ms

134.33 town?]E1
town]Ms

134.33 Trotter]E1
Hicks]Ms

134.33 Trotter]E1
Hicks]Ms

134.34 good-natured—she]
good-natured—She
]Ms

134.39 Tompkyns?" asks
Mamma.]E1
Tomkyns?" asks
Mama.]Ms

134.40 Tompkyns?]E1
Tomkyns?]Ms

135. 6 from]E1
[omit]]Ms

135. 8 sepoys]
Seapoys]Ms

135. 8 amiable]E1
aimiable]Ms

135. 9 Newcome—that's
]E1

Newcome—That's]Ms

135.11 ¶"You]E1
"You]Ms

135.26 jelly.]E1
Jelly.]Ms

135.28 there's]E1
There's]Ms

135.28 banker,]E1
banker]Ms

135.30 lodging-house]E1
lodging house]Ms

135.32 Street:—hers,]E1
Street:—Hers,]Ms

135.38 sepoys,]E1
Seapoys,]Ms

135.42 clenched]E1
clinched]Ms

135.46 shrieks]E1
shreiks]Ms

136. 1 it]
It]Ms

136. 2 circumstance;]E1
circumstance]Ms

136. 3 'Lieutenant Colonel
Newcome, C.B., a
]E1
'Lieut. Colonel
Newcome. C.B. A
]Ms

136. 3 officer]E1
Officer]Ms

136. 4 elder]R
younger]Ms

136. 6 inhabitants]E1
Inhabitants]Ms

136. 8 elderly relative]E1
Elderly Relative]Ms

136.13 *new comer himself*.]
new comer himself.
]E1
new come<r> himself.
]Ms

136.22 whose]E1
Whose]Ms

136.24 cloth]E1
Cloth]Ms

136.25 Pomposo,]E1
Pomposo]Ms

136.25 know,]E1
know]Ms

136.27 manufactories]
manufactures]Ms

136.28 received]E1
recieved]Ms

136.32 him—No, it's Vidler
the apothecary.]
him—No it's Fidler
the Apothecary.]Ms

136.38 gracious]E1
Gracious]Ms

136.44 election. But]
Election. but]Ms

[Begin Thackeray's hand]
137. 2 soldier,]E1
soldier]Ms

137. 3 manufactures—in
]E1
manufactures in]Ms

137. 4 North—but]E1
North, but]Ms

137. 7 son,]E1
son]Ms

137. 7 youth,]E1
youth]Ms

137. 8 environs]E1
environs,]Ms

137.19 O]E1
o]Ms

137.23 " 'PEEPING TOM.' "
[Note: The
remainder of this
chapter was added at
proof stage. The ms
continues without a
break with the next
chapter.]]E1
Peeping Tom.' "]Ms

[Begin Anne's hand]
139. 6 recorded. He]E1
recorded. ¶The
active gentleman
as before has been
stated was constantly
on the whirl to
visit one friend or
the other and his
boy's guardian and
the kind and aged
woman who had
been the mother
of his own earliest
days were among the
first persons in this
country whom he
hastened to embrace.
He]Ms

139. 8 Mail]E1
Mail whence
Newcome is distant
not many miles]Ms

139.13 post-chaising—the
]E1

post-chaising the
]Ms

139.13 country]E1
Country]Ms

139.19 came,]
came]Ms

139.20 good humour]E1
goodhumour]Ms

139.22 manufactories,]E1
manufacturies,]Ms

139.26 aforesaid,]E1
aforesaid]Ms

139.27 Colonel]E1
Colonels]Ms

139.31 old-fashioned]E1
old fashioned]Ms

140. 4 afterwards,—to]
afterwards—,to]Ms

140. 4 Grand Tour.]E1
grand tour.]Ms

140. 6 manufactories]
manufactures]Ms

140. 9 handwriting.]E1
hand writing.]Ms

140.12 to "Mrs.]E1
Mrs.]Ms

140.13 Row,"]E1
Row,]Ms

140.15 used—the Blue
House—was the
Roebuck,]E1
used the Blue house
was the Roe buck,
]Ms

140.16 Arms.]E1
Arms,]Ms

140.22 shakes,]E1
shakes]Ms

140.22 owned,]E1
owned]Ms

140.28 post-boys]
postboys]Ms

140.28 top-sawyer;]E1
top-Sawyer;]Ms

140.31 Baronet—their]E1
Baronet their]Ms

140.34 Liberals]E1
liberals]Ms

140.34 Arms.]E1
Arms. Scared by
the intelligence and
perhaps not liking
to meet the Buffs in
their stronghold at
the Arms,]Ms

140.35 agent,]E1
agent]Ms
140.35 act,]E1
act, waited for
the return of Mr.
Hookham his
partner who was
gone to Manchester
on business,]Ms
140.37 card.]E1
card. It will be time
to speak more fully
regarding Newcome
and its inhabitants
when we come to
have farther business
in that place.]Ms
141. 1 Bible]E1
bible]Ms
141. 4 whiskers.]E1
whiskers]Ms
141. 6 boy,]E1
boy]Ms
141.11 nurse, the]E1
nurse The]Ms
141.14 eyes]E1
eyes,]Ms
141.16 man's]E1
of man's]Ms
141.17 wherever he was,
]E1
where ever he was
]Ms
141.21 angels]E1
Angels]Ms
141.21 [noteThe next two
paragraphs, "Having
nothing . . . in the last
chapter." were added
at proof stage.]
141.24 He can spare but
that]R
That]Ms
142.26 bow-window]
bow window]Ms
142.27 unoccupied,]E1
unoccupied]Ms
142.29 within,]E1
within]Ms
142.35 Hannah:]E1
Hannah]Ms
142.36 week,]E1
week]Ms
142.39 shirts, she]
shirts. She]Ms
143. 1 natives,")]E1

natives")]Ms
143. 4 whipped,]
whipped]Ms
143. 4 pie-crusts]E1
pie crusts]Ms
143.11 as,]
as]Ms
143.12 Madeira,]E1
Madeira]Ms
143.17 card-case,]E1
card case,]Ms
143.17 chessmen,]E1
chess men,]Ms
143.19 Third]E1
third]Ms
143.21 sitting-room.]E1
sitting-room. Here
was another aging
woman, a grateful
recipient of Thomas
Newcome's gentle
Charity. May
those of us whom
fortune has endowed
liberally be able to
count such a client
or two, and to think
now and again of
a stricken wayfarer
helped and soothed
in his misfortune,
or a widow's cruise
replenished.]Ms
143.24 appeared, first,]E1
appeared first]Ms
143.25 and third,]E1
third]Ms
143.26 fourth,]E1
fourth]Ms
143.27 hand, fifth,]E1
hand fifth]Ms
143.29 Hannah, grinning,
]E1
Hannah grinning
]Ms
143.35 up,]E1
up]Ms
143.38 niece,]E1
niece]Ms
143.39 Camaralzaman]E1
Camaralzeman]Ms
143.40 artist:]E1
artist]Ms
143.42 abound,]E1
abound]Ms
[Begin Thackeray's hand]

144. 6 gold-leaf—as]E1
gold-leafs—as]Ms
144. 7 metal! As]E1
metal. Does not one
see sometimes in the
faces of the good
and charitable; the
just and pure those
expressions bright,
sweet and beatific,
those Insignia of
Love? it makes a
mean home bright
and pleasant: it
changes a dish of
herbs to a feast—it
causes a plain face
to look beautiful—as
]Ms
144. 7 task,]E1
task]Ms
144.19 [noteThe rest of
this paragraph, the
sketch, the next four
paragraphs, and
the fifth paragraph
through "beside him
during his visit."
were added in proof
stage.]
146.17 Hobson]
Hobson,]Ms
146.40 her]E1
Her]Ms
146.41 Préville's—when]E1
Préville's—When
]Ms
146.42 portait des bas
jaunes—I]
portoit des bas
jaunes.—I]Ms
146.45 night,]E1
night]Ms
147. 1 Look,]E1
Look]Ms
147. 8 sewing]E1
sowing]Ms
147.18 gloves,]E1
gloves]Ms
147.18 must, and]E1
must and perhaps
]Ms
148. 1 old-fashioned]E1
old fashioned]Ms
148. 1 fine]E1
nice]Ms
148. 9 Kean]

Keam]Ms

148.11 Kean, is]E1
Kean. Is]Ms

148.13 coats?"—Kean]E1
coats"—Kean]Ms

148.21 say,]E1
say]Ms

148.22 man]E1
man,]Ms

149. 1 IN WHICH MR.
SHERRICK LETS HIS
HOUSE IN FITZROY
SQUARE.]E1
[omit]]Ms

149. 2 place,]E1
place]Ms

[Begin Anne's hand]

149. 5 house.]E1
house; whose good
will he secured
by those means
of corruption to
which the kind soul
usually resorted
when dealing
with children;—
purchasing their
little votes by all
sorts of bribery
and treating; and
securing their
suffrages by every
kind of toy, picture
book, sweetmeat and
diversion.]Ms

149.18 see]E1
watch]Ms

149.24 audience? When
]E1
audience? The
great family Coach
was in waiting with
the flaming lamps,
the magnificent
horses and the huge
footman in powder
to convey this
happy party back
to Park Lane. Even
Miss Quigley the
governess forgot her
wrongs for that night
and owned to Lady
Jones's governess
next door that
Colonel Newcome's
behaviour to her
was that of a perfect

gentleman. As
for Ethel we have
stated that she and
her uncle fell in
love at first sight.
She showed her
Regard for him by
a thousand pretty
kindnesses, looks
and gestures. She
used to blush when
he came; her honest
eyes lighting up with
love and welcome
when she beheld
him, or when she
thought of him.
If she had had a
friend, a dear dear
darling friend as
most young ladies
of that age have I
have no doubt, she
would have covered
quires of letter paper
in discribing him,
But that blessing
had been denied
to Miss Ethel as
yet. She loved
Mamma of course
and Papa of course
too, but until Uncle
Newcome came it
seemed as if nobody
had been found
to love her. She
actually undertook
ornamental feminine
works in order to
make him presents.
She endowed him
with mysterious
book markers,
Cords for his watch,
anti macassars and
such like useful
articles. She learned
to net from the
housekeeper, in
order to make
Uncle Newcome a
purse, an immense
purse with the most
refulgent lapels and
the grandest gold
Rings. When]Ms

150. 2 schoolboy's tip? How
the kindness]E1
school boy's tip?
What a deal of

happiness can you
confer, worthy Sir
who have the coin to
spare with that little
piece of gold! How it
]Ms

150. 3 takes.]E1
takes,]Ms

150.13]E1
She made both uncle
and nephews fine
speeches upon the
occasion, warning
the discomfited elder
of the great evil
resulting from the
practice of giving
money to children;
of the sinfulness of
bribing their little
affections; creating
avaricious desires in
their young minds,
and so forth.]Ms

150.15 Lane.]E1
Lane, the goings
on in which house
formed the constant
subject of her
most virtuous
animadversion.]Ms

150.16 grown-up]E1
grown up]Ms

150.18 households.]E1
household.]Ms

150.24 a-piece]E1
apiece]Ms

150.25 pocket-money.]E1
pocket money.]Ms

150.29 Museum.]E1
museum.]Ms

150.31 exhibitions.]E1
exhibitions]Ms

150.34 Shakespeare,]E1
Shakespeare]Ms

151. 1 father? I]E1
father?—I]Ms

151. 4 sermon,]
sermon,:]Ms

151. 8 in loco parentis,]
'in loco parentis,']Ms

151.15 wife,]E1
wife]Ms

151.16 aristocracy.]
aristocracy]Ms

151.22 pocket-handkerchief.
¶Had]E1

pocket-handkerchief.
¶The little woman
had no idea as usual
but that she was
perfectly virtuous
and influenced by
the noblest motives.
No reasoning could
have convinced her
that she was jealous,
or vulgar, or wrong.
She never was wrong
in her own mind;
she was all humility,
honesty, simplicity;
and imbued with
the most virtuous
sentiments, and
uttering them
in fine language
for the benefit of
others. Considering
that she never
meddled with other
people's affairs, it
was wonderful how
well she knew them;
and, though she
went so seldom to
Park Lane, how
intimate she was with
all the transactions
which occurred in
that unlucky house.
The Colonel went
thither oftener than
he came to her—
of course—poor
dear Colonel! She
was afraid, afraid
that he had the
weakness of almost
all Englishmen—a
love for titles and
persons of rank
The Colonel took
the Park Lane
children to the
play;—Of course,
when people have
that unfortunate
weakness for rank
the commonest
artifice which
they employ is to
ingratiate themselves
with the children
of great families.
Did he ever ask to
take *her* children out

poor dear darlings.
Her father was but
a country lawyer
&c. &c. Meanwhile
the object of all this
sarcasm and scorn
and suspicion and
anger, was simply
the kindest soul
alive, and went to
see one kinswoman
often because her
home was pleasant;
and visited the other
seldom, because she
patronised him and
bored him. Very
likely the worthy
man had not made
the confession to
himself, but the
result was so. In
the one house he
was welcome and at
home in the other
he was received
with ceremoney
and a sermon:
and he could not
but percieve that
while Mrs. Hobson
was always never
alluding to Park
Lane Park Lane
left Mrs. Hobson,
and her doings and
her friends and her
parties, alone. ¶Had
]Ms

151.25 virtue.]E1
        virtue]Ms
151.27 Bey;]E1
        Bey]Ms
151.28 Rowe,]E1
        Rowe]Ms
151.28 Board of Control,
        ]E1
        board of Controle
        ]Ms
151.29 Rowe; the]E1
        Rowe, The]Ms
151.29 the]E1
        The]Ms
151.29 the]E1
        The]Ms
151.31 an]E1
        [omit]]Ms
152. 2 catalogue]E1

Catalogue]Ms
152. 3 habit]E1
        habits]Ms
152. 4 Control,]E1
        Controul,]Ms
152. 5 Ex-Governor]E1
        ExGovernor]Ms
152.18 shy.]
        shy,]Ms
152.24 farmer,]E1
        farmer]Ms
152.26 dear,]E1
        dear.]Ms
152.31 Newcome]
        N.]Ms
152.32 teapot,]E1
        teapot]Ms
152.33 have, I trust,]E1
        have I trust]Ms
152.38 family.]E1
        family. But I am
        a good man of
        business. I know a
        good horse, and I
        think I ain't a bad
        farmer.]Ms
152.39 dear.]E1
        Dear.]Ms
152.39 say,]E1
        say]Ms
152.40 her,]E1
        her]Ms
152.41 that;]E1
        that]Ms
152.43 City]
        city]Ms
152.43 house, No. 120,
        Fitzroy Square,]E1
        house]Ms
152.45 Indian]E1
        indian]Ms
153. 1 Newcome]E1
        Hobson]Ms
153. 2 friend. ¶The house
        ]E1
        friend. ¶He rides
        to the door of that
        handsome stone
        fronted, roomy,
        gloomy mansion
        Nos. 120. Fitzroy
        Square which Mr.
        Binnie and the
        Colonel had just
        engaged together.
        The house is so

spacious that there is
ample room for the
three establishments
which are about to
occupy it. There is a
large backparlour for
Mr. Binnie's library
which he has been
gathering with great
care for twenty years
past and which now
consists of several
thousand serviceable
volumes. This room
is considered to
be his own and
whenever he may
have a fancy to
retire to it, his
castle which no man
may enter. The
books which cover
the wall presently
make it the most
comfortable room in
the mansion. ¶The
house]Ms

153. 3 but,]
　　　　but]Ms

153. 3 owned,]E1
　　　　owned]Ms

153. 5 door,]E1
　　　　door]Ms

153. 8 corner.]E1
　　　　corner. Faint traces
　　　　of the ladies' school
　　　　still linger about
　　　　the mansion. In
　　　　the dingy upper
　　　　chambers are marks
　　　　against the walls
　　　　of many beds The
　　　　scholars ceased to
　　　　come the parlour
　　　　boarders did not pay.
　　　　The teachers could
　　　　not get their salaries,
　　　　]Ms

153.10 country]E1
　　　　country.]Ms

153.11 that]E1
　　　　hat]Ms

153.17 theatres,]E1
　　　　theatres]Ms

153.18 stories.]E1
　　　　stories—I do not
　　　　know in the least
　　　　who Mr. Sherrick's
　　　　father was.]Ms

153.19 Campion,]E1
　　　　[omit]]Ms

153.20 Wood,]E1
　　　　Wood]Ms

153.21 loud,]E1
　　　　aloud]Ms

153.23 bright-eyed]
　　　　bright eyed]Ms

153.25 ancestry,]E1
　　　　ancestory,]Ms

153.27 Binnie. ¶Mr.]E1
　　　　Binnie whom he
　　　　treated to a little
　　　　entertainment at
　　　　his lodgings. Mr.
　　　　Sherrick asked these
　　　　gentlemen to dinner
　　　　at St. John's Wood
　　　　where they met Lord
　　　　Bareacres. General
　　　　O'Locmy of the
　　　　Portuguese service.
　　　　Philip Barnes Lord
　　　　Kew's brother all
　　　　gentlemen of rank
　　　　and station and Mr.
　　　　Boss the celebrated
　　　　Bass singer. T. R.
　　　　D. L. and T. R. C.
　　　　G. and Galpin the
　　　　delightful ternor.
　　　　They had a very
　　　　pleasant evening.
　　　　A great deal of
　　　　after dinner music,
　　　　though the Colonel
　　　　steadfastly refused
　　　　to sing. Clive was
　　　　not of this dinner.
　　　　He and his friend
　　　　Digby finding better
　　　　amusement at the
　　　　play. ¶Well. The
　　　　result of this new
　　　　acquaintance was
　　　　that Mr. Sherrick
　　　　having a large and
　　　　commodious house.
　　　　No. 120. Fitzroy
　　　　Square. To let on
　　　　very reasonable
　　　　terms, Colonel
　　　　Newcome and Mr.
　　　　Binnie agreed to
　　　　take it between
　　　　them, and Mr.]Ms
　　　　[Begin Thackeray's hand]

154. 1 dear,]
　　　　dear]Ms

154. 3 hand,]E1
　　　　hand]Ms

154. 3 did,]E1
　　　　did]Ms

154. 5 taken,]E1
　　　　taken]Ms

154. 6 Clive,]E1
　　　　Clive]Ms

154. 6 Colonel,]E1
　　　　Colonel]Ms

154. 8 [Note: A portion
　　　　of manuscript (pp.
　　　　54.9-56.26) originally
　　　　meant to continue
　　　　at this point in
　　　　installment #5 (p.
　　　　154.8) was cut when
　　　　the installment
　　　　overflowed its
　　　　allotted 32 printed
　　　　pages. It was
　　　　inserted in #6 (text
　　　　corresponding to
　　　　pages 172.1-173.18
　　　　in this edition)
　　　　when copy for
　　　　that installment
　　　　ran short. The
　　　　transfer and some
　　　　revisions it entailed
　　　　were undertaken,
　　　　apparently, by
　　　　Percival Leigh in
　　　　Thackeray's absence
　　　　in Italy. The new
　　　　(published) order is
　　　　maintained in the
　　　　present edition.
　　　　Therefore, the
　　　　emendations for the
　　　　passage are listed
　　　　in the next number
　　　　at the beginning of
　　　　chapter 19, though
　　　　the manuscript
　　　　(the copy-text) puts
　　　　the passage at this
　　　　point.]

154. 8 house.]E1
　　　　house]Ms

154. 9 son,]
　　　　son]Ms

154.10 Binnie,]
　　　　Binnie]Ms

154.12 pot,]E1
　　　　pot]Ms

154.14 Schiedam.]

Schidan.]Ms

154.16 corner.]E1
corner for those
who read this
simple story may
understand how my
acquaintance with
Colonel Newcome
speedily ripened into
a friendship and
in what a sincere
regard I held him.
]Ms

154.20 blear-eyed boot-boy
to the rosy-cheeked
]E1
blear eyed boot boy
to the rosy cheeked
]Ms

154.22 postures—asleep,
]E1
postures asleep,]Ms

154.24 horseback—and]
horseback and]Ms

154.26 sketches.]E1
sketches]Ms

154.27 Clive,]
Grindley]Ms

154.28 over,]E1
over]Ms

154.28 Gandish's Drawing
Academy where, to
be sure,]
Gandishes drawing
academy where to be
sure]Ms

[Begin Thackeray's hand]

155. 1 A SCHOOL OF ART.
]E1
[omit]]Ms

155. 1 her]E1
its]Ms

155. 3 her]E1
its]Ms

155. 5 but]E1
[omit]]Ms

155. 6 accommodations]E1
accommodation]Ms

155.13 chairmen]E1
chair man]Ms

155.18 fashion]E1
Fashion]Ms

155.22 hair powdered,]E1
hair-powdered,]Ms

155.23 painter's]E1
Painter's]Ms

155.25 decadence:]E1
decadence]Ms

155.25 chooses]E1
Chooses]Ms

155.26 Bloomsbury, let us
say,]E1
Bloomsbury let us
say]Ms

156. 1 physicians]E1
Physicians]Ms

156. 2 look,]E1
look]Ms

156. 3 doctor's]E1
Doctor's]Ms

156. 4 physician]
Physician]Ms

156. 7 north window;]E1
north-window;]Ms

157.10 turn.]E1
turn.]Ms

157.13 the]E1
The]Ms

157.18 school-books]E1
school books]Ms

157.23 art *en règle*,]
Art *en règle*,]Ms

[Begin Anne's hand]

157.25 portrait-painter,
Alfred]E1
portrait painter,
Frederick]Ms

157.33 nymph-like]E1
nymph like]Ms

158. 5 capital, by Jove,]E1
capital by Jove]Ms

158. 7 sketch,]E1
sketch]Ms

158.13 now-a-days!—And]
now a days!—And
]Ms

158.14 sittings—the]
sittings—The]Ms

158.15 Cavalry—the]
Cavalry The]Ms

158.16 picture—it]
picture—It]Ms

158.16 declared,]E1
declared]Ms

158.24 course]E1
course,]Ms

158.34 humbug,]E1
hum-bugg]Ms

158.37 expense.]E1
expence.]Ms

159. 4 street-boys]E1
street boys]Ms

[Begin Thackeray's hand]

159. 5 then,]E1
then]Ms

159. 9 son,]
son]Ms

159.12 Jove,]E1
Jove]Ms

159.15 says, 'Hars est celare
Hartem,']E1
says Hars est celare
Hartem]Ms

159.16 wine,]E1
wine]Ms

160. 2 span. He]E1
span—He]Ms

160. 4 Mrs.]E1
the Mrs.]Ms

160. 5 best,]E1
best]Ms

160. 9 would:]E1
would]Ms

160. 9 Guys,]
Guys]Ms

160.12 Friars,]E1
Friars]Ms

160.14 steady, you know,
]E1
steady you know
]Ms

161. 6 arm,]E1
arm]Ms

161.15 Cowper,]E1
Cowper]Ms

161.16 lad. ¶"When the
British warrior
queen, / Bleeding
from the Roman
rods— [*line space*]
"Jolly verses! Haven't
I translated them
into Alcaics?" says
Clive, with a merry
laugh, and resumes
his history.]
lad. ¶'When the
British warrior
queen, / Bleeding
from the Roman
rods'— [*line space*]
"Jolly verses! Haven't
I translated them
into Alcaics?" says
Clive, with a merry
laugh, and resumes
his history.]E1

lad. ¶"When the
British Queen.
[*line space*] Trochaic
Tetrameter—*I*
remember:" and he
broke into a merry
laugh.]Ms

161.22 Gandish, you see,
was not]E1
Gandish you see was
]Ms

161.24 chicken,]E1
chicken]Ms

161.26 "'Admired.]
"'Admired]Ms

161.26 time. *Morning*]
time—*Morning*]Ms

161.27 it. My son as an
infant,]E1
it— My Son as an
Infant]Ms

161.28 Serpent, over the
piano. Fust]E1
Serpent over the
piano—Fust]Ms

161.29 *Non*]E1
non]Ms

162. 1 on,]E1
on]Ms

162. 6 first-rate]E1
first rate]Ms

162. 8 Babes in the Wood—
View]E1
babes in the wood—
View]Ms

162.10 Nelson—allegorical
]E1
Nelson—Allegorical
]Ms

162.13 antique. There's]E1
Antique there's]Ms

162.15 also from]E1
from also]Ms

162.21 'ut.]E1
'Ut.]Ms

162.23 burn,]E1
burn]Ms

162.26 background]E1
back ground]Ms

162.26 hopening,]E1
hopening]Ms

162.28 aperture,]E1
aperture]Ms

163. 1 lead you]E1
lead-you]Ms

163. 2 Gallery—Apollo,]E1

163. 2 Gallery—Apollo]Ms

163. 2 Hanadyomene,]E1
hanadyomene,]Ms

163. 3 Nimth, you see,]E1
Nimth you see]Ms

163. 6 *Vita*—' ¶"I]E1
Vita;' I]Ms

163.10 drawing-boards]E1
drawing]Ms

163.12 friend—what]E1
friend what]Ms

163.13 too,]E1
too]Ms

163.14 custos]E1
Custos]Ms

163.16 gentlemen.]
gentlemen]Ms

163.17 *est*—This]E1
est. —This]Ms

163.18 court yard]E1
Court Yard]Ms

163.18 studio,]E1
Studio,]Ms

163.21 ...'"]E1
..'"]Ms

163.25 in,]E1
in]Ms

163.25 'just a-going to
begin!'"]E1
just a going to
begin!"]Ms

163.28 master;]E1
Master;]Ms

[Begin Anne's hand]

163.31 drawing-board, a
poor mean-looking
]E1
drawing board, a
poor mean looking
]Ms

164.13 "out-and-outer,"]E1
"out and outer,"]Ms

164.16 red-haired]E1
red haired]Ms

165. 4 leck-spettles,]E1
leck spettles,]Ms

165. 8 the]E1
The]Ms

165.14 justice,]E1
justice]Ms

165.17 Prison and Hogarth
Painting Him, of the
Blowing]E1
prison and Hogarth
painting him, of the
blowing]Ms

165.19 Torture]E1
torture]Ms

165.19 Murder]E1
murder]Ms

165.20 Murder of Rizzio
]E1
murder of Rizio]Ms

165.31 academy,]E1
academy]Ms

[Begin Thackeray's hand]

166. 2 fellow-students]E1
fellow students]Ms

167. 1 NEW COMPANIONS.
]E1
[*omit*]]Ms

167. 5 gaiety]E1
gaiety,]Ms

167. 9 public-house]E1
public house]Ms

167.14 well-inclined]E1
well inclined]Ms

168. 1 studio,]E1
Studio,]Ms

168. 4 Oriental]E1
oriental]Ms

168. 6 way,]E1
way:]Ms

168. 7 Doocob, ady day idto
Vorder Street,"]E1
Doocob ady day idth
Vorder Street,"]Ms

168.11 "Yoicks!]E1
"Yoicks]Ms

168.12 brother,]E1
brother]Ms

168.13 theatre tickets]E1
theatre-tickets]Ms

168.21 M'Collop,]E1
M'Collop]Ms

168.24 junior scholars,]E1
Junior Scholars,]Ms

168.27 lithographic]E1
lithograph]Ms

168.29 school]E1
School]Ms

168.30 senior]E1
Senior]Ms

168.31 sweetstuff]E1
sweet stuff]Ms

168.36 arts of design—
Barker's;]E1
Arts of design—
Barkers;]Ms

169. 1 Gandishites.
　　　　Between]E1
　　　　Gandishites—
　　　　Between]Ms
169. 3 medallists;]E1
　　　　medallists]Ms
169. 4 student]E1
　　　　Student]Ms
169. 9 coffee house and
　　　　billiard-room,]E1
　　　　Coffee House and
　　　　Billiard-room,]Ms
169.11 Gandish's,]E1
　　　　Gandish's:]Ms
169.13 coffee-house]E1
　　　　Coffee-House]Ms
169.22 biceps,]E1
　　　　Biceps,]Ms
169.24 artists;]E1
　　　　Artists;]Ms
169.25 F.B.]E1
　　　　F.B.,]Ms
169.32 Gandish's, that
　　　　academy]E1
　　　　Gandish's that
　　　　Academy]Ms
170. 1 academy]E1
　　　　Academy]Ms
170. 5 club]E1
　　　　Club]Ms
[Begin Anne's hand]
170. 9 pupils.]E1
　　　　pupils,]Ms
170.10 horseback,]
　　　　horseback]Ms
170.12 did.]E1
　　　　did,]Ms
170.14 Junior,]E1
　　　　Junior]Ms
170.14 business,]E1
　　　　business]Ms
170.15 which,]E1
　　　　which]Ms
170.15 volume, one of the
　　　　]E1
　　　　volume one of The
　　　　]Ms
170.17 Dominicans]
　　　　Dominicains]Ms
170.21 Monarch—to]
　　　　Monarch to]Ms
170.29 proboscis;]
　　　　proboscis]Ms
170.31 bag,]
　　　　bag]Ms

170.32 hunchback]E1
　　　　hunch back]Ms
170.42 Old Hodge, he
　　　　avers,]E1
　　　　old Hodge, he avers
　　　　]Ms
170.43 college,]E1
　　　　College,]Ms
171. 9 Moss,]E1
　　　　Moss]Ms
171.11 shirt-studs, flaming
　　　　shirt-pins,]
　　　　shirtstuds, flaming
　　　　shirt pins,]Ms
171.12 generally,]E1
　　　　generally]Ms
171.17 drawing-board]E1
　　　　drawing board]Ms
[Begin Thackeray's hand]
171.29 Clive Newcome's
　　　　]E1
　　　　Clive-Newcome's
　　　　]Ms
171.36 bric-a-brac shop]E1
　　　　bric a brac-shop]Ms
171.36 two]
　　　　Two]Ms
171.37 gentlemen,]E1
　　　　gentlemen]Ms
171.37 old clothes-men,]E1
　　　　old-clothes-men,
　　　　]Ms
171.39 rack-punch]E1
　　　　rack punch]Ms
172.n1 [Note: The
　　　　beginning of this
　　　　chapter (172.1–
　　　　172.18) is taken from
　　　　manuscript pages
　　　　54.9-56.25 originally
　　　　intended for
　　　　number 5 (at 154.8).
　　　　Number 5 had too
　　　　much manuscript
　　　　and number 6
　　　　came up short.
　　　　Percival Leigh,
　　　　Thackeray's assistant
　　　　in London, moved
　　　　the passage in an
　　　　attempt to make
　　　　the installments
　　　　the right length.
　　　　That movement is
　　　　maintained in this
　　　　edition.]
172. 1 Our good Colonel's
　　　　house]E1

　　　　It]Ms
172. 5 ghastly.]E1
　　　　gahstly.]Ms
172. 8 conservatory,]E1
　　　　Conservatory,]Ms
172.11 cistern, the]E1
　　　　cistern. The]Ms
172.17 crockery—a]E1
　　　　crockery a]Ms
172.17 supplies,]E1
　　　　suplies]Ms
172.17 word,]E1
　　　　word]Ms
172.22 stair-carpets?]E1
　　　　staircarpets?]Ms
172.23 lumber:]
　　　　lumber.]Ms
172.23 camphor]E1
　　　　Camphor]Ms
172.24 Anything]
　　　　anything]Ms
172.26 splendour—a]
　　　　splendour a]Ms
172.26 glass—whereas]E1
　　　　glass whereas]Ms
172.28 breeches—and]E1
　　　　breeches and]Ms
172.29 bare—as]E1
　　　　bare as]Ms
173. 5 Street.]
　　　　Street]Ms
173. 9 Court, Temple,]E1
　　　　Court temple,]Ms
173.10 Fred Bayham.]E1
　　　　Dick Bahon.]Ms
173.10 Fred Bayham. Fred
　　　　Bayham]E1
　　　　Dick Bahon. Dick
　　　　Bahon]Ms
173.12 lately—and]E1
　　　　lately and]Ms
173.13 friends—is]E1
　　　　friends. Is]Ms
173.14 F.B.]E1
　　　　R.B.]Ms
173.15 F.B.]E1
　　　　R.B.]Ms
173.17 house,]E1
　　　　house]Ms
173.18 pleasant. He, who
　　　　]E1
　　　　pleasant. Our good
　　　　Colonel who]Ms

174. 4 seul]E1
Seul]Ms
174. 7 was,]E1
was]Ms
174. 8 son. "Look]E1
son—"Look]Ms
174. 9 say.]
say]Ms
174.12 upbraid'—There]
upbraid' There]Ms
174.17 artists.]E1
artists]Ms
175. 5 insignificance—
without, I trust,
]
insignificance—
Without I trust
]Ms
175.14 Academy. Surely
]E1
Academy.—Surely
]Ms
175.17 little,]E1
little]Ms
175.17 perhaps,]
perhaps]Ms
175.20 Hut (he]E1
hut he]Ms
175.20 subject) in 180–:
]E1
subject in 180[blank]:
]Ms
175.21 victory]E1
Victory]Ms
175.25 year. So]E1
year—So]Ms
175.28 piece."]E1
piece—"]Ms
175.38 anon. The]E1
anon—The]Ms
[Begin Anne's hand]
176. 4 performance,]
performance.]Ms
176. 5 professional]E1
professeonal]Ms
176. 6 puzzled, honest]
puzzled. Honest
]Ms
176. 9 her?—her]E1
her?—Her]Ms
176.14 commenced,]E1
commenced]Ms
176.16 sister-in-law]E1
sester]Ms
176.23 it.)]E1

it)]Ms
176.25 creature,]E1
creature]Ms
176.27 everything;]E1
everthing]Ms
176.32 coming,]E1
coming]Ms
176.32 She]E1
(She]Ms
176.33 fan.]E1
fan)]Ms
176.37 know,]E1
know]Ms
176.38 and Mr. McSheny,
the]E1
Mr. McSheng. The
]Ms
177. 2 you.]E1
you]Ms
177. 5 hodman,"]E1
Hodman,"]Ms
177. 9 announced,]E1
announced]Ms
177.15 court-dress]E1
Court dress]Ms
177.16 comers,]E1
comers]Ms
177.17 Quaker-like]E1
quakerlike]Ms
177.18 has,]E1
has]Ms
177.21 the]
The]Ms
177.23 into]E1
in to]Ms
177.23 foot,]E1
foot]Ms
177.23 is,]E1
is]Ms
[Begin Anne's hand]
177.25 mischievous]E1
mischeveous]Ms
177.30 arrive,—what]E1
arrive, What]Ms
177.31 Angels;]
Angels,]Ms
177.32 dessert.]E1
desert.]Ms
177.34 homely,]E1
homely]Ms
177.37 groups]E1
groupes]Ms
177.38 about,]E1
about]Ms
177.38 gentlemen,]E1

gentlemen]Ms
177.40 dam—let's]E1
Dam—let's]Ms
178. 2 button-hole,]E1
button hole,]Ms
178. 4 (and]E1
and]Ms
178. 5 elsewhere).]E1
elsewhere.]Ms
178. 6 dinner?]E1
Dinner?]Ms
178. 7 aunt, I know,]E1
aunt I know]Ms
[Begin Thackeray's hand]
178.10 companion;]
companion]Ms
178.11 harlequin. There's
]E1
Harlequin—There's
]Ms
178.12 drawing-master:]
drawing Master:
]Ms
178.13 must]E1
Must]Ms
178.24 Lords,]E1
Lords]Ms
178.30 waistcoat,]E1
waistcoat]Ms
178.36 carriage, the]E1
carriage—the]Ms
179. 9 spirit.]E1
Spirit.]Ms
179.10 portrait—Stockholm,
I think,]E1
portrait—Stockholm
I think]Ms
179.14 lordship's]E1
lordship]Ms
179.15 professor.]E1
Professor.]Ms
179.16 Elders,"]E1
elders,"]Ms
179.18 painted.]E1
painted]Ms
179.33 person,]E1
person]Ms
179.36 difficulty,]E1
difficulty]Ms
179.37 Gandish's,]E1
Gandish's]Ms
180. 1 CONTAINS MORE
PARTICULARS OF THE
COLONEL AND HIS
BRETHREN.]E1

an arm which has
]E1

203.27 shoulders,]R
shoulder,]E1

204. 6 rapt]R
wrapt]E1

205.33 *ami?'*]
ami?']E1

206.16 Bouillotte.]R
Bouilotte.]E1

207.37 'Jock]R
'Jack]E1

215.27 other.]R
other,]E1

215.29 compliments]R
comliments]E1

215.30 Lorraine':]
Lorraine:']E1

228.18 common-places]
common-/places]E1

229.35 you?":]
you?"]E1

230.37 songs.]R
songs,]E1

233.38 smooth]R
smoothe]E1

233.44 woman.]
woman,]E1

234.22 *Morning Press*]
Morning Press]E1

236.26 three]HM NY
the three]E1 R

240.34 her]R
her,]E1

242.27 attend]R
attends]E1

246.27 Calcutta.]R
Calcutta,]E1

259.34 billiards.]R
billiards,]E1

266. 2 number]R
mumber]E1

266.39 means]R
mean]E1

278.11 Kew.]
Kew,]E1

278.45 What do]
Do]E1

278.45 Jack Belsize]
Belsize, Jack Belsize
]E1

279.10 Frenchman]
Frenchmen]E1

[Begin Anne's hand]

281. 1 A RETREAT.]E1

[*omit*]]Ms

281.19 stirring,]E1
stirring]Ms

281.25 Seltzer-water]E1
Seltza water]Ms

281.26 gases]E1
gasses]Ms

281.26 air]E1
air,]Ms

281.29 was,]E1
was]Ms

281.34 Seltzer-water]E1
seltza water]Ms

282. 1 and]E1
[*omit*]]Ms

282. 3 labour;]E1
labour,]Ms

282. 8 boy;]E1
boy,]Ms

282. 9 doing;]E1
doing,]Ms

282.11 said, 'Clive,]E1
said Clive,]Ms

282.11 on.'"]E1
on."]Ms

282.13 pure-minded little
J.J.,]E1
pure minded little
J.J.]Ms

282.15 Exhibition. ¶"Are
]E1
exhibition. "Are]Ms

282.21 Hasdrubal."]E1
Hasdrubbal."]Ms

282.22 Hasdrubal]E1
Hasdrubbal]Ms

282.22 answered;]E1
answered]Ms

282.27 portent;]E1
portent]Ms

282.28 crony]E1
croney]Ms

282.29 him;]E1
him]Ms

282.29 word,]E1
word]Ms

282.34 carnation]E1
carnations]Ms

282.39 Assumption]E1
assumption]Ms

282.42 hymns]
Hymns]Ms

282.42 altars; and somewhat
as he worshipped
these masterpieces of

his art he admired
the beauty of Ethel.
]
altars; and,
somewhat as he
worshipped these
masterpieces of his
art he admired the
beauty of Ethel.]E1
altars.]Ms

283. 2 song;]E1
song]Ms

283. 7 painting-board,]E1
painting board,]Ms

283. 7 frequently,]E1
frequently]Ms

283. 8 manner,]E1
manner]Ms

283. 9 lungs— [*line space*]
"But]E1
lungs ¶"But]Ms

283.10 another's, she
never—can—be—
—mine."]
another's she
never—can—be—
—mine."]Ms

283.12 Night, the Grey
Mentor,]E1
night, the grey
mentor,]Ms

283.14 counsel:]
counsil:]Ms

283.19 the]E1
his]Ms

283.20 Only]E1
But]Ms

283.21 Bonn]E1
Bonn,]Ms

283.23 as]E1
was]Ms

283.27 self-denial]E1
self denial]Ms

283.28 remember,]E1
remember]Ms

283.30 "do you remember
]E1
"Do you remember"
]Ms

283.31 my]E1
"My]Ms

283.31 running away]E1
Running away"]Ms

283.32 waistcoat),]E1
waistcoat)]Ms

283.32 Asseer-Ghur?—"]E1
    Asseerghur?—"]Ms
283.35 siege of Asseer-
    Ghur,"]
    siege of Asseer-
    Ghur!"]E1
    battle of Asseerghur,"
    ]Ms
283.35 in]E1
    on]Ms
283.35 year 1803;]E1
    day]Ms
283.36 legs,]E1
    legs]Ms
283.36 you,]E1
    you]Ms
283.38 breeches,]E1
    breeches]Ms
284. 1 Sir. What]
    Sir—What]Ms
284. 3 about,]E1
    about]Ms
284. 3 Mahratta]E1
    ——]Ms
284. 4 run,]E1
    Run,]Ms
284. 5 Ridley.]E1
    Ridley,]Ms
284. 9 servant.]E1
    Servant.]Ms
284. 9 Asseer-Ghur."]E1
    Asseerghur."]Ms
284.12 "J.J.,]E1
    "J.J.]Ms
284.12 Asseer-Ghur.]E1
    Asseerghur.]Ms
284.16 labours.]E1
    labours,]Ms
284.17 De—No—God bless
    her,]E1
    De..No—God bless
    her]Ms
284.19 before,]E1
    before]Ms
285. 1 And if]E1
    If]Ms
285. 2 him,]E1
    him]Ms
285. 3 battle,]E1
    battle]Ms
285. 3 us, from]E1
    us in]Ms
285. 5 was,]E1
    was]Ms
285. 9 hotel,]E1

hotel]Ms
285.13 hour;]E1
    hour]Ms
285.15 then, laughing,]E1
    then laughing]Ms
    MS 28501 go,]E1
    go]Ms
285.19 Gothard,]E1
    Gothard]Ms
285.19 me,]E1
    me]Ms
285.22 Vett.?"]E1
    Vett?"]Ms
285.23 manner.]E1
    manner—]Ms
285.29 dragon.]E1
    Dragon.]Ms
285.30 carriage,]E1
    carriage]Ms
285.30 thing,]E1
    thing]Ms
285.31 two,]E1
    two]Ms
285.31 traps, you know,]E1
    traps you know]Ms
285.35 course,]E1
    course]Ms
285.38 Clive.]
    Clive,]E1
285.42 disagreeable]E1
    disagreable]Ms
286. 6 out, "can]E1
    out. "Can]Ms
286.11 ill-treated,]E1
    ill treated]Ms
286.12 towards]E1
    to wards]Ms
286.15 maintenance.]E1
    maintainance.]Ms
286.18 O, it]E1
    O It]Ms
286.19 shame,]E1
    shame]Ms
286.23 family,]E1
    family]Ms
286.24 Heavens!]
    Heavens]Ms
286.28 town,]E1
    town]Ms
286.29 clubs.]E1
    Clubs.]Ms
286.33 well,]E1
    well]Ms
286.38 DeLacy]
    Delacy]Ms

286.42 connexion:]E1
    connexion]Ms
286.43 remorse—annoyance
    ]E1
    remorse annoyance
    ]Ms
286.47 sorry,]E1
    sorry]Ms
287. 2 boat, you know,]E1
    boat you know]Ms
287. 3 everything, the
    elders]E1
    every thing The
    Elders]Ms
287. 4 agreeable]E1
    agreable]Ms
287. 6 tortures,]E1
    tortures]Ms
287.19 indeed, young fellow,
    ]E1
    indeed young fellow
    ]Ms
287.25 shindies]E1
    shintys]Ms
287.26 *apropos*]E1
    à propos]Ms
287.28 father,]E1
    father]Ms
287.30 and]E1
    And]Ms
287.33 conversation—"This
    ]
    conversation. "This
    ]Ms
287.35 billing—Pshaw!]E1
    billing—Pshaw]Ms
287.45 and]E1
    And]Ms
288. 2 if]
    If]Ms
288. 9 attorney-general,
    ]E1
    attorney general,
    ]Ms
288.13 itself,]E1
    itself]Ms
288.14 costermongers]
    Costermongers]Ms
288.16 handbasket."]E1
    hand basket."]Ms
288.19 was,]E1
    was.]MS
288.21 a]E1
    an]Ms

288.22 a-year: do]
a year: Do]Ms

288.29 opposite,]E1
opposite]Ms

288.33 parchment-covered
]E1
parchment covered
]Ms

288.33 well-known]E1
well known]Ms

288.35 promontory]E1
promontary]Ms

288.36 nose,]E1
nose]Ms

288.39 Kew,]E1
Kew]Ms

288.40 sizes,]E1
sizes]Ms

288.46 name,]E1
name]Ms

289. 1 chamber-door]
chamber door]Ms

289. 2 scoundrel]E1
scoundrell]Ms

289. 3 discomfiture]
discomfitiure]Ms

289. 5 mystery,]E1
mystery]Ms

289.11 supercilious "How de
dah"]
supecilious How de
dah]Ms

289.12 would have liked
]E1
was obliged]Ms

289.14 inspired]E1
inspirired]Ms

289.15 impartial,]E1
impartial]Ms

289.15 own,]E1
own]Ms

289.16 degree, to]E1
degree—to]Ms

289.18 betters,]E1
betters]Ms

289.22 "We were standing
apart from the
ladies," so Clive
narrated, "when
Barnes and I had
our little passage of
arms. He]E1
"He]Ms

289.24 before, and]E1
before," Clive said,
"and]Ms

289.26 beggar]E1
beggar,]Ms

289.28 oaths."]E1
oaths.]Ms

289.30 Barnes."]E1
Barnes:"]Ms

289.37 him." And]E1
him," and]Ms

289.41 good-natured: "no]
good-natured. "No
]Ms

289.42 Our young friend,
]E1
For our young friend
]Ms

289.42 premised,]E1
premised]Ms

290. 1 entering,]E1
entering]Ms

290. 4 a-whispering; and
then it]E1
a whispering; And
then It]Ms

290.14 Clive,]E1
Clive]Ms

290.19 fellow,]E1
fellow]Ms

290. 2 lonely—but—but]
lonely—But—But
]Ms

290.28 you with him]E1
him with you]Ms

290.32 spirit,]E1
spirit.]Ms

290.33 you; but Lady]E1
you, But lady]Ms

290.39 good-humour;]E1
goodhumour]Ms

290.43 talents—these]E1
talents these]Ms

291. 1 we—how]E1
we how]Ms

291. 8 matters,]E1
matters]Ms

291.21 Bogey]
Boguey]Ms

291.22 friend,]E1
friend]Ms

291.30 him—not]E1
him not]Ms

291.33 yesterday,]E1
yesterday]Ms

291.35 Finck]E1
Strumpf]Ms

291.37 lodgings,]E1

lodgings]Ms

291.38 tipsy]E1
tipsey]Ms

291.38 engaged,]E1
engaged]Ms

291.38 know,]E1
know]Ms

291.41 woman,]E1
woman]Ms

291.45 brats]
brats"]Ms

291.46 windows), You]
windows,) "You]Ms

292. 4 unconscious]E1
unconsious]Ms

292. 4 sister;]E1
sister]Ms

292. 5 says,]E1
says.]Ms

292. 7 until]E1
untill]Ms

292. 9 too,—that]
too,—That]Ms

292. 9 Miss—what]E1
miss what]Ms

292.12 surprised]E1
surprised.]Ms

292.14 And, indeed,]E1
And indeed]Ms

292.14 fact,]E1
fact]Ms

292.17 likely, Ethel,]E1
likely Ethel]Ms

292.18 circumstance,]E1
circumstance]Ms

292.19 cross-examination,
]E1
cross examination,
]Ms

292.20 grandmother,]E1
grandmother]Ms

292.23 wounded,]E1
wounded]Ms

292.24 Newcome]E1
Newcome,]Ms

292.26 cousin,]E1
cousin]Ms

292.27 imperturbable]E1
impurturbable]Ms

292.29 moment,]E1
moment]Ms

292.30 haughty—almost
]E1
haughty almost]Ms

292.31 entered,]E1
    entered]Ms
292.31 Countess's]E1
    Countesses]Ms
292.33 "Yes,]E1
    "Yes]Ms
292.34 Rome;]E1
    Rome]Ms
292.35 bless]E1
    Bless]Ms
292.36 "Good]
    "good]Ms
292.40 good]
    Good]Ms
292.40 roaring,]E1
    roaring]Ms
292.41 trowsers.]E1
    trowsers,]Ms
292.41 gaily,]E1
    gaily]Ms
292.43 faces,]E1
    faces]Ms
292.46 Est-ce]E1
    Est ce]Ms
292.47 Hôtel]E1
    Hotel]Ms
292.48 let's]E1
    Let's]Ms
293. 2 Indeed,]E1
    Indeed]Ms
293. 4 pine-clad]E1
    pine clad]Ms
293. 5 lime-tree]E1
    Lime tree]Ms
293. 5 Baden,]E1
    Baden]Ms
293. 5 booth]E1
    boothe]Ms
293. 8 Hôtel]E1
    Hotel]Ms
293. 8 of,]E1
    of]Ms
293.12 companions,]E1
    companions]Ms
293.12 horses,]E1
    horses]Ms
293.13 Ethel.]E1
    Ethel,]Ms
293.14 quiet]E1
    Quiet]Ms
293.15 out,]E1
    out]Ms
293.17 personage]E1
    personnage]Ms
293.18 too.]E1

too]Ms
293.19 carpet-bag,]E1
    carpet bag,]Ms
293.19 word,]E1
    word]Ms
293.21 Hôtel]E1
    Hotel]Ms
293.22 there]
    There]Ms
293.24 "Tiens,]E1
    "Tiens]Ms
293.25 "Yes,]E1
    "Yes]Ms
293.25 place,]E1
    place]Ms
293.28 Seigneur]E1
    seigneur]Ms
293.29 me:—affaires d'état,
    mon cher, affaires
    d'état."]E1
    me Affaires d'État,
    mon cher affaires
    d'État."]Ms
293.30 bag!"]E1
    bag,"]Ms
293.31 Princess]
    Princesse]Ms
293.33 Florac.]E1
    Florac]Ms
293.35 that?"]E1
    that"]Ms
293.36 Hôtel]E1
    Hotel]Ms
293.37 back,]E1
    back]Ms
293.37 face.]E1
    face,]Ms
293.39 handshaking,]
    handshaking]Ms
[Begin Thackeray's hand]
294. 9 le]E1
    Le]Ms
294.12 Q]
    Q.]Ms
294.12 Madame]E1
    Madame la Duchesse]Ms
294.12 travels,]E1
    Travels,]Ms
294.13 Crusaders,"]E1
    Crusaders."]Ms
294.14 Q]E1
    Q.]Ms
294.19 was,]E1
    was]Ms

294.20 Kew,]E1
    Kew]Ms
294.24 nothing,]E1
    nothing]Ms
294.26 opera:]
    Opera:]Ms
294.28 anchorites. She
    describes,]
    Anchorites. She
    describes]Ms
294.29 catastrophe,]
    Catastrophe]Ms
294.31 *apropos*]E1
    apropos]Ms
294.31 granaries,]E1
    granaries]Ms
294.32 old savage]
    old, savage,]Ms
295. 1 tyrant. They]E1
    tyrant.—they]Ms
295. 1 copy]E1
    Copy]Ms
295. 7 France]E1
    France [Begin Anne's
    hand] France]Ms
295. 8 *mariages*]E1
    marriages]Ms
295.11 de]E1
    [*omit*]]Ms
295.15 *étude d'avoué,*]E1
    Etude d'Avoue,]Ms
295.18 concluded]E1
    concluded,]Ms
295.20 personally]E1
    personnally]Ms
295.29 revolution—when]
    revolution—When
    ]Ms
295.32 Crusaders,—being]
    crusaders,—Being
    ]Ms
295.37 Cœur]E1
    Coeur]Ms
295.40 Dauphine]E1
    Dauphine,]Ms
295.43 hair,]E1
    hair]Ms
296. 3 d'Ivrys—the]
    d'Ivrys,—the]E1
    d'Ivrys and so on,—
    the]Ms
296. 8 you]E1
    You]Ms
296.12 cannot]E1

can not]Ms

296.13 years.]E1
       years,]Ms

296.14 himself,"]E1
       himself"]Ms

296.21 fists]E1
       fists,]Ms

296.23 peerage,]E1
       peerage]Ms

296.24 *terres.*]
       Terres.]Ms

296.25 nearest kinsman,
       ]E1
       cousin]Ms

296.34 pilgrimages]E1
       Pilgrimages]Ms

296.39 their]E1
       the]Ms

296.41 another,]E1
       another]Ms

296.42 nay,]E1
       nay]Ms

297. 5 Ennui,]E1
       Ennui]Ms

297. 6 Old]E1
       old]Ms

297. 6 Sea;]E1
       sea;]Ms

297. 9 d'Ivry,]E1
       d'Ivry]Ms

297.11 jealousy]E1
       Jealousy]Ms

297.13 rheumatism.
       Coming]E1
       Rheumatism coming
       ]Ms

297.14 innocent]E1
       Innocent]Ms

297.15 *convenance,*]
       convenance]Ms

[Begin Thackeray's hand]

297.26 d'Ivry,]E1
       d'Ivry]Ms

297.28 success.]E1
       success,]Ms

297.29 marriage,]E1
       marriage]Ms

297.30 saloons]E1
       Saloons]Ms

297.33 her.]E1
       her:]Ms

297.35 sombrero]E1
       Sombrero]Ms

297.37 she]E1
       She]Ms

297.38 sanguineous]E1
       sanguines]Ms

297.39 sacks,]E1
       Sacks,]Ms

297.42 writer, certainly
       immortal;]E1
       writer—certainly
       immortal]Ms

297.42 de]E1
       de.]Ms

297.43 *pensant,*]E1
       pensant]Ms

297.45 style,]
       style]Ms

297.46 Dumases]
       Dumass]Ms

298. 1 "M.]E1
       M.]Ms

298. 2 Monsieur,"]E1
       Monsieur,]Ms

298. 2 say, "when]E1
       say when]Ms

298. 2 forgotten."]E1
       forgotten.]Ms

298. 3 coulisses]E1
       Coulisses]Ms

298. 6 ¶For some little time
       ]E1
       ¶During the first
       years]Ms

298. 8 turn,]E1
       turn]Ms

298. 9 MADAME]E1
       MADAM]Ms

298.11 home, however,]E1
       home however]Ms

298.16 anything. M. le Duc,
       ]E1
       any thing. M. le.
       Duc]Ms

298.17 Goritz,]E1
       Goritz]Ms

298.21 into]E1
       in]Ms

298.21 *apropos*]E1
       apropos]Ms

298.22 nephew,]E1
       nephew]Ms

298.23 Florac,]E1
       Florac]Ms

298.26 owned—only]
       owned only]Ms

298.30 plump,]E1
       plump]Ms

298.33 mood,]E1

mood:]Ms

298.36 brother,]E1
       brother]Ms

298.36 Florac,]E1
       Florac]Ms

298.40 archiroyaliste,]E1
       Archiroyaliste,]Ms

298.40 Duchesse]E1
       Duchess d'Ivry]Ms

298.41 qu'il-y-a]E1
       qu'il y-a]Ms

299.11 Philippist,]E1
       Philipist,]Ms

299.15 Catholic:]
       Catholics:]Ms

299.16 mother,]E1
       mother]Ms

299.17 is,]E1
       is]Ms

299.18 *Une*]E1
       une]Ms

299.18 La]E1
       [*omit*]]Ms

299.19 side.]E1
       side]Ms

299.19 one. The]E1
       one—The]Ms

299.20 *Les*]E1
       les]Ms

299.27 payed]E1
       paid]Ms

299.32 Plantes. Since]E1
       Plantes—Since]Ms

299.35 loves, she says,]E1
       loves she says]Ms

299.38 Mauvais-ton,]
       Mauvais ton,]Ms

299.38 pianist,]E1
       Pianist]Ms

299.42 song!]E1
       Song!]Ms

299.43 *jonché*]E1
       Jonché]Ms

300. 7 governess,]E1
       Governess,]Ms

300. 8 compagnie—Miss]
       Compagnie—Miss
       ]Ms

300. 9 accent. But]E1
       accent—But]Ms

300.12 painter]E1
       Painter]Ms

300.14 desertion. [*line space*]
       ¶There]E1

desertion. There]Ms

[Begin Anne's hand]

300.17 story. The]E1
story—The]Ms

300.26 me,"]E1
me"]Ms

300.32 there,]E1
there]Ms

300.32 aspect, at present,]E1
aspect at present]Ms

300.36 confidentially,]E1
confidentially]Ms

[Begin Thackeray's hand]

300.44 ailes-de-pigeon, the old]E1
ailes-de-pigeon; the Old]Ms

300.45 cushion]E1
Cushion]Ms

301. 7 dynasty).]E1
Dynasty).]Ms

301. 9 society. He]E1
Society—He]Ms

301.10 names his lordship,]
names, his lordship]Ms

301.10 Kew]E1
Kew,]Ms

301.12 considerably)]E1
considerably,)]Ms

301.24 Duke. You]
Duke—You]Ms

301.26 Bad]E1
bad]Ms

301.30 attendants, La Reine]E1
attendants La reine]Ms

302. 6 forth,]E1
forth;]Ms

302.11 Cruchecassée]E1
Crûche Cassée]Ms

302.13 ladies—knowing]
ladies knowing]Ms

302.14 pocketed]E1
pocketted]Ms

302.17 Punter,]E1
Punter]Ms

302.19 army]E1
Army]Ms

302.21 Bagnères]E1

Vichy]Ms

302.25 Thompson, Cambridge Square, London,]E1
Smith, Cambridge Square London;]Ms

302.27 Thompson,]E1
Smith,]Ms

302.28 continental society." Might not he]E1
Continental society." Why he might]Ms

302.29 Jones']E1
Jones]Ms

302.30 slap-up]E1
slap up]Ms

302.30 panels]E1
pannels]Ms

302.30 coronet over?]E1
Coronet over!]Ms

302.33 schoolfellow, an attorney's]E1
Schoolfellow, an Attorney's]Ms

303. 1 Kiou!]E1
Kiou!]Ms

303. 4 earth,]E1
earth,]Ms

303. 9 daughter. "My]E1
daughter—"My]Ms

303.15 walks]E1
walks:]Ms

303.15 them]E1
them;]Ms

303.16 Punter, A.D.C.,]E1
Punter A.D.C.]Ms

303.16 tenderness).]
tenderness)]Ms

303.19 Mademoiselle]E1
Mademoiselle,]Ms

303.21 governess]E1
Governess]Ms

303.23 girl,]E1
girl]Ms

303.24 way.]E1
way,]Ms

303.26 children, Antoinette said,]E1
children. Antoinette said]Ms

303.29 cousin?]E1
Cousin?]Ms

303.30 better]E1
much better]Ms

[Begin Anne's hand]

303.33 angel,]E1
angel]Ms

303.35 cry,]E1
cry]Ms

303.42 her]E1
Her]Ms

303.44 câlineries]E1
calineries]Ms

304. 1 railed]E1
Railed]Ms

304. 6 Captain]E1
Colonel]Ms

304. 8 teeth?]E1
teeth,]Ms

304.10 me]
me,]Ms

304.12 Partez,]E1
Partez]Ms

305. 1 BARNES'S COURTSHIP.]E1
[omit]]Ms

305. 2 sister-in-law;]E1
sister-in-law,]Ms

305.12 life,]E1
life]Ms

305.15 common-place]E1
common place]Ms

305.20 hand,]E1
hand]Ms

305.20 nymph]E1
nymph,]Ms

305.21 eyes,]E1
eyes]Ms

305.22 girls,]E1
girls]Ms

305.22 possibly,]E1
possibly]Ms

305.24 mamma]E1
Mamma]Ms

305.28 mother;]E1
mother]Ms

306. 6 paroxysm and recovery. Madame]
paroxism and recovery—Madame]Ms

306.18 not. It]E1
not, it]Ms

306.21 neighbours,]E1
neighbours]Ms

306.23 society,]E1
society]Ms

306.23 truth;]E1

truth,]Ms
306.23 Some One Else]E1
some one else]Ms
306.25 pardon.]E1
pardon]Ms
306.27 stops!]E1
stops]Ms
306.28 odd-looking]E1
odd looking]Ms
306.31 o'clock;]E1
o'clock,]Ms
306.33 school-room]E1
schoolroom]Ms
306.34 business: if]E1
business. If]Ms
306.39 and]E1
[omit]]Ms
306.40 early.]
early,]Ms
306.42 Hussars, bottle-green]E1
Huzzars, bottle green]Ms
306.42 lace:]E1
lace,]Ms
306.44 conservative,]E1
conservative;]Ms
306.44 information,]E1
information]Ms
306.45 have. When]E1
have, when]Ms
307. 5 back, like Whittington. Isn't]E1
back like Whittington; is not]Ms
307. 7 months.]E1
many months.]Ms
307. 9 day, very likely,]E1
day very likely]Ms
307.12 reprobation:]
reprobation]Ms
307.12 prodigal—a]E1
prodigal, a]Ms
307.13 order—a]E1
order, a]Ms
307.31 place,]E1
place]Ms
307.34 glad]E1
glad,]Ms
307.34 gone,]E1
gone]Ms
307.34 especially;]E1
especially]Ms

307.37 Kew,]E1
Kew]Ms
307.38 character,]E1
character]Ms
307.40 "Yes,]E1
"Yes]Ms
307.40 fellow:"]E1
fellow,"]Ms
308. 2 said:]E1
said]Ms
308. 3 that]E1
That]Ms
308. 4 difficult,]E1
difficult]Ms
308. 5 dignity,]
dignity]Ms
308. 6 one,]
one]Ms
308. 6 conscientiously]E1
consienciously]Ms
308.10 Jack,]
Jack]Ms
308.10 summons,]
summons]Ms
308.18 that]E1
[omit]]Ms
308.19 entered]E1
entered,]Ms
308.21 Mamma,"]
Mamma"]Ms
308.31 lynx-eyed]E1
linx eyed]Ms
308.32 ceaselessly]E1
ceaslessly]Ms
308.33 fainting-fit]E1
fainting fit]Ms
308.33 malicious]
malicious,]Ms
308.35 Captain Belsize—Fiddle-dee-dee!]
Capt: Belsize—Fiddle dee dee!]Ms
308.41 peerage? Is]E1
peerage—Is]Ms
309. 9 replied]
replied,]Ms
309.10 shoulders, "Taisez vous,]E1
shoulders. "Taisez-vous,]Ms
309.10 vieille]E1
vielle]Ms
309.17 artist, and that]E1

artist and that.]Ms
309.21 Kew. "And]E1
Kew, "and]Ms
310. 3 republican.]E1
republican." [line space]]Ms
310. 7 the Countess]R
her mother]Ms
310.15 soul,]E1
soul]Ms
310.26 Why,]E1
Why]Ms
310.28 drawing-master]E1
drawing master]Ms
310.32 correspondence?]E1
correspondance?]Ms
310.33 know;]E1
know]Ms
310.42 concert-singers]E1
concert singers]Ms
311. 1 Kew;]E1
Kew]Ms
311. 4 fortune,]E1
fortune]Ms
311. 5 were,]E1
were]Ms
311. 5 began,]E1
began]Ms
311. 7 wit?]E1
wit]Ms
311.12 unkindly;]E1
unkindly]Ms
311.14 Turkish]E1
turkish]Ms
311.16 Circassian]E1
circassian]Ms
311.16 No,]E1
No]Ms
311.19 would,]E1
would]Ms
311.21 best,—I]E1
best. I]Ms
311.22 him.]E1
him]Ms
311.24 fly.]
fly,]Ms
311.26 soul,]E1
soul]Ms
311.26 kind; you]E1
kind, You]Ms
311.31 luncheon.]
luncheon,]Ms

311.32 world:—very good
looking]E1
world:—Very
goodlooking]Ms

311.33 temper,]E1
temper]Ms

311.34 marriage;]E1 MS
marriage]Ms

311.35 day. Why,]E1
day Why]Ms

311.35 cruelty;]E1
cruelty]Ms

311.37 termagant]E1
termagrant]Ms

311.38 after-days]E1
after days]Ms

311.41 too,]E1
too]Ms

311.41 least,]E1
least]Ms

311.41 good-humoured.
She]E1
good-humoured she
]Ms

312. 1 willing.]E1
willing]Ms

312. 2 dear? Because]E1
dear, because]Ms

312.10 conscious]E1
consious]Ms

312.11 admired. Meanwhile
]E1
admired meanwhile
]Ms

316. 1 Cruchecassée]
Crûche-Cassée]E1

316.18 Cruchecassée]
Crûche-/Cassée]E1

317. 4 wisdom.]R
wisdom]E1

318. 4 Ethel]
Ethel,]R
Ethel chose to
appear in a toilette
the very grandest
and finest which she
had ever assumed,
]E1

318. 6 world, chose to
appear in a toilette
the very grandest
and finest which she
had ever assumed.
]R
world.]E1

318.17 Fifth]R NY

Fourth]E1

321.16 committed.]R NY
committed,]E1

322.13 *voulez-vous?*]
voulez vous?]E1

322.24 pleased.]R
pleased,]E1

325.17 "if]R
"If]E1

326.45 Méri.]R
Méri]E1

328. 2 ball-room;]
ball-/room;]E1

328.48 "il]
"Il]E1

329.46 "C'est]
"C'èst]E1

330.20 loyal.]R
loyal.]E1

331. 6 good-natured]
good-/natured]E1

331.37 play-room.]
play-/room.]E1

332.10 entendez-vous,]
entendez vous,]E1

341.10 Capuchin,]R
capuchin,]E1

344. 3 heart]R
heart,]E1

344.28 countrywoman]R
contrywoman]E1

344.43 Chanticlere]
Chanticleer]E1

Vol. II.

6.49 Clive.]HM
Clive,]E1

11.07 was]R
were]E1

16.18 Mrs.]R
Mr.]E1

17.41 woman,]HM R
women,]E1

17.49 woman]HM R
women]E1

18.39 Bundelcund]R
Bumdlecund]E1

30.01 INJURED INNOCENCE.
[*line space*] ¶FROM
CLIVE NEWCOME,
ESQ., TO LIEUT.-
COL. NEWCOME,
C.B. ¶"BRIGHTON,
June 12. 18— ¶"MY
DEAREST FATHER,—As
]E1
¶From Clive
Newcome, Esq.,

to Lieut Colonel
Newcome C.B.
¶"Brighton June 12.
18— ¶My dearest
Father. As]Ms

31.05 have, I hope,]E1
have I hope]Ms

31.15 three months. At
Rome, however,]E1
three months—it
so happened there
was another fellow
running away for the
same reason, Captain
Belsize whom you
may remember—
We groaned and
moaned together
for a month and
consoled each other
as best we might.
Then we parted, and
I and J.J. went to
Rome; then]Ms

31.17 season]E1
Roman season]Ms

31.27 Brighton,]E1
Brighton]Ms

31.27 train]E1
train,]Ms

31.28 waiting-room); and
]E1
waiting-room.) And
]Ms

31.30 the Royal]E1
a royal]Ms

31.33 scolding. Uncle]E1
scolding on my
return from abroad
and is as sulky and
angry and as proud
as old Lady Kew.
¶"Uncle]Ms

31.34 Madame de
Montcontour's,]E1
Mme. de
Montcontour's]Ms

31.35 h's,]E1
h's]Ms

31.39 Mack—well,]E1
Mack—well]Ms

31.40 attack]E1
attack,]Ms

31.40 word]E1
word,]Ms

32.03 quarter,]E1
quarter]Ms

32.10 always,]E1
alway]Ms

32.17 very haughtily]E1
[*omit*]]Ms
32.20 her china,]E1
up her chayny]Ms
32.20 Clive,]
Clive]Ms
32.21 anger]E1
furiousness]Ms
32.23 *this*]E1
this]Ms
32.27 smoke,]E1
smoke his cigar in
the Square,]Ms
32.30 half-past one. You
can]E1
half past one. You
are welcome to]Ms
32.34 goodness,]E1
Goodness,]Ms
32.35 at?]E1
at]Ms
32.36 at,]E1
it,]Ms
32.37 the]E1
and folding the table
]Ms
33.01 where]E1
confound it where
]Ms
33.01 to?"]E1
to?" exclaims the
youth.]Ms
33.06 bear it."]E1
abide it—Lar, Master
Clive! Down tu
Borhambury one day
in the shrobberee
when one of the
young gentlemen
was a courting your
poor mother, Miss
Ann—Lar bless us
you should ha seen
Miss Martha and
how she came on!
She never cude bear
it and never wude."
]Ms
33.07 playful]E1
playful but
imperious]Ms
33.09 in the railway]E1
as you did yesterday
in the Railway]Ms
33.11 [Page 4 of the *Ms* is
missing. Text from
"she is!" through
"innocent as you
are." is supplied
from the first
edition.]

34.21 world,]E1
world]Ms
34.34 beach. ¶So away
went Clive to walk
with his cousins, and
then]E1
beach; and their
attendants made him
a bow, among them
little Trimmer who
acknowledged him
quite respectfully,
and looked as
demure and
innocent as if she
had not caused all
this disturbance we
have been narrating.
With Sir Brian ill
and Lady Ann and
Ethel up-stairs of
course requiring
apartments for
themselves, how
could all these little
folks get room in
Miss Honeyman's
house and would
they not interrupt
their papa by their
noise? I think it
is most possible
that they and their
Governess were
at Thompson's
the lodgings next
door, from the bow-
windows of which
they could crow and
sing and make signs
to their elders in
the neighbouring
house—Thompson's
lodgings very clean
and nice now, how
different from the
same apartments
when the careless
Bugsby rented them!
¶So away went Clive
to walk with his
cousins—who told
him all their news
and how they had
got a new Governess,
such a funny little
kind old Governess,
much nicer than
Miss Quigley who
knew Clive too, and

her name was Miss
Cann—And they
all went forth on
to the Chain Pier,
and there some of
them went below
among the great
pier-beams with the
green waters tossing
and shimmering
below—a sight
of pleasure and
wonderment—and
there Clive smoked
that cigar which has
been waiting all this
while—and then he
went]Ms
35.05 shawl.]R
shawls.]Ms
35.10 collar. Clive]E1
collar—Clive]Ms
35.12 countenance. As for
Ethel,]E1
countenance—As for
Ethel]Ms
35.12 unconscious. So,
]E1
unconscious—So,
]Ms
35.23 number]E1
great number]Ms
35.23 them.]E1
them, and a leg of
mutton was roasting
for them in the
kitchen.]Ms
35.28 though there was
]E1
there was scarcely
]Ms
35.31 chap]E1
wild chap]Ms
35.42 news,]E1
news]Ms
36.10 "Really]
"really]Ms
36.12 now,]E1
now]Ms
36.13 remarked,]E1
remarked]Ms
36.13 honour,]E1
honour]Ms
36.15 nobleman]E1
nobleman,]Ms
36.15 Rackstraws]E1
[*omit*]]Ms
36.16 now,]E1
now]Ms

36.18 you:]E1
   you]Ms
36.19 season; we did now,
   ]E1
   season we did now
   ]Ms
36.20 yesterday,]E1
   yesterday]Ms
36.26 honour,]E1
   honour]Ms
36.27 horses, you know,
   ]E1
   horses you know
   ]Ms
36.30 honour.]E1
   honour,]Ms
36.31 Bloxam's,]E1
   Bloxam's]Ms
36.33 (that Crackthorpe
   ]E1
   (That Crackthorpe,
   ]Ms
36.34 grandson,]E1
   grandson]Ms
36.35 the—at]E1
   the at]Ms
36.37 spinner,]E1
   spinner]Ms
36.39 yes,]E1
   yes]Ms
36.42 curiosity,]E1
   curiosity]Ms
36.42 say,]E1
   say]Ms
37.02 Barber-Surgeon—a]
   Barber Surgeon—a
   ]Ms
37.12 lodging-houses!]E1
   lodging houses!]Ms
37.12 green,]E1
   green]Ms
37.17 horrid: really now,]
   horrid really now
   ]Ms
37.19 "Well—something
   ]E1
   "Well—Something
   ]Ms
37.23 passed]E1
   past]Ms
37.25 races, you know,]E1
   races you know]Ms
37.26 another—it's]E1
   another—It's]Ms
37.27 mother;]E1
   mother]Ms
37.28 lie]E1
   live quite]Ms
37.30 amused,]E1
   amused]Ms

37.38 blood,]E1
   blood]Ms
37.43 "Don't,]E1
   "Don't]Ms
37.43 Carton,]E1
   Carton]Ms
37.44 to-morrow,]E1
   to-morrow]Ms
37.45 Hm and Hmm,]
   hm and hmm]Ms
37.46 (The]E1
   (the]Ms
37.47 Blackcap]E1
   [blank space]]Ms
38.10 said;]E1
   said,]Ms
38.11 army]E1
   Army]Ms
38.15 balcony,]E1
   balcony;]Ms
38.22 be occupied]E1
   have to occupy
   herself]Ms
38.24 tête-à-tête with]E1
   tête-à- with]Ms
38.25 Ethel. ¶Clive's]E1
   Ethel. So Clive
   amused himself as
   best he might in
   the interim. He
   wrote that letter
   to his father. He
   sketched boats along
   the sea-shore; he
   walked to Hove and
   made a drawing
   of the Church
   there. He strove
   to pacify his aunt,
   Mrs. Honeyman, by
   jokes, conversation
   about his travels,
   talk about old
   times and acontrite
   and affectionate
   demeanour. Mrs.
   Honeyman received
   the poor lad's
   flatteries very gruffly
   and curtly: as she
   sate in her little
   back parlour: she
   perfectly understood
   that the young
   man's heart was
   on the first floor
   whilst his person
   encumbered her
   room down below.
   ¶The splendid

menials arrayed in
powder and plush
who adorned Sir
Brian's London
house, were not
brought down to the
Brighton lodgings.
Mrs. Honeyman said
with reason that her
house was too small
to accommodate
those big men. Her
cook must provide
Lady Ann's meals, if
her ladyship took the
lodgings; and Mrs.
Honeyman herself
made the currant
tarts prepared
the custards with
which she treated
the inmates of her
house. Mr. Kuhn
waited at table, and
Lady Ann's women-
servants being much
too fine ladies to
do any such work;
Hannah gave a
helping hand at the
dinner. ¶Clive's]Ms
38.27 likewise invited, and
   ]E1
   who had likewise
   been invited,]Ms
38.28 a]E1
   [omit]]Ms
39.04 Brown,]E1
   Brown]Ms
39.09 dinner,]E1
   dinner]Ms
39.13 childhood,]E1
   childhood]Ms
39.14 it,]E1
   it]Ms
39.21 cook]E1
   Cook]Ms
39.31 aunt,]E1
   aunt]Ms
39.39 interposed.]E1
   breaks out.]Ms
40.05 that]E1
   [omit]]Ms
40.13 shots]E1
   side shots]Ms
40.23 tart,]E1
   tart]Ms
40.27 next morning—was
   ]
   next tomorrow—was
   ]E1

next morning
—tomorrow—
[insertion not in
Thackeray's hand]—
was]Ms
40.31 lady. Then]E1
lady—Then]Ms
40.33 for]E1
to]Ms
40.36 dancing, I do,]E1
dancing I do]Ms
40.40 and get the
invitation for your
friend.]E1
your commission
(Peule! says Ethel
with a shrug of
her shoulder. —an
askance look at
Clive.—) [insertion
not in Thackeray's
hand]]Ms
41.04 now. She]E1
now—She]Ms
41.12 had hit. Then]E1
at hit—Then]Ms
41.13 town]E1
town:]Ms
41.22 "Good-night,"]E1
"Good night,"]Ms
41.26 nobleman,]E1
nobleman]Ms
41.28 were.]E1
are.]Ms
42.01 RETURNS TO SOME
OLD FRIENDS.]E1
[omit]]Ms
42.18 cliff?"]E1
Cliff?"]Ms
42.18 from]E1
to]Ms
42.19 railroad.]E1
Railroad.]Ms
42.21 her,]E1
her]Ms
42.22 cliff?"]E1
Cliff?"]Ms
42.27 me,]E1
me]Ms
42.28 and]E1
And]Ms
42.29 young]E1
Young]Ms
43.01 Counsellor.]
Councillor.]Ms
43.04 airs—O]
airs—o]Ms
43.06 say, There!]E1
say there!]Ms
43.17 lightning. The]E1

lightning—The]Ms
43.23 gods]E1
Gods]Ms
43.24 night,]E1
night]Ms
43.24 honour,]E1
honour]Ms
43.26 woke]E1
came and woke]Ms
43.30 army," said Clive,
]E1
Army," said Clive
with another
ingenuous blush;
]Ms
43.31 them. O I would like
to cut my head off
as well as my hair!"
]E1
off the facial
ornaments. Do you
know old Gandish
called upon me three
days ago with a pair
of mustachios, and
yesterday I saw
a little fellow by
the name of Moss
swaggering about
Brighton pier with
another pair? You
remember Moss? O
I would like to cut
my head off as well
as my hair! I'm mad
about this woman—
mad about her!"
And he bit the backs
of his hands, fired
off twenty vollies of
cigar-smoke: dashed
the cigar into the
fireplace, drank
off tumbler after
tumbler of water and
gave other marks of
distraction.]Ms
43.33 friend.]E1
friend, coming to the
point.]Ms
44.02 win]E1
wine]Ms
44.04 "I]E1
"Well I]Ms
44.04 me,]E1
me]Ms
44.05 moment,]E1
moment]Ms
44.14 said,]E1
said]Ms

44.19 Clive's]E1
the]Ms
44.22 me—she]E1
me—She]Ms
44.25 was]
Was]Ms
44.25 counsel]E1
council]Ms
44.30 her;]E1
her,]Ms
44.31 silk robes,]E1
silk-robes,]Ms
44.34 grumbling,]E1
grumbling]Ms
44.42 seen]
seen,]E1
seem]Ms
45.02 nose)]
nose,)]Ms
45.03 &c. A]E1
&c.—A]Ms
45.07 famous]E1
certain famous]Ms
45.11 she,]E1
she, the dear
innocent,]Ms
45.23 them?]E1
these?]Ms
45.24 Mackenzie]E1
Mackenzie,]Ms
45.30 company." That]E1
good company"—
That]Ms
45.41 said,]
said]Ms
46.01 claret-jug]E1
Claret-jug]Ms
46.02 Mrs.]E1
the radiant Mrs.
]Ms
46.03 smiles, Clive]E1
smiles to us, Clive
who sate next me
]Ms
46.05 face]E1
face I thought,]Ms
46.06 followed]E1
followed out of the
room]Ms
46.06 mamma.]E1
bustling mamma.
]Ms
46.09 Thank]E1
F.B. owns to a
partiality for—thank
]Ms
46.13 hear,]E1
hear]Ms
46.17 a-piece."]E1
a piece."]Ms

46.22 to spare]E1
at present to spare.
]Ms
46.22 Odessa]E1
O'dessa]Ms
46.27 "You,]E1
"You]Ms
46.30 notice,"]E1
notice:"]Ms
46.31 gusto.]E1
gusto,]Ms
46.33 both,]E1
both]Ms
46.33 them,]E1
them]Ms
46.34 sent]E1
sent an order for
]Ms
46.35 funded]E1
banked it, Sir—
funded]Ms
47.04 possessions,]E1
possessions]Ms
47.24 finished,]E1
finished]Ms
47.32 man marry this]E1
one marry this little
]Ms
47.33 yonder,]E1
yonder]Ms
47.34 easy-going]
easy going]Ms
47.34 philosopher. Here's
]E1
philosopher—Here's
]Ms
47.36 except, I grant you,
]E1
except I grant you
]Ms
47.39 fashion, thank my
stars—I]E1
fashion thank my
Stars—I]Ms
47.41 frequent operas]E1
go to Operas]Ms
47.45 taken,]E1
taken]Ms
48.08 visit.]E1
visit—a footman
as brazen and
implacable as the
knocker itself
announcing that her
ladyship and Miss
Newcome were just
gone out.]Ms
48.15 me]E1
me again]Ms
48.16 lady]E1

lady to caper]Ms
48.16 Marquis.]E1
noble Marquis.]Ms
48.17 evening—as]E1
evening as]Ms
48.20 graciousness; on
other nights her
ladyship would
pass and no more
recognise him than
the servant who
opened the door. ¶If
]E1
graciousness, smile
and ask him how
his studies were
going on, and if he
had heard from his
father and regret
that she was not at
home when he called
once. On other
nights her ladyship
would pass and no
more recognise him
than the servant who
opened the door. ¶If
]Ms
48.24 exclusion,]E1
exclusion]Ms
48.27 street?]E1
street as though he
would crop the roses
and geraniums in
the balconies?]Ms
48.28 opera,]E1
Opera,]Ms
48.32 is,]E1
is]Ms
48.33 vicar's]E1
Vicar's]Ms
48.34 and]E1
[omit]]Ms
49.03 Groom of the Stole,
don't you know, to
stand,]E1
groom of the Stole
don't you know to
stand]Ms
49.04 could,]
could]Ms
49.07 broomstick,]E1
broomstick]Ms
49.07 sheep-faced]E1
sheep faced]Ms
49.14 Ethel, saving your
presence,]E1
Ethel saving your
presence]Ms
49.15 her this cutlet.]E1

him this Cutlet.]Ms
49.16 slut,]E1
Slut,]Ms
49.16 Mag,]E1
Mag]Ms
49.17 cutlet,]E1
cutlet]Ms
49.18 won't,]E1
won't]Ms
49.18 Why,]
Why]Ms
49.19 him (I]E1
him, I]Ms
49.20 psalm-singin')—do]
psalm singin'—do
]Ms
49.33 dowager]E1
Dowager]Ms
49.39 things,]E1
things]Ms
50.06 satirist—to whom
Butts:]E1
Satirist—to whom
Butts.]Ms
50.08 pots. I say, I]E1
pots—I say—I]Ms
50.11 months;]E1
months]Ms
50.11 play—so is Frank
too,]
play.—so is Frank too
]Ms
50.12 boy. So]E1
boy—So]Ms
50.15 the old]E1
that the old]Ms
50.15 relenting, and]E1
relenting and that
]Ms
50.16 again—Jack's]E1
again—especially as
Jack's]Ms
50.16 now,]
now]Ms
50.17 Susan,]
Susan]Ms
50.18 Jack, though," cries
another. And]E1
Jack though—" cries
another—And]Ms
50.21 are,]E1
are]Ms
50.21 conversation,]E1
conversation]Ms
50.26 Jack's]E1
his]Ms
50.32 Row,]E1
Row]Ms
50.39 corps.]E1
Corps.]Ms

50.42 dresses,]E1
    dresses]Ms
50.43 infantry,—nay,]E1
    infantry,—nay]Ms
50.44 Life Guardsmen]E1
    Life-Guardsmen]Ms
50.45 Street]
    St.]Ms
51.02 curly-whiskered]E1
    curly whiskered]Ms
51.04 Finch,]E1
    Runt Finch,]Ms
51.06 A.R.A.,]E1
    A.R.A.]Ms
51.08 turned down,]E1
    turned-down,]Ms
51.09 Scowler?]E1
    Mr. Scowler?]Ms
51.11 bit,]E1
    bit]Ms
51.12 vigorous]E1
    vigourous]Ms
51.16 company,]E1
    company]Ms
51.16 artist—Smee,]E1
    artist—Smee]Ms
52.07 society,]E1
    company,]Ms
52.15 kind]E1
    precious]Ms
52.17 thieves (though]E1
    thieves—(though
    ]Ms
52.19 company),]E1
    company)]Ms
52.22 yonder,]E1
    yonder]Ms
52.25 be,—I]E1
    be—I]Ms
52.28 shall]E1
    may]Ms
52.31 self-satisfied]E1
    self satisfied]Ms
53.07 corporeal,]E1
    corporeal]Ms
53.11 other]E1
    [omit]]Ms
53.13 are,]E1
    are]Ms
53.16 claret.]E1
    Claret.]Ms
53.18 character,]E1
    character]Ms
53.20 letters, chiefly from
    females,]E1
    letters chiefly from
    females]Ms
53.28 Pendennis—would
    ]E1
    Pendennis would
    ]Ms

53.29 Parish. He]E1
    Parish—He]Ms
53.30 being,]E1
    being]Ms
53.30 say,]E1
    say]Ms
53.36 occupy,]E1
    occupy]Ms
53.36 promoted,]E1
    promoted]Ms
53.41 then.]E1
    them.]Ms
54.01 this]NY
    his]Ms E1 R
54.02 him,]E1
    him.]Ms
54.04 church—at]E1
    Church—at]Ms
54.05 Sawders—by]E1
    Sawders, by]Ms
54.08 vacant]E1
    Vacant]Ms
54.13 owes]E1
    ows]Ms
54.14 has]E1
    had]Ms
54.21 a]E1
    the]Ms
54.23 Italy,]E1
    Italy]Ms
54.25 thirsty—having]E1
    thirsty having]Ms
54.27 chop—and]E1
    chop, and]Ms
55.04 it,]
    it]Ms
55.04 hurdy-gurdy?']E1
    hurdy gurdy?' says
    he for he still swears
    in a very reckless
    manner.]Ms
55.05 'you]E1
    'You]Ms
55.06 church music, and
    church]
    Church music, and
    Church]Ms
55.07 organ-loft,]
    organ loft]Ms
55.09 you]E1
    [omit]]Ms
55.09 split—why]E1
    struck—why]Ms
55.10 more]E1
    so]Ms
55.13 immensely,]E1
    immensely]Ms
55.16 lamps,]E1
    lamps]Ms
55.18 mean, again:—and

    Charles Honeyman,
    ]
    mean again:—and
    Charles Honeyman
    ]Ms
55.22 old,]E1
    old]Ms
55.26 now,]E1
    now]Ms
55.28 your uncle]E1
    him]Ms
55.29 Street.]E1
    St.]Ms
55.31 O'Curraghs,]
    O'Curraghs]Ms
55.34 P.M.G.,]
    P. M. G.,]Ms
55.40 Sir:]
    Sir, and]Ms
56.01 pellets;]E1
    pellets,]Ms
56.16 place,]E1
    place]Ms
56.19 be,—I]E1
    be, I]Ms
56.21 forehead,]E1
    forehead]Ms
56.29 market-gardener
    ]E1
    market gardener
    ]Ms
56.30 window]E1
    window, a bargain
    ]Ms
56.32 faint]E1
    pink,]Ms
56.33 organ-loft]E1
    organ-/loft]Ms
56.33 mediæval]E1
    Mediæval]Ms
56.39 David,]E1
    Saul,]Ms
56.45 talents, and]E1
    talents—and]Ms
57.02 Sherrick:]E1
    Sherrick]Ms
57.03 to]E1
    [omit]]Ms
57.05 levity,]E1
    levity]Ms
57.09 organ]
    Organ]Ms
57.09 footmen. Surely that
    powdered one in
    livery]E1
    footmen—Surely
    that Powdered one
    in yellow]Ms
57.10 colours?]E1

livery?]Ms
57.12 church]E1
Church]Ms
57.13 Honeyman,]E1
Honeyman]Ms
57.20 ear. She]E1
ear—She]Ms
57.21 belozenged]E1
bepainted]Ms
57.26 rattling]E1
jingling]Ms
57.27 aisle.]E1
Aisle.]Ms
57.29 husband, I suppose,
]E1
husband I suppose
]Ms
57.32 Fetlock—no, Lady
Fetlock—a]
Fetlock—no Lady
Fetlock—A]Ms
57.33 lady,]E1
lady]Ms
57.35 seven—no, nine—
with]E1
seven—no nine with
]Ms
57.35 Princess.—Julia]
Princess—Julia]Ms
57.40 fellow—excuse]
fellow excuse]Ms
57.41 is,]E1
is]Ms
58.03 glass,]E1
glass]Ms
58.04 Newcome,]E1
Newcome]Ms
58.07 reverend gent]E1
Reverend Gent]Ms
58.12 man,]E1
man]Ms
58.12 boy,]E1
boy]Ms
58.13 face.]E1
handsome face.]Ms
58.17 continues,]E1
continues]Ms
58.18 ——"]E1
[blank]."]Ms
58.19 alone;]E1
alone]Ms
58.21 called]E1
sooner called]Ms
59.02 folks,]E1
folks]Ms
59.04 "Thursday,]E1
"Thursday]Ms
59.04 Thursday,]E1
Thursday]Ms
59.06 like]E1

like particklar]Ms
59.07 cucumber?—no,]
cucumber?—no]Ms
59.08 me, you know I'm
thankful!"]E1
me you know I
am—a—thankful!"
]Ms
59.11 Mendelssohn]E1
Mendelsohn]Ms
59.11 next?]E1
next,]Ms
59.19 Clive]E1
Clive,]Ms
59.20 Rosherville),]E1
Rosherville)]Ms
59.24 himself,]E1
himself]Ms
59.25 least,]E1
least]Ms
59.25 No,]E1
No]Ms
59.26 on]E1
[omit]]Ms
59.28 day—and]
day—And]Ms
59.29 there]
they're]Ms E1
59.30 man—ill, I suppose,
]E1
man—ill I suppose
]Ms
59.37 Colonel's,]E1
Colonel's]Ms
59.42 side-table]
side table]Ms
59.43 chimney-glass]E1
chimney glass]Ms
59.45 clear-sighted]
clear sighted]Ms
60.01 double-faced,]E1
double faced,]Ms
60.06 doubly uneasy. In
fine,]E1
double uneasy. In
fine]Ms
60.07 but]
But]Ms
60.07 family,]E1
family]Ms
60.15 sake," remarks Mr.
Binnie.]E1
sake."]Ms
60.17 Rosey,]E1
Rosey]Ms
60.21 won't,]E1
won't]Ms
60.29 her]E1
[omit]]Ms
60.33 night]E1

night and]Ms
60.36 back]E1
the back]Ms
60.37 why,]
why]Ms
60.38 it]E1
Master Clive's absurd
infatuation]Ms
60.44 "O, thank]E1
"O Thank]Ms
61.03 a fine Scotch Italian,
]E1
an Italian with a fine
Edinburgh accent,
]Ms
61.04 ragazza]E1
[omit]]Ms
61.12 brougham.]E1
Brougham.]Ms
61.15 Betsy,]E1
Betsy]Ms
61.19 Smacker, Lessee"
(who]
Smacker Lessee"
who]Ms
61.27 double-frontispiece]
double frontispiece
]Ms
61.28 the benefit of the
poor; and (2)
reclining upon
straw, the leanest of
invalids.]E1
benefit the poor and
2 reclining upon
Straw—the leanest
of Invalids.]Ms
61.29 Longlegs,]E1
Lonlegs]Ms
61.30 Prayers; a Tale for
Children by a Lady,
]
prayers—a tale for
children by a lady
]Ms
61.32 Early Days by
Charles Honeyman,
]
early days by Charles
Honeyman]Ms
61.33 Yes,]E1
Yes]Ms
61.38 evening,]E1
evening]Ms
61.42 prettier]E1
many prettier girls
]Ms
62.05 Clive;]E1
Clive,]Ms
62.06 Old]E1

old]Ms
62.08 men,]E1
men pretty well:
]Ms
62.11 "What,]E1
"What]Ms
62.14 Kew, who's]E1
Kew who,]Ms
62.22 performance]E1
-'formance]Ms
62.23 gal, that is;]E1
gal that is]Ms
62.26 opera,]E1
opera]Ms
62.31 is,]E1
is]Ms
62.33 young]E1
[omit]]Ms
62.34 Rosey?"—]E1
Rosey—"]Ms
62.35 "Yes,]E1
"Yes]Ms
62.35 handsome,]E1
handsome and
has such decided
features,]Ms
63.06 friendly,]E1
friendly and was so
pleased with this
drawing]Ms
63.06 was]E1
was now]Ms
63.09 sitting,]E1
sitting]Ms
63.12 studio,]E1
Studio,]Ms
63.13 Gazette,]
Gazette]Ms
63.14 "CONVERSION]E1
"CONVERSION]Ms
63.16 likely,]E1
likely]Ms
63.27 niece. They liked the
music,]E1
niece: as they liked
the music]Ms
63.30 praising me; and
]E1
always praising me;
and always]Ms
63.31 know,]E1
know]Ms
63.35 any]E1
is any]Ms
64.01 A STAG OF TEN.]E1
[omit]]Ms
64.16 talking, and]E1
heard]Ms
65.13 small-pox,]E1
small pox,]Ms

65.20 person, I say,]E1
person I say]Ms
65.21 unless there were
]E1
unless, there are
]Ms
65.34 instance, the]E1
instance,—the]Ms
65.37 to,]E1
to]Ms
65.43 morning,]E1
morning]Ms
66.05 name. Many]E1
name—Many]Ms
66.09 away. But]E1
away—But]Ms
66.09 Dieu!]E1
Dieu!,]Ms
66.20 school-room]E1
school room]Ms
66.27 them,]E1
them]Ms
66.31 object.]E1
object:]Ms
66.35 success,]E1
success]Ms
66.39 Crackthorpe,]E1
Crackthorpe]Ms
66.40 condition,]E1
condition]Ms
66.41 offices),]E1
offices,)]Ms
66.44 houses—the]
houses.—the]Ms
66.44 them,]E1
them]Ms
67.05 tuft-hunter]E1
tuft hunter]Ms
67.24 Whatdyoucallem's.
]E1
Whatdyoucallem's:
]Ms
67.25 Suchandsuch Castle
]
Sucandsuch castle
]Ms
67.26 guests,]E1
guests]Ms
67.27 company. These]E1
company—These
]Ms
67.31 almost,]E1
almost]Ms
67.33 where,]E1
where]Ms
67.34 deer,]E1
deer]Ms
67.37 come—not]E1
come not]Ms
67.39 party,]E1

party]Ms
68.11 there]E1
that there]Ms
68.14 O,]E1
O]Ms
68.16 fiddle-faddle]E1
fiddle faddle]Ms
68.24 knew quite well]E1
felt well enough]Ms
68.25 that]E1
that,]Ms
68.37 chalk]E1
Clive's chalk]Ms
68.38 Crackthorpe]E1
Butts]Ms
68.40 room, no. 1246,]
room no. 1246]Ms
68.41 Officer—viz.,
Augustus Butts,]
Officer,—viz.,
Augustus Butts,]E1
Officer—viz
Frederick
Crackthorpe,]Ms
68.42 Honeyman,]E1
Honeyman]Ms
69.01 refused; Mr. Binnie,
]E1
refused Mr. Binnie
]Ms
69.02 heads, however,]E1
heads however]Ms
69.04 said,]E1
said]Ms
69.11 Bank]
bank]Ms
69.15 professor]
Professor]Ms
69.16 Polka.]E1
polka.]Ms
69.19 instructor]E1
Instructor]Ms
69.20 oaths and phrases
]E1
oaths, and phrases,
]Ms
69.20 he]NY
she]Ms E1 R
69.21 famous),]E1
famous,)]Ms
69.24 sovereign]E1
Sovereign]Ms
69.25 Tuileries,]E1
Tuilleries,]Ms
69.26 visited,]E1
visited]Ms
69.33 salons. Madame de
Florac,]E1
Salons. Madame de
Florac]Ms

69.34 own,]E1
    own]Ms
69.37 talked,]E1
    talked]Ms
69.39 Marshal,]E1
    Marshal]Ms
69.40 charming]E1
    Charming]Ms
69.42 Kew]E1
    Kew,]Ms
69.46 Newcome. She]E1
    Newcome—She]Ms
70.01 *ami;"*]E1
    ami,"]Ms
70.02 fondly, as tenderly,
    ]E1
    fondly as tenderly
    ]Ms
70.03 eyes—O]
    eyes! O]E1
    eyes—o]Ms
70.10 lose,]E1
    lose]Ms
70.11 love? Forty]E1
    love?—Forty]Ms
71.01 THE HÔTEL DE
    FLORAC.]E1
    [*omit*]]Ms
71.04 doctor,]E1
    Doctor,]Ms
71.04 director]
    Director]Ms
71.10 school.]E1
    School.]Ms
71.14 Cordélier,]R
    Cordelier,]Ms
71.26 every]
    Every]Ms
71.34 looking-glass]
    looking glass]Ms
72.02 mirror,]E1
    mirror]Ms
72.08 turns,]E1
    turns]Ms
72.12 door-pannels—
    nymphs]
    doors-pannels—
    nymphs]Ms
72.14 Newcome,]
    Newcome]Ms
72.14 Manchester,]
    Manchester]Ms
72.15 say]E1
    [*omit*]]Ms
72.21 *Gazette*, knowing]E1
    Gazette. Knowing
    ]Ms
72.22 periodical. When
    ]E1
    periodical Thomas
    Newcome had

ordered Messrs.
Smith and Elder, his
booksellers, to send
half a dozen copies
weekly friends of his
whom he pointed
out—(and "twelve
copies of any book
which Mr. Pendennis
publishes you will
be sure to send out
to me in India,"said
the good Colonel
on going away.) so
that honest Jack
Seedham living on
little more than his
his lieutenant's half
pay at Culhampton,
Tom Skinner in the
same station of life at
Bury St., Edmunds:
Miss Featherstone,
Laurel House
Academy, Taunton
Dean Somersetshire:
(where Charley
Bayford's poor girls
were, who was killed
in Burleigh) and
Madame Madame la
Comtesse de Florac,
a son hotel, Rue
St., Dominique St.,
Germain à Paris,
became readers
of our paper for
many years without
any expense to
themselves. ¶When
]Ms
72.29 her]E1
    Her]Ms
72.31 surprised]E1
    surprised there]Ms
73.01 mind, wrote M.
    l'Abbé,]E1
    mind wrote M.
    l'Abbé]Ms
73.11 Tuileries]E1
    Tuilleries]Ms
73.14 T.]E1
    S.]Ms
73.16 time. Sam]E1
    time or, I cannot be
    certain of this fact, a
    Deputy Lieutenant's
    uniform. Sam.]Ms
73.17 Bart.,]E1
    Bart,]Ms

73.18 majesty;]E1
    Majesty;]Ms
73.27 deputy lieutenant's
    uniform. ¶If]E1
    deputy-lieutenant's
    Uniform; Mrs.
    Mackenzie I know
    was wild for going
    and to present
    Rosey; and that
    James Binnie, Esq.,
    of the Bengal Civil
    Service should
    appear at St. James's
    "on his return from
    India." But James
    declined to wear
    tights and a sword
    and bag; he said that
    his gracious Queen
    could live very
    comfortably without
    seeing him dressed
    up like a Tom-noddy.
    Such were James's
    disrespectful notions
    about Court dresses
    and ceremonies. ¶If
    ]Ms
73.33 account—would]E1
    account would]Ms
73.34 Anglo-Continental
    ]E1
    Anglo Continental
    ]Ms
73.36 Montcontour, &c.
    &c.,]E1
    Montcontour &c. &c.
    ]Ms
73.40 Square]E1
    Squar]Ms
73.41 dissenting]E1
    Dissenting]Ms
74.02 landlord]E1
    land]Ms
74.07 Higg,]E1
    Higg]Ms
74.08 London,]E1
    London]Ms
74.08 Anglo-Continental.
    ]E1
    Anglo Continental.
    ]Ms
74.15 at]E1
    At]Ms
74.18 government.]E1
    Government.]Ms
74.20 visits]E1
    visit]Ms

74.21 still,]E1
    still]Ms
74.26 Princesse.]E1
    Princess]Ms
74.32 atélier]E1
    Atélier]Ms
74.35 board,]E1
    board]Ms
74.36 wilt]E1
    will]Ms
74.39 garçon, my son: thy
    ]E1
    garcon, my son Thy
    ]Ms
74.42 louis]E1
    Louis]Ms
74.43 Religion,]E1
    Religion]Ms
75.05 dancing,]E1
    dancing]Ms
75.13 le]E1
    le.]Ms
75.13 M.]E1
    M]Ms
75.17 family, perhaps,]E1
    family perhaps]Ms
75.20 soothe,]E1
    watch,]Ms
75.24 centered]R
    centred]Ms
75.28 youth,]E1
    youth;]Ms
75.30 respect,—everything
    ]E1
    respect everything
    ]Ms
75.32 disappointment,]E1
    disappointment]Ms
75.33 tears,]E1
    tears]Ms
75.46 sufferance]E1
    sufferance,]Ms
76.02 rather]E1
    [omit]]Ms
76.03 dependants and
    society,]E1
    dependents and
    Society,]Ms
76.06 in]E1
    in all]Ms
76.12 strong-winged]E1
    strong winged]Ms
76.15 circumstances,]E1
    circumstances]Ms
76.20 she]E1
    [omit]]Ms
76.22 Florac, blushing,
    ]E1
    Florac blushing]Ms
76.35 daughter is—and]

daughter—and]Ms
76.38 lawyers,]E1
    lawyers]Ms
76.44 hump-back]
    hump back]Ms
77.03 daughters. Which
    ]E1
    daughters—Which
    ]Ms
77.04 hump-back,]E1
    hump back,]Ms
77.08 she]E1
    She]Ms
77.10 not]E1
    whilst not]Ms
77.10 statesmen]E1
    Statesmen]Ms
77.11 French,]E1
    French]Ms
77.12 Europe,—who]E1
    Europe, who]Ms
77.12 at St.]E1
    at]Ms
77.13 Schoenbrunn,—
    naturally]E1
    Schoenbrunn,
    naturally]Ms
77.17 hotel;]E1
    Hotel;]Ms
77.22 hotel to hotel]
    Hotel to Hotel]Ms
77.38 first,]E1
    first]Ms
77.41 *Meess*]E1
    meess]Ms
77.43 them,]E1
    them]Ms
77.44 times," Paul said; "*à*
    ]E1
    times—" Paul said—
    "*à*]Ms
78.01 engaged, Florac]E1
    engaged—Florac
    ]Ms
78.02 Théâtre des Variétés,
    ]E1
    Theatre des variétés,
    ]Ms
78.04 club:]
    Club:]Ms
78.04 Louqsor—she]E1
    Louqsor—She]Ms
78.05 Louqsor—she]E1
    Louqsor. She]Ms
78.09 which,]E1
    which]Ms
78.10 turn,]E1
    turn.]Ms
78.11 language,]E1
    language]Ms

78.14 a]E1
    a a]Ms
78.22 yourself,]E1
    yourself]Ms
78.35 himself,]E1
    himself]Ms
78.40 much,]E1
    much]Ms
78.43 thee"—Clive]E1
    thee."—Clive]Ms
78.44 feel—am]E1
    feel am]Ms
79.05 garden,]E1
    garden]Ms
79.06 salute the]E1
    pay his respects to
    those]Ms
79.07 come?]E1
    come? When
    Madame de Florac
    in her first talk with
    the young lady spoke
    to her with such
    special tenderness
    and kindness, told
    her how her Uncle
    Thomas Newcome
    had spoken of her,
    and offered her
    friendship to the
    young girl; it may be
    that Miss Newcome
    half divined what
    was in her new
    friend's heart,and
    that something
    respecting Clive
    was lurking there.
    She embraced
    this proffered
    friendship with
    such uncommon
    eagerness: she
    found that quiet old
    house and garden so
    exceedingly pleasant;
    that she was always
    going to see Madame
    de Préville.]Ms
79.09 insist,]E1
    insist]Ms
79.09 doubt,]E1
    doubt]Ms
79.16 readers,]E1
    reader,]Ms
79.16 seasons—can]
    seasons—Can]Ms
79.20 India,]E1
    India]Ms
79.21 room,]E1

room]Ms
79.27 acquaintance,]E1
    acquaintance]Ms
79.31 monster, I say,]E1
    monster I say]Ms
79.34 toddle,]E1
    toddle]Ms
79.35 square,]E1
    Square]Ms
79.36 *dracones,*]E1
    dracones]Ms
80.02 expected.]E1
    expected, or had the
    least idea of.]Ms
80.05 Ah,]E1
    Ah]Ms
81.01 CONTAINS TWO OR
    THREE ACTS OF A
    LITTLE COMEDY.]E1
    [*omit*]]Ms
81.06 conversations as is,
    indeed,]E1
    conversations, as is
    indeed]Ms
81.17 perhaps]E1
    parts]Ms
81.20 in]E1
    the romancer, in
    ]Ms
81.21 depicts]E1
    traces]Ms
81.21 beings]E1
    charac beings]Ms
81.25 megatherium]E1
    Megatheriun]Ms
81.28 that]E1
    the]Ms
81.29 Triton]E1
    triton]Ms
81.29 moss-eaten]E1
    moss eaten]Ms
82.09 place.]E1
    place in.]Ms
82.09 at]E1
    on]Ms
82.14 powder,]E1
    powder]Ms
82.17 down,]
    down;]Ms
82.22 "How]E1
    how]Ms
82.23 Convent-garden,"
    ]E1
    Convent-garden]Ms
82.31 succession, sold the
    hotel]E1
    sold the Hotel]Ms
82.35 Yes—if]
    Yes—If]Ms
82.35 season]

Season]Ms
82.36 balls,]E1
    balls;]Ms
82.37 Sant Onofrio,]E1
    [*blank*]]Ms
82.38 died:]E1
    died]Ms
82.45 *new*]E1
    now]Ms
83.08 lady—no,]E1
    lady—no]Ms
83.11 taunts]E1
    tauntes]Ms
83.14 *you?*]E1
    you?]Ms
83.15 willingly?]E1
    willingly.]Ms
83.16 about,]E1
    about]Ms
83.18 so.—Those]E1
    so—Those]Ms
83.19 n'est-ce pas?]
    n'est-ce pas?]Ms E1
83.20 dessins?]E1
    desseins?]Ms
83.23 maisons—et]E1
    maisons,—et]Ms
83.23 encore—où est
    bonne Maman? [*Exit*
    ]E1
    encore—ou est
    bonne Maman? (*exit*
    ]Ms
83.24 *alley.*]E1
    alley.)]Ms
83.26 geography]E1
    Geography]Ms
83.32 silk,]E1
    silk]Ms
83.33 princess]
    Princess]Ms
83.33 box—because——]
    box—because]Ms
83.36 'Why and because.'
    ]E1
    Why and because.
    ]Ms
83.39 do,]E1
    do]Ms
83.42 *Clive.* Now]E1
    Now]Ms
84.02 you,]E1
    you]Ms
84.14 man's—no,]E1
    man's—no]Ms
84.17 ill-educated—I]E1
    ill educated—I]Ms
84.22 jealous—you
    gentlemen say so—
    (*Hurriedly.*)]

jealous You
    gentlemen say so—
    Hurriedly.]Ms
84.24 Tuileries,]
    Tuilleries,]Ms
84.26 d'Aguesseau.]E1
    d'Aguesseau]Ms
84.27 you—resembles]E1
    you resembles]Ms
84.31 moment. [*Exeunt*
    ]E1
    moment. *Exeunt*]Ms
84.32 *house.* [*line
    space*] [*centered*]
    CONVERSATION II.—
    Scene I. [*line space*]
    Miss Newcome arrives
    in Lady Kew's carriage,
    which enters the court
    of the Hôtel de Florac.
    [*line space*]]E1
    house. [*centered*]
    CONVERSATION II.
    Scene I.]Ms
84.38 le]E1
    le.]Ms
84.40 me,]E1
    me]Ms
84.45 (*Bell rings.*)]E1
    (*bell rings*)]Ms
85.03 Vicomtesse. [*Exit*
    old SAINT JEAN *to the*
    carriage: a Lackey
    ]E1
    Vicomtesse. *Exit old*
    Saint Jean—to the
    carriage a lackey]Ms
85.06 *Lackey.*]E1
    lackey.]Ms
85.07 (MISS]E1
    MISS]Ms
85.08 Princesse.) ¶*The
    Lackey (to the Servants*
    ]E1
    Princesse. ¶*The lackey*
    to the servants]Ms
85.09 box).]E1
    box.]Ms
85.11 say,]E1
    say]Ms
85.12 night,]E1
    night]Ms
85.15 carriage, not by no
    means, could]E1
    carriage Not by no
    means Could]Ms
85.17 scruy!]
    scruy]Ms
85.20 *Lackey.* We, Munseer.
    (*He*]E1

Lackey We, Munseer.
He]Ms
85.21 *landing-place.*) [*Exit*]
landing place, exit
]Ms
85.24 curricle,]E1
curricle]Ms
86.01 Billy?]E1
Billy and give her
a link or two more
curb.]Ms
86.02 feller,]E1
feller]Ms
86.03 park,]
park]Ms
86.04 Why,]E1
Why]Ms
86.05 be]E1
[*omit*]]Ms
86.07 Backystopper.]E1
Backeystopper.]Ms
86.12 *Tommy.*]E1
Thomy]Ms
86.15 'ouse]E1
'Ouse]Ms
86.19 hopen—no,]E1
hopen—no]Ms
86.20 (*He lapses into silence.*)
]E1
He lapses into silence.
]Ms
86.25 every morning—
blind hookey,
shampaign,]
every morning; blind
hookey, shampaign,
]E1
o'clock every
morning—blind
Hookey Shampaign
]Ms
86.31 him,]E1
him]Ms
86.33 *Lackey.*]E1
Lackey]Ms
86.33 Buzfuz]E1
Buzfus]Ms
86.34 Sangjang's]E1
Sang jang's]Ms
86.36 time,]E1
time]Ms
86.38 [*Exit Lackey.*]E1
[*omit*]]Ms
86.42 *Lackey.* (*who re-enters*).
]E1
Lacquey (*who reenters*).
]Ms
86.43 corner.]
corner]Ms
86.44 [*Exeunt Servants.* [*line
space*] [centered]

SCENE2. [*line space*]
¶*Ethel.*]
exeunt Servants.
[centered] SCENE 2.
¶ETHEL.]Ms
87.02 here—that]E1
here that]Ms
87.04 go,]
go]Ms
87.07 you?]E1
you]Ms
87.11 how,]E1
how]Ms
87.11 says,]E1
says]Ms
87.12 thankful]E1
sure I am thankful
]Ms
87.12 wasn't,]E1
wasn't]Ms
87.21 flatteries, so tired, O
]
flatteries, so tired,
oh,]
flatteries so tired o
]Ms
87.24 conversions;]E1
conversions,]Ms
87.30 sister,]E1
sister]Ms
87.34 him,]E1
him]Ms
87.35 hot-tempered]E1
hot tempered]Ms
87.39 me,]E1
me]Ms
87.39 Highgate's father
]E1
Highgate]Ms
87.41 against it.]E1
it against it.]Ms
87.42 bank, I believe: and
]E1
bank I believe: And
]Ms
87.43 debts]E1
old debts]Ms
87.44 bank,]E1
bank]Ms
88.08 vanity]E1
vanity,]Ms
88.10 opera]
Opera]Ms
88.11 O,]E1
o]Ms
88.15 Thursday—please
]E1
Thursday please
]Ms
88.17 night—I]E1

night I]Ms
88.19 me,]E1
me]Ms
88.22 velvet,]E1
velvet]Ms
88.23 dear. [*Exit*]E1
dear. *exit*]Ms
88.30 copying,]E1
copying]Ms
88.43 think—that]E1
think—That]Ms
88.45 Countess]
countess]Ms
88.45 in [*line space*]
[centered]
CONVERSATION III.
¶*Madame de Florac (at
work*).]E1
in [centered]
CONVERSATION III.
¶Madame de Florac.
(at work)]Ms
89.03 *Madame de F.*]E1
Mme. de Florac.]Ms
89.06 speak,]E1
speak]Ms
89.11 had]E1
[*omit*]]Ms
89.15 negotiations were
broken—my]
negociations were
broken—My]Ms
89.22 almost,]E1
almost]Ms
89.29 you,]E1
you]Ms
89.35 dying—*n'est-ce pas*—
and]
dying *n'est-ce-pas*—
and]Ms
89.37 so,]E1
so]Ms
89.38 love]E1
love each other]Ms
89.39 an]E1
the]Ms
90.08 surmise,]E1
surmise]Ms
90.09 thinking, perhaps,
]E1
thinking perhaps
]Ms
90.13 and—(*Here*]E1
and . . (—*Here*]Ms
90.16 evenings,]E1
evenings]Ms
90.16 liking—here this
vision, we say,]E1
liking—Here this
vision we say]Ms

90.18 father,]E1
father]Ms
90.23 Oh,]E1
Oh]Ms
90.26 very]E1
very very]Ms
90.26 never, almost,]E1
never almost]Ms
90.27 us,]E1
us]Ms
90.33 clever,]E1
clever]Ms
90.35 flatterers—O,]
flatterers—o]Ms
90.40 dresses;]E1
dresses]Ms
90.40 jewels;]E1
jewels]Ms
90.43 say, Why not?—and
to-night—yes,]E1
say Why not?—and
to-night—yes]Ms
90.44 wicked,]E1
wicked]Ms
90.47 ashamed—yes,]E1
ashamed yes]Ms
91.04 court and "Sir
Brian's" Papa and
"Your ladyship's"]
Court and Sir Brian's
Papa and your
ladyship's]Ms
91.06 uncle,]E1
uncle]Ms
91.09 usher]E1
Usher]Ms
91.11 different,]E1
different]Ms
91.19 *Ethel. (looking*]E1
Ethel looking]Ms
91.19 *Florac).*]E1
Florac.]Ms
91.21 *fraises!* (MADAME]
fraises!—(MADAME
]Ms
91.22 *gentleman with a
drawing-board under
his arm.)*]E1
*gentleman, with a
drawing board under
his arm.*]Ms
91.24 Claive! [(*Exit* SAINT
JEAN.]E1
Claive! (*exit* SAINT
JEAN.)]Ms
91.34 asked]E1
asked me]Ms
91.35 (*surveying the sketch*).
]E1
Surveying the sketch.
]Ms

91.36 chef-d'œuvre? ¶*Clive
(kisses her hand).*]E1
chef-dœuvre? ¶*Clive,
kisses her hand.*]Ms
91.39 clergyman,]E1
Clergyman,]Ms
91.41 He has a]E1
Hm! He is the
Surgeon—a]Ms
91.43 (*tossing*]E1
(*tossing*]Ms
91.43 Mackenzie's,]E1
Mackenzie's]Ms
91.45 though.]E1
though.]Ms
92.01 cheeks; china-blue
]E1
cheeks: China blue
]Ms
92.03 (*She*]E1
She]Ms
92.04 *court.*) ¶*Clive (to the
Countess).*]E1
*Court— ¶Clive to the
Countess.*]Ms
92.06 to Miss Newcome.
¶*Madame de F. (aside).*
]E1
with Miss Newcome.
¶*The Countess aside.*
]Ms
92.07 is]E1
is for]Ms
92.08 entendez-vous?]E1
entendez vous?]Ms
92.08 again. If]E1
again if]Ms
92.09 Encore! (*He*]E1
Encor! He]Ms
92.09 *again.*)]E1
again.]Ms
92.10 does]E1
Does]Ms
92.11 court-yard]E1
Court yard]Ms
92.16 Brougham.]E1
Brogham.]Ms
92.16 anywhere?]E1
any where?]Ms
92.19 le]E1
le.]Ms
92.19 de]E1
de.]Ms
92.25 night, for instance,
]E1
night for instance
]Ms
92.27 say,]E1
say]Ms
92.28 dance, waltzing with
M.]E1

dance waltzing with
M]Ms
92.30 she]E1
She]Ms
92.31 evening;]E1
evening]Ms
92.31 midnight,]E1
midnight]Ms
92.38 since.]E1
since.]Ms
92.39 gone. ¶*Miss*]E1
gone. *Miss*]Ms
92.43 than]E1
than that]Ms
93.10 been]E1
been now]Ms
93.13 turn?]E1
your turn?]Ms
93.14 only,]E1
only]Ms
93.14 the]E1
that]Ms
93.14 very,]E1
very]Ms
93.15 home,]E1
home]Ms
93.16 this]E1
[*omit*]]Ms
93.18 O, dry them,]E1
O dry them]Ms
93.19 you,]E1
you]Ms
93.20 they—they]E1
they they]Ms
93.20 proud, not angry,
]E1
proud not angry
]Ms
93.21 sister,]E1
sister]Ms
93.25 the]E1
The]Ms
93.31 anything, *n'est-ce*]E1
anything *n'est ce*]Ms
93.32 Earl. He]E1
Earl—He]Ms
93.33 leg,]E1
leg]Ms
93.33 song. It is peace-
time,]E1
Song. It is
peacetime,]Ms
93.35 me, he said,]E1
me he said]Ms
93.36 diplomacy,]E1
Diplomacy]Ms
93.38 think; or would he,
]E1

think or would he
]Ms
93.40 (musing). Barnes
would not, perhaps,
]E1
musing. Barnes
would not perhaps
]Ms
94.08 genius?—Yes,]E1
genius?—Yes]Ms
94.10 you, if]E1
you if,]Ms
94.12 O,]E1
O]Ms
94.15 arrival,]E1
arrival]Ms
94.15 country,]E1
Country]Ms
94.16 Farin——]E1
Farin . .]Ms
94.17 please,]E1
please]Ms
94.18 world,]E1
world]Ms
94.21 his]E1
His]Ms
94.27 Tuileries]E1
Tuilleries]Ms
94.29 Ambassador,]
Ambassador]Ms
94.37 (with a sigh).]E1
with a sigh.]Ms
94.38 its]E1
it's]Ms
95.06 others'. ¶Ethel. Yes,
]E1
other's. ¶Ethel. Yes
]Ms
95.13 so,]E1
so]Ms
95.17 queen]E1
Queen]Ms
95.18 happy, I think,]E1
happy I think]Ms
95.19 men,]E1
men]Ms
95.24 me, perhaps,]E1
me perhaps]Ms
95.26 more, or]E1
more—or]Ms
95.26 again, never—you
]E1
again never—You
]Ms
95.31 kind, too,]E1
kind too]Ms
95.34 but]E1
but very]Ms
95.39 (CLIVE]
CLIVE]Ms

95.39 after Miss]E1
after MISS]Ms
95.41 salon,]E1
salon]Ms
95.42 door.]E1
door;]Ms
95.43 hands.)]E1
hands.]Ms
95.44 (She]E1
She]Ms
95.44 looks.)]
looks.]Ms
96.01 Clive (very steadily).
Yes. ¶Madame]E1
Clive. very steadily.
Yes. Madame]Ms
96.03 organ]E1
music organs]Ms
96.03 Convent?]
convent?]Ms E1
96.06 (He]E1
He]Ms
96.08 O]E1
o]Ms
98.24 borough,]R
Borough,]Ms
99.17 dining-room,]E1
dining-/room,]Ms
101.40 Pall Mall Gazette]
"Pall Mall Gazette"
]Ms
103.25 prosperity—that]E1
prosperity that]Ms
103.26 &]E1
and]Ms
103.29 men,]E1
men]Ms
103.38 and, of course,]E1
and of course]Ms
103.44 common]E1
Common]Ms
103.45 wool,]E1
wool]Ms
103.45 colony]E1
Colony]Ms
103.47 copper-mines]E1
Copper-mines]Ms
104.03 &]E1
and]Ms
104.04 markets—The]
markets—the]Ms
104.10 dividend]E1
Dividend]Ms
104.11 cent]
Cent]Ms
104.11 capital:]E1
Capital:]Ms
104.11 copper]E1
Copper]Ms
104.12 to]E1

[omit]]Ms
104.14 became]E1
beca]Ms
104.15 friends, James
Binnie who]
friends, James
Binnie, who]E1
friends James Binnie
wh]Ms
104.16 time,]E1
time; and Samuel
Sherrick, Esq.;]Ms
104.16 shareholders,]E1
shareholders]Ms
104.23 note share,]E1
share]Ms
104.28 chambers,]E1
Chambers in the
Albany,]Ms
104.29 private,]E1
private]Ms
104.30 her]E1
her,]Ms
104.35 occasion).]E1
occasion.)]Ms
104.36 returned]E1
came back]Ms
104.39 Cashmere]E1
cashmere]Ms
105.01 CONTAINS AT LEAST
SIX MORE COURSES
AND TWO DESSERTS.
¶THE]E1
Chapter 11 ¶The
]Ms
105.02 over,]E1
over]Ms
105.03 apartments,]E1
apartments]Ms
150.07 couples,]E1
couples]Ms
105.10 Barnes]E1
Brian]Ms
105.12 to]E1
[omit]]Ms
105.16 No—she]E1
no—she]Ms
105.19 Barnes]E1
Brian]Ms
105.24 Mr. Pendennis.]E1
Mr. Pendennis.]Ms
105.28 Mrs. Pendennis.]E1
Mrs. Pendennis.
]Ms
106.04 Pendennis.]E1
Pendennis.]Ms
106.05 Mrs. P.]
Mrs. P.]Ms
106.06 Pendennis.]E1
Pendennis.]Ms

106.09 *Mrs. P.*]E1
    Mrs. P.]Ms
106.10 know.]E1
    know]Ms
106.11 sexes). One]E1
    sexes.) 'One]Ms
106.12 O]E1
    o]Ms
106.13 *Pendennis.*]E1
    Pendennis.]Ms
106.14 *Mrs. P.*]E1
    Mrs. P.]Ms
106.20 *Pendennis.*]E1
    Pendennis.]Ms
106.21 "That]E1
    that]Ms
106.21 Pendennis." ¶*Mrs. P.*
    ]E1
    Pendennis. ¶Mrs. P.
    ]Ms
106.27 *Pendennis.*]E1
    Pendennis.]Ms
106.27 *sait* . . . ¶*Mrs. P.*
    ]E1
    sait. . ¶Mrs. P.]Ms
106.31 gallantry! ¶*Pendennis.*
    What? ¶*Mrs. P.*]E1
    gallantry ¶Pendennis.
    What? ¶Mrs. P.]Ms
106.35 for—— ¶*Pendennis.*
    For what? ¶*Mrs. P.*
    ]E1
    for ¶Pendennis. For
    what?. ¶Mrs. P.]Ms
106.38 sneeringly]E1
    roughly]Ms
106.39 *Pendennis.*]E1
    Pendennis.]Ms
106.40 to-day;]E1
    to-day.]Ms
106.42 present,]E1
    present]Ms
106.44 *Mrs. P.*]E1
    Mrs. P.]Ms
106.44 Newcome, was he?
    ¶*Pendennis.*]E1
    Newcome was he?
    ¶Pendennis.]Ms
107.03 then, a younger son,
    ]E1
    then a younger son
    ]Ms
107.07 into]E1
    in to]Ms
107.10 *Mrs. P.*]E1
    Mrs. Pendennis.
    ]Ms
107.11 ¶And]E1
    And]Ms
107.12 silent,]E1

silent]Ms
107.13 right;]E1
    right]Ms
107.14 aggravating. Indeed
    ]
    aggravating—Indeed
    ]Ms
108.14 dukes and marquises
    ]E1
    Dukes and
    Marquises]Ms
108.15 baron in this realm.
    "Lord Highgate
    sweet]E1
    Baron in this realm
    "Lord Highgate
    Sweet]Ms
108.20 Crackthorpe, Lord
    Highgate, and Lady
    Clara,]E1
    Crackthorpe Lord
    Highgate and Lady
    Clara]Ms
108.21 bankeress]E1
    Bankeress]Ms
108.22 much)]
    much;)]Ms
108.26 well,]E1
    well]Ms
108.29 *Banquière*]E1
    banquière]Ms
108.34 us (Lady Clara
    Newcome's) Lord
    ]E1
    us—Lady Clara
    Newcome's—Lord
    ]Ms
108.40 us,]E1
    us]Ms
108.41 she]E1
    She]Ms
111.13 and even]NY
    even and]E1 R
111.16 day.]
    day,]E1
112.01 CLIVE IN NEW
    QUARTERS. ¶MY wife
    ]E1
    ¶With Clive my fair
    critic]Ms
112.01 with Clive]E1
    [*omit*]]Ms
112.21 me]E1
    us]Ms
112.24 glasses,]E1
    glasses]Ms
113.04 Blackmore.]E1
    Blackmore]Ms
113.05 indigo and wool and
    copper and sicca]

Indigo and Wool
and Copper and
Sicca]Ms
133.07 Blackmore. Dear
Cousin Barnes is for
ever asking me to
dinner: I might call
Lady Clara Clara
if I liked, as Sam
Newcome does in
Brianstone Square.
You can't think
how kind they are
to me there. My
aunt reproaches
me tenderly for
not going there
oftener—it's not very
good fun dining in
Brianstone Square, is
it? And she praises
my Cousin Maria
to me—you should
hear my aunt praise
her! I have to take
Maria down to
dinner; to sit by
the piano and listen
to her songs in all
languages. Do you
know Maria can
sing Hungarian and
Polish, besides your
common German,
Spanish, and Italian.
Those I have a
tour *other* agents,
Baynes and Jolly's—
Baynes's that is in
the Regent's Park,
where the girls are
prettier and just as
civil to me as at Aunt
Hobson's." And here
Clive would amuse
us by the accounts
which he gave us
of the snares which
the Misses Baynes,
those young syrens
of Regent's Park,
set for him; of the
songs which they
sang to enchant him,
the albums in which
they besought him to
draw—the thousand
winning ways which
they employed to
bring him into their

cave in York Terrace.
But neither Circe's
smiles nor Calypso's
blandishments
had any effect on
him; his ears were
stopped to their
music, and his eyes
rendered dull to
their charms by
those of the flighty
young enchantress
with whom my
wife had of late
made acquaintance.
¶Capitalist though
he was, our young
fellow was still]E1
Blackmore." Howbeit
our young fellow,
Capitalist though he
was, was]Ms

113.32 Gandish himself,
when Clive paid
a visit to that
illustrious artist's
Academy, received
his former pupil
as if the young
fellow had been a
sovereign prince
almost, accompanied
him to his horse, and
would have held
his stirrup as he
mounted, whilst the
beautiful daughters
of the house waved
adieus to him from
the parlour-window.
To the young men
assembled in his
studio, Gandish
was never tired of
talking about Clive.
The Professor would
take occasion to
inform them that
he had been to visit
his distinguished
young friend, Mr.
Newcome, son of
Colonel Newcome;
that last evening he
had been present
at an elegant
entertainment at
Mr. Newcome's
new apartments.
Clive's drawings

were hung up in
Gandish's gallery,
and pointed out to
visitors by the worthy
Professor. On one or
two occasions I was
allowed to become a
bachelor again, and
participate in these
jovial meetings. How
guilty my coat was
on my return home;
how haughty the
looks of the mistress
of my house, as she
bade Martha carry
away the obnoxious
garment! How
grand F. B. used
to be as president
of Clive's smoking
party, where he laid
down the law, talked
the most talk, sang
the jolliest song, and
consumed the most
drink of all the jolly
talkers and drinkers!
Clive's popularity
rose prodigiously;
not only youngsters,
but old practitioners
of the fine arts,
lauded his talents.
]E1
[omit]]Ms

114.13 parties,]E1
parties]Ms
115.02 easel at sun-rise,]E1
card at sun rise,]Ms
115.04 dark]E1
Dark]Ms
115.07 short-comings]E1
short comings]Ms
115.09 Sometimes]E1
Some times]Ms
115.10 of]E1
at]Ms
115.11 Why,]
Why]Ms
115.12 best,]E1
best]Ms
115.16 Street.]E1
St.]Ms
115.16 poney,]E1
poney]Ms
115.17 Toby,]E1
Toby]Ms
115.20 general?]E1
General?]Ms

115.24 objects,]E1
objects]Ms
115.26 me,]E1
me]Ms
115.32 afterwards,]E1
afterwards]Ms
115.34 you, I daresay, but
then, O]E1
you I daresay but
then, o]Ms
115.41 entirely,]E1
entirely]Ms
115.41 own,]E1
own]Ms
116.15 fling,]E1
fling]Ms
116.15 Clive,]E1
Clive]Ms
116.23 you. When]E1
you—When]Ms
116.44 thinking,]E1
thinking]Ms
116.45 children,]E1
children]Ms
116.47 sacred, went]E1
sacred—went]Ms
117.04 Sacred]E1
sacred]Ms
117.08 subject,]E1
subject]Ms
117.11 pleasures,]E1
pleasures]Ms
117.13 unspeakable, a
perfect faith,]E1
unspeakable a
perfect faith]Ms
117.13 offer?]E1
offer her?]Ms
117.16 Newcome,]E1
Newcome]Ms
117.17 far distant.]E1
very far away.]Ms
117.20 the good man]E1
his good father]Ms
117.25 pale,]E1
pale]Ms
117.26 the]E1
his]Ms
117.27 him good: it was
]E1
him—much]Ms
117.29 springs]E1
Springs]Ms
117.31 wanted]E1
wanted or for a book
she wanted]Ms
117.34 Laura]E1
She]Ms
117.36 Clavering,]E1
Clavering]Ms

117.36 tittle-tattle and
stupid inhabitants,
]E1
tittle-tattle, and
stupid inhabitants
]Ms
121.42 are]HM NY
were]E1
122.35 cheroot]R
cheeroot]Ms
127.01 FAMILY SECRETS.]E1
[*omit*]]Ms
127.02 tea-pot]E1
tea pot]Ms
127.19 smoke,]E1
smoke]Ms
127.26 little——"]E1
little"]Ms
127.30 Kew?"]E1
Kew"]Ms
127.31 and]E1
[*omit*]]Ms
127.31 Christmas]E1
Xmas]Ms
127.32 shameful,]E1
shameful]Ms
128.01 of——"]E1
of"]Ms
128.03 wanted,]E1
wanted]Ms
128.11 gentle,]
gentle]Ms
128.11 to reason]
to reason]Ms
128.17 her,]E1
her]Ms
128.19 not,]E1
not]Ms
128.21 fool,]E1
fool]Ms
128.25 devil. In]E1
devil in]Ms
128.26 her. If]E1
her—If]Ms
128.33 teeth.]E1
teeth,]Ms
128.36 "*Bon Dieu!*]E1
"Bon Dieu!]Ms
128.44 "No,]E1
"No —— him,"]Ms
129.10 die,]E1
die]Ms
129.14 Frank, I am told,
]E1
Frank I am told]Ms
129.21 it. And]
it—And]Ms
129.22 bygones,]E1
bygones]Ms
129.26 to—"]E1

to."]Ms
129.29 upper-regions]
upper-regions,]Ms
129.38 O,]
O]Ms
129.39 again;]E1
again]Ms
129.39 to a little shooting-
box.]E1
a little shooting box.
]Ms
129.40 women—allow]E1
women—Allow]Ms
129.42 boarding-school]E1
boarding School]Ms
129.42 Elysées]E1
Élysées]Ms
129.44 Follington,]E1
Follington]Ms
130.04 *galant*]E1
gallant]Ms
130.05 family,]
family]Ms
130.11 interest—but]
Interest—but]Ms
130.18 painter,]E1
painter]Ms
130.31 apothecary]E1
Apothecary]Ms
130.35 grandson—yes,]
grandson—yes]Ms
130.37 so,]E1
so]Ms
130.38 bed. Go]E1
bed—Go]Ms
130.41 older?"]E1
older? . ."]Ms
130.44 Barnes?"]E1
Barnes"]Ms
131.08 Grandmamma,]
Grandmamma]Ms
131.11 brougham]E1
Brougham]Ms
131.14 heart-burning,]E1
heart burning,]Ms
131.18 grandmother,]E1
grandmother]Ms
131.19 sister-in-law, Lady
Kew said,]E1
sister-in-law Lady
Kew said]Ms
131.21 *tête-à-tête*]
tête-a-tête]Ms E1
131.29 constituents.]E1
Constituents.]Ms
131.30 of]E1
[*omit*]]Ms
131.31 news,]E1
news]Ms
131.39 do,]

do]Ms
131.39 they]E1
the]Ms
131.40 with]E1
with with]Ms
132.06 Scotland," replies
]E1
Scotland—"replies
]Ms
132.07 life—as]E1
life as]Ms
132.25 Cornhill]E1
CornHill]Ms
132.29 of]E1
[*omit*]]Ms
132.30 cotton]E1
Cotton]Ms
132.31 says—" ¶"It's]E1
says" ¶"—It's]Ms
132.32 them.]E1
them]Ms
132.33 if—"]E1
if "]Ms
132.35 good]E1
any good]Ms
132.35 him,]E1
him]Ms
132.38 in—Cornhill, isn't
]E1
in—Cornhill. Isn't
]Ms
132.39 can. She]E1
can—She]Ms
133.12 kind,]E1
kind]Ms
133.14 Street but Barnes,
]E1
Street, but Barnes
]Ms
133.15 count,]E1
count]Ms
133.17 friend,]E1
friend]Ms
133.19 affectionate—   E.
]E1
affectionate, E.]Ms
133.20 *o'clock.*"]E1
o'clock.]Ms
133.34 bewildered,]E1
bewildered]Ms
133.38 so,]E1
so]Ms
134.09 Florac's—"I]
Florac's—I]Ms
134.10 "we]E1
they]Ms
134.10 meet there.]E1
meet.]Ms
134.15 her," &c.]E1
her."—&c.]Ms

134.16 attacked,]E1
 attacked]Ms
134.17 her]E1
 [*omit*]]Ms
134.22 the one I like best to
 talk to! Does he not
 ]E1
 I like to talk best to!
 Does not he]Ms
134.30 "He]E1
 He]Ms
134.30 absent,"]E1
 absent,]Ms
134.31 "Shall]E1
 Shall]Ms
134.32 her?" I]E1
 her?—I]Ms
134.35 followed by]E1
 and]Ms
134.37 opinion)—Lady]E1
 opinion) —Lady
 ]Ms
134.42 house.]E1
 house:]Ms
135.03 simple]E1
 simple;]Ms
135.05 comment,]E1
 comment]Ms
135.09 London,]E1
 London]Ms
135.10 secret,]E1
 secret]Ms
135.10 lies,]E1
 lies]Ms
135.22 that]E1
 on that]Ms
135.22 town,]E1
 town]Ms
135.23 Club,]E1
 club]Ms
135.30 morning—all]E1
 morning—All]Ms
135.31 I—I]
 I I]Ms
135.32 in," he said—"quite
 ]E1
 in—" he said—
 "quite]Ms
135.32 Kew,]E1
 Kew]Ms
135.35 Colonel,]E1
 Colonel]Ms
135.36 North—at—at]
 North—At—at]Ms
135.41 Barnes.
 ¶"Confounded]E1
 Barnes.
 "Confounded]Ms
136.08 ——, and was &c.,
 ]E1

and was &c.]Ms
136.12 oath,]E1
 oath]Ms
136.15 brings. Then]E1
 brings—Then]Ms
136.16 forth,]E1
 forth]Ms
136.17 City-wards,]E1
 city wards,]Ms
136.18 once]E1
 once in]Ms
136.19 twice]E1
 twice or thrice]Ms
136.20 the]E1
 [*omit*]]Ms
136.23 aweary,]E1
 a weary]Ms
136.26 country-house]E1
 country house]Ms
137.01 IN WHICH KINSMEN
 FALL OUT.]E1
 [*omit*]]Ms
137.06 disappointments,
 ]E1
 disappoints]Ms
137.28 re-illume]E1
 reillume]Ms
137.29 strong,]E1
 strong]Ms
138.11 gods]E1
 Gods]Ms
138.15 spirits rebel and,]
 spirits, rebels and
 ]Ms
138.19 right-minded]E1
 right minded]Ms
138.21 indifference; allure,
 dismiss,]E1
 indifference allure,
 dismiss]Ms
138.39 granddaughter,]E1
 grand-daughter,]Ms
138.40 herself. Meanwhile,
 ]E1
 herself: Meanwhile
 ]Ms
138.43 subject,]E1
 subject;]Ms
138.48 marriage,]E1
 marriage]Ms
138.49 determined,]
 determined]Ms
139.02 mercy!]E1
 mercy]Ms
139.07 but—but]
 but but]Ms
139.10 background.]
 back ground.]Ms
139.15 off]E1
 of]Ms

139.18 "Sir Brian the
 Templar."]E1
 Sir Brian the
 Templar.]Ms
139.27 she]E1
 She]Ms
139.28 "Captain]E1
 "Captain]Ms
139.31 Plainways,"]E1
 [blank]]Ms
139.35 Clive, he said,]E1
 Clive he said]Ms
140.06 love affair,"]E1
 love-affair,"]Ms
140.10 which,]E1
 which]Ms
140.11 happiness,]E1
 happiness]Ms
140.14 suburb), "and]E1
 suburb) and]Ms
140.14 I]E1
 "I]Ms
140.22 of—will]E1
 of will]Ms
140.23 Henchman,]E1
 Henchman]Ms
140.24 Marquis,]E1
 Marquis]Ms
140.30 quarrel,]E1
 quarrel,:]Ms
140.38 brat. There]E1
 brat—There]Ms
140.39 shop-lifters]E1
 shop lifters]Ms
141.06 fellow-collegians,
 ]E1
 fellow collegians,
 ]Ms
141.13 schools]E1
 Schools]Ms
141.18 women—O]E1
 women—o]Ms
141.31 master's]E1
 Master's]Ms
141.32 college]E1
 College]Ms
141.39 is,]E1
 is]Ms
141.40 potentate)—a]E1
 potentate-—)—a]Ms
141.41 and]E1
 the]Ms
141.44 company]E1
 companies]Ms
141.46 know,]E1
 know]Ms
141.47 things, you know,
 ]E1
 things you know
 ]Ms

142.06 handsome]E1
        beautiful]Ms
142.11 talent,]E1
        talent]Ms
142.23 drawing-room. They
        ogled]E1
        drawing-room—
        They ogld]Ms
142.38 appears,]E1
        appears]Ms
142.40 society generally,
        ]E1
        Society generally
        ]Ms
143.02 northern]E1
        Northern]Ms
143.06 hand. [line
        space] ¶"Rue St.
        Dominique, St.
        Germain. Paris, 10
        Fev. [line space]]
        hand. ¶"Rue St.
        Dominique St.
        Germain. Paris 10
        Fev.]Ms
143.11 unlock,]E1
        unlock]Ms
144.14 de Florac.]E1
        E. de Florac.]Ms
143.25 wounded; ah,]E1
        wounded Ah]Ms
143.34 all, all noble
        Montagnards.]E1
        all all noble
        montagnards.]Ms
143.36 project, very foolish,
        ]E1
        project very foolish
        ]Ms
144.02 company,—I]E1
        company I]Ms
144.04 happiness;]E1
        happiness]Ms
144.07 crimes,]E1
        crimes]Ms
144.09 for, do you see,]E1
        for do you see]Ms
144.10 did]E1
        did I did]Ms
144.11 Spring,]
        Spring]Ms
144.16 [line space] ¶Clive
        ]E1
        ¶Clive]Ms
144.23 daughters, as we
        have said,]E1
        daughters]Ms
144.24 girls.]E1
        girls since last we
        saw them.]Ms

144.24 back-boarded]
        back-/boarded]Ms
144.28 tenderness:]E1
        tenderness]Ms
144.30 are,]E1
        are]Ms
144.31 confessed,]E1
        confessed]Ms
144.31 education,]E1
        education]Ms
144.34 the meal]E1
        meal]Ms
144.35 drawing-room,]E1
        drawing-room
        whither]Ms
144.40 O]E1
        o]Ms
144.40 accent,]E1
        accent]Ms
145.01 Colonel. He was—O
        ]E1
        Colonel He was.—O
        ]Ms
145.10 peerage, open at
        ]E1
        peerage open at,
        ]Ms
145.14 Earl, &c. &c.]E1
        Earl) &c. &c.—]Ms
145.24 news, my dear
        Colonel?"]E1
        news my dear
        Colonel"]Ms
146.04 brief,]E1
        brief]Ms
146.04 said:—]E1
        said]Ms
146.06 Yes,]E1
        Yes]Ms
146.08 brother (and a great,
        great deal better),
        ]E1
        brother, (and a great
        great deal better)
        ]Ms
146.12 which]E1
        that]Ms
146.14 T. N.]E1
        T.N.]Ms
146.15 E.N.]E1
        E.N.]Ms
146.19 him:]E1
        him]Ms
146.21 nephew,]E1
        nephew]Ms
146.25 Change,]E1
        'Change,]Ms
146.25 time,]E1
        time]Ms
146.30 half-brother]E1

        half brother]Ms
146.33 Barnes's,]E1
        Barnes's]Ms
146.38 time,]E1
        time]Ms
146.39 remarks, his half-
        brother]E1
        remarks his half
        brother]Ms
146.42 satisfaction.]E1
        satisfaction]Ms
146.44 entered,]E1
        entered]Ms
147.05 asked]E1
        ask]Ms
147.11 amazement.]E1
        amusement.]Ms
147.16 mind, I say,]E1
        mind I say]Ms
147.25 you,]E1
        you]Ms
147.26 clerk—"Stop,]
        Clerk—"Stop,]Ms
147.33 Newcome]
        Newcome,]Ms
147.35 front),]E1
        front)]Ms
147.39 west end]E1
        West End]Ms
147.43 Colonel]E1
        colonel]Ms
148.06 himself,]E1
        himself]Ms
148.11 discomfiture;]E1
        discomfiture]Ms
148.13 Colonel,]E1
        Colonel]Ms
148.14 long,]E1
        long]Ms
148.16 Sam Newcome,]E1
        Sam. Newcome]Ms
148.17 Cambridge,]E1
        Cambridge]Ms
148.18 Barnes. ¶Of]E1
        Barnes having had
        the devil's own ill
        luck at blind hookey.
        Of]Ms
148.21 Having been treated
        very ill by the
        committee in a
        complaint which
        he made about the
        Club-cookery,]E1
        [omit]]Ms
148.24 club.]E1
        Club.]Ms
148.31 St., Feb. 15, 18—
        ]E1
        St. Feb 15. 18—
        ]Ms

148.33 to-day]E1
to-day,]Ms
148.41 ("There]
"There]Ms
148.41 fight,]E1
fight]Ms
148.43 mind.")]
mind."]Ms
149.02 man,]E1
man: that]Ms
149.02 one]E1
One]Ms
149.06 through]E1
through to]Ms
149.20 "Yours, &c.,]E1
"Yours &c.]Ms
149.26 you,]E1
you]Ms
149.36 regiment,]E1
regiment]Ms
149.37 eyes, almost—the]
eyes almost the]Ms
149.44 mare's,]E1
mare's]Ms
149.45 Stop,]E1
Stop]Ms
149.46 pocket-book,]E1
pocket]Ms
149.46 pocket-book]E1
pocket book]Ms
150.01 inscribed,]E1
inscribed]Ms
150.02 fellow—Colonel—no,
———]
fellow—Colonel—no
—]Ms
150.03 Colonel, on
horseback,]E1
Colonel on
horseback]Ms
150.04 follows:— [line space]
]E1
follows. ¶"Clive
Newcome, Esq., to
Sir Barnes Newcome
Newcome Bart.
¶]Ms
150.10 and]E1
[omit]]Ms
150.23 reply,]E1
reply]Ms
150.27 &c., &c." [line space]
]E1
&c. &c."]Ms
150.28 countenance,]E1
countenance]Ms
150.30 affair.]E1
Affair.]Ms
150.31 him, I think,]E1
him I think]Ms

150.35 poulet?"]E1
froulet?"]Ms
150.37 him,]E1
him]Ms
150.38 shot. Dammy!—but
]
shot dammy!—but
]Ms
151.02 him]E1
him,]Ms
151.14 me,]E1
me]Ms
151.14 for me,]E1
for,]Ms
151.16 accommodation,]E1
accommodation]Ms
151.17 policeman.]E1
policeman—]Ms
151.24 [line space] ¶When
]E1
¶When]Ms
151.30 Scott's:— [line space]
¶"He]E1
Scott's. ¶He]Ms
151.32 river-shore;]
river-shore]Ms
151.34 more,]
more]Ms
151.36 more."]E1
more.]Ms
151.38 "Adieu]E1
the Chorus Adieu
]Ms
151.39 more, / My dear!
]E1
more / My dear]Ms
151.41 more!"]E1
more!]Ms
151.42 painter,]E1
painter]Ms
152.05 dear,]E1
dear]Ms
152.05 he, "what]E1
he. "What]Ms
153.01 HAS A TRAGICAL
ENDING.]E1
[omit]]Ms
153.04 easel a crumpled
paper,]E1
easel, a crumpled
paper]Ms
153.05 now,]E1
now;]Ms
153.18 attempted,]E1
attempted]Ms
153.24 insolence, enmity
and ill-will.]
insolence enmity and
ill will.]Ms
153.27 "Pooh!]E1

"Pooh]Ms
153.27 that,"]E1
that;"]Ms
153.28 declined: in fact,
]E1
declined in fact]Ms
153.30 war,]E1
war]Ms
154.06 near; or,]E1
near or]Ms
154.07 them,]E1
them]Ms
154.09 Nature's]E1
nature's]Ms
154.15 town—is]E1
town is]Ms
154.16 children—don't]E1
children don't]Ms
154.17 rank—could]E1
rank, could]Ms
154.26 who,]E1
who]Ms
154.26 time,]E1
time]Ms
154.30 the]E1
this]Ms
154.34 Batters,]E1
I[blank]]Ms
154.36 spring he]E1
Spring Mr. [blank]
]Ms
154.39 one,]E1
one]Ms
154.39 Batters,]E1
[blank],]Ms
155.03 ourselves]E1
our selves]Ms
155.10 my]E1
thy]Ms
155.11 of-course, he said,]
of-course he said
]Ms
155.12 large,]E1
large]Ms
155.13 that]
That]Ms
155.16 much]E1
very much]Ms
155.17 good-nature]
good-nature,]Ms
155.18 and, depend on it,]
and depend on it
]Ms
155.26 departed. [line space]
]E1
departed.]Ms
155.33 younger]R
youngest]Ms
155.33 charmed, no doubt,
]E1

charmed no doubt]Ms

156.05 lads,]E1
lads]Ms

156.05 splendid,]E1
splendid]Ms

156.11 Al,"]
Al."]Ms

156.11 cousin. Seeing]E1
cousin—seeing]Ms

156.13 haughty.]E1
haughty]Ms

156.18 nobleman. Looking]E1
nobleman—Looking]Ms

156.20 her, grave and beautiful,]E1
her grave and beautiful]Ms

156.24 house. Lady]E1
house—Lady]Ms

156.28 Unwittingly]R
Unwillingly]Ms

156.34 houses?" "When]
houses? When]Ms

157.01 trodden, grunted out,]E1
trodden grunted out]Ms

157.04 George. Ethel]E1
George—Ethel]Ms

157.07 her—just]
her—Just]Ms

159.01 BARNES'S SKELETON CLOSET.]E1
[omit]]Ms

159.07 saffron-coloured]
saffron coloured]Ms

159.16 flock,]E1
flock]Ms

159.27 gravestone,]
grave stone,]Ms

159.31 conquests,—who]
conquests—who]E1
triumphs,—who]Ms

160.17 mother!" Here]E1
mother"—Here]Ms

160.20 fourscore]E1
four score]Ms

160.21 vanity—let]
vanity—Let]Ms

160.24 velvet-palled]E1
velvet palled]Ms

160.26 account. Look]E1
account—Look]Ms

160.26 the shell;—the]E1
yonder shell. The]Ms

160.27 countenance;]E1

countenance,]Ms

160.28 Farintosh;]E1
Farintosh,]Ms

160.29 carriage);]E1
carriage)]Ms

160.32 dead.]E1
dead]Ms

160.35 unjust. We]E1
unjust—We]Ms

160.37 over,]E1
over]Ms

161.01 demise, Mr. Rood (that]E1
demise Mr. Rood (That]Ms

161.03 man)]E1
man,)]Ms

161.05 marriage projects]E1
marriage-projects]Ms

161.13 trusteeship;]E1
trusteeship,]Ms

161.13 respectful:]E1
respectful,]Ms

161.27 mistress,]E1
mistress]Ms

161.34 talk,]E1
talk]Ms

161.40 Newcome:]E1
Newcome]Ms

161.42 bonnet,]E1
bonnet]Ms

161.46 clear-sighted]E1
clearsighted]Ms

162.03 fume; "what]E1
fume, "What]Ms

162.09 we]E1
We]Ms

162.11 its]E1
it's]Ms

162.19 once,]E1
once]Ms

162.21 Ethel,]E1
Ethel]Ms

162.21 woman,]E1
woman]Ms

162.27 more:]E1
more]Ms

162.35 Laura—O Laura,]
Laura—o Laura]Ms

162.36 without]E1
with out]Ms

162.37 "Why."]E1
"Why".]Ms

162.44 its]E1
it's]Ms

163.01 outside]E1
out side]Ms

163.06 SLOWCOME]E1

SLOWCOME]Ms

163.07 Queen)—not]E1
Queen)—Not]Ms

163.09 apothecary,]E1
Apothecary,]Ms

163.11 proprietor]E1
Proprietor]Ms

163.14 from]E1
from persons even more humble than]Ms

163.14 we shall arrive]E1
we must get the meaning of that "Why?" which Mrs. Laura did not choose to interpret. We must suborn kitchen-maids forsooth. We must converse with Ladies' maids: we must interrogate Doctor's boys: and then we shall arrive]Ms

163.25 school-boys and school-girls,]E1
school boys and schoolgirls,]Ms

163.33 playing]E1
playing at marbles]Ms

163.36 go]
Go]Ms

164.02 Uncompromising]E1
Uncomprising]Ms

164.03 Low]E1
low]Ms

164.05 everybody]E1
every body]Ms

164.10 North),]E1
North)]Ms

164.14 speeches]E1
official speeches]Ms

164.14 forefathers,]E1
forefather's]Ms

164.21 and]E1
or]Ms

164.24 and]E1
or]Ms

164.26 Everybody]E1
Every body]Ms

164.31 and,]
and]Ms

164.31 Newcome,]E1
Newcome]Ms

164.34 Leger,]E1
Ledger,]Ms

164.37 known,]

known]Ms
164.39 more;]E1
more]Ms
165.03 angry:]E1
angry]Ms
165.17 'em.]
'em,]Ms
165.18 Parliament]E1
parliament]Ms
165.20 races,]E1
Races,]Ms
165.21 missionaries;]E1
Missionaries;]Ms
165.25 sides,]E1
sides]Ms
165.31 market,]E1
market]Ms
165.38 Taplow—one]
Taplow. one]Ms
165.39 maid: the]E1
maid—the]Ms
165.40 at]E1
of]Ms
166.14 grief? Quite]
grief—Quite]Ms
166.36 martyr, I say,]E1
martyr I say]Ms
167.27 dinner-party]
dinner party]Ms
167.28 banker]E1
Banker]Ms
167.28 somebody;]E1
somebody,]Ms
167.30 Commons),]E1
Commons)]Ms
168.01 whether]
Whether]Ms
168.01 more]E1
most]Ms
168.07 Italy—went]E1
Italy, went]Ms
168.07 Venice]E1
Venice,]Ms
168.08 world—the]E1
world the]Ms
168.10 the Danube]NY
Danube]Ms E1 R
168.16 have liked to join]E1
like to have joined]Ms
168.18 fellow traveller.]E1
companion.]Ms
168.36 god-papa,]
God papa,]Ms
168.37 humiliating,]E1
humiliating]Ms
168.37 consolatory,]E1
consolatory]Ms
169.01 company,]E1

company]Ms
169.06 absent,]E1
absent]Ms
169.14 kindly;]E1
kindly]Ms
169.22 off,]E1
off]Ms
169.33 city.]E1
City.]Ms
170.02 judge,]E1
judge]Ms
170.02 and,]E1
and]Ms
170.04 Goby),]E1
Goby)]Ms
170.04 thought]E1
thought,]Ms
170.06 included,]E1
included]Ms
170.12 Archduke]E1
ArchDuke]Ms
170.19 chum]E1
Chum]Ms
170.42 bouquet? on]E1
bouquet—On]Ms
170.46 "Scalps—O]
"Scalps—o]Ms
171.08 bouquet.]E1
bouquet]Ms
171.12 "Dinner, dinner!"]E1
"Dinner Dinner!"]Ms
171.13 arm;]E1
arm,]Ms
171.15 [line space] ¶Our]E1
¶Our]Ms
171.30 Scheldt]R
Scheld]Ms
171.32 maître-d'hôtel.]E1
maitre-d'hotel.]Ms
171.42 obedience,]E1
obedience]Ms
171.43 marriage.]E1
marriage]Ms
171.43 point.)]E1
point)]Ms
172.02 so—well,]E1
so—well]Ms
172.11 so,]E1
so]Ms
172.12 as]E1
a]Ms
172.12 day.]E1
day:]Ms
172.15 is—what]E1
is—What]Ms
172.22 better,]E1
better]Ms
172.25 again—"But]E1

again. "But]Ms
172.27 Rosey,]E1
Rosey]Ms
172.37 who]E1
Who]Ms
172.41 champagne]E1
Champagne]Ms
173.01 ROSEBURY AND
NEWCOME]E1
[omit]]Ms
173.28 New Town, as
everybody knows,
]E1
New-town as every
body knows]Ms
173.29 railway]E1
Railway]Ms
173.31 Park]
park]Ms
173.34 viaduct of the New
Town]E1
Viaduct of the New-
town]Ms
174.02 New Town]E1
Newtown]Ms
174.14 Quakers—many]E1
quakers—many]Ms
174.17 clergy, you see,]E1
clergy you see]Ms
174.17 county families.]E1
county-families.]Ms
174.24 family,]E1
family]Ms
174.25 that]
'that]Ms
174.25 well, we say,]E1
well we say]Ms
174.29 billiard-marker]E1
billiard marker]Ms
174.38 nay,]E1
nay]Ms
174.42 carriage-and-four]
carriage and four
]Ms
175.01 Green;]E1
green;]Ms
175.03 head-gear]E1
bonnets]Ms
175.05 Park-people]
Park people]Ms
175.06 them,]E1
them]Ms
175.07 costermonger]
Costermonger]Ms
175.10 déjeuner]E1
Déjeuner]Ms
175.13 in the drawing-room
]
in the drawing-room,
]E1

on the drawing-room
table]Ms
175.18 table]
table.]Ms
175.20 open French]E1
open-french]Ms
175.21 sixpence,]E1
sixpence]Ms
175.23 door." "How]E1
door. How]Ms
175.24 lest]E1
[omit]]Ms
175.25 should]E1
would]Ms
176.05 Ethel]
Ethel]Ms
176.10 music-book,]E1
music book,]Ms
176.10 altar-cloth,]E1
altar cloth,]Ms
176.12 Park-people]
'Park People']Ms
176.21 D.D.,]E1
D.D.]Ms
176.28 stables]E1
stables,]Ms
176.32 be]E1
[omit]]Ms
176.37 prince."]
Prince."]Ms
176.37 (who]
who]Ms
176.40 Tom]E1
Tom,]Ms
177.01 here—if]E1
here—If]Ms
177.02 boots,]E1
boots]Ms
177.05 Florac said simply,
]E1
Florac, said simply
]Ms
177.06 Jowls]
Jowls.]Ms
177.07 est]E1
[omit]]Ms
177.18 arrived,]E1
arrived]Ms
177.19 asserted,]E1
asserted]Ms
177.20 apartments,—with]
apartments,—with
]Ms
177.23 brave:—he]
brave:—He]Ms
177.23 maître-d'hotel—
"Frédéric!]
maitre d'hotel—
"Frederick!]Ms
177.25 Frédéric.]

Frederic.]Ms
177.29 à]
a]Ms
177.30 Anglais, vois tu, mon
ami," continued]E1
Anglais vois tu mon
ami"—continued
]Ms
177.32 dinner—my]E1
dinner—My]Ms
177.34 Heuh!"—he]
Heuh!"—He]Ms
177.34 he]E1
He]Ms
177.36 embracive,]E1
embracive]Ms
177.38 nursery]E1
Nursery]Ms
178.01 then]E1
then indeed]Ms
179.05 Independent]E1
Examiner]Ms
179.20 Boulevard,]E1
Boulevard]Ms
179.24 in]E1
[omit]]Ms
179.27 quasi-Gothic]E1
quasi Gothic]Ms
179.30 alone,]E1
alone and alone,
]Ms
179.35 Year,]
Year]Ms
180.03 lodge-gates]E1
lodge-/gates]Ms
180.06 woman—one]
woman—One]Ms
180.08 Arms,]E1
arms,]Ms
180.25 drive. As]E1
drive—as]Ms
180.25 friend,]E1
friend?]Ms
180.26 me. When]E1
me: when]Ms
180.26 by,]E1
by]Ms
180.29 Taplow]E1
[blank]]Ms
180.30 Florac, "Don't]E1
Florac—"Don't]Ms
180.32 Florac, "where]E1
Florac—"where]Ms
180.39 gage—"]E1
gage—."]Ms
180.41 is,]E1
is]Ms
180.43 Harris.]
Harris—]E1
Hampton.]Ms

181.02 board."]E1
bard."]Ms
181.04 'tis]E1
'Tis]Ms
181.04 lie. My good Mr.
Harris, why]E1
lie.—My good Mr.
Hampton. Why]Ms
181.06 too.]E1
too,]Ms
181.07 Taplow's]E1
[blank]]Ms
181.08 re-entered]E1
reentered]Ms
181.09 Harris]E1
Hampton]Ms
181.11 hotel. The]E1
hotel—The]Ms
181.19 Harris,]
Harris]E1
Hampton,]Ms
181.25 We]E1
He]Ms
181.26 contrast,]E1
contrast]Ms
181.28 Florac.]E1
he.]Ms
181.36 cross-examination,
]E1
cross examination,
]Ms
182.02 her]E1
her her]Ms
182.12 his]E1
her]Ms
182.16 below,]E1
below]Ms
182.19 sometimes]E1
some times]Ms
182.26 winter morning:
]E1
winter-morning:
]Ms
182.33 Laura]E1
Eh bien? She]Ms
182.33 why,]E1
why]Ms
182.36 say," whispered]E1
say"—whispered
]Ms
182.37 shoulder;]E1
shoulder]Ms
182.38 hoped—I]
hoped I]Ms
183.02 boy to her—that the
]E1
Helen to her little
girl, that the two
]Ms
183.10 conservatory]

Conservatory]Ms

183.16 No, never—and]
No—never.—and
]Ms

183.19 dreams,]E1
dreams]Ms

183.20 O,]E1
o]Ms

183.21 that. Let]E1
that—Let]Ms

183.22 that,]E1
that]Ms

183.23 never,]
never]Ms

183.24 said,]E1
said]Ms

183.24 too—O]
too—o]Ms

183.25 said,]E1
said]Ms

183.26 time]E1
[omit]]Ms

183.30 there.' I]E1
there'—I]Ms

183.31 Arthur, that]E1
Arthur—that]Ms

183.43 sometimes.]E1
some times.]Ms

183.45 creature.]E1
Creature.]Ms

184.02 solitude.]E1
solitude]Ms

184.02 her, I think—and—
O—I]E1
her I think—and—
o—I]Ms

184.05 him,]E1
him]Ms

184.17 "Indeed,]E1
"Indeed]Ms

184.21 galley?"]E1
galley"]Ms

184.25 there. [line space]
]E1
there.]Ms

184.35 the wretched,]E1
the wretched,]Ms

184.38 morning,]E1
morning]Ms

184.41 [line space] ¶This]E1
¶This]Ms

184.42 dinner-time,]E1
dinner time,]Ms

184.43 ladies. ¶I]E1
ladies. I]Ms

184.45 remain,]E1
remain]Ms

184.45 it,]E1
it]Ms

185.03 the]E1

The]Ms

185.14 union,]E1
union]Ms

185.25 Bishop]E1
smug Bishop]Ms

185.31 myself,]E1
myself]Ms

185.31 simplicity,]E1
simplicity]Ms

185.31 believe]E1
beleive]Ms

185.32 guileless]E1
guiless]Ms

185.34 Harris]E1
Hampton]Ms

185.36 "Parbleu! No;"]E1
"Parbleu No,"]Ms

185.36 his,]E1
his]Ms

185.41 miserable;]E1
miserable,]Ms

186.04 night]E1
night,]Ms

186.05 raised),]E1
raised)]Ms

186.06 evening,]E1
evening]Ms

186.10 friend! what a
Joseph!"]E1
friend, what a
Joseph,"]Ms

186.13 angel!"]E1
angel—"]Ms

186.14 said;]E1
said]Ms

186.17 auxiliary]E1
auxillary]Ms

186.18 landlord]E1
Landlord]Ms

186.18 supply; indeed,]E1
supply indeed]Ms

186.20 game, &c.,]E1
game &c.]Ms

186.21 Highgate,]E1
Highgate]Ms

186.26 Robert;]E1
Robert,]Ms

186.28 note,]E1
note]Ms

186.31 truth,]E1
truth]Ms

186.31 and]E1
And]Ms

186.32 effectual]E1
more effectual]Ms

186.33 thought of making it,
]E1
though of making it
]Ms

186.38 ale.]E1

Ale.]Ms

186.44 auctioneer,]E1
Auctioneer,]Ms

186.45 reporter now editor
]
Reporter now Editor
]Ms

186.45 apothecary]
Apothecary]Ms

187.04 now;]E1
now,]Ms

187.04 course,]E1
course]Ms

187.06 partner—a]E1
partner a]Ms

187.08 nightwork]E1
night work]Ms

187.10 straightway]E1
straight way]Ms

187.11 partner. "From
Rosebury? The
Princess ill]E1
partner "From
Rosebury, the
Princess Ill]Ms

187.13 day-time. Confound
]E1
day time—Confound
]Ms

187.14 retour,]
retour]Ms

187.16 French,]E1
french,]Ms

187.16 "you're]E1
"You're]Ms

187.23 him,]E1
him.]Ms

187.30 John,]E1
John]Ms

187.36 Harris,]E1
Harris]Ms

187.39 brandy-and-water,
"it's]E1
brandy and water.
"It's]Ms

187.41 pocket-handkerchiefs
]E1
pocket handkerchiefs
]Ms

187.42 coronet."]E1
coronet, Potts."]Ms

187.44 place.]E1
place]Ms

187.45 hotel]
Hotel]Ms

188.03 passer-by]E1
passer by]Ms

188.05 previously:]E1
previously,]Ms

188.07 me."]E1

me,"]Ms

188.10 softness; "your]E1
softness. "Your]Ms

188.11 her.]E1
her]Ms

188.12 hasn't]E1
has n't]Ms

188.13 one—one—except]
one—one except]Ms

188.19 Rooster, forsooth,]E1
Rooster forsooth]Ms

188.24 it,]E1
it now,]Ms

188.24 now, the old hag—a]E1
now the old hag—— a]Ms

188.32 sea,]E1
sea]Ms

188.33 him,]E1
him]Ms

188.34 her:—strikes]
her:—Strikes]Ms

188.42 go]E1
go out]Ms

189.07 still,]E1
still]Ms

189.08 name,]E1
name]Ms

189.16 Florac.]E1
Florac—]Ms

189.18 sermons. My]E1
sermons—My]Ms

189.21 kindness, never! In]E1
kindness never—in]Ms

189.24 us,]E1
us]Ms

190.01 "ONE MORE
UNFORTUNATE."]E1
[omit]]Ms

190.15 of]E1
after]Ms

190.18 Highgate,]E1
Highgate]Ms

190.21 more.]E1
more:]Ms

190.25 coming. Lord]E1
coming—Lord]Ms

190.29 to]E1
with]Ms

190.32 know,]E1
know that]Ms

191.01 nurses,]E1
nurses;]Ms

191.02 bedsides]E1

bed sides]Ms

191.09 many were ready to
attend]E1
twenty were in
attendance]Ms

191.12 she]E1
She]Ms

191.15 the]E1
her]Ms

191.15 children,]E1
children,,]Ms

191.25 arrived with]E1
brought him]Ms

191.25 Newcome,]E1
Newcome']Ms

191.27 him, and]E1
him and this]Ms

191.33 leaves,]E1
leaves]Ms

191.43 the]E1
that]Ms

192.02 testimony,]E1
testimony]Ms

192.03 much. For]E1
much for]Ms

192.07 I,]E1
I]Ms

192.07 occurring,]E1
occurring]Ms

192.11 "The]E1
"the]Ms

192.14 be,]E1
be]Ms

192.20 Harris,]E1
Harris]Ms

192.20 called,]E1
called]Ms

192.26 merely,]E1
merely]Ms

192.34 Belsize]E1
And before Barnes
could answer, Belsize
]Ms

192.35 pavement. The]E1
pavement—The]Ms

192.40 Taplow, aghast,]E1
Taplow aghast]Ms

192.43 me." And]E1
me"—And]Ms

192.45 inns,]E1
Inns,]Ms

193.03 Speers]
[omit]]Ms

193.05 On the next day,
]E1
In the evening,]Ms

193.11 shortly]E1
an hour]Ms

193.17 continued. What
]E1

continued—What
]Ms

193.17 day, with a servant
]E1
day with a servants
]Ms

193.25 necessary]E1
necessary,]Ms

193.31 business—nay,
pleasure—it]E1
business nay
pleasure it]Ms

193.40 harangue. At]E1
harangue—At]Ms

194.01 well-known]E1
well known]Ms

194.02 of the tribunal and
the punishment]
†and the
punishment↓ of the
tribunal]Ms

194.03 the]E1
The]Ms

194.07 father,]E1
father]Ms

194.09 conduct,]E1
conduct]Ms

194.10 twenty]E1
fifty living]Ms

194.14 cruelty had]E1
cruelty—had]Ms

194.18 in vain for bread,
]E1
in-vain for bread
]Ms

194.19 life. Why]E1
life—Why]Ms

194.21 on—between]
on, between]E1
on—So between]Ms

194.34 asylum,]E1
asylum]Ms

194.38 goes]E1
passes]Ms

194.38 Malice]
malice]Ms

194.42 her,]E1
her]Ms

195.03 equals,]E1
equals]Ms

195.04 kind,]E1
kind]Ms

195.05 her,]E1
her]Ms

195.23 name]E1
name which]Ms

195.37 bishops,]E1
Bishops,]Ms

196.01 IN WHICH ACHILLES
LOSES BRISEIS.]E1

[*omit*]]Ms
196.11 During the period
of his London and
Parisian dissipations
his poor mother
did not venture to
remonstrate with
her young prodigal,
but shut her eyes,
not daring to open
them on his wild
courses. As for the
friends of his person
and house, many of
whom were portly
elderly gentlemen,
their affection for
the young Marquis
was so extreme
that there was no
company into which
their fidelity would
not lead them to
follow him; and
you might see him
dancing at Mabille
with veteran aides-
de-camp looking
on, or disporting
with opera dancers
at a Trois-Frères
banquet, which some
old gentleman of
his father's age had
taken the pains to
order. If his lordship
Count Almaviva
wants a friend to
carry the lanthorn or
to hold the ladder;
do you suppose
there are not many
most respectable
men in society who
will act Figaro?
When Farintosh]E1
When he]Ms
196.29 ladyships' hangers
on]E1
ladyship's hangers
]Ms
196.30 kinsmen,]E1
kinsmen]Ms
196.32 honour,]E1
honour]Ms
197.01 was,]
was]Ms
197.02 men,]E1
men]Ms
197.04 lady-mother]

lady mother]Ms
197.05 toadies]E1
Toadys]Ms
197.07 comments]E1
sentiments]Ms
197.16 toad-eaters]E1
toad eaters]Ms
197.20 ensuing]E1
ensueing]Ms
197.35 life—excitement]E1
life excitement]Ms
197.36 D—rking, with Lord
H—gate;]E1
D—king, with Lord
H—gate]Ms
197.38 B—nes]E1
B—ns]Ms
197.38 say,]E1
say]Ms
197.40 Perigord pie,]
Perigord-pie,]E1
erigord pie,]Ms
197.43 it.]E1
of it.]Ms
198.09 souls,]E1
souls]Ms
198.18 more]E1
more cigars]Ms
198.37 room,]E1
room]Ms
198.43 remember?]E1
remember?:]Ms
198.44 friend—what]
friend—What]Ms
199.04 here,]E1
here]Ms
199.05 No? Poor]E1
No?—Poor]Ms
199.16 sun.]E1
Sun.]Ms
199.17 Ratcatcher,]E1
Ratcatcher]Ms
199.18 order. Do]E1
order—Do]Ms
199.20 mine. Besides]E1
mine—Besides]Ms
199.27 best-plucked]E1
best-/plucked]Ms
199.28 creature, by Jove,
]E1
creature by Jove]Ms
199.32 different—she]
different—She]Ms
199.39 said,]E1
said]Ms
200.11 (in both languages),
]E1
in both languages,)
]Ms
200.14 cetera. Don't]

cetera—Don't]Ms
200.20 that]E1
that they]Ms
200.23 likewise]
likewise,]E1
too]Ms
200.24 O]E1
o]Ms
200.34 the]E1
her]Ms
201.04 valet,]E1
Valet,]Ms
201.04 captains]E1
Captains]Ms
201.10 son [*line space*]
¶"DEAR MADAM]E1
son. ¶"Dear Madam.
]Ms
201.11 hand-writing),]E1
hand-writing.)]Ms
201.27 "ETHEL NEWCOME."
]
"Ethel Newcome."
]Ms
201.29 family misfortune
]E1
family-misfortune
]Ms
201.32 Rosebury; do,]E1
Rosebury do]Ms
201.33 can, pray,]E1
can pray]Ms
201.34 to]E1
[*omit*]]Ms
201.39 very day of]E1
day after]Ms
202.08 already,]E1
already]Ms
202.12 Now she thought of
]E1
She insisted on]Ms
202.13 then feared lest she
should be ill received
]E1
being received not
very graciously]Ms
202.14 him. So at home
Lady Ann remained,
]E1
him—home Lady
Ann returned]Ms
202.16 at]E1
on]Ms
202.19 Brian—the]
Brians—the]Ms
202.25 her: and]E1
her so that]Ms
202.29 morrow]E1
third day]Ms
202.39 maledictions growled

about Sir Barnes's
]E1
maledictory
expressions growled
about his]Ms
203.01 poney-carriage]
poney carriage]Ms
203.02 *her*]E1
her]Ms
203.13 lodge gate]E1
Lodge Gate]Ms
203.17 market-place,]E1
Market-place,]Ms
203.21 villainy,]E1
villainy]Ms
203.24 enemy. [*line space*]
]E1
enemy.]Ms
204.05 fond),]
fond)]Ms
204.15 souls]E1
Souls]Ms
204.19 shepherd]E1
Shepherd]Ms
204.22 herself,]E1
herself]Ms
204.26 that]E1
[*omit*]]Ms
204.28 spent, she said,]E1
spent she said]Ms
204.33 superiority,]E1
superiority]Ms
204.37 her,]E1
her]Ms
204.37 him,]E1
him]Ms
204.40 almost,]E1
almost]Ms
204.44 much—who]E1
much, who]Ms
205.01 talk,]E1
talk]Ms
205.03 Why,]E1
Why]Ms
205.09 house,']E1
house with them,'
]Ms
205.16 him,]E1
him]Ms
205.20 early? I]E1
early?—I]Ms
205.22 grandmother,]E1
grandmother]Ms
205.22 subject,]E1
subject]Ms
205.40 too, in the]E1
too in]Ms
205.41 Burrs,]E1
[blank]]Ms
205.43 parks]E1

Parks]Ms
206.02 odious."' ¶I would
not willingly
interrupt the
narrative,but]E1
odious. [footnote]
*In order not
to interrupt the
narrative]Ms
206.04 (which]E1
which]Ms
206.05 manner),]E1
manner,]Ms
206.07 drawing-room]E1
dressing-room]Ms
206.07 at? We did not tell
our hostess that
poor Ethel and her
grandmother had
been accused of
doing the very same
thing, for which she
found fault with the
Misses Burr. Miss
Newcome thought
herself quite innocent,
or how should she
have cried out at the
naughty behaviour
of other people?
]E1
at.[end footnote]
]Ms
206.12 went, however,'
resumed my wife's
young penitent, 'it
]E1
went however,' it
]Ms
206.24 it—not]E1
it—not (here Miss
Ethel laughed)—not
]Ms
206.24 rank. (Here Miss
Ethel laughed.)]E1
rank.]Ms
206.25 we—every]
we every]Ms
206.28 him,]E1
him]Ms
206.30 character,]E1
character]Ms
206.34 him;]E1
him,]Ms
207.04 pity, God help her,
]E1
pity God help her
]Ms
207.05 days;—as]E1
days—as]Ms

207.08 by]E1
of my]Ms
207.09 myself,]E1
myself]Ms
207.10 is, as it were,]E1
is as it were]Ms
207.13 go]E1
go go]Ms
207.16 I]E1
And I]Ms
207.19 church the
clergyman]E1
Church the
Clergyman]Ms
207.20 face. [*line space*]]E1
face.]Ms
208.04 discomfited]E1
discomfitted]Ms
208.09 Potts.]E1
Potts]Ms
208.18 straightway]E1
straight way]Ms
208.22 Speers,]E1
[blank]]Ms
208.25 she]
She]Ms
208.35 meal,]E1
meal]Ms
208.37 china,]E1
China,]Ms
208.40 Ethel]
Edith]Ms
208.42 Ethel.]E1
Edith.]Ms
208.44 Ethel?"]E1
Edith?"]Ms
208.45 Ethel]E1
Edith]Ms
209.18 so—so,]
so—so]Ms
209.21 them, I own,]E1
them I own]Ms
209.22 men.]E1
men]Ms
209.44 marriages,]
marriages]Ms
210.06 now.]E1
this]Ms
210.15 be.]E1
be,]Ms
210.18 but, O!]
but, oh!]E1
but o]Ms
210.22 career,]E1
career]Ms
210.22 who]E1
that]Ms
210.23 royal]E1
Royal]Ms
210.26 Confessor,]E1

Confessor]Ms
210.26 . . ."]E1
. ."]Ms
210.26 disbelieve]E1
Disbelieve]Ms
210.32 am ashamed,"]E1
was humiliated,"
]Ms
210.33 is,]E1
is]Ms
210.38 *n'est-ce*]E1
n'est ce]Ms
210.43 mind. And I've
given up every
thing—everything—
and have broken off
with my old habits
and—and things you
know—and intend to
lead a regular life—
and will never go to
Tattersall's again; nor
bet a shilling; nor
touch another cigar
if you like—that is, if
you don't like; for I
love you so, Ethel—I
do, with all my heart
I do!" ¶"You are very
generous and kind,
Lord Farintosh,"
Ethel said. "It is
myself, not you,
I doubt. O! I am
humiliated to make
such a confession!"
¶"How humiliated?"
Ethel withdrew the
hand which the
young nobleman
endeavoured to
seize. ¶"If," she
continued, "if]E1
mind. ¶"But if]Ms
211.10 speak,—and]E1
speak, and]Ms
211.16 faults]E1
fault]Ms
211.19 ashamed]E1
ashamed and
humiliated]Ms
211.20 so."]E1
it."]Ms
211.26 me,]E1
me]Ms
211.27 what]E1
What]Ms
211.28 so,]E1
so]Ms
211.29 it—do]E1

it—Do]Ms
212.10 burst forth]E1
broke out]Ms
212.12 confidante:]
Confidante:]Ms
212.16 affair. [*line space*]
]E1
affair.]Ms
212.19 knew]E1
knew,]Ms
213.01 IN WHICH WE WRITE
TO THE COLONEL.
]E1
[*omit*]]Ms
213.16 Barnes,]E1
Barnes]Ms
213.17 affairs,]E1
affairs]Ms
213.18 attorney, Mr. Speers,
]E1
attorney Mr. [blank]
]Ms
213.19 the]E1
that]Ms
213.23 intelligence,]E1
intelligence]Ms
213.25 railway]E1
Railway]Ms
213.26 bank]E1
Bank]Ms
213.28 lodge]E1
Lodge]Ms
213.29 trembling,]E1
trembling]Ms
213.29 employer,]E1
employer]Ms
213.30 the]E1
[*omit*]]Ms
213.31 house]E1
House]Ms
214.10 leave,]E1
leave]Ms
214.16 said:—]E1
said.]Ms
214.23 *language,*—he]E1
language he]Ms
214.25 *course*]E1
course,]Ms
214.26 Clarykin sends a
thousand]E1
Clary kin sends *1000*
]Ms
214.27 affectionate,—E. N.
¶Will]E1
affectionate E.N. Will
]Ms
214.31 Pendennis,]E1
Pendennis]Ms
214.41 mind,]E1
mind]Ms

214.42 themselves,—nay,
enjoy possibly,]E1
themselves, nay
enjoy possibly]Ms
214.44 out,]E1
out]Ms
214.45 clear handwriting,
]E1
clearly handwriting
]Ms
215.05 plainly]E1
plainly,]Ms
215.09 . . ."—and]
. ."—and]Ms
215.14 handwriting,]E1
hand-writing,]Ms
215.15 guilt:]E1
guilt.]Ms
215.18 nightcaps]E1
night-caps]Ms
215.21 way, you see,]E1
way you see]Ms
215.22 letter.)]E1
letter.]Ms
215.31 nightcap—and]E1
night-cap—and]Ms
215.33 about, under]E1
about. Under]Ms
215.40 *letter?"*]E1
letter?"]Ms
215.42 No;]E1
No]Ms
216.05 now——"]E1
now"]Ms
216.10 Colonel—though
]E1
Colonel though]Ms
216.10 it—tell]E1
it. Tell]Ms
216.15 no—O]E1
no—o]Ms
216.15 cross-examining]E1
cross examining]Ms
216.27 she]E1
She]Ms
216.27 conspiracy, too;]E1
conspiracy too]Ms
216.34 prize; and]E1
prize;—and]Ms
217.01 IN WHICH WE ARE
INTRODUCED TO A
NEW NEWCOME.]E1
[*omit*]]Ms
217.09 previous, and that
the Colonel seemed
to be in the highest
spirits. High spirits
about what?]E1
previous.]Ms
217.24 homilies]E1

homelies]Ms
217.25 knees,]E1
knees]Ms
217.28 worldliness]E1
worldiness]Ms
217.31 open,]E1
open]Ms
217.32 once, to Highgate,
]E1
once to Highgate
]Ms
217.32 Farintosh,]E1
Farintosh]Ms
218.07 Kew—Mrs.]E1
Kew Mrs.]Ms
218.12 did]E1
will]Ms
218.17 the]E1
his]Ms
218.18 its head,]E1
it's head]Ms
218.20 world,]E1
world]Ms
218.26 wit, nor talents,]E1
wit nor talents]Ms
218.34 man, as we know,
]E1
man as we know
]Ms
218.35 hardly,]E1
hardly]Ms
218.37 hands]E1
hand]Ms
218.42 traffic]E1
traffick]Ms
219.02 our's—to]E1
ours—to]Ms
219.07 Ethel's]E1
Edith's]Ms
219.09 visits]E1
visit]Ms
219.17 She whispered to
me in her kind
way that she would
give a guinea, that
she would, to see a
certain couple made
happy together; that
they were born for
one another, that
they were; she was
for having me go off
to fetch Clive: but
who was I to act as
Hymen's messenger;
or to interpose in
such delicate family
affairs? ¶All this
while Sir Barnes
Newcome, Bart.,]E1

Barnes meanwhile
]Ms
219.24 ended,]E1
ended]Ms
219.24 Term,]
Term]Ms
219.31 little]E1
the little]Ms
219.33 in]E1
into]Ms
219.33 her,]E1
her]Ms
219.37 missionary
magazines,]E1
Missionary
Magazines,]Ms
219.37 travel and history
]E1
Travel and History
]Ms
220.11 wondered,]E1
wondered]Ms
220.20 doting,]E1
doting]Ms
220.24 "O,]
"O]Ms
220.30 [line space] ¶"MY DEAR
OLD MASON.]
¶My dear old Mason.
]Ms
220.35 too, and who
proposes to be
happier still before
any very long time is
over.]E1
too.]Ms
220.39 Battle]E1
battle]Ms
221.09 [line space] ¶Keziah
]E1
¶Keziah]Ms
221.19 news,]E1
news]Ms
222.01 MR. AND MRS. CLIVE
NEWCOME.]E1
[omit]]Ms
222.07 impaired]E1
impared]Ms
222.21 beauty,]E1
beauty]Ms
222.21 humour,]E1
humour]Ms
222.29 in this reticence;
and,]E1
this reticence and
]Ms
222.30 remorse,]E1
remorse]Ms
222.32 constant,]E1
constant]Ms

223.04 Newcome. She]E1
Newcome—She]Ms
223.08 Fairoaks]E1
Fair Oaks]Ms
223.09 children]E1
children,]Ms
223.10 dear),]
dear)]Ms
223.10 skill—there]
skill—There]Ms
223.11 rest, and she]E1
rest and she,]Ms
223.15 form,]E1
form]Ms
223.17 been,]E1
been]Ms
223.21 him,]E1
him]Ms
223.22 indignation,]E1
indignation]Ms
223.25 horror]E1
horor]Ms
223.28 ill-used]E1
ill used]Ms
223.31 servants]E1
servants,]Ms
223.31 Ethel]E1
Ether]Ms
223.32 fiery]E1
firy]Ms
223.34 tyranny: besides,
]E1
tyranny, besides]Ms
223.35 wily]E1
wiley]Ms
223.40 maintenance]E1
maintainance]Ms
223.45 income.]E1
income]Ms
223.45 hers,]E1
hers]Ms
224.03 servants.]E1
servants]Ms
224.07 neighbours,]E1
neighbours]Ms
224.10 thought;]E1
thought,]Ms
224.11 ostentation; was
awe-striken]E1
ostentation, was awe
striken]Ms
224.12 poverty]E1
the Poverty]Ms
224.13 compels]E1
compells]Ms
224.14 creeds, who
elsewhere]E1
creeds who else
where]Ms
224.15 continually,]E1

continually]Ms
224.16 it,]
it]Ms
224.16 master.]E1
master]Ms
224.17 day,—our young
London lady,]E1
day, Our young
London lady]Ms
224.19 these—threading]
these. threading
]Ms
224.22 heart-stricken]E1
heart stricken]Ms
224.26 to]E1
[omit]]Ms
224.28 Miss]E1
[omit]]Ms
224.29 ball-room? If]E1
ball-room, if]Ms
224.30 bear,]E1
bear]Ms
224.32 Clive]E1
Clive,]Ms
224.32 been lapsing]E1
been going]Ms
224.35 transferred]E1
transfered]Ms
224.37 him,]E1
him]Ms
224.39 asks,]E1
asks]Ms
224.42 harm—not]E1
harm not]Ms
224.43 Colonel,]E1
Colonel]Ms
225.06 decorum. "I]
decorum—"I]Ms
225.08 answered yes or no.
]E1
answred yes or no,
]Ms
225.09 care. Her]E1
care—Her]Ms
225.18 agreeable.]E1
agreable.]Ms
225.21 Her Majesty]E1
her majesty]Ms
225.25 Sir—for]
Sir. For]Ms
225.26 afterwards with
Rosey, who]E1
after wards with
Rosey. Who]Ms
225.32 Brussels,]E1
Brussels]Ms
225.34 Campaigner,]E1
Campaigner]Ms
225.34 which James had
meditated]E1

James had been
meditating]Ms
225.37 London,]E1
London]Ms
225.38 them,]E1
them]Ms
225.39 Tyburnian]E1
Tiburnian]Ms
225.44 every thing,]
everything,]Ms
225.45 carriage-makers]E1
carriage makers]Ms
226.01 creature]E1
creature,]Ms
226.03 qui-his]E1
qui his]Ms
226.04 homage;]
hommage]Ms
226.04 generals']E1
general's]Ms
226.09 Bays's]E1
Baizes]Ms
226.12 Park;]E1
park]Ms
226.13 round;]E1
round]Ms
226.15 other]E1
other.]Ms
226.16 Colonel's—now]
Colonel's now]Ms
226.19 one, I am sure,
could be]E1
one I am sure could
be entirely]Ms
226.22 blue-black]E1
blue black]Ms
226.23 judges, and the like,
]E1
judges and the like
]Ms
226.25 it—that]
it—That]Ms
226.26 entered,]E1
entered]Ms
226.27 a dainty]E1
dainty]Ms
226.27 pocket-handkerchief
]
pocket handkerchief
]Ms
226.29 group to group]
groupe to groupe
]Ms
226.30 Park, the Exhibition,
nay,]E1
park, the Exhibition,
nay]Ms
226.34 (save]E1
save]Ms
226.34 ago) had ever
seemed]E1

ago had ever been
]Ms
226.35 her—If]
her if]Ms
226.36 ailing,]E1
ailing]Ms
226.37 them:]E1
them]Ms
226.39 place: with]E1
place. With]Ms
226.39 replied.]
replied]Ms
226.40 at Musselburgh]
a Musselbourough
]Ms
226.41 Scotch]E1
scotch]Ms
226.44 condition,]E1
condition]Ms
226.44 suppose—when]E1
suppose—when]Ms
226.45 directors,]E1
directors]Ms
227.02 homage to him. His
brother Hobson,]E1
hommage to him—
His brother Hobson
]Ms
227.04 firm,]E1
firm]Ms
227.05 while.]
while]Ms
227.07 was such]E1
[omit]]Ms
227.11 lifetime—indeed]E1
life time—Indeed
]Ms
227.12 him—but]
him—But]Ms
227.12 interest, the]E1
interest—the]Ms
227.16 background]E1
back ground]Ms
227.16 group.]E1
groupe.]Ms
227.22 chariot wheel, have
sacrificed]
charriot wheel, have
sacrifised]Ms
227.25 girl—how]E1
girl. How]Ms
227.25 matter—had]E1
matter, had]Ms
227.27 himself. Was]E1
himself—Was]Ms
227.29 submission;]E1
submission]Ms
227.30 surely; he]E1
surely—he]Ms

227.31 heart, and]E1
heart—and]Ms
227.32 about. It]E1
about—It]Ms
227.38 children.]E1
children:]Ms
227.41 Well,]E1
Well]Ms
227.43 happy?]E1
happy]Ms
227.44 us,]E1
us]Ms
227.45 Pendennis,]E1
Pendennis]Ms
227.45 Briseis,]E1
Briseis]Ms
227.46 Warrington,]E1
Warrington]Ms
227.46 way,]E1
way]Ms
228.01 removed,]E1
removed]Ms
228.08 on]E1
in]Ms
228.09 negation. If Ethel
was not guiltless,
]E1
negation—If she was
not guiltless]Ms
228.10 guilty. He]E1
guilty he]Ms
228.11 palliations,]
palliations]Ms
228.12 rejected, and
deservedly rejected,
]E1
rejected and
deservedly rejected
]Ms
228.17 wife,]E1
wife]Ms
228.17 better,]E1
better]Ms
228.22 it,]E1
it]Ms
228.24 worthy,]E1
worthy]Ms
228.26 watched]E1
waited]Ms
228.27 loathsome]E1
loathesome]Ms
228.28 opinion; and Clive—
with]
opinion and Clive
with]Ms
228.34 countenance,]E1
countenance]Ms
228.35 attempted,]E1
attempted]Ms
228.38 a]E1

[omit]]Ms
228.39 Forgiveness? Pshaw!
Are]E1
Forgiveness. Pshaw
are]Ms
228.40 leading-strings?]E1
leading strings?]Ms
229.01 something]E1
somthing]Ms
229.05 part,]E1
part]Ms
229.07 you." And]E1
you," and a]Ms
229.07 over,]E1
over]Ms
230.01 MRS. CLIVE AT HOME.
]E1
[omit]]Ms
230.19 Bays's]
Baizes]Ms
230.24 'Change]
change]Ms
230.25 Bank,]E1
bank,]Ms
230.30 London,]E1
London]Ms
230.32 house]E1
House]Ms
230.35 place,]E1
place]Ms
231.06 Colonel,]E1
Colonel]Ms
231.07 way, that whatever
]E1
way that what ever
]Ms
231.08 house;]E1
house,]Ms
231.09 advantageous;]E1
advantageous,]Ms
231.11 consignments to
Hobson]E1
consignments to
Hobson and]Ms
231.13 acquaintances,]E1
acquaintances]Ms
231.18 Barnes,]E1
Barnes.]Ms
231.24 company,]
company]Ms
231.25 conducted]E1
conducted,]Ms
231.26 England,]E1
England.]Ms
231.27 muddle-headed]E1
muddle headed]Ms
231.27 white,]E1
white]Ms
231.29 them]E1
them,]Ms

231.30 house]E1
house in the city
]Ms
231.31 come]E1
have come]Ms
231.37 party;]E1
party]Ms
231.41 other,]E1
other]Ms
231.41 co-partners,]E1
co-partners]Ms
231.42 London]E1
Londo]Ms
231.43 Company, were
overruled]E1
Company were over
ruled]Ms
231.44 City;]E1
city,]Ms
232.05 Bayham, I
remember,]E1
Bayham I remember
]Ms
232.12 uttered,]E1
utterred,]Ms
232.13 Company—what]
company—what]Ms
232.15 taking]E1
though a director
too, taking]Ms
232.21 inherit.]E1
inherit:]Ms
232.28 people,]E1
people]Ms
232.30 marriage some
friends]E1
marriage. Some
friends of Colonel
Thomas Newcome
C.B.]Ms
232.32 tree,]E1
tree]Ms
232.32 dexterously]E1
dextrously]Ms
232.35 howitzer,]E1
Howatzar,]Ms
232.36 Britannia,]E1
Britania,]Ms
232.37 figures:]E1
figures,]Ms
232.38 Art,]
Art]Ms
232.39 year, as well as to
Fred. Bayham's
noble speech in
the course of the
evening, when it was
exhibited. The East
and its wars, and
its heroes, Assaye

and Seringapatam
('and Lord Lake
and Laswaree too,'
calls out the Colonel
greatly elated) tiger-
hunting palanquins,
Juggernaut,
elephants, the
burning of widows—
all passed before us
in F. B.'s splendid
oration. He spoke
of the product of
the Indian forest,
the palm-tree, the
cocoa-nut tree, the
banyan tree. Palms
the Colonel had
already brought back
with him, the palms
of valour, won in the
field of war (cheers).
Cocoa-nut trees he
had never seen,
though he had heard
wonders related
regarding the milky
contents of their
fruit. Here at any
rate was one tree of
the kind, under the
branches of which he
humbly trusted often
to repose—and, if
he might be so bold
as to carry on the
Eastern metaphor, he
would say, knowing
the excellence of
the Colonel's claret
and the splendour of
his hospitality, that
he would prefer a
cocoa-nut day at the
Colonel's to a banyan
day anywhere else.
Whilst F. B.'s speech
went on, I]E1
year. I]Ms

233.10 apropos]E1
    a propos]Ms
233.12 another,]E1
    another]Ms
233.13 gloomy. When]E1
    gloomy when]Ms
233.13 world,]E1
    world]Ms
233.17 it. How different
    it was from the
    old Fitzroy Square

mansion with
its ramshackle
furniture, and spoils
of brokers' shops,
and Tottenham-
court Road odds and
ends! An Oxford
Street upholsterer
had been let loose
in the yet virgin
chambers; and that
inventive genius
had decorated them
with all the wonders
his fancy could
devise. Roses and
Cupids quivered
on the ceilings, up
to which golden
arabesques crawled
from the walls; your
face (handsome
or otherwise) was
reflected by countless
looking-glasses,
so multiplied and
arranged as, as it
were, to carry you
into the next street.
You trod on velvet,
pausing with respect
in the centre of
the carpet, where
Rosey's cypher was
worked in the sweet
flowers which bear
her name.What
delightful crooked
legs the chairs
had! What corner-
cupboards there
were filled with
Dresden gimcracks,
which it was a part
of this little woman's
business in life to
purchase! What
étagères, and bon-
bonnières, and
chiffonnières! What
awfully bad pastels
there were on the
walls! What frightful
Boucher and Lancret
shepherds and
shepherdesses leered
over the portières!
What velvet-
bound volumes,
mother-of-pearl

albums, inkstands
representing beasts
of the field, prie-
dieux chairs, and
wonderful nick-
nacks I can recollect!
There was the
most magnificent
piano, though Rosey
seldom sang any
of her six songs
now; and when
she kept her couch
at a certain most
interesting period,
the good Colonel,
ever anxious to
procure amusement
for his darling, asked
whether she would
not like a barrel-
organ grinding fifty
or sixty favourite
pieces, which a
bearer could turn?
And he mentioned
how Windus, of
their regiment,
who loved music
exceedingly, had a
very fine instrument
of this kind out to
Barrackpore in the
year 1810, and relays
of barrels by each
ship with all the new
tunes from Europe.
The]E1
    it—The]Ms
233.44 together,]E1
    together]Ms
234.02 silent;]E1
    silent.]Ms
234.03 times,]E1
    times]Ms
234.04 J.J.,]E1
    J.J.]Ms
234.06 appearance]E1
    appearance,]Ms
234.08 somehow]
    some how]Ms
234.10 house. There]E1
    house—There]Ms
234.10 the]E1
    a]Ms
234.11 painter; Warrington,
    the cynic;]E1
    painter—Warrington,
    the cynic]Ms
234.14 great,]E1

great]Ms
234.14 set,]E1
       set.]Ms
234.15 visiting-book]
       visiting book]Ms
234.16 round,]E1
       round]Ms
234.16 Newcome, and
       Colonel Newcome;—
       the]E1
       Newcome Colonel
       Newcome. The]Ms
234.21 stories (the]E1
       stories—(the]Ms
234.23 student-days]E1
       student days]Ms
234.24 get on in]E1
       fit into]Ms
234.25 balls,]E1
       balls]Ms
234.25 foreheads,]E1
       forheads]Ms
234.28 dance, making woful
       blunders, however,
       ]E1
       dance making woful
       blunders however
       ]Ms
234.30 overdrink]E1
       over drink]Ms
234.36 beard,]E1
       beard.]Ms
234.36 Red]E1
       red]Ms
234.39 coldly.]E1
       coldly,]Ms
234.41 *gatherum*,]E1
       gatherum]Ms
234.41 parties,]E1
       parties]Ms
234.42 Poins]
       Poins,]E1
       Poyns]Ms
235.06 horseman—was]E1
       horseman—Was]Ms
235.08 sufferance;]E1
       sufferance,]Ms
235.08 fellow,]E1
       fellow]Ms
235.11 days,]E1
       days]Ms
235.12 son,]E1
       son]Ms
235.15 lightly]E1
       likely]Ms
235.16 division;]E1
       division]Ms
235.17 because,]E1
       because]Ms
235.18 again,]E1

again]Ms
235.20 handsome]E1
       splendid]Ms
235.23 amassed a]E1
       a master]Ms
235.23 Clive,]E1
       Clive]Ms
235.24 education,]E1
       education]Ms
235.27 Company; had]E1
       Company—Had]Ms
235.28 affairs; went]E1
       affairs—Went]Ms
235.29 painting-room,]E1
       painting-room]Ms
235.30 brushes!]E1
       brushes]Ms
235.32 Rosey,]
       Rosey]Ms
235.34 furrows]E1
       furroughs]Ms
235.39 easel]
       easle]Ms
235.40 acquaintances, stories
       ]E1
       acquaintances—
       stories]Ms
235.40 concert, practise
       artless smiles]E1
       concert—practise
       artless smiles,]Ms
235.41 bouderies, tears
       perhaps,]
       bouderies—tears
       perhaps]Ms
235.42 reconciliation.]E1
       reconciliation]Ms
235.43 she,]E1
       she]Ms
235.43 heart,]E1
       heart]Ms
236.01 her; the thought
       came]E1
       her the thought
       would come]Ms
236.01 straight-way]
       straight way]Ms
236.03 truth; the shoe was a
       ]E1
       truth the shoe—a
       ]Ms
236.07 agreeably.]E1
       agreably.]Ms
236.08 door;]E1
       door]Ms
236.10 carriage. The]E1
       carriage—The]Ms
236.11 (where]E1
       where]Ms
236.11 Picardy]E1

Piccardy]Ms
236.12 agreeable]E1
       agreable]Ms
236.12 him) and]E1
       him. And]Ms
236.13 intimate; but woe is
       me,]E1
       intimate, but wo is
       me]Ms
236.14 time:]E1
       time]Ms
236.18 Rosey!]E1
       Rosey]Ms
236.23 exploits; not]E1
       exploits. Not]Ms
236.26 butler,]E1
       Butler,]Ms
236.31 lady,]E1
       lady.]Ms
236.33 her. The]E1
       her—The]Ms
236.34 which,]E1
       which]Ms
236.35 dressing-room,]E1
       dressing-room]Ms
236.36 drawing-room,]E1
       drawing-room]Ms
236.37 ended,]E1
       ended]Ms
236.38 establishment,]E1
       establishment]Ms
236.39 fled back]E1
       fled—back]Ms
236.40 afterwards,]E1
       afterwards]Ms
236.41 said.]E1
       said]Ms
236.44 so—she]
       so—She]Ms
236.44 day,]E1
       day]Ms
236.45 Scotland, till
       Grandmamma]
       Scotland till
       Grandmama]Ms
237.01 Brussels,]E1
       Brussels]Ms
237.05 tantrums]E1
       tantrums and]Ms
237.05 Brussels]E1
       at Brussels]Ms
237.06 waists,]E1
       waists]Ms
237.08 women—this]E1
       women—This]Ms
237.12 kindly. "You]E1
       kindly, "you]Ms
237.13 mother, would you?"
       ¶"O,]E1
       mother would you?"
       ¶"O]Ms

237.16 day.]E1
    long day.]Ms
237.19 young gentleman in
    question,]E1
    gentleman in
    question]Ms
237.20 hansom]
    Handsome]Ms
237.21 Flag, Pall Mall,]E1
    Flag Pall Mall]Ms
237.22 Othello-like]
    Othello like]Ms
237.22 Cassio]E1
    cashier]Ms
238.01 ABSIT OMEN.]E1
    [omit]]Ms
238.09 together;]E1
    together]Ms
238.10 Bank]E1
    bank]Ms
238.11 commission]E1
    commision]Ms
238.27 Bayham]E1
    Bayham,]Ms
238.32 F.B., who]E1
    F.B.]Ms
238.32 affairs, discoursed
    ]E1
    affairs. Decoursed
    ]Ms
239.04 variegated.]E1
    varigated.]Ms
239.05 Honeyman.]E1
    Honeyman]Ms
239.07 maintain]E1
    maintain,]Ms
239.08 world;]E1
    world]Ms
239.09 nabobs.]E1
    nabobs,]Ms
239.14 maid]E1
    maid in]Ms
239.15 yachts]E1
    yatchs]Ms
239.15 Howbeit,]E1
    How be it]Ms
239.17 acquaintance,]E1
    acquaintance]Ms
239.21 sports.]E1
    sports]Ms
239.22 children.]E1
    children]Ms
239.23 merry;]E1
    merry]Ms
239.25 argosy]E1
    argose]Ms
239.27 yellow-faced]E1
    yellowfaced]Ms
239.33 "No,"]E1
    "No."]Ms

239.33 happened,]E1
    happened]Ms
239.36 crew—she]E1
    crew. She]Ms
239.36 nobly—who]E1
    nobly, and]Ms
239.41 congregate,]E1
    congregate]Ms
239.43 Leadenhall.—The]
    Leaden Hall.—The
    ]Ms
239.46 India.]E1
    India. [line space]
    ]Ms
240.01 thunderclap]E1
    thunder clap]Ms
240.03 shareholders]E1
    share holders]Ms
240.04 board-room was
    besieged]E1
    Board-Room was
    beseiged]Ms
240.05 bills]E1
    Bills]Ms
240.06 evening,]E1
    evening]Ms
240.06 henceforward,]
    hence-/forward,]Ms
240.07 Fog]R
    Fob]Ms
240.09 do honour to]E1
    meet]Ms
240.11 believe]E1
    beleive]Ms
240.16 look out]E1
    lookout,]Ms
240.18 yacht."]E1
    yatch."]Ms
240.20 occurrence]E1
    occurence]Ms
240.21 occasioned,]E1
    occasioned.]Ms
240.28 rupture between
    Hobson's family]E1
    rupture, between
    Hobson's family,]Ms
240.33 son]E1
    own son]Ms
240.36 whole]E1
    [omit]]Ms
240.37 his]E1
    [omit]]Ms
240.37 how, ever]E1
    how Ever]Ms
241.04 kinsman]E1
    kinsmen]Ms
241.05 angered]E1
    changed]Ms
241.06 disposition;]E1
    disposition]Ms

241.09 us?]E1
    ourselves]Ms
241.16 describe,]E1
    describe]Ms
241.17 Clive's father; whilst
    ]E1
    Clive and his father.
    Whilst]Ms
241.19 me,]E1
    me]Ms
241.19 he was]
    they were]Ms
241.24 say,]E1
    say]Ms
241.30 right. It]E1
    right, it]Ms
241.31 others. It]E1
    others—It]Ms
241.32 injury,]E1
    injury]Ms
241.32 it. The]E1
    it, the]Ms
241.34 the Colonel's]E1
    Clive's]Ms
241.35 enemy's]E1
    enemies']Ms
241.36 he]E1
    Clive]Ms
241.38 I]E1
    He has been led
    in this affair by his
    father—I]Ms
242.07 Banking House]E1
    Bankinghouse]Ms
242.10 Directors]E1
    directors]Ms
242.11 published;]E1
    published]Ms
242.12 had refused its
    drafts;]E1
    refused its draughts,
    but]Ms
242.13 Company]E1
    company]Ms
242.19 mentioned,]E1
    mentioned]Ms
242.22 book:]E1
    book]Ms
242.22 street:]E1
    street]Ms
242.23 was, in his idea,]E1
    was in his idea]Ms
242.26 it. "They]E1
    it "they]Ms
242.27 mine."]E1
    mine,"]Ms
242.34 Bank]E1
    bank]Ms
242.36 hot-headed]E1
    hot headed]Ms

242.37 Hindostanee—who]
Hindostanee—Who
]Ms
242.39 wily]E1
wiley]Ms
242.43 ago,]E1
ago]Ms
243.01 business, begad,]E1
business begad]Ms
243.07 personage]E1
personnage]Ms
243.08 give]E1
to give]Ms
243.11 full, nay,]E1
full nay]Ms
243.13 worthy,]E1
worthy]Ms
244.01 IN WHICH MRS. CLIVE
COMES INTO HER
FORTUNE.]E1
[omit]]Ms
244.08 Company.]E1
company.]Ms
244.10 it! He]E1
it—He]Ms
244.12 wrong—Absurd! If]
wrong—Absurd—If
]Ms
244.18 Company]E1
company]Ms
244.19 answer.]E1
answer]Ms
244.20 conscientiously he
thought so—never
]E1
consienciously he
thought so—Never
]Ms
244.21 been formed solely
]E1
solely been formed
]Ms
244.22 dragoon]E1
Dragoon]Ms
244.24 He, forsooth,]E1
He forsooth]Ms
244.24 it!]E1
it.]Ms
244.24 Companies]E1
companies]Ms
244.29 Hobson,]E1
Hobson]Ms
245.01 while he was on
the Continent—
confound the
Continent,]E1
during. his absence
on the continent—
Confound the
continent]Ms

245.03 received his brother's
excuses,]E1
recieved his brother's
excuses]Ms
245.07 knowledge. We
understand that sort
]E1
knowledge we
understand that kind
]Ms
245.08 last]E1
[omit]]Ms
245.10 had?"]E1
had—"]Ms
245.11 laugh. It]E1
laugh—It]Ms
245.13 confused. The]E1
confused—The]Ms
245.14 hall]E1
Hall]Ms
245.16 testimonial—the]
testimonial—The
]Ms
245.17 in]E1
with]Ms
245.17 banquets—the]
banquets—The]Ms
245.20 gloomy.]E1
gloomy,]Ms
245.20 F.B.,]E1
F.B.]Ms
245.23 falling, falling. ¶"I
]E1
falling falling. "I
]Ms
245.25 like]E1
[omit]]Ms
245.27 ship! You]E1
ship you]Ms
245.29 Ratray,]E1
Ratray]Ms
245.29 Europe,]E1
Europe]Ms
245.30 state. Shares]E1
state—Share]Ms
245.31 liver. Must come
home—the]E1
liver must come
home the]Ms
245.33 director,]E1
of the Indian
directors,]Ms
245.34 gentlemen, as we
know,]E1
gentlemen as we
know]Ms
245.39 crop. The]E1
crop, the]Ms
245.40 good-humour.]E1
good-/humour.]Ms

245.41 defections,]E1
defections]Ms
245.41 unpleasantries,]E1
unpleasantrys,]Ms
246.03 Mamma,]E1
Mama]Ms
246.04 styled]E1
stiled]Ms
246.06 simple-minded]E1
simple minded]Ms
246.07 feeling,]E1
feeling]Ms
246.08 Howbeit]E1
How be it]Ms
246.10 them,]E1
them]Ms
246.11 moiety]E1
moity]Ms
246.13 her, the truth is,]E1
her the truth is]Ms
246.14 good-humoured.
]E1
good-humoured]Ms
246.16 caresses;]E1
caresses]Ms
246.19 neat-handed,]E1
neathanded,]Ms
246.21 Mamma,]E1
Mamma]Ms
246.23 Newcome. Possibly
]E1
Newcome possibly
]Ms
246.24 Mamma,]E1
Mama,]Ms
246.26 least. She]E1
least she]Ms
246.27 face,]E1
face]Ms
246.28 with]E1
(with]Ms
246.29 said,]E1
said]Ms
246.29 why,]E1
why]Ms
246.31 add,]
add]Ms
246.32 (otherwise]
otherwise]Ms
246.33 statement),]
statement,]Ms
246.36 proposals,]E1
proposals]Ms
246.37 girl,]E1
girl]Ms
246.40 Mamma and,]
Mama and]Ms
246.40 Campaigner,]E1
Campaigner]Ms
246.41 house,]E1

house]Ms
246.42 Court,]E1
Court]Ms
246.42 husband]E1
husband,]Ms
246.43 side? No]E1
side no]Ms
247.01 warbled; and he]E1
warbled]Ms
247.02 in; and at]E1
in]Ms
247.03 face;—the]E1
face, the]Ms
247.09 philosopher;]E1
philosopher]Ms
247.11 bedside;]E1
bedside,]Ms
247.11 divine.]E1
Divine.]Ms
247.12 500£, thrice]E1
500£ Double]Ms
247.14 M'Craw,]E1
McCraw]Ms
247.16 M'Craw's, own
sermons;—let]E1
McCraw's, own
sermons, let]Ms
247.20 M'Craw's]E1
McCraw's]Ms
247.23 and only now
becoming visible to
human ken though
existent for ever and
ever?]E1
only now their
existence for ever
and ever becoming
visible to human ken
]Ms
247.25 yet perceive]
yet perceive]E1
perceive]Ms
247.29 me, when, fancying
that]E1
me. When fancying
]Ms
247.30 consolation,]
consolation]Ms
247.32 dress. Clive,]E1
dress—Clive]Ms
247.34 sincere.]E1
sincere]Ms
247.39 Clive,]E1
Clive]Ms
248.01 Clive, by]E1
Clive. By]Ms
248.01 wife,]E1
wife]Ms
248.01 Clive; the little lady
]E1

Clive. The little
Lady]Ms
248.04 a-year]
a year]Ms
248.06 own;]E1
own]Ms
248.10 Newcome,]E1
Newcome]Ms
248.10 inheritance,]E1
inheritance]Ms
248.11 shares]
Shares]Ms
248.11 stock,]
stock]Ms
248.12 shareholders]
share holders]Ms
248.14 personage]E1
personnage]Ms
248.16 her; she]
her She]Ms
248.17 dinner.]E1
dinner]Ms
248.18 countenance;]E1
countenance]Ms
248.18 o'er]E1
ore]Ms
248.19 said,]E1
said]Ms
248.24 To]E1
to]Ms
248.24 used,]E1
used]Ms
248.25 days,]E1
days]Ms
248.25 gentlemen.]E1
gentlemen]Ms
248.28 powerful]E1
powerful,]Ms
248.28 bank,]E1
bank]Ms
248.31 Leadenhall Street]
Leaden Hall St.]Ms
248.35 Bombay lawyer]
Bambay Lawyer]Ms
248.37 Newcome, very
formidable
personages]E1
Newcome very
formidable
personnages]Ms
248.44 equal. The]E1
equal the]Ms
248.46 wishes]E1
wishes,]Ms
249.01 Howbeit]
How be it]Ms
249.02 and,]E1
and]Ms
249.03 Calcutta, the]
Calcutta. The]Ms

249.05 home]E1
home,]Ms
249.10 year, when]E1
year. When]Ms
249.10 town;]E1
town,]Ms
249.15 personage.]E1
personnage.]Ms
249.16 instructive,]E1
instructive]Ms
249.20 possessions;—the
]E1
possessions. The
]Ms
249.27 interest,]E1
interest]Ms
249.28 knew,]
knew]Ms
249.29 benefactor—kissed]
benefactor, kissed
]Ms
249.31 son:]E1
son,]Ms
249.41 Parliament.]E1
Parliament]Ms
249.42 Court of Directors]
court of directors
]Ms
250.05 out,]E1
out]Ms
250.09 his]E1
my]Ms
250.14 it. Ministers]E1
it—Ministers]Ms
250.14 majority—cannot
]E1
majority cannot]Ms
250.28 circumstances; wears
]E1
circumstances. Wears
]Ms
250.33 Athenæum. 1. for
the]E1
Athenæum—The
]Ms
250.34 Home, and 2.]E1
home, and 2]Ms
250.35 denomination,]
denomination]Ms
250.36 Newcome Newcome,
Bart.,]E1
Newcome, Newcome
Park,]Ms
250.37 instant. No. 1, The
]E1
instant no. 1 the
]Ms
250.37 23rd]
23]Ms
250.37 Childhood:]

Childhood]Ms
250.38 2, The Poetry]E1
2 The poetry]Ms
250.39 Affections:]
Affections.]Ms
250.41 him.]E1
him]Ms
250.43 him,]E1
him]Ms
250.45 part,]E1
part.]Ms
251.01 country;]E1
country]Ms
251.02 we]E1
[omit]]Ms
251.03 see,]E1
see]Ms
251.08 her?"—says]
her"—says]Ms
251.09 eyebrows;]E1
eyebrows]Ms
251.13 interruption.]E1
interruption—]Ms
251.15 Newcome; since]E1
Newcome. Since]Ms
251.19 likely,]E1
likely]Ms
251.20 it.]E1
it]Ms
251.35 twenty. It]E1
twenty—It]Ms
251.38 main chance]
main-chance]Ms
251.42 hop-o-my-thumb]E1
hop o my thumb]Ms
251.47 count. But]E1
count—But]Ms
252.02 wife,]E1
wife]Ms
252.02 her.]E1
her,]Ms
252.03 says." And]E1
says," and]Ms
252.06 quasi-satirical comment upon that]E1
quasi sanctified satirical comment upon]Ms
252.11 moody, biting his nails,]
moody biting his nails]Ms
252.13 which,]E1
which]Ms
252.17 Jove,]E1
Jove]Ms

252.22 son delightedly on the shoulder.]E1
son delighted on the Shoulder.]Ms
252.24 Sir;]E1
Sir,]Ms
255.24 them."]NY
them?"]E1
them!"]R
260.06 Newcome's]
Newcomes's]E1
262.01 NEWCOME AND LIBERTY.]E1
[omit]]Ms
262.04 midnight]E1
Midnight]Ms
262.19 cups,]E1
cups]Ms
262.21 another,]E1
another]Ms
262.23 Potts—at]
Potts at]Ms
262.25 gold-laced]E1
gold laced]Ms
262.30 Ha!]E1
ha!]Ms
263.13 Barnes,]E1
Barnes]Ms
263.18 practice! exceedingly]E1
practice!— exceedingly]Ms
263.19 swindling]E1
Swindling]Ms
263.27 man,]E1
man]Ms
263.28 counsel,]E1
council,]Ms
263.29 remarks]E1
insinuates]Ms
263.35 legislators]E1
Legislators]Ms
263.48 past.]E1
past]Ms
264.03 touch. His]E1
touch—His]Ms
264.08 household]E1
house hold]Ms
264.12 people!" ¶"I]R
people! I]E1
265.39 Independent,]
Independent]E1
266.02 Independent, for one, says]
Independent for one, says,]Ms
266.14 wrongs.]E1
wrongs]Ms
266.17 himself]E1
[omit]]Ms

266.26 a sad look]E1
sad looks]Ms
266.29 son.]E1
Son.]Ms
267.23 Sentinel]
Sentinel,]E1
267.24 sepoy]
seapoy]E1
267.30 illustrious]
illustrious,]E1
267.30 heroes (ironical cheers).]
heroes, (ironical cheers.)]E1
268.01 A LETTER AND A RECONCILIATION.]E1
[omit]]Ms
268.01 Miss Ethel Newcome to Mrs. Pendennis. ¶DEAREST LAURA.]
Miss Ethel Newcome to Mrs. Pendennis. ¶Dearest Laura.]Ms
268.16 very]E1
very very]Ms
268.17 church]E1
Church]Ms
268.18 "Is]E1
Is]Ms
268.18 with]E1
well with]Ms
268.23 balcony]E1
Balcony]Ms
268.25 him]E1
[omit]]Ms
268.27 me,]E1
me]Ms
268.29 although]E1
though]Ms
269.01 amend him; but]E1
amend—but]Ms
269.04 cousin:]
Cousin:]Ms
269.06 old]E1
Old]Ms
269.09 laughed,]E1
laughed]Ms
269.13 sweet-looking]E1
sweet looking]Ms
269.14 then. He]E1
then—He]Ms
269.16 I]E1
I I]Ms
269.16 daresay,]E1
daresay]Ms
269.19 him,]E1
him]Ms
269.26 Farintosh. He]E1

Farintosh—He]Ms

269.32 me;]E1
    me,]Ms

269.34 were,]E1
    were]Ms

269.37 me,]E1
    me]Ms

269.40 Egbert,]E1
    Egbert]Ms

269.41 say,]E1
    say]Ms

269.41 orders;]E1
    orders]Ms

269.44 Alice;]E1
    [blank];]Ms

269.45 indeed, I think,]E1
    indeed I think]Ms

269.45 Mumford,]E1
    [blank],]Ms

270.03 [Ms missing]]Ms

270.19 his, a Mr.
    Warrington,]E1
    his a Mr. Warrington
    ]Ms

270.22 sad, sentimental,
    ]E1
    sad sentimental]Ms

270.27 again.—E.N."]E1
    again E.N."]Ms

270.40 half-satisfied]E1
    half satisfied]Ms

271.01 friend]E1
    Friend]Ms

271.02 tired)]E1
    tired]Ms

271.02 Jolly]E1
    jolly]Ms

271.03 Room]
    Rooms]Ms

271.03 Colonel,]E1
    Colonel]Ms

271.03 business,]E1
    business]Ms

271.06 introduction;]E1
    introduction]Ms

271.08 time,]E1
    time]Ms

271.15 hand, came into]E1
    hand came in to]Ms

271.24 I!"]E1
    I."]Ms

271.38 even]E1
    think ever]Ms

271.40 him,]E1
    him]Ms

272.08 did,]E1
    [omit]]Ms

272.12 car passes over us.
    You]E1
    Car passes over
    us—You]Ms

272.13 Father."]
    Father"]Ms

272.23 you. You]E1
    you—You]Ms

272.24 would]E1
    [omit]]Ms

272.26 quarrel. And]E1
    quarrel—And]Ms

272.32 days, and how he
    ]E1
    d and how]Ms

272.44 will.]E1
    will]Ms

273.05 burst]E1
    great burst]Ms

277.05 parties:—O,]E1
    parties:—o,]Ms

277.32 Parliament;]E1
    parliament;]Ms

277.36 present]E1
    [omit]]Ms

278.01 him]E1
    him,]Ms

278.13 defiance.]
    defiance,]E1

280.41 it]R
    [omit]]E1

282.44 voted]R
    and votes]E1

285.22 Mackenzie—bade
    ]E1
    Mackenzie bade]Ms

285.28 grand-mamma.]E1
    grandmamma.—
    ]Ms

285.30 cocoa-nut]E1
    Cocoa nut]Ms

285.32 ominous-looking
    ]E1
    ominous looking
    ]Ms

285.34 With the City
    manager came the
    City manager's
    friends, whose jokes
    passed gaily round,
    and who kept the
    conversation to
    themselves. Once
    I had the happiness
    to meet Mr. Ratray,
    who had returned,
    filled with rupees
    from the Indian
    bank; who told us
    many anecdotes
    of the splendour
    of Rummun Lall
    at Calcutta, who
    complimented the

Colonel on his fine
house and grand
dinners with sinister
good humour. Those
compliments did not
seem to please our
poor friend, that
familiarity choked
him.]E1
    [omit]]Ms

285.43 aristocracy,]E1
    Aristocracy,]Ms

286.06 City—that]E1
    city—that]Ms

286.10 well-known firm
    of money-lending
    solicitors,]E1
    well known firm
    of money lending
    Solicitors,]Ms

286.24 court]E1
    Court]Ms

286.26 Old Woman of
    Banbury Cross—still
    ]E1
    old woman of
    Banbury Cross—Still
    ]Ms

286.30 there,]E1
    there]Ms

286.36 F.B.,]E1
    F.B.]Ms

286.37 beer—fairly]E1
    beer fairly]Ms

286.43 solicitors]E1
    Solicitors]Ms

286.43 since,]E1
    since]Ms

287.02 them,]E1
    them]Ms

287.04 mahogany-coloured
    ]E1
    mahogany coloured
    ]Ms

287.09 attorney—and]
    Attorney—and]Ms

287.17 benefactor!]
    benefactor!—]E1
    benefactors!]Ms

287.19 *I*]E1
    I]Ms

287.23 herewith,]E1
    here with,]Ms

287.33 *Solvuntur*]E1
    Solvanta]Ms

288.04 similar]E1
    [omit]]Ms

288.06 Member]E1
    member]Ms

288.06 borough]E1
 Bough]Ms
288.06 name, the]E1
 name. The]Ms
288.08 cholera]E1
 Cholera]Ms
288.08 Barrackpore]R
 Barackpore.]E1
 Bharapore.]Ms
288.13 columns]E1
 Columns]Ms
288.18 society]E1
 Society]Ms
288.19 college]
 College]Ms
288.21 banking companies]
 Banking Companies
 ]Ms
288.22 knights]E1
 Knights]Ms
288.22 Court]E1
 Court.]Ms
288.23 Sudder]E1
 Sudder.]Ms
288.24 (the]E1
 the]Ms
288.25 Council): all]E1
 Council. All]Ms
288.25 there. As carriage
 after carriage]E1
 then as carriages
 after carriages]Ms
288.26 were]E1
 [omit]]Ms
288.35 India,]E1
 India]Ms
288.36 bills]E1
 Bills]Ms
288.37 Court.]E1
 Court.——]Ms
288.38 Calcutta,]E1
 Calcutta]Ms
288.39 merchant prince]E1
 Merchant Prince
 ]Ms
289.01 rupees]
 Rupees]Ms
289.03 Condor]E1
 Condons]Ms
289.04 comedy characters
 at the Chowringhee
 ]E1
 Comedy Characters
 at the Chowrugher
 ]Ms
289.12 catastrophe]E1
 Catastrophe]Ms
289.16 bills of which,]
 Bills of which]Ms
289.17 correspondents,]E1

Correspondents]Ms
289.19 Burrumpooter.]E1
 Burrumpoota.—
 ]Ms
289.20 chapter]
 Chapter]Ms
289.22 chariots]
 Chariots]Ms
289.23 her]E1
 are]Ms
289.26 cocoa-nut]
 Cocoa-nut]Ms
289.27 curtains]E1
 Curtains]Ms
289.30 bedstead]E1
 bed]Ms
289.31 have]E1
 has]Ms
289.33 regiment]E1
 Regiment]Ms
289.38 attend]E1
 go to]Ms
290.01 that]E1
 [omit]]Ms
291.01 IN WHICH MRS. CLIVE
 NEWCOME'S CARRIAGE
 IS ORDERED.]E1
 Chap.]Ms
291.06 common]E1
 Common]Ms
291.10 Colonel having]E1
 Colonel—having
 ]Ms
291.11 him,]E1
 him]Ms
291.12 touch,]E1
 touch]Ms
291.14 betake himself]
 betake himself,]E1
 be taken]Ms
291.16 bankruptcy]E1
 Bankruptcy]Ms
291.23 Thomas Newcome
 ]E1
 He]Ms
291.28 person]E1
 one]Ms
291.30 disaster,]E1
 disaster]Ms
292.01 and I came to
 London, and were
 urgent with similar
 offers. Our]E1
 drove from Rosebury
 and came to London
 with similar offers—
 Our]Ms
292.02 F.B.,]E1
 F.B.]Ms
292.03 voice,]E1

 voice]Ms
292.10 and]E1
 [omit]]Ms
292.15 almost,]E1
 almost]Ms
292.17 said.]E1
 said]Ms
292.18 man."]E1
 man.——]Ms
292.19 bankruptcy,"]E1
 Bankruptcy,"]Ms
292.24 certificate.]E1
 Certificate.]Ms
292.25 conduct]E1
 Conduct]Ms
292.26 law]E1
 Law]Ms
292.29 his wife]E1
 Mrs. ——]Ms
292.31 day?]E1
 day?—]Ms
292.37 Mackenzie,]E1
 Mackenzie.]Ms
292.38 son-in-law]R
 daughter]Ms E1
292.38 Josey's]E1
 Jose's]Ms
292.38 Mr. Smee, R. A.,
 ]E1
 Mrs. R.A.]Ms
292.41 me,]E1
 me]Ms
292.42 own emotion—but]
 own emotion—but,
 ]E1
 only notion—but
 ]Ms
293.04 debt]E1
 Debt]Ms
293.11 Tom's]E1
 Thom's]Ms
293.11 dinner]E1
 Dinner]Ms
293.17 bills]E1
 Bills]Ms
293.22 common]E1
 Common]Ms
293.27 Flag,]E1
 flag,]Ms
293.31 ball—she]E1
 Ball she]Ms
293.30 ball—just]E1
 Ball—just]Ms
293.31 week, out]E1
 week. Out]Ms
293.32 merchant]E1
 Merchant]Ms
293.33 ball,]E1
 ball]Ms
294.07 a]E1

the]Ms
294.08 hand.]E1
hand.—]Ms
294.17 family. On hearing
these news,]E1
family; on hearing
which,]Ms
294.17 company was not
desirable,]E1
Company was not
desirable]Ms
294.19 cabman]E1
Cabman]Ms
294.27 retire]E1
to retire]Ms
294.30 biscuit;]R
buscuit;]Ms E1
295.14 would,]E1
would]Ms
295.17 *whom,*]E1
whom,]Ms
295.18 *instant*]
instant,]E1
instant]Ms
295.19 *honourable*]E1
honourable]Ms
295.20 own,]E1
own]Ms
295.22 follow,]E1
[*omit*]]Ms
295.26 *rights*]
rights,]E1
rights]Ms
295.27 *unkind*]
unkind,]E1
unkind]Ms
295.27 *wicked*]
wicked,]E1
wicked]Ms
295.27 *unnatural*]
unnatural,]E1
unnatural]Ms
295.28 bread.]E1
bread.——]Ms
295.32 again,]E1
again]Ms
295.37 *cheated* so—yes
cheated—if]
cheated so, yes *cheated,*
if]E1
cheated so—yes
cheated—if]Ms
295.38 alive.]E1
alive.——]Ms
295.40 widow's]E1
widow whose]Ms
295.45 sorrow-stricken]E1
sorrow stricken]Ms
296.04 terror-stricken]E1
terror stricken]Ms

296.04 reason.]E1
reason.—]Ms
296.05 them,]E1
them]Ms
296.05 dismay,]E1
dismay]Ms
296.07 house, as elsewhere,
]E1
house as elsewhere
]Ms
296.07 creditors']E1
Creditors']Ms
296.14 know."]E1
know."——]Ms
296.16 a-piece]
a piece]Ms
296.17 screams,]E1
screams]Ms
296.21 consolation.]E1
consolation.—]Ms
296.28 *duty*]E1
duty]Ms
296.28 *religion*—and]E1
religion—and]Ms
296.29 *unprotected* and *robbed*
and *cheated*]
unprotected, and
robbed, and *cheated,*
]E1
unprotected and
robbed and cheated
]Ms
296.30 *single day*]E1
single day]Ms
296.31 *robbed* in it,]E1
robbed in it]Ms
296.35 *hide* our *heads*]E1
hide our heads]Ms
296.36 *painters*]
painters,]E1
painters]Ms
296.39 England."]E1
England.—]Ms
296.43 rogue. No,]E1
rogue—No,]Ms
297.01 now,]E1
now]Ms
297.02 removed. Clive]E1
removed.—Clive
]Ms
297.05 prosperity.]E1
prosperity.—]Ms
297.09 *celeres quatit pennas,*
]E1
celeris quatit pennas
]Ms
297.10 Grey Friars *resigno
quæ*]
Greyfriars *resigno quæ*
]E1

Greyfriars *resigno qui*
]Ms
297.10 *mea*]E1
meâ]Ms
297.11 *pauperiem*]E1
paupestiem]Ms
297.11 *quæro.*"]E1
quaro"]Ms
297.12 wine,]E1
wine]Ms
297.13 well-known]E1
well known]Ms
297.15 love,]E1
love]Ms
297.15 voice]E1
Voice]Ms
297.17 days.]E1
days.—]Ms
297.18 mind,]
mind]Ms
297.19 misfortunes,]E1
misfortunes]Ms
297.29 it.]E1
it.—]Ms
297.32 would]E1
used to]Ms
297.35 Rosey's,]E1
Rosey's]Ms
297.36 order, please,]E1
order please]Ms
297.36 good,]E1
good]Ms
297.38 out—we]E1
out—We]Ms
297.39 daresay. And]
daresay—And]Ms
297.41 a petara]E1
[blank]]Ms
297.42 vanities, you know,
]E1
vanities you know
]Ms
297.45 anna, by Jove,]
anna by Jove]Ms
297.46 creditors."]
Creditors."]Ms
298.04 hand. We]E1
hand—We]Ms
298.05 fellow-servants]E1
fellow servants]Ms
298.05 places,]E1
places]Ms
298.05 you,]E1
you]Ms
298.06 merit. Great]E1
merit—Great]Ms
298.06 family—we]E1
family—We]Ms
298.11 catastrophe]
Catastrophe]Ms

298.13 secret.]E1
　　　secret.—]Ms
298.14 women's apartments,
　　　looking with but
　　　little regret, I
　　　daresay, round those
　　　cheerless nuptial
　　　chambers with all
　　　their gaudy fittings;
　　　the fine looking-
　　　glasses, in which
　　　poor Rosey's little
　　　person had been
　　　reflected; the silken
　　　curtains under which
　　　he had lain by the
　　　poor child's side,
　　　wakeful and lonely.
　　　Here]E1
　　　women's apartments
　　　where]Ms
298.21 that;]E1
　　　that.]Ms
298.22 pearly]E1
　　　purly]Ms
298.25 ejaculations,]E1
　　　ejaculations]Ms
298.31 lady's]E1
　　　ladies]Ms
298.32 too,]E1
　　　too]Ms
298.33 affidavits,]E1
　　　affidavits]Ms
298.33 wife,]E1
　　　wife]Ms
298.34 assent.]E1
　　　assent.—]Ms
298.36 nonsense!" Clive,
　　　]E1
　　　nonsense"! Clive
　　　]Ms
298.37 Obeying this grim
　　　summons, the
　　　fluttering women
　　　produced the
　　　keys, and the black
　　　box was opened
　　　before him. ¶The
　　　box was found to
　　　contain a number of
　　　objects which Clive
　　　pronounced to be by
　　　no means necessary
　　　to his wife's and
　　　child's existence.]E1
　　　[omit]]Ms
298.45 box,]E1
　　　box]Ms
299.01 say,]E1
　　　say]Ms

299.01 (the]E1
　　　the]Ms
299.02 behind)—all]E1
　　　behind—All]Ms
299.05 into fierce laughter
　　　]E1
　　　laughing]Ms
299.07 infant.]E1
　　　infant]Ms
299.09 husband,]E1
　　　husband]Ms
299.10 her,]E1
　　　her]Ms
299.12 Even the
　　　Campaigner could
　　　not make head
　　　against Clive's stern
　　　resolution; and the
　　　incipient insurrection
　　　of the maids and
　　　the mistresses was
　　　quelled by his spirit.
　　　The lady's maid,
　　　a flighty creature,
　　　received her wages
　　　and took her leave:
　　　but the nurse could
　　　not find it in her
　　　heart to quit her
　　　little nursling so
　　　suddenly, and
　　　accompanied Clive's
　　　household in the
　　　journey upon which
　　　those poor folks were
　　　bound.]E1
　　　[omit]]Ms
299.18 reached]E1
　　　reach]Ms
299.19 daughter's; a]E1
　　　daughter's. A]Ms
299.20 tea-spoons—baby's]
　　　tea spoons—baby's
　　　]Ms
299.21 velvet-bound]E1
　　　velvet bound]Ms
299.22 articles,]E1
　　　Article]Ms
299.22 them,]E1
　　　them]Ms
299.23 own.]E1
　　　own.—]Ms
299.25 coachman]E1
　　　Coachman]Ms
299.27 bow,]E1
　　　bow]Ms
299.30 cab]E1
　　　Cab]Ms
299.31 ship]E1
　　　Ship]Ms

299.32 journey, no doubt,
　　　]E1
　　　journey no doubt
　　　]Ms
299.34 committed]E1
　　　comitted]Ms
300.01 BELISARIUS.]E1
　　　Chap.]Ms
300.03 place,]E1
　　　place]Ms
300.16 sketchings,]E1
　　　sketchings]Ms
300.20 loved;]E1
　　　loved]Ms
300.23 committee]E1
　　　Committee]Ms
300.24 Boat"]E1
　　　Boat" [line space]]Ms
300.24 walls]
　　　Walls]Ms
300.25 critic]E1
　　　Critic]Ms
300.27 artist demanded;
　　　and,]E1
　　　Artist demanded—
　　　and]Ms
300.29 disposal, the]E1
　　　disposal—the]Ms
300.30 gratitude,]E1
　　　gratitude]Ms
301.01 studio.]E1
　　　studio.—]Ms
301.03 we]E1
　　　We]Ms
301.05 creditors]E1
　　　Creditors]Ms
301.07 one occasion,]E1
　　　some occasion]Ms
301.08 City,]E1
　　　City]Ms
301.08 Sherrick. Affairs]E1
　　　Sherrick—Affairs
　　　]Ms
301.12 sigh;]E1
　　　sigh]Ms
301.14 advice,]E1
　　　advice]Ms
301.17 man;—but]E1
　　　man—; but]Ms
301.20 Bank,]E1
　　　Bank]Ms
301.22 lawyers, commission,
　　　premium, life-
　　　insurance,—you
　　　]
　　　lawyers commission
　　　premium life
　　　insurance,—you]Ms
301.24 Coffee-house]E1
　　　Coffee-House]Ms

301.26 bankruptcy]E1
    Bankruptcy]Ms
301.31 rascal]E1
    d—d]Ms
301.32 cock's]E1
    Cock's]Ms
301.33 Whittlesea's chapel
    too,]E1
    Wittlesea's trapple
    too,]Ms
301.33 Hang]E1
    D—n]Ms
301.33 Levant."]E1
    Levant."—]Ms
301.34 speech,]E1
    speech]Ms
301.39 Hobson]E1
    H]Ms
302.05 relief.]E1
    relief.—]Ms
302.08 Laura.]E1
    Laura]Ms
302.01 Clive. Our]E1
    Clive.—Our]Ms
302.18 Boulogne]E1
    Bologne]Ms
302.20 speedily,]E1
    speedily]Ms
302.21 grass-grown]E1
    grass grown]Ms
302.26 day. I strolled]E1
    Day. I walked]Ms
302.33 walls—few]E1
    walls—Few]Ms
302.33 ruminating]E1
    rankling]Ms
302.36 red-cheeked]E1
    red cheeked]Ms
302.41 had been]E1
    [omit]]Ms
303.02 voice.]E1
    voice]Ms
303.04 now—Boy]
    now—boy]Ms
303.09 said]E1
    said that]Ms
303.10 home,]E1
    home]Ms
303.10 clock]E1
    Clock]Ms
303.14 "Poor]E1
    "poor]Ms
303.15 Pen,]E1
    Pen.]Ms
303.17 I,]E1
    I]Ms
303.17 part,]E1
    part]Ms
303.18 Campaigner.]E1
    Campaigner.—]Ms

303.20 company really
    prospers,]E1
    Company really
    prospers]Ms
303.21 think,]E1
    think]Ms
303.21 companies]E1
    Companies]Ms
303.24 Exhibition,]
    Exhibition.]Ms
303.26 Belisarius and Obolus
    ]
    Belisarius and
    Obolus]Ms
303.28 kindness]E1
    great kindness]Ms
303.31 India.]E1
    India]Ms
303.33 were]E1
    was]Ms
303.35 friends.]E1
    friends.—]Ms
304.02 Rosey.]
    Rosey.—]Ms
304.04 prospects,]E1
    prospects]Ms
304.06 own, in fact,]E1
    own in fact]Ms
304.16 favour. God]E1
    favour—God]Ms
304.20 gives]E1
    give]Ms
304.25 Campai—Mrs.]E1
    Camp—and Mrs.
    ]Ms
304.26 you,]E1
    you.]Ms
304.30 a-year]E1
    a year]Ms
304.34 Clive. What]E1
    Clive—What]Ms
304.35 Why,]E1
    Why]Ms
304.41 Arthur.]E1
    Author.]Ms
304.42 down——there,]E1
    down—there]Ms
304.44 powers."]E1
    powers."—]Ms
305.01 old]E1
    [omit]]Ms
305.02 lodgings,]E1
    lodgings]Ms
305.06 apartments and]E1
    apartments—and
    ]Ms
305.07 reduced:]E1
    reduced]Ms
305.10 homely, pretty]E1
    homely—pretty]Ms

305.13 salon.]E1
    [omit]]Ms
305.13 command,]E1
    command]Ms
305.14 condescend]E1
    condescend]Ms
305.17 mother-in-law's not
    ]E1
    mother-in-law's—not
    ]Ms
305.21 Mackenzie.]E1
    Mackenzie.—]Ms
305.27 the]E1
    her]Ms
305.29 cod]E1
    Cod]Ms
305.29 doctor. Heaven]E1
    doctor—Heaven]Ms
305.30 paid,]
    paid]Ms
305.30 medicines,]
    medicines]Ms
305.31 imprudence—the]E1
    imprudence—the
    ]Ms
305.31 designing
    imprudence—and
    extravagance—and
    folly]
    designing imprudence,
    and extravagance, and
    folly]E1
    disingenuous
    imprudence—and
    extravagance—and
    folly]Ms
305.34 house,]E1
    house]Ms
305.35 end,]E1
    end]Ms
305.38 some]E1
    some]Ms
306.01 other]E1
    other]Ms
306.02 mother's blessings]E1
    mother's blessings
    ]Ms
306.04 Colonel,]E1
    Colonel]Ms
306.05 immense sums]E1
    immense sums]Ms
306.06 country,]E1
    country]Ms
306.11 paté]E1
    pate]Ms
306.15 pastry-cook's for]E1
    pastry cook's from
    ]Ms
306.13 him,]
    him]Ms

306.15 Colonel,]
　　　　Colonel]Ms
307.01 IN WHICH BELISARIUS
　　　　RETURNS FROM EXILE.
　　　　]E1
　　　　Chap.]Ms
307.02 des]E1
　　　　de]Ms
307.10 confidants]E1
　　　　a confidantes]Ms
307.10 affairs,]E1
　　　　affairs]Ms
307.19 father,]E1
　　　　father]Ms
307.21 Rosey,]E1
　　　　Rosey]Ms
307.22 nature,]E1
　　　　nature]Ms
307.27 sufficient]E1
　　　　sufficent]Ms
307.31 prosperity]E1
　　　　prosperity,]Ms
307.32 has]E1
　　　　as]Ms
307.32 unfortunately—a
　　　　]E1
　　　　unfortunately—A
　　　　]Ms
308.06 boughs]E1
　　　　bows]Ms
308.09 coarse-minded]E1
　　　　coarse minded]Ms
308.11 world—when]E1
　　　　world When]Ms
308.13 tyrant,]E1
　　　　tyrant]Ms
308.15 spirit,]E1
　　　　spirit]Ms
308.18 ears,]E1
　　　　ears]Ms
308.20 infant,]E1
　　　　infant]Ms
308.21 blest]
　　　　blst]Ms
308.23 choice society]E1
　　　　Choice Society]Ms
308.23 captains, captains']
　　　　Captains, Captains'
　　　　]Ms
308.23 stockbrokers']
　　　　Stockbrokers']Ms
308.25 councils—and]
　　　　Councils—and]Ms
308.28 Colonel,]E1
　　　　Colonel]Ms
308.28 previously,]E1
　　　　previously]Ms
308.29 levanting
　　　　auctioneer's]E1
　　　　Levantine
　　　　Auctioneer's]Ms

308.32 Clive;]E1
　　　　Clive]Ms
308.35 without]E1
　　　　with]Ms
308.37 him,]E1
　　　　him]Ms
308.40 money,"]E1
　　　　Money,"]Ms
308.42 persecution.]E1
　　　　persecution.—]Ms
309.02 close]E1
　　　　Close]Ms
309.11 emotion that]E1
　　　　emotion—but]Ms
309.13 jibes,]E1
　　　　jibes]Ms
309.13 see,]E1
　　　　see]Ms
309.14 whip. "He]E1
　　　　whip—"He]Ms
309.17 himself:]E1
　　　　himself]Ms
309.20 Bank,]E1
　　　　Bank]Ms
309.21 him. Great God!
　　　　]E1
　　　　him, great God]Ms
309.22 do—what]E1
　　　　do—What]Ms
309.23 paroxysm]E1
　　　　paroxyism]Ms
309.26 me,]E1
　　　　me]Ms
309.26 drawings,]E1
　　　　drawings]Ms
309.27 our]E1
　　　　or]Ms
309.30 broken—you]E1
　　　　broken—You]Ms
309.31 myself,]E1
　　　　myself]Ms
309.32 drawings]E1
　　　　drawing]Ms
309.33 chambers]
　　　　Chambers]Ms
309.36 it."]E1
　　　　it."—]Ms
309.39 indulged,]E1
　　　　indulged]Ms
309.40 into]E1
　　　　out in]Ms
310.01 exhibit).]
　　　　exhibit)]Ms
310.07 Boulogne,]E1
　　　　Boulogne]Ms
310.08 practise of economy,
　　　　]E1
　　　　practice of economy
　　　　]Ms
310.09 destitution.*]E1

　　　　destitution.—*]Ms
310.f* away,]E1
　　　　away]Ms
310.f* previously, sundry
　　　　]E1
　　　　previously Sundry
　　　　]Ms
310.14 owe. My colourman
　　　　]E1
　　　　owe—My Colorman
　　　　]Ms
310.17 the]E1
　　　　[omit]]Ms
310.18 colourman's]E1
　　　　Colourman's]Ms
310.21 that,]E1
　　　　that]Ms
310.22 here,]E1
　　　　here]Ms
310.23 a-year."]
　　　　a year."—]Ms
310.25 giver]E1
　　　　giver himself]Ms
310.30 you."]E1
　　　　you."—]Ms
310.31 friend,]E1
　　　　friend]Ms
310.32 des Bains,]E1
　　　　de Bain]Ms
310.33 appeared]E1
　　　　appeared clearly
　　　　]Ms
310.35 him.—And]
　　　　him—And]Ms
310.35 Colonel, too,]E1
　　　　Colonel too]Ms
310.36 Campaigner,]E1
　　　　Campaigner]Ms
310.40 guests—may]E1
　　　　guests—May]Ms
310.42 friends.—It]E1
　　　　friends—It]Ms
310.42 state]E1
　　　　State]Ms
311.02 away.]E1
　　　　away.—]Ms
311.04 breakfast]E1
　　　　breakfast on the]Ms
311.04 coffee-room]E1
　　　　Coffee-room]Ms
311.07 countenance]E1
　　　　Countenance]Ms
311.11 chestnut]
　　　　chesnut]Ms
311.15 neck—all]
　　　　neck—All]Ms
311.17 capitalist's]E1
　　　　Capitalist's]Ms
311.18 Campaigner.—]

campaigner.—]Ms

311.21 children—and then,
]E1
Children—and then
]Ms

311.22 expected,]E1
expected]Ms

311.22 business,]E1
business]Ms

311.25 *I*]E1
I]Ms

311.26 Newcome.]E1
Newcome.—]Ms

311.28 gentleman;]E1
gentleman]Ms

311.29 darling]E1
Darling]Ms

311.29 muddle-headed
creature,]E1
muddle headed
creature]Ms

311.31 condition—the]
Condition—the]Ms

311.32 calf's-foot]E1
calfsfoot]Ms

311.32 cods-liver]
cods liver]Ms

311.35 it,]E1
it]Ms

311.36 heaven]E1
Heaven]Ms

311.39 donation to herself.
]E1
sum of money to
herself.—]Ms

311.40 of money]E1
[*omit*]]Ms

311.40 pocket-book,]E1
pocket book,]Ms

311.42 tradesmen,]E1
tradesmen]Ms

312.02 London.]E1
London.—]Ms

312.10 hotel bill]
Hotel Bill]Ms

312.11 London.]E1
London.—]Ms

312.12 here to divulge]
here to divulge,]E1
hereto divulged]Ms

312.13 making]E1
maturing]Ms

312.16 to]E1
to be able to]Ms

312.17 case—but]
Case—but]Ms

312.18 Colonel,]E1
Colonel]Ms

312.19 bankruptcy,]E1
bankruptcy]Ms

312.20 statement, of course,
]E1
statement of course
]Ms

312.21 Colonel. He]E1
Colonel—He]Ms

312.23 everybody—was]E1
every body—was
]Ms

312.30 proposal,]E1
proposal]Ms

312.31 large,]E1
large]Ms

312.31 Had]E1
Have]Ms

312.39 proposal.]E1
proposal.—]Ms

312.41 kind,]E1
kind]Ms

312.41 sure,]E1
sure]Ms

312.44 adopt—*trade, she*]E1
adopt—*trade* she
]Ms

313.02 better.]E1
better.—]Ms

313.03 town,]E1
town.]Ms

313.09 departure,]E1
departure]Ms

313.09 eagerly,]E1
eagerly]Ms

313.10 it]E1
so it]Ms

313.10 otherwise. The]E1
otherwise—the]Ms

313.16 Rosey, she]E1
Rosey She]Ms

313.16 me,]E1
me]Ms

313.19 children]E1
Children]Ms

313.23 boa-constrictor,
doomed—
fluttering—
fascinated—scared
]E1
boa-constrictor
doomed—
fluttering—
fascinated—Scared
]Ms

313.23 pavid]
pavied]Ms

313.26 hour. I]E1
hour—I]Ms

313.44 hand,]
hand]E1

316.12 Alfred Smee,]
— Smee,]E1

318.27 value.]E1
value—]Ms

318.43 kindness—bestowing
]R
kindness—taking
]Ms

318.44 you;]E1
you,]Ms

318.45 Edition?]E1
Edition?—]Ms

319.10 so—and]R
so, and]Ms

319.28 justice,]E1
justice]Ms

319.29 his]E1
his own]Ms

319.32 a]E1
[*omit*]]Ms

319.37 wife, the]E1
wife—the]Ms

320.01 Pendennis,]E1
Pendennis]Ms

320.01 foot,]E1
foot]Ms

325.15 benefactions,]
benefacfactions,]E1

330.23 Grandmamma" * *]
grandmamma." * *
]E1

334.27 Hall]
hall]E1

334.41 avons-nous]
avons nous]E1

336.36 itself]NY
herself]E1 R

341.23 canvas."I]E1
canvass—"I]Ms

341.28 that: and]E1
that—And]Ms

341.29 doctors]E1
Doctors]Ms

341.35 now! and]E1
now!—and]Ms

341.36 fee,]E1
fee]Ms

342.01 skinned]E1
Skinned]Ms

342.03 Doctor]E1
Doctor, Doctor
Quackenboss,]Ms

342.04 that]E1
of that]Ms

342.06 Quackenboss]E1
Quackenbosse,]Ms

342.11 into the studio]E1
in to the Studio,]Ms

342.12 him]E1
her]Ms

342.12 curtsey.]E1
Curtsey.]Ms

342.16 morning. Bring]E1
morning—Bring]Ms
342.21 Clive; "and]E1
Clive—"and]Ms
342.24 Friars. It]E1
Friars—It]Ms
342.25 Rosa,]E1
Rosa]Ms
342.36 aristocracy,]E1
Aristocracy,]Ms
342.42 Campaigner,]E1
Campaigner]Ms
343.03 dinner,]E1
dinner]Ms
343.07 him; he]E1
him—He]Ms
343.08 Clive. "Will]E1
Clive—"Will]Ms
343.12 mince-pie.]E1
mince pie.]Ms
343.22 Boy.]E1
Boy:]Ms
343.34 mince-pies,]E1
mince-pies]Ms
343.36 or]E1
[omit]]Ms
343.37 he]E1
which he]Ms
343.38 the]E1
The]Ms
343.42 freshness]E1
freshness was gone]Ms
344.02 so]E1
so very]Ms
344.09 might, speaking]E1
might speaking,]Ms
344.10 affectation,]E1
affectation]Ms
344.11 gentlemen, he said,]E1
gentlemen he said]Ms
344.13 sadly,]E1
sadly]Ms
344.18 church every day,]E1
Church every day]Ms
344.21 imprudence,]E1
imprudence]Ms
344.22 chapel]E1
Chapel]Ms
344.32 brother,]E1
brothers,]Ms
344.38 studio, where smoking]E1
Studio, where Smoking]Ms

345.03 was]E1
was looking]Ms
345.12 him.]E1
him]Ms
345.14 besides,]E1
besides]Ms
345.20 me—(she]E1
me—(She]Ms
345.21 thinking, you know,]E1
thinking you know]Ms
345.23 at all,]E1
all]Ms
345.25 me,]E1
me]Ms
345.29 with]E1
for]Ms
345.31 chambers]E1
Chambers]Ms
345.37 wife. Why,]E1
wife, why,]Ms
346.01 I,]E1
I]Ms
346.01 aware,]E1
aware]Ms
346.05 other,]E1
other]Ms
346.10 him, I think,]E1
him I think]Ms
346.13 Newcome,]E1
Newcome]Ms
346.21 done,]E1
done]Ms
346.25 said. "I]E1
said—"I]Ms
346.29 upbraiding]E1
up braiding]Ms
346.33 mine,]E1
mine]Ms
346.44 poverty. Do]E1
poverty—Do]Ms
347.04 background]E1
back ground]Ms
347.08 chair—his worn-out]E1
chair—worn-out]Ms
347.12 friends—and, Miss Newcome, as]E1
friends—and Miss Newcome—as]Ms
347.22 money,]E1
money]Ms
347.25 a]E1
[omit]]Ms
347.26 Newcome,]E1
Newcome]Ms
347.27 Newcome,]E1
Newcome]Ms
347.27 £6,000]E1

6000£:]Ms
347.28 Newcome,]E1
Newcome]Ms
347.29 servant]E1
Servant]Ms
348.01 OLD FRIENDS COME TOGETHER.]E1
THE READER IS INVITED TO TWO DINNERS.]Ms
348.01 Snowhill,]E1
Snow hill,]Ms
348.05 Cistercian]E1
Cistercean]Ms
348.06 Friars.]E1
Friars]Ms
348.16 brethren.]E1
bretheren.]Ms
348.17 open:]E1
open]Ms
348.17 room;]E1
room,]Ms
348.20 round]E1
round round]Ms
348.22 mantel-piece:]E1
mantel piece:]Ms
348.24 there; she]E1
there She]Ms
348.29 handsome,]E1
handsome]Ms
348.30 while. "O Miss!"]E1
while, "O. Miss!,"]Ms
348.33 himself;]E1
himself]Ms
349.01 companion]E1
companion,]Ms
349.02 Bible.]E1
Bible,]Ms
349.04 Brethren,]E1
Bretheren,]Ms
349.05 career, once bright,]E1
career once bright]Ms
349.07 din]E1
din,]Ms
349.09 said. Would]E1
said, would]Ms
349.10 Newcome]E1
Newcome,]Ms
349.14 upstairs]E1
up-stairs]Ms
349.16 sofa]E1
sopha]Ms
349.18 ladies,]E1
ladies]Ms
349.19 Newcome.]E1
Newcome,]Ms
349.20 "That]E1

"that]Ms

349.21 Hospital, Sir!]
    hospital, Sir!,]Ms

349.26 Grey Friars.]E1
    Grey-Friars.]Ms

349.28 helpless child,]E1
    helpless-child,]Ms

349.29 hospital!]E1
    Hospital!]Ms

349.30 money:—he]
    money:—He]Ms

349.30 he]
    He]Ms

349.31 yourself,]E1
    your self,]Ms

349.34 child,]E1
    child]Ms

349.35 Rosa,]E1
    Rosa]Ms

349.36 sofa,]E1
    sopha below]Ms

349.43 prosperity,]Ms
    prosperity]Ms

349.46 gentleman;]E1
    gentleman]Ms

350.04 Grey Friars]E1
    Grey-Friars]Ms

350.09 "Ethel;"]E1
    "Ethel,"]Ms

350.11 Rosa]E1
    Rosa,]Ms

350.11 table-cover]E1
    table cover]Ms

350.17 Campaigner,]E1
    Campaigner]Ms

350.18 niece.]E1
    niece,]Ms

350.19 head;]E1
    head]Ms

350.24 opened,]E1
    opened]Ms

350.31 shoulder.]E1
    shoulder,]Ms

350.32 kneeling]E1
    keeling]Ms

350.34 over.]E1
    over,]Ms

350.37 boy]E1
    Boy]Ms

350.38 took place]
    took-place]Ms

350.40 Mackenzie]E1
    MacKenzie]Ms

350.43 cried—cried]E1
    cried cried]Ms

350.43 break. Ah me!]E1
    break Ah! me,]Ms

350.44 pent-up feeling!]E1
    pent up feeling]Ms

350.45 ground;]E1

ground,]Ms

350.45 boy]E1
    Boy]Ms

351.02 said]
    said.]Ms

351.03 exhibit,]E1
    exhibit]Ms

351.05 hearts,]E1
    hearts.]Ms

351.12 mind;]E1
    mind,]Ms

351.13 Rosa,]E1
    Rosa]Ms

351.18 intelligent,]E1
    intelligent]Ms

351.19 her]E1
    [omit]]Ms

351.23 mother,]E1
    mother]Ms

351.26 Sir,]E1
    Sir]Ms

351.38 visit;]E1
    visit]Ms

351.38 "An]E1
    An]Ms

351.39 housemaid?"]E1
    housemaid?]Ms

351.40 dog]E1
    Dog]Ms

351.42 qualities]E1
    qualities,]Ms

351.42 re-entered]E1
    reentered]Ms

351.43 remembered]E1
    remembered,]Ms

352.01 perceive]E1
    percieve]Ms

352.03 drawings,]E1
    drawings]Ms

352.12 longer—you]
    longer—You]Ms

352.12 like; you]E1
    like, You]Ms

352.14 drum]E1
    Drum]Ms

352.16 "Besides,]E1
    "Besides]Ms

352.23 letter,]E1
    letter]Ms

352.25 since,]E1
    since]Ms

352.25 Newcome,]E1
    Newcome]Ms

352.27 death,]E1
    death]Ms

352.28 enclosed a copy,]E1
    inclosed a copy.]Ms

352.29 through.]E1
    through]Ms

352.30 countenance,]E1

countenance]Ms

352.31 document,]E1
    document]Ms

352.35 it.]E1
    it;]Ms

352.36 who—who]E1
    who—who,]Ms

352.38 lawyer,]E1
    lawyer.]Ms

352.44 do,]E1
    do]Ms

352.48 sepoys and
    artillery—the sepoys
    and artillery]
    Seapoys and
    Artillery—the
    seapoys and Artillery
    ]Ms

353.01 convoy]E1
    Convoy]Ms

353.03 Clive. The]E1
    Clive, the]Ms

353.06 "I]E1
    "I]Ms

353.06 Grey Friars,—after
    chapel, you know.
    Do you]E1
    Grey-Friars,—after
    chapel you know do
    You]Ms

353.08 public-house in
    Cistercian Lane—
    The]E1
    public house in
    Cistercean Lane—the
    ]Ms

353.09 weren't]E1
    wern't]Ms

353.10 Heaven. A]E1
    Heaven—A]Ms

353.10 boy,]E1
    boy.]Ms

353.10 flogged me,]E1
    flogged, me]Ms

353.15 Arthur," he
    whispered;]E1
    Arthur." he
    whispered,]Ms

353.28 it. When]E1
    it—When]Ms

353.29 him;]E1
    him,]Ms

353.30 Mackenzie,]
    Mackenzie]Ms

353.46 fancying]E1
    fancying,]Ms

354.06 mantel-piece]E1
    mantelpiece]Ms

354.10 to]E1
    at]Ms

354.11 said, Yes,]E1
　　　　said Yes.]Ms
354.14 majestic]
　　　　majestec]Ms
354.17 carve]E1
　　　　carve upon]Ms
354.19 beef? Three]E1
　　　　beef, three]Ms
354.24 said,]E1
　　　　said]Ms
354.28 yesterday;]E1
　　　　yesterday,]Ms
354.30 already]E1
　　　　already,]Ms
354.35 ill]E1
　　　　ill,]Ms
354.35 sweetbread]E1
　　　　sweet bread]Ms
354.39 Clive,]E1
　　　　poor Clive,]Ms
354.43 plum-pudding,]E1
　　　　plumb-pudding,]Ms
354.44 mince-pies]
　　　　mince pies]Ms
354.45 thought,]E1
　　　　thought]Ms
355.03 shrieked]E1
　　　　shreeked]Ms
355.04 it.]E1
　　　　it]Ms
355.06 mince-pies,]E1
　　　　mince pies,]Ms
355.07 yourself]E1
　　　　your self]Ms
355.08 night,]E1
　　　　night]Ms
355.14 let]E1
　　　　[omit]]Ms
355.19 go,]E1
　　　　go]Ms
355.25 paper—see]
　　　　paper—See]Ms
355.25 waiting-woman]E1
　　　　waiting woman]Ms
355.27 table,]E1
　　　　table]Ms
355.29 policeman]E1
　　　　police man]Ms
355.32 doubt,]E1
　　　　doubt]Ms
355.35 fell]E1
　　　　fell down]Ms
355.36 moment,]E1
　　　　moment]Ms
355.41 money;—me]E1
　　　　money, me]Ms
356.04 robbed,]E1
　　　　robbed]Ms
356.07 more; go]E1
　　　　more, Go]Ms

356.08 never,]E1
　　　　never]Ms
356.09 God!]E1
　　　　God]Ms
356.14 you fiend!]E1
　　　　You Fiend!]Ms
356.17 suffer—what]E1
　　　　suffer—What]Ms
356.20 scene.]E1
　　　　Scene,]Ms
356.22 fiend,]E1
　　　　fiend]Ms
356.22 lady.]E1
　　　　lady]Ms
356.31 boy]E1
　　　　Boy]Ms
356.35 him]E1
　　　　him,]Ms
356.42 word;]E1
　　　　word]Ms
357.01 morning.]E1
　　　　morning,]Ms
357.07 busy, I suppose,]E1
　　　　busy I suppose]Ms
357.07 bed,"]E1
　　　　bed:"]Ms
357.11 grandson]E1
　　　　grandson laid]Ms
358.01 IN WHICH THE
　　　　COLONEL SAYS
　　　　"ADSUM" WHEN HIS
　　　　NAME IS CALLED.]E1
　　　　[omit]]Ms
358.02 never]E1
　　　　never more]Ms
358.25 Queen's]
　　　　Queen]Ms E1
358.26 express-train]E1
　　　　Express-train]Ms
358.33 robe-de-chambre
　　　　]E1
　　　　robe de chambre
　　　　]Ms
359.02 band-box]E1
　　　　band box]Ms
359.19 tongue,]E1
　　　　tongue]Ms
359.26 her, no doubt,]E1
　　　　her no doubt]Ms
359.29 Cashmere shawl]E1
　　　　cashmere Shawl]Ms
359.33 go,"]E1
　　　　go:"]Ms
359.41 "Madam,]E1
　　　　"Woman,]Ms
360.01 whom, no doubt,
　　　　]E1
　　　　whom no doubt]Ms
360.03 shoulders)—that]
　　　　shoulders) that]E1

　　　　shoulder)—that]Ms
360.10 Captain]E1
　　　　captain]Ms
360.11 dared]E1
　　　　dared]Ms
360.11 so."]E1
　　　　so;"]Ms
360.18 strongly,]E1
　　　　strongly]Ms
360.22 nurse]E1
　　　　Nurse]Ms
360.27 moment.]E1
　　　　moment]Ms
360.32 tidings. The]
　　　　tidings, the]Ms
360.45 ill—he]
　　　　ill—He]Ms
361.08 him. The bell began
　　　　]E1
　　　　him—the bell
　　　　beginning]Ms
361.15 more;]E1
　　　　more,]Ms
361.17 schoolmaster]E1
　　　　school-Master]Ms
361.22 twilight]E1
　　　　twi-light]Ms
361.28 husband,]E1
　　　　husband.]Ms
361.42 [line space]]E1
　　　　[omit]]Ms
361.44 newspaper]E1
　　　　Newspaper]Ms
361.46 son]E1
　　　　Son]Ms
362.01 Street,]E1
　　　　Street]Ms
362.04 censure—yet]E1
　　　　censure, Yet]Ms
362.11 him]E1
　　　　[omit]]Ms
362.13 earth]E1
　　　　Earth]Ms
362.15 cemetery]E1
　　　　Cemetery]Ms
362.27 snow]E1
　　　　Snow]Ms
362.29 City.]E1
　　　　City]Ms
362.39 spring.]E1
　　　　Spring.]Ms
362.40 chamber, luckily
　　　　vacant,]E1
　　　　chamber luckily
　　　　vacant]Ms
362.41 Colonel's,]E1
　　　　Colonel's]Ms
362.45 religion,]E1
　　　　Religion,]Ms
363.01 he]E1

He]Ms

363.09 gown-boy]E1
Gown Boy]Ms

363.14 him!"]E1
him—that Codd
Colonel wants to see
him!":]Ms

363.14 gown-boy]E1
Gownboy]Ms

363.17 school,]E1
School,]Ms

363.23 gown-boys]
GownBoys]Ms

363.25 gown-boy;]E1
Gownboy;]Ms

363.29 sweetness. He]E1
sweetness—He]Ms

363.33 care-worn]E1
care worn]Ms

363.34 Léonore:]
Léonore;]E1
Eleanore:]Ms

363.40 boy]E1
Boy]Ms

363.45 otherwise]E1
other wise]Ms

364.10 books;]E1
books]Ms

364.13 Red Cow?]E1
Red-Cow?]Ms

364.18 hopes, raised
sometimes,]E1
hopes raised
sometimes]Ms

364.21 there. One]E1
there—One]Ms

364.22 gown-boy]E1
Gown boy]Ms

364.23 awe-stricken]E1
awe stricken]Ms

364.25 cricket match]E1
cricket-match]Ms

364.25 green,]E1
Green,]Ms

364.29 hand;]E1
hand]Ms

364.31 *I, curre,*]E1
I curre]Ms

364.31 gown-boy!]E1
Gown boy!]Ms

364.34 command, spoke
Hindostanee as if to
his men. Then]E1
command and
murmured Threes
about and Charge—
then]Ms

364.37 nurse]E1
Nurse]Ms

365.02 awhile—then]

a while—then]Ms

365.03 still—once]
still—Once]Ms

365.04 heart-rending]E1
heart rending]Ms

365.04 "Léonore, Léonore!"
]E1
"Eleanore Eleanore!"
]Ms

365.08 chapel]E1
Chapel]Ms

365.11 said "Adsum!"]E1
said ¶"Adsum!"]Ms

365.12 school]
School]Ms

365.16 Switzerland,]E1
Switzerland]Ms

365.18 three and twenty
]E1
three-and-twenty
]Ms

365.24 (———) which]E1
which (———)]Ms

365.28 anybody]E1
any body]Ms

365.30 Eurydice,]E1
Euridice,]Ms

365.31 mentioned—how]
mentioned—How
]Ms2
mentioned. How
]Ms1

365.36 kills Lady Glenlivat,
at]Ms2
killed Lady
Farintosh's mother
]Ms1

365.37 one page]E1
page ( )]Ms

365.37 at another—but]
at another; but]E1
page ( )—but]Ms

366.14 Ethel. ¶Again,
why did Pendennis
introduce]E1
Ethel. Nor can
we judge much of
her likeness by Mr.
Doyle's etchings
in the present
volumes, for where
the Heroine has
been introduced,
our our provoking
English Timanthes
has turned her
face away, and only
shown the public a
head of hair. ¶Some
would like to know

from Mr. Pendennis
why he introduced
]Ms

366.22 lifetime;]E1
life time;]Ms

366.24 godfather]E1
Godfather]Ms

366.29 apropos]E1
apropos.]Ms

366.30 artful, for]E1
artful,—for]Ms

366.30 died, don't]E1
died—don't]Ms

366.31 week?)—annoying
]E1
week?) annoying
]Ms

366.33 (O]
(o]Ms

366.33 upstarts]E1
Upstarts]Ms

366.33 fable-land—the]
fable-land—The]Ms

367.03 absolutely. He]E1
absolutely—He]Ms

367.12 PARIS, 28 JUNE,]E1
Paris 28 June.]Ms

End-line Hyphenated Compounds

The following compound words are ambiguously hyphenated at the ends of lines in the present edition. They are listed here in the form they would have taken on a single line. Other words hyphenated at ends of lines in this edition are considered unambiguous, either always taken as single words or always hyphenated. "Mother-in-law" for example is always hyphenated, but "dex-/trous" never is. The conventions for hyphenation indicated on pages 419–20 of the Textual History are not repeated here.

Vol.I
3.22 steel-trap
7.19 greenhorn
12.19 cloth-factors
13.31 fresh-coloured
15.10 savoury-birds
43.41 Derby-day
50.29 stepmother
54.33 public-house
73.18 outstretched
77.20 neighbourhood
84.38 setting-room
90.26 householder
93.40 neighbourhood
96.6 nobleman
104.31 chimney-piece
105.29 downright
105.46 footmen's
111.39 paint-box
113.27 steam-packet
122.13 pen-knife
136.21 Grindpauper
142.11 lodge-gates
142.26 bow-window
145.35 sea-shore
198.8 tip-top
213.13 afternoon
217.6 pine-apple

223.14 safeguard
228.18 common-places
231.16 sea-side
261.38 midnight
262.39 hand-writing
266.27 clergyman
268.9 midnight
274.14 pot-house
280.6 moonlight
288.6 alderman's
314.1 head-ache
325.7 post-box
331.5 ball-room
334.13 Frenchman
336.8 birthplace
341.31 newspaper
352.22 undertake
359.13 Frenchman

Vol.II
46.9 back-hander
48.26 cab-horse
51.12 life-like
73.42 waistcoats
99.20 side-board
107.40 love-making
109.26 hairdresser
116.8 household
133.49 outstretched

146.17 overflowed
150.16 falsehood
156.2 ball-room
160.19 matronhood
173.8 holydays
173.22 farm-houses
194.19 bridegroom
196.4 upwards
201.4 body-guard
202.32 housekeeper
216.7 match-makers
226.31 waistcoat
230.21 browbeaten
238.26 homewards
242.16 shareholders
248.12 shareholders
269.5 afterwards
289.30 bedstead
299.22 henceforward
308.6 cocoa-nut
308.23 stockbroker's
310.26 midnight
311.9 forehead
318.20 common-places
327.26 ante-chapel
333.2 pig-tail
359.8 landlady

Appendix: Installment No. 6 Re-edited

As explained in "Textual History and Editorial Methods" (pp. 410–16), there is unresolved disagreement over the evidence concerning the variants between the manuscript and the first edition for intallment 6. It is not known if Thackeray had any hand in producing the first edition variants. The installment is edited in the main body of this volume with the assumption that Thackeray was unable to make proof corrections. The following re-editing of the installment is based on the assumption that Thackeray is the source of most if not all of those changes.

Chapter XVII.

A SCHOOL OF ART.

BRITISH art either finds her[1] peculiar nourishment in melancholy, and loves to fix her[2] abode in desert-places, or it may be her purse is but[3] slenderly furnished, and she is forced to put up with accommodations rejected by more prosperous callings. Some of the most dismal quarters of the town are colonised by her disciples and professors. In walking through streets which may have been gay and polite[4] when ladies' chairmen jostled each other on the pavement, and link-boys with their torches lighted the beaux over the mud; who has not remarked[5] the artist's invasion of those regions once devoted to fashion and gaiety? Centre windows of drawing rooms[6] are enlarged so as to reach up into bed-rooms—bed-rooms where Lady Betty has had her hair powdered, and where the painter's north-light now takes possession of the place which her toilet-table occupied a hundred years ago. There are degrees in decadence: after the Fashion chooses to emigrate[7] and retreats from Soho and Bloomsbury, let us say, to Cavendish Square, physicians come and occupy

---

[1] her *E1*] its *Ms*
[2] her *E1*] its *Ms*
[3] is but *E1*] is *Ms*
[4] polite *E1*] polite in days *Ms*
[5] remarked *E1*] marked *Ms*
[6] drawing rooms *E1*] drawing-room floors *Ms*
[7] to emigrate, *E1*] another quarter *Ms*

the vacant houses; which still have a respectable look, the windows being cleaned and the knockers and plates kept bright, and the doctor's carriage rolling round the square,[8] almost as fine as the countess's which has whisked away her ladyship to other regions.[9] A boarding-house mayhap succeeds[1] the physician, who has followed after his sick folks into the new country:[2] then Dick Tinto comes with his dingy brass plate, and breaks in his north window; and sets up his sitter's throne. I love his honest moustache and jaunty velvet-jacket; his queer figure; his queer vanities; his kind heart. Why should he not suffer his ruddy ringlets to fall over his shirt-collar?[3] Why should he deny himself his velvet?[4] it is but a kind[5] of fustian which costs him eighteen-pence[6] a yard. He is naturally what he is,[7] and breaks out into costume as spontaneously[8] as a bird sings or a bulb bears[9] a tulip. And as Dick under yonder terrific appearance of waving cloak, bristling beard, and shadowy sombrero[1] is a good kindly simple creature got up at a very cheap rate: so his life is consistent with his dress;[2] he gives his genius a darkling swagger and a romantic envelope; which, being removed, you find not a bravo but a kind chirping Soul, not a moody poet avoiding mankind for the better[3] company of his own great thoughts, but a jolly little chap who has an aptitude for painting brocade gowns, a bit[4] of armour (with figures inside them): or trees and cattle, or gondolas and buildings or what not;—an instinct for the picturesque which exhibits itself in his works and outwardly on his person—beyond this, a gentle creature loving his friends, his cups, feasts, merry-makings[5] and all good things. The kindest folks alive I have found among those scowling whiskeradoes. They open oysters with their yataghans, toast muffins on their rapiers; and fill their Venice glasses with half-and-half: If they have money in their lean purses, be sure they have a friend to share it: What innocent gaiety,[6] jovial suppers on thread-bare cloths and wonderful songs after! What pathos, merriment, humour does not a man enjoy,

---

8 carriage ... square, *E1*] carriage *Ms*

9 whisked ... regions. *E1*] wheeled away elsewhere:—the physician rolls away presently after her ladyship. *Ms*

1 mayhap succeeds *E1*] succeeds *Ms*

2 physician, who has ... country: and *E1*] physician, and *Ms*

3 shirt-collar? *E1*] falling collar? Why should he not wear a hat like Guy Fawkes and a beard like the Saracen Snow Hill? *Ms*

4 his velvet? *E1*] velvet? *Ms*

5 but a kind *E1*] only a sort *Ms*

6 costs him eighteen-pence *E1*] costs eighteen pence *Ms*

7 is naturally what he is, *E1*] cannot help himself: *Ms*

8 as spontaneously *E1*] naturally *Ms*

9 bears *E1*] produces *Ms*

1 of waving ... sombrero, *E1*] of bristling beard, waving cloak, and shadowy sombrero *Ms*

2 dress; he gives *E1*] dress: he clothes his honest ideas in whiskers penny-velvet and Guy Fawkes hats, he gives *Ms*

3 better *E1*] nobler *Ms*

4 a bit *E1*] and bits *Ms*

5 merrymakings, *E1*] children, merry-makings *Ms*

6 gaiety, what *E1*] gaiety! What genuine human kindness, what *Ms*

who frequents their company!—Mr. Clive Newcome, who has long since shaved his beard, who has become a family man, and has seen the world in a thousand different phases, avers that his life as an art student at home and abroad was the pleasantest part of his whole existence. It may not be more amusing in the telling, than the chronicle of a feast, or the accurate report of two lovers' conversation: but the biographer having brought his hero to this period of his life, is bound to relate it, before passing[7] to other occurrences which are to be narrated in their turn.

We may be sure the boy had many conversations with his affectionate guardian as to the profession which he should follow. As regarded mathematical and classical learning the elder Newcome was forced to admit that out of every hundred boys there were fifty as clever as his own, and at least fifty more industrious: the army in time of peace Colonel Newcome thought a bad trade for a young fellow so fond of ease and pleasure as his son:[8] his delight in the pencil was manifest to all. Were not his[9] schoolbooks full of caricatures of the masters: whilst his tutor Grindley was lecturing him did he not draw Grindley instinctively under[1] his very nose? A painter Clive was determined to be and nothing else; and Clive,[2] being then some[3] sixteen years of age, began to study the art,[4] *en règle*, under the eminent Mr. Gandish of Soho.

It was that well-known portrait-painter, Alfred Smee, Esq., R. A., who recommended Gandish's to Colonel Newcome one day when the two gentlemen met at dinner at Lady Anne Newcome's table.[5] Mr. Smee happened to examine some of Clive's drawings which the young fellow had executed for his cousins. Clive[6] found no better amusement than in making[7] pictures for them and would cheerfully pass evening after evening in that diversion. He had made a thousand sketches of Ethel before a year was over: a year every day of which seemed to increase the attractions of the fair young creature, develop her nymph-like form and give her figure fresh graces. Also of course Clive drew Alfred and the nursery in general;[8] Aunt Ann and the Blenheim spaniels, Mr. Kuhn and[9] his earrings, the majestic John bringing in the coalscuttle;[1] and all persons or objects in that establishment with which he was familiar. "What a genius the lad has!" the complimentary Mr. Smee averred, "What a force and individuality there is in all his drawings! Look at his horses, capital, by Jove, capital![2] and Al-

[7] relate it, before passing *E1*] describe it before he passes *Ms*
[8] son: *E1*] son was: *Ms*
[9] all. Were not his *E1*] all eyes: were not all his *Ms*
[1] under *E1*] and under *Ms*
[2] else; and Clive, *E1*] else: The father acquiesced in the lad's decision; and Clive *Ms*
[3] some *E1*] about *Ms*
[4] the art, *E1*] the rudiments of the art *Ms*
[5] met at dinner ... table. *E1*] met at Lady Ann's table. *Ms*
[6] his cousins. Clive *E1*] his little cousins; he *Ms*
[7] than in making *E1*] than making *Ms*
[8] nursery in general, *E1*] nursery; *Ms*
[9] and *E1*] with *Ms*
[1] coal-scuttle, and *E1*] coalscuttle; the melancholy Miss Quigley; *Ms*
[2] his horses! capital, by Jove, *E1*] these horses, capital by Jove *Ms*

fred on his poney and Miss Ethel in her Spanish hat with her hair flowing
in the wind! I must take this sketch, I positively must now—and show it to
Landseer." And the courtly artist daintily enveloped the drawing in a sheet
of paper and put it away in his hat and vowed subsequently that the great
painter had been delighted with the young man's performance. Smee was
not only charmed with Clive's skill as an artist but thought his head would
be an admirable one to paint. Such a rich complexion! such fine tones in
his hair! such eyes! to see real blue eyes was so rare now-a-days!—And the
Colonel too!—if the Colonel would but give him a few sittings—the grey[3]
uniform of the Bengal Cavalry—the silver lace—the little bit of red ribbon just to warm up the picture—it was seldom, Mr. Smee declared, that
an artist could get such an opportunity for colour. With our hideous vermilion uniforms there was no chance of doing anything. Rubens himself
could scarcely manage scarlet. Look at the horseman in Cuyp's famous
picture at the Louvre! The red was a positive blot upon the whole picture. There was nothing like French grey and silver. All which did not
prevent Mr. Smee from painting Sir Brian in a flaring deputy-lieutenant's
uniform and entreating all military men whom he met to sit to him in scarlet. Clive Newcome the Academician[4] succeeded in painting, of course for
mere friendship's sake and because he liked the subject, though he could
not refuse the cheque which Colonel Newcome sent him for the frame and
picture; but[5] no cajoleries could induce the old campaigner to sit to any
artist save one. He said he should be ashamed to pay fifty guineas for the
likeness of his homely face. He jocularly proposed to James Binnie to have
his head put on[6] the canvas, and Mr. Smee enthusiastically caught at the
idea: but honest James winked his droll eyes saying his was a beauty that
did not want any paint, and when Mr. Smee took his leave after dinner
in Fitzroy Square where this conversation was held, James Binnie hinted
that the Academician was no better than an old humbug, in which surmise
he was probably not altogether incorrect. Certain young men who frequented the kind Colonel's house were also somewhat of this opinion; and
made endless jokes at the painter's expense. Smee[7] plastered his sitters
with adulation, as methodically as he covered his canvas. He waylaid gentlemen at dinner; he inveigled unsuspecting folks into his studio, and had
their heads off their shoulders before they were aware. One day on our
way from the Temple through Howland Street to the Colonel's house, we
beheld Major-General Sir Thomas de Boots in full uniform[8] rushing from
Smee's door to his brougham. The coachman was absent refreshing himself at a neighbouring tap. The little street-boys cheered and hurrayed Sir
Thomas, as he sat arrayed in gold and scarlet in his chariot. He blushed
purple when he beheld us: no artist would have dared to imitate those

[3] the gray *E1*] The French grey *Ms*
[4] Newcome the Academician *E1*] Newcome, Mr. Smee *Ms*
[5] picture; but *E1*] the picture. But *Ms*
[6] on *E1*] upon *Ms*
[7] the painter's expense. Smee *E1*] the portrait painter's expence. He *Ms*
[8] full uniform *E1*] full fig *Ms*

purple[9] tones: he was one of the numberless victims of Mr. Smee.

One day then, day to be noted with a white stone, Colonel Newcome with his son and Mr. Smee, R.A.,[1] walked from the Colonel's[2] house to Gandish's which was not far removed thence: and young Clive who was a perfect mimic, described to his friends, and illustrated as his wont was by diagrams, the interview which he had with that Professor. "By Jove, you must see Gandish's, Pen," cries[3] Clive, "Gandish is worth the whole world. Come and be an art student—you'll find such jolly fellows there—Gandish calls it Hart-student, and says, 'Hars est celare Hartem,' by Jove he does. He treated us to[4] a little Latin as he brought out a cake and a bottle of wine, you know.

"The Governor was splendid, Sir. He wore gloves, you know he only puts 'em on on Parade days; and turned out for the occasion[5] spick and span. He ought to be a general officer—he looks like a Field Marshal, don't he? You should have seen him bowing to[6] Mrs. Gandish and the Miss Gandishes dressed all in their best, round the cake-tray![7] He takes his glass of wine and[8] sweeps them all round with a bow. 'I hope, young ladies,' says he, 'you don't often go into the students' room—I am afraid

[9] purple *E1*] violet *Ms*
[1] Newcome, with . . . R.A., *E1*] Newcome and his son with Mr. Smee R.A. *Ms*
[2] the Colonel's *E1*] their *Ms*
[3] cries *E1*] says *Ms*
[4] treated us to *E1*] gave us *Ms*
[5] out for the occasion *E1*] out *Ms*
[6] to Mrs. Gandish *E1*] to the Mrs. Gandish *Ms*
[7] cake-tray! *E1*] tray with the cake! *Ms*
[8] and sweeps *E1*] and he sweeps *Ms*

the young gentlemen would leave off looking at the statues, if *you* came in.' And so they would: for you never saw such Guys, but the dear old boy fancies every woman is a beauty.

"'Mr. Smee, you are looking at my pictur of Boadishia?' says Gandish (wouldn't he have caught it for his quantities at Grey Friars, that's all?)—

"'Yes—ah—yes,' says Mr. Smee,[9] putting his hand over his eyes and standing before it—looking steady, you know, as if he was going to see whereabouts he should hit Boadishia.

"'It was painted when you were a young man—four year before you were an Associate, Smee. It ad some success in its time and there's good pints about that picture—Gandish goes on. 'But[1] I never could get my[2] price for it: and here it hangs in my own room—Igh Art won't do in this country, Colonel, it's a melancholy fact.'

"'High Art—I should think it *is* high Art,' whispers old Smee, 'fourteen feet high at least'—and then out loud he says: 'The picture[3] has very fine points in it,[4] Gandish, as you say—Foreshortening of that arm, capital—capital—That red drapery carried off into the right of the picture, very skilfully managed.'

"'It's not like portrait painting, Smee—High Art,' says Gandish. 'The models of the hancient Britons in that pictur alone cost me thirty pound, when I was a struggling man; and had just married my Betsey[5] here. You reckonise Boadishia, Colonel: with the Roman elmet, cuirass and javeling of the period—all studied from the hantique, Sir—the glorious hantique.'

"'All but Boadicea,' says Father, 'She[6] remains always young.' And he began to speak the lines out of Cowper, he did, waving his stick like an old trump, and famous they[7] are," cries the lad.

> 'When the British warrior queen,
>   Bleeding from the Roman rods'—

"Jolly verses! Haven't I translated them into Alcaics?" says Clive, with[8] a merry laugh, and resumes his history.[9]

"'O, I *must*[1] have those verses in my album!' cries one of the young ladies. 'Did you compose them, Colonel Newcome?' But Gandish, you see, is never[2] thinking about any works but his own: and goes on. 'Study of my eldest daughter, exhibited 1816.'

"'No Pa—not '16,' cries Miss Gandish. 'She don't look like a chicken, I can tell you.'

"'Admired,' Gandish goes on, never heeding her,—I[3] can show you what the papers said of it at the time. *Morning Chronicle* and *Examiner* spoke most ighly of it. My son as an infant, Ercules Stranglin the Serpent, over the piano. Fust conception of my pictur of *Non Hangli sed Hangeli*.'

"'For which I can guess who were the angels that sate,' says Father— upon my word that old Governor. He is[4] a little too strong.[5] But Mr. Gandish listened no more to him than to Mr. Smee; and went on, buttering himself all over, as I have read the Hottentots do. 'Myself at thirty-three years of age!' says he, pointing to a portrait of a gentleman in leather breeches and mahogany boots; 'I could have been a portrait[6] painter, Mr. Smee.'

"'Indeed it was lucky for some of us[7] you devoted yourself to high art, Gandish,' says Mr. Smee; and sips the wine and puts it down again making a face;—it wasn't first-rate tipple you see.

"'Two girls,' continues that indomitable Mr. Gandish. 'Highdea for Babes in the Wood—View of Pæstum taken on the spot by myself when travelling with the late lamented Hearl of Kew—Beauty, Valour, Commerce and Liberty condoling with Britannia on the death of Admiral

[6] She *E1*] who *Ms*

[7] famous they *E1*] famous verses they *Ms*

[8] When the British warrior queen, ...Clive, with *E1*] When the [blank] <Roman> †British↓ Queen. [double space] Trochaic Tetrameter—*I* remember," and he broke into *Ms* [Thackeray remembered accurately that it was trochaic tetrameter, but left a blank in the manuscript to indicate that his memory failed about the exact wording.]

[9] laugh, and resumes his history. *E1*] laugh. *Ms*

[1] *must E1*] must *Ms*

[2] ladies. ...never *E1*] ladies—but Gandish you see was *Ms*

[3] 'Admired,' Gandish ...her,—I *E1*] 'Admired. I *Ms*

[4] is *E1*] goes *Ms*

[5] strong. *E1*] strong! *Ms*

[6] on, buttering ...portrait *E1*] on 'Myself at thirty three years of age—I could have been a portrait *Ms*

[7] for some of us *E1*] for us *Ms*

Viscount Nelson—[8] allegorical piece, drawn at a very early age, after Trafalgar—Mr. Fuseli saw that piece, Sir,[9] when I was a student of the Academy, and said to me, Young man, stick to[1] the antique. There's nothing like it—Those were 'is[2] very words. If you do me the favour to walk into the Hatrium you'll remark my great pictur also from English Istory—an English Historical painter, Sir, should be employed chiefly in English History. That's what *I* would have done. Why ain't there temples for us, where the people might read their History at a glance and without knowing how to read? Why is my Alfred 'anging up in this 'all? because there is no patronage for a man who devotes himself to Igh Art. You know the anecdote, Colonel? King Alfred flying from the Danes took refuge in a neaterd's 'Ut. The rustic's[3] wife told him to bake a cake and the Fugitive Sovering set down to his ignoble task, and forgitting it in the cares of State let the cake burn, on which the woman struck him—The moment chose[4] is when she is lifting her 'and to deliver the blow—The King receives it with majesty mingled with meekness—In the background the door of the 'ut is open,[5] letting in the royal[6] officers to announce[7] the Danes are defeated. The daylight breaks in at the aperture, signifying the dawning of 'Ope. That story, Sir, which I found in my researches in Istory has since become so popular, Sir, that hundreds of artists have painted it, hundreds! I who discovered the legend, have my pictur—here—'

"'Now, Colonel,' says the showman, 'let me let me[8] lead you through the Statue Gallery—Apollo, you see—the Venus Hanadyomene, the glorious Venus of the Louvre, which I saw in 1814, Colonel, in its glory—the[9] Laocoon—my friend Gibson's Nimth, you see, is the only Figure I admit amongst the Antiques—now up this stair to the Students' room, where I trust my young friend Mr. Newcome will labour assiduously. *Ars longa est,* Mr. Newcome, *Vita*—'

"I[1] trembled," Clive said, "lest my father should introduce a certain favourite quotation beginning *'Ingenuas didicisso'*—but he refrained and we went into the room, where a score of students were assembled, who all looked away from their drawing-boards as we entered.[2]

"'Here will be your place, Mr. Newcome,' says the Professor, 'and[3] here that of your young friend—what did you say was his name?' I told him Ridley—for my dear old governor has promised to pay for J.J. too, you

---

8 death ... Nelson— *E1*] Fall of Nelson— *Ms*
9 piece, sir, *E1*] piece *Ms*
1 Young man, stick to *E1*] Mr. Gandish, study *Ms*
2 'is *E1*] his *Ms*
3 rustic's *E1*] shepherd's *Ms*
4 chose *E1*] chosen *Ms*
5 of the 'ut is open, *E1*] is hopening *Ms*
6 royal *E1*] king's *Ms*
7 announce *E1*] say *Ms*
8 here!' "'Now ... me *E1*] here—now, Colonel, let me *Ms*
9 Louvre, which ... glory—the *E1*] Louvre, the *Ms*
1 *Vita*—' ¶"I *E1*] *Vita*; I *Ms*
2 drawing-boards as we entered. *E1*] drawing at the New Comer. *Ms*
3 Newcome,' says the Professor, 'and *E1*] Newcome, and *Ms*

know. 'Mr. Chivers is the senior pupil and custos of the room in the habsence of my son.[4] Mr. Chivers, Mr. Newcome—gentlemen, Mr. Newcome, a new pupil. My son, Charles Gandish—Colonel Newcome. Assiduity, gentlemen, assiduity.[5] *Ars longa, Vita brevis et linea recta brevissima est*—This way, Colonel, down these steps across the court yard to my own studio. There, gentlemen,' and[6] pulling aside a curtain Gandish says, 'There! ...'"

"And what was the masterpiece behind it? we ask of Clive,[7] after we have done laughing at his imitation.

"Hand round the hat, J.J.!" cries Clive. "Now, ladies and gentlemen, pay your money!—Now walk in, for the performance is 'just a-going to begin!'" Nor would the rogue ever tell us what Gandish's curtained picture[8] was.

Not a successful painter, Mr. Gandish was an excellent master; and regarding all artists save one perhaps, a good critic. Clive and his friend J.J. came soon after, and commenced their studies under him.[9] The one took his humble seat at the drawing-board, a poor mean-looking lad with worn[1] clothes, downcast features, a figure almost deformed; the other adorned by good health, good looks, and the best of tailors; ushered into the studio

with his father and Mr. Smee as his aides-de-camp on his entry; and previously announced there with all the eloquence of honest Gandish. "I bet he's 'ad cake and wine," says one youthful student, of an epicurean and satirical

[4] of my son. *E1*] of myself or my son. *Ms*
[5] Assiduity, gentlemen, assiduity. *E1*] Assiduity gentlemen. Assiduity gentlemen. *Ms*
[6] studio. There, gentlemen,' and *E1*] Studio, where I beg to ave your opinion of a little work on which I am at present occupied. There gentlemen!' and *Ms*
[7] masterpiece ... Clive, *E1*] work Clive?" we ask *Ms*
[8] picture *E1*] masterpiece *Ms*
[9] under him. *E1*] together. *Ms*
[1] worn clothes *E1*] worn out clothes *Ms*

GANDISH'S

turn. "I bet he might have it every day if he liked." In fact Gandish was always handing him sweetmeats of compliments and cordials of approbation. He had coat sleeves with silk linings—he had studs in his shirt. How different was the texture and colour of that garment, to the sleeves Bob Grimes displayed when he took his coat off to put on his working-jacket! Horses used actually[2] to come for him to Gandish's door which was situated in a certain lofty street in Soho. The Miss G.'s would smile at him from the parlour window as he mounted and rode splendidly off,[3] and those opposition beauties, the Miss Levisons, daughters of the professor of dancing over the way, seldom failed to greet the young gentleman with an admiring ogle from their great black eyes. Master Clive was pronounced an "out-and-outer," a "swell and no mistake," and complimented with scarce one dissentient voice by the simple academy at[4] Gandish's. Besides he drew very well: there could be no doubt about that. Caricatures of the students of course were passing constantly among them, and in[5] revenge for one which a[6] huge red-haired Scotch student, Mr. Sandy[7] M'Collop, had made of John James, Clive perpetrated a picture of Sandy which set the whole[8] room in a roar; and when the Caledonian giant uttered satirical remarks against the assembled company averring that they were a parcel of sneaks, a set of leck-spettles, and using epithets[9] still more vulgar, Clive slipped[1] off his fine silk-sleeved[2] coat in an instant, invited Mr. M'Collop into the back yard, instructed him in a science which the lad[3] himself had acquired at Grey Friars, and administered two black eyes to Sandy,[4] which prevented the young artist from seeing for some days after the head of the Laocoon which he was copying.[5] The Scotchman's superior weight and age might have given the combat a different conclusion, had it endured long after Clive's brilliant opening attack with his right and left. But Professor Gandish came out of his painting-room at the sound of battle, and could scarcely[6] credit his own eyes when he saw[7] those of poor M'Collop so

---

2 deformed; the other ... used actually *E1*] deformed. He was the butt of the young students round about him. His face and person were caricatured by those jovial young satirists, a score of times, before he had been a week in the school: whereas Clive arrived splendid in fine raiment with his father and Mr. Smee as aides de camp on the first day; Mr. Gandish showing them over his establishment and having previously informed Mrs. Gandish and the Miss Gandishes and all the Gentlemen of the academy of the wealth and fashion of his pupil. Horses actually used *Ms*

3 off, *E1*] away: *Ms*

4 acadamy at *E1*] acadamy assembled at *Ms*

5 that. Caricatures ... in *E1*] that. In *Ms*

6 one which a *E1*] a caricature which that *Ms*

7 Mr. Sandy *E1*] Sandy *Ms*

8 whole *E1*] pupils' *Ms*

9 using epithets *E1*] using other epithets *Ms*

1 slipped *E1*] pulled *Ms*

2 fine silk-sleeved coat *E1*] coat *Ms*

3 the lad *E1*] Clive *Ms*

4 administered two black eyes to Sandy, *E1*] administered to him two black eyes *Ms*

5 seeing for some days after the head ... copying. *E1*] seeing the head ... copying, for some days after. *Ms*

6 scarcely *E1*] hardly *Ms*

7 saw *E1*] beheld *Ms*

darkened. To do the Scotchman[8] justice, he bore Clive no rancour. They became friends then: and afterwards at Rome whither they subsequently went to pursue their studies. The fame of Mr. M'Collop as an artist has long since been established. His pictures of Lord Lovat in Prison and Hogarth Painting Him, of the Blowing up of the Kirk of Field (painted for M'Collop of M'Collop), of the Torture of the Covenanters, the Murder of the Regent, the Murder of Rizzio and other historical pieces all of course from Scotch history, have established his reputation in South as well as in North Britain. No one would suppose from the gloomy character of his works that Sandy M'Collop is one of the most jovial souls alive. Within six months after their little difference Clive and he were the greatest of[9] friends and it was by the former's suggestion that Mr. James Binnie gave Sandy his first commission who[1] selected the cheerful subject of the young Duke of Rothsay starving in prison.

During this period Mr. Clive assumed the *toga virilis* and beheld with inexpressible satisfaction the first growth of those mustachios which have since given him such a marked[2] appearance. Being at Gandish's and so near the dancing academy, what must he do but take lessons in the Terpsichorean art too, making himself as popular with the dancing folks as with the drawing folks and the jolly king[3] of his company every where. He gave entertainments to his fellow-students in the Upper Chambers in Fitzroy Square which were devoted to his use, inviting his father and Mr. Binnie to these parties now and then. And songs were sung, and pipes were smoked, and many a pleasant supper eaten: There was no stint, but no excess. No young man was ever seen to quit those apartments "the worse" as it is called, for liquor. Fred Bayham's uncle the bishop, could not be more decorous than F.B. as he left the Colonel's house, for[4] the Colonel made that one of the conditions of his son's hospitality, that nothing like intoxication should ensue from it. The good gentleman did not frequent the parties of the juniors: he saw that his presence rather silenced the young men; and left them to themselves confiding in Clive's parole, and went away to play his honest rubber of whist[5] at the Club; and many a time he heard[6] the young fellows' steps[7] tramping by his bedchamber-door, as he lay wakeful[8] happy to think his[9] son was happy.

[8] of poor ...Scotchman *E1*] of Mr. M'Collop. The young Scotchman was a generous enemy: to do him *Ms*
[9] greatest of *E1*] greatest *Ms*
[1] commission, who *E1*] commission for which he *Ms*
[2] marked *E1*] martial *Ms*
[3] jolly king *E1*] jolly young King *Ms*
[4] called, for liquor. ...house, for *E1*] called 'for drink'—for *Ms*
[5] rubber of whist *E1*] rubber *Ms*
[6] time he heard *E1*] time heard *Ms*
[7] fellow's steps *E1*] fellows' departing steps *Ms*
[8] wakeful within, *E1*] within *Ms*
[9] think his *E1*] think that his *Ms*

Chapter XVIII.

NEW COMPANIONS.

LIVE used to give droll[1] accounts of the young disciples at Gandish's; who were of various ages and conditions, and in whose company the young fellow took his place with that good-temper and gaiety which have seldom deserted him in life and have put him at ease wherever his fate has led him. He is in truth as much at home in a fine drawing-room as in a public-house parlour; and can talk as pleasantly to the polite mistress of the mansion, as to the jolly landlady dispensing her drinks from her bar. Not one of the Gandishites but was after a while well-inclined to the young fellow; from Mr. Chivers the senior pupil, down to the little imp Harry Hooker who knew as much mischief at twelve years old, and could draw as cleverly as many a student of five-and-twenty; and Bob Trotter the diminutive fag of the studio who ran on all the young men's errands, and fetched them in apples, oranges and walnuts. Clive opened his eyes with wonder when he first beheld these simple feasts, and the pleasure with which some of the young men partook of them. They were addicted to polonies: they did not disguise their love for Banbury cakes: they made bets in ginger-beer and gave and took the odds in that frothing liquor. There was a young Hebrew amongst the pupils, upon whom his brother students used playfully to press ham-sandwiches, pork sausages and the like. This young man (who has risen to great wealth subsequently, and was bankrupt only three months since) actually brought[2] cocoa-nuts, and sold them at a profit amongst the lads. His pockets were never without pencil-cases, French chalk, garnet-brooches for which he was willing to bargain. He behaved very rudely to Gandish, who seemed to be afraid before him. It was whispered that the Professor was not altogether easy in his circumstances, and that the elder Moss had some mysterious hold over him. Honeyman and Bayham who once came to see Clive at the studio, seemed each

[1] give droll *E1*] give us droll *Ms*
[2] brought *Ms*] bought *E1*

disturbed at beholding young Moss (seated there making a copy of the Marsyas). "Pa knows both those gents," he informed Clive afterwards with a wicked twinkle of his Oriental eyes. "Step in, Mr. Newcome, any day you are passing down Wardour Street; and see if you don't want[3] any thing in our way." (He pronounced the words in his own way: saying, "Step id Bister Doocob, ady day idto Vorder Street," &c.) This young gentleman could get tickets for almost all the theatres, which he gave or sold; and gave splendid accounts at Gandish's of the brilliant masquerades. Clive was greatly diverted at beholding Mr. Moss at one of these entertainments, dressed in a scarlet coat and top-boots, and calling out, "Yoicks! Hark forward!" fitfully to another Orientalist his younger brother, attired like a midshipman. Once Clive bought a half-dozen of theatre-tickets from Mr. Moss, which he distributed to the young fellows of the studio—but when this nice young man tried farther to tempt him on the next day, "Mr. Moss," Clive said to him[4] with much dignity, "I am very much obliged to you for your offer, but when I go to the play, I prefer paying at the door."[5]

Mr. Chivers[6] used to sit in one corner of the room occupied over a lithographic stone. He was an uncouth and peevish young man; for ever finding fault with the younger pupils, whose butt he was. Next in rank and age was M'Collop, before named: and these two were at first more than usually harsh and captious with Clive, whose prosperity offended them; and whose dandyfied manners, free and easy ways, and evident influence over the younger scholars,[7] gave umbrage to these elderly[8] apprentices. Clive at first returned Mr. Chivers war for war, controlment for controlment: but when he found[9] Chivers was the son of a helpless widow; that he maintained her by his lithographic vignettes for the music-sellers, and by the scanty remuneration of some lessons which he gave at a school at Highgate:—when Clive saw or fancied he saw, the lonely senior eyeing with hungry eyes,[1] the luncheons of cheese and bread and sweetstuff[2] which the young lads of the studio enjoyed, I promise you Mr. Clive's wrath against Chivers was speedily turned into compassion and kindness,[3] and he sought, and no doubt found, means of feeding Chivers without offending his testy independence.

Nigh to Gandish's was and perhaps is another establishment for teaching the arts of design—Barker's; which had the additional dignity of a Life and Costume Academy; frequented by a class of students more[4] advanced than those of Gandish's.[5]   Between these and the Barkerites there was a con-

---

[3] you don't want *E1*] you want *Ms*
[4] said to him *E1*] said *Ms*
[5] door." *Ms*] doors." *E1*
[6] Mr. Chivers *E1*] The Senior Student, Mr. Chivers, *Ms*
[7] younger scholars, *E1*] Junior Scholars, *Ms*
[8] these elderly *E1*] these laborious elderly *Ms*
[9] he found *E1*] the lad found that *Ms*
[1] eyes, *E1*] glances *Ms*
[2] cheese and bread, and sweetstuff, *E1*] bread and cheese and sweet stuff *Ms*
[3] compassion and kindness, *E1*] kindness and compassion, *Ms*
[4] students more *E1*] students usually more *Ms*
[5] those of Gandish's. *E1*] the Gandishites. *Ms*

stant[6] rivalry and emulation in and out of doors. Gandish sent more pupils
to the Royal Academy: Gandish had brought up three medallists; and the
last R.A. student sent to Rome was a Gandishite. Barker on the contrary
scorned and loathed Trafalgar Square; and laughed at its Art.[7] Barker exhibited in Pall Mall and Suffolk Street. He laughed at old Gandish and his
pictures, made minced-meat of his *Angli and Angeli,* and tore King Alfred
and his muffin to pieces. The young men of the respective schools used to
meet at Lundy's coffee-house and billiard-room, and smoke there and do
battle. Before Clive and his friend J.J. came to Gandish's, the Barkerites
were having the best of that constant match which the two academies were
playing. Fred Bayham who knew every coffee-house in town; and whose
initials were scored on a thousand tavern-doors; was for a while a constant[8]
visitor at Lundy's—played pool with the young men, did not disdain to
dip his beard into their porter-pots when invited to partake of their drink,
treated them handsomely when he was in cash himself; and was an hon-
ourary member of Barker's Academy. Nay when the Guardsman was not
forthcoming, who was standing for one of Barker's heroic pictures; Bayham bared his immense arms, and brawny shoulders; and stood as Prince
Edward with Philippa sucking the poisoned wound. He would take his
friends up to the picture in[9] the Exhibition, and proudly point to it. "Look
at that biceps, Sir, and now look at this—That's Barker's masterpiece, Sir,
and that's the muscle of F.B., Sir." In no company was F.B. greater than
in the society of the artists; in whose smoky haunts and airy parlours he
might often be found. It was from F.B., that Clive heard of Mr. Chivers's
struggles and honest industry—A great deal of shrewd advice could F.B.
give on occasion: and many a kind action and gentle office of charity was
this[1] jolly outlaw known to do and cause to be done. His advice to Clive
was most edifying at this time of our young gentleman's life, and he owns
that he was kept from much mischief by this queer counsellor.

A few months after Clive and J.J. had entered at Gandish's, that academy
began to hold its own against its rival. The[2] silent young disciple was pronounced to be a genius. His copies were beautiful in delicacy and finish.
His designs were exquisite for grace and richness of fancy. Mr. Gandish
took to himself the[3] credit for J.J.'s genius: Clive ever and fondly acknowledged the benefit he got from his friend's taste[4] and bright enthusiasm
and sure skill. As for Clive, if he was successful in the academy he was
doubly victorious out of it. His person was handsome his courage high,
his gaiety and frankness delightful and winning. His money was plenty,
and he spent it like a young king. He could speedily beat all the club at
Lundy's at billiards: and give points to the redoubted F.B. himself. He
sang a famous song at their jolly supper-parties: and J.J. had no greater

[6] a constant *E1*] constant *Ms*
[7] its art. *E1*] its Art, and pretensions. *Ms*
[8] constant *E1*] pretty constant *Ms*
[9] in *E1*] at *Ms*
[1] this *E1*] the *Ms*
[2] The *E1*] That *Ms*
[3] the *E1*] all the *Ms*
[4] friend's taste *E1*] friend's skill and taste *Ms*

delight than to listen to his fresh voice: and watch the young conqueror at the billiard-table where the balls seemed to obey him.

Clive was not the most docile of Mr. Gandish's pupils.[5] If he had not come to the studio on horseback, several of the young students averred, Gandish would not always have been praising him and quoting him as that professor certainly did. It must be confessed that the young ladies read the history of Clive's uncle in the Book of Baronets and that Gandish junr., probably[6] with an eye to business, made a design of a picture in which, according to that veracious volume, one of the Newcomes was represented as going cheerfully to the stake at Smithfield, surrounded by some very ill-favoured Dominicans whose arguments did not appear to make the least impression upon the martyr of the Newcome family. Sandy M'Collop devised a counter picture wherein the barber surgeon of King Edward the Confessor was drawn operating upon the beard of that monarch—to which piece of satire, Clive gallantly replied by a design representing Sawney Bean M'Collop, chief of the clan of that name, descending from his mountains into Edinburgh and his astonishment at beholding a pair of breeches for the first time. These playful jokes passed constantly amongst the young men of Gandish's studio. There was no one there who was not caricatured in one way or another.[7] He whose eyes looked not very straight was depicted with a most awful squint. The youth whom nature had endowed with somewhat lengthy nose was drawn by the caricaturists with a prodigious proboscis; little Bobby Moss the young Hebrew artist from Wardour Street was delineated with three hats and an old clothes bag, nor were poor J.J.'s round shoulders spared until Clive indignantly remonstrated at the hideous hunchback pictures which the boys[8] made of his friend and vowed[9] it was a shame to make jokes at such a deformity.

Our friend, if the truth must be told regarding him, though one of the most frank generous and kind-hearted persons, is of a nature somewhat haughty and imperious, and very likely the course of life which he now led and the society which he was compelled to keep served to increase some original defects in his character and to fortify a certain disposition to think well of himself with which his enemies not unjustly reproach him. He has been known very pathetically to lament that he was withdrawn from school too early, where a couple of years' further course of thrashings from his tyrant, Old Hodge, he avers, would have done him good. He laments that he was not sent to college, where if a young man receives no other discipline, at least he acquires that of meeting with his equals in society, and of assuredly finding his betters: whereas[1] in poor Mr. Gandish's Studio of Art, our young gentleman scarcely found a comrade that was not in one way or other his flatterer, his inferior, his honest or dishonest admirer. The influence of his family's rank and wealth acted more or less on all those

---

[5] pupils. *E1*] young pupils. *Ms*
[6] junr., probably *E1*] Junior possibly *Ms*
[7] another. *E1*] other. *Ms*
[8] boys *E1*] lads *Ms*
[9] vowed *E1*] vowed that *Ms*
[1] betters: whereas *E1*] betters. Whereas *Ms*

simple folks,[2] who would run on his errands, and vied with each other in winning the young nabob's favour. His very goodness of heart rendered him a more easy prey to their flattery, and his kind and jovial disposition led him into company from which he had been much better away. I am afraid that artful young Moss, whose parents dealt in pictures furniture jimcracks and jewellery, victimised Clive sadly with rings and chains, shirt-studs and flaming shirt-pins, and such vanities: which the poor young rogue locked up in his desk generally, only venturing to wear them when he was out of his father's sight or[3] of Mr. Binnie's whose shrewd eyes watched him very keenly.

Mr. Clive used to leave home every day shortly after noon when he was supposed to betake himself to Gandish's studio: but was the young gentleman always at the drawing-board copying from the antique when his father supposed him to be so devotedly[4] engaged? I fear his place was sometimes vacant. His friend J.J. worked every day and all day; many a time the steady little student remarked his patron's absence and no doubt gently remonstrated with him; but when Clive did come to his work he executed it with remarkable skill and rapidity; and Ridley was too fond of him to say a word at home regarding the shortcomings of the youthful scapegrace. Candid readers may sometimes have heard their friend Tom's mother lament that her darling was working too hard at College: or Harry's sisters express their anxiety lest his too rigorous attendance in Chambers (after which he will persist in sitting up all night reading those dreary law books which cost such an immense sum of money) should undermine dear Henry's health: and to such acute persons a word is sufficient to indicate young Mr. Clive Newcome's proceedings. Meanwhile his father, who knew no more of the world than Harry's simple sisters or Tom's fond mother, never doubted[5] that all Clive's doings were right, and that his boy was the best of boys.

"If that young man goes on as charmingly as he has begun," Clive's cousin Barnes Newcome said of his kinsman, "he will be a paragon. I saw him last night at Vauxhall in company with young Moss, whose father does bills, and keeps the bric-a-brac shop in Wardour Street; two or three other gentlemen, probably young old clothes-men, who had concluded for the day the labours of the bag, joined Mr. Newcome and his friend, and they partook of rack-punch in an arbour. He is a delightful youth, Cousin Clive, and I feel sure is about to be an honour to our family."

2 folks, who *E1*] folks. He had two or three humble friends *Ms*
3 or *E1*] and *Ms*
4 supposed . . . devotedly *E1*] thought he was so severely *Ms*
5 doubted that *E1*] doubted but that *Ms*

Chapter XIX.

THE COLONEL AT HOME.[6]

UR good Colonel's house had[1] received a coat of paint, which like Madame Latour's rouge in her latter days only served to make her careworn face look more ghastly. The kitchens were gloomy. The stables were gloomy. Great black passages, cracked conservatory, dilapidated bathroom with melancholy waters moaning[2] and fizzing from the cistern, the great large blank stone staircase were all so many melancholy features in the general countenance of the house, but the Colonel thought it perfectly cheerful and pleasant and furnished it[3] in his rough and ready way. One day a cartload of chairs, the next a waggon full of fenders, fire irons and glass and crockery—a quantity of supplies, in a word, he poured into the place. There were[4] a yellow curtain in the back drawing-room and green curtains in the front. The carpet was an immense bargain bought dirt cheap, Sir, at a sale in Euston Square. He was against the purchase of a carpet for the stairs. What was the good of it? What did men want with stair-carpets? His own apartment contained a wonderful assortment of lumber: shelves which he nailed himself, old Indian garments, camphor trunks. What did he want with gewgaws. Anything was good enough for an old soldier. But the spare bedroom was endowed with all sorts of splendour—a bed as big as a general's tent, a cheval glass—whereas the Colonel shaved in a little cracked mirror which cost him no more than King Stephen's breeches—and a handsome new carpet, while the boards of the Colonel's bedchamber were as bare—as bare as old Miss Scragg's shoulders which would be so much more comfortable were they covered up. Mr. Binnie's bedchamber was neat snug and appropriate. And Clive had a study and bedroom at the top of the house

[6] The first paragraph and the first two sentences of the second paragraph of this chapter were originally intended for the last page of chapter 16, but were moved to this point when installment No. 5 overflowed and No. 6 ran short of copy.

[1] OUR good Colonel's house had *E1*] It had *Ms*

[2] moaning *E1*] mourning *Ms*

[3] pleasant, and furnished it *E1*] pleasant and set about furnishing it *Ms*

[4] were *E1*] was *Ms*

which he was allowed to furnish entirely according to his own taste. How he and Ridley revelled in Wardour Street. What delightful coloured prints of hunting, racing and beautiful ladies did they not purchase, mount with their own hands, cut out for screens, frame and glaze and hang up on the walls. When the rooms were ready they gave a party inviting the Colonel and Mr. Binnie by note of hand, two gentlemen from Lamb Court, Temple, Mr. Honeyman and Fred Bayham. We must have Fred Bayham. Fred Bayham frankly asked, "Is Mr. Sherrick with whom you have become rather intimate lately—and mind you I say nothing but I recommend strangers in London to be cautious about their friends—is Mr. Sherrick coming to you, young 'un, because if he is F.B. must respectfully decline."

Mr. Sherrick was not invited and accordingly F.B. came. But Sherrick was invited on other days and a very queer society did our honest Colonel gather together in that queer house, so dreary, so dingy, so comfortless, so pleasant.[5]

Our good Colonel who was one of the most hospitable men alive, loved to have his friends around[6] him; and it must be confessed that the evening-parties now occasionally given in Fitzroy Square were[7] of the oddest assemblage of people—the correct East India gentlemen from Hanover Square: the artists, Clive's friends, gentlemen of all ages with all sorts of beards, in every variety of costume; now and again a stray schoolfellow from Grey Friars who stared, as well he might, at the company in which he found himself—Sometimes a few ladies were brought to these entertainments. The immense politeness of the good host compensated some of them, for the strangeness of his[8] company. They had never seen such odd-looking hairy men as those young artists nor such wonderful women as Colonel Newcome assembled together. He was good to all old maids, and poor widows. Retired Captains with large families of daughters found in him their best friend. He sent carriages to fetch them and bring them back from the suburbs where they dwelt. Gandish, Mrs. Gandish and the four Miss Gandishes in scarlet robes were constant attendants at[9] the Colonel's soirées. "I delight, Sir, in the 'ospitality[1] of my distinguished military friend," Mr. Gandish would say: "the Harmy has always been my passion. I served in the Soho Volunteers three years myself—till the conclusion of the war, Sir, till the conclusion of the war."

It was a great sight to see Mr. Frederick Bayham engaged in the waltz or the quadrille with some of the elderly houris at the Colonel's parties. F.B., like a good-natured F.B. as he was, always chose the plainest women as[2] partners and entertained them with profound compliments and sumptuous conversation. The Colonel likewise danced quadrilles with the utmost gravity. Waltzing had been invented long since his time: but he

---

5 Here ends the passage originally intended for Chapter 16.
6 friends around *E1*] friends constantly around *Ms*
7 were *E1*] were composed *Ms*
8 his *E1*] the *Ms*
9 at *E1*] of *Ms*
1 'ospitality *E1*] hospitality *Ms*
2 as *E1*] for *Ms*

practiced[3] quadrilles when they first came in about 1817 in Calcutta. To
see him leading up a little old maid, and bowing to her when the dance
was ended, and performing Cavalier seul with stately simplicity—was a
sight indeed to remember. If Clive Newcome had not such a fine sense
of humour: he would have blushed for his father's simplicity—As it was,
the elder's guileless goodness and childlike[4] trustfulness endeared him
immensely to his son. "Look at the old boy, Pendennis," he would say.
"Look at him leading up that old Miss Tidswell to the piano. Doesn't
he do it like an old Duke? I lay a wager[5] she thinks she is going to be
my mother-in-law—all the women are in love with him, young and old.
'Should he upbraid' There she goes—'I'll own that he'll[6] prevail, And sing
as sweetly as a nigh-tin-gale'! O you old warbler! Look at Father's old
head bobbing up and down! Wouldn't he do for Sir Roger de Coverley?
How do you do, Uncle Charles—I say, M'Collop, how gets[7] on the Duke
of Whatdyecallem starving in the Castle—Gandish says it's very good."
The lad retires to a group of artists. Mr. Honeyman comes up, with a

faint smile playing on his features like moonlight on the façade of Lady
Whittlesea's chapel.

"These parties are the most singular I have ever seen," whispers Honey-

---

[3] he practiced *E1*] he had practiced *Ms*
[4] childlike *E1*] childish *Ms*
[5] wager *E1*] guinea *Ms*
[6] he'll *E1*] he *Ms*
[7] gets *E1*] goes *Ms*

man.[8] "In entering one of these assemblies one is struck with[9] the immensity of London; and with[1] the sense of one's own insignificance—without, I trust, departing from my clerical character, nay from my very avocation as Incumbent of a London Chapel—I have seen a good deal of the world—And here is an assemblage, no doubt of most respectable persons on scarce one of whom I ever set eyes till this evening. Where does my good brother find such characters?[2]

"That," says Mr. Honeyman's interlocutor, "is the celebrated[3] though neglected artist, Professor Gandish, whom nothing but jealousy has kept out of the Royal Academy. Surely you have heard of the Great Gandish."

"Indeed I am ashamed to confess my ignorance—But a clergyman busy with his duties, knows little, perhaps too little,[4] of the Fine Arts."

"Gandish, Sir, is one of the greatest geniuses on whom our[5] ungrateful country ever trampled. He exhibited his first celebrated picture of Alfred in the Neatherd's Hut (he says he is the first who ever touched that subject) in 180–: but Lord Nelson's death and victory of Trafalgar occupied the public attention at that time, and Gandish's work went unnoticed. In the year 1816 he painted his great work of Boadicea. You see her before you, that lady in yellow with a light front and a turban. Boadicea became Mrs. Gandish in that year. So late as '27 he brought before the world his 'Non Angli sed Angeli'—two of the angels are yonder in sea green dresses, the Misses Gandish—the youth in Berlin[6] gloves was the little male angelus[7] of that piece."

"How come you to know all this, you strange man?" says[8] Mr. Honeyman.

"Simply because Gandish has told me twenty times. He tells the story to everybody every time he sees them. He told it to-day at dinner. Boadicea and the angels[9] came afterwards."

"Satire! Satire! Mr. Pendennis!" says the divine holding up a reproving finger of lavender kid. "Beware of a wicked wit!—But when a man has that tendency—I know how difficult it is to restrain! My dear Colonel, good evening! You have a great reception to-night. That gentleman's bass voice is very fine. Mr. Pendennis and I were admiring it.[1] The Wolf is a song admirably adapted to show its capabilities."

Mr. Gandish's autobiography had occupied the whole time after the retirement of the ladies from Colonel Newcome's dinner-table. Mr. Hobson Newcome had been asleep during the performance, Sir Curry Baughton

---

8 whispers Honeyman. *E1*] Honeyman whispers. *Ms*
9 with *E1*] by *Ms*
1 with *E1*] by *Ms*
2 characters? ¶That," *E1*] characters. Who can be that extraordinary man with the collars of his shirt turned down who is just now going to sing?" *Ms*
3 "is the celebrated, *E1*] "that is the celebrated *Ms*
4 little, perhaps too little, *E1*] little, too little perhaps *Ms*
5 our *E1*] an *Ms*
6 in Berlin *E1*] in the Berlin *Ms*
7 angelus *E1*] Angel *Ms*
8 says *E1*] asks *Ms*
9 angels *E1*] Angeli *Ms*
1 it. *E1*] it anon— *Ms*

and one or two of the Colonel's professional and military guests silent and puzzled, honest Mr. Binnie with his shrewd good-humoured face sipping his claret as usual and delivering a sly joke now and again to the gentlemen at his end of the table. Mrs. Newcome had sat by him in sulky dignity. Was it that Lady Baughton's diamonds offended her?—her ladyship and her daughter being attired in great splendour for a court ball which they were to attend that evening. Was she hurt because *she* was not invited to that Royal Entertainment?[2] As these festivities were to take[3] place at an early hour the ladies bidden were obliged to quit the Colonel's house before the[4] evening party commenced, from which Lady Ann declared she was quite vexed to be obliged to run away.

Lady Ann Newcome had been as gracious on this occasion as her sister-in-law had been out of humour. Everything pleased her in the house. She had no idea that there were such fine houses in that quarter of the town. She thought the dinner so very nice. That Mr. Binnie such a good-humoured looking gentleman. That stout gentleman with his collars turned down like Lord Byron, so exceedingly clever and full of information. A celebrated artist, was he? (Courtly Mr. Smee had his own opinion upon that point but did not utter it.) All those artists are so eccentric and amusing and clever! Before dinner she insisted upon seeing Clive's den with its pictures and casts and pipes. "You horrid young wicked creature, have you began to smoke already?" she asks as she admires[5] his room. She admired everthing; nothing could exceed her satisfaction.

The sisters-in-law kissed on meeting with that cordiality so delightful to witness in sisters who dwell together in unity. It was, "My dear Maria, what an age since I have seen you!" "My dear Ann, our occupations are so engrossing, our circles are so different!" in a languid response from the other. "Sir Brian is not coming, I suppose? Now Colonel!" She turns in a frisky manner towards him and taps her fan. "Did I not tell you Sir Brian would not come?"

"He is kept at the House of Commons, my dear. Those dreadful committees.[6] He was quite vexed at not being able to come."

"I know, I know, dear Ann. There are always excuses to gentlemen in Parliament. I have received many such. Mr. Shaloo and Mr.[7] McSheny, the leaders of our party often and often disappoint me. I *knew* Brian would not come. *My* husband came down[8] from Marble Head on purpose this morning. Nothing would have induced *us* to give up our brother's party."

"I believe you. I did come down[9] from Marble Head this morning, and I was four hours in the hay-field before I came away, and in the city till five and I've been to look at a horse afterwards at Tattersall's, and I'm as hungry as a hunter and as tired as a hodman," says Mr. Newcome with

[2] Entertainment? *E1*] Entertainment while others were asked. *Ms*
[3] were to take *E1*] take *Ms*
[4] the *E1*] his *Ms*
[5] asks, as she admires *E1*] asked as she admired *Ms*
[6] committees. *E1*] committees you know. *Ms*
[7] Shaloo and Mr. *E1*] Shaloo Mr. *Ms*
[8] came down *E1*] came *Ms*
[9] come down *E1*] come *Ms*

his hands in his pockets. "How do you do, Mr. Pendennis. Maria, you remember Mr. Pendennis, don't you?"

"Perfectly," replies the languid Maria. Mr. Gandish, Colonel Topham, Major M'Cracken are announced, and then in diamonds, feathers and splendour, Lady Baughton and Miss Baughton who are going to the Queen's Ball and Sir Curry Baughton not quite in his deputy-lieutenant's uniform as yet, looking very shy in a pair of blue trowsers with a glistering stripe of silver down the seams. Clive looks with wonder and delight at these ravishing ladies rustling in fresh brocades, with feathers, diamonds and every magnificence. Aunt Ann has not her court-dress on as yet, and Aunt Maria blushes as she beholds the new comers, having thought fit to attire herself in a high dress with a Quaker-like simplicity and a pair of gloves more than ordinarily dingy. The pretty little foot she has, it is true, and sticks it out from habit; but what is Mrs. Newcome's foot compared with that sweet little chaussure which[1] Miss Baughton exhibits and withdraws; the shiny[2] white satin slipper, the pink[3] stocking which ever and anon peeps from the rustling folds of her robe and timidly retires into its covert? That foot, light as it is, crushes Mrs. Newcome. No wonder she winces and is angry. There are some mischievous persons who rather like to witness that discomfiture. All Mr. Smee's flatteries that day failed to soothe her. She was in the state in which his canvasses sometimes are when he cannot paint on them.

What happened to her alone in the drawing-room when the ladies invited to the dinner had departed and those convoked to the soirée began to arrive,—what happened to her or to them I do not like to think. The Gandishes arrived first, Boadicea and the Angels; we judged so from the fact that young Mr. Gandish came blushing into the dessert. Name after name was announced of persons of whom Mrs. Newcome knew nothing. The young and the old, the pretty and homely, they were all in their best dresses and no doubt stared at Mrs. Newcome so obstinately plain in her attire. When we came upstairs from dinner we found her seated entirely by herself tapping her fan at the fireplace; timid groups of persons were round about, waiting for the irruption of the gentlemen, until the pleasure should begin. Mr. Newcome who came upstairs yawning was heard to say to his wife, "O dam—let's cut," and they went downstairs and waited until their carriage had arrived[4] when they quitted Fitzroy Square.

Mr. Barnes Newcome presently arrived looking particularly smart and lively, with a large flower in his button-hole, and leaning on the arm of a friend. "How doyoudo, Pendennis," he says with a peculiarly dandyfied air. "Did you dine here? you look as if you dined[5] here (and Barnes certainly as if he had dined elsewhere). I was only asked to the cold soirée. Who did you have for dinner? You had my mamma and the Baughtons, and my uncle and aunt, I know, for they are down below in the library waiting for the carriage. He is asleep and she is as sulky as a bear."

[1] which *E1*] which the lovely *Ms*
[2] shiny *E1*] sheeny, *Ms*
[3] the pink *E1*] the dazzling pink *Ms*
[4] had arrived, *E1*] arrived *Ms*
[5] dined *E1*] had dined *Ms*

"Why did Mrs. Newcome say I should find nobody I knew up here?" asks Barnes's companion; "on the contrary there are lots of fellows I know. There's Fred Bayham dancing like a harlequin. There's old Gandish who used to be my drawing-master: and my Brighton friends, your uncle and cousin, Barnes. What relations are they to me? must be some relations. Fine fellow your cousin."

"Hm!" growls Barnes, "very fine boy, not spoiled[6] at all, not fond of flattery, not surrounded by toadies, not fond of drink—delightful boy. See yonder! the young fellow is in conversation with his most intimate friend, a little crooked fellow, with long hair. Do you know who he is? He is the son of old Todmorden's butler: upon my life it's true."

"And suppose it is, what the deuce do I care?" cries Lord Kew. "A man must be somebody's son: Who can be more respectable than a butler?[7] When I am a middle-aged man, I hope humbly I shall look like a butler myself. Suppose you were to put ten of Gunter's men into the House of Lords, do you mean to say that[8] they would not look as well as any average ten peers in the House? Look at Lord Westcot. He is exactly like a butler. That's why the country has such confidence in him. I never dine with him but I fancy he ought to be at the sideboard. Here comes that insufferable little old Smee. How do you do, Mr. Smee."

Mr. Smee smiles his sweetest smile—With his rings, diamond shirt studs and red velvet waistcoat, there are few more elaborate middle-aged[9] bucks than Alfred Smee. "How do you do, my dear lord," cries this bland one. "Who would ever have thought of seeing your lordship here?"

"Why the deuce not, Mr. Smee?" asks Lord Kew abruptly. "Is it wrong to come here? I have been in the house only five minutes, and three people have said the same thing to me—Mrs. Newcome who is sitting downstairs in a rage waiting for her carriage, the condescending Barnes, and yourself—Why do *you* come here, Smee? How are you, Mr. Gandish. How do the fine arts go?"

"Your lordship's kindness in asking for them[1] will cheer them if anything will," says Mr. Gandish. "Your noble family has always patronised them. I am proud to be reckonised by your lordship in this house; where the distinguished father of one of my pupils entertains us this evening. A most promising young man, is young Mr. Clive—talents for a hamateur really most remarkable."

"Excellent upon my word, excellent," cries Mr. Smee. "I'm not an animal-painter myself and perhaps don't think much of that branch of the profession, but it seems to me the young fellow draws horses with the most wonderful spirit. I hope Lady Walham is very well and that she was satisfied with her son's portrait—Stockholm, I think, your brother is appointed to? I wish I might be allowed to paint the elder as well as the younger brother, my lord."

[6] spoiled *Ms*] spirited *E1*
[7] Who can . . . butler? *mistakenly inserted in E1 before* "A man
[8] say that *E1*] say *Ms*
[9] elaborate middle-aged *E1*] elaborate and killing middle-aged *Ms*
[1] asking for them *E1*] asking *Ms*

"I am an historical painter but whenever Lord Kew is painted I hope his lordship will think of the old servant of his lordship's family, Charles Gandish," cries the professor.

"I am like Susannah between the two Elders," says Lord Kew. "Let my innocence alone, Smee. Mr. Gandish, don't persecute my modesty with your addresses. I won't be painted. I am not a fit subject for a historical painter, Mr. Gandish."

"Halcibiades sate to Praxiteles and Pericles to Phidjas," remarks Gandish.

"The cases are not quite similar," says Lord Kew languidly. "You are no doubt fully equal to Praxiteles;[2] but I don't see my resemblance to[3] the other party. I should not look well as a hero: and Smee could not paint me handsome enough."

"I would try, my dear lord," cries Mr. Smee.

"I know you would, my dear fellow," Lord Kew answered looking at the painter with a lazy scorn in his eyes. "Where is Colonel Newcome, Mr. Gandish?" Mr. Gandish replied that our gallant Ost was dancing a quadrille in the next room; and the young gentleman walked on towards that apartment to pay his respects to the giver of the evening's entertainment.

Newcome's[4] behaviour to the young peer was ceremonious but not in the least servile. He saluted the other's superior rank, not his person, as he turned the guard out for a general officer. He never could be brought to be otherwise than cold and grave in his behaviour to John James: nor was it without difficulty, when young Ridley and his son became pupils at Gandish's, he could be induced to invite the former to his parties. "An artist is any man's equal," he said. "I have no prejudices of that sort, and think that Sir Joshua Reynolds and Doctor Johnson were fit company for any person of whatever rank. But a young man whose father may have to wait behind me at dinner should not be brought into my company." Clive compromised the dispute with a laugh. "First," says he, "I will wait till I am asked and then I promise I will not go to dine with Lord Todmorden."

---

[2] Praxiteles; *E1*] Praxiteles, Gandish; *Ms*
[3] to *E1*] to—to *Ms*
[4] ¶Newcome's *E1*] [no paragraph break] Newcome's *Ms*

Chapter XX.

CONTAINS MORE PARTICULARS OF THE COLONEL AND HIS BRETHERN.

Clive's amusements,[1] studies or occupations, such as they were, filled his day pretty completely, and caused the young gentleman's time to pass rapidly and pleasantly, his father, it must be owned, had no such resources, and the good Colonel's idleness hung[2] heavily upon him. He submitted very kindly to this infliction, however, as he would have done to any other for Clive's sake: and though he may have wished himself back with his regiment again, and engaged in the pursuits in which his[3] life had been spent; he chose to consider these desires as very selfish and blameable on his part; and sacrificed them resolutely for his son's welfare. The young fellow, I daresay, gave his parent no more credit for his[4] long self-denial than many other children award to their's. We take such life-offerings as our due commonly. The old French satirist avers that in a love affair, there is usually one person who loves, and the other *qui se laisse aimer:* it is only in later days perhaps, when the treasures of love are spent, and the kind hand cold which ministered them, that we remember how tender it was; how soft to soothe;[5] how eager to shield; how ready to support and caress. The ears may no longer hear, which would have received our words of thanks so delightedly. Let us hope those fruits of Love, though tardy, are yet not all too late; and though we bring our Tribute of reverence and gratitude, it may be[6] to a gravestone; there is an acceptance even there, for the stricken heart's oblation of fond remorse, contrite memories and pious tears. I am thinking of the love of Clive Newcome's father for him; (and perhaps, young reader, that of yours and mine for ourselves[7])—how the old man lay awake, and devised kindnesses, and gave his all for the love of his son; and the young man took, and spent, and slept, and made merry.

[1] amusements, *E1*] pleasures, *Ms*
[2] hung *E1*] hung rather *Ms*
[3] his *E1*] all his *Ms*
[4] his *E1*] this *Ms*
[5] soothe; *E1*] caress; *Ms*
[6] be *E1*] be but *Ms*
[7] that of yours and mine for ourselves *E1*] of yours and mine *Ms*

Did we not say at our tale's commencement that all stories were old? Careless prodigals and anxious elders have been from the beginning;—and so may love and repentance and forgiveness endure even till the end.

The stifling fogs, the slippery mud, the dun-dreary November mornings when the Regent's Park where the Colonel took his early walk was wrapped in yellow mist; must have been a melancholy exchange for the splendour of Eastern sunrise and the invigorating gallop at dawn, to which, for so many years of his life, Thomas Newcome had accustomed himself. His obstinate habit of early waking accompanied him to England, and occasioned the despair of his London domestics, who if Master wasn't so awful early would have found no fault with him, for a gentleman as gives less trouble to his servants; as scarcely ever rings the bell for hisself; as will brush his own clothes; as will even boil his own shaving water, in the little Hetna which he keeps[8] up in his dressing-room; as pays so regular, and[9] never looks twice at the accounts;—such a man deserved to be loved[1] by his household; and I daresay comparisons were made between him and his son, who do ring the bells; and scold if his boots ain't nice; and horder about like a young lord. But Clive though imperious was very liberal and good-humoured; and not the worse[2] served because he insisted upon exerting his youthful authority. As for friend Binnie, he had a hundred pursuits of his own which made his time pass very comfortably. He had all the lectures at the British Institution; he had the Geographical Society, the Asiatic Society, and the Political-Economy Club; and though he talked year after year of going to visit his relations in Scotland; the months and seasons passed away and his feet still beat the London pavement.

In spite of the cold reception[3] his brothers gave him, duty was duty, and Colonel Newcome still proposed or hoped to be well with the female members of the Newcome family. And having, as we have said, plenty of time on his hands: and, living at no very great distance from either of his brothers' town-houses; when their wives were in London, the elder Newcome was for paying them pretty constant visits. But after the good gentleman had called twice or thrice[4] upon his sister-in-law in Brianstone Square; bringing, as was his wont, a present for this little niece, or a book for that: Mrs. Newcome with her usual virtue gave him to understand that the occupations of an English matron, who besides her multifarious family duties, had her own intellectual culture to mind, would not allow her to pass the[5] mornings in idle gossip; and of course took great credit to herself for having so rebuked him. "I am not above instruction at *any* age," says she thanking Heaven (or complimenting it rather for having created a being so virtuous and humble-minded). "When Professor Schroff comes, I sit with my children and take lessons in German—and I say my verbs with Maria and Tommy[6] in the same class." Yes, with curtsies and fine speeches,

[8] keeps *E1*] keep *Ms*
[9] and *E1*] and as *Ms*
[1] loved *E1*] beloved *Ms*
[2] worse *E1*] worse liked or *Ms*
[3] reception *E1*] reception which *Ms*
[4] thrice *E1*] thrice in the forenoon *Ms*
[5] the *E1*] her *Ms*
[6] Tommy *E1*] Fanny *Ms*

she actually bowed her brother out of doors: and the honest gentleman meekly left her, though with bewilderment as he thought[7] of the different hospitality to which he had been accustomed in the East; where no friend's house was ever closed to him; where no neighbour was so busy but he had time to make Thomas Newcome welcome.

When Hobson Newcome's boys came home for their holydays their kind uncle was for treating them to the sights of the town—but here virtue again interposed[8] and laid its interdict upon pleasure. "Thank[9] you very much, my dear Colonel," says Virtue: "there never was surely such a kind affectionate unselfish creature as you are, and so indulgent[1] for children—but my boys and yours are brought up on a *very different* plan—Excuse me for saying that I do not think it is adviseable that they should even see too much of each other. Clive's company is not good for them."

"Great Heavens, Maria!" cries the Colonel starting up, "do you mean that my boy's society is not good enough for any boy alive."

Maria turned very red. She had said not more than she meant but more than she meant to say. "My dear Colonel! How hot we are! How angry you Indian gentlemen become with us poor women! Your boy is much older than mine. He lives with Artists—with all sorts of eccentric people. Our children are bred on *quite a different plan.*[2] Hobson will succeed his father in the bank; and dear Samuel I trust will go into the Church—I told you before, the views I had regarding the boys:[3] but it was most kind of you to think of them—most generous and kind."[4]

"That nabob of ours' is a queer fish," Hobson Newcome remarked to his nephew Barnes.[5] "He's as proud as Lucifer, he's always taking huff about one thing[6] or the other. He went off in a fume[7] the other night[8] because your aunt objected to his taking the boys to the play. She don't like their going to the play—My mother didn't either. Your aunt[9] is a woman who is uncommon[1] wide awake I can tell you."

"I always knew, Sir, that my[2] aunt was perfectly aware of the time of the[3] day," says Barnes with a bow.[4]

"And then the Colonel flies out about his boy, and says[5] that my wife

---

[7] gentlemen meekly ... he thought *E1*] gentlemen as he meekly left her, thought with bewilderment *Ms*

[8] virtue again interposed *E1*] again Virtue interfered *Ms*

[9] "Thank *E1*] 'I thank *Ms*

[1] indulgent *E1*] dangerous *Ms*

[2] bred on *quite a different plan. E1*] bred in quite a different fashion. *Ms*

[3] the boys: *E1*] the darling boys: *Ms*

[4] generous and kind." *E1*] kind and generous." *Ms*

[5] nephew Barnes. *E1*] nephew. *Ms*

[6] one thing *E1*] something *Ms*

[7] fume *E1*] fury *Ms*

[8] night *E1*] day *Ms*

[9] My mother didn't either. Your aunt *E1*] Your Aunt *Ms*

[1] uncommon *E1*] deuced *Ms*

[2] that my *E1*] my *Ms*

[3] of the *E1*] of *Ms*

[4] Barnes with a bow. *E1*] Barnes. *Ms*

[5] says *E1*] said *Ms*

insulted him—I used to like that boy. Before his father came he was a good lad enough—a jolly brave[6] little fellow."

"I confess I did not know Mr. Clive[7] at that interesting period of his existence," remarks Barnes.

"But since he has taken this mad-cap freak[8] of turning painter," the uncle continues, "there's no understanding the chap. Did you ever see such a set of fellows as the Colonel had got together at his party the other night? Dirty chaps in velvet coats and beards? They looked like a set of mountebanks. And this young Clive is going to turn painter—"

"Very advantageous[9] thing for the family. He'll do our pictures for nothing.[1] I always said he was a darling boy," simpered[2] Barnes.

"Darling Jackass!" growled out the senior.[3] "Confound it, why doesn't my brother set him up in some respectable business?[4] I ain't proud. *I* haven't married an earl's daughter—no offence to you, Barnes—"

"Not at all, Sir. I[5] can't help it[6] if my grandfather is a gentleman," says[7] Barnes with a fascinating[8] smile.

The uncle laughs—"I mean, I don't care what a fellow is if he is a good fellow. But a painter! Hang it—a painter's no trade at all. I don't fancy seeing one of our family sticking up pictures for sale—I don't like it, Barnes—"

"Hush! here[9] comes his distinguished friend, Mr. Pendennis," whispers Barnes: and the uncle growling out, "Dam all literary fellows—all artists—the whole lot of them!" turns away. Barnes waves three languid fingers of recognition towards Pendennis: and when the uncle and nephew have moved out of the club newspaper room, little Tom Eaves comes up and tells the present reporter every word of their conversation.[1]

Very soon Mrs. Newcome announced that their Indian brother found the society of Brianstone Square very[2] little to his taste as indeed how should he, being a man of a good harmless disposition certainly but of small intellectual culture? It could not be helped. She had done *her* utmost to make him welcome and grieved that their pursuits were not more congenial.[3] She heard that he was much more intimate in Park Lane. Possibly the superior rank of Lady Ann's family might present charms to Colonel

[6] jolly brave *E1*] jolly little brave *Ms*

[7] I confess . . . Clive *E1*] I didn't know him *Ms*

[8] mad-cap freak *E1*] mad-freak *Ms*

[9] advantageous *E1*] nice *Ms*

[1] family. He'll . . . nothing. *E1*] family, Sir. *Ms*

[2] simpered *E1*] says *Ms*

[3] growled out the senior. *E1*] cries Mr. Hodson. *Ms*

[4] business? *E1*] trade. *Ms*

[5] Barnes." ¶"Not at all, Sir. I *E1*] Barnes—' ¶I *Ms*

[6] it if *E1*] it you know if *Ms*

[7] gentleman," says *E1*] gentleman, Sir,' says *Ms*

[8] with a fascinating *E1*] with a bow and a fascinating *Ms*

[9] "Hush! here *E1*] Here *Ms*

[1] fellows—all . . . conversation. *E1*] fellows, and artists the whole lot of 'em,' turns away: and little Tom Eaves who has overheard the conversation at the Club repeats it with embellishments to the present reporter. *Ms*

[2] very little *E1*] little *Ms*

[3] more congenial. *E1*] congenial. *Ms*

Newcome who fell asleep at her assemblies.[4] His boy, she was afraid, was leading the most *irregular* life. He was growing a pair of mustachios: and going about with all sorts of wild associates. She found no fault—who was she to find fault with *any one*? But she had been compelled to hint that *her* children must not be too intimate with him.—And so between one brother who meant[5] no unkindness, and another who was all affection and good will, this undoubting woman created difference, distrust, disklike which might[6] one day possibly[7] lead to open rupture. The wicked are wicked no doubt; and they go astray, and they fall, and they come by their deserts: but who can tell[8] the mischief which the very virtuous do?[9]

To her[1] sister-in-law, Lady Ann, the Colonel's society was more welcome. The affectionate gentleman never tired of doing kindnesses to his brother's many children; and as Mr. Clive's pursuits now separated him a good deal from his father, the Colonel, not perhaps without a sigh that Fate should so separate him from the society which he loved best in the world, consoled himself as best he might with his nephews and nieces, especially with Ethel for whom his *belle passion*, conceived at first sight, never diminished. "If Uncle Newcome had a hundred children," Ethel said, who was rather jealous of disposition, "he would spoil them all." He found a fine occupation in breaking a pretty little horse for her; of which he made her a present—and there was no horse in the park that was so handsome,[2] and surely no girl who looked more beautiful, than Ethel Newcome[3] with her broad hat and red[4] ribbon, with her thick black locks waving round her bright face, galloping along the ride on Bhurtpore. Occasionally Clive was at[5] their riding parties; when the Colonel would fall back, and fondly survey the young[6] people cantering side by side over the grass: but by a tacit convention it was arranged that the cousins should be but seldom together; the Colonel might be his niece's companion; and no one could receive him with a more joyous welcome; but when Mr. Clive made his appearance with his father at the Park Lane door, a certain *gêne* was visible in Miss Ethel: who would never mount except with Colonel Newcome's assistance: and who, especially after Mr. Clive's famous mustachios made their appearance, rallied him and remonstrated with him regarding those ornaments—and treated him with much distance and dignity.[7] She asked him if he was going into the Army?—She could not understand how any but military men could wear mustachios; and then she looked fondly and archly at her uncle, and said she liked none that were not grey.

[4] assemblies. *E1*] assembly. *Ms*
[5] who meant *E1*] who at least meant *Ms*
[6] difference, ... might *E1*] distrust, difference, dislike which *Ms*
[7] possibly *E1*] was possibly to *Ms*
[8] tell *E1*] measure *Ms*
[9] [double space] *E1*] [normal space] *Ms*
[1] her *E1*] his *Ms*
[2] so handsome, *E1*] handsomer, *Ms*
[3] Ethel Newcome *E1*] Ethel *Ms*
[4] hat and red *E1*] hat, and her red *Ms*
[5] at *E1*] of *Ms*
[6] the young *E1*] the two young *Ms*
[7] dignity. *E1*] ceremony. *Ms*

Clive set her down as a very haughty aristocratic spoiled young creature. If he had been in love with her, no doubt he would have sacrificed
even those beloved new-born whiskers for the charmer. Had he not already bought on credit the necessary implements in a fine dressing-case
from young Moss? But he was not in love with her: otherwise he would
have found a thousand opportunities of riding with her, walking with her,
meeting her in spite of all prohibitions tacit or expressed, all governesses,
guardians, mamma's punctilios, and kind hints from friends. For a while
Mr. Clive thought himself in love with his cousin; than whom no more
beautiful young girl could be seen in any park, ball or drawing-room: and
he drew a hundred pictures of her; and discoursed about her beauties to
J.J. who fell in love with her on hearsay. But at this time Mademoiselle
Saltarelli was dancing at Drury Lane Theatre, and it certainly may be said
that Clive's first love was bestowed upon that beauty:[8] whose picture of
course he drew in most of her favourite characters: and for whom his passion lasted until the end of the season: when her 'night' was announced,
tickets to be had at the theatre or of Mademoiselle Saltarelli, Buckingham Street, Strand. Then it was that with[9] a throbbing heart and a five
pound note to engage places for the houri's benefit; Clive beheld Madame
Rogomme, Mademoiselle Saltarelli's mother, who entertained him in the
French language in a dark parlour smelling of onions. And oh! issuing from the adjoining dining-room (where was a dingy vision of a feast
and pewter-pots upon a darkling tablecloth)—could that lean, scraggy, old,
beetle-browed, yellow face,[1] who cried "Où es tu donc, Maman?" with such
a shrill nasal voice—could that elderly vixen, be the blooming and divine
Saltarelli? Clive drew her picture as she was; and a likeness of Madame Rogomme, her mamma. A Mosaic youth, profusely jewelled, and scented at

once with tobacco and Eau de Cologne, occupied Clive's stall, on Mademoiselle Saltarelli's night. It was young Mr. Moss of Gandish's to whom

---

[8] beauty: *E1*] beauty, whom he worshipped chastely from the pit-benches: *Ms*
[9] that with *E1*] that going with *Ms*
[1] yellow face, *E1*] yellow-faced, *Ms*

Newcome ceded his place: and who laughed (as he always did[2] at Clive's[3] jokes,) when the latter told the story of his interview with the dancer. "Paid five pound to see that woman. I would have took you behind the scenes (or *beide* the *seeds,* Mr. Moss said) and showed her to you for dothig!" Did he take Clive behind the scenes?—Over this part of the young gentleman's life without implying the least harm to him, for have not others been behind the scenes, and can there be any more[4] dreary objects than those whitened and raddled old women who shudder at the slips?—over this stage of Clive Newcome's life we may surely drop the curtain.

It is pleasanter to contemplate that kind old face of Clive's father, that sweet young blushing lady by his side as the two ride homewards at sunset: the grooms behind in quiet conversation about horses,[5] as men never tire of[6] talking about horses. Ethel wants to know about battles: about lovers' lamps which she has read of in *Lallah Rookh.* "Have you ever seen them, Uncle, floating down the Ganges of a night?"—about Indian widows—"Did you actually see one burning, and hear her scream as you rode up?"— She wonders whether he will tell her anything about Clive's mother: how she must have loved Uncle Newcome! Ethel can't bear somehow to think that her name was Mrs. Casey—perhaps he was very fond of her; though he scarcely ever mentions her name. She was nothing like that good old funny Miss Honeyman at Brighton. Who could the person be?—a person that[7] her uncle knew ever so long ago—a French lady, whom her uncle says Ethel often resembles? That is why he speaks French so well. He can recite pages out of Racine. Perhaps it was the French lady who taught him. And he was not very happy at the Hermitage, (though Grandpapa was a very kind good man): and he upset Papa in a little carriage, and was wild, and got into disgrace, and was sent[8] to India? He could not have been very bad, Ethel thinks looking at him with her honest eyes. Last week he went to the Drawing-Room and Papa presented him. His uniform of grey and silver was quite old: yet[9] he looked much grander than Sir Brian in his new deputy-lieutenant's dress. "Next year when I am presented you must come too, Sir," says Ethel. "I insist upon it,[1] you must come too."

"I will order a new uniform, Ethel," says her uncle.

The girl laughs. "When little Egbert took hold of your sword, Uncle, and asked you[2] how many people you had killed, do[3] you know I had the same question in my mind? And I thought when you went to the Drawing-Room, perhaps the King will knight him. But instead he knighted mamma's apothecary, Sir Danby Jilks,—that horrid little man: and I won't have you knighted any more."

[2] always did *E1*] did *Ms*

[3] at Clive's *E1*] at all Clive's *Ms*

[4] any more *E1*] more *Ms*

[5] conversation about horses, *E1*] conversation; talking about horses *Ms*

[6] of *E1*] in *Ms*

[7] be?—a person that *E1*] be, a lady whom *Ms*

[8] carriage, and . . . sent *E1*] carriage and got into disgrace and was wild, and was sent *Ms*

[9] old, yet *E1*] old: but yet *Ms*

[1] it, *E1*] it that *Ms*

[2] asked you *E1*] asked *Ms*

[3] killed, do *E1*] killed with it—Do *Ms*

"Have you killed many Men with this Sword, Uncle?"

"I hope Egbert won't ask Sir Danby Jilks, how many people *he* has killed," says the Colonel laughing. But thinking this joke too severe upon Sir Danby and the profession he forthwith apologises by narrating many anecdotes he knows to the credit of surgeons—how when the fever broke out on board their ship going to India: their surgeon devoted himself to the safety of the crew; and died himself leaving directions for the treatment of the patients when he was gone: what heroism the doctors showed during the cholera in India; and what courage he had seen some of them exhibit in action, attending the wounded men[4] under the hottest fire, and exposing themselves as readily as the bravest troops. Ethel declares that her uncle always will talk of[5] other people's courage, and never say a word about his own. "And the only reason," she says, "which made me like that odious Sir Thomas de Boots; who laughs so, and looks so red, and pays such horrid compliments to all ladies: was that he praised you, Uncle, at Newcome last year, when Barnes—when he came to us at Christmas. Why did you not come? Mamma and I went to see your old nurse; and we found her such a nice old lady." So the pair talk kindly on, riding homewards through the pleasant summer twilight. Mamma had[6] gone out to dinner; and there were cards for three parties afterwards. "O how I wish it was next year!" says Miss Ethel.

Many a splendid assembly, and many a brilliant next year will the ardent and hopeful young creature enjoy: but in the midst of her splendours and triumphs, buzzing flatterers, conquered rivals, prostrate admirers; no doubt she will think sometimes of that quiet season, before the world began for her; and that dear old friend on whose arm she leaned while she was yet a young girl.

The Colonel comes to Park Street early in the afternoon when the mistress of the house, surrounded by her little ones, is administering dinner to them. He behaves with splendid courtesy to Miss Quigley, the governess, and makes a point of taking wine with her, and of making a most profound bow during that ceremony. Miss Quigley cannot help thinking Colonel Newcome's bow very fine. She has an idea that his late Majesty must have bowed in that way: she flutteringly imparts this opinion to Lady Ann's maid; who tells her mistress, who tells Miss Ethel, who watches the Colonel the next time he takes wine with Miss Quigley: and they[7] laugh, and then Ethel tells him; so that the gentleman and the governess have to blush ever after when they drink wine together. When she is walking with her little charges in the Park, (or in that[8] before-mentioned paradise[9] nigh to Apsley House) faint signals of welcome appear on[1] her wan cheeks. She knows the dear Colonel amongst a thousand horsemen. If Ethel makes for her uncle purses, guard-chains, antimacassars and the like beautiful and useful articles, I believe it is in reality Miss Quigley who does four-fifths

---

[4] wounded men *E1*] wounded *Ms*
[5] of *E1*] about *Ms*
[6] had *E1*] has *Ms*
[7] and they *E1*] and then they *Ms*
[8] in that *E1*] their *Ms*
[9] paradise *E1*] reserved Paradise *Ms*
[1] on *E1*] in *Ms*

of the work,—as she sits alone in the[2] school-room—high, high up in that lone house, when the little ones are long since asleep, before her dismal little tea-tray, and[3] her little desk, containing her mother's letters and her mementos of home.

There are of course numberless fine parties in Park Lane, where the Colonel knows he would be very welcome. But if there be grand assemblies,[4] he does not care to come. "I like to go to the club best," he says to Lady Ann. "We talk there as you do here about persons; and about Jack marrying and Tom dying and so forth. But we have known Jack and Tom all our lives and so are interested in talking about them, just as you are in speaking of your own friends and habitual society. They are people whose names I have sometimes read in the newspaper, but whom I never thought of meeting until I came to your house. What has an old fellow like me to say to your young dandies, or old dowagers?"

"Mamma is very odd, and sometimes very captious, my dear Colonel," said Lady Ann with a blush—"She suffers so frightfully from tic, that we are all[5] bound to pardon her."[6]

Truth to tell, old Lady Kew had been particularly rude to Colonel Newcome and Clive; Ethel's birthday befel in the spring, on which occasion[7] she was wont[8] to have a juvenile assembly; chiefly of girls of her own age and condition, who came accompanied by a few governesses; and they played and sang their little duets and choruses together; and enjoyed a gentle refection of sponge-cakes, jellies, tea and the like. The Colonel, who was invited to this little party, sent a fine present to his favourite, Ethel; and Clive and his friend J.J. made a funny series of drawings representing the life of a young lady, as they imagined it—and drawing her progress, from her cradle upwards; now engaged with her doll, then with her dancing-master; now marching in her back-board, now crying over her German lessons; and dressed[9] for her first ball finally, and bestowing her hand upon a dandy of preternatural ugliness,[1] who was kneeling at her feet as the happy man. This picture was the delight of the laughing happy girls—except perhaps the little cousins from Brianstone Square, who were invited to Ethel's party; but were so overpowered by the prodigious new dresses in which their mamma had attired them; that they could admire nothing but their rustling pink frocks, their enormous sashes, their lovely new silk stockings.

Lady Kew coming to London attended on[2] the party: and presented her grand-daughter with a sixpenny pincushion. The Colonel had sent

---

[2] the *E1*] her *Ms*

[3] tea-tray, and *E1*] tea-tray, with her poor little work-baskets, *Ms*

[4] if there be grand assemblies, *E1*] to these grand assemblies *Ms*

[5] are all *E1*] all are *Ms*

[6] pardon her." *E1*] pardon her—" ¶"Poor dear old lady!" cries the Colonel. "It was not what she said to me, but what she said about Clive that hurt me. I am sure I should not have replied so hastily had I known she was in pain." *Ms*

[7] occasion *E1*] anniversary *Ms*

[8] wont *E1*] accustomed *Ms*

[9] and dressed *E1*] dressed *Ms*

[1] ugliness, *E1*] hideousness, *Ms*

[2] attended on *E1*] attended *Ms*

Ethel a beautiful little gold watch and chain. Her aunt had complimented her with that refreshing work, "Alison's History of Europe," richly bound— Lady Kew's pincushion made rather a poor figure among the gifts; whence probably arose her ladyship's ill-humour.

Ethel's grandmother became exceedingly testy, when, the Colonel arriving, Ethel ran up to him and thanked him for the beautiful watch in return for which she gave him a kiss: which I daresay amply repaid Colonel Newcome; and shortly after him, Mr. Clive arrived, looking uncommonly handsome, with that smart little beard and mustachio, with which nature had recently gifted him. As he entered, all the girls who had been admiring his pictures began to clap their hands. Mr. Clive Newcome blushed and looked none the worse for that indication of modesty.

Lady Kew had met Colonel Newcome a half-dozen times at her daughter's house: but on this occasion she had quite forgotten him, for when the Colonel made her a bow, her ladyship regarded him steadily, and beckoning her daughter to her, asked who the gentleman was who has[3] just kissed Ethel? Trembling as she always did before her mother, Lady Ann explained. Lady Kew said "O": and left Colonel Newcome blushing and rather *embarrassé de sa personne* before her.

With the clapping of hands that[4] greeted Clive's arrival, the Countess was by no means more good-humoured—Not aware of her wrath, the young fellow who had also previously been presented to her, came forward presently to make her his compliments. "Pray, who are you?" she said looking at[5] him very earnestly[6] in the face.—He told her his name.

"Hm," said Lady Kew. "I have heard of you and I have heard very little good of you."

"Will your ladyship please to give me your informant?" cried out Colonel Newcome. Barnes Newcome who had condescended to attend his sister's little fête, and had been languidly watching the frolics of the young people, looked very much alarmed.

---

[3] has *E1*] had *Ms*
[4] that *E1*] which *Ms*
[5] looking at *E1*] looking *Ms*
[6] earnestly *E1*] calmly *Ms*